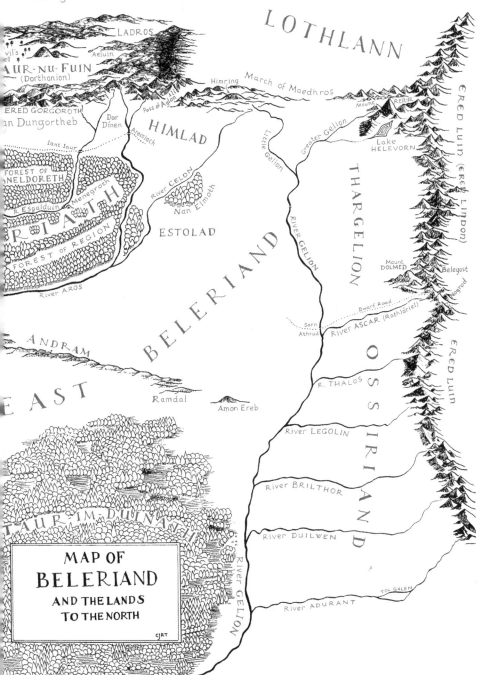

N FAUGLITH
(Ard-galen)

LOTHLANN

LADROS

vil's
ell
Aeluin

AUR-NU-FUIN
(Dorthonion)

Himring    March of Maedhros

ERED GORGOROTH
an Dungortheb

Dor
Dínen

Aglon

HIMLAD

Pass of Aglon

Mount RERIR

Lake
HELEVORN

ERED LUIN (ERED LINDON)

Iant Iaur

Aros Iach

FOREST OF
NELDORETH

River CELON

Little Gelion

Greater Gelion

R. Esgalduin

Menegroth

Nan Elmoth

THARGELION

Mount
DOLMED

Belegost

RIATH

FOREST OF REGION

ESTOLAD

River GELION

River AROS

BELERIAND

Dwarf Road

Sarn
Athrad

River ASCAR (Rathlóriel)

Nogrod

ERED Luin

ANDRAM

Ramdal

Amon Ereb

R. THALOS

O

S

S

I

R

I

A

N

D

EAST

River LEGOLIN

River BRILTHOR

TAUR-IM-DUINATH

River DUILWEN

River GELION

TOL GALEN

MAP OF
BELERIAND
AND THE LANDS
TO THE NORTH

River ADURANT

CJRT

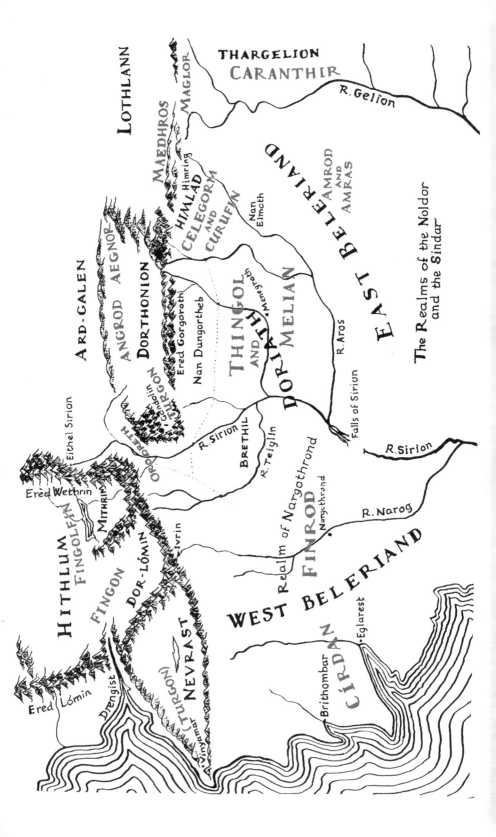

# THE SILMARILLION

J. R. R. TOLKIEN

# QUENTA SILMARILLION
(The History of the Silmarils)

together with

## AINULINDALË
(The Music of the Ainur)

and

## VALAQUENTA
(Account of the Valar)

To which is appended
## AKALLABÊTH
(The Downfall of Númenor)

and

# OF THE RINGS OF POWER AND
# THE THIRD AGE

# J. R. R. TOLKIEN

# The Silmarillion

edited by
## CHRISTOPHER TOLKIEN

HarperCollins*Publishers*

HarperCollins*Publishers* Ltd
1 London Bridge Street
London SE1 9GF

HarperCollins*Publishers*
Macken House, 39/40 Mayor Street Upper
Dublin 1, D01 C9W8, Ireland

www.tolkien.co.uk
www.tolkienestate.com

This hardback edition 2023
1

First published in Great Britain by
George Allen & Unwin (Publishers) Ltd 1977,
and by HarperCollins*Publishers* 1992

# FOREWORD

*The Silmarillion*, now published four years after the death of its author, is an account of the Elder Days, or the First Age of the World. In *The Lord of the Rings* were narrated the great events at the end of the Third Age; but the tales of *The Silmarillion* are legends deriving from a much deeper past, when Morgoth, the first Dark Lord, dwelt in Middle-earth, and the High Elves made war upon him for the recovery of the Silmarils.

Not only, however, does *The Silmarillion* relate the events of a far earlier time than those of *The Lord of the Rings*; it is also, in all the essentials of its conception, far the earlier work. Indeed, although it was not then called *The Silmarillion*, it was already in being half a century ago; and in battered notebooks extending back to 1917 can still be read the earliest versions, often hastily pencilled, of the central stories of the mythology. But it was never published (though some indication of its content could be gleaned from *The Lord of the Rings*), and throughout my father's long life he never abandoned it, nor ceased even in his last years to work on it. In all that time *The Silmarillion*, considered simply as a large narrative structure, underwent relatively little radical change; it became long ago a fixed tradition, and background to later writings. But it was far indeed from being a fixed text, and did not remain unchanged even in certain fundamental ideas concerning the nature of the world it portrays; while the same legends came to be retold in longer and shorter forms, and in different styles. As the years passed the changes and variants, both in detail and in larger perspectives, became so complex, so pervasive, and so many-layered that a final and definitive version seemed unattainable. Moreover the old legends ('old' now not only in their derivation from the remote First Age, but also in terms of my father's life) became the vehicle and depository of his profoundest reflections. In his later writing mythology and poetry sank down behind his theological and philosophical preoccupations: from which arose incompatibilities of tone.

On my father's death it fell to me to try to bring the work into publishable form. It became clear to me that to attempt to present, within the covers of a single book, the diversity of the materials—to show *The Silmarillion* as in truth a continuing and evolving creation extending over more than half a century—would in fact lead only to confusion and the submerging of what is essential. I set myself there-

fore to work out a single text, selecting and arranging in such a way
as seemed to me to produce the most coherent and internally self-
consistent narrative. In this work the concluding chapters (from the
death of Túrin Turambar) introduced peculiar difficulties, in that
they had remained unchanged for many years, and were in some
respects in serious disharmony with more developed conceptions in
other parts of the book.

A complete consistency (either within the compass of *The Silmarillion* itself or between *The Silmarillion* and other published writings
of my father's) is not to be looked for, and could only be achieved, if
at all, at heavy and needless cost. Moreover, my father came to
conceive *The Silmarillion* as a compilation, a compendious narrative,
made long afterwards from sources of great diversity (poems, and
annals, and oral tales) that had survived in agelong tradition; and this
conception has indeed its parallel in the actual history of the book, for
a great deal of earlier prose and poetry does underlie it, and it is to
some extent a compendium in fact and not only in theory. To this may
be ascribed the varying speed of the narrative and fullness of detail in
different parts, the contrast (for example) of the precise recollections
of place and motive in the legend of Túrin Turambar beside the high
and remote account of the end of the First Age, when Thangorodrim
was broken and Morgoth overthrown; and also some differences of
tone and portrayal, some obscurities, and, here and there, some lack
of cohesion. In the case of the *Valaquenta*, for instance, we have to
assume that while it contains much that must go back to the earliest
days of the Eldar in Valinor, it was remodelled in later times; and
thus explain its continual shifting of tense and viewpoint, so that the
divine powers seem now present and active in the world, now remote,
a vanished order known only to memory.

The book, though entitled as it must be *The Silmarillion*, contains
not only the *Quenta Silmarillion*, or *Silmarillion* proper, but also four
other short works. The *Ainulindalë* and *Valaquenta*, which are given
at the beginning, are indeed closely associated with *The Silmarillion*;
but the *Akallabêth* and *Of the Rings of Power*, which appear at the end,
are (it must be emphasised) wholly separate and independent. They
are included according to my father's explicit intention; and by their
inclusion the entire history is set forth from the Music of the Ainur
in which the world began to the passing of the Ringbearers from the
Havens of Mithlond at the end of the Third Age.

The number of names that occur in the book is very large, and I
have provided a full index; but the number of persons (Elves and
Men) who play an important part in the narrative of the First Age is

very much smaller, and all of these will be found in the genealogical tables. In addition I have provided a table setting out the rather complex naming of the different Elvish peoples ; a note on the pronunciation of Elvish names, and a list of some of the chief elements found in these names ; and a map. It may be noted that the great mountain range in the east, Ered Luin or Ered Lindon, the Blue Mountains, appears in the extreme west of the map in *The Lord of the Rings*. In the body of the book there is a smaller map: the intention of this is to make clear at a glance where lay the kingdoms of the Elves after the return of the Noldor to Middle-earth. I have not burdened the book further with any sort of commentary or annotation. There is indeed a wealth of unpublished writing by my father concerning the Three Ages, narrative, linguistic, historical, and philosophical, and I hope that it will prove possible to publish some of this at a later date.

In the difficult and doubtful task of preparing the text of the book I was very greatly assisted by Guy Kay, who worked with me in 1974–1975.

*Christopher Tolkien*

# CONTENTS

*Tables*

*Genealogies:*
> I The House of Finwë
> II The Descendants of Olwë and Elwë
> III The House of Bëor
> IV and V The House of Hador and The People
> of Haleth

*The Sundering of the Elves*

# AINULINDALË

# AINULINDALË

## The Music of the Ainur

There was Eru, the One, who in Arda is called Ilúvatar; and he made first the Ainur, the Holy Ones, that were the offspring of his thought, and they were with him before aught else was made. And he spoke to them, propounding to them themes of music; and they sang before him, and he was glad. But for a long while they sang only each alone, or but few together, while the rest hearkened; for each comprehended only that part of the mind of Ilúvatar from which he came, and in the understanding of their brethren they grew but slowly. Yet ever as they listened they came to deeper understanding, and increased in unison and harmony.

And it came to pass that Ilúvatar called together all the Ainur and declared to them a mighty theme, unfolding to them things greater and more wonderful than he had yet revealed; and the glory of its beginning and the splendour of its end amazed the Ainur, so that they bowed before Ilúvatar and were silent.

Then Ilúvatar said to them : 'Of the theme that I have declared to you, I will now that ye make in harmony together a Great Music. And since I have kindled you with the Flame Imperishable, ye shall show forth your powers in adorning this theme, each with his own thoughts and devices, if he will. But I will sit and hearken, and be glad that through you great beauty has been wakened into song.'

Then the voices of the Ainur, like unto harps and lutes, and pipes and trumpets, and viols and organs, and like unto countless choirs singing with words, began to fashion the theme of Ilúvatar to a great music; and a sound arose of endless interchanging melodies woven in harmony that passed beyond hearing into the depths and into the heights, and the places of the dwelling of Ilúvatar were filled to overflowing, and the music and the echo of the music went out into the Void, and it was not void. Never since have the Ainur made any music like to this music, though it has been said that a greater still shall be made before Ilúvatar by the choirs of the Ainur and the Children of Ilúvatar after the end of days. Then the themes of Ilúvatar shall be played aright, and take Being in the moment of their utterance, for all shall then understand fully his intent in their part, and each shall know the comprehension of each, and Ilúvatar shall give to their thoughts the secret fire, being well pleased.

But now Ilúvatar sat and hearkened, and for a great while it seemed good to him, for in the music there were no flaws. But as the theme progressed, it came into the heart of Melkor to interweave matters of his own imagining that were not in accord with the theme of Ilúvatar ; for he sought therein to increase the power and glory of the part assigned to himself. To Melkor among the Ainur had been given the greatest gifts of power and knowledge, and he had a share in all the gifts of his brethren. He had gone often alone into the void places seeking the Imperishable Flame ; for desire grew hot within him to bring into Being things of his own, and it seemed to him that Ilúvatar took no thought for the Void, and he was impatient of its emptiness. Yet he found not the Fire, for it is with Ilúvatar. But being alone he had begun to conceive thoughts of his own unlike those of his brethren.

Some of these thoughts he now wove into his music, and straightway discord arose about him, and many that sang nigh him grew despondent, and their thought was disturbed and their music faltered ; but some began to attune their music to his rather than to the thought which they had at first. Then the discord of Melkor spread ever wider, and the melodies which had been heard before foundered in a sea of turbulent sound. But Ilúvatar sat and hearkened until it seemed that about his throne there was a raging storm, as of dark waters that made war one upon another in an endless wrath that would not be assuaged.

Then Ilúvatar arose, and the Ainur perceived that he smiled ; and he lifted up his left hand, and a new theme began amid the storm, like and yet unlike to the former theme, and it gathered power and had new beauty. But the discord of Melkor rose in uproar and contended with it, and again there was a war of sound more violent than before, until many of the Ainur were dismayed and sang no longer, and Melkor had the mastery. Then again Ilúvatar arose, and the Ainur perceived that his countenance was stern ; and he lifted up his right hand, and behold! a third theme grew amid the confusion, and it was unlike the others. For it seemed at first soft and sweet, a mere rippling of gentle sounds in delicate melodies ; but it could not be quenched, and it took to itself power and profundity. And it seemed at last that there were two musics progressing at one time before the seat of Ilúvatar, and they were utterly at variance. The one was deep and wide and beautiful, but slow and blended with an immeasurable sorrow, from which its beauty chiefly came. The other had now achieved a unity of its own; but it was loud, and vain, and endlessly repeated; and it had little harmony, but rather a clamorous unison as of many trumpets braying upon a few notes. And it essayed to drown the other music by the violence of its voice, but it seemed that its most triumphant notes were taken by the other and woven into its own solemn pattern.

In the midst of this strife, whereat the halls of Ilúvatar shook and a tremor ran out into the silences yet unmoved, Ilúvatar arose a third time, and his face was terrible to behold. Then he raised up both his hands, and in one chord, deeper than the Abyss, higher than the Firmament, piercing as the light of the eye of Ilúvatar, the Music ceased.

Then Ilúvatar spoke, and he said: 'Mighty are the Ainur, and mightiest among them is Melkor; but that he may know, and all the Ainur, that I am Ilúvatar, those things that ye have sung, I will show them forth, that ye may see what ye have done. And thou, Melkor, shalt see that no theme may be played that hath not its uttermost source in me, nor can any alter the music in my despite. For he that attempteth this shall prove but mine instrument in the devising of things more wonderful, which he himself hath not imagined.'

Then the Ainur were afraid, and they did not yet comprehend the words that were said to them; and Melkor was filled with shame, of which came secret anger. But Ilúvatar arose in splendour, and he went forth from the fair regions that he had made for the Ainur; and the Ainur followed him.

But when they were come into the Void, Ilúvatar said to them: 'Behold your Music!' And he showed to them a vision, giving to them sight where before was only hearing; and they saw a new World made visible before them, and it was globed amid the Void, and it was sustained therein, but was not of it. And as they looked and wondered this World began to unfold its history, and it seemed to them that it lived and grew. And when the Ainur had gazed for a while and were silent, Ilúvatar said again: 'Behold your Music! This is your minstrelsy; and each of you shall find contained herein, amid the design that I set before you, all those things which it may seem that he himself devised or added. And thou, Melkor, wilt discover all the secret thoughts of thy mind, and wilt perceive that they are but a part of the whole and tributary to its glory.'

And many other things Ilúvatar spoke to the Ainur at that time, and because of their memory of his words, and the knowledge that each has of the music that he himself made, the Ainur know much of

what was, and is, and is to come, and few things are unseen by them.
Yet some things there are that they cannot see, neither alone nor
taking counsel together; for to none but himself has Ilúvatar revealed
all that he has in store, and in every age there come forth things that
are new and have no foretelling, for they do not proceed from the past.
And so it was that as this vision of the World was played before them,
the Ainur saw that it contained things which they had not thought.
And they saw with amazement the coming of the Children of Ilúvatar,
and the habitation that was prepared for them; and they perceived
that they themselves in the labour of their music had been busy with
the preparation of this dwelling, and yet knew not that it had any
purpose beyond its own beauty. For the Children of Ilúvatar were
conceived by him alone; and they came with the third theme, and
were not in the theme which Ilúvatar propounded at the beginning,
and none of the Ainur had part in their making. Therefore when they
beheld them, the more did they love them, being things other than
themselves, strange and free, wherein they saw the mind of Ilúvatar
reflected anew, and learned yet a little more of his wisdom, which
otherwise had been hidden even from the Ainur.

Now the Children of Ilúvatar are Elves and Men, the Firstborn and
the Followers. And amid all the splendours of the World, its vast
halls and spaces, and its wheeling fires, Ilúvatar chose a place for
their habitation in the Deeps of Time and in the midst of the innumerable stars. And this habitation might seem a little thing to those
who consider only the majesty of the Ainur, and not their terrible
sharpness; as who should take the whole field of Arda for the foundation of a pillar and so raise it until the cone of its summit were more
bitter than a needle; or who consider only the immeasurable vastness
of the World, which still the Ainur are shaping, and not the minute
precision to which they shape all things therein. But when the Ainur
had beheld this habitation in a vision and had seen the Children of
Ilúvatar arise therein, then many of the most mighty among them
bent all their thought and their desire towards that place. And of
these Melkor was the chief, even as he was in the beginning the
greatest of the Ainur who took part in the Music. And he feigned,
even to himself at first, that he desired to go thither and order all
things for the good of the Children of Ilúvatar, controlling the turmoils of the heat and the cold that had come to pass through him.
But he desired rather to subdue to his will both Elves and Men,
envying the gifts with which Ilúvatar promised to endow them; and
he wished himself to have subjects and servants, and to be called
Lord, and to be a master over other wills.

But the other Ainur looked upon this habitation set within the vast spaces of the World, which the Elves call Arda, the Earth; and their hearts rejoiced in light, and their eyes beholding many colours were filled with gladness; but because of the roaring of the sea they felt a great unquiet. And they observed the winds and the air, and the matters of which Arda was made, of iron and stone and silver and gold and many substances: but of all these water they most greatly praised. And it is said by the Eldar that in water there lives yet the echo of the Music of the Ainur more than in any substance else that is in this Earth; and many of the Children of Ilúvatar hearken still unsated to the voices of the Sea, and yet know not for what they listen.

Now to water had that Ainu whom the Elves call Ulmo turned his thought, and of all most deeply was he instructed by Ilúvatar in music. But of the airs and winds Manwë most had pondered, who is the noblest of the Ainur. Of the fabric of Earth had Aulë thought, to whom Ilúvatar had given skill and knowledge scarce less than to Melkor; but the delight and pride of Aulë is in the deed of making, and in the thing made, and neither in possession nor in his own mastery; wherefore he gives and hoards not, and is free from care, passing ever on to some new work.

And Ilúvatar spoke to Ulmo, and said: 'Seest thou not how here in this little realm in the Deeps of Time Melkor hath made war upon thy province? He hath bethought him of bitter cold immoderate, and yet hath not destroyed the beauty of thy fountains, nor of thy clear pools. Behold the snow, and the cunning work of frost! Melkor hath devised heats and fire without restraint, and hath not dried up thy desire nor utterly quelled the music of the sea. Behold rather the height and glory of the clouds, and the everchanging mists; and listen to the fall of rain upon the Earth! And in these clouds thou art drawn nearer to Manwë, thy friend, whom thou lovest.'

Then Ulmo answered: 'Truly, Water is become now fairer than my heart imagined, neither had my secret thought conceived the snowflake, nor in all my music was contained the falling of the rain. I will seek Manwë, that he and I may make melodies for ever to thy delight!' And Manwë and Ulmo have from the beginning been allied, and in all things have served most faithfully the purpose of Ilúvatar.

But even as Ulmo spoke, and while the Ainur were yet gazing upon this vision, it was taken away and hidden from their sight; and it seemed to them that in that moment they perceived a new thing, Darkness, which they had not known before except in thought. But they had become enamoured of the beauty of the vision and engrossed in the unfolding of the World which came there to being, and their minds were filled with it; for the history was incomplete and the circles of time not full-wrought when the vision was taken away. And some have said that the vision ceased ere the fulfilment of the Dominion of Men and the fading of the Firstborn; wherefore, though the Music is over all, the Valar have not seen as with sight the Later Ages or the ending of the World.

Then there was unrest among the Ainur; but Ilúvatar called to them, and said: 'I know the desire of your minds that what ye have seen should verily be, not only in your thought, but even as ye yourselves are, and yet other. Therefore I say: *Eä! Let these things Be!* And I will send forth into the Void the Flame Imperishable, and it shall be at the heart of the World, and the World shall Be; and those of you that will may go down into it.' And suddenly the Ainur saw afar off a light, as it were a cloud with a living heart of flame; and they knew that this was no vision only, but that Ilúvatar had made a new thing: Eä, the World that Is.

Thus it came to pass that of the Ainur some abode still with Ilúvatar beyond the confines of the World; but others, and among them many of the greatest and most fair, took the leave of Ilúvatar and descended into it. But this condition Ilúvatar made, or it is the necessity of their love, that their power should thenceforward be contained and bounded in the World, to be within it for ever, until it is complete, so that they are its life and it is theirs. And therefore they are named the Valar, the Powers of the World.

But when the Valar entered into Eä they were at first astounded and at a loss, for it was as if naught was yet made which they had seen in vision, and all was but on point to begin and yet unshaped, and it was dark. For the Great Music had been but the growth and flowering of thought in the Timeless Halls, and the Vision only a foreshowing; but now they had entered in at the beginning of Time, and the Valar perceived that the World had been but foreshadowed and foresung, and they must achieve it. So began their great labours in wastes unmeasured and unexplored, and in ages uncounted and forgotten, until in the Deeps of Time and in the midst of the vast halls of Eä there came to be that hour and that place where was made the habitation of the Children of Ilúvatar. And in this work the chief part was taken by Manwë and Aulë and Ulmo; but Melkor too was there from the first, and he meddled in all that was done, turning it if he might to his own desires and purposes; and he kindled great fires. When therefore Earth was yet young and full of flame Melkor coveted it, and he said to the other Valar : 'This shall be my own kingdom ; and I name it unto myself !'

But Manwë was the brother of Melkor in the mind of Ilúvatar, and he was the chief instrument of the second theme that Ilúvatar had raised up against the discord of Melkor ; and he called unto himself many spirits both greater and less, and they came down into the fields of Arda and aided Manwë, lest Melkor should hinder the fulfilment of their labour for ever, and Earth should wither ere it flowered. And Manwë said unto Melkor : 'This kingdom thou shalt not take for thine own, wrongfully, for many others have laboured here no less than thou.' And there was strife between Melkor and the other Valar ; and for that time Melkor withdrew and departed to other regions and did there what he would ; but he did not put the desire of the Kingdom of Arda from his heart.

Now the Valar took to themselves shape and hue ; and because they were drawn into the World by love of the Children of Ilúvatar, for whom they hoped, they took shape after that manner which they had beheld in the Vision of Ilúvatar, save only in majesty and splendour. Moreover their shape comes of their knowledge of the visible World, rather than of the World itself ; and they need it not, save only as we use raiment, and yet we may be naked and suffer no loss of our being. Therefore the Valar may walk, if they will, unclad, and then even the Eldar cannot clearly perceive them, though they be present. But when they desire to clothe themselves the Valar take upon them forms some as of male and some as of female ; for that difference of temper they had even from their beginning, and it is but bodied forth in the choice of each, not made by the choice, even as with us male and female may be shown by the raiment but is not made thereby. But the shapes wherein the Great Ones array themselves are not at all times like to the shapes of the kings and queens of the Children of Ilúvatar ; for at times they may clothe themselves in their own thought, made visible in forms of majesty and dread.

And the Valar drew unto them many companions, some less, some well nigh as great as themselves, and they laboured together in the ordering of the Earth and the curbing of its tumults. Then Melkor saw what was done, and that the Valar walked on Earth as powers visible, clad in the raiment of the World, and were lovely and glorious to see, and blissful, and that the Earth was becoming as a garden for their delight, for its turmoils were subdued. His envy grew then the greater within him ; and he also took visible form, but because of his mood and the malice that burned in him that form was dark and terrible. And he descended upon Arda in power and majesty greater

than any other of the Valar, as a mountain that wades in the sea and
has its head above the clouds and is clad in ice and crowned with
smoke and fire; and the light of the eyes of Melkor was like a flame
that withers with heat and pierces with a deadly cold.

Thus began the first battle of the Valar with Melkor for the dominion of Arda; and of those tumults the Elves know but little. For what
has here been declared is come from the Valar themselves, with whom
the Eldalië spoke in the land of Valinor, and by whom they were instructed; but little would the Valar ever tell of the wars before the
coming of the Elves. Yet it is told among the Eldar that the Valar
endeavoured ever, in despite of Melkor, to rule the Earth and to prepare it for the coming of the Firstborn; and they built lands and
Melkor destroyed them; valleys they delved and Melkor raised them
up; mountains they carved and Melkor threw them down; seas they
hollowed and Melkor spilled them; and naught might have peace or
come to lasting growth, for as surely as the Valar began a labour so
would Melkor undo it or corrupt it. And yet their labour was not all
in vain; and though nowhere and in no work was their will and purpose wholly fulfilled, and all things were in hue and shape other than
the Valar had at first intended, slowly nonetheless the Earth was
fashioned and made firm. And thus was the habitation of the Children
of Ilúvatar established at the last in the Deeps of Time and amidst the
innumerable stars.

# VALAQUENTA

# VALAQUENTA

## Account of the Valar and Maiar
## according to the lore of the
## Eldar

In the beginning Eru, the One, who in the Elvish tongue is named
Ilúvatar, made the Ainur of his thought; and they made a great
Music before him. In this Music the World was begun; for Ilúvatar
made visible the song of the Ainur, and they beheld it as a light in the
darkness. And many among them became enamoured of its beauty,
and of its history which they saw beginning and unfolding as in a
vision. Therefore Ilúvatar gave to their vision Being, and set it amid
the Void, and the Secret Fire was sent to burn at the heart of the
World; and it was called Eä.

Then those of the Ainur who desired it arose and entered into the
World at the beginning of Time; and it was their task to achieve it,
and by their labours to fulfil the vision which they had seen. Long
they laboured in the regions of Eä, which are vast beyond the thought
of Elves and Men, until in the time appointed was made Arda, the
Kingdom of Earth. Then they put on the raiment of Earth and
descended into it, and dwelt therein.

## Of the Valar

The Great among these spirits the Elves name the Valar, the Powers
of Arda, and Men have often called them gods. The Lords of the
Valar are seven; and the Valier, the Queens of the Valar, are seven
also. These were their names in the Elvish tongue as it was spoken in
Valinor, though they have other names in the speech of the Elves in
Middle-earth, and their names among Men are manifold. The names
of the Lords in due order are: Manwë, Ulmo, Aulë, Oromë, Mandos,
Lórien, and Tulkas; and the names of the Queens are: Varda,
Yavanna, Nienna, Estë, Vairë, Vána, and Nessa. Melkor is counted

no longer among the Valar, and his name is not spoken upon Earth.

Manwë and Melkor were brethren in the thought of Ilúvatar. The mightiest of those Ainur who came into the World was in his beginning Melkor; but Manwë is dearest to Ilúvatar and understands most clearly his purposes. He was appointed to be, in the fullness of time, the first of all Kings: lord of the realm of Arda and ruler of all that dwell therein. In Arda his delight is in the winds and the clouds, and in all the regions of the air, from the heights to the depths, from the utmost borders of the Veil of Arda to the breezes that blow in the grass. Súlimo he is surnamed, Lord of the Breath of Arda. All swift birds, strong of wing, he loves, and they come and go at his bidding.

With Manwë dwells Varda, Lady of the Stars, who knows all the regions of Eä. Too great is her beauty to be declared in the words of Men or of Elves; for the light of Ilúvatar lives still in her face. In light is her power and her joy. Out of the deeps of Eä she came to the aid of Manwë; for Melkor she knew from before the making of the Music and rejected him, and he hated her, and feared her more than all others whom Eru made. Manwë and Varda are seldom parted, and they remain in Valinor. Their halls are above the everlasting snow, upon Oiolossë, the uttermost tower of Taniquetil, tallest of all the mountains upon Earth. When Manwë there ascends his throne and looks forth, if Varda is beside him, he sees further than all other eyes, through mist, and through darkness, and over the leagues of the sea. And if Manwë is with her, Varda hears more clearly than all other ears the sound of voices that cry from east to west, from the hills and the valleys, and from the dark places that Melkor has made upon Earth. Of all the Great Ones who dwell in this world the Elves hold Varda most in reverence and love. Elbereth they name her, and they call upon her name out of the shadows of Middle-earth, and uplift it in song at the rising of the stars.

Ulmo is the Lord of Waters. He is alone. He dwells nowhere long, but moves as he will in all the deep waters about the Earth or under the Earth. He is next in might to Manwë, and before Valinor was made he was closest to him in friendship; but thereafter he went seldom to the councils of the Valar, unless great matters were in debate. For he kept all Arda in thought, and he has no need of any resting-place. Moreover he does not love to walk upon land, and will seldom clothe himself in a body after the manner of his peers. If the Children of Eru beheld him they were filled with a great dread; for the arising of the King of the Sea was terrible, as a mounting wave that strides to the land, with dark helm foam-crested and raiment of mail shimmering from silver down into shadows of green. The trumpets of Manwë are loud, but Ulmo's voice is deep as the deeps of the ocean which he only has seen.

Nonetheless Ulmo loves both Elves and Men, and never abandoned them, not even when they lay under the wrath of the Valar. At times he will come unseen to the shores of Middle-earth, or pass far inland up firths of the sea, and there make music upon his great horns, the Ulumúri, that are wrought of white shell; and those to whom that music comes hear it ever after in their hearts, and longing for the sea never leaves them again. But mostly Ulmo speaks to those who dwell in Middle-earth with voices that are heard only as the music of water. For all seas, lakes, rivers, fountains and springs are in his government; so that the Elves say that the spirit of Ulmo runs in all the veins of the world. Thus news comes to Ulmo, even in the deeps, of all the needs and griefs of Arda, which otherwise would be hidden from Manwë.

Aulë has might little less than Ulmo. His lordship is over all the substances of which Arda is made. In the beginning he wrought much in fellowship with Manwë and Ulmo; and the fashioning of all lands was his labour. He is a smith and a master of all crafts, and he delights in works of skill, however small, as much as in the mighty building of old. His are the gems that lie deep in the Earth and the gold that is fair in the hand, no less than the walls of the mountains and the basins of the sea. The Noldor learned most of him, and he was ever their friend. Melkor was jealous of him, for Aulë was most like himself in thought and in powers; and there was long strife between them, in which Melkor ever marred or undid the works of Aulë, and Aulë grew weary in repairing the tumults and disorders of Melkor. Both, also, desired to make things of their own that should be new and unthought of by others, and delighted in the praise of their skill. But Aulë remained faithful to Eru and submitted all that he did to his will; and he did not envy the works of others, but sought and gave counsel. Whereas Melkor spent his spirit in envy and hate, until at last he could make nothing save in mockery of the thought of others, and all their works he destroyed if he could.

The spouse of Aulë is Yavanna, the Giver of Fruits. She is the lover of all things that grow in the earth, and all their countless forms she holds in her mind, from the trees like towers in forests long ago to the moss upon stones or the small and secret things in the mould. In reverence Yavanna is next to Varda among the Queens of the Valar. In the form of a woman she is tall, and robed in green; but at times she takes other shapes. Some there are who have seen her standing like a tree under heaven, crowned with the Sun; and from all its branches there spilled a golden dew upon the barren earth, and it grew green with corn; but the roots of the tree were in the waters of Ulmo, and the winds of Manwë spoke in its leaves. Kementári, Queen of the Earth, she is surnamed in the Eldarin tongue.

The Fëanturi, masters of spirits, are brethren, and they are called most often Mandos and Lórien. Yet these are rightly the names of the places of their dwelling, and their true names are Námo and Irmo.

Námo the elder dwells in Mandos, which is westward in Valinor. He is the keeper of the Houses of the Dead, and the summoner of the spirits of the slain. He forgets nothing; and he knows all things that shall be, save only those that lie still in the freedom of Ilúvatar. He is the Doomsman of the Valar; but he pronounces his dooms and his judgements only at the bidding of Manwë. Vairë the Weaver is his spouse, who weaves all things that have ever been in Time into her storied webs, and the halls of Mandos that ever widen as the ages pass are clothed with them.

Irmo the younger is the master of visions and dreams. In Lórien are his gardens in the land of the Valar, and they are the fairest of all places in the world, filled with many spirits. Estë the gentle, healer of hurts and of weariness, is his spouse. Grey is her raiment; and rest is her gift. She walks not by day, but sleeps upon an island in the tree-shadowed lake of Lórellin. From the fountains of Irmo and Estë all those who dwell in Valinor draw refreshment; and often the Valar come themselves to Lórien and there find repose and easing of the burden of Arda.

Mightier than Estë is Nienna, sister of the Fëanturi; she dwells alone. She is acquainted with grief, and mourns for every wound that Arda has suffered in the marring of Melkor. So great was her sorrow, as the Music unfolded, that her song turned to lamentation long before its end, and the sound of mourning was woven into the themes of the World before it began. But she does not weep for herself; and those who hearken to her learn pity, and endurance in hope. Her halls are west of West, upon the borders of the world; and she comes seldom to the city of Valimar where all is glad. She goes rather to the halls of Mandos, which are near to her own; and all those who wait in Mandos cry to her, for she brings strength to the spirit and turns sorrow to wisdom. The windows of her house look outward from the walls of the world.

Greatest in strength and deeds of prowess is Tulkas, who is surnamed Astaldo, the Valiant. He came last to Arda, to aid the Valar in the first battles with Melkor. He delights in wrestling and in contests of strength; and he rides no steed, for he can outrun all things that go on feet, and he is tireless. His hair and beard are golden, and his flesh ruddy; his weapons are his hands. He has little heed for either the past or the future, and is of no avail as a counsellor, but is a hardy friend. His spouse is Nessa, the sister of Oromë, and she also is lithe and fleetfooted. Deer she loves, and they follow her train whenever she goes in the wild; but she can outrun them, swift as an arrow with the wind in her hair. In dancing she delights, and she dances in Valimar on lawns of never-fading green.

Oromë is a mighty lord. If he is less strong than Tulkas, he is more dreadful in anger; whereas Tulkas laughs ever, in sport or in war, and even in the face of Melkor he laughed in battles before the Elves were born. Oromë loved the lands of Middle-earth, and he left them unwillingly and came last to Valinor; and often of old he passed back east over the mountains and returned with his host to the hills and the plains. He is a hunter of monsters and fell beasts, and he delights in horses and in hounds; and all trees he loves, for which reason he is called Aldaron, and by the Sindar Tauron, the Lord of Forests. Nahar is the name of his horse, white in the sun, and shining silver at night. The Valaróma is the name of his great horn, the sound of which is like the upgoing of the Sun in scarlet, or the sheer lightning cleaving the clouds. Above all the horns of his host it was heard in the woods that Yavanna brought forth in Valinor; for there Oromë would train his folk and his beasts for the pursuit of the evil creatures of Melkor. The spouse of Oromë is Vána, the Ever-young; she is the younger sister of Yavanna. All flowers spring as she passes and open if she glances upon them; and all birds sing at her coming.

These are the names of the Valar and the Valier, and here is told in brief their likenesses, such as the Eldar beheld them in Aman. But fair and noble as were the forms in which they were manifest to the Children of Ilúvatar, they were but a veil upon their beauty and their power. And if little is here said of all that the Eldar once knew, that is as nothing compared with their true being, which goes back into regions and ages far beyond our thought. Among them Nine were of chief power and reverence; but one is removed from their number, and Eight remain, the Aratar, the High Ones of Arda: Manwë and Varda, Ulmo, Yavanna and Aulë, Mandos, Nienna, and Oromë. Though Manwë is their King and holds their allegiance under Eru, in majesty they are peers, surpassing beyond compare all others, whether of the Valar and the Maiar, or of any other order that Ilúvatar has sent into Eä.

# Of the Maiar

With the Valar came other spirits whose being also began before the World, of the same order as the Valar but of less degree. These are the Maiar, the people of the Valar, and their servants and helpers. Their number is not known to the Elves, and few have names in any of the tongues of the Children of Ilúvatar; for though it is otherwise in Aman, in Middle-earth the Maiar have seldom appeared in form visible to Elves and Men.

Chief among the Maiar of Valinor whose names are remembered in the histories of the Elder Days are Ilmarë, the handmaid of Varda, and Eönwë, the banner-bearer and herald of Manwë, whose might in arms is surpassed by none in Arda. But of all the Maiar Ossë and Uinen are best known to the Children of Ilúvatar.

Ossë is a vassal of Ulmo, and he is master of the seas that wash the shores of Middle-earth. He does not go in the deeps, but loves the coasts and the isles, and rejoices in the winds of Manwë; for in storm he delights, and laughs amid the roaring of the waves. His spouse is Uinen, the Lady of the Seas, whose hair lies spread through all waters under sky. All creatures she loves that live in the salt streams, and all weeds that grow there; to her mariners cry, for she can lay calm upon the waves, restraining the wildness of Ossë. The Númenóreans lived long in her protection, and held her in reverence equal to the Valar.

Melkor hated the Sea, for he could not subdue it. It is said that in the making of Arda he endeavoured to draw Ossë to his allegiance, promising to him all the realm and power of Ulmo, if he would serve him. So it was that long ago there arose great tumults in the sea that wrought ruin to the lands. But Uinen, at the prayer of Aulë, restrained Ossë and brought him before Ulmo; and he was pardoned and re-turned to his allegiance, to which he has remained faithful. For the most part; for the delight in violence has never wholly departed from him, and at times he will rage in his wilfulness without any command from Ulmo his lord. Therefore those who dwell by the sea or go up in ships may love him, but they do not trust him.

Melian was the name of a Maia who served both Vána and Estë; she dwelt long in Lórien, tending the trees that flower in the gardens of Irmo, ere she came to Middle-earth. Nightingales sang about her wherever she went.

Wisest of the Maiar was Olórin. He too dwelt in Lórien, but his ways took him often to the house of Nienna, and of her he learned pity and patience.

Of Melian much is told in the *Quenta Silmarillion*. But of Olórin that tale does not speak; for though he loved the Elves, he walked among them unseen, or in form as one of them, and they did not know whence came the fair visions or the promptings of wisdom that he put into their hearts. In later days he was the friend of all the Children of Ilúvatar, and took pity on their sorrows; and those who listened to him awoke from despair and put away the imaginations of darkness.

# Of the Enemies

Last of all is set the name of Melkor, He who arises in Might. But that name he has forfeited; and the Noldor, who among the Elves suffered most from his malice, will not utter it, and they name him Morgoth, the Dark Enemy of the World. Great might was given to him by Ilúvatar, and he was coëval with Manwë. In the powers and knowledge of all the other Valar he had part, but he turned them to evil purposes, and squandered his strength in violence and tyranny. For he coveted Arda and all that was in it, desiring the kingship of Manwë and dominion over the realms of his peers.

From splendour he fell through arrogance to contempt for all things save himself, a spirit wasteful and pitiless. Understanding he turned to subtlety in perverting to his own will all that he would use, until he became a liar without shame. He began with the desire of Light, but when he could not possess it for himself alone, he descended through fire and wrath into a great burning, down into Darkness. And darkness he used most in his evil works upon Arda, and filled it with fear for all living things.

Yet so great was the power of his uprising that in ages forgotten he contended with Manwë and all the Valar, and through long years in Arda held dominion over most of the lands of the Earth. But he was not alone. For of the Maiar many were drawn to his splendour in the days of his greatness, and remained in that allegiance down into his darkness; and others he corrupted afterwards to his service with lies and treacherous gifts. Dreadful among these spirits were the Valaraukar, the scourges of fire that in Middle-earth were called the Balrogs, demons of terror.

Among those of his servants that have names the greatest was that spirit whom the Eldar called Sauron, or Gorthaur the Cruel. In his beginning he was of the Maiar of Aulë, and he remained mighty in the lore of that people. In all the deeds of Melkor the Morgoth upon Arda, in his vast works and in the deceits of his cunning, Sauron had a part, and was only less evil than his master in that for long he served another and not himself. But in after years he rose like a shadow of Morgoth and a ghost of his malice, and walked behind him on the same ruinous path down into the Void.

# HERE ENDS THE VALAQUENTA

# QUENTA SILMARILLION

*The History of the
Silmarils*

# Chapter 1

# OF THE BEGINNING OF DAYS

It is told among the wise that the First War began before Arda was full-shaped, and ere yet there was anything that grew or walked upon earth; and for long Melkor had the upper hand. But in the midst of the war a spirit of great strength and hardihood came to the aid of the Valar, hearing in the far heaven that there was battle in the Little Kingdom; and Arda was filled with the sound of his laughter. So came Tulkas the Strong, whose anger passes like a mighty wind, scattering cloud and darkness before it; and Melkor fled before his wrath and his laughter, and forsook Arda, and there was peace for a long age. And Tulkas remained and became one of the Valar of the Kingdom of Arda; but Melkor brooded in the outer darkness, and his hate was given to Tulkas for ever after.

In that time the Valar brought order to the seas and the lands and the mountains, and Yavanna planted at last the seeds that she had long devised. And since, when the fires were subdued or buried beneath the primeval hills, there was need of light, Aulë at the prayer of Yavanna wrought two mighty lamps for the lighting of the Middle-earth which he had built amid the encircling seas. Then Varda filled the lamps and Manwë hallowed them, and the Valar set them upon high pillars, more lofty far than are any mountains of the later days. One lamp they raised near to the north of Middle-earth, and it was named Illuin; and the other was raised in the south, and it was named Ormal; and the light of the Lamps of the Valar flowed out over the Earth, so that all was lit as it were in a changeless day.

Then the seeds that Yavanna had sown began swiftly to sprout and to burgeon, and there arose a multitude of growing things great and small, mosses and grasses and great ferns, and trees whose tops were crowned with cloud as they were living mountains, but whose feet were wrapped in a green twilight. And beasts came forth and dwelt in the grassy plains, or in the rivers and the lakes, or walked in the shadows of the woods. As yet no flower had bloomed nor any bird had sung, for these things waited still their time in the bosom of Yavanna; but wealth there was of her imagining, and nowhere more rich than in the midmost parts of the Earth, where the light of both the Lamps met and blended. And there upon the Isle of Almaren in the Great Lake was the first dwelling of the Valar when all things

35

were young, and new-made green was yet a marvel in the eyes of the makers; and they were long content.

Now it came to pass that while the Valar rested from their labours, and watched the growth and unfolding of the things that they had devised and begun, Manwë ordained a great feast; and the Valar and all their host came at his bidding. But Aulë and Tulkas were weary; for the craft of Aulë and the strength of Tulkas had been at the service of all without ceasing in the days of their labour. And Melkor knew of all that was done, for even then he had secret friends and spies among the Maiar whom he had converted to his cause; and far off in the darkness he was filled with hatred, being jealous of the work of his peers, whom he desired to make subject to himself. Therefore he gathered to himself spirits out of the halls of Eä that he had perverted to his service, and he deemed himself strong. And seeing now his time he drew near again to Arda, and looked down upon it, and the beauty of the Earth in its Spring filled him the more with hate.

Now therefore the Valar were gathered upon Almaren, fearing no evil, and because of the light of Illuin they did not perceive the shadow in the north that was cast from afar by Melkor; for he was grown dark as the Night of the Void. And it is sung that in that feast of the Spring of Arda Tulkas espoused Nessa the sister of Oromë, and she danced before the Valar upon the green grass of Almaren.

Then Tulkas slept, being weary and content, and Melkor deemed that his hour had come. And he passed therefore over the Walls of the Night with his host, and came to Middle-earth far in the north; and the Valar were not aware of him.

Now Melkor began the delving and building of a vast fortress, deep under Earth, beneath dark mountains where the beams of Illuin were cold and dim. That stronghold was named Utumno. And though the Valar knew naught of it as yet, nonetheless the evil of Melkor and the blight of his hatred flowed out thence, and the Spring of Arda was marred. Green things fell sick and rotted, and rivers were choked with weeds and slime, and fens were made, rank and poisonous, the breeding place of flies; and forests grew dark and perilous, the haunts of fear; and beasts became monsters of horn and ivory and dyed the earth with blood. Then the Valar knew indeed that Melkor was at work again, and they sought for his hiding place. But Melkor, trusting in the strength of Utumno and the might of his servants, came forth suddenly to war, and struck the first blow, ere the Valar were prepared; and he assailed the lights of Illuin and Ormal, and cast down their pillars and broke their lamps. In the overthrow of the mighty pillars lands were broken and seas arose in tumult; and when the lamps were spilled destroying flame was poured out over the Earth. And the shape of Arda and the symmetry of its waters and its lands was marred in that time, so that the first designs of the Valar were never after restored.

In the confusion and the darkness Melkor escaped, though fear fell upon him; for above the roaring of the seas he heard the voice of Manwë as a mighty wind, and the earth trembled beneath the feet of Tulkas. But he came to Utumno ere Tulkas could overtake him; and there he lay hid. And the Valar could not at that time overcome him, for the greater part of their strength was needed to restrain the tumults of the Earth, and to save from ruin all that could be saved of their labour; and afterwards they feared to rend the Earth again, until they knew where the Children of Ilúvatar were dwelling, who were yet to come in a time that was hidden from the Valar.

Thus ended the Spring of Arda. The dwelling of the Valar upon Almaren was utterly destroyed, and they had no abiding place upon the face of the Earth. Therefore they departed from Middle-earth and went to the Land of Aman, the westernmost of all lands upon the borders of the world; for its west shores looked upon the Outer Sea, that is called by the Elves Ekkaia, encircling the Kingdom of Arda. How wide is that sea none know but the Valar; and beyond it are the Walls of the Night. But the east shores of Aman were the uttermost end of Belegaer, the Great Sea of the West; and since Melkor was returned to Middle-earth and they could not yet overcome him, the Valar fortified their dwelling, and upon the shores of the sea they raised the Pelóri, the Mountains of Aman, highest upon Earth. And above all the mountains of the Pelóri was that height upon whose summit Manwë set his throne. Taniquetil the Elves name that holy mountain, and Oiolossë Everlasting Whiteness, and Elerrína Crowned with Stars, and many names beside; but the Sindar spoke of it in their later tongue as Amon Uilos. From their halls upon Taniquetil Manwë and Varda could look out across the Earth even into the furthest East.

Behind the walls of the Pelóri the Valar established their domain in that region which is called Valinor; and there were their houses, their gardens, and their towers. In that guarded land the Valar gathered great store of light and all the fairest things that were saved from the ruin; and many others yet fairer they made anew, and Valinor became more beautiful even than Middle-earth in the Spring of Arda; and it was blessed, for the Deathless dwelt there, and there naught faded nor withered, neither was there any stain upon flower or leaf in that land, nor any corruption or sickness in anything that lived; for the very stones and waters were hallowed.

And when Valinor was full-wrought and the mansions of the Valar were established, in the midst of the plain beyond the mountains they built their city, Valmar of many bells. Before its western gate there was a green mound, Ezellohar, that is named also Corollairë; and Yavanna hallowed it, and she sat there long upon the green grass and sang a song of power, in which was set all her thought of things that grow in the earth. But Nienna thought in silence, and watered the mould with tears. In that time the Valar were gathered together to hear the song of Yavanna, and they sat silent upon their thrones of council in the Máhanaxar, the Ring of Doom near to the golden gates of Valmar; and Yavanna Kementári sang before them and they watched.

And as they watched, upon the mound there came forth two slender shoots; and silence was over all the world in that hour, nor was there any other sound save the chanting of Yavanna. Under her song the saplings grew and became fair and tall, and came to flower; and thus there awoke in the world the Two Trees of Valinor. Of all things which Yavanna made they have most renown, and about their fate all the tales of the Elder Days are woven.

The one had leaves of dark green that beneath were as shining silver, and from each of his countless flowers a dew of silver light was ever falling, and the earth beneath was dappled with the shadows of his fluttering leaves. The other bore leaves of a young green like the new-opened beech; their edges were of glittering gold. Flowers swung upon her branches in clusters of yellow flame, formed each to a glowing horn that spilled a golden rain upon the ground; and from the blossom of that tree there came forth warmth and a great light. Telperion the one was called in Valinor, and Silpion, and Ninquelótë, and many other names; but Laurelin the other was, and Malinalda, and Culúrien, and many names in song beside.

In seven hours the glory of each tree waxed to full and waned again to naught; and each awoke once more to life an hour before the other ceased to shine. Thus in Valinor twice every day there came a gentle hour of softer light when both trees were faint and their gold and silver beams were mingled. Telperion was the elder of the trees and came first to full stature and to bloom; and that first hour in which he shone, the white glimmer of a silver dawn, the Valar reckoned not into the tale of hours, but named it the Opening Hour, and counted from it the ages of their reign in Valinor. Therefore at the sixth hour

of the First Day, and of all the joyful days thereafter, until the
Darkening of Valinor, Telperion ceased his time of flower; and at the
twelfth hour Laurelin her blossoming. And each day of the Valar in
Aman contained twelve hours, and ended with the second mingling
of the lights, in which Laurelin was waning but Telperion was waxing.
But the light that was spilled from the trees endured long, ere it was
taken up into the airs or sank down into the earth; and the dews of
Telperion and the rain that fell from Laurelin Varda hoarded in great
vats like shining lakes, that were to all the land of the Valar as wells
of water and of light. Thus began the Days of the Bliss of Valinor;
and thus began also the Count of Time.

But as the ages drew on to the hour appointed by Ilúvatar for the
coming of the Firstborn, Middle-earth lay in a twilight beneath the
stars that Varda had wrought in the ages forgotten of her labours in
Eä. And in the darkness Melkor dwelt, and still often walked abroad,
in many shapes of power and fear, and he wielded cold and fire,
from the tops of the mountains to the deep furnaces that are beneath
them; and whatsoever was cruel or violent or deadly in those days is
laid to his charge.

From the beauty and bliss of Valinor the Valar came seldom over
the mountains to Middle-earth, but gave to the land beyond the
Pelóri their care and their love. And in the midst of the Blessed
Realm were the mansions of Aulë, and there he laboured long. For
in the making of all things in that land he had the chief part, and he
wrought there many beautiful and shapely works both openly and in
secret. Of him comes the lore and knowledge of the Earth and of all
things that it contains: whether the lore of those that make not, but
seek only for the understanding of what is, or the lore of all craftsmen:
the weaver, the shaper of wood, and the worker in metals; and the
tiller and husbandman also, though these last and all that deal with
things that grow and bear fruit must look also to the spouse of Aulë,
Yavanna Kementári. Aulë it is who is named the Friend of the
Noldor, for of him they learned much in after days, and they are the
most skilled of the Elves; and in their own fashion, according to the
gifts which Ilúvatar gave to them, they added much to his teaching,
delighting in tongues and in scripts, and in the figures of broidery, of
drawing, and of carving. The Noldor also it was who first achieved
the making of gems; and the fairest of all gems were the Silmarils,
and they are lost.

But Manwë Súlimo, highest and holiest of the Valar, sat upon the
borders of Aman, forsaking not in his thought the Outer Lands. For

his throne was set in majesty upon the pinnacle of Taniquetil, the highest of the mountains of the world, standing upon the margin of the sea. Spirits in the shape of hawks and eagles flew ever to and from his halls; and their eyes could see to the depths of the seas, and pierce the hidden caverns beneath the world. Thus they brought word to him of well nigh all that passed in Arda; yet some things were hidden even from the eyes of Manwë and the servants of Manwë, for where Melkor sat in his dark thought impenetrable shadows lay.

Manwë has no thought for his own honour, and is not jealous of his power, but rules all to peace. The Vanyar he loved best of all the Elves, and of him they received song and poetry; for poetry is the delight of Manwë, and the song of words is his music. His raiment is blue, and blue is the fire of his eyes, and his sceptre is of sapphire, which the Noldor wrought for him; and he was appointed to be the vicegerent of Ilúvatar, King of the world of Valar and Elves and Men, and the chief defence against the evil of Melkor. With Manwë dwelt Varda the most beautiful, she who in the Sindarin tongue is named Elbereth, Queen of the Valar, maker of the stars; and with them were a great host of spirits in blessedness.

But Ulmo was alone, and he abode not in Valinor, nor ever came thither unless there were need for a great council; he dwelt from the beginning of Arda in the Outer Ocean, and still he dwells there. Thence he governs the flowing of all waters, and the ebbing, the courses of all rivers and the replenishment of springs, the distilling of all dews and rain in every land beneath the sky. In the deep places he gives thought to music great and terrible; and the echo of that music runs through all the veins of the world in sorrow and in joy; for if joyful is the fountain that rises in the sun, its springs are in the wells of sorrow unfathomed at the foundations of the Earth. The Teleri learned much of Ulmo, and for this reason their music has both sadness and enchantment. Salmar came with him to Arda, he who made the horns of Ulmo that none may ever forget who once has heard them; and Ossë and Uinen also, to whom he gave the government of the waves and the movements of the Inner Seas, and many other spirits beside. And thus it was by the power of Ulmo that even under the darkness of Melkor life coursed still through many secret lodes, and the Earth did not die; and to all who were lost in that darkness or wandered far from the light of the Valar the ear of Ulmo was ever open; nor has he ever forsaken Middle-earth, and whatsoever may since have befallen of ruin or of change he has not ceased to take thought for it, and will not until the end of days.

And in that time of dark Yavanna also was unwilling utterly to forsake the Outer Lands; for all things that grow are dear to her, and she mourned for the works that she had begun in Middle-earth but Melkor had marred. Therefore leaving the house of Aulë and the flowering meads of Valinor she would come at times and heal the hurts of Melkor; and returning she would ever urge the Valar to that war with his evil dominion that they must surely wage ere the coming of the Firstborn. And Oromë tamer of beasts would ride too at whiles in the darkness of the unlit forests; as a mighty hunter he came with spear and bow, pursuing to the death the monsters and fell creatures of the kingdom of Melkor, and his white horse Nahar shone like silver in the shadows. Then the sleeping earth trembled at the beat of his golden hooves, and in the twilight of the world Oromë would sound the Valaróma his great horn upon the plains of Arda; whereat the mountains echoed, and the shadows of evil fled away, and Melkor himself quailed in Utumno, foreboding the wrath to come. But even as Oromë passed the servants of Melkor would gather again; and the lands were filled with shadows and deceit.

Now all is said concerning the manner of the Earth and its rulers in the beginning of days, and ere the world became such as the Children of Ilúvatar have known it. For Elves and Men are the Children of Ilúvatar; and since they understood not fully that theme by which the Children entered into the Music, none of the Ainur dared to add anything to their fashion. For which reason the Valar are to these kindreds rather their elders and their chieftains than their masters; and if ever in their dealings with Elves and Men the Ainur have endeavoured to force them when they would not be guided, seldom has this turned to good, howsoever good the intent. The dealings of the Ainur have indeed been mostly with the Elves, for Ilúvatar made them more like in nature to the Ainur, though less in might and stature; whereas to Men he gave strange gifts.

For it is said that after the departure of the Valar there was silence, and for an age Ilúvatar sat alone in thought. Then he spoke and said: 'Behold I love the Earth, which shall be a mansion for the Quendi and the Atani! But the Quendi shall be the fairest of all earthly creatures, and they shall have and shall conceive and bring forth more beauty than all my Children; and they shall have the greater bliss in this world. But to the Atani I will give a new gift.' Therefore he willed that the hearts of Men should seek beyond the world and should find no rest therein; but they should have a virtue to shape their life, amid the powers and chances of the world, beyond the Music of the Ainur, which is as fate to all things else; and of their operation everything should be, in form and deed, completed, and the world fulfilled unto the last and smallest.

But Ilúvatar knew that Men, being set amid the turmoils of the powers of the world, would stray often, and would not use their gifts in harmony; and he said: 'These too in their time shall find that all that they do redounds at the end only to the glory of my work.' Yet the Elves believe that Men are often a grief to Manwë, who knows most of the mind of Ilúvatar; for it seems to the Elves that Men resemble Melkor most of all the Ainur, although he has ever feared and hated them, even those that served him.

It is one with this gift of freedom that the children of Men dwell only a short space in the world alive, and are not bound to it, and depart soon whither the Elves know not. Whereas the Elves remain until the end of days, and their love of the Earth and all the world is more single and more poignant therefore, and as the years lengthen ever more sorrowful. For the Elves die not till the world dies, unless they are slain or waste in grief (and to both these seeming deaths they are subject); neither does age subdue their strength, unless one grow weary of ten thousand centuries; and dying they are gathered to the halls of Mandos in Valinor, whence they may in time return. But the sons of Men die indeed, and leave the world; wherefore they are called the Guests, or the Strangers. Death is their fate, the gift of Ilúvatar, which as Time wears even the Powers shall envy. But Melkor has cast his shadow upon it, and confounded it with darkness, and brought forth evil out of good, and fear out of hope. Yet of old the Valar declared to the Elves in Valinor that Men shall join in the Second Music of the Ainur; whereas Ilúvatar has not revealed what he purposes for the Elves after the World's end, and Melkor has not discovered it.

# Chapter 2

# OF AULË AND YAVANNA

It is told that in their beginning the Dwarves were made by Aulë in the darkness of Middle-earth; for so greatly did Aulë desire the coming of the Children, to have learners to whom he could teach his lore and his crafts, that he was unwilling to await the fulfilment of the designs of Ilúvatar. And Aulë made the Dwarves even as they still are, because the forms of the Children who were to come were unclear to his mind, and because the power of Melkor was yet over the Earth; and he wished therefore that they should be strong and unyielding. But fearing that the other Valar might blame his work, he wrought in secret: and he made first the Seven Fathers of the Dwarves in a hall under the mountains in Middle-earth.

Now Ilúvatar knew what was done, and in the very hour that Aulë's work was complete, and he was pleased, and began to instruct the Dwarves in the speech that he had devised for them, Ilúvatar spoke to him; and Aulë heard his voice and was silent. And the voice of Ilúvatar said to him: 'Why hast thou done this? Why dost thou attempt a thing which thou knowest is beyond thy power and thy authority? For thou hast from me as a gift thy own being only, and no more; and therefore the creatures of thy hand and mind can live only by that being, moving when thou thinkest to move them, and if thy thought be elsewhere, standing idle. Is that thy desire?'

Then Aulë answered: 'I did not desire such lordship. I desired things other than I am, to love and to teach them, so that they too might perceive the beauty of Eä, which thou hast caused to be. For it seemed to me that there is great room in Arda for many things that might rejoice in it, yet it is for the most part empty still, and dumb. And in my impatience I have fallen into folly. Yet the making of things is in my heart from my own making by thee; and the child of little understanding that makes a play of the deeds of his father may do so without thought of mockery, but because he is the son of his father. But what shall I do now, so that thou be not angry with me for ever? As a child to his father, I offer to thee these things, the work of the hands which thou hast made. Do with them what thou wilt. But should I not rather destroy the work of my presumption?'

Then Aulë took up a great hammer to smite the Dwarves; and he wept. But Ilúvatar had compassion upon Aulë and his desire, because of his humility; and the Dwarves shrank from the hammer and were afraid, and they bowed down their heads and begged for mercy. And the voice of Ilúvatar said to Aulë: 'Thy offer I accepted even as it was made. Dost thou not see that these things have now a life of their own, and speak with their own voices? Else they would not have flinched from thy blow, nor from any command of thy will.' Then Aulë cast down his hammer and was glad, and he gave thanks to Ilúvatar, saying: 'May Eru bless my work and amend it!'

But Ilúvatar spoke again and said: 'Even as I gave being to the thoughts of the Ainur at the beginning of the World, so now I have taken up thy desire and given to it a place therein; but in no other way will I amend thy handiwork, and as thou hast made it, so shall it be. But I will not suffer this: that these should come before the Firstborn of my design, nor that thy impatience should be rewarded. They shall sleep now in the darkness under stone, and shall not come forth until the Firstborn have awakened upon Earth; and until that time thou and they shall wait, though long it seem. But when the time comes I will awaken them, and they shall be to thee as children; and often strife shall arise between thine and mine, the children of my adoption and the children of my choice.'

Then Aulë took the Seven Fathers of the Dwarves, and laid them to rest in far-sundered places; and he returned to Valinor, and waited while the long years lengthened.

Since they were to come in the days of the power of Melkor, Aulë made the Dwarves strong to endure. Therefore they are stone-hard, stubborn, fast in friendship and in enmity, and they suffer toil and hunger and hurt of body more hardily than all other speaking peoples; and they live long, far beyond the span of Men, yet not for ever. Aforetime it was held among the Elves in Middle-earth that dying the Dwarves returned to the earth and the stone of which they were made; yet that is not their own belief. For they say that Aulë the Maker, whom they call Mahal, cares for them, and gathers them to Mandos in halls set apart; and that he declared to their Fathers of old that Ilúvatar will hallow them and give them a place among the Children in the End. Then their part shall be to serve Aulë and to aid him in the remaking of Arda after the Last Battle. They say also that the Seven Fathers of the Dwarves return to live again in their own kin and to bear once more their ancient names: of whom Durin was the most renowned in after ages, father of that kindred most friendly to the Elves, whose mansions were at Khazad-dûm.

Now when Aulë laboured in the making of the Dwarves he kept this

OF AULË AND YAVANNA

work hidden from the other Valar; but at last he opened his mind to Yavanna and told her of all that had come to pass. Then Yavanna said to him: 'Eru is merciful. Now I see that thy heart rejoiceth, as indeed it may; for thou hast received not only forgiveness but bounty. Yet because thou hiddest this thought from me until its achievement, thy children will have little love for the things of my love. They will love first the things made by their own hands, as doth their father. They will delve in the earth, and the things that grow and live upon the earth they will not heed. Many a tree shall feel the bite of their iron without pity.'

But Aulë answered: 'That shall also be true of the Children of Ilúvatar; for they will eat and they will build. And though the things of thy realm have worth in themselves, and would have worth if no Children were to come, yet Eru will give them dominion, and they shall use all that they find in Arda: though not, by the purpose of Eru, without respect or without gratitude.'

'Not unless Melkor darken their hearts,' said Yavanna. And she was not appeased, but grieved in heart, fearing what might be done upon Middle-earth in days to come. Therefore she went before Manwë, and she did not betray the counsel of Aulë, but she said: 'King of Arda, is it true, as Aulë hath said to me, that the Children when they come shall have dominion over all the things of my labour, to do as they will therewith?'

'It is true,' said Manwë. 'But why dost thou ask, for thou hadst no need of the teaching of Aulë?'

Then Yavanna was silent and looked into her own thought. And she answered: 'Because my heart is anxious, thinking of the days to come. All my works are dear to me. Is it not enough that Melkor should have marred so many? Shall nothing that I have devised be free from the dominion of others?'

'If thou hadst thy will what wouldst thou reserve?' said Manwë. 'Of all thy realm what dost thou hold dearest?'

'All have their worth,' said Yavanna, 'and each contributes to the worth of the others. But the *kelvar* can flee or defend themselves, whereas the *olvar* that grow cannot. And among these I hold trees dear. Long in the growing, swift shall they be in the felling, and unless they pay toll with fruit upon bough little mourned in their passing. So I see in my thought. Would that the trees might speak on behalf of all things that have roots, and punish those that wrong them!'

'This is a strange thought,' said Manwë.

'Yet it was in the Song,' said Yavanna. 'For while thou wert in the heavens and with Ulmo built the clouds and poured out the rains, I lifted up the branches of great trees to receive them, and some sang to Ilúvatar amid the wind and the rain.'

Then Manwë sat silent, and the thought of Yavanna that she had put into his heart grew and unfolded; and it was beheld by Ilúvatar. Then it seemed to Manwë that the Song rose once more about him, and he heeded now many things therein that though he had heard them he had not heeded before. And at last the Vision was renewed, but it was not now remote, for he was himself within it, and yet he saw that all was upheld by the hand of Ilúvatar; and the hand entered in, and from it came forth many wonders that had until then been hidden from him in the hearts of the Ainur.

Then Manwë awoke, and he went down to Yavanna upon Ezellohar, and he sat beside her beneath the Two Trees. And Manwë said: 'O Kementári, Eru hath spoken, saying: "Do then any of the Valar suppose that I did not hear all the Song, even the least sound of the least voice? Behold! When the Children awake, then the thought of Yavanna will awake also, and it will summon spirits from afar, and they will go among the *kelvar* and the *olvar*, and some will dwell therein, and be held in reverence, and their just anger shall be feared. For a time: while the Firstborn are in their power, and while the Secondborn are young." But dost thou not now remember, Kementári, that thy thought sang not always alone? Did not thy thought and mine meet also, so that we took wing together like great birds that soar above the clouds? That also shall come to be by the heed of Ilúvatar, and before the Children awake there shall go forth with wings like the wind the Eagles of the Lords of the West.'

Then Yavanna was glad, and she stood up, reaching her arms towards the heavens, and she said: 'High shall climb the trees of Kementári, that the Eagles of the King may house therein!'

But Manwë rose also, and it seemed that he stood to such a height that his voice came down to Yavanna as from the paths of the winds.

'Nay,' he said, 'only the trees of Aulë will be tall enough. In the mountains the Eagles shall house, and hear the voices of those who call upon us. But in the forests shall walk the Shepherds of the Trees.'

Then Manwë and Yavanna parted for that time, and Yavanna returned to Aulë; and he was in his smithy, pouring molten metal into a mould. 'Eru is bountiful,' she said. 'Now let thy children beware! For there shall walk a power in the forests whose wrath they will arouse at their peril.'

'Nonetheless they will have need of wood,' said Aulë, and he went on with his smith-work.

# Chapter 3

# OF THE COMING OF THE ELVES
# AND THE CAPTIVITY OF MELKOR

Through long ages the Valar dwelt in bliss in the light of the Trees
beyond the Mountains of Aman, but all Middle-earth lay in a twilight
under the stars. While the Lamps had shone, growth began there
which now was checked, because all was again dark. But already the
oldest living things had arisen: in the seas the great weeds, and on
earth the shadow of great trees; and in the valleys of the night-clad
hills there were dark creatures old and strong. To those lands and
forests the Valar seldom came, save only Yavanna and Oromë; and
Yavanna would walk there in the shadows, grieving because the
growth and promise of the Spring of Arda was stayed. And she set
a sleep upon many things that had arisen in the Spring, so that they
should not age, but should wait for a time of awakening that yet
should be.

But in the north Melkor built his strength, and he slept not, but
watched, and laboured; and the evil things that he had perverted
walked abroad, and the dark and slumbering woods were haunted by
monsters and shapes of dread. And in Utumno he gathered his
demons about him, those spirits who first adhered to him in the days
of his splendour, and became most like him in his corruption: their
hearts were of fire, but they were cloaked in darkness, and terror
went before them; they had whips of flame. Balrogs they were named
in Middle-earth in later days. And in that dark time Melkor bred
many other monsters of divers shapes and kinds that long troubled
the world; and his realm spread now ever southward over Middle-
earth.

And Melkor made also a fortress and armoury not far from the
north-western shores of the sea, to resist any assault that might come
from Aman. That stronghold was commanded by Sauron, lieutenant
of Melkor; and it was named Angband.

It came to pass that the Valar held council, for they became troubled
by the tidings that Yavanna and Oromë brought from the Outer
Lands; and Yavanna spoke before the Valar, saying: 'Ye mighty of
Arda, the Vision of Ilúvatar was brief and soon taken away, so that
maybe we cannot guess within a narrow count of days the hour

47

appointed. Yet be sure of this: the hour approaches, and within this age our hope shall be revealed, and the Children shall awake. Shall we then leave the lands of their dwelling desolate and full of evil? Shall they walk in darkness while we have light? Shall they call Melkor lord while Manwë sits upon Taniquetil?'

And Tulkas cried: 'Nay! Let us make war swiftly! Have we not rested from strife overlong, and is not our strength now renewed? Shall one alone contest with us for ever?'

But at the bidding of Manwë Mandos spoke, and he said: 'In this age the Children of Ilúvatar shall come indeed, but they come not yet. Moreover it is doom that the Firstborn shall come in the darkness, and shall look first upon the stars. Great light shall be for their waning. To Varda ever shall they call at need.'

Then Varda went forth from the council, and she looked out from the height of Taniquetil, and beheld the darkness of Middle-earth beneath the innumerable stars, faint and far. Then she began a great labour, greatest of all the works of the Valar since their coming into Arda. She took the silver dews from the vats of Telperion, and therewith she made new stars and brighter against the coming of the Firstborn; wherefore she whose name out of the deeps of time and the labours of Eä was Tintallë, the Kindler, was called after by the Elves Elentári, Queen of the Stars. Carnil and Luinil, Nénar and Lumbar, Alcarinquë and Elemmírë she wrought in that time, and many other of the ancient stars she gathered together and set as signs in the heavens of Arda: Wilwarin, Telumendil, Soronúmë, and Anarríma; and Menelmacar with his shining belt, that forebodes the Last Battle that shall be at the end of days. And high in the north as a challenge to Melkor she set the crown of seven mighty stars to swing, Valacirca, the Sickle of the Valar and sign of doom.

It is told that even as Varda ended her labours, and they were long, when first Menelmacar strode up the sky and the blue fire of Helluin flickered in the mists above the borders of the world, in that hour the Children of the Earth awoke, the Firstborn of Ilúvatar. By the starlit mere of Cuiviénen, Water of Awakening, they rose from the sleep of Ilúvatar; and while they dwelt yet silent by Cuiviénen their eyes beheld first of all things the stars of heaven. Therefore they have ever loved the starlight, and have revered Varda Elentári above all the Valar.

In the changes of the world the shapes of lands and of seas have been broken and remade; rivers have not kept their courses, neither have mountains remained steadfast; and to Cuiviénen there is no returning. But it is said among the Elves that it lay far off in the east of Middle-earth, and northward, and it was a bay in the Inland Sea of Helcar; and that sea stood where aforetime the roots of the mountain of Illuin had been before Melkor overthrew it. Many waters flowed down thither from heights in the east, and the first sound that was heard by the Elves was the sound of water flowing, and the sound of water falling over stone.

Long they dwelt in their first home by the water under stars, and they walked the Earth in wonder; and they began to make speech and to give names to all things that they perceived. Themselves they named the Quendi, signifying those that speak with voices; for as yet they had met no other living things that spoke or sang.

And on a time it chanced that Oromë rode eastward in his hunting, and he turned north by the shores of Helcar and passed under the shadows of the Orocarni, the Mountains of the East. Then on a sudden Nahar set up a great neighing, and stood still. And Oromë wondered and sat silent, and it seemed to him that in the quiet of the land under the stars he heard afar off many voices singing.

Thus it was that the Valar found at last, as it were by chance, those whom they had so long awaited. And Oromë looking upon the Elves was filled with wonder, as though they were beings sudden and marvellous and unforeseen; for so it shall ever be with the Valar. From without the World, though all things may be forethought in music or foreshown in vision from afar, to those who enter verily into Eä each in its time shall be met at unawares as something new and unforetold.

In the beginning the Elder Children of Ilúvatar were stronger and greater than they have since become; but not more fair, for though the beauty of the Quendi in the days of their youth was beyond all other beauty that Ilúvatar has caused to be, it has not perished, but lives in the West, and sorrow and wisdom have enriched it. And Oromë loved the Quendi, and named them in their own tongue Eldar, the people of the stars; but that name was after borne only by those who followed him upon the westward road.

Yet many of the Quendi were filled with dread at his coming; and this was the doing of Melkor. For by after-knowledge the wise declare that Melkor, ever watchful, was first aware of the awakening of the Quendi, and sent shadows and evil spirits to spy upon them and waylay them. So it came to pass, some years ere the coming of Oromë, that if any of the Elves strayed far abroad, alone or few together, they would often vanish, and never return; and the Quendi said that the Hunter had caught them, and they were afraid. And indeed the most ancient songs of the Elves, of which echoes are

remembered still in the West, tell of the shadow-shapes that walked
in the hills above Cuiviénen, or would pass suddenly over the stars;
and of the dark Rider upon his wild horse that pursued those that
wandered to take them and devour them. Now Melkor greatly hated
and feared the riding of Oromë, and either he sent indeed his dark
servants as riders, or he set lying whispers abroad, for the purpose
that the Quendi should shun Oromë, if ever they should meet.

Thus it was that when Nahar neighed and Oromë indeed came
among them, some of the Quendi hid themselves, and some fled and
were lost. But those that had courage, and stayed, perceived swiftly
that the Great Rider was no shape out of darkness; for the light of
Aman was in his face, and all the noblest of the Elves were drawn
towards it.

But of those unhappy ones who were ensnared by Melkor little is
known of a certainty. For who of the living has descended into the
pits of Utumno, or has explored the darkness of the counsels of
Melkor? Yet this is held true by the wise of Eressëa, that all those of
the Quendi who came into the hands of Melkor, ere Utumno was
broken, were put there in prison, and by slow arts of cruelty were
corrupted and enslaved; and thus did Melkor breed the hideous
race of the Orcs in envy and mockery of the Elves, of whom they were
afterwards the bitterest foes. For the Orcs had life and multiplied
after the manner of the Children of Ilúvatar; and naught that had
life of its own, nor the semblance of life, could ever Melkor make
since his rebellion in the Ainulindalë before the Beginning: so say
the wise. And deep in their dark hearts the Orcs loathed the Master
whom they served in fear, the maker only of their misery. This it may
be was the vilest deed of Melkor, and the most hateful to Ilúvatar.

Oromë tarried a while among the Quendi, and then swiftly he rode
back over land and sea to Valinor and brought the tidings to Valmar;
and he spoke of the shadows that troubled Cuiviénen. Then the
Valar rejoiced, and yet they were in doubt amid their joy; and they
debated long what counsel it were best to take for the guarding of
the Quendi from the shadow of Melkor. But Oromë returned at once
to Middle-earth and abode with the Elves.

Manwë sat long in thought upon Taniquetil, and he sought the
counsel of Ilúvatar. And coming then down to Valmar he summoned
the Valar to the Ring of Doom, and thither came even Ulmo from
the Outer Sea.

Then Manwë said to the Valar: 'This is the counsel of Ilúvatar
in my heart: that we should take up again the mastery of Arda, at

whatsoever cost, and deliver the Quendi from the shadow of Melkor.'
Then Tulkas was glad; but Aulë was grieved, foreboding the hurts
of the world that must come of that strife. But the Valar made ready
and came forth from Aman in strength of war, resolving to assault
the fortresses of Melkor and make an end. Never did Melkor forget
that this war was made for the sake of the Elves, and that they were
the cause of his downfall. Yet they had no part in those deeds, and
they know little of the riding of the might of the West against the
North in the beginning of their days.

Melkor met the onset of the Valar in the North-west of Middle-
earth, and all that region was much broken. But the first victory of
the hosts of the West was swift, and the servants of Melkor fled
before them to Utumno. Then the Valar passed over Middle-earth,
and they set a guard over Cuiviénen; and thereafter the Quendi knew
nothing of the great Battle of the Powers, save that the Earth shook
and groaned beneath them, and the waters were moved, and in the
north there were lights as of mighty fires. Long and grievous was the
siege of Utumno, and many battles were fought before its gates of
which naught but the rumour is known to the Elves. In that time the
shape of Middle-earth was changed, and the Great Sea that sundered
it from Aman grew wide and deep; and it broke in upon the coasts
and made a deep gulf to the southward. Many lesser bays were made
between the Great Gulf and Helcaraxë far in the north, where
Middle-earth and Aman came nigh together. Of these the Bay of Balar
was the chief; and into it the mighty river Sirion flowed down from
the new-raised highlands northwards: Dorthonion, and the mountains
about Hithlum. The lands of the far north were all made desolate in
those days; for there Utumno was delved exceeding deep, and its pits
were filled with fires and with great hosts of the servants of Melkor.

But at the last the gates of Utumno were broken and the halls
unroofed, and Melkor took refuge in the uttermost pit. Then
Tulkas stood forth as champion of the Valar and wrestled with him,
and cast him upon his face; and he was bound with the chain Angainor
that Aulë had wrought, and led captive; and the world had peace for
a long age.

Nonetheless the Valar did not discover all the mighty vaults and
caverns hidden with deceit far under the fortresses of Angband and
Utumno. Many evil things still lingered there, and others were
dispersed and fled into the dark and roamed in the waste places of
the world, awaiting a more evil hour; and Sauron they did not find.

But when the Battle was ended and from the ruin of the North
great clouds arose and hid the stars, the Valar drew Melkor back to

Valinor, bound hand and foot, and blindfold; and he was brought to
the Ring of Doom. There he lay upon his face before the feet of
Manwë and sued for pardon; but his prayer was denied, and he was
cast into prison in the fastness of Mandos, whence none can escape,
neither Vala, nor Elf, nor mortal Man. Vast and strong are those
halls, and they were built in the west of the land of Aman. There was
Melkor doomed to abide for three ages long, before his cause should
be tried anew, or he should plead again for pardon.

Then again the Valar were gathered in council, and they were
divided in debate. For some, and of those Ulmo was the chief, held
that the Quendi should be left free to walk as they would in Middle-
earth, and with their gifts of skill to order all the lands and heal their
hurts. But the most part feared for the Quendi in the dangerous
world amid the deceits of the starlit dusk; and they were filled moreover with the love of the beauty of the Elves and desired their fellowship. At the last, therefore, the Valar summoned the Quendi to Valinor,
there to be gathered at the knees of the Powers in the light of the
Trees for ever; and Mandos broke his silence, saying: 'So it is
doomed.' From this summons came many woes that afterwards befell.

But the Elves were at first unwilling to hearken to the summons,
for they had as yet seen the Valar only in their wrath as they went to
war, save Oromë alone; and they were filled with dread. Therefore
Oromë was sent again to them, and he chose from among them
ambassadors who should go to Valinor and speak for their people;
and these were Ingwë, Finwë, and Elwë, who afterwards were kings.
And coming they were filled with awe by the glory and majesty of
the Valar, and desired greatly the light and splendour of the Trees.
Then Oromë brought them back to Cuiviénen, and they spoke
before their people, and counselled them to heed the summons of
the Valar and remove into the West.

Then befell the first sundering of the Elves. For the kindred of
Ingwë, and the most part of the kindreds of Finwë and Elwë, were
swayed by the words of their lords, and were willing to depart and
follow Oromë; and these were known ever after as the Eldar, by the
name that Oromë gave to the Elves in the beginning, in their own
tongue. But many refused the summons, preferring the starlight and
the wide spaces of Middle-earth to the rumour of the Trees; and
these are the Avari, the Unwilling, and they were sundered in that
time from the Eldar, and met never again until many ages were past.

The Eldar prepared now a great march from their first homes in
the east; and they were arrayed in three hosts. The smallest host and
the first to set forth was led by Ingwë, the most high lord of all the

Elvish race. He entered into Valinor and sits at the feet of the Powers, and all Elves revere his name; but he came never back, nor looked again upon Middle-earth. The Vanyar were his people; they are the Fair Elves, the beloved of Manwë and Varda, and few among Men have spoken with them.

Next came the Noldor, a name of wisdom, the people of Finwë. They are the Deep Elves, the friends of Aulë; and they are renowned in song, for they fought and laboured long and grievously in the northern lands of old.

The greatest host came last, and they are named the Teleri, for they tarried on the road, and were not wholly of a mind to pass from the dusk to the light of Valinor. In water they had great delight, and those that came at last to the western shores were enamoured of the sea. The Sea-elves therefore they became in the land of Aman, the Falmari, for they made music beside the breaking waves. Two lords they had, for their numbers were great: Elwë Singollo (which signifies Greymantle) and Olwë his brother.

These were the three kindreds of the Eldalië, who passing at length into the uttermost West in the days of the Trees are called the Calaquendi, Elves of the Light. But others of the Eldar there were who set out indeed upon the westward march, but became lost upon the long road, or turned aside, or lingered on the shores of Middle-earth; and these were for the most part of the kindred of the Teleri, as is told hereafter. They dwelt by the sea, or wandered in the woods and mountains of the world, yet their hearts were turned towards the West. Those Elves the Calaquendi call the Úmanyar, since they came never to the land of Aman and the Blessed Realm; but the Úmanyar and the Avari alike they call the Moriquendi, Elves of the Darkness, for they never beheld the Light that was before the Sun and Moon.

It is told that when the hosts of the Eldalië departed from Cuiviénen Oromë rode at their head upon Nahar, his white horse shod with gold; and passing northward about the Sea of Helcar they turned towards the west. Before them great clouds hung still black in the North above the ruins of war, and the stars in that region were hidden. Then not a few grew afraid and repented, and turned back, and are forgotten.

Long and slow was the march of the Eldar into the west, for the leagues of Middle-earth were uncounted, and weary and pathless. Nor did the Eldar desire to hasten, for they were filled with wonder at all that they saw, and by many lands and rivers they wished to abide; and though all were yet willing to wander, many feared rather their journey's end than hoped for it. Therefore whenever Oromë departed, having at times other matters to heed, they halted and went forward no more, until he returned to guide them. And it came to pass after many years of journeying in this manner that the Eldar took their course through a forest, and they came to a great river, wider than any they had yet seen; and beyond it were mountains whose sharp horns seemed to pierce the realm of the stars. This river, it is said, was even the river which was after called Anduin the Great, and was ever the frontier of the west-lands of Middle-earth. But the mountains were the Hithaeglir, the Towers of Mist upon the borders of Eriador; yet they were taller and more terrible in those days, and were reared by Melkor to hinder the riding of Oromë. Now the Teleri abode long on the east bank of that river and wished to remain there, but the Vanyar and the Noldor passed over it, and Oromë led them into the passes of the mountains. And when Oromë was gone forward the Teleri looked upon the shadowy heights and were afraid.

Then one arose in the host of Olwë, which was ever the hindmost on the road; Lenwë he was called. He forsook the westward march, and led away a numerous people, southwards down the great river, and they passed out of the knowledge of their kin until long years were past. Those were the Nandor; and they became a people apart, unlike their kin, save that they loved water, and dwelt most beside falls and running streams. Greater knowledge they had of living things, tree and herb, bird and beast, than all other Elves. In after years Denethor, son of Lenwë, turned again west at last, and led a part of that people over the mountains into Beleriand ere the rising of the Moon.

At length the Vanyar and the Noldor came over Ered Luin, the Blue Mountains, between Eriador and the westernmost land of Middle-earth, which the Elves after named Beleriand; and the foremost companies passed over the Vale of Sirion and came down to the shores of the Great Sea between Drengist and the Bay of Balar. But when they beheld it great fear came upon them, and many withdrew into the woods and highlands of Beleriand. Then Oromë departed, and returned to Valinor to seek the counsel of Manwë, and left them.

And the host of the Teleri passed over the Misty Mountains, and crossed the wide lands of Eriador, being urged on by Elwë Singollo, for he was eager to return to Valinor and the Light that he had beheld; and he wished not to be sundered from the Noldor, for he had great friendship with Finwë their lord. Thus after many years the Teleri also came at last over Ered Luin into the eastern regions of Beleriand. There they halted, and dwelt a while beyond the River Gelion.

# Chapter 4

# OF THINGOL AND MELIAN

Melian was a Maia, of the race of the Valar. She dwelt in the gardens of Lórien, and among all his people there were none more beautiful than Melian, nor more wise, nor more skilled in songs of enchantment. It is told that the Valar would leave their works, and the birds of Valinor their mirth, that the bells of Valmar were silent and the fountains ceased to flow, when at the mingling of the lights Melian sang in Lórien. Nightingales went always with her, and she taught them their song; and she loved the deep shadows of the great trees. She was akin before the World was made to Yavanna herself; and in that time when the Quendi awoke beside the waters of Cuiviénen she departed from Valinor and came to the Hither Lands, and there she filled the silence of Middle-earth before the dawn with her voice and the voices of her birds.

Now when their journey was near its end, as has been told, the people of the Teleri rested long in East Beleriand, beyond the River Gelion; and at that time many of the Noldor still lay to the westward, in those forests that were afterwards named Neldoreth and Region. Elwë, lord of the Teleri, went often through the great woods to seek out Finwë his friend in the dwellings of the Noldor; and it chanced on a time that he came alone to the starlit wood of Nan Elmoth, and there suddenly he heard the song of nightingales. Then an enchantment fell on him, and he stood still; and afar off beyond the voices of the *lómelindi* he heard the voice of Melian, and it filled all his heart with wonder and desire. He forgot then utterly all his people and all the purposes of his mind, and following the birds under the shadow of the trees he passed deep into Nan Elmoth and was lost. But he came at last to a glade open to the stars, and there Melian stood; and out of the darkness he looked at her, and the light of Aman was in her face.

She spoke no word; but being filled with love Elwë came to her and took her hand, and straightway a spell was laid on him, so that they stood thus while long years were measured by the wheeling stars above them; and the trees of Nan Elmoth grew tall and dark before they spoke any word.

Thus Elwë's folk who sought him found him not, and Olwë took the kingship of the Teleri and departed, as is told hereafter. Elwë

Singollo came never again across the sea to Valinor so long as he lived, and Melian returned not thither while their realm together lasted; but of her there came among both Elves and Men a strain of the Ainur who were with Ilúvatar before Eä. In after days he became a king renowned, and his people were all the Eldar of Beleriand; the Sindar they were named, the Grey-elves, the Elves of the Twilight, and King Greymantle was he, Elu Thingol in the tongue of that land. And Melian was his Queen, wiser than any child of Middle-earth; and their hidden halls were in Menegroth, the Thousand Caves, in Doriath. Great power Melian lent to Thingol, who was himself great among the Eldar; for he alone of all the Sindar had seen with his own eyes the Trees in the day of their flowering, and king though he was of Úmanyar, he was not accounted among the Moriquendi, but with the Elves of the Light, mighty upon Middle-earth. And of the love of Thingol and Melian there came into the world the fairest of all the Children of Ilúvatar that was or shall ever be.

# Chapter 5

# OF ELDAMAR AND THE PRINCES OF THE ELDALIË

In time the hosts of the Vanyar and the Noldor came to the last western shores of the Hither Lands. In the north these shores, in the ancient days after the Battle of the Powers, bent ever westward, until in the northernmost parts of Arda only a narrow sea divided Aman, upon which Valinor was built, from the Hither Lands; but this narrow sea was filled with grinding ice, because of the violence of the frosts of Melkor. Therefore Oromë did not lead the hosts of the Eldalië into the far north, but brought them to the fair lands about the River Sirion, that afterwards were named Beleriand; and from those shores whence first the Eldar looked in fear and wonder on the Sea there stretched an ocean, wide and dark and deep, between them and the Mountains of Aman.

Now Ulmo, by the counsel of the Valar, came to the shores of Middle-earth and spoke with the Eldar who waited there, gazing on the dark waves; and because of his words and the music which he made for them on his horns of shell their fear of the sea was turned rather to desire. Therefore Ulmo uprooted an island which long had stood alone amid the sea, far from either shore, since the tumults of the fall of Illuin; and with the aid of his servants he moved it, as it were a mighty ship, and anchored it in the Bay of Balar, into which Sirion poured his water. Then the Vanyar and the Noldor embarked upon that isle, and were drawn over the sea, and came at last to the long shores beneath the Mountains of Aman; and they entered Valinor and were welcomed to its bliss. But the eastern horn of the island, which was deep-grounded in the shoals off the mouths of Sirion, was broken asunder and remained behind; and that, it is said, was the Isle of Balar, to which afterwards Ossë often came.

But the Teleri remained still in Middle-earth, for they dwelt in East Beleriand far from the sea, and they heard not the summons of Ulmo until too late; and many searched still for Elwë their lord, and without him they were unwilling to depart. But when they learned that Ingwë and Finwë and their peoples were gone, then many of the Teleri pressed on to the shores of Beleriand, and dwelt thereafter near the Mouths of Sirion, in longing for their friends that had departed; and they took Olwë, Elwë's brother, to be their king. Long they remained by the coasts of the western sea, and Ossë and Uinen came to them and befriended them; and Ossë instructed them, sitting upon a rock near to the margin of the land, and of him they learned all manner of sea-lore and sea-music. Thus it came to be that the Teleri, who were from the beginning lovers of water, and the fairest singers of all the Elves, were after enamoured of the seas, and their songs were filled with the sound of waves upon the shore.

When many years had passed, Ulmo hearkened to the prayers of the Noldor and of Finwë their king, who grieved at their long sundering from the Teleri, and besought him to bring them to Aman, if they would come. And most of them proved now willing indeed; but great was the grief of Ossë when Ulmo returned to the coasts of Beleriand, to bear them away to Valinor; for his care was for the seas of Middle-earth and the shores of the Hither Lands, and he was ill-pleased that the voices of the Teleri should be heard no more in his domain. Some he persuaded to remain; and those were the Falathrim, the Elves of the Falas, who in after days had dwellings at the havens of Brithombar and Eglarest, the first mariners in Middle-earth and the first makers of ships. Círdan the Shipwright was their lord.

The kinsfolk and friends of Elwë Singollo also remained in the Hither Lands, seeking him yet, though they would fain have departed to Valinor and the light of the Trees, if Ulmo and Olwë had been willing to tarry longer. But Olwë would be gone; and at last the main host of the Teleri embarked upon the isle, and Ulmo drew them far away. Then the friends of Elwë were left behind; and they called themselves Eglath, the Forsaken People. They dwelt in the woods and hills of Beleriand, rather than by the sea, which filled them with sorrow; but the desire of Aman was ever in their hearts.

But when Elwë awoke from his long trance, he came forth from Nan Elmoth with Melian, and they dwelt thereafter in the woods in the midst of the land. Greatly though he had desired to see again the light of the Trees, in the face of Melian he beheld the light of Aman as in an unclouded mirror, and in that light he was content. His people gathered about him in joy, and they were amazed; for fair and noble as he had been, now he appeared as it were a lord of the Maiar, his hair as grey silver, tallest of all the Children of Ilúvatar; and a high doom was before him.

Now Ossë followed after the host of Olwë, and when they were come to the Bay of Eldamar (which is Elvenhome) he called to them; and they knew his voice, and begged Ulmo to stay their voyage. And

Ulmo granted their request, and at his bidding Ossë made fast the island and rooted it to the foundations of the sea. Ulmo did this the more readily, for he understood the hearts of the Teleri, and in the council of the Valar he had spoken against the summons, thinking that it were better for the Quendi to remain in Middle-earth. The Valar were little pleased to learn what he had done; and Finwë grieved when the Teleri came not, and yet more when he learned that Elwë was forsaken, and knew that he should not see him again, unless it were in the halls of Mandos. But the island was not moved again, and stood there alone in the Bay of Eldamar; and it was called Tol Eressëa, the Lonely Isle. There the Teleri abode as they wished under the stars of heaven, and yet within sight of Aman and the deathless shore; and by that long sojourn apart in the Lonely Isle was caused the sundering of their speech from that of the Vanyar and the Noldor.

To these the Valar had given a land and a dwelling-place. Even among the radiant flowers of the Tree-lit gardens of Valinor they longed still at times to see the stars; and therefore a gap was made in the great walls of the Pelóri, and there in a deep valley that ran down to the sea the Eldar raised a high green hill: Túna it was called. From the west the light of the Trees fell upon it, and its shadow lay ever eastward; and to the east it looked towards the Bay of Elvenhome, and the Lonely Isle, and the Shadowy Seas. Then through the Calacirya, the Pass of Light, the radiance of the Blessed Realm streamed forth, kindling the dark waves to silver and gold, and it touched the Lonely Isle, and its western shore grew green and fair. There bloomed the first flowers that ever were east of the Mountains of Aman.

Upon the crown of Túna the city of the Elves was built, the white walls and terraces of Tirion; and the highest of the towers of that city was the Tower of Ingwë, Mindon Eldaliéva, whose silver lamp shone far out into the mists of the sea. Few are the ships of mortal Men that have seen its slender beam. In Tirion upon Túna the Vanyar and the Noldor dwelt long in fellowship. And since of all things in Valinor they loved most the White Tree, Yavanna made for them a tree like to a lesser image of Telperion, save that it did not give light of its own being; Galathilion it was named in the Sindarin tongue. This tree was planted in the courts beneath the Mindon and there flourished, and its seedlings were many in Eldamar. Of these one was afterwards planted in Tol Eressëa, and it prospered there, and was named Celeborn; thence came in the fullness of time, as is elsewhere told, Nimloth, the White Tree of Númenor.

Manwë and Varda loved most the Vanyar, the Fair Elves; but the

Noldor were beloved of Aulë, and he and his people came often among them. Great became their knowledge and their skill; yet even greater was their thirst for more knowledge, and in many things they soon surpassed their teachers. They were changeful in speech, for they had great love of words, and sought ever to find names more fit for all things that they knew or imagined. And it came to pass that the masons of the house of Finwë, quarrying in the hills after stone (for they delighted in the building of high towers), first discovered the earth-gems, and brought them forth in countless myriads; and they devised tools for the cutting and shaping of gems, and carved them in many forms. They hoarded them not, but gave them freely, and by their labour enriched all Valinor.

The Noldor afterwards came back to Middle-earth, and this tale tells mostly of their deeds; therefore the names and kinship of their princes may here be told, in that form which these names later bore in the tongue of the Elves of Beleriand.

Finwë was King of the Noldor. The sons of Finwë were Fëanor, and Fingolfin, and Finarfin; but the mother of Fëanor was Míriel Serindë, whereas the mother of Fingolfin and Finarfin was Indis of the Vanyar.

Fëanor was the mightiest in skill of word and of hand, more learned than his brothers; his spirit burned as a flame. Fingolfin was the strongest, the most steadfast, and the most valiant. Finarfin was the fairest, and the most wise of heart; and afterwards he was a friend of the sons of Olwë, lord of the Teleri, and had to wife Eärwen, the swan-maiden of Alqualondë, Olwë's daughter.

The seven sons of Fëanor were Maedhros the tall; Maglor the mighty singer, whose voice was heard far over land and sea; Celegorm the fair, and Caranthir the dark; Curufin the crafty, who inherited most his father's skill of hand; and the youngest Amrod and Amras, who were twin brothers, alike in mood and face. In later days they were great hunters in the woods of Middle-earth; and a hunter also was Celegorm, who in Valinor was a friend of Oromë, and often followed the Vala's horn.

The sons of Fingolfin were Fingon, who was afterwards King of the Noldor in the north of the world, and Turgon, lord of Gondolin; their sister was Aredhel the White. She was younger in the years of the Eldar than her brothers; and when she was grown to full stature and beauty she was tall and strong, and loved much to ride and hunt in the forests. There she was often in the company of the sons of Fëanor, her kin; but to none was her heart's love given. Ar-Feiniel she was called, the White Lady of the Noldor, for she was pale, though her hair was dark, and she was never arrayed but in silver and white.

The sons of Finarfin were Finrod the faithful (who was afterwards named Felagund, Lord of Caves), Orodreth, Angrod, and Aegnor; these four were as close in friendship with the sons of Fingolfin as though they were all brothers. A sister they had, Galadriel, most beautiful of all the house of Finwë; her hair was lit with gold as though it had caught in a mesh the radiance of Laurelin.

Here must be told how the Teleri came at last to the land of Aman. Through a long age they dwelt in Tol Eressëa; but slowly their hearts were changed, and were drawn towards the light that flowed out over the sea to the Lonely Isle. They were torn between the love of the music of the waves upon their shores, and the desire to see again their kindred and to look upon the splendour of Valinor; but in the end desire of the light was the stronger. Therefore Ulmo, submitting to the will of the Valar, sent to them Ossë, their friend, and he though grieving taught them the craft of ship-building; and when their ships were built he brought them as his parting gift many strong-winged swans. Then the swans drew the white ships of the Teleri over the windless sea; and thus at last and latest they came to Aman and the shores of Eldamar.

There they dwelt, and if they wished they could see the light of the Trees, and could tread the golden streets of Valmar and the crystal stairs of Tirion upon Túna, the green hill; but most of all they sailed in their swift ships on the waters of the Bay of Elvenhome, or walked in the waves upon the shore with their hair gleaming in the light beyond the hill. Many jewels the Noldor gave them, opals and diamonds and pale crystals, which they strewed upon the shores and scattered in the pools; marvellous were the beaches of Elendë in those days. And many pearls they won for themselves from the sea, and their halls were of pearl, and of pearl were the mansions of Olwë at Alqualondë, the Haven of the Swans, lit with many lamps. For that was their city, and the haven of their ships; and those were made in the likeness of swans, with beaks of gold and eyes of gold and jet. The gate of that harbour was an arch of living rock sea-carved; and it lay upon the confines of Eldamar, north of the Calacirya, where the light of the stars was bright and clear.

As the ages passed the Vanyar grew to love the land of the Valar and the full light of the Trees, and they forsook the city of Tirion upon Túna, and dwelt thereafter upon the mountain of Manwë, or about the plains and woods of Valinor, and became sundered from the Noldor. But the memory of Middle-earth under the stars remained in the hearts of the Noldor, and they abode in the Calacirya, and in the hills and valleys within sound of the western sea; and though many of them went often about the land of the Valar, making far journeys in search of the secrets of land and water and all living things, yet the peoples of Túna and Alqualondë drew together in those days. Finwë was king in Tirion and Olwë in Alqualondë; but Ingwë was ever held the High King of all the Elves. He abode thereafter at the feet of Manwë upon Taniquetil.

Fëanor and his sons abode seldom in one place for long, but travelled far and wide upon the confines of Valinor, going even to the borders of the Dark and the cold shores of the Outer Sea, seeking the unknown. Often they were guests in the halls of Aulë; but Celegorm went rather to the house of Oromë, and there he got great knowledge of birds and beasts, and all their tongues he knew. For all living things that are or have been in the Kingdom of Arda, save only the fell and evil creatures of Melkor, lived then in the land of Aman; and there also were many other creatures that have not been seen upon Middle-earth, and perhaps never now shall be, since the fashion of the world was changed.

## Chapter 6

# OF FËANOR AND THE
# UNCHAINING OF MELKOR

Now the Three Kindreds of the Eldar were gathered at last in Valinor, and Melkor was chained. This was the Noontide of the Blessed Realm, the fullness of its glory and its bliss, long in tale of years, but in memory too brief. In those days the Eldar became full-grown in stature of body and of mind, and the Noldor advanced ever in skill and knowledge; and the long years were filled with their joyful labours, in which many new things fair and wonderful were devised. Then it was that the Noldor first bethought them of letters, and Rúmil of Tirion was the name of the loremaster who first achieved fitting signs for the recording of speech and song, some for graving upon metal or in stone, others for drawing with brush or with pen.

In that time was born in Eldamar, in the house of the King in Tirion upon the crown of Túna, the eldest of the sons of Finwë, and the most beloved. Curufinwë was his name, but by his mother he was called Fëanor, Spirit of Fire; and thus he is remembered in all the tales of the Noldor.

Míriel was the name of his mother, who was called Serindë, because of her surpassing skill in weaving and needlework; for her hands were more skilled to fineness than any hands even among the Noldor. The love of Finwë and Míriel was great and glad, for it began in the Blessed Realm in the Days of Bliss. But in the bearing of her son Míriel was consumed in spirit and body; and after his birth she yearned for release from the labour of living. And when she had named him, she said to Finwë: 'Never again shall I bear child; for strength that would have nourished the life of many has gone forth into Fëanor.'

Then Finwë was grieved, for the Noldor were in the youth of their days, and he desired to bring forth many children into the bliss of Aman; and he said: 'Surely there is healing in Aman? Here all weariness can find rest.' But when Míriel languished still, Finwë sought the counsel of Manwë, and Manwë delivered her to the care of Irmo in Lórien. At their parting (for a little while as he thought) Finwë was sad, for it seemed an unhappy chance that the mother should depart and miss the beginning at least of the childhood days of her son.

'It is indeed unhappy,' said Míriel, 'and I would weep, if I were not so weary. But hold me blameless in this, and in all that may come after.'

She went then to the gardens of Lórien and lay down to sleep; but though she seemed to sleep, her spirit indeed departed from her body, and passed in silence to the halls of Mandos. The maidens of Estë tended the body of Míriel, and it remained unwithered; but she did not return. Then Finwë lived in sorrow; and he went often to the gardens of Lórien, and sitting beneath the silver willows beside the body of his wife he called her by her names. But it was unavailing; and alone in all the Blessed Realm he was deprived of joy. After a while he went to Lórien no more.

All his love he gave thereafter to his son; and Fëanor grew swiftly, as if a secret fire were kindled within him. He was tall, and fair of face, and masterful, his eyes piercingly bright and his hair raven-dark; in the pursuit of all his purposes eager and steadfast. Few ever changed his courses by counsel, none by force. He became of all the Noldor, then or after, the most subtle in mind and the most skilled in hand. In his youth, bettering the work of Rúmil, he devised those letters which bear his name, and which the Eldar used ever after; and he it was who, first of the Noldor, discovered how gems greater and brighter than those of the Earth might be made with skill. The first gems that Fëanor made were white and colourless, but being set under starlight they would blaze with blue and silver fires brighter than Helluin; and other crystals he made also, wherein things far away could be seen small but clear, as with the eyes of the eagles of Manwë. Seldom were the hands and mind of Fëanor at rest.

While still in his early youth he wedded Nerdanel, the daughter of a great smith named Mahtan, among those of the Noldor most dear to Aulë; and of Mahtan he learned much of the making of things in metal and in stone. Nerdanel also was firm of will, but more patient than Fëanor, desiring to understand minds rather than to master them, and at first she restrained him when the fire of his heart grew too hot; but his later deeds grieved her, and they became estranged. Seven sons she bore to Fëanor; her mood she bequeathed in part to some of them, but not to all.

Now it came to pass that Finwë took as his second wife Indis the Fair. She was a Vanya, close kin of Ingwë the High King, golden-haired and tall, and in all ways unlike Míriel. Finwë loved her greatly, and was glad again. But the shadow of Míriel did not depart from the house of Finwë, nor from his heart; and of all whom he loved Fëanor had ever the chief share of his thought.

The wedding of his father was not pleasing to Fëanor; and he had no great love for Indis, nor for Fingolfin and Finarfin, her sons. He lived apart from them, exploring the land of Aman, or busying himself with the knowledge and the crafts in which he delighted. In those unhappy things which later came to pass, and in which Fëanor was the leader, many saw the effect of this breach within the house of Finwë, judging that if Finwë had endured his loss and been content with the fathering of his mighty son, the courses of Fëanor would have been otherwise, and great evil might have been prevented; for the sorrow and the strife in the house of Finwë is graven in the memory of the Noldorin Elves. But the children of Indis were great and glorious, and their children also; and if they had not lived the history of the Eldar would have been diminished.

Now even while Fëanor and the craftsmen of the Noldor worked with delight, foreseeing no end to their labours, and while the sons of Indis grew to their full stature, the Noontide of Valinor was drawing to its close. For it came to pass that Melkor, as the Valar had decreed, completed the term of his bondage, dwelling for three ages in the duress of Mandos, alone. At length, as Manwë had promised, he was brought again before the thrones of the Valar. Then he looked upon their glory and their bliss, and envy was in his heart; he looked upon the Children of Ilúvatar that sat at the feet of the Mighty, and hatred filled him; he looked upon the wealth of bright gems, and he lusted for them; but he hid his thoughts, and postponed his vengeance.

Before the gates of Valmar Melkor abased himself at the feet of Manwë and sued for pardon, vowing that if he might be made only the least of the free people of Valinor he would aid the Valar in all their works, and most of all in the healing of the many hurts that he had done to the world. And Nienna aided his prayer; but Mandos was silent.

Then Manwë granted him pardon; but the Valar would not yet suffer him to depart beyond their sight and vigilance, and he was constrained to dwell within the gates of Valmar. But fair-seeming were all the words and deeds of Melkor in that time, and both the Valar and the Eldar had profit from his aid and counsel, if they sought it; and therefore in a while he was given leave to go freely about the land, and it seemed to Manwë that the evil of Melkor was cured. For Manwë was free from evil and could not comprehend it, and he knew that in the beginning, in the thought of Ilúvatar, Melkor had been even as he; and he saw not to the depths of Melkor's heart, and did not perceive that all love had departed from him for ever. But Ulmo was not deceived, and Tulkas clenched his hands whenever he saw Melkor his foe go by; for if Tulkas is slow to wrath he is slow also to forget. But they obeyed the judgement of Manwë; for those who will defend authority against rebellion must not themselves rebel.

Now in his heart Melkor most hated the Eldar, both because they were fair and joyful and because in them he saw the reason for the arising of the Valar, and his own downfall. Therefore all the more did he feign love for them and seek their friendship, and he offered them the service of his lore and labour in any great deed that they would do. The Vanyar indeed held him in suspicion, for they dwelt in the light of the Trees and were content; and to the Teleri he gave small heed, thinking them of little worth, tools too weak for his designs. But the Noldor took delight in the hidden knowledge that he could reveal to them; and some hearkened to words that it would have been better for them never to have heard. Melkor indeed declared afterwards that Fëanor had learned much art from him in secret, and had been instructed by him in the greatest of all his works; but he lied in his lust and his envy, for none of the Eldalië ever hated Melkor more than Fëanor son of Finwë, who first named him Morgoth; and snared though he was in the webs of Melkor's malice against the Valar he held no converse with him and took no counsel from him. For Fëanor was driven by the fire of his own heart only, working ever swiftly and alone; and he asked the aid and sought the counsel of none that dwelt in Aman, great or small, save only and for a little while of Nerdanel the wise, his wife.

# Chapter 7

## OF THE SILMARILS AND THE UNREST OF THE NOLDOR

In that time were made those things that afterwards were most renowned of all the works of the Elves. For Fëanor, being come to his full might, was filled with a new thought, or it may be that some shadow of foreknowledge came to him of the doom that drew near; and he pondered how the light of the Trees, the glory of the Blessed Realm, might be preserved imperishable. Then he began a long and secret labour, and he summoned all his lore, and his power, and his subtle skill; and at the end of all he made the Silmarils.

As three great jewels they were in form. But not until the End, when Fëanor shall return who perished ere the Sun was made, and sits now in the Halls of Awaiting and comes no more among his kin; not until the Sun passes and the Moon falls, shall it be known of what substance they were made. Like the crystal of diamonds it appeared, and yet was more strong than adamant, so that no violence could mar it or break it within the Kingdom of Arda. Yet that crystal was to the Silmarils but as is the body to the Children of Ilúvatar: the house of its inner fire, that is within it and yet in all parts of it, and is its life. And the inner fire of the Silmarils Fëanor made of the blended light of the Trees of Valinor, which lives in them yet, though the Trees have long withered and shine no more. Therefore even in the darkness of the deepest treasury the Silmarils of their own radiance shone like the stars of Varda; and yet, as were they indeed living things, they rejoiced in light and received it and gave it back in hues more marvellous than before.

All who dwelt in Aman were filled with wonder and delight at the work of Fëanor. And Varda hallowed the Silmarils, so that thereafter no mortal flesh, nor hands unclean, nor anything of evil will might touch them, but it was scorched and withered; and Mandos foretold that the fates of Arda, earth, sea, and air, lay locked within them. The heart of Fëanor was fast bound to these things that he himself had made.

Then Melkor lusted for the Silmarils, and the very memory of their radiance was a gnawing fire in his heart. From that time forth, inflamed by this desire, he sought ever more eagerly how he should destroy Fëanor and end the friendship of the Valar and the Elves;

but he dissembled his purposes with cunning, and nothing of his malice could yet be seen in the semblance that he wore. Long was he at work, and slow at first and barren was his labour. But he that sows lies in the end shall not lack of a harvest, and soon he may rest from toil indeed while others reap and sow in his stead. Ever Melkor found some ears that would heed him, and some tongues that would enlarge what they had heard; and his lies passed from friend to friend, as secrets of which the knowledge proves the teller wise. Bitterly did the Noldor atone for the folly of their open ears in the days that followed after.

When he saw that many leaned towards him, Melkor would often walk among them, and amid his fair words others were woven, so subtly that many who heard them believed in recollection that they arose from their own thought. Visions he would conjure in their hearts of the mighty realms that they could have ruled at their own will, in power and freedom in the East; and then whispers went abroad that the Valar had brought the Eldar to Aman because of their jealousy, fearing that the beauty of the Quendi and the makers' power that Ilúvatar had bequeathed to them would grow too great for the Valar to govern, as the Elves waxed and spread over the wide lands of the world.

In those days, moreover, though the Valar knew indeed of the coming of Men that were to be, the Elves as yet knew naught of it; for Manwë had not revealed it to them. But Melkor spoke to them in secret of Mortal Men, seeing how the silence of the Valar might be twisted to evil. Little he knew yet concerning Men, for engrossed with his own thought in the Music he had paid small heed to the Third Theme of Ilúvatar; but now the whisper went among the Elves that Manwë held them captive, so that Men might come and supplant them in the kingdoms of Middle-earth, for the Valar saw that they might more easily sway this short-lived and weaker race, defrauding the Elves of the inheritance of Ilúvatar. Small truth was there in this, and little have the Valar ever prevailed to sway the wills of Men; but many of the Noldor believed, or half believed, the evil words.

Thus ere the Valar were aware, the peace of Valinor was poisoned. The Noldor began to murmur against them, and many became filled with pride, forgetting how much of what they had and knew came to them in gift from the Valar. Fiercest burned the new flame of desire for freedom and wider realms in the eager heart of Fëanor; and Melkor laughed in his secrecy, for to that mark his lies had been addressed, hating Fëanor above all, and lusting ever for the Silmarils.

But these he was not suffered to approach; for though at great feasts Fëanor would wear them, blazing on his brow, at other times they were guarded close, locked in the deep chambers of his hoard in Tirion. For Fëanor began to love the Silmarils with a greedy love, and grudged the sight of them to all save to his father and his seven sons; he seldom remembered now that the light within them was not his own.

High princes were Fëanor and Fingolfin, the elder sons of Finwë, honoured by all in Aman; but now they grew proud and jealous each of his rights and his possessions. Then Melkor set new lies abroad in Eldamar, and whispers came to Fëanor that Fingolfin and his sons were plotting to usurp the leadership of Finwë and of the elder line of Fëanor, and to supplant them by the leave of the Valar; for the Valar were ill-pleased that the Silmarils lay in Tirion and were not committed to their keeping. But to Fingolfin and Finarfin it was said: 'Beware! Small love has the proud son of Míriel ever had for the children of Indis. Now he has become great, and he has his father in his hand. It will not be long before he drives you forth from Túna!'

And when Melkor saw that these lies were smouldering, and that pride and anger were awake among the Noldor, he spoke to them concerning weapons; and in that time the Noldor began the smithying of swords and axes and spears. Shields also they made displaying the tokens of many houses and kindreds that vied one with another; and these only they wore abroad, and of other weapons they did not speak, for each believed that he alone had received the warning. And Fëanor made a secret forge, of which not even Melkor was aware; and there he tempered fell swords for himself and for his sons, and made tall helms with plumes of red. Bitterly did Mahtan rue the day when he taught to the husband of Nerdanel all the lore of metalwork that he had learned of Aulë.

Thus with lies and evil whisperings and false counsel Melkor kindled the hearts of the Noldor to strife; and of their quarrels came at length the end of the high days of Valinor and the evening of its ancient glory. For Fëanor now began openly to speak words of rebellion against the Valar, crying aloud that he would depart from Valinor back to the world without, and would deliver the Noldor from thraldom, if they would follow him.

Then there was great unrest in Tirion, and Finwë was troubled; and he summoned all his lords to council. But Fingolfin hastened to his halls and stood before him, saying: 'King and father, wilt thou not restrain the pride of our brother, Curufinwë, who is called the

Spirit of Fire, all too truly? By what right does he speak for all our people, as if he were King? Thou it was who long ago spoke before the Quendi, bidding them accept the summons of the Valar to Aman. Thou it was that led the Noldor upon the long road through the perils of Middle-earth to the light of Eldamar. If thou dost not now repent of it, two sons at least thou hast to honour thy words.'

But even as Fingolfin spoke, Fëanor strode into the chamber, and he was fully armed: his high helm upon his head, and at his side a mighty sword. 'So it is, even as I guessed,' he said. 'My half-brother would be before me with my father, in this as in all other matters.' Then turning upon Fingolfin he drew his sword, crying: 'Get thee gone, and take thy due place!'

Fingolfin bowed before Finwë, and without word or glance to Fëanor he went from the chamber. But Fëanor followed him, and at the door of the king's house he stayed him; and the point of his bright sword he set against Fingolfin's breast. 'See, half-brother!' he said. 'This is sharper than thy tongue. Try but once more to usurp my place and the love of my father, and maybe it will rid the Noldor of one who seeks to be the master of thralls.'

These words were heard by many, for the house of Finwë was in the great square beneath the Mindon; but again Fingolfin made no answer, and passing through the throng in silence he went to seek Finarfin his brother.

Now the unrest of the Noldor was not indeed hidden from the Valar, but its seed had been sown in the dark; and therefore, since Fëanor first spoke openly against them, they judged that he was the mover of discontent, being eminent in self-will and arrogance, though all the Noldor had become proud. And Manwë was grieved, but he watched and said no word. The Valar had brought the Eldar to their land freely, to dwell or to depart; and though they might judge departure to be folly, they might not restrain them from it. But now the deeds of Fëanor could not be passed over, and the Valar were angered and dismayed; and he was summoned to appear before them at the gates of Valmar, to answer for all his words and deeds. There also were summoned all others who had any part in this matter, or any knowledge of it; and Fëanor standing before Mandos in the Ring of Doom was commanded to answer all that was asked of him. Then at last the root was laid bare, and the malice of Melkor revealed; and straightway Tulkas left the council to lay hands upon him and bring him again to judgement. But Fëanor was not held guiltless, for he it was that had broken the peace of Valinor and drawn his sword upon his kinsman; and Mandos said to him: 'Thou speakest of thraldom. If thraldom it be, thou canst not escape it; for Manwë is King of Arda, and not of Aman only. And this deed was unlawful, whether in Aman or not in Aman. Therefore this doom is now made: for twelve years thou shalt leave Tirion where this threat was uttered. In that time take counsel with thyself, and remember who and what thou art. But after that time this matter shall be set in peace and held redressed, if others will release thee.'

Then Fingolfin said: 'I will release my brother.' But Fëanor spoke no word in answer, standing silent before the Valar. Then he turned and left the council, and departed from Valmar.

With him into banishment went his seven sons, and northward in Valinor they made a strong place and treasury in the hills; and there at Formenos a multitude of gems were laid in hoard, and weapons also, and the Silmarils were shut in a chamber of iron. Thither also came Finwë the King, because of the love that he bore to Fëanor; and Fingolfin ruled the Noldor in Tirion. Thus the lies of Melkor were made true in seeming, though Fëanor by his own deeds had brought this thing to pass; and the bitterness that Melkor had sown endured, and lived still long afterwards between the sons of Fingolfin and Fëanor.

Now Melkor, knowing that his devices had been revealed, hid himself and passed from place to place as a cloud in the hills; and Tulkas sought for him in vain. Then it seemed to the people of Valinor that the light of the Trees was dimmed, and the shadows of all standing things grew longer and darker in that time.

It is told that for a time Melkor was not seen again in Valinor, nor was any rumour heard of him, until suddenly he came to Formenos, and spoke with Fëanor before his doors. Friendship he feigned with cunning argument, urging him to his former thought of flight from the trammels of the Valar; and he said: 'Behold the truth of all that I have spoken, and how thou art banished unjustly. But if the heart of Fëanor is yet free and bold as were his words in Tirion, then I will aid him, and bring him far from this narrow land. For am I not Vala also? Yea, and more than those who sit in pride in Valimar; and I have ever been a friend to the Noldor, most skilled and most valiant of the people of Arda.'

Now Fëanor's heart was still bitter at his humiliation before Mandos, and he looked at Melkor in silence, pondering if indeed he might yet trust him so far as to aid him in his flight. And Melkor, seeing that Fëanor wavered, and knowing that the Silmarils held his heart in thrall, said at the last: 'Here is a strong place, and well guarded; but think not that the Silmarils will lie safe in any treasury within the realm of the Valar!'

But his cunning overreached his aim; his words touched too deep, and awoke a fire more fierce than he designed; and Fëanor looked upon Melkor with eyes that burned through his fair semblance and pierced the cloaks of his mind, perceiving there his fierce lust for the Silmarils. Then hate overcame Fëanor's fear, and he cursed Melkor and bade him be gone, saying: 'Get thee gone from my gate, thou jail-crow of Mandos!' And he shut the doors of his house in the face of the mightiest of all the dwellers in Eä.

Then Melkor departed in shame, for he was himself in peril, and he saw not his time yet for revenge; but his heart was black with anger. And Finwë was filled with great fear, and in haste he sent messengers to Manwë in Valmar.

Now the Valar were sitting in council before their gates, fearing the lengthening of the shadows, when the messengers came from Formenos. At once Oromë and Tulkas sprang up, but even as they set out in pursuit messengers came from Eldamar, telling that Melkor had fled through the Calacirya, and from the hill of Túna the Elves had seen him pass in wrath as a thundercloud. And they said that thence he had turned northward, for the Teleri in Alqualondë had seen his shadow going by their haven towards Araman.

Thus Melkor departed from Valinor, and for a while the Two Trees shone again unshadowed, and the land was filled with light. But the Valar sought in vain for tidings of their enemy; and as a cloud far off that looms ever higher, borne upon a slow cold wind, a doubt now marred the joy of all the dwellers in Aman, dreading they knew not what evil that yet might come.

## Chapter 8

# OF THE DARKENING OF VALINOR

When Manwë heard of the ways that Melkor had taken, it seemed plain to him that he purposed to escape to his old strongholds in the north of Middle-earth; and Oromë and Tulkas went with all speed northward, seeking to overtake him if they might, but they found no trace or rumour of him beyond the shores of the Teleri, in the unpeopled wastes that drew near to the Ice. Thereafter the watch was redoubled along the northern fences of Aman; but to no purpose, for ere ever the pursuit set out Melkor had turned back, and in secrecy passed away far to the south. For he was yet as one of the Valar, and could change his form, or walk unclad, as could his brethren; though that power he was soon to lose for ever.

Thus unseen he came at last to the dark region of Avathar. That narrow land lay south of the Bay of Eldamar, beneath the eastern feet of the Pelóri, and its long and mournful shores stretched away into the south, lightless and unexplored. There, beneath the sheer walls of the mountains and the cold dark sea, the shadows were deepest and thickest in the world; and there in Avathar, secret and unknown, Ungoliant had made her abode. The Eldar knew not whence she came; but some have said that in ages long before she descended from the darkness that lies about Arda, when Melkor first looked down in envy upon the Kingdom of Manwë, and that in the beginning she was one of those that he corrupted to his service. But she had disowned her Master, desiring to be mistress of her own lust, taking all things to herself to feed her emptiness; and she fled to the south, escaping the assaults of the Valar and the hunters of Oromë, for their vigilance had ever been to the north, and the south was long unheeded. Thence she had crept towards the light of the Blessed Realm; for she hungered for light and hated it.

In a ravine she lived, and took shape as a spider of monstrous form, weaving her black webs in a cleft of the mountains. There she sucked up all light that she could find, and spun it forth again in dark nets of strangling gloom, until no light more could come to her abode; and she was famished.

Now Melkor came to Avathar and sought her out; and he put on again the form that he had worn as the tyrant of Utumno: a dark Lord, tall and terrible. In that form he remained ever after. There in the

73

black shadows, beyond the sight even of Manwë in his highest halls, Melkor with Ungoliant plotted his revenge. But when Ungoliant understood the purpose of Melkor, she was torn between lust and great fear; for she was loath to dare the perils of Aman and the power of the dreadful Lords, and she would not stir from her hiding. Therefore Melkor said to her: 'Do as I bid; and if thou hunger still when all is done, then I will give thee whatsoever thy lust may demand. Yea, with both hands.' Lightly he made this vow, as he ever did; and he laughed in his heart. Thus did the great thief set his lure for the lesser.

A cloak of darkness she wove about them when Melkor and Ungoliant set forth: an Unlight, in which things seemed to be no more, and which eyes could not pierce, for it was void. Then slowly she wrought her webs: rope by rope from cleft to cleft, from jutting rock to pinnacle of stone, ever climbing upwards, crawling and clinging, until at last she reached the very summit of Hyarmentir, the highest mountain in that region of the world, far south of great Taniquetil. There the Valar were not vigilant; for west of the Pelóri was an empty land in twilight, and eastward the mountains looked out, save for forgotten Avathar, only upon the dim waters of the pathless sea.

But now upon the mountain-top dark Ungoliant lay; and she made a ladder of woven ropes and cast it down, and Melkor climbed upon it and came to that high place, and stood beside her, looking down upon the Guarded Realm. Below them lay the woods of Oromë, and westward shimmered the fields and pastures of Yavanna, gold beneath the tall wheat of the gods. But Melkor looked north, and saw afar the shining plain, and the silver domes of Valmar gleaming in the mingling of the lights of Telperion and Laurelin. Then Melkor laughed aloud, and leapt swiftly down the long western slopes; and Ungoliant was at his side, and her darkness covered them.

Now it was a time of festival, as Melkor knew well. Though all tides and seasons were at the will of the Valar, and in Valinor there was no winter of death, nonetheless they dwelt then in the Kingdom of Arda, and that was but a small realm in the halls of Eä, whose life is Time, which flows ever from the first note to the last chord of Eru. And even as it was then the delight of the Valar (as is told in the *Ainulindalë*) to clothe themselves as in a vesture in the forms of the Children of Ilúvatar, so also did they eat and drink, and gather the fruits of Yavanna from the Earth, which under Eru they had made.

Therefore Yavanna set times for the flowering and the ripening of all things that grew in Valinor; and at each first gathering of fruits

Manwë made a high feast for the praising of Eru, when all the peoples of Valinor poured forth their joy in music and song upon Taniquetil. This now was the hour, and Manwë decreed a feast more glorious than any that had been held since the coming of the Eldar to Aman. For though the escape of Melkor portended toils and sorrows to come, and indeed none could tell what further hurts would be done to Arda ere he could be subdued again, at this time Manwë designed to heal the evil that had arisen among the Noldor; and all were bidden to come to his halls upon Taniquetil, there to put aside the griefs that lay between their princes, and forget utterly the lies of their Enemy.

There came the Vanyar, and there came the Noldor of Tirion, and the Maiar were gathered together, and the Valar were arrayed in their beauty and majesty; and they sang before Manwë and Varda in their lofty halls, or danced upon the green slopes of the Mountain that looked west towards the Trees. In that day the streets of Valmar were empty, and the stairs of Tirion were silent; and all the land lay sleeping in peace. Only the Teleri beyond the mountains still sang upon the shores of the sea; for they recked little of seasons or times, and gave no thought to the cares of the Rulers of Arda, or the shadow that had fallen on Valinor, for it had not touched them, as yet.

One thing only marred the design of Manwë. Fëanor came indeed, for him alone Manwë had commanded to come; but Finwë came not, nor any others of the Noldor of Formenos. For said Finwë: 'While the ban lasts upon Fëanor my son, that he may not go to Tirion, I hold myself unkinged, and I will not meet my people.' And Fëanor came not in raiment of festival, and he wore no ornament, neither silver nor gold nor any gem; and he denied the sight of the Silmarils to the Valar and the Eldar, and left them locked in Formenos in their chamber of iron. Nevertheless he met Fingolfin before the throne of Manwë, and was reconciled, in word; and Fingolfin set at naught the unsheathing of the sword. For Fingolfin held forth his hand, saying: 'As I promised, I do now. I release thee, and remember no grievance.'

Then Fëanor took his hand in silence; but Fingolfin said: 'Half-brother in blood, full brother in heart will I be. Thou shalt lead and I will follow. May no new grief divide us.'

'I hear thee,' said Fëanor. 'So be it.' But they did not know the meaning that their words would bear.

It is told that even as Fëanor and Fingolfin stood before Manwë there came the mingling of the lights, when both Trees were shining, and the silent city of Valmar was filled with a radiance of silver and gold. And in that very hour Melkor and Ungoliant came hastening over the fields of Valinor, as the shadow of a black cloud upon the wind fleets over the sunlit earth; and they came before the green mound Ezellohar. Then the Unlight of Ungoliant rose up even to the roots of the Trees, and Melkor sprang upon the mound; and with his black spear he smote each Tree to its core, wounded them deep, and their sap poured forth as it were their blood, and was spilled upon the ground. But Ungoliant sucked it up, and going then from Tree to Tree she set her black beak to their wounds, till they were drained; and the poison of Death that was in her went into their tissues and withered them, root, branch, and leaf; and they died. And still she thirsted, and going to the Wells of Varda she drank them dry; but Ungoliant belched forth black vapours as she drank, and swelled to a shape so vast and hideous that Melkor was afraid.

So the great darkness fell upon Valinor. Of the deeds of that day much is told in the *Aldudénië*, that Elemmírë of the Vanyar made and is known to all the Eldar. Yet no song or tale could contain all the grief and terror that then befell. The Light failed; but the Darkness that followed was more than loss of light. In that hour was made a Darkness that seemed not lack but a thing with being of its own: for it was indeed made by malice out of Light, and it had power to pierce the eye, and to enter heart and mind, and strangle the very will.

Varda looked down from Taniquetil, and beheld the Shadow soaring up in sudden towers of gloom; Valmar had foundered in a deep sea of night. Soon the Holy Mountain stood alone, a last island in a world that was drowned. All song ceased. There was silence in Valinor, and no sound could be heard, save only from afar there came on the wind through the pass of the mountains the wailing of the Teleri like the cold cry of gulls. For it blew chill from the East in that hour, and the vast shadows of the sea were rolled against the walls of the shore.

But Manwë from his high seat looked out, and his eyes alone pierced through the night, until they saw a Darkness beyond dark which they could not penetrate, huge but far away, moving now northward with great speed; and he knew that Melkor had come and gone.

Then the pursuit was begun; and the earth shook beneath the horses of the host of Oromë, and the fire that was stricken from the hooves of Nahar was the first light that returned to Valinor. But so soon as any came up with the Cloud of Ungoliant the riders of the Valar were blinded and dismayed, and they were scattered, and went they knew not whither; and the sound of the Valaróma faltered and failed. And Tulkas was as one caught in a black net at night, and he stood powerless and beat the air in vain. But when the Darkness had passed, it was too late: Melkor had gone whither he would, and his vengeance was achieved.

# *Chapter* 9

# OF THE FLIGHT OF THE NOLDOR

After a time a great concourse gathered about the Ring of Doom; and the Valar sat in shadow, for it was night. But the stars of Varda now glimmered overhead, and the air was clear; for the winds of Manwë had driven away the vapours of death and rolled back the shadows of the sea. Then Yavanna arose and stood upon Ezellohar, the Green Mound, but it was bare now and black; and she laid her hands upon the Trees, but they were dead and dark, and each branch that she touched broke and fell lifeless at her feet. Then many voices were lifted in lamentation; and it seemed to those that mourned that they had drained to the dregs the cup of woe that Melkor had filled for them. But it was not so.

Yavanna spoke before the Valar, saying: 'The Light of the Trees has passed away, and lives now only in the Silmarils of Fëanor. Foresighted was he! Even for those who are mightiest under Ilúvatar there is some work that they may accomplish once, and once only. The Light of the Trees I brought into being, and within Eä I can do so never again. Yet had I but a little of that light I could recall life to the Trees, ere their roots decay; and then our hurt should be healed, and the malice of Melkor be confounded.'

Then Manwë spoke and said: 'Hearest thou, Fëanor son of Finwë, the words of Yavanna? Wilt thou grant what she would ask?'

There was long silence, but Fëanor answered no word. Then Tulkas cried: 'Speak, O Noldo, yea or nay! But who shall deny Yavanna? And did not the light of the Silmarils come from her work in the beginning?'

But Aulë the Maker said: 'Be not hasty! We ask a greater thing than thou knowest. Let him have peace yet awhile.'

But Fëanor spoke then, and cried bitterly: 'For the less even as for the greater there is some deed that he may accomplish but once only; and in that deed his heart shall rest. It may be that I can unlock my jewels, but never again shall I make their like; and if I must break them, I shall break my heart, and I shall be slain; first of all the Eldar in Aman.'

'Not the first,' said Mandos, but they did not understand his word; and again there was silence, while Fëanor brooded in the dark. It seemed to him that he was beset in a ring of enemies, and the words

78

of Melkor returned to him, saying that the Silmarils were not safe, if the Valar would possess them. 'And is he not Vala as are they,' said his thought, 'and does he not understand their hearts? Yea, a thief shall reveal thieves!' Then he cried aloud: 'This thing I will not do of free will. But if the Valar will constrain me, then shall I know indeed that Melkor is of their kindred.'

Then Mandos said: 'Thou hast spoken.' And Nienna arose and went up onto Ezellohar, and cast back her grey hood, and with her tears washed away the defilements of Ungoliant; and she sang in mourning for the bitterness of the world and the Marring of Arda.

But even as Nienna mourned, there came messengers from Formenos, and they were Noldor and bore new tidings of evil. For they told how a blind Darkness came northward, and in the midst walked some power for which there was no name, and the Darkness issued from it. But Melkor also was there, and he came to the house of Fëanor, and there he slew Finwë King of the Noldor before his doors, and spilled the first blood in the Blessed Realm; for Finwë alone had not fled from the horror of the Dark. And they told that Melkor had broken the stronghold of Formenos, and taken all the jewels of the Noldor that were hoarded in that place; and the Silmarils were gone.

Then Fëanor rose, and lifting up his hand before Manwë he cursed Melkor, naming him *Morgoth*, the Black Foe of the World; and by that name only was he known to the Eldar ever after. And he cursed also the summons of Manwë and the hour in which he came to Taniquetil, thinking in the madness of his rage and grief that had he been at Formenos his strength would have availed more than to be slain also, as Melkor had purposed. Then Fëanor ran from the Ring of Doom, and fled into the night; for his father was dearer to him than the Light of Valinor or the peerless works of his hands; and who among sons, of Elves or of Men, have held their fathers of greater worth?

Many there grieved for the anguish of Fëanor, but his loss was not his alone; and Yavanna wept by the mound, in fear that the Darkness should swallow the last rays of the Light of Valinor for ever. For though the Valar did not yet understand fully what had befallen, they perceived that Melkor had called upon some aid that came from beyond Arda. The Silmarils had passed away, and all one it may seem whether Fëanor had said yea or nay to Yavanna; yet had he said yea at the first, before the tidings came from Formenos, it may be that his after deeds would have been other than they were. But now the doom of the Noldor drew near.

Meanwhile Morgoth escaping from the pursuit of the Valar came to the wastes of Araman. This land lay northward between the Mountains of the Pelóri and the Great Sea, as Avathar lay to the south; but Araman was a wider land, and between the shores and the mountains were barren plains, ever colder as the Ice drew nearer. Through this region Morgoth and Ungoliant passed in haste, and so came through the great mists of Oiomúrë to the Helcaraxë, where the strait between Araman and Middle-earth was filled with grinding ice; and he crossed over, and came back at last to the north of the Outer Lands. Together they went on, for Morgoth could not elude Ungoliant, and her cloud was still about him, and all her eyes were upon him; and they came to those lands that lay north of the Firth of Drengist. Now Morgoth was drawing near to the ruins of Angband, where his great western stronghold had been; and Ungoliant perceived his hope, and knew that here he would seek to escape from her, and she stayed him, demanding that he fulfil his promise.

'Blackheart!' she said. 'I have done thy bidding. But I hunger still.'

'What wouldst thou have more?' said Morgoth. 'Dost thou desire all the world for thy belly? I did not vow to give thee that. I am its Lord.'

'Not so much,' said Ungoliant. 'But thou hast a great treasure from Formenos; I will have all that. Yea, with both hands thou shalt give it.'

Then perforce Morgoth surrendered to her the gems that he bore with him, one by one and grudgingly; and she devoured them, and their beauty perished from the world. Huger and darker yet grew Ungoliant, but her lust was unsated. 'With one hand thou givest,' she said; 'with the left only. Open thy right hand.'

In his right hand Morgoth held close the Silmarils, and though they were locked in a crystal casket, they had begun to burn him, and his hand was clenched in pain; but he would not open it. 'Nay!' he said. 'Thou hast had thy due. For with my power that I put into thee thy work was accomplished. I need thee no more. These things thou shalt not have, nor see. I name them unto myself for ever.'

But Ungoliant had grown great, and he less by the power that had gone out of him; and she rose against him, and her cloud closed about him, and she enmeshed him in a web of clinging thongs to strangle him. Then Morgoth sent forth a terrible cry, that echoed in the mountains. Therefore that region was called Lammoth; for the echoes of his voice dwelt there ever after, so that any who cried aloud in that land awoke them, and all the waste between the hills and the sea was filled with a clamour as of voices in anguish. The cry of Morgoth in that hour was the greatest and most dreadful that was ever heard in the northern world; the mountains shook, and the earth trembled, and rocks were riven asunder. Deep in forgotten places that cry was heard. Far beneath the ruined halls of Angband, in vaults to which the Valar in the haste of their assault had not descended, Balrogs lurked still, awaiting ever the return of their Lord; and now swiftly they arose, and passing over Hithlum they came to Lammoth as a tempest of fire. With their whips of flame they smote asunder the webs of Ungoliant, and she quailed, and turned to flight, belching black vapours to cover her; and fleeing from the north she went down into Beleriand, and dwelt beneath Ered Gorgoroth, in that dark valley that was after called Nan Dungortheb, the Valley of Dreadful Death, because of the horror that she bred there. For other foul creatures of spider form had dwelt there since the days of the delving of Angband, and she mated with them, and devoured them; and even after Ungoliant herself departed, and went whither she would into the forgotten south of the world, her offspring abode there and wove their hideous webs. Of the fate of Ungoliant no tale tells. Yet some have said that she ended long ago, when in her uttermost famine she devoured herself at last.

And thus the fear of Yavanna that the Silmarils would be swallowed up and fall into nothingness did not come to pass; but they remained in the power of Morgoth. And he being freed gathered again all his servants that he could find, and came to the ruins of Angband. There he delved anew his vast vaults and dungeons, and above their gates he reared the threefold peaks of Thangorodrim, and a great reek of dark smoke was ever wreathed about them. There countless became the hosts of his beasts and his demons, and the race of the Orcs, bred long before, grew and multiplied in the bowels of the earth. Dark now fell the shadow on Beleriand, as is told hereafter; but in Angband Morgoth forged for himself a great crown of iron, and he called himself King of the World. In token of this he set the Silmarils in his crown. His hands were burned black by the touch of those hallowed jewels, and black they remained ever after; nor was he ever free from the pain of the burning, and the anger of the pain. That crown he never took from his head, though its weight became a deadly weariness. Never but once only did he depart for a while secretly from his domain in the North; seldom indeed did he leave the deep places of his fortress, but governed his armies from his northern throne. And once only also did he himself wield weapon, while his realm lasted.

For now, more than in the days of Utumno ere his pride was

humbled, his hatred devoured him, and in the domination of his servants and the inspiring of them with lust of evil he spent his spirit. Nonetheless his majesty as one of the Valar long remained, though turned to terror, and before his face all save the mightiest sank into a dark pit of fear.

Now when it was known that Morgoth had escaped from Valinor and pursuit was unavailing, the Valar remained long seated in darkness in the Ring of Doom, and the Maiar and the Vanyar stood beside them and wept; but the Noldor for the most part returned to Tirion and mourned for the darkening of their fair city. Through the dim ravine of the Calacirya fogs drifted in from the shadowy seas and mantled its towers, and the lamp of the Mindon burned pale in the gloom.

Then suddenly Fëanor appeared in the city and called on all to come to the high court of the King upon the summit of Túna; but the doom of banishment that had been laid upon him was not yet lifted, and he rebelled against the Valar. A great multitude gathered swiftly, therefore, to hear what he would say; and the hill and all the stairs and streets that climbed upon it were lit with the light of many torches that each one bore in hand. Fëanor was a master of words, and his tongue had great power over hearts when he would use it; and that night he made a speech before the Noldor which they ever remembered. Fierce and fell were his words, and filled with anger and pride; and hearing them the Noldor were stirred to madness. His wrath and his hate were given most to Morgoth, and yet well nigh all that he said came from the very lies of Morgoth himself; but he was distraught with grief for the slaying of his father, and with anguish for the rape of the Silmarils. He claimed now the kingship of all the Noldor, since Finwë was dead, and he scorned the decrees of the Valar.

'Why, O people of the Noldor,' he cried, 'why should we longer serve the jealous Valar, who cannot keep us nor even their own realm secure from their Enemy? And though he be now their foe, are not they and he of one kin? Vengeance calls me hence, but even were it otherwise I would not dwell longer in the same land with the kin of my father's slayer and of the thief of my treasure. Yet I am not the only valiant in this valiant people. And have ye not all lost your King? And what else have ye not lost, cooped here in a narrow land between the mountains and the sea?

'Here once was light, that the Valar begrudged to Middle-earth, but now dark levels all. Shall we mourn here deedless for ever, a shadow-folk, mist-haunting, dropping vain tears in the thankless sea? Or shall we return to our home? In Cuiviénen sweet ran the waters under unclouded stars, and wide lands lay about, where a free people might walk. There they lie still and await us who in our folly forsook them. Come away! Let the cowards keep this city!'

Long he spoke, and ever he urged the Noldor to follow him and by their own prowess to win freedom and great realms in the lands of the East, before it was too late; for he echoed the lies of Melkor, that the Valar had cozened them and would hold them captive so that Men might rule in Middle-earth. Many of the Eldar heard then for the first time of the Aftercomers. 'Fair shall the end be,' he cried, 'though long and hard shall be the road! Say farewell to bondage! But say farewell also to ease! Say farewell to the weak! Say farewell to your treasures! More still shall we make. Journey light: but bring with you your swords! For we will go further than Oromë, endure longer than Tulkas: we will never turn back from pursuit. After Morgoth to the ends of the Earth! War shall he have and hatred undying. But when we have conquered and have regained the Silmarils, then we and we alone shall be lords of the unsullied Light, and masters of the bliss and beauty of Arda. No other race shall oust us!'

Then Fëanor swore a terrible oath. His seven sons leapt straight-way to his side and took the selfsame vow together, and red as blood shone their drawn swords in the glare of the torches. They swore an oath which none shall break, and none should take, by the name even of Ilúvatar, calling the Everlasting Dark upon them if they kept it not; and Manwë they named in witness, and Varda, and the hallowed mountain of Taniquetil, vowing to pursue with vengeance and hatred to the ends of the World Vala, Demon, Elf or Man as yet unborn, or any creature, great or small, good or evil, that time should bring forth unto the end of days, whoso should hold or take or keep a Silmaril from their possession.

Thus spoke Maedhros and Maglor and Celegorm, Curufin and Caranthir, Amrod and Amras, princes of the Noldor; and many quailed to hear the dread words. For so sworn, good or evil, an oath may not be broken, and it shall pursue oathkeeper and oathbreaker to the world's end. Fingolfin and Turgon his son therefore spoke against Fëanor, and fierce words awoke, so that once again wrath came near to the edge of swords. But Finarfin spoke softly, as was his wont, and sought to calm the Noldor, persuading them to pause and ponder ere deeds were done that could not be undone; and Orodreth, alone of his sons, spoke in like manner. Finrod was with Turgon, his friend; but Galadriel, the only woman of the Noldor to stand that day tall and valiant among the contending princes, was eager to be gone. No oaths she swore, but the words of Fëanor concerning Middle-earth had kindled in her heart, for she yearned to see the wide unguarded lands and to rule there a realm at her own will. Of like mind with Galadriel was Fingon Fingolfin's son, being moved also by Fëanor's words, though he loved him little; and with Fingon stood as they ever did Angrod and Aegnor, sons of Finarfin. But these held their peace and spoke not against their fathers.

At length after long debate Fëanor prevailed, and the greater part of the Noldor there assembled he set aflame with the desire of new things and strange countries. Therefore when Finarfin spoke yet again for heed and delay, a great shout went up: 'Nay, let us be gone!' And straightway Fëanor and his sons began to prepare for the marching forth.

Little foresight could there be for those who dared to take so dark a road. Yet all was done in over-haste; for Fëanor drove them on, fearing lest in the cooling of their hearts his words should wane and other counsels yet prevail; and for all his proud words he did not forget the power of the Valar. But from Valmar no message came, and Manwë was silent. He would not yet either forbid or hinder Fëanor's purpose; for the Valar were aggrieved that they were charged with evil intent to the Eldar, or that any were held captive by them against their will. Now they watched and waited, for they did not yet believe that Fëanor could hold the host of the Noldor to his will.

And indeed when Fëanor began the marshalling of the Noldor for their setting-out, then at once dissension arose. For though he had brought the assembly in a mind to depart, by no means all were of a mind to take Fëanor as King. Greater love was given to Fingolfin and his sons, and his household and the most part of the dwellers in Tirion refused to renounce him, if he would go with them; and thus at the last as two divided hosts the Noldor set forth upon their bitter road. Fëanor and his following were in the van, but the greater host came behind under Fingolfin; and he marched against his wisdom, because Fingon his son so urged him, and because he would not be sundered from his people that were eager to go, nor leave them to the rash counsels of Fëanor. Nor did he forget his words before the throne of Manwë. With Fingolfin went Finarfin also and for like reasons; but most loath was he to depart. And of all the Noldor in Valinor, who were grown now to a great people, but one tithe refused to take the road: some for the love that they bore to the Valar (and to Aulë not least), some for the love of Tirion and the many things that they had made; none for fear of peril by the way.

But even as the trumpet sang and Fëanor issued from the gates of Tirion a messenger came at last from Manwë, saying: 'Against the folly of Fëanor shall be set my counsel only. Go not forth! For the hour is evil, and your road leads to sorrow that ye do not foresee. No aid will the Valar lend you in this quest; but neither will they hinder you; for this ye shall know: as ye came hither freely, freely shall ye depart. But thou Fëanor Finwë's son, by thine oath art exiled. The lies of Melkor thou shalt unlearn in bitterness. Vala he is, thou saist. Then thou hast sworn in vain, for none of the Valar canst thou overcome now or ever within the halls of Eä, not though Eru whom thou namest had made thee thrice greater than thou art.'

But Fëanor laughed, and spoke not to the herald, but to the Noldor, saying: 'So! Then will this valiant people send forth the heir of their King alone into banishment with his sons only, and return to their bondage? But if any will come with me, I say to them: Is sorrow foreboded to you? But in Aman we have seen it. In Aman we have come through bliss to woe. The other now we will try: through sorrow to find joy; or freedom, at the least.'

Then turning to the herald he cried: 'Say this to Manwë Súlimo, High King of Arda: if Fëanor cannot overthrow Morgoth, at least he delays not to assail him, and sits not idle in grief. And it may be that Eru has set in me a fire greater than thou knowest. Such hurt at the least will I do to the Foe of the Valar that even the mighty in the Ring of Doom shall wonder to hear it. Yea, in the end they shall follow me. Farewell!'

In that hour the voice of Fëanor grew so great and so potent that even the herald of the Valar bowed before him as one full-answered, and departed; and the Noldor were over-ruled. Therefore they continued their march; and the House of Fëanor hastened before them along the coasts of Elendë: not once did they turn their eyes back to Tirion on the green hill of Túna. Slower and less eagerly came the host of Fingolfin after them. Of those Fingon was the foremost; but at the rear went Finarfin and Finrod, and many of the noblest and wisest of the Noldor; and often they looked behind them to see their fair city, until the lamp of the Mindon Eldaliéva was lost in the night. More than any others of the Exiles they carried thence memories of the bliss they had forsaken, and some even of the things that they had made there they took with them: a solace and a burden on the road.

Now Fëanor led the Noldor northward, because his first purpose was to follow Morgoth. Moreover Túna beneath Taniquetil was set nigh to the girdle of Arda, and there the Great Sea was immeasurably wide, whereas ever northward the sundering seas grew narrower, as the wasteland of Araman and the coasts of Middle-earth drew together. But as the mind of Fëanor cooled and took counsel he perceived over-late that all these great companies would never overcome the long leagues to the north, nor cross the seas at the last, save with the aid of ships; yet it would need long time and toil to build so great a fleet, even were there any among the Noldor skilled in that craft. He resolved now therefore to persuade the Teleri, ever friends to the Noldor, to join with them; and in his rebellion he thought that thus the bliss of Valinor might be further diminished and his power for war upon Morgoth be increased. He hastened then to Alqualondë, and spoke to the Teleri as he had spoken before in Tirion.

But the Teleri were unmoved by aught that he could say. They were grieved indeed at the going of their kinsfolk and long friends, but would rather dissuade them than aid them; and no ship would they lend, nor help in the building, against the will of the Valar. As for themselves, they desired now no other home but the strands of Eldamar, and no other lord than Olwë, prince of Alqualondë. And he had never lent ear to Morgoth, nor welcomed him to his land, and he trusted still that Ulmo and the other great among the Valar would redress the hurts of Morgoth, and that the night would pass yet to a new dawn.

Then Fëanor grew wrathful, for he still feared delay; and hotly he spoke to Olwë. 'You renounce your friendship, even in the hour of our need,' he said. 'Yet you were glad indeed to receive our aid when you came at last to these shores, fainthearted loiterers, and wellnigh emptyhanded. In huts on the beaches would you be dwelling still, had not the Noldor carved out your haven and toiled upon your walls.'

But Olwë answered: 'We renounce no friendship. But it may be the part of a friend to rebuke a friend's folly. And when the Noldor welcomed us and gave us aid, otherwise then you spoke: in the land of Aman we were to dwell for ever, as brothers whose houses stand side by side. But as for our white ships: those you gave us not. We learned not that craft from the Noldor, but from the Lords of the Sea; and the white timbers we wrought with our own hands, and the white sails were woven by our wives and our daughters. Therefore we will neither give them nor sell them for any league or friendship. For I say to you, Fëanor son of Finwë, these are to us as are the gems of the Noldor: the work of our hearts, whose like we shall not make again.'

Thereupon Fëanor left him, and sat in dark thought beyond the walls of Alqualondë, until his host was assembled. When he judged that his strength was enough, he went to the Haven of the Swans and began to man the ships that were anchored there and to take them away by force. But the Teleri withstood him, and cast many of the Noldor into the sea. Then swords were drawn, and a bitter fight was fought upon the ships, and about the lamplit quays and piers of the Haven, and even upon the great arch of its gate. Thrice the people of Fëanor were driven back, and many were slain upon either side; but the vanguard of the Noldor were succoured by Fingon with the foremost of the host of Fingolfin, who coming up found a battle joined and their own kin falling, and rushed in before they knew rightly the cause of the quarrel; some thought indeed that the Teleri had sought to waylay the march of the Noldor at the bidding of the Valar.

Thus at last the Teleri were overcome, and a great part of their mariners that dwelt in Alqualondë were wickedly slain. For the Noldor were become fierce and desperate, and the Teleri had less strength, and were armed for the most part but with slender bows. Then the Noldor drew away their white ships and manned their oars as best they might, and rowed them north along the coast. And Olwë called upon Ossë, but he came not, for it was not permitted by the Valar that the flight of the Noldor should be hindered by force. But Uinen wept for the mariners of the Teleri; and the sea rose in wrath against the slayers, so that many of the ships were wrecked and those in them drowned. Of the Kinslaying at Alqualondë more is told in that lament which is named *Noldolantë*, the Fall of the Noldor, that Maglor made ere he was lost.

Nonetheless the greater part of the Noldor escaped, and when the storm was past they held on their course, some by ship and some by land; but the way was long and ever more evil as they went forward. After they had marched for a great while in the unmeasured night, they came at length to the northern confines of the Guarded Realm, upon the borders of the empty waste of Araman which were mountainous and cold. There they beheld suddenly a dark figure standing high upon a rock that looked down upon the shore. Some say that it was Mandos himself, and no lesser herald of Manwë. And they heard a loud voice, solemn and terrible, that bade them stand and give ear. Then all halted and stood still, and from end to end of the hosts of the Noldor the voice was heard speaking the curse and prophecy which is called the Prophecy of the North, and the Doom of the Noldor. Much it foretold in dark words, which the Noldor understood not until the woes indeed after befell them; but all heard the curse that was uttered upon those that would not stay nor seek the doom and pardon of the Valar.

'Tears unnumbered ye shall shed; and the Valar will fence Valinor against you, and shut you out, so that not even the echo of your lamentation shall pass over the mountains. On the House of Fëanor the wrath of the Valar lieth from the West unto the uttermost East, and upon all that will follow them it shall be laid also. Their Oath shall drive them, and yet betray them, and ever snatch away the very treasures that they have sworn to pursue. To evil end shall all things turn that they begin well; and by treason of kin unto kin, and the fear of treason, shall this come to pass. The Dispossessed shall they be for ever.

'Ye have spilled the blood of your kindred unrighteously and have stained the land of Aman. For blood ye shall render blood, and beyond Aman ye shall dwell in Death's shadow. For though Eru appointed to you to die not in Eä, and no sickness may assail you, yet slain ye may be, and slain ye shall be: by weapon and by torment and by grief; and your houseless spirits shall come then to Mandos. There long shall ye abide and yearn for your bodies, and find little pity though all whom ye have slain should entreat for you. And those that endure in Middle-earth and come not to Mandos shall grow weary of the world as with a great burden, and shall wane, and become as shadows of regret before the younger race that cometh after. The Valar have spoken.'

Then many quailed; but Fëanor hardened his heart and said: 'We have sworn, and not lightly. This oath we will keep. We are threatened with many evils, and treason not least; but one thing is not said: that we shall suffer from cowardice, from cravens or the fear of cravens. Therefore I say that we will go on, and this doom I add: the deeds that we shall do shall be the matter of song until the last days of Arda.'

But in that hour Finarfin forsook the march, and turned back, being filled with grief, and with bitterness against the House of Fëanor, because of his kinship with Olwë of Alqualondë; and many of his people went with him, retracing their steps in sorrow, until they beheld once more the far beam of the Mindon upon Túna still shining in the night, and so came at last to Valinor. There they received the pardon of the Valar, and Finarfin was set to rule the remnant of the Noldor in the Blessed Realm. But his sons were not with him, for they would not forsake the sons of Fingolfin; and all Fingolfin's folk went forward still, feeling the constraint of their kinship and the will of Fëanor, and fearing to face the doom of the Valar, since not all of them had been guiltless of the Kinslaying at Alqualondë. Moreover Fingon and Turgon were bold and fiery of heart, and loath to abandon any task to which they had put their hands until the bitter end, if bitter it must be. So the main host held on, and swiftly the evil that was foretold began its work.

The Noldor came at last far into the north of Arda; and they saw the first teeth of the ice that floated in the sea, and knew that they were drawing nigh to the Helcaraxë. For between the land of Aman that in the north curved eastward, and the east-shores of Endor (which is Middle-earth) that bore westward, there was a narrow strait, through which the chill waters of the Encircling Sea and the waves of Belegaer flowed together, and there were vast fogs and mists of deathly cold, and the sea-streams were filled with clashing hills of ice and the grinding of ice deep-sunken. Such was the Helcaraxë, and there none yet had dared to tread save the Valar only and Ungoliant.

Therefore Fëanor halted and the Noldor debated what course they should now take. But they began to suffer anguish from the cold, and the clinging mists through which no gleam of star could pierce; and many repented of the road and began to murmur, especially those that followed Fingolfin, cursing Fëanor, and naming him as the cause of all the woes of the Eldar. But Fëanor, knowing all that was said, took counsel with his sons; and two courses only they saw to escape from Araman and come into Endor: by the straits or by ship. But the Helcaraxë they deemed impassable, whereas the ships were too few. Many had been lost upon their long journey, and there remained now not enough to bear across all the great host together; yet none were willing to abide upon the western coast while others were ferried first: already the fear of treachery was awake among the Noldor. Therefore it came into the hearts of Fëanor and his sons to seize all the ships and depart suddenly; for they had retained the mastery of the fleet since the battle of the Haven, and it was manned only by those who had fought there and were bound to Fëanor. And as though it came at his call, there sprang up a wind from the north-west, and Fëanor slipped away secretly with all whom he deemed true to him, and went aboard, and put out to sea, and left Fingolfin in Araman. And since the sea was there narrow, steering east and somewhat south he passed over without loss, and first of all the Noldor set foot once more upon the shores of Middle-earth; and the landing of Fëanor was at the mouth of the firth which was called Drengist and ran into Dor-lómin.

But when they were landed, Maedhros the eldest of his sons, and on a time the friend of Fingon ere Morgoth's lies came between, spoke to Fëanor, saying: 'Now what ships and rowers will you spare to return, and whom shall they bear hither first? Fingon the valiant?'

Then Fëanor laughed as one fey, and he cried: 'None and none! What I have left behind I count now no loss; needless baggage on the road it has proved. Let those that cursed my name, curse me still, and whine their way back to the cages of the Valar! Let the ships burn!' Then Maedhros alone stood aside, but Fëanor caused fire to be set to the white ships of the Teleri. So in that place which was called Losgar at the outlet of the Firth of Drengist ended the fairest vessels that ever sailed the sea, in a great burning, bright and terrible. And Fingolfin and his people saw the light afar off, red beneath the clouds; and they knew that they were betrayed. This was the firstfruits of the Kinslaying and the Doom of the Noldor.

Then Fingolfin seeing that Fëanor had left him to perish in Araman or return in shame to Valinor was filled with bitterness; but he desired now as never before to come by some way to Middle-earth, and meet Fëanor again. And he and his host wandered long in misery, but their valour and endurance grew with hardship; for they were a mighty people, the elder children undying of Eru Ilúvatar, but new-come from the Blessed Realm, and not yet weary with the weariness of Earth. The fire of their hearts was young, and led by Fingolfin and his sons, and by Finrod and Galadriel, they dared to pass into the bitterest North; and finding no other way they endured at last the terror of the Helcaraxë and the cruel hills of ice. Few of the deeds of the Noldor thereafter surpassed that desperate crossing in hardihood or woe. There Elenwë the wife of Turgon was lost, and many others perished also; and it was with a lessened host that Fingolfin set foot at last upon the Outer Lands. Small love for Fëanor or his sons had those that marched at last behind him, and blew their trumpets in Middle-earth at the first rising of the Moon.

## Chapter 10

# OF THE SINDAR

Now as has been told the power of Elwë and Melian increased in Middle-earth, and all the Elves of Beleriand, from the mariners of Círdan to the wandering hunters of the Blue Mountains beyond the River Gelion, owned Elwë as their lord; Elu Thingol he was called, King Greymantle, in the tongue of his people. They are called the Sindar, the Grey-elves of starlit Beleriand; and although they were Moriquendi, under the lordship of Thingol and the teaching of Melian they became the fairest and the most wise and skilful of all the Elves of Middle-earth. And at the end of the first age of the Chaining of Melkor, when all the Earth had peace and the glory of Valinor was at its noon, there came into the world Lúthien, the only child of Thingol and Melian. Though Middle-earth lay for the most part in the Sleep of Yavanna, in Beleriand under the power of Melian there was life and joy, and the bright stars shone as silver fires; and there in the forest of Neldoreth Lúthien was born, and the white flowers of *niphredil* came forth to greet her as stars from the earth.

It came to pass during the second age of the captivity of Melkor that Dwarves came over the Blue Mountains of Ered Luin into Beleriand. Themselves they named Khazâd, but the Sindar called them Naugrim, the Stunted People, and Gonnhirrim, Masters of Stone. Far to the east were the most ancient dwellings of the Naugrim, but they had delved for themselves great halls and mansions, after the manner of their kind, in the eastern side of Ered Luin; and those cities were named in their own tongue Gabilgathol and Tumunzahar. To the north of the great height of Mount Dolmed was Gabilgathol, which the Elves interpreted in their tongue Belegost, that is Mickleburg; and southward was delved Tumunzahar, by the Elves named Nogrod, the Hollowbold. Greatest of all the mansions of the Dwarves was Khazad-dûm, the Dwarrowdelf, Hadhodrond in the Elvish tongue, that was afterwards in the days of its darkness called Moria; but it was far off in the Mountains of Mist beyond the wide leagues of Eriador, and to the Eldar came but as a name and a rumour from the words of the Dwarves of the Blue Mountains.

From Nogrod and Belegost the Naugrim came forth into Beleriand; and the Elves were filled with amazement, for they had believed themselves to be the only living things in Middle-earth that spoke with words or wrought with hands, and that all others were but birds and beasts. But they could understand no word of the tongue of the Naugrim, which to their ears was cumbrous and unlovely; and few ever of the Eldar have achieved the mastery of it. But the Dwarves were swift to learn, and indeed were more willing to learn the Elven-tongue than to teach their own to those of alien race. Few of the Eldar went ever to Nogrod and Belegost, save Eöl of Nan Elmoth and Maeglin his son; but the Dwarves trafficked into Beleriand, and they made a great road that passed under the shoulders of Mount Dolmed and followed the course of the River Ascar, crossing Gelion at Sarn Athrad, the Ford of Stones, where battle after befell. Ever cool was the friendship between the Naugrim and the Eldar, though much profit they had one of the other; but at that time those griefs that lay between them had not yet come to pass, and King Thingol welcomed them. But the Naugrim gave their friendship more readily to the Noldor in after days than to any others of Elves and Men, because of their love and reverence for Aulë; and the gems of the Noldor they praised above all other wealth. In the darkness of Arda already the Dwarves wrought great works, for even from the first days of their Fathers they had marvellous skill with metals and with stone; but in that ancient time iron and copper they loved to work, rather than silver or gold.

Now Melian had much foresight, after the manner of the Maiar; and when the second age of the captivity of Melkor had passed, she counselled Thingol that the Peace of Arda would not last for ever. He took thought therefore how he should make for himself a kingly dwelling, and a place that should be strong, if evil were to awake again in Middle-earth; and he sought aid and counsel of the Dwarves of Belegost. They gave it willingly, for they were unwearied in those days and eager for new works; and though the Dwarves ever de-manded a price for all that they did, whether with delight or with toil, at this time they held themselves paid. For Melian taught them much that they were eager to learn, and Thingol rewarded them with many fair pearls. These Círdan gave to him, for they were got in great number in the shallow waters about the Isle of Balar; but the Naugrim had not before seen their like, and they held them dear. One there was as great as a dove's egg, and its sheen was as starlight on the foam of the sea; Nimphelos it was named, and the chieftain of the Dwarves of Belegost prized it above a mountain of wealth.

Therefore the Naugrim laboured long and gladly for Thingol, and devised for him mansions after the fashion of their people, delved

deep in the earth. Where the Esgalduin flowed down, and parted
Neldoreth from Region, there rose in the midst of the forest a rocky
hill, and the river ran at its feet. There they made the gates of the
hall of Thingol, and they built a bridge of stone over the river, by
which alone the gates could be entered. Beyond the gates wide
passages ran down to high halls and chambers far below that were
hewn in the living stone, so many and so great that that dwelling
was named Menegroth, the Thousand Caves.

But the Elves also had part in that labour, and Elves and Dwarves
together, each with their own skill, there wrought out the visions of
Melian, images of the wonder and beauty of Valinor beyond the Sea.
The pillars of Menegroth were hewn in the likeness of the beeches
of Oromë, stock, bough, and leaf, and they were lit with lanterns of
gold. The nightingales sang there as in the gardens of Lórien; and
there were fountains of silver, and basins of marble, and floors of
many-coloured stones. Carven figures of beasts and birds there ran
upon the walls, or climbed upon the pillars, or peered among the
branches entwined with many flowers. And as the years passed
Melian and her maidens filled the halls with woven hangings wherein
could be read the deeds of the Valar, and many things that had
befallen in Arda since its beginning, and shadows of things that were
yet to be. That was the fairest dwelling of any king that has ever been
east of the Sea.

And when the building of Menegroth was achieved, and there was
peace in the realm of Thingol and Melian, the Naugrim yet came
ever and anon over the mountains and went in traffic about the lands;
but they went seldom to the Falas, for they hated the sound of the
sea and feared to look upon it. To Beleriand there came no other
rumour or tidings of the world without.

But as the third age of the captivity of Melkor drew on, the
Dwarves became troubled, and they spoke to King Thingol, saying
that the Valar had not rooted out utterly the evils of the North, and
now the remnant, having long multiplied in the dark, were coming
forth once more and roaming far and wide. 'There are fell beasts,'
they said, 'in the land east of the mountains, and your ancient
kindred that dwell there are flying from the plains to the hills.'

And ere long the evil creatures came even to Beleriand, over passes
in the mountains, or up from the south through the dark forests.
Wolves there were, or creatures that walked in wolf-shapes, and other
fell beings of shadow; and among them were the Orcs, who afterwards wrought ruin in Beleriand: but they were yet few and wary,
and did but smell out the ways of the land, awaiting the return of

their lord. Whence they came, or what they were, the Elves knew not then, thinking them perhaps to be Avari who had become evil and savage in the wild; in which they guessed all too near, it is said.

Therefore Thingol took thought for arms, which before his people had not needed, and these at first the Naugrim smithied for him; for they were greatly skilled in such work, though none among them surpassed the craftsmen of Nogrod, of whom Telchar the smith was greatest in renown. A warlike race of old were all the Naugrim, and they would fight fiercely against whomsoever aggrieved them: servants of Melkor, or Eldar, or Avari, or wild beasts, or not seldom their own kin, Dwarves of other mansions and lordships. Their smithcraft indeed the Sindar soon learned of them; yet in the tempering of steel alone of all crafts the Dwarves were never outmatched even by the Noldor, and in the making of mail of linked rings, which was first contrived by the smiths of Belegost, their work had no rival.

At this time therefore the Sindar were well-armed, and they drove off all creatures of evil, and had peace again; but Thingol's armouries were stored with axes and with spears and swords, and tall helms, and long coats of bright mail; for the hauberks of the Dwarves were so fashioned that they rusted not but shone ever as if they were new-burnished. And that proved well for Thingol in the time that was to come.

Now as has been told, one Lenwë of the host of Olwë forsook the march of the Eldar at that time when the Teleri were halted by the shores of the Great River upon the borders of the westlands of Middle-earth. Little is known of the wanderings of the Nandor, whom he led away down Anduin: some, it is said, dwelt age-long in the woods of the Vale of the Great River, some came at last to its mouths and there dwelt by the Sea, and yet others passing by Ered Nimrais, the White Mountains, came north again and entered the wilderness of Eriador between Ered Luin and the far Mountains of Mist. Now these were a woodland people and had no weapons of steel, and the coming of the fell beasts of the North filled them with great fear, as the Naugrim declared to King Thingol in Menegroth. Therefore Denethor, the son of Lenwë, hearing rumour of the might of Thingol and his majesty, and of the peace of his realm, gathered such host of his scattered people as he could, and led them over the mountains into Beleriand. There they were welcomed by Thingol, as kin long lost that return, and they dwelt in Ossiriand, the Land of Seven Rivers.

Of the long years of peace that followed after the coming of

Denethor there is little tale. In those days, it is said, Daeron the Minstrel, chief loremaster of the kingdom of Thingol, devised his Runes; and the Naugrim that came to Thingol learned them, and were well-pleased with the device, esteeming Daeron's skill higher than did the Sindar, his own people. By the Naugrim the *Cirth* were taken east over the mountains and passed into the knowledge of many peoples; but they were little used by the Sindar for the keeping of records, until the days of the War, and much that was held in memory perished in the ruins of Doriath. But of bliss and glad life there is little to be said, before it ends; as works fair and wonderful, while still they endure for eyes to see, are their own record, and only when they are in peril or broken for ever do they pass into song.

In Beleriand in those days the Elves walked, and the rivers flowed, and the stars shone, and the night-flowers gave forth their scents; and the beauty of Melian was as the noon, and the beauty of Lúthien was as the dawn in spring. In Beleriand King Thingol upon his throne was as the lords of the Maiar, whose power is at rest, whose joy is as an air that they breathe in all their days, whose thought flows in a tide untroubled from the heights to the deeps. In Beleriand still at times rode Oromë the great, passing like a wind over the mountains, and the sound of his horn came down the leagues of the starlight, and the Elves feared him for the splendour of his countenance and the great noise of the onrush of Nahar; but when the Valaróma echoed in the hills, they knew well that all evil things were fled far away.

But it came to pass at last that the end of bliss was at hand, and the noontide of Valinor was drawing to its twilight. For as has been told and as is known to all, being written in lore and sung in many songs, Melkor slew the Trees of the Valar with the aid of Ungoliant, and escaped, and came back to Middle-earth. Far to the north befell the strife of Morgoth and Ungoliant; but the great cry of Morgoth echoed through Beleriand, and all its people shrank for fear; for though they knew not what it foreboded, they heard then the herald of death. Soon afterwards Ungoliant fled from the north and came into the realm of King Thingol, and a terror of darkness was about her; but by the power of Melian she was stayed, and entered not into Neldoreth, but abode long time under the shadow of the precipices in which Dorthonion fell southward. And they became known as Ered Gorgoroth, the Mountains of Terror, and none dared go thither, or pass nigh them; there life and light were strangled, and there all waters were poisoned. But Morgoth, as has before been told, re-turned to Angband, and built it anew, and above its doors he reared the reeking towers of Thangorodrim; and the gates of Morgoth were but one hundred and fifty leagues distant from the bridge of Menegroth: far and yet all too near.

Now the Orcs that multiplied in the darkness of the earth grew strong and fell, and their dark lord filled them with a lust of ruin and death; and they issued from Angband's gates under the clouds that Morgoth sent forth, and passed silently into the highlands of the north. Thence on a sudden a great army came into Beleriand and assailed King Thingol. Now in his wide realm many Elves wandered free in the wild, or dwelt at peace in small kindreds far sundered; and only about Menegroth in the midst of the land, and along the Falas in the country of the mariners, were there numerous peoples. But the Orcs came down upon either side of Menegroth, and from camps in the east between Celon and Gelion, and west in the plains between Sirion and Narog, they plundered far and wide; and Thingol was cut off from Círdan at Eglarest. Therefore he called upon Denethor; and the Elves came in force from Region beyond Aros and from Ossiriand, and fought the first battle in the Wars of Beleriand. And the eastern host of the Orcs was taken between the armies of the Eldar, north of the Andram and midway between Aros and Gelion, and there they were utterly defeated, and those that fled north from the great slaughter were waylaid by the axes of the Naugrim that issued from Mount Dolmed: few indeed returned to Angband.

But the victory of the Elves was dear-bought. For those of Ossiriand were light-armed, and no match for the Orcs, who were shod with iron and iron-shielded and bore great spears with broad blades; and Denethor was cut off and surrounded upon the hill of Amon Ereb. There he fell and all his nearest kin about him, before the host of Thingol could come to his aid. Bitterly though his fall was avenged, when Thingol came upon the rear of the Orcs and slew them in heaps, his people lamented him ever after and took no king again. After the battle some returned to Ossiriand, and their tidings filled the remnant of their people with great fear, so that thereafter they came never forth in open war, but kept themselves by wariness and secrecy; and they were called the Laiquendi, the Green-elves, because of their raiment of the colour of leaves. But many went north and entered the guarded realm of Thingol, and were merged with his people.

And when Thingol came again to Menegroth he learned that the Orc-host in the west was victorious, and had driven Círdan to the rim of the sea. Therefore he withdrew all his people that his summons could reach within the fastness of Neldoreth and Region, and Melian put forth her power and fenced all that dominion round about with an unseen wall of shadow and bewilderment: the Girdle of Melian, that none thereafter could pass against her will or the will of King Thingol, unless one should come with a power greater than that of Melian the Maia. And this inner land, which was long named Eglador, was after called Doriath, the guarded kingdom, Land of the Girdle. Within it there was yet a watchful peace; but without there was peril and great fear, and the servants of Morgoth roamed at will, save in the walled havens of the Falas.

But new tidings were at hand, which none in Middle-earth had foreseen, neither Morgoth in his pits nor Melian in Menegroth; for no news came out of Aman, whether by messenger, or by spirit, or by vision in dream, after the death of the Trees. In this same time Fëanor came over the Sea in the white ships of the Teleri, and landed in the Firth of Drengist, and there burned the ships at Losgar.

## Chapter 11

# OF THE SUN AND MOON AND THE HIDING OF VALINOR

It is told that after the flight of Melkor the Valar sat long unmoved upon their thrones in the Ring of Doom; but they were not idle, as Fëanor declared in the folly of his heart. For the Valar may work many things with thought rather than with hands, and without voices in silence they may hold council one with another. Thus they held vigil in the night of Valinor, and their thought passed back beyond Eä and forth to the End; yet neither power nor wisdom assuaged their grief, and the knowing of evil in the hour of its being. And they mourned not more for the death of the Trees than for the marring of Fëanor: of the works of Melkor one of the most evil. For Fëanor was made the mightiest in all parts of body and mind, in valour, in endurance, in beauty, in understanding, in skill, in strength and in subtlety alike, of all the Children of Ilúvatar, and a bright flame was in him. The works of wonder for the glory of Arda that he might otherwise have wrought only Manwë might in some measure conceive. And it was told by the Vanyar who held vigil with the Valar that when the messengers declared to Manwë the answers of Fëanor to his heralds, Manwë wept and bowed his head. But at that last word of Fëanor: that at the least the Noldor should do deeds to live in song for ever, he raised his head, as one that hears a voice far off, and he said: 'So shall it be! Dear-bought those songs shall be accounted, and yet shall be well-bought. For the price could be no other. Thus even as Eru spoke to us shall beauty not before conceived be brought into Eä, and evil yet be good to have been.'

But Mandos said: 'And yet remain evil. To me shall Fëanor come soon.'

But when at last the Valar learned that the Noldor had indeed passed out of Aman and were come back into Middle-earth, they arose and began to set forth in deeds those counsels which they had taken in thought for the redress of the evils of Melkor. Then Manwë bade Yavanna and Nienna to put forth all their powers of growth and healing; and they put forth all their powers upon the Trees. But the tears of Nienna availed not to heal their mortal wounds; and for a long while Yavanna sang alone in the shadows. Yet even as hope failed and her song faltered, Telperion bore at last upon a leafless bough one great flower of silver, and Laurelin a single fruit of gold.

These Yavanna took; and then the Trees died, and their lifeless stems stand yet in Valinor, a memorial of vanished joy. But the flower and the fruit Yavanna gave to Aulë, and Manwë hallowed them, and Aulë and his people made vessels to hold them and preserve their radiance: as is said in the *Narsilion*, the Song of the Sun and Moon. These vessels the Valar gave to Varda, that they might become lamps of heaven, outshining the ancient stars, being nearer to Arda; and she gave them power to traverse the lower regions of Ilmen, and set them to voyage upon appointed courses above the girdle of the Earth from the West unto the East and to return.

These things the Valar did, recalling in their twilight the darkness of the lands of Arda; and they resolved now to illumine Middle-earth and with light to hinder the deeds of Melkor. For they remembered the Avari that remained by the waters of their awakening, and they did not utterly forsake the Noldor in exile; and Manwë knew also that the hour of the coming of Men was drawn nigh. And it is said indeed that, even as the Valar made war upon Melkor for the sake of the Quendi, so now for that time they forbore for the sake of the Hildor, the Aftercomers, the younger Children of Ilúvatar. For so grievous had been the hurts of Middle-earth in the war upon Utumno that the Valar feared lest even worse should now befall; whereas the Hildor should be mortal, and weaker than the Quendi to withstand fear and tumult. Moreover it was not revealed to Manwë where the beginning of Men should be, north, south, or east. Therefore the Valar sent forth light, but made strong the land of their dwelling.

Isil the Sheen the Vanyar of old named the Moon, flower of Telperion in Valinor; and Anar the Fire-golden, fruit of Laurelin, they named the Sun. But the Noldor named them also Rána, the Wayward, and Vása, the Heart of Fire, that awakens and consumes; for the Sun was set as a sign for the awakening of Men and the waning of the Elves, but the Moon cherishes their memory.

The maiden whom the Valar chose from among the Maiar to guide the vessel of the Sun was named Arien, and he that steered the island of the Moon was Tilion. In the days of the Trees Arien had tended the golden flowers in the gardens of Vána, and watered them with the bright dews of Laurelin; but Tilion was a hunter of the company of Oromë, and he had a silver bow. He was a lover of silver, and when he would rest he forsook the woods of Oromë, and going into Lórien he lay in dream by the pools of Estë, in Telperion's flickering beams;

and he begged to be given the task of tending for ever the last Flower of Silver. Arien the maiden was mightier than he, and she was chosen because she had not feared the heats of Laurelin, and was unhurt by them, being from the beginning a spirit of fire, whom Melkor had not deceived nor drawn to his service. Too bright were the eyes of Arien for even the Eldar to look on, and leaving Valinor she forsook the form and raiment which like the Valar she had worn there, and she was as a naked flame, terrible in the fullness of her splendour.

Isil was first wrought and made ready, and first rose into the realm of the stars, and was the elder of the new lights, as was Telperion of the Trees. Then for a while the world had moonlight, and many things stirred and woke that had waited long in the sleep of Yavanna. The servants of Morgoth were filled with amazement, but the Elves of the Outer Lands looked up in delight; and even as the Moon rose above the darkness in the west, Fingolfin let blow his silver trumpets and began his march into Middle-earth, and the shadows of his host went long and black before them.

Tilion had traversed the heaven seven times, and thus was in the furthest east, when the vessel of Arien was made ready. Then Anar arose in glory, and the first dawn of the Sun was like a great fire upon the towers of the Pelóri: the clouds of Middle-earth were kindled, and there was heard the sound of many waterfalls. Then indeed Morgoth was dismayed, and he descended into the uttermost depths of Angband, and withdrew his servants, sending forth great reek and dark cloud to hide his land from the light of the Daystar.

Now Varda purposed that the two vessels should journey in Ilmen and ever be aloft, but not together; each should pass from Valinor into the east and return, the one issuing from the west as the other turned from the east. Thus the first of the new days were reckoned after the manner of the Trees, from the mingling of the lights when Arien and Tilion passed in their courses, above the middle of the Earth. But Tilion was wayward and uncertain in speed, and held not to his appointed path; and he sought to come near to Arien, being drawn by her splendour, though the flame of Anar scorched him, and the island of the Moon was darkened.

Because of the waywardness of Tilion, therefore, and yet more because of the prayers of Lórien and Estë, who said that sleep and rest had been banished from the Earth, and the stars were hidden, Varda changed her counsel, and allowed a time wherein the world should still have shadow and half-light. Anar rested therefore a while in Valinor, lying upon the cool bosom of the Outer Sea; and Evening, the time of the descent and resting of the Sun, was the hour of greatest light and joy in Aman. But soon the Sun was drawn down by the servants of Ulmo, and went then in haste under the Earth, and so came unseen to the east and there mounted the heaven again, lest night be over-long and evil walk under the Moon. But by Anar the waters of the Outer Sea were made hot and glowed with coloured fire, and Valinor had light for a while after the passing of Arien. Yet as she journeyed under the Earth and drew towards the east the glow faded and Valinor was dim, and the Valar mourned then most for the death of Laurelin. At dawn the shadows of the Mountains of Defence lay heavy on the Blessed Realm.

Varda commanded the Moon to journey in like manner, and passing under Earth to arise in the east, but only after the Sun had descended from heaven. But Tilion went with uncertain pace, as yet he goes, and was still drawn towards Arien, as he shall ever be; so that often both may be seen above the Earth together, or at times it will chance that he comes so nigh that his shadow cuts off her brightness and there is a darkness amid the day.

Therefore by the coming and going of Anar the Valar reckoned the days thereafter until the Change of the World. For Tilion tarried seldom in Valinor, but more often would pass swiftly over the western land, over Avathar, or Araman, or Valinor, and plunge in the chasm beyond the Outer Sea, pursuing his way alone amid the grots and caverns at the roots of Arda. There he would often wander long, and late would return.

Still therefore, after the Long Night, the light of Valinor was greater and fairer than upon Middle-earth; for the Sun rested there, and the lights of heaven drew nearer to Earth in that region. But neither the Sun nor the Moon can recall the light that was of old, that came from the Trees before they were touched by the poison of Ungoliant. That light lives now in the Silmarils alone.

But Morgoth hated the new lights, and was for a while confounded by this unlooked-for stroke of the Valar. Then he assailed Tilion, sending spirits of shadow against him, and there was strife in Ilmen beneath the paths of the stars; but Tilion was victorious. And Arien Morgoth feared with a great fear, but dared not come nigh her, having indeed no longer the power; for as he grew in malice, and sent forth from himself the evil that he conceived in lies and creatures of wickedness, his might passed into them and was dispersed, and he himself became ever more bound to the earth, unwilling to issue from his dark strongholds. With shadows he hid himself and his servants from Arien, the glance of whose eyes they could not long endure;

and the lands near his dwelling were shrouded in fumes and great clouds.

But seeing the assault upon Tilion the Valar were in doubt, fearing what the malice and cunning of Morgoth might yet contrive against them. Being unwilling to make war upon him in Middle-earth, they remembered nonetheless the ruin of Almaren; and they resolved that the like should not befall Valinor. Therefore at that time they fortified their land anew, and they raised up the mountain-walls of the Pelóri to sheer and dreadful heights, east, north, and south. Their outer sides were dark and smooth, without foothold or ledge, and they fell in great precipices with faces hard as glass, and rose up to towers with crowns of white ice. A sleepless watch was set upon them, and no pass led through them, save only at the Calacirya: but that pass the Valar did not close, because of the Eldar that were faithful, and in the city of Tirion upon the green hill Finarfin yet ruled the remnant of the Noldor in the deep cleft of the mountains. For all those of elven-race, even the Vanyar and Ingwë their lord, must breathe at times the outer air and the wind that comes over the sea from the lands of their birth; and the Valar would not sunder the Teleri wholly from their kin. But in the Calacirya they set strong towers and many sentinels, and at its issue upon the plains of Valmar a host was encamped, so that neither bird nor beast nor elf nor man, nor any creature beside that dwelt in Middle-earth, could pass that leaguer.

And in that time also, which songs call *Nurtalë Valinóreva*, the Hiding of Valinor, the Enchanted Isles were set, and all the seas about them were filled with shadows and bewilderment. And these isles were strung as a net in the Shadowy Seas from the north to the south, before Tol Eressëa, the Lonely Isle, is reached by one sailing west. Hardly might any vessel pass between them, for in the dangerous sounds the waves sighed for ever upon dark rocks shrouded in mist. And in the twilight a great weariness came upon mariners and a loathing of the sea; but all that ever set foot upon the islands were there entrapped, and slept until the Change of the World. Thus it was that as Mandos foretold to them in Araman the Blessed Realm was shut against the Noldor; and of the many messengers that in after days sailed into the West none came ever to Valinor—save one only: the mightiest mariner of song.

# Chapter 12

# OF MEN

The Valar sat now behind their mountains at peace; and having given light to Middle-earth they left it for long untended, and the lordship of Morgoth was uncontested save by the valour of the Noldor. Most in mind Ulmo kept the exiles, who gathered news of the Earth through all the waters.

From this time forth were reckoned the Years of the Sun. Swifter and briefer are they than the long Years of the Trees in Valinor. In that time the air of Middle-earth became heavy with the breath of growth and mortality, and the changing and ageing of all things was hastened exceedingly; life teemed upon the soil and in the waters in the Second Spring of Arda, and the Eldar increased, and beneath the new Sun Beleriand grew green and fair.

At the first rising of the Sun the Younger Children of Ilúvatar awoke in the land of Hildórien in the eastward regions of Middle-earth; but the first Sun arose in the West, and the opening eyes of Men were turned towards it, and their feet as they wandered over the Earth for the most part strayed that way. The Atani they were named by the Eldar, the Second People; but they called them also Hildor, the Followers, and many other names: Apanónar, the After-born, Engwar, the Sickly, and Fírimar, the Mortals; and they named them the Usurpers, the Strangers, and the Inscrutable, the Self-cursed, the Heavy-handed, the Night-fearers, the Children of the Sun. Of Men little is told in these tales, which concern the Eldest Days before the waxing of mortals and the waning of the Elves, save of those fathers of men, the Atanatári, who in the first years of the Sun and Moon wandered into the North of the world. To Hildórien there came no Vala to guide Men, or to summon them to dwell in Valinor; and Men have feared the Valar, rather than loved them, and have not understood the purposes of the Powers, being at variance with them, and at strife with the world. Ulmo nonetheless took thought for them, aiding the counsel and will of Manwë; and his messages came often to them by stream and flood. But they have not skill in such matters, and still less had they in those days before they had mingled with the Elves. Therefore they loved the waters, and their hearts were stirred, but they understood not the messages. Yet it is told that ere long they met Dark Elves in many places, and were befriended by them; and Men became the companions and disciples in their childhood of these ancient folk, wanderers of the Elven-race who never set out upon the paths to Valinor, and knew of the Valar only as a rumour and a distant name.

Morgoth had then not long come back into Middle-earth, and his power went not far abroad, and was moreover checked by the sudden coming of great light. There was little peril in the lands and hills; and there new things, devised long ages before in the thought of Yavanna and sown as seed in the dark, came at last to their budding and their bloom. West, North, and South the children of Men spread and wandered, and their joy was the joy of the morning before the dew is dry, when every leaf is green.

But the dawn is brief and the day full often belies its promise; and now the time drew on to the great wars of the powers of the North, when Noldor and Sindar and Men strove against the hosts of Morgoth Bauglir, and went down in ruin. To this end the cunning lies of Morgoth that he sowed of old, and sowed ever anew among his foes, and the curse that came of the slaying at Alqualondë, and the oath of Fëanor, were ever at work. Only a part is here told of the deeds of those days, and most is said of the Noldor, and the Silmarils, and the mortals that became entangled in their fate. In those days Elves and Men were of like stature and strength of body, but the Elves had greater wisdom, and skill, and beauty; and those who had dwelt in Valinor and looked upon the Powers as much surpassed the Dark Elves in these things as they in turn surpassed the people of mortal race. Only in the realm of Doriath, whose queen Melian was of the kindred of Valar, did the Sindar come near to match the Calaquendi of the Blessed Realm.

Immortal were the Elves, and their wisdom waxed from age to age, and no sickness nor pestilence brought death to them. Their bodies indeed were of the stuff of Earth, and could be destroyed; and in those days they were more like to the bodies of Men, since they had not so long been inhabited by the fire of their spirit, which consumes them from within in the courses of time. But Men were more frail, more easily slain by weapon or mischance, and less easily healed; subject to sickness and many ills; and they grew old and died. What may befall their spirits after death the Elves know not. Some say that they too go to the halls of Mandos; but their place of waiting there is not that of the Elves, and Mandos under Ilúvatar alone save Manwë knows whither they go after the time of recollection in those silent halls beside the Outer Sea. None have ever come back from the mansions of the dead, save only Beren son of Barahir, whose hand had touched a Silmaril; but he never spoke afterward to mortal Men. The fate of Men after death, maybe, is not in the hands of the Valar, nor was all foretold in the Music of the Ainur.

In after days, when because of the triumph of Morgoth Elves and Men became estranged, as he most wished, those of the Elven-race that lived still in Middle-earth waned and faded, and Men usurped the sunlight. Then the Quendi wandered in the lonely places of the great lands and the isles, and took to the moonlight and the starlight, and to the woods and caves, becoming as shadows and memories, save those who ever and anon set sail into the West and vanished from Middle-earth. But in the dawn of years Elves and Men were allies and held themselves akin, and there were some among Men that learned the wisdom of the Eldar, and became great and valiant among the captains of the Noldor. And in the glory and beauty of the Elves, and in their fate, full share had the offspring of elf and mortal, Eärendil, and Elwing, and Elrond their child.

# Chapter 13

# OF THE RETURN OF THE NOLDOR

It has been told that Fëanor and his sons came first of the Exiles to Middle-earth, and landed in the waste of Lammoth, the Great Echo, upon the outer shores of the Firth of Drengist. And even as the Noldor set foot upon the strand their cries were taken up into the hills and multiplied, so that a clamour as of countless mighty voices filled all the coasts of the North; and the noise of the burning of the ships at Losgar went down the winds of the sea as a tumult of great wrath, and far away all who heard that sound were filled with wonder.

Now the flames of that burning were seen not only by Fingolfin, whom Fëanor had deserted in Araman, but also by the Orcs and the watchers of Morgoth. No tale has told what Morgoth thought in his heart at the tidings that Fëanor, his bitterest foe, had brought a host out of the West. It may be that he feared him little, for he had as yet no proof of the swords of the Noldor; and soon it was seen that he purposed to drive them back into the sea.

Under the cold stars before the rising of the Moon the host of Fëanor went up the long Firth of Drengist that pierced the Echoing Hills of Ered Lómin, and passed thus from the shores into the great land of Hithlum; and they came at length to the long lake of Mithrim, and upon its northern shore made their encampment in the region that bore the same name. But the host of Morgoth, aroused by the tumult of Lammoth and the light of the burning at Losgar, came through the passes of Ered Wethrin, the Mountains of Shadow, and assailed Fëanor on a sudden, before his camp was full-wrought or put in defence; and there on the grey fields of Mithrim was fought the Second Battle in the Wars of Beleriand. Dagor-nuin-Giliath it is named, the Battle-under-Stars, for the Moon had not yet risen; and it is renowned in song. The Noldor, outnumbered and taken at unawares, were yet swiftly victorious; for the light of Aman was not yet dimmed in their eyes, and they were strong and swift, and deadly in anger, and their swords were long and terrible. The Orcs fled before them, and they were driven forth from Mithrim with great slaughter, and hunted over the Mountains of Shadow into the great plain of Ard-galen, that lay northward of Dorthonion. There the armies of Morgoth that had passed south into the Vale of Sirion and beleaguered Círdan in the Havens of the Falas came up to their aid, and were caught in their ruin. For Celegorm, Fëanor's son, having news of them, waylaid them with a part of the Elven-host, and coming down upon them out of the hills near Eithel Sirion drove them into the Fen of Serech. Evil indeed were the tidings that came at last to Angband, and Morgoth was dismayed. Ten days that battle lasted, and from it returned of all the hosts that he had prepared for the conquest of Beleriand no more than a handful of leaves.

Yet cause he had for great joy, though it was hidden from him for a while. For Fëanor, in his wrath against the Enemy, would not halt, but pressed on behind the remnant of the Orcs, thinking so to come at Morgoth himself; and he laughed aloud as he wielded his sword, rejoicing that he had dared the wrath of the Valar and the evils of the road, that he might see the hour of his vengeance. Nothing did he know of Angband or the great strength of defence that Morgoth had so swiftly prepared; but even had he known it would not have deterred him, for he was fey, consumed by the flame of his own wrath. Thus it was that he drew far ahead of the van of his host; and seeing this the servants of Morgoth turned to bay, and there issued from Angband Balrogs to aid them. There upon the confines of Dor Daedeloth, the land of Morgoth, Fëanor was surrounded, with few friends about him. Long he fought on, and undismayed, though he was wrapped in fire and wounded with many wounds; but at the last he was smitten to the ground by Gothmog, Lord of Balrogs, whom Ecthelion after slew in Gondolin. There he would have perished, had not his sons in that moment come up with force to his aid; and the Balrogs left him, and departed to Angband.

Then his sons raised up their father and bore him back towards Mithrim. But as they drew near to Eithel Sirion and were upon the upward path to the pass over the mountains, Fëanor bade them halt; for his wounds were mortal, and he knew that his hour was come. And looking out from the slopes of Ered Wethrin with his last sight he beheld far off the peaks of Thangorodrim, mightiest of the towers of Middle-earth, and knew with the foreknowledge of death that no power of the Noldor would ever overthrow them; but he cursed the name of Morgoth thrice, and laid it upon his sons to hold to their oath, and to avenge their father. Then he died; but he had neither burial nor tomb, for so fiery was his spirit that as it sped his body fell to ash, and was borne away like smoke; and his likeness has never again appeared in Arda, neither has his spirit left the halls of Mandos. Thus ended the mightiest of the Noldor, of whose deeds came both their greatest renown and their most grievous woe.

Now in Mithrim there dwelt Grey-elves, folk of Beleriand that had wandered north over the mountains, and the Noldor met them with gladness, as kinsfolk long sundered; but speech at first was not easy between them, for in their long severance the tongues of the Cala-quendi in Valinor and of the Moriquendi in Beleriand had drawn far apart. From the Elves of Mithrim the Noldor learned of the power of Elu Thingol, King in Doriath, and the girdle of enchantment that fenced his realm; and tidings of these great deeds in the north came south to Menegroth, and to the havens of Brithombar and Eglarest. Then all the Elves of Beleriand were filled with wonder and with hope at the coming of their mighty kindred, who thus returned un-looked-for from the West in the very hour of their need, believing in-deed at first that they came as emissaries of the Valar to deliver them.

But even in the hour of the death of Fëanor an embassy came to his sons from Morgoth, acknowledging defeat, and offering terms, even to the surrender of a Silmaril. Then Maedhros the tall, the eldest son, persuaded his brothers to feign to treat with Morgoth, and to meet his emissaries at the place appointed; but the Noldor had as little thought of faith as had he. Wherefore each embassy came with greater force than was agreed; but Morgoth sent the more, and there were Balrogs. Maedhros was ambushed, and all his company were slain; but he himself was taken alive by the command of Morgoth, and brought to Angband.

Then the brothers of Maedhros drew back, and fortified a great camp in Hithlum; but Morgoth held Maedhros as hostage, and sent word that he would not release him unless the Noldor would forsake their war, returning into the West, or else departing far from Beleriand into the South of the world. But the sons of Fëanor knew that Morgoth would betray them, and would not release Maedhros, whatsoever they might do; and they were constrained also by their oath, and might not for any cause forsake the war against their Enemy. Therefore Morgoth took Maedhros and hung him from the face of a precipice upon Thangorodrim, and he was caught to the rock by the wrist of his right hand in a band of steel.

Now rumour came to the camp in Hithlum of the march of Fingolfin and those that followed him, who had crossed the Grinding Ice; and all the world lay then in wonder at the coming of the Moon. But as the host of Fingolfin marched into Mithrim the Sun rose flaming in the West; and Fingolfin unfurled his blue and silver banners, and blew his horns, and flowers sprang beneath his marching feet, and the ages of the stars were ended. At the uprising of the great light the servants of Morgoth fled into Angband, and Fingolfin passed unopposed through the fastness of Dor Daedeloth while his foes hid beneath the earth. Then the Elves smote upon the gates of Angband, and the challenge of their trumpets shook the towers of Thangorodrim; and Maedhros heard them amid his torment and cried aloud, but his voice was lost in the echoes of the stone.

But Fingolfin, being of other temper than Fëanor, and wary of the wiles of Morgoth, withdrew from Dor Daedeloth and turned back towards Mithrim, for he had heard tidings that there he should find the sons of Fëanor, and he desired also to have the shield of the Mountains of Shadow while his people rested and grew strong; for he had seen the strength of Angband, and thought not that it would fall to the sound of trumpets only. Therefore coming at length to Hithlum he made his first camp and dwelling by the northern shores of Lake Mithrim. No love was there in the hearts of those that followed Fingolfin for the House of Fëanor, for the agony of those that endured the crossing of the Ice had been great, and Fingolfin held the sons the accomplices of their father. Then there was peril of strife between the hosts; but grievous as were their losses upon the road, the people of Fingolfin and of Finrod son of Finarfin were still more numerous than the followers of Fëanor, and these now withdrew before them, and removed their dwelling to the southern shore; and the lake lay between them. Many of Fëanor's people indeed repented of the burning at Losgar, and were filled with amazement at the valour that had brought the friends whom they had abandoned over the Ice of the North; and they would have welcomed them, but they dared not, for shame.

Thus because of the curse that lay upon them the Noldor achieved nothing, while Morgoth hesitated, and the dread of light was new and strong upon the Orcs. But Morgoth arose from thought, and seeing the division of his foes he laughed. In the pits of Angband he caused vast smokes and vapours to be made, and they came forth from the reeking tops of the Iron Mountains, and afar off they could be seen in Mithrim, staining the bright airs in the first mornings of the world. A wind came out of the east, and bore them over Hithlum, darkening the new Sun; and they fell, and coiled about the fields and hollows, and lay upon the waters of Mithrim, drear and poisonous.

Then Fingon the valiant, son of Fingolfin, resolved to heal the feud that divided the Noldor, before their Enemy should be ready for war; for the earth trembled in the Northlands with the thunder of the forges of Morgoth underground. Long before, in the bliss of Valinor, before Melkor was unchained, or lies came between them, Fingon had been close in friendship with Maedhros; and though he knew not yet that Maedhros had not forgotten him at the burning of the ships, the thought of their ancient friendship stung his heart. Therefore he dared a deed which is justly renowned among the feats of the princes of the Noldor: alone, and without the counsel of any, he set forth in search of Maedhros; and aided by the very darkness that Morgoth had made he came unseen into the fastness of his foes. High upon the shoulders of Thangorodrim he climbed, and looked in despair upon the desolation of the land; but no passage or crevice could he find through which he might come within Morgoth's stronghold. Then in defiance of the Orcs, who cowered still in the dark vaults beneath the earth, he took his harp and sang a song of Valinor that the Noldor made of old, before strife was born among the sons of Finwë; and his voice rang in the mournful hollows that had never heard before aught save cries of fear and woe.

Thus Fingon found what he sought. For suddenly above him far and faint his song was taken up, and a voice answering called to him. Maedhros it was that sang amid his torment. But Fingon climbed to the foot of the precipice where his kinsman hung, and then could go no further; and he wept when he saw the cruel device of Morgoth. Maedhros therefore, being in anguish without hope, begged Fingon to shoot him with his bow; and Fingon strung an arrow, and bent his bow. And seeing no better hope he cried to Manwë, saying: 'O King to whom all birds are dear, speed now this feathered shaft, and recall some pity for the Noldor in their need!'

His prayer was answered swiftly. For Manwë to whom all birds are dear, and to whom they bring news upon Taniquetil from Middle-earth, had sent forth the race of Eagles, commanding them to dwell in the crags of the North, and to keep watch upon Morgoth; for Manwë still had pity for the exiled Elves. And the Eagles brought news of much that passed in those days to the sad ears of Manwë. Now, even as Fingon bent his bow, there flew down from the high airs Thorondor, King of Eagles, mightiest of all birds that have ever been, whose outstretched wings spanned thirty fathoms; and staying Fingon's hand he took him up, and bore him to the face of the rock where Maedhros hung. But Fingon could not release the hell-wrought bond upon his wrist, nor sever it, nor draw it from the stone. Again therefore in his pain Maedhros begged that he would slay him; but Fingon cut off his hand above the wrist, and Thorondor bore them back to Mithrim.

There Maedhros in time was healed; for the fire of life was hot within him, and his strength was of the ancient world, such as those possessed who were nurtured in Valinor. His body recovered from his torment and became hale, but the shadow of his pain was in his heart; and he lived to wield his sword with left hand more deadly than his right had been. By this deed Fingon won great renown, and all the Noldor praised him; and the hatred between the houses of Fingolfin and Fëanor was assuaged. For Maedhros begged forgiveness for the desertion in Araman; and he waived his claim to kingship over all the Noldor, saying to Fingolfin: 'If there lay no grievance between us, lord, still the kingship would rightly come to you, the eldest here of the house of Finwë, and not the least wise.' But to this his brothers did not all in their hearts agree.

Therefore even as Mandos foretold the House of Fëanor were called the Dispossessed, because the overlordship passed from it, the elder, to the house of Fingolfin, both in Elendë and in Beleriand, and because also of the loss of the Silmarils. But the Noldor being again united set a watch upon the borders of Dor Daedeloth, and Angband was beleaguered from west, and south, and east; and they sent forth messengers far and wide to explore the countries of Beleriand, and to treat with the people that dwelt there.

Now King Thingol welcomed not with a full heart the coming of so many princes in might out of the West, eager for new realms; and he would not open his kingdom, nor remove its girdle of enchantment, for wise with the wisdom of Melian he trusted not that the restraint of Morgoth would endure. Alone of the princes of the Noldor those of Finarfin's house were suffered to pass within the confines of Doriath; for they could claim close kinship with King Thingol himself, since their mother was Eärwen of Alqualondë, Olwë's daughter.

Angrod son of Finarfin was the first of the Exiles to come to Menegroth, as messenger of his brother Finrod, and he spoke long with the King, telling him of the deeds of the Noldor in the north, and of their numbers, and of the ordering of their force; but being true, and wisehearted, and thinking all griefs now forgiven, he spoke no word concerning the kinslaying, nor of the manner of the exile of the Noldor and the oath of Fëanor. King Thingol hearkened to the words of Angrod; and ere he went he said to him: 'Thus shall you speak for me to those that sent you. In Hithlum the Noldor have leave to dwell, and in the highlands of Dorthonion, and in the lands east of Doriath that are empty and wild; but elsewhere there are many of my people, and I would not have them restrained of their freedom, still less ousted from their homes. Beware therefore how you princes of the West bear yourselves; for I am the Lord of Beleriand,

and all who seek to dwell there shall hear my word. Into Doriath none shall come to abide but only such as I call as guests, or who seek me in great need.'

Now the lords of the Noldor held council in Mithrim, and thither came Angrod out of Doriath, bearing the message of King Thingol. Cold seemed its welcome to the Noldor, and the sons of Fëanor were angered at the words; but Maedhros laughed, saying: 'A king is he that can hold his own, or else his title is vain. Thingol does but grant us lands where his power does not run. Indeed Doriath alone would be his realm this day, but for the coming of the Noldor. Therefore in Doriath let him reign, and be glad that he has the sons of Finwë for his neighbours, not the Orcs of Morgoth that we found. Elsewhere it shall go as seems good to us.'

But Caranthir, who loved not the sons of Finarfin, and was the harshest of the brothers and the most quick to anger, cried aloud: 'Yea more! Let not the sons of Finarfin run hither and thither with their tales to this Dark Elf in his caves! Who made them our spokesmen to deal with him? And though they be come indeed to Beleriand, let them not so swiftly forget that their father is a lord of the Noldor, though their mother be of other kin.'

Then Angrod was wrathful and went forth from the council. Maedhros indeed rebuked Caranthir; but the greater part of the Noldor, of both followings, hearing his words were troubled in heart, fearing the fell spirit of the sons of Fëanor that it seemed would ever be like to burst forth in rash word or violence. But Maedhros restrained his brothers, and they departed from the council, and soon afterwards they left Mithrim and went eastward beyond Aros to the wide lands about the Hill of Himring. That region was named thereafter the March of Maedhros; for northwards there was little defence of hill or river against assault from Angband. There Maedhros and his brothers kept watch, gathering all such people as would come to them, and they had few dealings with their kinsfolk westward, save at need. It is said indeed that Maedhros himself devised this plan, to lessen the chances of strife, and because he was very willing that the chief peril of assault should fall upon himself; and he remained for his part in friendship with the houses of Fingolfin and Finarfin, and would come among them at times for common counsel. Yet he also was bound by the oath, though it slept now for a time.

Now the people of Caranthir dwelt furthest east beyond the upper waters of Gelion, about Lake Helevorn under Mount Rerir and to the southward; and they climbed the heights of Ered Luin and looked eastward in wonder, for wild and wide it seemed to them were the lands of Middle-earth. And thus it was that Caranthir's people came upon the Dwarves, who after the onslaught of Morgoth and the coming of the Noldor had ceased their traffic into Beleriand. But though either people loved skill and were eager to learn, no great love was there between them; for the Dwarves were secret and quick to resentment, and Caranthir was haughty and scarce concealed his scorn for the unloveliness of the Naugrim, and his people followed their lord. Nevertheless since both peoples feared and hated Morgoth they made alliance, and had of it great profit; for the Naugrim learned many secrets of craft in those days, so that the smiths and masons of Nogrod and Belegost became renowned among their kin, and when the Dwarves began again to journey into Beleriand all the traffic of the dwarf-mines passed first through the hands of Caranthir, and thus great riches came to him.

When twenty years of the Sun had passed, Fingolfin King of the Noldor made a great feast; and it was held in the spring near to the pools of Ivrin, whence the swift river Narog rose, for there the lands were green and fair at the feet of the Mountains of Shadow that shielded them from the north. The joy of that feast was long remembered in later days of sorrow; and it was called Mereth Aderthad, the Feast of Reuniting. Thither came many of the chieftains and people of Fingolfin and Finrod; and of the sons of Fëanor Maedhros and Maglor, with warriors of the eastern March; and there came also great numbers of the Grey-elves, wanderers of the woods of Beleriand and folk of the Havens, with Círdan their lord. There came even Green-elves from Ossiriand, the Land of Seven Rivers, far off under the walls of the Blue Mountains; but out of Doriath there came but two messengers, Mablung and Daeron, bearing greetings from the King.

At Mereth Aderthad many counsels were taken in good will, and oaths were sworn of league and friendship; and it is told that at this feast the tongue of the Grey-elves was most spoken even by the Noldor, for they learned swiftly the speech of Beleriand, whereas the Sindar were slow to master the tongue of Valinor. The hearts of the Noldor were high and full of hope, and to many among them it seemed that the words of Fëanor had been justified, bidding them seek freedom and fair kingdoms in Middle-earth; and indeed there followed after long years of peace, while their swords fenced Beleriand from the ruin of Morgoth, and his power was shut behind his gates. In those days there was joy beneath the new Sun and Moon, and all the land was glad; but still the Shadow brooded in the north.

And when again thirty years had passed, Turgon son of Fingolfin left Nevrast where he dwelt and sought out Finrod his friend upon the island of Tol Sirion, and they journeyed southward along the river, being weary for a while of the northern mountains; and as they journeyed night came upon them beyond the Meres of Twilight beside the waters of Sirion, and they slept upon his banks beneath the summer stars. But Ulmo coming up the river laid a deep sleep upon them and heavy dreams; and the trouble of the dreams remained after they awoke, but neither said aught to the other, for their memory was not clear, and each believed that Ulmo had sent a message to him alone. But unquiet was upon them ever after, and doubt of what should befall, and they wandered often alone in untrodden lands, seeking far and wide for places of hidden strength; for it seemed to each that he was bidden to prepare for a day of evil, and to establish a retreat, lest Morgoth should burst from Angband and overthrow the armies of the North.

Now on a time Finrod and Galadriel his sister were the guests of Thingol their kinsman in Doriath. Then Finrod was filled with wonder at the strength and majesty of Menegroth, its treasuries and armouries and its many-pillared halls of stone; and it came into his heart that he would build wide halls behind ever-guarded gates in some deep and secret place beneath the hills. Therefore he opened his heart to Thingol, telling him of his dreams; and Thingol spoke to him of the deep gorge of the River Narog, and the caves under the High Faroth in its steep western shore, and when he departed he gave him guides to lead him to that place of which few yet knew. Thus Finrod came to the Caverns of Narog, and began to establish there deep halls and armouries after the fashion of the mansions of Menegroth; and that stronghold was called Nargothrond. In that labour Finrod was aided by the Dwarves of the Blue Mountains; and they were rewarded well, for Finrod had brought more treasures out of Tirion than any other of the princes of the Noldor. And in that time was made for him the Nauglamír, the Necklace of the Dwarves, most renowned of their works in the Elder Days. It was a carcanet of gold, and set therein were gems uncounted from Valinor; but it had a power within it so that it rested lightly on its wearer as a strand of flax, and whatsoever neck it clasped it sat always with grace and loveliness.

There in Nargothrond Finrod made his home with many of his people, and he was named in the tongue of the Dwarves Felagund, Hewer of Caves; and that name he bore thereafter until his end. But Finrod Felagund was not the first to dwell in the caves beside the River Narog.

Galadriel his sister went not with him to Nargothrond, for in Doriath dwelt Celeborn, kinsman of Thingol, and there was great love between them. Therefore she remained in the Hidden Kingdom, and abode with Melian, and of her learned great lore and wisdom concerning Middle-earth.

But Turgon remembered the city set upon a hill, Tirion the fair with its tower and tree, and he found not what he sought, but returned to Nevrast, and sat in peace in Vinyamar by the shores of the sea. And in the next year Ulmo himself appeared to him, and bade him go forth again alone into the Vale of Sirion; and Turgon went forth, and by the guidance of Ulmo he discovered the hidden vale of Tumladen in the Encircling Mountains, in the midst of which there was a hill of stone. Of this he spoke to none as yet, but returned once more to Nevrast, and there began in his secret counsels to devise the plan of a city after the manner of Tirion upon Túna, for which his heart yearned in exile.

Now Morgoth, believing the report of his spies that the lords of the Noldor were wandering abroad with little thought of war, made trial of the strength and watchfulness of his enemies. Once more, with little warning, his might was stirred, and suddenly there were earthquakes in the north, and fire came from fissures in the earth, and the Iron Mountains vomited flame; and Orcs poured forth across the plain of Ard-galen. Thence they thrust down the Pass of Sirion in the west, and in the east they burst through the land of Maglor, in the gap between the hills of Maedhros and the outliers of the Blue Mountains. But Fingolfin and Maedhros were not sleeping, and while others sought out the scattered bands of Orcs that strayed in Beleriand and did great evil they came upon the main host from either side as it was assaulting Dorthonion; and they defeated the servants of Morgoth, and pursuing them across Ard-galen destroyed them utterly, to the least and last, within sight of Angband's gates. That was the third great battle of the Wars of Beleriand, and it was named Dagor Aglareb, the Glorious Battle.

A victory it was, and yet a warning; and the princes took heed of it, and thereafter drew closer their leaguer, and strengthened and ordered their watch, setting the Siege of Angband, which lasted wellnigh four hundred years of the Sun. For a long time after Dagor Aglareb no servant of Morgoth would venture from his gates, for they feared the lords of the Noldor; and Fingolfin boasted that save by treason among themselves Morgoth could never again burst from the leaguer of the Eldar, nor come upon them at unawares. Yet the

Noldor could not capture Angband, nor could they regain the Silmarils; and war never wholly ceased in all that time of the Siege, for Morgoth devised new evils, and ever and anon he would make trial of his enemies. Nor could the stronghold of Morgoth be ever wholly encircled; for the Iron Mountains, from whose great curving wall the towers of Thangorodrim were thrust forward, defended it upon either side, and were impassable to the Noldor, because of their snow and ice. Thus in his rear and to the north Morgoth had no foes, and by that way his spies at times went out, and came by devious routes into Beleriand. And desiring above all to sow fear and disunion among the Eldar, he commanded the Orcs to take alive any of them that they could and bring them bound to Angband; and some he so daunted by the terror of his eyes that they needed no chains more, but walked ever in fear of him, doing his will wherever they might be. Thus Morgoth learned much of all that had befallen since the rebellion of Fëanor, and he rejoiced, seeing therein the seed of many dissensions among his foes.

When nearly one hundred years had run since the Dagor Aglareb, Morgoth endeavoured to take Fingolfin at unawares (for he knew of the vigilance of Maedhros); and he sent forth an army into the white north, and they turned west and again south and came down the coasts to the Firth of Drengist, by the route that Fingolfin followed from the Grinding Ice. Thus they would enter into the realm of Hithlum from the west; but they were espied in time, and Fingon fell upon them among the hills at the head of the Firth, and most of the Orcs were driven into the sea. This was not reckoned among the great battles, for the Orcs were not in great number, and only a part of the people of Hithlum fought there. But thereafter there was peace for many years, and no open assault from Angband, for Morgoth perceived now that the Orcs unaided were no match for the Noldor; and he sought in his heart for new counsel.

Again after a hundred years Glaurung, the first of the Urulóki, the fire-drakes of the North, issued from Angband's gates by night. He was yet young and scarce half-grown, for long and slow is the life of the dragons, but the Elves fled before him to Ered Wethrin and Dorthonion in dismay; and he defiled the fields of Ard-galen. Then Fingon prince of Hithlum rode against him with archers on horse-back, and hemmed him round with a ring of swift riders; and Glaurung could not endure their darts, being not yet come to his full armoury, and he fled back to Angband, and came not forth again for many years. Fingon won great praise, and the Noldor rejoiced; for few foresaw the full meaning and threat of this new thing. But Morgoth was ill-pleased that Glaurung had disclosed himself over-soon; and after his defeat there was the Long Peace of wellnigh two hundred years. In all that time there were but affrays on the marches, and all Beleriand prospered and grew rich. Behind the guard of their armies in the north the Noldor built their dwellings and their towers, and many fair things they made in those days, and poems and histories and books of lore. In many parts of the land the Noldor and the Sindar became welded into one people, and spoke the same tongue; though this difference remained between them, that the Noldor had the greater power of mind and body, and were the mightier warriors and sages, and they built with stone, and loved the hill-slopes and open lands. But the Sindar had the fairer voices and were more skilled in music, save only Maglor son of Fëanor, and they loved the woods and the riversides; and some of the Grey-elves still wandered far and wide without settled abode, and they sang as they went.

# Chapter 14

# OF BELERIAND AND ITS REALMS

This is the fashion of the lands into which the Noldor came, in the north of the western regions of Middle-earth, in the ancient days; and here also is told of the manner in which the chieftains of the Eldar held their lands and the leaguer upon Morgoth after the Dagor Aglareb, the third battle in the Wars of Beleriand.

In the north of the world Melkor had in the ages past reared Ered Engrin, the Iron Mountains, as a fence to his citadel of Utumno; and they stood upon the borders of the regions of everlasting cold, in a great curve from east to west. Behind the walls of Ered Engrin in the west, where they bent back northwards, Melkor built another fortress, as a defence against assault that might come from Valinor; and when he came back to Middle-earth, as has been told, he took up his abode in the endless dungeons of Angband, the Hells of Iron, for in the War of the Powers the Valar, in their haste to overthrow him in his great stronghold of Utumno, did not wholly destroy Angband nor search out all its deep places. Beneath Ered Engrin he made a great tunnel, which issued south of the mountains; and there he made a mighty gate. But above this gate, and behind it even to the mountains, he piled the thunderous towers of Thangorodrim, that were made of the ash and slag of his subterranean furnaces, and the vast refuse of his tunnellings. They were black and desolate and exceedingly lofty; and smoke issued from their tops, dark and foul upon the northern sky. Before the gates of Angband filth and desolation spread southward for many miles over the wide plain of Ard-galen; but after the coming of the Sun rich grass arose there, and while Angband was besieged and its gates shut there were green things even among the pits and broken rocks before the doors of hell.

To the west of Thangorodrim lay Hísilómë, the Land of Mist, for so it was named by the Noldor in their own tongue because of the clouds that Morgoth sent thither during their first encampment; Hithlum it became in the tongue of the Sindar that dwelt in those regions. It was a fair land while the Siege of Angband lasted, although its air was cool and winter there was cold. In the west it was bounded by Ered Lómin, the Echoing Mountains that marched near the sea; and in the east and south by the great curve of Ered Wethrin, the Shadowy Mountains, that looked across Ard-galen and the Vale of Sirion.

Fingolfin and Fingon his son held Hithlum, and the most part of Fingolfin's folk dwelt in Mithrim about the shores of the great lake; to Fingon was assigned Dor-lómin, that lay to the west of the Mountains of Mithrim. But their chief fortress was at Eithel Sirion in the east of Ered Wethrin, whence they kept watch upon Ard-galen; and their cavalry rode upon that plain even to the shadow of Thangorodrim, for from few their horses had increased swiftly, and the grass of Ard-galen was rich and green. Of those horses many of the sires came from Valinor, and they were given to Fingolfin by Maedhros in atonement of his losses, for they had been carried by ship to Losgar.

West of Dor-lómin, beyond the Echoing Mountains, which south of the Firth of Drengist marched inland, lay Nevrast, that signifies the Hither Shore in the Sindarin tongue. That name was given at first to all the coastlands south of the Firth, but afterwards only to the land whose shores lay between Drengist and Mount Taras. There for many years was the realm of Turgon the wise, son of Fingolfin, bounded by the sea, and by Ered Lómin, and by the hills which continued the walls of Ered Wethrin westward, from Ivrin to Mount Taras, which stood upon a promontory. By some Nevrast was held to belong rather to Beleriand than to Hithlum, for it was a milder land, watered by the wet winds from the sea and sheltered from the cold north winds that blew over Hithlum. It was a hollow land, surrounded by mountains and great coast-cliffs higher than the plains behind, and no river flowed thence; and there was a great mere in the midst of Nevrast, with no certain shores, being encircled by wide marshes. Linaewen was the name of that mere, because of the multitude of birds that dwelt there, of such as love tall reeds and shallow pools. At the coming of the Noldor many of the Grey-elves lived in Nevrast near to the coasts, and especially about Mount Taras in the south-west; for to that place Ulmo and Ossë had been wont to come in days of old. All that people took Turgon for their lord, and the mingling of the Noldor and the Sindar came to pass soonest there; and Turgon dwelt long in those halls that he named Vinyamar, under Mount Taras beside the sea.

South of Ard-galen the great highland named Dorthonion stretched for sixty leagues from west to east; great pine forests it bore, especially on its northern and western sides. By gentle slopes from the plain it rose to a bleak and lofty land, where lay many tarns at the feet of bare tors whose heads were higher than the peaks of Ered Wethrin; but southward where it looked towards Doriath it fell

suddenly in dreadful precipices. From the northern slopes of Dorthonion Angrod and Aegnor, sons of Finarfin, looked out over the
fields of Ard-galen, and were the vassals of their brother Finrod, lord
of Nargothrond; their people were few, for the land was barren, and
the great highlands behind were deemed to be a bulwark that
Morgoth would not lightly seek to cross.

Between Dorthonion and the Shadowy Mountains there was a
narrow vale, whose sheer walls were clad with pines; but the vale
itself was green, for the River Sirion flowed through it, hastening
towards Beleriand. Finrod held the Pass of Sirion, and upon the isle
of Tol Sirion in the midst of the river he built a mighty watch-tower,
Minas Tirith; but after Nargothrond was made he committed that
fortress mostly to the keeping of Orodreth his brother.

Now the great and fair country of Beleriand lay on either side of the
mighty river Sirion, renowned in song, which rose at Eithel Sirion
and skirted the edge of Ard-galen ere he plunged through the pass,
becoming ever fuller with the streams of the mountains. Thence he
flowed south for one hundred and thirty leagues, gathering the waters
of many tributaries, until with a mighty flood he reached his many
mouths and sandy delta in the Bay of Balar. And following Sirion
from north to south there lay upon the right hand in West Beleriand
the Forest of Brethil between Sirion and Teiglin, and then the realm
of Nargothrond, between Teiglin and Narog. And the River Narog
rose in the falls of Ivrin in the southern face of Dor-lómin, and
flowed some eighty leagues ere he joined Sirion in Nan-tathren, the
Land of Willows. South of Nan-tathren was a region of meads filled
with many flowers, where few folk dwelt; and beyond lay the
marshes and isles of reed about the mouths of Sirion, and the sands
of his delta empty of all living things save birds of the sea.

But the realm of Nargothrond extended also west of Narog to the
River Nenning, that reached the sea at Eglarest; and Finrod became
the overlord of all the Elves of Beleriand between Sirion and the sea,
save only in the Falas. There dwelt those of the Sindar who still
loved ships, and Círdan the shipbuilder was their lord; but between
Círdan and Finrod there was friendship and alliance, and with the
aid of the Noldor the havens of Brithombar and Eglarest were built
anew. Behind their great walls they became fair towns and harbours
with quays and piers of stone. Upon the cape west of Eglarest Finrod
raised the tower of Barad Nimras to watch the western sea, though
needlessly, as it proved; for at no time ever did Morgoth essay to
build ships or to make war by sea. Water all his servants shunned,
and to the sea none would willingly go nigh, save in dire need. With

the aid of the Elves of the Havens some of the folk of Nargothrond built new ships, and they went forth and explored the great Isle of Balar, thinking there to prepare a last refuge, if evil came; but it was not their fate that they should ever dwell there.

Thus the realm of Finrod was the greatest by far, though he was the youngest of the great lords of the Noldor, Fingolfin, Fingon, and Maedhros, and Finrod Felagund. But Fingolfin was held overlord of all the Noldor, and Fingon after him, though their own realm was but the northern land of Hithlum; yet their people were the most hardy and valiant, most feared by the Orcs and most hated by Morgoth.

Upon the left hand of Sirion lay East Beleriand, at its widest a hundred leagues from Sirion to Gelion and the borders of Ossiriand; and first, between Sirion and Mindeb, lay the empty land of Dimbar under the peaks of the Crissaegrim, abode of eagles. Between Mindeb and the upper waters of Esgalduin lay the no-land of Nan Dungortheb; and that region was filled with fear, for upon its one side the power of Melian fenced the north march of Doriath, but upon the other side the sheer precipices of Ered Gorgoroth, Mountains of Terror, fell down from high Dorthonion. Thither, as was earlier told, Ungoliant had fled from the whips of the Balrogs, and there she dwelt a while, filling the ravines with her deadly gloom, and there still, when she had passed away, her foul offspring lurked and wove their evil nets; and the thin waters that spilled from Ered Gorgoroth were defiled, and perilous to drink, for the hearts of those that tasted them were filled with shadows of madness and despair. All living things else shunned that land, and the Noldor would pass through Nan Dungortheb only at great need, by paths near to the borders of Doriath and furthest from the haunted hills. That way was made long before, in the time ere Morgoth returned to Middle-earth; and if one fared upon it he came eastwards to Esgalduin, where still there stood in the days of the Siege the stone bridge of Iant Iaur. Thence he passed through Dor Dínen, the Silent Land, and crossing the Arossiach (which signifies the Fords of Aros) came to the north marches of Beleriand, where dwelt the sons of Fëanor.

Southward lay the guarded woods of Doriath, abode of Thingol the Hidden King, into whose realm none passed save by his will. Its northern and lesser part, the Forest of Neldoreth, was bounded east and south by the dark river Esgalduin, which bent westward in the midst of the land; and between Aros and Esgalduin lay the denser and greater woods of Region. Upon the southern bank of Esgalduin, where it turned westward towards Sirion, were the Caves of

Menegroth; and all Doriath lay east of Sirion save for a narrow region of woodland between the meeting of Teiglin and Sirion and the Meres of Twilight. By the people of Doriath this wood was called Nivrim, the West March; great oak-trees grew there, and it also was encompassed within the Girdle of Melian, that so some portion of Sirion which she loved in reverence of Ulmo should be wholly under the power of Thingol.

In the south-west of Doriath, where Aros flowed into Sirion, lay great pools and marshes on either side of the river, which halted there in his course and strayed in many channels. That region was named Aelin-uial, the Twilight Meres, for they were wrapped in mists, and the enchantment of Doriath lay over them. Now all the northern part of Beleriand sloped southward to this point and then for a while was plain, and the flood of Sirion was stayed. But south of Aelin-uial the land fell suddenly and steeply; and all the lower fields of Sirion were divided from the upper fields by this fall, which to one looking from the south northward appeared as an endless chain of hills running from Eglarest beyond Narog in the west to Amon Ereb in the east, within far sight of Gelion. Narog came through these hills in a deep gorge, and flowed over rapids but had no fall, and on its western bank the land rose into the great wooded highlands of Taur-en-Faroth. On the west side of this gorge, where the short and foaming stream Ringwil tumbled headlong into Narog from the High Faroth, Finrod established Nargothrond. But some twenty-five leagues east of the gorge of Nargothrond Sirion fell from the north in a mighty fall below the Meres, and then he plunged suddenly underground into great tunnels that the weight of his falling waters delved; and he issued again three leagues southward with great noise and smoke through rocky arches at the foot of the hills which were called the Gates of Sirion.

This dividing fall was named Andram, the Long Wall, from Nargothrond to Ramdal, the Wall's End, in East Beleriand. But in the east it became ever less sheer, for the vale of Gelion sloped steadily southward, and Gelion had neither fall nor rapids throughout his course, but was ever swifter than was Sirion. Between Ramdal and Gelion there stood a single hill of great extent and gentle slopes, but seeming mightier than it was, for it stood alone; and that hill was named Amon Ereb. Upon Amon Ereb died Denethor, lord of the Nandor that dwelt in Ossiriand, who marched to the aid of Thingol against Morgoth in those days when the Orcs first came down in force, and broke the starlit peace of Beleriand; and upon that hill Maedhros dwelt after the great defeat. But south of the Andram,

between Sirion and Gelion, was a wild land of tangled forest in which
no folk went, save here and there a few Dark Elves wandering; Taur-
im-Duinath it was named, the Forest between the Rivers.

Gelion was a great river; and he rose in two sources and had at
first two branches; Little Gelion that came from the Hill of Himring,
and Greater Gelion that came from Mount Rerir. From the meeting of
his arms he flowed south for forty leagues before he found his tributaries; and before he found the sea he was twice as long as Sirion,
though less wide and full, for more rain fell in Hithlum and Dorthonion, whence Sirion drew his waters, than in the east. From Ered
Luin flowed the six tributaries of Gelion: Ascar (that was after
named Rathlóriel), Thalos, Legolin, Brilthor, Duilwen, and Adurant,
swift and turbulent streams, falling steeply from the mountains; and
between Ascar in the north and Adurant in the south, and between
Gelion and Ered Luin, lay the far green country of Ossiriand, the
Land of Seven Rivers. Now at a point nearly midway in its course the
stream of Adurant divided and then joined again; and the island that
its waters enclosed was named Tol Galen, the Green Isle. There
Beren and Lúthien dwelt after their return.

In Ossiriand dwelt the Green-elves, in the protection of their
rivers; for after Sirion Ulmo loved Gelion above all the waters of the
western world. The woodcraft of the Elves of Ossiriand was such that
a stranger might pass through their land from end to end and see
none of them. They were clad in green in spring and summer, and
the sound of their singing could be heard even across the waters of
Gelion; wherefore the Noldor named that country Lindon, the land
of music, and the mountains beyond they named Ered Lindon, for
they first saw them from Ossiriand.

East of Dorthonion the marches of Beleriand were most open to
attack, and only hills of no great height guarded the vale of Gelion
from the north. In that region, upon the March of Maedhros and in
the lands behind, dwelt the sons of Fëanor with many people; and
their riders passed often over the vast northern plain, Lothlann the
wide and empty, east of Ard-galen, lest Morgoth should attempt any
sortie towards East Beleriand. The chief citadel of Maedhros was
upon the Hill of Himring, the Ever-cold; and that was wide-
shouldered, bare of trees, and flat upon its summit, surrounded by
many lesser hills. Between Himring and Dorthonion there was a pass,
exceeding steep upon the west, and that was the Pass of Aglon, and
was a gate unto Doriath; and a bitter wind blew ever through it from

the north. But Celegorm and Curufin fortified Aglon and held it with
great strength, and all the land of Himlad southward between the
River Aros that rose in Dorthonion and his tributary Celon that came
from Himring.

Between the arms of Gelion was the ward of Maglor, and here in
one place the hills failed altogether; there it was that the Orcs came
into East Beleriand before the Third Battle. Therefore the Noldor
held strength of cavalry in the plains at that place; and the people
of Caranthir fortified the mountains to the east of Maglor's Gap.
There Mount Rerir, and about it many lesser heights, stood out from
the main range of Ered Lindon westward; and in the angle between
Rerir and Ered Lindon there was a lake, shadowed by mountains on
all sides save the south. That was Lake Helevorn, deep and dark, and
beside it Caranthir had his abode; but all the great land between
Gelion and the mountains, and between Rerir and the River Ascar,
was called by the Noldor Thargelion, which signifies the Land beyond
Gelion, or Dor Caranthir, the Land of Caranthir; and it was here
that the Noldor first met the Dwarves. But Thargelion was before
called by the Grey-elves Talath Rhúnen, the East Vale.

Thus the sons of Fëanor under Maedhros were the lords of East
Beleriand, but their people were in that time mostly in the north of
the land, and southward they rode only to hunt in the greenwoods.
But there Amrod and Amras had their abode, and they came seldom
northward while the Siege lasted; and there also other of the Elf-
lords would ride at times, even from afar, for the land was wild but
very fair. Of these Finrod Felagund came most often, for he had great
love of wandering, and he came even into Ossiriand, and won the
friendship of the Green-elves. But none of the Noldor went ever
over Ered Lindon, while their realm lasted; and little news and late
came into Beleriand of what passed in the regions of the East.

## Chapter 15

# OF THE NOLDOR IN BELERIAND

It has been told how by the guidance of Ulmo Turgon of Nevrast discovered the hidden vale of Tumladen; and that (as was after known) lay east of the upper waters of Sirion, in a ring of mountains tall and sheer, and no living thing came there save the eagles of Thorondor. But there was a deep way under the mountains delved in the darkness of the world by waters that flowed out to join the streams of Sirion; and this way Turgon found, and so came to the green plain amid the mountains, and saw the island-hill that stood there of hard smooth stone; for the vale had been a great lake in ancient days. Then Turgon knew that he had found the place of his desire, and he resolved to build there a fair city, a memorial of Tirion upon Túna; but he returned to Nevrast, and remained there in peace, though he pondered ever in his thought how he should accomplish his design.

Now after the Dagor Aglareb the unquiet that Ulmo set in his heart returned to him, and he summoned many of the hardiest and most skilled of his people, and led them secretly to the hidden vale, and there they began the building of the city that Turgon had devised; and they set a watch all about it, that none might come upon their work from without, and the power of Ulmo that ran in Sirion protected them. But Turgon dwelt still for the most part in Nevrast, until it came to pass that at last the city was full-wrought, after two and fifty years of secret toil. It is said that Turgon appointed its name to be Ondolindë in the speech of the Elves of Valinor, the Rock of the Music of Water, for there were fountains upon the hill; but in the Sindarin tongue the name was changed, and it became Gondolin, the Hidden Rock. Then Turgon prepared to depart from Nevrast and leave his halls in Vinyamar beside the sea; and there Ulmo came to him once again, and spoke with him. And he said: 'Now thou shalt go at last to Gondolin, Turgon; and I will maintain my power in the Vale of Sirion, and in all the waters therein, so that none shall mark thy going, nor shall any find there the hidden entrance against thy will. Longest of all the realms of the Eldalië shall Gondolin stand against Melkor. But love not too well the work of thy hands and the devices of thy heart; and remember that the true hope of the Noldor lieth in the West and cometh from the Sea.'

And Ulmo warned Turgon that he also lay under the Doom of

Mandos, which Ulmo had no power to remove. 'Thus it may come
to pass,' he said, 'that the curse of the Noldor shall find thee too ere
the end, and treason awake within thy walls. Then they shall be
in peril of fire. But if this peril draweth nigh indeed, then even from
Nevrast one shall come to warn thee, and from him beyond ruin and
fire hope shall be born for Elves and Men. Leave therefore in this
house arms and a sword, that in years to come he may find them,
and thus shalt thou know him, and not be deceived.' And Ulmo
declared to Turgon of what kind and stature should be the helm and
mail and sword that he left behind.

Then Ulmo returned to the sea, and Turgon sent forth all his
people, even to a third part of the Noldor of Fingolfin's following,
and a yet greater host of the Sindar; and they passed away, company
by company, secretly, under the shadows of Ered Wethrin, and they
came unseen to Gondolin, and none knew whither they had gone.
And last of all Turgon arose, and went with his household silently
through the hills, and passed the gates in the mountains, and they
were shut behind him.

Through many long years none passed inward thereafter, save
Húrin and Huor only; and the host of Turgon came never forth again
until the Year of Lamentation after three hundred and fifty years
and more. But behind the circle of the mountains the people of
Turgon grew and throve, and they put forth their skill in labour
unceasing, so that Gondolin upon Amon Gwareth became fair indeed
and fit to compare even with Elven Tirion beyond the sea. High and
white were its walls, and smooth its stairs, and tall and strong was
the Tower of the King. There shining fountains played, and in the
courts of Turgon stood images of the Trees of old, which Turgon
himself wrought with elven-craft; and the Tree which he made of
gold was named Glingal, and the Tree whose flowers he made of
silver was named Belthil. But fairer than all the wonders of Gondolin
was Idril, Turgon's daughter, she that was called Celebrindal, the
Silver-foot, whose hair was as the gold of Laurelin before the coming
of Melkor. Thus Turgon lived long in bliss; but Nevrast was desolate, and remained empty of living folk until the ruin of Beleriand.

Now while the city of Gondolin was building in secret, Finrod
Felagund wrought in the deep places of Nargothrond; but Galadriel
his sister dwelt, as has been told, in Thingol's realm in Doriath. And
at times Melian and Galadriel would speak together of Valinor and
the bliss of old; but beyond the dark hour of the death of the Trees
Galadriel would not go, but ever fell silent. And on a time Melian

said: 'There is some woe that lies upon you and your kin. That I can see in you, but all else is hidden from me; for by no vision or thought can I perceive anything that passed or passes in the West: a shadow lies over all the land of Aman, and reaches far out over the sea. Why will you not tell me more?'

'For that woe is past,' said Galadriel; 'and I would take what joy is here left, untroubled by memory. And maybe there is woe enough yet to come, though still hope may seem bright.'

Then Melian looked in her eyes, and said: 'I believe not that the Noldor came forth as messengers of the Valar, as was said at first: not though they came in the very hour of our need. For they speak never of the Valar, nor have their high lords brought any message to Thingol, whether from Manwë, or Ulmo, or even from Olwë the King's brother, and his own folk that went over the sea. For what cause, Galadriel, were the high people of the Noldor driven forth as exiles from Aman? Or what evil lies on the sons of Fëanor that they are so haughty and so fell? Do I not strike near the truth?'

'Near,' said Galadriel; 'save that we were not driven forth, but came of our own will, and against that of the Valar. And through great peril and in despite of the Valar for this purpose we came: to take vengeance upon Morgoth, and regain what he stole.'

Then Galadriel spoke to Melian of the Silmarils, and of the slaying of King Finwë at Formenos; but still she said no word of the Oath, nor of the Kinslaying, nor of the burning of the ships at Losgar. But Melian said: 'Now much you tell me, and yet more I perceive. A darkness you would cast over the long road from Tirion, but I see evil there, which Thingol should learn for his guidance.'

'Maybe,' said Galadriel; 'but not of me.'

And Melian spoke then no more of these matters with Galadriel; but she told to King Thingol all that she had heard of the Silmarils. 'This is a great matter,' she said, 'greater indeed than the Noldor themselves understand; for the Light of Aman and the fate of Arda lie locked now in these things, the work of Fëanor, who is gone. They shall not be recovered, I foretell, by any power of the Eldar; and the world shall be broken in battles that are to come, ere they are wrested from Morgoth. See now! Fëanor they have slain, and many another, as I guess; but first of all the deaths they have brought and yet shall bring was Finwë your friend. Morgoth slew him, ere he fled from Aman.'

Then Thingol was silent, being filled with grief and foreboding; but at length he said: 'Now at last I understand the coming of the Noldor out of the West, at which I wondered much before. Not to

our aid did they come (save by chance); for those that remain in
Middle-earth the Valar will leave to their own devices, until the
uttermost need. For vengeance and redress of their loss the Noldor
came. Yet all the more sure shall they be as allies against Morgoth,
with whom it is not now to be thought that they shall ever make
treaty.'

But Melian said: 'Truly for these causes they came; but for others
also. Beware of the sons of Fëanor! The shadow of the wrath of the
Valar lies upon them; and they have done evil, I perceive, both in
Aman and to their own kin. A grief but lulled to sleep lies between
the princes of the Noldor.'

And Thingol answered: 'What is that to me? Of Fëanor I have
heard but report, which makes him great indeed. Of his sons I hear
little to my pleasure; yet they are likely to prove the deadliest foes of
our foe.'

'Their swords and their counsels shall have two edges,' said
Melian; and afterwards they spoke no more of this matter.

It was not long before whispered tales began to pass among the
Sindar concerning the deeds of the Noldor ere they came to Beleriand.
Certain it is whence they came, and the evil truth was enhanced and
poisoned by lies; but the Sindar were yet unwary and trustful of
words, and (as may well be thought) Morgoth chose them for this
first assault of his malice, for they knew him not. And Círdan, hearing
these dark tales, was troubled; for he was wise, and perceived swiftly
that true or false they were put about at this time through malice,
though the malice he deemed was that of the princes of the Noldor,
because of the jealousy of their houses. Therefore he sent messengers
to Thingol to tell all that he had heard.

It chanced that at that time the sons of Finarfin were again the
guests of Thingol, for they wished to see their sister Galadriel. Then
Thingol, being greatly moved, spoke in anger to Finrod, saying: 'Ill
have you done to me, kinsman, to conceal so great matters from me.
For now I have learned of all the evil deeds of the Noldor.'

But Finrod answered: 'What ill have I done you, lord? Or what
evil deed have the Noldor done in all your realm to grieve you?
Neither against your kingship nor against any of your people have
they thought evil or done evil.'

'I marvel at you, son of Eärwen,' said Thingol, 'that you would
come to the board of your kinsman thus red-handed from the slaying
of your mother's kin, and yet say naught in defence, nor yet seek any
pardon!'

Then Finrod was greatly troubled, but he was silent, for he could not defend himself, save by bringing charges against the other princes of the Noldor; and that he was loath to do before Thingol. But in Angrod's heart the memory of the words of Caranthir welled up again in bitterness, and he cried: 'Lord, I know not what lies you have heard, nor whence; but we came not red-handed. Guiltless we came forth, save maybe of folly, to listen to the words of fell Fëanor, and become as if besotted with wine, and as briefly. No evil did we do on our road, but suffered ourselves great wrong; and forgave it. For this we are named tale-bearers to you and treasonable to the Noldor: untruly as you know, for we have of our loyalty been silent before you, and thus earned your anger. But now these charges are no longer to be borne, and the truth you shall know.'

Then Angrod spoke bitterly against the sons of Fëanor, telling of the blood at Alqualondë, and the Doom of Mandos, and the burning of the ships at Losgar. And he cried: 'Wherefore should we that endured the Grinding Ice bear the name of kinslayers and traitors?'

'Yet the shadow of Mandos lies on you also,' said Melian. But Thingol was long silent ere he spoke. 'Go now!' he said. 'For my heart is hot within me. Later you may return, if you will; for I will not shut my doors for ever against you, my kindred, that were ensnared in an evil that you did not aid. With Fingolfin and his people also I will keep friendship, for they have bitterly atoned for such ill as they did. And in our hatred of the Power that wrought all this woe our griefs shall be lost. But hear my words! Never again in my ears shall be heard the tongue of those who slew my kin in Alqualondë! Nor in all my realm shall it be openly spoken, while my power endures. All the Sindar shall hear my command that they shall neither speak with the tongue of the Noldor nor answer to it. And all such as use it shall be held slayers of kin and betrayers of kin unrepentant.'

Then the sons of Finarfin departed from Menegroth with heavy hearts, perceiving how the words of Mandos would ever be made true, and that none of the Noldor that followed after Fëanor could escape from the shadow that lay upon his house. And it came to pass even as Thingol had spoken; for the Sindar heard his word, and thereafter throughout Beleriand they refused the tongue of the Noldor, and shunned those that spoke it aloud; but the Exiles took the Sindarin tongue in all their daily uses, and the High Speech of the West was spoken only by the lords of the Noldor among themselves. Yet that speech lived ever as a language of lore, wherever any of that people dwelt.

It came to pass that Nargothrond was full-wrought (and yet Turgon
still dwelt in the halls of Vinyamar), and the sons of Finarfin were
gathered there to a feast; and Galadriel came from Doriath and dwelt
a while in Nargothrond. Now King Finrod Felagund had no wife,
and Galadriel asked him why this should be; but foresight came upon
Felagund as she spoke, and he said: 'An oath I too shall swear, and
must be free to fulfil it, and go into darkness. Nor shall anything of
my realm endure that a son should inherit.'

But it is said that not until that hour had such cold thoughts ruled
him; for indeed she whom he had loved was Amarië of the Vanyar,
and she went not with him into exile.

# Chapter 16

# OF MAEGLIN

Aredhel Ar-Feiniel, the White Lady of the Noldor, daughter of Fingolfin, dwelt in Nevrast with Turgon her brother, and she went with him to the Hidden Kingdom. But she wearied of the guarded city of Gondolin, desiring ever the longer the more to ride again in the wide lands and to walk in the forests, as had been her wont in Valinor; and when two hundred years had passed since Gondolin was full-wrought, she spoke to Turgon and asked leave to depart. Turgon was loath to grant this, and long denied her; but at the last he yielded, saying: 'Go then, if you will, though it is against my wisdom, and I forebode that ill will come of it both to you and to me. But you shall go only to seek Fingon, our brother; and those that I send with you shall return hither to Gondolin as swiftly as they may.'

But Aredhel said: 'I am your sister and not your servant, and beyond your bounds I will go as seems good to me. And if you begrudge me an escort, then I will go alone.'

Then Turgon answered: 'I grudge you nothing that I have. Yet I desire that none shall dwell beyond my walls who know the way hither; and if I trust you, my sister, others I trust less to keep guard on their tongues.'

And Turgon appointed three lords of his household to ride with Aredhel, and he bade them lead her to Fingon in Hithlum, if they might prevail upon her. 'And be wary,' he said; 'for though Morgoth be yet hemmed in the North there are many perils in Middle-earth of which the Lady knows nothing.' Then Aredhel departed from Gondolin, and Turgon's heart was heavy at her going.

But when she came to the Ford of Brithiach in the River Sirion she said to her companions: 'Turn now south and not north, for I will not ride to Hithlum; my heart desires rather to find the sons of Fëanor, my friends of old.' And since she could not be dissuaded they turned south as she commanded, and sought admittance into Doriath. But the march-wardens denied them; for Thingol would suffer none of the Noldor to pass the Girdle, save his kinsfolk of the house of Finarfin, and least of all those that were friends of the sons of Fëanor. Therefore the march-wardens said to Aredhel: 'To the land of Celegorm for which you seek, Lady, you may by no means pass through the realm of King Thingol; you must ride beyond the

Girdle of Melian, to the south or to the north. The speediest way is by the paths that lead east from the Brithiach through Dimbar and along the north-march of this kingdom, until you pass the Bridge of Esgalduin and the Fords of Aros, and come to the lands that lie behind the Hill of Himring. There dwell, as we believe, Celegorm and Curufin, and it may be that you will find them; but the road is perilous.'

Then Aredhel turned back and sought the dangerous road between the haunted valleys of Ered Gorgoroth and the north fences of Doriath; and as they drew near to the evil region of Nan Dungortheb the riders became enmeshed in shadows, and Aredhel strayed from her companions and was lost. They sought long for her in vain, fearing that she had been ensnared, or had drunk from the poisoned streams of that land; but the fell creatures of Ungoliant that dwelt in the ravines were aroused and pursued them, and they hardly escaped with their lives. When at last they returned and their tale was told there was great sorrow in Gondolin; and Turgon sat long alone, enduring grief and anger in silence.

But Aredhel, having sought in vain for her companions, rode on, for she was fearless and hardy of heart, as were all the children of Finwë; and she held on her way, and crossing Esgalduin and Aros came to the land of Himlad between Aros and Celon where Celegorm and Curufin dwelt in those days, before the breaking of the Siege of Angband. At that time they were from home, riding with Caranthir east in Thargelion; but the people of Celegorm welcomed her and bade her stay among them with honour until their lord's return. There for a while she was content, and had great joy in wandering free in the woodlands; but as the year lengthened and Celegorm did not return, she became restless again, and took to riding alone ever further abroad, seeking for new paths and untrodden glades. Thus it chanced in the waning of the year that Aredhel came to the south of Himlad, and passed over Celon; and before she was aware she was enmeshed in Nan Elmoth.

In that wood in ages past Melian walked in the twilight of Middle-earth when the trees were young, and enchantment lay upon it still. But now the trees of Nan Elmoth were the tallest and darkest in all Beleriand, and there the sun never came; and there Eöl dwelt, who was named the Dark Elf. Of old he was of the kin of Thingol, but he was restless and ill at ease in Doriath, and when the Girdle of Melian was set about the Forest of Region where he dwelt he fled thence to Nan Elmoth. There he lived in deep shadow, loving the night and the twilight under the stars. He shunned the Noldor, holding them to blame for the return of Morgoth, to trouble the quiet of Beleriand; but for the Dwarves he had more liking than any other of the Elvenfolk of old. From him the Dwarves learned much of what passed in the lands of the Eldar.

Now the traffic of the Dwarves down from the Blue Mountains followed two roads across East Beleriand, and the northern way, going towards the Fords of Aros, passed nigh to Nan Elmoth; and there Eöl would meet the Naugrim and hold converse with them. And as their friendship grew he would at times go and dwell as guest in the deep mansions of Nogrod or Belegost. There he learned much of metalwork, and came to great skill therein; and he devised a metal as hard as the steel of the Dwarves, but so malleable that he could make it thin and supple; and yet it remained resistant to all blades and darts. He named it *galvorn*, for it was black and shining like jet, and he was clad in it whenever he went abroad. But Eöl, though stooped by his smithwork, was no Dwarf, but a tall Elf of a high kin of the Teleri, noble though grim of face; and his eyes could see deep into shadows and dark places. And it came to pass that he saw Aredhel Ar-Feiniel as she strayed among the tall trees near the borders of Nan Elmoth, a gleam of white in the dim land. Very fair she seemed to him, and he desired her; and he set his enchantments about her so that she could not find the ways out, but drew ever nearer to his dwelling in the depths of the wood. There were his smithy, and his dim halls, and such servants as he had, silent and secret as their master. And when Aredhel, weary with wandering, came at last to his doors, he revealed himself; and he welcomed her, and led her into his house. And there she remained; for Eöl took her to wife, and it was long ere any of her kin heard of her again.

It is not said that Aredhel was wholly unwilling, nor that her life in Nan Elmoth was hateful to her for many years. For though at Eöl's command she must shun the sunlight, they wandered far together under the stars or by the light of the sickle moon; or she might fare alone as she would, save that Eöl forbade her to seek the sons of Fëanor, or any others of the Noldor. And Aredhel bore to Eöl a son in the shadows of Nan Elmoth, and in her heart she gave him a name in the forbidden tongue of the Noldor, Lómion, that signifies Child of the Twilight; but his father gave him no name until he was twelve years old. Then he called him Maeglin, which is Sharp Glance, for he perceived that the eyes of his son were more piercing than his own, and his thought could read the secrets of hearts beyond the mist of words.

As Maeglin grew to full stature he resembled in face and form rather his kindred of the Noldor, but in mood and mind he was the son of his father. His words were few save in matters that touched him near, and then his voice had a power to move those that heard him and to overthrow those that withstood him. He was tall and black-haired; his eyes were dark, yet bright and keen as the eyes of the Noldor, and his skin was white. Often he went with Eöl to the cities of the Dwarves in the east of Ered Lindon, and there he learned eagerly what they would teach, and above all the craft of finding the ores of metals in the mountains.

Yet it is said that Maeglin loved his mother better, and if Eöl were abroad he would sit long beside her and listen to all that she could tell him of her kin and their deeds in Eldamar, and of the might and valour of the princes of the House of Fingolfin. All these things he laid to heart, but most of all that which he heard of Turgon, and that he had no heir; for Elenwë his wife perished in the crossing of the Helcaraxë, and his daughter Idril Celebrindal was his only child.

In the telling of these tales there was awakened in Aredhel a desire to see her own kin again, and she marvelled that she had grown weary of the light of Gondolin, and the fountains in the sun, and the green sward of Tumladen under the windy skies of spring; moreover she was often alone in the shadows when both her son and her husband were away. Of these tales also grew the first quarrels of Maeglin and Eöl. For by no means would his mother reveal to Maeglin where Turgon dwelt, nor by what means one might come thither, and he bided his time, trusting yet to wheedle the secret from her, or per-haps to read her unguarded mind; but ere that could be done he desired to look on the Noldor and speak with the sons of Fëanor, his kin, that dwelt not far away. But when he declared his purpose to Eöl, his father was wrathful. 'You are of the house of Eöl, Maeglin, my son,' he said, 'and not of the Golodhrim. All this land is the land of the Teleri, and I will not deal nor have my son deal with the slayers of our kin, the invaders and usurpers of our homes. In this you shall obey me, or I will set you in bonds.' And Maeglin did not answer, but was cold and silent, and went abroad no more with Eöl; and Eöl mistrusted him.

It came to pass that at the midsummer the Dwarves, as was their custom, bade Eöl to a feast in Nogrod; and he rode away. Now Maeglin and his mother were free for a while to go where they wished, and they rode often to the eaves of the wood, seeking the sunlight; and desire grew hot in Maeglin's heart to leave Nan Elmoth for ever. Therefore he said to Aredhel: 'Lady, let us depart while there is time! What hope is there in this wood for you or for me? Here we are held in bondage, and no profit shall I find here; for I have learned all that my father has to teach, or that the Naugrim will reveal to me. Shall we not seek for Gondolin? You shall be my guide, and I will be your guard!'

Then Aredhel was glad, and looked with pride upon her son; and telling the servants of Eöl that they went to seek the sons of Fëanor they departed and rode away to the north eaves of Nan Elmoth. There they crossed the slender stream of Celon into the land of Himlad and rode on to the Fords of Aros, and so westward along the fences of Doriath.

Now Eöl returned out of the east sooner than Maeglin had foreseen, and found his wife and his son but two days gone; and so great was his anger that he followed after them even by the light of day. As he entered the Himlad he mastered his wrath and went warily, remembering his danger, for Celegorm and Curufin were mighty lords who loved Eöl not at all, and Curufin moreover was of perilous mood; but the scouts of Aglon had marked the riding of Maeglin and Aredhel to the Fords of Aros, and Curufin perceiving that strange deeds were afoot came south from the Pass and encamped near the Fords. And before Eöl had ridden far across the Himlad he was waylaid by the riders of Curufin, and taken to their lord.

Then Curufin said to Eöl: 'What errand have you, Dark Elf, in my lands? An urgent matter, perhaps, that keeps one so sun-shy abroad by day.'

And Eöl knowing his peril restrained the bitter words that arose in his mind. 'I have learned, Lord Curufin,' he said, 'that my son and my wife, the White Lady of Gondolin, have ridden to visit you while I was from home; and it seemed to me fitting that I should join them on this errand.'

Then Curufin laughed at Eöl, and he said: 'They might have found their welcome here less warm than they hoped, had you accompanied them; but it is no matter, for that was not their errand. It is not two days since they passed over the Arossiach, and thence rode swiftly westward. It seems that you would deceive me; unless indeed you yourself have been deceived.'

And Eöl answered: 'Then, lord, perhaps you will give me leave to go, and discover the truth of this matter.'

'You have my leave, but not my love,' said Curufin. 'The sooner you depart from my land the better will it please me.'

Then Eöl mounted his horse, saying: 'It is good, Lord Curufin, to find a kinsman thus kindly at need. I will remember it when I return.'

Then Curufin looked darkly upon Eöl. 'Do not flaunt the title of your wife before me,' he said. 'For those who steal the daughters of the Noldor and wed them without gift or leave do not gain kinship with their kin. I have given you leave to go. Take it, and be gone. By the laws of the Eldar I may not slay you at this time. And this counsel I add: return now to your dwelling in the darkness of Nan Elmoth; for my heart warns me that if you now pursue those who love you no more, never will you return thither.'

Then Eöl rode off in haste, and he was filled with hatred of all the Noldor; for he perceived now that Maeglin and Aredhel were fleeing to Gondolin. And driven by anger and the shame of his humiliation he crossed the Fords of Aros and rode hard upon the way that they had gone before; but though they knew not that he followed them, and he had the swiftest steed, he came never in sight of them until they reached the Brithiach, and abandoned their horses. Then by ill fate they were betrayed; for the horses neighed loudly, and Eöl's steed heard them, and sped towards them; and Eöl saw from afar the white raiment of Aredhel, and marked which way she went, seeking the secret path into the mountains.

Now Aredhel and Maeglin came to the Outer Gate of Gondolin and the Dark Guard under the mountains; and there she was received with joy, and passing through the Seven Gates she came with Maeglin to Turgon upon Amon Gwareth. Then the King listened with wonder to all that Aredhel had to tell; and he looked with liking upon Maeglin his sister-son, seeing in him one worthy to be accounted among the princes of the Noldor.

'I rejoice indeed that Ar-Feiniel has returned to Gondolin,' he said, 'and now more fair again shall my city seem than in the days when I deemed her lost. And Maeglin shall have the highest honour in my realm.'

Then Maeglin bowed low and took Turgon for lord and king, to do all his will; but thereafter he stood silent and watchful, for the bliss and splendour of Gondolin surpassed all that he had imagined from the tales of his mother, and he was amazed by the strength of the city and the hosts of its people, and the many things strange and beautiful that he beheld. Yet to none were his eyes more often drawn than to Idril the King's daughter, who sat beside him; for she was golden as the Vanyar, her mother's kindred, and she seemed to him as the sun from which all the King's hall drew its light.

But Eöl, following after Aredhel, found the Dry River and the secret path, and so creeping in by stealth he came to the Guard, and was taken and questioned. And when the Guard heard that he claimed

Aredhel as wife they were amazed, and sent a swift messenger to the City; and he came to the King's hall.

'Lord,' he cried, 'the Guard have taken captive one that came by stealth to the Dark Gate. Eöl he names himself, and he is a tall Elf, dark and grim, of the kindred of the Sindar; yet he claims the Lady Aredhel as his wife, and demands to be brought before you. His wrath is great and he is hard to restrain; but we have not slain him as your law commands.'

Then Aredhel said: 'Alas! Eöl has followed us, even as I feared. But with great stealth was it done; for we saw and heard no pursuit as we entered upon the Hidden Way.' Then she said to the messenger: 'He speaks but the truth. He is Eöl, and I am his wife, and he is the father of my son. Slay him not, but lead him hither to the King's judgement, if the King so wills.'

And so it was done; and Eöl was brought to Turgon's hall and stood before his high seat, proud and sullen. Though he was amazed no less than his son at all that he saw, his heart was filled the more with anger and with hate of the Noldor. But Turgon treated him with honour, and rose up and would take his hand; and he said: 'Welcome, kinsman, for so I hold you. Here you shall dwell at your pleasure, save only that you must here abide and depart not from my kingdom; for it is my law that none who finds the way hither shall depart.'

But Eöl withdrew his hand. 'I acknowledge not your law,' he said. 'No right have you or any of your kin in this land to seize realms or to set bounds, either here or there. This is the land of the Teleri, to which you bring war and all unquiet, dealing ever proudly and unjustly. I care nothing for your secrets and I came not to spy upon you, but to claim my own: my wife and my son. Yet if in Aredhel your sister you have some claim, then let her remain; let the bird go back to the cage, where soon she will sicken again, as she sickened before. But not so Maeglin. My son you shall not withhold from me. Come, Maeglin son of Eöl! Your father commands you. Leave the house of his enemies and the slayers of his kin, or be accursed!' But Maeglin answered nothing.

Then Turgon sat in his high seat holding his staff of doom, and in a stern voice spoke: 'I will not debate with you, Dark Elf. By the swords of the Noldor alone are your sunless woods defended. Your freedom to wander there wild you owe to my kin; and but for them long since you would have laboured in thraldom in the pits of Angband. And here I am King; and whether you will it or will it not, my doom is law. This choice only is given to you: to abide here, or to die here; and so also for your son.'

Then Eöl looked into the eyes of King Turgon, and he was not daunted, but stood long without word or movement while a still silence fell upon the hall; and Aredhel was afraid, knowing that he was perilous. Suddenly, swift as serpent, he seized a javelin that he held hid beneath his cloak and cast it at Maeglin, crying: 'The second choice I take and for my son also! You shall not hold what is mine!'

But Aredhel sprang before the dart, and it smote her in the shoulder; and Eöl was overborne by many and set in bonds, and led away, while others tended Aredhel. But Maeglin looking upon his father was silent.

It was appointed that Eöl should be brought on the next day to the King's judgement; and Aredhel and Idril moved Turgon to mercy. But in the evening Aredhel sickened, though the wound had seemed little, and she fell into the darkness, and in the night she died; for the point of the javelin was poisoned, though none knew it until too late.

Therefore when Eöl was brought before Turgon he found no mercy; and they led him forth to the Caragdûr, a precipice of black rock upon the north side of the hill of Gondolin, there to cast him down from the sheer walls of the city. And Maeglin stood by and said nothing; but at the last Eöl cried out: 'So you forsake your father and his kin, ill-gotten son! Here shall you fail of all your hopes, and here may you yet die the same death as I.'

Then they cast Eöl over the Caragdûr, and so he ended, and to all in Gondolin it seemed just; but Idril was troubled, and from that day she mistrusted her kinsman. But Maeglin prospered and grew great among the Gondolindrim, praised by all, and high in the favour of Turgon; for if he would learn eagerly and swiftly all that he might, he had much also to teach. And he gathered about him all such as had the most bent to smithcraft and mining; and he sought in the Echoriath (which are the Encircling Mountains), and found rich lodes of ore of divers metals. Most he prized the hard iron of the mine of Anghabar in the north of the Echoriath, and thence he got a wealth of forged metal and of steel, so that the arms of the Gondolindrim were made ever stronger and more keen; and that stood them in good stead in the days to come. Wise in counsel was Maeglin and wary, and yet hardy and valiant at need. And that was seen in after days: for when in the dread year of the Nirnaeth Arnoediad Turgon opened his leaguer and marched forth to the help of Fingon in the north, Maeglin would not remain in Gondolin as regent of the King, but went to the war and fought beside Turgon, and proved fell and fearless in battle.

Thus all seemed well with the fortunes of Maeglin, who had risen to be mighty among the princes of the Noldor, and greatest save one in the most renowned of their realms. Yet he did not reveal his heart; and though not all things went as he would he endured it in silence, hiding his mind so that few could read it, unless it were Idril Cele-brindal. For from his first days in Gondolin he had borne a grief, ever worsening, that robbed him of all joy: he loved the beauty of Idril and desired her, without hope. The Eldar wedded not with kin so near, nor ever before had any desired to do so. And however that might be, Idril loved Maeglin not at all; and knowing his thought of her she loved him the less. For it seemed to her a thing strange and crooked in him, as indeed the Eldar ever since have deemed it: an evil fruit of the Kinslaying, whereby the shadow of the curse of Mandos fell upon the last hope of the Noldor. But as the years passed still Maeglin watched Idril, and waited, and his love turned to dark-ness in his heart. And he sought the more to have his will in other matters, shirking no toil or burden, if he might thereby have power.

Thus it was in Gondolin; and amid all the bliss of that realm, while its glory lasted, a dark seed of evil was sown.

# Chapter 17

## OF THE COMING OF MEN INTO THE WEST

When three hundred years and more were gone since the Noldor came to Beleriand, in the days of the Long Peace, Finrod Felagund lord of Nargothrond journeyed east of Sirion and went hunting with Maglor and Maedhros, sons of Fëanor. But he wearied of the chase and passed on alone towards the mountains of Ered Lindon that he saw shining afar; and taking the Dwarf-road he crossed Gelion at the ford of Sarn Athrad, and turning south over the upper streams of Ascar, he came into the north of Ossiriand.

In a valley among the foothills of the mountains, below the springs of Thalos, he saw lights in the evening, and far off he heard the sound of song. At this he wondered much, for the Green-elves of that land lit no fires, nor did they sing by night. At first he feared that a raid of Orcs had passed the leaguer of the North, but as he drew near he perceived that it was not so; for the singers used a tongue that he had not heard before, neither that of Dwarves nor of Orcs. Then Felagund, standing silent in the night-shadow of the trees, looked down into the camp, and there he beheld a strange people.

Now these were a part of the kindred and following of Bëor the Old, as he was afterwards called, a chieftain among Men. After many lives of wandering out of the East he had led them at last over the Blue Mountains, the first of the race of Men to enter Beleriand; and they sang because they were glad, and believed that they had escaped from all perils and had come at last to a land without fear.

Long Felagund watched them, and love for them stirred in his heart; but he remained hidden in the trees until they had all fallen asleep. Then he went among the sleeping people, and sat beside their dying fire where none kept watch; and he took up a rude harp which Bëor had laid aside, and he played music upon it such as the ears of Men had not heard; for they had as yet no teachers in the art, save only the Dark Elves in the wild lands.

Now men awoke and listened to Felagund as he harped and sang, and each thought that he was in some fair dream, until he saw that his fellows were awake also beside him; but they did not speak or stir while Felagund still played, because of the beauty of the music and the wonder of the song. Wisdom was in the words of the Elven-king, and the hearts grew wiser that hearkened to him; for the things of which he sang, of the making of Arda, and the bliss of Aman beyond the shadows of the Sea, came as clear visions before their eyes, and his Elvish speech was interpreted in each mind according to its measure.

Thus it was that Men called King Felagund, whom they first met of all the Eldar, Nóm, that is Wisdom, in the language of that people, and after him they named his folk Nómin, the Wise. Indeed they believed at first that Felagund was one of the Valar, of whom they had heard rumour that they dwelt far in the West; and this was (some say) the cause of their journeying. But Felagund dwelt among them and taught them true knowledge, and they loved him, and took him for their lord, and were ever after loyal to the house of Finarfin.

Now the Eldar were beyond all other peoples skilled in tongues; and Felagund discovered also that he could read in the minds of Men such thoughts as they wished to reveal in speech, so that their words were easily interpreted. It is said also that these Men had long had dealings with the Dark Elves east of the mountains, and from them had learned much of their speech; and since all the languages of the Quendi were of one origin, the language of Bëor and his folk resembled the Elven-tongue in many words and devices. It was not long therefore before Felagund could hold converse with Bëor; and while he dwelt with him they spoke much together. But when he questioned him concerning the arising of Men and their journeys, Bëor would say little; and indeed he knew little, for the fathers of his people had told few tales of their past and a silence had fallen upon their memory. 'A darkness lies behind us,' Bëor said; 'and we have turned our backs upon it, and we do not desire to return thither even in thought. Westwards our hearts have been turned, and we believe that there we shall find Light.'

But it was said afterwards among the Eldar that when Men awoke in Hildórien at the rising of the Sun the spies of Morgoth were watchful, and tidings were soon brought to him; and this seemed to him so great a matter that secretly under shadow he himself departed from Angband, and went forth into Middle-earth, leaving to Sauron the command of the War. Of his dealings with Men the Eldar indeed knew nothing, at that time, and learnt but little afterwards; but that a darkness lay upon the hearts of Men (as the shadow of the Kinslaying and the Doom of Mandos lay upon the Noldor) they perceived clearly even in the people of the Elf-friends whom they first knew. To corrupt or destroy whatsoever arose new and fair was ever the chief desire of Morgoth; and doubtless he had this purpose also in his errand: by fear and lies to make Men the foes of the Eldar, and bring them up out of the east against Beleriand. But this design was slow to ripen, and was never wholly achieved; for Men (it is said) were at first very few in number, whereas Morgoth grew afraid of the growing power and union of the Eldar and came back to Angband, leaving behind at that time but few servants, and those of less might and cunning.

Now Felagund learned from Bëor that there were many other Men of like mind who were also journeying westward. 'Others of my own kin have crossed the Mountains,' he said, 'and they are wandering not far away; and the Haladin, a people from whom we are sundered in speech, are still in the valleys on the eastern slopes, awaiting tidings before they venture further. There are yet other Men, whose tongue is more like to ours, with whom we had had dealings at times. They were before us on the westward march, but we passed them; for they are a numerous people, and yet keep together and move slowly, being all ruled by one chieftain whom they call Marach.'

Now the Green-elves of Ossiriand were troubled by the coming of Men, and when they heard that a lord of the Eldar from over the Sea was among them they sent messengers to Felagund. 'Lord,' they said, 'if you have power over these newcomers, bid them return by the ways that they came, or else to go forward. For we desire no strangers in this land to break the peace in which we live. And these folk are hewers of trees and hunters of beasts; therefore we are their unfriends, and if they will not depart we shall afflict them in all ways that we can.'

Then by the advice of Felagund Bëor gathered all the wandering families and kindreds of his people, and they removed over Gelion, and took up their abode in the lands of Amrod and Amras, upon the east banks of the Celon south of Nan Elmoth, near to the borders of Doriath; and the name of that land thereafter was Estolad, the Encampment. But when after a year had passed Felagund wished to return to his own country, Bëor begged leave to come with him; and he remained in the service of the King of Nargothrond while his life lasted. In this way he got his name, Bëor, whereas his name before had been Balan; for Bëor signified 'Vassal' in the tongue of his people. The rule of his folk he committed to Baran his elder son; and he did not return again to Estolad.

Soon after the departure of Felagund the other Men of whom Bëor had spoken came also into Beleriand. First came the Haladin; but meeting the unfriendship of the Green-elves they turned north and dwelt in Thargelion, in the country of Caranthir son of Fëanor; there for a time they had peace, and the people of Caranthir paid little heed to them. In the next year Marach led his people over the mountains; they were a tall and warlike folk, marching in ordered companies, and the Elves of Ossiriand hid themselves and did not waylay them. But Marach, hearing that the people of Bëor were dwelling in a green and fertile land, came down the Dwarf-road, and settled in the country south and east of the dwellings of Baran son of Bëor; and there was great friendship between those peoples.

Felagund himself often returned to visit Men; and many other Elves out of the west-lands, both Noldor and Sindar, journeyed to Estolad, being eager to see the Edain, whose coming had long been foretold. Now Atani, the Second People, was the name given to Men in Valinor in the lore that told of their coming; but in the speech of Beleriand that name became Edain, and it was there used only of the three kindreds of the Elf-friends.

Fingolfin, as King of all the Noldor, sent messengers of welcome to them; and then many young and eager men of the Edain went away and took service with the kings and lords of the Eldar. Among them was Malach son of Marach, and he dwelt in Hithlum for fourteen years; and he learned the Elven-tongue and was given the name of Aradan.

The Edain did not long dwell content in Estolad, for many still desired to go westward; but they did not know the way. Before them lay the fences of Doriath, and southward lay Sirion and its impassable fens. Therefore the kings of the three houses of the Noldor, seeing hope of strength in the sons of Men, sent word that any of the Edain that wished might remove and come to dwell among their people. In this way the migration of the Edain began: at first little by little, but later in families and kindreds, they arose and left Estolad, until after some fifty years many thousands had entered the lands of the Kings. Most of these took the long road northwards, until the ways became well known to them. The people of Bëor came to Dorthonion and dwelt in lands ruled by the house of Finarfin. The people of Aradan (for Marach his father remained in Estolad until his death) for the most part went on westward; and some came to Hithlum, but Magor son of Aradan and many of the people passed down Sirion into Beleriand and dwelt a while in the vales of the southern slopes of Ered Wethrin.

It is said that in all these matters none save Finrod Felagund took counsel with King Thingol, and he was ill pleased, both for that reason, and because he was troubled by dreams concerning the

coming of Men, ere ever the first tidings of them were heard. Therefore he commanded that Men should take no lands to dwell in save
in the north, and that the princes whom they served should be
answerable for all that they did; and he said: 'Into Doriath shall no
Man come while my realm lasts, not even those of the house of Bëor
who serve Finrod the beloved.' Melian said nothing to him at that
time, but afterwards she said to Galadriel: 'Now the world runs on
swiftly to great tidings. And one of Men, even of Bëor's house, shall indeed come, and the Girdle of Melian shall not restrain him, for doom
greater than my power shall send him; and the songs that shall spring
from that coming shall endure when all Middle-earth is changed.'

But many Men remained in Estolad, and there was still a mingled
people living there long years after, until in the ruin of Beleriand
they were overwhelmed or fled back into the East. For beside the old
who deemed that their wandering days were over there were not a
few who desired to go their own ways, and they feared the Eldar and
the light of their eyes; and then dissensions awoke among the Edain,
in which the shadow of Morgoth may be discerned, for certain it is
that he knew of the coming of Men into Beleriand and of their
growing friendship with the Elves.

The leaders of discontent were Bereg of the house of Bëor, and
Amlach, one of the grandsons of Marach; and they said openly: 'We
took long roads, desiring to escape the perils of Middle-earth and the
dark things that dwell there; for we heard that there was Light in the
West. But now we learn that the Light is beyond the Sea. Thither
we cannot come where the Gods dwell in bliss. Save one; for the
Lord of the Dark is here before us, and the Eldar, wise but fell, who
make endless war upon him. In the North he dwells, they say; and
there is the pain and death from which we fled. We will not go that
way.'

Then a council and assembly of Men was called, and great numbers
came together. And the Elf-friends answered Bereg, saying: 'Truly
from the Dark King come all the evils from which we fled; but he
seeks dominion over all Middle-earth, and whither now shall we
turn and he will not pursue us? Unless he be vanquished here, or
at least held in leaguer. Only by the valour of the Eldar is he restrained, and maybe it was for this purpose, to aid them at need,
that we were brought into this land.'

To this Bereg answered: 'Let the Eldar look to it! Our lives are
short enough.' But there arose one who seemed to all to be Amlach
son of Imlach, speaking fell words that shook the hearts of all who

heard him: 'All this is but Elvish lore, tales to beguile newcomers that are unwary. The Sea has no shore. There is no Light in the West. You have followed a fool-fire of the Elves to the end of the world! Which of you has seen the least of the Gods? Who has beheld the Dark King in the North? Those who seek the dominion of Middle-earth are the Eldar. Greedy for wealth they have delved in the earth for its secrets and have stirred to wrath the things that dwell beneath it, as they have ever done and ever shall. Let the Orcs have the realm that is theirs, and we will have ours. There is room in the world, if the Eldar will let us be!'

Then those that listened sat for a while astounded, and a shadow of fear fell on their hearts; and they resolved to depart far from the lands of the Eldar. But afterwards Amlach returned among them, and denied that he had been present at their debate or had spoken such words as they reported; and there was doubt and bewilderment among Men. Then the Elf-friends said: 'You will now believe this at least: there is indeed a Dark Lord, and his spies and emissaries are among us; for he fears us, and the strength that we may give to his foes.'

But some still answered: 'He hates us, rather, and ever the more the longer we dwell here, meddling in his quarrel with the Kings of the Eldar, to no gain of ours.' Many therefore of those that yet remained in Estolad made ready to depart; and Bereg led a thousand of the people of Bëor away southwards, and they passed out of the songs of those days. But Amlach repented, saying: 'I have now a quarrel of my own with this Master of Lies, which will last to my life's end'; and he went away north and entered the service of Maedhros. But those of his people who were of like mind with Bereg chose a new leader, and they went back over the mountains into Eriador, and are forgotten.

During this time the Haladin remained in Thargelion and were content. But Morgoth, seeing that by lies and deceits he could not yet wholly estrange Elves and Men, was filled with wrath, and endeavoured to do Men what hurt he could. Therefore he sent out an Orc-raid, and passing east it escaped the leaguer, and came in stealth back over Ered Lindon by the passes of the Dwarf-road, and fell upon the Haladin in the southern woods of the land of Caranthir.

Now the Haladin did not live under the rule of lords or many together, but each homestead was set apart and governed its own affairs, and they were slow to unite. But there was among them a man named Haldad, who was masterful and fearless; and he gathered all the brave men that he could find, and retreated to the angle of land between Ascar and Gelion, and in the utmost corner he built a stockade across from water to water; and behind it they led all the women and children that they could save. There they were besieged, until their food was gone.

Haldad had twin children: Haleth his daughter, and Haldar his son; and both were valiant in the defence, for Haleth was a woman of great heart and strength. But at last Haldad was slain in a sortie against the Orcs; and Haldar, who rushed out to save his father's body from their butchery, was hewn down beside him. Then Haleth held the people together, though they were without hope; and some cast themselves in the rivers and were drowned. But seven days later, as the Orcs made their last assault and had already broken through the stockade, there came suddenly a music of trumpets, and Caranthir with his host came down from the north and drove the Orcs into the rivers.

Then Caranthir looked kindly upon Men and did Haleth great honour; and he offered her recompense for her father and brother. And seeing, over late, what valour there was in the Edain, he said to her: 'If you will remove and dwell further north, there you shall have the friendship and protection of the Eldar, and free lands of your own.'

But Haleth was proud, and unwilling to be guided or ruled, and most of the Haladin were of like mood. Therefore she thanked Caranthir, but answered: 'My mind is now set, lord, to leave the shadow of the mountains, and go west, whither others of our kin have gone.' When therefore the Haladin had gathered all whom they could find alive of their folk who had fled wild into the woods before the Orcs, and had gleaned what remained of their goods in their burned homesteads, they took Haleth for their chief; and she led them at last to Estolad, and there dwelt for a time.

But they remained a people apart, and were ever after known to Elves and Men as the People of Haleth. Haleth remained their chief while her days lasted, but she did not wed, and the headship afterwards passed to Haldan son of Haldar her brother. Soon however Haleth desired to move westward again; and though most of her people were against this counsel, she led them forth once more; and they went without help or guidance of the Eldar, and passing over Celon and Aros they journeyed in the perilous land between the Mountains of Terror and the Girdle of Melian. That land was even then not yet so evil as it after became, but it was no road for mortal Men to take without aid, and Haleth only brought her people through it with hardship and loss, constraining them to go forward by the strength of her will. At last they crossed over the Brithiach, and many bitterly repented of their journey; but there was now no returning. Therefore in new lands they went back to their old life as best they could; and they dwelt in free homesteads in the woods of Talath Dirnen beyond Teiglin, and some wandered far into the realm of Nargothrond. But there were many who loved the Lady Haleth and wished to go whither she would, and dwell under her rule; and these she led into the Forest of Brethil, between Teiglin and Sirion. Thither in the evil days that followed many of her scattered folk returned.

Now Brethil was claimed as part of his realm by King Thingol, though it was not within the Girdle of Melian, and he would have denied it to Haleth; but Felagund, who had the friendship of Thingol, hearing of all that had befallen the People of Haleth, obtained this grace for her: that she should dwell free in Brethil, upon the condition only that her people should guard the Crossings of Teiglin against all enemies of the Eldar, and allow no Orcs to enter their woods. To this Haleth answered: 'Where are Haldad my father, and Haldar my brother? If the King of Doriath fears a friendship between Haleth and those who have devoured her kin, then the thoughts of the Eldar are strange to Men.' And Haleth dwelt in Brethil until she died; and her people raised a green mound over her in the heights of the forest, Tûr Haretha, the Ladybarrow, Haudh-en-Arwen in the Sindarin tongue.

In this way it came to pass that the Edain dwelt in the lands of the Eldar, some here, some there, some wandering, some settled in kindreds or small peoples; and the most part of them soon learned the Grey-elven tongue, both as a common speech among themselves and because many were eager to learn the lore of the Elves. But after a time the Elf-kings, seeing that it was not good for Elves and Men to dwell mingled together without order, and that Men needed lords of their own kind, set regions apart where Men could live their own lives, and appointed chieftains to hold these lands freely. They were the allies of the Eldar in war, but marched under their own leaders. Yet many of the Edain had delight in the friendship of the Elves, and dwelt among them for so long as they had leave; and the young men often took service for a time in the hosts of the kings.

Now Hador Lórindol, son of Hathol, son of Magor, son of Malach Aradan, entered the household of Fingolfin in his youth, and was loved by the King. Fingolfin therefore gave to him the lordship of Dor-lómin, and into that land he gathered most of the people of his kin, and became the mightiest of the chieftains of the Edain. In his house only the Elven-tongue was spoken; but their own speech was not forgotten, and from it came the common tongue of Númenor. But in Dorthonion the lordship of the people of Bëor and the country of Ladros was given to Boromir, son of Boron, who was the grandson of Bëor the Old.

The sons of Hador were Galdor and Gundor; and the sons of Galdor were Húrin and Huor; and the son of Húrin was Túrin the Bane of Glaurung; and the son of Huor was Tuor, father of Eärendil the Blessed. The son of Boromir was Bregor, whose sons were Bregolas and Barahir; and the sons of Bregolas were Baragund and Belegund. The daughter of Baragund was Morwen, the mother of Túrin, and the daughter of Belegund was Rían, the mother of Tuor. But the son of Barahir was Beren One-hand, who won the love of Lúthien Thingol's daughter, and returned from the Dead; from them came Elwing the wife of Eärendil, and all the Kings of Númenor after.

All these were caught in the net of the Doom of the Noldor; and they did great deeds which the Eldar remember still among the histories of the Kings of old. And in those days the strength of Men was added to the power of the Noldor, and their hope was high; and Morgoth was straitly enclosed, for the people of Hador, being hardy to endure cold and long wandering, feared not at times to go far into the north and there keep watch upon the movements of the Enemy. The Men of the Three Houses throve and multiplied, but greatest among them was the house of Hador Goldenhead, peer of Elven-lords. His people were of great strength and stature, ready in mind, bold and steadfast, quick to anger and to laughter, mighty among the Children of Ilúvatar in the youth of Mankind. Yellow-haired they were for the most part, and blue-eyed; but not so was Túrin, whose mother was Morwen of the house of Bëor. The Men of that house were dark or brown of hair, with grey eyes; and of all Men they were most like to the Noldor and most loved by them; for they were eager of mind, cunning-handed, swift in understanding, long in memory, and they were moved sooner to pity than to laughter. Like to them were the woodland folk of Haleth, but they were of lesser stature, and less eager for lore. They used few words, and did not love great concourse of men; and many among them delighted in solitude, wandering free in the greenwoods while the wonder of the lands of the Eldar was new upon them. But in the realms of the West their time was brief and their days unhappy.

The years of the Edain were lengthened, according to the reckoning of Men, after their coming to Beleriand; but at last Bëor the

Old died when he had lived three and ninety years, for four and forty of which he had served King Felagund. And when he lay dead, of no wound or grief, but stricken by age, the Eldar saw for the first time the swift waning of the life of Men, and the death of weariness which they knew not in themselves; and they grieved greatly for the loss of their friends. But Bëor at the last had relinquished his life willingly and passed in peace; and the Eldar wondered much at the strange fate of Men, for in all their lore there was no account of it, and its end was hidden from them.

Nonetheless the Edain of old learned swiftly of the Eldar all such art and knowledge as they could receive, and their sons increased in wisdom and skill, until they far surpassed all others of Mankind, who dwelt still east of the mountains and had not seen the Eldar, nor looked upon the faces that had beheld the Light of Valinor.

# Chapter 18

# OF THE RUIN OF BELERIAND AND THE FALL OF FINGOLFIN

Now Fingolfin, King of the North, and High King of the Noldor, seeing that his people were become numerous and strong, and that the Men allied to them were many and valiant, pondered once more an assault upon Angband; for he knew that they lived in danger while the circle of the siege was incomplete, and Morgoth was free to labour in his deep mines, devising what evils none could foretell ere he should reveal them. This counsel was wise according to the measure of his knowledge; for the Noldor did not yet comprehend the fullness of the power of Morgoth, nor understand that their unaided war upon him was without final hope, whether they hasted or delayed. But because the land was fair and their kingdoms wide, most of the Noldor were content with things as they were, trusting them to last, and slow to begin an assault in which many must surely perish were it in victory or in defeat. Therefore they were little disposed to hearken to Fingolfin, and the sons of Fëanor at that time least of all. Among the chieftains of the Noldor Angrod and Aegnor alone were of like mind with the King; for they dwelt in regions whence Thangorodrim could be descried, and the threat of Morgoth was present to their thought. Thus the designs of Fingolfin came to naught, and the land had peace yet for a while.

But when the sixth generation of Men after Bëor and Marach were not yet come to full manhood, it being then four hundred years and five and fifty since the coming of Fingolfin, the evil befell that he had long dreaded, and yet more dire and sudden than his darkest fear. For Morgoth had long prepared his force in secret, while ever the malice of his heart grew greater, and his hatred of the Noldor more bitter; and he desired not only to end his foes but to destroy also and defile the lands that they had taken and made fair. And it is said that his hate overcame his counsel, so that if he had but endured to wait longer, until his designs were full, then the Noldor would have perished utterly. But on his part he esteemed too lightly the valour of the Elves, and of Men he took yet no account.

There came a time of winter, when night was dark and without moon; and the wide plain of Ard-galen stretched dim beneath the cold stars, from the hill-forts of the Noldor to the feet of Thangorodrim. The watchfires burned low, and the guards were few; on the plain few were waking in the camps of the horsemen of Hithlum. Then suddenly Morgoth sent forth great rivers of flame that ran down swifter than Balrogs from Thangorodrim, and poured over all the plain; and the Mountains of Iron belched forth fires of many poisonous hues, and the fume of them stank upon the air, and was deadly. Thus Ard-galen perished, and fire devoured its grasses; and it became a burned and desolate waste, full of a choking dust, barren and lifeless. Thereafter its name was changed, and it was called Anfauglith, the Gasping Dust. Many charred bones had there their roofless grave; for many of the Noldor perished in that burning, who were caught by the running flame and could not fly to the hills. The heights of Dorthonion and Ered Wethrin held back the fiery torrents, but their woods upon the slopes that looked towards Angband were all kindled, and the smoke wrought confusion among the defenders. Thus began the fourth of the great battles, Dagor Bragollach, the Battle of Sudden Flame.

In the front of that fire came Glaurung the golden, father of dragons, in his full might; and in his train were Balrogs, and behind them came the black armies of the Orcs in multitudes such as the Noldor had never before seen or imagined. And they assaulted the fortresses of the Noldor, and broke the leaguer about Angband, and slew wherever they found them the Noldor and their allies, Grey-elves and Men. Many of the stoutest of the foes of Morgoth were destroyed in the first days of that war, bewildered and dispersed and unable to muster their strength. War ceased not wholly ever again in Beleriand; but the Battle of Sudden Flame is held to have ended with the coming of spring, when the onslaught of Morgoth grew less.

Thus ended the Siege of Angband; and the foes of Morgoth were scattered and sundered one from another. The most part of the Grey-elves fled south and forsook the northern war; many were received into Doriath, and the kingdom and strength of Thingol grew greater in that time, for the power of Melian the queen was woven about his borders and evil could not yet enter that hidden realm. Others took refuge in the fortresses by the sea, and in Nargothrond; and some fled the land and hid themselves in Ossiriand, or passing the mountains wandered homeless in the wild. And rumour of the war and the breaking of the siege reached the ears of Men in the east of Middle-earth.

The sons of Finarfin bore most heavily the brunt of the assault, and Angrod and Aegnor were slain; beside them fell Bregolas lord of the house of Bëor, and a great part of the warriors of that people. But Barahir the brother of Bregolas was in the fighting further westward, near to the Pass of Sirion. There King Finrod Felagund, hastening from the south, was cut off from his people and surrounded with small company in the Fen of Serech; and he would have been slain or taken, but Barahir came up with the bravest of his men and rescued him, and made a wall of spears about him; and they cut their way out of the battle with great loss. Thus Felagund escaped, and returned to his deep fortress of Nargothrond; but he swore an oath of abiding friendship and aid in every need to Barahir and all his kin, and in token of his vow he gave to Barahir his ring. Barahir was now by right lord of the house of Bëor, and he returned to Dorthonion; but most of his people fled from their homes and took refuge in the fastness of Hithlum.

So great was the onslaught of Morgoth that Fingolfin and Fingon could not come to the aid of the sons of Finarfin; and the hosts of Hithlum were driven back with great loss to the fortresses of Ered Wethrin, and these they hardly defended against the Orcs. Before the walls of Eithel Sirion fell Hador the Golden-haired, defending the rearguard of his lord Fingolfin, being then sixty and six years of age, and with him fell Gundor his younger son, pierced with many arrows; and they were mourned by the Elves. Then Galdor the Tall took the lordship of his father. And because of the strength and height of the Shadowy Mountains, which withstood the torrent of fire, and by the valour of the Elves and the Men of the North, which neither Orc nor Balrog could yet overcome, Hithlum remained unconquered, a threat upon the flank of Morgoth's attack; but Fingolfin was sundered from his kinsmen by a sea of foes.

For the war had gone ill with the sons of Fëanor, and well nigh all the east marches were taken by assault. The Pass of Aglon was forced, though with great cost to the hosts of Morgoth; and Celegorm and Curufin being defeated fled south and west by the marches of Doriath, and coming at last to Nargothrond sought harbour with Finrod Felagund. Thus it came to pass that their people swelled the strength of Nargothrond; but it would have been better, as was after seen, if they had remained in the east among their own kin. Maedhros did deeds of surpassing valour, and the Orcs fled before his face; for since his torment upon Thangorodrim his spirit burned like a white fire within, and he was as one that returns from the dead. Thus the great fortress upon the Hill of Himring could not be taken, and many of the most valiant that remained, both of the people of Dorthonion and of the east marches, rallied there to Maedhros; and for a while he closed once more the Pass of Aglon, so that the Orcs could not enter Beleriand by that road. But they overwhelmed the riders of the people of Fëanor upon Lothlann, for Glaurung came thither, and passed through Maglor's Gap, and destroyed all the land between the arms of Gelion. And the Orcs took the fortress upon the west slopes of Mount Rerir, and ravaged all Thargelion, the land of Caranthir; and they defiled Lake Helevorn. Thence they passed over Gelion with fire and terror and came far into East Beleriand. Maglor joined Maedhros upon Himring; but Caranthir fled and joined the remnant of his people to the scattered folk of the hunters, Amrod and Amras, and they retreated and passed Ramdal in the south. Upon Amon Ereb they maintained a watch and some strength of war, and they had aid of the Green-elves; and the Orcs came not into Ossiriand, nor to Taur-im-Duinath and the wilds of the south.

Now news came to Hithlum that Dorthonion was lost and the sons of Finarfin overthrown, and that the sons of Fëanor were driven from their lands. Then Fingolfin beheld (as it seemed to him) the utter ruin of the Noldor, and the defeat beyond redress of all their houses; and filled with wrath and despair he mounted upon Rochallor his great horse and rode forth alone, and none might restrain him. He passed over Dor-nu-Fauglith like a wind amid the dust, and all that beheld his onset fled in amaze, thinking that Oromë himself was come: for a great madness of rage was upon him, so that his eyes shone like the eyes of the Valar. Thus he came alone to Angband's gates, and he sounded his horn, and smote once more upon the brazen doors, and challenged Morgoth to come forth to single combat. And Morgoth came.

That was the last time in those wars that he passed the doors of his stronghold, and it is said that he took not the challenge willingly; for though his might was greatest of all things in this world, alone of the Valar he knew fear. But he could not now deny the challenge before the face of his captains; for the rocks rang with the shrill music of Fingolfin's horn, and his voice came keen and clear down into the depths of Angband; and Fingolfin named Morgoth craven, and lord of slaves. Therefore Morgoth came, climbing slowly from his subterranean throne, and the rumour of his feet was like thunder underground. And he issued forth clad in black armour; and he stood before the King like a tower, iron-crowned, and his vast shield, sable unblazoned, cast a shadow over him like a stormcloud. But Fingolfin gleamed beneath it as a star; for his mail was overlaid with silver, and his blue shield was set with crystals; and he drew his sword Ringil, that glittered like ice.

Then Morgoth hurled aloft Grond, the Hammer of the Under-world, and swung it down like a bolt of thunder. But Fingolfin sprang aside, and Grond rent a mighty pit in the earth, whence smoke and fire darted. Many times Morgoth essayed to smite him, and each time Fingolfin leaped away, as a lightning shoots from under a dark cloud; and he wounded Morgoth with seven wounds, and seven times Morgoth gave a cry of anguish, whereat the hosts of Angband fell upon their faces in dismay, and the cries echoed in the Northlands.

But at the last the King grew weary, and Morgoth bore down his shield upon him. Thrice he was crushed to his knees, and thrice arose again and bore up his broken shield and stricken helm. But the earth was all rent and pitted about him, and he stumbled and fell backward before the feet of Morgoth; and Morgoth set his left foot upon his neck, and the weight of it was like a fallen hill. Yet with his last and desperate stroke Fingolfin hewed the foot with Ringil, and the blood gushed forth black and smoking and filled the pits of Grond.

Thus died Fingolfin, High King of the Noldor, most proud and valiant of the Elven-kings of old. The Orcs made no boast of that duel at the gate; neither do the Elves sing of it, for their sorrow is too deep. Yet the tale of it is remembered still, for Thorondor King of Eagles brought the tidings to Gondolin, and to Hithlum afar off. And Morgoth took the body of the Elven-king and broke it, and would cast it to his wolves; but Thorondor came hasting from his eyrie among the peaks of the Crissaegrim, and he stooped upon Morgoth and marred his face. The rushing of the wings of Thorondor was like the noise of the winds of Manwë, and he seized the body in his mighty talons, and soaring suddenly above the darts of the Orcs he bore the King away. And he laid him upon a mountain-top that looked from the north upon the hidden valley of Gondolin; and Turgon coming built a high cairn over his father. No Orc dared ever after to pass over the mount of Fingolfin or draw nigh his tomb, until the doom of Gondolin was come and treachery was born among his kin. Morgoth went ever halt of one foot after that day, and the pain of his wounds could not be healed; and in his face was the scar that Thorondor made.

Great was the lamentation in Hithlum when the fall of Fingolfin became known, and Fingon in sorrow took the lordship of the house of Fingolfin and the kingdom of the Noldor; but his young son Ereinion (who was after named Gil-galad) he sent to the Havens.

Now Morgoth's power overshadowed the Northlands; but Barahir would not flee from Dorthonion, and remained contesting the land foot by foot with his enemies. Then Morgoth pursued his people to the death, until few remained; and all the forest of the northward slopes of that land was turned little by little into a region of such dread and dark enchantment that even the Orcs would not enter it unless need drove them, and it was called Deldúwath, and Taur-nu-Fuin, The Forest under Nightshade. The trees that grew there after the burning were black and grim, and their roots were tangled, groping in the dark like claws; and those who strayed among them became lost and blind, and were strangled or pursued to madness by phantoms of terror. At last so desperate was the case of Barahir that Emeldir the Manhearted his wife (whose mind was rather to fight beside her son and her husband than to flee) gathered together all the women and children that were left, and gave arms to those that would bear them; and she led them into the mountains that lay behind, and so by perilous paths, until they came at last with loss and misery to Brethil. Some were there received among the Haladin, but some passed on over the mountains to Dor-lómin and the people of Galdor, Hador's son; and among those were Rían, daughter of Belegund, and Morwen, who was named Eledhwen, that is Elfsheen, daughter of Baragund. But none ever saw again the men that they had left. For these were slain one by one, until at last only twelve men remained to Barahir: Beren his son, and Baragund and Belegund his nephews, the sons of Bregolas, and nine faithful servants of his house whose names were long remembered in the songs of the Noldor: Radhruin and Dairuin they were, Dagnir and Ragnor, Gildor and Gorlim the unhappy, Arthad and Urthel, and Hathaldir the young. Outlaws without hope they became, a desperate band that could not escape and would not yield, for their dwellings were destroyed, and their wives and children captured, slain, or fled. From Hithlum there came neither news nor help, and Barahir and his men were hunted like wild beasts; and they retreated to the barren highland above the forest, and wandered among the tarns and rocky moors of that region, furthest from the spies and spells of Morgoth. Their bed was the heather and their roof the cloudy sky.

For nigh on two years after the Dagor Bragollach the Noldor still defended the western pass about the sources of Sirion, for the power of Ulmo was in that water, and Minas Tirith withstood the Orcs. But at length, after the fall of Fingolfin, Sauron, greatest and most terrible of the servants of Morgoth, who in the Sindarin tongue was named Gorthaur, came against Orodreth, the warden of the tower upon Tol Sirion. Sauron was become now a sorcerer of dreadful power, master of shadows and of phantoms, foul in wisdom, cruel in strength, misshaping what he touched, twisting what he ruled, lord of werewolves; his dominion was torment. He took Minas Tirith by assault, for a dark cloud of fear fell upon those that defended it; and Orodreth was driven out, and fled to Nargothrond. Then Sauron made it into a watchtower for Morgoth, a stronghold of evil, and a menace; and the fair isle of Tol Sirion became accursed, and it was called Tol-in-Gaurhoth, the Isle of Werewolves. No living creature could pass through that vale that Sauron did not espy from the tower where he sat. And Morgoth held now the western pass, and his terror filled the fields and woods of Beleriand. Beyond Hithlum he pursued his foes relentlessly, and he searched out their hiding-places and took their strongholds one by one. The Orcs growing ever bolder wandered at will far and wide, coming down Sirion in the west and Celon in the east, and they encompassed Doriath; and they harried the lands so that beast and bird fled before them, and silence and desolation spread steadily from the North. Many of the Noldor and the Sindar they took captive and led to Angband, and made them thralls, forcing them to use their skill and their knowledge in the service of Morgoth. And Morgoth sent out his spies, and they were clad in false forms and deceit was in their speech; they made lying promises of reward, and with cunning words sought to arouse fear and jealousy among the peoples, accusing their kings and chieftains of greed, and of treachery one to another. And because of the curse of the Kinslaying at Alqualondë these lies were often believed; and indeed as the time darkened they had a measure of truth, for the hearts and minds of the Elves of Beleriand became clouded with despair and fear. But ever the Noldor feared most the treachery of those of their own kin, who had been thralls in Angband; for Morgoth used some of these for his evil purposes, and feigning to give them liberty sent them abroad, but their wills were chained to his, and they strayed only to come back to him again. Therefore if any of his captives escaped in truth, and returned to their own people, they had little welcome, and wandered alone outlawed and desperate.

To Men Morgoth feigned pity, if any would hearken to his messages, saying that their woes came only of their servitude to the rebel Noldor, but at the hands of the rightful Lord of Middle-earth they would get honour and a just reward of valour, if they would leave rebellion. But few men of the Three Houses of the Edain would give ear to him, not even were they brought to the torment of Angband.

Therefore Morgoth pursued them with hatred; and he sent his messengers over the mountains.

It is told that at this time the Swarthy Men came first into Beleriand. Some were already secretly under the dominion of Morgoth, and came at his call; but not all, for the rumour of Beleriand, of its lands and waters, of its wars and riches, went now far and wide, and the wandering feet of Men were ever set westward in those days. These Men were short and broad, long and strong in the arm; their skins were swart or sallow, and their hair was dark as were their eyes. Their houses were many, and some had greater liking for the Dwarves of the mountains than for the Elves. But Maedhros, knowing the weakness of the Noldor and the Edain, whereas the pits of Angband seemed to hold store inexhaustible and ever-renewed, made alliance with these new-come Men, and gave his friendship to the greatest of their chieftains, Bór and Ulfang. And Morgoth was well content; for this was as he had designed. The sons of Bór were Borlad, Borlach, and Borthand; and they followed Maedhros and Maglor, and cheated the hope of Morgoth, and were faithful. The sons of Ulfang the Black were Ulfast, and Ulwarth, and Uldor the accursed; and they followed Caranthir and swore allegiance to him, and proved faithless.

There was small love between the Edain and the Easterlings, and they met seldom; for the newcomers abode long in East Beleriand, but Hador's folk were shut in Hithlum, and Bëor's house was well-nigh destroyed. The People of Haleth were at first untouched by the northern war, for they dwelt to the southward in the Forest of Brethil; but now there was battle between them and the invading Orcs, for they were stout-hearted men and would not lightly forsake the woods that they loved. And amid the tale of defeats of that time the deeds of the Haladin are remembered with honour: for after the taking of Minas Tirith the Orcs came through the western pass, and maybe would have ravaged even to the mouths of Sirion; but Halmir lord of the Haladin sent swift word to Thingol, for he had friendship with the Elves that guarded the borders of Doriath. Then Beleg Strongbow, chief of the marchwardens of Thingol, brought great strength of the Sindar armed with axes into Brethil; and issuing from the deeps of the forest Halmir and Beleg took an Orc-legion at unawares and destroyed it. Thereafter the black tide out of the North was stemmed in that region, and the Orcs dared not cross the Teiglin for many years after. The People of Haleth dwelt yet in watchful peace in the Forest of Brethil, and behind their guard the Kingdom of Nargothrond had respite, and mustered its strength.

At this time Húrin and Huor, the sons of Galdor of Dor-lómin, were dwelling with the Haladin, for they were akin. In the days before the Dagor Bragollach those two houses of the Edain were joined at a great feast, when Galdor and Glóredhel the children of Hador Goldenhead were wedded to Hareth and Haldír the children of Halmir lord of the Haladin. Thus it was that the sons of Galdor were fostered in Brethil by Haldir their uncle, according to the custom of Men in that time; and they went both to that battle with the Orcs, even Huor, for he would not be restrained, though he was but thirteen years old. But being with a company that was cut off from the rest they were pursued to the Ford of Brithiach, and there they would have been taken or slain but for the power of Ulmo, that was still strong in Sirion. A mist arose from the river and hid them from their enemies, and they escaped over the Brithiach into Dimbar, and wandered among the hills beneath the sheer walls of the Crissaegrim, until they were bewildered in the deceits of that land and knew not the way to go on or to return. There Thorondor espied them, and he sent two of his eagles to their aid; and the eagles bore them up and brought them beyond the Encircling Mountains to the secret vale of Tumladen and the hidden city of Gondolin, which no Man yet had seen.

There Turgon the King received them well, when he learned of their kin; for messages and dreams had come to him up Sirion from the sea, from Ulmo, Lord of Waters, warning him of woe to come and counselling him to deal kindly with the sons of the house of Hador, from whom help should come to him at need. Húrin and Huor dwelt as guests in the King's house for well nigh a year; and it is said that in this time Húrin learned much lore of the Elves, and understood also something of the counsels and purposes of the King. For Turgon took great liking for the sons of Galdor, and spoke much with them; and he wished indeed to keep them in Gondolin out of love, and not only for his law that no stranger, be he Elf or Man, who found the way to the secret kingdom and looked upon the city should ever depart again, until the King should open the leaguer, and the hidden people should come forth.

But Húrin and Huor desired to return to their own people and share in the wars and griefs that now beset them. And Húrin said to Turgon: 'Lord, we are but mortal Men, and unlike the Eldar. They may endure for long years awaiting battle with their enemies in some far distant day; but for us the time is short, and our hope and strength soon wither. Moreover we did not find the road to Gondolin, and indeed we do not know surely where this city stands; for we were

brought in fear and wonder by the high ways of the air, and in mercy
our eyes were veiled.' Then Turgon granted his prayer, and he said:
'By the way that you came you have leave to depart, if Thorondor
is willing. I grieve at this parting; yet in a little while, as the Eldar
account it, we may meet again.'

But Maeglin, the King's sister-son, who was mighty in Gondolin,
grieved not at all at their going, though he begrudged them the
favour of the King, for he had no love for any of the kindred of Men;
and he said to Húrin: 'The King's grace is greater than you know,
and the law is become less stern than aforetime; or else no choice
would be given you but to abide here to your life's end.'

Then Húrin answered him: 'The King's grace is great indeed; but
if our word is not enough, then we will swear oaths to you.' And the
brothers swore never to reveal the counsels of Turgon, and to keep
secret all that they had seen in his realm. Then they took their leave,
and the eagles coming bore them away by night, and set them down
in Dor-lómin before the dawn. Their kinsfolk rejoiced to see them,
for messengers from Brethil had reported that they were lost; but
they would not declare even to their father where they had been,
save that they were rescued in the wilderness by the eagles that
brought them home. But Galdor said: 'Did you then dwell a year in
the wild? Or did the eagles house you in their eyries? But you found
food and fine raiment, and return as young princes, not as waifs of
the wood.' And Húrin answered: 'Be content that we have returned;
for only under an oath of silence was this permitted.' Then Galdor
questioned them no more, but he and many others guessed at the
truth; and in time the strange fortune of Húrin and Huor reached
the ears of the servants of Morgoth.

Now when Turgon learned of the breaking of the leaguer of Angband he would not suffer any of his own people to issue forth to war;
for he deemed that Gondolin was strong, and the time not yet ripe
for its revealing. But he believed also that the ending of the Siege
was the beginning of the downfall of the Noldor, unless aid should
come; and he sent companies of the Gondolindrim in secret to the
mouths of Sirion and the Isle of Balar. There they built ships, and
set sail into the uttermost West upon Turgon's errand, seeking for
Valinor, to ask for pardon and aid of the Valar; and they besought
the birds of the sea to guide them. But the seas were wild and wide,
and shadow and enchantment lay upon them; and Valinor was hidden. Therefore none of the messengers of Turgon came into the West,
and many were lost and few returned; but the doom of Gondolin
drew nearer.

Rumour came to Morgoth of these things, and he was unquiet amid his victories; and he desired greatly to learn tidings of Felagund and Turgon. For they had vanished out of knowledge, and yet were not dead; and he feared what they might yet accomplish against him. Of Nargothrond he knew indeed the name, but neither its place nor its strength; and of Gondolin he knew nothing, and the thought of Turgon troubled him the more. Therefore he sent forth ever more spies into Beleriand; but he recalled the main hosts of the Orcs to Angband, for he perceived that he could not yet make a final and victorious battle until he had gathered new strength, and that he had not measured rightly the valour of the Noldor nor the might in arms of the Men that fought beside them. Great though his victory had been in the Bragollach and in the years after, and grievous the harm that he had done to his enemies, his own loss had been no less; and though he held Dorthonion and the Pass of Sirion, the Eldar recovering from their first dismay began now to regain what they had lost. Thus Beleriand in the south had a semblance of peace again for a few brief years; but the forges of Angband were full of labour.

When seven years had passed since the Fourth Battle, Morgoth renewed his assault, and he sent a great force against Hithlum. The attack on the passes of the Shadowy Mountains was bitter, and in the siege of Eithel Sirion Galdor the tall, Lord of Dor-lómin, was slain by an arrow. That fortress he held on behalf of Fingon the High King; and in that same place his father Hador Lórindol died but a little time before. Húrin his son was then newly come to manhood, but he was great in strength both of mind and body; and he drove the Orcs with heavy slaughter from Ered Wethrin, and pursued them far across the sands of Anfauglith.

But King Fingon was hard put to it to hold back the army of Angband that came down from the north; and battle was joined upon the very plains of Hithlum. There Fingon was outnumbered; but the ships of Círdan sailed in great strength up the Firth of Drengist, and in the hour of need the Elves of the Falas came upon the host of Morgoth from the west. Then the Orcs broke and fled, and the Eldar had the victory, and their horsed archers pursued them even into the Iron Mountains.

Thereafter Húrin son of Galdor ruled the house of Hador in Dor-lómin, and served Fingon. Húrin was of less stature than his fathers, or his son after him; but he was tireless and enduring in body, lithe and swift after the manner of his mother's kin, Hareth of the Haladin. His wife was Morwen Eledhwen, daughter of Baragund of the house of Bëor, she who fled from Dorthonion with Rían daughter of Bele-gund and Emeldir the mother of Beren.

In that time also the outlaws of Dorthonion were destroyed, as is told hereafter; and Beren son of Barahir alone escaping came hardly into Doriath.

## Chapter 19

# OF BEREN AND LÚTHIEN

Among the tales of sorrow and of ruin that come down to us from the darkness of those days there are yet some in which amid weeping there is joy and under the shadow of death light that endures. And of these histories most fair still in the ears of the Elves is the tale of Beren and Lúthien. Of their lives was made the Lay of Leithian, Release from Bondage, which is the longest save one of the songs concerning the world of old; but here the tale is told in fewer words and without song.

It has been told that Barahir would not forsake Dorthonion, and there Morgoth pursued him to the death, until at last there remained to him only twelve companions. Now the forest of Dorthonion rose southward into mountainous moors; and in the east of those high-lands there lay a lake, Tarn Aeluin, with wild heaths about it, and all that land was pathless and untamed, for even in the days of the Long Peace none had dwelt there. But the waters of Tarn Aeluin were held in reverence, for they were clear and blue by day and by night were a mirror for the stars; and it was said that Melian herself had hallowed that water in days of old. Thither Barahir and his outlaws withdrew, and there made their lair, and Morgoth could not discover it. But the rumour of the deeds of Barahir and his companions went far and wide; and Morgoth commanded Sauron to find them and destroy them.

Now among the companions of Barahir was Gorlim son of Angrim. His wife was named Eilinel, and their love was great, ere evil befell. But Gorlim returning from the war upon the marches found his house plundered and forsaken, and his wife gone; whether slain or taken he knew not. Then he fled to Barahir, and of his companions he was the most fierce and desperate; but doubt gnawed his heart, thinking that perhaps Eilinel was not dead. At times he would depart alone and secretly, and visit his house that still stood amid the fields and woods he had once possessed; and this became known to the servants of Morgoth.

On a time of autumn he came in the dusk of evening, and drawing near he saw as he thought a light at the window; and coming warily he looked within. There he saw Eilinel, and her face was worn with grief and hunger, and it seemed to him that he heard her voice lamenting that he had forsaken her. But even as he cried aloud the light was blown out in the wind; wolves howled, and on his shoulders he felt suddenly the heavy hands of Sauron's hunters. Thus Gorlim was ensnared; and taking him to their camp they tormented him, seeking to learn the hidings of Barahir and all his ways. But nothing would Gorlim tell. Then they promised him that he should be released and restored to Eilinel, if he would yield; and being at last worn with pain, and yearning for his wife, he faltered. Then straightway they brought him into the dreadful presence of Sauron; and Sauron said: 'I hear now that thou wouldst barter with me. What is thy price?'

And Gorlim answered that he should find Eilinel again, and with her be set free; for he thought that Eilinel also had been made captive.

Then Sauron smiled, saying: 'That is a small price for so great a treachery. So shall it surely be. Say on!'

Now Gorlim would have drawn back, but daunted by the eyes of Sauron he told at last all that he would know. Then Sauron laughed; and he mocked Gorlim, and revealed to him that he had seen only a phantom devised by wizardry to entrap him; for Eilinel was dead. 'Nonetheless I will grant thy prayer,' said Sauron; 'and thou shalt go to Eilinel, and be set free of my service.' Then he put him cruelly to death.

In this way the hiding of Barahir was revealed, and Morgoth drew his net about it; and the Orcs coming in the still hours before dawn surprised the Men of Dorthonion and slew them all, save one. For Beren son of Barahir had been sent by his father on a perilous errand to spy upon the ways of the Enemy, and he was far afield when the lair was taken. But as he slept benighted in the forest he dreamed that carrion-birds sat thick as leaves upon bare trees beside a mere, and blood dripped from their beaks. Then Beren was aware in his dream of a form that came to him across the water, and it was a wraith of Gorlim; and it spoke to him declaring his treachery and death, and bade him make haste to warn his father.

Then Beren awoke, and sped through the night, and came back to the lair of the outlaws on the second morning. But as he drew near the carrion-birds rose from the ground and sat in the alder-trees beside Tarn Aeluin, and croaked in mockery.

There Beren buried his father's bones, and raised a cairn of boulders above him, and swore upon it an oath of vengeance. First therefore he pursued the Orcs that had slain his father and his kinsmen, and he found their camp by night at Rivil's Well above the Fen of Serech, and because of his woodcraft he came near to their fire unseen. There their captain made boast of his deeds, and he held up the hand of Barahir that he had cut off as a token for Sauron that their mission was fulfilled; and the ring of Felagund was on that hand. Then Beren sprang from behind a rock, and slew the captain, and taking the hand and the ring he escaped, being defended by fate; for the Orcs were dismayed, and their arrows wild.

Thereafter for four years more Beren wandered still upon Dorthonion, a solitary outlaw; but he became the friend of birds and beasts, and they aided him, and did not betray him, and from that time forth he ate no flesh nor slew any living thing that was not in the service of Morgoth. He did not fear death, but only captivity, and being bold and desperate he escaped both death and bonds; and the deeds of lonely daring that he achieved were noised abroad throughout Beleriand, and the tale of them came even into Doriath. At length Morgoth set a price upon his head no less than the price upon the head of Fingon, High King of the Noldor; but the Orcs fled rather at the rumour of his approach than sought him out. Therefore an army was sent against him under the command of Sauron; and Sauron brought werewolves, fell beasts inhabited by dreadful spirits that he had imprisoned in their bodies.

All that land was now become filled with evil, and all clean things were departing from it; and Beren was pressed so hard that at last he was forced to flee from Dorthonion. In time of winter and snow he forsook the land and grave of his father, and climbing into the high regions of Gorgoroth, the Mountains of Terror, he descried afar the land of Doriath. There it was put into his heart that he would go down into the Hidden Kingdom, where no mortal foot had yet trodden.

Terrible was his southward journey. Sheer were the precipices of Ered Gorgoroth, and beneath their feet were shadows that were laid before the rising of the Moon. Beyond lay the wilderness of Dungortheb, where the sorcery of Sauron and the power of Melian came together, and horror and madness walked. There spiders of the fell race of Ungoliant abode, spinning their unseen webs in which all living things were snared; and monsters wandered there that were born in the long dark before the Sun, hunting silently with many eyes. No food for Elves or Men was there in that haunted land, but death only. That journey is not accounted least among the great deeds of Beren, but he spoke of it to no one after, lest the horror return into his mind; and none know how he found a way, and so came by paths that no Man nor Elf else ever dared to tread to the borders of Doriath. And he passed through the mazes that Melian wove about the kingdom of Thingol, even as she had foretold; for a great doom lay upon him.

It is told in the Lay of Leithian that Beren came stumbling into Doriath grey and bowed as with many years of woe, so great had been the torment of the road. But wandering in the summer in the woods of Neldoreth he came upon Lúthien, daughter of Thingol and Melian, at a time of evening under moonrise, as she danced upon the unfading grass in the glades beside Esgalduin. Then all memory of his pain departed from him, and he fell into an enchantment; for Lúthien was the most beautiful of all the Children of Ilúvatar. Blue was her raiment as the unclouded heaven, but her eyes were grey as the starlit evening; her mantle was sewn with golden flowers, but her hair was dark as the shadows of twilight. As the light upon the leaves of trees, as the voice of clear waters, as the stars above the mists of the world, such was her glory and her loveliness; and in her face was a shining light.

But she vanished from his sight; and he became dumb, as one that is bound under a spell, and he strayed long in the woods, wild and wary as a beast, seeking for her. In his heart he called her Tinúviel, that signifies Nightingale, daughter of twilight, in the Grey-elven tongue, for he knew no other name for her. And he saw her afar as leaves in the winds of autumn, and in winter as a star upon a hill, but a chain was upon his limbs.

There came a time near dawn on the eve of spring, and Lúthien danced upon a green hill; and suddenly she began to sing. Keen, heart-piercing was her song as the song of the lark that rises from the gates of night and pours its voice among the dying stars, seeing the sun behind the walls of the world; and the song of Lúthien released the bonds of winter, and the frozen waters spoke, and flowers sprang from the cold earth where her feet had passed.

Then the spell of silence fell from Beren, and he called to her, crying Tinúviel; and the woods echoed the name. Then she halted in wonder, and fled no more, and Beren came to her. But as she looked on him, doom fell upon her, and she loved him; yet she slipped from his arms and vanished from his sight even as the day was breaking. Then Beren lay upon the ground in a swoon, as one slain at once by bliss and grief; and he fell into a sleep as it were into an abyss of shadow, and waking he was cold as stone, and his heart barren and forsaken. And wandering in mind he groped as one that is stricken with sudden blindness, and seeks with hands to grasp the vanished light. Thus he began the payment of anguish for the fate that was laid on him; and in his fate Lúthien was caught, and being immortal she shared in his mortality, and being free received his chain; and her anguish was greater than any other of the Eldalië has known.

Beyond his hope she returned to him where he sat in darkness, and long ago in the Hidden Kingdom she laid her hand in his. Thereafter often she came to him, and they went in secret through the woods together from spring to summer; and no others of the Children of Ilúvatar have had joy so great, though the time was brief.

But Daeron the minstrel also loved Lúthien, and he espied her meetings with Beren, and betrayed them to Thingol. Then the King was filled with anger, for Lúthien he loved above all things, setting her above all the princes of the Elves; whereas mortal Men he did not even take into his service. Therefore he spoke in grief and amazement to Lúthien; but she would reveal nothing, until he swore an oath to her that he would neither slay Beren nor imprison him. But he sent his servants to lay hands on him and lead him to Menegroth as a malefactor; and Lúthien forestalling them led Beren herself before the throne of Thingol, as if he were an honoured guest.

Then Thingol looked upon Beren in scorn and anger; but Melian was silent. 'Who are you,' said the King, 'that come hither as a thief, and unbidden dare to approach my throne?'

But Beren being filled with dread, for the splendour of Menegroth and the majesty of Thingol were very great, answered nothing. Therefore Lúthien spoke, and said: 'He is Beren son of Barahir, lord of Men, mighty foe of Morgoth, the tale of whose deeds is become a song even among the Elves.'

'Let Beren speak!' said Thingol. 'What would you here, unhappy mortal, and for what cause have you left your own land to enter this, which is forbidden to such as you? Can you show reason why my power should not be laid on you in heavy punishment for your insolence and folly?'

Then Beren looking up beheld the eyes of Lúthien, and his glance went also to the face of Melian; and it seemed to him that words were put into his mouth. Fear left him, and the pride of the eldest house of Men returned to him; and he said: 'My fate, O King, led me hither, through perils such as few even of the Elves would dare. And here I have found what I sought not indeed, but finding I would possess for ever. For it is above all gold and silver, and beyond all jewels. Neither rock, nor steel, nor the fires of Morgoth, nor all the powers of the Elf-kingdoms, shall keep from me the treasure that I desire. For Lúthien your daughter is the fairest of all the Children of the World.'

Then silence fell upon the hall, for those that stood there were astounded and afraid, and they thought that Beren would be slain. But Thingol spoke slowly, saying: 'Death you have earned with these words; and death you should find suddenly, had I not sworn an oath in haste; of which I repent, baseborn mortal, who in the realm of Morgoth has learnt to creep in secret as his spies and thralls.'

Then Beren answered: 'Death you can give me earned or unearned; but the names I will not take from you of baseborn, nor spy, nor thrall. By the ring of Felagund, that he gave to Barahir my father on the battlefield of the North, my house has not earned such names from any Elf, be he king or no.'

His words were proud, and all eyes looked upon the ring; for he held it now aloft, and the green jewels gleamed there that the Noldor had devised in Valinor. For this ring was like to twin serpents, whose eyes were emeralds, and their heads met beneath a crown of golden flowers, that the one upheld and the other devoured; that was the badge of Finarfin and his house. Then Melian leaned to Thingol's side, and in whispered counsel bade him forgo his wrath. 'For not by you,' she said, 'shall Beren be slain; and far and free does his fate lead him in the end, yet it is wound with yours. Take heed!'

But Thingol looked in silence upon Lúthien; and he thought in his heart: 'Unhappy Men, children of little lords and brief kings, shall such as these lay hands on you, and yet live?' Then breaking the silence he said: 'I see the ring, son of Barahir, and I perceive that you are proud, and deem yourself mighty. But a father's deeds, even had his service been rendered to me, avail not to win the daughter of Thingol and Melian. See now! I too desire a treasure that is withheld. For rock and steel and the fires of Morgoth keep the jewel that I would possess against all the powers of the Elf-kingdoms. Yet I hear you say that bonds such as these do not daunt you. Go your way therefore! Bring to me in your hand a Silmaril from Morgoth's crown; and then, if she will, Lúthien may set her hand in yours. Then you shall have my jewel; and though the fate of Arda lie within the Silmarils, yet you shall hold me generous.'

Thus he wrought the doom of Doriath, and was ensnared within the curse of Mandos. And those that heard these words perceived that Thingol would save his oath, and yet send Beren to his death; for they knew that not all the power of the Noldor, before the Siege was broken, had availed even to see from afar the shining Silmarils of Fëanor. For they were set in the Iron Crown, and treasured in Angband above all wealth; and Balrogs were about them, and countless swords, and strong bars, and unassailable walls, and the dark majesty of Morgoth.

But Beren laughed. 'For little price,' he said, 'do Elven-kings sell their daughters: for gems, and things made by craft. But if this be your will, Thingol, I will perform it. And when we meet again my hand shall hold a Silmaril from the Iron Crown; for you have not looked the last upon Beren son of Barahir.'

Then he looked in the eyes of Melian, who spoke not; and he bade farewell to Lúthien Tinúviel, and bowing before Thingol and Melian he put aside the guards about him, and departed from Menegroth alone.

Then at last Melian spoke, and she said to Thingol: 'O King, you have devised cunning counsel. But if my eyes have not lost their sight, it is ill for you, whether Beren fail in his errand, or achieve it. For you have doomed either your daughter, or yourself. And now is Doriath drawn within the fate of a mightier realm.'

But Thingol answered: 'I sell not to Elves or Men those whom I love and cherish above all treasure. And if there were hope or fear that Beren should come ever back alive to Menegroth, he should not have looked again upon the light of heaven, though I had sworn it.'

But Lúthien was silent, and from that hour she sang not again in Doriath. A brooding silence fell upon the woods, and the shadows lengthened in the kingdom of Thingol.

It is told in the Lay of Leithian that Beren passed through Doriath unhindered, and came at length to the region of the Twilight Meres, and the Fens of Sirion; and leaving Thingol's land he climbed the hills above the Falls of Sirion, where the river plunged underground with great noise. Thence he looked westward, and through the mist and rains that lay upon those hills he saw Talath Dirnen, the Guarded Plain, stretching between Sirion and Narog; and beyond he descried afar the highlands of Taur-en-Faroth that rose above Nargothrond. And being destitute, without hope or counsel, he turned his feet thither.

Upon all that plain the Elves of Nargothrond kept unceasing watch; and every hill upon its borders was crowned with hidden towers, and through all its woods and fields archers ranged secretly and with great craft. Their arrows were sure and deadly, and nothing crept there against their will. Therefore, ere Beren had come far upon his road, they were aware of him, and his death was nigh. But knowing his danger he held ever aloft the ring of Felagund; and though he saw no living thing, because of the stealth of the hunters, he felt that he was watched, and cried often aloud: 'I am Beren son of Barahir, friend of Felagund. Take me to the King!'

Therefore the hunters slew him not, but assembling they waylaid
him, and commanded him to halt. But seeing the ring they bowed
before him, though he was in evil plight, wild and wayworn; and
they led him northward and westward, going by night lest their
paths should be revealed. For at that time there was no ford or
bridge over the torrent of Narog before the gates of Nargothrond;
but further to the north, where Ginglith joined Narog, the flood was
less, and crossing there and turning again southward the Elves
led Beren under the light of the moon to the dark gates of their
hidden halls.

Thus Beren came before King Finrod Felagund; and Felagund
knew him, needing no ring to remind him of the kin of Bëor and of
Barahir. Behind closed doors they sat, and Beren told of the death of
Barahir, and of all that had befallen him in Doriath; and he wept,
recalling Lúthien and their joy together. But Felagund heard his tale
in wonder and disquiet; and he knew that the oath he had sworn was
come upon him for his death, as long before he had foretold to Galadriel. He spoke then to Beren in heaviness of heart. 'It is plain that
Thingol desires your death; but it seems that this doom goes beyond
his purpose, and that the Oath of Fëanor is again at work. For the
Silmarils are cursed with an oath of hatred, and he that even names
them in desire moves a great power from slumber; and the sons of
Fëanor would lay all the Elf-kingdoms in ruin rather than suffer any
other than themselves to win or possess a Silmaril, for the Oath drives
them. And now Celegorm and Curufin are dwelling in my halls; and
though I, Finarfin's son, am King, they have won a strong power in
the realm, and lead many of their own people. They have shown
friendship to me in every need, but I fear that they will show neither
love nor mercy to you, if your quest be told. Yet my own oath holds;
and thus we are all ensnared.'

Then King Felagund spoke before his people, recalling the deeds
of Barahir, and his vow; and he declared that it was laid upon him to
aid the son of Barahir in his need, and he sought the help of his
chieftains. Then Celegorm arose amid the throng, and drawing his
sword he cried: 'Be he friend or foe, whether demon of Morgoth, or
Elf, or child of Men, or any other living thing in Arda, neither law,
nor love, nor league of hell, nor might of the Valar, nor any power of
wizardry, shall defend him from the pursuing hate of Fëanor's sons,
if he take or find a Silmaril and keep it. For the Silmarils we alone
claim, until the world ends.'

Many other words he spoke, as potent as were long before in
Tirion the words of his father that first inflamed the Noldor to

rebellion. And after Celegorm Curufin spoke, more softly but with no less power, conjuring in the minds of the Elves a vision of war and the ruin of Nargothrond. So great a fear did he set in their hearts that never after until the time of Túrin would any Elf of that realm go into open battle; but with stealth and ambush, with wizardry and venomed dart, they pursued all strangers, forgetting the bonds of kinship. Thus they fell from the valour and freedom of the Elves of old, and their land was darkened.

And now they murmured that Finarfin's son was not as a Vala to command them, and they turned their faces from him. But the curse of Mandos came upon the brothers, and dark thoughts arose in their hearts, thinking to send forth Felagund alone to his death, and to usurp, it might be, the throne of Nargothrond; for they were of the eldest line of the princes of the Noldor.

And Felagund seeing that he was forsaken took from his head the silver crown of Nargothrond and cast it at his feet, saying: 'Your oaths of faith to me you may break, but I must hold my bond. Yet if there be any on whom the shadow of our curse has not yet fallen, I should find at least a few to follow me, and should not go hence as a beggar that is thrust from the gates.' There were ten that stood by him; and the chief of them, who was named Edrahil, stooping lifted the crown and asked that it be given to a steward until Felagund's return. 'For you remain my king, and theirs,' he said, 'whatever betide.'

Then Felagund gave the crown of Nargothrond to Orodreth his brother to govern in his stead; and Celegorm and Curufin said nothing, but they smiled and went from the halls.

On an evening of autumn Felagund and Beren set out from Nargothrond with their ten companions; and they journeyed beside Narog to his source in the Falls of Ivrin. Beneath the Shadowy Mountains they came upon a company of Orcs, and slew them all in their camp by night; and they took their gear and their weapons. By the arts of Felagund their own forms and faces were changed into the likeness of Orcs; and thus disguised they came far upon their northward road, and ventured into the western pass, between Ered Wethrin and the highlands of Taur-nu-Fuin. But Sauron in his tower was ware of them, and doubt took him; for they went in haste, and stayed not to report their deeds, as was commanded to all the servants of Morgoth that passed that way. Therefore he sent to waylay them, and bring them before him.

Thus befell the contest of Sauron and Felagund which is renowned.

For Felagund strove with Sauron in songs of power, and the power of
the King was very great; but Sauron had the mastery, as is told in
the Lay of Leithian:

> He chanted a song of wizardry,
> Of piercing, opening, of treachery,
> Revealing, uncovering, betraying.
> Then sudden Felagund there swaying
> Sang in answer a song of staying,
> Resisting, battling against power,
> Of secrets kept, strength like a tower,
> And trust unbroken, freedom, escape;
> Of changing and of shifting shape,
> Of snares eluded, broken traps,
> The prison opening, the chain that snaps.
>    Backwards and forwards swayed their song.
> Reeling and foundering, as ever more strong
> The chanting swelled, Felagund fought,
> And all the magic and might he brought
> Of Elvenesse into his words.
> Softly in the gloom they heard the birds
> Singing afar in Nargothrond,
> The sighing of the Sea beyond,
> Beyond the western world, on sand,
> On sand of pearls in Elvenland.
>    Then the gloom gathered; darkness growing
> In Valinor, the red blood flowing
> Beside the Sea, where the Noldor slew
> The Foamriders, and stealing drew
> Their white ships with their white sails
> From lamplit havens. The wind wails,
> The wolf howls. The ravens flee.
> The ice mutters in the mouths of the Sea.
> The captives sad in Angband mourn.
> Thunder rumbles, the fires burn—
> And Finrod fell before the throne.

Then Sauron stripped from them their disguise, and they stood
before him naked and afraid. But though their kinds were revealed,
Sauron could not discover their names or their purposes.

He cast them therefore into a deep pit, dark and silent, and threatened to slay them cruelly, unless one would betray the truth to him.

From time to time they saw two eyes kindled in the dark, and a were-wolf devoured one of the companions; but none betrayed their lord.

In the time when Sauron cast Beren into the pit a weight of horror came upon Lúthien's heart; and going to Melian for counsel she learned that Beren lay in the dungeons of Tol-in-Gaurhoth without hope of rescue. Then Lúthien, perceiving that no help would come from any other on earth, resolved to fly from Doriath and come herself to him; but she sought the aid of Daeron, and he betrayed her purpose to the King. Then Thingol was filled with fear and wonder; and because he would not deprive Lúthien of the lights of heaven, lest she fail and fade, and yet would restrain her, he caused a house to be built from which she should not escape. Not far from the gates of Menegroth stood the greatest of all the trees in the Forest of Neldoreth; and that was a beech-forest and the northern half of the kingdom. This mighty beech was named Hírilorn, and it had three trunks, equal in girth, smooth in rind, and exceeding tall; no branches grew from them for a great height above the ground. Far aloft between the shafts of Hírilorn a wooden house was built, and there Lúthien was made to dwell; and the ladders were taken away and guarded, save only when the servants of Thingol brought her such things as she needed.

It is told in the Lay of Leithian how she escaped from the house in Hírilorn; for she put forth her arts of enchantment, and caused her hair to grow to great length, and of it she wove a dark robe that wrapped her beauty like a shadow, and it was laden with a spell of sleep. Of the strands that remained she twined a rope, and she let it down from her window; and as the end swayed above the guards that sat beneath the tree they fell into a deep slumber. Then Lúthien climbed from her prison, and shrouded in her shadowy cloak she escaped from all eyes, and vanished out of Doriath.

It chanced that Celegorm and Curufin went on a hunt through the Guarded Plain; and this they did because Sauron, being filled with suspicion, sent forth many wolves into the Elf-lands. Therefore they took their hounds and rode forth; and they thought that ere they returned they might also hear tidings concerning King Felagund. Now the chief of the wolfhounds that followed Celegorm was named Huan. He was not born in Middle-earth, but came from the Blessed Realm; for Oromë had given him to Celegorm long ago in Valinor, and there he had followed the horn of his master, before evil came. Huan followed Celegorm into exile, and was faithful; and thus he too came under the doom of woe set upon the Noldor, and it was decreed that he should meet death, but not until he encountered the mightiest wolf that would ever walk the world.

Huan it was that found Lúthien flying like a shadow surprised by the daylight under the trees, when Celegorm and Curufin rested a while near to the western eaves of Doriath; for nothing could escape the sight and scent of Huan, nor could any enchantment stay him, and he slept not, neither by night nor day. He brought her to Celegorm, and Lúthien, learning that he was a prince of the Noldor and a foe of Morgoth, was glad; and she declared herself, casting aside her cloak. So great was her sudden beauty revealed beneath the sun that Celegorm became enamoured of her; but he spoke her fair, and promised that she would find help in her need, if she returned with him now to Nargothrond. By no sign did he reveal that he knew already of Beren and the quest, of which she told, nor that it was a matter which touched him near.

Thus they broke off the hunt and returned to Nargothrond, and Lúthien was betrayed; for they held her fast, and took away her cloak, and she was not permitted to pass the gates or to speak with any save the brothers, Celegorm and Curufin. For now, believing that Beren and Felagund were prisoners beyond hope of aid, they purposed to let the King perish, and to keep Lúthien, and force Thingol to give her hand to Celegorm. Thus they would advance their power, and become the mightiest of the princes of the Noldor. And they did not purpose to seek the Silmarils by craft or war, or to suffer any others to do so, until they had all the might of the Elf-kingdoms under their hands. Orodreth had no power to withstand them, for they swayed the hearts of the people of Nargothrond; and Celegorm sent messengers to Thingol urging his suit.

But Huan the hound was true of heart, and the love of Lúthien had fallen upon him in the first hour of their meeting; and he grieved at her captivity. Therefore he came often to her chamber; and at night he lay before her door, for he felt that evil had come to Nargothrond. Lúthien spoke often to Huan in her loneliness, telling of Beren, who was the friend of all birds and beasts that did not serve Morgoth; and Huan understood all that was said. For he comprehended the speech of all things with voice; but it was permitted to him thrice only ere his death to speak with words.

Now Huan devised a plan for the aid of Lúthien; and coming at a time of night he brought her cloak, and for the first time he spoke, giving her counsel. Then he led her by secret ways out of Nargothrond, and they fled north together; and he humbled his pride and suffered her to ride upon him in the fashion of a steed, even as the

Orcs did at times upon great wolves. Thus they made great speed, for Huan was swift and tireless.

In the pits of Sauron Beren and Felagund lay, and all their companions were now dead; but Sauron purposed to keep Felagund to the last, for he perceived that he was a Noldo of great might and wisdom, and he deemed that in him lay the secret of their errand. But when the wolf came for Beren, Felagund put forth all his power, and burst his bonds; and he wrestled with the werewolf, and slew it with his hands and teeth; yet he himself was wounded to the death. Then he spoke to Beren, saying: 'I go now to my long rest in the timeless halls beyond the seas and the Mountains of Aman. It will be long ere I am seen among the Noldor again; and it may be that we shall not meet a second time in death or life, for the fates of our kindreds are apart. Farewell!' He died then in the dark, in Tol-in-Gaurhoth, whose great tower he himself had built. Thus King Finrod Felagund, fairest and most beloved of the house of Finwë, redeemed his oath; but Beren mourned beside him in despair.

In that hour Lúthien came, and standing upon the bridge that led to Sauron's isle she sang a song that no walls of stone could hinder. Beren heard, and he thought that he dreamed; for the stars shone above him, and in the trees nightingales were singing. And in answer he sang a song of challenge that he had made in praise of the Seven Stars, the Sickle of the Valar that Varda hung above the North as a sign for the fall of Morgoth. Then all strength left him and he fell down into darkness.

But Lúthien heard his answering voice, and she sang then a song of greater power. The wolves howled, and the isle trembled. Sauron stood in the high tower, wrapped in his black thought; but he smiled hearing her voice, for he knew that it was the daughter of Melian. The fame of the beauty of Lúthien and the wonder of her song had long gone forth from Doriath; and he thought to make her captive and hand her over to the power of Morgoth, for his reward would be great.

Therefore he sent a wolf to the bridge. But Huan slew it silently. Still Sauron sent others one by one; and one by one Huan took them by the throat and slew them. Then Sauron sent Draugluin, a dread beast, old in evil, lord and sire of the werewolves of Angband. His might was great; and the battle of Huan and Draugluin was long and fierce. Yet at length Draugluin escaped, and fleeing back into the tower he died before Sauron's feet; and as he died he told his master: 'Huan is there!' Now Sauron knew well, as did all in that land, the fate that was decreed for the hound of Valinor, and it came into his thought that he himself would accomplish it. Therefore he took upon himself the form of a werewolf, and made himself the mightiest that had yet walked the world; and he came forth to win the passage of the bridge.

So great was the horror of his approach that Huan leaped aside. Then Sauron sprang upon Lúthien; and she swooned before the menace of the fell spirit in his eyes and the foul vapour of his breath. But even as he came, falling she cast a fold of her dark cloak before his eyes; and he stumbled, for a fleeting drowsiness came upon him. Then Huan sprang. There befell the battle of Huan and Wolf-Sauron, and the howls and baying echoed in the hills, and the watchers on the walls of Ered Wethrin across the valley heard it afar and were dismayed.

But no wizardry nor spell, neither fang nor venom, nor devil's art nor beast-strength, could overthrow Huan of Valinor; and he took his foe by the throat and pinned him down. Then Sauron shifted shape, from wolf to serpent, and from monster to his own accustomed form; but he could not elude the grip of Huan without forsaking his body utterly. Ere his foul spirit left its dark house, Lúthien came to him, and said that he should be stripped of his raiment of flesh, and his ghost be sent quaking back to Morgoth; and she said: 'There everlastingly thy naked self shall endure the torment of his scorn, pierced by his eyes, unless thou yield to me the mastery of thy tower.'

Then Sauron yielded himself, and Lúthien took the mastery of the isle and all that was there; and Huan released him. And immediately he took the form of a vampire, great as a dark cloud across the moon, and he fled, dripping blood from his throat upon the trees, and came to Taur-nu-Fuin, and dwelt there, filling it with horror.

Then Lúthien stood upon the bridge, and declared her power: and the spell was loosed that bound stone to stone, and the gates were thrown down, and the walls opened, and the pits laid bare; and many thralls and captives came forth in wonder and dismay, shielding their eyes against the pale moonlight, for they had lain long in the darkness of Sauron. But Beren came not. Therefore Huan and Lúthien sought him in the isle; and Lúthien found him mourning by Felagund. So deep was his anguish that he lay still, and did not hear her feet. Then thinking him already dead she put her arms about him and fell into a dark forgetfulness. But Beren coming back to the light out of the pits of despair lifted her up, and they looked again upon one another; and the day rising over the dark hills shone upon them.

They buried the body of Felagund upon the hill-top of his own isle, and it was clean again; and the green grave of Finrod Finarfin's son, fairest of all the princes of the Elves, remained inviolate, until the land was changed and broken, and foundered under destroying seas. But Finrod walks with Finarfin his father beneath the trees in Eldamar.

Now Beren and Lúthien Tinúviel went free again and together walked through the woods renewing for a time their joy; and though winter came it hurt them not, for flowers lingered where Lúthien went, and the birds sang beneath the snowclad hills. But Huan being faithful went back to Celegorm his master; yet their love was less than before.

There was tumult in Nargothrond. For thither now returned many Elves that had been prisoners in the isle of Sauron; and a clamour arose that no words of Celegorm could still. They lamented bitterly the fall of Felagund their king, saying that a maiden had dared that which the sons of Fëanor had not dared to do; but many perceived that it was treachery rather than fear that had guided Celegorm and Curufin. Therefore the hearts of the people of Nargothrond were released from their dominion, and turned again to the house of Finarfin; and they obeyed Orodreth. But he would not suffer them to slay the brothers, as some desired, for the spilling of kindred blood by kin would bind the curse of Mandos more closely upon them all. Yet neither bread nor rest would he grant to Celegorm and Curufin within his realm, and he swore that there should be little love between Nargothrond and the sons of Fëanor thereafter.

'Let it be so!' said Celegorm, and there was a light of menace in his eyes; but Curufin smiled. Then they took horse and rode away like fire, to find if they might their kindred in the east. But none would go with them, not even those that were of their own people; for all perceived that the curse lay heavily upon the brothers, and that evil followed them. In that time Celebrimbor the son of Curufin repudiated the deeds of his father, and remained in Nargothrond; yet Huan followed still the horse of Celegorm his master.

Northward they rode, for they intended in their haste to pass through Dimbar, and along the north marches of Doriath, seeking the swiftest road to Himring, where Maedhros their brother dwelt; and still they might hope with speed to traverse it, since it lay close to Doriath's borders, shunning Nan Dungortheb and the distant menace of the Mountains of Terror.

Now it is told that Beren and Lúthien came in their wandering into the Forest of Brethil, and drew near at last to the borders of Doriath.

Then Beren took thought of his vow; and against his heart he resolved, when Lúthien was come again within the safety of her own land, to set forth once more. But she was not willing to be parted from him again, saying: 'You must choose, Beren, between these two: to relinquish the quest and your oath and seek a life of wandering upon the face of the earth; or to hold to your word and challenge the power of darkness upon its throne. But on either road I shall go with you, and our doom shall be alike.'

Even as they spoke together of these things, walking without heed of aught else, Celegorm and Curufin rode up, hastening through the forest; and the brothers espied them and knew them from afar. Then Celegorm turned his horse, and spurred it upon Beren, purposing to ride him down; but Curufin swerving stooped and lifted Lúthien to his saddle, for he was a strong and cunning horseman. Then Beren sprang from before Celegorm full upon the speeding horse of Curufin that had passed him; and the Leap of Beren is renowned among Men and Elves. He took Curufin by the throat from behind, and hurled him backward, and they fell to the ground together. The horse reared and fell, but Lúthien was flung aside, and lay upon the grass.

Then Beren throttled Curufin; but death was near him, for Celegorm rode upon him with a spear. In that hour Huan forsook the service of Celegorm, and sprang upon him, so that his horse swerved aside, and would not approach Beren because of the terror of the great hound. Celegorm cursed both hound and horse, but Huan was unmoved. Then Lúthien rising forbade the slaying of Curufin; but Beren despoiled him of his gear and weapons, and took his knife, Angrist. That knife was made by Telchar of Nogrod, and hung sheathless by his side; iron it would cleave as if it were green wood. Then Beren lifting Curufin flung him from him, and bade him walk now back to his noble kinsfolk, who might teach him to turn his valour to worthier use. 'Your horse,' he said, 'I keep for the service of Lúthien, and it may be accounted happy to be free of such a master.'

Then Curufin cursed Beren under cloud and sky. 'Go hence,' he said, 'unto a swift and bitter death.' Celegorm took him beside him on his horse, and the brothers made then as if to ride away; and Beren turned away and took no heed of their words. But Curufin, being filled with shame and malice, took the bow of Celegorm and shot back as they went; and the arrow was aimed at Lúthien. Huan leaping caught it in his mouth; but Curufin shot again, and Beren sprang before Lúthien, and the dart smote him in the breast.

It is told that Huan pursued the sons of Fëanor, and they fled in fear; and returning he brought to Lúthien a herb out of the forest. With that leaf she staunched Beren's wound, and by her arts and by her love she healed him; and thus at last they returned to Doriath. There Beren, being torn between his oath and his love, and knowing Lúthien to be now safe, arose one morning before the sun, and committed her to the care of Huan; then in great anguish he departed while she yet slept upon the grass.

He rode northward again with all speed to the Pass of Sirion, and coming to the skirts of Taur-nu-Fuin he looked out across the waste of Anfauglith and saw afar the peaks of Thangorodrim. There he dismissed the horse of Curufin, and bade it leave now dread and servitude and run free upon the green grass in the lands of Sirion. Then being now alone and upon the threshold of the final peril he made the Song of Parting, in praise of Lúthien and the lights of heaven; for he believed that he must now say farewell to both love and light. Of that song these words were part:

> *Farewell sweet earth and northern sky,*
> *for ever blest, since here did lie*
> *and here with lissom limbs did run*
> *beneath the Moon, beneath the Sun,*
> *Lúthien Tinúviel*
> *more fair than mortal tongue can tell.*
> *Though all to ruin fell the world*
> *and were dissolved and backward hurled*
> *unmade into the old abyss,*
> *yet were its making good, for this—*
> *the dusk, the dawn, the earth, the sea—*
> *that Lúthien for a time should be.*

And he sang aloud, caring not what ear should overhear him, for he was desperate and looked for no escape.

But Lúthien heard his song, and she sang in answer, as she came through the woods unlooked for. For Huan, consenting once more to be her steed, had borne her swiftly hard upon Beren's trail. Long he had pondered in his heart what counsel he could devise for the lightening of the peril of these two whom he loved. He turned aside therefore at Sauron's isle, as they ran northward again, and he took thence the ghastly wolf-hame of Draugluin, and the bat-fell of Thuringwethil. She was the messenger of Sauron, and was wont to fly in vampire's form to Angband; and her great fingered wings were barbed at each joint's end with an iron claw. Clad in these dreadful garments Huan and Lúthien ran through Taur-nu-Fuin, and all things fled before them.

Beren seeing their approach was dismayed; and he wondered, for he had heard the voice of Tinúviel, and he thought it now a phantom for his ensnaring. But they halted and cast aside their disguise, and Lúthien ran towards him. Thus Beren and Lúthien met again between the desert and the wood. For a while he was silent, and was glad; but after a space he strove once more to dissuade Lúthien from her journey.

'Thrice now I curse my oath to Thingol,' he said, 'and I would that he had slain me in Menegroth, rather than I should bring you under the shadow of Morgoth.'

Then for the second time Huan spoke with words; and he counselled Beren, saying: 'From the shadow of death you can no longer save Lúthien, for by her love she is now subject to it. You can turn from your fate and lead her into exile, seeking peace in vain while your life lasts. But if you will not deny your doom, then either Lúthien, being forsaken, must assuredly die alone, or she must with you challenge the fate that lies before you—hopeless, yet not certain. Further counsel I cannot give, nor may I go further on your road. But my heart forebodes that what you find at the Gate I shall myself see. All else is dark to me; yet it may be that our three paths lead back to Doriath, and we may meet before the end.'

Then Beren perceived that Lúthien could not be divided from the doom that lay upon them both, and he sought no longer to dissuade her. By the counsel of Huan and the arts of Lúthien he was arrayed now in the hame of Draugluin, and she in the winged fell of Thuringwethil. Beren became in all things like a werewolf to look upon, save that in his eyes there shone a spirit grim indeed but clean; and horror was in his glance as he saw upon his flank a bat-like creature clinging with creased wings. Then howling under the moon he leaped down the hill, and the bat wheeled and flittered above him.

They passed through all perils, until they came with the dust of their long and weary road upon them to the drear dale that lay before the Gate of Angband. Black chasms opened beside the road, whence forms as of writhing serpents issued. On either hand the cliffs stood as embattled walls, and upon them sat carrion fowl crying with fell voices. Before them was the impregnable Gate, an arch wide and dark at the foot of the mountain; above it reared a thousand feet of precipice.

There dismay took them, for at the gate was a guard of whom no tidings had yet gone forth. Rumour of he knew not what designs abroad among the princes of the Elves had come to Morgoth, and ever down the aisles of the forest was heard the baying of Huan, the great hound of war, whom long ago the Valar unleashed. Then Morgoth recalled the doom of Huan, and he chose one from among the whelps of the race of Draugluin; and he fed him with his own hand upon living flesh, and put his power upon him. Swiftly the wolf grew, until he could creep into no den, but lay huge and hungry before the feet of Morgoth. There the fire and anguish of hell entered into him, and he became filled with a devouring spirit, tormented, terrible, and strong. Carcharoth, the Red Maw, he is named in the tales of those days, and Anfauglir, the Jaws of Thirst. And Morgoth set him to lie unsleeping before the doors of Angband, lest Huan come.

Now Carcharoth espied them from afar, and he was filled with doubt; for news had long been brought to Angband that Draugluin was dead. Therefore when they approached he denied them entry, and bade them stand; and he drew near with menace, scenting something strange in the air about them. But suddenly some power, descended from of old from divine race, possessed Lúthien, and casting back her foul raiment she stood forth, small before the might of Carcharoth, but radiant and terrible. Lifting up her hand she commanded him to sleep, saying: 'O woe-begotten spirit, fall now into dark oblivion, and forget for a while the dreadful doom of life.' And Carcharoth was felled, as though lightning had smitten him.

Then Beren and Lúthien went through the Gate, and down the labyrinthine stairs; and together wrought the greatest deed that has been dared by Elves or Men. For they came to the seat of Morgoth in his nethermost hall, that was upheld by horror, lit by fire, and filled with weapons of death and torment. There Beren slunk in wolf's form beneath his throne; but Lúthien was stripped of her disguise by the will of Morgoth, and he bent his gaze upon her. She was not daunted by his eyes; and she named her own name, and offered her service to sing before him, after the manner of a minstrel. Then Morgoth looking upon her beauty conceived in his thought an evil lust, and a design more dark than any that had yet come into his heart since he fled from Valinor. Thus he was beguiled by his own malice, for he watched her, leaving her free for a while, and taking secret pleasure in his thought. Then suddenly she eluded his sight, and out of the shadows began a song of such surpassing loveliness, and of such blinding power, that he listened perforce; and a blindness came upon him, as his eyes roamed to and fro, seeking her.

All his court were cast down in slumber, and all the fires faded and were quenched; but the Silmarils in the crown on Morgoth's head blazed forth suddenly with a radiance of white flame; and the burden of that crown and of the jewels bowed down his head, as though the world were set upon it, laden with a weight of care, of fear, and of desire, that even the will of Morgoth could not support. Then Lúthien catching up her winged robe sprang into the air, and her voice came dropping down like rain into pools, profound and dark. She cast her cloak before his eyes, and set upon him a dream, dark as the Outer Void where once he walked alone. Suddenly he fell, as a hill sliding in avalanche, and hurled like thunder from his throne lay prone upon the floors of hell. The iron crown rolled echoing from his head. All things were still.

As a dead beast Beren lay upon the ground; but Lúthien touching him with her hand aroused him, and he cast aside the wolf-hame. Then he drew forth the knife Angrist; and from the iron claws that held it he cut a Silmaril.

As he closed it in his hand, the radiance welled through his living flesh, and his hand became as a shining lamp; but the jewel suffered his touch and hurt him not. It came then into Beren's mind that he would go beyond his vow, and bear out of Angband all three of the Jewels of Fëanor; but such was not the doom of the Silmarils. The knife Angrist snapped, and a shard of the blade flying smote the cheek of Morgoth. He groaned and stirred, and all the host of Angband moved in sleep.

Then terror fell upon Beren and Lúthien, and they fled, heedless and without disguise, desiring only to see the light once more. They were neither hindered nor pursued, but the Gate was held against their going out; for Carcharoth had arisen from sleep, and stood now in wrath upon the threshold of Angband. Before they were aware of him, he saw them, and sprang upon them as they ran.

Lúthien was spent, and she had not time nor strength to quell the wolf. But Beren strode forth before her, and in his right hand he held aloft the Silmaril. Carcharoth halted, and for a moment was afraid. 'Get you gone, and fly!' cried Beren; 'for here is a fire that shall consume you, and all evil things.' And he thrust the Silmaril before the eyes of the wolf.

But Carcharoth looked upon that holy jewel and was not daunted, and the devouring spirit within him awoke to sudden fire; and gaping he took suddenly the hand within his jaws, and he bit it off at the wrist. Then swiftly all his inwards were filled with a flame of anguish, and the Silmaril seared his accursed flesh. Howling he fled before them, and the walls of the valley of the Gate echoed with the clamour of his torment. So terrible did he become in his madness that all the creatures of Morgoth that abode in that valley, or were upon any of the roads that led thither, fled far away; for he slew all living things that stood in his path, and burst from the North with ruin upon the world. Of all the terrors that came ever into Beleriand ere Angband's fall the madness of Carcharoth was the most dreadful; for the power of the Silmaril was hidden within him.

Now Beren lay in a swoon within the perilous Gate, and death drew nigh him, for there was venom on the fangs of the wolf. Lúthien with her lips drew out the venom, and she put forth her failing power to staunch the hideous wound. But behind her in the depths of Angband the rumour grew of great wrath aroused. The hosts of Morgoth were awakened.

Thus the quest of the Silmaril was like to have ended in ruin and despair; but in that hour above the wall of the valley three mighty birds appeared, flying northward with wings swifter than the wind. Among all birds and beasts the wandering and need of Beren had been noised, and Huan himself had bidden all things watch, that they might bring him aid. High above the realm of Morgoth Thorondor and his vassals soared, and seeing now the madness of the Wolf and Beren's fall they came swiftly down, even as the powers of Angband were released from the toils of sleep.

Then they lifted up Lúthien and Beren from the earth, and bore them aloft into the clouds. Below them suddenly thunder rolled, lightnings leaped upward, and the mountains quaked. Fire and smoke belched forth from Thangorodrim, and flaming bolts were hurled far abroad, falling ruinous upon the lands; and the Noldor in Hithlum trembled. But Thorondor took his way far above the earth, seeking the high roads of heaven, where the sun daylong shines unveiled and the moon walks amid the cloudless stars. Thus they passed swiftly over Dor-nu-Fauglith, and over Taur-nu-Fuin, and came above the hidden valley of Tumladen. No cloud nor mist lay there, and looking down Lúthien saw far below, as a white light starting from a green jewel, the radiance of Gondolin the fair where Turgon dwelt. But she wept, for she thought that Beren would surely die; he spoke no word, nor opened his eyes, and knew thereafter nothing of his flight. And at the last the eagles set them down upon the borders of Doriath; and they were come to that same dell whence Beren had stolen in despair and left Lúthien asleep.

There the eagles laid her at Beren's side and returned to the peaks of Crissaegrim and their high eyries; but Huan came to her, and together they tended Beren, even as before when she healed him of the wound that Curufin gave to him. But this wound was fell and poisonous. Long Beren lay, and his spirit wandered upon the dark borders of death, knowing ever an anguish that pursued him from dream to dream. Then suddenly, when her hope was almost spent, he woke again, and looked up, seeing leaves against the sky; and he heard beneath the leaves singing soft and slow beside him Lúthien Tinúviel. And it was spring again.

Thereafter Beren was named Erchamion, which is the One-handed; and suffering was graven in his face. But at last he was drawn back to life by the love of Lúthien, and he arose, and together they walked in the woods once more. And they did not hasten from that place, for it seemed fair to them. Lúthien indeed was willing to wander in the wild without returning, forgetting house and people and all the glory of the Elf-kingdoms, and for a time Beren was content; but he could not for long forget his oath to return to Menegroth, nor would he withhold Lúthien from Thingol for ever. For he held by the law of Men, deeming it perilous to set at naught the will of the father, save at the last need; and it seemed also to him unfit that one so royal and fair as Lúthien should live always in the woods, as the rude hunters among Men, without home or honour or the fair things which are the delight of the queens of the Eldalië. Therefore after a while he persuaded her, and their footsteps forsook the houseless lands; and he passed into Doriath, leading Lúthien home. So their doom willed it.

Upon Doriath evil days had fallen. Grief and silence had come upon all its people when Lúthien was lost. Long they had sought for her in vain. And it is told that in that time Daeron the minstrel of Thingol strayed from the land, and was seen no more. He it was that made music for the dance and song of Lúthien, before Beren came to Doriath; and he had loved her, and set all his thought of her in his music. He became the greatest of all the minstrels of the Elves east of the Sea, named even before Maglor son of Fëanor. But seeking for Lúthien in despair he wandered upon strange paths, and passing over the mountains he came into the East of Middle-earth, where for many ages he made lament beside dark waters for Lúthien, daughter of Thingol, most beautiful of all living things.

In that time Thingol turned to Melian; but now she withheld her counsel from him, saying that the doom that he had devised must work to its appointed end, and that he must wait now upon time. But Thingol learned that Lúthien had journeyed far from Doriath, for messages came secretly from Celegorm, as has been told, saying that

Felagund was dead, and Beren was dead, but Lúthien was in Nargothrond, and that Celegorm would wed her. Then Thingol was wrathful, and he sent forth spies, thinking to make war upon Nargothrond;
and thus he learned that Lúthien was again fled, and that Celegorm
and Curufin were driven from Nargothrond. Then his counsel was
in doubt, for he had not the strength to assail the seven sons of
Fëanor; but he sent messengers to Himring to summon their aid in
seeking for Lúthien, since Celegorm had not sent her to the house of
her father, nor had he kept her safely.

But in the north of his realm his messengers met with a peril
sudden and unlooked for: the onslaught of Carcharoth, the Wolf of
Angband. In his madness he had run ravening from the north, and
passing at length over Taur-nu-Fuin upon its eastern side he came
down from the sources of Esgalduin like a destroying fire. Nothing
hindered him, and the might of Melian upon the borders of the land
stayed him not; for fate drove him, and the power of the Silmaril
that he bore to his torment. Thus he burst into the inviolate woods of
Doriath, and all fled away in fear. Alone of the messengers Mablung,
chief captain of the King, escaped, and he brought the dread tidings
to Thingol.

Even in that dark hour Beren and Lúthien returned, hastening
from the west, and the news of their coming went before them like a
sound of music borne by the wind into dark houses where men sit
sorrowful. They came at last to the gates of Menegroth, and a great
host followed them. Then Beren led Lúthien before the throne of
Thingol her father; and he looked in wonder upon Beren, whom he
had thought dead; but he loved him not, because of the woes that
he had brought upon Doriath. But Beren knelt before him, and said:
'I return according to my word. I am come now to claim my own.'

And Thingol answered: 'What of your quest, and of your vow?'

But Beren said: 'It is fulfilled. Even now a Silmaril is in my hand.'

Then Thingol said: 'Show it to me!'

And Beren put forth his left hand, slowly opening its fingers; but
it was empty. Then he held up his right arm; and from that hour he
named himself Camlost, the Empty-handed.

Then Thingol's mood was softened; and Beren sat before his
throne upon the left, and Lúthien upon the right, and they told all the
tale of the Quest, while all there listened and were filled with amazement. And it seemed to Thingol that this Man was unlike all other
mortal Men, and among the great in Arda, and the love of Lúthien
a thing new and strange; and he perceived that their doom might not
be withstood by any power of the world. Therefore at the last he

yielded his will, and Beren took the hand of Lúthien before the throne of her father.

But now a shadow fell upon the joy of Doriath at the return of Lúthien the fair; for learning of the cause of the madness of Carcharoth the people grew the more afraid, perceiving that his danger was fraught with dreadful power because of the holy jewel, and hardly might be overthrown. And Beren, hearing of the onslaught of the Wolf, understood that the Quest was not yet fulfilled.

Therefore, since daily Carcharoth drew nearer to Menegroth, they prepared the Hunting of the Wolf; of all pursuits of beasts whereof tales tell the most perilous. To that chase went Huan the Hound of Valinor, and Mablung of the Heavy Hand, and Beleg Strongbow, and Beren Erchamion, and Thingol King of Doriath. They rode forth in the morning and passed over the River Esgalduin; but Lúthien remained behind at the gates of Menegroth. A dark shadow fell upon her and it seemed to her that the sun had sickened and turned black.

The hunters turned east and north, and following the course of the river they came at last upon Carcharoth the Wolf in a dark valley, down the northern side whereof Esgalduin fell in a torrent over steep falls. At the foot of the falls Carcharoth drank to ease his consuming thirst, and he howled, and thus they were aware of him. But he, espying their approach, rushed not suddenly to attack them. It may be that the devil's cunning of his heart awoke, being for a moment eased of his pain by the sweet waters of Esgalduin; and even as they rode towards him he slunk aside into a deep brake, and there lay hid. But they set a guard about all that place, and waited, and the shadows grew long in the forest.

Beren stood beside Thingol, and suddenly they were aware that Huan had left their side. Then a great baying awoke in the thicket; for Huan becoming impatient and desiring to look upon this wolf had gone in alone to dislodge him. But Carcharoth avoided him, and bursting from the thorns leaped suddenly upon Thingol. Swiftly Beren strode before him with a spear, but Carcharoth swept it aside and felled him, biting at his breast. In that moment Huan leaped from the thicket upon the back of the Wolf, and they fell together fighting bitterly; and no battle of wolf and hound has been like to it, for in the baying of Huan was heard the voice of the horns of Oromë and the wrath of the Valar, but in the howls of Carcharoth was the hate of Morgoth and malice crueller than teeth of steel; and the rocks were rent by their clamour and fell from on high and choked the falls of Esgalduin. There they fought to the death; but Thingol gave no heed, for he knelt by Beren, seeing that he was sorely hurt.

Huan in that hour slew Carcharoth; but there in the woven woods of Doriath his own doom long spoken was fulfilled, and he was wounded mortally, and the venom of Morgoth entered into him. Then he came, and falling beside Beren spoke for the third time with words; and he bade Beren farewell before he died. Beren spoke not, but laid his hand upon the head of the hound, and so they parted.

Mablung and Beleg came hastening to the King's aid, but when they looked upon what was done they cast aside their spears and wept. Then Mablung took a knife and ripped up the belly of the Wolf; and within he was wellnigh all consumed as with a fire, but the hand of Beren that held the jewel was yet incorrupt. But when Mablung reached forth to touch it, the hand was no more, and the Silmaril lay there unveiled, and the light of it filled the shadows of the forest all about them. Then quickly and in fear Mablung took it and set it in Beren's living hand; and Beren was aroused by the touch of the Silmaril, and held it aloft, and bade Thingol receive it. 'Now is the Quest achieved,' he said, 'and my doom full-wrought'; and he spoke no more.

They bore back Beren Camlost son of Barahir upon a bier of branches with Huan the wolfhound at his side; and night fell ere they returned to Menegroth. At the feet of Hírilorn the great beech Lúthien met them walking slow, and some bore torches beside the bier. There she set her arms about Beren, and kissed him, bidding him await her beyond the Western Sea; and he looked upon her eyes ere the spirit left him. But the starlight was quenched and darkness had fallen even upon Lúthien Tinúviel. Thus ended the Quest of the Silmaril; but the Lay of Leithian, Release from Bondage, does not end.

For the spirit of Beren at her bidding tarried in the halls of Mandos, unwilling to leave the world, until Lúthien came to say her last farewell upon the dim shores of the Outer Sea, whence Men that die set out never to return. But the spirit of Lúthien fell down into darkness, and at the last it fled, and her body lay like a flower that is suddenly cut off and lies for a while unwithered on the grass.

Then a winter, as it were the hoar age of mortal Men, fell upon Thingol. But Lúthien came to the halls of Mandos, where are the appointed places of the Eldalië, beyond the mansions of the West upon the confines of the world. There those that wait sit in the shadow of their thought. But her beauty was more than their beauty, and her sorrow deeper than their sorrows; and she knelt before Mandos and sang to him.

The song of Lúthien before Mandos was the song most fair that ever in words was woven, and the song most sorrowful that ever the world shall hear. Unchanged, imperishable, it is sung still in Valinor beyond the hearing of the world, and listening the Valar are grieved. For Lúthien wove two themes of words, of the sorrow of the Eldar and the grief of Men, of the Two Kindreds that were made by Ilúvatar to dwell in Arda, the Kingdom of Earth amid the innumerable stars. And as she knelt before him her tears fell upon his feet like rain upon the stones; and Mandos was moved to pity, who never before was so moved, nor has been since.

Therefore he summoned Beren, and even as Lúthien had spoken in the hour of his death they met again beyond the Western Sea. But Mandos had no power to withhold the spirits of Men that were dead within the confines of the world, after their time of waiting; nor could he change the fates of the Children of Ilúvatar. He went therefore to Manwë, Lord of the Valar, who governed the world under the hand of Ilúvatar; and Manwë sought counsel in his inmost thought, where the will of Ilúvatar was revealed.

These were the choices that he gave to Lúthien. Because of her labours and her sorrow, she should be released from Mandos, and go to Valimar, there to dwell until the world's end among the Valar, forgetting all griefs that her life had known. Thither Beren could not come. For it was not permitted to the Valar to withhold Death from him, which is the gift of Ilúvatar to Men. But the other choice was this: that she might return to Middle-earth, and take with her Beren, there to dwell again, but without certitude of life or joy. Then she would become mortal, and subject to a second death, even as he; and ere long she would leave the world for ever, and her beauty become only a memory in song.

This doom she chose, forsaking the Blessed Realm, and putting aside all claim to kinship with those that dwell there; that thus whatever grief might lie in wait, the fates of Beren and Lúthien might be joined, and their paths lead together beyond the confines of the world. So it was that alone of the Eldalië she has died indeed, and left the world long ago. Yet in her choice the Two Kindreds have been joined; and she is the forerunner of many in whom the Eldar see yet, though all the world is changed, the likeness of Lúthien the beloved, whom they have lost.

## Chapter 20

# OF THE FIFTH BATTLE: NIRNAETH
# ARNOEDIAD

It is said that Beren and Lúthien returned to the northern lands of Middle-earth, and dwelt together for a time as living man and woman; and they took up again their mortal form in Doriath. Those that saw them were both glad and fearful; and Lúthien went to Menegroth and healed the winter of Thingol with the touch of her hand. But Melian looked in her eyes and read the doom that was written there, and turned away; for she knew that a parting beyond the end of the world had come between them, and no grief of loss has been heavier than the grief of Melian the Maia in that hour. Then Beren and Lúthien went forth alone, fearing neither thirst nor hunger; and they passed beyond the River Gelion into Ossiriand, and dwelt there in Tol Galen the green isle, in the midst of Adurant, until all tidings of them ceased. The Eldar afterwards called that country Dor Firn-i-Guinar, the Land of the Dead that Live; and there was born Dior Aranel the beautiful, who was after known as Dior Eluchíl, which is Thingol's Heir. No mortal man spoke ever again with Beren son of Barahir; and none saw Beren or Lúthien leave the world, or marked where at last their bodies lay.

In those days Maedhros son of Fëanor lifted up his heart, perceiving that Morgoth was not unassailable; for the deeds of Beren and Lúthien were sung in many songs throughout Beleriand. Yet Morgoth would destroy them all, one by one, if they could not again unite, and make new league and common council; and he began those counsels for the raising of the fortunes of the Eldar that are called the Union of Maedhros.

Yet the oath of Fëanor and the evil deeds that it had wrought did injury to the design of Maedhros, and he had less aid than should have been. Orodreth would not march forth at the word of any son of Fëanor, because of the deeds of Celegorm and Curufin; and the Elves of Nargothrond trusted still to defend their hidden stronghold by secrecy and stealth. Thence came only a small company, following Gwindor son of Guilin, a very valiant prince; and against the will of Orodreth he went to the northern war, because he grieved for the loss of Gelmir his brother in the Dagor Bragollach. They took the badge of the house of Fingolfin, and marched beneath the banners of Fingon; and they came never back, save one.

From Doriath came little help. For Maedhros and his brothers, being constrained by their oath, had before sent to Thingol and reminded him with haughty words of their claim, summoning him to yield the Silmaril, or become their enemy. Melian counselled him to surrender it; but the words of the sons of Fëanor were proud and threatening, and Thingol was filled with anger, thinking of the anguish of Lúthien and the blood of Beren whereby the jewel had been won, despite the malice of Celegorm and Curufin. And every day that he looked upon the Silmaril the more he desired to keep it for ever; for such was its power. Therefore he sent back the messengers with scornful words. Maedhros made no answer, for he had now begun to devise the league and union of the Elves; but Celegorm and Curufin vowed openly to slay Thingol and destroy his people, if they came victorious from war, and the jewel were not surrendered of free will. Then Thingol fortified the marches of his realm, and went not to war, nor any out of Doriath save Mablung and Beleg, who were unwilling to have no part in these great deeds. To them Thingol gave leave to go, so long as they served not the sons of Fëanor; and they joined themselves to the host of Fingon.

But Maedhros had the help of the Naugrim, both in armed force and in great store of weapons; and the smithies of Nogrod and Belegost were busy in those days. And he gathered together again all his brothers and all the people who would follow them; and the Men of Bór and Ulfang were marshalled and trained for war, and they summoned yet more of their kinsfolk out of the East. Moreover in the west Fingon, ever the friend of Maedhros, took counsel with Himring, and in Hithlum the Noldor and the Men of the house of Hador prepared for war. In the forest of Brethil Halmir, lord of the People of Haleth, gathered his men, and they whetted their axes; but Halmir died ere the war came, and Haldir his son ruled that people. And to Gondolin also the tidings came, to Turgon, the hidden king.

But Maedhros made trial of his strength too soon, ere his plans were full-wrought; and though the Orcs were driven out of all the northward regions of Beleriand, and even Dorthonion was freed for a while, Morgoth was warned of the uprising of the Eldar and the Elf-friends, and took counsel against them. Many spies and workers of treason he sent forth among them, as he was the better able now to do, for the faithless Men of his secret allegiance were yet deep in the secrets of the sons of Fëanor.

At length Maedhros, having gathered all the strength that he could of Elves and Men and Dwarves, resolved to assault Angband from east and west; and he purposed to march with banners displayed in open force over Anfauglith. But when he had drawn forth, as he hoped, the armies of Morgoth in answer, then Fingon should issue forth from the passes of Hithlum; and thus they thought to take the might of Morgoth as between anvil and hammer, and break it to pieces. And the signal for this was to be the firing of a great beacon in Dorthonion.

On the appointed day, on the morning of Midsummer, the trumpets of the Eldar greeted the rising of the sun; and in the east was raised the standard of the sons of Fëanor, and in the west the standard of Fingon, High King of the Noldor. Then Fingon looked out from the walls of Eithel Sirion, and his host was arrayed in the valleys and the woods upon the east of Ered Wethrin, well hid from the eyes of the Enemy; but he knew that it was very great. For there all the Noldor of Hithlum were asssembled, together with Elves of the Falas and Gwindor's company from Nargothrond, and he had great strength of Men: upon the right were the host of Dor-lómin and all the valour of Húrin and Huor his brother, and to them had come Haldir of Brethil with many men of the woods.

Then Fingon looked towards Thangorodrim, and there was a dark cloud about it, and a black smoke went up; and he knew that the wrath of Morgoth was aroused, and that their challenge was accepted. A shadow of doubt fell upon Fingon's heart; and he looked eastwards, seeking if he might see with elven-sight the dust of Anfauglith rising beneath the hosts of Maedhros. He knew not that Maedhros was hindered in his setting-forth by the guile of Uldor the accursed, who deceived him with false warnings of assault from Angband.

But now a cry went up, passing up the wind from the south from vale to vale, and Elves and Men lifted their voices in wonder and joy. For unsummoned and unlooked for Turgon had opened the leaguer of Gondolin, and was come with an army ten thousand strong, with bright mail and long swords and spears like a forest. Then when Fingon heard afar the great trumpet of Turgon his brother, the shadow passed and his heart was uplifted, and he shouted aloud: '*Utúlie'n aurë! Aiya Eldalië ar Atanatári, utúlie'n aurë!* The day has come! Behold, people of the Eldar and Fathers of Men, the day has come!' And all those who heard his great voice echo in the hills answered crying: '*Auta i lómë!* The night is passing!'

Now Morgoth, who knew much of what was done and designed by his enemies, chose his hour, and trusting in his treacherous servants to hold back Maedhros and prevent the union of his foes he sent a force seeming great (and yet but part of all that he had made ready) towards Hithlum; and they were clad all in dun raiment and showed no naked steel, and thus were already far over the sands of Anfauglith before their approach was seen.

Then the hearts of the Noldor grew hot, and their captains wished to assail their foes upon the plain; but Húrin spoke against it, and bade them beware of the guile of Morgoth, whose strength was always greater than it seemed, and his purpose other than he revealed. And though the signal of the approach of Maedhros came not, and the host grew impatient, Húrin urged them still to await it, and to let the Orcs break themselves in assault upon the hills.

But the Captain of Morgoth in the west had been commanded to draw out Fingon swiftly from his hills by whatever means he could. He marched on therefore until the front of his battle was drawn up before the stream of Sirion, from the walls of the fortress of Eithel Sirion to the inflowing of Rivil at the Fen of Serech; and the outposts of Fingon could see the eyes of their enemies. But there was no answer to his challenge, and the taunts of the Orcs faltered as they looked upon the silent walls and the hidden threat of the hills. Then the Captain of Morgoth sent out riders with tokens of parley, and they rode up before the outworks of the Barad Eithel. With them they brought Gelmir son of Guilin, that lord of Nargothrond whom they had captured in the Bragollach; and they had blinded him. Then the heralds of Angband showed him forth, crying: 'We have many more such at home, but you must make haste if you would find them; for we shall deal with them all when we return even so.' And they hewed off Gelmir's hands and feet, and his head last, within sight of the Elves, and left him.

By ill chance, at that place in the outworks stood Gwindor of Nargothrond, the brother of Gelmir. Now his wrath was kindled to madness, and he leapt forth on horseback, and many riders with him; and they pursued the heralds and slew them, and drove on deep into the main host. And seeing this all the host of the Noldor was set on fire, and Fingon put on his white helm and sounded his trumpets, and all the host of Hithlum leapt forth from the hills in sudden onslaught. The light of the drawing of the swords of the Noldor was like a fire in a field of reeds; and so fell and swift was their onset that almost the designs of Morgoth went astray. Before the army that he sent westward could be strengthened it was swept away, and the banners of Fingon passed over Anfauglith and were raised before the walls of Angband. Ever in the forefront of that battle went

Gwindor and the Elves of Nargothrond, and even now they could not be restrained; and they burst through the Gate and slew the guards upon the very stairs of Angband, and Morgoth trembled upon his deep throne, hearing them beat upon his doors. But they were trapped there, and all were slain save Gwindor only, whom they took alive; for Fingon could not come to their aid. By many secret doors in Thangorodrim Morgoth had let issue forth his main host that he held in waiting, and Fingon was beaten back with great loss from the walls.

Then in the plain of Anfauglith, on the fourth day of the war, there began Nirnaeth Arnoediad, Unnumbered Tears, for no song or tale can contain all its grief. The host of Fingon retreated over the sands, and Haldir lord of the Haladin was slain in the rearguard; with him fell most of the Men of Brethil, and came never back to their woods. But on the fifth day as night fell, and they were still far from Ered Wethrin, the Orcs surrounded the host of Hithlum, and they fought until day, pressed ever closer. In the morning came hope, when the horns of Turgon were heard as he marched up with the main host of Gondolin; for they had been stationed southward guarding the Pass of Sirion, and Turgon restrained most of his people from the rash onslaught. Now he hastened to the aid of his brother; and the Gondolindrim were strong and clad in mail, and their ranks shone like a river of steel in the sun.

Now the phalanx of the guard of the King broke through the ranks of the Orcs, and Turgon hewed his way to the side of his brother; and it is told that the meeting of Turgon with Húrin, who stood beside Fingon, was glad in the midst of battle. Then hope was renewed in the hearts of the Elves; and in that very time, at the third hour of morning, the trumpets of Maedhros were heard at last coming up from the east, and the banners of the sons of Fëanor assailed the enemy in the rear. Some have said that even then the Eldar might have won the day, had all their hosts proved faithful; for the Orcs wavered, and their onslaught was stayed, and already some were turning to flight. But even as the vanguard of Maedhros came upon the Orcs, Morgoth loosed his last strength, and Angband was emptied. There came wolves, and wolfriders, and there came Balrogs, and dragons, and Glaurung father of dragons. The strength and terror of the Great Worm were now great indeed, and Elves and Men withered before him; and he came between the hosts of Maedhros and Fingon and swept them apart.

Yet neither by wolf, nor by Balrog, nor by Dragon, would Morgoth have achieved his end, but for the treachery of Men. In this hour the plots of Ulfang were revealed. Many of the Easterlings turned and fled, their hearts being filled with lies and fear; but the sons of Ulfang went over suddenly to Morgoth and drove in upon the rear of the sons of Fëanor, and in the confusion that they wrought they came near to the standard of Maedhros. They reaped not the reward that Morgoth promised them, for Maglor slew Uldor the accursed, the leader in treason, and the sons of Bór slew Ulfast and Ulwarth ere they themselves were slain. But new strength of evil Men came up that Uldor had summoned and kept hidden in the eastern hills, and the host of Maedhros was assailed now on three sides, and it broke, and was scattered, and fled this way and that. Yet fate saved the sons of Fëanor, and though all were wounded none were slain, for they drew together, and gathering a remnant of the Noldor and the Naugrim about them they hewed a way out of the battle and escaped far away towards Mount Dolmed in the east.

Last of all the eastern force to stand firm were the Dwarves of Belegost, and thus they won renown. For the Naugrim withstood fire more hardily than either Elves or Men, and it was their custom moreover to wear great masks in battle hideous to look upon; and those stood them in good stead against the dragons. And but for them Glaurung and his brood would have withered all that was left of the Noldor. But the Naugrim made a circle about him when he assailed them, and even his mighty armour was not full proof against the blows of their great axes; and when in his rage Glaurung turned and struck down Azaghâl, Lord of Belegost, and crawled over him, with his last stroke Azaghâl drove a knife into his belly, and so wounded him that he fled the field, and the beasts of Angband in dismay followed after him. Then the Dwarves raised up the body of Azaghâl and bore it away; and with slow steps they walked behind singing a dirge in deep voices, as it were a funeral pomp in their country, and gave no heed more to their foes; and none dared to stay them.

But now in the western battle Fingon and Turgon were assailed by a tide of foes thrice greater than all the force that was left to them. Gothmog, Lord of Balrogs, high-captain of Angband, was come; and he drove a dark wedge between the Elvenhosts, surrounding King Fingon, and thrusting Turgon and Húrin aside towards the Fen of Serech. Then he turned upon Fingon. That was a grim meeting. At last Fingon stood alone with his guard dead about him; and he fought with Gothmog, until another Balrog came behind and cast a thong of fire about him. Then Gothmog hewed him with his black axe, and a white flame sprang up from the helm of Fingon as it was cloven. Thus fell the High King of the Noldor; and they beat him into the dust with their maces, and his banner, blue and silver, they trod into the mire of his blood.

The field was lost; but still Húrin and Huor and the remnant of the house of Hador stood firm with Turgon of Gondolin, and the hosts of Morgoth could not yet win the Pass of Sirion. Then Húrin spoke to Turgon, saying: 'Go now, lord, while time is! For in you lives the last hope of the Eldar, and while Gondolin stands Morgoth shall still know fear in his heart.'

But Turgon answered: 'Not long now can Gondolin be hidden; and being discovered it must fall.'

Then Huor spoke and said: 'Yet if it stands but a little while, then out of your house shall come the hope of Elves and Men. This I say to you, lord, with the eyes of death: though we part here for ever, and I shall not look on your white walls again, from you and from me a new star shall arise. Farewell!'

And Maeglin, Turgon's sister-son, who stood by, heard these words, and did not forget them; but he said nothing.

Then Turgon took the counsel of Húrin and Huor, and summoning all that remained of the host of Gondolin and such of Fingon's people as could be gathered he retreated towards the Pass of Sirion; and his captains Ecthelion and Glorfindel guarded the flanks to right and left, so that none of the enemy should pass them by. But the Men of Dor-lómin held the rearguard, as Húrin and Huor desired; for they did not wish in their hearts to leave the Northlands, and if they could not win back to their homes, there they would stand to the end. Thus was the treachery of Uldor redressed; and of all the deeds of war that the fathers of Men wrought in behalf of the Eldar, the last stand of the Men of Dor-lómin is most renowned.

So it was that Turgon fought his way southward, until coming behind the guard of Húrin and Huor he passed down Sirion and escaped; and he vanished into the mountains and was hidden from the eyes of Morgoth. But the brothers drew the remnant of the Men of the house of Hador about them, and foot by foot they withdrew, until they came behind the Fen of Serech, and had the stream of Rivil before them. There they stood and gave way no more.

Then all the hosts of Angband swarmed against them, and they bridged the stream with their dead, and encircled the remnant of Hithlum as a gathering tide about a rock. There as the sun westered on the sixth day, and the shadow of Ered Wethrin grew dark, Huor fell pierced with a venomed arrow in his eye, and all the valiant Men of Hador were slain about him in a heap; and the Orcs hewed their heads and piled them as a mound of gold in the sunset.

Last of all Húrin stood alone. Then he cast aside his shield, and wielded an axe two-handed; and it is sung that the axe smoked in the black blood of the troll-guard of Gothmog until it withered, and each time that he slew Húrin cried: '*Aurë entuluva!* Day shall come again!' Seventy times he uttered that cry; but they took him at last alive, by the command of Morgoth, for the Orcs grappled him with their hands, which clung to him still though he hewed off their arms; and ever their numbers were renewed, until at last he fell buried beneath them. Then Gothmog bound him and dragged him to Angband with mockery.

Thus ended Nirnaeth Arnoediad, as the sun went down beyond the sea. Night fell in Hithlum, and there came a great storm of wind out of the West.

Great was the triumph of Morgoth, and his design was accomplished in a manner after his own heart; for Men took the lives of Men, and betrayed the Eldar, and fear and hatred were aroused among those that should have been united against him. From that day the hearts of the Elves were estranged from Men, save only those of the Three Houses of the Edain.

The realm of Fingon was no more; and the sons of Fëanor wandered as leaves before the wind. Their arms were scattered, and their league broken; and they took to a wild and woodland life beneath the feet of Ered Lindon, mingling with the Green-elves of Ossiriand, bereft of their power and glory of old. In Brethil some few of the Haladin yet dwelt in the protection of their woods, and Handir son of Haldir was their lord; but to Hithlum came back never one of Fingon's host, nor any of the Men of Hador's house, nor any tidings of the battle and the fate of their lords. But Morgoth sent thither the Easterlings that had served him, denying them the rich lands of Beleriand which they coveted; and he shut them in Hithlum and forbade them to leave it. Such was the reward he gave them for their treachery to Maedhros: to plunder and harass the old and the women and the children of Hador's people. The remnant of the Eldar of Hithlum were taken to the mines of the north and laboured there as thralls, save some that eluded him and escaped into the wilds and the mountains.

The Orcs and the wolves went freely through all the North, and came ever further southward into Beleriand, even as far as Nantathren, the Land of Willows, and the borders of Ossiriand, and none were safe in field or wild. Doriath indeed remained, and the halls of Nargothrond were hidden; but Morgoth gave small heed to them, either because he knew little of them, or because their hour was not yet come in the deep purposes of his malice. Many now fled to the Havens and took refuge behind Círdan's walls, and the mariners passed up and down the coast and harried the enemy with swift landings. But in the next year, ere the winter was come, Morgoth sent great strength over Hithlum and Nevrast, and they came down the rivers Brithon and Nenning and ravaged all the Falas, and besieged the walls of Brithombar and Eglarest. Smiths and miners and makers of fire they brought with them, and they set up great engines; and valiantly though they were resisted they broke the walls at last. Then the Havens were laid in ruin, and the tower of Barad Nimras cast down; and the most part of Círdan's people were slain or enslaved. But some went aboard ship and escaped by sea; and among them was Ereinion Gil-galad, the son of Fingon, whom his father had sent to the Havens after the Dagor Bragollach. This remnant sailed with Círdan south to the Isle of Balar, and they made a refuge for all that could come thither; for they kept a foothold also at the Mouths of Sirion, and there many light and swift ships lay hid in the creeks and waters where the reeds were dense as a forest.

And when Turgon heard of this he sent again his messengers to Sirion's mouths, and besought the aid of Círdan the Shipwright. At the bidding of Turgon Círdan built seven swift ships, and they sailed out into the West; but no tidings of them came ever back to Balar, save of one, and the last. The mariners of that ship toiled long in the sea, and returning at last in despair they foundered in a great storm within sight of the coasts of Middle-earth; but one of them was saved by Ulmo from the wrath of Ossë, and the waves bore him up, and cast him ashore in Nevrast. His name was Voronwë; and he was one of those that Turgon sent forth as messengers from Gondolin.

Now the thought of Morgoth dwelt ever upon Turgon; for Turgon had escaped him, of all his foes that one whom he most desired to take or to destroy. And that thought troubled him, and marred his victory, for Turgon of the mighty house of Fingolfin was now by right King of all the Noldor; and Morgoth feared and hated the house of Fingolfin, because they had the friendship of Ulmo his foe, and because of the wounds that Fingolfin gave him with his sword. And most of all his kin Morgoth feared Turgon; for of old in Valinor his eye had lighted upon him, and whenever he drew near a shadow had fallen on his spirit, foreboding that in some time that yet lay hidden, from Turgon ruin should come to him.

Therefore Húrin was brought before Morgoth, for Morgoth knew that he had the friendship of the King of Gondolin; but Húrin defied him, and mocked him. Then Morgoth cursed Húrin and Morwen and their offspring, and set a doom upon them of darkness and sorrow; and taking Húrin from prison he set him in a chair of stone upon a high place of Thangorodrim. There he was bound by the power of Morgoth, and Morgoth standing beside him cursed him again; and he said: 'Sit now there; and look out upon the lands where evil and despair shall come upon those whom thou lovest. Thou hast dared to mock me, and to question the power of Melkor, Master of the fates of Arda. Therefore with my eyes thou shalt see, and with my ears thou shalt hear; and never shalt thou move from this place until all is fulfilled unto its bitter end.'

And even so it came to pass; but it is not said that Húrin asked ever of Morgoth either mercy or death, for himself or for any of his kin.

By the command of Morgoth the Orcs with great labour gathered all the bodies of those who had fallen in the great battle, and all their harness and weapons, and piled them in a great mound in the midst of Anfauglith; and it was like a hill that could be seen from afar. Haudh-en-Ndengin the Elves named it, the Hill of Slain, and Haudh-en-Nirnaeth, the Hill of Tears. But grass came there and grew again long and green upon that hill, alone in all the desert that Morgoth made; and no creature of Morgoth trod thereafter upon the earth beneath which the swords of the Eldar and the Edain crumbled into rust.

# Chapter 21

# OF TÚRIN TURAMBAR

Rían, daughter of Belegund, was the wife of Huor, son of Galdor; and she was wedded to him two months before he went with Húrin his brother to the Nirnaeth Arnoediad. When no tidings came of her lord she fled into the wild; but she was aided by the Grey-elves of Mithrim, and when her son Tuor was born they fostered him. Then Rían departed from Hithlum, and going to the Haudh-en-Ndengin she laid herself down upon it and died.

Morwen, daughter of Baragund, was the wife of Húrin, Lord of Dor-lómin; and their son was Túrin, who was born in the year that Beren Erchamion came upon Lúthien in the Forest of Neldoreth. A daughter they had also who was called Lalaith, which is Laughter, and she was beloved by Túrin her brother; but when she was three years old there came a pestilence to Hithlum, borne on an evil wind out of Angband, and she died.

Now after the Nirnaeth Arnoediad Morwen abode still in Dor-lómin, for Túrin was but eight years old, and she was again with child. Those days were evil; for the Easterlings that came into Hithlum despised the remnant of the people of Hador, and they oppressed them, and took their lands and their goods, and enslaved their children. But so great was the beauty and majesty of the Lady of Dor-lómin that the Easterlings were afraid, and dared not to lay hands upon her or her household; and they whispered among themselves, saying that she was perilous, and a witch skilled in magic and in league with the Elves. Yet she was now poor and without aid, save that she was succoured secretly by a kinswoman of Húrin named Aerin, whom Brodda, an Easterling, had taken as his wife; and Morwen feared greatly that Túrin would be taken from her and enslaved. Therefore it came into her heart to send him away in secret, and to beg King Thingol to harbour him, for Beren son of Barahir was her father's kinsman, and he had been moreover a friend of Húrin, ere evil befell. Therefore in the autumn of the Year of Lamentation Morwen sent Túrin forth over the mountains with two aged servants, bidding them find entry, if they could, into the kingdom of Doriath. Thus was the fate of Túrin woven, which is fulltold in that lay that is called *Narn i Hîn Húrin*, the Tale of the Children of Húrin, and is the longest of all the lays that speak of those days. Here that tale is told in brief, for it is woven with the fate of the Silmarils and of the Elves; and it is called the Tale of Grief, for it is sorrowful, and in it are revealed most evil works of Morgoth Bauglir.

In the first beginning of the year Morwen gave birth to her child, the daughter of Húrin; and she named her Nienor, which is Mourning. But Túrin and his companions passing through great perils came at last to the borders of Doriath; and there they were found by Beleg Strongbow, chief of the marchwardens of King Thingol, who led them to Menegroth. Then Thingol received Túrin, and took him even to his own fostering, in honour of Húrin the Steadfast; for Thingol's mood was changed towards the houses of the Elf-friends. Thereafter messengers went north to Hithlum, bidding Morwen leave Dor-lómin and return with them to Doriath; but still she would not leave the house in which she had dwelt with Húrin. And when the Elves departed she sent with them the Dragon-helm of Dor-lómin, greatest of the heirlooms of the house of Hador.

Túrin grew fair and strong in Doriath, but he was marked with sorrow. For nine years he dwelt in Thingol's halls, and during that time his grief grew less; for messengers went at times to Hithlum, and returning they brought better tidings of Morwen and Nienor. But there came a day when the messengers did not return out of the north, and Thingol would send no more. Then Túrin was filled with fear for his mother and his sister, and in grimness of heart he went before the King and asked for mail and sword; and he put on the Dragon-helm of Dor-lómin and went out to battle on the marches of Doriath, and became the companion in arms of Beleg Cúthalion.

And when three years had passed, Túrin returned again to Menegroth; but he came from the wild, and was unkempt, and his gear and garments were wayworn. Now one there was in Doriath, of the people of the Nandor, high in the counsels of the King; Saeros was his name. He had long begrudged to Túrin the honour he received as Thingol's fosterson; and seated opposite to him at the board he taunted him, saying: 'If the Men of Hithlum are so wild and fell, of what sort are the women of that land? Do they run like deer clad only in their hair?' Then Túrin in great anger took up a drinking-vessel, and cast it at Saeros; and he was grievously hurt.

On the next day Saeros waylaid Túrin as he set out from Menegroth to return to the marches; but Túrin overcame him, and set him to run naked as a hunted beast through the woods. Then Saeros fleeing in terror before him fell into the chasm of a stream, and his body was broken on a great rock in the water. But others coming saw what was done, and Mablung was among them; and he bade Túrin return with him to Menegroth and abide the judgement of the King, seeking his pardon. But Túrin, deeming himself now an outlaw and fearing to be held captive, refused Mablung's bidding, and turned swiftly away; and passing through the Girdle of Melian he came into the woods west of Sirion. There he joined himself to a band of such houseless and desperate men as could be found in those evil days lurking in the wild; and their hands were turned against all who came in their path, Elves and Men and Orcs.

But when all that had befallen was told and searched out before Thingol, the King pardoned Túrin, holding him wronged. In that time Beleg Strongbow returned from the north marches and came to Menegroth, seeking him; and Thingol spoke to Beleg, saying: 'I grieve, Cúthalion; for I took Húrin's son as my son, and so he shall remain, unless Húrin himself should return out of the shadows to claim his own. I would not have any say that Túrin was driven forth unjustly into the wild, and gladly would I welcome him back; for I loved him well.'

And Beleg answered: 'I will seek Túrin until I find him, and I will bring him back to Menegroth, if I can; for I love him also.'

Then Beleg departed from Menegroth, and far across Beleriand he sought in vain for tidings of Túrin through many perils.

But Túrin abode long among the outlaws, and became their captain; and he named himself Neithan, the Wronged. Very warily they dwelt in the wooded lands south of Teiglin; but when a year had passed since Túrin fled from Doriath, Beleg came upon their lair by night. It chanced that at that time Túrin was gone from the camp; and the outlaws seized Beleg and bound him, and treated him cruelly, for they feared him as a spy of the King of Doriath. But Túrin returning and seeing what was done, was stricken with remorse for all their evil and lawless deeds; and he released Beleg, and they renewed their friendship, and Túrin foreswore thenceforward war or plunder against all save the servants of Angband.

Then Beleg told Túrin of King Thingol's pardon; and he sought to persuade him by all means that he might to return with him to Doriath, saying that there was great need of his strength and valour on the north marches of the realm. 'Of late the Orcs have found a way down out of Taur-nu-Fuin,' he said; 'they have made a road through the Pass of Anach.'

'I do not remember it,' said Túrin.

'Never did we go so far from the borders,' said Beleg. 'But you have seen the peaks of the Crissaegrim far off, and to the east the dark walls of the Gorgoroth. Anach lies between, above the high springs of Mindeb, a hard and dangerous road; yet many come by it now, and Dimbar which used to be in peace is falling under the Black Hand, and the Men of Brethil are troubled. We are needed there.'

But in the pride of his heart Túrin refused the pardon of the King, and the words of Beleg were of no avail to change his mood. And he for his part urged Beleg to remain with him in the lands west of Sirion; but that Beleg would not do, and he said: 'Hard you are, Túrin, and stubborn. Now the turn is mine. If you wish indeed to have the Strongbow beside you, look for me in Dimbar; for thither I shall return.'

On the next day Beleg set out, and Túrin went with him a bowshot from the camp; but he said nothing. 'Is it farewell, then, son of Húrin?' said Beleg. Then Túrin looked out westward, and he saw far off the great height of Amon Rûdh; and unwitting of what lay before him he answered: 'You have said, seek me in Dimbar. But I say, seek for me on Amon Rûdh! Else, this is our last farewell.' Then they parted, in friendship, yet in sadness.

Now Beleg returned to the Thousand Caves, and coming before Thingol and Melian he told them of all that had befallen, save only of his evil handling by Túrin's companions. Then Thingol sighed, and he said: 'What more would Túrin have me do?'

'Give me leave, lord,' said Beleg, 'and I will guard him and guide him as I may; then no man shall say that elven-words are lightly spoken. Nor would I wish to see so great a good run to nothing in the wild.'

Then Thingol gave Beleg leave to do as he would; and he said: 'Beleg Cúthalion! For many deeds you have earned my thanks; but not the least is the finding of my fosterson. At this parting ask for any gift, and I will not deny it to you.'

'I ask then for a sword of worth,' said Beleg; 'for the Orcs come now too thick and close for a bow only, and such blade as I have is no match for their armour.'

'Choose from all that I have,' said Thingol, 'save only Aranrúth, my own.'

Then Beleg chose Anglachel; and that was a sword of great worth, and it was so named because it was made of iron that fell from heaven as a blazing star; it would cleave all earth-delved iron. One other sword only in Middle-earth was like to it. That sword does not enter into this tale, though it was made of the same ore by the same smith; and that smith was Eöl the Dark Elf, who took Aredhel Turgon's sister to wife. He gave Anglachel to Thingol as fee, which he begrudged, for leave to dwell in Nan Elmoth; but its mate Anguirel he kept, until it was stolen from him by Maeglin, his son.

But as Thingol turned the hilt of Anglachel towards Beleg, Melian looked at the blade; and she said: 'There is malice in this sword. The dark heart of the smith still dwells in it. It will not love the hand it serves; neither will it abide with you long.'

'Nonetheless I will wield it while I may,' said Beleg.

'Another gift I will give to you, Cúthalion,' said Melian, 'that shall be your help in the wild, and the help also of those whom you choose.' And she gave him store of *lembas*, the waybread of the Elves, wrapped in leaves of silver, and the threads that bound it were sealed at the knots with the seal of the Queen, a wafer of white wax shaped as a single flower of Telperion; for according to the customs of the Eldalië the keeping and giving of *lembas* belonged to the Queen alone. In nothing did Melian show greater favour to Túrin than in this gift; for the Eldar had never before allowed Men to use this waybread, and seldom did so again.

Then Beleg departed with these gifts from Menegroth and went back to the north marches, where he had his lodges, and many friends. Then in Dimbar the Orcs were driven back, and Anglachel rejoiced to be unsheathed; but when the winter came, and war was stilled, suddenly his companions missed Beleg, and he returned to them no more.

Now when Beleg parted from the outlaws and returned into Doriath, Túrin led them away westward out of Sirion's vale; for they grew weary of their life without rest, ever watchful and in fear of pursuit, and they sought for a safer lair. And it chanced at a time of evening that they came upon three Dwarves, who fled before them; but one that lagged behind was seized and thrown down, and a man of the company took his bow and let fly an arrow at the others as they vanished in the dusk. Now the dwarf that they had taken was named Mîm; and he pleaded for his life before Túrin, and offered as ransom to lead them to his hidden halls which none might find without his aid. Then Túrin pitied Mîm, and spared him; and he said: 'Where is your house?'

Then Mîm answered: 'High above the lands lies the house of Mîm, upon the great hill; Amon Rûdh is that hill called now, since the Elves changed all the names.'

Then Túrin was silent, and he looked long upon the dwarf; and at last he said: 'You shall bring us to that place.'

On the next day they set out thither, following Mîm to Amon

Rûdh. Now that hill stood upon the edge of the moorlands that rose between the vales of Sirion and Narog, and high above the stony heath it reared its crown; but its steep grey head was bare, save for the red *seregon* that mantled the stone. And as the men of Túrin's band drew near, the sun westering broke through the clouds, and fell upon the crown; and the *seregon* was all in flower. Then one among them said: 'There is blood on the hill-top.'

But Mîm led them by secret paths up the steep slopes of Amon Rûdh; and at the mouth of his cave he bowed to Túrin, saying: 'Enter into Bar-en-Danwedh, the House of Ransom; for so it shall be called.'

And now there came another dwarf bearing light to greet him, and they spoke together, and passed swiftly down into the darkness of the cave; but Túrin followed after, and came at length to a chamber far within, lit by dim lamps hanging upon chains. There he found Mîm kneeling at a stone couch beside the wall, and he tore his beard, and wailed, crying one name unceasingly; and on the couch there lay a third. But Túrin entering stood beside Mîm, and offered him aid. Then Mîm looked up at him, and said: 'You can give no aid. For this is Khîm, my son; and he is dead, pierced by an arrow. He died at sunset. Ibun my son has told me.'

Then pity rose in Túrin's heart, and he said to Mîm: 'Alas! I would recall that shaft, if I could. Now Bar-en-Danwedh this house shall be called in truth; and if ever I come to any wealth, I will pay you a ransom of gold for your son, in token of sorrow, though it gladden your heart no more.'

Then Mîm rose, and looked long at Túrin. 'I hear you,' he said. 'You speak like a dwarf-lord of old; and at that I marvel. Now my heart is cooled, though it is not glad; and in this house you may dwell, if you will; for I will pay my ransom.'

So began the abiding of Túrin in the hidden house of Mîm upon Amon Rûdh; and he walked on the greensward before the mouth of the cave, and looked out east, and west, and north. Northward he looked, and descried the Forest of Brethil climbing green about Amon Obel in its midst, and thither his eyes were drawn ever and again, he knew not why; for his heart was set rather to the north-west, where league upon league away on the skirts of the sky it seemed to him that he could glimpse the Mountains of Shadow, the walls of his home. But at evening Túrin looked west into the sunset, as the sun rode down red into the hazes above the distant coasts, and the Vale of Narog lay deep in the shadows between.

In the time that followed Túrin spoke much with Mîm, and sitting

with him alone he listened to his lore and the tale of his life. For
Mîm came of Dwarves that were banished in ancient days from the
great Dwarf-cities of the east, and long before the return of Morgoth
they wandered westward into Beleriand; but they became diminished
in stature and in smith-craft, and they took to lives of stealth, walking
with bowed shoulders and furtive steps. Before the Dwarves of
Nogrod and Belegost came west over the mountains the Elves of
Beleriand knew not what these others were, and they hunted them,
and slew them; but afterwards they let them alone, and they were
called Noegyth Nibin, the Petty-Dwarves, in the Sindarin tongue.
They loved none but themselves, and if they feared and hated the
Orcs, they hated the Eldar no less, and the Exiles most of all; for
the Noldor, they said, had stolen their lands and their homes. Long
ere King Finrod Felagund came over the Sea, the caves of Nargothrond were discovered by them, and by them its delving was begun;
and beneath the crown of Amon Rûdh, the Bald Hill, the slow hands
of the Petty-Dwarves had bored and deepened the caves through the
long years that they dwelt there, untroubled by the Grey-elves of
the woods. But now at last they had dwindled and died out of Middle-
earth, all save Mîm and his two sons; and Mîm was old even in the
reckoning of Dwarves, old and forgotten. And in his halls the smithies
were idle, and the axes rusted, and their name was remembered only
in ancient tales of Doriath and Nargothrond.

But when the year drew on to midwinter, snow came down from
the north heavier than they had known it in the river-vales, and Amon
Rûdh was covered deep; and they said that the winters worsened in
Beleriand as the power of Angband grew. Then only the hardiest
dared stir abroad; and some fell sick, and all were pinched with
hunger. But in the dim dusk of a winter's day there appeared suddenly among them a man, as it seemed, of great bulk and girth,
cloaked and hooded in white; and he walked up to the fire without a
word. And when men sprang up in fear, he laughed, and threw back
his hood, and beneath his wide cloak he bore a great pack; and in the
light of the fire Túrin looked again on the face of Beleg Cúthalion.

Thus Beleg returned once more to Túrin, and their meeting was
glad; and with him he brought out of Dimbar the Dragon-helm of
Dor-lómin, thinking that it might lift Túrin's thought again above his
life in the wilderness as the leader of a petty company. But still
Túrin would not return to Doriath; and Beleg yielding to his love
against his wisdom remained with him, and did not depart, and in
that time he laboured much for the good of Túrin's company. Those
that were hurt or sick he tended, and gave to them the *lembas* of

Melian; and they were quickly healed, for though the Grey-elves were less in skill and knowledge than the Exiles from Valinor, in the ways of the life of Middle-earth they had a wisdom beyond the reach of Men. And because Beleg was strong and enduring, farsighted in mind as in eye, he came to be held in honour among the outlaws; but the hatred of Mîm for the Elf that had come into Bar-en-Danwedh grew ever greater, and he sat with Ibun his son in the deepest shadows of his house, speaking to none. But Túrin paid now little heed to the Dwarf; and when winter passed, and spring came, they had sterner work to do.

Who knows now the counsels of Morgoth? Who can measure the reach of his thought, who had been Melkor, mighty among the Ainur of the Great Song, and sat now, a dark lord upon a dark throne in the North, weighing in his malice all the tidings that came to him, and perceiving more of the deeds and purposes of his enemies than even the wisest of them feared, save only Melian the Queen? To her often the thought of Morgoth reached out, and there was foiled.

And now again the might of Angband was moved; and as the long fingers of a groping hand the forerunners of his armies probed the ways into Beleriand. Through Anach they came, and Dimbar was taken, and all the north marches of Doriath. Down the ancient road they came that led through the long defile of Sirion, past the isle where Minas Tirith of Finrod had stood, and so through the land between Malduin and Sirion, and on through the eaves of Brethil to the Crossings of Teiglin. Thence the road went on into the Guarded Plain; but the Orcs did not go far upon it, as yet, for there dwelt now in the wild a terror that was hidden, and upon the red hill were watchful eyes of which they had not been warned. For Túrin put on again the Helm of Hador; and far and wide in Beleriand the whisper went, under wood and over stream and through the passes of the hills, saying that the Helm and Bow that had fallen in Dimbar had arisen again beyond hope. Then many who went leaderless, dispossessed but undaunted, took heart again, and came to seek the Two Captains. Dor-Cúarthol, the Land of Bow and Helm, was in that time named all the region between Teiglin and the west march of Doriath; and Túrin named himself anew, Gorthol, the Dread Helm, and his heart was high again. In Menegroth, and in the deep halls of Nargothrond, and even in the hidden realm of Gondolin, the fame of the deeds of the Two Captains was heard; and in Angband also they were known. Then Morgoth laughed, for now by the Dragon-helm was Húrin's son revealed to him again; and ere long Amon Rûdh was ringed with spies.

In the waning of the year Mîm the Dwarf and Ibun his son went out from Bar-en-Danwedh to gather roots in the wild for their winter store; and they were taken captive by Orcs. Then for a second time Mîm promised to guide his enemies by the secret paths to his home on Amon Rûdh; but yet he sought to delay the fulfilment of his promise, and demanded that Gorthol should not be slain. Then the Orc-captain laughed, and he said to Mîm: 'Assuredly Túrin son of Húrin shall not be slain.'

Thus was Bar-en-Danwedh betrayed, for the Orcs came upon it by night at unawares, guided by Mîm. There many of Túrin's company were slain as they slept; but some fleeing by an inner stair came out upon the hill-top, and there they fought until they fell, and their blood flowed out upon the *seregon* that mantled the stone. But a net was cast over Túrin as he fought, and he was enmeshed in it, and overcome, and led away.

And at length when all was silent again Mîm crept out of the shadows of his house; and as the sun rose over the mists of Sirion he stood beside the dead men on the hill-top. But he perceived that not all those that lay there were dead; for by one his gaze was returned, and he looked in the eyes of Beleg the Elf. Then with hatred long-stored Mîm stepped up to Beleg, and drew forth the sword Anglachel that lay beneath the body of one that had fallen beside him; but Beleg stumbling up seized back the sword and thrust it at the Dwarf, and Mîm in terror fled wailing from the hill-top. And Beleg cried after him: 'The vengeance of the house of Hador will find you yet!'

Now Beleg was sorely wounded, but he was mighty among the Elves of Middle-earth, and he was moreover a master of healing. Therefore he did not die, and slowly his strength returned; and he sought in vain among the dead for Túrin, to bury him. But he found him not; and then he knew that Húrin's son was yet alive, and taken to Angband.

With little hope Beleg departed from Amon Rûdh and set out northward, towards the Crossings of Teiglin, following in the track of the Orcs; and he crossed over the Brithiach and journeyed through Dimbar towards the Pass of Anach. And now he was not far behind them, for he went without sleeping, whereas they had tarried on their road, hunting in the lands and fearing no pursuit as they came northward; and not even in the dreadful woods of Taur-nu-Fuin did he swerve from the trail, for the skill of Beleg was greater than any that have been in Middle-earth. But as he passed by night through that evil land he came upon one lying asleep at the foot of a great dead tree; and Beleg staying his steps beside the sleeper saw that it was an Elf. Then he spoke to him, and gave him *lembas*, and asked him what fate had brought him to that terrible place; and he named himself Gwindor, son of Guilin.

Grieving Beleg looked upon him; for Gwindor was now but a bent and fearful shadow of his former shape and mood, when in the Nirnaeth Arnoediad that lord of Nargothrond rode with rash courage to the very doors of Angband, and there was taken. For few of the Noldor whom Morgoth captured were put to death, because of their skill in forging and in mining for metals and gems; and Gwindor was not slain, but put to labour in the mines of the North. By secret tunnels known only to themselves the mining Elves might sometimes escape; and thus it came to pass that Beleg found him, spent and bewildered in the mazes of Taur-nu-Fuin.

And Gwindor told him that as he lay and lurked among the trees he·saw a great company of Orcs passing northwards, and wolves went with them; and among them was a Man, whose hands were chained, and they drove him onward with whips. 'Very tall he was,' said Gwindor, 'as tall as are the Men from the misty hills of Hithlum.' Then Beleg told him of his own errand in Taur-nu-Fuin; and Gwindor sought to dissuade him from his quest, saying that he would but join Túrin in the anguish that awaited him. But Beleg would not abandon Túrin, and despairing himself he aroused hope again in Gwindor's heart; and together they went on, following the Orcs until they came out of the forest on the high slopes that ran down to the barren dunes of Anfauglith. There within sight of the peaks of Thangorodrim the Orcs made their encampment in a bare dell as the light of day was failing, and setting wolf-sentinels all about they fell to carousing. A great storm rode up out of the west, and lightning glittered on the Shadowy Mountains far away, as Beleg and Gwindor crept towards the dell.

When all in the camp were sleeping Beleg took his bow, and in the darkness shot the wolf-sentinels, one by one and silently. Then in great peril they entered in, and they found Túrin fettered hand and foot and tied to a withered tree; and all about him knives that had been cast at him were embedded in the trunk, and he was senseless in a sleep of great weariness. But Beleg and Gwindor cut the bonds that held him, and lifting him they carried him out of the dell; yet they could bear him no further than to a thicket of thorn-trees a little way above. There they laid him down; and now the storm drew very near. Beleg drew his sword Anglachel, and with it he cut the fetters that bound Túrin; but fate was that day more strong, for the blade slipped as he cut the shackles, and Túrin's foot was pricked.

Then he was aroused into a sudden wakefulness of rage and fear, and seeing one bending over him with naked blade he leapt up with a great cry, believing that Orcs were come again to torment him; and grappling with him in the darkness he seized Anglachel, and slew Beleg Cúthalion thinking him a foe.

But as he stood, finding himself free, and ready to sell his life dearly against imagined foes, there came a great flash of lightning above them; and in its light he looked down on Beleg's face. Then Túrin stood stonestill and silent, staring on that dreadful death, knowing what he had done; and so terrible was his face, lit by the lightning that flickered all about them, that Gwindor cowered down upon the ground and dared not raise his eyes.

But now in the dell beneath the Orcs were aroused, and all the camp was in a tumult; for they feared the thunder that came out of the west, believing that it was sent against them by the great Enemies beyond the Sea. Then a wind arose, and great rains fell, and torrents swept down from the heights of Taur-nu-Fuin; and though Gwindor cried out to Túrin, warning him of their utmost peril, he made no answer, but sat unmoving and unweeping in the tempest beside the body of Beleg Cúthalion.

When morning came the storm was passed away eastward over Lothlann, and the sun of autumn rose hot and bright; but believing that Túrin would have fled far away from that place and all trace of his flight be washed away, the Orcs departed in haste without longer search, and far off Gwindor saw them marching away over the steaming sands of Anfauglith. Thus it came to pass that they returned to Morgoth emptyhanded, and left behind them the son of Húrin, who sat crazed and unwitting on the slopes of Taur-nu-Fuin, bearing a burden heavier than their bonds.

Then Gwindor roused Túrin to aid him in the burial of Beleg, and he rose as one that walked in sleep; and together they laid Beleg in a shallow grave, and placed beside him Belthronding his great bow, that was made of black yew-wood. But the dread sword Anglachel Gwindor took, saying that it were better that it should take vengeance on the servants of Morgoth than lie useless in the earth; and he took also the *lembas* of Melian to strengthen them in the wild.

Thus ended Beleg Strongbow, truest of friends, greatest in skill of all that harboured in the woods of Beleriand in the Elder Days, at the hand of him whom he most loved; and that grief was graven on the face of Túrin and never faded. But courage and strength were renewed in the Elf of Nargothrond, and departing from Taur-nu-Fuin he led Túrin far away. Never once as they wandered together on long and grievous paths did Túrin speak, and he walked as one without wish or purpose, while the year waned and winter drew on over the northern lands. But Gwindor was ever beside him to guard him and guide him; and thus they passed westward over Sirion and came at length to Eithel Ivrin, the springs whence Narog rose beneath the Mountains of Shadow. There Gwindor spoke to Túrin, saying: 'Awake, Túrin son of Húrin Thalion! On Ivrin's lake is endless laughter. She is fed from crystal fountains unfailing, and guarded from defilement by Ulmo, Lord of Waters, who wrought her beauty in ancient days.' Then Túrin knelt and drank from that water; and suddenly he cast himself down, and his tears were unloosed at last, and he was healed of his madness.

There he made a song for Beleg, and he named it *Laer Cú Beleg*, the Song of the Great Bow, singing it aloud heedless of peril. And Gwindor gave the sword Anglachel into his hands, and Túrin knew that it was heavy and strong and had great power; but its blade was black and dull and its edges blunt. Then Gwindor said: 'This is a strange blade, and unlike any that I have seen in Middle-earth. It mourns for Beleg even as you do. But be comforted; for I return to Nargothrond of the house of Finarfin, and you shall come with me, and be healed and renewed.'

'Who are you?' said Túrin.

'A wandering Elf, a thrall escaped, whom Beleg met and comforted,' said Gwindor. 'Yet once I was Gwindor son of Guilin, a lord of Nargothrond, until I went to the Nirnaeth Arnoediad, and was enslaved in Angband.'

'Then have you seen Húrin son of Galdor, the warrior of Dorlómin?' said Túrin.

'I have not seen him,' said Gwindor. 'But rumour of him runs through Angband that he still defies Morgoth; and Morgoth has laid a curse upon him and all his kin.'

'That I do believe,' said Túrin.

And now they arose, and departing from Eithel Ivrin they journeyed southward along the banks of Narog, until they were taken by scouts of the Elves and brought as prisoners to the hidden stronghold. Thus did Túrin come to Nargothrond.

At first his own people did not know Gwindor, who went out young and strong, and returned now seeming as one of the aged among mortal Men, because of his torments and his labours; but Finduilas daughter of Orodreth the King knew him and welcomed him, for she had loved him before the Nirnaeth, and so greatly did Gwindor

love her beauty that he named her Faelivrin, which is the gleam of
the sun on the pools of Ivrin. For Gwindor's sake Túrin was admitted with him into Nargothrond, and he dwelt there in honour.
But when Gwindor would tell his name, Túrin checked him, saying:
'I am Agarwaen the son of Úmarth (which is the Bloodstained, son
of Ill-fate), a hunter in the woods'; and the Elves of Nargothrond
questioned him no more.

   In the time that followed Túrin grew high in favour with Orodreth,
and well-nigh all hearts were turned to him in Nargothrond. For he
was young, and only now reached his full manhood; and he was in
truth the son of Morwen Eledhwen to look upon: dark-haired and
pale-skinned, with grey eyes, and his face more beautiful than any
other among mortal Men, in the Elder Days. His speech and bearing
were that of the ancient kingdom of Doriath, and even among the
Elves he might be taken for one from the great houses of the Noldor;
therefore many called him Adanedhel, the Elf-Man. The sword
Anglachel was forged anew for him by cunning smiths of Nargothrond, and though ever black its edges shone with pale fire; and he
named it Gurthang, Iron of Death. So great was his prowess and
skill in warfare on the confines of the Guarded Plain that he himself
became known as Mormegil, the Black Sword; and the Elves said:
'The Mormegil cannot be slain, save by mischance, or an evil arrow
from afar.' Therefore they gave him dwarf-mail, to guard him; and
in a grim mood he found also in the armouries a dwarf-mask all
gilded, and he put it on before battle, and his enemies fled before
his face.

   Then the heart of Finduilas was turned from Gwindor and against
her will her love was given to Túrin; but Túrin did not perceive
what had befallen. And being torn in heart Finduilas became sorrowful; and she grew wan and silent. But Gwindor sat in dark thought;
and on a time he spoke to Finduilas, saying: 'Daughter of the house
of Finarfin, let no grief lie between us; for though Morgoth has laid
my life in ruin, you still I love. Go whither love leads you; yet beware! It is not fitting that the Elder Children of Ilúvatar should wed
with the Younger; nor is it wise, for they are brief, and soon pass, to
leave us in widowhood while the world lasts. Neither will fate suffer
it, unless it be once or twice only, for some high cause of doom that
we do not perceive. But this Man is not Beren. A doom indeed lies
on him, as seeing eyes may well read in him, but a dark doom. Enter
not into it! And if you will, your love shall betray you to bitterness
and death. For hearken to me! Though he be indeed *agarwaen* son of
*úmarth*, his right name is Túrin son of Húrin, whom Morgoth holds

in Angband, and whose kin he has cursed. Doubt not the power of Morgoth Bauglir! Is it not written in me?'

Then Finduilas sat long in thought; but at the last she said only: 'Túrin son of Húrin loves me not; nor will.'

Now when Túrin learnt from Finduilas of what had passed, he was wrathful, and he said to Gwindor: 'In love I hold you for rescue and safe-keeping. But now you have done ill to me, friend, to betray my right name, and call my doom upon me, from which I would lie hid.'

But Gwindor answered: 'The doom lies in yourself, not in your name.'

When it became known to Orodreth that the Mormegil was in truth the son of Húrin Thalion he gave him great honour, and Túrin became mighty among the people of Nargothrond. But he had no liking for their manner of warfare, of ambush and stealth and secret arrow, and he yearned for brave strokes and battle in the open; and his counsels weighed with the King ever the longer the more. In those days the Elves of Nargothrond forsook their secrecy and went openly to battle, and great store of weapons were made; and by the counsel of Túrin the Noldor built a mighty bridge over the Narog from the Doors of Felagund, for the swifter passage of their arms. Then the servants of Angband were driven out of all the land between Narog and Sirion eastward, and westward to the Nenning and the desolate Falas; and though Gwindor spoke ever against Túrin in the council of the King, holding it an ill policy, he fell into dishonour and none heeded him, for his strength was small and he was no longer forward in arms. Thus Nargothrond was revealed to the wrath and hatred of Morgoth; but still at Túrin's prayer his true name was not spoken, and though the fame of his deeds came into Doriath and to the ears of Thingol, rumour spoke only of the Black Sword of Nargothrond.

In that time of respite and hope, when because of the deeds of the Mormegil the power of Morgoth was stemmed west of Sirion, Morwen fled at last from Dor-lómin with Nienor her daughter, and adventured the long journey to Thingol's halls. There new grief awaited her, for she found Túrin gone, and to Doriath there had come no tidings since the Dragon-helm had vanished from the lands west of Sirion; but Morwen remained in Doriath with Nienor as guests of Thingol and Melian, and were treated with honour.

Now it came to pass, when four hundred and ninety-five years had passed since the rising of the Moon, in the spring of the year, there

came to Nargothrond two Elves, named Gelmir and Arminas; they
were of Angrod's people, but since the Dagor Bragollach they dwelt
in the south with Círdan the Shipwright. From their far journeys
they brought tidings of a great mustering of Orcs and evil creatures
under the eaves of Ered Wethrin and in the Pass of Sirion; and they
told also that Ulmo had come to Círdan, giving warning that great
peril drew nigh to Nargothrond.

'Hear the words of the Lord of Waters!' said they to the King.
'Thus he spoke to Círdan the Shipwright: "The Evil of the North has
defiled the springs of Sirion, and my power withdraws from the
fingers of the flowing waters. But a worse thing is yet to come forth.
Say therefore to the Lord of Nargothrond: Shut the doors of the
fortress and go not abroad. Cast the stones of your pride into the loud
river, that the creeping evil may not find the gate."'

Orodreth was troubled by the dark words of the messengers, but
Túrin would by no means hearken to these counsels, and least of all
would he suffer the great bridge to be cast down; for he was become
proud and stern, and would order all things as he wished.

Soon afterwards Handir Lord of Brethil was slain, for the Orcs
invaded his land, and Handir gave them battle; but the Men of
Brethil were worsted, and driven back into their woods. And in the
autumn of the year, biding his hour, Morgoth loosed upon the people
of Narog the great host that he had long prepared; and Glaurung the
Urulóki passed over Anfauglith, and came thence into the north
vales of Sirion and there did great evil. Under the shadows of Ered
Wethrin he defiled the Eithel Ivrin, and thence he passed into the
realm of Nargothrond, and burned the Talath Dirnen, the Guarded
Plain, between Narog and Teiglin.

Then the warriors of Nargothrond went forth, and tall and terrible
on that day looked Túrin, and the heart of the host was upheld, as he
rode on the right hand of Orodreth. But greater far was the host of
Morgoth than any scouts had told, and none but Túrin defended by his
dwarf-mask could withstand the approach of Glaurung; and the
Elves were driven back and pressed by the Orcs into the field of
Tumhalad, between Ginglith and Narog, and there they were
penned. On that day all the pride and host of Nargothrond withered
away; and Orodreth was slain in the forefront of the battle, and
Gwindor son of Guilin was wounded to the death. But Túrin came
to his aid, and all fled before him; and he bore Gwindor out of the
rout, and escaping into a wood there laid him on the grass.

Then Gwindor said to Túrin: 'Let bearing pay for bearing! But
ill-fated was mine, and vain is thine; for my body is marred beyond

healing, and I must leave Middle-earth. And though I love thee, son
of Húrin, yet I rue the day that I took thee from the Orcs. But for thy
prowess and thy pride, still I should have love and life, and Nargothrond should yet stand a while. Now if thou love me, leave me!
Haste thee to Nargothrond, and save Finduilas. And this last I say
to thee: she alone stands between thee and thy doom. If thou fail
her, it shall not fail to find thee. Farewell!'

Then Túrin sped back to Nargothrond, mustering such of the rout
as he met with on the way; and the leaves fell from the trees in a great
wind as they went, for the autumn was passing to a dire winter. But
the host of the Orcs and Glaurung the Dragon were there before him,
and they came suddenly, ere those that were left on guard were aware
of what had befallen on the field of Tumhalad. In that day the bridge
over Narog proved an evil; for it was great and mightily made and
could not swiftly be destroyed, and the enemy came readily over the
deep river, and Glaurung came in full fire against the Doors of Felagund, and overthrew them, and passed within.

And even as Túrin came up the dreadful sack of Nargothrond was
well nigh achieved. The Orcs had slain or driven off all that remained
in arms, and were even then ransacking the great halls and chambers,
plundering and destroying; but those of the women and maidens
that were not burned or slain they had herded on the terraces before
the doors, as slaves to be taken into Morgoth's thraldom. Upon this
ruin and woe Túrin came, and none could withstand him; or would
not, though he struck down all before him, and passed over the
bridge, and hewed his way towards the captives.

And now he stood alone, for the few that followed him had fled.
But in that moment Glaurung issued from the gaping doors, and lay
behind, between Túrin and the bridge. Then suddenly he spoke, by
the evil spirit that was in him, saying: 'Hail, son of Húrin. Well
met!'

Then Túrin sprang about, and strode against him, and the edges of
Gurthang shone as with flame; but Glaurung withheld his blast, and
opened wide his serpent-eyes and gazed upon Túrin. Without fear
Túrin looked into them as he raised up the sword; and straightway
he fell under the binding spell of the lidless eyes of the dragon, and
was halted moveless. Then for a long time he stood as one graven of
stone; and they two were alone, silent before the doors of Nargothrond. But Glaurung spoke again, taunting Túrin, and he said:
'Evil have been all thy ways, son of Húrin. Thankless fosterling, outlaw, slayer of thy friend, thief of love, usurper of Nargothrond, captain
foolhardy, and deserter of thy kin. As thralls thy mother and thy sister

live in Dor-lómin, in misery and want. Thou art arrayed as a prince, but they go in rags; and for thee they yearn, but thou carest not for that. Glad may thy father be to learn that he hath such a son; as learn he shall.' And Túrin being under the spell of Glaurung hearkened to his words, and he saw himself as in a mirror misshapen by malice, and loathed that which he saw.

And while he was yet held by the eyes of the dragon in torment of mind, and could not stir, the Orcs drove away the herded captives, and they passed nigh to Túrin and crossed over the bridge. Among them was Finduilas, and she cried out to Túrin as she went; but not until her cries and the wailing of the captives was lost upon the northward road did Glaurung release Túrin, and he might not stop his ears against that voice that haunted him after.

Then suddenly Glaurung withdrew his glance, and waited; and Túrin stirred slowly, as one waking from a hideous dream. Then coming to himself he sprang upon the dragon with a cry. But Glaurung laughed, saying: 'If thou wilt be slain, I will slay thee gladly. But small help will that be to Morwen and Nienor. No heed didst thou give to the cries of the Elf-woman. Wilt thou deny also the bond of thy blood?'

But Túrin drawing back his sword stabbed at the dragon's eyes; and Glaurung coiling back swiftly towered above him, and said: 'Nay! At least thou art valiant; beyond all whom I have met. And they lie who say that we of our part do not honour the valour of foes. See now! I offer thee freedom. Go to thy kin, if thou canst. Get thee gone! And if Elf or Man be left to make tale of these days, then surely in scorn they will name thee, if thou spurnest this gift.'

Then Túrin, being yet bemused by the eyes of the dragon, as were he treating with a foe that could know pity, believed the words of Glaurung; and turning away he sped over the bridge. But as he went Glaurung spoke behind him, saying in a fell voice: 'Haste thee now, son of Húrin, to Dor-lómin! Or perhaps the Orcs shall come before thee, once again. And if thou tarry for Finduilas, then never shalt thou see Morwen again, and never at all shalt thou see Nienor thy sister; and they will curse thee.'

But Túrin passed away on the northward road, and Glaurung laughed once more, for he had accomplished the errand of his Master. Then he turned to his own pleasure, and sent forth his blast, and burned all about him. But all the Orcs that were busy in the sack he routed forth, and drove them away, and denied them their plunder even to the last thing of worth. The bridge then he broke down and cast into the foam of Narog; and being thus secure he gathered all the hoard and riches of Felagund and heaped them, and lay upon them in the innermost hall, and rested a while.

And Túrin hastened along the ways to the north, through the lands now desolate between Narog and Teiglin, and the Fell Winter came down to meet him; for in that year snow fell ere autumn was passed, and spring came late and cold. Ever it seemed to him as he went that he heard the cries of Finduilas, calling his name by wood and hill, and great was his anguish; but his heart being hot with the lies of Glaurung, and seeing ever in his mind the Orcs burning the house of Húrin or putting Morwen and Nienor to torment, he held on his way, and turned never aside.

At last worn by haste and the long road (for forty leagues and more had he journeyed without rest) he came with the first ice of winter to the pools of Ivrin, where before he had been healed. But they were now but a frozen mire, and he could drink there no more.

Thus he came hardly by the passes of Dor-lómin, through bitter snows from the north, and found again the land of his childhood. Bare and bleak it was; and Morwen was gone. Her house stood empty, broken and cold; and no living thing dwelt nigh. Therefore Túrin departed, and came to the house of Brodda the Easterling, he that had to wife Aerin, Húrin's kinswoman; and there he learned of an old servant that Morwen was long gone, for she had fled with Nienor out of Dor-lómin, none but Aerin knew where.

Then Túrin strode to Brodda's table, and seizing him he drew his sword, and demanded that he be told whither Morwen had gone; and Aerin declared to him that she went to Doriath to seek her son. 'For the lands were freed then from evil,' she said, 'by the Black Sword of the south, who now has fallen, they say.' Then Túrin's eyes were opened, and the last threads of Glaurung's spell were loosed; and for anguish, and wrath at the lies that had deluded him, and hatred of the oppressors of Morwen, a black rage seized him, and he slew Brodda in his hall, and other Easterlings that were his guests. Thereafter he fled out into the winter, a hunted man; but he was aided by some that remained of Hador's people and knew the ways of the wild, and with them he escaped through the falling snow and came to an outlaws' refuge in the southern mountains of Dor-lómin. Thence Túrin passed again from the land of his childhood, and returned to Sirion's vale. His heart was bitter, for to Dor-lómin he had brought only greater woe upon the remnant of his people, and they were glad of his going; and this comfort alone he had: that by the prowess of the Black Sword the ways to Doriath had been laid open to Morwen.

And he said in his thought: 'Then those deeds wrought not evil to all. And where else might I have better bestowed my kin, even had I come sooner? For if the Girdle of Melian be broken, then last hope is ended. Nay, it is better indeed as things be; for a shadow I cast wheresoever I come. Let Melian keep them! And I will leave them in peace unshadowed for a while.'

Now Túrin coming down from Ered Wethrin sought for Finduilas in vain, roaming the woods beneath the mountains, wild and wary as a beast; and he waylaid all the roads that went north to the Pass of Sirion. But he was too late; for all the trails had grown old, or were washed away by the winter. Yet thus it was that passing southwards down Teiglin Túrin came upon some of the Men of Brethil that were surrounded by Orcs; and he delivered them, for the Orcs fled from Gurthang. He named himself Wildman of the Woods, and they besought him to come and dwell with them; but he said that he had an errand yet unachieved, to seek Finduilas, Orodreth's daughter of Nargothrond. Then Dorlas, the leader of those woodmen, told the grievous tidings of her death. For the Men of Brethil had waylaid at the Crossings of Teiglin the Orc-host that led the captives of Nargothrond, hoping to rescue them; but the Orcs had at once cruelly slain their prisoners, and Finduilas they pinned to a tree with a spear. So she died, saying at the last: 'Tell the Mormegil that Finduilas is here.' Therefore they had laid her in a mound near that place, and named it Haudh-en-Elleth, the Mound of the Elf-maid.

Túrin bade them lead him thither, and there he fell down into a darkness of grief that was near death. Then Dorlas by his black sword, the fame whereof had come even into the deeps of Brethil, and by his quest of the King's daughter, knew that this Wildman was indeed the Mormegil of Nargothrond, whom rumour said was the son of Húrin of Dor-lómin. Therefore the woodmen lifted him up, and bore him away to their homes. Now those were set in a stockade upon a high place in the forest, Ephel Brandir upon Amon Obel; for the People of Haleth were now dwindled by war, and Brandir son of Handir who ruled them was a man of gentle mood, and lame also from childhood, and he trusted rather in secrecy than in deeds of war to save them from the power of the North. Therefore he feared the tidings that Dorlas brought, and when he beheld the face of Túrin as he lay on the bier a cloud of foreboding lay on his heart. Nonetheless being moved by his woe he took him into his own house and tended him, for he had skill in healing. And with the beginning of spring Túrin cast off his darkness, and grew hale again; and he arose, and he thought that he would remain in Brethil hidden, and put his shadow behind him, forsaking the past. He took therefore a new name, Turambar, which in the High-elven speech signified Master of Doom; and he besought the woodmen to forget that he was a stranger among them or ever bore any other name. Nonetheless he would not wholly leave deeds of war; for he could not endure that the Orcs should come to the Crossings of Teiglin or draw nigh to Haudh-en-Elleth, and he made that a place of dread for them, so that they shunned it. But he laid his black sword by, and wielded rather the bow and the spear.

Now new tidings came to Doriath concerning Nargothrond, for some that had escaped from the defeat and the sack, and had survived the Fell Winter in the wild, came at last to Thingol seeking refuge; and the march-wardens brought them to the King. And some said that all the enemy had withdrawn northwards, and others that Glaurung abode still in the halls of Felagund; and some said that the Mormegil was slain, and others that he was cast under a spell by the dragon and dwelt there yet, as one changed to stone. But all declared that it was known to many in Nargothrond ere the end that the Mormegil was none other than Túrin son of Húrin of Dor-lómin.

Then Morwen was distraught, and refusing the counsel of Melian she rode forth alone into the wild to seek her son, or some true tidings of him. Thingol therefore sent Mablung after her, with many hardy march-wards, to find her and guard her, and to learn what news they might; but Nienor was bidden to remain behind. Yet the fearlessness of her house was hers; and in an evil hour, in hope that Morwen would return when she saw that her daughter would go with her into peril, Nienor disguised herself as one of Thingol's people, and went with that ill-fated riding.

They came upon Morwen by the banks of Sirion, and Mablung besought her to return to Menegroth; but she was fey, and would not be persuaded. Then also the coming of Nienor was revealed, and despite Morwen's command she would not go back; and Mablung perforce brought them to the hidden ferries at the Meres of Twilight, and they passed over Sirion. And after three days' journeying they came to Amon Ethir, the Hill of Spies, that long ago Felagund had caused to be raised with great labour, a league before the doors of Nargothrond. There Mablung set a guard of riders about Morwen and her daughter, and forbade them to go further. But he, seeing from the hill no sign of any enemy, went down with his scouts to the Narog, as stealthily as they could go.

But Glaurung was aware of all that they did, and he came forth in heat of wrath, and lay into the river; and a vast vapour and foul reek went up, in which Mablung and his company were blinded and lost. Then Glaurung passed east over Narog.

Seeing the onset of the dragon the guards upon Amon Ethir sought to lead Morwen and Nienor away, and fly with them with all speed back eastwards; but the wind bore the blank mists upon them, and their horses were maddened by the dragon-stench, and were ungovernable, and ran this way and that, so that some were dashed against trees and were slain, and others were borne far away. Thus the ladies were lost, and of Morwen indeed no sure tidings came ever to Doriath after. But Nienor, being thrown by her steed, yet unhurt, made her way back to Amon Ethir, there to await Mablung, and came thus above the reek into the sunlight; and looking westward she stared straight into the eyes of Glaurung, whose head lay upon the hill-top.

Her will strove with him for a while, but he put forth his power, and having learned who she was he constrained her to gaze into his eyes, and he laid a spell of utter darkness and forgetfulness upon her, so that she could remember nothing that had ever befallen her, nor her own name, nor the name of any other thing; and for many days she could neither hear, nor see, nor stir by her own will. Then Glaurung left her standing alone upon Amon Ethir, and went back to Nargothrond.

Now Mablung, who greatly daring had explored the halls of Felagund when Glaurung left them, fled from them at the approach of the dragon, and returned to Amon Ethir. The sun sank and night fell as he climbed the hill, and he found none there save Nienor, standing alone under the stars as an image of stone. No word she spoke or heard, but would follow, if he took up her hand. Therefore in great grief he led her away, though it seemed to him vain; for they were both like to perish, succourless in the wild.

But they were found by three of Mablung's companions, and slowly they journeyed northward and eastward towards the fences of the land of Doriath beyond Sirion, and the guarded bridge nigh to the inflowing of Esgalduin. Slowly the strength of Nienor returned as they drew nearer to Doriath; but still she could not speak or hear, and walked blindly as she was led. But even as they drew near the fences at last she closed her staring eyes, and would sleep; and they laid her down, and rested also, unheedfully, for they were utterly outworn. There they were assailed by an Orc-band, such as now roamed often as nigh the fences of Doriath as they dared. But Nienor in that hour recovered hearing and sight, and being awakened by the cries of the Orcs she sprang up in terror, and fled ere they could come to her.

Then the Orcs gave chase, and the Elves after; and they overtook the Orcs and slew them ere they could harm her, but Nienor escaped them. For she fled as in a madness of fear, swifter than a deer, and tore off all her clothing as she ran, until she was naked; and she passed out of their sight, running northward, and though they sought her long they found her not, nor any trace of her. And at last Mablung in despair returned to Menegroth and told the tidings. Then Thingol and Melian were filled with grief; but Mablung went forth, and sought long in vain for tidings of Morwen and Nienor.

But Nienor ran on into the woods until she was spent, and then fell, and slept, and awoke; and it was a sunlit morning, and she rejoiced in light as it were a new thing, and all things else that she saw seemed new and strange, for she had no names for them. Nothing did she remember save a darkness that lay behind her, and a shadow of fear; therefore she went warily as a hunted beast, and became famished, for she had no food and knew not how to seek it. But coming at last to the Crossings of Teiglin she passed over, seeking the shelter of the great trees of Brethil, for she was afraid, and it seemed to her that the darkness was overtaking her again from which she had fled.

But it was a great storm of thunder that came up from the south, and in terror she cast herself down upon the mound of Haudh-en-Elleth, stopping her ears from the thunder; but the rain smote her and drenched her, and she lay like a wild beast that is dying. There Turambar found her, as he came to the Crossings of Teiglin, having heard rumour of Orcs that roamed near; and seeing in a flare of lightning the body as it seemed of a slain maiden lying upon the mound of Finduilas he was stricken to the heart. But the woodmen lifted her up, and Turambar cast his cloak about her, and they took her to a lodge nearby, and warmed her, and gave her food. And as soon as she looked upon Turambar she was comforted, for it seemed to her that she had found at last something that she had sought in her darkness; and she would not be parted from him. But when he asked her concerning her name and her kin and her misadventure, then she became troubled as a child that perceives that something is demanded but cannot understand what it may be; and she wept. Therefore Turambar said: 'Do not be troubled. The tale shall wait. But I will give you a name, and I will call you Níniel, Tear-maiden.' And at that name she shook her head, but said: Níniel. That was the first word she spoke after her darkness, and it remained her name among the woodmen ever after.

On the next day they bore her towards Ephel Brandir; but when

they came to Dimrost, the Rainy Stair, where the tumbling stream
of Celebros fell towards Teiglin, a great shuddering came upon her,
wherefore afterwards that place was called Nen Girith, the Shuddering Water. Ere she came to the home of the woodmen upon Amon
Obel she was sick of a fever; and long she lay thus, tended by the
women of Brethil, and they taught her language as to an infant. But
ere the autumn came by the skill of Brandir she was healed of her
sickness, and she could speak; but nothing did she remember of the
time before she was found by Turambar on the mound of Haudh-en-
Elleth. And Brandir loved her; but all her heart was given to Turambar.

In that time the woodmen were not troubled by the Orcs, and
Turambar went not to war, and there was peace in Brethil. His heart
turned to Níniel, and he asked her in marriage; but for that time she
delayed in spite of her love. For Brandir foreboded he knew not what,
and sought to restrain her, rather for her sake than his own or
rivalry with Turambar; and he revealed to her that Turambar was
Túrin son of Húrin, and though she knew not the name a shadow
fell upon her mind.

But when three years were passed since the sack of Nargothrond
Turambar asked Níniel again, and vowed that now he would wed
her, or else go back to war in the wild. And Níniel took him with joy,
and they were wedded at the midsummer, and the woodmen of
Brethil made a great feast. But ere the end of the year Glaurung sent
Orcs of his dominion against Brethil; and Turambar sat at home
deedless, for he had promised to Níniel that he would go to battle
only if their homes were assailed. But the woodmen were worsted,
and Dorlas upbraided him that he would not aid the people that he
had taken for his own. Then Turambar arose and brought forth again
his black sword, and he gathered a great company of the Men of
Brethil, and they defeated the Orcs utterly. But Glaurung heard
tidings that the Black Sword was in Brethil, and he pondered what
he heard, devising new evil.

In the spring of the year after Níniel conceived, and she became
wan and sad; and at the same time there came to Ephel Brandir the
first rumours that Glaurung had issued from Nargothrond. Then
Turambar sent out scouts far afield, for now he ordered things as he
would, and few gave heed to Brandir. As it drew near to summer
Glaurung came to the borders of Brethil, and lay near the west shores
of Teiglin; and then there was great fear among the woodfolk, for it
was now plain that the Great Worm would assail them and ravage
their land, and not pass by, returning to Angband, as they had hoped.

They sought therefore the counsel of Turambar; and he counselled them that it was vain to go against Glaurung with all their force, for only by cunning and good fortune could they defeat him. He offered therefore himself to seek the dragon on the borders of the land, and bade the rest of the people to remain at Ephel Brandir, but to prepare for flight. For if Glaurung had the victory, he would come first to the woodmen's homes to destroy them, and they could not hope to withstand him; but if they then scattered far and wide, then many might escape, for Glaurung would not take up his dwelling in Brethil, and would return soon to Nargothrond.

Then Turambar asked for companions willing to aid him in his peril; and Dorlas stood forth, but no others. Therefore Dorlas upbraided the people, and spoke scorn of Brandir, who could not play the part of the heir of the house of Haleth; and Brandir was shamed before his people, and was bitter at heart. But Hunthor, kinsman of Brandir, asked his leave to go in his stead. Then Turambar said farewell to Níniel, and she was filled with fear and foreboding, and their parting was sorrowful; but Turambar set out with his two companions and went to Nen Girith.

Then Níniel being unable to endure her fear, and unwilling to wait in the Ephel tidings of Turambar's fortune, set forth after him, and a great company went with her. At this Brandir was filled all the more with dread, and he sought to dissuade her and the people that would go with her from this rashness, but they heeded him not. Therefore he renounced his lordship, and all love for the people that had scorned him, and having naught left but his love for Níniel he girt himself with a sword and went after her; but being lame he fell far behind.

Now Turambar came to Nen Girith at sundown, and there he learned that Glaurung lay on the brink of the high shores of Teiglin, and was like to move when night fell. Then he called those tidings good; for the dragon lay at Cabed-en-Aras, where the river ran in a deep and narrow gorge that a hunted deer might overleap, and Turambar thought that he would seek no further, but would attempt to pass over the gorge. Therefore he purposed to creep down at dusk, and descend into the ravine under night, and cross over the wild water; and then to climb up the further cliff, and so come to the dragon beneath his guard.

This counsel he took, but the heart of Dorlas failed when they came to the races of Teiglin in the dark, and he dared not attempt the perilous crossing, but drew back and lurked in the woods, burdened with shame. Turambar and Hunthor, nonetheless, crossed over in safety, for the loud roaring of the water drowned all other sounds, and Glaurung slept. But ere the middle-night the dragon roused, and with a great noise and blast cast his forward part across the chasm, and began to draw his bulk after. Turambar and Hunthor were well-nigh overcome by the heat and the stench, as they sought in haste for a way up to come at Glaurung; and Hunthor was slain by a great stone that was dislodged from on high by the passage of the dragon, and smote him on the head and cast him into the river. So he ended, of the house of Haleth not the least valiant.

Then Turambar summoned all his will and courage and climbed the cliff alone, and came beneath the dragon. Then he drew Gurthang, and with all the might of his arm, and of his hate, he thrust it into the soft belly of the Worm, even up to the hilts. But when Glaurung felt his death-pang, he screamed, and in his dreadful throe he heaved up his bulk and hurled himself across the chasm, and there lay lashing and coiling in his agony. And he set all in a blaze about him, and beat all to ruin, until at last his fires died, and he lay still.

Now Gurthang had been wrested from Turambar's hand in the throe of Glaurung, and it clave to the belly of the dragon. Turambar therefore crossed the water once more, desiring to recover his sword and to look upon his foe; and he found him stretched at his length, and rolled upon one side, and the hilts of Gurthang stood in his belly. Then Turambar seized the hilts and set his foot upon the belly, and cried in mockery of the dragon and his words at Nargothrond: 'Hail, Worm of Morgoth! Well met again! Die now and the darkness have thee! Thus is Túrin son of Húrin avenged.'

Then he wrenched out the sword, but a spout of black blood followed it, and fell on his hand, and the venom burned it. And thereupon Glaurung opened his eyes and looked upon Turambar with such malice that it smote him as a blow; and by that stroke and the anguish of the venom he fell into a dark swoon, and lay as one dead, and his sword was beneath him.

The screams of Glaurung rang in the woods, and came to the people that waited at Nen Girith; and when those that looked forth heard them, and saw afar the ruin and burning that the dragon made, they deemed that he had triumphed and was destroying those that assailed him. And Níniel sat and shuddered beside the falling water, and at the voice of Glaurung her darkness crept upon her again, so that she could not stir from that place of her own will.

Even so Brandir found her, for he came to Nen Girith at last, limping wearily; and when he heard that the dragon had crossed the river and had beaten down his foes, his heart yearned towards Níniel in pity. Yet he thought also: 'Turambar is dead, but Níniel lives. Now it may be that she will come with me, and I will lead her away, and so we shall escape from the dragon together.' After a while therefore he stood by Níniel, and he said: 'Come! It is time to go. If you will, I will lead you.' And he took her hand, and she arose silently, and followed him; and in the darkness none saw them go.

But as they went down the path to the Crossings the moon rose, and cast a grey light on the land, and Níniel said: 'Is this the way?' And Brandir answered that he knew no way, save to flee as they might from Glaurung, and escape into the wild. But Níniel said: 'The Black Sword was my beloved and my husband. To seek him only do I go. What else could you think?' And she sped on before him. Thus she came towards the Crossings of Teiglin and beheld Haudh-en-Elleth in the white moonlight, and great dread came on her. Then with a cry she turned away, casting off her cloak, and fled southward along the river, and her white raiment shone in the moon.

Thus Brandir saw her from the hill-side, and turned to cross her path, but he was still behind her when she came to the ruin of Glaurung nigh the brink of Cabed-en-Aras. There she saw the dragon lying, but she heeded him not, for a man lay beside him; and she ran to Turambar, and called his name in vain. Then finding that his hand was burned she washed it with tears and bound it about with a strip of her raiment, and she kissed him and cried on him again to awake. Thereat Glaurung stirred for the last time ere he died, and he spoke with his last breath, saying: 'Hail, Nienor, daughter of Húrin. We meet again ere the end. I give thee joy that thou hast found thy brother at last. And now thou shalt know him: a stabber in the dark, treacherous to foes, faithless to friends, and a curse unto his kin, Túrin son of Húrin! But the worst of all his deeds thou shalt feel in thyself.'

Then Glaurung died, and the veil of his malice was taken from her, and she remembered all the days of her life. Looking down upon Túrin she cried: 'Farewell, O twice beloved! *A Túrin Turambar turun ambartanen*: master of doom by doom mastered! O happy to be dead!' Then Brandir who had heard all, standing stricken upon the edge of ruin, hastened towards her; but she ran from him distraught with horror and anguish, and coming to the brink of Cabed-en-Aras she cast herself over, and was lost in the wild water.

Then Brandir came and looked down, and turned away in horror; and though he no longer desired life, he could not seek death in that roaring water. And thereafter no man looked again upon Cabed-en-Aras, nor would any beast or bird come there, nor any tree grow; and it was named Cabed Naeramarth, the Leap of Dreadful Doom.

But Brandir made his way back to Nen Girith, to bring tidings to the people; and he met Dorlas in the woods, and slew him: the first blood that ever he had spilled, and the last. And he came to Nen Girith, and men cried to him: 'Have you seen her? For Níniel is gone.'

And he answered: 'Níniel is gone for ever. The Dragon is dead, and Turambar is dead; and those tidings are good.' The people murmured at these words, saying that he was crazed; but Brandir said: 'Hear me to the end! Níniel the beloved is also dead. She cast herself into Teiglin, desiring life no more; for she learned that she was none other than Nienor daughter of Húrin of Dor-lómin, ere her forgetfulness came upon her, and that Turambar was her brother, Túrin son of Húrin.'

But even as he ceased, and the people wept, Túrin himself came before them. For when the dragon died, his swoon left him, and he fell into a deep sleep of weariness. But the cold of the night troubled him, and the hilts of Gurthang drove into his side, and he awoke. Then he saw that one had tended his hand, and he wondered much that he was left nonetheless to lie upon the cold ground; and he called, and hearing no answer he went in search of aid, for he was weary and sick.

But when the people saw him they drew back in fear, thinking that it was his unquiet spirit; and he said: 'Nay, be glad; for the Dragon is dead, and I live. But wherefore have you scorned my counsel, and come into peril? And where is Níniel? For her I would see. And surely you did not bring her from her home?'

Then Brandir told him that it was so, and Níniel was dead. But the wife of Dorlas cried out: 'Nay, lord, he is crazed. For he came here saying that you were dead, and he called it good tidings. But you live.'

Then Turambar was wrathful, and believed that all Brandir said or did was done in malice towards himself and Níniel, begrudging their love; and he spoke evilly to Brandir, calling him Club-foot. Then Brandir reported all that he had heard, and named Níniel Nienor daughter of Húrin, and he cried out upon Turambar with the last words of Glaurung, that he was a curse unto his kin and to all that harboured him.

Then Turambar fell into a fury, for in those words he heard the feet of his doom overtaking him; and he charged Brandir with leading Níniel to her death, and publishing with delight the lies of Glaurung, if indeed he devised them not himself. Then he cursed Brandir, and slew him; and he fled from the people into the woods. But after a while his madness left him, and he came to Haudh-en-Elleth, and there sat, and pondered all his deeds. And he cried upon Finduilas to bring him counsel; for he knew not whether he would do now more ill to go to Doriath to seek his kin, or to forsake them for ever and seek death in battle.

And even as he sat there Mablung with a company of Grey-elves came over the Crossings of Teiglin, and he knew Túrin, and hailed him, and was glad indeed to find him yet living; for he had learned of the coming forth of Glaurung and that his path led to Brethil, and also he had heard report that the Black Sword of Nargothrond now dwelt there. Therefore he came to give warning to Túrin, and help if need be; but Túrin said: 'You come too late. The Dragon is dead.'

Then they marvelled, and gave him great praise; but he cared nothing for it, and said: 'This only I ask: give me news of my kin, for in Dor-lómin I learned that they had gone to the Hidden Kingdom.'

Then Mablung was dismayed, but needs must tell to Túrin how Morwen was lost, and Nienor cast into a spell of dumb forgetfulness, and how she escaped them upon the borders of Doriath and fled northwards. Then at last Túrin knew that doom had overtaken him, and that he had slain Brandir unjustly; so that the words of Glaurung were fulfilled in him. And he laughed as one fey, crying: 'This is a bitter jest indeed!' But he bade Mablung go, and return to Doriath, with curses upon it. 'And a curse too upon your errand!' he cried. 'This only was wanting. Now comes the night.'

Then he fled from them like the wind, and they were amazed, wondering what madness had seized him; and they followed after him. But Túrin far out-ran them; and he came to Cabed-en-Aras, and heard the roaring of the water, and saw that all the leaves fell sere from the trees, as though winter had come. There he drew forth his sword, that now alone remained to him of all his possessions, and he said: 'Hail Gurthang! No lord or loyalty dost thou know, save the hand that wieldeth thee. From no blood wilt thou shrink. Wilt thou therefore take Túrin Turambar, wilt thou slay me swiftly?'

And from the blade rang a cold voice in answer: 'Yea, I will drink thy blood gladly, that so I may forget the blood of Beleg my master, and the blood of Brandir slain unjustly. I will slay thee swiftly.'

Then Túrin set the hilts upon the ground, and cast himself upon the point of Gurthang, and the black blade took his life. But Mablung and the Elves came and looked on the shape of Glaurung lying dead, and upon the body of Túrin, and they grieved; and when Men of Brethil came thither, and they learned the reasons of Túrin's madness and death, they were aghast; and Mablung said bitterly: 'I also have been meshed in the doom of the Children of Húrin, and thus with my tidings have slain one that I loved.'

Then they lifted up Túrin, and found that Gurthang had broken asunder. But Elves and Men gathered there great store of wood, and they made a mighty burning, and the Dragon was consumed to ashes. Túrin they laid in a high mound where he had fallen, and the shards of Gurthang were laid beside him. And when all was done, the Elves sang a lament for the Children of Húrin, and a great grey stone was set upon the mound, and thereon was carven in runes of Doriath:

TÚRIN TURAMBAR DAGNIR GLAURUNGA

and beneath they wrote also:

NIENOR NÍNIEL

But she was not there, nor was it ever known whither the cold waters of Teiglin had taken her.

# Chapter 22

# OF THE RUIN OF DORIATH

So ended the tale of Túrin Turambar; but Morgoth did not sleep nor rest from evil, and his dealings with the house of Hador were not yet ended. Against them his malice was unsated, though Húrin was under his eye, and Morwen wandered distraught in the wild.

Unhappy was the lot of Húrin; for all that Morgoth knew of the working of his malice Húrin knew also, but lies were mingled with the truth, and aught that was good was hidden or distorted. In all ways Morgoth sought most to cast an evil light on those things that Thingol and Melian had done, for he hated them, and feared them. When therefore he judged the time to be ripe, he released Húrin from his bondage, bidding him go whither he would; and he feigned that in this he was moved by pity as for an enemy utterly defeated. But he lied, for his purpose was that Húrin should still further his hatred for Elves and Men, ere he died.

Then little though he trusted the words of Morgoth, knowing indeed that he was without pity, Húrin took his freedom, and went forth in grief, embittered by the words of the Dark Lord; and a year was now gone since the death of Túrin his son. For twenty-eight years he had been captive in Angband, and he was grown grim to look upon. His hair and beard were white and long, but he walked unbowed, bearing a great black staff; and he was girt with a sword. Thus he passed into Hithlum, and tidings came to the chieftains of the Easterlings that there was a great riding of captains and black soldiers of Angband over the sands of Anfauglith, and with them came an old man, as one that was held in high honour. Therefore they did not lay hands on Húrin, but let him walk at will in those lands; in which they were wise, for the remnant of his own people shunned him, because of his coming from Angband as one in league and honour with Morgoth.

Thus his freedom did but increase the bitterness of Húrin's heart; and he departed from the land of Hithlum and went up into the mountains. Thence he descried far off amid the clouds the peaks of the Crissaegrim, and he remembered Turgon; and he desired to come again to the hidden realm of Gondolin. He went down therefore from Ered Wethrin, and he knew not that the creatures of Morgoth watched all his steps; and crossing over the Brithiach he passed into

Dimbar, and came to the dark feet of the Echoriath. All the land was cold and desolate, and he looked about him with little hope, standing at the foot of a great fall of stones beneath a sheer rock-wall; and he knew not that this was all that was now left to see of the old Way of Escape: the Dry River was blocked, and the arched gate was buried. Then Húrin looked up to the grey sky, thinking that he might once more descry the eagles, as he had done long ago in his youth; but he saw only the shadows blown from the east, and clouds swirling about the inaccessible peaks, and he heard only the wind hissing over the stones.

But the watch of the great eagles was now redoubled, and they marked Húrin well, far below, forlorn in the fading light; and straightway Thorondor himself, since the tidings seemed great, brought word to Turgon. But Turgon said: 'Does Morgoth sleep? You were mistaken.'

'Not so,' said Thorondor. 'If the Eagles of Manwë were wont to err thus, then long ago, lord, your hiding would have been in vain.'

'Then your words bode ill,' said Turgon; 'for they can bear but one meaning. Even Húrin Thalion has surrendered to the will of Morgoth. My heart is shut.'

But when Thorondor was gone, Turgon sat long in thought, and he was troubled, remembering the deeds of Húrin of Dor-lómin; and he opened his heart, and sent to the eagles to seek for Húrin, and to bring him if they might to Gondolin. But it was too late, and they never saw him again in light or in shadow.

For Húrin stood in despair before the silent cliffs of the Echoriath, and the westering sun, piercing the clouds, stained his white hair with red. Then he cried aloud in the wilderness, heedless of any ears, and he cursed the pitiless land; and standing at last upon a high rock he looked towards Gondolin and called in a great voice: 'Turgon, Turgon, remember the Fen of Serech! O Turgon, will you not hear in your hidden halls?' But there was no sound save the wind in the dry grasses. 'Even so they hissed in Serech at the sunset,' he said; and as he spoke the sun went behind the Mountains of Shadow, and a darkness fell about him, and the wind ceased, and there was silence in the waste.

Yet there were ears that heard the words that Húrin spoke, and report of all came soon to the Dark Throne in the north; and Morgoth smiled, for he knew now clearly in what region Turgon dwelt, though because of the eagles no spy of his could yet come within sight of the land behind the Encircling Mountains. This was the first evil that the freedom of Húrin achieved.

As darkness fell Húrin stumbled from the rock, and fell into a heavy sleep of grief. But in his sleep he heard the voice of Morwen lamenting, and often she spoke his name; and it seemed to him that her voice came out of Brethil. Therefore when he awoke with the coming of day he arose, and went back to the Brithiach; and passing along the eaves of Brethil he came at a time of night to the Crossings of Teiglin. The night-sentinels saw him, but they were filled with dread, for they thought that they saw a ghost out of some ancient battle-mound that walked with darkness about it; and therefore Húrin was not stayed, and he came at last to the place of the burning of Glaurung, and saw the tall stone standing near the brink of Cabed Naeramarth.

But Húrin did not look at the stone, for he knew what was written there; and his eyes had seen that he was not alone. Sitting in the shadow of the stone there was a woman, bent over her knees; and as Húrin stood there silent she cast back her tattered hood and lifted her face. Grey she was and old, but suddenly her eyes looked into his, and he knew her; for though they were wild and full of fear, that light still gleamed in them that long ago had earned for her the name Eledhwen, proudest and most beautiful of mortal women in the days of old.

'You come at last,' she said. 'I have waited too long.'

'It was a dark road. I have come as I could,' he answered.

'But you are too late,' said Morwen. 'They are lost.'

'I know it,' he said. 'But you are not.'

But Morwen said: 'Almost. I am spent. I shall go with the sun. Now little time is left: if you know, tell me! How did she find him?'

But Húrin did not answer, and they sat beside the stone, and did not speak again; and when the sun went down Morwen sighed and clasped his hand, and was still; and Húrin knew that she had died. He looked down at her in the twilight and it seemed to him that the lines of grief and cruel hardship were smoothed away. 'She was not conquered,' he said; and he closed her eyes, and sat unmoving beside her as the night drew down. The waters of Cabed Naeramarth roared on, but he heard no sound, and he saw nothing, and felt nothing, for his heart was stone within him. But there came a chill wind that drove sharp rain into his face; and he was roused, and anger rose in him like smoke, mastering reason, so that all his desire was to seek vengeance for his wrongs and for the wrongs of his kin, accusing in his anguish all those who ever had dealings with them. Then he rose up, and he made a grave for Morwen above Cabed Naeramarth on the west side of the stone; and upon it he cut these words: *Here lies also Morwen Eledhwen.*

It is told that a seer and harp-player of Brethil named Glirhuin
made a song, saying that the Stone of the Hapless should not be
defiled by Morgoth nor ever thrown down, not though the sea
should drown all the land; as after indeed befell, and still Tol Morwen stands alone in the water beyond the new coasts that were made
in the days of the wrath of the Valar. But Húrin does not lie there,
for his doom drove him on, and the Shadow still followed him.

Now Húrin crossed over Teiglin and passed southwards down the
ancient road that led to Nargothrond; and he saw far off to the eastward the lonely height of Amon Rûdh, and knew what had befallen
there. At length he came to the banks of Narog, and ventured the
passage of the wild river upon the fallen stones of the bridge, as
Mablung of Doriath had ventured it before him; and he stood before
the broken Doors of Felagund, leaning upon his staff.

Here it must be told that after the departure of Glaurung Mîm the
Petty-Dwarf had found his way to Nargothrond, and crept within the
ruined halls; and he took possession of them, and sat there fingering
the gold and the gems, letting them run ever through his hands, for
none came nigh to despoil him, from dread of the spirit of Glaurung
and his very memory. But now one had come, and stood upon the
threshold; and Mîm came forth, and demanded to know his purpose.
But Húrin said: 'Who are you, that would hinder me from entering
the house of Finrod Felagund?'

Then the Dwarf answered: 'I am Mîm; and before the proud ones
came from over the Sea, Dwarves delved the halls of Nulukkizdîn.
I have but returned to take what is mine; for I am the last of my
people.'

'Then you shall enjoy your inheritance no longer,' said Húrin; 'for
I am Húrin son of Galdor, returned out of Angband, and my son was
Túrin Turambar, whom you have not forgotten; and he it was that
slew Glaurung the Dragon, who wasted these halls where now you
sit; and not unknown is it to me by whom the Dragon-helm of Dor-
lómin was betrayed.'

Then Mîm in great fear besought Húrin to take what he would, but
to spare his life; but Húrin gave no heed to his prayer, and slew him
there before the doors of Nargothrond. Then he entered in, and stayed
a while in that dreadful place, where the treasures of Valinor lay
strewn upon the floors in darkness and decay; but it is told that when
Húrin came forth from the wreck of Nargothrond and stood again
beneath the sky he bore with him out of all that great hoard but one
thing only.

Now Húrin journeyed eastward, and he came to the Meres of Twi-light above the Falls of Sirion; and there he was taken by the Elves that guarded the western marches of Doriath, and brought before King Thingol in the Thousand Caves. Then Thingol was filled with wonder and grief when he looked on him, and knew that grim and aged man for Húrin Thalion, the captive of Morgoth; but he greeted him fairly and showed him honour. Húrin made no answer to the King, but drew forth from beneath his cloak that one thing which he had taken with him out of Nargothrond; and that was no lesser treasure than the Nauglamír, the Necklace of the Dwarves, that was made for Finrod Felagund long years before by the craftsmen of Nogrod and Belegost, most famed of all their works in the Elder Days, and prized by Finrod while he lived above all the treasures of Nargothrond. And Húrin cast it at the feet of Thingol with wild and bitter words.

'Receive thou thy fee,' he cried, 'for thy fair keeping of my children and my wife! For this is the Nauglamír, whose name is known to many among Elves and Men; and I bring it to thee out of the dark-ness of Nargothrond, where Finrod thy kinsman left it behind him when he set forth with Beren son of Barahir to fulfil the errand of Thingol of Doriath!'

Then Thingol looked upon the great treasure, and knew it for the Nauglamír, and well did he understand Húrin's intent; but being filled with pity he restrained his wrath, and endured Húrin's scorn. And at the last Melian spoke, and said: 'Húrin Thalion, Morgoth hath bewitched thee; for he that seeth through Morgoth's eyes, will-ing or unwilling, seeth all things crooked. Long was Túrin thy son fostered in the halls of Menegroth, and shown love and honour as the son of the King; and it was not by the King's will nor by mine that he came never back to Doriath. And afterwards thy wife and thy daughter were harboured here with honour and goodwill; and we sought by all means that we might to dissuade Morwen from the road to Nargothrond. With the voice of Morgoth thou dost now upbraid thy friends.'

And hearing the words of Melian Húrin stood moveless, and he gazed long into the eyes of the Queen; and there in Menegroth, defended still by the Girdle of Melian from the darkness of the Enemy, he read the truth of all that was done, and tasted at last the fullness of woe that was measured for him by Morgoth Bauglir. And he spoke no more of what was past, but stooping lifted up the Nauglamír from where it lay before Thingol's chair, and he gave it to him, saying: 'Receive now, lord, the Necklace of the Dwarves, as

a gift from one who has nothing, and as a memorial of Húrin of Dor-
lómin. For now my fate is fulfilled, and the purpose of Morgoth
achieved; but I am his thrall no longer.'

Then he turned away, and passed out from the Thousand Caves,
and all that saw him fell back before his face; and none sought to
withstand his going, nor did any know whither he went. But it is said
that Húrin would not live thereafter, being bereft of all purpose and
desire, and cast himself at last into the western sea; and so ended the
mightiest of the warriors of mortal Men.

But when Húrin was gone from Menegroth, Thingol sat long in
silence, gazing upon the great treasure that lay upon his knees; and it
came into his mind that it should be remade, and in it should be set
the Silmaril. For as the years passed Thingol's thought turned unceasingly to the jewel of Fëanor, and became bound to it, and he
liked not to let it rest even behind the doors of his inmost treasury;
and he was minded now to bear it with him always, waking and sleeping.

In those days the Dwarves still came on their journeys into Beleri-
and from their mansions in Ered Lindon, and passing over Gelion
at Sarn Athrad, the Ford of Stones, they travelled the ancient road to
Doriath; for their skill in the working of metal and stone was very
great, and there was much need of their craft in the halls of Menegroth. But they came now no longer in small parties as aforetime, but
in great companies well armed for their protection in the perilous
lands between Aros and Gelion; and they dwelt in Menegroth at such
times in chambers and smithies set apart for them. At that very time
great craftsmen of Nogrod were lately come into Doriath; and the
King therefore summoning them declared his desire, that if their skill
were great enough they should remake the Nauglamír, and in it set
the Silmaril. Then the Dwarves looked upon the work of their fathers,
and they beheld with wonder the shining jewel of Fëanor; and they
were filled with a great lust to possess them, and carry them off to
their far homes in the mountains. But they dissembled their mind, and
consented to the task.

Long was their labour; and Thingol went down alone to their deep
smithies, and sat ever among them as they worked. In time his desire
was achieved, and the greatest of the works of Elves and Dwarves
were brought together and made one; and its beauty was very great,
for now the countless jewels of the Nauglamír did reflect and cast
abroad in marvellous hues the light of the Silmaril amidmost. Then
Thingol, being alone among them, made to take it up and clasp it

about his neck; but the Dwarves in that moment withheld it from him, and demanded that he yield it up to them, saying: 'By what right does the Elvenking lay claim to the Nauglamír, that was made by our fathers for Finrod Felagund who is dead? It has come to him but by the hand of Húrin the Man of Dor-lómin, who took it as a thief out of the darkness of Nargothrond.' But Thingol perceived their hearts, and saw well that desiring the Silmaril they sought but a pretext and fair cloak for their true intent; and in his wrath and pride he gave no heed to his peril, but spoke to them in scorn, saying: 'How do ye of uncouth race dare to demand aught of me, Elu Thingol, Lord of Beleriand, whose life began by the waters of Cuiviénen years uncounted ere the fathers of the stunted people awoke?' And standing tall and proud among them he bade them with shameful words be gone unrequited out of Doriath.

Then the lust of the Dwarves was kindled to rage by the words of the King; and they rose up about him, and laid hands on him, and slew him as he stood. So died in the deep places of Menegroth Elwë Singollo, King of Doriath, who alone of all the Children of Ilúvatar was joined with one of the Ainur; and he who, alone of the Forsaken Elves, had seen the light of the Trees of Valinor, with his last sight gazed upon the Silmaril.

Then the Dwarves taking the Nauglamír passed out of Menegroth and fled eastwards through Region. But tidings went swiftly through the forest, and few of that company came over Aros, for they were pursued to the death as they sought the eastward road; and the Nauglamír was retaken, and brought back in bitter grief to Melian the Queen. Yet two there were of the slayers of Thingol who escaped from the pursuit on the eastern marches, and returned at last to their city far off in the Blue Mountains; and there in Nogrod they told somewhat of all that had befallen, saying that the Dwarves were slain in Doriath by command of the Elvenking, who thus would cheat them of their reward.

Then great was the wrath and lamentation of the Dwarves of Nogrod for the death of their kin and their great craftsmen, and they tore their beards, and wailed; and long they sat taking thought for vengeance. It is told that they asked aid from Belegost, but it was denied them, and the Dwarves of Belegost sought to dissuade them from their purpose; but their counsel was unavailing, and ere long a great host came forth from Nogrod, and crossing over Gelion marched westward through Beleriand.

Upon Doriath a heavy change had fallen. Melian sat long in silence beside Thingol the King, and her thought passed back into the star-lit years and to their first meeting among the nightingales of Nan Elmoth in ages past; and she knew that her parting from Thingol was the forerunner of a greater parting, and that the doom of Doriath was drawing nigh. For Melian was of the divine race of the Valar, and she was a Maia of great power and wisdom; but for love of Elwë Singollo she took upon herself the form of the Elder Children of Ilúvatar, and in that union she became bound by the chain and tram-mels of the flesh of Arda. In that form she bore to him Lúthien Tinúviel; and in that form she gained a power over the substance of Arda, and by the Girdle of Melian was Doriath defended through long ages from the evils without. But now Thingol lay dead, and his spirit had passed to the halls of Mandos; and with his death a change came also upon Melian. Thus it came to pass that her power was withdrawn in that time from the forests of Neldoreth and Region, and Esgalduin the enchanted river spoke with a different voice, and Doriath lay open to its enemies.

Thereafter Melian spoke to none save to Mablung only, bidding him take heed to the Silmaril, and to send word speedily to Beren and Lúthien in Ossiriand; and she vanished out of Middle-earth, and passed to the land of the Valar beyond the western sea, to muse upon her sorrows in the gardens of Lórien, whence she came, and this tale speaks of her no more.

Thus it was that the host of the Naugrim crossing over Aros passed unhindered into the woods of Doriath; and none withstood them, for they were many and fierce, and the captains of the Grey-elves were cast into doubt and despair, and went hither and thither purposeless. But the Dwarves held on their way, and passed over the great bridge, and entered into Menegroth; and there befell a thing most grievous among the sorrowful deeds of the Elder Days. For there was battle in the Thousand Caves, and many Elves and Dwarves were slain; and it has not been forgotten. But the Dwarves were victorious, and the halls of Thingol were ransacked and plundered. There fell Mablung of the Heavy Hand before the doors of the treasury wherein lay the Nauglamír; and the Silmaril was taken.

At that time Beren and Lúthien yet dwelt in Tol Galen, the Green Isle, in the River Adurant, southernmost of the streams that falling from Ered Lindon flowed down to join with Gelion; and their son Dior Eluchíl had to wife Nimloth, kinswoman of Celeborn, prince of Doriath, who was wedded to the Lady Galadriel. The sons of Dior and Nimloth were Eluréd and Elurín; and a daughter also was born to them, and she was named Elwing, which is Star-spray, for she was born on a night of stars, whose light glittered in the spray of the waterfall of Lanthir Lamath beside her father's house.

Now word went swiftly among the Elves of Ossiriand that a great host of Dwarves bearing gear of war had come down out of the mountains and passed over Gelion at the Ford of Stones. These tidings came soon to Beren and Lúthien; and in that time also a messenger came to them out of Doriath telling of what had befallen there. Then Beren arose and left Tol Galen, and summoning to him Dior his son they went north to the River Ascar; and with them went many of the Green-elves of Ossiriand.

Thus it came to pass that when the Dwarves of Nogrod, returning from Menegroth with diminished host, came again to Sarn Athrad, they were assailed by unseen enemies; for as they climbed up Gelion's banks burdened with the spoils of Doriath, suddenly all the woods were filled with the sound of elven-horns, and shafts sped upon them from every side. There very many of the Dwarves were slain in the first onset; but some escaping from the ambush held together, and fled eastwards towards the mountains. And as they climbed the long slopes beneath Mount Dolmed there came forth the Shepherds of the Trees, and they drove the Dwarves into the shadowy woods of Ered Lindon: whence, it is said, came never one to climb the high passes that led to their homes.

In that battle by Sarn Athrad Beren fought his last fight, and himself slew the Lord of Nogrod, and wrested from him the Necklace of the Dwarves; but he dying laid his curse upon all the treasure. Then Beren gazed in wonder on the selfsame jewel of Fëanor that he had cut from Morgoth's iron crown, now shining set amid gold and gems by the cunning of the Dwarves; and he washed it clean of blood in the waters of the river. And when all was finished the treasure of Doriath was drowned in the River Ascar, and from that time the river was named anew, Rathlóriel, the Goldenbed; but Beren took the Nauglamír and returned to Tol Galen. Little did it ease the grief of Lúthien to learn that the Lord of Nogrod was slain and many Dwarves beside; but it is said and sung that Lúthien wearing that necklace and that immortal jewel was the vision of greatest beauty and glory that has ever been outside the realm of Valinor; and for a little while the Land of the Dead that Live became like a vision of the land of the Valar, and no place has been since so fair, so fruitful, or so filled with light.

Now Dior Thingol's heir bade farewell to Beren and Lúthien, and departing from Lanthir Lamath with Nimloth his wife he came to

Menegroth, and abode there; and with them went their young sons
Eluréd and Elurín, and Elwing their daughter. Then the Sindar
received them with joy, and they arose from the darkness of their
grief for fallen kin and King and for the departure of Melian; and
Dior Eluchíl set himself to raise anew the glory of the kingdom of
Doriath.

There came a night of autumn, and when it grew late, one came and
smote upon the doors of Menegroth, demanding admittance to the
King. He was a lord of the Green-elves hastening from Ossiriand, and
the door-wards brought him to where Dior sat alone in his chamber;
and there in silence he gave to the King a coffer, and took his leave.
But in that coffer lay the Necklace of the Dwarves, wherein was set
the Silmaril; and Dior looking upon it knew it for a sign that Beren
Erchamion and Lúthien Tinúviel had died indeed, and gone where
go the race of Men to a fate beyond the world.

Long did Dior gaze upon the Silmaril, which his father and mother
had brought beyond hope out of the terror of Morgoth; and his
grief was great that death had come upon them so soon. But the
wise have said that the Silmaril hastened their end; for the flame
of the beauty of Lúthien as she wore it was too bright for mortal
lands.

Then Dior arose, and about his neck he clasped the Nauglamír;
and now he appeared as the fairest of all the children of the world,
of threefold race: of the Edain, and of the Eldar, and of the Maiar of
the Blessed Realm.

But now the rumour ran among the scattered Elves of Beleriand
that Dior Thingol's heir wore the Nauglamír, and they said: 'A
Silmaril of Fëanor burns again in the woods of Doriath'; and the
oath of the sons of Fëanor was waked again from sleep. For while
Lúthien wore the Necklace of the Dwarves no Elf would dare to assail
her; but now hearing of the renewal of Doriath and of Dior's pride
the seven gathered again from wandering, and they sent to him to
claim their own.

But Dior returned no answer to the sons of Fëanor; and Celegorm
stirred up his brothers to prepare an assault upon Doriath. They
came at unawares in the middle of winter, and fought with Dior in
the Thousand Caves; and so befell the second slaying of Elf by Elf.
There fell Celegorm by Dior's hand, and there fell Curufin, and dark
Caranthir; but Dior was slain also, and Nimloth his wife, and the
cruel servants of Celegorm seized his young sons and left them to

starve in the forest. Of this Maedhros indeed repented, and sought for them long in the woods of Doriath; but his search was unavailing, and of the fate of Eluréd and Elurín no tale tells.

Thus Doriath was destroyed, and never rose again. But the sons of Fëanor gained not what they sought; for a remnant of the people fled before them, and with them was Elwing Dior's daughter, and they escaped, and bearing with them the Silmaril they came in time to the mouths of the River Sirion by the sea.

# Chapter 23

# OF TUOR AND THE FALL OF GONDOLIN

It has been told that Huor the brother of Húrin was slain in the Battle of Unnumbered Tears; and in the winter of that year Rían his wife bore a child in the wilds of Mithrim, and he was named Tuor, and was taken to foster by Annael of the Grey-elves, who yet lived in those hills. Now when Tuor was sixteen years old the Elves were minded to leave the caves of Androth where they dwelt, and to make their way secretly to the Havens of Sirion in the distant south; but they were assailed by Orcs and Easterlings before they made good their escape, and Tuor was taken captive and enslaved by Lorgan, chief of the Easterlings of Hithlum. For three years he endured that thraldom, but at the end of that time he escaped; and returning to the caves of Androth he dwelt there alone, and did such great hurt to the Easterlings that Lorgan set a price upon his head.

But when Tuor had lived thus in solitude as an outlaw for four years, Ulmo set it in his heart to depart from the land of his fathers, for he had chosen Tuor as the instrument of his designs; and leaving once more the caves of Androth he went westwards across Dor-lómin, and found Annon-in-Gelydh, the Gate of the Noldor, which the people of Turgon built when they dwelt in Nevrast long years before. Thence a dark tunnel led beneath the mountains, and issued into Cirith Ninniach, the Rainbow Cleft, through which a turbulent water ran towards the western sea. Thus it was that Tuor's flight from Hithlum was marked by neither Man nor Orc, and no knowledge of it came to the ears of Morgoth.

And Tuor came into Nevrast, and looking upon Belegaer the Great Sea he was enamoured of it, and the sound of it and the longing for it were ever in his heart and ear, and an unquiet was on him that took him at last into the depths of the realms of Ulmo. Then he dwelt in Nevrast alone, and the summer of that year passed, and the doom of Nargothrond drew near; but when the autumn came he saw seven great swans flying south, and he knew them for a sign that he had tarried overlong, and he followed their flight along the shores of the sea. Thus he came at length to the deserted halls of Vinyamar beneath Mount Taras, and he entered in, and found there the shield and hauberk, and the sword and helm, that Turgon had left there by the command of Ulmo long before; and he arrayed himself in those arms, and went down to the shore. But there came a great storm out of the west, and out of that storm Ulmo the Lord of Waters arose in majesty and spoke to Tuor as he stood beside the sea. And Ulmo bade him depart from that place and seek out the hidden kingdom of Gondolin; and he gave Tuor a great cloak, to mantle him in shadow from the eyes of his enemies.

But in the morning when the storm was passed, Tuor came upon an Elf standing beside the walls of Vinyamar; and he was Voronwë, son of Aranwë, of Gondolin, who sailed in the last ship that Turgon sent into the West. But when that ship returning at last out of the deep ocean foundered in the great storm within sight of the coasts of Middle-earth, Ulmo took him up, alone of all its mariners, and cast him onto the land near Vinyamar; and learning of the command laid upon Tuor by the Lord of Waters Voronwë was filled with wonder, and did not refuse him his guidance to the hidden door of Gondolin. Therefore they set out together from that place, and as the Fell Winter of that year came down upon them out of the north they went warily eastward under the eaves of the Mountains of Shadow.

At length they came in their journeying to the Pools of Ivrin, and looked with grief on the defilement wrought there by the passage of Glaurung the Dragon; but even as they gazed upon it they saw one going northward in haste, and he was a tall Man, clad in black, and bearing a black sword. But they knew not who he was, nor anything of what had befallen in the south; and he passed them by, and they said no word.

And at the last by the power that Ulmo set upon them they came to the hidden door of Gondolin, and passing down the tunnel they reached the inner gate, and were taken by the guard as prisoners. Then they were led up the mighty ravine of Orfalch Echor, barred by seven gates, and brought before Ecthelion of the Fountain, the warden of the great gate at the end of the climbing road; and there Tuor cast aside his cloak, and from the arms that he bore from Vinyamar it was seen that he was in truth one sent by Ulmo. Then Tuor looked down upon the fair vale of Tumladen, set as a green jewel amid the encircling hills; and he saw far off upon the rocky height of Amon Gwareth Gondolin the great, city of seven names, whose fame and glory is mightiest in song of all dwellings of the Elves in the Hither Lands. At the bidding of Ecthelion trumpets were blown on the towers of the great gate, and they echoed in the hills; and far off but clear there came a sound of answering trumpets blown upon the white walls of the city, flushed with the rose of dawn upon the plain.

Thus it was that the son of Huor rode across Tumladen, and came to the gate of Gondolin; and passing up the wide stairways of the city he was brought at last to the Tower of the King, and looked upon the images of the Trees of Valinor. Then Tuor stood before Turgon son of Fingolfin, High King of the Noldor, and upon the King's right hand there stood Maeglin his sister-son, but upon his left hand sat Idril Celebrindal his daughter; and all that heard the voice of Tuor marvelled, doubting that this were in truth a Man of mortal race, for his words were the words of the Lord of Waters that came to him in that hour. And he gave warning to Turgon that the Curse of Mandos now hastened to its fulfilment, when all the works of the Noldor should perish; and he bade him depart, and abandon the fair and mighty city that he had built, and go down Sirion to the sea.

Then Turgon pondered long the counsel of Ulmo, and there came into his mind the words that were spoken to him in Vinyamar: 'Love not too well the work of thy hands and the devices of thy heart; and remember that the true hope of the Noldor lieth in the West, and cometh from the Sea.' But Turgon was become proud, and Gondolin as beautiful as a memory of Elven Tirion, and he trusted still in its secret and impregnable strength, though even a Vala should gainsay it; and after the Nirnaeth Arnoediad the people of that city desired never again to mingle in the woes of Elves and Men without, nor to return through dread and danger into the West. Shut behind their pathless and enchanted hills they suffered none to enter, though he fled from Morgoth hate-pursued; and tidings of the lands beyond came to them faint and far, and they heeded them little. The spies of Angband sought for them in vain; and their dwelling was as a rumour, and a secret that none could find. Maeglin spoke ever against Tuor in the councils of the King, and his words seemed the more weighty in that they went with Turgon's heart; and at the last he rejected the bidding of Ulmo and refused his counsel. But in the warning of the Vala he heard again the words that were spoken before the departing Noldor on the coast of Araman long ago; and the fear of treason was wakened in Turgon's heart. Therefore in that time the very entrance to the hidden door in the Encircling Mountains was caused to be blocked up; and thereafter none went ever forth from Gondolin on any errand of peace or war, while that city stood. Tidings were brought by Thorondor Lord of Eagles of the fall of Nargothrond, and after of the slaying of Thingol and of Dior his heir, and of the ruin of Doriath; but Turgon shut his ear to word of the woes without, and vowed to march never at the side of any son of

Fëanor; and his people he forbade ever to pass the leaguer of the hills.

And Tuor remained in Gondolin, for its bliss and its beauty and the wisdom of its people held him enthralled; and he became mighty in stature and in mind, and learned deeply of the lore of the exiled Elves. Then the heart of Idril was turned to him, and his to her; and Maeglin's secret hatred grew ever greater, for he desired above all things to possess her, the only heir of the King of Gondolin. But so high did Tuor stand in the favour of the King that when he had dwelt there for seven years Turgon did not refuse him even the hand of his daughter; for though he would not heed the bidding of Ulmo, he perceived that the fate of the Noldor was wound with the one whom Ulmo had sent; and he did not forget the words that Huor spoke to him before the host of Gondolin departed from the Battle of Un-numbered Tears.

Then there was made a great and joyful feast, for Tuor had won the hearts of all that people, save only of Maeglin and his secret following; and thus there came to pass the second union of Elves and Men.

In the spring of the year after was born in Gondolin Eärendil Halfelven, the son of Tuor and Idril Celebrindal; and that was five hundred years and three since the coming of the Noldor to Middle-earth. Of surpassing beauty was Eärendil, for a light was in his face as the light of heaven, and he had the beauty and the wisdom of the Eldar and the strength and hardihood of the Men of old; and the Sea spoke ever in his ear and heart, even as with Tuor his father.

Then the days of Gondolin were yet full of joy and peace; and none knew that the region wherein the Hidden Kingdom lay had been at last revealed to Morgoth by the cries of Húrin, when standing in the wilderness beyond the Encircling Mountains and finding no entrance he called on Turgon in despair. Thereafter the thought of Morgoth was bent unceasing on the mountainous land between Anach and the upper waters of Sirion, whither his servants had never passed; yet still no spy or creature out of Angband could come there because of the vigilance of the eagles, and Morgoth was thwarted in the fulfilment of his designs. But Idril Celebrindal was wise and far-seeing, and her heart misgave her, and foreboding crept upon her spirit as a cloud. Therefore in that time she let prepare a secret way, that should lead down from the city and passing out beneath the surface of the plain issue far beyond the walls, northward of Amon Gwareth; and she contrived it that the work was known but to few, and no whisper of it came to Maeglin's ears.

Now on a time, when Eärendil was yet young, Maeglin was lost. For he, as has been told, loved mining and quarrying after metals above all other craft; and he was master and leader of the Elves who worked in the mountains distant from the city, seeking after metals for their smithying of things both of peace and war. But often Maeglin went with few of his folk beyond the leaguer of the hills, and the King knew not that his bidding was defied; and thus it came to pass, as fate willed, that Maeglin was taken prisoner by Orcs, and brought to Angband. Maeglin was no weakling or craven, but the torment wherewith he was threatened cowed his spirit, and he purchased his life and freedom by revealing to Morgoth the very place of Gondolin and the ways whereby it might be found and assailed. Great indeed was the joy of Morgoth, and to Maeglin he promised the lordship of Gondolin as his vassal, and the possession of Idril Celebrindal, when the city should be taken; and indeed desire for Idril and hatred for Tuor led Maeglin the easier to his treachery, most infamous in all the histories of the Elder Days. But Morgoth sent him back to Gondolin, lest any should suspect the betrayal, and so that Maeglin should aid the assault from within, when the hour came; and he abode in the halls of the King with smiling face and evil in his heart, while the darkness gathered ever deeper upon Idril.

At last, in the year when Eärendil was seven years old, Morgoth was ready, and he loosed upon Gondolin his Balrogs, and his Orcs, and his wolves; and with them came dragons of the brood of Glaurung, and they were become now many and terrible. The host of Morgoth came over the northern hills where the height was greatest and the watch least vigilant, and it came at night upon a time of festival, when all the people of Gondolin were upon the walls to await the rising sun, and sing their songs at its uplifting; for the morrow was the great feast that they named the Gates of Summer. But the red light mounted the hills in the north and not in the east; and there was no stay in the advance of the foe until they were beneath the very walls of Gondolin, and the city was beleaguered without hope. Of the deeds of desperate valour there done, by the chieftains of the noble houses and their warriors, and not least by Tuor, much is told in *The Fall of Gondolin*: of the battle of Ecthelion of the Fountain with Gothmog Lord of Balrogs in the very square of the King, where each slew the other, and of the defence of the tower of Turgon by the people of his household, until the tower was overthrown; and mighty was its fall and the fall of Turgon in its ruin.

Tuor sought to rescue Idril from the sack of the city, but Maeglin had laid hands on her, and on Eärendil; and Tuor fought with Maeglin on the walls, and cast him far out, and his body as it fell smote the rocky slopes of Amon Gwareth thrice ere it pitched into the flames below. Then Tuor and Idril led such remnants of the people of Gondolin as they could gather in the confusion of the burning down the secret way which Idril had prepared; and of that passage the captains of Angband knew nothing, and thought not that any fugitives would take a path towards the north and the highest parts of the mountains and the nighest to Angband. The fume of the burning, and the steam of the fair fountains of Gondolin withering in the flame of the dragons of the north, fell upon the vale of Tumladen in mournful mists; and thus was the escape of Tuor and his company aided, for there was still a long and open road to follow from the tunnel's mouth to the foothills of the mountains. Nonetheless they came thither, and beyond hope they climbed, in woe and misery, for the high places were cold and terrible, and they had among them many that were wounded, and women and children.

There was a dreadful pass, Cirith Thoronath it was named, the Eagles' Cleft, where beneath the shadow of the highest peaks a narrow path wound its way; on the right hand it was walled by a precipice, and on the left a dreadful fall leapt into emptiness. Along that narrow way their march was strung, when they were ambushed by Orcs, for Morgoth had set watchers all about the encircling hills; and a Balrog was with them. Then dreadful was their plight, and hardly would they have been saved by the valour of yellow-haired Glorfindel, chief of the House of the Golden Flower of Gondolin, had not Thorondor come timely to their aid.

Many are the songs that have been sung of the duel of Glorfindel with the Balrog upon a pinnacle of rock in that high place; and both fell to ruin in the abyss. But the eagles coming stooped upon the Orcs, and drove them shrieking back; and all were slain or cast into the deeps, so that rumour of the escape from Gondolin came not until long after to Morgoth's ears. Then Thorondor bore up Glorfindel's body out of the abyss, and they buried him in a mound of stones beside the pass; and a green turf came there, and yellow flowers bloomed upon it amid the barrenness of stone, until the world was changed.

Thus led by Tuor son of Huor the remnant of Gondolin passed over the mountains, and came down into the Vale of Sirion; and fleeing southward by weary and dangerous marches they came at length to Nan-tathren, the Land of Willows, for the power of Ulmo yet ran in the great river, and it was about them. There they rested a while, and were healed of their hurts and weariness; but their

sorrow could not be healed. And they made a feast in memory of
Gondolin and of the Elves that had perished there, the maidens, and
the wives, and the warriors of the King; and for Glorfindel the
beloved many were the songs they sang, under the willows of Nan-
tathren in the waning of the year. There Tuor made a song for Eärendil his son, concerning the coming of Ulmo the Lord of Waters to the
shores of Nevrast aforetime; and the sea-longing woke in his heart,
and in his son's also. Therefore Idril and Tuor departed from Nan-
tathren, and went southwards down the river to the sea; and they
dwelt there by the mouths of Sirion, and joined their people to the
company of Elwing Dior's daughter, that had fled thither but a little
while before. And when the tidings came to Balar of the fall of
Gondolin and the death of Turgon, Ereinion Gil-galad son of Fingon was named High King of the Noldor in Middle-earth.

But Morgoth thought that his triumph was fulfilled, recking little
of the sons of Fëanor, and of their oath, which had harmed him
never and turned always to his mightiest aid; and in his black thought
he laughed, regretting not the one Silmaril that he had lost, for by
it as he deemed the last shred of the people of the Eldar should
vanish from Middle-earth and trouble it no more. If he knew of the
dwelling by the waters of Sirion, he gave no sign, biding his time,
and waiting upon the working of oath and lie. Yet by Sirion and the
sea there grew up an Elven-folk, the gleanings of Doriath and Gondolin; and from Balar the mariners of Círdan came among them, and
they took to the waves and the building of ships, dwelling ever nigh
to the coasts of Arvernien, under the shadow of Ulmo's hand.

And it is said that in that time Ulmo came to Valinor out of the
deep waters, and spoke there to the Valar of the need of the Elves;
and he called on them to forgive them, and rescue them from the
overmastering might of Morgoth, and win back the Silmarils, wherein
alone now bloomed the light of the Days of Bliss when the Two
Trees still shone in Valinor. But Manwë moved not; and of the
counsels of his heart what tale shall tell? The wise have said that the
hour was not yet come, and that only one speaking in person for the
cause of both Elves and Men, pleading for pardon on their misdeeds
and pity on their woes, might move the counsels of the Powers; and
the oath of Fëanor perhaps even Manwë could not loose, until it
found its end, and the sons of Fëanor relinquished the Silmarils,
upon which they had laid their ruthless claim. For the light which lit
the Silmarils the Valar themselves had made.

In those days Tuor felt old age creep upon him, and ever a longing for the deeps of the Sea grew stronger in his heart. Therefore he built a great ship, and he named it Eärrámë, which is Sea-Wing; and with Idril Celebrindal he set sail into the sunset and the West, and came no more into any tale or song. But in after days it was sung that Tuor alone of mortal Men was numbered among the elder race, and was joined with the Noldor, whom he loved; and his fate is sundered from the fate of Men.

# Chapter 24

# OF THE VOYAGE OF EÄRENDIL AND THE WAR OF WRATH

Bright Eärendil was then lord of the people that dwelt nigh to Sirion's mouths; and he took to wife Elwing the fair, and she bore to him Elrond and Elros, who are called the Half-elven. Yet Eärendil could not rest, and his voyages about the shores of the Hither Lands eased not his unquiet. Two purposes grew in his heart, blended as one in longing for the wide Sea: he sought to sail thereon, seeking after Tuor and Idril who returned not; and he thought to find perhaps the last shore, and bring ere he died the message of Elves and Men to the Valar in the West, that should move their hearts to pity for the sorrows of Middle-earth.

Now Eärendil became fast in friendship with Círdan the Shipwright, who dwelt on the Isle of Balar with those of his people who escaped from the sack of the Havens of Brithombar and Eglarest. With the aid of Círdan Eärendil built Vingilot, the Foam-flower, fairest of the ships of song; golden were its oars and white its timbers, hewn in the birchwoods of Nimbrethil, and its sails were as the argent moon. In the *Lay of Eärendil* is many a thing sung of his adventures in the deep and in lands untrodden, and in many seas and in many isles; but Elwing was not with him, and she sat in sorrow by the mouths of Sirion.

Eärendil found not Tuor nor Idril, nor came he ever on that journey to the shores of Valinor, defeated by shadows and enchantment, driven by repelling winds, until in longing for Elwing he turned homeward towards the coast of Beleriand. And his heart bade him haste, for a sudden fear had fallen on him out of dreams; and the winds that before he had striven with might not now bear him back as swift as his desire.

Now when first the tidings came to Maedhros that Elwing yet lived, and dwelt in possession of the Silmaril by the mouths of Sirion, he repenting of the deeds in Doriath withheld his hand. But in time the knowledge of their oath unfulfilled returned to torment him and his brothers, and gathering from their wandering hunting-paths they sent messages to the Havens of friendship and yet of stern demand. Then Elwing and the people of Sirion would not yield the jewel which Beren had won and Lúthien had worn, and for which Dior the fair was slain; and least of all while Eärendil their lord was on the sea, for it seemed to them that in the Silmaril lay the healing and the blessing that had come upon their houses and their ships. And so there came to pass the last and cruellest of the slayings of Elf by Elf; and that was the third of the great wrongs achieved by the accursed oath.

For the sons of Fëanor that yet lived came down suddenly upon the exiles of Gondolin and the remnant of Doriath, and destroyed them. In that battle some of their people stood aside, and some few rebelled and were slain upon the other part aiding Elwing against their own lords (for such was the sorrow and confusion in the hearts of the Eldar in those days); but Maedhros and Maglor won the day, though they alone remained thereafter of the sons of Fëanor, for both Amrod and Amras were slain. Too late the ships of Círdan and Gil-galad the High King came hasting to the aid of the Elves of Sirion; and Elwing was gone, and her sons. Then such few of that people as did not perish in the assault joined themselves to Gil-galad, and went with him to Balar; and they told that Elros and Elrond were taken captive, but Elwing with the Silmaril upon her breast had cast herself into the sea.

Thus Maedhros and Maglor gained not the jewel; but it was not lost. For Ulmo bore up Elwing out of the waves, and he gave her the likeness of a great white bird, and upon her breast there shone as a star the Silmaril, as she flew over the water to seek Eärendil her beloved. On a time of night Eärendil at the helm of his ship saw her come towards him, as a white cloud exceeding swift beneath the moon, as a star over the sea moving in strange course, a pale flame on wings of storm. And it is sung that she fell from the air upon the timbers of Vingilot, in a swoon, nigh unto death for the urgency of her speed, and Eärendil took her to his bosom; but in the morning with marvelling eyes he beheld his wife in her own form beside him with her hair upon his face, and she slept.

Great was the sorrow of Eärendil and Elwing for the ruin of the havens of Sirion, and the captivity of their sons, and they feared that they would be slain; but it was not so. For Maglor took pity upon Elros and Elrond, and he cherished them, and love grew after between them, as little might be thought; but Maglor's heart was sick and weary with the burden of the dreadful oath.

Yet Eärendil saw now no hope left in the lands of Middle-earth, and he turned again in despair and came not home, but sought back once more to Valinor with Elwing at his side. He stood now most often at the prow of Vingilot, and the Silmaril was bound upon his brow; and ever its light grew greater as they drew into the West. And the wise have said that it was by reason of the power of that holy jewel that they came in time to waters that no vessels save those of the Teleri had known; and they came to the Enchanted Isles and escaped their enchantment; and they came into the Shadowy Seas and passed their shadows, and they looked upon Tol Eressëa the Lonely Isle, but tarried not; and at the last they cast anchor in the Bay of Eldamar, and the Teleri saw the coming of that ship out of the East and they were amazed, gazing from afar upon the light of the Silmaril, and it was very great. Then Eärendil, first of living Men, landed on the immortal shores; and he spoke there to Elwing and to those that were with him, and they were three mariners who had sailed all the seas besides him: Falathar, Erellont, and Aerandir were their names. And Eärendil said to them: 'Here none but myself shall set foot, lest you fall under the wrath of the Valar. But that peril I will take on myself alone, for the sake of the Two Kindreds.'

But Elwing answered: 'Then would our paths be sundered for ever; but all thy perils I will take on myself also.' And she leaped into the white foam and ran towards him; but Eärendil was sorrowful, for he feared the anger of the Lords of the West upon any of Middle-earth that should dare to pass the leaguer of Aman. And there they bade farewell to the companions of their voyage, and were taken from them for ever.

Then Eärendil said to Elwing: 'Await me here; for one only may bring the message that it is my fate to bear.' And he went up alone into the land, and came into the Calacirya, and it seemed to him empty and silent; for even as Morgoth and Ungoliant came in ages past, so now Eärendil had come at a time of festival, and wellnigh all the Elvenfolk were gone to Valimar, or were gathered in the halls of Manwë upon Taniquetil, and few were left to keep watch upon the walls of Tirion.

But some there were who saw him from afar, and the great light that he bore; and they went in haste to Valimar. But Eärendil climbed the green hill of Túna and found it bare; and he entered into the streets of Tirion, and they were empty; and his heart was heavy, for he feared that some evil had come even to the Blessed Realm. He walked in the deserted ways of Tirion, and the dust upon his raiment and his shoes was a dust of diamonds, and he shone and glistened as he climbed the long white stairs. And he called aloud in many tongues, both of Elves and Men, but there were none to answer him. Therefore he turned back at last towards the sea; but even as he took the shoreward road one stood upon the hill and called to him in a great voice, crying:

'Hail Eärendil, of mariners most renowned, the looked for that cometh at unawares, the longed for that cometh beyond hope! Hail Eärendil, bearer of light before the Sun and Moon! Splendour of the Children of Earth, star in the darkness, jewel in the sunset, radiant in the morning!'

That voice was the voice of Eönwë, herald of Manwë, and he came from Valimar, and summoned Eärendil to come before the Powers of Arda. And Eärendil went into Valinor and to the halls of Valimar, and never again set foot upon the lands of Men. Then the Valar took counsel together, and they summoned Ulmo from the deeps of the sea; and Eärendil stood before their faces, and delivered the errand of the Two Kindreds. Pardon he asked for the Noldor and pity for their great sorrows, and mercy upon Men and Elves and succour in their need. And his prayer was granted.

It is told among the Elves that after Eärendil had departed, seeking Elwing his wife, Mandos spoke concerning his fate; and he said: 'Shall mortal Man step living upon the undying lands, and yet live?' But Ulmo said: 'For this he was born into the world. And say unto me: whether is he Eärendil Tuor's son of the line of Hador, or the son of Idril, Turgon's daughter, of the Elven-house of Finwë?' And Mandos answered: 'Equally the Noldor, who went wilfully into exile, may not return hither.'

But when all was spoken, Manwë gave judgement, and he said: 'In this matter the power of doom is given to me. The peril that he ventured for love of the Two Kindreds shall not fall upon Eärendil, nor shall it fall upon Elwing his wife, who entered into peril for love of him; but they shall not walk again ever among Elves or Men in the Outer Lands. And this is my decree concerning them: to Eärendil and to Elwing, and to their sons, shall be given leave each to choose freely to which kindred their fates shall be joined, and under which kindred they shall be judged.'

Now when Eärendil was long time gone Elwing became lonely and afraid; and wandering by the margin of the sea she came near to Alqualondë, where lay the Telerin fleets. There the Teleri befriended her, and they listened to her tales of Doriath and Gondolin and the griefs of Beleriand, and they were filled with pity and wonder; and there Eärendil returning found her, at the Haven of the Swans. But ere long they were summoned to Valimar; and there the decree of the Elder King was declared to them.

Then Eärendil said to Elwing: 'Choose thou, for now I am weary of the world.' And Elwing chose to be judged among the Firstborn Children of Ilúvatar, because of Lúthien; and for her sake Eärendil chose alike, though his heart was rather with the kindred of Men and the people of his father. Then at the bidding of the Valar Eönwë went to the shore of Aman, where the companions of Eärendil still remained, awaiting tidings; and he took a boat, and the three mariners were set therein, and the Valar drove them away into the East with a great wind. But they took Vingilot, and hallowed it, and bore it away through Valinor to the uttermost rim of the world; and there it passed through the Door of Night and was lifted up even into the oceans of heaven.

Now fair and marvellous was that vessel made, and it was filled with a wavering flame, pure and bright; and Eärendil the Mariner sat at the helm, glistening with dust of elven-gems, and the Silmaril was bound upon his brow. Far he journeyed in that ship, even into the starless voids; but most often was he seen at morning or at evening, glimmering in sunrise or sunset, as he came back to Valinor from voyages beyond the confines of the world.

On those journeys Elwing did not go, for she might not endure the cold and the pathless voids, and she loved rather the earth and the sweet winds that blow on sea and hill. Therefore there was built for her a white tower northward upon the borders of the Sundering Seas; and thither at times all the sea-birds of the earth repaired. And it is said that Elwing learned the tongues of birds, who herself had once worn their shape; and they taught her the craft of flight, and her wings were of white and silver-grey. And at times, when Eärendil returning drew near again to Arda, she would fly to meet him, even as she had flown long ago, when she was rescued from the sea. Then the far-sighted among the Elves that dwelt in the Lonely Isle would see her like a white bird, shining, rose-stained in the sunset, as she soared in joy to greet the coming of Vingilot to haven.

Now when first Vingilot was set to sail in the seas of heaven, it rose unlooked for, glittering and bright; and the people of Middle-earth beheld it from afar and wondered, and they took it for a sign, and called it Gil-Estel, the Star of High Hope. And when this new star was seen at evening, Maedhros spoke to Maglor his brother, and he said: 'Surely that is a Silmaril that shines now in the West?'

And Maglor answered: 'If it be truly the Silmaril which we saw cast into the sea that rises again by the power of the Valar, then let us be glad; for its glory is seen now by many, and is yet secure from all evil.' Then the Elves looked up, and despaired no longer; but Morgoth was filled with doubt.

Yet it is said that Morgoth looked not for the assault that came upon him from the West; for so great was his pride become that he deemed that none would ever again come with open war against him.

Moreover he thought that he had for ever estranged the Noldor from the Lords of the West, and that content in their blissful realm the Valar would heed no more his kingdom in the world without; for to him that is pitiless the deeds of pity are ever strange and beyond reckoning. But the host of the Valar prepared for battle; and beneath their white banners marched the Vanyar, the people of Ingwë, and those also of the Noldor who never departed from Valinor, whose leader was Finarfin the son of Finwë. Few of the Teleri were willing to go forth to war, for they remembered the slaying at the Swanhaven, and the rape of their ships; but they hearkened to Elwing, who was the daughter of Dior Eluchíl and come of their own kindred, and they sent mariners enough to sail the ships that bore the host of Valinor east over the sea. Yet they stayed aboard their vessels, and none of them set foot upon the Hither Lands.

Of the march of the host of the Valar to the north of Middle-earth little is said in any tale; for among them went none of those Elves who had dwelt and suffered in the Hither Lands, and who made the histories of those days that still are known; and tidings of these things they only learned long afterwards from their kinsfolk in Aman. But at the last the might of Valinor came up out of the West, and the challenge of the trumpets of Eönwë filled the sky; and Beleriand was ablaze with the glory of their arms, for the host of the Valar were arrayed in forms young and fair and terrible, and the mountains rang beneath their feet.

The meeting of the hosts of the West and of the North is named the Great Battle, and the War of Wrath. There was marshalled the whole power of the Throne of Morgoth, and it had become great beyond count, so that Anfauglith could not contain it; and all the North was aflame with war.

But it availed him not. The Balrogs were destroyed, save some few that fled and hid themselves in caverns inaccessible at the roots of the earth; and the uncounted legions of the Orcs perished like straw in a great fire, or were swept like shrivelled leaves before a burning wind. Few remained to trouble the world for long years after. And such few as were left of the three houses of the Elf-friends, Fathers of Men, fought upon the part of the Valar; and they were avenged in those days for Baragund and Barahir, Galdor and Gundor, Huor and Húrin, and many others of their lords. But a great part of the sons of Men, whether of the people of Uldor or others new-come out of the east, marched with the Enemy; and the Elves do not forget it.

Then, seeing that his hosts were overthrown and his power dispersed, Morgoth quailed, and he dared not to come forth himself. But he loosed upon his foes the last desperate assault that he had prepared, and out of the pits of Angband there issued the winged dragons, that had not before been seen; and so sudden and ruinous was the onset of that dreadful fleet that the host of the Valar was driven back, for the coming of the dragons was with great thunder, and lightning, and a tempest of fire.

But Eärendil came, shining with white flame, and about Vingilot were gathered all the great birds of heaven and Thorondor was their captain, and there was battle in the air all the day and through a dark night of doubt. Before the rising of the sun Eärendil slew Ancalagon the Black, the mightiest of the dragon-host, and cast him from the sky; and he fell upon the towers of Thangorodrim, and they were broken in his ruin. Then the sun rose, and the host of the Valar prevailed, and well-nigh all the dragons were destroyed; and all the pits of Morgoth were broken and unroofed, and the might of the Valar descended into the deeps of the earth. There Morgoth stood at last at bay, and yet unvaliant. He fled into the deepest of his mines, and sued for peace and pardon; but his feet were hewn from under him, and he was hurled upon his face. Then he was bound with the chain Angainor which he had worn aforetime, and his iron crown they beat into a collar for his neck, and his head was bowed upon his knees. And the two Silmarils which remained to Morgoth were taken from his crown, and they shone unsullied beneath the sky; and Eönwë took them, and guarded them.

Thus an end was made of the power of Angband in the North, and the evil realm was brought to naught; and out of the deep prisons a multitude of slaves came forth beyond all hope into the light of day, and they looked upon a world that was changed. For so great was the fury of those adversaries that the northern regions of the western world were rent asunder, and the sea roared in through many chasms, and there was confusion and great noise; and rivers perished or found new paths, and the valleys were upheaved and the hills trod down; and Sirion was no more.

Then Eönwë as herald of the Elder King summoned the Elves of Beleriand to depart from Middle-earth. But Maedhros and Maglor would not hearken, and they prepared, though now with weariness and loathing, to attempt in despair the fulfilment of their oath; for they would have given battle for the Silmarils, were they withheld, even against the victorious host of Valinor, even though they stood alone against all the world. And they sent a message therefore to

Eönwë, bidding him yield up now those jewels which of old Fëanor their father made and Morgoth stole from him.

But Eönwë answered that the right to the work of their father, which the sons of Fëanor formerly possessed, had now perished, because of their many and merciless deeds, being blinded by their oath, and most of all because of their slaying of Dior and the assault upon the Havens. The light of the Silmarils should go now into the West, whence it came in the beginning; and to Valinor must Maedhros and Maglor return, and there abide the judgement of the Valar, by whose decree alone would Eönwë yield the jewels from his charge. Then Maglor desired indeed to submit, for his heart was sorrowful, and he said: 'The oath says not that we may not bide our time, and it may be that in Valinor all shall be forgiven and forgot, and we shall come into our own in peace.'

But Maedhros answered that if they returned to Aman but the favour of the Valar were withheld from them, then their oath would still remain, but its fulfilment be beyond all hope; and he said: 'Who can tell to what dreadful doom we shall come, if we disobey the Powers in their own land, or purpose ever to bring war again into their holy realm?'

Yet Maglor still held back, saying: 'If Manwë and Varda themselves deny the fulfilment of an oath to which we named them in witness, is it not made void?'

And Maedhros answered: 'But how shall our voices reach to Ilúvatar beyond the Circles of the World? And by Ilúvatar we swore in our madness, and called the Everlasting Darkness upon us, if we kept not our word. Who shall release us?'

'If none can release us,' said Maglor, 'then indeed the Everlasting Darkness shall be our lot, whether we keep our oath or break it; but less evil shall we do in the breaking.'

Yet he yielded at last to the will of Maedhros, and they took counsel together how they should lay hands on the Silmarils. And they disguised themselves, and came in the night to the camp of Eönwë, and crept into the place where the Silmarils were guarded; and they slew the guards, and laid hands on the jewels. Then all the camp was raised against them, and they prepared to die, defending themselves until the last. But Eönwë would not permit the slaying of the sons of Fëanor; and departing unfought they fled far away. Each of them took to himself a Silmaril, for they said: 'Since one is lost to us, and but two remain, and we two alone of our brothers, so is it plain that fate would have us share the heirlooms of our father.'

But the jewel burned the hand of Maedhros in pain unbearable;

and he perceived that it was as Eönwë had said, and that his right thereto had become void, and that the oath was vain. And being in anguish and despair he cast himself into a gaping chasm filled with fire, and so ended; and the Silmaril that he bore was taken into the bosom of the Earth.

And it is told of Maglor that he could not endure the pain with which the Silmaril tormented him; and he cast it at last into the Sea, and thereafter he wandered ever upon the shores, singing in pain and regret beside the waves. For Maglor was mighty among the singers of old, named only after Daeron of Doriath; but he came never back among the people of the Elves. And thus it came to pass that the Silmarils found their long homes: one in the airs of heaven, and one in the fires of the heart of the world, and one in the deep waters.

In those days there was a great building of ships upon the shores of the Western Sea; and thence in many a fleet the Eldar set sail into the West, and came never back to the lands of weeping and of war. And the Vanyar returned beneath their white banners, and were borne in triumph to Valinor; but their joy in victory was diminished, for they returned without the Silmarils from Morgoth's crown, and they knew that those jewels could not be found or brought together again unless the world be broken and remade.

And when they came into the West the Elves of Beleriand dwelt upon Tol Eressëa, the Lonely Isle, that looks both west and east; whence they might come even to Valinor. They were admitted again to the love of Manwë and the pardon of the Valar; and the Teleri forgave their ancient grief, and the curse was laid to rest.

Yet not all the Eldalië were willing to forsake the Hither Lands where they had long suffered and long dwelt; and some lingered many an age in Middle-earth. Among those were Círdan the Shipwright, and Celeborn of Doriath, with Galadriel his wife, who alone remained of those who led the Noldor to exile in Beleriand. In Middle-earth dwelt also Gil-galad the High King, and with him was Elrond Half-elven, who chose, as was granted to him, to be numbered among the Eldar; but Elros his brother chose to abide with Men. And from these brethren alone has come among Men the blood of the Firstborn and a strain of the spirits divine that were before Arda; for they were the sons of Elwing, Dior's daughter, Lúthien's son, child of Thingol and Melian; and Eärendil their father was the son of Idril Celebrindal, Turgon's daughter of Gondolin.

But Morgoth himself the Valar thrust through the Door of Night beyond the Walls of the World, into the Timeless Void; and a guard is set for ever on those walls, and Eärendil keeps watch upon the ramparts of the sky. Yet the lies that Melkor, the mighty and accursed, Morgoth Bauglir, the Power of Terror and of Hate, sowed in the hearts of Elves and Men are a seed that does not die and cannot be destroyed; and ever and anon it sprouts anew, and will bear dark fruit even unto the latest days.

Here ends the SILMARILLION. If it has passed from the high and the beautiful to darkness and ruin, that was of old the fate of Arda Marred; and if any change shall come and the Marring be amended, Manwë and Varda may know; but they have not revealed it, and it is not declared in the dooms of Mandos.

# AKALLABÊTH

# AKALLABÊTH

## The Downfall of Númenor

It is said by the Eldar that Men came into the world in the time of the Shadow of Morgoth, and they fell swiftly under his dominion; for he sent his emissaries among them, and they listened to his evil and cunning words, and they worshipped the Darkness and yet feared it. But there were some that turned from evil and left the lands of their kindred, and wandered ever westward; for they had heard a rumour that in the West there was a light which the Shadow could not dim. The servants of Morgoth pursued them with hatred, and their ways were long and hard; yet they came at last to the lands that look upon the Sea, and they entered Beleriand in the days of the War of the Jewels. The Edain these were named in the Sindarin tongue; and they became friends and allies of the Eldar, and did deeds of great valour in the war against Morgoth.

Of them was sprung, upon the side of his fathers, Bright Eärendil; and in the *Lay of Eärendil* it is told how at the last, when the victory of Morgoth was almost complete, he built his ship Vingilot, that Men called Rothinzil, and voyaged upon the unsailed seas, seeking ever for Valinor; for he desired to speak before the Powers on behalf of the Two Kindreds, that the Valar might have pity on them and send them help in their uttermost need. Therefore by Elves and Men he is called Eärendil the Blessed, for he achieved his quest after long labours and many perils, and from Valinor there came the host of the Lords of the West. But Eärendil came never back to the lands that he had loved.

In the Great Battle when at last Morgoth was overthrown and Thangorodrim was broken, the Edain alone of the kindreds of Men fought for the Valar, whereas many others fought for Morgoth. And after the victory of the Lords of the West those of the evil Men who were not destroyed fled back into the east, where many of their race were still wandering in the unharvested lands, wild and lawless, refusing alike the summons of the Valar and of Morgoth. And the evil Men came among them, and cast over them a shadow of fear, and they took them for kings. Then the Valar forsook for a time the Men of Middle-earth who had refused their summons and had taken the friends of Morgoth to be their masters; and Men dwelt in darkness and were troubled by many evil things that Morgoth had devised in the days of his dominion: demons, and dragons, and misshapen beasts, and the unclean Orcs that are mockeries of the Children of Ilúvatar. And the lot of Men was unhappy.

But Manwë put forth Morgoth and shut him beyond the World in the Void that is without; and he cannot himself return again into the World, present and visible, while the Lords of the West are still enthroned. Yet the seeds that he had planted still grew and sprouted, bearing evil fruit, if any would tend them. For his will remained and guided his servants, moving them ever to thwart the will of the Valar and to destroy those that obeyed them. This the Lords of the West knew full well. When therefore Morgoth had been thrust forth, they held council concerning the ages that should come after. The Eldar they summoned to return into the West, and those that hearkened to the summons dwelt in the Isle of Eressëa; and there is in that land a haven that is named Avallónë, for it is of all cities the nearest to Valinor, and the tower of Avallónë is the first sight that the mariner beholds when at last he draws nigh to the Undying Lands over the leagues of the Sea. To the Fathers of Men of the three faithful houses rich reward also was given. Eönwë came among them and taught them; and they were given wisdom and power and life more enduring than any others of mortal race have possessed. A land was made for the Edain to dwell in, neither part of Middle-earth nor of Valinor, for it was sundered from either by a wide sea; yet it was nearer to Valinor. It was raised by Ossë out of the depths of the Great Water, and it was established by Aulë and enriched by Yavanna; and the Eldar brought thither flowers and fountains out of Tol Eressëa. That land the Valar called Andor, the Land of Gift; and the Star of Eärendil shone bright in the West as a token that all was made ready, and as a guide over the sea; and Men marvelled to see that silver flame in the paths of the Sun.

Then the Edain set sail upon the deep waters, following the Star; and the Valar laid a peace upon the sea for many days, and sent sunlight and a sailing wind, so that the waters glittered before the eyes of the Edain like rippling glass, and the foam flew like snow before the stems of their ships. But so bright was Rothinzil that even at morning Men could see it glimmering in the West, and in the cloudless night it shone alone, for no other star could stand beside it. And setting their course towards it the Edain came at last over leagues of sea and saw afar the land that was prepared for them, Andor, the Land of

Gift, shimmering in a golden haze. Then they went up out of the sea
and found a country fair and fruitful, and they were glad. And they
called that land Elenna, which is Starwards; but also Anadûnê,
which is Westernesse, Númenórë in the High Eldarin tongue.

This was the beginning of that people that in the Grey-elven speech
are called the Dúnedain: the Númenóreans, Kings among Men. But
they did not thus escape from the doom of death that Ilúvatar had
set upon all Mankind, and they were mortal still, though their years
were long, and they knew no sickness, ere the shadow fell upon them.
Therefore they grew wise and glorious, and in all things more like
to the Firstborn than any other of the kindreds of Men; and they were
tall, taller than the tallest of the sons of Middle-earth; and the light
of their eyes was like the bright stars. But their numbers increased
only slowly in the land, for though daughters and sons were born to
them, fairer than their fathers, yet their children were few.

Of old the chief city and haven of Númenor was in the midst of its
western coasts, and it was called Andúnië because it faced the sunset.
But in the midst of the land was a mountain tall and steep, and it was
named the Meneltarma, the Pillar of Heaven, and upon it was a high
place that was hallowed to Eru Ilúvatar, and it was open and unroofed,
and no other temple or fane was there in the land of the Númenóreans. At the feet of the mountain were built the tombs of the Kings,
and hard by upon a hill was Armenelos, fairest of cities, and there
stood the tower and the citadel that was raised by Elros son of Eärendil, whom the Valar appointed to be the first King of the Dúnedain.

Now Elros and Elrond his brother were descended from the Three
Houses of the Edain, but in part also both from the Eldar and the
Maiar; for Idril of Gondolin and Lúthien daughter of Melian were
their foremothers. The Valar indeed may not withdraw the gift of
death, which comes to Men from Ilúvatar, but in the matter of the
Half-elven Ilúvatar gave to them the judgement; and they judged
that to the sons of Eärendil should be given choice of their own destiny. And Elrond chose to remain with the Firstborn, and to him the
life of the Firstborn was granted. But to Elros, who chose to be a
king of Men, still a great span of years was allotted, many times that
of the Men of Middle-earth; and all his line, the kings and lords of
the royal house, had long life even according to the measure of the
Númenóreans. But Elros lived five hundred years, and ruled the
Númenóreans four hundred years and ten.

Thus the years passed, and while Middle-earth went backward and
light and wisdom faded, the Dúnedain dwelt under the protection of
the Valar and in the friendship of the Eldar, and they increased in

stature both of mind and body. For though this people used still their own speech, their kings and lords knew and spoke also the Elven tongue, which they had learned in the days of their alliance, and thus they held converse still with the Eldar, whether of Eressëa or of the westlands of Middle-earth. And the loremasters among them learned also the High Eldarin tongue of the Blessed Realm, in which much story and song was preserved from the beginning of the world; and they made letters and scrolls and books, and wrote in them many things of wisdom and wonder in the high tide of their realm, of which all is now forgot. So it came to pass that, beside their own names, all the lords of the Númenóreans had also Eldarin names; and the like with the cities and fair places that they founded in Númenor and on the shores of the Hither Lands.

For the Dúnedain became mighty in crafts, so that if they had had the mind they could easily have surpassed the evil kings of Middle-earth in the making of war and the forging of weapons; but they were become men of peace. Above all arts they nourished ship-building and sea-craft, and they became mariners whose like shall never be again since the world was diminished; and voyaging upon the wide seas was the chief feat and adventure of their hardy men in the gallant days of their youth.

But the Lords of Valinor forbade them to sail so far westward that the coasts of Númenor could no longer be seen; and for long the Dúnedain were content, though they did not fully understand the purpose of this ban. But the design of Manwë was that the Númenóreans should not be tempted to seek for the Blessed Realm, nor desire to overpass the limits set to their bliss, becoming enamoured of the immortality of the Valar and the Eldar and the lands where all things endure.

For in those days Valinor still remained in the world visible, and there Ilúvatar permitted the Valar to maintain upon Earth an abiding place, a memorial of that which might have been if Morgoth had not cast his shadow on the world. This the Númenóreans knew full well; and at times, when all the air was clear and the sun was in the east, they would look out and descry far off in the west a city white-shining on a distant shore, and a great harbour and a tower. For in those days the Númenóreans were far-sighted; yet even so it was only the keenest eyes among them that could see this vision, from the Meneltarma, maybe, or from some tall ship that lay off their western coast as far as it was lawful for them to go. For they did not dare to break the Ban of the Lords of the West. But the wise among them knew that this distant land was not indeed the Blessed Realm of

Valinor, but was Avallónë, the haven of the Eldar upon Eressëa, easternmost of the Undying Lands. And thence at times the First-born still would come sailing to Númenor in oarless boats, as white birds flying from the sunset. And they brought to Númenor many gifts: birds of song, and fragrant flowers, and herbs of great virtue. And a seedling they brought of Celeborn, the White Tree that grew in the midst of Eressëa; and that was in its turn a seedling of Gala-thilion the Tree of Túna, the image of Telperion that Yavanna gave to the Eldar in the Blessed Realm. And the tree grew and blossomed in the courts of the King in Armenelos; Nimloth it was named, and flowered in the evening, and the shadows of night it filled with its fragrance.

Thus it was that because of the Ban of the Valar the voyages of the Dúnedain in those days went ever eastward and not westward, from the darkness of the North to the heats of the South, and beyond the South to the Nether Darkness; and they came even into the inner seas, and sailed about Middle-earth and glimpsed from their high prows the Gates of Morning in the East. And the Dúnedain came at times to the shores of the Great Lands, and they took pity on the forsaken world of Middle-earth; and the Lords of Númenor set foot again upon the western shores in the Dark Years of Men, and none yet dared to withstand them. For most of the Men of that age that sat under the Shadow were now grown weak and fearful. And coming among them the Númenóreans taught them many things. Corn and wine they brought, and they instructed Men in the sowing of seed and the grinding of grain, in the hewing of wood and the shaping of stone, and in the ordering of their life, such as it might be in the lands of swift death and little bliss.

Then the Men of Middle-earth were comforted, and here and there upon the western shores the houseless woods drew back, and Men shook off the yoke of the offspring of Morgoth, and unlearned their terror of the dark. And they revered the memory of the tall Sea-kings, and when they had departed they called them gods, hoping for their return; for at that time the Númenóreans dwelt never long in Middle-earth, nor made there as yet any habitation of their own. Eastward they must sail, but ever west their hearts returned.

Now this yearning grew ever greater with the years; and the Númenóreans began to hunger for the undying city that they saw from afar, and the desire of everlasting life, to escape from death and the ending of delight, grew strong upon them; and ever as their power and glory grew greater their unquiet increased. For though the Valar had rewarded the Dúnedain with long life, they could not take from them the weariness of the world that comes at last, and they died, even their kings of the seed of Eärendil; and the span of their lives was brief in the eyes of the Eldar. Thus it was that a shadow fell upon them: in which maybe the will of Morgoth was at work that still moved in the world. And the Númenóreans began to murmur, at first in their hearts, and then in open words, against the doom of Men, and most of all against the Ban which forbade them to sail into the West.

And they said among themselves: 'Why do the Lords of the West sit there in peace unending, while we must die and go we know not whither, leaving our home and all that we have made? And the Eldar die not, even those that rebelled against the Lords. And since we have mastered all seas, and no water is so wild or so wide that our ships cannot overcome it, why should we not go to Avallónë and greet there our friends?'

And some there were who said: 'Why should we not go even to Aman, and taste there, were it but for a day, the bliss of the Powers? Have we not become mighty among the people of Arda?'

The Eldar reported these words to the Valar, and Manwë was grieved, seeing a cloud gather on the noon-tide of Númenor. And he sent messengers to the Dúnedain, who spoke earnestly to the King, and to all who would listen, concerning the fate and fashion of the world.

'The Doom of the World,' they said, 'One alone can change who made it. And were you so to voyage that escaping all deceits and snares you came indeed to Aman, the Blessed Realm, little would it profit you. For it is not the land of Manwë that makes its people deathless, but the Deathless that dwell therein have hallowed the land; and there you would but wither and grow weary the sooner, as moths in a light too strong and steadfast.'

But the King said: 'And does not Eärendil, my forefather, live? Or is he not in the land of Aman?'

To which they answered: 'You know that he has a fate apart, and was adjudged to the Firstborn who die not; yet this also is his doom that he can never return again to mortal lands. Whereas you and your people are not of the Firstborn, but are mortal Men as Ilúvatar made you. Yet it seems that you desire now to have the good of both kindreds, to sail to Valinor when you will, and to return when you please to your homes. That cannot be. Nor can the Valar take away the gifts of Ilúvatar. The Eldar, you say, are unpunished, and even those who rebelled do not die. Yet that is to them neither reward nor punishment, but the fulfilment of their being. They cannot escape, and are bound to this world, never to leave it so long as it lasts, for its life is theirs. And you are punished for the rebellion of Men, you say, in which you had small part, and so it is that you die. But that was not at first appointed for a punishment. Thus you escape, and leave the world, and are not bound to it, in hope or in weariness. Which of us therefore should envy the others?'

And the Númenóreans answered: 'Why should we not envy the Valar, or even the least of the Deathless? For of us is required a blind trust, and a hope without assurance, knowing not what lies before us in a little while. And yet we also love the Earth and would not lose it.'

Then the Messengers said: 'Indeed the mind of Ilúvatar concerning you is not known to the Valar, and he has not revealed all things that are to come. But this we hold to be true, that your home is not here, neither in the Land of Aman nor anywhere within the Circles of the World. And the Doom of Men, that they should depart, was at first a gift of Ilúvatar. It became a grief to them only because coming under the shadow of Morgoth it seemed to them that they were surrounded by a great darkness, of which they were afraid; and some grew wilful and proud and would not yield, until life was reft from them. We who bear the ever-mounting burden of the years do not clearly understand this; but if that grief has returned to trouble you, as you say, then we fear that the Shadow arises once more and grows again in your hearts. Therefore, though you be the Dúnedain, fairest of Men, who escaped from the Shadow of old and fought valiantly against it, we say to you: Beware! The will of Eru may not be gainsaid; and the Valar bid you earnestly not to withhold the trust to which you are called, lest soon it become again a bond by which you are constrained. Hope rather that in the end even the least of your desires shall have fruit. The love of Arda was set in your hearts by Ilúvatar, and he does not plant to no purpose. Nonetheless, many ages of Men unborn may pass ere that purpose is made known; and to you it will be revealed and not to the Valar.'

These things took place in the days of Tar-Ciryatan the Ship-builder, and of Tar-Atanamir his son; and they were proud men, eager for wealth, and they laid the men of Middle-earth under tribute, taking now rather than giving. It was to Tar-Atanamir that the Messengers came; and he was the thirteenth King, and in his day the Realm of Númenor had endured for more than two thousand years, and was come to the zenith of its bliss, if not yet of its power. But Atanamir was ill pleased with the counsel of the Messengers and gave little heed to it, and the greater part of his people followed him; for they wished still to escape death in their own day, not waiting upon hope. And Atanamir lived to a great age, clinging to his life beyond the end of all joy; and he was the first of the Númenóreans to do this, refusing to depart until he was witless and unmanned, and denying to his son the kingship at the height of his days. For the Lords of Númenor had been wont to wed late in their long lives and to depart and leave the mastery to their sons when these were come to full stature of body and mind.

Then Tar-Ancalimon, son of Atanamir, became King, and he was of like mind; and in his day the people of Númenor became divided. On the one hand was the greater party, and they were called the King's Men, and they grew proud and were estranged from the Eldar and the Valar. And on the other hand was the lesser party, and they were called the Elendili, the Elf-friends; for though they remained loyal indeed to the King and the House of Elros, they wished to keep the friendship of the Eldar, and they hearkened to the counsel of the Lords of the West. Nonetheless even they, who named themselves the Faithful, did not wholly escape from the affliction of their people, and they were troubled by the thought of death.

Thus the bliss of Westernesse became diminished; but still its might and splendour increased. For the kings and their people had not yet abandoned wisdom, and if they loved the Valar no longer at least they still feared them. They did not dare openly to break the Ban or to sail beyond the limits that had been appointed. Eastwards still they steered their tall ships. But the fear of death grew ever darker upon them, and they delayed it by all means that they could; and they began to build great houses for their dead, while their wise men laboured unceasingly to discover if they might the secret of recalling life, or at the least of the prolonging of Men's days. Yet they achieved only the art of preserving incorrupt the dead flesh of Men, and they filled all the land with silent tombs in which the thought of death was enshrined in the darkness. But those that lived turned the more eagerly to pleasure and revelry, desiring ever more goods and more riches; and after the days of Tar-Ancalimon the offering of the first fruits to Eru was neglected, and men went seldom any more to the Hallow upon the heights of Meneltarma in the midst of the land.

Thus it came to pass in that time that the Númenóreans first made great settlements upon the west shores of the ancient lands; for their own land seemed to them shrunken, and they had no rest or content therein, and they desired now wealth and dominion in Middle-earth, since the West was denied. Great harbours and strong towers they made, and there many of them took up their abode; but they appeared now rather as lords and masters and gatherers of tribute than as helpers and teachers. And the great ships of the Númenóreans were borne east on the winds and returned ever laden, and the power and majesty of their kings were increased; and they drank and they feasted and they clad themselves in silver and gold.

In all this the Elf-friends had small part. They alone came now ever to the north and the land of Gil-galad, keeping their friendship with the Elves and lending them aid against Sauron; and their haven was Pelargir above the mouths of Anduin the Great. But the King's Men sailed far away to the south; and the lordships and strong-holds that they made have left many rumours in the legends of Men.

In this Age, as is elsewhere told, Sauron arose again in Middle-earth, and grew, and turned back to the evil in which he was nurtured by Morgoth, becoming mighty in his service. Already in the days of Tar-Minastir, the eleventh King of Númenor, he had fortified the land of Mordor and had built there the Tower of Barad-dûr, and thereafter he strove ever for the dominion of Middle-earth, to become a king over all kings and as a god unto Men. And Sauron hated the Númenóreans, because of the deeds of their fathers and their ancient alliance with the Elves and allegiance to the Valar; nor did he forget the aid that Tar-Minastir had rendered to Gil-galad of old, in that time when the One Ring was forged and there was war between Sauron and the Elves in Eriador. Now he learned that the kings of Númenor had increased in power and splendour, and he hated them the more; and he feared them, lest they should invade his lands and wrest from him the dominion of the East. But for a long time he did not dare to challenge the Lords of the Sea, and he withdrew from the coasts.

Yet Sauron was ever guileful, and it is said that among those whom he ensnared with the Nine Rings three were great lords of Númenór-ean race. And when the Úlairi arose that were the Ring-wraiths, his servants, and the strength of his terror and mastery over Men had grown exceedingly great, he began to assail the strong places of the Númenóreans upon the shores of the sea.

In those days the Shadow grew deeper upon Númenor; and the lives of the Kings of the House of Elros waned because of their re-bellion, but they hardened their hearts the more against the Valar. And the nineteenth king took the sceptre of his fathers, and he ascended the throne in the name of Adûnakhor, Lord of the West, forsaking the Elven-tongues and forbidding their use in his hearing. Yet in the Scroll of Kings the name Herunúmen was inscribed in the High-elven speech, because of ancient custom, which the kings feared to break utterly, lest evil befall. Now this title seemed to the Faithful over-proud, being the title of the Valar; and their hearts were sorely tried between their loyalty to the House of Elros and their reverence of the appointed Powers. But worse was yet to come. For Ar-Gimilzôr the twenty-second king was the greatest enemy of the Faithful. In his day the White Tree was untended and began to decline; and he forbade utterly the use of the Elven-tongues, and punished those that welcomed the ships of Eressëa, that still came secretly to the west-shores of the land.

Now the Elendili dwelt mostly in the western regions of Númenor; but Ar-Gimilzôr commanded all that he could discover to be of this party to remove from the west and dwell in the east of the land; and there they were watched. And the chief dwelling of the Faithful in the later days was thus nigh to the harbour of Rómenna; thence many set sail to Middle-earth, seeking the northern coasts where they might speak still with the Eldar in the kingdom of Gil-galad. This was known to the kings, but they hindered it not, so long as the Elendili departed from their land and did not return; for they desired to end all friendship between their people and the Eldar of Eressëa, whom they named the Spies of the Valar, hoping to keep their deeds and their counsels hidden from the Lords of the West. But all that they did was known to Manwë, and the Valar were wroth with the Kings of Númenor, and gave them counsel and protection no more; and the ships of Eressëa came never again out of the sunset, and the havens of Andúnië were forlorn.

Highest in honour after the house of the kings were the Lords of Andúnië; for they were of the line of Elros, being descended from Silmarien, daughter of Tar-Elendil the fourth king of Númenor. And these lords were loyal to the kings, and revered them; and the Lord of Andúnië was ever among the chief councillors of the Sceptre. Yet also from the beginning they bore especial love to the Eldar and reverence for the Valar; and as the Shadow grew they aided the Faithful as they could. But for long they did not declare themselves openly, and sought rather to amend the hearts of the lords of the Sceptre with wiser counsels.

There was a lady Inzilbêth, renowned for her beauty, and her mother was Lindórië, sister of Eärendur, the Lord of Andúnië in the days of Ar-Sakalthôr father of Ar-Gimilzôr. Gimilzôr took her to wife, though this was little to her liking, for she was in heart one of the Faithful, being taught by her mother; but the kings and their sons were grown proud and not to be gainsaid in their wishes. No love was there between Ar-Gimilzôr and his queen, or between their sons. Inziladûn, the elder, was like his mother in mind as in body; but Gimilkhâd, the younger, went with his father, unless he were yet prouder and more wilful. To him Ar-Gimilzôr would have yielded the sceptre rather than to the elder son, if the laws had allowed.

But when Inziladûn acceded to the sceptre, he took again a title in the Elven-tongue as of old, calling himself Tar-Palantir, for he was far-sighted both in eye and in mind, and even those that hated him feared his words as those of a true-seer. He gave peace for a while to the Faithful; and he went once more at due seasons to the Hallow of Eru upon the Meneltarma, which Ar-Gimilzôr had forsaken. The White Tree he tended again with honour; and he prophesied, saying that when the Tree perished, then also would the line of the Kings come to its end. But his repentance was too late to appease the anger of the Valar with the insolence of his fathers, of which the greater part of his people did not repent. And Gimilkhâd was strong and ungentle, and he took the leadership of those that had been called the King's Men and opposed the will of his brother as openly as he dared, and yet more in secret. Thus the days of Tar-Palantir became darkened with grief; and he would spend much of his time in the west, and there ascended often the ancient tower of King Minastir upon the hill of Oromet nigh to Andúnië, whence he gazed westward in yearning, hoping to see, maybe, some sail upon the sea. But no ship came ever again from the West to Númenor, and Avallónë was veiled in cloud.

Now Gimilkhâd died two years before his two hundredth year (which was accounted an early death for one of Elros' line even in its waning), but this brought no peace to the King. For Pharazôn son of Gimilkhâd had become a man yet more restless and eager for wealth and power than his father. He had fared often abroad, as a leader in the wars that the Númenóreans made then in the coastlands of Middle-earth, seeking to extend their dominion over Men; and thus he had won great renown as a captain both by land and by sea. Therefore when he came back to Númenor, hearing of his father's death, the hearts of the people were turned to him; for he brought with him great wealth, and was for the time free in his giving.

And it came to pass that Tar-Palantir grew weary of grief and died. He had no son, but a daughter only, whom he named Míriel in the Elven-tongue; and to her now by right and the laws of the Númenóreans came the sceptre. But Pharazôn took her to wife against her will, doing evil in this and evil also in that the laws of Númenor did not permit the marriage, even in the royal house, of those more nearly akin than cousins in the second degree. And when they were wedded, he seized the sceptre into his own hand, taking the title of Ar-Pharazôn (Tar-Calion in the Elven-tongue); and the name of his queen he changed to Ar-Zimraphel.

The mightiest and proudest was Ar-Pharazôn the Golden of all those that had wielded the Sceptre of the Sea-Kings since the foundation of Númenor; and three and twenty Kings and Queens had ruled the Númenóreans before, and slept now in their deep tombs under the mount of Meneltarma, lying upon beds of gold.

And sitting upon his carven throne in the city of Armenelos in the glory of his power, he brooded darkly, thinking of war. For he had learned in Middle-earth of the strength of the realm of Sauron, and of his hatred of Westernesse. And now there came to him the masters of ships and captains returning out of the East, and they reported that Sauron was putting forth his might, since Ar-Pharazôn had gone back from Middle-earth, and he was pressing down upon the cities by the coasts; and he had taken now the title of King of Men, and declared his purpose to drive the Númenóreans into the sea, and destroy even Númenor, if that might be.

Great was the anger of Ar-Pharazôn at these tidings, and as he pondered long in secret, his heart was filled with the desire of power unbounded and the sole dominion of his will. And he determined without counsel of the Valar, or the aid of any wisdom but his own, that the title of King of Men he would himself claim, and would compel Sauron to become his vassal and his servant; for in his pride he deemed that no king should ever arise so mighty as to vie with the Heir of Eärendil. Therefore he began in that time to smithy great hoard of weapons, and many ships of war he built and stored them with his arms; and when all was made ready he himself set sail with his host into the East.

And men saw his sails coming up out of the sunset, dyed as with scarlet and gleaming with red and gold, and fear fell upon the dwellers by the coasts, and they fled far away. But the fleet came at last to that place that was called Umbar, where was the mighty haven of the Númenóreans that no hand had wrought. Empty and silent were all the lands about when the King of the Sea marched upon Middle-earth. For seven days he journeyed with banner and trumpet, and he came to a hill, and he went up, and he set there his pavilion and his throne; and he sat him down in the midst of the land, and the tents of his host were ranged all about him, blue, golden, and white, as a field of tall flowers. Then he sent forth heralds, and he commanded Sauron to come before him and swear to him fealty.

And Sauron came. Even from his mighty tower of Barad-dûr he

came, and made no offer of battle. For he perceived that the power
and majesty of the Kings of the Sea surpassed all rumour of them, so
that he could not trust even the greatest of his servants to withstand
them; and he saw not his time yet to work his will with the Dúnedain.
And he was crafty, well skilled to gain what he would by subtlety
when force might not avail. Therefore he humbled himself before
Ar-Pharazôn and smoothed his tongue; and men wondered, for all
that he said seemed fair and wise.

   But Ar-Pharazôn was not yet deceived, and it came into his mind
that, for the better keeping of Sauron and of his oaths of fealty, he
should be brought to Númenor, there to dwell as a hostage for himself and all his servants in Middle-earth. To this Sauron assented
as one constrained, yet in his secret thought he received it gladly, for
it chimed indeed with his desire. And Sauron passed over the sea
and looked upon the land of Númenor, and on the city of Armenelos
in the days of its glory, and he was astounded; but his heart within
was filled the more with envy and hate.

   Yet such was the cunning of his mind and mouth, and the strength
of his hidden will, that ere three years had passed he had become
closest to the secret counsels of the King; for flattery sweet as honey
was ever on his tongue, and knowledge he had of many things yet
unrevealed to Men. And seeing the favour that he had of their lord
all the councillors began to fawn upon him, save one alone, Amandil
lord of Andúnië. Then slowly a change came over the land, and the
hearts of the Elf-friends were sorely troubled, and many fell away
out of fear; and although those that remained still called themselves
the Faithful, their enemies named them rebels. For now, having the
ears of men, Sauron with many arguments gainsaid all that the Valar
had taught; and he bade men think that in the world, in the east and
even in the west, there lay yet many seas and many lands for their
winning, wherein was wealth uncounted. And still, if they should at
the last come to the end of those lands and seas, beyond all lay the
Ancient Darkness. 'And out of it the world was made. For Darkness
alone is worshipful, and the Lord thereof may yet make other worlds
to be gifts to those that serve him, so that the increase of their power
shall find no end.'

   And Ar-Pharazôn said: 'Who is the Lord of the Darkness?'

   Then behind locked doors Sauron spoke to the King, and he lied,
saying: 'It is he whose name is not now spoken; for the Valar have
deceived you concerning him, putting forward the name of Eru, a
phantom devised in the folly of their hearts, seeking to enchain Men
in servitude to themselves. For they are the oracle of this Eru, which

speaks only what they will. But he that is their master shall yet prevail, and he will deliver you from this phantom; and his name is Melkor, Lord of All, Giver of Freedom, and he shall make you stronger then they.'

Then Ar-Pharazôn the King turned back to the worship of the Dark, and of Melkor the Lord thereof, at first in secret, but ere long openly and in the face of his people; and they for the most part followed him. Yet there dwelt still a remnant of the Faithful, as has been told, at Rómenna and in the country near, and other few there were here and there in the land. The chief among them, to whom they looked for leading and courage in evil days, was Amandil, councillor of the King, and his son Elendil, whose sons were Isildur and Anárion, then young men by the reckoning of Númenor. Amandil and Elendil were great ship-captains; and they were of the line of Elros Tar-Minyatur, though not of the ruling house to whom belonged the crown and the throne in the city of Armenelos. In the days of their youth together Amandil had been dear to Pharazôn, and though he was of the Elf-friends he remained in his council until the coming of Sauron. Now he was dismissed, for Sauron hated him above all others in Númenor. But he was so noble, and had been so mighty a captain of the sea, that he was still held in honour by many of the people, and neither the King nor Sauron dared to lay hands on him as yet.

Therefore Amandil withdrew to Rómenna, and all that he trusted still to be faithful he summoned to come thither in secret; for he feared that evil would now grow apace, and all the Elf-friends were in peril. And so it soon came to pass. For the Meneltarma was utterly deserted in those days; and though not even Sauron dared to defile the high place, yet the King would let no man, upon pain of death, ascend to it, not even those of the Faithful who kept Ilúvatar in their hearts. And Sauron urged the King to cut down the White Tree, Nimloth the Fair, that grew in his courts, for it was a memorial of the Eldar and of the light of Valinor.

At the first the King would not assent to this, since he believed that the fortunes of his house were bound up with the Tree, as was forespoken by Tar-Palantir. Thus in his folly he who now hated the Eldar and the Valar vainly clung to the shadow of the old allegiance of Númenor. But when Amandil heard rumour of the evil purpose of Sauron he was grieved to the heart, knowing that in the end Sauron would surely have his will. Then he spoke to Elendil and the sons of Elendil, recalling the tale of the Trees of Valinor; and Isildur said no word, but went out by night and did a deed for which he was afterwards renowned. For he passed alone in disguise to Armenelos and to the courts of the King, which were now forbidden to the Faithful; and he came to the place of the Tree, which was forbidden to all by the orders of Sauron, and the Tree was watched day and night by guards in his service. At that time Nimloth was dark and bore no bloom, for it was late in the autumn, and its winter was nigh; and Isildur passed through the guards and took from the Tree a fruit that hung upon it, and turned to go. But the guard was aroused, and he was assailed, and fought his way out, receiving many wounds; and he escaped, and because he was disguised it was not discovered who had laid hands on the Tree. But Isildur came at last hardly back to Rómenna and delivered the fruit to the hands of Amandil, ere his strength failed him. Then the fruit was planted in secret, and it was blessed by Amandil; and a shoot arose from it and sprouted in the spring. But when its first leaf opened then Isildur, who had lain long and come near to death, arose and was troubled no more by his wounds.

None too soon was this done; for after the assault the King yielded to Sauron and felled the White Tree, and turned then wholly away from the allegiance of his fathers. But Sauron caused to be built upon the hill in the midst of the city of the Númenóreans, Armenelos the Golden, a mighty temple; and it was in the form of a circle at the base, and there the walls were fifty feet in thickness, and the width of the base was five hundred feet across the centre, and the walls rose from the ground five hundred feet, and they were crowned with a mighty dome. And that dome was roofed all with silver, and rose glittering in the sun, so that the light of it could be seen afar off; but soon the light was darkened, and the silver became black. For there was an altar of fire in the midst of the temple, and in the topmost of the dome there was a louver, whence there issued a great smoke. And the first fire upon the altar Sauron kindled with the hewn wood of Nimloth, and it crackled and was consumed; but men marvelled at the reek that went up from it, so that the land lay under a cloud for seven days, until slowly it passed into the west.

Thereafter the fire and smoke went up without ceasing; for the power of Sauron daily increased, and in that temple, with spilling of blood and torment and great wickedness, men made sacrifice to Melkor that he should release them from Death. And most often from among the Faithful they chose their victims; yet never openly on the charge that they would not worship Melkor, the Giver of Freedom, rather was cause sought against them that they hated the King and were his rebels, or that they plotted against their kin, devising lies and poisons. These charges were for the most part false; yet those were bitter days, and hate brings forth hate.

But for all this Death did not depart from the land, rather it came sooner and more often, and in many dreadful guises. For whereas aforetime men had grown slowly old, and had laid them down in the end to sleep, when they were weary at last of the world, now madness and sickness assailed them; and yet they were afraid to die and go out into the dark, the realm of the lord that they had taken; and they cursed themselves in their agony. And men took weapons in those days and slew one another for little cause; for they were become quick to anger, and Sauron, or those whom he had bound to himself, went about the land setting man against man, so that the people murmured against the King and the lords, or against any that had aught that they had not; and the men of power took cruel revenge.

Nonetheless for long it seemed to the Númenóreans that they prospered, and if they were not increased in happiness, yet they grew more strong, and their rich men ever richer. For with the aid and counsel of Sauron they multiplied their possessions, and they devised engines, and they built ever greater ships. And they sailed now with power and armoury to Middle-earth, and they came no longer as bringers of gifts, nor even as rulers, but as fierce men of war. And they hunted the men of Middle-earth and took their goods and enslaved them, and many they slew cruelly upon their altars. For they built in their fortresses temples and great tombs in those days; and men feared them, and the memory of the kindly kings of the ancient days faded from the world and was darkened by many a tale of dread.

Thus Ar-Pharazôn, King of the Land of the Star, grew to the mightiest tyrant that had yet been in the world since the reign of Morgoth, though in truth Sauron ruled all from behind the throne. But the years passed, and the King felt the shadow of death approach, as his days lengthened; and he was filled with fear and wrath. Now came the hour that Sauron had prepared and long had awaited. And Sauron spoke to the King, saying that his strength was now so great that he might think to have his will in all things, and be subject to no command or ban.

And he said: 'The Valar have possessed themselves of the land where there is no death; and they lie to you concerning it, hiding it as best they may, because of their avarice, and their fear lest the Kings of Men should wrest from them the deathless realm and rule the world in their stead. And though, doubtless, the gift of life unending is not for all, but only for such as are worthy, being men of might and pride and great lineage, yet against all justice is it done that this gift, which is his due, should be withheld from the King of Kings, Ar-Pharazôn, mightiest of the sons of Earth, to whom Manwë alone can be compared, if even he. But great kings do not brook denials, and take what is their due.'

Then Ar-Pharazôn, being besotted, and walking under the shadow of death, for his span was drawing towards its end, hearkened to Sauron; and he began to ponder in his heart how he might make war upon the Valar. He was long preparing this design, and he spoke not openly of it, yet it could not be hidden from all. And Amandil, becoming aware of the purposes of the King, was dismayed and filled with a great dread, for he knew that Men could not vanquish the Valar in war, and that ruin must come upon the world, if this war were not stayed. Therefore he called his son, Elendil, and he said to him:

'The days are dark, and there is no hope for Men, for the Faithful are few. Therefore I am minded to try that counsel which our fore-father Eärendil took of old, to sail into the West, be there ban or no, and to speak to the Valar, even to Manwë himself, if may be, and beseech his aid ere all is lost.'

'Would you then betray the King?' said Elendil. 'For you know well the charge that they make against us, that we are traitors and spies, and that until this day it has been false.'

'If I thought that Manwë needed such a messenger,' said Amandil, 'I would betray the King. For there is but one loyalty from which no man can be absolved in heart for any cause. But it is for mercy upon Men and their deliverance from Sauron the Deceiver that I would plead, since some at least have remained faithful. And as for the Ban, I will suffer in myself the penalty, lest all my people should become guilty.'

'But what think you, my father, is like to befall those of your house whom you leave behind, when your deed becomes known?'

'It must not become known,' said Amandil. 'I will prepare my going in secret, and I will set sail into the east, whither daily the ships depart from our havens; and thereafter, as wind and chance may allow, I will go about, through south or north, back into the west, and seek what I may find. But for you and your folk, my son, I counsel that you should prepare yourselves other ships, and put aboard all such things as your hearts cannot bear to part with; and when the ships are ready, you should lie in the haven of Rómenna, and give out among men that you purpose, when you see your time, to follow me into the east. Amandil is no longer so dear to our kinsman upon the throne that he will grieve over much, if we seek to depart, for a season or for good. But let it not be seen that you intend to take many men, or he will be troubled, because of the war that he now plots, for which he will need all the force that he may gather. Seek out the Faithful that are known still to be true, and let them join you in secret, if they are willing to go with you, and share in your design.'

'And what shall that design be?' said Elendil.

'To meddle not in the war, and to watch,' answered Amandil. 'Until I return I can say no more. But it is most like that you shall fly from the Land of the Star with no star to guide you; for that land is defiled. Then you shall lose all that you have loved, foretasting death in life, seeking a land of exile elsewhere. But east or west the Valar alone can say.'

Then Amandil said farewell to all his household, as one that is about to die. 'For,' said he, 'it may well prove that you will see me never again; and that I shall show you no such sign as Eärendil showed long ago. But hold you ever in readiness, for the end of the world that we have known is now at hand.'

It is said that Amandil set sail in a small ship at night, and steered first eastward, and then went about and passed into the west. And he took with him three servants, dear to his heart, and never again were they heard of by word or sign in this world, nor is there any tale or guess of their fate. Men could not a second time be saved by any such embassy, and for the treason of Númenor there was no easy absolving.

But Elendil did all that his father had bidden, and his ships lay off the east coast of the land; and the Faithful put aboard their wives and their children, and their heirlooms, and great store of goods. Many things there were of beauty and power, such as the Númenóreans had contrived in the days of their wisdom, vessels and jewels, and scrolls of lore written in scarlet and black. And Seven Stones they had, the gift of the Eldar; but in the ship of Isildur was guarded the young tree, the scion of Nimloth the Fair. Thus Elendil held himself in readiness, and did not meddle in the evil deeds of those days; and ever he looked for a sign that did not come. Then he journeyed in secret to the western shores and gazed out over the sea, for sorrow and yearning were upon him, and he greatly loved his father. But naught could he descry save the fleets of Ar-Pharazôn gathering in the havens of the west.

Now aforetime in the isle of Númenor the weather was ever apt to the needs and liking of Men: rain in due season and ever in measure; and sunshine, now warmer, now cooler, and winds from the sea. And when the wind was in the west, it seemed to many that it was filled with a fragrance, fleeting but sweet, heart-stirring, as of flowers that bloom for ever in undying meads and have no names on mortal shores. But all this was now changed; for the sky itself was darkened, and there were storms of rain and hail in those days, and violent winds; and ever and anon a great ship of the Númenóreans would founder and return not to haven, though such a grief had not till then befallen them since the rising of the Star. And out of the west there would come at times a great cloud in the evening, shaped as it were an eagle, with pinions spread to the north and the south; and slowly it would loom up, blotting out the sunset, and then uttermost night would fall upon Númenor. And some of the eagles bore lightning beneath their wings, and thunder echoed between sea and cloud.

Then men grew afraid. 'Behold the Eagles of the Lords of the West!' they cried. 'The Eagles of Manwë are come upon Númenor!' And they fell upon their faces.

Then some few would repent for a season, but others hardened their hearts, and they shook their fists at heaven, saying: 'The Lords of the West have plotted against us. They strike first. The next blow shall be ours!' These words the King himself spoke, but they were devised by Sauron.

Now the lightnings increased and slew men upon the hills, and in the fields, and in the streets of the city; and a fiery bolt smote the dome of the Temple and shore it asunder, and it was wreathed in flame. But the Temple itself was unshaken, and Sauron stood there upon the pinnacle and defied the lightning and was unharmed; and in that hour men called him a god and did all that he would. When therefore the last portent came they heeded it little. For the land shook under them, and a groaning as of thunder underground was mingled with the roaring of the sea, and smoke issued from the peak of the Meneltarma. But all the more did Ar-Pharazôn press on with his armament.

In that time the fleets of the Númenóreans darkened the sea upon the west of the land, and they were like an archipelago of a thousand isles; their masts were as a forest upon the mountains, and their sails like a brooding cloud; and their banners were golden and black. And all things waited upon the word of Ar-Pharazôn; and Sauron withdrew into the inmost circle of the Temple, and men brought him victims to be burned.

Then the Eagles of the Lords of the West came up out of the dayfall, and they were arrayed as for battle, advancing in a line the end of which diminished beyond sight; and as they came their wings spread ever wider, grasping the sky. But the West burned red behind them, and they glowed beneath, as though they were lit with a flame of great anger, so that all Númenor was illumined as with a smouldering fire; and men looked upon the faces of their fellows, and it seemed to them that they were red with wrath.

Then Ar-Pharazôn hardened his heart, and he went aboard his mighty ship, Alcarondas, Castle of the Sea. Many-oared it was and many-masted, golden and sable; and upon it the throne of Ar-Pharazôn was set. Then he did on his panoply and his crown, and let raise his standard, and he gave the signal for the raising of the anchors; and in that hour the trumpets of Númenor outrang the thunder.

Thus the fleets of the Númenóreans moved against the menace of the West; and there was little wind, but they had many oars and many strong slaves to row beneath the lash. The sun went down, and there came a great silence. Darkness fell upon the land, and the sea was still, while the world waited for what should betide. Slowly the fleets passed out of the sight of the watchers in the havens, and their lights faded, and night took them; and in the morning they were gone. For a wind arose in the east and it wafted them away; and they broke the Ban of the Valar, and sailed into forbidden seas, going up with war against the Deathless, to wrest from them everlasting life within the Circles of the World.

But the fleets of Ar-Pharazôn came up out of the deeps of the sea and encompassed Avallónë and all the isle of Eressëa, and the Eldar mourned, for the light of the setting sun was cut off by the cloud of the Númenóreans. And at last Ar-Pharazôn came even to Aman, the Blessed Realm, and the coasts of Valinor; and still all was silent, and doom hung by a thread. For Ar-Pharazôn wavered at the end, and almost he turned back. His heart misgave him when he looked upon the soundless shores and saw Taniquetil shining, whiter than snow, colder than death, silent, immutable, terrible as the shadow of the light of Ilúvatar. But pride was now his master, and at last he left his ship and strode upon the shore, claiming the land for his own, if none should do battle for it. And a host of the Númenóreans encamped in might about Túna, whence all the Eldar had fled.

Then Manwë upon the Mountain called upon Ilúvatar, and for that time the Valar laid down their government of Arda. But Ilúvatar showed forth his power, and he changed the fashion of the world; and a great chasm opened in the sea between Númenor and the Deathless Lands, and the waters flowed down into it, and the noise and smoke of the cataracts went up to heaven, and the world was shaken. And all the fleets of the Númenóreans were drawn down into the abyss, and they were drowned and swallowed up for ever. But Ar-Pharazôn the King and the mortal warriors that had set foot upon the land of Aman were buried under falling hills: there it is said that they lie imprisoned in the Caves of the Forgotten, until the Last Battle and the Day of Doom.

But the land of Aman and Eressëa of the Eldar were taken away and removed beyond the reach of Men for ever. And Andor, the Land of Gift, Númenor of the Kings, Elenna of the Star of Eärendil, was utterly destroyed. For it was nigh to the east of the great rift, and its foundations were overturned, and it fell and went down into darkness, and is no more. And there is not now upon Earth any place abiding where the memory of a time without evil is preserved. For Ilúvatar cast back the Great Seas west of Middle-earth, and the Empty Lands east of it, and new lands and new seas were made; and the world was diminished, for Valinor and Eressëa were taken from it into the realm of hidden things.

In an hour unlooked for by Men this doom befell, on the nine and thirtieth day since the passing of the fleets. Then suddenly fire burst from the Meneltarma, and there came a mighty wind and a tumult of the earth, and the sky reeled, and the hills slid, and Númenor went down into the sea, with all its children and its wives and its maidens and its ladies proud; and all its gardens and its halls and its towers, its tombs and its riches, and its jewels and its webs and its things painted and carven, and its laughter and its mirth and its music, its wisdom and its lore: they vanished for ever. And last of all the mounting wave, green and cold and plumed with foam, climbing over the land, took to its bosom Tar-Míriel the Queen, fairer than silver or ivory or pearls. Too late she strove to ascend the steep ways of the Meneltarma to the holy place; for the waters overtook her, and her cry was lost in the roaring of the wind.

But whether or no it were that Amandil came indeed to Valinor and Manwë hearkened to his prayer, by grace of the Valar Elendil and his sons and their people were spared from the ruin of that day. For Elendil had remained in Rómenna, refusing the summons of the King when he set forth to war; and avoiding the soldiers of Sauron that came to seize him and drag him to the fires of the Temple, he went aboard his ship and stood off from the shore, waiting on the time. There he was protected by the land from the great draught of the sea that drew all towards the abyss, and afterwards he was sheltered from the first fury of the storm. But when the devouring wave

rolled over the land and Númenor toppled to its fall, then he would
have been overwhelmed and would have deemed it the lesser grief
to perish, for no wrench of death could be more bitter than the loss
and agony of that day; but the great wind took him, wilder than any
wind that Men had known, roaring from the west, and it swept his
ships far away; and it rent their sails and snapped their masts,
hunting the unhappy men like straws upon the water.

Nine ships there were: four for Elendil, and for Isildur three, and
for Anárion two; and they fled before the black gale out of the twilight of doom into the darkness of the world. And the deeps rose
beneath them in towering anger, and waves like unto mountains
moving with great caps of writhen snow bore them up amid the
wreckage of the clouds, and after many days cast them away upon the
shores of Middle-earth. And all the coasts and seaward regions of the
western world suffered great change and ruin in that time; for the
seas invaded the lands, and shores foundered, and ancient isles were
drowned, and new isles were uplifted; and hills crumbled and rivers
were turned into strange courses.

Elendil and his sons after founded kingdoms in Middle-earth; and
though their lore and craft was but an echo of that which had been
ere Sauron came to Númenor, yet very great it seemed to the wild
men of the world. And much is said in other lore of the deeds of the
heirs of Elendil in the age that came after, and of their strife with
Sauron that not yet was ended.

For Sauron himself was filled with great fear at the wrath of the
Valar, and the doom that Eru laid upon sea and land. It was greater
far than aught he had looked for, hoping only for the death of the
Númenóreans and the defeat of their proud king. And Sauron, sitting
in his black seat in the midst of the Temple, had laughed when he
heard the trumpets of Ar-Pharazôn sounding for battle; and again he
had laughed when he heard the thunder of the storm; and a third
time, even as he laughed at his own thought, thinking what he would
do now in the world, being rid of the Edain for ever, he was taken
in the midst of his mirth, and his seat and his temple fell into the
abyss. But Sauron was not of mortal flesh, and though he was robbed
now of that shape in which he had wrought so great an evil, so that
he could never again appear fair to the eyes of Men, yet his spirit arose
out of the deep and passed as a shadow and a black wind over the
sea, and came back to Middle-earth and to Mordor that was his
home. There he took up again his great Ring in Barad-dûr, and dwelt
there, dark and silent, until he wrought himself a new guise, an image

of malice and hatred made visible; and the Eye of Sauron the Terrible few could endure.

But these things come not into the tale of the Drowning of Númenor, of which now all is told. And even the name of that land perished, and Men spoke thereafter not of Elenna, nor of Andor the Gift that was taken away, nor of Númenórë on the confines of the world; but the exiles on the shores of the sea, if they turned towards the West in the desire of their hearts, spoke of Mar-nu-Falmar that was whelmed in the waves, Akallabêth the Downfallen, Atalantë in the Eldarin tongue.

Among the Exiles many believed that the summit of the Meneltarma, the Pillar of Heaven, was not drowned for ever, but rose again above the waves, a lonely island lost in the great waters; for it had been a hallowed place, and even in the days of Sauron none had defiled it. And some there were of the seed of Eärendil that afterwards sought for it, because it was said among loremasters that the farsighted men of old could see from the Meneltarma a glimmer of the Deathless Land. For even after the ruin the hearts of the Dúnedain were still set westwards; and though they knew indeed that the world was changed, they said: 'Avallónë is vanished from the Earth and the Land of Aman is taken away, and in the world of this present darkness they cannot be found. Yet once they were, and therefore they still are, in true being and in the whole shape of the world as at first it was devised.'

For the Dúnedain held that even mortal Men, if so blessed, might look upon other times than those of their bodies' life; and they longed ever to escape from the shadows of their exile and to see in some fashion the light that dies not; for the sorrow of the thought of death had pursued them over the deeps of the sea. Thus it was that great mariners among them would still search the empty seas, hoping to come upon the Isle of Meneltarma, and there to see a vision of things that were. But they found it not. And those that sailed far came only to the new lands, and found them like to the old lands, and subject to death. And those that sailed furthest set but a girdle about the Earth and returned weary at last to the place of their beginning; and they said: 'All roads are now bent.'

Thus in after days, what by the voyages of ships, what by lore and star-craft, the kings of Men knew that the world was indeed made round, and yet the Eldar were permitted still to depart and to come to the Ancient West and to Avallónë, if they would. Therefore the loremasters of Men said that a Straight Road must still be, for those that were permitted to find it. And they taught that, while the new world fell away, the old road and the path of the memory of the West still went on, as it were a mighty bridge invisible that passed through the air of breath and of flight (which were bent now as the world was bent), and traversed Ilmen which flesh unaided cannot endure, until it came to Tol Eressëa, the Lonely Isle, and maybe even beyond, to Valinor, where the Valar still dwell and watch the unfolding of the story of the world. And tales and rumours arose along the shores of the sea concerning mariners and men forlorn upon the water who, by some fate or grace or favour of the Valar, had entered in upon the Straight Way and seen the face of the world sink below them, and so had come to the lamplit quays of Avallónë, or verily to the last beaches on the margin of Aman, and there had looked upon the White Mountain, dreadful and beautiful, before they died.

# OF THE
# RINGS OF POWER
# AND THE
# THIRD AGE

# OF THE RINGS OF POWER AND THE
# THIRD AGE

## in which these tales come to
## their end

Of old there was Sauron the Maia, whom the Sindar in Beleriand named Gorthaur. In the beginning of Arda Melkor seduced him to his allegiance, and he became the greatest and most trusted of the servants of the Enemy, and the most perilous, for he could assume many forms, and for long if he willed he could still appear noble and beautiful, so as to deceive all but the most wary.

When Thangorodrim was broken and Morgoth overthrown, Sauron put on his fair hue again and did obeisance to Eönwë, the herald of Manwë, and abjured all his evil deeds. And some hold that this was not at first falsely done, but that Sauron in truth repented, if only out of fear, being dismayed by the fall of Morgoth and the great wrath of the Lords of the West. But it was not within the power of Eönwë to pardon those of his own order, and he commanded Sauron to return to Aman and there receive the judgement of Manwë. Then Sauron was ashamed, and he was unwilling to return in humiliation and to receive from the Valar a sentence, it might be, of long servitude in proof of his good faith; for under Morgoth his power had been great. Therefore when Eönwë departed he hid himself in Middle-earth; and he fell back into evil, for the bonds that Morgoth had laid upon him were very strong.

In the Great Battle and the tumults of the fall of Thangorodrim there were mighty convulsions in the earth, and Beleriand was broken and laid waste; and northward and westward many lands sank beneath the waters of the Great Sea. In the east, in Ossiriand, the walls of Ered Luin were broken, and a great gap was made in them towards the south, and a gulf of the sea flowed in. Into that gulf the River Lhûn fell by a new course, and it was called therefore the Gulf of Lhûn. That country had of old been named Lindon by the Noldor, and this name it bore thereafter; and many of the Eldar still dwelt there, lingering, unwilling yet to forsake Beleriand where they had fought and laboured long. Gil-galad son of Fingon was their king, and with him was Elrond Half-elven, son of Eärendil the Mariner and brother of Elros first king of Númenor.

Upon the shores of the Gulf of Lhûn the Elves built their havens, and named them Mithlond; and there they held many ships, for the harbourage was good. From the Grey Havens the Eldar ever and anon set sail, fleeing from the darkness of the days of Earth; for by the mercy of the Valar the Firstborn could still follow the Straight Road and return, if they would, to their kindred in Eressëa and Valinor beyond the encircling seas.

Others of the Eldar there were who crossed the mountains of Ered Luin in that age and passed into the inner lands. Many of these were Teleri, survivors of Doriath and Ossiriand; and they established realms among the Silvan Elves in woods and mountains far from the sea, for which nonetheless they ever yearned in their hearts. Only in Eregion, which Men called Hollin, did Elves of Noldorin race establish a lasting realm beyond the Ered Luin. Eregion was nigh to the great mansions of the Dwarves that were named Khazad-dûm, but by the Elves Hadhodrond, and afterwards Moria. From Ost-in-Edhil, the city of the Elves, the highroad ran to the west gate of Khazad-dûm, for a friendship arose between Dwarves and Elves, such as has never elsewhere been, to the enrichment of both those peoples. In Eregion the craftsmen of the Gwaith-i-Mírdain, the People of the Jewel-smiths, surpassed in cunning all that have ever wrought, save only Fëanor himself; and indeed greatest in skill among them was Celebrimbor, son of Curufin, who was estranged from his father and remained in Nargothrond when Celegorm and Curufin were driven forth, as is told in the *Quenta Silmarillion*.

Elsewhere in Middle-earth there was peace for many years; yet the lands were for the most part savage and desolate, save only where the people of Beleriand came. Many Elves dwelt there indeed, as they had dwelt through the countless years, wandering free in the wide lands far from the Sea; but they were Avari, to whom the deeds of Beleriand were but a rumour and Valinor only a distant name. And in the south and in the further east Men multiplied; and most of them turned to evil, for Sauron was at work.

Seeing the desolation of the world, Sauron said in his heart that the Valar, having overthrown Morgoth, had again forgotten Middle-earth; and his pride grew apace. He looked with hatred on the Eldar, and he feared the Men of Númenor who came back at whiles in their ships to the shores of Middle-earth; but for long he dissembled his mind and concealed the dark designs that he shaped in his heart.

Men he found the easiest to sway of all the peoples of the Earth; but long he sought to persuade the Elves to his service, for he knew that the Firstborn had the greater power; and he went far and wide among them, and his hue was still that of one both fair and wise. Only to Lindon he did not come, for Gil-galad and Elrond doubted him and his fair-seeming, and though they knew not who in truth he was they would not admit him to that land. But elsewhere the Elves received him gladly, and few among them hearkened to the messengers from Lindon bidding them beware; for Sauron took to himself the name of Annatar, the Lord of Gifts, and they had at first much profit from his friendship. And he said to them: 'Alas, for the weakness of the great! For a mighty king is Gil-galad, and wise in all lore is Master Elrond, and yet they will not aid me in my labours. Can it be that they do not desire to see other lands become as blissful as their own? But wherefore should Middle-earth remain for ever desolate and dark, whereas the Elves could make it as fair as Eressëa, nay even as Valinor? And since you have not returned thither, as you might, I perceive that you love this Middle-earth, as do I. Is it not then our task to labour together for its enrichment, and for the raising of all the Elven-kindreds that wander here untaught to the height of that power and knowledge which those have who are beyond the Sea?'

It was in Eregion that the counsels of Sauron were most gladly received, for in that land the Noldor desired ever to increase the skill and subtlety of their works. Moreover they were not at peace in their hearts, since they had refused to return into the West, and they desired both to stay in Middle-earth, which indeed they loved, and yet to enjoy the bliss of those that had departed. Therefore they hearkened to Sauron, and they learned of him many things, for his knowledge was great. In those days the smiths of Ost-in-Edhil surpassed all that they had contrived before; and they took thought, and they made Rings of Power. But Sauron guided their labours, and he was aware of all that they did; for his desire was to set a bond upon the Elves and to bring them under his vigilance.

Now the Elves made many rings; but secretly Sauron made One Ring to rule all the others, and their power was bound up with it, to be subject wholly to it and to last only so long as it too should last. And much of the strength and will of Sauron passed into that One Ring; for the power of the Elven-rings was very great, and that which should govern them must be a thing of surpassing potency; and

Sauron forged it in the Mountain of Fire in the Land of Shadow. And while he wore the One Ring he could perceive all the things that were done by means of the lesser rings, and he could see and govern the very thoughts of those that wore them.

But the Elves were not so lightly to be caught. As soon as Sauron set the One Ring upon his finger they were aware of him; and they knew him, and perceived that he would be master of them, and of all that they wrought. Then in anger and fear they took off their rings. But he, finding that he was betrayed and that the Elves were not deceived, was filled with wrath; and he came against them with open war, demanding that all the rings should be delivered to him, since the Elven-smiths could not have attained to their making without his lore and counsel. But the Elves fled from him; and three of their rings they saved, and bore them away, and hid them.

Now these were the Three that had last been made, and they possessed the greatest powers. Narya, Nenya, and Vilya, they were named, the Rings of Fire, and of Water, and of Air, set with ruby and adamant and sapphire; and of all the Elven-rings Sauron most desired to possess them, for those who had them in their keeping could ward off the decays of time and postpone the weariness of the world. But Sauron could not discover them, for they were given into the hands of the Wise, who concealed them and never again used them openly while Sauron kept the Ruling Ring. Therefore the Three remained unsullied, for they were forged by Celebrimbor alone, and the hand of Sauron had never touched them; yet they also were subject to the One.

From that time war never ceased between Sauron and the Elves; and Eregion was laid waste, and Celebrimbor slain, and the doors of Moria were shut. In that time the stronghold and refuge of Imladris, that Men called Rivendell, was founded by Elrond Half-elven; and long it endured. But Sauron gathered into his hands all the remaining Rings of Power; and he dealt them out to the other peoples of Middle-earth, hoping thus to bring under his sway all those that desired secret power beyond the measure of their kind. Seven rings he gave to the Dwarves; but to Men he gave nine, for Men proved in this matter as in others the readiest to his will. And all those rings that he governed he perverted, the more easily since he had a part in their making, and they were accursed, and they betrayed in the end all those that used them. The Dwarves indeed proved tough and hard to tame; they ill endure the domination of others, and the thoughts of their hearts are hard to fathom, nor can they be turned to shadows. They used their rings only for the getting of wealth; but wrath and an overmastering greed of gold were kindled in their hearts, of which evil enough after came to the profit of Sauron. It is said that the foundation of each of the Seven Hoards of the Dwarf-kings of old was a golden ring; but all those hoards long ago were plundered and the Dragons devoured them, and of the Seven Rings some were consumed in fire and some Sauron recovered.

Men proved easier to ensnare. Those who used the Nine Rings became mighty in their day, kings, sorcerers, and warriors of old. They obtained glory and great wealth, yet it turned to their undoing. They had, as it seemed, unending life, yet life became unendurable to them. They could walk, if they would, unseen by all eyes in this world beneath the sun, and they could see things in worlds invisible to mortal men; but too often they beheld only the phantoms and delusions of Sauron. And one by one, sooner or later, according to their native strength and to the good or evil of their wills in the beginning, they fell under the thraldom of the ring that they bore and under the domination of the One, which was Sauron's. And they became for ever invisible save to him that wore the Ruling Ring, and they entered into the realm of shadows. The Nazgûl were they, the Ringwraiths, the Enemy's most terrible servants; darkness went with them, and they cried with the voices of death.

Now Sauron's lust and pride increased, until he knew no bounds, and he determined to make himself master of all things in Middle-earth, and to destroy the Elves, and to compass, if he might, the downfall of Númenor. He brooked no freedom nor any rivalry, and he named himself Lord of the Earth. A mask he still could wear so that if he wished he might deceive the eyes of Men, seeming to them wise and fair. But he ruled rather by force and fear, if they might avail; and those who perceived his shadow spreading over the world called him the Dark Lord and named him the Enemy; and he gathered again under his government all the evil things of the days of Morgoth that remained on earth or beneath it, and the Orcs were at his command and multiplied like flies. Thus the Black Years began, which the Elves call the Days of Flight. In that time many of the Elves of Middle-earth fled to Lindon and thence over the seas never to return; and many were destroyed by Sauron and his servants. But in Lindon Gil-galad still maintained his power, and Sauron dared not as yet to pass the Mountains of Ered Luin nor to assail the Havens; and Gil-galad was aided by the Númenóreans. Elsewhere Sauron reigned, and those who would be free took refuge in the fastnesses of wood and mountain, and ever fear pursued them. In the east and south well nigh all Men were under his dominion, and they grew strong in those days and built many towns and walls of stone, and they were numerous and fierce in war and armed with iron. To them Sauron was both king and god; and they feared him exceedingly, for he surrounded his abode with fire.

Yet there came at length a stay in the onslaught of Sauron upon the westlands. For, as is told in the *Akallabêth,* he was challenged by the might of Númenor. So great was the power and splendour of the Númeróreans in the noontide of their realm that the servants of Sauron would not withstand them, and hoping to accomplish by cunning what he could not achieve by force, he left Middle-earth for a while and went to Númenor as a hostage of Tar-Calion the King. And there he abode, until at the last by his craft he had corrupted the hearts of most of that people, and set them at war with the Valar, and so compassed their ruin, as he had long desired. But that ruin was more terrible than Sauron had foreseen, for he had forgotten the might of the Lords of the West in their anger. The world was broken, and the land was swallowed up, and the seas rose over it, and Sauron himself went down into the abyss. But his spirit arose and fled back on a dark wind to Middle-earth, seeking a home. There he found that the power of Gil-galad had grown great in the years of his absence, and it was spread now over wide regions of the north and west, and had passed beyond the Misty Mountains and the Great River even to the borders of Greenwood the Great, and was drawing nigh to the strong places where once he had dwelt secure. Then Sauron withdrew to his fortress in the Black Land and meditated war.

In that time those of the Númenóreans who were saved from destruction fled eastward, as is told in the *Akallabêth.* The chief of these were Elendil the Tall and his sons, Isildur and Anárion. Kinsmen of the King they were, descendants of Elros, but they had been unwilling to listen to Sauron, and had refused to make war on the Lords of the West. Manning their ships with all who remained faithful they forsook the land of Númenor ere ruin came upon it. They were mighty men and their ships were strong and tall, but the tempests overtook them, and they were borne aloft on hills of water even to the clouds, and they descended upon Middle-earth like birds of the storm.

Elendil was cast up by the waves in the land of Lindon, and he was befriended by Gil-galad. Thence he passed up the River Lhûn, and beyond Ered Luin he established his realm, and his people dwelt in many places in Eriador about the courses of the Lhûn and the Baranduin; but his chief city was at Annúminas beside the water of

Lake Nenuial. At Fornost upon the North Downs also the Númenóreans dwelt, and in Cardolan, and in the hills of Rhudaur; and towers
they raised upon Emyn Beraid and upon Amon Sûl; and there remain many barrows and ruined works in those places, but the towers
of Emyn Beraid still look towards the sea.

Isildur and Anárion were borne away southwards, and at the last
they brought their ships up the Great River Anduin, that flows out of
Rhovanion into the western sea in the Bay of Belfalas; and they
established a realm in those lands that were after called Gondor,
whereas the Northern Kingdom was named Arnor. Long before in
the days of their power the mariners of Númenor had established a
haven and strong places about the mouths of Anduin, in despite of
Sauron in the Black Land that lay nigh upon the east. In the later
days to this haven came only the Faithful of Númenor, and many
therefore of the folk of the coastlands in that region were in whole or
in part akin to the Elf-friends and the people of Elendil, and they
welcomed his sons. The chief city of this southern realm was Osgiliath, through the midst of which the Great River flowed; and the
Númenóreans built there a great bridge, upon which there were
towers and houses of stone wonderful to behold, and tall ships came
up out of the sea to the quays of the city. Other strong places they
built also upon either hand: Minas Ithil, the Tower of the Rising
Moon, eastward upon a shoulder of the Mountains of Shadow as a
threat to Mordor; and to the westward Minas Anor, the Tower of the
Setting Sun, at the feet of Mount Mindolluin, as a shield against the
wild men of the dales. In Minas Ithil was the house of Isildur, and
in Minas Anor the house of Anárion, but they shared the realm between them and their thrones were set side by side in the Great Hall
of Osgiliath. These were the chief dwellings of the Númenóreans in
Gondor, but other works marvellous and strong they built in the land
in the days of their power, at the Argonath, and at Aglarond, and at
Erech; and in the circle of Angrenost, which Men called Isengard,
they made the Pinnacle of Orthanc of unbreakable stone.

Many treasures and great heirlooms of virtue and wonder the
Exiles had brought from Númenor; and of these the most renowned
were the Seven Stones and the White Tree. The White Tree was
grown from the fruit of Nimloth the Fair that stood in the courts of
the King at Armenelos in Númenor, ere Sauron burned it; and
Nimloth was in its turn descended from the Tree of Tirion, that was
an image of the Eldest of Trees, White Telperion which Yavanna
caused to grow in the land of the Valar. The Tree, memorial of the
Eldar and of the light of Valinor, was planted in Minas Ithil before

the house of Isildur, since he it was that had saved the fruit from destruction; but the Stones were divided.

Three Elendil took, and his sons each two. Those of Elendil were set in towers upon Emyn Beraid, and upon Amon Sûl, and in the city of Annúminas. But those of his sons were at Minas Ithil and Minas Anor, and at Orthanc and in Osgiliath. Now these Stones had this virtue that those who looked therein might perceive in them things far off, whether in place or in time. For the most part they revealed only things near to another kindred Stone, for the Stones each called to each; but those who possessed great strength of will and of mind might learn to direct their gaze whither they would. Thus the Númenóreans were aware of many things that their enemies wished to conceal, and little escaped their vigilance in the days of their might.

It is said that the towers of Emyn Beraid were not built indeed by the Exiles of Númenor, but were raised by Gil-galad for Elendil, his friend; and the Seeing Stone of Emyn Beraid was set in Elostirion, the tallest of the towers. Thither Elendil would repair, and thence he would gaze out over the sundering seas, when the yearning of exile was upon him; and it is believed that thus he would at whiles see far away even the Tower of Avallónë upon Eressëa, where the Master-stone abode, and yet abides. These stones were gifts of the Eldar to Amandil, father of Elendil, for the comfort of the Faithful of Númenor in their dark days, when the Elves might come no longer to that land under the shadow of Sauron. They were called the Palantíri, those that watch from afar; but all those that were brought to Middle-earth long ago were lost.

Thus the Exiles of Númenor established their realms in Arnor and in Gondor; but ere many years had passed it became manifest that their enemy, Sauron, had also returned. He came in secret, as has been told, to his ancient kingdom of Mordor beyond the Ephel Dúath, the Mountains of Shadow, and that country marched with Gondor upon the east. There above the valley of Gorgoroth was built his fortress vast and strong, Barad-dûr, the Dark Tower; and there was a fiery mountain in that land that the Elves named Orodruin. Indeed for that reason Sauron had set there his dwelling long before, for he used the fire that welled there from the heart of the earth in his sorceries and in his forging; and in the midst of the Land of Mordor he had fashioned the Ruling Ring. There now he brooded in the dark, until he had wrought for himself a new shape; and it was terrible, for his fair semblance had departed for ever when he was cast into the abyss at the drowning of Númenor. He took up again the great Ring and clothed himself in power; and the malice of the Eye of Sauron few even of the great among Elves and Men could endure.

Now Sauron prepared war against the Eldar and the Men of Westernesse, and the fires of the Mountain were wakened again. Wherefore seeing the smoke of Orodruin from afar, and perceiving that Sauron had returned, the Númenóreans named that mountain anew Amon Amarth, which is Mount Doom. And Sauron gathered to him great strength of his servants out of the east and the south; and among them were not a few of the high race of Númenor. For in the days of the sojourn of Sauron in that land the hearts of well nigh all its people had been turned towards darkness. Therefore many of those who sailed east in that time and made fortresses and dwellings upon the coasts were already bent to his will, and they served him still gladly in Middle-earth. But because of the power of Gil-galad these renegades, lords both mighty and evil, for the most part took up their abodes in the southlands far away; yet two there were, Herumor and Fuinur, who rose to power among the Haradrim, a great and cruel people that dwelt in the wide lands south of Mordor beyond the mouths of Anduin.

When therefore Sauron saw his time he came with great force against the new realm of Gondor, and he took Minas Ithil, and he destroyed the White Tree of Isildur that grew there. But Isildur escaped, and taking with him a seedling of the Tree he went with his wife and his sons by ship down the River, and they sailed from the mouths of Anduin seeking Elendil. Meanwhile Anárion held Osgiliath against the Enemy, and for that time drove him back to the mountains; but Sauron gathered his strength again, and Anárion knew that unless help should come his kingdom would not long stand.

Now Elendil and Gil-galad took counsel together, for they perceived that Sauron would grow too strong and would overcome all his enemies one by one, if they did not unite against him. Therefore they made that League which is called the Last Alliance, and they marched east into Middle-earth gathering a great host of Elves and Men; and they halted for a while at Imladris. It is said that the host that was there assembled was fairer and more splendid in arms than any that has since been seen in Middle-earth, and none greater has been mustered since the host of the Valar went against Thangorodrim.

From Imladris they crossed the Misty Mountains by many passes and marched down the River Anduin, and so came at last upon the host of Sauron on Dagorlad, the Battle Plain, which lies before the gate of the Black Land. All living things were divided in that day, and some of every kind, even of beasts and birds, were found in either host, save the Elves only. They alone were undivided and followed Gil-galad. Of the Dwarves few fought upon either side; but the kindred of Durin of Moria fought against Sauron.

The host of Gil-galad and Elendil had the victory, for the might of the Elves was still great in those days, and the Númenóreans were strong and tall, and terrible in their wrath. Against Aeglos the spear of Gil-galad none could stand; and the sword of Elendil filled Orcs and Men with fear, for it shone with the light of the sun and of the moon, and it was named Narsil.

Then Gil-galad and Elendil passed into Mordor and encompassed the stronghold of Sauron; and they laid siege to it for seven years, and suffered grievous loss by fire and by the darts and bolts of the Enemy, and Sauron sent many sorties against them. There in the valley of Gorgoroth Anárion son of Elendil was slain, and many others. But at the last the siege was so strait that Sauron himself came forth; and he wrestled with Gil-galad and Elendil, and they both were slain, and the sword of Elendil broke under him as he fell. But Sauron also was thrown down, and with the hilt-shard of Narsil Isildur cut the Ruling Ring from the hand of Sauron and took it for his own. Then Sauron was for that time vanquished, and he forsook his body, and his spirit fled far away and hid in waste places; and he took no visible shape again for many long years.

Thus began the Third Age of the World, after the Eldest Days and the Black Years; and there was still hope in that time and the memory of mirth, and for long the White Tree of the Eldar flowered in the courts of the Kings of Men, for the seedling which he had saved Isildur planted in the citadel of Anor in memory of his brother, ere he departed from Gondor. The servants of Sauron were routed and dispersed, yet they were not wholly destroyed; and though many Men turned now from evil and became subject to the heirs of Elendil, yet many more remembered Sauron in their hearts and hated the kingdoms of the West. The Dark Tower was levelled to the ground, yet its foundations remained, and it was not forgotten. The Númenóreans indeed set a guard upon the land of Mordor, but none dared dwell there because of the terror of the memory of Sauron, and because of the Mountain of Fire that stood nigh to Barad-dûr; and the valley of Gorgoroth was filled with ash. Many of the Elves and many of the Númenóreans and of Men who were their allies had perished in the Battle and the Siege; and Elendil the Tall and Gil-galad the

High King were no more. Never again was such a host assembled, nor was there any such league of Elves and Men; for after Elendil's day the two kindreds became estranged.

The Ruling Ring passed out of the knowledge even of the Wise in that age; yet it was not unmade. For Isildur would not surrender it to Elrond and Círdan who stood by. They counselled him to cast it into the fire of Orodruin nigh at hand, in which it had been forged, so that it should perish, and the power of Sauron be for ever diminished, and he should remain only as a shadow of malice in the wilderness. But Isildur refused this counsel, saying: 'This I will have as weregild for my father's death, and my brother's. Was it not I that dealt the Enemy his death-blow?' And the Ring that he held seemed to him exceedingly fair to look on; and he would not suffer it to be destroyed. Taking it therefore he returned at first to Minas Anor, and there planted the White Tree in memory of his brother Anárion. But soon he departed, and after he had given counsel to Meneldil, his brother's son, and had committed to him the realm of the south, he bore away the Ring, to be an heirloom of his house, and marched north from Gondor by the way that Elendil had come; and he forsook the South Kingdom, for he purposed to take up his father's realm in Eriador, far from the shadow of the Black Land.

But Isildur was overwhelmed by a host of Orcs that lay in wait in the Misty Mountains; and they descended upon him at unawares in his camp between the Greenwood and the Great River, nigh to Loeg Ningloron, the Gladden Fields, for he was heedless and set no guard, deeming that all his foes were overthrown. There well nigh all his people were slain, and among them were his three elder sons, Elendur, Aratan, and Ciryon; but his wife and his youngest son, Valandil, he had left in Imladris when he went to the war. Isildur himself escaped by means of the Ring, for when he wore it he was invisible to all eyes; but the Orcs hunted him by scent and slot, until he came to the River and plunged in. There the Ring betrayed him and avenged its maker, for it slipped from his finger as he swam, and it was lost in the water. Then the Orcs saw him as he laboured in the stream, and they shot him with many arrows, and that was his end. Only three of his people came ever back over the mountains after long wandering; and of these one was Ohtar his esquire, to whose keeping he had given the shards of the sword of Elendil.

Thus Narsil came in due time to the hand of Valandil, Isildur's heir, in Imladris; but the blade was broken and its light was extinguished, and it was not forged anew. And Master Elrond foretold that this would not be done until the Ruling Ring should be found

again and Sauron should return; but the hope of Elves and Men was
that these things might never come to pass.

Valandil took up his abode in Annúminas, but his folk were diminished, and of the Númenóreans and of the Men of Eriador there
remained now too few to people the land or to maintain all the places
that Elendil had built; in Dagorlad, and in Mordor, and upon the
Gladden Fields many had fallen. And it came to pass after the days
of Eärendur, the seventh king that followed Valandil, that the Men
of Westernesse, the Dúnedain of the North, became divided into
petty realms and lordships, and their foes devoured them one by
one. Ever they dwindled with the years, until their glory passed,
leaving only green mounds in the grass. At length naught was left
of them but a strange people wandering secretly in the wild, and other
men knew not their homes nor the purpose of their journeys, and save
in Imladris, in the house of Elrond, their ancestry was forgotten.
Yet the shards of the sword were cherished during many lives of Men
by the heirs of Isildur; and their line, from father to son, remained
unbroken.

In the south the realm of Gondor endured, and for a time its
splendour grew, until it recalled the wealth and majesty of Númenor
ere it fell. High towers the people of Gondor built, and strong places,
and havens of many ships; and the Winged Crown of the Kings of
Men was held in awe by people of many lands and tongues. For many
a year the White Tree grew before the King's house in Minas Anor,
the seed of that tree which Isildur brought out of the deeps of the
sea from Númenor; and the seed before that came from Avallónë,
and before that from Valinor in the Day before days when the world
was young.

Yet at the last, in the wearing of the swift years of Middle-earth,
Gondor waned, and the line of Meneldil son of Anárion failed. For
the blood of the Númenóreans became much mingled with that of
other men, and their power and wisdom was diminished, and their
life-span was shortened, and the watch upon Mordor slumbered.
And in the days of Telemnar, the third and twentieth of the line of
Meneldil, a plague came upon dark winds out of the east, and it smote
the King and his children, and many of the people of Gondor
perished. Then the forts on the borders of Mordor were deserted, and
Minas Ithil was emptied of its people; and evil entered again into
the Black Land secretly, and the ashes of Gorgoroth were stirred
as by a cold wind, for dark shapes gathered there. It is said that
these were indeed the Úlairi, whom Sauron called the Nazgûl,
the Nine Ringwraiths that had long remained hidden, but returned

now to prepare the ways of their Master, for he had begun to grow again.

And in the days of Eärnil they made their first stroke, and they came by night out of Mordor over the passes of the Mountains of Shadow, and took Minas Ithil for their abode; and they made it a place of such dread that none dared to look upon it. Thereafter it was called Minas Morgul, the Tower of Sorcery; and Minas Morgul was ever at war with Minas Anor in the west. Then Osgiliath, which in the waning of the people had long been deserted, became a place of ruins and a city of ghosts. But Minas Anor endured, and it was named anew Minas Tirith, the Tower of Guard; for there the kings caused to be built in the citadel a white tower, very tall and fair, and its eye was upon many lands. Proud still and strong was that city, and in it the White Tree still flowered for a while before the house of the Kings; and there the remnant of the Númenóreans still defended the passage of the River against the terrors of Minas Morgul and against all the enemies of the West, Orcs and monsters and evil Men; and thus the lands behind them, west of Anduin, were protected from war and destruction.

Still Minas Tirith endured after the days of Eärnur, son of Eärnil, and the last King of Gondor. He it was that rode alone to the gates of Minas Morgul to meet the challenge of the Morgul-lord; and he met him in single combat, but he was betrayed by the Nazgûl and taken alive into the city of torment, and no living man saw him ever again. Now Eärnur left no heir, but when the line of the Kings failed the Stewards of the house of Mardil the Faithful ruled the city and its ever-shrinking realm; and the Rohirrim, the Horsemen of the North, came and dwelt in the green land of Rohan, which before was named Calenardhon and was a part of the kingdom of Gondor; and the Rohirrim aided the Lords of the City in their wars. And northward, beyond the Falls of Rauros and the Gates of Argonath, there were as yet other defences, powers more ancient of which Men knew little, against whom the things of evil did not dare to move, until in the ripening of time their dark lord, Sauron, should come forth again. And until that time was come, never again after the days of Eärnil did the Nazgûl dare to cross the River or to come forth from their city in shape visible to Men.

In all the days of the Third Age, after the fall of Gil-galad, Master Elrond abode in Imladris, and he gathered there many Elves, and other folk of wisdom and power from among all the kindreds of Middle-earth, and he preserved through many lives of Men the

memory of all that had been fair; and the house of Elrond was a
refuge for the weary and the oppressed, and a treasury of good counsel and wise lore. In that house were harboured the Heirs of Isildur,
in childhood and old age, because of the kinship of their blood with
Elrond himself, and because he knew in his wisdom that one should
come of their line to whom a great part was appointed in the last
deeds of that Age. And until that time came the shards of Elendil's
sword were given into the keeping of Elrond, when the days of the
Dúnedain darkened and they became a wandering people.

In Eriador Imladris was the chief dwelling of the High Elves; but
at the Grey Havens of Lindon there abode also a remnant of the
people of Gil-galad the Elvenking. At times they would wander into
the lands of Eriador, but for the most part they dwelt near the shores
of the sea, building and tending the elven-ships wherein those of the
Firstborn who grew weary of the world set sail into the uttermost
West. Círdan the Shipwright was lord of the Havens and mighty
among the Wise.

Of the Three Rings that the Elves had preserved unsullied no open
word was ever spoken among the Wise, and few even of the Eldar
knew where they were bestowed. Yet after the fall of Sauron their
power was ever at work, and where they abode there mirth also dwelt
and all things were unstained by the griefs of time. Therefore ere the
Third Age was ended the Elves perceived that the Ring of Sapphire
was with Elrond, in the fair valley of Rivendell, upon whose house the
stars of heaven most brightly shone; whereas the Ring of Adamant
was in the Land of Lórien where dwelt the Lady Galadriel. A queen
she was of the woodland Elves, the wife of Celeborn of Doriath, yet
she herself was of the Noldor and remembered the Day before days
in Valinor, and she was the mightiest and fairest of all the Elves that
remained in Middle-earth. But the Red Ring remained hidden until
the end, and none save Elrond and Galadriel and Círdan knew to
whom it had been committed.

Thus it was that in two domains the bliss and beauty of the Elves
remained still undiminished while that Age endured: in Imladris;
and in Lothlórien, the hidden land between Celebrant and Anduin,
where the trees bore flowers of gold and no Orc or evil thing dared
ever come. Yet many voices were heard among the Elves foreboding
that, if Sauron should come again, then either he would find the
Ruling Ring that was lost, or at the best his enemies would discover
it and destroy it; but in either chance the powers of the Three must
then fail and all things maintained by them must fade, and so the
Elves should pass into the twilight and the Dominion of Men begin.

And so indeed it has since befallen: the One and the Seven and the Nine are destroyed; and the Three have passed away, and with them the Third Age is ended, and the Tales of the Eldar in Middle-earth draw to their close. Those were the Fading Years, and in them the last flowering of the Elves east of the Sea came to its winter. In that time the Noldor walked still in the Hither Lands, mightiest and fairest of the children of the world, and their tongues were still heard by mortal ears. Many things of beauty and wonder remained on earth in that time, and many things also of evil and dread: Orcs there were and trolls and dragons and fell beasts, and strange creatures old and wise in the woods whose names are forgotten; Dwarves still laboured in the hills and wrought with patient craft works of metal and stone that none now can rival. But the Dominion of Men was preparing and all things were changing, until at last the Dark Lord arose in Mirkwood again.

Now of old the name of that forest was Greenwood the Great, and its wide halls and aisles were the haunt of many beasts and of birds of bright song; and there was the realm of King Thranduil under the oak and the beech. But after many years, when well nigh a third of that age of the world had passed, a darkness crept slowly through the wood from the southward, and fear walked there in shadowy glades; fell beasts came hunting, and cruel and evil creatures laid there their snares.

Then the name of the forest was changed and Mirkwood it was called, for the nightshade lay deep there, and few dared to pass through, save only in the north where Thranduil's people still held the evil at bay. Whence it came few could tell, and it was long ere even the Wise could discover it. It was the shadow of Sauron and the sign of his return. For coming out of the wastes of the East he took up his abode in the south of the forest, and slowly he grew and took shape there again; in a dark hill he made his dwelling and wrought there his sorcery, and all folk feared the Sorcerer of Dol Guldur, and yet they knew not at first how great was their peril.

Even as the first shadows were felt in Mirkwood there appeared in the west of Middle-earth the Istari, whom Men called the Wizards. None knew at that time whence they were, save Círdan of the Havens, and only to Elrond and to Galadriel did he reveal that they came over the Sea. But afterwards it was said among the Elves that they were messengers sent by the Lords of the West to contest the power of Sauron, if he should arise again, and to move Elves and Men and all living things of good will to valiant deeds. In the likeness of Men they appeared, old but vigorous, and they changed little with the years, and aged but slowly, though great cares lay on them; great wisdom they had, and many powers of mind and hand. Long they journeyed far and wide among Elves and Men, and held converse also with beasts and with birds; and the peoples of Middle-earth gave to them many names, for their true names they did not reveal. Chief among them were those whom the Elves called Mithrandir and Curunír, but Men in the North named Gandalf and Saruman. Of these Curunír was the eldest and came first, and after him came Mithrandir and Radagast, and others of the Istari who went into the east of Middle-earth, and do not come into these tales. Radagast was the friend of all beasts and birds; but Curunír went most among Men, and he was subtle in speech and skilled in all the devices of smithcraft. Mithrandir was closest in counsel with Elrond and the Elves. He wandered far in the North and West and made never in any land any lasting abode; but Curunír journeyed into the East, and when he returned he dwelt at Orthanc in the Ring of Isengard, which the Númenóreans made in the days of their power.

Ever most vigilant was Mithrandir, and he it was that most doubted the darkness in Mirkwood, for though many deemed that it was wrought by the Ringwraiths, he feared that it was indeed the first shadow of Sauron returning; and he went to Dol Guldur, and the Sorcerer fled from him, and there was a watchful peace for a long while. But at length the Shadow returned and its power increased; and in that time was first made the Council of the Wise that is called the White Council, and therein were Elrond and Galadriel and Círdan, and other lords of the Eldar, and with them were Mithrandir and Curunír. And Curunír (that was Saruman the White) was chosen to be their chief, for he had most studied the devices of Sauron of old. Galadriel indeed had wished that Mithrandir should be the head of the Council, and Saruman begrudged them that, for his pride and desire of mastery was grown great; but Mithrandir refused the office, since he would have no ties and no allegiance, save to those who sent him, and he would abide in no place nor be subject to any summons. But Saruman now began to study the lore of the Rings of Power, their making and their history.

Now the Shadow grew ever greater, and the hearts of Elrond and Mithrandir darkened. Therefore on a time Mithrandir at great peril went again to Dol Guldur and the pits of the Sorcerer, and he discovered the truth of his fears, and escaped. And returning to Elrond he said:

'True, alas, is our guess. This is not one of the Úlairi, as many have long supposed. It is Sauron himself who has taken shape again and now grows apace; and he is gathering again all the Rings to his hand; and he seeks ever for news of the One, and of the Heirs of Isildur, if they live still on earth.'

And Elrond answered: 'In the hour that Isildur took the Ring and would not surrender it, this doom was wrought, that Sauron should return.'

'Yet the One was lost,' said Mithrandir, 'and while it still lies hid, we can master the Enemy, if we gather our strength and tarry not too long.'

Then the White Council was summoned; and Mithrandir urged them to swift deeds, but Curunír spoke against him, and counselled them to wait yet and to watch.

'For I believe not,' said he, 'that the One will ever be found again in Middle-earth. Into Anduin it fell, and long ago, I deem, it was rolled to the Sea. There it shall lie until the end, when all this world is broken and the deeps are removed.'

Therefore naught was done at that time, though Elrond's heart misgave him, and he said to Mithrandir: 'Nonetheless I forebode that the One will yet be found, and then war will arise again, and in that war this Age will be ended. Indeed in a second darkness it will end, unless some strange chance deliver us that my eyes cannot see.'

'Many are the strange chances of the world,' said Mithrandir, 'and help oft shall come from the hands of the weak when the Wise falter.'

Thus the Wise were troubled, but none as yet perceived that Curunír had turned to dark thoughts and was already a traitor in heart: for he desired that he and no other should find the Great Ring, so that he might wield it himself and order all the world to his will. Too long he had studied the ways of Sauron in hope to defeat him, and now he envied him as a rival rather than hated his works. And he deemed that the Ring, which was Sauron's, would seek for its master as he became manifest once more; but if he were driven out again, then it would lie hid. Therefore he was willing to play with peril and let Sauron be for a time, hoping by his craft to forestall both his friends and the Enemy, when the Ring should appear.

He set a watch upon the Gladden Fields; but soon he discovered that the servants of Dol Guldur were searching all the ways of the River in that region. Then he perceived that Sauron also had learned of the manner of Isildur's end, and he grew afraid and withdrew to Isengard and fortified it; and ever he probed deeper into the lore of the Rings of Power and the art of their forging. But he spoke of none of this to the Council, hoping still that he might be the first to hear news of the Ring. He gathered a great host of spies, and many of these were birds; for Radagast lent him his aid, divining naught of his treachery, and deeming that this was but part of the watch upon the Enemy.

But ever the shadow in Mirkwood grew deeper, and to Dol Guldur evil things repaired out of all the dark places of the world; and they were united again under one will, and their malice was directed against the Elves and the survivors of Númenor. Therefore at last the Council was again summoned and the lore of the Rings was much debated; but Mithrandir spoke to the Council, saying:

'It is not needed that the Ring should be found, for while it abides on earth and is not unmade, still the power that it holds will live, and Sauron will grow and have hope. The might of the Elves and the Elf-friends is less now than of old. Soon he will be too strong for you, even without the Great Ring; for he rules the Nine, and of the Seven he has recovered three. We must strike.'

To this Curunír now assented, desiring that Sauron should be thrust from Dol Guldur, which was nigh to the River, and should have leisure to search there no longer. Therefore, for the last time, he aided the Council, and they put forth their strength; and they assailed Dol Guldur, and drove Sauron from his hold, and Mirkwood for a brief while was made wholesome again.

But their stroke was too late. For the Dark Lord had foreseen it, and he had long prepared all his movements; and the Úlairi, his Nine Servants, had gone before him to make ready for his coming. Therefore his flight was but a feint, and he soon returned, and ere the Wise could prevent him he re-entered his kingdom in Mordor and reared once again the dark towers of Barad-dûr. And in that year the White Council met for the last time, and Curunír withdrew to Isengard, and took counsel with none save himself.

Orcs were mustering, and far to the east and the south the wild peoples were arming. Then in the midst of gathering fear and the rumour of war the foreboding of Elrond was proved true, and the One Ring was indeed found again, by a chance more strange than even Mithrandir had foreseen; and it was hidden from Curunír and from Sauron. For it had been taken from Anduin long ere they sought for it, being found by one of the small fisher-folk that dwelt by the River, ere the Kings failed in Gondor; and by its finder it was brought beyond search into dark hiding under the roots of the mountains. There it dwelt, until even in the year of the assault upon Dol Guldur it was found again, by a wayfarer, fleeing into the depths of the earth from the pursuit of the Orcs, and passed into a far distant country, even to the land of the Periannath, the Little People, the Halflings, who dwelt in the west of Eriador. And ere that day they had been held of small account by Elves and by Men, and neither Sauron nor any of the Wise save Mithrandir had in all their counsels given thought to them.

Now by fortune and his vigilance Mithrandir first learned of the Ring, ere Sauron had news of it; yet he was dismayed and in doubt. For too great was the evil power of this thing for any of the Wise to wield, unless like Curunír he wished himself to become a tyrant and a dark lord in his turn; but neither could it be concealed from Sauron for ever, nor could it be unmade by the craft of the Elves. Therefore with the help of the Dúnedain of the North Mithrandir set a watch upon the land of the Periannath and bided his time. But Sauron had many ears, and soon he heard rumour of the One Ring, which above all things he desired, and he sent forth the Nazgûl to take it. Then war was kindled, and in battle with Sauron the Third Age ended even as it had begun.

But those who saw the things that were done in that time, deeds of valour and wonder, have elsewhere told the tale of the War of the Ring, and how it ended both in victory unlooked for and in sorrow long foreseen. Here let it be said that in those days the Heir of Isildur arose in the North, and he took the shards of the sword of Elendil, and in Imladris they were reforged; and he went then to war, a great captain of Men. He was Aragorn son of Arathorn, the nine and thirtieth heir in the right line from Isildur, and yet more like to Elendil than any before him. Battle there was in Rohan, and Curunír the traitor was thrown down and Isengard broken; and before the City of Gondor a great field was fought, and the Lord of Morgul, Captain of Sauron, there passed into darkness; and the Heir of Isildur led the host of the West to the Black Gates of Mordor.

In that last battle were Mithrandir, and the sons of Elrond, and the King of Rohan, and lords of Gondor, and the Heir of Isildur with the Dúnedain of the North. There at the last they looked upon death and defeat, and all their valour was in vain; for Sauron was too strong. Yet in that hour was put to the proof that which Mithrandir had spoken, and help came from the hands of the weak when the Wise faltered. For, as many songs have since sung, it was the Periannath, the Little People, dwellers in hillsides and meadows, that brought them deliverance.

For Frodo the Halfling, it is said, at the bidding of Mithrandir took on himself the burden, and alone with his servant he passed through peril and darkness and came at last in Sauron's despite even to Mount Doom; and there into the Fire where it was wrought he cast the Great Ring of Power, and so at last it was unmade and its evil consumed.

Then Sauron failed, and he was utterly vanquished and passed away like a shadow of malice; and the towers of Barad-dûr crumbled in ruin, and at the rumour of their fall many lands trembled. Thus peace came again, and a new Spring opened on earth; and the Heir of Isildur was crowned King of Gondor and Arnor, and the might of the Dúnedain was lifted up and their glory renewed. In the courts of Minas Anor the White Tree flowered again, for a seedling was found by Mithrandir in the snows of Mindolluin that rose tall and white above the City of Gondor; and while it still grew there the Elder Days were not wholly forgotten in the hearts of the Kings.

Now all these things were achieved for the most part by the counsel and vigilance of Mithrandir, and in the last few days he was revealed as a lord of great reverence, and clad in white he rode into battle; but not until the time came for him to depart was it known that he had long guarded the Red Ring of Fire. At the first that Ring had been entrusted to Círdan, Lord of the Havens; but he had surrendered it to Mithrandir, for he knew whence he came and whither at last he would return.

'Take now this Ring,' he said; 'for thy labours and thy cares will be heavy, but in all it will support thee and defend thee from weariness. For this is the Ring of Fire, and herewith, maybe, thou shalt rekindle hearts to the valour of old in a world that grows chill. But as for me, my heart is with the Sea, and I will dwell by the grey shores, guarding the Havens until the last ship sails. Then I shall await thee.'

White was that ship and long was it a-building, and long it awaited the end of which Círdan had spoken. But when all these things were done, and the Heir of Isildur had taken up the lordship of Men, and the dominion of the West had passed to him, then it was made plain that the power of the Three Rings also was ended, and to the Firstborn the world grew old and grey. In that time the last of the Noldor set sail from the Havens and left Middle-earth for ever. And latest of all the Keepers of the Three Rings rode to the Sea, and Master Elrond took there the ship that Círdan had made ready. In the twilight of autumn it sailed out of Mithlond, until the seas of the Bent World fell away beneath it, and the winds of the round sky troubled it no more, and borne upon the high airs above the mists of the world it passed into the Ancient West, and an end was come for the Eldar of story and of song.

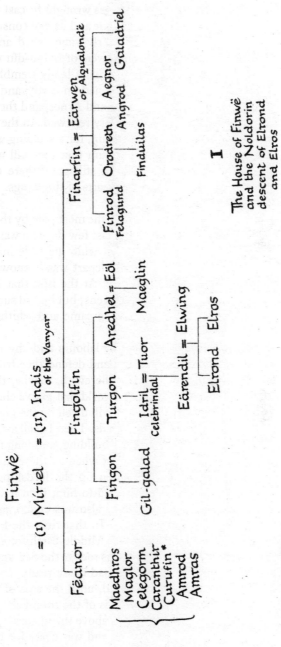

I

The House of Finwë
and the Noldorin
descent of Elrond
and Elros

Finwë

= (I) Míriel    = (II) Indis of the Vanyar

Fëanor                    Fingolfin                    Finarfin = Eärwen of Alqualondë

Maedhros                  Fingon    Turgon    Aredhel = Eöl    Finrod    Orodreth    Aegnor    Galadriel
Maglor                                                              Felagund              Angrod
Celegorm                  Gil-galad    Idril = Tuor    Maeglin                Finduilas
Caranthir                              Celebrindal
Curufin *
Amrod                                  Eärendil = Elwing
Amras
                                       Elrond    Elros

* father of Celebrimbor

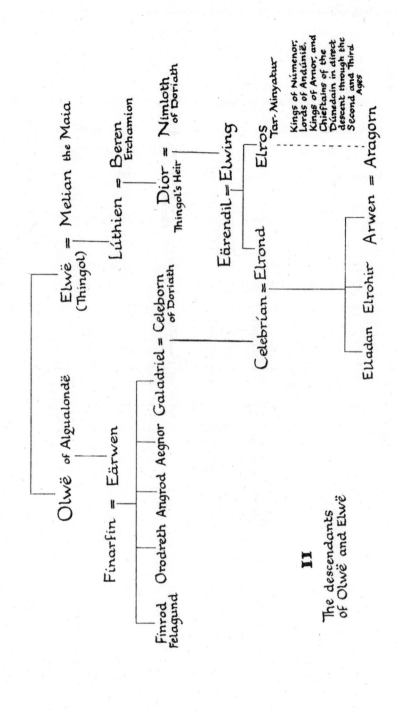

Olwë of Alqualondë — Elwë (Thingol) = Melian the Maia

Finarfin = Eärwen

Finrod Felagund   Orodreth   Angrod   Aegnor   Galadriel = Celeborn of Doriath

Lúthien = Beren Erchamion

Dior = Nimloth of Doriath
Thingol's Heir

Eärendil = Elwing

Celebrían = Elrond          Elros Tar-Minyatur

Kings of Númenor, Lords of Andúnië, Kings of Arnor, and Chieftains of the Dúnedain in direct descent through the Second and Third Ages

Elladan   Elrohir   Arwen = Aragorn

II

The descendants of Olwë and Elwë

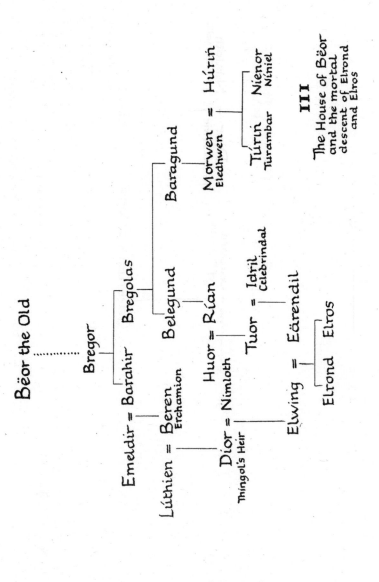

III

The House of Bëor
and the mortal
descent of Elrond
and Elros

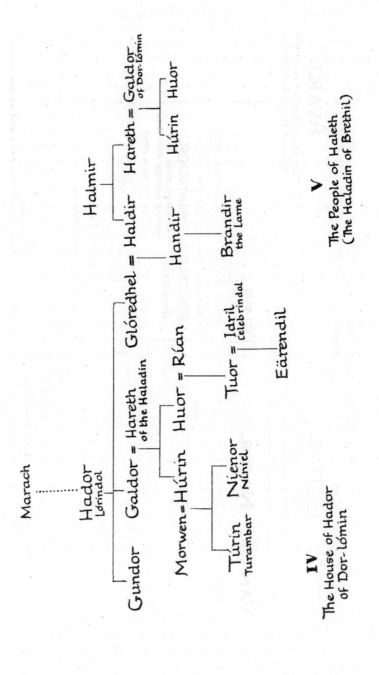

Marach

Hador
Lórindol

Gundor     Galdor = Hareth          Glóredhel = Haldir          Halmir          Hareth = Galdor
                    of the Haladin                                                            of Dor-lómin

Morwen = Húrin     Huor = Rían                    Handir                    Húrin     Huor

Túrin     Nienor                    Tuor = Idril                    Brandir
Turambar  Níniel                           Celebrindal                  the Lame

                                    Eärendil

**IV**

The House of Hador
of Dor-lómin

**V**

The People of Haleth
(The Haladin of Brethil)

# QUENDI
The Elves

## ELDAR
Elves of the Great Journey from Cuiviénen

## AVARI
'The unwilling': Elves who refused the Great Journey

### VANYAR
All went to Aman

### NOLDOR
All went to Aman

**Those that went to Aman**

## CALAQUENDI
'Elves of the Light' (High Elves)
(They came to Aman in the days of the Two Trees)

### TELERI

**Those that remained in Beleriand:**

## SINDAR
Grey-elves

**Those that left the march of the Teleri east of the Misty Mts.:**

## NANDOR
of whom some afterwards entered Beleriand:

## LAIQUENDI
Green-elves of Ossiriand

## ÚMANYAR
The Eldar who were 'not of Aman'

## MORIQUENDI
'Elves of the Darkness'
(They never saw the Light of the Trees)

---

The Sundering of the Elves and some of the names given to their divisions

# NOTE ON PRONUNCIATION

The following note is intended simply to clarify a few main features in the pronunciation of names in the Elvish languages, and is by no means exhaustive. For full information on the subject see *The Lord of the Rings* Appendix E.

## CONSONANTS

C        always has the value of *k*, never of *s*; thus *Celeborn* is '*Keleborn*', not '*Seleborn*'. In a few cases, as *Tulkas*, *Kementári* a *k* has been used in the spelling in this book.

CH     always has the value of *ch* in Scotch *loch* or German *buch*, never that of *ch* in English *church*. Examples are *Carcharoth*, *Erchamion*.

DH     is always used to represent the sound of a voiced ('soft') *th* in English, that is the *th* in *then*, not the *th* in *thin*. Examples are *Maedhros*, *Aredhel*, *Haudh-en-Arwen*.

G        always has the sound of English *g* in *get*; thus *Region*, *Eregion* are not pronounced like English *region*, and the first syllable of *Ginglith* is as in English *begin*, not as in *gin*.

           Consonants written twice are pronounced long; thus *Yavanna* has the long *n* heard in English *unnamed*, *penknife*, not the short *n* in *unaimed*, *penny*.

## VOWELS

AI      has the sound of English *eye*; thus the second syllable of *Edain* is like English *dine*, not *Dane*.

AU     has the value of English *ow* in *town*; thus the first syllable of *Aulë* is like English *owl*, and the first syllable of *Sauron* is like English *sour*, not *sore*.

EI       as in *Teiglin* has the sound of English *grey*.

IE       should not be pronounced as in English *piece*, but with both the vowels *i* and *e* sounded, and run together; thus *Ni-enna*, not '*Neena*'.

UI      as in *Uinen* has the sound of English *ruin*.

AE     as in *Aegnor*, *Nirnaeth*, and OE as in *Noegyth*, *Loeg*, are combinations of the individual vowels, *a-e*, *o-e*, but *ae* may be pronounced in the same way as *ai*, and *oe* as in English *toy*.

EA and EO  are not run together, but constitute two syllables; these combinations are written *ëa* and *ëo* (or, when they begin names, *Eä* and *Eö*: *Eärendil*, *Eönwë*).

Ú            in names like *Húrin*, *Túrin*, *Túna* should be pronounced *oo*; thus '*Toorin*', not '*Tyoorin*'.

ER, IR, UR  before a consonant (as in *Nerdanel*, *Círdan*, *Gurthang*) or at the end of a word (as in *Ainur*) should not be pronounced as in English *fern*, *fir*, *fur*, but as in English *air*, *eer*, *oor*.

E            at the end of words is always pronounced as a distinct vowel, and in this position is written *ë*. It is likewise always pronounced in the middle of words like *Celeborn*, *Menegroth*.

A circumflex accent in stressed monosyllables in Sindarin denotes the particularly long vowel heard in such words (thus *Hîn Húrin*); but in Adúnaic (Númenórean) and Khuzdul (Dwarvish) names the circumflex is simply used to denote long vowels.

# INDEX

Since the number of names in the book is very large, this index provides, in addition to page-references, a short statement concerning each person and place. These statements are not epitomes of all that is said in the text, and for most of the central figures in the narrative are kept extremely brief; but such an index is inevitably bulky, and I have reduced its size in various ways.

The chief of these concerns the fact that very often the English translation of an Elvish name is also used as the name independently; thus for example the dwelling of King Thingol is called both *Menegroth* and 'The Thousand Caves' (and also both together). In most such cases I have combined the Elvish name and its translated meaning under one entry, with the result that the page-references are not restricted to the name that appears as the heading (e.g., those under *Echoriath* include those to 'Encircling Mountains'). The English renderings are given separate headings, but only with a simple direction to the main entry, and only if they occur independently. Words in inverted commas are translations; many of these occur in the text (as *Tol Eressëa* 'the Lonely Isle'), but I have added a great many others. Information about some names that are not translated is contained in the Appendix.

With the many titles and formal expressions in English whose Elvish originals are not given, such as 'the Elder King' and 'the Two Kindreds', I have been selective, but the great majority are registered. The references are in intention complete (and sometimes include pages where the subject of the entry occurs but is not actually mentioned by name) except in a very few cases where the name occurs very frequently indeed, as *Beleriand*, *Valar*. Here the word *passim* is used, but selected references are given to important passages; and in the entries for some of the Noldorin princes the many occurrences of the name that relate only to their sons or their houses have been eliminated.

References to *The Lord of the Rings* are by title of the volume, book, and chapter.

*Aegnor*   The fourth son of Finarfin, who with his brother Angrod held the northern slopes of Dorthonion; slain in the Dagor Bragollach. The name means 'Fell Fire'. 61, 84, 120, 150–1

*Aelin-uial*   'Meres of Twilight', where Aros flowed into Sirion. 114, 122, 168, 217, 231

*Aerandir*   'Sea-wanderer', one of the three mariners who accompanied Eärendil on his voyages. 248

*Aerin*   A kinswoman of Húrin in Dor-lómin; taken as wife by Brodda the Easterling; aided Morwen after the Nirnaeth Arnoediad. 198, 215

*Aftercomers*   The Younger Children of Ilúvatar, Men; translation of *Hildor*. 83, 99

*Agarwaen*   'Blood-stained', name given to himself by Túrin when he came to Nargothrond. 210

*Aglarond*   'The Glittering Cavern' of Helm's Deep in Ered Nimrais (see *The Two Towers* III 8). 291

*Aglon*   'The Narrow Pass', between Dorthonion and the heights to the west of Himring. 123–4, 135, 152–3

*Ainulindalë*   'The Music of the Ainur', also called *The (Great) Music*, *The (Great) Song*. 15–20, 25–6, 28, 41–2, 45–6, 50, 68, 74, 105, 205. Also the name of the account of Creation said to have been composed by Rúmil of Tirion in the Elder Days. 74

*Ainur*   'The Holy Ones' (singular *Ainu*); the first beings created by Ilúvatar, the 'order' of the Valar and Maiar, made before Eä. 15–20, 25–6, 41–2, 44, 46, 56, 105, 205, 233

*Akallabêth*   'The Downfallen', Adûnaic (Númenórean) word equivalent in meaning to Quenya *Atalantë*. 281   Also the title of the account of the Downfall of Númenor. 290

*Alcarinquë*   'The Glorious', name of a star. 48

*Alcarondas*   The great ship of Ar-Pharazôn in which he sailed to Aman. 278

*Aldaron*   'Lord of Trees', a Quenya name of the Vala Oromë; cf. *Tauron*. 29

*Aldudénië*   'Lament for the Two Trees', made by a Vanyarin Elf named Elemmírë. 76

*Almaren*   The first abode of the Valar in Arda, before the second onslaught of Melkor: an isle in a great lake in the midst of Middle-earth. 35–7, 102

*Alqualondë*   'Haven of the Swans', the chief city and haven of the Teleri on the shores of Aman. 60–2, 72, 86–7, 89, 104, 111, 129, 156, 249, 251

*Aman*   'Blessed, free from evil', the name of the land in the West, beyond the Great Sea, in which the Valar dwelt after they had left the Isle of Almaren. Often referred to as *the Blessed Realm*. *Passim*; see especially 37, 62, 264

*Amandil*   'Lover of Aman'; the last lord of Andúnië in Númenor, descendant of Elros and father of Elendil; set out on a voyage to Valinor and did not return. 271–3, 275–6, 279, 292

*Anfauglir*   A name of the wolf Carcharoth, translated in the text as 'Jaws of Thirst'. 180

*Anfauglith*   Name of the plain of Ard-galen after its desolation by Morgoth in the Battle of Sudden Flame; translated in the text as 'the Gasping Dust'. Cf. *Dor-nu-Fauglith*. 151, 160, 178, 190–2, 197, 207–8, 212, 227, 251

*Angainor*   The chain wrought by Aulë with which Melkor was twice bound. 51, 252

*Angband*   'Iron Prison, Hell of Iron', the great dungeon-fortress of Morgoth in the Northwest of Middle-earth. *Passim*; see especially 47, 81, 95–6, 118, 179. *The Siege of Angband* 115–16, 118, 121, 124, 132, 150–1, 159, 167

*Anghabar*   'Iron-delvings', a mine in the Encircling Mountains about the plain of Gondolin. 138

*Anglachel*   The sword made from meteoric iron that Thingol received from Eöl and which he gave to Beleg; after its reforging for Túrin named *Gurthang*. 201–2, 206–10

*Angrenost*   'Iron Fortress', Númenórean fortress on the west borders of Gondor, afterwards inhabited by the wizard Curunír (Saruman); see *Isengard*. 291

*Angrim*   Father of Gorlim the Unhappy. 162

*Angrist*   'Iron-cleaver', the knife made by Telchar of Nogrod, taken from Curufin by Beren and used by him to cut the Silmaril from Morgoth's crown. 177, 181

*Angrod*   The third son of Finarfin, who with his brother Aegnor held the northern slopes of Dorthonion; slain in the Dagor Bragollach. 61, 84, 111–12, 120, 129, 150–1, 212

*Anguirel*   Eöl's sword, made of the same metal as Anglachel. 202

*Annael*   Grey-elf of Mithrim, fosterfather of Tuor. 238

*Annatar*   'Lord of Gifts', name given to himself by Sauron in the Second Age, in that time when he appeared in a fair form among the Eldar who remained in Middle-earth. 287

*Annon-in-Gelydh*   'Gate of the Noldor', entrance to a subterranean watercourse in the western hills of Dor-lómin, leading to Cirith Ninniach. 238

*Annúminas*   'Tower of the West' (i.e. of Westernesse, Númenor); city of the Kings of Arnor beside Lake Nenuial. 290, 292, 296

*Anor*   See *Minas Anor*.

*Apanónar*   'The Afterborn', an Elvish name for Men. 103

*Aradan*   Sindarin name of Malach, son of Marach. 143, 147

*Aragorn*   The thirty-ninth Heir of Isildur in the direct line; King of the reunited realms of Arnor and Gondor after the War of the Ring; wedded Arwen, daughter of Elrond. 303. Called *the Heir of Isildur* 303–4

*Araman*   Barren wasteland on the coast of Aman, between the Pelóri and the Sea, extending northward to the Helcaraxë. 72, 80, 86–7, 89–90, 101–2, 106, 111, 240

*Aranel* Name of Dior Thingol's Heir. 188

*Aranrúth* 'King's Ire', the name of Thingol's sword. Aranrúth survived the ruin of Doriath and was possessed by the Kings of Númenor. 201

*Aranwë* Elf of Gondolin, father of Voronwë. 239

*Aratan* Second son of Isildur, slain with him at the Gladden Fields. 295

*Aratar* 'The Exalted', the eight Valar of greatest power. 29

*Arathorn* Father of Aragorn. 303

*Arda* 'The Realm', name of the Earth as the Kingdom of Manwë. *Passim*; see especially 19, 22

*Ard-galen* The great grassy plain north of Dorthonion, called after its desolation *Anfauglith* and *Dor-nu-Fauglith*. The name means 'the Green Region'; cf. *Calen-ardhon* (Rohan). 106, 115–16, 118–20, 123, 150–1

*Aredhel* 'Noble Elf', the sister of Turgon of Gondolin, who was ensnared by Eöl in Nan Elmoth and bore to him Maeglin; called also *Ar-Feiniel*, the White Lady of the Noldor, the White Lady of Gondolin. 60, 131–8, 201

*Ar-Feiniel* See *Aredhel*.

*Ar-Gimilzôr* Twenty-second King of Númenor, persecutor of the Elendili. 268–9

*Argonath* 'King-stones', the Pillars of the Kings, great carvings of Isildur and Anárion on the Anduin at the entrance to the northern bounds of Gondor (see *The Fellowship of the Ring* II 9). 291, 297

*Arien* A Maia, chosen by the Valar to guide the vessel of the Sun. 99–101

*Armenelos* City of the Kings in Númenor. 261, 263, 270–3, 291

*Arminas* See *Gelmir* (2).

*Arnor* 'Land of the King', the northern realm of the Númenóreans in Middle-earth, established by Elendil after his escape from the Drowning of Númenor. 291–2, 304

*Aros* The southern river of Doriath. 96, 112, 121–2, 124, 132, 146, 232–4

*Arossiach* The Fords of Aros, near the north-eastern edge of Doriath. 121, 132–3, 135–6

*Ar-Pharazôn* 'The Golden', twenty-fourth and last King of Númenor; named in Quenya *Tar-Calion*; captor of Sauron, by whom he was seduced; commander of the great fleet that went against Aman. 269–80

*Ar-Sakalthôr* Father of Ar-Gimilzôr. 268

*Arthad* One of the twelve companions of Barahir on Dorthonion. 155

*Arvernien* The coastlands of Middle-earth west of Sirion's mouths. Cf. Bilbo's song at Rivendell: 'Eärendil was a mariner that tarried in Arvernien . . .' (*The Fellowship of the Ring* II 1). 244

*Ar-Zimraphel* See *Míriel* (2).

*Ascar*   The most northerly of the tributaries of Gelion in Ossiriand (after-wards called *Rathlóriel*). The name means 'rushing, impetuous'. 92, 123–4, 140, 146, 235

*Astaldo*   'The Valiant', name of the Vala Tulkas. 28

*Atalantë*   'The Downfallen', Quenya word equivalent in meaning to *Akallabêth*. 281

*Atanamir*   See *Tar-Atanamir*.

*Atanatári*   'Fathers of Men'; see *Atani*. 103, 190

*Atani*   'The Second People', Men (singular *Atan*). For the origin of the name see 143. Since in Beleriand for a long time the only Men known to the Noldor and Sindar were those of the Three Houses of the Elf-friends, this name (in the Sindarin form *Adan*, plural *Edain*) became specially associated with them, so that it was seldom applied to other Men who came later to Beleriand, or who were reported to be dwelling beyond the Mountains. But in the speech of Ilúvatar (41) the mean-ing is 'Men (in general)'. 41, 103, 143; *Edain* 143–4, 146–9, 156–8, 195, 197, 236, 259–61, 280

*Aulë*   A Vala, one of the Aratar, the smith and master of crafts, spouse of Yavanna; see especially 27, 39, and for his making of the Dwarves 43 ff.   19–20, 25, 27, 29–30, 32, 35–6, 39, 41, 43–6, 51, 53, 60, 62, 64, 69, 78, 84, 92, 99, 260

*Avallónë*   Haven and city of the Eldar on Tol Eressëa, so named, according to the *Akallabêth*, 'for it is of all cities the nearest to Valinor'. 260, 263–4, 269, 278, 281–2, 292, 296

*Avari*   'The Unwilling, the Refusers', the name given to all those Elves who refused to join the westward march from Cuiviénen. See *Eldar* and *Dark Elves*. 52–3, 94, 99, 286

*Avathar*   'The Shadows', the forsaken land on the coast of Aman south of the Bay of Eldamar, between the Pelóri and the Sea, where Melkor met Ungoliant. 73–4, 80, 101

*Azaghâl*   Lord of the Dwarves of Belegost; wounded Glaurung in the Nirnaeth Arnoediad, and was killed by him. 193

*Balan*   The name of Bëor the Old before he took service with Finrod. 142

*Balar*   The great bay to the south of Beleriand into which the river Sirion flowed. 51, 54, 57, 120   Also the isle in the bay, said to have been the eastern horn of Tol Eressëa that broke away, where Círdan and Gil-galad dwelt after the Nirnaeth Arnoediad. 57, 92, 121, 159, 196, 244, 246–7

*Balrog*   'Demon of Might', Sindarin form (Quenya *Valarauko*) of the name of the demons of fire that served Morgoth. 31, 47, 81, 107–8, 121, 151–2, 167, 192–3, 242–3, 251

*Barad-dûr*   'The Dark Tower' of Sauron in Mordor. 267, 270, 280, 292, 294, 302, 304

*Barad Eithel*   'Tower of the Well', the fortress of the Noldor at Eithel Sirion. 191

*Barad Nimras* 'White Horn Tower', raised by Finrod Felagund on the cape west of Eglarest. 120, 196

*Baragund* Father of Morwen the wife of Húrin; nephew of Barahir and one of his twelve companions on Dorthonion. 148, 155, 160, 198, 251

*Barahir* Father of Beren; rescued Finrod Felagund in the Dagor Bragollach, and received from him his ring; slain on Dorthonion. For the later history of the ring of Barahir, which became an heirloom of the House of Isildur, see *The Lord of the Rings* Appendix A (I, iii). 105, 148, 152, 154–5, 161–4, 166–9, 186, 188, 198, 231, 251

*Baran* Elder son of Bëor the Old. 142–3

*Baranduin* 'The Brown River' in Eriador, flowing into the Sea south of the Blue Mountains; the Brandywine of the Shire in *The Lord of the Rings.* 290

*Bar-en-Danwedh* 'House of Ransom', the name that Mîm the Dwarf gave to his dwelling on Amon Rûdh when he yielded it to Túrin. 203, 205–6

*Battles of Beleriand* The first battle: 96. The second battle (the Battle-under-Stars): see *Dagor-nuin-Giliath.* The third battle (the Glorious Battle): see *Dagor Aglareb.* The fourth battle (the Battle of Sudden Flame): see *Dagor Bragollach.* The fifth battle (Unnumbered Tears): see *Nirnaeth Arnoediad. The Great Battle:* 251–2

*Bauglir* A name of Morgoth: 'the Constrainer'. 104, 199, 211, 231, 255

*Beleg* A great archer and chief of the marchwardens of Doriath; called *Cúthalion* 'Strongbow'; friend and companion of Túrin, by whom he was slain. 157, 185–6, 189, 199–202, 204–9, 225

*Belegaer* 'The Great Sea' of the West, between Middle-earth and Aman. Named *Belegaer* 37, 89, 238; but very frequently called *the (Great) Sea*, also *the Western Sea* and *the Great Water.*

*Belegost* 'Great Fortress', one of the two cities of the Dwarves in the Blue Mountains; translation into Sindarin of Dwarvish *Gabilgathol.* See *Mickleburg.* 91–2, 94, 113, 133, 189, 193, 204, 231, 233

*Belegund* Father of Rían the wife of Huor; nephew of Barahir and one of his twelve companions on Dorthonion. 148, 155, 161, 198

*Beleriand* The name was said to have signified 'the country of Balar', and to have been given at first to the lands about the mouths of Sirion that faced the Isle of Balar. Later the name spread to include all the ancient coast of the Northwest of Middle-earth south of the Firth of Drengist, and all the inner lands south of Hithlum and eastwards to the feet of the Blue Mountains, divided by the river Sirion into East and West Beleriand. Beleriand was broken in the turmoils at the end of the First Age, and invaded by the sea, so that only Ossiriand (Lindon) remained. *Passim*; see especially 120–4, 252, 285–6

*Belfalas* Region on the southern coast of Gondor looking on to the great bay of the same name; *Bay of Belfalas* 291

*Belthil* 'Divine radiance', the image of Telperion made by Turgon in Gondolin. 126

*Belthronding*   The bow of Beleg Cúthalion, which was buried with him.
  208

*Bëor*   Called the Old; leader of the first Men to enter Beleriand; vassal of
  Finrod Felagund; progenitor of the House of Bëor (called also *the
  Eldest House of Men* and *the First House of the Edain*); see *Balan*.
  140–3, 148–50, 169.  *House of, People of, Bëor* 143–5, 148, 152, 157,
  160–1

*Bereg*   Grandson of Baran son of Bëor the Old (this is not stated in the
  text); a leader of dissension among the Men of Estolad; went back over
  the mountains into Eriador. 144–5

*Beren*   Son of Barahir; cut a Silmaril from Morgoth's crown to be the
  bride-price of Lúthien Thingol's daughter, and was slain by Carcharoth the wolf of Angband; but returning from the dead, alone of
  mortal Men, lived afterwards with Lúthien on Tol Galen in Ossiriand,
  and fought with the Dwarves at Sarn Athrad. Great-grandfather of
  Elrond and Elros and ancestor of the Númenórean Kings. Called
  also *Camlost*, *Erchamion*, and *One-hand*. 105, 123, 148, 155, 161–70,
  172–89, 198, 210, 231, 234–5, 246

*Black Land*   See *Mordor*.

*Black Sword*   See *Mormegil*.

*Black Years*   See 289, 294

*Blessed Realm*   See *Aman*.

*Blue Mountains*   See *Ered Luin* and *Ered Lindon*.

*Bór*   A chieftain of the Easterlings, follower with his three sons of
  Maedhros and Maglor. 157, 189.  *Sons of Bór* 193

*Borlach*   One of the three sons of Bór; slain with his brothers in the Nirnaeth Arnoediad. 157

*Borlad*   One of the three sons of Bór; see *Borlach*.

*Boromir*   Great-grandson of Bëor the Old, grandfather of Barahir father
  of Beren; first lord of Ladros. 148

*Boron*   Father of Boromir. 148

*Borthand*   One of the three sons of Bór; see *Borlach*.

*Bragollach*   See *Dagor Bragollach*.

*Brandir*   Called the Lame; ruler of the People of Haleth after the death of
  Handir his father; enamoured of Nienor; slain by Túrin. 216, 220–5

*Bregolas*   Father of Baragund and Belegund; slain in the Dagor Bragollach. 148, 151, 155

*Bregor*   Father of Barahir and Bregolas. 148

*Brethil*   The forest between the rivers Teiglin and Sirion, dwelling-place
  of the Haladin (the People of Haleth). 120, 147, 155, 157–9, 176, 189–
  90, 192, 195, 201, 203, 205, 212, 216, 219–21, 225–6, 229–30

*Bridge of Esgalduin*   See *Iant Iaur*.

*Brilthor*   'Glittering Torrent', the fourth of the tributaries of Gelion in
  Ossiriand. 123

*Brithiach*   The ford over Sirion north of the Forest of Brethil. 131–2, 136,
  147, 158, 206, 227, 229

*Celegorm*   The third son of Fëanor, called the Fair; until the Dagor Bragollach lord of the region of Himlad with Curufin his brother; dwelt in Nargothrond and imprisoned Lúthien; master of Huan the wolfhound; slain by Dior in Menegroth. 60, 62, 83, 107, 124, 131–2, 135, 152, 169–70, 172–3, 176–7, 183–4, 188–9, 236, 286

*Celon*   River flowing southwest from the Hill of Himring, a tributary of Aros. The name means 'stream flowing down from heights'. 96, 124, 132, 135, 142, 146, 156

*Children of Ilúvatar*   Also *Children of Eru*: translations of *Híni Ilúvataro*, *Eruhíni*; the Firstborn and the Followers, Elves and Men. Also *The Children, Children of the Earth, Children of the World. Passim*; see especially 18, 41

*Círdan*   'The Shipwright'; Telerin Elf, lord of the Falas (coasts of West Beleriand); at the destruction of the Havens after the Nirnaeth Arnoediad escaped with Gil-galad to the Isle of Balar; during the Second and Third Ages keeper of the Grey Havens in the Gulf of Lhûn; at the coming of Mithrandir entrusted to him Narya, the Ring of Fire. 58, 91–2, 96, 107, 113, 120, 128, 160, 196, 212, 244, 246–7, 254, 295, 298–300, 304

*Cirith Ninniach*   'Rainbow Cleft', by which Tuor came to the Western Sea; see *Annon-in-Gelydh*. 238

*Cirith Thoronath*   'Eagles' Cleft', a high pass in the mountains north of Gondolin, where Glorfindel fought with a Balrog and fell into the abyss. 243

*Cirth*   The Runes, first devised by Daeron of Doriath. 95

*Ciryon*   Third son of Isildur, slain with him at the Gladden Fields. 295

*Corollairë*   'The Green Mound' of the Two Trees in Valinor; also called *Ezellohar*. 38

*Crissaegrim*   The mountain-peaks south of Gondolin, where were the eyries of Thorondor. 121, 154, 158, 182, 200, 227

*Crossings of Teiglin*   In the southwest of the Forest of Brethil, where the old road southward from the Pass of Sirion crossed the Teiglin. 147, 205–6, 216–17, 219, 223, 225, 229

*Cuiviénen*   'Water of Awakening', the lake in Middle-earth where the first Elves awoke, and where they were found by Oromë. 48, 50–3, 55, 83, 99, 233

*Culúrien*   A name of Laurelin. 38

*Curufin*   The fifth son of Fëanor, called the Crafty; father of Celebrimbor. For the origin of his name see *Fëanor*; and for his history see *Celegorm*. 60, 83, 124, 132, 135–6, 152, 169–70, 172–3, 176–8, 183–4, 188–9, 236, 286

*Curufinwë*   See *Fëanor*. 63, 69

*Curunír*   'The one of cunning devices', Elvish name of Saruman, one of the Istari (Wizards). 300–3

*Cúthalion*   'Strongbow'; see *Beleg*.

*Dol Guldur* 'Hill of Sorcery', fastness of the Necromancer (Sauron) in southern Mirkwood in the Third Age. 299–302

*Dolmed* 'Wet Head', a great mountain in the Ered Luin, near the Dwarf-cities of Nogrod and Belegost. 91–2, 96, 193, 235

*Dor Caranthir* 'Land of Caranthir'; see *Thargelion*. 124, 145, 153

*Dor-Cúarthol* 'Land of Bow and Helm', name of the country defended by Beleg and Túrin from their lair on Amon Rûdh. 205

*Dor Daedeloth* 'Land of the Shadow of Horror', the land of Morgoth in the north. 107, 109, 111

*Dor Dínen* 'The Silent Land', where nothing dwelt, between the upper waters of Esgalduin and Aros. 121

*Dor Firn-i-Guinar* 'Land of the Dead that Live', name of that region in Ossiriand where Beren and Lúthien dwelt after their return. 188, 235

*Doriath* 'Land of the Fence' (*Dor Iâth*), referring to the Girdle of Melian, earlier called Eglador; the kingdom of Thingol and Melian in the forests of Neldoreth and Region, ruled from Menegroth on the river Esgalduin. Also called *the Hidden Kingdom. Passim*; see especially 97, 121–2

*Dorlas* A Man of the Haladin in Brethil; went with Túrin and Hunthor to the attack on Glaurung, but withdrew in fear; slain by Brandir the Lame. 216, 220–1, 224  The wife of Dorlas, not named, 224

*Dor-lómin* Region in the south of Hithlum, the territory of Fingon, given as a fief to the House of Hador; the home of Húrin and Morwen. 89, 119–20, 147, 155, 158–60, 190, 194, 198–9, 204, 209, 211, 214–17, 224–5, 228, 230, 232–3, 238  *The Lady of Dor-lómin*: Morwen. 198

*Dor-nu-Fauglith* 'Land under Choking Ash'; see *Anfauglith*. 153, 182

*Dorthonion* 'Land of Pines', the great forested highlands on the northern borders of Beleriand, afterwards called Taur-nu-Fuin. Cf. Tree-beard's song in *The Two Towers* III 4: 'To the pine-trees upon the highland of Dorthonion I climbed in the Winter . . .' 51, 95, 106, 111, 115–16, 119–21, 123–4, 143, 148, 151–3, 155, 160–4, 189–90

*Dragon-helm of Dor-lómin* Heirloom of the House of Hador, worn by Túrin; also called *the Helm of Hador*. 199, 204–5, 211, 230

*Dragons* 192–3, 242–3, 252, 260, 289, 299

*Drauglin* The great werewolf slain by Huan at Tol-in-Gaurhoth, and in whose form Beren entered Angband. 174, 178–80

*Drengist* The long firth that pierced Ered Lómin, the west-fence of Hithlum. 54, 80, 89–90, 97, 100, 116, 119, 160

*Dry River* The river that once flowed out under the Encircling Mountains from the primeval lake where was afterwards Tumladen, the plain of Gondolin. 136, 228

*Duilwen* The fifth of the tributaries of Gelion in Ossiriand. 123

*Dúnedain* 'The Edain of the West'; see *Númenóreans*.

*Dungortheb* See *Nan Dungortheb*.

*Durin* Lord of the Dwarves of Khazad-dûm (Moria). 44, 294

*Dwarf-road* Road leading down into Beleriand from the cities of Nogrod

*Eglador*   The former name of Doriath, before it was encompassed by the
Girdle of Melian; probably connected with the name *Eglath*. 97

*Eglarest*   The southern of the Havens of the Falas on the coast of Beleri-
and. 58, 96, 108, 120, 122, 196, 246

*Eglath*   'The Forsaken People', name given to themselves by the Telerin
Elves who remained in Beleriand seeking for Elwë (Thingol) when the
main host of the Teleri departed to Aman. 58, 233

*Eilinel*   The wife of Gorlim the Unhappy. 162–3

*Eithel Ivrin*   'Ivrin's Well', the source of the river Narog beneath Ered
Wethrin. 209, 212

*Eithel Sirion*   'Sirion's Well', in the eastern face of Ered Wethrin, where
was the great fortress of Fingolfin and Fingon (see *Barad Eithel*). 107,
119–20, 152, 160, 190–1

*Ekkaia*   Elvish name of the Outer Sea, encircling Arda; referred to also as
*the Outer Ocean* and *the Encircling Sea*. 37, 40, 50, 62, 89, 100–1,
104, 186

*Elbereth*   The usual name of Varda in Sindarin, 'Star-Queen'; cf. *Elentári*.
26, 40

*Eldalië*   'The Elven-folk', used as equivalent to *Eldar*. 22, 53, 57, 66, 125,
166, 183, 186–7, 190, 202, 254

*Eldamar*   'Elvenhome', the region of Aman in which the Elves dwelt;
also the great Bay of the same name. 58–9, 61, 63, 69–70, 72–3, 86,
134, 176, 248

*Eldar*   According to Elvish legend the name *Eldar* 'People of the Stars'
was given to all the Elves by the Vala Oromë (49). It came however to
be used to refer only to the Elves of the Three Kindreds (Vanyar,
Noldor, and Teleri) who set out on the great westward march from
Cuiviénen (whether or not they remained in Middle-earth), and to
exclude the Avari. The Elves of Aman, and all Elves who ever dwelt
in Aman, were called the High Elves (*Tareldar*) and Elves of the Light
(*Calaquendi*); see *Dark Elves*, *Úmanyar*. *Passim*; see entry *Elves*.

*Eldarin*   Of the Eldar; used in reference to the language(s) of the Eldar.
The occurrences of the term in fact refer to Quenya, also called *High
Eldarin* and *High-elven*; see *Quenya*.

*Elder Days*   The First Age; also called *the Eldest Days*. 30, 38, 103, 114,
208, 210, 231, 234, 242, 294, 304

*Elder King*   Manwë. 249, 252

*Eledhwen*   See *Morwen*.

*Elemmírë* (*1*)   Name of a star. 48

*Elemmírë* (*2*)   Vanyarin Elf, maker of the *Aldudénië*, the Lament for the
Two Trees. 76

*Elendë*   A name of Eldamar. 61, 85, 111

*Elendil*   Called the Tall; son of Amandil, last lord of Andúnië in Númenor,
descended from Eärendil and Elwing but not of the direct line of the
Kings; escaped with his sons Isildur and Anárion from the Drowning
of Númenor and founded the Númenórean realms in Middle-earth;

the hosts of the Teleri on the westward journey from Cuiviénen, until he was lost in Nan Elmoth; afterwards Lord of the Sindar, ruling in Doriath with Melian; received the Silmaril from Beren; slain in Menegroth by the Dwarves. Called (*Elu*) *Thingol* in Sindarin. See *Dark Elves, Thingol*. 52–5, 57–9, 91, 233–4

*Elwing* Daughter of Dior, who escaping from Doriath with the Silmaril wedded Eärendil at the Mouths of Sirion and went with him to Valinor; mother of Elrond and Elros. The name means 'Star-spray'; see *Lanthir Lamath*. 105, 148, 235–7, 244, 246–51, 254

*Emeldir* Called the Man-hearted; wife of Barahir and mother of Beren; led the women and children of the House of Bëor from Dorthonion after the Dagor Bragollach. (She was herself also a descendant of Bëor the Old, and her father's name was Beren; this is not stated in the text.) 155, 161

*Emyn Beraid* 'The Tower Hills' in the west of Eriador; see *Elostirion*. 291–2

*Enchanted Isles* The islands set by the Valar in the Great Sea eastwards of Tol Eressëa at the time of the Hiding of Valinor. 102, 248

*Encircling Mountains* See *Echoriath*.

*Encircling Sea* See *Ekkaia*.

*Endor* 'Middle Land', Middle-earth. 89

*Engwar* 'The Sickly', one of the Elvish names for Men. 103

*Eöl* Called the Dark Elf; the great smith who dwelt in Nan Elmoth, and took Aredhel Turgon's sister to wife; friend of the Dwarves; maker of the sword Anglachel (Gurthang); father of Maeglin; put to death in Gondolin. 92, 132–8, 201

*Eönwë* One of the mightiest of the Maiar; called the Herald of Manwë; leader of the host of the Valar in the attack on Morgoth at the end of the First Age. 30, 249–54, 260, 285

*Ephel Brandir* 'The encircling fence of Brandir', dwellings of the Men of Brethil upon Amon Obel; also called *the Ephel*. 216, 219–21

*Ephel Dúath* 'Fence of Shadow', the mountain-range between Gondor and Mordor; also called *the Mountains of Shadow*. 291–2, 297

*Erchamion* 'One-handed', the name of Beren after his escape from Angband. 183, 185, 198, 236

*Erech* A hill in the west of Gondor, where was the Stone of Isildur (see *The Return of the King* V 2). 291

*Ered Engrin* 'The Iron Mountains' in the far north. 109, 115–16, 118, 151, 160

*Ered Gorgoroth* 'The Mountains of Terror', northward of Nan Dungortheb; also called *the Gorgoroth*. 81, 95, 121, 132, 146, 164, 176, 201

*Ered Lindon* 'The Mountains of Lindon', another name for *Ered Luin*, the Blue Mountains. 123–4, 134, 140, 145, 195, 232, 234–5

*Ered Lómin* 'The Echoing Mountains', forming the west-fence of Hithlum. 106, 118–19

*Ered Luin* 'The Blue Mountains', also called *Ered Lindon*. After the destruction at the end of the First Age Ered Luin formed the north-western coastal range of Middle-earth. 54, 91, 94, 112–15, 123, 133, 140, 233, 285–6, 289–90

*Ered Nimrais* The White Mountains (*nimrais* 'white horns'), the great range from east to west south of the Misty Mountains. 94

*Ered Wethrin* 'The Mountains of Shadow', 'The Shadowy Mountains', the great curving range bordering Dor-nu-Fauglith (Ard-galen) on the west and forming the barrier between Hithlum and West Beleriand. 106–7, 109, 113, 116, 118–20, 126, 143, 151–2, 160, 170, 175, 190, 192, 194, 203, 207, 209, 212, 216, 227–8, 239

*Eregion* 'Land of Holly' (called by Men *Hollin*); Noldorin realm in the Second Age at the western feet of the Misty Mountains, where the Elven Rings were made. 286–8

*Ereinion* 'Scion of Kings', the son of Fingon, known always by his surname *Gil-galad*. 154, 196, 244

*Erellont* One of the three mariners who accompanied Eärendil on his voyages. 248

*Eressëa* See *Tol Eressëa*.

*Eriador* The land between the Misty Mountains and the Blue, in which lay the Kingdom of Arnor (and also the Shire of the Hobbits). 54, 91, 94, 145, 267, 290, 295–6, 298, 303

*Eru* 'The One', 'He that is Alone': Ilúvatar. 15, 25–7, 29, 44–6, 74–5, 85, 88, 90, 98, 261, 265–6, 269, 271, 280; also in *Children of Eru*.

*Esgalduin* The river of Doriath, dividing the forests of Neldoreth and Region, and flowing into Sirion. The name means 'River under Veil'. 93, 121, 132, 165, 184–5, 218, 234

*Estë* One of the Valier, the spouse of Irmo (Lórien); her name means 'Rest'. 25, 28, 30, 63, 99–100.

*Estolad* The land south of Nan Elmoth where the Men of the followings of Bëor and Marach dwelt after they crossed the Blue Mountains into Beleriand; translated in the text as 'the Encampment'. 142–6

*Ezellohar* The Green Mound of the Two Trees of Valinor; also called *Corollairë*. 38, 46, 76, 78–9

*Faelivrin* Name given to Finduilas by Gwindor. 210
*Faithful, The* See *Elendili*.
*Falas* The western coasts of Beleriand, south of Nevrast. 58, 93, 96–7, 107, 120, 160, 190, 196, 211

*Falathar* One of the three mariners who accompanied Eärendil on his voyages. 248

*Falathrim* The Telerin Elves of the Falas, whose lord was Círdan. 58

*Falmari* The Sea-elves; name of the Teleri who departed from Middle-earth and went into the West. 53

*Fëanor* Eldest son of Finwë (the only child of Finwë and Míriel), half-brother of Fingolfin and Finarfin; greatest of the Noldor, and leader in their rebellion; deviser of the Fëanorian script; maker of the

Silmarils; slain in Mithrim in the Dagor-nuin-Giliath. His name was *Curufinwë* (*curu* 'skill'), and he gave this name to his fifth son, Curufin; but he was himself known always by his mother's name for him, *Fëanáro* 'Spirit of Fire', which was given the Sindarin form *Fëanor*. Chapters V-IX and XIII *passim*; see especially 60, 63-4, 66, 98. Elsewhere his name occurs chiefly in *the sons of Fëanor*.

*Fëanturi* 'Masters of Spirits', the Valar Námo (Mandos) and Irmo (Lórien). 28

*Felagund* The name by which King Finrod was known after the establishment of Nargothrond; it was Dwarvish in origin (*felak-gundu* 'cave-hewer', but translated in the text as 'Lord of Caves', 61). For references see *Finrod*.

*Finarfin* The third son of Finwë, the younger of Fëanor's half-brothers; remained in Aman after the Exile of the Noldor and ruled the remnant of his people in Tirion. Alone among the Noldorin princes he and his descendants had golden hair, derived from his mother Indis, who was a Vanyarin Elf (see *Vanyar*). 60, 65, 69-70, 83-5, 88, 102, 167, 176, 251. Many other occurrences of the name of Finarfin relate to his sons or his people.

*Finduilas* Daughter of Orodreth, loved by Gwindor; captured in the sack of Nargothrond, and killed by Orcs at the Crossings of Teiglin. 209-11, 213-16, 225

*Fingolfin* The second son of Finwë, the elder of Fëanor's half-brothers; High King of the Noldor in Beleriand, dwelling in Hithlum; slain by Morgoth in single combat. 60, 65, 69-71, 75, 83-4, 89-90, 100, 106, 108-9, 111, 113, 115-16, 119, 121, 129, 143, 147, 150, 152-5, 196. Many other occurrences of the name of Fingolfin relate to his sons or his people.

*Fingon* The eldest son of Fingolfin, called the Valiant; rescued Maedhros from Thangorodrim; High King of the Noldor after the death of his father; slain by Gothmog in the Nirnaeth Arnoediad. 60, 84-5, 87, 89-90, 109-11, 116, 119, 121, 131, 138, 152, 154, 160, 164, 189-96, 244, 286

*Finrod* The eldest son of Finarfin, called 'the Faithful' and 'the Friend of Men'. Founder and King of Nargothrond, whence his name *Felagund*; encountered in Ossiriand the first Men to cross the Blue Mountains; rescued by Barahir in the Dagor Bragollach; redeemed his oath to Barahir by accompanying Beren on his quest; slain in defence of Beren in the dungeons of Tol-in-Gaurhoth. The following references include those to *Felagund* used alone: 61, 83, 85, 90, 109, 111, 113-14, 120-2, 124, 126, 128-30, 140-4, 147, 149, 152, 160, 164, 167-76, 184, 204, 211, 213, 215, 217-18, 230-1, 233

*Finwë* Leader of the Noldor on the westward journey from Cuiviénen; King of the Noldor in Aman; father of Fëanor, Fingolfin, and Finarfin; slain by Morgoth at Formenos. 52-5, 57-66, 69-72, 75, 79, 82, 127; other references are to his sons or his house.

*Fírimar* 'Mortals', one of the Elvish names for Men. 103

*Firstborn, The* The Elder Children of Ilúvatar, the Elves. 18, 20, 22, 39, 41, 44, 46, 48, 249, 254, 261, 263–4, 286–7, 298, 304

*Followers, The* The Younger Children of Ilúvatar, Men; translation of *Hildor*. 18

*Ford of Stones* See *Sarn Athrad*.

*Fords of Aros* See *Arossiach*.

*Formenos* 'Northern Fortress', the stronghold of Fëanor and his sons in the north of Valinor, built after the banishment of Fëanor from Tirion. 71–2, 75, 79–80, 127

*Fornost* 'Northern Fortress', Númenórean city on the North Downs in Eriador. 291

*Forsaken Elves* See *Eglath*.

*Frodo* The Ringbearer. 303

*Fuinur* A renegade Númenórean who became mighty among the Haradrim at the end of the Second Age. 293


*Gabilgathol* See *Belegost*. 91

*Galadriel* Daughter of Finarfin and sister of Finrod Felagund; one of the leaders of the Noldorin rebellion against the Valar; wedded Celeborn of Doriath and with him remained in Middle-earth after the end of the First Age; keeper of Nenya, the Ring of Water, in Lothlórien. 61, 83–4, 90, 114–15, 126–8, 130, 144, 169, 234, 254, 298–300

*Galathilion* The White Tree of Tirion, the image of Telperion made by Yavanna for the Vanyar and the Noldor. 59, 263, 291

*Galdor* Called the Tall; son of Hador Lórindol and lord of Dor-lómin after him; father of Húrin and Huor; slain at Eithel Sirion. 148, 152, 155, 158–60, 198, 209, 230, 251

*galvorn* The metal devised by Eöl. 133

*Gandalf* The name among Men of Mithrandir, one of the Istari (Wizards); see *Olórin*. 300

*Gates of Summer* A great festival of Gondolin, on the eve of which the city was assaulted by the forces of Morgoth. 242

*Gelion* The great river of East Beleriand, rising in Himring and Mount Rerir and fed by the rivers of Ossiriand flowing down from the Blue Mountains. 54–5, 91–2, 96, 112, 121–4, 140, 142, 146, 153, 188, 232–5

*Gelmir* (1) Elf of Nargothrond, brother of Gwindor, captured in the Dagor Bragollach and afterwards put to death in front of Eithel Sirion, as a provocation to its defenders, before the Nirnaeth Arnoediad. 188, 191

*Gelmir* (2) Elf of the people of Angrod, who with Arminas came to Nargothrond to warn Orodreth of its peril. 212

*Gildor* One of the twelve companions of Barahir on Dorthonion. 155

*Gil-Estel* 'Star of Hope', Sindarin name for Eärendil bearing the Silmaril in his ship Vingilot. 250

*Gil-galad* 'Star of Radiance', the name by which Ereinion son of Fingon was afterwards known. After the death of Turgon he become the last High King of the Noldor in Middle-earth, and remained in Lindon after the end of the First Age; leader with Elendil of the Last Alliance of Men and Elves and slain with him in combat with Sauron. 154, 196, 244, 247, 254, 267–8, 286–7, 289–90, 292–4, 297–8

**Gimilkhâd**   Younger son of Ar-Gimilzôr and Inzilbêth and father of Ar-Pharazôn, the last King of Númenor. 269

**Gimilzôr**   See *Ar-Gimilzôr*.

**Ginglith**   River in West Beleriand flowing into the Narog above Nargothrond. 169, 212

**Gladden Fields**   Partial translation of *Loeg Ningloron*; the great stretches of reeds and iris (gladden) in and about the Anduin, where Isildur was slain and the One Ring lost. 295–6, 301

**Glaurung**   The first of the Dragons of Morgoth, called *the Father of Dragons*; in the Dagor Bragollach, the Nirnaeth Arnoediad, and the Sack of Nargothrond; cast his spell upon Túrin and upon Nienor; slain by Túrin at Cabed-en-Aras. Called also *the Great Worm* and *the Worm of Morgoth*. 116–17, 148, 151, 153, 192–3, 212–15, 217–18, 220–6, 229–30, 239, 242

**Glingal**   'Hanging Flame', the image of Laurelin made by Turgon in Gondolin. 126

**Glirhuin**   A minstrel of Brethil. 230

**Glóredhel**   Daughter of Hador Lórindol of Dor-lómin and sister of Galdor; wedded Haldir of Brethil. 158

**Glorfindel**   Elf of Gondolin, who fell to his death in Cirith Thoronath in combat with a Balrog after the escape from the sack of the city. The name means 'Golden-haired'. 194, 243–4

**Golodhrim**   The Noldor. *Golodh* was the Sindarin form of Quenya *Noldo*, and *-rim* a collective plural ending; cf. *Annon-in-Gelydh*, the Gate of the Noldor. 134

**Gondolin**   'The Hidden Rock' (see *Ondolindë*), secret city of King Turgon surrounded by the Encircling Mountains (Echoriath). 60, 107, 125–6, 131–2, 134–6, 138–9, 154, 158–60, 182, 189–90, 192, 194, 196–7, 205, 227–8, 239–44, 247, 249, 254, 261

**Gondolindrim**   The people of Gondolin. 138, 159, 192

**Gondor**   'Land of Stone', name of the southern Númenórean kingdom in Middle-earth, established by Isildur and Anárion. 291–7, 302–4. *City of Gondor*: Minas Tirith. 304

**Gonnhirrim**   'Masters of Stone', a Sindarin name for the Dwarves. 91

**Gorgoroth** (*1*)   See *Ered Gorgoroth*.

**Gorgoroth** (*2*)   A plateau in Mordor, between the converging Mountains of Shadow and Mountains of Ash. 292, 294, 296

**Gorlim**   Called the Unhappy; one of the twelve companions of Barahir on Dorthonion, who was ensnared by a phantom of his wife Eilinel and revealed to Sauron the hiding-place of Barahir. 155, 162–3

**Gorthaur**   The name of Sauron in Sindarin. 32, 155, 285

*House of, People of, Hador* 148, 157-8, 160, 189, 194-5, 198-9, 206, 215, 227, 249. *Helm of Hador*: see *Dragon-helm of Dor-lómin*.

*Haladin* The second people of Men to enter Beleriand; afterwards called the *People of Haleth*, dwelling in the Forest of Brethil, also *the Men of Brethil*. 142, 145-6, 155, 157-8, 160, 192, 195

*Haldad* Leader of the Haladin in their defence against the attack on them by Orcs in Thargelion, and slain there; father of the Lady Haleth. 145-7

*Haldan* Son of Haldar; leader of the Haladin after the death of the Lady Haleth. 146

*Haldar* Son of Haldad of the Haladin, and brother of the Lady Haleth; slain with his father in the Orc-raid on Thargelion. 146-7

*Haldir* Son of Halmir of Brethil; wedded Glóredhel, daughter of Hador of Dor-lómin; slain in the Nirnaeth Arnoediad. 158, 189-90, 192, 195

*Haleth* Called the Lady Haleth; leader of the Haladin (who were named from her the People of Haleth) from Thargelion to the lands west of Sirion. 146-7. *House of, People of, Haleth* 146-8, 157, 189, 216, 221-2

*Half-elven* Translation of Sindarin *Peredhel*, plural *Peredhil*, applied to Elrond and Elros, 246, 254, 261, 286, 288; and to Eärendil, 241

*Halflings* Translation of *Periannath* (Hobbits). 303

*Halls of Awaiting* The Halls of Mandos. 67

*Halmir* Lord of the Haladin, son of Haldan; with Beleg of Doriath defeated the Orcs that came south from the Pass of Sirion after the Dagor Bragollach. 157-8, 189

*Handir* Son of Haldir and Glóredhel, father of Brandir the Lame; lord of the Haladin after Haldir's death; slain in Brethil in battle with Orcs. 195, 212, 216

*Haradrim* The Men of Harad ('the South'), the lands south of Mordor. 293

*Hareth* Daughter of Halmir of Brethil; wedded Galdor of Dor-lómin; mother of Húrin and Huor. 158, 160

*Hathaldir* Called the Young; one of the twelve companions of Barahir on Dorthonion. 155

*Hathol* Father of Hador Lórindol. 147

*Haudh-en-Arwen* 'The Ladybarrow', the burial-mound of Haleth in the Forest of Brethil. 147

*Haudh-en-Elleth* The mound in which Finduilas was buried, near the Crossings of Teiglin. 216-17, 219-20, 223, 225

*Haudh-en-Ndengin* 'The Mound of Slain' in the desert of Anfauglith, where were piled the bodies of the Elves and Men that died in the Nirnaeth Arnoediad. 197-8

*Haudh-en-Nirnaeth* 'The Mound of Tears', another name of *Haudh-en-Ndengin*. 197

*Havens, The* Brithombar and Eglarest on the coast of Beleriand: 107, 113, 121, 154, 196. The Havens of Sirion at the end of the First Age: 238, 246-7, 253. The Grey Havens (*Mithlond*) in the Gulf of Lhûn:

289, 298-9, 304. Alqualondë, the Haven of the Swans or Swanhaven, is also called simply *The Haven*: 87, 89

*Helcar*  The Inland Sea in the northeast of Middle-earth, where once stood the mountain of the lamp of Illuin; the mere of Cuiviénen where the first Elves awoke is described as a bay in this sea. 49, 53

*Helcaraxë*  The strait between Araman and Middle-earth; also referred to as *the Grinding Ice*. 51, 57, 80, 89-90, 108, 116, 129, 134

*Helevorn*  'Black Glass', a lake in the north of Thargelion, below Mount Rerir, where Caranthir dwelt. 112, 124, 153

*Helluin*  The star Sirius. 48, 64

*Herumor*  A renegade Númenórean who became mighty among the Haradrim at the end of the Second Age. 293

*Herunúmen*  'Lord of the West', Quenya name of Ar-Adûnakhor. 267

*Hidden Kingdom*  Name given both to Doriath, 115, 164, 166, 225, and to Gondolin, 131, 241

*High-elven*  See *Quenya*.

*High Elves*  See *Eldar*. 298

*High Faroth*  See *Taur-en-Faroth*.

*Hildor*  'The Followers', 'The Aftercomers', Elvish name for Men, as the Younger Children of Ilúvatar. 99, 103

*Hildórien*  The land in the east of Middle-earth where the first Men (*Hildor*) awoke. 103, 141

*Himlad*  'Cool Plain', the region where Celegorm and Curufin dwelt south of the Pass of Aglon. 124, 132, 135

*Himring*  The great hill west of Maglor's Gap on which was the stronghold of Maedhros; translated in the text as 'Ever-cold'. 112, 123-4, 132, 152-3, 176, 184, 189

*Hírilorn*  The great beech-tree in Doriath with three trunks, in which Lúthien was imprisoned. The name means 'Tree of the Lady'. 172, 186

*Hísilómë*  'Land of Mist', Quenya name of Hithlum. 118

*Hithaeglir*  'Line of Misty Peaks': the Misty Mountains, or Mountains of Mist. (The form *Hithaeglin* on the map to *The Lord of the Rings* is an error.) 54, 91, 94, 290, 293, 295

*Hither Lands*  Middle-earth (also called *the Outer Lands*). 55, 57-8, 239, 246, 251, 254, 262, 299

*Hithlum*  'Land of Mist' (see 118), the region bounded on the east and south by Ered Wethrin and on the west by Ered Lómin; see *Hísilómë*. 51, 81, 106, 108-9, 111, 116, 118-19, 121, 123, 131, 143, 151-7, 160, 182, 189-92, 194-6, 198-9, 207, 227, 238

*Hollin*  See *Eregion*. 286

*Hollowbold*  Translation of *Nogrod*: 'hollow dwelling' (early English *bold*, noun related to the verb *build*). 91

*Huan*  The great wolfhound of Valinor that Oromë gave to Celegorm; friend and helper of Beren and Lúthien; slew and slain by Carcharoth. The name means 'great dog, hound'. 172-80, 182, 185-6

*Hunthor*  A Man of the Haladin in Brethil who accompanied Túrin in his attack on Glaurung at Cabed-en-Aras and was killed there by a falling stone. 221-2

*Huor*  Son of Galdor of Dor-lómin, husband of Rían and father of Tuor; went to Gondolin with Húrin his brother; slain in the Nirnaeth Arnoediad. 126, 148, 158, 190, 194, 198, 238, 240-1, 243, 251

*Húrin*  Called *Thalion* 'the Steadfast', 'the Strong'; son of Galdor of Dor-lómin, husband of Morwen and father of Túrin and Nienor; lord of Dor-lómin, vassal of Fingon. Went with Huor his brother to Gondolin; captured by Morgoth in the Nirnaeth Arnoediad and set upon Thangorodrim for many years; after his release slew Mîm in Nargothrond and brought the Nauglamîr to King Thingol. 126, 148, 158-60, 190-201, 205-6, 208-11, 213-17, 220, 222-4, 226-33, 238, 241, 251

*Hyarmentir*  The highest mountain in the regions south of Valinor. 74

*Iant Iaur*  'The Old Bridge' over the Esgalduin on the northern borders of Doriath; also called *the Bridge of Esgalduin*. 121, 132

*Ibun*  One of the sons of Mîm the Petty-dwarf. 203, 205-6

*Idril*  Called *Celebrindal* 'Silverfoot'; the daughter (and only child) of Turgon and Elenwë; wife of Tuor, mother of Eärendil, with whom she escaped from Gondolin to the Mouths of Sirion; departed thence with Tuor into the West. 126, 134, 136, 138-9, 240-3, 245-6, 249, 254, 261

*Illuin*  One of the Lamps of the Valar made by Aulë. Illuin stood in the northern part of Middle-earth, and after the overthrow of the mountain by Melkor the Inland Sea of Helcar was formed there. 35-6, 49, 57

*Ilmarë*  A Maia, the handmaid of Varda. 30

*Ilmen*  The region above the air where the stars are. 99-101, 282

*Ilúvatar*  'Father of All', Eru. 15-21, 25-6, 28-9, 31, 39-44, 46-50, 56, 66, 68, 78, 83, 90, 104, 187, 253, 261-2, 264-5, 272, 278-9

*Imlach*  Father of Amlach. 144

*Imladris*  'Rivendell' (literally, 'Deep Dale of the Cleft'), Elrond's dwelling in a valley of the Misty Mountains. 288, 293, 295-8, 303

*Indis*  Vanyarin Elf, close kin of Ingwë; second wife of Finwë, mother of Fingolfin and Finarfin. 60, 64-5, 69

*Ingwë*  Leader of the Vanyar, the first of the three hosts of the Eldar on the westward journey from Cuiviénen. In Aman he dwelt upon Taniquetil, and was held High King of all the Elves. 52-3, 57, 59, 62, 64, 102, 251

*Inziladûn*  Elder son of Ar-Gimilzôr and Inzilbêth; afterwards named *Tar-Palantir*. 269

*Inzilbêth*  Queen of Ar-Gimilzôr; of the house of the lords of Andúnië. 268

*Irmo*  The Vala usually named Lórien, the place of his dwelling. *Irmo* means 'Desirer' or 'Master of Desire'. 28, 30, 63

*Iron Mountains*   See *Ered Engrin.*

*Isengard*   Translation (to represent the language of Rohan) of the Elvish name *Angrenost.* 291, 300–3

*Isil*   Quenya name of the Moon. 99–100

*Isildur*   Elder son of Elendil, who with his father and his brother Anárion escaped from the Drowning of Númenor and founded in Middle-earth the Númenórean realms in exile; lord of Minas Ithil; cut the Ruling Ring from Sauron's hand; slain by Orcs in the Anduin when the Ring slipped from his finger. 272–3, 276, 279–80, 290–6, 301. *Heirs of Isildur* 298, 301.   *Heir of Isildur* = Aragorn 303–4

*Istari*   The Wizards. See *Curunír, Saruman; Mithrandir, Gandalf, Olórin; Radagast.* 299–300

*Ivrin*   The lake and falls beneath Ered Wethrin where the river Narog rose. 119, 209. *Pools of Ivrin* 113, 210, 215, 239. *Falls of Ivrin* 120, 170. See *Eithel Ivrin.*

*kelvar*   An Elvish word retained in the speeches of Yavanna and Manwë in Chapter II: 'animals, living things that move'. 45–6

*Kementári*   'Queen of the Earth', a title of Yavanna. 28, 38–9, 46

*Khazâd*   The name of the Dwarves in their own language (*Khuzdul*). 91

*Khazad-dûm*   The great mansions of the Dwarves of Durin's race in the Misty Mountains (*Hadhodrond, Moria*). See *Khazâd; dûm* is probably a plural or collective, meaning 'excavations, halls, mansions'. 44, 91, 286

*Khîm*   Son of Mîm the Petty-dwarf, slain by one of Túrin's outlaw band. 203

*King's Men*   Númenóreans hostile to the Eldar and the Elendili. 266–7, 269

*Kinslaying, The*   The slaying of the Teleri by the Noldor at Alqualondë. 87, 89–90, 104, 111, 127, 129, 139, 141, 156

*Ladros*   The lands to the northeast of Dorthonion that were granted by the Noldorin Kings to the Men of the House of Bëor. 148

*Laer Cú Beleg*   'The Song of the Great Bow', made by Túrin at Eithel Ivrin in memory of Beleg Cúthalion. 209

*Laiquendi*   'The Green-elves' of Ossiriand. 96

*Lalaith*   'Laughter', daughter of Húrin and Morwen who died in childhood. 198

*Lammoth*   'The Great Echo', region north of the Firth of Drengist, named from the echoes of Morgoth's cry in his struggle with Ungoliant. 80–1, 106

*Land of Shadow*   See *Mordor.*

*Land of the Dead that Live*   See *Dor Firn-i-Guinar.*

*Land of the Star*   Númenor. 274, 276

*Lanthir Lamath*   'Waterfall of Echoing Voices', where Dior had his house in Ossiriand, and after which his daughter Elwing ('Star-spray') was named. 235

*Last Alliance*  The league made at the end of the Second Age between Elendil and Gil-galad to defeat Sauron. 293

*Laurelin*  'Song of Gold', the younger of the Two Trees of Valinor. 38–9, 61, 74, 99–101, 126

*Lay of Leithian*  The long poem concerning the lives of Beren and Lúthien from which the prose account in *The Silmarillion* was derived. *Leithian* is translated 'Release from Bondage'. 162, 165, 168, 171–2, 186

*Legolin*  The third of the tributaries of Gelion in Ossiriand. 123

*lembas*  Sindarin name of the waybread of the Eldar (from earlier *lennmbass* 'journey-bread'; in Quenya *coimas* 'life-bread'). 202, 204, 207–8

*Lenwë*  The leader of the Elves from the host of the Teleri who refused to cross the Misty Mountains on the westward journey from Cuiviénen (the Nandor); father of Denethor. 54, 94

*Lhûn*  River in Eriador flowing into the sea in the Gulf of Lhûn. 285–6, 290

*Linaewen*  'Lake of birds', the great mere in Nevrast. 119

*Lindon*  A name of Ossiriand in the First Age; see 123. After the tumults at the end of the First Age the name Lindon was retained for the lands west of the Blue Mountains that still remained above the Sea: 285, 287, 289–90, 298

*Lindórië*  Mother of Inzilbêth. 268

*Little Gelion*  One of the two tributary branches of the river Gelion in the north, rising in the Hill of Himring. 123

*Loeg Ningloron*  'Pools of the golden water-flowers'; see *Gladden Fields*.

*lómelindi*  Quenya word meaning 'dusk-singers', nightingales. 55

*Lómion*  'Son of Twilight', the Quenya name that Aredhel gave to Maeglin. 133

*Lonely Isle*  See *Tol Eressëa*.

*Lord of Waters*  See *Ulmo*.

*Lords of the West*  See *Valar*.

*Lórellin*  The lake in Lórien in Valinor where the Vala Estë sleeps by day. 28

*Lorgan*  Chief of the Easterling Men in Hithlum after the Nirnaeth Arnoediad, by whom Tuor was enslaved. 238

*Lórien (1)*  The name of the gardens and dwelling-place of the Vala Irmo, who was himself usually called Lórien. 25, 28, 30, 55, 63–4, 93, 99–100, 234

*Lórien (2)*  The land ruled by Celeborn and Galadriel between the rivers Celebrant and Anduin. Probably the original name of this land was altered to the form of the Quenya name Lórien of the gardens of the Vala Irmo in Valinor. In Lothlórien the Sindarin word *loth* 'flower' is prefixed. 298

*Lórindol*  'Goldenhead'; see *Hador*.

*Malinalda* 'Tree of Gold', a name of Laurelin. 38

*Mandos* The place of the dwelling in Aman of the Vala properly called Námo, the Judge, though this name was seldom used, and he himself was usually referred to as Mandos. Named as Vala: 25, 28–9, 48, 52, 65, 67, 70–2, 78–9, 87, 98, 102, 104, 111, 129, 186–7, 249, 255. Named as the place of his dwelling (including *Halls of Mandos*; also *Halls of Awaiting, Houses of the Dead*): 28, 42, 44, 52, 59, 64–5, 67, 88, 104, 107, 186–7, 234. With reference to the Doom of the Noldor and the Curse of Mandos: 125–6, 129, 139, 141, 167, 170, 176, 240

*Manwë* The chief of the Valar, called also *Súlimo, the Elder King, the Ruler of Arda. Passim*; see especially 21, 26, 39–40, 65–6, 110

*Marach* Leader of the third host of Men to enter Beleriand, ancestor of Hador Lórindol. 142–4, 150

*March of Maedhros* The open lands to the north of the headwaters of the river Gelion, held by Maedhros and his brothers against attack on East Beleriand; also called *the eastern March*. 112–13, 123

*Mardil* Called the Faithful; the first Ruling Steward of Gondor. 297

*Mar-nu-Falmar* 'The Land under the Waves', name of Númenor after the Downfall. 281

*Melian* A Maia, who left Valinor and came to Middle-earth; afterwards the Queen of King Thingol in Doriath, about which she set a girdle of enchantment, the Girdle of Melian; mother of Lúthien, and fore-mother of Elrond and Elros. 30–1, 55–6, 58, 91–3, 95, 97, 104, 111, 115, 121–2, 126–9, 132, 144, 146–7, 151, Chapter XIX *passim*, 188–9, Chapters XXI, XXII *passim*, 254, 261

*Melkor* The Quenya name for the great rebellious Vala, the beginning of evil, in his origin the mightiest of the Ainur; afterwards named *Morgoth, Bauglir, the Dark Lord, the Enemy*, etc. The meaning of *Melkor* was 'He who arises in Might'; the Sindarin form was *Belegûr*, but it was never used, save in a deliberately altered form *Belegurth* 'Great Death'. *Passim* (after the rape of the Silmarils usually called *Morgoth*); see especially 16, 18, 31, 50, 65–6, 81–2, 101, 205, 260

*Men* See especially 41–2, 68, 103–4, 140–2, 149, 259, 264–5; and see also *Atani, Children of Ilúvatar, Easterlings*.

*Menegroth* 'The Thousand Caves', the hidden halls of Thingol and Melian on the river Esgalduin in Doriath; see especially 93. 56, 93–4, 96–7, 108, 111, 114, 122, 129, 166, 168, 172, 179, 183–6, 188, 199–202, 205, 217, 219, 231–6

*Meneldil* Son of Anárion, King of Gondor. 295–6

*Menelmacar* 'Swordsman of the Sky', the constellation Orion. 48

*Meneltarma* 'Pillar of Heaven', the mountain in the midst of Númenor, upon whose summit was the Hallow of Eru Ilúvatar. 261–2, 266, 269–70, 272, 277, 279, 281

*Meres of Twilight* See *Aelin-uial*.

*Mereth Aderthad* The 'Feast of Reuniting' held by Fingolfin near the Pools of Ivrin. 113

*Mickleburg* Translation of *Belegost*: 'great fortress'. 91

*Middle-earth* The lands to the east of the Great Sea; also called *the Hither Lands*, *the Outer Lands*, *the Great Lands*, and *Endor*. *Passim*.

*Mîm* The Petty-dwarf, in whose house (*Bar-en-Danwedh*) on Amon Rûdh Túrin dwelt with the outlaw band, and by whom their lair was betrayed to the Orcs; slain by Húrin in Nargothrond. 202–6, 230

*Minas Anor* 'Tower of the Sun' (also simply *Anor*), afterwards called Minas Tirith; the city of Anárion, at the feet of Mount Mindolluin. 291–2, 294–7, 304

*Minas Ithil* 'Tower of the Moon', afterwards called Minas Morgul; the city of Isildur, built on a shoulder of the Ephel Dúath. 291–3, 296–7

*Minas Morgul* 'Tower of Sorcery' (also simply *Morgul*), name of Minas Ithil after its capture by the Ringwraiths. 297, 303

*Minastir* See *Tar-Minastir*.

*Minas Tirith* (1) 'Tower of Watch', built by Finrod Felagund on Tol Sirion; see *Tol-in-Gaurhoth*. 120, 155–7, 205

*Minas Tirith* (2) Later name of Minas Anor. 297. Called *the City of Gondor* 304

*Mindeb* A tributary of Sirion, between Dimbar and the Forest of Neldoreth. 121, 201

*Mindolluin* 'Towering Blue-head', the great mountain behind Minas Anor. 291, 304

*Mindon Eldaliéva* 'Lofty Tower of the Eldalië', the tower of Ingwë in the city of Tirion; also simply *the Mindon*. 59, 70, 82, 85, 88

*Míriel* (1) The first wife of Finwë, mother of Fëanor; died after Fëanor's birth. Called Serindë 'the Broideress'. 60, 63–4, 69

*Míriel* (2) Daughter of Tar-Palantir, forced into marriage by Ar-Pharazôn, and as his queen named *Ar-Zimraphel*; also called *Tar-Míriel*. 269, 279

*Mirkwood* See *Greenwood the Great*.

*Misty Mountains* See *Hithaeglir*.

*Mithlond* 'The Grey Havens', harbours of the Elves on the Gulf of Lhûn; also referred to as *the Havens*. 286, 289, 298–9, 304

*Mithrandir* 'The Grey Pilgrim', Elvish name of Gandalf (Olórin), one of the Istari (Wizards). 300–4

*Mithrim* The name of the great lake in the east of Hithlum, and also of the region about it and of the mountains to the west, separating Mithrim from Dor-lómin. The name was orginally that of the Sindarin Elves who dwelt there. 106–10, 112, 119, 198, 238

*Mordor* 'The Black Land', also called *the Land of Shadow*; Sauron's realm east of the mountains of the Ephel Dúath. 267, 280, 288, 290–7, 302–3

*Morgoth* 'The Black Enemy', name of Melkor, first given to him by

Fëanor after the rape of the Silmarils. 31–2, 66, 79 and thereafter *passim*. See *Melkor*.

*Morgul*   See *Minas Morgul*.

*Moria*   'The Black Chasm', later name for Khazad-dûm (Hadhodrond). 91, 286, 288, 294

*Moriquendi*   'Elves of the Darkness'; see *Dark Elves*. 53, 56, 91, 108

*Mormegil*   'The Black Sword', name given to Túrin as captain of the host of Nargothrond; see *Gurthang*. 210–11, 215–17, 220, 223, 225

*Morwen*   Daughter of Baragund (nephew of Barahir, the father of Beren); wife of Húrin and mother of Túrin and Nienor; called *Eledhwen* (translated in the text as 'Elfsheen') and *the Lady of Dor-lómin*. 148, 155, 160, 197–9, 210–11, 214–15, 217–19, 225, 227, 229, 231

*Mountain of Fire*   See Orodruin.

*Mountains*: *of Aman*, *of Defence*, see *Pelóri*; *of the East*, see *Orocarni*; *of Iron*, see *Ered Engrin*; *of Mist*, see *Hithaeglir*; *of Mithrim*, see *Mithrim*; *of Shadow*, see *Ered Wethrin* and *Ephel Dúath*; *of Terror*, see *Ered Gorgoroth*.

*Mount Doom*   See *Amon Amarth*.

*Music of the Ainur*   See *Ainulindalë*.


*Nahar*   The horse of the Vala Oromë, said by the Eldar to be so named on account of his voice. 29, 41, 49–50, 53, 76, 95

*Námo*   A Vala, one of the Aratar; usually named *Mandos*, the place of his dwelling. *Námo* means 'Ordainer, Judge'. 28

*Nandor*   Said to mean 'Those who turn back': the Nandor were those Elves from the host of the Teleri who refused to cross the Misty Mountains on the westward journey from Cuiviénen, but of whom a part, led by Denethor, came long afterwards over the Blue Mountains and dwelt in Ossiriand (the Green-elves). 54, 94, 122, 199

*Nan Dungortheb*   Also *Dungortheb*; translated in the text as 'Valley of Dreadful Death'. The valley between the precipices of Ered Gorgoroth and the Girdle of Melian. 81, 121, 132, 164, 176

*Nan Elmoth*   The forest east of the river Celon where Elwë (Thingol) was enchanted by Melian and lost; afterwards the dwelling-place of Eöl. 55, 58, 92, 132–6, 142, 202, 234

*Nan-tathren*   'Willow-vale', translated as 'the Land of Willows', where the river Narog flowed into Sirion. In Treebeard's song in *The Two Towers* III 4 Quenya forms of the name are used: *in the willow-meads of Tasarinan*; *Nan-tasarion*. 120, 195, 243–4

*Nargothrond*   'The great underground fortress on the river Narog', founded by Finrod Felagund and destroyed by Glaurung; also the realm of Nargothrond extending east and west of the Narog. 114–15, 120–2, 126, 130, 140, 142, 147, 151–2, 156–7, 160, 168–71, 173, 176, 184, 188, 190–2, 195, Chapter XXI *passim*, 230–1, 233, 238, 240, 286

*Narn i Hîn Húrin*   'The Tale of the Children of Húrin', the long lay from which Chapter XXI was derived; ascribed to the poet Dírhavel, a

Túrin; spell-bound by Glaurung at Nargothrond and in ignorance of her past wedded Túrin in Brethil in her name Níniel; cast herself into the Teiglin. 199, 211, 214–15, 217–26

*Nimbrethil*  Birch-woods in Arvernien in the south of Beleriand. Cf. Bilbo's song at Rivendell: 'He built a boat of timber felled in Nimbrethil to journey in . . .' (*The Fellowship of the Ring* II 1). 246

*Nimloth* (*1*)  The White Tree of Númenor, of which a fruit taken by Isildur before it was felled grew into the White Tree of Minas Ithil. *Nimloth* 'White Blossom' is the Sindarin form of Quenya *Ninquelótë*, one of the names of Telperion. 59, 263, 268–9, 272–3, 276, 291

*Nimloth* (*2*)  Elf of Doriath who wedded Dior Thingol's Heir; mother of Elwing; slain in Menegroth in the attack by the sons of Fëanor. 234–6

*Nimphelos*  The great pearl given by Thingol to the lord of the Dwarves of Belegost. 92

*Níniel*  'Tear-maiden', the name that Túrin, ignorant of their relationship, gave to his sister; see *Nienor*.

*Ninquelótë*  'White Blossom', a name of Telperion; see *Nimloth* (*1*). 38

*niphredil*  A white flower that bloomed in Doriath in starlight when Lúthien was born. It grew also on Cerin Amroth in Lothlórien (*The Fellowship of the Ring* II 6, 8). 91

*Nirnaeth Arnoediad*  'Tears Unnumbered' (also simply *the Nirnaeth*), the name given to the ruinous fifth battle in the Wars of Beleriand. 138, 192, 195, 198, 207, 209, 238, 240–1

*Nivrim*  That part of Doriath that lay on the west bank of Sirion. 122

*Noegyth Nibin*  'Petty-dwarves' (see also under *Dwarves*). 204, 230

*Nogrod*  One of the two cities of the Dwarves in the Blue Mountains; translation into Sindarin of Dwarvish *Tumunzahar*. See *Hollowbold*. 91–2, 94, 113, 133–4, 177, 189, 204, 231–3, 235

*Noldolantë*  'The Fall of the Noldor', a lament made by Maglor son of Fëanor. 87

*Noldor*  The Deep Elves, the second host of the Eldar on the westward journey from Cuiviénen, led by Finwë. The name (Quenya *Noldo*, Sindarin *Golodh*) meant 'the Wise' (but wise in the sense of possessing knowledge, not in the sense of possessing sagacity, sound judgement). For the language of the Noldor see *Quenya*. *Passim*; see especially 39, 53, 60, 62–3, 117, 287

*Nóm, Nómin*  'Wisdom' and 'the Wise', the names that the Men of Bëor's following gave to Finrod and his people in their own tongue. 141

*North Downs*  In Eriador, where was built the Númenórean city of Fornost. 291

*Nulukkizdîn*  Dwarvish name of Nargothrond. 230

*Númenor*  (In full Quenya form *Númenórë*, 261, 281.) 'Westernesse', 'Westland', the great island prepared by the Valar as a dwelling-place for the Edain after the ending of the First Age. Called also *Anadûnê*,

*Ossë* A Maia, vassal of Ulmo, with whom he entered the waters of Arda; lover and instructor of the Teleri. 30, 40, 57–9, 61, 87, 119, 196, 260

*Ossiriand* 'Land of Seven Rivers' (these being Gelion and its tributaries flowing down from the Blue Mountains), the land of the Green-elves. Cf. Treebeard's song in *The Two Towers* III 4: 'I wandered in Summer in the elm-woods of Ossiriand. Ah! the light and the music in the Summer by the Seven Rivers of Ossir!' See *Lindon*. 94, 96, 113, 121–4, 140, 142–3, 151, 153, 188, 195, 234–6, 285–6

*Ost-in-Edhil* 'Fortress of the Eldar', the city of the Elves in Eregion. 286–7

*Outer Lands* Middle-earth (also called *the Hither Lands*). 39, 41, 47, 80, 90, 100, 249

*Outer Sea* See *Ekkaia*.


*Palantíri* 'Those that watch from afar', the seven Seeing Stones brought by Elendil and his sons from Númenor; made by Fëanor in Aman (see 64, and *The Two Towers* III 11). 276, 291–2

*Pelargir* 'Garth of Royal Ships', the Númenórean haven above the delta of Anduin. 267

*Pelóri* 'The fencing or defensive heights', called also *the Mountains of Aman* and *the Mountains of Defence*, raised by the Valar after the destruction of their dwelling on Almaren; ranging in a crescent from north to south, close to the eastern shores of Aman. 37, 39, 47, 57, 59, 73–4, 80, 100–2, 174

*People of Haleth* See *Haladin* and *Haleth*.

*Periannath* The Halflings (Hobbits). 303

*Petty-dwarves* Translation of *Noegyth Nibin*. See also under *Dwarves*.

*Pharazôn* See *Ar-Pharazôn*.

*Prophecy of the North* The Doom of the Noldor, uttered by Mandos on the coast of Araman. 87


*Quendi* Original Elvish name for Elves (of every kind, including the Avari), meaning 'Those that speak with voices'. 41, 49–52, 55, 59, 68, 70, 99, 105, 141

*Quenta Silmarillion* 'The History of the Silmarils.' 286

*Quenya* The ancient tongue, common to all Elves, in the form that it took in Valinor; brought to Middle-earth by the Noldorin exiles, but abandoned by them as a daily speech, especially after the edict of King Thingol against its use; see especially 113, 129. Not named as such in this book, but referred to as *Eldarin*, 28, 262, 281; *High Eldarin*, 261–2; *High-elven*, 217, 267; *the tongue of Valinor*, 113; *the speech of the Elves of Valinor*, 125; *the tongue of the Noldor*, 129, 133; *the High Speech of the West*, 129


*Radagast* One of the Istari (Wizards). 300, 302

*Radhruin* One of the twelve companions of Barahir on Dorthonion. 155

*Sarn Athrad*  'Ford of Stones', where the Dwarf-road from Nogrod and Belegost crossed the river Gelion. 92, 140, 232, 235

*Saruman*  'Man of Skill', the name among Men of *Curunír* (which it translates), one of the Istari (Wizards). 300

*Sauron*  'The Abhorred' (in Sindarin called *Gorthaur*); greatest of the servants of Melkor, in his origin a Maia of Aulë. 32, 47, 51, 141, 155–6, 162–4, 170–2, 174–6, 178, 267, 270–5, 277, 279–81, 285–304

*Secondborn, The*  The Younger Children of Ilúvatar, Men. 46

*Seeing Stones*  See *Palantíri*.

*Serech*  The great fen north of the Pass of Sirion, where the river Rivil flowed in from Dorthonion. 107, 152, 163, 191, 193–4, 228

*seregon*  'Blood of Stone', a plant with deep red flowers that grew on Amon Rûdh. 203, 206

*Serindë*  'The Broideress'; see *Míriel* (1).

*Seven Fathers of the Dwarves*  See *Dwarves*.

*Seven Stones*  See *Palantíri*.

*Shadowy Mountains*  See *Ered Wethrin*.

*Shepherds of the Trees*  Ents. 46, 235

*Sickle of the Valar*  See *Valacirca*.

*Silmarien*  Daughter of Tar-Elendil, the fourth King of Númenor; mother of the first lord of Andúnië and ancestress of Elendil and his sons Isildur and Anárion. 268

*Silmarils*  The three jewels made by Fëanor before the destruction of the Two Trees of Valinor, and filled with their light; see especially 67. 39, 67–9, 71–2, 75, 78–83, 101, 104–5, 108, 111, 116, 127, 167–9, 173, 181–2, 184–6, 189, 199, 232–7, 244, 246–8, 250, 252–4

*Silpion*  A name of Telperion. 38

*Silvan Elves*  Also called *Woodland Elves*. They appear to have been in origin those Nandorin Elves who never passed west of the Misty Mountains, but remained in the Vale of Anduin and in Greenwood the Great; see *Nandor*. 286, 298

*Sindar*  The Grey-elves. The name was applied to all the Elves of Telerin origin whom the returning Noldor found in Beleriand, save for the Green-elves of Ossiriand. The Noldor may have devised this name because the first Elves of this origin whom they met with were in the north, under the grey skies and mists about Lake Mithrim (see *Mithrim*); or perhaps because the Grey-elves were not of the Light (of Valinor) nor yet of the Dark (Avari), but were *Elves of the Twilight* (56). But it was held to refer to Elwë's name *Thingol* (Quenya *Sindacollo*, *Singollo* 'Grey-cloak'), since he was acknowledged high king of all the land and its peoples. The Sindar called themselves *Edhil*, plural *Edhel*. 29, 37, 56, 91, 94–5, 104, 108, 113, 117–20, 124, 126, 128–9, 137, 143, 151, 156–7, 198, 204–5, 225, 234, 236, 238, 285

*Sindarin*  The Elvish tongue of Beleriand, derived from the common Elvish speech but greatly changed through long ages from Quenya of Valinor; acquired by the Noldorin exiles in Beleriand (see 113, 129).

*Tar-Minyatur*   Name of Elros Half-elven as first King of Númenor. 272

*Tar-Míriel*   See *Míriel* (2).

*Tarn Aeluin*   The lake on Dorthonion where Barahir and his companions made their lair, and where they were slain. 162–3

*Tar-Palantir*   Twenty-third King of Númenor, who repented of the ways of the Kings, and took his name in Quenya: 'He who looks afar'. See *Inziladûn.* 269, 272

*Taur-en-Faroth*   The wooded highlands to the west of the river Narog above Nargothrond; also called *the High Faroth.* 114, 122, 168

*Taur-im-Duinath*   'The Forest between Rivers', name of the wild country south of the Andram between Sirion and Gelion. 123, 153

*Taur-nu-Fuin*   Later name of Dorthonion: 'the Forest under Night'. Cf. *Deldúwath.* 155, 170, 175, 178–9, 182, 184, 200, 206–8

*Tauron*   'The Forester' (translated in the *Valaquenta* 'Lord of Forests'), a name of Oromë among the Sindar. Cf. *Aldaron.* 29

*Teiglin*   A tributary of Sirion, rising in Ered Wethrin and bounding the Forest of Brethil on the south; see also *Crossings of Teiglin.* 120, 122, 147, 157, 200, 205, 212, 215–16, 220–1, 224, 226, 230

*Telchar*   The most renowned of the smiths of Nogrod, the maker of Angrist and (according to Aragorn in *The Two Towers* III 6) of Narsil. 94, 177

*Telemnar*   Twenty-sixth King of Gondor. 296

*Teleri*   The third and greatest of the three hosts of the Eldar on the westward journey from Cuiviénen, led by Elwë (Thingol) and Olwë. Their own name for themselves was *Lindar,* the Singers; the name *Teleri,* the Last-comers, the Hindmost, was given to them by those before them on the march. Many of the Teleri did not leave Middle-earth; the Sindar and the Nandor were Telerin Elves in origin. 40, 53–5, 57–61, 66, 72–3, 75, 86–7, 90, 94, 97, 102, 133–4, 137, 248–9, 251, 254, 286

*Telperion*   The elder of the Two Trees of Valinor. 38–9, 48, 59, 74, 99–100, 202, 263, 291. Called *the White Tree* 59

*Telumendil*   Name of a constellation. 48

*Thalion*   'Steadfast, Strong'; see *Húrin.*

*Thalos*   The second of the tributaries of Gelion in Ossiriand. 123, 140

*Thangorodrim*   'Mountains of Tyranny', reared by Morgoth above Angband; broken down in the Great Battle at the end of the First Age. 81, 96, 107–10, 116, 118–19, 150–2, 178, 182, 190, 192, 197, 207, 252, 259, 285, 293

*Thargelion*   'The Land beyond Gelion', between Mount Rerir and the river Ascar, where Caranthir dwelt; called also *Dor Caranthir* and *Talath Rhûnen.* 124, 132, 143, 145, 153

*Thingol*   'Grey-cloak', 'Grey-mantle' (in Quenya *Sindacollo, Singollo*), the name by which Elwë, leader with his brother Olwë of the host of the Teleri from Cuiviénen and afterwards King of Doriath, was known in Beleriand; also called *the Hidden King.* See *Elwë.* 56, 91–7,

# APPENDIX

## ELEMENTS IN QUENYA AND SINDARIN NAMES

These notes have been compiled for those who take an interest in the Eldarin languages, and *The Lord of the Rings* is extensively drawn upon for illustration. They are necessarily very compressed, giving an air of certainty and finality that is not altogether justified; and they are very selective, this depending both on considerations of length and the limitations of the editor's knowledge. The headings are not arranged systematically by roots or in Quenya or Sindarin forms, but somewhat arbitrarily, the aim being to make the component elements of names as readily identifiable as possible.

*adan*    (plural *Edain*) in *Adanedhel, Aradan, Dúnedain*. For its meaning and history see *Atani* in the Index.

*aelin*    'lake, pool' in *Aelin-uial*; cf. *lin* (*1*).

*aglar*    'glory, brilliance' in *Dagor Aglareb, Aglarond*. The form in Quenya, *alkar*, has transposition of the consonants: to Sindarin *aglareb* corresponds *Alkarinquë*. The root is *kal*- 'shine', q.v.

*aina*    'holy' in *Ainur, Ainulindalë*.

*alda*    'tree' (Quenya) in *Aldaron, Aldudenië, Malinalda*, corresponding to Sindarin *galadh* (seen in *Caras Galadon* and the *Galadrim* of Lothlórien).

*alqua*    'swan' (Sindarin *alph*) in *Alqualondë*; from a root *alak*- 'rushing' occurring also in *Ancalagon*.

*amarth*    'doom' in *Amon Amarth, Cabed Naeramarth, Úmarth*, and in the Sindarin form of Túrin's name 'Master of Doom', *Turamarth*. The Quenya form of the word appears in *Turambar*.

*amon*    'hill', a Sindarin word occurring as the first element of many names; plural *emyn* in *Emyn Beraid*.

*anca*    'jaws' in *Ancalagon* (for the second element in this name see *alqua*).

*an(d)*    'long' in *Andram, Anduin*; also in *Anfalas* ('Langstrand') in Gondor, *Cair Andros* ('ship of long-foam') an island in Anduin, and *Angerthas* 'long rune-rows'.

*andúnë*    'sunset, west' in *Andúnië*, to which corresponds in Sindarin *annûn*, cf. *Annúminas*, and *Henneth Annûn* 'window of the sunset' in Ithilien. The ancient root of these words, *ndu*, meaning 'down, from on high', appears also in Quenya *númen* 'the way of the sunset, west' and in Sindarin *dûn* 'west', cf. *Dúnedain*. Adûnaic *adûn* in *Adûnakhor*, *Anadûnê* was a loan from Eldarin speech.

*anga*    'iron', Sindarin *ang*, in *Angainor, Angband, Anghabar, Anglachel*,

*Angrist, Angrod, Anguirel, Gurthang; angren* 'of iron' in *Angrenost,* plural *engrin* in *Ered Engrin.*

*anna* 'gift' in *Annatar, Melian, Yavanna;* the same stem in *Andor* 'Land of Gift'.

*annon* 'great door or gate', plural *ennyn,* in *Annon-in-Gelydh;* cf. *Morannon* the 'Black Gate' of Mordor and *Sirannon* the 'Gate-stream' of Moria.

*ar-* 'beside, outside' (whence Quenya *ar* 'and', Sindarin *a*), probably in *Araman* 'outside Aman'; cf. also (*Nirnaeth*) *Arnoediad* '(Tears) without reckoning'.

*ar(a)-* 'high, noble, royal' appears in a great many names, as *Aradan, Aredhel, Argonath, Arnor,* etc.; extended stem *arat-* appearing in *Aratar,* and in *aráto* 'champion, eminent man', e.g. *Angrod* from *Angaráto* and *Finrod* from *Findaráto;* also *aran* 'king' in *Aranrúth. Ereinion* 'scion of kings' (name of Gil-galad) has the plural of *aran;* cf. *Fornost Erain* 'Norbury of the Kings' in Arnor. The prefix *Ar-* of the Adûnaic names of the Kings of Númenor was derived from this.

*arien* (the Maia of the Sun) is derived from a root *as-* seen also in Quenya *árë* 'sunlight'.

*atar* 'father' in *Atanatári* (see *Atani* in Index), *Ilúvatar.*

*band* 'prison, duress' in *Angband;* from original *mbando,* of which the Quenya form appears in *Mandos* (Sindarin *Angband*=Quenya *Angamando*).

*bar* 'dwelling' in *Bar-en-Danwedh.* The ancient word *mbár* (Quenya *már,* Sindarin *bar*) meant the 'home' both of persons and of peoples, and thus appears in many place-names, as *Brithombar, Dimbar* (the first element of which means 'sad, gloomy'), *Eldamar, Val(i)mar, Vinyamar, Mar-nu-Falmar. Mardil,* name of the first of the Ruling Stewards of Gondor, means 'devoted to the house' (i.e. of the Kings).

*barad* 'tower' in *Barad-dûr, Barad Eithel, Barad Nimras;* the plural in *Emyn Beraid.*

*beleg* 'mighty' in *Beleg, Belegaer, Belegost, Laer Cú Beleg.*

*bragol* 'sudden' in *Dagor Bragollach.*

*brethil* probably means 'silver birch'; cf. *Nimbrethil* the birchwoods in Arvernien, and *Fimbrethil,* one of the Entwives.

*brith* 'gravel' in *Brithiach, Brithombar, Brithon.*

*(For many names beginning with C see entries under K)*

*calen* (*galen*) the usual Sindarin word for 'green', in *Ard-galen, Tol Galen, Calenardhon;* also in *Parth Galen* ('Green Sward') beside Anduin and *Pinnath Gelin* ('Green Ridges') in Gondor. See *kal-.*

*cam* (from *kambā*) 'hand', but specifically of the hand held cupped in the attitude of receiving or holding, in *Camlost, Erchamion.*

*carak-* This root is seen in Quenya *carca* 'fang', of which the Sindarin form *carch* occurs in *Carcharoth*, and also in *Carchost* ('Fang Fort', one of the Towers of the Teeth at the entrance to Mordor). Cf. *Caragdûr*, *Carach Angren* ('Iron Jaws', the rampart and dike guarding the entrance to Udûn in Mordor), and *Helcaraxë*.

*caran* 'red', Quenya *carnë*, in *Caranthir, Carnil, Orocarni*; also in *Caradhras*, from *caran-rass*, the 'Red-horn' in the Misty Mountains, and *Carnimírië* 'red-jewelled', the rowan-tree in Treebeard's song. The translation of *Carcharoth* in the text as 'Red Maw' must depend on association with this word; see *carak-*.

*celeb* 'silver' (Quenya *telep, telpë*, as in *Telperion*) in *Celeborn, Celebrant, Celebros. Celebrimbor* means 'silver-fist', from the adjective *celebrin* 'silver' (meaning not 'made of silver' but 'like silver, in hue or worth') and *paur* (Quenya *quárë*) 'fist', often used to mean 'hand'; the Quenya form of the name was *Telperinquar. Celebrindal* has *celebrin* and *tal*, *dal* 'foot'.

*coron* 'mound' in *Corollairë* (also called *Coron Oiolairë*, which latter word appears to mean 'Ever-summer', cf. *Oiolossë*); cf. *Cerin Amroth*, the great mound in Lothlórien.

*cú* 'bow' in *Cúthalion, Dor Cúarthol, Laer Cú Beleg*.

*cuivië* 'awakening' in *Cuiviénen* (Sindarin *Nen Echui*). Other derivatives of the same root are *Dor Firn-i-Guinar; coirë*, the first beginning of Spring, Sindarin *echuir, The Lord of the Rings* Appendix D; and *coimas* 'life-bread', Quenya name of *lembas*.

*cul-* 'golden-red' in *Culúrien*.

*curu* 'skill' in *Curufin(wë), Curunír*.


*dae* 'shadow' in *Dor Daedeloth*, and perhaps in *Daeron*.

*dagor* 'battle'; the root is *ndak-*, cf. *Haudh-en-Ndengin*. Another derivative is *Dagnir* (*Dagnir Glaurunga* 'Glaurung's Bane').

*del* 'horror' in *Deldúwath; deloth* 'abhorrence' in *Dor Daedeloth*.

*dîn* 'silent' in *Dor Dínen*; cf. *Rath Dínen*, the Silent Street in Minas Tirith, and *Amon Dîn*, one of the beacon-hills of Gondor.

*dol* 'head' in *Lórindol*; often applied to hills and mountains, as in *Dol Guldur, Dolmed, Mindolluin* (also *Nardol*, one of the beacon-hills of Gondor, and *Fanuidhol*, one of the Mountains of Moria).

*dôr* 'land' (i.e. dry land as opposed to sea) was derived from *ndor*; it occurs in many Sindarin names, as *Doriath, Dorthonion, Eriador, Gondor, Mordor*, etc. In Quenya the stem was blended and confused with a quite distinct word *nórë* meaning 'people'; in origin *Valinórë* was strictly 'the people of the Valar', but *Valandor* 'the land of the Valar', and similarly *Númen(n)órë* 'people of the West', but *Númendor* 'land of the West'. Quenya *Endor* 'Middle-earth' was from *ened* 'middle' and *ndor*; this in Sindarin became *Ennor* (cf. *ennorath* 'middle lands' in the chant *A Elbereth Gilthoniel*).

*draug* 'wolf in *Draugluin*.

*dú* 'night, dimness' in *Delduwath, Ephel Dúath*. Derived from earlier *dōmē*, whence Quenya *lómë*; thus Sindarin *dúlin* 'nightingale' corresponds to *lómelindë*.

*duin* '(long) river' in *Anduin, Baranduin, Esgalduin, Malduin, Taur-im-Duinath*.

*dûr* 'dark' in *Barad-dûr, Caragdûr, Dol Guldur*; also in *Durthang* (a castle in Mordor).

*ëar* 'sea' (Quenya) in *Eärendil, Eärrámë*, and many other names. The Sindarin word *gaer* (in *Belegaer*) is apparently derived from the same original stem.

*echor* in *Echoriath* 'Encircling Mountains' and *Orfalch Echor*; cf. *Rammas Echor* 'the great wall of the outer circle' about the Pelennor Fields at Minas Tirith.

*edhel* 'elf' (Sindarin) in *Adanedhel, Aredhel, Glóredhel, Ost-in-Edhil*; also in *Peredhil* 'Half-elven'.

*eithel* 'well' in *Eithel Ivrin, Eithel Sirion, Barad Eithel*; also in *Mitheithel*, the river Hoarwell in Eriador (named from its source). See *kel-*.

*êl, elen* 'star'. According to Elvish legend, *ele* was a primitive exclamation 'behold!' made by the Elves when they first saw the stars. From this origin derived the ancient words *êl* and *elen*, meaning 'star', and the adjectives *elda* and *elena*, meaning 'of the stars'. These elements appear in a great many names. For the later use of the name *Eldar* see the Index. The Sindarin equivalent of *Elda* was *Edhel* (plural *Edhil*), q.v.; but the strictly corresponding form was *Eledh*, which occurs in *Eledhwen*.

*er* 'one, alone', in *Amon Ereb* (cf. *Erebor*, the Lonely Mountain), *Erchamion, Eressëa, Eru*.

*ereg* 'thorn, holly' in *Eregion, Region*.

*esgal* 'screen, hiding' in *Esgalduin*.

*falas* 'shore, line of surf' (Quenya *falassë*) in *Falas, Belfalas*; also *Anfalas* in Gondor. Cf. *Falathar, Falathrim*. Another derivative from the root was Quenya *falma* '(crested) wave', whence *Falmari, Mar-nu-Falmar*.

*faroth* is derived from a root meaning 'hunt, pursue'; in the Lay of Leithian the *Taur-en-Faroth* above Nargothrond are called 'the Hills of the Hunters'.

*faug-* 'gape' in *Anfauglir, Anfauglith, Dor-nu-Fauglith*.

*fëa* 'spirit' in *Fëanor, Fëanturi*.

*fin-* 'hair' in *Finduilas, Fingon, Finrod, Glorfindel*.

*formen* 'north' (Quenya) in *Formenos*; Sindarin *forn* (also *for, forod*) in *Fornost*.

*fuin* 'gloom, darkness' (Quenya *huinë*) in *Fuinur, Taur-nu-Fuin*.

*gaer* 'sea' in *Belegaer* (and in *Gaerys*, Sindarin name of Ossë). Said to derive from the stem *gaya* 'awe, dread', and to have been the name made for the vast and terrifying Great Sea when the Eldar first came to its shores.

*gaur* 'werewolf' (from a root *ngwaw-* 'howl') in *Tol-in-Gaurhoth*.

*gil* 'star' in *Dagor-nuin-Giliath*, *Osgiliath* (*giliath* 'host of stars'); *Gil-Estel*, *Gil-galad*.

*girith* 'shuddering' in *Nen Girith*; cf. also *Girithron*, name of the last month of the year in Sindarin (*The Lord of the Rings* Appendix D).

*glîn* 'gleam' (particularly applied to the eyes) in *Maeglin*.

*golodh* is the Sindarin form of Quenya *Noldo*; see *gûl*. Plural *Golodhrim*, and *Gelydh* (in *Annon-in-Gelydh*).

*gond* 'stone' in *Gondolin*, *Gondor*, *Gonnhirrim*, *Argonath*, *seregon*. The name of the hidden city of King Turgon was devised by him in Quenya as *Ondolindë* (Quenya *ondo*=Sindarin *gond*, and *lindë* 'singing, song'); but it was known always in legend in the Sindarin form *Gondolin*, which was probably interpreted as *gond-dolen* 'Hidden Rock'.

*gor* 'horror, dread' in *Gorthaur*, *Gorthol*; *goroth* of the same meaning, with reduplicated *gor*, in *Gorgoroth*, *Ered Gorgoroth*.

*groth* (*grod*) 'delving, underground dwelling' in *Menegroth*, *Nogrod* (probably also in *Nimrodel*, 'lady of the white cave'). *Nogrod* was originally *Novrod* 'hollow delving' (hence the translation *Hollowbold*), but was altered under the influence of *naug* 'dwarf'.

*gûl* 'sorcery' in *Dol Guldur*, *Minas Morgul*. This word was derived from the same ancient stem *ngol-* that appears in *Noldor*; cf. Quenya *nólë* 'long study, lore, knowledge'. But the Sindarin word was darkened in sense by its frequent use in the compound *morgul* 'black arts'.

*gurth* 'death' in *Gurthang* (see also *Melkor* in the Index).

*gwaith* 'people' in *Gwaith-i-Mírdain*; cf. *Enedwaith* 'Middle-folk', name of the land between the Greyflood and the Isen.

*gwath, wath* 'shadow' in *Delduwath*, *Ephel Dúath*; also in *Gwathló*, the river Greyflood in Eriador. Related forms in *Ered Wethrin*, *Thuringwethil*. (This Sindarin word referred to dim light, not to the shadows of objects cast by light: these were called *morchaint* 'dark shapes'.)

*hadhod* in *Hadhodrond* (translation of *Khazad-dûm*) was a rendering of *Khazâd* into Sindarin sounds.

*haudh* 'mound' in *Haudh-en-Arwen*, *Haudh-en-Elleth*, etc.

*heru* 'lord' in *Herumor*, *Herunúmen*; Sindarin *hîr* in *Gonnhirrim*, *Rohirrim*, *Barahir*; *híril* 'lady' in *Hírilorn*.

*him* 'cool' in *Himlad* (and *Himring*?).

*híni* 'children' in *Eruhíni* 'Children of Eru'; *Narn i Hîn Húrin*.

*hîth* 'mist' in *Hithaeglir*, *Hithlum* (also in *Nen Hithoel*, a lake in Anduin). *Hithlum* is Sindarin in form, adapted from the Quenya name *Hísilómë* given by the Noldorin exiles (Quenya *hísië* 'mist', cf. *Hísimë*, the name of the eleventh month of the year, *The Lord of the Rings* Appendix D).

*hoth* 'host, horde' (nearly always in a bad sense) in *Tol-in-Gaurhoth*; also in *Loss(h)oth*, the Snowmen of Forochel (*The Lord of the Rings* Appendix A (I, iii)) and *Glamhoth* 'din-horde', a name for Orcs.

*hyarmen* 'south' (Quenya) in *Hyarmentir*; Sindarin *har-, harn, harad*.

*iâ* 'void, abyss' in *Moria*.
*iant* 'bridge' in *Iant Iaur*.
*iâth* 'fence' in *Doriath*.
*iaur* 'old' in *Iant Iaur*; cf. the Elvish name of Bombadil, *Iarwain*.
*ilm-* This stem appears in *Ilmen, Ilmarë*, and also in *Ilmarin* ('mansion of the high airs', the dwelling of Manwë and Varda upon Oiolossë).
*ilúvë* 'the whole, the all' in *Ilúvatar*.

*kal- (gal-)* This root, meaning 'shine', appears in *Calacirya, Calaquendi, Tar-calion; galvorn, Gil-galad, Galadriel*. The last two names have no connexion with Sindarin *galadh* 'tree', although in the case of Galadriel such a connexion was often made, and the name altered to *Galadhriel*. In the High-elven speech her name was *Al(a)táriel*, derived from *alata* 'radiance' (Sindarin *galad*) and *riel* 'garlanded maiden' (from a root *rig-* 'twine, wreathe'): the whole meaning 'maiden crowned with a radiant garland', referring to her hair. *calen (galen)* 'green' is etymologically 'bright', and derives from this root; see also *aglar*.

*káno* 'commander': this Quenya word is the origin of the second element in *Fingon* and *Turgon*.

*kel-* 'go away', of water 'flow away, flow down', in *Celon*; from *et-kelē* 'issue of water, spring' was derived, with transposition of the consonants, Quenya *ehtelë*, Sindarin *eithel*.

*kemen* 'earth' in *Kementári*; a Quenya word referring to the earth as a flat floor beneath *menel*, the heavens.

*khelek-* 'ice' in *Helcar, Helcaraxë* (Quenya *helka* 'icy, ice-cold'). But in *Helevorn* the first element is Sindarin *heledh* 'glass', taken from Khuzdul *kheled* (cf. *Kheled-zâram* 'Mirrormere'); *Helevorn* means 'black glass' (cf. *galvorn*).

*khil-* 'follow' in *Hildor, Hildórien, Eluchil*.

*kir-* 'cut, cleave' in *Calacirya, Cirth, Angerthas, Cirith (Ninniach, Thoronath)*. From the sense 'pass swiftly through' was derived Quenya *círya* 'sharp-prowed ship' (cf. English *cutter*), and this meaning appears also in *Círdan, Tar-Ciryatan*, and no doubt in the name of Isildur's son *Ciryon*.

*lad* 'plain, valley' in *Dagorlad, Himlad*; *imlad* a narrow valley with steep sides, in *Imladris* (cf. also *Imlad Morgul* in the Ephel Dúath).

*laurë* 'gold' (but of light and colour, not of the metal) in *Laurelin*; the Sindarin forms in *Glóredhel, Glorfindel, Loeg Ningloron, Lórindol, Rathlóriel.*

*lhach* 'leaping flame' in *Dagor Bragollach*, and probably in *Anglachel* (the sword made by Eöl of meteoric iron).

*lin* (1) 'pool, mere' in *Linaewen* (which contains *aew* (Quenya *aiwë*) 'small bird'), *Teiglin*; cf. *aelin.*

*lin-* (2) This root, meaning 'sing, make a musical sound', occurs in *Ainulindalë, Laurelin, Lindar, Lindon, Ered Lindon, lómelindi.*

*lith* 'ash' in *Anfauglith, Dor-nu-Fauglith*; also in *Ered Lithui*, the Ashen Mountains, forming the northern border of Mordor, and *Lithlad* 'Plain of Ashes' at the feet of Ered Lithui.

*lok-* 'bend, loop' in *Urulóki* (Quenya *(h)lókë* 'snake, serpent', Sindarin *lhûg*).

*lóm* 'echo' in *Dor-lómin, Ered Lómin*; related are *Lammoth, Lanthir Lamath.*

*lómë* 'dusk' in *Lómion, lómelindi*; see *dú.*

*londë* 'land-locked haven' in *Alqualondë*; the Sindarin form *lond (lonn)* in *Mithlond.*

*los* 'snow' in *Oiolossë* (Quenya *oio* 'ever' and *lossë* 'snow, snow-white'); Sindarin *loss* in *Amon Uilos* and *Aeglos.*

*loth* 'flower' in *Lothlórien, Nimloth*; Quenya *lótë* in *Ninquelótë, Vingilótë.*

*luin* 'blue' in *Ered Luin, Helluin, Luinil, Mindolluin.*


*maeg* 'sharp, piercing' (Quenya *maika*) in *Maeglin.*

*mal-* 'gold' in *Malduin, Malinalda*; also in *mallorn*, and in the Field of *Cormallen*, which means 'golden circle' and was named from the *culumalda* trees that grew there (see *cul-*).

*mān-* 'good, blessed, unmarred' in *Aman, Manwë*; derivatives of *Aman* in *Amandil, Araman, Úmanyar.*

*mel-* 'love' in *Melian* (from *Melyanna* 'dear gift'); this stem is seen also in the Sindarin word *mellon* 'friend' in the inscription on the West-gate of Moria.

*men* 'way' in *Númen, Hyarmen, Rómen, Formen.*

*menel* 'the heavens' in *Meneldil, Menelmacar, Meneltarma.*

*mereth* 'feast' in *Mereth Aderthad*; also in *Merethrond*, the Hall of Feasts in Minas Tirith.

*minas* 'tower' in *Annúminas, Minas Anor, Minas Tirith*, etc. The same stem occurs in other words referring to isolated, prominent, things, e.g. *Mindolluin, Mindon*; probably related is Quenya *minya* 'first' (cf. *Tar-Minyatur*, the name of Elros as first King of Númenor).

*mîr* 'jewel' (Quenya *mírë*) in *Elemmírë, Gwaith-i-Mírdain, Míriel, Nauglamír, Tar-Atanamir.*

*mith* 'grey' in *Mithlond, Mithrandir, Mithrim*; also in *Mitheithel*, the river Hoarwell in Eriador.

*mor* 'dark' in *Mordor, Morgoth, Moria, Moriquendi, Mormegil, Morwen*, etc.

*moth* 'dusk' in *Nan Elmoth*.


*nan(d)* 'valley' in *Nan Dungortheb, Nan Elmoth, Nan Tathren*.

*nár* 'fire' in *Narsil, Narya*; present also in the original forms of *Aegnor* (*Aikanáro* 'Sharp Flame' or 'Fell Fire') and *Fëanor* (*Fëanáro* 'Spirit of Fire'). The Sindarin form was *naur*, as in *Sammath Naur*, the Chambers of Fire in Orodruin. Derived from the same ancient root (*a*)*nar* was the name of the Sun, Quenya *Anar* (also in *Anárion*), Sindarin *Anor* (cf. *Minas Anor, Anórien*).

*naug* 'dwarf' in *Naugrim*; see also *Nogrod* in entry *groth*. Related is another Sindarin word for 'dwarf', *nogoth*, plural *noegyth* (*Noegyth Nibin* 'Petty-dwarves') and *nogothrim*.

*-(n)dil* is a very frequent ending of personal names, *Amandil, Eärendil* (shortened *Eärnil*), *Elendil, Mardil*, etc.; it implies 'devotion', 'disinterested love' (see *Mardil* in entry *bar*).

*-(n)dur* in names such as *Eärendur* (shortened *Eärnur*) is similar in meaning to *-(n)dil*.

*neldor* 'beech' in *Neldoreth*; but it seems that this was properly the name of Hírilorn, the great beech-tree with three trunks (*neldë* 'three' and *orn*).

*nen* 'water', used of lakes, pools, and lesser rivers, in *Nen Girith, Nenning, Nenuial, Nenya*; *Cuiviénen, Uinen*; also in many names in *The Lord of the Rings*, as *Nen Hithoel, Bruinen, Emyn Arnen, Núrnen. Nîn* 'wet' in *Loeg Ningloron*; also in *Nindalf*.

*nim* 'white' (from earlier *nimf, nimp*) in *Nimbrethil, Nimloth, Nimphelos, niphredil* (*niphred* 'pallor'), *Barad Nimras, Ered Nimrais*. The Quenya form was *ninquë*; thus *Ninquelótë* = *Nimloth*. Cf. also *Taniquetil*.


*orn* 'tree' in *Celeborn, Hírilorn*; cf. *Fangorn* 'Treebeard', and *mallorn*, plural *mellyrn*, the trees of Lothlórien.

*orod* 'mountain' in *Orodruin, Thangorodrim*; *Orocarni, Oromet*. Plural *ered* in *Ered Engrin, Ered Lindon*, etc.

*os(t)* 'fortress' in *Angrenost, Belegost, Formenos, Fornost, Mandos, Nargothrond* (from *Narog-ost-rond*), *Os(t)giliath, Ost-in-Edhil*.


*palan* (Quenya) 'far and wide' in *palantíri, Tar-Palantir*.

*pel-* 'go round, encircle' in *Pelargir, Pelóri*, and in the *Pelennor*, the 'fenced land' of Minas Tirith; also in *Ephel Brandir, Ephel Dúath* (*ephel* from *et-pel* 'outer fence').

*quen-* (*quet-*) 'say, speak' in *Quendi* (*Calaquendi, Laiquendi, Moriquendi*), *Quenya, Valaquenta, Quenta Silmarillion.* The Sindarin forms have *p* (or *b*) for *qu*; e.g. *pedo* 'speak' in the inscription on the West-gate of Moria, corresponding to the Quenya stem *quet-*, and Gandalf's words before the gate, *lasto beth lammen* 'listen to the words of my tongue', where *beth* 'word' corresponds to Quenya *quetta.*

*ram*    'wall' (Quenya *ramba*) in *Andram, Ramdal*; also in *Rammas Echor*, the wall about the Pelennor Fields at Minas Tirith.

*ran-*   'wander, stray' in *Rána*, the Moon, and in *Mithrandir, Aerandir*; also in the river *Gilraen* in Gondor.

*rant*   'course' in the river-names *Adurant* (with *adu* 'double') and *Celebrant* ('Silverlode').

*ras*    'horn' in *Barad Nimras*, also in *Caradhras* ('Redhorn') and *Methedras* ('Last Peak') in the Misty Mountains; plural *rais* in *Ered Nimrais.*

*rauko*  'demon' in *Valaraukar*; Sindarin *raug, rog* in *Balrog.*

*ril*    'brilliance' in *Idril, Silmaril*; also in *Andúril* (the sword of Aragorn) and in *mithril* (Moria-silver). Idril's name in Quenya form was *Itarillë* (or *Itarildë*), from a stem *ita-* 'sparkle'.

*rim*    'great number, host' (Quenya *rimbë*) was commonly used to form collective plurals, as *Golodhrim, Mithrim* (see the Index), *Naugrim, Thangorodrim*, etc.

*ring*   'cold, chill' in *Ringil, Ringwil, Himring*; also in the river *Ringló* in Gondor, and in *Ringarë*, Quenya name of the last month of the year (*The Lord of the Rings* Appendix D).

*ris*    'cleave' appears to have blended with the stem *kris-* of similar meaning (a derivative of the root *kir-* 'cleave, cut', q.v.); hence *Angrist* (also *Orcrist* 'Orc-cleaver', the sword of Thorin Oakenshield), *Crissaegrim, Imladris.*

*roch*   'horse' (Quenya *rokko*) in *Rochallor, Rohan* (from *Rochand* 'land of horses'), *Rohirrim*; also in *Roheryn* 'horse of the lady' (cf. *heru*), Aragorn's horse, which was so called because given to him by Arwen (*The Return of the King* V 2).

*rom-*   A stem used of the sound of trumpets and horns which appears in *Oromë* and *Valaróma*; cf. *Béma*, the name of this Vala in the language of Rohan as translated into Anglo-Saxon in *The Lord of the Rings* Appendix A (II): Anglo-Saxon *bēme* 'trumpet'.

*rómen*  'uprising, sunrise, east' (Quenya) in *Rómenna*. The Sindarin words for 'east', *rhûn* (in *Talath Rhúnen*) and *amrûn*, were of the same origin.

*rond*   meant a vaulted or arched roof, or a large hall or chamber so roofed; so *Nargothrond* (see *ost*), *Hadhodrond, Aglarond.* It could be applied to the heavens, hence the name *Elrond* 'star-dome'.

*ros*    'foam, spindrift, spray' in *Celebros, Elros, Rauros*; also in *Cair Andros*, an island in the river Anduin.

*ruin* 'red flame' (Quenya *rúnya*) in *Orodruin*.
*rûth* 'anger' in *Aranrúth*.


*sarn* '(small) stone' in *Sarn Athrad* (*Sarn Ford* on the Brandywine is a
half-translation of this); also in *Sarn Gebir* ('stone-spikes': *ceber*,
plural *cebir* 'stakes'), rapids in the river Anduin. A derivative is *Serni*,
a river in Gondor.
*sereg* 'blood' (Quenya *serkë*) in *seregon*.
*sil-* (and variant *thil-*) 'shine (with white or silver light)' in *Belthil*,
*Galathilion, Silpion*, and in Quenya *Isil*, Sindarin *Ithil*, the Moon
(whence *Isildur, Narsil*; *Minas Ithil, Ithilien*). The Quenya word
*Silmarilli* is said to derive from the name *silima* that Fëanor gave to
the substance from which they were made.
*sîr* 'river', from root *sir-* 'flow', in *Ossiriand* (the first element is from
the stem of the numeral 'seven', Quenya *otso*, Sindarin *odo*), *Sirion*;
also in *Sirannon* (the 'Gate-stream' of Moria) and *Sirith* ('a flowing',
as *tirith* 'watching' from *tir*), a river in Gondor. With change of *s* to
*h* in the middle of words it is present in *Minhiriath* 'between the
rivers', the region between the Brandywine and the Greyflood; in
*Nanduhirion* 'vale of dim streams', the Dimrill Dale (see *nan(d)* and
*dú*); and in *Ethir Anduin*, the outflow or delta of Anduin (from *et-sîr*).
*súl* 'wind' in *Amon Súl, Súlimo*; cf. *súlimë*, Quenya name of the third
month of the year (*The Lord of the Rings* Appendix D).


*tal* (*dal*) 'foot' in *Celebrindal*, and with the meaning 'end' in *Ramdal*.
*talath* 'flat lands, plain' in *Talath Dirnen, Talath Rhúnen*.
*tar-* 'high' (Quenya *tára* 'lofty'), prefix of the Quenya names of the
Númenórean Kings; also in *Annatar*. Feminine *tári* 'she that is high,
Queen' in *Elentári, Kementári*. Cf. *tarma* 'pillar' in *Meneltarma*.
*tathar* 'willow'; adjective *tathren* in *Nan-tathren*; Quenya *tasarë* in
*Tasarinan, Nan-tasarion* (see *Nan-tathren* in the Index).
*taur* 'wood, forest' (Quenya *taurë*) in *Tauron, Taur-im-Duinath, Taur-nu-
Fuin*.
*tel-* 'finish, end, be last' in *Teleri*.
*thalion* 'strong, dauntless' in *Cúthalion, Thalion*.
*thang* 'oppression' in *Thangorodrim*, also in *Durthang* (a castle in Mordor).
Quenya *sanga* meant 'press, throng', whence *Sangahyando* 'Throng-
cleaver', name of a man in Gondor (*The Lord of the Rings* Appendix A
(I, iv)).
*thar-* 'athwart, across' in *Sarn Athrad, Thargelion*; also in *Tharbad* (from
*thara-pata* 'crossway') where the ancient road from Arnor and Gondor
crossed the Greyflood.
*thaur* 'abominable, abhorrent' in *Sauron* (from *Thauron*), *Gorthaur*.

*thin(d)* 'grey' in *Thingol*; Quenya *sinda* in *Sindar*, *Singollo* (*Sindacollo: collo* 'cloak').

*thôl* 'helm' in *Dor Cúarthol*, *Gorthol*.

*thôn* 'pine-tree' in *Dorthonion*.

*thoron* 'eagle' in *Thorondor* (Quenya *Sorontar*), *Cirith Thoronath*. The Quenya form is perhaps present in the constellation-name *Soronúmë*.

*til* 'point, horn' in *Taniquetil*, *Tilion* ('the Horned'); also in *Celebdil* 'Silvertine', one of the Mountains of Moria.

*tin-* 'sparkle' (Quenya *tinta* 'cause to sparkle', *tinwë* 'spark') in *Tintallë*; also in *tindómë* 'starry twilight' (*The Lord of the Rings* Appendix D), whence *tindómerel* 'daughter of the twilight', a poetic name for the nightingale (Sindarin *Tinúviel*). It appears also in Sindarin *ithildin* 'starmoon', the substance of which the devices on the West-gate of Moria were made.

*tir* 'watch, watch over' in *Minas Tirith*, *palantíri*, *Tar-Palantir*, *Tirion*.

*tol* 'isle' (rising with sheer sides from the sea or from a river) in *Tol Eressëa*, *Tol Galen*, etc.

*tum* 'valley' in *Tumhalad*, *Tumladen*; Quenya *tumbo* (cf. Treebeard's *tumbalemorna* 'black deep valley', *The Two Towers* III 4). Cf. *Utumno*, Sindarin *Udûn* (Gandalf in Moria named the Balrog 'Flame of Udûn'), a name afterwards used of the deep dale in Moria between the Morannon and the Isenmouthe.

*tur* 'power, mastery' in *Turambar*, *Turgon*, *Túrin*, *Fëanturi*, *Tar-Minyatur*.


*uial* 'twilight' in *Aelin-uial*, *Nenuial*.

*ur-* 'heat, be hot' in *Urulóki*; cf. *Urimë* and *Urui*, Quenya and Sindarin names of the eighth month of the year (*The Lord of the Rings* Appendix D). Related is the Quenya word *aurë* 'sunlight, day' (cf. Fingon's cry before the Nirnaeth Arnoediad), Sindarin *aur*, which in the form *Or-* is prefixed to the names of the days of the week.


*val-* 'power' in *Valar*, *Valacirca*, *Valaquenta*, *Valaraukar*, *Val(i)mar*, *Valinor*. The original stem was *bal-*, preserved in Sindarin *Balan*, plural *Belain*, the Valar, and in *Balrog*.


*wen* 'maiden' is a frequent ending, as in *Eärwen*, *Morwen*.

*wing* 'foam, spray' in *Elwing*, *Vingelot* (and only in these two names).


*yávë* 'fruit' (Quenya) in *Yavanna*; cf. *Yavannië*, Quenya name of the ninth month of the year, and *yávië* 'autumn' (*The Lord of the Rings* Appendix D).

# THE BOOK OF LOST TALES

## PART II

THE HISTORY OF MIDDLE-EARTH

I
THE BOOK OF LOST TALES, PART ONE

II
THE BOOK OF LOST TALES, PART TWO

III
THE LAYS OF BELERIAND

IV
THE SHAPING OF MIDDLE-EARTH

V
THE LOST ROAD AND OTHER WRITINGS

VI
THE RETURN OF THE SHADOW

VII
THE TREASON OF ISENGARD

VIII
THE WAR OF THE RING

IX
SAURON DEFEATED

X
MORGOTH'S RING

XI
THE WAR OF THE JEWELS

XII
THE PEOPLES OF MIDDLE-EARTH

J. R. R. TOLKIEN

# The
# Book of Lost Tales

## PART II

Christopher Tolkien

HarperCollins*Publishers*

HarperCollins*Publishers* Ltd
1 London Bridge Street
London SE1 9GF

HarperCollins*Publishers*
Macken House, 39/40 Mayor Street Upper
Dublin 1, D01 C9W8, Ireland

www.tolkien.co.uk
www.tolkienestate.com

This hardback edition 2023
1

First published in Great Britain by
George Allen & Unwin (Publishers) Ltd 1984,
and by HarperCollins*Publishers* 1991

# CONTENTS

# PREFACE

This second part of *The Book of Lost Tales* is arranged on the same lines and with the same intentions as the first part, as described in the Foreword to it, pages 10–11. References to the first part are given in the form 'I. 240', to the second as 'p. 240', except where a reference is made to both, e.g. 'I. 222, II. 292'.

As before, I have adopted a consistent (if not necessarily 'correct') system of accentuation for names; and in the cases of *Mim* and *Niniel*, written thus throughout, I give *Mîm* and *Níniel*.

The two pages from the original manuscripts are reproduced with the permission of the Bodleian Library, Oxford, and I wish to express my thanks to the staff of the Department of Western Manuscripts at the Bodleian for their assistance. The correspondence of the original pages to the printed text in this book is as follows:

(1) The page from the manuscript of *The Tale of Tinúviel*. Upper part: printed text page 24 (7 lines up, *the sorest dread*) to page 25 (line 3, *so swiftly.*"). Lower part: printed text page 25 (11 lines up, *the harsh voice*) to page 26 (line 7, *but Tevildo*).

(2) The page from the manuscript of *The Fall of Gondolin*. Upper part: printed text page 189 (line 12, *"Now," therefore said Galdor* to line 20 *if no further.*"). Lower part: printed text page 189 (line 27, *But the others, led by one Legolas Greenleaf*) to page 190 (line 11, *leaving the main company to follow he*).

For differences in the printed text of *The Fall of Gondolin* from the page reproduced see page 201, notes 34–36, and page 203, *Bad Uthwen*; some other small differences not referred to in the notes are also due to later changes made to the text B of the Tale (see pages 146–7).

These pages illustrate the complicated 'jigsaw' of the manuscripts of the *Lost Tales* described in the Foreword to Part I, page 10.

The third volume in this 'History' will contain the alliterative *Lay of the Children of Húrin* (*c*.1918–1925) and the *Lay of Leithian* (1925–1931), together with the commentary on a part of the latter by C. S. Lewis, and the rewriting of the poem that my father embarked on after the completion of *The Lord of the Rings*.

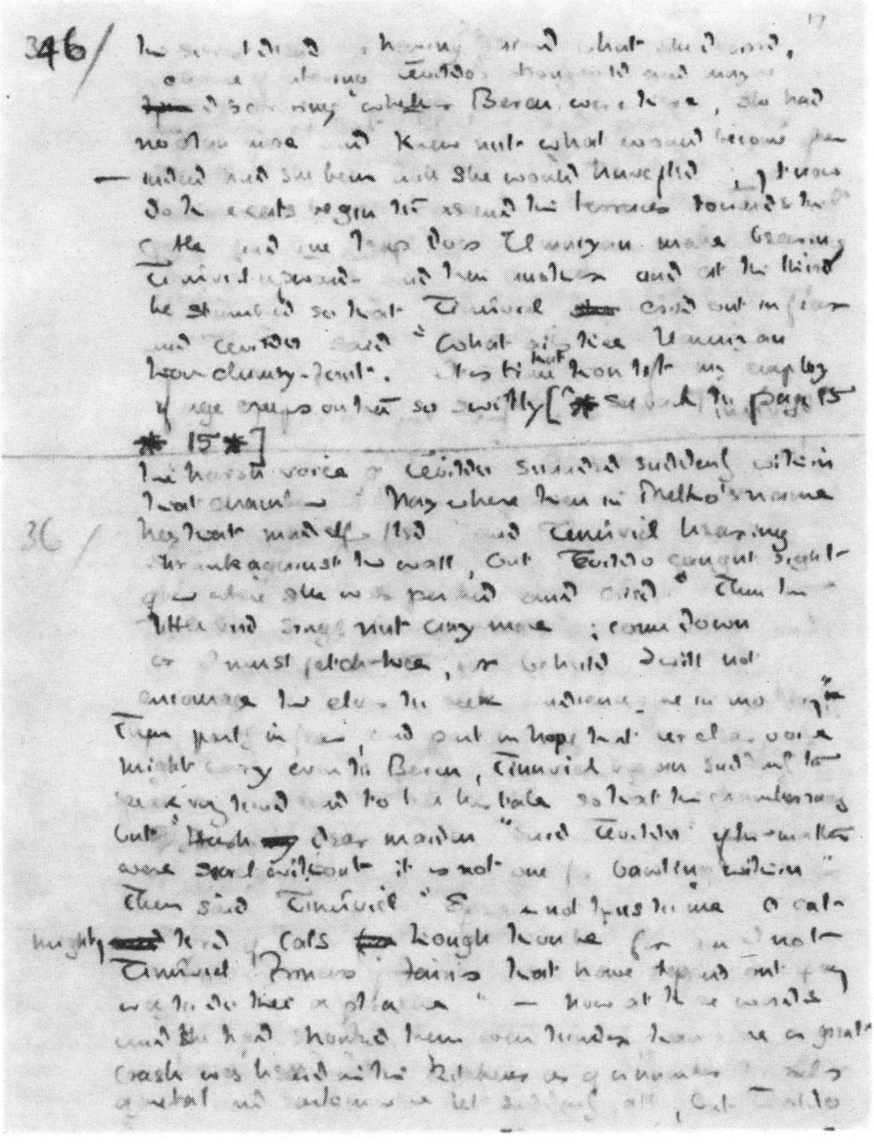

A page from the *Tale of Tinúviel*

"Now therefore" said Galdor "we must get as far hence
toward the encircling Mountains ere dawn come upon us,
and that gives us great space of time albeit it is winter."
Thereat rose a dissension for a member said that it were folly
to make for Cristhorn as Tuor proposed. "The sun," say
they "will be up long ere we win the foothills and we shall
be o'erwhelmed in the plain ~~those orcas and those demons,
nor may a host o'erwhelm as we fare in~~"
~~And make us and those yet were here for making~~
~~Bad Uswen the way of escape now further~~
Let us fare to Bad Uswen the way of escape for that is
but half the journeying, and our weary and our wounded
may hope to win so far ~~and~~ no further.

But others, led by Legolas Greenleaf of the house the
Tree who knew all that plain by day or by dark, and was
night-sighted made ~~a~~ speed for all their weariness over
the vale, and halted only after a great march. Then was
all the earth spread with the grey light of that sad dawn that
looked no more on the beauty of Gondolin. Out the plain was full of mists
— and that was a marvel for no mist came there ever before, and
this perchance had to do with the doom of the fountain of the king. Again
they rose and covered by the vapours tarried long past dawn
safely, till they were already far, or for any to espy them in those
misty airs from the hill or ~~the~~ from the ruined walls.
Now the Mountains were on that side seven leagues save a
mile from Gondolin and Cristhorn the Cleft of Eagles another
league up toward coming from the beginning of the mountains where
they were now yet two leagues and part of a third from the pass, and
very weary thereto. By now the sun hung
~~the~~ well above a saddle in the eastward hills,
and she was very red and great; and the mists with them were
lifted, but the ruins of Gondolin were utterly hidden as in a cloud
Behold ~~then~~ at the chasms of the cars they saw, but half a league
away, a knot of men that fled on foot — and these were pursued
by a strange cavalry, for on great wolves rode ~~so~~ Orcs, as they
thought, brandishing spears. Then said Tuor: Lo! here ~~are~~
is Cristhorn my son and my men of the wing and they are in
sore straits." Forthwith he chose fifty of the men that were
least weary, and leaving the main company to follow, he

A page from the tale of *The Fall of Gondolin*

# I

# THE TALE OF TINÚVIEL

The *Tale of Tinúviel* was written in 1917, but the earliest extant text is
later, being a manuscript in ink over an erased original in pencil; and in
fact my father's rewriting of this tale seems to have been one of the last
completed elements in the *Lost Tales* (see I. 203–4).

There is also a typescript version of the *Tale of Tinúviel*, later than the
manuscript but belonging to the same 'phase' of the mythology: my
father had the manuscript before him and changed the text as he went
along. Significant differences between the two versions of the tale are
given on pp. 41 ff.

In the manuscript the tale is headed: 'Link to the Tale of Tinúviel, also
the Tale of Tinúviel.' The *Link* begins with the following passage:

'Great was the power of Melko for ill,' said Eriol, 'if he could indeed
destroy with his cunning the happiness and glory of the Gods and
Elves, darkening the light of their dwelling and bringing all their love
to naught. This must surely be the worst deed that ever he has done.'

'Of a truth never has such evil again been done in Valinor,' said
Lindo, 'but Melko's hand has laboured at worse things in the world,
and the seeds of his evil have waxen since to a great and terrible
growth.'

'Nay,' said Eriol, 'yet can my heart not think of other griefs, for
sorrow at the destruction of those most fair Trees and the darkness of
the world.'

This passage was struck out, and is not found in the typescript text,
but it reappears in almost identical form at the end of *The Flight of the
Noldoli* (I. 169). The reason for this was that my father decided that the
*Tale of the Sun and Moon*, rather than *Tinúviel*, should follow *The
Darkening of Valinor* and *The Flight of the Noldoli* (see I. 203–4,
where the complex question of the re-ordering of the *Tales* at this point is
discussed). The opening words of the next part of the *Link*, 'Now in the
days soon after the telling of this tale', referred, when they were written,
to the tale of *The Darkening of Valinor* and *The Flight of the Noldoli*;
but it is never made plain to what tale they were to refer when *Tinúviel*
had been removed from its earlier position.

The two versions of the *Link* are at first very close, but when Eriol
speaks of his own past history they diverge. For the earlier part I give
the typescript text alone, and when they diverge I give them both in

succession. All discussion of this story of Eriol's life is postponed to Chapter VI.

Now in the days soon after the telling of this tale, behold, winter approached the land of Tol Eressëa, for now had Eriol forgetful of his wandering mood abode some time in old Kortirion. Never in those months did he fare beyond the good tilth that lay without the grey walls of that town, but many a hall of the kindreds of the Inwir and the Teleri received him as their glad guest, and ever more skilled in the tongues of the Elves did he become, and more deep in knowledge of their customs, of their tales and songs.

Then was winter come sudden upon the Lonely Isle, and the lawns and gardens drew on a sparkling mantle of white snows; their fountains were still, and all their bare trees silent, and the far sun glinted pale amid the mist or splintered upon facets of long hanging ice. Still fared Eriol not away, but watched the cold moon from the frosty skies look down upon Mar Vanwa Tyaliéva, and when above the roofs the stars gleamed blue he would listen, yet no sound of the flutes of Timpinen heard he now; for the breath of summer is that sprite, and or ever autumn's secret presence fills the air he takes his grey magic boat, and the swallows draw him far away.

Even so Eriol knew laughter and merriment and musics too, and song, in the dwellings of Kortirion – even Eriol the wanderer whose heart before had known no rest. Came now a grey day, and a wan afternoon, but within was firelight and good warmth and dancing and merry children's noise, for Eriol was making a great play with the maids and boys in the Hall of Play Regained. There at length tired with their mirth they cast themselves down upon the rugs before the hearth, and a child among them, a little maid, said: 'Tell me, O Eriol, a tale!'

'What then shall I tell, O Vëannë?' said he, and she, clambering upon his knee, said: 'A tale of Men and of children in the Great Lands, or of thy home – and didst thou have a garden there such as we, where poppies grew and pansies like those that grow in my corner by the Arbour of the Thrushes?'

I give now the manuscript version of the remainder of the *Link* passage:

Then Eriol told her of his home that was in an old town of Men girt with a wall now crumbled and broken, and a river ran thereby over which a castle with a great tower hung. 'A very high tower indeed,' said he, 'and the moon climbed high or ever he thrust his face above it.' 'Was it then as high as Ingil's Tirin?' said Vëannë, but Eriol said that that he could not guess, for 'twas very many years agone since he had seen that castle or its tower, for 'O Vëannë,' said he, 'I lived there but a while, and not after I was grown to be a boy. My father came of a coastward folk, and the love of the sea that I had never seen was in my bones, and my father whetted my desire, for he told me tales that his father had told him before. Now my mother died in a cruel and hungry siege of that old town, and my father was slain in bitter fight about the walls, and in the end I Eriol escaped to the shoreland of the Western Sea, and mostly have lived upon the bosom of the waves or by its side since those far days.'

Now the children about were filled with sadness at the sorrows that fell on those dwellers in the Great Lands, and at the wars and death, and Vëannë clung to Eriol, saying: 'O Melinon, go never to a war – or hast thou ever yet?'

'Aye, often enough,' said Eriol, 'but not to the great wars of the earthly kings and mighty nations which are cruel and bitter, and many fair lands and lovely things and even women and sweet maids such as thou Vëannë Melinir are whelmed by them in ruin; yet gallant affrays have I seen wherein small bands of brave men do sometimes meet and swift blows are dealt. But behold, why speak we of these things, little one; wouldst not hear rather of my first ventures on the sea?'

Then was there much eagerness alight, and Eriol told them of his wanderings about the western havens, of the comrades he made and the ports he knew, of how he was wrecked upon far western islands until at last upon one lonely one he came on an ancient sailor who gave him shelter, and over a fire within his lonely cabin told him strange tales of things beyond the Western Seas, of the Magic Isles and that most lonely one that lay beyond. Long ago had he once sighted it shining afar off, and after had he sought it many a day in vain.

'Ever after,' said Eriol, 'did I sail more curiously about the western isles seeking more stories of the kind, and thus it is indeed that after many great voyages I came myself by the blessing of the Gods to Tol Eressëa in the end – wherefore I now sit here talking to thee, Vëannë, till my words have run dry.'

Then nonetheless did a boy, Ausir, beg him to tell more of ships and the sea, but Eriol said: 'Nay – still is there time ere Ilfiniol ring the gong for evening meat: come, one of you children, tell me a tale that you have heard!' Then Vëannë sat up and clapped her hands, saying: 'I will tell you the Tale of Tinúviel.'

The typescript version of this passage reads as follows:

Then Eriol told of his home of long ago, that was in an ancient town of Men girt with a wall now crumbled and broken, for the folk that dwelt there had long known days of rich and easy peace. A river ran thereby, o'er which a castle with a great tower hung. 'There dwelt a mighty duke,' said he, 'and did he gaze from the topmost battlements never might he see the bounds of his wide domain, save where far to east the blue shapes of the great mountains lay – yet was that tower held the most lofty that stood in the lands of Men.' 'Was it as high as great Ingil's Tirin?' said Vëannë, but said Eriol: 'A very high tower indeed was it, and the moon climbed far or ever he thrust his face above it, yet may I not now guess how high, O Vëannë, for 'tis many years agone since last I saw that castle or its steep tower. War fell suddenly on that town amid its slumbrous peace, nor were its crumbled walls able to withstand the onslaught of the wild men from the Mountains of the East. There perished my mother in that cruel and hungry siege, and my father was slain fighting bitterly about the walls in the last sack. In those far days was I not yet war-high, and a bondslave was I made.

'Know then that my father was come of a coastward folk ere he wandered to that place, and the longing for the sea that I had never seen was in my bones; which often had my father whetted, telling me tales of the wide waters and recalling lore that he had learned of his father aforetime. Small need to tell of my travail thereafter in thraldom, for in the end I brake my bonds and got me to the shoreland of the Western Sea – and mostly have I lived upon the bosom of its waves or by its side since those old days.'

Now hearing of the sorrows that fell upon the dwellers in the Great Lands, the wars and death, the children were filled with sadness, and Vëannë clung to Eriol, saying: 'O Melinon, go thou never to a war – or hast thou ever yet?'

'Aye, often enough,' said Eriol, 'yet not to the great wars of the earthly kings and mighty nations, which are cruel and bitter, whelming in their ruin all the beauty both of the earth and of those fair things that men fashion with their hands in times of peace – nay, they spare not sweet women and tender maids, such as thou, Vëannë Melinir, for then are men drunk with wrath and the lust of blood, and Melko fares abroad. But gallant affrays have I seen wherein brave men did sometimes meet, and swift blows were dealt, and strength of body and of heart was proven – but, behold, why speak we of these things, little one? Wouldst not hear rather of my ventures on the sea?'

Then was there much eagerness alight, and Eriol told them of his first wanderings about the western havens, of the comrades he made, and the ports he knew; of how he was one time wrecked upon far western islands and there upon a lonely eyot found an ancient mariner who dwelt for ever solitary in a cabin on the shore, that he had fashioned of the timbers of his boat. 'More wise was he,' said Eriol, 'in all matters of the sea than any other I have met, and much of wizardry was there in his lore. Strange things he told me of regions far beyond the Western Sea, of the Magic Isles and that most lonely one that lies behind. Once long ago, he said, he had sighted it glimmering afar off, and after had he sought it many a day in vain. Much lore he taught me of the hidden seas, and the dark and trackless waters, and without this never had I found this sweetest land, or this dear town or the Cottage of Lost Play – yet it was not without long and grievous search thereafter, and many a weary voyage, that I came myself by the blessing of the Gods to Tol Eressëa at the last – wherefore I now sit here talking to thee, Vëannë, till my words have run dry.'

Then nevertheless did a boy, Ausir, beg him to tell more of ships and the sea, saying: 'For knowest thou not, O Eriol, that that ancient mariner beside the lonely sea was none other than Ulmo's self, who appeareth not seldom thus to those voyagers whom he loves – yet he who has spoken with Ulmo must have many a tale to tell that will not be stale in the ears even of those that dwell here in Kortirion.' But Eriol at that time believed not that saying of Ausir's, and said: 'Nay, pay me your debt ere Ilfrin ring the gong for evening meat – come, one of you shall tell me a tale that you have heard.'

Then did Vëannë sit up and clap her hands, crying: 'I will tell thee the Tale of Tinúviel.'

★

## The Tale of Tinúviel

I give now the text of the *Tale of Tinúviel* as it appears in the manuscript. The *Link* is not in fact distinguished or separated in any way from the tale proper, and Vëannë makes no formal opening to it.

'Who was then Tinúviel?' said Eriol. 'Know you not?' said Ausir; 'Tinúviel was the daughter of Tinwë Linto.' 'Tinwelint', said Vëannë, but said the other: "'Tis all one, but the Elves of this house who love the tale do say Tinwë Linto, though Vairë hath said that Tinwë alone is his right name ere he wandered in the woods.'

'Hush thee, Ausir,' said Vëannë, 'for it is my tale and I will tell it to Eriol. Did I not see Gwendeling and Tinúviel once with my own eyes when journeying by the Way of Dreams in long past days?'[1]

'What was Queen Wendelin like (for so do the Elves call her),[2] O Vëannë, if thou sawest her?' said Ausir.

'Slender and very dark of hair,' said Vëannë, 'and her skin was white and pale, but her eyes shone and seemed deep, and she was clad in filmy garments most lovely yet of black, jet-spangled and girt with silver. If ever she sang, or if she danced, dreams and slumbers passed over your head and made it heavy. Indeed she was a sprite that escaped from Lórien's gardens before even Kôr was built, and she wandered in the wooded places of the world, and nightingales went with her and often sang about her. It was the song of these birds that smote the ears of Tinwelint, leader of that tribe of the Eldar that after were the Solosimpi the pipers of the shore, as he fared with his companions behind the horse of Oromë from Palisor. Ilúvatar had set a seed of music in the hearts of all that kindred, or so Vairë saith, and she is of them, and it blossomed after very wondrously, but now the song of Gwendeling's nightingales was the most beautiful music that Tinwelint had ever heard, and he strayed aside for a moment, as he thought, from the host, seeking in the dark trees whence it might come.

And it is said that it was not a moment he hearkened, but many years, and vainly his people sought him, until at length they followed Oromë and were borne upon Tol Eressëa far away, and he saw them never again. Yet after a while as it seemed to him he came upon Gwendeling lying in a bed of leaves gazing at the stars above her and hearkening also to her birds. Now Tinwelint stepping softly stooped and looked upon her, thinking "Lo, here is a fairer being even than the most beautiful of my own folk" – for indeed Gwendeling was not elf or woman but of the children of the Gods; and bending further to touch a tress of her hair he snapped a twig with his foot. Then Gwendeling was up and away laughing softly, sometimes singing distantly or dancing ever just before him, till a swoon of fragrant slumbers fell upon him and he fell face downward neath the trees and slept a very great while.

Now when he awoke he thought no more of his people (and indeed it had been vain, for long now had those reached Valinor) but desired only to see the twilight-lady; but she was not far, for she had remained nigh at hand and watched over him. More of their story I know not, O Eriol, save that in the end she became his wife, for Tinwelint and Gwendeling very long indeed were king and queen of the Lost Elves of Artanor or the Land Beyond, or so it is said here.

Long, long after, as thou knowest, Melko brake again into the world from Valinor, and all the Eldar both those who remained in the dark or had been lost upon the march from Palisor and those Noldoli too who fared back into the world after him seeking their stolen treasury fell beneath his power as thralls. Yet it is told that many there were who escaped and wandered in the woods and empty places, and of these many a wild and woodland clan rallied beneath King Tinwelint. Of those the most were Ilkorindi – which is to say Eldar that never had beheld Valinor or the Two Trees or dwelt in Kôr – and eerie they were and strange beings, knowing little of light or loveliness or of musics save it be dark songs and chantings of a rugged wonder that faded in the wooded places or echoed in deep caves. Different indeed did they become when the Sun arose, and indeed before that already were their numbers mingled with a many wandering Gnomes, and wayward sprites too there were of Lórien's host that dwelt in the courts of Tinwelint, being followers of Gwendeling, and these were not of the kindreds of the Eldalië.

Now in the days of Sunlight and Moonsheen still dwelt Tinwelint in Artanor, and nor he nor the most of his folk went to the Battle of Unnumbered Tears, though that story toucheth not this tale. Yet was his lordship greatly increased after that unhappy field by fugitives that fled to his protection. Hidden was his dwelling from the vision and knowledge of Melko by the magics of Gwendeling the fay, and she wove spells about the paths thereto that none but the Eldar might tread them easily, and so was the king secured from all dangers save it be treachery alone. Now his halls were builded in a deep cavern of great size, and they were nonetheless a kingly and a fair abode. This cavern was in the heart of the mighty forest of Artanor that is the mightiest of forests, and a stream ran before its doors, but none could enter that portal save across the stream, and a bridge spanned it narrow and well-guarded. Those places were not ill albeit the Iron Mountains were not utterly distant beyond whom lay Hisilómë where dwelt Men, and thrall-Noldoli laboured, and few free-Eldar went.

Lo, now I will tell you of things that happened in the halls of Tinwelint after the arising of the Sun indeed but long ere the unforgotten Battle of Unnumbered Tears. And Melko had not completed his designs nor had he unveiled his full might and cruelty.

Two children had Tinwelint then, Dairon and Tinúviel, and Tinúviel was a maiden, and the most beautiful of all the maidens of the hidden Elves, and indeed few have been so fair, for her mother was a fay, a daughter of the Gods; but Dairon was then a boy strong and merry, and above all things he delighted to play upon a pipe of reeds or other woodland instruments, and he is named now among the three most magic players of the Elves, and the others are Tinfang Warble and Ivárë who plays beside the sea. But Tinúviel's joy was rather in the dance, and no names are set with hers for the beauty and subtlety of her twinkling feet.

Now it was the delight of Dairon and Tinúviel to fare away from the cavernous palace of Tinwelint their father and together spend long times amid the trees. There often would Dairon sit upon a tussock or a tree-root and make music while Tinúviel danced thereto, and when she danced to the playing of Dairon more lissom was she than Gwendeling, more magical than Tinfang Warble neath the moon, nor may any see such lilting save be it only in the rose gardens of Valinor where Nessa dances on the lawns of never-fading green.

Even at night when the moon shone pale still would they play and dance, and they were not afraid as I should be, for the rule of Tinwelint and of Gwendeling held evil from the woods and Melko troubled them not as yet, and Men were hemmed beyond the hills.

Now the place that they loved the most was a shady spot, and elms grew there, and beech too, but these were not very tall, and some chestnut trees there were with white flowers, but the ground was moist and a great misty growth of hemlocks rose beneath the trees. On a time of June they were playing there, and the white umbels of the hemlocks were like a cloud about the boles of the trees, and there Tinúviel danced until the evening faded late, and there were many white moths abroad. Tinúviel being a fairy minded them not as many of the children of Men do, although she loved not beetles, and spiders will none of the Eldar touch because of Ungweliantë – but now the white moths flittered about her head and Dairon trilled an eerie tune, when suddenly that strange thing befell.

Never have I heard how Beren came thither over the hills; yet was he braver than most, as thou shalt hear, and 'twas the love of wandering maybe alone that had sped him through the terrors of the Iron Mountains until he reached the Lands Beyond.

Now Beren was a Gnome, son of Egnor the forester who hunted in the darker places³ in the north of Hisilómë. Dread and suspicion was between the Eldar and those of their kindred that had tasted the slavery of Melko, and in this did the evil deeds of the Gnomes at the Haven of the Swans revenge itself. Now the lies of Melko ran among Beren's folk so that they believed evil things of the secret Elves, yet now did he see Tinúviel dancing in the twilight, and Tinúviel was in a silver-pearly dress, and her bare white feet were twinkling among the hemlock-stems. Then Beren cared not whether she were Vala or Elf or child of Men and crept near to see; and he leant against a young elm that grew upon a mound so that he might look down into the little glade where she was dancing, for the enchantment made him faint. So slender was she and so fair that at length he stood heedlessly in the open the better to gaze upon her, and at that moment the full moon came brightly through the boughs and Dairon caught sight of Beren's face. Straightway did he perceive that he was none of their folk, and all the Elves of the woodland thought of the Gnomes of Dor Lómin as treacherous creatures, cruel and faithless, wherefore Dairon dropped his instrument and crying "Flee, flee, O Tinúviel, an enemy walks this wood" he was gone swiftly through the trees. Then Tinúviel in her amaze followed not straightway, for she understood not his words at once, and knowing she could not run or leap so hardily as her brother she slipped suddenly down among the white hemlocks and hid herself beneath a very tall flower with many spreading leaves; and here she looked in her white raiment like a spatter of moonlight shimmering through the leaves upon the floor.

Then Beren was sad, for he was lonely and was grieved at their fright, and he looked for Tinúviel everywhere about, thinking her not fled. Thus suddenly did he lay his hand upon her slender arm beneath the leaves, and with a cry she started away from him and flitted as fast as she could in the wan light, in and about the tree-trunks and the hemlock-stalks. The tender touch of her arm made Beren yet more eager than before to find her, and he followed swiftly and yet not swiftly enough, for in the end she escaped him, and reached the dwellings of her father in fear; nor did she dance alone in the woods for many a day after.

This was a great sorrow to Beren, who would not leave those places, hoping to see that fair elfin maiden dance yet again, and he wandered in the wood growing wild and lonely for many a day and searching for Tinúviel. By dawn and dusk he sought her, but ever more hopefully when the moon shone bright. At last one night he caught a sparkle afar off, and lo, there she was dancing alone on a little treeless knoll and Dairon was not there. Often and often she came there after and danced and sang to herself, and sometimes Dairon would be nigh, and then Beren watched from the wood's edge afar, and sometimes he was away and Beren crept then closer. Indeed for long Tinúviel knew of his coming and feigned otherwise, and for long her fear had departed by reason of the wistful hunger of his face lit by the moonlight; and she saw that he was kind and in love with her beautiful dancing.

Then Beren took to following Tinúviel secretly through the woods even to the entrance of the cave and the bridge's head, and when she was gone in he would cry across the stream, softly saying "Tinúviel", for he had caught the name from Dairon's lips; and although he knew it not Tinúviel often hearkened from within the shadows of the cavernous doors and laughed softly or smiled. At length one day as she danced alone he stepped out more boldly and said to her: "Tinúviel, teach me to dance." "Who art thou?" said she. "Beren. I am from across the Bitter Hills." "Then if thou wouldst dance, follow me," said the maiden, and she danced before Beren away, and away into the woods, nimbly and yet not so fast that he could not follow, and ever and anon she would look back and laugh at him stumbling after, saying "Dance, Beren, dance! as they dance beyond the Bitter Hills!" In this way they came by winding paths to the abode of Tinwelint, and Tinúviel beckoned Beren beyond the stream, and he followed her wondering down into the cave and the deep halls of her home.

When however Beren found himself before the king he was abashed, and of the stateliness of Queen Gwendeling he was in great awe, and behold when the king said: "Who art thou that stumbleth into my halls unbidden?" he had nought to say. Tinúviel answered therefore for him, saying: "This, my father, is Beren, a wanderer from beyond the hills, and he would learn to dance as the Elves of Artanor can dance," and she laughed, but the king frowned when he heard whence Beren came, and he said: "Put away thy light words, my child, and say has this wild Elf of the shadows sought to do thee any harm?"

"Nay, father," said she, "and I think there is not evil in his heart at all, and be thou not harsh with him, unless thou desirest to see thy daughter Tinúviel weep, for more wonder has he at my dancing than any that I have known." Therefore said Tinwelint now: "O Beren son of the Noldoli, what dost thou desire of the Elves of the wood ere thou returnest whence thou camest?"

So great was the amazed joy of Beren's heart when Tinúviel spake thus for him to her father that his courage rose within him, and his adventurous spirit that had brought him out of Hisilómë and over the Mountains of Iron awoke again, and looking boldly upon Tinwelint he said: "Why, O king, I desire thy daughter Tinúviel, for she is the fairest and most sweet of all maidens I have seen or dreamed of."

Then was there a silence in the hall, save that Dairon laughed, and all who heard were astounded, but Tinúviel cast down her eyes, and the king glancing at the wild and rugged aspect of Beren burst also into laughter, whereat Beren flushed for shame, and Tinúviel's heart was sore for him. "Why! wed my Tinúviel fairest of the maidens of the world, and become a prince of the woodland Elves – 'tis but a little boon for a stranger to ask," quoth Tinwelint. "Haply I may with right ask somewhat in return. Nothing great shall it be, a token only of thy esteem. Bring me a Silmaril from the Crown of Melko, and that day Tinúviel weds thee, an she will."

Then all in that place knew that the king treated the matter as an uncouth jest, having pity on the Gnome, and they smiled, for the fame of the Silmarils of Fëanor was now great throughout the world, and the Noldoli had told tales of them, and many that had escaped from Angamandi had seen them now blazing lustrous in the iron crown of Melko. Never did this crown leave his head, and he treasured those jewels as his eyes, and no one in the world, or fay or elf or man, could hope ever to set finger even on them and live. This indeed did Beren know, and he guessed the meaning of their mocking smiles, and aflame with anger he cried: "Nay, but 'tis too small a gift to the father of so sweet a bride. Strange nonetheless seem to me the customs of the woodland Elves, like to the rude laws of the folk of Men, that thou shouldst name the gift unoffered, yet lo! I Beren, a huntsman of the Noldoli,[4] will fulfil thy small desire," and with that he burst from the hall while all stood astonished; but Tinúviel wept suddenly. "'Twas ill done, O my father," she cried, "to send one to his death with thy sorry jesting – for now methinks he will attempt the deed, being maddened by thy scorn, and Melko will slay him, and none will look ever again with such love upon my dancing."

Then said the king: "'Twill not be the first of Gnomes that Melko has slain and for less reason. It is well for him that he lies not bound here in grievous spells for his trespass in my halls and for his insolent speech"; yet Gwendeling said nought, neither did she chide Tinúviel or question her sudden weeping for this unknown wanderer.

Beren however going from before the face of Tinwelint was carried by his wrath far through the woods, until he drew nigh to the lower hills and treeless lands that warned of the approach of the bleak Iron Mountains. Only then did he feel his weariness and stay his march, and thereafter did his greater travails begin. Nights of deep despondency were his and he saw no hope whatever in his quest, and indeed there was little, and soon, as he followed the Iron Mountains till he drew nigh to the terrible regions of Melko's abode, the greatest fears assailed him. Many poisonous snakes were in those places and wolves roamed about, and more fearsome still were the wandering bands of the goblins and the Orcs – foul broodlings of Melko who fared abroad doing his evil work, snaring and capturing beasts, and Men, and Elves, and dragging them to their lord.

Many times was Beren near to capture by the Orcs, and once he escaped the jaws of a great wolf only after a combat wherein he was armed but with an ashen club, and other perils and adventures did he know each day of his wandering to Angamandi. Hunger and thirst too tortured him often, and often he would have turned back had not that been well nigh as perilous as going on; but the voice of Tinúviel pleading with Tinwelint echoed in his heart, and at night time it seemed to him that his heart heard her sometimes weeping softly for him far away in the woodlands of her home: – and this was indeed true.

One day he was driven by great hunger to search amid a deserted camping of some Orcs for scraps of food, but some of these returned unawares and took him prisoner, and they tormented him but did not slay him, for their captain seeing his strength, worn though he was with hardships, thought that Melko might perchance be pleasured if he was brought before him and might set him to some heavy thrall-work in his mines or in his smithies. So came it that Beren was dragged before Melko, and he bore a stout heart within him nonetheless, for it was a belief among his father's kindred that the power of Melko would not abide for ever, but the Valar would hearken at last to the tears of the Noldoli, and would arise and bind Melko and open Valinor once more to the weary Elves, and great joy should come back upon Earth.

Melko however looking upon him was wroth, asking how a Gnome, a thrall by birth of his, had dared to fare away into the woods unbidden, but Beren answered that he was no runagate but came of a kindred of Gnomes that dwelt in Aryador and mingled much there among the folk of Men. Then was Melko yet more angry, for he sought ever to destroy the friendship and intercourse of Elves and Men, and said that evidently here was a plotter of deep treacheries against Melko's lordship, and one worthy of the tortures of the Balrogs; but Beren seeing his peril answered: "Think not, O most mighty Ainu Melko, Lord of the World, that this can be true, for an it were then should I not be here unaided and alone. No friendship has Beren son of Egnor for the kindred of Men; nay indeed, wearying utterly of the lands infested by that folk he has wandered out of Aryador. Many a great tale has my father made to me aforetime of thy splendour and glory, wherefore, albeit I am no renegade thrall, I do desire nothing so much as to serve thee in what small manner I may," and Beren said therewith that he was a great trapper of small animals and a snarer of birds, and had become lost in the hills in these pursuits until after much wandering he had come into strange lands, and even had not the Orcs seized him he would indeed have had no other rede of safety but to approach the majesty of Ainu Melko and beg him to grant him some humble office – as a winner of meats for his table perchance.

Now the Valar must have inspired that speech, or perchance it was a spell of cunning words cast on him in compassion by Gwendeling, for indeed it saved his life, and Melko marking his hardy frame believed him, and was willing to accept him as a thrall of his kitchens. Flattery savoured ever sweet in the nostrils of that Ainu, and for all his unfathomed wisdom many a lie of those whom he despised deceived him, were they clothed sweetly in words of praise; therefore now he gave orders for Beren to be made a thrall of Tevildo Prince of Cats*. Now Tevildo was a

---

* Footnote in the manuscript: *Tifil (Bridhon) Miaugion or Tevildo (Vardo) Meoita.*

mighty cat − the mightiest of all − and possessed of an evil sprite, as some say, and he was in Melko's constant following; and that cat had all cats subject to him, and he and his subjects were the chasers and getters of meat for Melko's table and for his frequent feasts. Wherefore is it that there is hatred still between the Elves and all cats even now when Melko rules no more, and his beasts are become of little account.

When therefore Beren was led away to the halls of Tevildo, and these were not utterly distant from the place of Melko's throne, he was much afraid, for he had not looked for such a turn in things, and those halls were ill-lighted and were full of growling and of monstrous purrings in the dark. All about shone cats' eyes glowing like green lamps or red or yellow where Tevildo's thanes sat waving and lashing their beautiful tails, but Tevildo himself sat at their head and he was a mighty cat and coal-black and evil to look upon. His eyes were long and very narrow and slanted, and gleamed both red and green, but his great grey whiskers were as stout and as sharp as needles. His purr was like the roll of drums and his growl like thunder, but when he yelled in wrath it turned the blood cold, and indeed small beasts and birds were frozen as to stone, or dropped lifeless often at the very sound. Now Tevildo seeing Beren narrowed his eyes until they seemed to shut, and said: "I smell dog", and he took dislike to Beren from that moment. Now Beren had been a lover of hounds in his own wild home.

"Why," said Tevildo, "do ye dare to bring such a creature before me, unless perchance it is to make meat of him?" But those who led Beren said: "Nay, 'twas the word of Melko that this unhappy Elf wear out his life as a catcher of beasts and birds in Tevildo's employ." Then indeed did Tevildo screech in scorn and said: "Then in sooth was my lord asleep or his thoughts were settled elsewhere, for what use think ye is a child of the Eldar to aid the Prince of Cats and his thanes in the catching of birds or of beasts − as well had ye brought some clumsy-footed Man, for none are there either of Elves or Men that can vie with us in our pursuit." Nonetheless he set Beren to a test, and he bade him go catch three mice, "for my hall is infested with them," said he. This indeed was not true, as might be imagined, yet a certain few there were − a very wild, evil, and magic kind that dared to dwell there in dark holes, but they were larger than rats and very fierce, and Tevildo harboured them for his own private sport and suffered not their numbers to dwindle.

Three days did Beren hunt them, but having nothing wherewith to devise a trap (and indeed he did not lie to Melko saying that he had cunning in such contrivances) he hunted in vain getting nothing better than a bitten finger for all his labour. Then was Tevildo scornful and in great anger, but Beren got no harm of him or his thanes at that time because of Melko's bidding other than a few scratches. Evil however were his days thereafter in the dwellings of Tevildo. They made him a scullion, and his days passed miserably in the washing of floors and vessels, in the scrubbing of tables and the hewing of wood and the drawing of water. Often too would he be set to the turning of spits whereon birds and fat mice were daintily roasted for the cats, yet seldom did he get food or sleep himself, and he became haggard and unkempt, and wished often that never straying out of Hisilómë he had not even caught sight of the vision of Tinúviel.

Now that fair maiden wept for a very great while after Beren's departure and danced no more about the woods, and Dairon grew angry and could not understand her, but she had grown to love the face of Beren peeping through the branches and the crackle of his feet as they followed her through the wood; and his voice that called wistfully "Tinúviel, Tinúviel" across the stream before her father's doors she longed to hear again, and she would not now dance when Beren was fled to the evil halls of Melko and maybe had already perished. So bitter did this thought become at last that that most tender maiden went to her mother, for to her father she dared not go nor even suffer him to see her weep.

"O Gwendeling, my mother," said she, "tell me of thy magic, if thou canst, how doth Beren fare. Is all yet well with him?" "Nay," said Gwendeling. "He lives indeed, but in an evil captivity, and hope is dead in his heart, for behold, he is a slave in the power of Tevildo Prince of Cats."

"Then," said Tinúviel, "I must go and succour him, for none else do I know that will."

Now Gwendeling laughed not, for in many matters she was wise, and forewise, yet it was a thing unthought in a mad dream that any Elf, still less a maiden, the daughter of the king, should fare untended to the halls of Melko, even in those earlier days before the Battle of Tears when Melko's power had not grown great and he veiled his designs and spread his net of lies. Wherefore did Gwendeling softly bid her not to speak such folly; but Tinúviel said: "Then must thou plead with my father for aid, that he send warriors to Angamandi and demand the freedom of Beren from Ainu Melko."

This indeed did Gwendeling do, of love for her daughter, and so wroth was Tinwelint that Tinúviel wished that never had her desire been made known; and Tinwelint bade her nor speak nor think of Beren more, and swore he would slay him an he trod those halls again. Now then Tinúviel pondered much what she might do, and going to Dairon she begged him to aid her, or indeed to fare away with her to Angamandi an he would; but Dairon thought with little love of Beren, and he said: "Wherefore should I go into the direst peril that there is in the world for the sake of a wandering Gnome of the woods? Indeed I have no love for him, for he has destroyed our play together, our music and our dancing." But Dairon moreover told the king of what Tinúviel had desired of him — and this he did not of ill intent but fearing lest Tinúviel fare away to her death in the madness of her heart.

Now[5] when Tinwelint heard this he called Tinúviel and said: "Wherefore, O maiden of mine, does thou not put this folly away from thee, and seek to do my bidding?" But Tinúviel would not answer, and the king bade her promise him that neither would she think more on Beren, nor would she seek in her folly to follow after him to the evil lands whether alone or tempting any of his folk with her. But Tinúviel said that the first she would not promise and the second only in part, for she would not tempt any of the folk of the woodlands to go with her.

Then was her father mightily angry, and beneath his anger not a little amazed and afraid, for he loved Tinúviel; but this was the plan he devised, for he might not shut his daughter for ever in the caverns where only a dim and flickering light ever came. Now above the portals of his cavernous hall was a steep slope falling to the river, and there grew mighty beeches; and one there was that was named Hirilorn, the Queen of Trees, for she was very mighty, and so deeply cloven was her bole that it seemed as if three shafts sprang from the ground together and they were of like size, round and straight, and their grey rind was smooth as silk, unbroken by branch or twig for a very great height above men's heads.

Now Tinwelint let build high up in that strange tree, as high as men could fashion their longest ladders to reach, a little house of wood, and it was above the first branches and was sweetly veiled in leaves. Now that house had three corners and three windows in each wall, and at each corner was one of the shafts of Hirilorn. There then did Tinwelint bid Tinúviel dwell until she would

consent to be wise, and when she fared up the ladders of tall pine
these were taken from beneath and no way had she to get down
again. All that she required was brought to her, and folk would
scale the ladders and give her food or whatever else she wished for,
and then descending again take away the ladders, and the king
promised death to any who left one leaning against the tree or who
should try by stealth to place one there at night. A guard therefore
was set nigh the tree's foot, and yet came Dairon often thither in
sorrow at what he had brought to pass, for he was lonely without
Tinúviel; but Tinúviel had at first much pleasure in her house
among the leaves, and would gaze out of her little window while
Dairon made his sweetest melodies beneath.

But one night a dream of the Valar came to Tinúviel and she
dreamt of Beren, and her heart said: "Let me be gone to seek him
whom all others have forgot"; and waking, the moon was shining
through the trees, and she pondered very deeply how she might
escape. Now Tinúviel daughter of Gwendeling was not ignorant
of magics or of spells, as may well be believed, and after much
thought she devised a plan. The next day she asked those who
came to her to bring, if they would, some of the clearest water of
the stream below, "but this," she said, "must be drawn at midnight
in a silver bowl, and brought to my hand with no word spoken,"
and after that she desired wine to be brought, "but this," she said,
"must be borne hither in a flagon of gold at noon, and he who
brings it must sing as he comes," and they did as they were bid,
but Tinwelint was not told.

Then said Tinúviel, "Go now to my mother and say to her that
her daughter desires a spinning wheel to pass her weary hours,"
but Dairon secretly she begged fashion her a tiny loom, and he
did this even in the little house of Tinúviel in the tree. "But
wherewith will you spin and wherewith weave?" said he; and
Tinúviel answered: "With spells and magics," but Dairon knew
not her design, nor said more to the king or to Gwendeling.

Now Tinúviel took the wine and water when she was alone, and
singing a very magical song the while, she mingled them together,
and as they lay in the bowl of gold she sang a song of growth, and as
they lay in the bowl of silver she sang another song, and the names
of all the tallest and longest things upon Earth were set in that
song; the beards of the Indravangs, the tail of Karkaras, the body
of Glorund, the bole of Hirilorn, and the sword of Nan she
named, nor did she forget the chain Angainu that Aulë and Tulkas
made or the neck of Gilim the giant, and last and longest of all she

spake of the hair of Uinen the lady of the sea that is spread through all the waters. Then did she lave her head with the mingled water and wine, and as she did so she sang a third song, a song of uttermost sleep, and the hair of Tinúviel which was dark and finer than the most delicate threads of twilight began suddenly to grow very fast indeed, and after twelve hours had passed it nigh filled the little room, and then Tinúviel was very pleased and she lay down to rest; and when she awoke the room was full as with a black mist and she was deep hidden under it, and lo! her hair was trailing out of the windows and blowing about the tree boles in the morning. Then with difficulty she found her little shears and cut the threads of that growth nigh to her head, and after that her hair grew only as it was wont before.

Then was the labour of Tinúviel begun, and though she laboured with the deftness of an Elf long was she spinning and longer weaving still, and did any come and hail her from below she bid them be gone, saying: "I am abed, and desire only to sleep," and Dairon was much amazed, and called often up to her, but she did not answer.

Now of that cloudy hair Tinúviel wove a robe of misty black soaked with drowsiness more magical far than even that one that her mother had worn and danced in long long ago before the Sun arose, and therewith she covered her garments of shimmering white, and magic slumbers filled the airs about her; but of what remained she twisted a mighty strand, and this she fastened to the bole of the tree within her house, and then was her labour ended, and she looked out of her window westward to the river. Already the sunlight was fading in the trees, and as dusk filled the woods she began a song very soft and low, and as she sung she cast out her long hair from the window so that its slumbrous mist touched the heads and faces of the guards below, and they listening to her voice fell suddenly into a fathomless sleep. Then did Tinúviel clad in her garments of darkness slip down that rope of hair light as a squirrel, and away she danced to the bridge, and before the bridgewards could cry out she was among them dancing; and as the hem of her black robe touched them they fell asleep, and Tinúviel fled very far away as fast as her dancing feet would flit.

Now when the escape of Tinúviel reached the ears of Tinwelint great was his mingled grief and wrath, and all his court was in uproar, and all the woods ringing with the search, but Tinúviel was already far away drawing nigh to the gloomy foothills where the Mountains of Night begin; and 'tis said that Dairon following after her became utterly lost, and came never back to Elfinesse, but turned towards Palisor, and there plays⁶ subtle magic musics still, wistful and lonely in the woods and forests of the south.

Yet ere long as Tinúviel went forward a sudden dread overtook her at the thought of what she had dared to do and what lay before; then did she turn back for a while, and she wept, wishing Dairon was with her, and it is said that he indeed was not far off, but was wandering lost in the great pines, the Forest of Night, where afterward Túrin slew Beleg by mishap.⁷ Nigh was Tinúviel now to those places, but she entered not that dark region, and regaining heart pressed on, and by reason of the greater magic of her being and because of the spell of wonder and of sleep that fared about her no such dangers assailed her as did Beren before; yet was it a long and evil and weary journey for a maiden to tread.

Now is it to be told to thee, Eriol, that in those days Tevildo had but one trouble in the world, and that was the kindred of the Dogs. Many indeed of these were neither friends nor foes of the Cats, for they had become subject to Melko and were as savage and cruel as any of his animals; indeed from the most cruel and most savage he bred the race of wolves, and they were very dear indeed to him. Was it not the great grey wolf Karkaras Knife-fang, father of wolves, who guarded the gates of Angamandi in those days and long had done so? Many were there however who would neither bow to Melko nor live wholly in fear of him, but dwelt either in the dwellings of Men and guarded them from much evil that had otherwise befallen them or roamed the woods of Hisilómë or passing the mountainous places fared even at times into the region of Artanor and the lands beyond and to the south.

Did ever any of these view Tevildo or any of his thanes or subjects, then there was a great baying and a mighty chase, and albeit seldom was any cat slain by reason of their skill in climbing and in hiding and because of the protecting might of Melko, yet was great enmity between them, and some of those hounds were held in dread among the cats. None however did Tevildo fear, for he was as strong as any among them, and more agile and more swift save only than Huan Captain of Dogs. So swift was Huan that on a time he had tasted the fur of Tevildo, and though Tevildo had paid him for that with a gash from his great claws, yet was the pride of the Prince of Cats unappeased and he lusted to do a great harm to Huan of the Dogs.

Great therefore was the good fortune that befell Tinúviel in meeting with Huan in the woods, although at first she was mortally afraid and fled. But Huan overtook her in two leaps, and speaking soft and deep the tongue of the Lost Elves he bid her be not afraid, and "Wherefore," said he, "do I see an Elfin maiden, and one most fair, wandering alone so nigh to the abodes of the Ainu of Evil? Knowst thou not these are very evil places to be in, little one, even with a companion, and they are death to the lonely?"

"That know I," said she, "and I am not here for the love of wayfaring, but I seek only Beren."

"What knowest thou then," said Huan, "of Beren – or indeed meanest thou Beren son of the huntsman of the Elves, Egnor bo-Rimion, a friend of mine since very ancient days?"

"Nay, I know not even whether my Beren be thy friend, for I seek only Beren from beyond the Bitter Hills, whom I knew in the woods near to my father's home. Now is he gone, and my mother Gwendeling says of her wisdom that he is a thrall in the cruel house of Tevildo Prince of Cats; and whether this be true or yet worse be now befallen him I do not know, and I go to discover him – though plan I have none."

"Then will I make thee one," said Huan, "but do thou trust in me, for I am Huan of the Dogs, chief foe of Tevildo. Rest thee now with me a while within the shadows of the wood, and I will think deeply."

Then Tinúviel did as he said, and indeed she slept long while Huan watched, for she was very weary. But after a while awakening she said: "Lo, I have tarried over long. Come, what is thy thought, O Huan?"

And Huan said: "A dark and difficult matter is this, and no other rede can I devise but this. Creep now if thou hast the heart to the abiding place of that Prince while the sun is high, and Tevildo and the most of his household drowze upon the terraces before his gates. There discover in what manner thou mayst whether Beren be indeed within, as thy mother said to thee. Now I will lie not far hence in the woods, and thou wilt do me a pleasure and aid thy own desires an going before Tevildo, be Beren there or be he not, thou tellest him how thou hast stumbled upon Huan of the Dogs lying sick in the woods at this place. Do not indeed direct him hither, for thou must guide him, if it may be, thyself. Then wilt thou see what I contrive for thee and for Tevildo. Methinks that bearing such tidings Tevildo will not entreat thee ill within his halls nor seek to hold thee there."

In this way did Huan design both to do Tevildo a hurt, or perchance if it might so be to slay him, and to aid Beren whom he guessed in truth to be that Beren son of Egnor whom the hounds of Hisilómë loved. Indeed hearing the name of Gwendeling and knowing thereby that this maiden was a princess of the woodland fairies he was eager to aid her, and his heart warmed to her sweetness.

Now Tinúviel taking heart stole near to the halls of Tevildo, and Huan wondered much at her courage, following unknown to her, as far as he might for the success of his design. At length however she passed beyond his sight, and leaving the shelter of the trees came to a region of long grass dotted with bushes that sloped ever upward toward a shoulder of the hills. Now upon that rocky spur the sun shone, but over all the hills and mountains at its back a black cloud brooded, for there was Angamandi; and Tinúviel fared on not daring to look up at that gloom, for fear oppressed her, and as she went the ground rose and the grass grew more scant and rock-strewn until it came even to a cliff, sheer of one side, and there upon a stony shelf was the castle of Tevildo. No pathway led thereto, and the place where it stood fell towards the woods in terrace after terrace so that none might reach its gates save by many great leaps, and those became ever steeper as the castle drew more nigh. Few were the windows of the house and upon the ground there were none – indeed the very gate was in the air where in the dwellings of Men are wont to be the windows of the upper floor; but the roof had many wide and flat spaces open to the sun.

Now does Tinúviel wander disconsolate upon the lowest terrace and look in dread at the dark house upon the hill, when behold, she came at a bend in the rock upon a lone cat lying in the sun and seemingly asleep. As she approached he opened a yellow eye and blinked at her, and thereupon rising and stretching he stepped up to her and said: "Whither away, little maid – dost not know that you trespass on the sunning ground of his highness Tevildo and his thanes?"

Now Tinúviel was very much afraid, but she made as bold an answer as she was able, saying: "That know I, my lord" – and this pleased the old cat greatly, for he was in truth only Tevildo's doorkeeper – "but I would indeed of your goodness be brought to Tevildo's presence now – nay, even if he sleeps," said she, for the doorkeeper lashed his tail in astonished refusal. "I have words of immediate import for his private ear. Lead me to him, my lord," she pleaded, and thereat the cat purred so loudly that she dared to stroke his ugly head, and this was much larger than her own, being greater than that of any dog that is now on Earth. Thus entreated,

Umuiyan, for such was his name, said: "Come then with me," and
seizing Tinúviel suddenly by her garments at the shoulder to her
great terror he tossed her upon his back and leaped upon the
second terrace. There he stopped, and as Tinúviel scrambled
from his back he said: "Well is it for thee that this afternoon my
lord Tevildo lieth upon this lowly terrace far from his house, for a
great weariness and a desire for sleep has come upon me, so that I
fear me I should not be willing to carry thee much farther"; now
Tinúviel was robed in her robe of sable mist.

So saying Umuiyan* yawned mightily and stretched himself
before he led her along that terrace to an open space, where upon a
wide couch of baking stones lay the horrible form of Tevildo
himself, and both his evil eyes were shut. Going up to him the
doorcat Umuiyan spoke in his ear softly, saying: "A maiden awaits
thy pleasure, my lord, who hath news of importance to deliver to
thee, nor would she take my refusal." Then did Tevildo angrily
lash his tail, half opening an eye – "What is it – be swift," said he,
"for this is no hour to come desiring audience of Tevildo Prince of
Cats."

"Nay, lord," said Tinúviel trembling, "be not angry; nor do I
think that thou wilt when thou hearest, yet is the matter such that
it were better not even whispered here where the breezes blow,"
and Tinúviel cast a glance as it were of apprehension toward the
woods.

"Nay, get thee gone," said Tevildo, "thou smellest of dog, and
what news of good came ever to a cat from a fairy that had had
dealings with the dogs?"

"Why, sir, that I smell of dogs is no matter of wonder, for I have
just escaped from one – and it is indeed of a certain very mighty
dog whose name thou knowest that I would speak." Then up sat
Tevildo and opened his eyes, and he looked all about him, and
stretched three times, and at last bade the doorcat lead Tinúviel
within; and Umuiyan caught her upon his back as before. Now
was Tinúviel in the sorest dread, for having gained what she
desired, a chance of entering Tevildo's stronghold and maybe of
discovering whether Beren were there, she had no plan more, and
knew not what would become of her – indeed had she been able
she would have fled; yet now do those cats begin to ascend the
terraces towards the castle, and one leap does Umuiyan make
bearing Tinúviel upwards and then another, and at the third he

* Written above *Umuiyan* here is the name *Gumniow*, enclosed within brackets.

stumbled so that Tinúviel cried out in fear, and Tevildo said: "What ails thee, Umuiyan, thou clumsy-foot? It is time that thou left my employ if age creeps on thee so swiftly." But Umuiyan said: "Nay, lord, I know not what it is, but a mist is before mine eyes and my head is heavy," and he staggered as one drunk, so that Tinúviel slid from his back, and thereupon he laid him down as if in a dead sleep; but Tevildo was wroth and seized Tinúviel and none too gently, and himself bore her to the gates. Then with a mighty leap he sprang within, and bidding that maiden alight he set up a yell that echoed fearsomely in the dark ways and passages. Forthwith they hastened to him from within, and some he bid descend to Umuiyan and bind him and cast him from the rocks "on the northern side where they fall most sheer, for he is of no use more to me," he said, "for age has robbed him of his sureness of foot"; and Tinúviel quaked to hear the ruthlessness of this beast. But even as he spake he himself yawned and stumbled as with a sudden drowziness, and he bid others to lead Tinúviel away to a certain chamber within, and that was the one where Tevildo was accustomed to sit at meat with his greatest thanes. It was full of bones and smelt evilly; no windows were there and but one door; but a hatchway gave from it upon the great kitchens, and a red light crept thence and dimly lit the place.

Now so adread was Tinúviel when those catfolk left her there that she stood a moment unable to stir, but soon becoming used to the darkness she looked about and espying the hatchway that had a wide sill she sprang thereto, for it was not over high and she was a nimble Elf. Now gazing therethrough, for it was ajar, she saw the wide vaulted kitchens and the great fires that burnt there, and those that toiled always within, and the most were cats – but behold, there by a great fire stooped Beren, and he was grimed with labour, and Tinúviel sat and wept, but as yet dared nothing. Indeed even as she sat the harsh voice of Tevildo sounded suddenly within that chamber: "Nay, where then in Melko's name has that mad Elf fled," and Tinúviel hearing shrank against the wall, but Tevildo caught sight of her where she was perched and cried: "Then the little bird sings not any more; come down or I must fetch thee, for behold, I will not encourage the Elves to seek audience of me in mockery."

Then partly in fear, and part in hope that her clear voice might carry even to Beren, Tinúviel began suddenly to speak very loud and to tell her tale so that the chambers rang; but "Hush, dear maiden," said Tevildo, "if the matter were secret without it is not one for bawling within." Then said Tinúviel: "Speak not thus to me, O cat, mighty Lord of Cats though thou be, for am I not Tinúviel Princess of Fairies that have stepped out of my way to do thee a pleasure?" Now at those words, and she had shouted them even louder than before, a great crash was heard in the kitchens as of a number of vessels of metal and earthenware let suddenly fall, but Tevildo snarled: "There trippeth that fool Beren the Elf. Melko rid me of such folk" – yet Tinúviel, guessing that Beren had heard and been smitten with astonishment, put aside her fears and repented her daring no longer. Tevildo nonetheless was very wroth at her haughty words, and had he not been minded first to discover what good he might get from her tale, it had fared ill with Tinúviel straightway. Indeed from that moment was she in great peril, for Melko and all his vassals held Tinwelint and his folk as outlaws, and great was their joy to ensnare them and cruelly entreat them, so that much favour would Tevildo have gained had he taken Tinúviel before his lord. Indeed, so soon as she named herself, this did he purpose to do when his own business had been done, but of a truth his wits were drowzed that day, and he forgot to marvel more why Tinúviel sat perched upon the sill of the hatchway; nor did he think more of Beren, for his mind was bent only to the tale Tinúviel bore to him. Wherefore said he, dissembling his evil mood, "Nay, Lady, be not angry, but come, delay whetteth my desire – what is it that thou hast for my ears, for they twitch already."

But Tinúviel said: "There is a great beast, rude and violent, and his name is Huan" – and at that name Tevildo's back curved, and his hair bristled and crackled, and the light of his eyes was red – "and," she went on, "it seems to me a shame that such a brute be suffered to infest the woods so nigh even to the abode of the powerful Prince of Cats, my lord Tevildo"; but Tevildo said: "Nor is he suffered, and cometh never there save it be by stealth."

"Howso that may be," said Tinúviel, "there he is now, yet methinks that at last may his [life] be brought utterly to an end, for lo, as I was going through the woods I saw where a great animal lay upon the ground moaning as in sickness – and behold, it was Huan, and some evil spell or malady has him in its grip, and still he lies helpless in a dale not a mile westward in the woods from this hall. Now with this perhaps I would not have troubled your ears, had not the brute when I approached to succour him snarled upon me and essayed to bite me, and meseems that such a creature deserves whatever come to him."

Now all this that Tinúviel spake was a great lie in whose devising Huan had guided her, and maidens of the Eldar are not wont to fashion lies; yet have I never heard that any of the Eldar blamed her therein nor Beren afterward, and neither do I, for Tevildo was an evil cat and Melko the wickedest of all beings, and Tinúviel was in dire peril at their hands. Tevildo however, himself a great and skilled liar, was so deeply versed in the lies and subtleties of all the beasts and creatures that he seldom knew whether to believe what was said to him or not, and was wont to disbelieve all things save those he wished to believe true, and so was he often deceived by the more honest. Now the story of Huan and his helplessness so pleased him that he was fain to believe it true, and determined at least to test it; yet at first he feigned indifference, saying this was a small matter for such secrecy and might have been spoken outside without further ado. But Tinúviel said she had not thought that Tevildo Prince of Cats needed to learn that the ears of Huan heard the slightest sounds a league away, and the voice of a cat further than any sound else.

Now therefore Tevildo sought to discover from Tinúviel under pretence of mistrusting her tale where exactly Huan might be found, but she made only vague answers, seeing in this her only hope of escaping from the castle, and at length Tevildo, overcome by curiosity and threatening evil things if she should prove false, summoned two of his thanes to him, and one was Oikeroi, a fierce and warlike cat. Then did the three set out with Tinúviel from that place, but Tinúviel took off her magical garment of black and folded it, so that for all its size and density it appeared no more than the smallest kerchief (for so was she able), and thus was she borne down the terraces upon the back of Oikeroi without mishap, and no drowziness assailed her bearer. Now crept they through the woods in the direction she had named, and soon does Tevildo smell dog and bristles and lashes his great tail, but after he climbs a lofty tree and looks down from thence into that dale that Tinúviel had shown to them. There he does indeed see the great form of Huan lying prostrate groaning and moaning, and he comes down in much glee and haste, and indeed in his eagerness he forgets Tinúviel, who now in great fear for Huan lies hidden in a bank of fern. The design of Tevildo and his two companions was to enter that dale silently from different quarters and so come all suddenly upon Huan unawares and slay him, or if he were too stricken to make fight to make sport of him and torment him. This did they now, but even as they leapt out upon him Huan sprang up into the air with a mighty baying, and his jaws closed in the back close to the neck of that cat Oikeroi, and Oikeroi died; but the other thane fled howling up a great tree, and so was Tevildo left alone face to face with Huan, and such an encounter was not much to his mind, yet was Huan upon him too swiftly for flight, and they fought fiercely in that glade, and the noise that Tevildo made was very hideous; but at length Huan had him by the throat, and that cat might well have perished had not his claws as he struck out blindly pierced Huan's eye. Then did Huan give tongue, and Tevildo screeching fearsomely got himself loose with a great wrench and leapt up a tall and smooth tree that stood by, even as his companion had done. Despite his grievous hurt Huan now leaps beneath that tree baying mightily, and Telvido curses him and casts evil words upon him from above.

Then said Huan: "Lo, Tevildo, these are the words of Huan whom thou thoughtest to catch and slay helpless as the miserable mice it is thy wont to hunt – stay for ever up thy lonely tree and bleed to death of thy wounds, or come down and feel again my teeth. But if neither are to thy liking, then tell me where is Tinúviel Princess of Fairies and Beren son of Egnor, for these are my friends. Now these shall be set as ransom against thee – though it be valuing thee far over thy worth."

"As for that cursed Elf, she lies whimpering in the ferns yonder, an my ears mistake not," said Tevildo, "and Beren methinks is being soundly scratched by Miaulë my cook in the kitchens of my castle for his clumsiness there an hour ago."

"Then let them be given to me in safety," said Huan, "and thou mayest return thyself to thy halls and lick thyself unharmed."

"Of a surety my thane who is here with me shall fetch them for thee," said Tevildo, but growled Huan: "Ay, and fetch also all thy tribe and the hosts of the Orcs and the plagues of Melko. Nay, I am no fool; rather shalt thou give Tinúviel a token and she shall fetch Beren, or thou shalt stay here if thou likest not the other way." Then was Tevildo forced to cast down his golden collar – a token no cat dare dishonour, but Huan said: "Nay, more yet is needed, for this will arouse all thy folk to seek thee," and this Tevildo knew and had hoped. So was it that in the end weariness and hunger and fear prevailed upon that proud cat, a prince of the service of Melko, to reveal the secret of the cats and the spell that Melko had entrusted to him; and those were words of magic whereby the stones of his evil house were held together, and whereby he held all beasts of the catfolk under his sway, filling them with an evil power beyond their nature; for long has it been said that Tevildo was an evil fay in beastlike shape. When therefore he had told it Huan laughed till the woods rang, for he knew that the days of the power of the cats were over.

Now sped Tinúviel with the golden collar of Tevildo back to the lowest terrace before the gates, and standing she spake the spell in her clear voice. Then behold, the air was filled with the voices of cats and the house of Tevildo shook; and there came therefrom a host of indwellers and they were shrunk to puny size and were afeared of Tinúviel, who waving the collar of Tevildo spake before them certain of the words that Tevildo had said in her hearing to Huan, and they cowered before her. But she said: "Lo, let all those of the folk of the Elves or of the children of Men that are bound within these halls be brought forth," and behold, Beren was brought forth, but of other thralls there were none, save only Gimli, an aged Gnome, bent in thraldom and grown blind, but whose hearing was the keenest that has been in the world, as all songs say. Gimli came leaning upon a stick and Beren aided him, but Beren was clad in rags and haggard, and he had in his hand a great knife he had caught up in the kitchen, fearing some new ill when the house shook and all the voices of the cats were heard; but when he beheld Tinúviel standing amid the host of cats that shrank from her and saw the great collar of Tevildo, then was he[8] amazed utterly, and knew not what to think. But Tinúviel was very glad, and spoke saying: "O Beren from beyond the Bitter Hills, wilt thou now dance with me – but let it not be here." And she led Beren far away, and all those cats set up a howling and wailing, so that Huan and Tevildo heard it in the woods, but none followed or molested them, for they were afraid, and the magic of Melko was fallen from them.

This indeed they rued afterward when Tevildo returned home followed by his trembling comrade, for Tevildo's wrath was terrible, and he lashed his tail and dealt blows at all who stood nigh. Now Huan of the dogs, though it might seem a folly, when Beren and Tinúviel came to that glade had suffered that evil Prince to return without further war, but the great collar of gold he had set about his own neck, and at this was Tevildo more angry than all else, for a great magic of strength and power lay therein. Little to Huan's liking was it that Tevildo lived still, but now no longer did he fear the cats, and that tribe has fled before the dogs ever since, and the dogs hold them still in scorn since the humbling of Tevildo in the woods nigh Angamandi; and Huan has not done any greater deed. Indeed afterward Melko heard all and he cursed Tevildo and his folk and banished them, nor have they since that day had lord or master or any friend, and their voices wail and screech for their hearts are very lonely and bitter and full of loss, yet there is only darkness therein and no kindliness.

At the time however whereof the tale tells it was Tevildo's chief desire to recapture Beren and Tinúviel and to slay Huan, that he might regain the spell and magic he had lost, for he was in great fear of Melko, and he dared not seek his master's aid and reveal his defeat and the betrayal of his spell. Unwitting of this Huan feared those places, and was in great dread lest those doings come swiftly to Melko's ear, as did most things that came to pass in the world; wherefore now Tinúviel and Beren wandered far away with Huan, and they became great in friendship with him, and in that life Beren grew strong again and his thraldom fell from him, and Tinúviel loved him.

Yet wild and rugged and very lonely were those days, for never a face of Elf or of Man did they see, and Tinúviel grew at last to long sorely for Gwendeling her mother and the songs of sweet magic she was used to sing to her children as twilight fell in the woodlands by their ancient halls. Often she half fancied she heard the flute of Dairon her brother, in pleasant glades' wherein they sojourned, and her heart grew heavy. At length she said to Beren and to Huan: "I must return home," and now is it Beren's heart that is overcast with sorrow, for he loved that life in the woods with the dogs (for by now many others had become joined to Huan), yet not if Tinúviel were not there.

Nonetheless said he: "Never may I go back with thee to the land of Artanor – nor come there ever after to seek thee, sweet Tinúviel, save only bearing a Silmaril; nor may that ever now be achieved, for am I not a fugitive from the very halls of Melko, and in danger of the most evil pains do any of his servants spy me." Now this he said in the grief of his heart at parting with Tinúviel, and she was torn in mind, abiding not the thought of leaving Beren nor yet of living ever thus in exile. So sat she a great while in sad thought and she spoke not, but Beren sat nigh and at length said: "Tinúviel, one thing only can we do – go get a Silmaril"; and she sought thereupon Huan, asking his aid and advice, but he was very grave and saw nothing but folly in the matter. Yet in the end Tinúviel begged of him the fell of Oikeroi that he slew in the affray of the glade; now Oikeroi was a very mighty cat and Huan carried that fell with him as a trophy.

Now doth Tinúviel put forth her skill and fairy-magic, and she
sews Beren into this fell and makes him to the likeness of a great
cat, and she teaches him how to sit and sprawl, to step and bound
and trot in the semblance of a cat, till Huan's very whiskers
bristled at the sight, and thereat Beren and Tinúviel laughed.
Never however could Beren learn to screech or wail or to purr like
any cat that ever walked, nor could Tinúviel awaken a glow in the
dead eyes of the catskin – "but we must put up with that," said she,
"and thou hast the air of a very noble cat if thou but hold thy
tongue."

Then did they bid farewell to Huan and set out for the halls of
Melko by easy journeys, for Beren was in great discomfort and
heat within the fur of Oikeroi, and Tinúviel's heart became lighter
awhile than it had been for long, and she stroked Beren or pulled
his tail, and Beren was angry because he could not lash it in answer
as fiercely as he wished. At length however they drew near to
Angamandi, as indeed the rumblings and deep noises, and the
sound of mighty hammerings of ten thousand smiths labouring
unceasingly, declared to them. Nigh were the sad chambers where
the thrall-Noldoli laboured bitterly under the Orcs and goblins
of the hills, and here the gloom and darkness was great so that
their hearts fell, but Tinúviel arrayed her once more in her dark
garment of deep sleep. Now the gates of Angamandi were of iron
wrought hideously and set with knives and spikes, and before
them lay the greatest wolf the world has ever seen, even Karkaras
Knife-fang who had never slept; and Karkaras growled when he
saw Tinúviel approach, but of the cat he took not much heed, for
he thought little of cats and they were ever passing in and out.

"Growl not, O Karkaras," said she, "for I go to seek my lord
Melko, and this thane of Tevildo goeth with me as escort." Now
the dark robe veiled all her shimmering beauty, and Karkaras was
not much troubled in mind, yet nonetheless he approached as was
his wont to snuff the air of her, and the sweet fragrance of the
Eldar that garment might not hide. Therefore straightway did
Tinúviel begin a magic dance, and the black strands of her dark
veil she cast in his eyes so that his legs shook with a drowziness and
he rolled over and was asleep. But not until he was fast in dreams
of great chases in the woods of Hisilómë when he was yet a whelp
did Tinúviel cease, and then did those twain enter that black
portal, and winding down many shadowy ways they stumbled at
length into the very presence of Melko.

In that gloom Beren passed well enough as a very thane of

Tevildo, and indeed Oikeroi had aforetime been much about the halls of Melko, so that none heeded him and he slunk under the very chair of the Ainu unseen, but the adders and evil things there lying set him in great fear so that he durst not move.

Now all this fell out most fortunately, for had Tevildo been with Melko their deceit would have been discovered — and indeed of that danger they had thought, not knowing that Tevildo sat now in his halls and knew not what to do should his discomfiture become noised in Angamandi; but behold, Melko espieth Tinúviel and saith: "Who art thou that flittest about my halls like a bat? How camest thou in, for of a surety thou dost not belong here?"

"Nay, that I do not yet," saith Tinúviel, "though I may perchance hereafter, of thy goodness, my lord Melko. Knowest thou not that I am Tinúviel daughter of Tinwelint the outlaw, and he hath driven me from his halls, for he is an overbearing Elf and I give not my love at his command."

Now in truth was Melko amazed that the daughter of Tinwelint came thus of her free will to his dwelling, Angamandi the terrible, and suspecting something untoward he asked what was her desire: "for knowest thou not," saith he, "that there is no love here for thy father or his folk, nor needst thou hope for soft words and good cheer from me."

"So hath my father said," saith she, "but wherefore need I believe him? Behold, I have a skill of subtle dances, and I would dance now before you, my lord, for then methinks I might readily be granted some humble corner of your halls wherein to dwell until such times as you should call for the little dancer Tinúviel to lighten your cares."

"Nay," saith Melko, "such things are little to my mind; but as thou hast come thus far to dance, dance, and after we will see," and with that he leered horribly, for his dark mind pondered some evil.

Then did Tinúviel begin such a dance as neither she nor any other sprite or fay or elf danced ever before or has done since, and after a while even Melko's gaze was held in wonder. Round the hall she fared, swift as a swallow, noiseless as a bat, magically beautiful as only Tinúviel ever was, and now she was at Melko's side, now before him, now behind, and her misty draperies touched his face and waved before his eyes, and the folk that sat about the walls or stood in that place were whelmed one by one in sleep, falling down into deep dreams of all that their ill hearts desired.

Beneath his chair the adders lay like stones, and the wolves before his feet yawned and slumbered, and Melko gazed on enchanted, but he did not sleep. Then began Tinúviel to dance a yet swifter dance before his eyes, and even as she danced she sang in a voice very low and wonderful a song which Gwendeling had taught her long ago, a song that the youths and maidens sang beneath the cypresses of the gardens of Lórien when the Tree of Gold had waned and Silpion was gleaming. The voices of nightingales were in it, and many subtle odours seemed to fill the air of that noisome place as she trod the floor lightly as a feather in the wind; nor has any voice or sight of such beauty ever again been seen there, and Ainu Melko for all his power and majesty succumbed to the magic of that Elf-maid, and indeed even the eyelids of Lórien had grown heavy had he been there to see. Then did Melko fall forward drowzed, and sank at last in utter sleep down from his chair upon the floor, and his iron crown rolled away.

Suddenly Tinúviel ceased. In the hall no sound was heard save of slumbrous breath; even Beren slept beneath the very seat of Melko, but Tinúviel shook him so that he awoke at last. Then in fear and trembling he tore asunder his disguise and freeing himself from it leapt to his feet. Now does he draw that knife that he had from Tevildo's kitchens and he seizes the mighty iron crown, but Tinúviel could not move it and scarcely might the thews of Beren avail to turn it. Great is the frenzy of their fear as in that dark hall of sleeping evil Beren labours as noiselessly as may be to prise out a Silmaril with his knife. Now does he loosen the great central jewel and the sweat pours from his brow, but even as he forces it from the crown lo! his knife snaps with a loud crack.

Tinúviel smothers a cry thereat and Beren springs away with the one Silmaril in his hand, and the sleepers stir and Melko groans as though ill thoughts disturbed his dreams, and a black look comes upon his sleeping face. Content now with that one flashing gem those twain fled desperately from the hall, stumbling wildly down many dark passages till from the glimmering of grey light they knew they neared the gates – and behold! Karkaras lies across the threshold, awake once more and watchful.

Straightway Beren thrust himself before Tinúviel although she said him nay, and this proved in the end ill, for Tinúviel had not time to cast her spell of slumber over the beast again, ere seeing Beren he bared his teeth and growled angrily. "Wherefore this surliness, Karkaras?" said Tinúviel. "Wherefore this Gnome[10] who entered not and yet now issueth in haste?" quoth Knife-fang, and with that he leapt upon Beren, who struck straight between the wolf's eyes with his fist, catching for his throat with the other hand.

Then Karkaras seized that hand in his dreadful jaws, and it was the hand wherein Beren clasped the blazing Silmaril, and both hand and jewel Karkaras bit off and took into his red maw. Great was the agony of Beren and the fear and anguish of Tinúviel, yet even as they expect to feel the teeth of the wolf a new thing strange and terrible comes to pass. Behold now that Silmaril blazeth with a white and hidden fire of its own nature and is possessed of a fierce and holy magic – for did it not come from Valinor and the blessed realms, being fashioned with spells of the Gods and Gnomes before evil came there; and it doth not tolerate the touch of evil flesh or of unholy hand. Now cometh it into the foul body of Karkaras, and suddenly that beast is burnt with a terrible anguish and the howling of his pain is ghastly to hear as it echoeth in those rocky ways, so that all that sleeping court within awakes. Then did Tinúviel and Beren flee like the wind from the gates, yet was Karkaras far before them raging and in madness as a beast pursued by Balrogs; and after when they might draw breath Tinúviel wept over the maimed arm of Beren kissing it often, so that behold it bled not, and pain left it, and was healed by the tender healing of her love; yet was Beren ever after surnamed among all folk Ermabwed the One-handed, which in the language of the Lonely Isle is Elmavoitë.

Now however must they bethink them of escape – if such may be their fortune, and Tinúviel wrapped part of her dark mantle about Beren, and so for a while flitting by dusk and dark amid the hills they were seen by none, albeit Melko had raised all his Orcs of terror against them; and his fury at the rape of that jewel was greater than the Elves had ever seen it yet.

Even so it seems soon to them that the net of the hunters drew ever more tightly upon them, and though they had reached the edge of the more familiar woods and passed the glooms of the forest of Taurfuin, still were there many leagues of peril yet to pass between them and the caverns of the king, and even did they reach ever there it seemed like they would but draw the chase behind them thither and Melko's hate upon all that woodland folk. So great indeed was the hue and cry that Huan learnt of it far away, and he marvelled much at the daring of those twain, and still more that ever they had escaped from Angamandi.

Now goes he with many dogs through the woods hunting Orcs

and thanes of Tevildo, and many hurts he got thus, and many of them he slew or put to fear and flight, until one even at dusk the Valar brought him to a glade in that northward region of Artanor that was called afterward Nan Dumgorthin, the land of the dark idols, but that is a matter that concerns not this tale. Howbeit it was even then a dark land and gloomy and foreboding, and dread wandered beneath its lowering trees no less even than in Taurfuin; and those two Elves Tinúviel and Beren were lying therein weary and without hope, and Tinúviel wept but Beren was fingering his knife.

Now when Huan saw them he would not suffer them to speak or to tell any of their tale, but straightway took Tinúviel upon his mighty back and bade Beren run as best he could beside him, "for," said he, "a great company of the Orcs are drawing swiftly hither, and wolves are their trackers and their scouts." Now doth Huan's pack run about them, and they go very swiftly along quick and secret paths towards the homes of the folk of Tinwelint far away. Thus was it that they eluded the host of their enemies, but had nonetheless many an encounter afterward with wandering things of evil, and Beren slew an Orc that came nigh to dragging off Tinúviel, and that was a good deed. Seeing then that the hunt still pressed them close, once more did Huan lead them by winding ways, and dared not yet straightly to bring them to the land of the woodland fairies. So cunning however was his leading that at last after many days the chase fell far away, and no longer did they see or hear anything of the bands of Orcs; no goblins waylaid them nor did the howling of any evil wolves come upon the airs at night, and belike that was because already they had stepped within the circle of Gwendeling's magic that hid the paths from evil things and kept harm from the regions of the woodelves.

Then did Tinúviel breathe freely once more as she had not done since she fled from her father's halls, and Beren rested in the sun far from the glooms of Angband until the last bitterness of thraldom left him. Because of the light falling through green leaves and the whisper of clean winds and the song of birds once more are they wholly unafraid.

At last came there nevertheless a day whereon waking out of a deep slumber Beren started up as one who leaves a dream of happy things coming suddenly to his mind, and he said: "Farewell, O Huan, most trusty comrade, and thou, little Tinúviel, whom I love, fare thee well. This only I beg of thee, get thee now straight to the safety of thy home, and may good Huan lead thee. But I – lo,

I must away into the solitude of the woods, for I have lost that
Silmaril which I had, and never dare I draw near to Angamandi
more, wherefore neither will I enter the halls of Tinwelint." Then
he wept to himself, but Tinúviel who was nigh and had hearkened
to his musing came beside him and said: "Nay, now is my heart
changed," and if thou dwellest in the woods, O Beren Ermabwed,
then so will I, and if thou wilt wander in the wild places there will I
wander also, or with thee or after thee: – yet never shall my father
see me again save only if thou takest me to him." Then indeed was
Beren glad at her sweet words, and fain would he have dwelt with
her as a huntsman of the wild, but his heart smote him for all that
she had suffered for him, and for her he put away his pride.
Indeed she reasoned with him, saying it would be folly to be
stubborn, and that her father would greet them with nought but
joy, being glad to see his daughter yet alive – and "maybe," said
she, "he will have shame that his jesting has given thy fair hand to
the jaws of Karkaras." But Huan also she implored to return with
them a space, for "my father owes thee a very great reward, O
Huan," saith she, "an he loves his daughter at all."

So came it that those three set forward once again together, and
came at last back to the woodlands that Tinúviel knew and loved
nigh to the dwellings of her folk and to the deep halls of her home.
Yet even as they approach they find fear and tumult among that
people such as had not been for a long age, and asking some that
wept before their doors they learned that ever since the day of
Tinúviel's secret flight ill-fortune had befallen them. Lo, the king
had been distraught with grief and had relaxed his ancient wariness
and cunning; indeed his warriors had been sent hither and thither
deep into the unwholesome woods searching for that maiden, and
many had been slain or lost for ever, and war there was with
Melko's servants about all their northern and eastern borders, so
that the folk feared mightily lest that Ainu upraise his strength
and come utterly to crush them and Gwendeling's magic have not
the strength to withhold the numbers of the Orcs. "Behold,"
said they, "now is the worst of all befallen, for long has Queen
Gwendeling sat aloof and smiled not nor spoken, looking as it were
to a great distance with haggard eyes, and the web of her magic has
blown thin about the woods, and the woods are dreary, for Dairon
comes not back, neither is his music heard ever in the glades.
Behold now the crown of all our evil tidings, for know that there
has broken upon us raging from the halls of Evil a great grey wolf
filled with an evil spirit, and he fares as though lashed by some

hidden madness, and none are safe. Already has he slain many as he runs wildly snapping and yelling through the woods, so that the very banks of the stream that flows before the king's halls has become a lurking-place of danger. There comes the awful wolf oftentimes to drink, looking as the evil Prince himself with bloodshot eyes and tongue lolling out, and never can he slake his desire for water as though some inward fire devours him."

Then was Tinúviel sad at the thought of the unhappiness that had come upon her folk, and most of all was her heart bitter at the story of Dairon, for of this she had not heard any murmur before. Yet could she not wish Beren had come never to the lands of Artanor, and together they made haste to Tinwelint; and already to the Elves of the wood it seemed that the evil was at an end now that Tinúviel was come back among them unharmed. Indeed they scarce had hoped for that.

In great gloom do they find King Tinwelint, yet suddenly is his sorrow melted to tears of gladness, and Gwendeling sings again for joy when Tinúviel enters there and casting away her raiment of dark mist she stands before them in her pearly radiance of old. For a while all is mirth and wonder in that hall, and yet at length the king turns his eyes to Beren and says: "So thou hast returned too – bringing a Silmaril, beyond doubt, in recompense for all the ill thou hast wrought my land; or an thou hast not, I know not wherefore thou art here."

Then Tinúviel stamped her foot and cried so that the king and all about him wondered at her new and fearless mood: "For shame, my father – behold, here is Beren the brave whom thy jesting drove into dark places and foul captivity and the Valar alone saved from a bitter death. Methinks 'twould rather befit a king of the Eldar to reward him than revile him."

"Nay," said Beren, "the king thy father hath the right. Lord," said he, "I have a Silmaril in my hand even now."

"Show me then," said the king in amaze.

"That I cannot," said Beren, "for my hand is not here"; and he held forth his maimed arm.

Then was the king's heart turned to him by reason of his stout and courteous demeanour, and he bade Beren and Tinúviel relate to him all that had befallen either of them, and he was eager to hearken, for he did not fully comprehend the meaning of Beren's words. When however he had heard all yet more was his heart turned to Beren, and he marvelled at the love that had awakened in the heart of Tinúviel so that she had done greater deeds and more daring than any of the warriors of his folk.

"Never again," said he, "O Beren I beg of thee, leave this court nor the side of Tinúviel, for thou art a great Elf and thy name will ever be great among the kindreds." Yet Beren answered him proudly, and said: "Nay, O King, I hold to my word and thine, and I will get thee that Silmaril or ever I dwell in peace in thy halls." And the king entreated him to journey no more into the dark and unknown realms, but Beren said: "No need is there thereof, for behold that jewel is even now nigh to thy caverns," and he made clear to Tinwelint that that beast that ravaged his land was none other than Karkaras, the wolfward of Melko's gates – and this was not known to all, but Beren knew it taught by Huan, whose cunning in the reading of track and slot was greatest among all the hounds, and therein are none of them unskilled. Huan indeed was with Beren now in the halls, and when those twain spoke of a chase and a great hunt he begged to be in that deed; and it was granted gladly. Now do those three prepare themselves to harry that beast, that all the folk be rid of the terror of the wolf, and Beren kept his word, bringing a Silmaril to shine once more in Elfinesse. King Tinwelint himself led that chase, and Beren was beside him, and Mablung the heavy-handed, chief of the king's thanes, leaped up and grasped a spear[12] – a mighty weapon captured in battle with the distant Orcs – and with those three stalked Huan mightiest of dogs, but others they would not take according to the desire of the king, who said: "Four is enough for the slaying even of the Hell-wolf" – but only those who had seen knew how fearsome was that beast, nigh as large as a horse among Men, and so great was the ardour of his breath that it scorched whatsoever it touched. About the hour of sunrise they set forth, and soon after Huan espied a new slot beside the stream, not far from the king's doors, "and," quoth he, "this is the print of Karkaras." Thereafter they followed that stream all day, and at many places its banks were new-trampled and torn and the water of the pools that lay about it was fouled as though some beasts possessed of madness had rolled and fought there not long before.

Now sinks the sun and fades beyond the western trees and darkness is creeping down from Hisilómë so that the light of the forest dies. Even so come they to a place where the spoor swerves from the stream or perchance is lost in its waters and Huan may no longer follow it; and here therefore they encamp, sleeping in turns beside the stream, and the early night wears away.

Suddenly in Beren's watch a sound of great terror leaped up
from far away – a howling as of seventy maddened wolves – then
lo! the brushwood cracks and saplings snap as the terror draweth
near, and Beren knows that Karkaras is upon them. Scarce had he
time to rouse the others, and they were but just sprung up and
half-awake, when a great form loomed in the wavering moonlight
filtering there, and it was fleeing like one mad, and its course was
bent towards the water. Thereat Huan gave tongue, and straightway the beast swerved aside towards them, and foam was dripping
from his jaws and a red light shining from his eyes, and his face
was marred with mingled terror and with wrath. No sooner did he
leave the trees than Huan rushed upon him fearless of heart, but
he with a mighty leap sprang right over that great dog, for all his
fury was kindled suddenly against Beren whom he recognized as
he stood behind, and to his dark mind it seemed that there was the
cause of all his agony. Then Beren thrust swiftly upward with a
spear into his throat, and Huan leapt again and had him by a hind
leg, and Karkaras fell as a stone, for at that same moment the
king's spear found his heart, and his evil spirit gushed forth and
sped howling faintly as it fared over the dark hills to Mandos; but
Beren lay under him crushed beneath his weight. Now they roll
back that carcase and fall to cutting it open, but Huan licks Beren's
face whence blood is flowing. Soon is the truth of Beren's words
made clear, for the vitals of the wolf are half-consumed as though
an inner fire had long been smouldering there, and suddenly the
night is filled with a wondrous lustre, shot with pale and secret
colours, as Mablung[13] draws forth the Silmaril. Then holding it
out he said: "Behold O King,"[14] but Tinwelint said: "Nay, never
will I handle it save only if Beren give it to me." But Huan said:
"And that seems like never to be, unless ye tend him swiftly, for
methinks he is hurt sorely"; and Mablung and the king were
ashamed.

Therefore now they raised Beren gently up and tended him and
washed him, and he breathed, but he spoke not nor opened his
eyes, and when the sun arose and they had rested a little they bore
him as softly as might be upon a bier of boughs back through the
woodlands; and nigh midday they drew near the homes of the folk
again, and then were they deadly weary, and Beren had not moved
nor spoken, but groaned thrice.

There did all the people flock to meet them when their approach
was noised among them, and some bore them meat and cool drinks
and salves and healing things for their hurts, and but for the harm

that Beren had met great indeed had been their joy. Now then they covered the leafy boughs whereon he lay with soft raiment, and they bore him away to the halls of the king, and there was Tinúviel awaiting them in great distress; and she fell upon Beren's breast and wept and kissed him, and he awoke and knew her, and after Mablung gave him that Silmaril, and he lifted it above him gazing at its beauty, ere he said slowly and with pain: "Behold, O King, I give thee the wondrous jewel thou didst desire, and it is but a little thing found by the wayside, for once methinks thou hadst one beyond thought more beautiful, and she is now mine." Yet even as he spake the shadows of Mandos lay upon his face, and his spirit fled in that hour to the margin of the world, and Tinúviel's tender kisses called him not back.'

    Then did Vëannë suddenly cease speaking, and Eriol sadly said: 'A tale of ruth for so sweet a maid to tell'; but behold, Vëannë wept, and not for a while did she say: 'Nay, that is not all the tale; but here endeth all that I rightly know,' and other children there spake, and one said: 'Lo, I have heard that the magic of Tinúviel's tender kisses healed Beren, and recalled his spirit from the gates of Mandos, and long time he dwelt among the Lost Elves wandering the glades in love with sweet Tinúviel.' But another said: 'Nay, that was not so, O Ausir, and if thou wilt listen I will tell the true and wondrous tale; for Beren died there in Tinúviel's arms even as Vëannë has said, and Tinúviel crushed with sorrow and finding no comfort or light in all the world followed him swiftly down those dark ways that all must tread alone. Now her beauty and tender loveliness touched even the cold heart of Mandos, so that he suffered her to lead Beren forth once more into the world, nor has this ever been done since to Man or Elf, and many songs and stories are there of the prayer of Tinúviel before the throne of Mandos that I remember not right well. Yet said Mandos to those twain: "Lo, O Elves, it is not to any life of perfect joy that I dismiss you, for such may no longer be found in all the world where sits Melko of the evil heart – and know ye that ye will become mortal even as Men, and when ye fare hither again it will be for ever, unless the Gods summon you indeed to Valinor." Nonetheless those twain departed hand in hand, and they fared together through the northern woods, and oftentimes were they seen dancing magic dances down the hills, and their name became heard far and wide.'
    And thereat that boy ceased, and Vëannë said: 'Aye, and they

did more than dance, for their deeds afterward were very great, and many tales are there thereof that thou must hear, O Eriol Melinon, upon another time of tale-telling. For those twain it is that stories name i·Cuilwarthon, which is to say the dead that live again, and they became mighty fairies in the lands about the north of Sirion. Behold now all is ended – and doth it like thee?' But Eriol said: 'Indeed 'tis a wondrous tale, such as I looked not to hear from the lips of the little maids of Mar Vanwa Tyaliéva,' but Vëannë answered him: 'Nay, but I fashioned it not with words of myself; but it is dear to me – and indeed all the children know of the deeds that it relates – and I have learned it by heart, reading it in the great books, and I do not comprehend all that is set therein.'

'Neither do I,' said Eriol – but suddenly cried Ausir: 'Behold, Eriol, Vëannë has never told thee what befell Huan; nor how he would take no rewards from Tinwelint nor dwell nigh him, but wandered forth again grieving for Tinúviel and Beren. On a time he fell in with Mablung[15] who aided in the chase, and was now fallen much to hunting in lonely parts; and the twain hunted together as friends until the days of Glorund the Drake and of Túrin Turambar, when once more Huan found Beren and played his part in the great deeds of the Nauglafring, the Necklace of the Dwarves.'

'Nay, how could I tell all this,' said Vëannë, 'for behold it is time for the evening meat already'; and soon after the great gong rang.

### The second version of the Tale of Tinúviel

As already mentioned (p. 3), there exists a revised version of part of the tale in a typescript (made by my father). This follows the manuscript version closely or very closely on the whole, and in no way alters the style or air of the former; it is therefore unnecessary to give this second version *in extenso*. But the typescript does in places introduce interesting changes, and these are given below (the pages of the corresponding passages in the manuscript version are given in the margin).

The title in the typescript (which begins with the *Link* passage already given, pp. 4–7) was originally 'The Tale of Tynwfiel, Princess of Dor Athro', which was changed to 'The Tale of Tinúviel, the Dancer of Doriath'.

(8)  'Who then was Tinúviel?' said Eriol. 'Knowst thou not,' said Ausir, 'she was the daughter of Singoldo, king of Artanor?' 'Hush

thee, Ausir,' said Vëannë, 'this is my tale, and 'tis a tale of the
Gnomes, wherefore I beg that thou fill not Eriol's ear with thy
Elfin names. Lo! I will tell this tale only, for did I not see Melian
and Tinúviel once long ago with my own eyes when journeying by
the Way of Dreams?'

'What then was Queen Melian like,' quoth Eriol, 'if thou hast
seen her, O Vëannë?'

'Slender and very dark of hair,' said she, 'and her skin was white
and pale, but her eyes shone seeming to hold great depths. Clad
she was in filmy garments most lovely yet of the hue of night,
jet-spangled and girt with silver. If ever she sang or if ever
she danced, dreams and slumbers passed over the heads of those
that were nigh, making them heavy as it were with a strong wine
of sleep. Indeed she was a sprite that, escaping from Lórien's
gardens before even Kôr was built, wandered in the wild places of
the world and in every lonely wood. Nightingales fared with her
singing about her as she went – and 'twas the song of these birds
that smote the ears of Thingol as he marched at the head of that
second[16] tribe of the Eldaliё which afterward became the Shoreland Pipers, the Solosimpi of the Isle. Now had they come a great
way from dim Palisor, and wearily the companies laboured behind
the swift-footed horse of Oromë, wherefore the music of the magic
birds of Melian seemed to him full of all solace, more beautiful
than other melodies of Earth, and he strayed aside for a moment,
as he thought, from the host, seeking in the dark trees whence it
might come.

And it is said that it was not a moment that he hearkened, but
many years, and vainly his people sought him, until at length they
must perforce follow Oromë upon Tol Eressëa, and be borne
thereon far away leaving him listening to the birds enchanted in
the woods of Aryador. That was the first sorrow of the Solosimpi,
that after were many; but Ilúvatar in memory of Thingol set a seed
of music in the hearts of that folk above all kindreds of the Earth
save only the Gods, and after, as all story tells, it blossomed
wondrously upon the isle and in glorious Valinor.

Little sorrow, however, had Thingol; for after a little, as him
seemed, he came upon Melian lying on a bed of leaves . . .

*

(9)     Long thereafter, as now thou knowest, Melko brake once more
into the world from Valinor, and wellnigh all beings therein came
under his foul thraldom; nor were the Lost Elves free, nor the
errant Gnomes that wandered the mountainous places seeking
their stolen treasury. Yet some few there were that led by mighty
kings still defied that evil one in fast and hidden places, and if

Turgon King of Gondolin was the most glorious of these, for a while the most mighty and the longest free was Thingol of the Woods.

Now in the after-days of Sunshine and Moonsheen still dwelt Thingol in Artanor and ruled a numerous and hardy folk drawn from all the tribes of ancient Elfinesse – for neither he nor his people went to the dread Battle of Unnumbered Tears – a matter which toucheth not this tale. Yet was his lordship greatly increased after that most bitter field by fugitives seeking a leader and a home. Hidden was his dwelling thereafter from the vision and knowledge of Melko by the cunning magics of Melian the fay, and she wove spells about all the paths that led thereto, so that none but the children of the Eldalië might tread them without straying. Thus was the king guarded against all evils save treachery alone; his halls were builded in a deep cavern, vaulted immeasurable, that knew no other entrance than a rocky door, mighty, pillared with stone, and shadowed by the loftiest and most ancient trees in all the shaggy forests of Artanor. A great stream was there that fared a dark and silent course in the deep woods, and this flowed wide and swift before that doorway, so that all who would enter that portal must first cross a bridge hung by the Noldoli of Thingol's service across that water – and narrow it was and strongly guarded. In no wise ill were those forest lands, although not utterly distant were the Iron Mountains and black Hisilómë beyond them where dwelt the strange race of Men, and thrall-Noldoli laboured, and few free-Eldar went.

Two children had Thingol then, Dairon and Tinúviel . . .

\*

(10)    'her mother was a fay, a child of Lórien' for manuscript 'her mother was a fay, a daughter of the Gods'.

\*

(11)    'Now Beren was a Gnome, son of Egnor the forester' as in manuscript; but *Egnor* changed to *Barahir*. This however was a much later and as it were casual change; Beren's father was still Egnor in 1925.    \*

(11)    Manuscript version 'and all the Elves of the woodland thought of the Gnomes of Dor Lómin as treacherous creatures, cruel and faithless' is omitted in the typescript.

\*

(13)    *Angband* for manuscript *Angamandi*, and throughout.

\*

(14)   Many a combat and an escape had he in those days, and he slew
therein more than once both wolf and the Orc that rode thereon
with nought but an ashen club that he bore; and other perils and
adventures . . .

*

(15)   But Melko looking wroth upon him asked: "How hast thou, O
thrall, dared to fare thus out of the land where thy folk dwells at
my behest, and to wander in the great woods unbidden, leaving
the labours to which thou hast been set?" Then answered Beren
that he was no runagate thrall, but came of a kindred of the
Gnomes that dwelt in Aryador where were many of the folk of
Men. Then was Melko yet more wroth, saying: "Here have we a
plotter of deep treacheries against Melko's lordship, and one
worthy of the tortures of the Balrogs" – for he sought ever to
destroy the friendship and intercourse of Elves and Men, lest they
forget the Battle of Unnumbered Tears and once more arise in
wrath against him. But Beren seeing his peril answered: "Think
not, O most mighty Belcha Morgoth (for such be his names
among the Gnomes), that could be so; for, an it were, then should
I not be here unaided and alone. No friendship has Beren son of
Egnor for the kindred of Men; nay indeed, wearying utterly of the
lands infested by that folk he has wandered out of Aryador.
Whither then should he go but to Angband? For many a great tale
has his father made to him aforetime of thy splendour and thy
glory. Lo, lord, albeit I am no renegade thrall, still do I desire
nothing so much as to serve thee in what small manner I may."
Little of truth was therein, and indeed his father Egnor was the
chiefest foe of Melko in all the kin of the Gnomes that still were
free, save only Turgon king of Gondolin and the sons of Fëanor,
and long days of friendship had he known with the folk of Men,
what time he was brother in arms to Úrin the steadfast; but in
those days he bore another name and Egnor was nought for
Melko. The truth, however, did Beren then tell, saying that he
was a great huntsman, swift and cunning to shoot or snare or to
outrun all birds and beasts. "I was lost unawares in a part of the
hills that were not known to me, O lord," he said, "the while I was
hunting; and wandering far I came to strange lands and knew no
other rede of safety save to fare to Angband, that all can find who
see the black hills of the north from afar. I would myself have fared
to thee and begged of thee some humble office (as a winner of
meats for thy table, perchance) had not these Orcs seized me and
tormented me unjustly."
       Now the Valar must have inspired that speech, or maybe it was
a spell of cunning words cast upon him in compassion by Melian as
he fled from the hall; for indeed it saved his life . . .

Subsequently a part of this passage was emended on the typescript, to read:

... and long days of friendship had he known with the folk of
Men (as had Beren himself thereafter as brother in arms to Úrin
the Steadfast); but in those days the Orcs named him Rog the
Fleet, and the name of Egnor was nought to Melko.

At the same time the words 'Now the Valar must have inspired
that speech' were changed to 'Now the Valar inspired that speech'.

\*

(15)    Thus was Beren set by Melko as a thrall to The Prince of Cats,
whom the Gnomes have called Tiberth Bridhon Miaugion, but
the Elves Tevildo.

Subsequently *Tiberth* appears for MS *Tevildo* throughout,
and in one place the full name *Tiberth Bridhon Miaugion* appears
again. In the MS the Gnomish name is *Tifil*.

\*

(17)    ... getting nought but a bitten finger for his toil. Then was
Tiberth wroth, and said: "Thou hast lied to my lord, O Gnome,
and art fitter to be a scullion than a huntsman, who canst not catch
even the mice about my halls." Evil thereafter were his days in the
power of Tiberth; for a scullion they made him, and unending
labour he had in the hewing of wood and drawing of water, and in
the menial services of that noisome abode. Often too was he
tormented by the cats and other evil beasts of their company, and
when, as happened at whiles, there was an Orc-feast in those halls,
he would ofttimes be set to the roasting of birds and other meats
upon spits before the mighty fires in Melko's dungeons, until he
swooned for the overwhelming heat; yet he knew himself fortunate
beyond all hope in being yet alive among those cruel foes of Gods
and Elves. Seldom got he food or sleep himself, and he became
haggard and half-blind, so that he wished often that never straying
out of the wild free places of Hisilómë he had not even caught sight
afar off of the vision of Tinúviel.

\*

(17)    But Melian laughed not, nor said aught thereto; for in many
things was she wise and forewise – yet nonetheless it was a thing
unthought in a mad dream that any Elf, still less a maiden, the
daughter of that king who had longest defied Melko, should fare
alone even to the borders of that sorrowful country amid which
lies Angband and the Hells of Iron. Little love was there between
the woodland Elves and the folk of Angband even in those days
before the Battle of Unnumbered Tears when Melko's power was
not grown to its full, and he veiled his designs, and spread his net

of lies. "No help wilt thou get therein of me, little one," said she; "for even if magic and destiny should bring thee safe out of that foolhardiness, yet should many and great things come thereof, and on some many sorrows, and my rede is that thou tell never thy father of thy desire."

But this last word of Melian's did Thingol coming unaware overhear, and they must perforce tell him all, and he was so wroth when he heard it that Tinúviel wished that never had her thoughts been revealed even to her mother.

*

(18)    Indeed I have no love for him, for he has destroyed our play together, our music and our dancing." But Tinúviel said: "I ask it not for him, but for myself, and for that very play of ours together aforetime." And Dairon said: "And for thy sake I say thee nay"; and they spake no more thereof together, but Dairon told the king of what Tinúviel had desired of him, fearing lest that dauntless maiden fare away to her death in the madness of her heart.

*

(18)    . . . he might not shut his daughter for ever in the caves, where the light was only that of torches dim and flickering.

*

(19)    The names of all the tallest and longest things upon Earth were set in that song: the beards of the Indrafangs, the tail of Carcaras, the body of Glorund the drake, the bole of Hirilorn, and the sword of Nan she named, nor did she forget the chain Angainu that Aulë and Tulkas made, or the neck of Gilim the giant that is taller than many elm trees; . . .

*Carcaras* is spelt thus subsequently in the typescript.

*

(20)    . . . as fast as her dancing feet would flit.

Now when the guards awoke it was late in the morning, and they fled away nor dared to bear the tidings to their lord; and Dairon it was bore word of the escape of Tinúviel to Thingol, for he had met the folk that ran in amazement from the ladders which each morning were lifted to her door. Great was the mingled grief and wrath of the king, and all the deep places of his court were in uproar, and all the woods were ringing with the search; but Tinúviel was already far away dancing madly through the dark woods towards the gloomy foothills and the Mountains of Night. 'Tis said that Dairon sped swiftest and furthest in pursuit, but was wrapped in the deceit of those far places, and became utterly lost, and came never back to Elfinesse, but turned towards Palisor; and there he plays subtle magic musics still, wistful and lonely in the woods and forests of the south.

Now fared Tinúviel forward, and a sudden dread overtook her at the thought of what she had dared to do, and of what lay before her. Then did she turn back for a while, and wept, wishing that Dairon were with her. It is said that he was not indeed at that time far off, and wandered lost in Taurfuin, the Forest of Night, where after Túrin slew Beleg by mishap. Nigh was Tinúviel to those evil places; but she entered not that dark region, and the Valar set a new hope in her heart, so that she pressed on once more.

*

(21)    Seldom was any of the cats slain indeed; for in those days they were mightier far in valour and in strength than they have been since those things befell that thou art soon to learn, mightier even than the tawny cats of the southern lands where the sun burns hot. No less too was their skill in climbing and in hiding, and their fleetness was that of an arrow, yet were the free dogs of the northern woods marvellously valiant and knew no fear, and great enmity was between them, and some of those hounds were held in dread even by the greatest of the cats. None, however, did Tiberth fear save only Huan the lord of the Hounds of Hisilómë. So swift was Huan that on a time he had fallen upon Tiberth as he hunted alone in the woods, and pursuing him had overtaken him and nigh rent the fur of his neck from him ere he was rescued by a host of Orcs that heard his cries. Huan got him many hurts in that battle ere he won away, but the wounded pride of Tiberth lusted ever for his death.

Great therefore was the good fortune that befell Tinúviel in meeting with Huan in the woods; and this she did in a little glade nigh to the forest's borders, where the first grasslands begin that are nourished by the upper waters of the river Sirion. Seeing him she was mortally afraid and turned to flee; but in two swift leaps Huan overtook her. Speaking softly the deep tongue of the Lost Elves he bade her be not afeared, and "wherefore," said he, "do I see an Elfin maiden, and one most fair, wandering thus nigh to the places of the Prince of Evil Heart?

*

(22)    What is thy thought, O Huan?"

"Little counsel have I for thee," said he, "save that thou goest with all speed back to Artanor and thy father's halls, and I will accompany thee all the way, until those lands be reached that the magic of Melian the Queen does encompass." "That will I never do," said she, "while Beren liveth here, forgotten of his friends." "I thought that such would be thy answer," said he, "but if thou wilt still go forward with thy mad quest, then no counsel have I for thee save a desperate and a perilous one: we must make now all speed towards the ill places of Tiberth's abiding that are yet far off. I will guide thee thither by the most secret ways, and when we are come there thou must creep alone, if thou hast the heart, to the dwelling of that prince at an hour nigh noon when he and most of his household lie drowsing upon the terraces before his gates. There thou mayst perchance discover, if fortune is very kind, whether Beren be indeed within that ill place as thy mother said to thee. But lo, I will lie not far from the foot of the mount whereon Tiberth's hall is built, and thou must say to Tiberth so soon as thou seest him, be Beren there or be he not, that thou hast stumbled upon Huan of the Dogs lying sick of great wounds in a withered dale without his gates. Fear not overmuch, for herein wilt thou both do my pleasure and further thine own desires, as well as may be; nor do I think that when Tiberth hears thy tidings thou wilt be in any peril thyself for a time. Only do thou not direct him to the place that I shall show to thee; thou must offer to guide him thither thyself. Thus thou shalt get free again of his evil house, and shalt see what I contrive for the Prince of Cats." Then did Tinúviel shudder at the thought of what lay before, but she said that this rede would she sooner take than to return home, and they set forth straightway by secret pathways through the woods, and by winding trails over the bleak and stony lands that lay beyond.

At last on a day at morn they came to a wide dale hollowed like a bowl among the rocks. Deep were its sides, but nought grew there save low bushes of scanty leaves and withered grass. "This is the Withered Dale that I spake of," said Huan. "Yonder is the cave where the great

Here the typescript version of the *Tale of Tinúviel* ends, at the foot of a page. I think it is improbable that any more of this version was made.

## NOTES

1   For earlier references to Olórë Mallë, the Way of Dreams, see I.18, 27; 211, 225.

2   The distinction made here between the Elves (who call the queen *Wendelin*) and, by implication, the Gnomes (who call her

*Gwendeling*) is even more explicit in the typescript version, p. 42
("'tis a tale of the *Gnomes*, wherefore I beg that thou fill not Eriol's
ears with thy *Elfin* names') and p. 45 ('The Prince of Cats, whom the
*Gnomes* have called Tiberth Bridhon Miaugion, but the *Elves*
Tevildo'). See I.50–1.

3   The manuscript as originally written read: 'Now Beren was a
Gnome, son of a thrall of Melko's, some have said, that laboured in
the darker places . . .' See note 4.

4   The manuscript as originally written read: 'I Beren of the Noldoli,
son of Egnor the huntsman . . .' See note 3.

5   From this point, and continuing to the words 'forests of the south'
on p. 21, the text is written on detached pages placed in the notebook. There is no rejected material corresponding to this passage. It
is possible that it existed, and was removed from the book and lost;
but, though the book is in a decayed state, it does not seem that any
pages were removed here, and I think it more likely that my father
simply found himself short of space, as he wrote over the original,
erased, version, and (almost certainly) expanded it as he went.

6   The text as originally written read: 'came never back to Ellu, but
plays . . .' (for *Ellu* see *Changes to Names* below). As a result of the
interpolation 'but turned towards Palisor' Palisor is placed in the
south of the world. In the tale of *The Coming of the Elves* (I.114)
Palisor is called 'the midmost region' (see also the drawing of
the 'World-Ship', I.84), and it seems possible that the word
'south' should have been changed; but it remains in the typescript
(p. 47).

7   The *Tale of Turambar*, though composed after the *Tale of Tinúviel*,
was in existence when *Tinúviel* was rewritten (see p. 69).

8   From 'amazed utterly' to 'if Tinúviel were not there' (p. 30) the text
is written on an inserted page; see note 5 – here also the underlying
textual situation is obscure.

9   A short passage of earlier text in pencil becomes visible here,
ending: '. . . and Tinúviel grew to long sorely for Wendelin her
mother and for the sight of Linwë and for Kapalen making music in
pleasant glades.' *Kapalen* must be a name preceding *Tifanto*, itself
preceding *Dairon* (see *Changes to Names* below).

10   *this Gnome*: original reading *this man*. This was a slip, but a
significant slip (see p. 52), in all probability. It is possible that 'man'
was used here, as occasionally elsewhere (e.g. p. 18 'as high as men
could fashion their longest ladders', where the reference is to the
Elves of Artanor), to mean 'male Elf', but in that case there would
seem no reason to change it.

11   Struck out here in the manuscript: 'Beren of the Hills'.

12   'Mablung the heavy-handed, chief of the king's thanes, leaped up
and grasped a spear' replaced the original reading 'Tifanto cast aside
his pipe and grasped a spear'. Originally the name of Tinúviel's

brother was *Tifanto* throughout the tale. See notes 13–15, and the Commentary, p. 59.

13  *Mablung* replaced *Tifanto*, and again immediately below; see note 12.

14  'O King' replaced 'O father'; see note 12.

15  In this place *Mablung* was the form as first written; see the Commentary, p. 59.

16  It is essential to the narrative of the Coming of the Elves that the Solosimpi were the third and last of the three tribes; 'second' here can only be a slip, if a surprising one.

Changes made to names in
*The Tale of Tinúviel*

(i)  Manuscript Version

*Ilfiniol* < *Elfriniol*. In the typescript text the name is *Ilfrin*. See pp. 201–2.

*Tinwë Linto, Tinwelint*  In the opening passage of the tale (p. 8), where Ausir and Vëannë differ on the forms of Tinwelint's name, the MS is very confused and it is impossible to understand the succeeding stages. Throughout the tale, as originally written, Vëannë calls Tinwelint *Tinto Ellu* or *Ellu*, but in the argument at the beginning it is Ausir who calls him *Tinto Ellu* while Vëannë calls him *Tinto'ellon*. *(Tinto) Ellu* is certainly an 'Elvish' form, but it is corrected throughout the tale to the Gnomish *Tinwelint*, while Ausir's *Tinto Ellu* at the beginning is corrected to *Tinwë Linto*. (At the third occurrence of *Tinwë* in the opening passage the name as originally written was *Linwë*: see I.130.)

In the tales of *The Coming of the Elves* and *The Theft of Melko* in Part One *Ellu* is the name of the second lord of the Solosimpi chosen in Tinwelint's place (afterwards Olwë), but at both occurrences (I.120, 141) this is a later addition (I.130 note 5, 155). Many years later *Ellu* again became Thingol's name (Sindarin *Elu Thingol*, Quenya *Elwë Singollo*, in *The Silmarillion*).

*Gwendeling*  As the tale was originally written, *Wendelin* was the name throughout (*Wendelin* is found in tales given in Part One, emended from *Tindriel*: I.106–7, 131). It was later changed throughout to the Gnomish form *Gwendeling* (found in the early Gnomish dictionary, I.273, itself changed later to *Gwedhiling*) except in the mouth of Ausir, who uses the 'Elvish' form *Wendelin* (p. 8).

*Dairon*  < *Tifanto* throughout. For the change of *Tifanto* > *Mablung* at the end of the tale (notes 12–14 above) see the Commentary, p. 59, and for the name *Kapalen* preceding *Tifanto* see note 9.

*Dor Lómin*  < *Aryador* (p. 11). In the tale of *The Coming of the*

*Elves* it is said (I.119) that Aryador was the name of Hisilómë among Men; for *Dor Lómin – Hisilómë* see I.112. At subsequent occurrences in this tale *Aryador* was not changed.

*Angband* was originally twice written, and in one of these cases it was changed to *Angamandi*, in the other (p. 35) allowed to stand; in all other instances *Angamandi* was the form first written. In the manuscript version of the tale Vëannë does not make consistent use of Gnomish or 'Elvish' forms: thus she says *Tevildo* (not *Tifil*), *Angamandi, Gwendeling* (< *Wendelin*), *Tinwelint* (< *Tinto* (*Ellu*)). In the typescript version, on the other hand, Vëannë says *Tiberth, Angband, Melian* (< *Gwenethlin*), *Thingol* (< *Tinwelint*).

*Hirilorn, the Queen of Trees* < *Golosbrindi, the Queen of the Forest* (p. 18); *Hirilorn* < *Golosbrindi* at subsequent occurrences.

*Uinen* < *Onen* (or possibly *Únen*).

*Egnor bo-Rimion* < *Egnor go-Rimion*. In the tales previously given the patronymic prefix is *go-* (I.146, 155).

*Tinwelint* < *Tinthellon* (p. 35, the only case). Cf. *Tinto'ellon* mentioned above under *Tinwë Linto*.

*i·Cuilwarthon* < *i·Guilwarthon*.


(ii) Typescript Version

*Tinúviel* < *Tynwfiel* in the title and at every occurrence until the passage corresponding to MS version p. 11 'yet now did he see Tinúviel dancing in the twilight'; there and subsequently the form typed was *Tinúviel*.

*Singoldo* < *Tinwë Linto* (p. 41).

*Melian* < *Gwenethlin* at every occurrence until the passage corresponding to MS version p. 12 'the stateliness of Queen Gwendeling'; there and subsequently the form typed was *Melian*.

*Thingol* < *Tinwelint* at every occurrence until the passage corresponding to MS version p. 12 'by winding paths to the abode of Tinwelint'; there and subsequently the form typed was *Thingol*.

For *Egnor* > *Barahir* see p. 43.


Commentary on
*The Tale of Tinúviel*

§1.   *The primary narrative*

In this section I shall consider only the conduct of the main story, and leave for the moment such questions as the wider history implied in it, Tinwelint's people and his dwelling, or the geography of the lands that appear in the story.

The story of Beren's coming upon Tinúviel in the moonlit glade in its earliest recorded form (pp. 11–12) was never changed in its central image; and it should be noticed that the passage in *The Silmarillion* (p. 165) is an extremely concentrated and exalted rendering of the scene: many elements not mentioned there were never in fact lost. In a very late reworking of the passage in the *Lay of Leithian** the hemlocks and the white moths still appear, and Daeron the minstrel is present when Beren comes to the glade. But there are nonetheless the most remarkable differences; and the chief of these is of course that Beren was here no mortal Man, but an Elf, one of the Noldoli, and the absolutely essential element of the story of Beren and Lúthien is not present. It will be seen later (pp. 71–2, 139) that this was not originally so, however: in the now lost (because erased) first form of the *Tale of Tinúviel* he had been a Man (it is for this reason that I have said that the reading *man* in the manuscript (see p. 33 and note 10), later changed to *Gnome*, is a 'significant slip'). Several years after the composition of the tale in the form in which we have it he became a Man again, though at that time (1925–6) my father appears to have hesitated long on the matter of the elvish or mortal nature of Beren.

In the tale there is, necessarily, a quite different reason for the hostility and distrust shown to Beren in Artanor (Doriath) – namely that 'the Elves of the woodland thought of the Gnomes of Dor Lómin as treacherous creatures, cruel and faithless' (see below, p. 65). It seems clear that at this time the history of Beren and his father (Egnor) was only very sketchily devised; there is in any case no hint of the story of the outlaw band led by his father and its betrayal by Gorlim the Unhappy (*The Silmarillion* pp. 162ff.) before the first form of the *Lay of Leithian*, where the story appears fully formed (the Lay was in being to rather beyond this point by the late summer of 1925). But an association of Beren's father (changed to Beren himself) with Úrin (Húrin) as 'brother in arms' is mentioned in the typescript version of the tale (pp. 44–5); according to the latest of the outlines for *Gilfanon's Tale* (I.240) 'Úrin and Egnor marched with countless battalions' (against the forces of Melko).

In the old story, Tinúviel had no meetings with Beren before the day when he boldly accosted her at last, and it was at that very time that she led him to Tinwelint's cave; they were not lovers, Tinúviel knew nothing of Beren but that he was enamoured of her dancing, and it seems that she brought him before her father as a matter of courtesy, the natural thing to do. The betrayal of Beren to Thingol by Daeron (*The Silmarillion* p. 166) therefore has no place in the old story – there is nothing to betray; and indeed it is not shown in the tale that Dairon knew anything

---

* The long unfinished poem in rhyming couplets in which is told the story of Beren and Lúthien Tinúviel; composed in 1925-31, but parts of it substantially rewritten many years later.

whatsoever of Beren before Tinúviel led him into the cave, beyond having once seen his face in the moonlight.

Despite these radical differences in the narrative structure, it is remarkable how many features of the scene in Tinwelint's hall (pp. 12–13), when Beren stood before the king, endured, while all the inner significance was shifted and enlarged. To the beginning go back, for instance, Beren's abashment and silence, Tinúviel's answering for him, the sudden rising of his courage and uttering of his desire without preamble or hesitation. But the tone is altogether lighter and less grave than it afterwards became; in the jeering laughter of Tinwelint, who treats the matter as a jest and Beren as a benighted fool, there is no hint of what is explicit in the later story: 'Thus he wrought the doom of Doriath, and was ensnared within the curse of Mandos' (*The Silmarillion* p. 167). The Silmarils are indeed famous, and they have a holy power (p. 34), but the fate of the world is not bound up with them (*The Silmarillion* p. 67); Beren is an Elf, if of a feared and distrusted people, and his request lacks the deepest dimension of outrage; and he and Tinúviel are not lovers.

In this passage is the first mention of the Iron Crown of Melko, and the setting of the Silmarils in the Crown; and here again is a detail that was never lost: 'Never did this crown leave his head' (cf. *The Silmarillion* p. 81: 'That crown he never took from his head, though its weight became a deadly weariness').

But from this point Vëannë's story diverges in an altogether unexpected fashion from the later narrative. At no other place in the *Lost Tales* is the subsequent transformation more remarkable than in this, the precursor of the story of the capture of Beren and Felagund and their companions by Sauron the Necromancer, the imprisonment and death of all save Beren in the dungeons of Tol-in-Gaurhoth (the Isle of Werewolves in the river Sirion), and the rescue of Beren and overthrow of Sauron by Lúthien and Huan.

Most notably, what may be referred to as 'the Nargothrond Element' is entirely absent, and in so far as it already existed had as yet made no contact with the story of Beren and Tinúviel (for Nargothrond, not yet so named, at this period see pp. 81, 123–4). Beren has no ring of Felagund, he has no companions on his northward journey, and there is no relationship between (on the one hand) the story of his capture, his speech with Melko, and his dispatch to the house of Tevildo, and (on the other) the events of the later narrative whereby Beren and the band of Elves out of Nargothrond found themselves in Sauron's dungeon. Indeed, all the complex background of legend, of battles and rivalries, oaths and alliances, out of which the story of Beren and Lúthien arises in *The Silmarillion*, is very largely absent. The castle of the Cats 'is' the tower of Sauron on Tol-in-Gaurhoth, but only in the sense that it occupies the same 'space' in the narrative: beyond this there is no point in seeking even shadowy resemblances between the two establishments. The monstrous gormandising cats, their kitchens and their sunning terraces, and their engagingly Elvish-feline names (*Miaugion, Miaulë, Meoita*) all disappeared without trace. Did Tevildo? It would scarcely be true, I think, to say even that Sauron 'originated' in a cat: in the next phase of the legends the Necromancer (Thû) has no feline attributes. On the other hand it would be wrong to regard it as a simple matter of *replacement* (Thû stepping into the narrative place vacated by Tevildo) without any element of *transformation* of what was previously there. Tevildo's immediate successor is 'the Lord of Wolves', himself a werewolf, and he retains the Tevildo-trait of hating Huan more than any other creature in the world. Tevildo was 'an evil fay in beastlike shape' (p. 29); and the battle between the two great beasts, the hound against the werewolf (originally the hound against the demon in feline form) was never lost.

When the tale returns to Tinúviel in Artanor the situation is quite the reverse: for the story of her imprisonment in the house in Hirilorn and her escape from it never underwent any significant change. The passage in *The Silmarillion* (p. 172) is indeed very brief, but its lack of detail is due to compression rather than to omission based on dissatisfaction; the *Lay of Leithian*, from which the prose account in *The Silmarillion* directly derives, is in this passage so close, in point of narrative detail, to the *Tale of Tinúviel* as to be almost identical with it.

It may be observed that in this part of the story the earliest version had a strength that was diminished later, in that the duration of Tinúviel's imprisonment and her journey to Beren's rescue relates readily enough to that of Beren's captivity, which was intended by his captors to be unending; whereas in the later story there is a great deal of event and movement (with the addition of Lúthien's captivity in Nargothrond) to be fitted into the time when Beren was awaiting his death in the dungeon of the Necromancer.

While the strong element of 'explanatory' beast-fable (concerning cats and dogs) was to be entirely eliminated, and Tevildo Prince of Cats replaced by the Necromancer, Huan nonetheless remained from it as the great Hound of Valinor. His encounter with Tinúviel in the woods, her inability to escape from him, and indeed his love for her from the moment of their meeting (suggested in the tale, p. 23, explicit in *The Silmarillion* p. 173), were already present, though the context of their encounter and the motives of Huan were wholly different from the absence of 'the Nargothrond Element' (Felagund, Celegorm and Curufin).

In the story of the defeat of Tevildo and the rescue of Beren the germ of the later legend is clearly seen, though for the most part only in broad structural resemblances. It is curious to observe that the loud speaking of Tinúviel sitting perched on the sill of the kitchen hatch in the castle of the Cats, so that Beren might hear, is the precursor of her singing on the bridge of Tol-in-Gaurhoth the song that Beren heard in his dungeon (*The Silmarillion* p. 174). Tevildo's intention to hand her over to Melko remained in Sauron's similar purpose (*ibid.*); the killing of the cat

Oikeroi (p. 28) is the germ of Huan's fight with Draugluin – the skin of Huan's dead opponent is put to the same use in either case (pp. 30–1, *The Silmarillion* pp. 178–9); the battle of Tevildo and Huan was to become that of Huan and Wolf-Sauron, and with essentially the same outcome: Huan released his enemy when he yielded the mastery of his dwelling. This last is very notable: the utterance by Tinúviel of the spell which bound stone to stone in the evil castle (p. 29). Of course, when this was written the castle of Tevildo was an adventitious feature in the story – it had no previous history: it was an evil place through and through, and the spell (deriving from Melko) that Tevildo was forced to reveal was the secret of Tevildo's own power over his creatures as well as the magic that held the stones together. With the entry of Felagund into the developing legend and the Elvish watchtower on Tol Sirion (*Minas Tirith: The Silmarillion* pp. 120, 155–6) captured by the Necromancer, the spell is displaced: for it cannot be thought to be the work of Felagund, who built the fortress, since if it had been he would have been able to pronounce it in the dungeon and bring the place down over their heads – a less evil way for them to die. This element in the legend remained, however, and is fully present in *The Silmarillion* (p. 175), though since my father did not actually say there that Sauron told Huan and Lúthien what the words were, but only that he 'yielded himself', one may miss the significance of what happened:

> And she said: 'There everlastingly thy naked self shall endure the torment of his scorn, pierced by his eyes, unless thou yield to me the mastery of thy tower.'
> Then Sauron yielded himself, and Lúthien took the mastery of the isle and all that was there. . . .
> Then Lúthien stood upon the bridge, and declared her power: and the spell was loosed that bound stone to stone, and the gates were thrown down, and the walls opened, and the pits laid bare.

Here again the actual matter of the narrative is totally different in the early and late forms of the legend: in *The Silmarillion* 'many thralls and captives came forth in wonder and dismay . . . for they had lain long in the darkness of Sauron', whereas in the tale the inmates who emerged from the shaken dwelling (other than Beren and the apparently inconsequent figure of the blind slave-Gnome Gimli) were a host of cats, reduced by the breaking of Tevildo's spell to 'puny size'. (If my father had used in the tale names other than Huan, Beren, and Tinúviel, and in the absence of all other knowledge, including that of authorship, it would not be easy to demonstrate from a simple comparison between this part of the Tale and the story as told in *The Silmarillion* that the resemblances were more than superficial and accidental.)

A more minor narrative point may be noticed here. The typescript version would presumably have treated the fight of Huan and Tevildo somewhat differently, for in the manuscript Tevildo and his companion can flee up great trees (p. 28), whereas in the typescript nothing grew in the Withered Dale (where Huan was to lie feigning sick) save 'low bushes of scanty leaves' (p. 48).

In the remainder of the story the congruence between early and late forms is far closer. The narrative structure in the tale may be summarised thus:

- Beren is attired for disguise in the fell of the dead cat Oikeroi.
- He and Tinúviel journey together to Angamandi.
- Tinúviel lays a spell of sleep on Karkaras the wolf-ward of Angamandi.
- They enter Angamandi, Beren slinks in his beast-shape beneath the seat of Melko, and Tinúviel dances before Melko.
- All the host of Angamandi and finally Melko himself are cast into sleep, and Melko's iron crown rolls from his head.
- Tinúviel rouses Beren, who cuts a Silmaril from the crown, and the blade snaps.
- The sleepers stir, and Beren and Tinúviel flee back to the gates, but find Karkaras awake again.
- Karkaras bites off Beren's outthrust hand holding the Silmaril.
- Karkaras becomes mad with the pain of the Silmaril in his belly, for the Silmaril is a holy thing and sears evil flesh.
- Karkaras goes raging south to Artanor.
- Beren and Tinúviel return to Artanor; they go before Tinwelint and Beren declares that a Silmaril is in his hand.
- The hunting of the wolf takes place, and Mablung the Heavy-handed is one of the hunters.
- Beren is slain by Karkaras, and is borne back to the cavern of Tinwelint on a bier of boughs; dying he gives the Silmaril to Tinwelint.
- Tinúviel follows Beren to Mandos, and Mandos permits them to return into the world.

Changing the catskin of Oikeroi to the wolfskin of Draugluin, and altering some other names, this would do tolerably well as a précis of the story in The Silmarillion! But of course it is devised as a summary of similarities. There are major differences as well as a host of minor ones that do not appear in it.

Again, most important is the absence of 'the Nargothrond Element'. When this combined with the Beren legend it introduced Felagund as Beren's companion, Lúthien's imprisonment in Nargothrond by Celegorm and Curufin, her escape with Huan the hound of Celegorm, and the attack on Beren and Lúthien as they returned from Tol-in-Gaurhoth by Celegorm and Curufin, now fleeing from Nargothrond (The Silmarillion pp. 173–4, 176–8).

The narrative after the conclusion of the episode of 'the Thraldom of
Beren' is conducted quite differently in the old story (pp. 30–1), in that
here Huan is with Beren and Tinúviel; Tinúviel longs for her home, and
Beren is grieved because he loves the life in the woods with the dogs, but
he resolves the impasse by determining to obtain a Silmaril, and though
Huan thinks their plan is folly he gives them the fell of Oikeroi, clad in
which Beren sets out with Tinúviel for Angamandi. In *The Silmarillion*
(p. 177) likewise, Beren, after long wandering in the woods with Lúthien
(though not with Huan), resolves to set forth again on the quest of the
Silmaril, but Lúthien's stance in the matter is different:

'You must choose, Beren, between these two: to relinquish the quest
and your oath and seek a life of wandering upon the face of the earth; or
to hold to your word and challenge the power of darkness upon its
throne. But on either road I shall go with you, and our doom shall be
alike.'

There then intervened the attack on Beren and Lúthien by Celegorm
and Curufin, when Huan, deserting his master, joined himself to them;
they returned together to Doriath, and when they got there Beren left
Lúthien sleeping and went back northwards by himself, riding Curufin's
horse. He was overtaken on the edge of Anfauglith by Huan bearing
Lúthien on his back and bringing from Tol-in-Gaurhoth the skins of
Draugluin and of Sauron's bat-messenger Thuringwethil (of whom in
the old story there is no trace); attired in these Beren and Lúthien went to
Angband. Huan is here their active counsellor.

The later legend is thus more full of movement and incident in this
part than is the *Tale of Tinúviel* (though the final form was not achieved
all at one stroke, as may be imagined); and in the *Silmarillion* form this is
the more marked from the fact that the account is a compression and a
summary of the long *Lay of Leithian*.*

In the *Tale of Tinúviel* the account of Beren's disguise is characteristi-
cally detailed: his instruction by Tinúviel in feline behaviour, his heat
and discomfort inside the skin. Tinúviel's disguise as a bat has however
not yet emerged, and whereas in *The Silmarillion* when confronted by

---

* Cf. Professor T. A. Shippey, *The Road to Middle-earth*, 1982, p. 193: 'In "Beren and
Lúthien" as a whole there is too much plot. The other side of that criticism is that on
occasion Tolkien has to be rather brisk with his own inventions. Celegorm wounds Beren,
and the hound Huan turns on his master and pursues him; "returning he brought to
Lúthien a herb out of the forest. With that leaf she staunched Beren's wound, and by her
arts and her love she healed him. . . ." The motif of the healing herb is a common one, the
centre for instance of the Breton *lai* of *Eliduc* (turned into *conte* by Marie de France). But
in that it occupies a whole scene, if not a whole poem. In *The Silmarillion* it appears only to
be dismissed in two lines, while Beren's wound is inflicted and healed in five. Repeatedly
one has this sense of summary . . .' This sense is eminently justified! In the *Lay of Leithian*
the wounding and the healing with the herb occupy some 64 lines. (Cf. my Foreword to
*The Silmarillion*, p. 8.)

Carcharoth she 'cast back her foul raiment' and 'commanded him to sleep', here she used once more the magical misty robe spun of her hair: 'the black strands of her dark veil she cast in his eyes' (p. 31). The indifference of Karkaras to the false Oikeroi contrasts with Carcharoth's suspicion of the false Druagluin, of whose death he had heard tidings: in the old story it is emphasised that no news of the discomfiture of Tevildo (and the death of Oikeroi) had yet reached Angamandi.

The encounter of Tinúviel with Melko is given with far more detail than in *The Silmarillion* (here much compressed from its source); notable is the phrase (p. 32) 'he leered horribly, for his dark mind pondered some evil', forerunner of that in *The Silmarillion* (p. 180):

> Then Morgoth looking upon her beauty conceived in his thought an evil lust, and a design more dark than any that had yet come into his heart since he fled from Valinor.

We are never told anything more explicit.

Whether Melko's words to Tinúviel, 'Who art thou that flittest about my halls like a bat?', and the description of her dancing 'noiseless as a bat', were the germ of her later bat-disguise cannot be said, though it seems possible.

The knife with which Beren cut the Silmaril from the Iron Crown has a quite different provenance in the *Tale of Tinúviel*, being a kitchen-knife that Beren took from Tevildo's castle (pp. 29, 33); in *The Silmarillion* it was Angrist, the famous knife made by Telchar which Beren took from Curufin. The sleepers of Angamandi are here disturbed by the sound of the snapping of the knife-blade; in *The Silmarillion* it is the shard flying from the snapped knife and striking Morgoth's cheek that makes him groan and stir.

There is a minor difference in the accounts of the meeting with the wolf as Beren and Tinúviel fled out. In *The Silmarillion* 'Lúthien was spent, and she had not time nor strength to quell the wolf'; in the tale it seems that she might have done so if Beren had not been precipitate. Much more important, there appears here for the first time the conception of the holy power of the Silmarils that burns unhallowed flesh.*

The escape of Tinúviel and Beren from Angamandi and their return to Artanor (pp. 34–6) is treated quite differently in the *Tale of Tinúviel*. In *The Silmarillion* (pp. 182–3) they were rescued by the Eagles and set down on the borders of Doriath; and far more is made of the healing of Beren's wound, in which Huan plays a part. In the old story Huan comes to them later, after their long southward flight on foot. In both accounts there is a discussion between them as to whether or not they should return to her father's hall, but it is quite differently conducted – in the tale it is she who persuades Beren to return, in *The Silmarillion* it is Beren who persuades her.

---

* In an early note there is a reference to 'the sacred Silmarils': I.169, note 2.

There is a curious feature in the story of the Wolf-hunt (pp. 38–9) which may be considered here (see p. 50, notes 12–15). At first, it was Tinúviel's brother who took part in the hunt with Tinwelint, Beren, and Huan, and his name is here *Tifanto*, which was the name throughout the tale before its replacement by *Dairon*.* Subsequently 'Tifanto' – without passing through the stage of 'Dairon' – was replaced by 'Mablung the heavy-handed, chief of the king's thanes', who here makes his first appearance, as the fourth member of the hunt. But earlier in the tale it is told that Tifanto > Dairon, leaving Artanor to seek Tinúviel, became utterly lost, 'and came never back to Elfinesse' (p. 21), and the loss of Tifanto > Dairon is referred to again when Beren and Tinúviel returned to Artanor (pp. 36–7).

Thus on the one hand Tifanto was lost, and it is a grief to Tinúviel on her return to learn of it, but on the other he was present at the Wolf-hunt. *Tifanto* was then changed to *Dairon* throughout the tale, except in the story of the Wolf-hunt, where *Tifanto* was replaced by a new character, *Mablung*. This shows that *Tifanto* was removed from the hunt before the change of name to *Dairon*, but does not explain how, under the name *Tifanto*, he was both lost in the wilds and present at the hunt. Since there is nothing in the MS itself to explain this puzzle, I can only conclude that my father did, in fact, write at first that Tifanto was lost and never came back, and also that he took part in the Wolf-hunt; but observing this contradiction he introduced Mablung in the latter rôle (and probably did this even before the tale was completed, since at the last appearance of Mablung his name was written thus, not emended from *Tifanto*: see note 15). It was subsequent to this that *Tifanto* was emended, wherever it still stood, to *Dairon*.

In the tale the hunt is differently managed from the story in *The Silmarillion* (where, incidentally, Beleg Strongbow was present). It is curious that all (including, as it appears, Huan!) save Beren were asleep when Karkaras came on them ('in Beren's watch', p. 39). In *The Silmarillion* Huan slew Carcharoth and was slain by him, whereas here Karkaras met his death from the king's spear, and the boy Ausir tells at the end that Huan lived on to find Beren again at the time of 'the great deeds of the Nauglafring' (p. 41). Of Huan's destiny, that he should not die 'until he encountered the mightiest wolf that would ever walk the world', and of his being permitted 'thrice only ere his death to speak with words' (*The Silmarillion* p. 173), there is nothing here.

The most remarkable feature of the *Tale of Tinúviel* remains the fact that in its earliest extant form Beren was an Elf; and in this connection very notable are the words of the boy at the end (p. 40):

* The idea that Timpinen (Tinfang Warble) was the son of Tinwelint and sister of Tinúviel (see I.106, note 1) had been abandoned. Tifanto/Dairon is now named with Tinfang and Ivárë as 'the three most magic players of the Elves' (p. 10).

Yet said Mandos to those twain: 'Lo, O Elves, it is not to any life of
perfect joy that I dismiss you, for such may no longer be found in all
the world where sits Melko of the evil heart – and know ye that *ye will
become mortal even as Men*, and when ye fare hither again it will be
for ever, unless the Gods summon you indeed to Valinor.'

In the tale of *The Coming of the Valar and the Building of Valinor*
there occurs the following passage (I.76; commentary I.90):

Thither [i.e. to Mandos] in after days fared the Elves of all the clans
who were by illhap slain with weapons or did die of grief for those that
were slain – and only so might the Eldar die, and then it was only for a
while. There Mandos spake their doom, and there they waited in the
darkness, dreaming of their past deeds, until such time as he appointed
when they might again be born into their children, and go forth to
laugh and sing again.

The same idea occurs in the tale of *The Music of the Ainur* (I.59). The
peculiar dispensation of Mandos in the case of Beren and Tinúviel as here
conceived is therefore that their whole 'natural' destiny as Elves was
changed: having died as Elves might die (from wounds or from grief)
they were not reborn as new beings, but returned from Mandos in their
own persons – yet now 'mortal even as Men'. The earliest eschatology is
too unclear to allow of a satisfactory interpretation of this 'mortality', and
the passage in *The Building of Valinor* on the fates of Men (I.77) is
particularly hard to understand (see the commentary on it, I.90ff.). But
it seems possible that the words 'even as Men' in the address of Mandos to
Beren and Tinúviel were included to stress the finality of whatever
second deaths they might undergo; their departure would be as final as
that of Men, there would be no second return in their own persons, and
no reincarnation. They will remain in Mandos ('when ye fare hither
again it will be for ever') – unless they are summoned by the Gods to
dwell in Valinor. These last words should probably be related to the
passage in *The Building of Valinor* concerning the fate of certain Men
(I.77):

Few are they and happy indeed for whom at a season doth Nornorë the
herald of the Gods set out. Then ride they with him in chariots or upon
good horses down into the vale of Valinor and feast in the halls of
Valmar, dwelling in the houses of the Gods until the Great End come.

§2.   *Places and peoples in the Tale of Tinúviel*

To consider first what can be learned of the geography of the Great
Lands from this tale: the early 'dictionary' of the Gnomish language

makes it clear that the meaning of *Artanor* was 'the Land Beyond', as it is interpreted in the text (p. 9). Several passages in the *Lost Tales* cast light on this expression. In an outline for Gilfanon's untold tale (I.240) the Noldoli exiled from Valinor

now fought for the first time with the Orcs and captured the pass of the Bitter Hills; thus they escaped from the Land of Shadows . . . They entered the Forest of Artanor and the Region of the Great Plains . . .

(which latter, I suggested, may be the forerunner of the later Talath Dirnen, the Guarded Plain of Nargothrond). The tale to follow Gilfanon's, according to the projected scheme (I.241), was to be that of Tinúviel, and this outline begins: 'Beren son of Egnor wandered out of Dor Lómin [i.e. Hisilómë, see I.112] into Artanor . . .' In the present tale, it is said that Beren came 'through the terrors of the Iron Mountains until he reached the Lands Beyond' (p. 11), and also (p. 21) that some of the Dogs 'roamed the woods of Hisilómë or passing the mountainous places fared even at times into the region of Artanor and the lands beyond and to the south'. And finally, in the *Tale of Turambar* (p. 72) there is a reference to 'the road over the dark hills of Hithlum into the great forests of the Land Beyond where in those days Tinwelint the hidden king had his abode'.

It is quite clear, then, that Artanor, afterwards called Doriath (which appears in the title to the typescript text of the *Tale of Tinúviel*, together with an earlier form *Dor Athro*, p. 41), lay in the original conception in much the same relation to Hisilómë (the Land of Shadow(s), Dor Lómin, Aryador) as does Doriath to Hithlum (Hisilómë) in *The Silmarillion*: to the south, and divided from it by a mountain-range, the Iron Mountains or Bitter Hills.

In commenting on the tale of *The Theft of Melko and the Darkening of Valinor* I have noticed (I.158–9) that whereas in the *Lost Tales* Hisilómë is declared to be beyond the Iron Mountains, it is also said (in the *Tale of Turambar*, p. 77) that these mountains were so named from Angband, the Hells of Iron, which lay beneath 'their northernmost fastnesses', and that therefore there seems to be a contradictory usage of the term 'Iron Mountains' within the *Lost Tales* – 'unless it can be supposed that these mountains were conceived as a continuous range, the southerly extension (the later Mountains of Shadow) forming the southern fence of Hisilómë, while the northern peaks, being above Angband, gave the range its name'.

Now in the *Tale of Tinúviel* Beren, journeying north from Artanor, 'drew nigh to the lower hills and treeless lands that warned of the approach of the bleak Iron Mountains' (p. 14). These he had previously traversed, coming out of Hisilómë; but now 'he followed the Iron Mountains till he drew nigh to the terrible regions of Melko's abode'.

This seems to support the suggestion that the mountains fencing Hisilómë from the Lands Beyond were continuous with those above Angband; and we may compare the little primitive map (I.81), where the mountain range *f* isolates Hisilómë (*g*): see I.112, 135. The implication is that 'dim' or 'black' Hisilómë had no defence against Melko.

There appear now also the Mountains of Night (pp. 20, 46–7), and it seems clear that the great pinewoods of Taurfuin, the Forest of Night, grew upon those heights (in *The Silmarillion* Dorthonion 'Land of Pines', afterwards named Taur-nu-Fuin). Dairon was lost there, but Tinúviel, though she passed near, did not enter 'that dark region'. There is nothing to show that it was not placed then as it was later – to the east of Ered Wethrin, the Mountains of Shadow. It is also at least possible that the description (in the manuscript version only, p. 23) of Tinúviel, on departing from Huan, leaving 'the shelter of the trees' and coming to 'a region of long grass' is a first intimation of the great plain of Ard-galen (called after its desolation Anfauglith and Dor-nu-Fauglith), especially if this is related to the passage in the typescript version telling of Tinúviel's meeting with Huan 'in a little glade nigh to the forest's borders, where the first grasslands begin that are nourished by the upper waters of the river Sirion' (p. 47).

After their escape from Angamandi Huan found Beren and Tinúviel 'in that northward region of Artanor that was called afterward Nan Dumgorthin, the land of the dark idols' (p. 35). In the Gnomish dictionary *Nan Dumgorthin* is defined as 'a land of dark forest east of Artanor where on a wooded mountain were hidden idols sacrificed to by some evil tribes of renegade men' (*dum* 'secret, not to be spoken', *dumgort*, *dungort* 'an (evil) idol'). In the *Lay of the Children of Húrin* in alliterative verse Túrin and his companion Flinding (later Gwindor), fleeing after the death of Beleg Strongbow, came to this land:

> There the twain enfolded     phantom twilight
> and dim mazes     dark, unholy,
> in Nan Dungorthin     where nameless gods
> have shrouded shrines     in shadows secret,
> more old than Morgoth     or the ancient lords
> the golden Gods     of the guarded West.
> But the ghostly dwellers     of that grey valley
> hindered nor hurt them,     and they held their course
> with creeping flesh     and quaking limb.
> Yet laughter at whiles     with lingering echo,
> as distant mockery     of demon voices
> there harsh and hollow     in the hushed twilight
> Flinding fancied,     fell, unwholesome . . .

There are, I believe, no other references to the gods of Nan Dumgorthin. In the poem the land was placed west of Sirion; and finally, as Nan

Dungortheb 'the Valley of Dreadful Death', it becomes in *The Silmarillion* (pp. 81, 121) a 'no-land' between the Girdle of Melian and Ered Gorgoroth, the Mountains of Terror. But the description of it in the *Tale of Tinúviel* as a 'northward region of Artanor' clearly does not imply that it lay within the protective magic of Gwendeling, and it seems that this 'zone' was originally less distinctly bounded, and less extensive, than 'the Girdle of Melian' afterwards became. Probably *Artanor* was conceived at this time as a great region of forest in the heart of which was Tinwelint's cavern, and only his immediate domain was protected by the power of the queen:

> Hidden was his dwelling from the vision and knowledge of Melko by the magics of Gwendeling the fay, and she wove spells about the paths thereto that none but the Eldar might tread them easily, and so was the king secured from all dangers save it be treachery alone. (p. 9).

It seems, also, that her protection was originally by no means so complete and so mighty a wall of defence as it became. Thus, although Orcs and wolves disappeared when Beren and Tinúviel 'stepped within the circle of Gwendeling's magic that hid the paths from evil things and kept harm from the regions of the woodelves' (p. 35), the fear is expressed that even if Beren and Tinúviel reached the cavern of King Tinwelint 'they would but draw the chase behind them thither' (p. 34), and Tinwelint's people feared that Melko would 'upraise his strength and come utterly to crush them and Gwendeling's magic have not the strength to withhold the numbers of the Orcs' (p. 36).

The picture of Menegroth beside Esgalduin, accessible only by the bridge (*The Silmarillion* pp. 92–3) goes back to the beginning, though neither cave nor river are named in the tale. But (as will be seen more emphatically in later tales in this book) Tinwelint, the wood-fairy in his cavern, had a long elevation before him, to become ultimately Thingol of the Thousand Caves ('the fairest dwelling of any king that has ever been east of the Sea'). In the beginning, Tinwelint's dwelling was not a subterranean city full of marvels, silver fountains falling into basins of marble and pillars carved like trees, but a rugged cave; and if in the typescript version the cave comes to be 'vaulted immeasureable', it is still illuminated only by the dim and flickering light of torches (pp. 43, 46).

There have been earlier references in the *Lost Tales* to Tinwelint and the place of his dwelling. In a passage added to, but then rejected from, the tale of *The Chaining of Melko* (I.106, note 1) it is said that he was lost in Hisilómë and met Wendelin there; 'loving her he was content to leave his folk and dance for ever in the shadows'. In *The Coming of the Elves* (I.115) 'Tinwë abode not long with his people, and yet 'tis said lives still lord of the scattered Elves of Hisilómë'; and in the same tale (I.118–19) the 'Lost Elves' were still there 'long after when Men were shut in Hisilómë by Melko', and Men called them the Shadow Folk, and feared them. But in the *Tale of Tinúviel* the conception has changed. Tinwelint is now a king ŕuling, not in Hisilómë, but in Artanor.* (It is not said where it was that he came upon Gwendeling.)

In the account (manuscript version only, see pp. 9, 42) of Tinwelint's people there is mention of Elves 'who remained in the dark'; and this obviously refers to Elves who never left the Waters of Awakening. (Of course those who were lost on the march from Palisor also never left 'the dark' (i.e. they never came to the light of the Trees), but the distinction made in this sentence is not between the darkness and the light but between those who *remained* and those who *set out*). On the emergence of this idea in the course of the writing of the *Lost Tales* see I.234. Of Tinwelint's subjects 'the most were Ilkorindi', and they must be those who 'had been lost upon the march from Palisor' (earlier, 'the Lost Elves of Hisilómë').

Here, a major difference in essential conception between the old legend and the form in *The Silmarillion* is apparent. These Ilkorindi of Tinwelint's following ('eerie and strange beings' whose 'dark songs and chantings . . . faded in the wooded places or echoed in deep caves') are described in terms applicable to the wild Avari ('the Unwilling') of *The Silmarillion*; but they are of course actually the precursors of the Grey-elves of Doriath. The term *Eldar* is here equivalent to *Elves* ('all the Eldar both *those who remained in the dark* or had been lost upon the march from Palisor') and is not restricted to those who made, or at least embarked on, the Great Journey; all were Ilkorindi – Dark Elves – if they never passed over the Sea. The later significance of the Great Journey in conferring 'Eldarin' status was an aspect of the elevation of the Grey-elves of Beleriand, bringing about a distinction of the utmost importance within the category of the *Moriquendi* or 'Elves of the Darkness' – the *Avari* (who were not Eldar) and the *Úmanyar* (the Eldar who were 'not of Aman'): see the table 'The Sundering of the Elves' given in *The Silmarillion*. Thus:

| | *Lost Tales* | | *Silmarillion* | | |
|---|---|---|---|---|---|
| | of Kôr | | Avari | | |
| Eldar | of the Great Lands (the Darkness): Ilkorindi | Eldar (of the Great Journey) | | of Aman | of Middle-earth (Úmanyar) |

But among Tinwelint's subjects there were also *Noldoli*, Gnomes. This matter is somewhat obscure, but at least it may be observed that the

---

* In the outlines for *Gilfanon's Tale* the 'Shadow Folk' of Hisilómë have ceased to be Elves and become 'fays' whose origin is unknown: I.237, 239.

manuscript and typescript versions of the *Tale of Tinúviel* do not envisage precisely the same situation.

The manuscript text is perhaps not perfectly explicit on the subject, but it is said (p. 9) that of Tinwelint's subjects '*the most* were Ilkorindi', and that before the rising of the Sun 'already were their numbers mingled with a many wandering Gnomes'. Yet Dairon fled from the apparition of Beren in the forest because 'all the Elves of the woodland thought of the Gnomes of Dor Lómin as treacherous creatures, cruel and faithless' (p. 11); and 'Dread and suspicion was between the Eldar and those of their kindred that had tasted the slavery of Melko, and in this did the evil deeds of the Gnomes at the Haven of the Swans revenge itself' (p. 11). The hostility of the Elves of Artanor to Gnomes was, then, specifically a hostility to the Gnomes of Hisilómë (Dor Lómin), who were suspected of being under the will of Melko (and this is probably a foreshadowing of the suspicion and rejection of Elves escaped from Angband described in *The Silmarillion* p. 156). In the manuscript it is said (p. 9) that *all* the Elves of the Great Lands (those who remained in Palisor, those who were lost on the march, and the Noldoli returned from Valinor) fell beneath the power of Melko, though many escaped and wandered in the wild; and as the manuscript text was first written (see p. 11 and note 3) Beren was 'son of a thrall of Melko's . . . that laboured in the darker places in the north of Hisilómë'. This conception seems reasonably clear, so far as it goes.

In the typescript version it is expressly stated that there were Gnomes 'in Tinwelint's service' (p. 43): the bridge over the forest river, leading to Tinwelint's door, was hung by them. It is not now stated that all the Elves of the Great Lands fell beneath Melko; rather there are named several centres of resistance to his power, in addition to Tinwelint/ Thingol in Artanor: Turgon of Gondolin, the Sons of Fëanor, and Egnor of Hisilómë (Beren's father) – one of the chiefest foes of Melko 'in all the kin of the Gnomes that still were free' (p. 44). Presumably this led to the exclusion in the typescript of the passage telling that the woodland Elves thought of the Gnomes of Dor Lómin as treacherous and faithless (see p. 43), while that concerning the distrust of those who had been Melko's slaves was retained. The passage concerning Hisilómë 'where dwelt Men, and thrall-Noldoli laboured, and few free-Eldar went' (p. 10) was also retained; but Hisilómë, in Beren's wish that he had never strayed out of it, becomes 'the wild free places of Hisilómë' (pp. 17, 45).

This leads to an altogether baffling question, that of the references to the Battle of Unnumbered Tears; and several of the passages just cited bear on it.

The story of 'The Travail of the Noldoli and the Coming of Mankind' that was to have been told by Gilfanon, but which after its opening pages most unhappily never got beyond the stage of outline projections, was to be followed by that of Beren and Tinúviel (see I. 241). After the Battle of Unnumbered Tears there is mention of the Thraldom of the Noldoli, the Mines of Melko, the Spell of Bottomless Dread, the shutting of Men in

Hisilómë, and *then* 'Beren son of Egnor wandered out of Dor Lómin into Artanor . . .' (In *The Silmarillion* the deeds of Beren and Lúthien preceded the Battle of Unnumbered Tears.)

Now in the *Tale of Tinúviel* there is a reference, in both versions, to the 'thrall-Noldoli' who laboured in Hisilómë and of Men dwelling there; and as the passage introducing Beren was first written in the manuscript his father was one of these slaves. It is said, again in both versions, that neither Tinwelint nor the most part of his people went to the battle, but that his lordship was greatly increased by fugitives from it (p. 9); and to the following statement that his dwelling was hidden by the magic of Gwendeling/Melian the typescript adds the word 'thereafter' (p. 43), i.e. after the Battle of Unnumbered Tears. In the changed passage in the typescript referring to Egnor he is one of the chiefest foes of Melko 'in all the kin of the Gnomes *that still were free*'.

All this seems to allow of only one conclusion: the events of the *Tale of Tinúviel* took place *after* the great battle; and this seems to be clinched by the express statement in the typescript: where the manuscript (p. 15) says that Melko 'sought ever to destroy the friendship and intercourse of Elves and Men', the second version adds (p. 44): *'lest they forget the Battle of Unnumbered Tears* and once more arise in wrath against him'.

It is very odd, therefore, that Vëannë should say at the beginning (in the manuscript only, p. 10 and see p. 43) that she will tell 'of things that happened in the halls of Tinwelint *after the arising of the Sun indeed but long ere the unforgotten Battle of Unnumbered Tears*'. (This in any case seems to imply a much longer period between the two events than is suggested in the outlines for *Gilfanon's Tale*: see I.242). This is repeated later (p. 17): 'it was a thing unthought . . . that any Elf . . . should fare untended to the halls of Melko, *even in those earlier days before the Battle of Tears* when Melko's power had not grown great . . .' But it is stranger still that this second sentence is retained in the typescript (p. 45). The typescript version has thus two inescapably contradictory statements:

Melko 'sought ever to destroy the friendship and intercourse of Elves and Men, lest they forget the Battle of Unnumbered Tears' (p. 44);

'Little love was there between the woodland Elves and the folk of Angband even in those days before the Battle of Unnumbered Tears' (p. 45).

Such a radical contradiction within a single text is in the highest degree unusual, perhaps unique, in all the writings concerned with the First Age. But I can see no way to explain it, other than simply accepting it as a radical contradiction; nor indeed can I explain those statements in both versions that the events of the tale took place *before* the battle, since virtually all indications point to the contrary.*

---

* In the *Tale of Turambar* the story of Beren and Tinúviel clearly and necessarily took place *before* the Battle of Unnumbered Tears (pp. 71–2, 140).

## §3. *Miscellaneous Matters*

### (i) *Morgoth*

Beren addresses Melko as 'most mighty Belcha Morgoth', which are said to be his names among the Gnomes (p. 44). In the Gnomish dictionary *Belcha* is given as the Gnomish form corresponding to *Melko* (see I.260), but *Morgoth* is not found in it: indeed this is the first and only appearance of the name in the *Lost Tales*. The element *goth* is given in the Gnomish dictionary with the meaning 'war, strife'; but if *Morgoth* meant at this period 'Black Strife' it is perhaps strange that Beren should use it in a flattering speech. A name-list made in the 1930s explains *Morgoth* as 'formed from his Orc-name *Goth* "Lord or Master" with *mor* "dark or black" prefixed', but it seems very doubtful that this etymology is valid for the earlier period. This name-list explains *Gothmog* 'Captain of Balrogs' as containing the same Orc-element ('Voice of *Goth* (Morgoth)'); but in the name-list to the tale of *The Fall of Gondolin* (p. 216) the name *Gothmog* is said to mean 'Strife-and-hatred' (*mog-* 'detest, hate' appears in the Gnomish dictionary), which supports the interpretation of *Morgoth* in the present tale as 'Black Strife'.*

### (ii) *Orcs and Balrogs*

Despite the reference to 'the wandering bands of the goblins *and* the Orcs' (p. 14, retained in the typescript version), the terms are certainly synonymous in the *Tale of Turambar*. The Orcs are described in the present tale (*ibid.*) as 'foul broodlings of Melko'. In the second version (p. 44) wolf-rider Orcs appear.

Balrogs, mentioned in the tale (p. 15), have appeared in one of the outlines for *Gilfanon's Tale* (I.241); but they had already played an important part in the earliest of the *Lost Tales*, that of *The Fall of Gondolin* (see pp. 212–13).

### (iii) *Tinúviel's 'lengthening spell'*

Of the 'longest things' named in this spell (pp. 19–20, 46) two, 'the sword of Nan' and 'the neck of Gilim the giant', seem now lost beyond recall, though they survived into the spell in the *Lay of Leithian*, where the sword of Nan is itself named, *Glend*, and Gilim is called 'the giant of

---

* Nothing is said in any text to suggest that Gothmog played such a role in relation to Morgoth as the interpretation 'Voice of *Goth*' implies, but nor is anything said to contradict it, and he was from the beginning an important figure in the evil realm and in especial relation to Melko (see p. 216). There is perhaps a reminiscence of 'the Voice of Morgoth' in 'the Mouth of Sauron', the Black Númenórean who was the Lieutenant of Barad-dûr (*The Return of the King* V. 10).

Eruman'. *Gilim* in the Gnomish dictionary means 'winter' (see I.260, entry *Melko*), which does not seem particularly appropriate: though a jotting, very difficult to read, in the little notebook used for memoranda in connection with the *Lost Tales* (see I.171) seems to say that Nan was a 'giant of summer of the South', and that he was like an elm.

The *Indravangs* (*Indrafangs* in the typescript) are the 'Longbeards'; this is said in the Gnomish dictionary to be 'a special name of the Nauglath or Dwarves' (see further the *Tale of the Nauglafring*, p. 247).

*Karkaras* (*Carcaras* in the typescript) 'Knife-fang' is named in the spell since he was originally conceived as the 'father of wolves, who guarded the gates of Angamandi in those days *and long had done so*' (p. 21). In *The Silmarillion* (p. 180) he has a different history: chosen by Morgoth 'from among the whelps of the race of Draugluin' and reared to be the death of Huan, he was set before the gates of Angband in that very time. In *The Silmarillion* (*ibid.*) Carcharoth is rendered 'the Red Maw', and this expression is used in the text of the tale (p. 34): 'both hand and jewel Karkaras bit off and took into his red maw'.

*Glorund* is the name of the dragon in the *Tale of Turambar* (*Glaurung* in *The Silmarillion*).

In the tale of *The Chaining of Melko* there is no suggestion that Tulkas had any part in the making of the chain (there in the form *Angaino*): I.100.

(iv)   *The influence of the Valar*

There is frequent suggestion that the Valar in some way exercised a direct influence over the minds and hearts of the distant Elves in the Great Lands. Thus it is said (p. 15) that the Valar must have inspired Beren's ingenious speech to Melko, and while this may be no more than a 'rhetorical' flourish, it is clear that Tinúviel's dream of Beren is meant to be accepted as 'a dream of the Valar' (p. 19). Again, 'the Valar set a new hope in her heart' (p. 47); and later in Vëannë's tale the Valar are seen as active 'fates', guiding the destinies of the characters – so the Valar 'brought' Huan to find Beren and Tinúviel in Nan Dumgorthin (p. 35), and Tinúviel says to Tinwelint that 'the Valar alone saved Beren from a bitter death' (p. 37).

# II

# TURAMBAR AND THE FOALÓKË

The *Tale of Turambar*, like that of *Tinúviel*, is a manuscript written in ink over a wholly erased original in pencil. But it seems certain that the *extant* form of *Turambar* preceded the *extant* form of *Tinúviel*. This can be deduced in more ways than one, but the order of composition is clearly exemplified in the forms of the name of the King of the Woodland Elves (Thingol). Throughout the manuscript of *Turambar* he was originally *Tintoglin* (and this appears also in the tale of *The Coming of the Elves*, where it was changed to *Tinwelint*, I.115, 131). A note on the manuscript at the beginning of the tale says: 'Tintoglin's name must be altered throughout to *Ellon* or *Tinthellon* = Q. *Ellu*', but the note was struck out, and all through the tale *Tintoglin* was in fact changed to *Tinwelint*.

Now in the *Tale of Tinúviel* the king's name was first given as *Ellu* (or *Tinto Ellu*), and once as *Tinthellon* (pp. 50–1); subsequently it was changed throughout to *Tinwelint*. It is clear that the direction to change *Tintoglin* to '*Ellon* or *Tinthellon* = Q. *Ellu*' belongs to the time when the *Tale of Tinúviel* was being, or had been, rewritten, and that the extant *Tale of Turambar* already existed.

There is also the fact that the rewritten *Tinúviel* was followed, at the same time of composition, by the first form of the 'interlude' in which Gilfanon appears (see I.203), whereas at the beginning of *Turambar* there is a reference to Ailios (who was replaced by Gilfanon) concluding the previous tale. On the different arrangement of the tale-telling at this point that my father subsequently introduced but failed to carry through see I.229–30. According to the earlier arrangement, Ailios told his tale on the first night of the feast of Turuhalmë or the Logdrawing, and Eltas followed with the *Tale of Turambar* on the second.

There is evidence that the *Tale of Turambar* was in existence at any rate by the middle of 1919. Humphrey Carpenter discovered a passage, written on a scrap of proof for the Oxford English Dictionary, in an early alphabet of my father's devising; and transliterating it he found it to be from this tale, not far from the beginning. He has told me that my father was using this version of the 'Alphabet of Rúmil' about June 1919 (see *Biography*, p. 100).

When then Ailios had spoken his fill the time for the lighting of candles was at hand, and so came the first day of Turuhalmë to an end; but on the second night Ailios was not there, and being asked by Lindo one Eltas began a tale, and said:

'Now all folk gathered here know that this is the story of Turambar and the Foalókë, and it is,' said he, 'a favourite tale among Men, and tells of very ancient days of that folk before the Battle of Tasarinan when first Men entered the dark vales of Hisilómë.

In these days many such stories do Men tell still, and more have they told in the past especially in those kingdoms of the North that once I knew. Maybe the deeds of other of their warriors have become mingled therein, and many matters beside that are not in the most ancient tale – but now I will tell to you the true and lamentable tale, and I knew it long ere I trod Olórë Mallë in the days before the fall of Gondolin.

In those days my folk dwelt in a vale of Hisilómë and that land did Men name Aryador in the tongues they then used, but they were very far from the shores of Asgon and the spurs of the Iron Mountains were nigh to their dwellings and great woods of very gloomy trees. My father said to me that many of our older men venturing afar had themselves seen the evil worms of Melko and some had fallen before them, and by reason of the hatred of our people for those creatures and of the evil Vala often was the story of Turambar and the Foalókë in their mouths – but rather after the fashion of the Gnomes did they say Turumart and the Fuithlug.

For know that before the Battle of Lamentation and the ruin of the Noldoli there dwelt a lord of Men named Úrin, and hearkening to the summons of the Gnomes he and his folk marched with the Ilkorindi against Melko, but their wives and children they left behind them in the woodlands, and with them was Mavwin wife of Úrin, and her son remained with her, for he was not yet war-high. Now the name of that boy was Túrin and is so in all tongues, but Mavwin do the Eldar call Mavoinë.

Now Úrin and his followers fled not from that battle as did most of the kindreds of Men, but many of them were slain fighting to the last, and Úrin was made captive. Of the Noldoli who fought there all the companies were slain or captured or fled away in rout, save that of Turondo (Turgon) only, and he and his folk cut a path for themselves out of that fray and come not into this tale. Nonetheless the escape of that great company marred the complete victory that otherwise had Melko won over his adversaries, and he desired very greatly to discover whither they had fled; and this he might not do, for his spies availed nothing, and no tortures at that time had power to force treacherous knowledge from the captive Noldoli.

Knowing therefore that the Elves of Kôr thought little of Men, holding them in scant fear or suspicion for their blindness and lack of skill, he would constrain Úrin to take up his employ and go seek after Turondo as a spy of Melko. To this however neither threats of torture nor promises of rich reward would bring Úrin to consent, for he said: "Nay, do as thou wilt, for to no evil work of thine wilt thou ever constrain me, O Melko, thou foe of Gods and Men."

"Of a surety," said Melko in anger, "to no work of mine will I bid thee again, nor yet will I force thee thereto, but upon deeds of mine that will be little to thy liking shalt thou sit here and gaze, nor be able to move foot or hand against them." And this was the torture he devised for the affliction of Úrin the Steadfast, and setting him in a lofty place of the mountains he stood beside him and cursed him and his folk with dread curses of the Valar, putting a doom of woe and a death of sorrow upon them; but to Úrin he gave a measure of vision, so that much of those things that befell his wife and children he might see and be helpless to aid, for magic held him in that high place. "Behold!" said Melko, "the life of Túrin thy son shall be accounted a matter for tears wherever Elves or Men are gathered for the telling of tales"; but Úrin said: "At least none shall pity him for this, that he had a craven for father."

Now after that battle Mavwin got her in tears into the land of Hithlum or Dor Lómin where all Men must now dwell by the word of Melko, save some wild few that yet roamed without. There was Nienóri born to her, but her husband Úrin languished in the thraldom of Melko, and Túrin being yet a small boy Mavwin knew not in her distress how to foster both him and his sister, for Úrin's men had all perished in the great affray, and the strange men who dwelt nigh knew not the dignity of the Lady Mavwin, and all that land was dark and little kindly.

The next short section of the text was struck through afterwards and replaced by a rider on an attached slip. The rejected passage reads:

At that time the rumour [*written above*: memory] of the deeds of Beren Ermabwed had become noised much in Dor Lómin, wherefore it came into the heart of Mavwin, for lack of better counsel, to send Túrin to the court of Tintoglin,[1] begging him to foster this orphan for the memory of Beren, and to teach him the wisdom of fays and of Eldar; now Egnor[2] was akin to Mavwin and he was the father of Beren the One-handed.

The replacement passage reads:

>    Amended passage to fit better with the story of Tinúviel and
>    the afterhistory of the Nauglafring:

The tale tells however that Úrin had been a friend of the Elves,
and in this he was different from many of his folk. Now great had
his friendship been with Egnor, the Elf of the greenwood, the
huntsman of the Gnomes, and Beren Ermabwed son of Egnor he
knew and had rendered him a service once in respect of Damrod
his son; but the deeds of Beren of the One Hand in the halls of
Tinwelint³ were remembered still in Dor Lómin. Wherefore it
came into the heart of Mavwin, for lack of other counsel, to send
Túrin her son to the court of Tinwelint, begging him to foster this
orphan for the memory of Úrin and of Beren son of Egnor.⁴

Very bitter indeed was that sundering, and for long [?time]
Túrin wept and would not leave his mother, and this was the first
of the many sorrows that befell him in life. Yet at length when his
mother had reasoned with him he gave way and prepared him in
anguish for that journey. With him went two old men, retainers
aforetime of his father Úrin, and when all was ready and the
farewells taken they turned their feet towards the dark hills, and
the little dwelling of Mavwin was lost in the trees, and Túrin blind
with tears could see her no more. Then ere they passed out of
earshot he cried out: "O Mavwin my mother, soon will I come
back to thee" – but he knew not that the doom of Melko lay
between them.
    Long and very weary and uncertain was the road over the dark
hills of Hithlum into the great forests of the Land Beyond where in
those days Tinwelint the hidden king had his abode; and Túrin
son of Úrin⁵ was the first of Men to tread that way, nor have many
trodden it since. In perils were Túrin and his guardians of wolves
and wandering Orcs that at that time fared even thus far from
Angband as the power of Melko waxed and spread over the
kingdoms of the North. Evil magics were about them, that often
missing their way they wandered fruitlessly for many days, yet in
the end did they win through and thanked the Valar therefor – yet
maybe it was but part of the fate that Melko wove about their feet,
for in after time Túrin would fain have perished as a child there in
the dark woods.
    Howso that may be, this was the manner of their coming to

Tinwelint's halls; for in the woodlands beyond the mountains they became utterly lost, until at length having no means of sustenance they were like to die, when they were discovered by a wood-ranger, a huntsman of the secret Elves, and he was called Beleg, for he was of great stature and girth as such was among that folk. Then Beleg led them by devious paths through many dark and lonely forestlands to the banks of that shadowed stream before the cavernous doors of Tinwelint's halls. Now coming before that king they were received well for the memory of Úrin the Steadfast, and when also the king heard of the bond tween Úrin and Beren the One-handed[6] and of the plight of that lady Mavwin his heart became softened and he granted her desire, nor would he send Túrin away, but rather said he: "Son of Úrin, thou shalt dwell sweetly in my woodland court, nor even so as a retainer, but behold as a second child of mine shalt thou be, and all the wisdoms of Gwedheling and of myself shalt thou be taught."

After a time therefore when the travellers had rested he despatched the younger of the two guardians of Túrin back unto Mavwin, for such was that man's desire to die in the service of the wife of Úrin, yet was an escort of Elves sent with him, and such comfort and magics for the journey as could be devised, and moreover these words did he bear from Tinwelint to Mavwin: "Behold O Lady Mavwin wife of Úrin the Steadfast, not for love nor for fear of Melko but of the wisdom of my heart and the fate of the Valar did I not go with my folk to the Battle of Unnumbered Tears, who now am become a safety and a refuge for all who fearing evil may find the secret ways that lead to the protection of my halls. Perchance now is there no other bulwark left against the arrogance of the Vala of Iron, for men say Turgon is not slain, but who knoweth the truth of it or how long he may escape? Now therefore shall thy son Túrin be fostered here as my own child until he is of age to succour thee – then, an he will, he may depart." More too he bid the Lady Mavwin, might she o'ercome the journey, fare back also to his halls, and dwell there in peace; but this when she heard she did not do, both for the tenderness of her little child Nienóri, and for that rather would she dwell poor among Men than live sweetly as an almsguest even among the woodland Elves. It may be too that she clung to that dwelling that Úrin had set her in ere he went to the great war, hoping still faintly for his return, for none of the messengers that had borne the lamentable tidings from that field might say that he was dead, reporting only that none knew where he might be – yet in truth those messengers were few and half-distraught, and now the years were slowly passing since the last blow fell on that most grievous day. Indeed in after days she yearned to look again upon Túrin, and maybe in the end, when Nienóri had grown, had cast aside her pride and fared over the hills, had not these become impassable for the might and great magic of Melko, who hemmed all Men in Hithlum and slew such as dared beyond its walls.

Thus came to pass the dwelling of Túrin in the halls of Tinwelint; and with him was suffered to dwell Gumlin the aged who had fared with him out of Hithlum, and had no heart or strength for the returning. Very much joy had he in that sojourn, yet did the sorrow of his sundering from Mavwin fall never quite away from him; great waxed his strength of body and the stoutness of his feats got him praise wheresoever Tinwelint was held as lord, yet he was a silent boy and often gloomy, and he got not love easily and fortune did not follow him, for few things that he desired greatly came to him and many things at which he laboured went awry. For nothing however did he grieve so much as the ceasing of all messengers between Mavwin and himself, when after a few years as has been told the hills became untraversable and the ways were shut. Now Túrin was seven years old when he fared to the woodland Elves, and seven years he dwelt there while tidings came ever and anon to him from his mother, so that he heard how his sister Nienóri grew to a slender maid and very fair, and how things grew better in Hithlum and his mother more in peace; and then all words ceased, and the years passed.

To ease his sorrow and the rage of his heart, that remembered always how Úrin and his folk had gone down in battle against Melko, Túrin was for ever ranging with the most warlike of the folk of Tinwelint far abroad, and long ere he was grown to first manhood he slew and took hurts in frays with the Orcs that prowled unceasingly upon the confines of the realm and were a menace to the Elves. Indeed but for his prowess much hurt had that folk sustained, and he held the wrath of Melko from them for many years, and after his days they were harassed sorely, and in the end must have been cast into thraldom had not such great and dread events befallen that Melko forgot them.

Now about the courts of Tinwelint there dwelt an Elf called Orgof, and he, as were the most of that king's folk, was an Ilkorin, yet he had Gnome-blood also. Of his mother's side he was nearly akin to the king himself, and was in some favour being a good

hunter and an Elf of prowess, yet was he somewhat loose with his
tongue and overweening by reason of his favour with the king; yet
of nothing was he so fain as of fine raiment and of jewels and of
gold and silver ornament, and was ever himself clad most bravely.
Now Túrin lying continually in the woods and travailing in far and
lonely places grew to be uncouth of raiment and wild of locks, and
Orgof made jest of him whensoever the twain sat at the king's
board; but Túrin said never a word to his foolish jesting, and
indeed at no time did he give much heed to words that were spoken
to him, and the eyes beneath his shaggy brows oftentimes looked
as to a great distance – so that he seemed to see far things and to
listen to sounds of the woodland that others heard not.

On a time Túrin sate at meat with the king, and it was that day
twelve years since he had gazed through his tears upon Mavwin
standing before the doors and weeping as he made his way among
the trees, until their stems had taken her from his sight, and he was
moody, speaking curt answers to those that sat nigh him, and most
of all to Orgof.

But this fool would not give him peace, making a laugh of his
rough clothes and tangled hair, for Túrin had then come new from
a long abiding in the woods, and at length he drew forth daintily a
comb of gold that he had and offered it to Túrin; and having
drunk well, when Túrin deigned not to notice him he said: "Nay,
an thou knowst not how to use a comb, hie thee back to thy
mother, for she perchance will teach thee – unless in sooth the
women of Hithlum be as ugly as their sons and as little kempt."
Then a fierce anger born of his sore heart and these words concerning the lady Mavwin blazed suddenly in Túrin's breast, so
that he seized a heavy drinking-vessel of gold that lay by his right
hand and unmindful of his strength he cast it with great force in
Orgof's teeth, saying: "Stop thy mouth therewith, fool, and prate
no more." But Orgof's face was broken and he fell back with great
weight, striking his head upon the stone of the floor and dragging
upon him the table and all its vessels, and he spake nor prated
again, for he was dead.

Then all men rose in silence, but Túrin, gazing aghast upon the
body of Orgof and the spilled wine upon his hand, turned on his
heel and strode into the night; and some that were akin to Orgof
drew their weapons half from their sheaths, yet none struck, for
the king gave no sign but stared stonily upon the body of Orgof,
and very great amaze was in his face. But Túrin laved his hands in
the stream without the doors and burst there into tears, saying:

"Lo! Is there a curse upon me, for all I do is ill, and now is it so turned that I must flee the house of my fosterfather an outlaw guilty of blood – nor look upon the faces of any I love again." And in his heart he dared not return to Hithlum lest his mother be bitterly grieved at his disgrace, or perchance he might draw the wrath of the Elves behind him to his folk; wherefore he got himself far away, and when men came to seek him he might not be found.

Yet they did not seek his harm, although he knew it not, for Tinwelint despite his grief and the ill deed pardoned him, and the most of his folk were with him in that, for Túrin had long held his peace or returned courtesy to the folly of Orgof, though stung often enough thereby, for that Elf being not a little jealous was used to barb his words; and now therefore the near kinsmen of Orgof were constrained by fear of Tinwelint and by many gifts to accept the king's doom.

Yet Túrin in unhappiness, believing the hand of all against him and the heart of the king become that of a foe, crept to the uttermost bounds of that woodland realm. There he hunted for his subsistence, being a good shot with the bow, yet he rivalled not the Elves at that, for rather at the wielding of the sword was he mightier than they. To him gathered a few wild spirits, and amongst them was Beleg the huntsman, who had rescued Gumlin and Túrin in the woods aforetime. Now in many adventures were those twain together, Beleg the Elf and Túrin the Man, which are not now told or remembered but which once were sung in many a place. With beast and with goblin they warred and fared at times into far places unknown to the Elves, and the fame of the hidden hunters of the marches began to be heard among Orcs and Elves, so that perchance Tinwelint would soon have become aware of the place of Túrin's abiding, had not upon a time all that band of Túrin's fallen into desperate encounter with a host of Orcs who outnumbered them three times. All were there slain save Túrin and Beleg, and Beleg escaped with wounds, but Túrin was overborne and bound, for such was the will of Melko that he be brought to him alive; for behold, dwelling in the halls of Linwë[7] about which had that fay Gwedheling the queen woven much magic and mystery and such power of spells as can come only from Valinor, whence indeed long time agone she once had brought them, Túrin had been lost out of his sight, and he feared lest he cheat the doom that was devised for him. Therefore now he purposed to entreat him grievously before the eyes of Úrin; but Úrin had called upon the Valar of the West, being taught much concerning them by the

Eldar of Kôr – the Gnomes he had encountered – and his words came, who shall say how, to Manwë Súlimo upon the heights of Taniquetil, the Mountain of the World. Nonetheless was Túrin dragged now many an evil league in sore distress, a captive of the pitiless Orcs, and they made slow journeying, for they followed ever the line of dark hills toward those regions where they rise high and gloomy and their heads are shrouded in black vapours. There are they called Angorodin or the Iron Mountains, for beneath the roots of their northernmost fastnesses lies Angband, the Hells of Iron, most grievous of all abodes – and thither were they now making laden with booty and with evil deeds.

Know then that in those days still was Hithlum and the Lands Beyond full of the wild Elves and of Noldoli yet free, fugitives of the old battle; and some wandered ever wearily, and others had secret and hidden abodes in caves or woodland fastnesses, but Melko sought untiringly after them and most pitilessly did he entreat them of all his thralls did he capture them. Orcs and dragons and evil fays were loosed against them and their lives were full of sorrow and travail, so that those who found not in the end the realms of Tinwelint nor the secret stronghold of the king of the city of stone* perished or were enslaved.

Noldoli too there were who were under the evil enchantments of Melko and wandered as in a dream of fear, doing his ill bidding, for the spell of bottomless dread was on them and they felt the eyes of Melko burn them from afar. Yet often did these sad Elves both thrall and free hear the voice of Ulmo in the streams or by the sea-marge where the waters of Sirion mingled with the waves; for Ulmo, of all the Valar, still thought of them most tenderly and designed with their slender aid to bring Melko's evil to ruin. Then remembering the blessedness of Valinor would they at times cast away their fear, doing good deeds and aiding both Elves and Men against the Lord of Iron.

Now was it that it came into the heart of Beleg the hunter of the Elves to seek after Túrin so soon as his own hurts were healed. This being done in no great number of days, for he had a skill of healing, he made all speed after the band of Orcs, and he had need of all his craft as tracker to follow that trail, for a band of the goblins of Melko go cunningly and very light. Soon was he far beyond any regions known to him, yet for love of Túrin he pressed on, and in this did he show courage greater than the most of that

* Gondolin.

woodland folk, and indeed there are none who may now measure
the depth of fear and anguish that Melko set in the hearts of Men
and of Elves in those sad days. Thus did it fall out that Beleg
became lost and benighted in a dark and perilous region so thick
with pines of giant growth that none but the goblins might find a
track, having eyes that pierced the deepest gloom, yet were many
even of these lost long time in those regions; and they were called
by the Noldoli Taurfuin, the Forest of Night. Now giving himself
up for lost Beleg lay with his back to a mighty tree and listened to
the wind in the gaunt tops of the forest many fathoms above him,
and the moaning of the night airs and the creaking of the branches
was full of sorrow and foreboding, and his heart became utterly
weary.

On a sudden he noticed a little light afar among the trees steady
and pale as it were of a glowworm very bright, yet thinking it
might scarce be glowworm in such a place he crept towards it.
Now the Noldoli that laboured in the earth and aforetime had skill
of crafts in metals and gems in Valinor were the most valued of the
thralls of Melko, and he suffered them not to stray far away, and so
it was that Beleg knew not that these Elves had little lanterns of
strange fashion, and they were of silver and of crystal and a flame
of a pale blue burnt forever within, and this was a secret and the
jewel-makers among them alone knew it nor would they reveal it
even to Melko, albeit many jewels and many magic lights they
were constrained to make for him.

Aided by these lamps the Noldoli fared much at night, and
seldom lost a path had they but once trodden it before. So it was
that drawing near Beleg beheld one of the hill-gnomes stretched
upon the needles beneath a great pine asleep, and his blue lantern
stood glimmering nigh his head. Then Beleg awakened him, and
that Elf started up in great fear and anguish, and Beleg learned
that he was a fugitive from the mines of Melko and named himself
Flinding bo-Dhuilin of an ancient house of the Gnomes. Now
falling into talk Flinding was overjoyed to have speech with a free
Noldo, and told many tales of his flight from the uttermost fastness
of the mines of Melko; and at length said he: "When I thought
myself all but free, lo, I strayed at night unwarily into the midmost
of an Orc-camp, and they were asleep and much spoil and weighted
packs they had, and many captive Elves I thought I descried: and
one there was that lay nigh to a trunk to which he was bound most
grievously, and he moaned and cried out bitterly against Melko,
calling on the names of Úrin and Mavwin; and though at that time

being a craven from long captivity I fled heedlessly, now do I marvel much, for who of the thralls of Angband has not known of Úrin the Steadfast who alone of Men defies Melko chained in torment upon a bitter peak?"

Then was Beleg in great eagerness and sprang to his feet shouting: "'Tis Túrin, fosterson of Tinwelint, even he whom I seek, who was the son of Úrin long ago. – Nay, lead me to this camp, O son of Duilin, and soon shall he be free," but Flinding was much afeared, saying: "Softer words, my Beleg, for the Orcs have ears of cats, and though a day's march lies between me and that encampment who knows whether they be not followed after."

Nonetheless hearing the story of Túrin from Beleg, despite his dread he consented to lead Beleg to that place, and long ere the sun rose on the day or its fainting beams crept into that dark forest they were upon the road, guided by the dancing light of Flinding's swinging lamp. Now it happened that in their journeying their paths crossed that of the Orcs who now were renewing their march, but in a direction other than that they had for long pursued, for now fearing the escape of their prisoner they made for a place where they knew the trees were thinner and a track ran for many a league easy to pursue; wherefore that evening, or ever they came to the spot that Flinding sought, they heard a shouting and a rough singing that was afar in the woods but drawing near; nor did they hide too soon ere the whole of that Orc-band passed nigh to them, and some of the captains were mounted upon small horses, and to one of these was Túrin tied by the wrists so that he must trot or be dragged cruelly. Then did Beleg and Flinding follow timorously after as dusk fell on the forest, and when that band encamped they lurked near until all was quiet save the moaning of the captives. Now Flinding covered his lamp with a pelt and they crept near, and behold the goblins slept, for it was not their wont to keep fire or watch in their bivouacs, and for guard they trusted to certain fierce wolves that went always with their bands as dogs with Men, but slept not when they camped, and their eyes shone like points of red light among the trees. Now was Flinding in sore dread, but Beleg bid him follow, and the two crept between the wolves at a point where there was a great gap between them, and as the luck of the Valar had it Túrin was lying nigh, apart from the others, and Beleg came unseen to his side and would cut his bonds, when he found his knife had dropped from his side in his creeping and his sword he had left behind without the camp. Therefore now, for they dare not risk the creeping forth and back

again, do Beleg and Flinding both stout men essay to carry him
sleeping soundly in utter weariness stealthily from the camp, and
this they did, and it has ever been thought a great feat, and few
have done the like in passing the wolf guards of the goblins and
despoiling their camps.

Now in the woods at no great distance from the camp they laid
him down, for they might not bear him further, seeing that he was
a Man and of greater stature than they;⁸ but Beleg fetched his
sword and would cut his bonds forthwith. The bonds about his
wrists he severed first and was cutting those upon the ankles when
blundering in the dark he pricked Túrin's foot deeply, and Túrin
awoke in fear. Now seeing a form bend over him in the gloom
sword in hand and feeling the smart of his foot he thought it was
one of the Orcs come to slay him or to torment him – and this they
did often, cutting him with knives or hurting him with spears; but
now Túrin feeling his hand free leapt up and flung all his weight
suddenly upon Beleg, who fell and was half-crushed, lying speechless on the ground; but Túrin at the same time seized the sword
and struck it through Beleg's throat or ever Flinding might know
what had betid. Then Túrin leapt back and shouting out curses
upon the goblins bid them come and slay him or taste of his sword,
for he fancied himself in the midst of their camp, and thought not
of flight but only of selling his life dear. Now would he have made
at Flinding, but that Gnome sprang back, dropping his lamp, so
that its cover slipped and the light of it shone forth, and he called
out in the tongue of the Gnomes that Túrin should hold his hand
and slay not his friends – then did Túrin hearing his speech pause,
and as he stood, by the light of the lamp he saw the white face of
Beleg lying nigh his feet with pierced throat, and he stood as one
stricken to stone, and such was the look upon his face that Flinding
dared not speak for a long while. Indeed little mind had he for
words, for by that light had he also seen the fate of Beleg and was
very bitter in heart. At length however it seemed to Flinding that
the Orcs were astir, and so it was, for the shouts of Túrin had come
to them; wherefore he said to Túrin: "The Orcs are upon us, let us
flee," but Túrin answered not, and Flinding shook him, bidding
him gather his wits or perish, and then Túrin did as he was bid but
yet as one dazed, and stooping he raised Beleg and kissed his
mouth.

Then did Flinding guide Túrin as well as he might swiftly from
those regions, and Túrin wandered with him following as he led,
and at length for a while they had shaken off pursuit and could

breathe again. Now then did Flinding have space to tell Túrin all he knew and of his meeting with Beleg, and the floods of Túrin's tears were loosed, and he wept bitterly, for Beleg had been his comrade often in many deeds; and this was the third anguish that befell Túrin, nor did he lose the mark of that sorrow utterly in all his life; and long he wandered with Flinding caring little whither he went, and but for that Gnome soon would he have been recaptured or lost, for he thought only of the stark face of Beleg the huntsman, lying in the dark forest slain by his hand even as he cut the bonds of thraldom from him.

In that time was Túrin's hair touched with grey, despite his few years. Long time however did Túrin and the Noldo journey together, and by reason of the magic of that lamp fared by night and hid by day and were lost in the hills, and the Orcs found them not.

Now in the mountains there was a place of caves above a stream, and that stream ran down to feed the river Sirion, but grass grew before the doors of the caves, and these were cunningly concealed by trees and such magics as those scattered bands that dwelt therein remembered still. Indeed at this time this place had grown to be a strong dwelling of the folk and many a fugitive swelled them, and there the ancient arts and works of the Noldoli came once more to life albeit in a rude and rugged fashion.

There was smithying in secret and forging of good weapons, and even fashioning of some fair things beside, and the women spun once more and wove, and at times was gold quarried privily in places nigh, where it was found, so that deep in those caverns might vessels of beauty be seen in the flame of secret lights, and old songs were faintly sung. Yet did the dwellers in the caves flee always before the Orcs and never give battle unless compelled by mischance or were they able to so entrap them that all might be slain and none escape alive; and this they did of policy that no tidings reach Melko of their dwelling nor might he suspect any numerous gathering of folk in those parts.

This place however was known to the Noldo Flinding who fared with Túrin; indeed he was once of that people long since, before the Orcs captured him and he was held in thraldom. Thither did he now wend being sure that the pursuit came no longer nigh them, yet went he nonetheless by devious ways, so that it was long ere they drew nigh to that region, and the spies and watchers of the Rodothlim (for so were that folk named) gave warning of their

approach, and the folk withdrew before them, such as were abroad
from their dwelling. Then they closed their doors and hoped that
the strangers might not discover their caves, for they feared and
mistrusted all unknown folk of whatever race, so evil were the
lessons of that dreadful time.

Now then Flinding and Túrin dared even to the caves' mouths,
and perceiving that these twain knew now the paths thereto the
Rodothlim sallied and made them prisoners and drew them within
their rocky halls, and they were led before the chief, Orodreth.
Now the free Noldoli at that time feared much those of their kin
who had tasted thraldom, for compelled by fear and torture and
spells much treachery had they wrought; even thus did the evil
deeds of the Gnomes at Cópas Alqalunten find vengeance,' setting
Gnome against Gnome, and the Noldoli cursed the day that ever
they first hearkened to the deceit of Melko, rueing utterly their
departure from the blessed realm of Valinor.

Nonetheless when Orodreth heard the tale of Flinding and
knew it to be true he welcomed him with joy back among the folk,
yet was that Gnome so changed by the anguish of his slavery that
few knew him again; but for Flinding's sake Orodreth hearkened
to the tale of Túrin, and Túrin told of his travails and named Úrin
as his sire, nor had the Gnomes yet forgot that name. Then was
the heart of Orodreth made kind and he bade them dwell among
the Rodothlim and be faithful to him. So came the sojourn of
Túrin among the people of the caves, and he dwelt with Flinding
bo-Dhuilin and laboured much for the good of the folk, and slew
many a wandering Orc, and did doughty deeds in their defence. In
return much did he learn of new wisdom from them, for memories
of Valinor burnt yet deep in their wild hearts, and greater still was
their wisdom than that of such Eldar as had seen never the blest
faces of the Gods.

Among that people was a very fair maiden and she was named
Failivrin, and her father was Galweg; and this Gnome had a liking
for Túrin and aided him much, and Túrin was often with him in
ventures and good deeds. Now many a tale of these did Galweg
make beside his hearth and Túrin was often at his board, and the
heart of Failivrin became moved at the sight of him, and wondered
often at his gloom and sadness, pondering what sorrow lay locked
in her breast, for Túrin went not gaily being weighted with the
death of Beleg that he felt upon his head, and he suffered not his
heart to be moved, although he was glad of her sweetness; but he
deemed himself an outlawed man and one burdened with a heavy

doom of ill. Therefore did Failivrin become sorrowful and wept in secret, and she grew so pale that folk marvelled at the whiteness and delicacy of her face and her bright eyes that shone therein.

Now came a time when the Orc-bands and the evil things of Melko drew ever nigher to the dwelling of this folk, and despite the good spells that ran in the stream beneath it seemed like that their abode would remain no longer hidden. It is said however that during all this time the dwelling of Túrin in the caves and his deeds among the Rodothlim were veiled from Melko's eyes, and that he infested not the Rodothlim for Túrin's sake nor out of design, but rather it was the ever increasing numbers of these creatures and their growing power and fierceness that brought them so far afield. Nonetheless the blindness and ill-fortune that he wove of old clung yet to Túrin, as may be seen.

Each day grew the brows of the chiefs of the Rodothlim more dark, and dreams came to them[10] bidding them arise and depart swiftly and secretly, seeking, if it might be, after Turgon, for with him might yet salvation be found for the Gnomes. Whispers too there were in the stream at eve, and those among them skilled to hear such voices added their foreboding at the councils of the folk. Now at these councils had Túrin won him a place by dint of many valorous deeds, and he gainsaid their fears, trusting in his strength, for he lusted ever for war with the creatures of Melko, and he upbraided the men of the folk, saying: "Lo! Ye have weapons of great excellence of workmanship, and yet are the most of them clean of your foes' blood. Remember ye the Battle of Uncounted Tears and forget not your folk that there fell, nor seek ever to flee, but fight and stand."

Now despite the wisdom of their wisest such bitter words confused their counsels and delayed them, and there were no few of the stout-hearted that found hope in them, being sad at the thought of abandoning those places where they had begun to make an abiding place of peace and goodliness; but Túrin begged Orodreth for a sword, and he had not wielded a sword since the slaying of Beleg, but rather had he been contented with a mighty club. Now then Orodreth let fashion for him a great sword, and it was made by magic to be utterly black save at its edges, and those were shining bright and sharp as but Gnome-steel may be. Heavy it was, and was sheathed in black, and it hung from a sable belt, and Túrin named it Gurtholfin the Wand of Death; and often that blade leapt in his hand of its own lust, and it is said that at times it spake dark words to him. Therewith did he now range the hills,

and slew unceasingly, so that Blacksword of the Rodothlim became
a name of terror to the Orcs, and for a great season all evil was
fended from the caverns of the Gnomes. Hence comes that name
of Túrin's among the Gnomes, calling him Mormagli or Mormakil
according to their speech, for these names signify black sword.

The greater however did Túrin's valour become so grew the
love of Failivrin more deep, and did men murmur against him in
his absence she spake for him, and sought ever to minister to him,
and her he treated ever courteously and happily, saying he had
found a fair sister in the Gnome-lands. By Túrin's deeds however
was the ancient counsel of the Rodothlim set aside and their abode
made known far and wide, nor was Melko ignorant of it, yet many
of the Noldoli now fled to them and their strength waxed and
Túrin was held in great honour among them. Then were days of
great happiness and for a while men lived openly again and might
fare far abroad from their homes in safety, and many boasted of
the salvation of the Noldoli, while Melko gathered in secret his
great hordes. These did he loose suddenly upon them at unawares,
and they gathered their warriors in great haste and went against
him, but behold, an army of Orcs descended upon them, and
wolves, and Orcs mounted upon wolves; and a great worm was
with them whose scales were polished bronze and whose breath
was a mingled fire and smoke, and his name was Glorund.[11] All the
men of the Rodothlim fell or were taken in that battle, for the foe
was numberless, and that was the most bitter affray since the evil
field of Nínin-Udathriol.* Orodreth was there sorely hurt and
Túrin bore him out of the fight ere yet all was ended, and with the
aid of Flinding whose wounds were not great[12] he got him to the
caves.

There died Orodreth, reproaching Túrin that he had ever
withstood his wise counsels, and Túrin's heart was bitter at the
ruin of the folk that was set to his account.[13] Then leaving Lord
Orodreth dead Túrin went to the places of Galweg's abiding, and
there was Failivrin weeping bitterly at the tidings of her father's
death, but Túrin sought to comfort her, and for the pain of
her heart and the sorrow of her father's death and of the ruin
of her folk she swooned upon his breast and cast her arms about

---

* At the bottom of the manuscript page is written:

'*Nieriltasinwa*   the battle of unnumbered tears
*Glorund   Laurundo* or *Undolaurë*'

Later *Glorund* and *Laurundo* were emended to *Glorunt* and *Laurunto*.

him. So deep was the ruth of Túrin's heart that in that hour he deemed he loved her very dearly; yet were now he and Flinding alone save for a few aged carles and dying men, and the Orcs having despoiled the field of dead were nigh upon them.

Thus stood Túrin before the doors with Gurtholfin in hand, and Flinding was beside him; and the Orcs fell on that place and ransacked it utterly, dragging out all the folk that lurked therein and all their goods, whatsoever of great or little worth might there lie hid. But Túrin denied the entrance of Galweg's dwelling to them, and they fell thick about him, until a company of their archers standing at a distance shot a cloud of arrows at him. Now he wore chainmail such as all the warriors of the Gnomes have ever loved and still do wear, yet it turned not all those ill shafts, and already was he sore hurt when Flinding fell pierced suddenly through the eye; and soon too had he met his death – and his weird had been the happier thereby – had not that great drake coming now upon the sack bidden them cease their shooting; but with the power of his breath he drove Túrin from those doors and with the magic of his eyes he bound him hand and foot.

Now those drakes and worms are the evillest creatures that Melko has made, and the most uncouth, yet of all are they the most powerful, save it be the Balrogs only. A great cunning and wisdom have they, so that it has been long said amongst Men that whosoever might taste the heart of a dragon would know all tongues of Gods or Men, of birds or beasts, and his ears would catch whispers of the Valar or of Melko such as never had he heard before. Few have there been that ever achieved a deed of such prowess as the slaying of a drake, nor might any even of such doughty ones taste their blood and live, for it is as a poison of fires that slays all save the most godlike in strength. Howso that may be, even as their lord these foul beasts love lies and lust after gold and precious things with a great fierceness of desire, albeit they may not use nor enjoy them.

Thus was it that this *lókë* (for so do the Eldar name the worms of Melko) suffered the Orcs to slay whom they would and to gather whom they listed into a very great and very sorrowful throng of women, maids, and little children, but all the mighty treasure that they had brought from the rocky halls and heaped glistering in the sun before the doors he coveted for himself and forbade them set finger on it, and they durst not withstand him, nor could they have done so an they would.

In that sad band stood Failivrin in horror, and she stretched out

her arms towards Túrin, but Túrin was held by the spell of the
drake, for that beast had a foul magic in his glance, as have many
others of his kind, and he turned the sinews of Túrin as it were to
stone, for his eye held Túrin's eye so that his will died, and he
could not stir of his own purpose, yet might he see and hear.

Then did Glorund taunt Túrin nigh to madness, saying that lo!
he had cast away his sword nor had the heart to strike a blow for his
friends – now Túrin's sword lay at his feet whither it had slipped
from his unnervéd grasp. Great was the agony of Túrin's heart
thereat, and the Orcs laughed at him, and of the captives some
cried bitterly against him. Even now did the Orcs begin to drive
away that host of thralls, and his heart broke at the sight, yet he
moved not; and the pale face of Failivrin faded afar, and her voice
was borne to him crying: "O Túrin Mormakil, where is thy heart;
O my beloved, wherefore dost thou forsake me?" So great then
became Túrin's anguish that even the spell of that worm might not
restrain it, and crying aloud he reached for the sword at his feet
and would wound the drake with it, but the serpent breathed a
foul and heated breath upon him, so that he swooned and thought
that it was death.

A long time thereafter, and the tale telleth not how long,
he came to himself, and he was lying gazing at the sun before
the doors, and his head rested against a heap of gold even as the
ransackers had left it. Then said the drake, who was hard by:
"Wonderest thou not wherefore I have withheld death from thee,
O Túrin Mormakil, who wast once named brave?" Then Túrin
remembered all his griefs and the evil that had fallen upon him,
and he said: "Taunt me not, foul worm, for thou knowest I would
die; and for that alone, methinks, thou slayest me not."

But the drake answered saying: "Know then this, O Túrin son
of Úrin, that a fate of evil is woven about thee, and thou mayst not
untangle thy footsteps from it whitherever thou goest. Yea indeed,
I would not have thee slain, for thus wouldst thou escape very
bitter sorrows and a weird of anguish." Then Túrin leaping
suddenly to his feet and avoiding that beast's baleful eye raised
aloft his sword and cried: "Nay, from this hour shall none name
me Túrin if I live. Behold, I will name me a new name and it shall
be Turambar!" Now this meaneth Conqueror of Fate, and the
form of the name in the Gnome-speech is Turumart. Then uttering
these words he made a second time at the drake, thinking indeed to
force the drake to slay him and to conquer his fate by death, but
the dragon laughed, saying: "Thou fool! An I would, I had slain

thee long since and could do so here and now, and if I will not thou
canst not do battle with me waking, for my eye can cast once more
the binding spell upon thee that thou stand as stone. Nay, get thee
gone, O Turambar Conqueror of Fate! First thou must meet thy
doom an thou wouldst o'ercome it." But Turambar was filled with
shame and anger, and perchance he had slain himself, so great was
his madness, although thus might he not hope that ever his spirit
would be freed from the dark glooms of Mandos or stray into the
pleasant paths of Valinor;[14] but amidst his misery he bethought
him of Failivrin's pallid face and he bowed his head, for the
thought came into his heart to seek back through all the woods
after her sad footsteps even be it to Angamandi and the Hills of
Iron. Maybe in that desperate venture he had found a kindly and
swift death or perchance an ill one, and maybe he had rescued
Failivrin and found happiness, yet not thus was he fated to earn
the name he had taken anew, and the drake reading his mind
suffered him not thus lightly to escape his tide of ill.

"Hearken to me, O son of Úrin," said he; "ever wast thou a
coward at heart, vaunting thyself falsely before men. Perchance
thou thinkest it a gallant deed to go follow after a maiden of strange
kin, recking little of thine own that suffer now terrible things?
Behold, Mavwin who loves thee long has eagerly awaited thy
return, knowing that thou hast found manhood a while ago, and
she looks for thy succour in vain, for little she knows that her son is
an outlaw stained with the blood of his comrades, a defiler of his
lord's table. Ill do men entreat her, and behold the Orcs infest now
those parts of Hithlum, and she is in fear and peril and her
daughter Nienóri thy sister with her."

Then was Turambar aflame with sorrow and with shame for the
lies of that worm were barbed with truth, and for the spell of his
eyes he believed all that was said. Therefore his old desire to see
once more Mavwin his mother and to look upon Nienóri whom he
had never seen since his first days[15] grew hot within him, and with
a heart torn with sorrow for the fate of Failivrin he turned his feet
towards the hills seeking Dor Lómin, and his sword was sheathed.
And truly is it said: "Forsake not for anything thy friends – nor
believe those who counsel thee to do so" – for of his abandoning of
Failivrin in danger that he himself could see came the very direst
evil upon him and all he loved; and indeed his heart was confounded and wavered, and he left those places in uttermost shame
and weariness. But the dragon gloated upon the hoard and lay
coiled upon it, and the fame of that great treasure of golden vessels

and of unwrought gold that lay by the caves above the stream fared far and wide about; yet the great worm slept before it, and evil thoughts he had as he pondered the planting of his cunning lies and the sprouting thereof and their growth and fruit, and fumes of smoke went up from his nostrils as he slept.

On a time therefore long afterward came Turambar with great travail into Hisilómë, and found at length the place of the abode of his mother, even the one whence he had been sundered as a child, but behold, it was roofless and the tilth about it ran wild. Then his heart smote him, but he learned of some that dwelt nigh that lighting on better days the Lady Mavwin had departed some years agone to places not far distant where was a great and prosperous dwelling of men, for that region of Hisilómë was fertile and men tilled the land somewhat and many had flocks and herds, though for the most part in the dark days after the great battle men feared to dwell in settled places and ranged the woods and hunted or fished, and so it was with those kindreds about the waters of Asgon whence after arose Tuor son of Peleg.

Hearing these words however Turambar was amazed, and questioned them concerning the wandering into those regions of Orcs and other fierce folk of Melko, but they shook their heads, and said that never had such creatures come hither deep into the land of Hisilómë.[16] "If thou wishest for Orcs then go to the hills that encompass our land about," said they, "and thou wilt not search long. Scarce may the wariest fare in and out so constant is their watch, and they infest the rocky gates of the land that the Children of Men be penned for ever in the Land of Shadows; but men say 'tis the will of Melko that they trouble us not here – and yet it seems to us that thou hast come from afar, and at this we marvel, for long is it since one from other lands might tread this way." Then Turambar was in perplexity at this and he doubted the deceit of the dragon's words, yet he went now in hope to the dwelling of men and the house of his mother, and coming upon homesteads of men he was easily directed thither. Now men looked strangely at his questioning, and indeed they had reason, yet were such as he spoke to in great awe and wonder at him and shrank back from speech with him, for his garb was of the wild woods and his hair was long and his face haggard and drawn as with unquenchable sorrows, and therein burnt fiercely his dark eyes beneath dark brows. A collar of fine gold he wore and his mighty sword was at his side, and men marvelled much at him;

and did any dare to question him he named himself Turambar son of the weary forest,* and that seemed but the more strange to them.

Now came he to the dwelling of Mavwin, and behold it was a fair house, but none dwelt there, and grass was high in the gardens, and there were no kine in the byres nor horses in the sheds, and the pastures about were silent and empty. Only the swallows had dwelling beneath the timbers of the eaves and these made a noise and a bustle as if departure for autumn was at hand, and Turambar sat before the carven doors and wept. And one who was passing on to other dwellings, for a track passed nigh to that homestead, espied him, and coming asked him his grief, and Turambar said that it was bitter for a son sundered for many years from his home to give up all that was dear and dare the dangers of the infested hills to find only the halls of his kindred empty when he returned at last.

"Nay, then this is a very trick of Melko's," said the other, "for of a truth here dwelt the Lady Mavwin wife of Úrin, and yet is she gone two years past very secretly and suddenly, and men say that she seeks her son who is lost, and that her daughter Nienóri goes with her, but I know not the story. This however I know, and many about here do likewise, and cry shame thereon, for know that the guardianship of all her goods and land she gave to Brodda, a man whom she trusted, and he is lord of these regions by men's consent and has to wife a kinswoman of hers. But now she is long away he has mingled her herds and flocks, small as they were, with his mighty ones, branding them with his own marks, yet the dwelling and stead of Mavwin he suffereth to fall to ruin, and men think ill of it but move not, for the power of Brodda has grown to be great."

Then Turambar begged him to set his feet upon the paths to Brodda's halls, and the man did as he desired, so that Turambar striding thither came upon them just as night fell and men sat to meat in that house. Great was the company that night and the light of many torches fell upon them, but the Lady Airin was not there, for men drank overmuch at Brodda's feasts and their songs were fierce and quarrels blazed about the hall, and those things she loved not. Now Turambar smote upon the gates and his heart was black and a great wrath was in him, for the words of the stranger before his mother's doors were bitter to him.

* A note on the manuscript referring to this name reads: '*Turumart go-Dhrauthodauros* [emended to *bo-Dhrauthodavros*] or *Turambar Rúsitaurion*.'

Then did some open to his knocking and Turambar strode into that hall, and Brodda bade him be seated and ordered wine and meats to be set before him, but Turambar would neither eat nor drink, so that men looking askance upon his sullenness asked him who he might be. Then Turambar stepping out into the midst of them before the high place where Brodda sat said: "Behold, 1 am Turambar son of the forest", and men laughed thereat, but Turambar's eyes were full of wrath. Then said Brodda in doubt: "What wilt thou of me, O son of the wild forest?" But Turambar said: "Lord Brodda, I am come to repay thy stewardship of others' goods," and silence fell in that place; but Brodda laughed, saying again: "But who art thou?" And thereupon Turambar leapt upon the high place and ere Brodda might foresee the act he drew Gurtholfin and seizing Brodda by the locks all but smote his head from off his body, crying aloud: "So dieth the rich man who addeth the widow's little to his much. Lo, men die not all in the wild woods, and am I not in truth the son of Úrin, who having sought back unto his folk findeth an empty hall despoiled." Then was there a great uproar in that hall, and indeed though he was burdened overmuch with his many griefs and wellnigh distraught, yet was this deed of Turambar violent and unlawful. Some were there nonetheless that would not unsheathe their weapons, saying that Brodda was a thief and died as one, but many there were that leapt with swords against Turambar and he was hard put to it, and one man he slew, and it was Orlin. Then came Airin of the long hair in great fear into the halls and at her voice men stayed their hands; but great was her horror when she saw the deeds that were done, and Turambar turned his face away and might not look upon her, for his wrath was grown cold and he was sick and weary.

But she hearing the tale said: "Nay, grieve not for me, son of Úrin, but for thyself; for my lord was a hard lord and cruel and unjust, and men might say somewhat in thy defence, yet behold thou hast slain him now at his board being his guest, and Orlin thou hast slain who is of thy mother's kin; and what shall be thy doom?" At those words some were silent and many shouted "death", but Airin said that it was not wholly in accord with the laws of that place, "for," said she, "Brodda was slain wrongfully, yet just was the wrath of the slayer, and Orlin too did he slay in defence, though it were in the hall of a feast. Yet now I fear that this man must get him swiftly from among us nor ever set foot upon these lands again, else shall any man slay him; but those lands and goods that were Úrin's shall Brodda's kin hold, save only do Mavwin and Nienóri return ever from their wandering, yet even so may Túrin son of Úrin inherit nor part nor parcel of them ever." Now this doom seemed just to all save Turambar, and they marvelled at the equity of Airin whose lord lay slain, and they guessed not at the horror of her life aforetime with that man; but Turambar cast his sword upon the floor and bade them slay him, yet they would not for the words of Airin whom they loved, and Airin suffered it not for the love of Mavwin, hoping yet to join those twain mother and son in happiness, and her doom she had made to satisfy men's anger and save Túrin from death. "Nay," said she, "three days do I give thee to get thee out of the land, wherefore go!" and Turambar lifting his sword wiped it, saying: "Would I were clean of his blood," and he went forth into the night. In the folly of his heart now did he deem himself cut off in truth for ever from Mavwin his mother, thinking that never again would any he loved be fain to look upon him. Then did he thirst for news of his mother and sister and of none might he ask, but wandered back over the hills knowing only that they sought him still perchance in the forests of the Lands Beyond, and no more did he know for a long while.

Of his wanderings thereafter has no tale told, save that after much roaming his sorrow grew dulled and his heart dead, until at last in places very far away many a journey beyond the river of the Rodothlim he fell in with some huntsmen of the woods, and these were Men. Some of that company were thanes of Úrin, or sons of them, and they had wandered darkly ever since that Battle of Tears, but now did Turambar join their number, and built his life anew so well as he might. Now that people had houses in a more smiling region of the woods in lands that were not utterly far from Sirion or the grassy hills of that river's middle course, and they were hardy men and bowed not to Melko, and Turambar got honour among them.

Now is it to tell that far other had matters fallen out with Mavwin than the Foalókë had said to Túrin, for her days turning to better she had peace and honour among the men of those regions. Nonetheless her grief at the loss of her son by reason of the cutting off of all messengers deepened only with the years, albeit Nienóri grew to a most fair and slender maid. At the time of Túrin's flight from the halls of Tinwelint she was already twelve[17] years old and tall and beautiful.

Now the tale tells not the number of days that Turambar

sojourned with the Rodothlim but these were very many, and during that time Nienóri grew to the threshold of womanhood, and often was there speech between her and her mother of Túrin that was lost. In the halls of Tinwelint too the memory of Túrin lived still, and there still abode Gumlin, now decrepit in years, who aforetime had been the guardian of Túrin's childhood upon that first journey to the Lands Beyond. Now was Gumlin white-haired and the years were heavy on him, but he longed sorely for a sight once more of the folk of Men and of the Lady Mavwin his mistress. On a time then Gumlin learnt of the withdrawal from the hills of the greater number of those Orc-bands and other fierce beings of Melko's that had for so long made them impassable to Elves and Men. Now for a space were the hills and the paths that led over them far and wide free of his evil, for Melko had at that time a great and terrible project afoot, and that was the destruction of the Rodothlim and of many dwellings of the Gnomes beside, that his spies had revealed,[18] yet all the folk of those regions breathed the freer for a while, though had they known all perchance they had not done so.

Then Gumlin the aged fell to his knees before Tinwelint and begged that he suffer him to depart homeward, that he might see his mistress of old ere death took him to the halls of Mandos – if indeed that lady had not fared thither before him. Then the king[19] said yea, and for his journey he gave him two guides for the succouring of his age; yet those three, Gumlin and the woodland Elves, made a very hard journey, for it was late winter, and yet would Gumlin by no means abide until spring should come.

Now as they drew nigh to that region of Hisilómë where aforetime Mavwin had dwelt and nigh where she dwelt yet a great snow fell, as happened oft in those parts on days that should rather have been ones of early spring. Therein was Gumlin whelmed, and his guides seeking aid came unawares upon Mavwin's house, and calling for aid of her were granted it. Then by the aid of the folk of Mavwin was Gumlin found and carried to the house and warmed back to life, and coming to himself at length he knew Mavwin and was very joyful.

Now when he was in part healed he told his tale to Mavwin, and as he recounted the years and the doughtiest of the feats of Túrin she was glad, but great was her sorrow and dismay at the tidings of his sundering from Linwë[20] and the manner of it, and going from Gumlin she wept bitterly. Indeed for long and since ever she knew that Túrin, an he lived, had grown to manhood she had wondered that he sought not back to her, and often dread had filled her heart lest attempting this he had perished in the hills; but now the truth was bitter to bear and she was desolate for a great while, nor might Nienóri comfort her.

Now by reason of the unkindness of the weather those guides that had brought Gumlin out of Tinwelint's realms abode as her guests until spring came, but with spring's first coming Gumlin died.

Then arose Mavwin and going to several of the chiefs of those places she besought their aid, telling them the tale of Túrin's fate as Gumlin had told it to her. But some laughed, saying she was deceived by the babblings of a dying man, and the most said that she was distraught with grief, and that it would be a fool's counsel to seek beyond the hills a man who had been lost for years agone: "nor," said they, "will we lend man or horse to such a quest, for all our love for thee, O Mavwin wife of Úrin."

Then Mavwin departed in tears but railed not at them, for she had scant hope in her plea and knew that wisdom was in their words. Nonetheless being unable to rest she came now to those guides of the Elves, who chafed already to be away beneath the sun; and she said to them: "Lead me now to your lord," and they would dissuade her, saying that the road was no road for a woman's feet to tread; yet she did not heed them. Rather did she beg of her friend whose name was Airin Faiglindra* (long-tressed) and was wed to Brodda a lord of that region, and rich and powerful, that Nienóri might be taken under the guardianship of her husband and all her goods thereto. This did Airin obtain of Brodda without great pleading, and when she knew this she would take farewell of her daughter; but her plan availed little, for Nienóri stood before her mother and said: "Either thou goest not, O Mavwin my mother, or go we both," nor would anything turn her from those words. Therefore in the end did both mother and daughter make them ready for that sore journey, and the guides murmured much thereat. Yet it so happened that the season which followed that bitter winter was very kindly, and despite the forebodings of the guides the four passed the hills and made their long journey with no greater evils than hunger and thirst.

Coming therefore at length before Tinwelint Mavwin cast herself down and wept, begging pardon for Túrin and compassion and aid for herself and Nienóri; but Tinwelint bade her arise and

* In the margin is written *Fírilanda*.

seat herself beside Gwedheling his queen, saying: "Long years ago was Túrin thy son forgiven, aye, even as he left these halls, and many a weary search have we made for him. No outlawry of mine was it that took him from this realm, but remorse and bitterness drew him to the wilds, and there, methinks, evil things o'ertook him, or an he lives yet I fear me it is in bondage to the Orcs." Then Mavwin wept again and implored the king to give her aid, for she said: "Yea verily I would fare until the flesh of my feet were worn away, if haply at the journey's end I might see the face of Túrin son of Úrin my well-beloved." But the king said that he knew not whither she might seek her son save in Angamandi, and thither he might not send any of his lieges, not though his heart were full of ruth for the sorrow of Úrin's folk. Indeed Tinwelint spoke but as he believed just, nor meant he to add to Mavwin's sorrow save only to restrain her from so mad and deadly a quest, but Mavwin hearing him spake no word more, and going from him went out into the woods and suffered no one to stay her, and only Nienóri followed her whithersoever she went.

Now the folk of Tinwelint looked with pity on those twain and with kindness, and secretly they watched them, and unbeknown kept much harm from them, so that the wandering ladies of the woods became familiar among them and dear to many, yet were they a sight of ruth, and folk swore hatred to Melko and his works who saw them pass. Thus came it that after many moons Mavwin fell in with a band of wandering Gnomes, and entering into discourse with them the tale was told to her of the Rodothlim, such as those Gnomes knew of it, and of the dwelling of Túrin among them. Of the whelming of that abode of folk by the hosts of Melko and by the dragon Glorund they told too, for those deeds were then new and their fame went far and wide. Now Túrin they named not by name, calling him Mormakil, a wild man who fled from the face of Tinwelint and escaped thereafter from the hands of the Orcs.

Then was the heart of Mavwin filled with hope and she questioned them more, but the Noldoli said that they had not heard that any came alive out of that ransacking save such as were haled to Angamandi, and then again was Mavwin's hope dashed low. Yet did she nonetheless get her back to the king's halls, and telling her tale besought his aid against the Foalókë. Now it was Mavwin's thought that perchance Túrin dwelt yet in the thraldom of the dragon and it might fall to them in some manner to liberate him, or again should the prowess of the king's men suffice then might

they slay the worm in vengeance for his evils, and so at his death
might he speak words of knowledge concerning the fate of Túrin,
were he indeed no longer nigh the caverns of the Rodothlim. Of
the mighty hoard that that worm guarded Mavwin recked little,
but she spake much of it to Tinwelint, even as the Noldoli had
spoken of it to her. Now the folk of Tinwelint were of the woodlands and had scant wealth, yet did they love fair and beauteous
things, gold and silver and gems, as do all the Eldar but the
Noldoli most of all; nor was the king of other mind in this, and his
riches were small, save it be for that glorious Silmaril that many a
king had given all his treasury contained if he might possess it.
   Therefore did Tinwelint answer: "Now shalt thou have aid, O
Mavwin most steadfast, and, openly I say it to thee, it is not for
hope of freeing Túrin thereby that I grant it to thee, for such hope
I do not see in this tale, but rather the death of hope. Yet it is a
truth that I have need and desire of treasury, and it may be that
such shall come to me by this venture; yet half of the spoil shalt
thou have O Mavwin for the memory of Úrin and Túrin, or else
shalt thou ward it for Nienóri thy daughter." Then said Mavwin:
"Nay, give me but a woodman's cot and my son," and the king
answered: "That I cannot, for I am but a king of the wild Elves,
and no Vala of the western isles."
   Then Tinwelint gathered a picked band of his warriors and
hunters and told them his bidding, and it seemed that the name of
the Foalókë was known already among them, and there were many
who could guide the band unto the regions of his dwelling, yet was
that name a terror to the stoutest and the places of his abode a land
of accursed dread. Now the ancient dwellings of the Rodothlim
were not utterly distant from the realm of Tinwelint, albeit far
enough, but the king said to Mavwin: "Bide now and Nienóri also
with me, and my men shall fare against the drake, and all that they
do and find in those places will they faithfully report," – and his
men said: "Yea, we will do thy bidding, O King," but fear stood in
their eyes.
   Then Mavwin seeing it said: "Yea, O King, let Nienóri my
daughter bide indeed at the feet of Gwedheling the Queen, but I
who care not an I die or live will go look upon the dragon and find
my son"; and Tinwelint laughed, yet Gwedheling and Nienóri
fearing that she spake no jest pled earnestly with her. But she was
as adamant, fearing lest this her last hope of rescuing Túrin come
to nought through the terror of Tinwelint's men, and none might
move her. "Of love, I know," said she, "come all the words ye

speak, yet give me rather a horse to ride and if ye will a sharp knife for my own death at need, and let me be gone." Now these words struck amazement into those Elves that heard, for indeed the wives and daughters of Men in those days were hardy and their youth lasted a great span, yet did this seem a madness to all.

Madder yet did it seem when Nienóri, seeing the obstinacy of her mother, said before them all: "Then I too will go; whither my mother Mavwin goeth thither more easily yet shall I, Nienóri daughter of Úrin, fare"; but Gwedheling said to the king that he allow it not, for she was a fay and perchance foresaw dimly what might be.

Then had Mavwin ended the dispute and departed from the king's presence into the woods, had not Nienóri caught at her robe and stayed her, and so did all plead with Mavwin, till at length it was agreed that the king send a strong party against the Foalókë and that Nienóri and Mavwin ride with them until the regions of the beast be found. Then should they seek a high place whence they might see something of the deeds yet in safety and secrecy, while the warriors crept upon the worm to slay it. Now of this high place a woodsman told, and often had he gazed therefrom upon the dwelling of the worm afar. At length was that band of dragon-slayers got ready, and they were mounted upon goodly horses swift and sure-going, albeit few of those beasts were possessed by the folk of the woods. Horses too were found for Nienóri and for Mavwin, and they rode at the head of the warriors, and folk marvelled much to see their bearing, for the men of Úrin and those amongst whom Nienóri was nurtured were much upon horses, and both knave and maid among them rode even in tender years.

After many days' going came now that cavalcade within view of a place that once had been a fair region, and through it a swift river ran over a rocky bed, and of one side was the brink of it high and tree-grown and of the other the land was more level and fertile and broad-swelling, but beyond the high bank of the river the hills drew close. Thither as they looked they saw that the land had become all barren and was blasted for a great distance about the ancient caverns of the Rodothlim, and the trees were crushed to the earth or snapped. Toward the hills a black heath stretched and the lands were scored with the great slots that that loathly worm made in his creeping.

Many are the dragons that Melko has loosed upon the world and some are more mighty than others. Now the least mighty — yet were they very great beside the Men of those days — are cold as is the nature of snakes and serpents, and of them a many having wings go with the uttermost noise and speed; but the mightier are hot and very heavy and slow-going, and some belch flame, and fire flickereth beneath their scales, and the lust and greed and cunning evil of these is the greatest of all creatures: and such was the Foalókë whose burning there set all the places of his habitation in waste and desolation. Already greater far had this worm waxen than in the days of the onslaught upon the Rodothlim, and greater too was his hoarded treasure, for Men and Elves and even Orcs he slew, or enthralled that they served him, bringing him food to slake his lust [?on] precious things, and spoils of their harryings to swell his hoard.

Now was that band aghast as they looked upon that region from afar, yet they prepared them for battle, and drawing lots sent one of their number with Nienóri and Mavwin to that high place[21] upon the confines of the withered land that had been named, and it was covered with trees, and might be reached by hidden paths. Even as those three rode thither and the warriors crept stealthily toward the caves, leaving their horses that were already in a sweat of fear, behold the Foalókë came from his lair, and sliding down the bank lay across the stream, as often was his wont. Straightway great fog and steams leapt up and a stench was mingled therein, so that that band was whelmed in vapours and well-nigh stifled, and they crying to one another in the mist displayed their presence to the worm; and he laughed aloud. At that most awful of all sounds of beasts they fled wildly in the mists, and yet they could not discover their horses, for these in an extremity of terror broke loose and fled.

Then Nienóri hearing far cries and seeing the great mist roll toward them from the river turned back with her mother to the place of sundering, and there alighting waited in great doubt. Suddenly came that blind mist upon them as they stood, and with it came flying madly the dim horses of the huntsmen. Then their own catching their terror trampled to death that Elf who was their escort as he caught at the flying bridles, and wild with fear they sped to the dark woods and never more bore Man or Elf upon their saddles; but Mavwin and Nienóri were left alone and succourless upon the borders of the places of fear. Very perilous indeed was their estate, and long they groped in the mist and knew not where they were nor saw they ever any of the band again, and only pale voices seemed to pass them by afar crying out as in dread, and then all was silent. Now did they cling together and being weary stumbled on heedless whither their steps might go, till on a sudden the sun gleamed thin above them, and hope returned to them; and behold the mists lifted and the airs became clearer and they stood not far from the river. Even now it smoked as it were hot, and behold the Foalókë lay there and his eyes were upon them.

No word did he speak nor did he move, but his baleful eye held their gaze until the strength seemed to leave their knees and their minds grew dim. Then did Nienóri drag herself by a might of will from that influence for a while, and "Behold," she cried, "O serpent of Melko, what wilt thou with us – be swift to say or do, for know that we seek not thee nor thy gold but one Túrin who dwelt here upon a time." Then said the drake, and the earth quaked at him: "Thou liest – glad had ye been at my death, and glad thy band of cravens who now flee gibbering in the woods might they have despoiled me. Fools and liars, liars and cravens, how shall ye slay or despoil Glorund the Foalókë, who ere his power had waxen slew the hosts of the Rodothlim and Orodreth their lord, devouring all his folk."

"Yet perchance," said Nienóri, "one Túrin got him from that fray and dwells still here beneath thy bonds, an he has not escaped thee and is now far hence," and this she said at a venture, hoping against hope, but said the evil one: "Lo! the names of all who dwelt here before the taking of the caves of my wisdom I know, and I say to thee that none who named himself Túrin went hence alive." And even so was Túrin's boast subtly turned against him, for these beasts love ever to speak thus, doubly playing with cunning words.[22]

"Then was Túrin slain in this evil place," said Mavwin, but the dragon answered: "Here did the name of Túrin fade for ever from the earth – but weep not, woman, for it was the name of a craven that betrayed his friends." "Foul beast, cease thy evil sayings," said Mavwin; "slayer of my son, revile not the dead, lest thine own bane come upon thee." "Less proud must be thy words, O Mavwin, an thou wilt escape torment or thy daughter with thee," did that drake answer, but Mavwin cried: "O most accursed, lo! I fear thee not. Take me an thou wilt to thy torments and thy bondage, for of a truth I desired thy death, but suffer only Nienóri my daughter to go back to the dwellings of Men: for she came hither constrained by me, and knowing not the purposes of our journey."

"Seek not to cajole me, woman," sneered that evil one. "Liever would I keep thy daughter and slay thee or send thee back to thy hovels, but I have need of neither of you." With those words he opened full his evil eyes, and a light shone in them, and Mavwin and Nienóri quaked beneath them and a swoon came upon their minds, and them seemed that they groped in endless tunnels of darkness, and there they found not one another ever again, and calling only vain echoes answered and there was no glimmer of light.

When however after a time that she remembered not the blackness left the mind of Nienóri, behold the river and the withered places of the Foalókë were no more about her, but the deep woodlands, and it was dusk. Now she seemed to herself to awake from dreams of horror nor could she recall them, but their dread hung dark behind her mind, and her memory of all past things was dimmed. So for a long while she strayed lost in the woods, and haply the spell alone kept life in her, for she hungered bitterly and was athirst, and by fortune it was summer, for her garments became torn and her feet unshod and weary, and often she wept, and she went she knew not whither.

Now on a time in an opening in the wood she descried a campment as it were of Men, and creeping nigh by reason of hunger to espy it she saw that they were creatures of a squat and unlovely stature that dwelt there, and most evil faces had they, and their voices and their laughter was as the clash of stone and metal. Armed they were with curved swords and bows of horn, and she was possessed with fear as she looked upon them, although she knew not that they were Orcs, for never had she seen those evil ones before. Now did she turn and flee, but was espied, and one let fly a shaft at her that quivered suddenly in a tree beside her as she ran, and others seeing that it was a woman young and fair gave chase whooping and calling hideously. Now Nienóri ran as best she might for the density of the wood, but soon was she spent and capture and dread thraldom was very near, when one came crashing through the woods as though in answer to her lamentable cries.

Wild and black was his hair yet streaked with grey, and his face was pale and marked as with deep sorrows of the past, and in his hand he bare a great sword whereof all but the very edge was black. Therewith he leapt against the following Orcs and hewed them, and they soon fled, being taken aback, and though some shot arrows at random amidst the trees they did little scathe, and five of them were slain.

Then sat Nienóri upon a stone and for weariness and the

lessened strain of fear sobs shook her and she could not speak; but her rescuer stood beside her awhile and marvelled at her fairness and that she wandered thus lonely in the woods, and at length he said: "O sweet maiden of the woods, whence comest thou, and what may be thy name?"

"Nay, these things I know not," said she. "Yet methinks I stray very far from my home and folk, and many very evil things have fallen upon me in the way, whereof nought but a cloud hangs upon my memory – nay, whence I am or whither I go I know not" – and she wept afresh, but that man spake, saying: "Then behold, I will call thee Níniel, or little one of tears," and thereat she raised her face towards his, and it was very sweet though marred with weeping, and she said with a look of wonderment: "Nay, not Níniel, not Níniel." Yet more might she not remember, and her face filled with distress, so that she cried: "Nay, who art thou, warrior of the woods; why troublest thou me?" "Turambar am I called," said he, "and no home nor kindred have I nor any past to think on, but I wander for ever," and again at that name that maiden's wonder stirred.

"Now," said Turambar, "dry thy tears, O Níniel, for thou hast come upon such safety as these woods afford. Lo, one am I now of a small folk of the forest, and a sweet dwelling in a clearing have we far from hence, but today as thy fortune would we fared a-hunting, – aye, and Orc-harrying too, for we are hard put to it to fend those evil ones from our homes."

Then did Níniel (for thus Turambar called her ever, and she learnt to call it her name) fare away with him to his comrades, and they asking little got them upon horses, and Turambar set Níniel before him, and thus they fared as swift as they might from the danger of the Orcs.

Now at the time of the affray of Turambar with the pursuing Orcs was half the day already spent, yet were they already leagues upon their way ere they dismounted once more, and it was then early night. Already at the sunset had it seemed to Níniel that the woods were lighter and less gloomy and the air less evil-laden than behind. Now did they make a camp in a glade and the stars shone clear above where the tree-roof was thin, but Níniel lay a little apart and they gave her many fells to keep her from the night chills, and thus she slept more softly than for many a night and the breezes kissed her face, but Turambar told his comrades of the meeting in the wood and they wondered who she might be or how she came wandering thither as one under a spell of blind forgetfulness.

Next day again they pressed on and so for many journeys more beside until at length weary and fain for rest they came one noon to a woodland stream, and this they followed for some way until, behold, they came to a place where it might be forded by reason of its shallowness and of the rocks that stood up in its course; but on their right it dived in a great fall and fell into a chasm, and Turambar pointing said: "Now are we nigh to home, for this is the fall of the Silver Bowl," but Níniel not knowing why was filled with a dread and could not look upon the loveliness of that foaming water. Now soon came they to places of thinner trees and to a slope whereon but few grew save here and there an ancient oak of great girth, and the grass about their feet was soft, for the clearing had been made many years and was very wide. There stood also a cluster of goodly houses of timber, and a tilth was about them and trees of fruit. To one of these houses that was adorned with strange rude carvings, and flowers bloomed bright about it, did Turambar lead now Níniel. "Behold," said he, "my abode—there an thou listest thou shalt abide for now, but methinks it is a lonely hall, and there be houses of this folk beside where there are maidens and womenfolk, and there wouldst thou liever and better be." So came it afterward that Nienóri dwelt with the wood-rangers,* and after a while entered the house of Bethos, a stout man who had fought though then but a boy in the Battle of Unnumbered Tears. Thence did he escape, but his wife was a Noldo-maiden, as the tale telleth, and very fair, and fair also were his sons and daughters save only his eldest son Tamar Lamefoot.

Now as the days passed Turambar grew to love Níniel very greatly indeed, and all the folk beside loved her for her great loveliness and sweetness, yet was she ever half-sorrowful and often distraught of mind, as one that seeks for something mislaid that soon she must discover, so that folk said: "Would that the Valar would lift the spell that lies upon Níniel." Nonetheless for the most part she was happy indeed among the folk and in the house of Bethos, and each day she grew ever fairer, and Tamar Lamefoot who was held of little account loved her though in vain.

Now came days when life once more seemed to contain joy to Turambar, and the bitterness of the past grew dim and far away, and a fresh love was in his heart. Then did he think to put his fate

---

* In the margin, apparently with reference to the word 'wood-rangers', is written *Vettar*.

for ever from him and live out his life there in the woodland homes with children about him, and looking upon Níniel he desired to wed her. Then did he often press his suit with her, yet though he was a man of valiance and renown she delayed him, saying nor yea nor no, yet herself she knew not why, for it seemed to her heart that she loved him deeply, fearing for him were he away, and knowing happiness when he was nigh.

Now it was a custom of that folk to obey a chief, and he was chosen by them from their stoutest men, and that office did he hold until of his own will he laid it down again being sick or gone in years, or were he slain. And at that time Bethos was their chief; but he was slain by evil luck in a foray not long after – for despite his years he still rode abroad – and it fell out that a new captain must be chosen. In the end then did they name Turambar, for his lineage, in that it was known among them that he was son of Úrin, was held in esteem among those stout rebels against Melko, whereas[23] he had beside become a very mighty man in all deeds and one of wisdom great beyond his years, by reason of his far wanderings and his dealings with the Elves.

Seeing therefore the love of their new chief for Níniel and thinking they knew that she loved him also in return, those men began to say how they would lief see their lord wed, and that it was folly to delay for no good cause; but this word came to the ears of Níniel, and at length she consented to be the wife of Turambar, and all were fain thereat. A goodly feast was made and there was song and mirth, and Níniel became lady of the woodland-rangers and dwelt thereafter in Turambar's house. There great was their happiness, though there lay at times a chill foreboding upon Níniel's heart, but Turambar was in joy and said in his heart: "'Twas well that I did name myself Turambar, for lo! I have overcome the doom of evil that was woven about my feet." The past he laid aside and to Níniel he spoke not overmuch of bygone things, save of his father and mother and the sister he had not seen, but always was Níniel troubled at such talk and he knew not why.[24] But of his flight from the halls of Tinwelint and the death of Beleg and of his seeking back to Hisilómë he said never a word, and the thought of Failivrin lay locked in his deepest heart wellnigh forgotten.

Naught ever might Níniel tell him of her days before, and did he ask her distress was written on her face as though he troubled the surface of dark dreams, and he grieved at times thereat, but it weighed not much upon him.

Now fare the days by and Níniel and Turambar dwell in peace, but Tamar Lamefoot wanders the woods thinking the world an ill and bitter place, and he loved Níniel very greatly nor might he stifle his love. But behold, in those days the Foalókë waxed fat, and having many bands of Noldoli and of Orcs subject to him he thought to extend his dominion far and wide. Indeed in many places in those days these beasts of Melko's did in like manner, setting up kingdoms of terror of their own that flourished beneath the evil mantle of Melko's lordship. So it was that the bands of Glorund the drake harried the folk of Tinwelint very grievously, and at length there came some nigh even to those woods and glades that were beloved of Turambar and his folk.

Now those woodmen fled not but dealt stoutly with their foes, and the wrath of Glorund the worm was very great when tidings were brought to him of a brave folk of Men that dwelt far beyond the river and that his marauders might not subdue them. It is told indeed that despite the cunning of his evil designs he did not yet know where was the dwelling of Turambar or of Nienóri; and of truth in those days it seemed that fortune smiled on Turambar awhile, for his people waxed and they became prosperous, and many escaped even from uttermost Hisilómë and came unto him, and store of wealth and good things he gathered, for all his battles brought him victory and booty. Like a king and queen did Turambar and Níniel become, and there was song and mirth in those glades of their dwelling, and much happiness in their halls. And Níniel conceived.[25]

Much of this did spies report to the Foalókë, and his wrath was terrible. Moreover his greed was mightily kindled, so that after pondering much he set a guard that he might trust to watch his dwelling and his treasury, and the captain of these was Mîm the dwarf.[26] Then leaving the caves and the places of his sleep he crossed the streams and drew into the woods, and they blazed before his face. Tidings of this came swiftly to Turambar, but he feared not as yet nor indeed heeded the tale much, for it was a very great way from the home of the woodmen to the caverns of the worm. But now sank Níniel's heart, and though she knew not wherefore a weight of dread and sorrow lay upon her, and seldom after the coming of that word did she smile, so that Turambar wondered and was sad.

Now draweth the Foalókë during that time through the deep woods and a path of desolation lies behind, and yet in his creeping a very great while passes, until, behold, suddenly a party of the woodmen come upon him unawares sleeping in the woods among the broken trees. Of these several were overcome by the noxious breath of the beast and after were slain; but two making their utmost speed brought tidings to their lord that the tale aforetime had not been vain, and indeed now was the drake crept even within the confines of his realm; and so saying they fell fainting before his feet.

Now the place where the dragon lay was low-lying and a little hill there was, not far distant, islanded among the trees but itself not much wooded, whence might be espied albeit afar off much of that region now torn by the passage of the drake. A stream there was too that ran through the forest in that part between the drake and the dwellings of the woodmen, but its course ran very nigh to the dragon and it was a narrow stream with banks deep-cloven and o'erhung with trees. Wherefore Turambar purposed now to take his stoutest men to that knoll and watch if they could the dragon's movements in secret, that perchance they might fall upon him at some disadvantage and contrive to slay him, for in this lay their best hope. This band he suffered not to be very great, and the rest at his bidding took arms and scoured about, fearing that hosts of the Orcs were come with the worm their lord. This indeed was not so, and he came alone trusting in his overwhelming power.

Now when Turambar made ready to depart then Níniel begged to ride beside him and he consented, for he loved her and it was his thought that if he fell and the drake lived then might none of that people be saved, and he would liever have Níniel by him, hoping perchance to snatch her at the least from the clutches of the worm, by death at his own or one of his liege's hands.

So rode forth together Turambar and Níniel, as that folk knew them, and behind were a score of good men. Now the distance to that knoll among the woods they compassed in a day's journey, and after them though it were against the bidding and counsel of Turambar there stole a great concourse of his folk, even women and children. The lure of a strange dread held them, and some thought to see a great fight, and others went with the rest thinking little, nor did any think to see what in the end their eyes saw; and they followed not far behind, for Turambar's party went slowly and warily. When first then Turambar suffered her to ride beside him Níniel was blither than for long she had been, and she brightened the foreboding of those men's hearts; but soon they came to a place not far from the foot of the knoll, and there her heart sank, and indeed a gloom fell upon all.

Yet very fair was that place, for here flowed that same stream that further down wound past the dragon's lair in a deep bed cloven deep into the earth; and it came rushing cold from the hills beyond the woodmen's homes, and it fell over a great fall where the water-worn rock jutted smooth and grey from amid the grass. Now this was the head of that force which the woodmen named the Silver Bowl, and aforetime Turambar and Níniel had passed it by, faring home first from the rescuing of Níniel. The height of that fall was very great and the waters had a loud and musical voice, splashing into a silver foam far below where they had worn a great hollow in the rocks; and this hollow was o'ershadowed by trees and bushes, but the sun gleamed through upon the spray; and about the head of the fall there was an open glade and a green sward where grew a wealth of flowers, and men loved that spot.

Here did Níniel of a sudden weep, and casting herself upon Turambar begged him tempt not fate but rather fly with her and all his folk, leading them into distant lands. But looking at her he said: "Nay, Níniel mine, nor thou nor I die this day, nor yet tomorrow, by the evil of the dragon or by the foemen's swords," but he knew not the fulfilment of his words; and hearing them Níniel quelled her weeping and was very still. Having therefore rested a while here those warriors afterward climbed the hill and Níniel fared with them. Afar off they might see from its summit a wide tract where all the trees were broken and the lands were hurt[27] and scorched and the earth black, yet nigh the edge of the trees that were still unharmed, and that was not far from the lip of the deep river-chasm, there arose a thin smoke of great blackness, and men said: "There lieth the worm."

Then were counsels of many a kind spoken upon that hill-top, and men feared to go openly against the dragon by day or by night or whether he waked or slept, and seeing their dread Turambar gave them a rede, and it was taken, and these were his words: "Well have ye said, O huntsmen of the woods, that not by day or by night shall men hope to take a dragon of Melko unawares, and behold this one hath made a waste about him, and the earth is beaten flat so that none may creep near and be hidden. Wherefore whoso hath the heart shall come with me and we will go down the rocks to the foot of the fall, and so gaining the path of the stream perchance we may come as nigh to the drake as may be. Then must we climb if we are able up under the near bank and so wait, for methinks the Foalókë will rest not much longer ere he draweth on towards our dwellings. Thus must he either cross this deep stream or turn far out of his ways, for he is grown too mighty to creep along its bed. Now I think not that he will turn aside, for it is but a ditch, a narrow rut filled with trickling water, to the great Foalókë of the golden caves. If however he belie my counsel and come not on by this path, some few of you must take courage in your hearts, striving to decoy him warily back across the stream, that there we who lie hid may give him his bane stabbing from beneath, for the armour of these vile worms is of little worth upon their bellies."

Now of that band were there but six that stood forward readily to go with Turambar, and he seeing that said that he had thought there were more than six brave men among his folk, yet after that he would not suffer any of the others to go with him, saying that better were the six without the hindrance of the fearful. Then did Turambar take farewell of Níniel and they kissed upon the hilltop, and it was then late afternoon, but Níniel's heart went as to stone with grief; and all that company descended to the head of Silver Bowl, and there she beheld her lord climb to the fall's bottom with his six companions. Now when he was vanished far below she spake bitterly to those who had dared not to go, and they for shame answered not but crept back unto the hill-top and gazed out towards the dragon's lair, and Níniel sat beside the water looking before her, and she wept not but was in anguish.

None stayed beside her save Tamar alone who had fared unbidden with that company, and he had loved her since first she dwelt in Bethos' halls, and once had thought to win her ere Turambar took her. The lameness of Tamar was with him from childhood, yet was he both wise and kindly, though held of little account among those folk, to whom strength was safety and valour the greatest pride of men. Now however did Tamar bear a sword, and many had scoffed at him for that, yet he took joy at the chance of guarding Níniel, albeit she noticed him not.

Now is it to tell that Turambar reached the place of his design after great labour in the rocky bed of the stream, and with his men clambered with difficulty up the steep side of that ravine. Just below the lip of it they were lodged in certain overhanging trees, and not far off they might hear the great breathing of the beast, and some of his companions fell in dread.

Already had darkness come and all the night they clung there, and there was a strange flickering where the dragon lay and dread noises and a quaking if he stirred, and when dawn came Turambar saw that he had but three companions, and he cursed the others for their cravenhood, nor doth any tale tell whither those unfaithful ones fled. On this day did all come to pass as Turambar had thought, for the drake bestirring himself drew slowly to the chasm's edge and turned not aside, but sought to overcreep it and come thus at the homes of the woodmen. Now the terror of his oncoming was very great, for the earth shook, and those three feared lest the trees that upheld them should loosen their roots and fall into the rocky stream below. The leaves too of those trees that grew nigh were shrivelled in the serpent's breath, yet were they not hurt because of the shelter of the bank.

At length did the drake reach the stream-edge and the sight of his evil head and dripping jaws was utterly hideous, and these they saw clearly and were in terror lest he too espy them, for he crossed not over at the spot where Turambar had chosen to lie hid because of the narrowness here of the chasm and its lesser depth. Rather he began to heave himself now across the ravine a little below them, and so slipping from their places Turambar and his men reached as swiftly as might be the stream's bed and came beneath the belly of the worm. Here was the heat so great and so vile the stench that his men were taken with a sore dread and durst not climb the bank again. Then in his wrath Turambar would have turned his sword against them, but they fled, and so was it that alone he scaled the wall until he came close beneath the dragon's body, and he reeled by reason of the heat and of the stench and clung to a stout bush.

Then abiding until a very vital and unfended spot was within stroke, he heaved up Gurtholfin his black sword and stabbed with all his strength above his head, and that magic blade of the Rodothlim went into the vitals of the dragon even to the hilt, and the yell of his death-pain rent the woods and all that heard it were aghast.

Then did that drake writhe horribly and the huge spires of his contortions were terrible to see, and all the trees he brake that stood nigh to the place of his agony. Almost had he crossed the chasm when Gurtholfin pierced him, and now he cast himself upon its farther bank and laid all waste about him, and lashed and coiled and made a yelling and a bellowing such that the stoutest blenched and turned to flee. Now those afar thought that this was the fearsome noise of battle betwixt the seven, Turambar and his comrades,[28] and little they hoped ever to see any of them return, and Níniel's heart died within her at the sounds; but below in the ravine those three cravens who had watched Turambar from afar fled now in terrror back towards the fall, and Turambar clung nigh to the lip of the chasm white and trembling, for he was spent.

At length did those noises of horror cease, and there arose a great smoking, for Glorund was dying. Then in utter hardihood did Turambar creep out alone from his hiding, for in the agony of the Foalókë his sword was dragged from his hand ere he might withdraw it, and he cherished Gurtholfin beyond all his possessions, for all things died, or man or beast, whom once its edges bit. Now Turambar saw where the dragon lay, and he was stretched out stiff upon his side, and Gurtholfin stood yet in his belly; but he breathed still.

Nonetheless Turambar creeping up set his foot upon his body and withdrew Gurtholfin hardly with all his strength, and as he did so he said in the triumph of his heart: "Now do we meet again, O Glorund, thou and I, Turambar, who was once named brave";[29] but even as he spake the evil blood spouted from that wound upon his hand and burnt it, and it was withered, so that for the sudden pain he cried aloud. Then the Foalókë opening his dread eyes looked upon him, and he fell in a swoon beside the drake and his sword was under him.

Thus did the day draw on and there came no tidings to the hill-top, nor could Níniel longer bear her anguish but arose and made as to leave that glade above the waterfall, and Tamar Lamefoot said: "What dost thou seek to do?" but she: "I would seek my lord and lay me in death beside him, for methinks he is dead", and he sought to dissuade her but without avail. And even as evening fell that fair lady crept through the woods and she would not that Tamar should follow her, but seeing that he did so she fled blindly through the trees, tearing her clothes and marring her face in places of thorny undergrowth, and Tamar being lame could not keep up with her. So fell night upon the woods and all was still, and a great dread for Níniel fell upon Tamar, so that he cursed his weakness and his heart was bitter, yet did he cease not to follow so swiftly as he might, and losing sight of her he bent his course towards that part of the forest nigh to the ravine where had been fought the worm's last fight, for indeed that might be perceived by the watchers on the hill. Now rose a bright moon when the night was old, and Tamar, wandering often alone far and wide from the woodmen's homes, knew those places, and came at last to the edge of that desolation that the dragon had made in his agony; but the moonlight was very bright, and staying among the bushes near the edge of that place Tamar heard and saw all that there betid.

Behold now Níniel had reached those places not long before

him, and straightway did she run fearless into the open for love of
her lord, and so found him lying with his withered hand in a swoon
across his sword; but the beast that lay hugely stretched beside she
heeded not at all, and falling beside Turambar she wept, and
kissed his face, and put salve upon his hand, for such she had
brought in a little box when first they sallied forth, fearing that
many hurts would be gotten ere men wended home.

Yet Turambar woke not at her touch, nor stirred, and she cried
aloud, thinking him now surely dead: "O Turambar, my lord,
awake, for the serpent of wrath is dead and I alone am near!" But
lo! at those words the drake stirred his last, and turning his baleful
eyes upon her ere he shut them for ever said: "O thou Nienóri
daughter of Mavwin, I give thee joy that thou hast found thy
brother at the last, for the search hath been weary – and now is he
become a very mighty fellow and a stabber of his foes unseen"; but
Nienóri sat as one stunned, and with that Glorund died, and with
his death the veil of his spells fell from her, and all her memory
grew crystal clear, neither did she forget any of those things that had
befallen her since first she fell beneath the magic of the worm; so
that her form shook with horror and anguish. Then did she start to
her feet, standing wanly in the moon, and looking upon Turambar
with wide eyes thus spake she aloud: "Then is thy doom spent at
last. Well art thou dead, O most unhappy," but distraught with
her woe suddenly she fled from that place and fared wildly away as
one mad whithersoever her feet led her.

But Tamar whose heart was numbed with grief and ruth followed
as he might, recking little of Turambar, for wrath at the fate of
Nienóri filled all his heart. Now the stream and the deep chasm lay
across her path, but it so chanced that she turned aside ere she
came to its banks and followed its winding course through stony
and thorny places until she came once again to the glade at the
head of the great roaring fall, and it was empty as the first grey
light of a new day filtered through the trees.

There did she stay her feet and standing spake as to herself: "O
waters of the forest whither do ye go? Wilt thou take Nienóri,
Nienóri daughter of Úrin, child of woe? O ye white foams, would
that ye might lave me clean – but deep, deep must be the waters
that would wash my memory of this nameless curse. O bear me
hence, far far away, where are the waters of the unremembering
sea. O waters of the forest whither do ye go?" Then ceasing
suddenly she cast herself over the fall's brink, and perished where
it foams about the rocks below; but at that moment the sun arose

above the trees and light fell upon the waters, and the waters roared unheeding above the death of Nienóri.

Now all this did Tamar behold, and to him the light of the new sun seemed dark, but turning from those places he went to the hill-top and there was already gathered a great concourse of folk, and among them were those three that had last deserted Turambar, and they made a story for the ears of the folk. But Tamar coming stood suddenly before them, and his face was terrible to see, so that a whisper ran among them: "He is dead"; but others said: "What then has befallen the little Níniel?" – but Tamar cried aloud: "Hear, O my people, and say if there is a fate like unto the one I tell unto thee, or a woe so heavy. Dead is the drake, but at his side lieth also Turambar dead, even he who was first called Túrin son of Úrin,[30] and that is well; aye very well," and folk murmured, wondering at his speech, and some said that he was mad. But Tamar said: "For know, O people, that Níniel the fair beloved of you all and whom I love dearer than my heart is dead, and the waters roar above her, for she has leapt o'er the falls of Silver Bowl desiring never more to see the light of day. Now endeth all that evil spell, now is the doom of the folk of Úrin terribly fulfilled, for she that ye called Níniel was even Nienóri daughter of Úrin, and this did she know or ever she died, and this did she tell to the wild woods, and their echo came to me."

At those words did the hearts of all who stood there break for sorrow and for dread, yet did none dare to go to the place of the anguish of that fair lady, for a sad spirit abideth there yet and none sets foot upon its sward; but a great remorse pierced the hearts of those three cravens, and creeping from the throng they went to seek their lord's body, and behold they found him stirring and alive, for when the dragon died the swoon had left him, and he slept a deep sleep of weariness, yet now was he awakening and was in pain. Even as those three stood by he spake and said "Níniel", and at that word they hid their faces for ruth and horror, and could not look upon his face, but afterward they roused him, and behold he was very fain of his victory; yet suddenly marking his hand he said: "Lo! one has been that has tended my hurt with skill – who think ye that it was?" – but they answered him not, for they guessed. Now therefore was Turambar borne weary and hurt back among his folk, and one sped before and cried that their lord lived, but men knew not if they were glad; and as he came among them many turned aside their faces to hide their hearts' perplexity and their tears, and none durst speak.

But Turambar said to those that stood nigh: "Where is Níniel, my Níniel – for I had thought to find her here in gladness – yet if she has returned rather to my halls then is it well", but those that heard could no longer restrain their weeping, and Turambar rose crying: "What new ill is this – speak, speak, my people, and torment me not!" But one said: "Níniel alas is dead my lord," but Turambar cried out bitterly against the Valar and his fate of woe, and at last another said: "Aye, she is dead, for she fell even into the depths of Silver Bowl," but Tamar who stood by muttered:"Nay, she cast herself thither." Then Turambar catching those words seized him by the arm and cried: "Speak, thou club-foot, speak, say what meaneth thy foul speech, or thou shalt lose thy tongue," for his misery was terrible to see.

Now was Tamar's heart in a great turmoil of pain for the dread things that he had seen and heard, and the long hopelessness of his love for Níniel, so did rage against Turambar kindle suddenly within him, and shaking off his touch he said: "A maid thou foundest in the wild woods and gave her a jesting name, that thou and all the folk called her Níniel, the little one of tears. Ill was that jest, Turambar, for lo! she has cast herself away blind with horror and with woe, desiring never to see thee again, and the name she named herself in death was Nienóri daughter of Úrin, child of woe, nor may all the waters of the Silver Bowl as they drop into the deep shed the full tale of tears o'er Níniel."

Then Turambar with a roar took his throat and shook him, saying: "Thou liest – thou evil son of Bethos" – but Tamar gasped "Nay, accursed one; so spake Glorund the drake, and Níniel hearing knew that it was true." But Turambar said: "Then go commune in Mandos with thy Glorund," and he slew him before the face of the people, and fared after as one mad, shouting "He lieth, he lieth"; and yet being free now of blindness and of dreams in his deep heart he knew that it was true and that now his weird was spent at last.

So did he leave the folk behind and drive heedless through the woods calling ever the name of Níniel, till the woods rang most dismally with that word, and his going led him by circuitous ways ever to the glade of Silver Bowl, and none had dared to follow him. There shone the sun of afternoon, and lo, were all the trees grown sere although it was high summer still, and noise there was as of dying autumn in the leaves. Withered were all the flowers and the grass, and the voice of the falling water was sadder than tears for the death of the white maiden Nienóri daughter of Úrin that there had been. There stood Turambar spent at last, and there he drew his sword, and said: "Hail, Gurtholfin, wand of death, for thou art all men's bane and all men's lives fain wouldst thou drink, knowing no lord or faith save the hand that wields thee if it be strong. Thee only have I now – slay me therefore and be swift, for life is a curse, and all my days are creeping foul, and all my deeds are vile, and all I love is dead." And Gurtholfin said: "That will I gladly do, for blood is blood, and perchance thine is not less sweet than many a one's that thou hast given me ere now"; and Turambar cast himself then upon the point of Gurtholfin, and the dark blade took his life.

But later some came timidly and bore him away and laid him in a place nigh, and raised a great mound over him, and thereafter some drew a great rock there with a smooth face, and on it were cut strange signs such as Turambar himself had taught them in dead days, bringing that knowledge from the caves of the Rodothlim, and that writing said:

> Turambar slayer of Glorund the Worm
> who also was Túrin Mormakil
> Son of Úrin of the Woods

and beneath that was carven the word "Níniel" (or child of tears); but she was not there, nor where the waters have laid her fair form doth any man know.'

Now thereupon did Eltas cease his speaking, and suddenly all who hearkened wept; but he said thereto: 'Yea, 'tis an unhappy tale, for sorrow hath fared ever abroad among Men and doth so still, but in the wild days were very terrible things done and suffered; and yet hath Melko seldom devised more cruelty, nor do I know a tale that is more pitiful.'

Then after a time some questioned him concerning Mavwin and Úrin and after happenings, and he said: 'Now of Mavwin hath no sure record been preserved like unto the tale of Túrin Turambar her son, and many things are said and some of them differ from one another; but this much can I tell to ye, that after those dread deeds the woodfolk had no heart for their abiding place and departed to other valleys of the wood, and yet did a few linger sadly nigh their old homes; and once came an aged dame wandering through the woods, and she chanced upon that carven rock. To her did one of those woodmen read the meaning of the signs, and he told her all the tale as he remembered it – but she was silent, and nor spoke nor moved. Then said he: "Thy heart is heavy, for it is a tale to move all men to tears." But she said: "Ay, sad indeed is my heart, for I am Mavwin, mother of those twain," and that man perceived that not yet had that long tale of sorrow reached its ending – but Mavwin arose and went out into the woods crying in anguish, and for long time she haunted that spot so that the woodman and his folk fled and came never back, and none may say whether indeed it was Mavwin that came there or her dark shade that sought not back to Mandos by reason of her great unhappiness.[31]

Yet it is said that all these dread happenings Úrin saw by the magic of Melko, and was continually tempted by that Ainu to yield to his will, and he would not; but when the doom of his folk was utterly fulfilled then did Melko think to use Úrin in another and more subtle way, and he released him from that high and bitter place where he had sat through many years in torment of heart. But Melko went to him and spoke evilly of the Elves to him, and especially did he accuse Tinwelint[32] of weakness and cravenhood. "Never can I comprehend," said he, "wherefore it is that there be still great and wise Men who trust to the friendship of the Elves, and becoming fools enough to resist my might do treble their folly in looking for sure help therein from Gnomes or Fairies. Lo, O Úrin, but for the faint heart of Tinwelint of the woodland how could my designs have come to pass, and perchance now had Nienóri lived and Mavwin thy wife had wept not, being glad for the recovery of her son. Go therefore, O foolish one, and return to eat the bitter bread of almsgiving in the halls of thy fair friends."

Then did Úrin bowed with years and sorrow depart unmolested from Melko's realms and came unto the better lands, but ever as he went he pondered Melko's saying and the cunning web of woven truth and falsity clouded his heart's eye, and he was very bitter in spirit. Now therefore he gathered to him a band of wild Elves,[33] and they were waxen a fierce and lawless folk that dwelt not with their kin, who thrust them into the hills to live or die as they might. On a time therefore Úrin led them to the caves of the Rodothlim, and behold the Orcs had fled therefrom at the death of Glorund, and one only dwelt there still, an old misshapen dwarf who sat ever on the pile of gold singing black songs of enchantment to himself. But none had come nigh till then to despoil him, for the terror of the drake lived longer than he, and none had ventured thither again for dread of the very spirit of Glorund the worm.[34] Now therefore when those Elves approached the dwarf stood before the doors of the cave that was once the abode of Galweg, and he cried: "What will ye with me, O outlaws of the hills?" But Úrin answered: "We come to take what is not thine." Then said that dwarf, and his name was Mîm: "O Úrin, little did I think to see thee, a lord of Men, with such a rabble. Hearken now to the words of Mîm the fatherless, and depart, touching not this gold no more than were it venomous fires. For has not Glorund lain long years upon it, and the evil of the drakes of Melko is on it, and no good can it bring to Man or Elf, but I, only I, can ward it, Mîm the dwarf, and by many a dark spell have I bound it to myself." Then Úrin wavered, but his men were wroth at that, so that he bid them seize it all, and Mîm stood by and watched, and he broke forth into terrible and evil curses. Thereat did Úrin smite him, saying: "We came but to take what was not thine – now for thy evil words we will take what is thine as well, even thy life."

But Mîm dying said unto Úrin: "Now Elves and Men shall rue this deed, and because of the death of Mîm the dwarf shall death follow this gold so long as it remain on Earth, and a like fate shall every part and portion share with the whole." And Úrin shuddered, but his folk laughed.

Now Úrin caused his followers to bear this gold to the halls of Tinwelint, and they murmured at that, but he said: "Are ye become as the drakes of Melko, that would lie and wallow in gold and seek no other joy? A sweeter life shall ye have in the court of that king of greed, an ye bear such treasury to him, than all the gold of Valinor can get you in the empty woods."

Now his heart was bitter against Tinwelint, and he desired to have a vengeance on him, as may be seen. So great was that hoard that great though Úrin's company might be scarce could they bear it to the caves of Tinwelint the king, and some 'tis said was left behind and some was lost upon the way, and evil has followed its finders for ever.

Yet in the end that laden host came to the bridge before the doors, and being asked by the guards Úrin said: "Say to the king that Úrin the Steadfast is come bearing gifts," and this was done. Then Úrin let bear all that magnificence before the king, but it was hidden in sacks or shut in boxes of rough wood; and Tinwelint greeted Úrin with joy and with amaze and bid him thrice welcome, and he and all his court arose in honour of that lord of Men; but Úrin's heart was blind by reason of his tormented years and of the lies of Melko, and he said: "Nay, O King, I do not desire to hear such words – but say only, where is Mavwin my wife, and knowest thou what death did Nienóri my daughter die?" And Tinwelint said that he knew not.

Then did Úrin fiercely tell that tale, and the king and all his folk about him hid their faces for great ruth, but Úrin said: "Nay,[35] had you such a heart as have the least of Men, never would they have been lost; but lo, I bring you now a payment in full for the troubles of your puny band that went against Glorund the drake, and deserting gave up my dear ones to his power. Gaze, O Tinwelint, sweetly on my gifts, for methinks the lustre of gold is all your heart contains."

Then did men cast down that treasury at the king's feet, uncovering it so that all that court were dazzled and amazed – but Úrin's men understood now what was forward and were little pleased. "Behold the hoard of Glorund," said Úrin, "bought by the death of Nienóri with the blood of Túrin slayer of the worm. Take it, O craven king, and be glad that some Men be brave to win thee riches."

Then were Úrin's words more than Tinwelint could endure, and he said: "What meanest thou, child of Men, and wherefore upbraidest thou me?[36] Long did I foster thy son and forgave him the evil of his deeds, and afterward thy wife I succoured, giving way against my counsel to her wild desires. Melko it is that hates thee and not I. Yet what is it to me – and wherefore dost thou of the uncouth race of Men endure to upbraid a king of the Eldalië? Lo! in Palisor my life began years uncounted before the first of Men awoke. Get thee gone, O Úrin, for Melko hath bewitched thee, and take thy riches with thee" – but he forebore to slay or to bind Úrin in spells, remembering his ancient valiance in the Eldar's cause.

Then Úrin departed, but would not touch the gold, and stricken in years he reached Hisilómë and died among Men, but his words living after him bred estrangement between Elves and Men. Yet it is said that when he was dead his shade fared into the woods seeking Mavwin, and long those twain haunted the woods about the fall of Silver Bowl bewailing their children. But the Elves of Kôr have told, and they know, that at last Úrin and Mavwin fared to Mandos, and Nienóri was not there nor Túrin their son. Turambar indeed had followed Nienóri along the black pathways to the doors of Fui, but Fui would not open to them, neither would Vefántur. Yet now the prayers of Úrin and Mavwin came even to Manwë, and the Gods had mercy on their unhappy fate, so that those twain Túrin and Nienóri entered into Fôs'Almir, the bath of flame, even as Urwendi and her maidens had done in ages past before the first rising of the Sun, and so were all their sorrows and stains washed away, and they dwelt as shining Valar among the blessed ones, and now the love of that brother and sister is very fair; but Turambar indeed shall stand beside Fionwë in the Great Wrack, and Melko and his drakes shall curse the sword of Mormakil.'

And so saying Eltas made an end, and none asked further.

## NOTES

1 The passage was rejected before the change of *Tintoglin* to *Tinwelint*; see p. 69.

2 Above the name *Egnor* is written 'Damrod the Gnome'; see Commentary, pp. 139–40.

3 Here and immediately below the name as first written was *Tinthellon*; this rider must belong to the same time as the note on the MS directing that *Tintoglin* be changed to *Ellon* or *Tinthellon* (p. 69). See note 32.

4 Associated with this replacement is a note on the manuscript reading: 'If Beren be a Gnome (as now in the story of Tinúviel) the references to Beren must be altered.' In the rejected passage Egnor father of Beren 'was akin to Mavwin', i.e. Egnor was a Man. See notes 5 and 6, and the Commentary, p. 139.

5 'Túrin son of Úrin': original reading 'Beren Ermabwed'. See notes 4 and 6.

6 Original reading 'and when also the king heard of the kinship between Mavwin and Beren'. See notes 4 and 5.

7 *Linwë (Tinto)* was the king's original 'Elvish' name, and belongs to the same 'layer' of names as *Tintoglin* (see I.115, 131). Its retention here (not changed to *Tinwë*) is clearly a simple oversight. See notes 19 and 20.

8 Original reading 'seeing that he was a Man of great size'.

9 With this passage cf. that in the *Tale of Tinúviel* p. 11, which is closely similar. That the passage in *Turambar* is the earlier (to be presumed in any case) is shown by the fact that that in *Tinúviel* is only relevant if Beren is a Gnome, not a Man (see note 4).

10 'dreams came to them': original reading 'dreams the Valar sent to them'.

11 'and his name was Glorund' was added later, as were the subsequent occurrences of the name on pp. 86, 94, 98; but from the first on p. 103 onwards *Glorund* appears in the manuscript as first written.

12 'with the aid of Flinding whose wounds were not great': original reading 'with the aid of a lightly wounded man'. All the subsequent references to Flinding in this passage were added.

13   Original reading 'Túrin's heart was bitter, and so it was that he and that other alone returned from that battle'. – In the phrase 'reproaching Túrin that he had ever withstood his wise counsels' 'ever' means 'always': Túrin had always resisted Orodreth's counsels.

14   Original reading 'although all folk at that time held such a deed grievous and cowardly'.

15   Original reading 'and to look upon Nienóri again'. This was emended to 'and to look upon Nienóri whom he had never seen'. The words 'since his first days' were added still later.

16   The following passage was struck out, apparently at the time of writing:

> "Indeed," said they, "it is the report of men of travel and rangers of the hills that for many and many moons have even the farthest marches been free of them and unwonted safe, and so have many men fared out of Hisilómë to the Lands Beyond." And this was the truth that during the life of Turambar as an exile from the court of Tintoglin or hidden amongst the Rothwarin Melko had troubled Hisilómë little and the paths thereto.

(*Rothwarin* was the original form throughout, replaced later by *Rodothlim*.) See p. 92, where the situation described in the rejected passage is referred to the earlier time (before the destruction of the Rodothlim) when Mavwin and Nienóri left Hisilómë.

17   Original reading 'twice seven'. When Túrin fled from the land of Tinwelint it was exactly 12 years since he had left his mother's house (p. 75), and Nienóri was born before that, but just how long before is not stated.

18   After 'a great and terrible project afoot' the original reading was 'the story of which entereth not into this tale'. I do not know whether this means that when my father first wrote here of Melko's 'project' he did not have the destruction of the Rodothlim in mind.

19   'the king': original reading 'Linwë'. See note 7.

20   *Linwë*: an oversight. See note 7.

21   'that high place': original reading 'a hill'.

22   This sentence, 'And even so was Túrin's boast . . .', was added in pencil later. The reference is to Túrin's naming himself *Turambar* – 'from this hour shall none name me Túrin if I live', p. 86.

23   This sentence, from 'for his lineage . . .' to approximately this point, is very lightly struck through. On the opposite page of the MS is hastily scribbled: 'Make Turambar never tell new folk of his lineage (will bury the past) – this avoids chance (as cert.) of Níniel hearing his lineage from any.' See Commentary, p. 131.

24   Against this sentence there is a pencilled question-mark in the margin. See note 23 and the Commentary, p. 131.

25   'And Níniel conceived' was added in pencil later. See Commentary, p. 135.

26   'and the captain of these was Mîm the dwarf' added afterwards in pencil. See Commentary p. 137.

27   The word *tract* may be read as *track*, and the word *hurt* (but with less probability) as *burnt*.

28   As it stands this sentence can hardly mean other than that the people thought that the men were fighting among themselves; but why should they think such a thing? More likely, my father inadvertently missed out the end of the sentence: 'betwixt the seven, Turambar and his comrades, and the dragon.'

29   Turambar refers to Glorund's words to him before the caves of the Rodothlim: 'O Túrin Mormakil, who wast once named brave' (p. 86).

30   These words, from 'even he who . . .', were added later in pencil. *Úrin* may also be read as *Húrin*.

31   From this point to the end of Eltas' tale the original text was struck through, and is followed in the manuscript book by two brief narrative outlines, these being rejected also. The text given here (from 'Yet it is said . . .') is found on slips placed in the book. For the rejected material see the Commentary, pp. 135–7.

32   Throughout the final portion of the text (that written on slips, see note 31) the king's name was first written *Tinthellon*, not *Tintoglin* (see note 3).

33   'Elves': original reading 'men'. The same change was made below ('Now therefore when those Elves approached'), and a little later 'men' was removed in two places ('his folk laughed', 'Úrin caused his followers to bear the gold', p. 114); but several occurrences of 'men' were retained, possibly through oversight, though 'men' is used of Elves very frequently in the *Tale of Turambar* (e.g. 'Beleg and Flinding both stout men', p. 80).

34   This sentence, from 'But none had come nigh . . .', was added later in pencil.

35   This sentence, from 'Then did Úrin fiercely . . .', was added later, replacing 'Then said Úrin: "Yet had you such a heart . . ."'

36   This sentence, from "What meanest thou . . .", replaces the original reading "Begone, and take thy filth with thee."

Changes made to names in<br>
The Tale of Turambar

*Fuithlug*   < *Fothlug* < *Fothlog*

*Nienóri*   At the first occurrence (p. 71) my father originally wrote *Nyenòre (Nienor)*. Afterwards he struck out *Nyenòre*, removed the brackets round *Nienor*, and added *-i*, giving *Nienori*. At subsequent occurrences the name was written both *Nienor* and

*Nienóri*, but *Nienor* was changed to *Nienóri* later throughout the
earlier part of the tale. Towards the end, and in the text written on
slips that concludes it, the form is *Nienor*. I have given *Nienóri*
throughout.

*Tinwelint*  <  *Tinthellon* (p. 72, twice). See p. 69 and note 3.
*Tinwelint* < *Tinthellon* also in the concluding portion of the text,
see note 32.

*Tinwelint*  <  *Tintoglin* throughout the tale, except as just noted
(where *Tinwelint* < *Tinthellon* in passages added later); see p. 69.

*Gwedheling*   <   *Gwendeling* at all occurrences (*Gwendeling* un-
changed at p. 76, but this is obviously an oversight: I read
*Gwedheling* in the text). In the Gnomish dictionary the form
*Gwendeling* was changed to *Gwedhiling*; see p. 50.

*Flinding bo-Dhuilin*  <  *Flinding go-Dhuilin*   This change, made at
the occurrence on p. 78, was not made at p. 82, but this was clearly
because the form was missed, and I read *bo-Dhuilin* in both cases;
the same change from *go-* to *bo-* in the *Tale of Tinúviel*, see p. 51.
The form *Dhuilin* is taken by the name when the patronymic is
prefixed (cf. *Duilin* p. 79).

*Rodothlim*  < *Rothwarin* at every occurrence.

*Gurtholfin*  <  *Gortholfin* at the first occurrences, but from p. 90
*Gurtholfin* was the form first written.

Commentary on
*The Tale of Turambar*

§1.  *The primary narrative*

In commenting on this long tale it is convenient to break it into short
sections. In the course of this commentary I frequently refer to the long
(though incomplete) prose narrative, the *Narn i Hîn Húrin*, given in
*Unfinished Tales* pp. 57 ff., often in preference to the briefer account in
*The Silmarillion*, chapter XXI; and in reference to the former I cite
'*Narn*' and the page-number in *Unfinished Tales*.

(i) *The capture of Úrin and Túrin's childhood in Hisilómë* (pp. 70–2).

At the outset of the tale, it would be interesting to know more of the
teller, Eltas. He is a puzzling figure: he seems to be a Man (he says that
'our people' called Turambar *Turumart* 'after the fashion of the Gnomes')
living in Hisilómë after the days of Turambar but before the fall of
Gondolin, and he 'trod Olórë Mallë', the Path of Dreams. Is he then a
child, one of 'the children of the fathers of the fathers of Men', who
'found Kôr and remained with the Eldar for ever' (*The Cottage of Lost
Play*, I. 19–20)?

The opening passage agrees in almost all essentials with the ultimate form of the story. Thus there go back to the beginning of the 'tradition' (or at least to its earliest extant form) the departure of Húrin to the Battle of Unnumbered Tears at the summons of the Noldor, while his wife (Mavwin = Morwen) and young son Túrin remained behind; the great stand of Húrin's men, and Húrin's capture by Morgoth; the reason for Húrin's torture (Morgoth's wish to learn the whereabouts of Turgon) and the mode of it, and Morgoth's curse; the birth of Nienor shortly after the great battle.

That Men were shut in Hisilómë (or Hithlum, the Gnomish form, which here first appears, equated with Dor Lómin, p. 71) after the Battle of Unnumbered Tears is stated in *The Coming of the Elves* (I.118) and in the last of the outlines for *Gilfanon's Tale* (I.241); later on this was transformed into the confinement of the treacherous Easterling Men in Hithlum (*The Silmarillion* p. 195), and their ill-treatment of the survivors of the House of Hador became an essential element in the story of Túrin's childhood. But in the *Tale of Turambar* the idea is already present that 'the strange men who dwelt nigh knew not the dignity of the Lady Mavwin'. It is not in fact clear where Úrin dwelt: it is said here that after the battle 'Mavwin got her in tears into the land of Hithlum or Dor Lómin where all Men must now dwell', which can only mean that she went there, on account of Melko's command, from wherever she had dwelt with Úrin before; on the other hand, a little later in the tale (p. 73), and in apparent contradiction to this, Mavwin would not accept the invitation of Tinwelint to come to Artanor partly because (it is suggested) 'she clung to that dwelling that Úrin had set her in *ere he went to the great war*'.

In the later story Morwen resolved to send Túrin away from fear that he would be enslaved by the Easterlings (*Narn* p. 70), whereas here all that is said is that Mavwin 'knew not in her distress how to foster both him and his sister' (which presumably reflects her poverty). This in turn reflects a further difference, namely that here Nienóri was born before Túrin's departure (but see p. 131); in the later legend he and his companions left Dor-lómin in the autumn of the Year of Lamentation and Nienor was born early in the following year – thus he had never seen her, even as an infant.

An important underlying difference is the absence in the tale of the motive that Húrin had himself visited Gondolin, a fact known to Morgoth and the reason for his being taken alive (*The Silmarillion* pp. 158–9, 196–7); this element in the story arose much later, when the founding of Gondolin was set far back and long before the Battle of Unnumbered Tears.

(ii)    *Túrin in Artanor* (pp. 72–6)

From the original story of Túrin's journey the two old men who accom-

panied him, one of whom returned to Mavwin while the older remained
with Túrin, were never lost; and the cry of Túrin as they set out
reappears in the *Narn* (p. 73): 'Morwen, Morwen, when shall I see you
again?'

Beleg was present from the beginning, as was the meaning of his name:
'he was called Beleg *for* he was of great stature' (see I.254, entry *Haloisi
velikë*, and the Appendix to *The Silmarillion*, entry *beleg*); and he
plays the same rôle in the old story, rescuing the travellers starving in the
forest and taking them to the king.

In the later versions there is no trace of the remarkable message sent by
Tinwelint to Mavwin, and indeed his curiously candid explanation, that
he held aloof from the Battle of Unnumbered Tears because in his
wisdom he foresaw that Artanor could become a refuge if disaster befell,
is hardly in keeping with his character as afterwards conceived. There
were of course quite other reasons for his conduct (*The Silmarillion*
p. 189). On the other hand, Mavwin's motives for not herself leaving
Hithlum remained unchanged (see the passage in the *Narn*, p. 70, where
the word 'almsguest' is an echo of the old tale); but the statement is
puzzling that Mavwin might, when Nienóri was grown, have put aside
her pride and passed over the mountains, had they not become impassable
– clearly suggesting that she never left Hithlum. Perhaps the meaning is,
however, that she might have made the journey *earlier* (while Túrin was
still in Artanor) than she in fact did (when for a time the ways became
easier, but Túrin had gone).

The character of Túrin as a boy reappears in every stroke of the
description in the *Narn* (p. 77):

It seemed that fortune was unfriendly to him, so that often what he
designed went awry, and what he desired he did not gain; neither did
he win friendship easily, for he was not merry, and laughed seldom,
and a shadow lay on his youth.

(It is a notable point that is added in the tale: 'at no time did he give
much heed to words that were spoken to him'). And the ending of all
word between Túrin and his mother comes about in the same way –
increased guard on the mountains (*Narn* p. 78).

While the story of Túrin and Saeros as told in *The Silmarillion*, and in
far more detail in the *Narn*, goes back in essentials to the *Tale of
Turambar*, there are some notable differences – the chief being that as
the story was first told Túrin's tormentor was slain outright by the
thrown drinking-cup. The later complications of Saeros' treacherous
assault on Túrin the following day and his chase to the death, of the trial
of Túrin in his absence for this deed and of the testimony of Nellas (this
last only in the *Narn*) are entirely absent, necessarily; nor does Mablung
appear – indeed it seems clear that Mablung first emerged at the end of
the *Tale of Tinúviel* (see p. 59). Some details survived (as the comb

which Orgof/Saeros offered tauntingly to Túrin, *Narn* p. 80), while others were changed or neglected (as that it was the anniversary of Túrin's departure from his home – though the figure of twelve years agrees with the later story, and that the king was present in the hall, contrast *Narn* p. 79). But the taunt that roused Túrin to murderous rage remained essentially the same, in that it touched on his mother; and the story was never changed that Túrin came into the hall tousled and roughly clad, and that he was mocked for this by his enemy.

Orgof is not greatly distinct from Saeros, if less developed. He was in the king's favour, proud, and jealous of Túrin; in the later story he was a Nandorin Elf while here he is an Ilkorin with some Gnomish blood (for Gnomes in Artanor see p. 65), but doubtless some peculiarity in his origin was part of the 'tradition'. In the old story he is explicitly a fop and a fool, and he is not given the motives of hatred for Túrin that are ascribed to him in the *Narn* (p. 77).

Though far simpler in narrative, the essential element of Túrin's ignorance of his pardon was present from the outset. The tale provides an explanation, not found later, of why Túrin did not, on leaving Artanor, return to Hithlum; cf. the *Narn* p. 87: 'to Dor-lómin he did not dare, for it was closely beset, and one man alone could not hope at that time, as he thought, to come through the passes of the Mountains of Shadow.'

Túrin's prowess against the Orcs during his sojourn in Artanor is given a more central or indeed unique importance in the tale ('he held the wrath of Melko from them for many years') especially as Beleg, his companion-in-arms in the later versions, is not here mentioned (and in this passage the power of the queen to withstand invasion of the kingdom seems again (see p. 63) less than it afterwards became).

(iii)    *Túrin and Beleg* (pp. 76–81)

That part of the Túrin saga following on his days in Artanor/Doriath underwent a large development later ('Túrin among the Outlaws'), and indeed my father never brought this part of the story to finality. In the oldest version there is a much more rapid development of the plot: Beleg joins Túrin's band, and the destruction of the band and capture of Túrin by the Orcs follows (in terms of the narrative) almost immediately. There is no mention of 'outlaws' but only of 'wild spirits', no long search for Túrin by Beleg, no capture and maltreatment of Beleg by the band, and no betrayal of the camp by a traitor (the part ultimately taken by Mîm the Dwarf). Beleg indeed (as already noticed) is not said to have been Túrin's companion in the earlier time, before the slaying of Orgof, and they only take up together after Túrin's self-imposed exile.

Beleg is called a Noldo (p. 78), and if this single reference is to be given full weight (and there seems no reason not to: it is explicit in the *Tale of Tinúviel* that there were Noldoli in Artanor, and Orgof had Gnomish

blood) then it is to be observed that Beleg as originally conceived was an
Elf of Kôr. He is not here marked out as a great bowman (neither his
name Cúthalion 'Strongbow' nor his great bow Belthronding appear); he
is described at his first appearance (p. 73) as 'a wood-ranger, a huntsman
of the secret Elves', but not as the chief of the marchwardens of the
realm.

But from the capture of Túrin to the death of Beleg the old tale was
scarcely changed afterwards in any really important respect, though
altered in many details: such as Beleg's shooting of the wolf-sentinels
silently in the darkness in the later story, and the flash of lightning that
illuminated Beleg's face – but the blue-shining lamps of the Noldor
appear again in much later writings: one was borne by the Elves Gelmir
and Arminas who guided Tuor through the Gate of the Noldor on his
journey to the sea (see *Unfinished Tales* pp. 22, 51 note 2). In my
father's painting (probably dating from 1927 or 1928) of the meeting
between Beleg and Flinding in Taur-nu-Fuin (reproduced in *Pictures
by J. R. R. Tolkien*, no. 37) Flinding's lamp is seen beside him. The plot
of the old story is very precisely contrived in such details as the reason for
the carrying of Túrin, still sleeping, out of the Orc-camp, and for Beleg's
using his sword, rather than a knife, to cut Túrin's bonds; perhaps also in
the crushing of Beleg by Túrin so that he was winded and could not speak
his name before Túrin gave him his death-blow.

The story of Túrin's madness after the slaying of Beleg, the guidance
of Gwindor, and the release of Túrin's tears at Eithel Ivrin, is here in
embryo. Of the peculiar nature of Beleg's sword there is no suggestion.

(iv)   *Túrin among the Rodothlim; Túrin and Glorund* (pp. 81–8)

In this passage is found (so far as written record goes, for it is
to be remembered that a wholly erased text underlies the manuscript)
the origin of Nargothrond, as yet unnamed. Among many remarkable
features the chief is perhaps that Orodreth was there before Felagund,
Lord of Caves, with whom in the later legend Nargothrond was identified,
as its founder and deviser. (In *The Silmarillion* Orodreth was one of
Finrod Felagund's brothers (the sons of Finarfin), to whom Felagund
gave the command of Minas Tirith on Tol Sirion after the making of
Nargothrond (p. 120), and Orodreth became King of Nargothrond after
Felagund's death.) In the tale this cave-dwelling of exiled Noldoli
is a simpler and rougher place, and (as is suggested) short-lived against
the overwhelming power of Melko; but, as so often, there were many
features that were never altered, even though in a crucial respect the
history of Nargothrond was to be greatly modified by contact with the
legend of Beren and Tinúviel. Thus the site was from the start 'above a
stream' (the later Narog) that 'ran down to feed the river Sirion', and as is
seen later (p. 96) the bank of the river on the side of the caves was higher
and the hills drew close: cf. *The Silmarillion* p. 114: 'the caves under the

High Faroth in its steep western shore'. The policy of secrecy and refusal of open war pursued by the Elves of Nargothrond was always an essential element (cf. *The Silmarillion* pp. 168, 170),* as was the overturning of that policy by the confidence and masterfulness of Túrin (though in the tale there is no mention of the great bridge that he caused to be built). Here, however, the fall of the redoubt is perhaps more emphatically attributed to Túrin, his coming there seen more simply as a curse, and the disaster as more inevitably proceeding from his unwisdom: at least in the fragments of this part of the *Narn* (pp. 155–7) Túrin's case against Gwindor, who argued for the continuation of secrecy, is seemingly not without substance, despite the outcome. But the essential story is the same: Túrin's policy revealed Nargothrond to Morgoth, who came against it with overwhelming strength and destroyed it.

In relation to the earliest version the roles of Flinding (Gwindor), Failivrin (Finduilas),† and Orodreth were to undergo a remarkable set of transferences. In the old tale Flinding had been of the Rodothlim before his capture and imprisonment in Angband, just as afterwards Gwindor came from Nargothrond (but with a great development in his story, see *The Silmarillion* pp. 188, 191–2), and on his return was so changed as to be scarcely recognisable (I pass over such enduring minor features as the taking of Túrin and Flinding/Gwindor prisoner on their coming to the caves). The beautiful Failivrin is already present, and her unrequited love for Túrin, but the complication of her former relation with Gwindor is quite absent, and she is not the daughter of Orodreth the King but of one Galweg (who was to disappear utterly). Flinding is not shown as opposed to Túrin's policies; and in the final battle he aids Túrin in bearing Orodreth out of the fight. Orodreth dies (after being carried back to the caves) reproaching Túrin for what he has brought to pass – as does Gwindor dying in *The Silmarillion* (p. 213), with the added bitterness of his relation with Finduilas. But Failivrin's father Galweg is slain in the battle, as is Finduilas' father Orodreth in *The Silmarillion*. Thus in the evolution of the legend Orodreth took over the rôle of Galweg, while Gwindor took over in part the rôle of Orodreth.

As I have noticed earlier, there is no mention in the tale of any peculiarity attaching to Beleg's sword, and though the Black Sword is already present it was made for Túrin on the orders of Orodreth, and its blackness and its shining pale edges were of its first making (see *The Silmarillion* pp. 209–10). Its power of speech ('it is said that at times it spake dark words to him') remained afterwards in its dreadful words to Túrin before his death (*Narn* p. 145) – a motive that appears already

---

* From the first of these passages it seems that when Beren came to Nargothrond the 'secret' policy was already pursued under Felagund; but from the second it seems that it came into being from the potent rhetoric of Curufin after Beren went there.

† In *The Silmarillion* she is named Finduilas, and the name Faelivrin 'which is the gleam of the sun on the pools of Ivrin' was given to her by Gwindor (pp. 209–10).

in the tale, p. 112; and Túrin's name derived from the sword (here *Mormagli*, *Mormakil*, later *Mormegil*) was already devised. But of Túrin's disguising of his true name in Nargothrond there is no suggestion: indeed it is explicitly stated that he said who he was.

Of Gelmir and Arminas and the warning they brought to Nargothrond from Ulmo (*Narn* pp. 159–62) the germ can perhaps be seen in the 'whispers in the stream at eve', which undoubtedly implies messages from Ulmo (see p. 77).

The dragon Glorund is named in the 'lengthening spell' in the *Tale of Tinúviel* (pp. 19, 46), but the actual name was only introduced in the course of the writing of the *Tale of Turambar* (see note 11). There is no suggestion that he had played any previous part in the history, or indeed that he was the first of his kind, the Father of Dragons, with a long record of evil already before the Sack of Nargothrond. Of great interest is the passage in which the nature of the dragons of Melko is defined: their evil wisdom, their love of lies and gold (which 'they may not use or enjoy'), and the knowledge of tongues that Men say would come from eating a dragon's heart (with evident reference to the legend in the Norse Edda of Sigurd Fafnisbane, who was enabled to understand, to his own great profit, the speech of birds when he ate the heart of the dragon Fafnir, roasting it on a spit).

The story of the sack of Nargothrond is somewhat differently treated in the old story, although the essentials were to remain of the driving away of Failivrin/Finduilas among the captives and of the powerlessness of Túrin to aid her, being spellbound by the dragon. Minor differences (such as the later arrival of Glorund on the scene: in *The Silmarillion* Túrin only came back to Nargothrond after Glaurung had entered the caves and the sack was 'well nigh achieved') and minor agreements (such as the denial of the plunder to the Orcs) may here be passed over; most interesting is the account of Túrin's words with the dragon. Here the whole issue of Túrin's escaping or not escaping his doom is introduced, and it is significant that he takes the name *Turambar* at this juncture, whereas in the later legend he takes it when he joins the Woodmen in Brethil, and less is made of it. The old version is far less powerfully and concisely expressed, and the dragon's words are less subtle and ingeniously untrue. Here too the moral is very explicitly pointed, that Túrin *should not* have abandoned Failivrin 'in danger that he himself could see' – does this not suggest that, even under the dragon's spell as he was, there was a weakness (a 'blindness', see p. 83) in Túrin which the dragon touched? As the story is told in *The Silmarillion* the moral would seem uncalled for: Túrin was opposed by an adversary too powerful for his mind and will.

There is here a remarkable passage in which suicide is declared a sin, depriving such a one of all hope 'that ever his spirit would be freed from the dark glooms of Mandos or stray into the pleasant paths of Valinor'. This seems to go with the perplexing passage in the tale of *The Coming of the Valar and the Building of Valinor* concerning the fates of Men: see p. 60.

Finally, it is strange that in the old story the gold and treasure was carried out from the caves by the Orcs and remained there (it 'lay by the caves above the stream'), and the dragon most uncharacteristically 'slept before it' in the open. In *The Silmarillion* Glaurung 'gathered all the hoard and riches of Felagund and heaped them, and lay upon them in the innermost hall'.

### (v)  *Túrin's return to Hithlum* (pp. 88–91)

In this passage the case is much as in previous parts of the tale: the large structure of the story was not greatly changed afterwards, but there are many important differences nonetheless.

In the *Tale of Turambar* it is clear that the house of Mavwin was not imagined as standing near to the hills or mountains that formed the barrier between Hithlum and the Lands Beyond: Túrin was told that never did Orcs 'come hither deep into the land of Hisilómë', in contrast to the *Narn* (p. 68), where 'Húrin's house stood in the south-east of Dor-lómin, and the mountains were near; Nen Lalaith indeed came down from a spring under the shadow of Amon Darthir, over whose shoulder there was a steep pass'. The removal of Mavwin from one house to another in Hithlum, visited in turn by Túrin as he sought for her, was afterwards rejected, to the improvement of the story. Here Túrin comes back to his old home in the late summer, whereas in *The Silmarillion* the fall of Nargothrond took place in the late autumn ('the leaves fell from the trees in a great wind as they went, for the autumn was passing to a dire winter,' p. 213) and Túrin came to Dor-lómin in the Fell Winter (p. 215).

The names Brodda and Airin (later spelled Aerin) remained; but Brodda is here the lord of the land, and Airin plays a more important part in the scene in the hall, dealing justice with vigour and wisdom, than she does later. It is not said here that she had been married by force, though her life with Brodda is declared to have been very evil; but of course the situation in the later narratives is far more clear-cut – the Men of Hithlum were 'Easterlings', 'Incomers' hostile to the Elves and the remnant of the House of Hador, whereas in the early story no differentiation is made among them, and indeed Brodda was 'a man whom Mavwin trusted'. The motive of Brodda's ill-treatment of Mavwin is already present, but only to the extent that he embezzled her goods after her departure; in the *Narn* it seems from Aerin's words to Túrin (p. 107) that the oppression of Morwen by Brodda and others was the cause of her going at last to Doriath. In the brief account in *The Silmarillion* (p. 215) it is not indeed made explicit that Brodda in particular deserved Túrin's hatred.

Túrin's conduct in the hall is in the tale essentially simpler: the true story has been told to him by a passer-by, he enters to exact vengeance on Brodda for thieving Mavwin's goods, and he does so with dispatch. As told in the *Narn*, where Túrin's eyes are only finally opened to the deception that has been practised upon him by the words of Aerin, who is present in the hall, his rage is more passionate, crazed, and bitter, and indeed more comprehensible: and the moral observation that Túrin's deed was 'violent and unlawful' is not made. The story of Airin's judgement on these doings, made in order to save Túrin, was afterwards removed; and Túrin's solitary departure was expanded, with the addition also of the firing of Brodda's hall by Aerin (*Narn* p. 109).

Some details survived all the changes: in the *Narn* Túrin still seizes Brodda by the hair, and just as in the tale his rage suddenly expired after the deed of violence ('his wrath was grown cold'), so in the *Narn* 'the fire of his rage was as ashes'. It may be noticed here that while in the old story Túrin does not rename himself so often, his tendency to do so is already present.

The story of how Túrin came among the Woodmen and delivered them from Orcs is not found in the *Tale of Turambar*; nor is there any mention of the Mound of Finduilas near the Crossings of Teiglin nor any account of her fate.

(vi)  *The return of Gumlin to Hithlum and the departure of Mavwin and Nienóri to Artanor* (pp. 91–3)

In the later story the elder of Túrin's guardians (Gumlin in the tale, Grithnir in the *Narn*) plays no part after his bringing Túrin to Doriath: it is only said that he stayed there till he died (*Narn* p. 74); and Morwen had no tidings out of Doriath before leaving her home – indeed she only learnt that Túrin had left Thingol's realm when she got there (*The Silmarillion* p. 211; cf. Aerin's words in the *Narn*, p. 107: 'She looked to find her son there awaiting her.') This whole section of the tale does no more than explain with what my father doubtless felt (since he afterwards rejected it almost in its entirety) to be unnecessary complication why Mavwin went to Tinwelint. I think it is clear, however, that the difference between the versions here depends on the different views of Mavwin's (Morwen's) condition in Hithlum. In the old story she is not suffering hardship and oppression; she trusts Brodda to the extent of entrusting not only her goods to him but even her daughter, and is said indeed to have 'peace and honour among the men of those regions'; the chieftains speak of the love they bear her. A motive for her departure is found in the coming of Gumlin and the news he brings of Túrin's flight from the lands of Tinwelint. In the later story, on the other hand, Brodda's character as tyrant and oppressor is extended, and it is Morwen's very plight at his hands that leads her to depart. (The news that came to Túrin in Doriath that 'Morwen's plight was eased' (*Narn* p. 77, cf. *The Silmarillion* p. 199) is probably a survival from the old story; nothing is said in the later narratives to explain how this came about, and ceased.) In either case her motive for leaving is coupled with the fact of the increased safety of the lands; but whereas in the later story the reason for this was the prowess of the Black Sword of Nargothrond, in the tale it was the 'great and terrible project' of Melko that was afoot – the assault on the caves of the Rodothlim (see note 18).

It is curious that in this passage Airin and Brodda are introduced as if for the first time. It is perhaps significant that the part of the tale extending from the dragon's words 'Hearken to me, O son of Úrin...' on p. 87 to '... fell to his knees before Tinwelint' on p. 92 was written in a separate part of the manuscript book: possibly this replaced an earlier text in which Brodda and Airin did not appear. But many such questions arise from the earliest manuscripts, and few can now be certainly unravelled.

(vii)   *Mavwin and Nienóri in Artanor and their meeting with Glorund* (pp. 93–9)

The next essential step in the development of the plot – the learning by Mavwin/Morwen of Túrin's sojourn in Nargothrond – is more neatly and naturally handled in *The Silmarillion* (p. 217) and the *Narn* (p. 112), where news is brought to Thingol by fugitives from the sack, in contrast to the *Tale of Turambar*, where Mavwin and Nienóri only learn of the destruction of the Elves of the Caves from a band of Noldoli while themselves wandering aimlessly in the forest. It is odd that these Noldoli did not name Túrin by his name but only as the *Mormakil*: it seems that they did not know who he was, but they knew enough of his history to make his identity plain to Mavwin. As noted above, Túrin declared his name and lineage to the Elves of the Caves. In the later narrative, on the other hand, Túrin did conceal it in Nargothrond, calling himself Agarwaen, but all those who brought news of the fall to Doriath 'declared that it was known to many in Nargothrond ere the end that the Mormegil was none other than Túrin son of Húrin of Dor-lómin'.

As often, unneeded complication in the early story was afterwards cleared away: thus the elaborate argumentation needed to get Tinwelint's warriors and Mavwin and Nienóri on the road together is gone from *The Silmarillion* and the *Narn*. In the tale the ladies and the Elvish warriors all set off together with the full intention that the former shall watch developments from a high place (afterwards Amon Ethir, the Hill of Spies); in the later story Morwen simply rides off, and the party of Elves, led by Mablung, follows after her, with Nienor among them in disguise.

Particularly notable is the passage in the tale in which Mavwin holds out the great gold-hoard of the Rodothlim as a bait to Tinwelint, and Tinwelint unashamedly admits that (as a wild Elf of the woods) it is this, not any hope of aiding Túrin, that moves him to send out a party. The majesty, power, and pride of Thingol rose with the development of the conception of the Grey-elves of Beleriand; as I have said earlier (p. 63) 'In the beginning, Tinwelint's dwelling was not a subterranean city full

of marvels . . . but a rugged cave', and here he is seen planning a foray to
augment his slender wealth in precious things – a far cry from the
description of his vast treasury in the *Narn* (p. 76):

Now Thingol had in Menegroth deep armouries filled with great
wealth of weapons: metal wrought like fishes' mail and shining like
water in the moon; swords and axes, shields and helms, wrought by
Telchar himself or by his master Gamil Zirak the old, or by elven-
wrights more skilful still. For some things he had received in gift that
came out of Valinor and were wrought by Fëanor in his mastery, than
whom no craftsman was greater in all the days of the world.

Great as are the differences from the later legend in the encounter with
the dragon, the stinking vapours raised by his lying in the river as the
cause of the miscarriage of the plan, the maddened flight of the horses,
and the enspelling of Nienor so that all memory of her past was lost, are
already present. Most striking perhaps of the many differences is the fact
that Mavwin was present at the conversation with Glorund; and of these
speeches there is no echo in the *Narn* (pp. 118–19), save that Nienor's
naming of Túrin as the object of their quest revealed her identity to the
dragon (this is explicit in the *Narn*, and may probably be surmised from
the tale). The peculiar tone of Glaurung in the later narrative, sneering
and curt, knowing and self-possessed, and unfathomably wicked, can be
detected already in the words of Glorund, but as he evolved he gained
immeasurably in dread by becoming more laconic.

The chief difference of structure lies in the total absence of the
'Mablung-element' from the tale, nor is there any foreshadowing of it.
There is no suggestion of an exploration of the sacked dwellings in the
dragon's absence (indeed he does not, as it appears, go any distance from
them); the purpose of the expedition from Artanor was expressly warlike
('a strong party against the Foalókë', 'they prepared them for battle'),
since Tinwelint had hopes of laying hands on the treasure, whereas
afterwards it became purely a scouting foray, for Thingol 'desired greatly
to know more of the fate of Nargothrond' (*Narn* p. 113).

A curious point is that though Mavwin and Nienóri were to be stationed
on the tree-covered 'high place' that was afterward called the Hill of
Spies, and where they were in fact so stationed in *The Silmarillion* and
the *Narn*, it seems that in the old story they never got there, but were
ensnared by Glorund where he lay in, or not far from, the river. Thus the
'high place' had in the event almost no significance in the tale.

(viii) *Turambar and Níniel* (pp. 99–102)

In the later legend Nienor was found by Mablung after her enspelling by
Glaurung, and with three companions he led her back towards the

borders of Doriath. The chase after Nienor by the band of Orcs (*Narn* p. 120) is present in the tale, but it does not have its later narrative function of leading to Nienor's flight and loss by Mablung and the other Elves (who do not appear): rather it leads directly to her rescue by Turambar, now dwelling among the Woodmen. In the *Narn* (p. 122) the Woodmen of Brethil did indeed come past the spot where they found her on their return from a foray against Orcs; but the circumstances of her finding are altogether different, most especially since there is in the tale no mention of the Haudh-en-Elleth, the Mound of Finduilas.

An interesting detail concerns Nienor's response to Turambar's naming her *Níniel*. In *The Silmarillion* and the *Narn* 'she shook her head, but said: Níniel'; in the present text she said: 'Not Níniel, not Níniel.' One has the impression that in the old story what impressed her darkened mind was only the resemblance of *Níniel* to her own forgotten name *Nienóri* (and of *Turambar* to *Túrin*), whereas in the later she both denied and in some way accepted the name *Níniel*.

An original element in the legend is the Woodmen's bringing of Níniel to a place ('Silver Bowl') where there was a great waterfall (afterwards Dimrost, the Rainy Stair, where the stream of Celebros 'fell towards Teiglin'): and these falls were near to the dwellings of the Woodmen – but the place where they found Níniel was much further off in the forest (several days' journey) than were the Crossings of Teiglin from Dimrost. When she came there she was filled with dread, a foreboding of what was to happen there afterwards, and this is the origin of her shuddering fit in the later narratives, from which the place was renamed Nen Girith, the Shuddering Water (see *Narn* p. 149, note 24).

The utter darkness imposed on Níniel's mind by the dragon's spell is less emphasized in the tale, and there is no suggestion that she needed to relearn her very language; but it is interesting to observe the recurrence in a changed context of the simile of 'one that seeks for something mislaid': in the *Narn* (p. 123) Níniel is said to have taken great delight in the relearning of words, 'as one that finds again treasures great and small that were mislaid'.

The lame man, here called Tamar, and his vain love of Níniel already appear; unlike his later counterpart Brandir he was not the chief of the Woodmen, but he was the son of the chief. He was also Half-elven! Most extraordinary is the statement that the wife of Bethos the chieftain and mother of Tamar was an Elf, a woman of the Noldoli: this is mentioned in passing, as if the great significance and rarity of the union of Elf and Mortal had not yet emerged – but in a Name-list associated with the tale of *The Fall of Gondolin* Eärendel is said to be 'the only being that is half of the kindred of the Eldalië and half of Men' (p. 215).*

---

* In a later rewriting of a passage in that tale (p. 164 and note 22) it is said of Tuor and Idril of Gondolin: 'Thus was first wed a child of Men with a daughter of Elfinesse, nor was Tuor the last.'

The initial reluctance of Níniel to receive Turambar's suit is given no explanation in the tale: the implication must be that some instinct, some subconscious appreciation of the truth, held her back. In *The Silmarillion* (p. 220)

> for that time she delayed in spite of her love. For Brandir foreboded he knew not what, and sought to restrain her, rather for her sake than his own or rivalry with Turambar; and he revealed to her that Turambar was Túrin son of Húrin, and though she knew not the name a shadow fell upon her mind.

In the final version as in the oldest, the Woodmen knew who Turambar was. My father's scribbled directions for the alteration of the story cited in note 23 ('Make Turambar never tell new folk of his lineage . . .') are puzzling: for since Níniel had lost all memory of her past she would not know the names Túrin son of Húrin even if it were told to her that Turambar was he. It is however possible that when my father wrote this he imagined Níniel's lost knowledge of herself and her family as being nearer the surface of her mind, and capable of being brought back by hearing the names – in contrast to the later story where she did not consciously recognise the name of Túrin even when Brandir told it to her. Clearly the question-mark against the reference in the text of the tale to Turambar's speaking to Níniel 'of his father and mother and the sister he had not seen' and Níniel's distress at his words (see note 24) depends on the same train of thought. The statement here that Turambar had never seen his sister is at variance with what is said earlier in the tale, that he did not leave Hithlum until after Nienóri's birth (p. 71); but my father was uncertain on this point, as is clearly seen from the succession of readings, changed back and forth between the two ideas, given in note 15.

(ix)   *The slaying of Glorund* (pp. 103–8)

In this section I follow the narrative of the tale as far as Túrin's swoon when the dying dragon opened his eyes and looked at him. Here the later story runs very close to the old, but there are many interesting differences.

In the tale Glorund is said to have had bands of both Orcs and Noldoli subject to him, but only the Orcs remained afterwards; cf. the *Narn* p. 125:

> Now the power and malice of Glaurung grew apace, and he waxed fat [cf. 'the Foalókë waxed fat'], and he gathered Orcs to him, and ruled as a dragon-King, and all the realm of Nargothrond that had been was laid under him.

The mention in the tale that Tinwelint's people were 'grievously harried' by Glorund's bands suggests once again that the magic of the Queen was no very substantial protection; while the statement that 'at length there came some [Orcs] nigh even to those woods and glades that were beloved of Turambar and his folk' seems at variance with Turambar's saying to Níniel earlier that 'we are hard put to it to fend those evil ones from our homes' (p. 100). There is no mention here of Turambar's pledge to Níniel that he would go to battle only if the homes of the Woodmen were assailed (*Narn* pp. 125–6); and there is no figure corresponding to Dorlas of the later versions. Tamar's character, briefly described (p. 106), is in accord so far as it goes with what is later told of Brandir, but the relationship of Brandir to Níniel, who called him her brother (*Narn* p. 124), had not emerged. The happiness and prosperity of the Woodmen under Turambar's chieftainship is much more strongly emphasized in the tale (afterwards he was not indeed the chieftain, at least not in name); and it leads in fact to Glorund's greed as a motive for his assault on them.

The topographical indications in this passage, important to the narrative, are readily enough accommodated to the later accounts, with one major exception: it is clear that in the old story the stream of the waterfall that fell down to the Silver Bowl was the same as that which ran through the gorge where Turambar slew Glorund:

Here flowed that same stream that further down wound past the dragon's lair [*lair* = the place where he was lying] in a deep bed cloven deep into the earth (p. 105).

Thus Turambar and his companions, as he said,

will go down the rocks to the foot of the fall, and so gaining the path of the stream perchance we may come as nigh to the drake as may be (*ibid.*).

In the final story, on the other hand, the falling stream (Celebros) was a tributary of Teiglin; cf. the *Narn* p. 127:

Now the river Teiglin . . . flowed down from Ered Wethrin swift as Narog, but at first between low shores, until after the Crossings, gathering power from other streams, it clove a way through the feet of the highlands upon which stood the Forest of Brethil. Thereafter it ran in deep ravines, whose great sides were like walls of rock, but pent at the bottom the waters flowed with great force and noise. And right in the path of Glaurung there lay now one of these gorges, by no means the deepest, but the narrowest, just north of the inflow of Celebros.

The pleasant place ('a green sward where grew a wealth of flowers')
survived; cf. the *Narn* p. 123: 'There was a wide greensward at the
head of the falls, and birches grew about it.' So also did the 'Silver
Bowl', though the name was lost: 'the stream [Celebros] went over a
lip of worn stone, and fell down by many foaming steps into a rocky bowl
far below' (*Narn, ibid.*; cf. the tale p. 105: 'it fell over a great fall where
the water-worn rock jutted smooth and grey from amid the grass'). The
'little hill' or 'knoll', 'islanded among the trees', from which Turambar
and his companions looked out is not so described in the *Narn*, but the
picture of a high place and lookout near the head of the falls remained, as
may be seen from the statement in the *Narn* (p. 123) that from Nen
Girith 'there was a wide view towards the ravines of Teiglin'; later (*Narn*
p. 128) it is said that it was Turambar's intention to 'ride to the high fall of
Nen Girith . . . whence he could look far across the lands'. It seems
certain, then, that the old image never faded, and was only a little
changed.

While in both old and late accounts a great concourse of the people
follow Turambar to the head of the falls against his bidding, in the late
his motive for commanding them not to come is explicit: they are to
remain in their homes and prepare for flight. Here on the other hand
Níniel rides with Turambar to the head of Silver Bowl and says farewell
to him there. But a detail of the old story survived: Turambar's words to
Níniel 'Nor thou nor I die this day, nor yet tomorrow, by the evil of the
dragon or by the foemen's swords' are closely paralleled by his words to
her in the *Narn* (p. 129): 'Neither you nor I shall be slain by this Dragon,
nor by any foe of the North'; and in the one account Níniel 'quelled her
weeping and was very still', while in the other she 'ceased to weep and fell
silent'. The situation is generally simpler in the tale, in that the Woodmen
are scarcely characterised; Tamar is not as Brandir the titular head of the
people, and this motive for bitterness against Turambar is absent, nor is
there a Dorlas to insult him or a Hunthor to rebuke Dorlas. Tamar is
however present with Níniel at the same point in the story, having girded
himself with a sword: 'and many scoffed at him for that', just as it is
afterwards said of Brandir that he had seldom done so before (*Narn*
p. 132).

Turambar here set out from the head of the falls with six companions,
all of whom proved in the end fainthearted, whereas later he had only
two, Dorlas and Hunthor, and Hunthor remained staunch, though killed
by a falling stone in the gorge. But the result is the same, in that
Turambar must climb the further cliff of the gorge alone. Here the
dragon remained where he lay near the brink of the cliff all night,
and only moved with the dawn, so that his death and the events that
immediately followed it took place by daylight. But in other respects
the killing of the dragon remained even in many details much as it
was originally written, more especially if comparison is made with the
*Narn* (p. 134), where there reappears the need for Turambar and his

companion(s) to move from their first station in order to come up directly under the belly of the beast (this is passed over in *The Silmarillion*).

Two notable points in this section remain to be mentioned; both are afterthoughts pencilled into the manuscript. In the one we meet for the first time Mîm the Dwarf as the captain of Glorund's guard over his treasure during his absence – a strange choice for the post, one would think. On this matter see p. 137 below. In the other it is said that Níniel conceived a child by Turambar, which, remarkably enough, is not said in the text as originally written; on this see p. 135.

### (x)   *The deaths of Túrin and Nienóri* (pp. 108–12)

In the conclusion of the story the structure remained the same from the old tale to the *Narn*: the moonlight, the tending of Turambar's burnt hand, the cry of Níniel that stirred the dragon to his final malice, the accusation by the dragon that Turambar was a stabber of foes unseen, Turambar's naming Tamar/Brandir 'Club-foot' and sending him to consort with the dragon in death, the sudden withering of the leaves at the place of Nienor's leap as if it were already the end of autumn, the invocation of Nienor to the waters and of Turambar to his sword, the raising of Túrin's mound and the inscription in 'strange signs' upon it. Many other features could be added. But there are also many differences; here I refer only to some of the most important.

Mablung being absent from the old story, it is only Turambar's intuition ('being free now of blindness' – the blindness that Melko 'wove of old', p. 83)* that informs him that Tamar was telling the truth. The slaying of Glaurung and all its aftermath is in the late story compassed in the course of a single night and the morning of the next day, whereas in the tale it is spread over two nights, the intervening day, and the morning of the second. Turambar is carried back to the people on the hill-top by the three deserters who had left him in the ravine, whereas in the late story he comes himself. (Of the slaying of Dorlas by Brandir there is no trace in the tale, and the taking of a sword by Tamar has no issue.)

Particularly interesting is the result of the changing of the place where Túrin and Nienóri died. In the tale there is only one river, and Níniel follows the stream up through the woods and casts herself over the falls of Silver Bowl (in the place afterwards called Nen Girith), and here too, in the glade above the falls, Turambar slew himself; in the developed story her death-leap was into the ravine of Teiglin at Cabed-en-Aras, the Deer's Leap, near the spot where Turambar lay beside Glaurung, and here Turambar's death took place also. Thus Níniel's sense of dread when she first came to Silver Bowl with the Woodmen who rescued her

---

\* Cf. his words to Mablung in the *Narn*, p. 144: 'For see, I am blind! Did you not know? Blind, blind, groping since childhood in a dark mist of Morgoth!'

(p. 101) foreboded her own death in that place, but in the changed story there is less reason for a foreknowledge of evil to come upon her there. But while the place was changed, the withering of the leaves remained, and the awe of the scene of their deaths, so that none would go to Cabed-en-Aras after, as they would not set foot on the grass above Silver Bowl.

The most remarkable feature of the earliest version of the story of Turambar and Níniel is surely that as my father first wrote it he did *not* say that she had conceived a child by him (note 25); and thus there is nothing in the old story corresponding to Glaurung's words to her: 'But the worst of all his deeds thou shalt feel in thyself' (*Narn* p. 138). The fact that above all accounts for Nienor's utter horror and despair was added to the tale later.

In concluding this long analysis of the *Tale of Turambar* proper the absence of place-names in the later part of it may be remarked. The dwelling of the Rodothlim is not named, nor the river that flowed past it; no name is given to the forest where the Woodmen dwelt, to their village, or even to the stream of such central importance at the end of the story (contrast Nargothrond, Narog, Tumhalad, Amon Ethir, Brethil, Amon Obel, Ephel Brandir, Teiglin, Celebros of the later narratives).

### §2.   *The further narrative of Eltas*
### *(after the death of Túrin)*

My father struck out the greater part of this continuation, allowing it to stand only as far as the words 'by reason of her great unhappiness' on p. 113 (see note 31). From the brief passage that was retained it is seen that the story of Morwen's coming to the stone on Túrin's mound goes back to the beginning, though in the later story she met Húrin there (*The Silmarillion*, p. 229).

The rejected part continues as follows:

Yet it is said also that when the doom of his folk was utterly fulfilled then was Úrin released by Melko, and bowed with age he fared back into the better lands. There did he gather some few to him, and they went and found the caverns of the Rothwarin [*earlier form for* Rodothlim, *see p.* 119] empty, and none guarded them, and a mighty treasury lay there still for none had found it, in that the terror of the drake lived longer than he and none had ventured thither again. But Úrin let bear the gold even before Linwë [i.e. Tinwelint], and casting it before his feet bade him bitterly to take his vile reward, naming him a craven by whose faint heart had much evil fallen to his house that might never have been; and in this began a new estrangement between Elves and Men, for Linwë was wroth at Úrin's words and bid him begone, for said he: "Long did I foster Túrin thy son and forgave him the evil of his deeds, and afterward thy wife I succoured, giving way against my counsel to her wild desires. Yet what is it to me – and wherefore dost thou, O son of the uncouth race of Men, endure to upbraid a king of the Eldalië, whose life began in Palisor ages uncounted before Men were born?" And then Úrin would have gone, but his men were not willing to leave the gold there, and a dissension arose between them and the Elves, and of this grew bitter blows, and Tintoglin [i.e. Tinwelint] might not stay them.

There then was Úrin's band slain in his halls, and they stained with their blood the dragon's hoard; but Úrin escaped and cursed that gold with a dread curse so that none might enjoy it, and he that held any part of it found evil and death to come of it. But Linwë hearing that curse caused the gold to be cast into a deep pool of the river before his doors, and not for very long did any see it again save for the Ring of Doom [*emended to:* the Necklace of the Dwarves], and that tale belongs not here, although therein did the evil of the worm Glorund find its last fulfilment.

(The last phrase is an addition to the text.) The remainder of this rejected narrative, concerning the final fates of Úrin and Mavwin and their children, is essentially the same as in the replacement text given on p. 115 ('Then Úrin departed . . .') and need not be given.

Immediately following the rejected narrative there is a short outline headed 'Story of the Nauglafring or the Necklace of the Dwarves', and this also was struck through. Here there is no mention of Úrin at all, but it is told that the Orcs (emended from *Gongs*, see I. 245 note 10) who guarded the treasury of Glorund went in search of him when he did not come back to the caves, and in their absence Tintoglin (i.e. Tinwelint), learning of Glorund's death, sent Elves to steal the hoard of the Rothwarin (i.e. Rodothlim). The Orcs returning cursed the thieves, and they cursed the gold also.

Linwë (i.e. Tinwelint) guarded the gold, and he had a great necklace made by certain Úvanimor (Nautar or Nauglath). (*Úvanimor* have been defined in an earlier tale as 'monsters, giants, and ogres', see I. 75, 236; *Nauglath* are Dwarves, I. 236). In this Necklace the Silmaril was set; but the curse of the gold was on him, and he defrauded them of part of their reward. The Nauglath plotted, and got aid of Men; Linwë was slain in a raid, and the gold carried away.

There follows another rejected outline, headed 'The Necklace of the Dwarves', and this combines features of the preceding outline with features of the rejected ending of Eltas' narrative (pp. 135–6). Here Úrin gathers a band of Elves and Men who are wild and fierce, and they go to the caves, which are lightly guarded because the 'Orqui' (i.e. Orcs) are abroad seeking Glorund. They carry off the treasure, and the Orcs returning curse it. Úrin casts the treasure before the king and reproaches him (saying that he might have sent a greater company to the caves to secure the treasure, if not to aid Mavwin in her distress); 'Tintoglin would not touch it and bid Úrin hold what he had won, but Úrin would depart with bitter words'. Úrin's men were not willing to leave it, and they sneaked back; there was an affray in the king's halls, and much blood was spilt on the gold. The outline concludes thus:

The Gongs sack Linwë's halls and Linwë is slain and the gold is carried far away. Beren Ermabwed falls upon them at a crossing of Sirion and the treasure is cast into the water, and with it the Silmaril of Fëanor. The Nauglath that dwell nigh dive after the gold but only one mighty necklace of gold (and that Silmaril is on it) do they find. This becomes a mark of their king.

These two outlines are partly concerned with the story of the Nauglafring and show my father pondering that story before he wrote it; there is no need to consider these elements here. It is evident that he was in great doubt as to the further course of the story after the release of Úrin – what happened to the dragon's hoard? Was it guarded or unguarded, and if guarded by whom? How did it come at last into Tinwelint's hands? Who cursed it, and at what point in the story? If it was Úrin and his band that seized it, were they Men or Elves or both?

In the final text, written on slips placed in the manuscript book and given above pp. 113–16, these questions were resolved thus: Úrin's band was at first Men, then changed to Elves (see note 33); the treasure was guarded by the dwarf Mîm, whom Úrin slew, and it was he who cursed the gold as he died; Úrin's band became a baggage-train to carry the treasure to Tinwelint in sacks and wooden boxes (and they got it to the bridge before the king's door in the heart of the forest without, apparently, any difficulty). In this text there is no hint of what happened to the treasure after Úrin's departure (because the *Tale of the Nauglafring* begins at that point).

Subsequent to the writing of the *Tale of Turambar* proper, my father inserted Mîm into the text at an earlier point in the story (see pp. 103, 118 note 26), making him the captain of the guard appointed by Glorund to watch the treasure in his absence; but whether this was written in before or after the appearance of Mîm at the end (pp. 113–14) – whether it represents a different idea, or is an explanation of how Mîm came to be there – I cannot say.

In *The Silmarillion* (pp. 230–2) the story is wholly changed, in that the treasure remained in Nargothrond, and Húrin after the slaying of Mîm (for a far better reason than that in the early narrative) brought nothing from it to Doriath save the Necklace of the Dwarves.

Of the astonishing feature at the end of Eltas' narrative (pp. 115–16) of the 'deification' of Túrin Turambar and Nienóri (and the refusal of the Gods of Death to open their doors to them) it must be said that nowhere is there any explanation given – though in much later versions of the mythology Túrin Turambar appears in the Last Battle and smites Morgoth with his black sword. The purifying bath into which Túrin and Nienóri entered, called *Fôs'Almir* in the final text, was in the rejected text named *Faurí*; in the *Tale of the Sun and Moon* it has been described (I.187), but is there given other names: *Tanyasalpë*, *Faskala-númen*, and *Faskalan*.

There remains one further scrap of text to be considered. The second of the rejected outlines given above (pp. 136–7) was written in ink over a pencilled outline that was *not* erased, and I have been able to disinter a good deal of it from beneath the later writing. The two passages have nothing to do with each other; for some reason my father did not trouble in this case to erase earlier writing. The underlying text, so far as I can make it out, reads:

Tirannë and Vainóni fall in with the evil magician Kurúki who gives them a baneful drink. They forget their names and wander distraught in the woods. Vainóni is lost. She meets Turambar who saves her from Orcs and aids in her search for her mother. They are wed and live in happiness. Turambar becomes lord of rangers of the woods and a harrier of the Orcs. He goes to seek out the Foalókë which ravages his land. The treasure-heap – and flight of his band. He slays the Foalókë and is wounded. Vainóni succours him, but the dragon in dying tells her all, lifting the veil Kurúki has set over them. Anguish of Turambar and Vainóni. She flees into the woods and casts herself over a waterfall. Madness of Turambar who dwells alone . . . . . . . . . Úrin escapes from Angamandi and seeks Tirannë. Turambar flees from him and falls upon his sword. . . . . . . . . . . . . . . . . . . . . . . . . Úrin builds a cairn and . . . . . . . . . . . doom of Melko. Tirannë dies of grief and Úrin reaches Hisilómë. . . . . . . . . . . . . . . . . . . . . . . . . . . . . . . . . . . .
Purification of Turambar and Vainóni who fare shining about the world and go with the hosts of Tulkas against Melko.

Detached jottings follow this, doubtless written at the same time:

Úrin escapes. Tirannë learns of Túrin. Both wander distraught . . . in the wood.
Túrin leaves Linwë for in a quarrel he slew one of Linwë's kin (accidentally).
Introduce Failivrin element into the story?
Turambar unable to fight because of Foalókë's eyes. Sees Failivrin depart.

This can only represent some of my father's very earliest meditations on the story of Túrin Turambar. (That it appears in the notebook at the *end* of the fully-written Tale may seem surprising, but he clearly used these books in a rather eccentric way.) Nienóri is here called *Vainóni*, and Mavwin *Tirannë*; the spell of forgetfulness is here laid by a magician named *Kurúki*, although it is the dragon who lifts the veil that the magician set over them. Túrin's two encounters with the dragon seem to have emerged from an original single one.

As I have mentioned before, the *Tale of Turambar*, like others of the *Lost Tales*, is written in ink over a wholly erased pencilled text, and the extant form of the tale is such that it could only be derived from a rougher draft preceding it; but the underlying text is so completely erased that there is no clue as to what stage it had reached in the development of the legend. It may well be – I think it is extremely probable – that in this outline concerning Vainóni, Tirannë, and Kurúki we glimpse by an odd chance a 'layer' in the Túrin-saga older even than the erased text underlying the extant version.

## §3.  *Miscellaneous Matters*

### (i)  *Beren*

The rejected passage given on p. 71, together with the marginal note 'If Beren be a Gnome (as now in the story of Tinúviel) the references to Beren must be altered' (note 4), is the basis for my assertion (p. 52) that in the earliest, now lost, form of the *Tale of Tinúviel* Beren was a Man. I have shown, I hope, that the extant form of the *Tale of Turambar* preceded the extant form of the *Tale of Tinúviel* (p. 69). Beren was a Man, *and akin to Mavwin*, when the extant *Turambar* was written; he became a Gnome in the extant *Tinúviel*; and this change was then written into *Turambar*. What the replacement passage on p. 72 does is to change the relation of Egnor and Beren from kinship with Úrin's wife to friendship with Úrin. (A correction to the typescript version of *Tinúviel*, p. 45, is later: making the comradeship of Úrin with Beren rather than with Egnor.) Two further changes to the text of Turambar consequent on the change in Beren from Man to Elf are given in notes 5 and 6. – It is interesting to observe that in the developed genealogy of *The Silmarillion*, when Beren was of course again a Man, he was also again akin to Morwen: for Beren was first cousin to Morwen's father Baragund.

In the rejected passage on p. 71 my father wrote against the name Egnor 'Damrod the Gnome' (note 2), and in the amended passage he wrote that Úrin had known Beren 'and had rendered him a service once in respect of Damrod his son'. There is no clue anywhere as to what this service may have been; but in the second of the 'schemes' for *The Book of Lost Tales* (see I.233–4) the outline for the *Tale of the Nauglafring* refers to the son of Beren and Tinúviel, the father of Elwing, by the name *Daimord*, although in the actual tale as written the son is as he was to remain *Dior*. Presumably *Daimord* is to be equated with *Damrod*.

I cannot explain the insertion of 'Damrod the Gnome' against 'Egnor' in the rejected passage – possibly it was no more than a passing idea, to give the name *Damrod* to Beren's father.

It may be noticed here that both the rejected and the replacement passages make it very clear that the events of the story of Beren and Tinúviel took place *before* the Battle of Unnumbered Tears; see pp. 65–6.

### (ii)  *The Battle of Tasarinan*

It is said at the beginning of the present tale (p. 70) that it 'tells of very ancient days of that folk [Men] before the Battle of Tasarinan when first Men entered the dark vales of Hisilómë'.

On the face of it this offers an extreme contradiction, since it is said many times that Men were shut in Hisilómë at the time of the Battle of Unnumbered Tears, and the *Tale of Turambar* takes place – must take place – after that battle. The solution lies, however, in an ambiguity in the sentence just cited. My father did not mean that this was a tale of Men in ancient days of that folk before they entered Hisilómë; he meant 'this is a tale of the ancient days *when* Men first entered Hisilómë – long before the Battle of Tasarinan'.

*Tasarinan* is the Land of Willows, *Nan-tathren* in *The Silmarillion*; the early word-lists or dictionaries give the 'Elvish' form *tasarin* 'willow' and the Gnomish *tathrin*.* The Battle of Tasarinan took place long after, in the course of the great expedition from Valinor for the release of the enslaved Noldoli in the Great Lands. See pp. 219–20.

### (iii)  *The geography of the Tale of Turambar*

The passage describing the route of the Orcs who captured Túrin (p. 77) seems to give further support to the idea that 'the mountains fencing Hisilómë from the Lands Beyond were continuous with those above Angband' (p. 62); for it is said here that the Orcs 'followed ever the line of dark hills toward those regions where they rise high and gloomy and their heads are shrouded in black vapours', and '*there* are they called Angorodin or the Iron Mountains, for beneath the roots of their northernmost fastnesses lies Angband'.

The site of the caves of the Rodothlim, agreeing well with what is said later of Nargothrond, has been discussed already (p. 123), as has the topography of the Silver Bowl and the ravine in which Turambar slew Glorund, in relation to the later Teiglin, Celebros, and Nen Girith (pp. 132–3). There are in addition some indications in the tale of how the caves of the Rodothlim related to Tinwelint's kingdom and to the land

---

* *Tasarinan* survived as the Quenya name without change: 'the willow-meads of Tasarinan' in Treebeard's song in *The Two Towers*, III.4.

where the Woodmen dwelt. It is said (p. 95) that 'the dwellings of the Rodothlim were not utterly distant from the realm of Tinwelint, albeit far enough'; while the Woodmen dwelt 'in lands that were not utterly far from Sirion or the grassy hills of that river's middle course' (p. 91), which may be taken to agree tolerably with the situation of the Forest of Brethil. The region where they lived is said in the same passage to have been 'very far away many a journey beyond the river of the Rodothlim', and Glorund's wrath was great when he heard of 'a brave folk of Men that dwelt far beyond the river' (p. 103); this also can be accommodated quite well to the developed geographical conception – Brethil was indeed a good distance beyond the river (Narog) for one setting out from Nargothrond.

My strong impression is that though the geography of the west of the Great Lands *may* have been still fairly vague, it already had, in many important respects, the same essential structure and relations as those seen on the map accompanying *The Silmarillion*.

## (iv) *The influence of the Valar*

As in the *Tale of Tinúviel* (see p. 68), in the *Tale of Turambar* also there are several references to the power of the Valar in the affairs of Men and Elves in the Great Lands – and to prayers, both of thanksgiving and request, addressed to them: thus Túrin's guardians 'thanked the Valar' that they accomplished the journey to Artanor (p. 72), and more remarkably, Úrin 'called upon the Valar of the West, being taught much concerning them by the Eldar of Kôr – the Gnomes he had encountered – and his words came, who shall say how, to Manwë Súlimo upon the heights of Taniquetil' (p. 77). (Úrin was already an 'Elf-friend', instructed by the Noldoli; cf. the replacement passage on p. 72.) Was his prayer 'answered'? Possibly this is the meaning of the very strange expression 'as the luck of the Valar had it' (p. 79), when Flinding and Beleg found Túrin lying near the point where they entered the Orc-camp.*

Dreams sent by the Valar came to the chieftains of the Rodothlim, though this was changed later and the reference to the Valar removed (p. 83 and note 10); the Woodmen said 'Would that the Valar would lift the spell that lies upon Níniel' (p. 101); and Túrin 'cried out bitterly against the Valar and his fate of woe' (p. 111).

An interesting reference to the Valar (and their power) occurs in Tinwelint's reply (p. 95) to Mavwin's words 'Give me but a woodman's cot and my son'. The king said: 'That I cannot, for I am but a king of the wild Elves, *and no Vala of the western isles*.' In the small part of *Gilfanon's Tale* that was actually written it is told (I.231) of the Dark Elves who remained in Palisor that they said that 'their brethren had gone

---

* The Gnomish dictionary has the entry: *gwalt* 'good luck – any providential occurrence or thought: "the luck of the Valar", *i·gwalt ne Vanion*' (I.272).

westward to the Shining Isles. There, said they, do the Gods dwell, and they called them the Great Folk of the West, and thought they dwelt on firelit islands in the sea.'

### (v)   Túrin's age

According to the *Tale of Turambar*, when Túrin left Mavwin he was seven years old, and it was after he had dwelt among the woodland Elves for seven years that all tidings from his home ceased (p. 74); in the *Narn* the corresponding years are eight and nine, and Túrin was seventeen, not fourteen, when 'his grief was renewed' (pp. 68, 76–7). It was exactly twelve years to the day of his departure from Mavwin when he slew Orgof and fled from Artanor (p. 75), when he was nineteen; in the *Narn* (p. 79) it was likewise twelve years since he left Hithlum when he hunted Saeros to his death, but he was twenty.

'The tale tells not the number of days that Turambar sojourned with the Rodothlim but these were very many, and during that time Nienóri grew to the threshold of womanhood' (pp. 91–2). Nienóri was seven years younger than Túrin: she was twelve when he fled from Artanor (*ibid.*). He cannot then have dwelt among the Rodothlim for more than (say) five or six years; and it is said that when he was chosen chieftain of the Woodmen he possessed 'wisdom great beyond his years'.

Bethos, chieftain of the Woodmen before Túrin, 'had fought *though then but a boy* in the Battle of Unnumbered Tears' (p. 101), but he was killed in a foray, since '*despite his years* he still rode abroad'. But it is impossible to relate Bethos' span (from 'a boy' at the Battle of Unnumbered Tears to his death on a foray at an age sufficiently ripe to be remarked on) to Túrin's; for the events after the destruction of the Rodothlim, culminating in Túrin's rescue of Níniel after her first encounter with Glorund, cannot cover any great length of time. What is clear and certain is that in the old story Túrin died when still a very young man. According to the precise dating provided in much later writing, he was 35 years old at his death.

### (vi)   The stature of Elves and Men

The Elves are conceived to be of slighter build and stature than Men: so Beleg 'was of great stature and girth *as such was among that folk*' (p. 73), and Túrin 'was a Man and of greater stature than they', i.e. Beleg and Flinding (p. 80) – this sentence being an emendation from 'he was a Man of great size' (note 8). See on this matter I. 32, 235.

### (vii)   Winged Dragons

At the end of *The Silmarillion* (p. 252) Morgoth 'loosed upon his foes the last desperate assault that he had prepared, and out of the pits of Angband there issued the winged dragons, that had not before been seen'. The suggestion is that winged dragons were a refinement of Morgoth's original design (embodied in Glaurung, Father of Dragons who went upon his belly). According to the *Tale of Turambar* (pp. 96–7), on the other hand, among Melko's many dragons some were smaller, cold like snakes, and of these many were flying creatures; while others, the mightier, were hot and heavy, fire-dragons, and these were unwinged. As already noted (p. 125) there is no suggestion in the tale that Glorund was the first of his kind.

# III

# THE FALL OF GONDOLIN

At the end of Eltas' account of Úrin's visit to Tinwelint and of the strange fates of Úrin and Mavwin, Túrin and Nienóri (p. 116), the manuscript written on loose sheets in fact continues with a brief interlude in which the further course of the tale-telling is discussed in Mar Vanwa Tyaliéva.

And so saying Eltas made an end, and none asked further. But Lindo bid all thank him for his tale, and thereto he said: 'Nay, if you will, there is much yet to tell concerning the gold of Glorund, and how the evil of that worm found its last fulfilment – but behold, that is the story of the Nauglafring or the Necklace of the Dwarves and must wait a while – and other stories of lighter and more happy things I have to tell if you would liefer listen to them.'

Then arose many voices begging Eltas to tell the tale of the Nauglafring on the morrow, but he said: 'Nay! For who here knows the full tale of Tuor and the coming of Eärendel, or who was Beren Ermabwed, and what were his deeds, for such things is it better to know rightly first.' And all said that Beren Ermabwed they knew well, but of the coming of Eärendel little enough had ever been told.

'And great harm is that,' said Lindo, 'for it is the greatest of the stories of the Gnomes, and even in this house is Ilfiniol son of Bronweg, who knows those deeds more truly than any that are now on Earth.'

About that time Ilfiniol the Gong-warden entered indeed, and Lindo said to him: 'Behold, O Littleheart son of Bronweg, it is the desire of all that you tell us the tales of Tuor and of Eärendel as soon as may be.' And Ilfiniol was fain of that, but said he: 'It is a mighty tale, and seven times shall folk fare to the Tale-fire ere it be rightly told; and so twined is it with those stories of the Nauglafring and of the Elf-march[1] that I would fain have aid in that telling of Ailios here and of Meril the Lady of the Isle, for long is it since she sought this house.'

Therefore were messengers sent on the next day to the *korin*[2] of high elms, and they said that Lindo and Vairë would fain see the face of their lady among them, for they purposed to make a festival and to hold a great telling of Elfin tales, ere Eriol their guest fared awhile to Tavrobel. So was it that for three days that room heard no more tales and the folk of Vanwa Tyaliéva made great preparations, but on the fourth night Meril fared there amid her company of maidens, and full of light and mirth was that place; but after the evening meat a great host sat before Tôn a Gwedrin,[3] and the maidens of Meril sang the most beautiful songs that island knew.[4]

And of those one did afterward Heorrenda turn to the language of his folk, and it is thus.[5]


But when those songs had fallen into silence then said Meril, who sate in the chair of Lindo: 'Come now, O Ilfiniol, begin thou the tale of tales, and tell it more fully than thou hast ever done.'

Then said Littleheart son of Bronweg . . . (Tale of Gondolin).

[sic]


This then is the *Link* between the *Tale of Turambar* and *The Fall of Gondolin* (an earlier 'preface' to the tale is given below). It seems that my father hesitated as to which tale was to follow *Turambar* (see note 4), but decided that it was time to introduce *The Fall of Gondolin*, which had been in existence for some time.

In this *Link*, Ailios (later Gilfanon) is present ('I would fain have aid . . . of Ailios here') at the end of Eltas' tale of Turambar, but at the beginning of Eltas' tale (p. 70) it is expressly said that he was not present that night. On the proposal that Eriol should 'fare awhile' to Tavrobel (as the guest of Gilfanon) see I.175.

The fact that Eltas speaks of the tale of Beren Ermabwed as if he did not know that it had only recently been told in Mar Vanwa Tyaliéva is no doubt to be explained by that tale not having been told before the Tale-fire (see pp. 4–7).

The teller of the tale of *The Fall of Gondolin*, Littleheart the Gong-warden of Mar Vanwa Tyaliéva, has appeared several times in the *Lost Tales*, and his Elvish name(s) have many different forms (see under *Changes made to names* at the end of the text of the tale). In *The Cottage of Lost Play* he is said (I.15) to be 'ancient beyond count', and to have 'sailed in Wingilot with Eärendel in that last voyage wherein they sought for Kôr'; and in the *Link* to *The Music of the Ainur* (I.46) he 'had a weather-worn face and blue eyes of great merriment, and was very slender and small, nor might one say if he were fifty or ten thousand'. He is a Gnome, the son of Bronweg/Voronwë (Voronwë of *The Silmarillion*) (I.48, 94).

*The texts of 'The Fall of Gondolin'*

The textual history of *The Fall of Gondolin*, if considered in detail, is extremely complex; but though I will set it out here, as I understand it, there is no need in fact for it to complicate the reading of the tale.

In the first place, there is a very difficult manuscript contained in two school exercise-books, where the title of the tale is *Tuor and the Exiles of Gondolin (which bringeth in the great tale of Eärendel)*. (This is the only title actually found in the early texts, but my father always later referred to it as *The Fall of Gondolin*.) This manuscript is (or rather, was) the original text of the tale, dating from 1916–17 (see I. 203 and *Unfinished Tales* p. 4), and I will call it here for convenience *Tuor A*. My father's treatment of it subsequently was unlike that of *Tinúviel* and *Turambar* (where the original text was erased and a new version written in its place); in this tale he did not set down a complete new text, but allowed a good deal of the old to stand, at least in the earlier part of it: as the revision progressed the rewriting in ink over the top of the pencilled text did become almost continuous, and though the pencil was not erased the ink effectively obliterates it. But even after the second version becomes continuous there are several places where the old narrative was not over-written but merely struck through, and remains legible. Thus, while *Tuor A* is on the same footing as *Tinúviel* and *Turambar* (and others of the *Lost Tales*) in that it is a later revision, a second version, my father's method in *Gondolin* allows it to be seen that here at least the revision was by no means a complete recasting (still less a re-imagining); for if those passages in the later parts of the tale which can still be compared in the two versions shew that he was following the old fairly closely, the same is quite probably true in those places where no comparison can be made.

From Tuor A, as it was *when all changes had been made to it* (i.e. when it was in the form that it has now), my mother made a fair copy (*Tuor B*), which considering the difficulty of the original is extremely exact, with only very occasional errors of transcription. I have said in *Unfinished Tales* (p. 5) that this copy was made 'apparently in 1917', but this now seems to me improbable.* Such conceptions as the Music of the Ainur, which is referred to by later addition in *Tuor A* (p. 163), *may* of course have been in my father's mind a good while before he wrote that tale in Oxford while working on the Dictionary (I. 45), but it seems more likely that the revision of *Tuor A* (and therefore also *Tuor B* copied from it after its revision) belongs to that period also.

Subsequently my father took his pencil to *Tuor B*, emending it fairly heavily, though mostly in the earlier part of the tale, and almost entirely

---

* Humphrey Carpenter in his *Biography* (p. 92) says that the tale 'was written out during Tolkien's convalescence at Great Haywood early in 1917', but he is doubtless referring to the original pencilled text of *Tuor A*.

for stylistic rather than narrative reasons; but these emendations, as will be seen, were not all made at the same time. Some of them are written out on separate slips, and of these several have on their reverse sides parts of an etymological discussion of certain Germanic words for the Butcher-bird or Shrike, material which appears in the Oxford Dictionary in the entry *Wariangle*. Taken with the fact that one of the slips with this material on the reverse clearly contains a direction for the shortening of the tale when delivered orally (see note 21), it is virtually certain that a good deal of the revision of *Tuor B* was made before my father read it to the Essay Club of Exeter College in the spring of 1920 (see *Unfinished Tales* p. 5).

That not all the emendations to *Tuor B* were made at the same time is shown by the existence of a typescript (*Tuor C*), without title, which extends only so far as 'your hill of vigilance against the evil of Melko' (p. 161). This was taken from *Tuor B* when some changes had been made to it, but not those which I deduce to have been made before the occasion when it was read aloud. An odd feature of this text is that blanks were left for many of the names, and only some were filled in afterwards. Towards the end of it there is a good deal of independent variation from *Tuor B*, but it is all of a minor character and none has narrative significance. I conclude that this was a side-branch that petered out.

The textual history can then be represented thus:

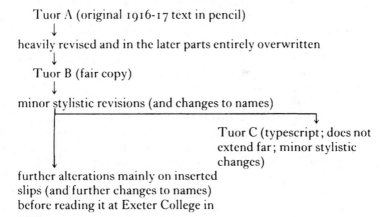

Tuor A (original 1916-17 text in pencil)
↓
heavily revised and in the later parts entirely overwritten
↓
Tuor B (fair copy)
↓
minor stylistic revisions (and changes to names)

Tuor C (typescript; does not extend far; minor stylistic changes)

further alterations mainly on inserted slips (and further changes to names) before reading it at Exeter College in 1920
(the text in this book)

Since the narrative itself underwent very little change of note in the course of this history (granted that substantial parts of the original text *Tuor A* are almost entirely illegible), the text that follows here is that of *Tuor B* in its final form, with some interesting earlier readings given in the Notes. It seems that my father did not check the fair copy *Tuor B* against the original, and did not in every case pick up the errors of transcription it contains; when he did, he emended them anew, according to the sense, and not by reference back to *Tuor A*. In a very few cases I have gone back to *Tuor A* where this is clearly correct (as 'a wall of water rose nigh to the cliff-top', p. 151, where *Tuor B* and the typescript *Tuor C* have 'high to the cliff-top').

Throughout the typescript Tuor is called *Tûr*. In *Tuor B* the name is sometimes emended from *Tuor* to *Tûr* in the earlier part of the tale (it appears as *Tûr* in the latest revisions), but by no means in every case. My father apparently decided to change the name but ultimately decided against it; and I give *Tuor* throughout.

An interesting document accompanies the Tale: this is a substantial though incomplete list of names (with explanations) that occur in it, now in places difficult or impossible to read. The names are given in alphabetical order but go only as far as L. Linguistic information from this list is incorporated in the Appendix on Names, but the head-note to the list may be cited here:

> Here is set forth by Eriol at the teaching of Bronweg's son Elfrith [*emended from* Elfriniel] or Littleheart (and he was so named for the youth and wonder of his heart) those names and words that are used in these tales from either the tongue of the Elves of Kôr as at that time spoken in the Lonely Isle, or from that related one of the Noldoli their kin whom they wrested from Melko.
>
> Here first are they which appear in *The Tale of Tuor and the Exiles of Gondolin*, first among these those ones in the Gnome-speech.

In *Tuor A* appear two versions (one struck out) of a short 'preface' to the tale by Littleheart which does not appear in *Tuor B*. The second version reads:

> Then said Littleheart son of Bronweg: 'Now the story that I tell is of the Noldoli, who were my father's folk, and belike the names will ring strange in your ears and familiar folk be called by names not before heard, for the Noldoli speak a curious tongue sweet still to my ears though not maybe to all the Eldar. Wise folk see it as close kin to Eldarissa, but it soundeth not so, and I know nought of such lore. Wherefore will I utter to you the right Eldar names where there be such, but in many cases there be none.
>     Know then,' said he, 'that

The earlier version (headed 'Link between *Tuor* and tale before') begins in the same way but then diverges:

> . . . and it is sweet to my ears still, though lest it be not so to all else of Eldar and Men here gathered I will use no more of it than I must, and that is in the names of those folk and things whereof the tale tells but

for which, seeing they passed away ere ever the rest of the Eldar came
from Kôr, the Elves have no true names. Know then,' said he, 'that
Tuor

This 'preface' thus connects to the opening of the tale. There here
appears, in the second version, the name *Eldarissa* for the language of
the *Eldar* or *Elves*, as opposed to *Noldorissa* (a term found in the
Name-list); on the distinction involved see I.50–1. With Littleheart's
words here compare what Rúmil said to Eriol about him (I.48):

'"Tongues and speeches," they will say, "one is enough for me" – and
thus said Littleheart the Gong-warden once upon a time: "Gnome-
speech," said he, "is enough for me – did not that one Eärendel and
Tuor and Bronweg my father (that mincingly ye miscall Voronwë)
speak it and no other?" Yet he had to learn the Elfin in the end, or be
doomed either to silence or to leave Mar Vanwa Tyaliéva . . .'

After these lengthy preliminaries I give the text of the Tale.

★

*Tuor and the Exiles of Gondolin*
*(which bringeth in the great tale of Eärendel)*

Then said Littleheart son of Bronweg: 'Know then that Tuor
was a man who dwelt in very ancient days in that land of the North
called Dor Lómin or the Land of Shadows, and of the Eldar the
Noldoli know it best.
Now the folk whence Tuor came wandered the forests and fells
and knew not and sang not of the sea; but Tuor dwelt not with
them, and lived alone about that lake called Mithrim, now hunting
in its woods, now making music beside its shores on his rugged
harp of wood and the sinews of bears. Now many hearing of the
power of his rough songs came from near and far to hearken to his
harping, but Tuor left his singing and departed to lonely places.
Here he learnt many strange things and got knowledge of the
wandering Noldoli, who taught him much of their speech and
lore; but he was not fated to dwell for ever in those woods.
Thereafter 'tis said that magic and destiny led him on a day
to a cavernous opening down which a hidden river flowed from
Mithrim. And Tuor entered that cavern seeking to learn its secret,
but the waters of Mithrim drove him forward into the heart of the

rock and he might not win back into the light. And this, 'tis said, was the will of Ulmo Lord of Waters at whose prompting the Noldoli had made that hidden way.

Then came the Noldoli to Tuor and guided him along dark passages amid the mountains until he came out in the light once more, and saw that the river flowed swiftly in a ravine of great depth with sides unscalable. Now Tuor desired no more to return but went ever forward, and the river led him always toward the west.[6]

The sun rose behind his back and set before his face, and where the water foamed among many boulders or fell over falls there were at times rainbows woven across the ravine, but at evening its smooth sides would glow in the setting sun, and for these reasons Tuor called it Golden Cleft or the Gully of the Rainbow Roof, which is in the speech of the Gnomes Glorfalc or Cris Ilbranteloth.

Now Tuor journeyed here for three days,[7]drinking the waters of the secret river and feeding on its fish; and these were of gold and blue and silver and of many wondrous shapes. At length the ravine widened, and ever as it opened its sides became lower and more rough, and the bed of the river more impeded with boulders against which the waters foamed and spouted. Long times would Tuor sit and gaze at the splashing water and listen to its voice, and then he would rise and leap onward from stone to stone singing as he went; or as the stars came out in the narrow strip of heaven above the gully he would raise echoes to answer the fierce twanging of his harp.

One day after a great journey of weary going Tuor at deep evening heard a cry, and he might not decide of what creature it came. Now he said: "It is a fay-creature", now, "Nay, 'tis but some small beast that waileth among the rocks"; or again it seemed to him that an unknown bird piped with a voice new to his ears and strangely sad − and because he had not heard the voice of any bird in all his wandering down Golden Cleft he was glad of the sound although it was mournful. On the next day at an hour of the morning he heard the same cry above his head, and looking up beheld three great white birds beating back up the gully on strong wing, and uttering cries like to the ones he had heard amid the dusk. Now these were the gulls, the birds of Ossë.[8]

In this part of that riverway there were islets of rock amid the currents, and fallen rocks fringed with white sand at the gully-side, so that it was ill-going, and seeking a while Tuor found a spot where he might with labour scale the cliffs at last. Then came a fresh wind against his face, and he said: "This is very good and like the drinking of wine," but he knew not that he was near the confines of the Great Sea.

As he went along above the waters that ravine again drew together and the walls towered up, so that he fared on a high cliff-top, and there came a narrow neck, and this was full of noise. Then Tuor looking downward saw the greatest of marvels, for it seemed that a flood of angry water would come up the narrows and flow back against the river to its source, but that water which had come down from distant Mithrim would still press on, and a wall of water rose nigh to the cliff-top, and it was crowned with foam and twisted by the winds. Then the waters of Mithrim were overthrown and the incoming flood swept roaring up the channel and whelmed the rocky islets and churned the white sand – so that Tuor fled and was afraid, who did not know the ways of the sea; but the Ainur put it into his heart to climb from the gully when he did, or had he been whelmed in the incoming tide, and that was a fierce one by reason of a wind from the west. Then Tuor found himself in a rugged country bare of trees, and swept by a wind coming from the set of the sun, and all the shrubs and bushes leaned to the dawn because of that prevalence of that wind. And here for a while he wandered till he came to the black cliffs by the sea and saw the ocean and its waves for the first time, and at that hour the sun sank beyond the rim of Earth far out to sea, and he stood on the cliff-top with outspread arms, and his heart was filled with a longing very great indeed. Now some say that he was the first of Men to reach the Sea and look upon it and know the desire it brings; but I know not if they say well.

In those regions he set up his abode, dwelling in a cove sheltered by great sable rocks, whose floor was of white sand, save when the high flood partly overspread it with blue water; nor did foam or froth come there save at times of the direst tempest. There long he sojourned alone and roamed about the shore or fared over the rocks at the ebb, marvelling at the pools and the great weeds, the dripping caverns and the strange sea-fowl that he saw and came to know; but the rise and fall of the water and the voice of the waves was ever to him the greatest wonder and ever did it seem a new and unimaginable thing.

Now on the quiet waters of Mithrim over which the voice of the duck or moorhen would carry far he had fared much in a small boat with a prow fashioned like to the neck of a swan, and this he had lost on the day of his finding the hidden river. On the sea he adventured not as yet, though his heart was ever egging him with a strange longing thereto, and on quiet evenings when the sun went down beyond the edge of the sea it grew to a fierce desire.

Timber he had that came down the hidden river; a goodly wood it was, for the Noldoli hewed it in the forests of Dor Lómin and floated it to him of a purpose. But he built not as yet aught save a dwelling in a sheltered place of his cove, which tales among the Eldar since name Falasquil. This by slow labour he adorned with fair carvings of the beasts and trees and flowers and birds that he knew about the waters of Mithrim, and ever among them was the Swan the chief, for Tuor loved this emblem and it became the sign of himself, his kindred and folk thereafter. There he passed a very great while until the loneliness of the empty sea got into his heart, and even Tuor the solitary longed for the voice of Men. Herewith the Ainur[9] had something to do: for Ulmo loved Tuor.

One morning while casting his eye along the shore – and it was then the latest days of summer – Tuor saw three swans flying high and strong from the northward. Now these birds he had not before seen in these regions, and he took them for a sign, and said: "Long has my heart been set on a journey far from here; lo! now at length I will follow these swans." Behold, the swans dropped into the water of his cove and there swimming thrice about rose again and winged slowly south along the coast, and Tuor bearing his harp and spear followed them.

'Twas a great day's journey Tuor put behind him that day; and he came ere evening to a region where trees again appeared, and the manner of the land through which he now fared differed greatly from those shores about Falasquil. There had Tuor known mighty cliffs beset with caverns and great spoutholes, and deep-walled coves, but from the cliff-tops a rugged land and flat ran bleakly back to where a blue rim far to the east spake of distant hills. Now however did he see a long and sloping shore and stretches of sand, while the distant hills marched ever nearer to the margin of the sea, and their dark slopes were clad with pine or fir and about their feet sprang birches and ancient oaks. From the feet of the hills fresh torrents rushed down narrow chasms and so found the shores and the salt waves. Now some of these clefts Tuor might not overleap, and often was it ill-going in these places, but still he laboured on, for the swans fared ever before him, now circling suddenly, now speeding forward, but never coming to earth, and the rush of their strong-beating wings encouraged him.

'Tis told that in this manner Tuor fared onward for a great

number of days, and that winter marched from the north somewhat speedier than he for all his tirelessness. Nevertheless came he
without scathe of beast or weather at a time of first spring to a river
mouth. Now here was the land less northerly and more kindly
than about the issuing of Golden Cleft, and moreover by a trend of
the coast was the sea now rather to the south of him than to the
west, as he could mark by the sun and stars; but he had kept his
right hand always to the sea.

This river flowed down a goodly channel and on its banks were
rich lands: grasses and moist meadow to the one side and tree-
grown slopes of the other; its waters met the sea sluggishly and
fought not as the waters of Mithrim in the north. Long tongues of
land lay islanded in its course covered with reeds and bushy
thicket, until further to seaward sandy spits ran out; and these
were places beloved by such a multitude of birds as Tuor had
nowhere yet encountered. Their piping and wailing and whistling
filled the air; and here amid their white wings Tuor lost sight of
the three swans, nor saw he them again.

Then did Tuor grow for a season weary of the sea, for the
buffeting of his travel had been sore. Nor was this without Ulmo's
devising, and that night the Noldoli came to him and he arose
from sleep. Guided by their blue lanterns he found a way beside
the river border, and strode so mightily inland that when dawn
filled the sky to his right hand lo! the sea and its voice were far
behind him, and the wind came from before him so that its odour
was not even in the air. Thus came he soon to that region that has
been called Arlisgion "the place of reeds", and this is in those lands
that are to the south of Dor Lómin and separated therefrom by the
Iron Mountains whose spurs run even to the sea. From those
mountains came this river, and of a great clearness and marvellous
chill were its waters even at this place. Now this is a river most
famous in the histories of Eldar and Noldoli and in all tongues is it
named Sirion. Here Tuor rested awhile until driven by desire he
arose once more to journey further and further by many days'
marches along the river borders. Full spring had not yet brought
summer when he came to a region yet more lovely. Here the song
of small birds shrilled about him with a music of loveliness, for
there are no birds that sing like the songbirds of the Land of
Willows; and to this region of wonder he had now come. Here the
river wound in wide curves with low banks through a great plain of
the sweetest grass and very long and green; willows of untold age
were about its borders, and its wide bosom was strewn with

waterlily leaves, whose flowers were not yet in the earliness of the year, but beneath the willows the green swords of the flaglilies were drawn, and sedges stood, and reeds in embattled array. Now there dwelt in these dark places a spirit of whispers, and it whispered to Tuor at dusk and he was loth to depart; and at morn for the glory of the unnumbered buttercups he was yet more loth, and he tarried.

Here saw he the first butterflies and was glad of the sight; and it is said that all butterflies and their kindred were born in the valley of the Land of Willows. Then came the summer and the time of moths and the warm evenings, and Tuor wondered at the multitude of flies, at their buzzing and the droning of the beetles and the hum of bees; and to all these things he gave names of his own, and wove the names into new songs on his old harp; and these songs were softer than his singing of old.

Then Ulmo grew in dread lest Tuor dwell for ever here and the great things of his design come not to fulfilment. Therefore he feared longer to trust Tuor's guidance to the Noldoli alone, who did service to him in secret, and out of fear of Melko wavered much. Nor were they strong against the magic of that place of willows, for very great was its enchantment. Did not even after the days of Tuor Noldorin and his Eldar come there seeking for Dor Lómin and the hidden river and the caverns of the Gnomes' imprisonment; yet thus nigh to their quest's end were like to abandon it? Indeed sleeping and dancing here, and making fair music of river sounds and the murmur of grass, and weaving rich fabrics of gossamer and the feathers of winged insects, they were whelmed by the goblins sped by Melko from the Hills of Iron and Noldorin made bare escape thence. But these things were not as yet.

Behold now Ulmo leapt upon his car before the doorway of his palace below the still waters of the Outer Sea; and his car was drawn by narwhal and sealion and was in fashion like a whale; and amidst the sounding of great conches he sped from Ulmonan. So great was the speed of his going that in days, and not in years without count as might be thought, he reached the mouth of the river. Up this his car might not fare without hurt to its water and its banks; therefore Ulmo, loving all rivers and this one more than most, went thence on foot, robed to the middle in mail like the scales of blue and silver fishes; but his hair was a bluish silver and his beard to his feet was of the same hue, and he bore neither helm nor crown. Beneath his mail fell the skirts of his kirtle of shimmering greens, and of what substance these were woven is not known, but whoso looked into the depths of their subtle colours seemed to behold the faint movements of deep waters shot with the stealthy lights of phosphorescent fish that live in the abyss. Girt was he with a rope of mighty pearls, and he was shod with mighty shoes of stone.

Thither he bore too his great instrument of music; and this was of strange design, for it was made of many long twisted shells pierced with holes. Blowing therein and playing with his long fingers he made deep melodies of a magic greater than any other among musicians hath ever compassed on harp or lute, on lyre or pipe, or instruments of the bow. Then coming along the river he sate among the reeds at twilight and played upon his thing of shells; and it was nigh to those places where Tuor tarried. And Tuor hearkened and was stricken dumb. There he stood knee-deep in the grass and heard no more the hum of insects, nor the murmur of the river borders, and the odour of flowers entered not into his nostrils; but he heard the sound of waves and the wail of sea-birds, and his soul leapt for rocky places and the ledges that reek of fish, for the splash of the diving cormorant and those places where the sea bores into the black cliffs and yells aloud.

Then Ulmo arose and spake to him and for dread he came near to death, for the depth of the voice of Ulmo is of the uttermost depth: even as deep as his eyes which are the deepest of all things. And Ulmo said: "O Tuor of the lonely heart, I will not that thou dwell for ever in fair places of birds and flowers; nor would I lead thee through this pleasant land,[10] but that so it must be. But fare now on thy destined journey and tarry not, for far from hence is thy weird set. Now must thou seek through the lands for the city of the folk called Gondothlim or the dwellers in stone, and the Noldoli shall escort thee thither in secret for fear of the spies of Melko. Words I will set to your mouth there, and there you shall abide awhile. Yet maybe thy life shall turn again to the mighty waters; and of a surety a child shall come of thee than whom no man shall know more of the uttermost deeps, be it of the sea or of the firmament of heaven." Then spake Ulmo also to Tuor some of his design and desire, but thereof Tuor understood little at that time and feared greatly.

Then Ulmo was wrapped in a mist as it were of sea air in those inland places, and Tuor, with that music in his ears, would fain return to the regions of the Great Sea; yet remembering his bidding turned and went inland along the river, and so fared till day. Yet he that has heard the conches of Ulmo hears them call him till death, and so did Tuor find.

When day came he was weary and slept till it was nigh dusk again, and the Noldoli came to him and guided him. So fared he many days by dusk and dark and slept by day, and because of this it came afterwards that he remembered not over well the paths that he traversed in those times. Now Tuor and his guides held on untiring, and the land became one of rolling hills and the river wound about their feet, and there were many dales of exceeding pleasantness; but here the Noldoli became ill at ease. "These," said they, "are the confines of those regions which Melko infesteth with his Goblins, the people of hate. Far to the north — yet alas not far enough, would they were ten thousand leagues — lie the Mountains of Iron where sits the power and terror of Melko, whose thralls we are. Indeed in this guiding of thee we do in secret from him, and did he know all our purposes the torment of the Balrogs would be ours."

Falling then into such fear the Noldoli soon after left him and he fared alone amid the hills, and their going proved ill afterwards, for "Melko has many eyes", 'tis said, and while Tuor fared with the Gnomes they took him twilight ways and by many secret tunnels through the hills. But now he became lost, and climbed often to the tops of knolls and hills scanning the lands about. Yet he might not see signs of any dwelling of folk, and indeed the city of the Gondothlim was not found with ease, seeing that Melko and his spies had not even yet discovered it. 'Tis said nonetheless that at this time those spies got wind thus that the strange foot of Man had been set in those lands, and that for that Melko doubled his craft and watchfulness.

Now when the Gnomes out of fear deserted Tuor, one Voronwë or Bronweg followed afar off despite his fear, when chiding availed not to enhearten the others. Now Tuor had fallen into a great weariness and was sitting beside the rushing stream, and the sea-longing was about his heart, and he was minded once more to follow this river back to the wide waters and the roaring waves. But this Voronwë the faithful came up with him again, and standing by his ear said: "O Tuor, think not but that thou shalt again one day see thy desire; arise now, and behold, I will not leave thee. I am not of the road-learned of the Noldoli, being a craftsman and maker of things made by hand of wood and of metal, and I joined not the band of escort till late. Yet of old have I heard whispers and sayings said in secret amid the weariness of thraldom, concerning a city where Noldoli might be free could they find the hidden way thereto; and we twain may without a doubt[11] find the road to the City of Stone, where is that freedom of the Gondothlim."

Know then that the Gondothlim were that kin of the Noldoli who alone escaped Melko's power when at the Battle of Unnumbered Tears he slew and enslaved their folk[12] and wove spells about them and caused them to dwell in the Hells of Iron, faring thence at his will and bidding only.

Long time did Tuor and Bronweg[13] seek for the city of that folk, until after many days they came upon a deep dale amid the hills. Here went the river over a very stony bed with much rush and noise, and it was curtained with a heavy growth of alders; but the walls of the dale were sheer, for they were nigh to some mountains which Voronwë knew not. There in the green wall that Gnome found an opening like a great door with sloping sides, and this was cloaked with thick bushes and long-tangled undergrowth; yet Voronwë's piercing sight might not be deceived. Nonetheless 'tis said that such a magic had its builders set about it (by aid of Ulmo whose power ran in that river even if the dread of Melko fared upon its banks) that none save of the blood of the Noldoli might light on it thus by chance; nor would Tuor have found it ever but for the steadfastness of that Gnome Voronwë.[14] Now the Gondothlim made their abode thus secret out of dread of Melko; yet even so no few of the braver Noldoli would slip down the river Sirion from those mountains, and if many perished so by Melko's evil, many finding this magic passage came at last to the City of Stone and swelled its people.

Greatly did Tuor and Voronwë rejoice to find this gate, yet entering they found there a way dark, rough-going, and circuitous; and long time they travelled faltering within its tunnels. It was full of fearsome echoes, and there a countless stepping of feet would come behind them, so that Voronwë became adread, and said: "It is Melko's goblins, the Orcs of the hills." Then would they run, falling over stones in the blackness, till they perceived it was but the deceit of the place. Thus did they come, after it seemed a measureless time of fearful groping, to a place where a far light glimmered, and making for this gleam they came to a gate like that by which they had entered, but in no way overgrown. Then they passed into the sunlight and could for a while see nought, but instantly a great gong sounded and there was a clash of armour, and behold, they were surrounded by warriors in steel.

Then they looked up and could see, and lo! they were at the foot of steep hills, and these hills made a great circle wherein lay a wide plain, and set therein, not rightly at the midmost but rather nearer to that place where they stood, was a great hill with a level top, and upon that summit rose a city in the new light of the morning.

Then Voronwë spake to the Guard of the Gondothlim, and his speech they comprehended, for it was the sweet tongue of the Gnomes.[15] Then spake Tuor also and questioned where they might be, and who might be the folk in arms who stood about, for he was somewhat in amaze and wondered much at the goodly fashion of their weapons. Then 'twas said to him by one of that company: "We are the guardians of the issue of the Way of Escape. Rejoice that ye have found it, for behold before you the City of Seven Names where all who war with Melko may find hope."

Then said Tuor: "What be those names?" And the chief of the Guard made answer: "'Tis said and 'tis sung: 'Gondobar am I called and Gondothlimbar, City of Stone and City of the Dwellers in Stone; Gondolin the Stone of Song and Gwarestrin am I named, the Tower of Guard, Gar Thurion or the Secret Place, for I am hidden from the eyes of Melko; but they who love me most greatly call me Loth, for like a flower am I, even Lothengriol the flower that blooms on the plain.' Yet," said he, "in our daily speech we speak and we name it mostly Gondolin." Then said Voronwë: "Bring us thither, for we fain would enter," and Tuor said that his heart desired much to tread the ways of that fair city.

Then said the chief of the Guard that they themselves must abide here, for there were yet many days of their moon of watch to pass, but that Voronwë and Tuor might pass on to Gondolin; and moreover that they would need thereto no guide, for "Lo, it stands fair to see and very clear, and its towers prick the heavens above the Hill of Watch in the midmost plain." Then Tuor and his companion fared over the plain that was of a marvellous level, broken but here and there by boulders round and smooth which lay amid a sward, or by pools in rocky beds. Many fair pathways lay across that plain, and they came after a day's light march to the foot of the Hill of Watch (which is in the tongue of the Noldoli Amon Gwareth). Then did they begin to ascend the winding stairways which climbed up to the city gate; nor might any one reach that city save on foot and espied from the walls. As the westward gate was golden in the last sunlight did they come to the long stair's head, and many eyes gazed[16] upon them from the battlements and towers.

But Tuor looked upon the walls of stone, and the uplifted towers, upon the glistering pinnacles of the town, and he looked upon the stairs of stone and marble, bordered by slender balustrades and cooled by the leap of threadlike waterfalls seeking the plain from the fountains of Amon Gwareth, and he fared as one in some dream of the Gods, for he deemed not such things were seen by men in the visions of their sleep, so great was his amaze at the glory of Gondolin.

Even so came they to the gates, Tuor in wonder and Voronwë in great joy that daring much he had both brought Tuor hither in the will of Ulmo and had himself thrown off the yoke of Melko for ever. Though he hated him no wise less, no longer did he dread that Evil One[17] with a binding terror (and of a sooth that spell which Melko held over the Noldoli was one of bottomless dread, so that he seemed ever nigh them even were they far from the Hells of Iron, and their hearts quaked and they fled not even when they could; and to this Melko trusted often).

Now is there a sally from the gates of Gondolin and a throng comes about these twain in wonder, rejoicing that yet another of the Noldoli has fled hither from Melko, and marvelling at the stature and the gaunt limbs of Tuor, his heavy spear barbed with fish bone and his great harp. Rugged was his aspect, and his locks were unkempt, and he was clad in the skins of bears. 'Tis written that in those days the fathers of the fathers of Men were of less stature than Men now are, and the children of Elfinesse of greater growth, yet was Tuor taller than any that stood there. Indeed the Gondothlim were not bent of back as some of their unhappy kin became, labouring without rest at delving and hammering for Melko, but small were they and slender and very lithe.[18] They were swift of foot and surpassing fair; sweet and sad were their mouths, and their eyes had ever a joy within quivering to tears; for in those times the Gnomes were exiles at heart, haunted with a desire for their ancient home that faded not. But fate and unconquerable eagerness after knowledge had driven them into far places, and now were they hemmed by Melko and must make their abiding as fair as they might by labour and by love.

How it came ever that among Men the Noldoli have been confused with the Orcs who are Melko's goblins, I know not, unless it be that certain of the Noldoli were twisted to the evil of Melko and mingled among these Orcs, for all that race were bred by Melko of the subterranean heats and slime. Their hearts were of granite and their bodies deformed; foul their faces which smiled not, but their laugh that of the clash of metal, and to nothing were they more fain than to aid in the basest of the purposes of Melko. The greatest hatred was between them and the Noldoli, who named them Glamhoth, or folk of dreadful hate.

Behold, the armed' guardians of the gate pressed back the thronging folk that gathered about the wanderers, and one among them spake saying: "This is a city of watch and ward, Gondolin on Amon Gwareth, where all may be free who are of true heart, but none may be free to enter unknown. Tell me then your names." But Voronwë named himself Bronweg of the Gnomes, come hither[19] by the will of Ulmo as guide to this son of Men; and Tuor said: "I am Tuor son of Peleg son of Indor of the house of the Swan of the sons of the Men of the North who live far hence, and I fare hither by the will of Ulmo of the Outer Oceans."

Then all who listened grew silent, and his deep and rolling voice held them in amaze, for their own voices were fair as the plash of fountains. Then a saying arose among them: "Lead him before the king."

Then did the throng return within the gates and the wanderers with them, and Tuor saw they were of iron and of great height and strength. Now the streets of Gondolin were paved with stone and wide, kerbed with marble, and fair houses and courts amid gardens of bright flowers were set about the ways, and many towers of great slenderness and beauty builded of white marble and carved most marvellously rose to the heaven. Squares there were lit with fountains and the home of birds that sang amid the branches of their aged trees, but of all these the greatest was that place where stood the king's palace, and the tower thereof was the loftiest in the city, and the fountains that played before the doors shot twenty fathoms and seven in the air and fell in a singing rain of crystal: therein did the sun glitter splendidly by day, and the moon most magically shimmered by night. The birds that dwelt there were of the whiteness of snow and their voices sweeter than a lullaby of music.

On either side of the doors of the palace were two trees, one that bore blossom of gold and the other of silver, nor did they ever fade, for they were shoots of old from the glorious Trees of Valinor that lit those places before Melko and Gloomweaver withered them: and those trees the Gondothlim named Glingol and Bansil.

Then Turgon king of Gondolin robed in white with a belt of gold, and a coronet of garnets was upon his head, stood before his doors and spake from the head of the white stairs that led thereto. "Welcome, O Man of the Land of Shadows. Lo! thy coming was set in our books of wisdom, and it has been written that there would come to pass many great things in the homes of the Gondothlim whenso thou faredst hither."

Then spake Tuor, and Ulmo set power in his heart and majesty in his voice. "Behold, O father of the City of Stone, I am bidden by him who maketh deep music in the Abyss, and who knoweth the mind of Elves and Men, to say unto thee that the days of Release draw nigh. There have come to the ears of Ulmo whispers of your dwelling and your hill of vigilance against the evil of Melko, and he is glad: but his heart is wroth and the hearts of the Valar are angered who sit in the mountains of Valinor and look upon the world from the peak of Taniquetil, seeing the sorrow of the thraldom of the Noldoli and the wanderings of Men; for Melko ringeth them in the Land of Shadows beyond hills of iron. Therefore have I been brought by a secret way to bid you number your hosts and prepare for battle, for the time is ripe."

Then spake Turgon: "That will I not do, though it be the words of Ulmo and all the Valar. I will not adventure this my people against the terror of the Orcs, nor emperil my city against the fire of Melko."

Then spake Tuor: "Nay, if thou dost not now dare greatly then will the Orcs dwell for ever and possess in the end most of the mountains of the Earth, and cease not to trouble both Elves and Men, even though by other means the Valar contrive hereafter to release the Noldoli; but if thou trust now to the Valar, though terrible the encounter, then shall the Orcs fall, and Melko's power be minished to a little thing."

But Turgon said that he was king of Gondolin and no will should force him against his counsel to emperil the dear labour of long ages gone; but Tuor said, for thus was he bidden by Ulmo who had feared the reluctance of Turgon: "Then am I bidden to say that men of the Gondothlim repair swiftly and secretly down the river Sirion to the sea, and there build them boats and go seek back to Valinor: lo! the paths thereto are forgotten and the highways faded from the world, and the seas and mountains are about it, yet still dwell there the Elves on the hill of Kôr and the Gods sit in Valinor, though their mirth is minished for sorrow and fear of Melko, and they hide their land and weave about it inaccessible magic that no evil come to its shores. Yet still might thy messengers win there and turn their hearts that they rise in wrath and smite Melko, and destroy the Hells of Iron that he has wrought beneath the Mountains of Darkness."

Then said Turgon: "Every year at the lifting of winter have messengers repaired swiftly and by stealth down the river that is called Sirion to the coasts of the Great Sea, and there builded them boats whereto have swans and gulls been harnessed or the strong wings of the wind, and these have sought back beyond the moon and sun to Valinor; but the paths thereto are forgotten and the highways faded from the world, and the seas and mountains are about it, and they that sit within in mirth reck little of the dread of Melko or the sorrow of the world, but hide their land and weave about it inaccessible magic, that no tidings of evil come ever to their ears. Nay, enough of my people have for years untold gone out to the wide waters never to return, but have perished in the deep places or wander now lost in the shadows that have no paths; and at the coming of next year no more shall fare to the sea, but rather will we trust to ourselves and our city for the warding off of Melko; and thereto have the Valar been of scant help aforetime."

Then Tuor's heart was heavy, and Voronwë wept; and Tuor sat by the great fountain of the king and its splashing recalled the music of the waves, and his soul was troubled by the conches of Ulmo and he would return down the waters of Sirion to the sea. But Turgon, who knew that Tuor, mortal as he was, had the favour of the Valar, marking his stout glance and the power of his voice sent to him and bade him dwell in Gondolin and be in his favour, and abide even within the royal halls if he would.

Then Tuor, for he was weary, and that place was fair, said yea; and hence cometh the abiding of Tuor in Gondolin. Of all Tuor's deeds among the Gondothlim the tales tell not, but 'tis said that many a time would he have stolen thence, growing weary of the concourses of folk, and thinking of empty forest and fell or hearing afar the sea-music of Ulmo, had not his heart been filled with love for a woman of the Gondothlim, and she was a daughter of the king.

Now Tuor learnt many things in those realms taught by Voronwë whom he loved, and who loved him exceeding greatly in return; or else was he instructed by the skilled men of the city and the wise men of the king. Wherefore he became a man far mightier than aforetime and wisdom was in his counsel; and many things became clear to him that were unclear before, and many things known that are still unknown to mortal Men. There he heard concerning that city of Gondolin and how

unstaying labour through ages of years had not sufficed to its
building and adornment whereat folk[20] travailed yet; of the delving of that hidden tunnel he heard, which the folk named the Way
of Escape, and how there had been divided counsels in that
matter, yet pity for the enthralled Noldoli had prevailed in the end
to its making; of the guard without ceasing he was told, that
was held there in arms and likewise at certain low places in the
encircling mountains, and how watchers dwelt ever vigilant on
the highest peaks of that range beside builded beacons ready
for the fire; for never did that folk cease to look for an onslaught
of the Orcs did their stronghold become known.

Now however was the guard of the hills maintained rather by
custom than necessity, for the Gondothlim had long ago with
unimagined toil levelled and cleared and delved all that plain
about Amon Gwareth, so that scarce Gnome or bird or beast or
snake could approach but was espied from many leagues off, for
among the Gondothlim were many whose eyes were keener than
the very hawks of Manwë Súlimo Lord of Gods and Elves who
dwells upon Taniquetil; and for this reason did they call that
vale Tumladin or the valley of smoothness. Now this great work
was finished to their mind, and folk were the busier about the
quarrying of metals and the forging of all manner of swords and
axes, spears and bills, and the fashioning of coats of mail,
byrnies and hauberks, greaves and vambraces, helms and shields.
Now 'twas said to Tuor that already the whole folk of Gondolin
shooting with bows without stay day or night might not expend
their hoarded arrows in many years, and that yearly their fear of
the Orcs grew the less for this.

There learnt Tuor of building with stone, of masonry and the
hewing of rock and marble; crafts of weaving and spinning,
broidure and painting, did he fathom, and cunning in metals.
Musics most delicate he there heard; and in these were they who
dwelt in the southern city the most deeply skilled, for there played
a profusion of murmuring founts and springs. Many of these
subtleties Tuor mastered and learned to entwine with his songs to
the wonder and heart's joy of all who heard. Strange stories of the
Sun and Moon and Stars, of the manner of the Earth and its
elements, and of the depths of heaven, were told to him; and the
secret characters of the Elves he learnt, and their speeches and old
tongues, and heard tell of Ilúvatar, the Lord for Always, who
dwelleth beyond the world, of the great music of the Ainur about
Ilúvatar's feet in the uttermost deeps of time, whence came the

making of the world and the manner of it, and all therein and their governance.[21]

Now for his skill and his great mastery over all lore and craft whatsoever, and his great courage of heart and body, did Tuor become a comfort and stay to the king who had no son; and he was beloved by the folk of Gondolin. Upon a time the king caused his most cunning artificers to fashion a suit of armour for Tuor as a great gift, and it was made of Gnome-steel overlaid with silver; but his helm was adorned with a device of metals and jewels like to two swan-wings, one on either side, and a swan's wing was wrought on his shield; but he carried an axe rather than a sword, and this in the speech of the Gondothlim he named Dramborleg, for its buffet stunned and its edge clove all armour.

A house was built for him upon the southern walls, for he loved the free airs and liked not the close neighbourhood of other dwellings. There it was his delight often to stand on the battlements at dawn, and folk rejoiced to see the new light catch the wings of his helm – and many murmured and would fain have backed him into battle with the Orcs, seeing that the speeches of those two, Tuor and Turgon, before the palace were known to many; but this matter went not further for reverence of Turgon, and because at this time in Tuor's heart the thought of the words of Ulmo seemed to have grown dim and far off.

Now came days when Tuor had dwelt among the Gondothlim many years. Long had he known and cherished a love for the king's daughter, and now was his heart full of that love. Great love too had Idril for Tuor, and the strands of her fate were woven with his even from that day when first she gazed upon him from a high window as he stood a way-worn suppliant before the palace of the king. Little cause had Turgon to withstand their love, for he saw in Tuor a kinsman of comfort and great hope. Thus was first wed a child of Men with a daughter of Elfinesse, nor was Tuor the last. Less bliss have many had than they, and their sorrow in the end was great. Yet great was the mirth of those days when Idril and Tuor were wed before the folk in Gar Ainion, the Place of the Gods, nigh to the king's halls. A day of merriment was that wedding to the city of Gondolin, and of [22] the greatest happiness to Tuor and Idril. Thereafter dwelt they in joy in that house upon the walls that looked out south over Tumladin, and this was good to the hearts of all in the city save Meglin alone. Now that Gnome was come of an ancient house, though now were its numbers less

than others, but he himself was nephew to the king by his mother
the king's sister Isfin; and that tale of Isfin and Eöl may not here be
told.[23]

Now the sign of Meglin was a sable Mole, and he was great
among quarrymen and a chief of the delvers after ore; and many of
these belonged to his house. Less fair was he than most of this
goodly folk, swart and of none too kindly mood, so that he won
small love, and whispers there were that he had Orc's blood in his
veins, but I know not how this could be true. Now he had bid
often with the king for the hand of Idril, yet Turgon finding her
very loth had as often said nay, for him seemed Meglin's suit was
caused as much by the desire of standing in high power beside the
royal throne as by love of that most fair maid. Fair indeed was
she and brave thereto; and the people called her Idril of the
Silver Feet* in that she went ever barefoot and bareheaded, king's
daughter as she was, save only at pomps of the Ainur; and Meglin
gnawed his anger seeing Tuor thrust him out.

In these days came to pass the fulfilment of the time of the
desire of the Valar and the hope of [the] Eldalië, for in great love
Idril bore to Tuor a son and he was called Eärendel. Now thereto
there are many interpretations both among Elves and Men, but
belike it was a name wrought of some secret tongue among the
Gondothlim[24] and that has perished with them from the dwellings
of the Earth.

Now this babe was of greatest beauty; his skin of a shining white
and his eyes of a blue surpassing that of the sky in southern lands –
bluer than the sapphires of the raiment of Manwë;[25] and the envy
of Meglin was deep at his birth, but the joy of Turgon and all the
people very great indeed.

Behold now many years have gone since Tuor was lost amid the
foothills and deserted by those Noldoli; yet many years too have
gone since to Melko's ears came first those strange tidings – faint
were they and various in form – of a Man wandering amid the
dales of the waters of Sirion. Now Melko was not much afraid of
the race of Men in those days of his great power, and for this
reason did Ulmo work through one of this kindred for the better
deceiving of Melko, seeing that no Valar and scarce any of the
Eldar or Noldoli might stir unmarked of his vigilance. Yet nonetheless foreboding smote that ill heart at the tidings, and he got
together a mighty army of spies: sons of the Orcs were there with

* Faintly pencilled above in *Tuor B: Idril Talceleb.*

eyes of yellow and green like cats that could pierce all glooms and
see through mist or fog or night; snakes that could go everywhither
and search all crannies or the deepest pits or the highest peaks,
listen to every whisper that ran in the grass or echoed in the hills;
wolves there were and ravening dogs and great weasels full of the
thirst of blood whose nostrils could take scent moons old through
running water, or whose eyes find among shingle footsteps that
had passed a lifetime since; owls came and falcons whose keen
glance might descry by day or night the fluttering of small birds in
all the woods of the world, and the movement of every mouse or
vole or rat that crept or dwelt throughout the Earth. All these he
summoned to his Hall of Iron, and they came in multitudes.
Thence he sent them over the Earth to seek this Man who had
escaped from the Land of Shadows, but yet far more curiously and
intently to search out the dwelling of the Noldoli that had escaped
his thraldom; for these his heart burnt to destroy or to enslave.

    Now while Tuor dwelt in happiness and in great increase of
knowledge and might in Gondolin, these creatures through the
years untiring nosed among the stones and rocks, hunted
the forests and the heaths, espied the airs and lofty places,
tracked all paths about the dales and plains, and neither let
nor stayed. From this hunt they brought a wealth of tidings to
Melko – indeed among many hidden things that they dragged
to light they discovered that Way of Escape whereby Tuor
and Voronwë entered aforetime. Nor had they done so save by
constraining some of the less stout of the Noldoli with dire threats
of torment to join in that great ransacking; for because of the
magic about that gate no folk of Melko unaided by the Gnomes
could come to it. Yet now they had pried of late far into its
tunnels and captured within many of the Noldoli creeping there to
flee from thraldom. They had scaled too the Encircling Hills*
at certain places and gazed upon the beauty of the city of
Gondolin and the strength of Amon Gwareth from afar; but into
the plain they could not win for the vigilance of its guardians and
the difficulty of those mountains. Indeed the Gondothlim were
mighty archers, and bows they made of a marvel of power.
Therewith might they shoot an arrow into heaven seven times as
far as could the best bowman among Men shoot at a mark upon the
ground; and they would have suffered no falcon to hover long over
their plain or snake to crawl therein; for they liked not creatures of
blood, broodlings of Melko.

    * Pencilled above in *Tuor B: Heborodin*.

Now in those days was Eärendel one year old when these ill tidings came to that city of the spies of Melko and how they encompassed the vale of Tumladin around. Then Turgon's heart was saddened, remembering the words of Tuor in past years before the palace doors; and he caused the watch and ward to be thrice strengthened at all points, and engines of war to be devised by his artificers and set upon the hill. Poisonous fires and hot liquids, arrows and great rocks, was he prepared to shoot down on any who would assail those gleaming walls; and then he abode as well content as might be, but Tuor's heart was heavier than the king's, for now the words of Ulmo came ever to his mind, and their purport and gravity he understood more deeply than of old; nor did he find any great comfort in Idril, for her heart boded more darkly even than his own.

Know then that Idril had a great power of piercing with her thought the darkness of the hearts of Elves and Men, and the glooms of the future thereto – further even than is the common power of the kindreds of the Eldalië; therefore she spake thus on a day to Tuor: "Know, my husband, that my heart misgives me for doubt of Meglin, and I fear that he will bring an ill on this fair realm, though by no means may I see how or when – yet I dread lest all that he knows of our doings and preparations become in some manner known to the Foe, so that he devise a new means of whelming us, against which we have thought of no defence. Lo! I dreamed on a night that Meglin builded a furnace, and coming at us unawares flung therein Eärendel our babe, and would after thrust in thee and me; but that for sorrow at the death of our fair child I would not resist."

And Tuor answered: "There is reason for thy fear, for neither is my heart good towards Meglin; yet is he the nephew of the king and thine own cousin, nor is there charge against him, and I see nought to do but to abide and watch."

But Idril said: "This is my rede thereto: gather thou in deep secret those delvers and quarrymen who by careful trial are found to hold least love for Meglin by reason of the pride and arrogance of his dealings among them. From these thou must choose trusty men to keep watch upon Meglin whenso he fares to the outer hills, yet I counsel thee to set the greater part of those in whose secrecy thou canst confide at a hidden delving, and to devise with their aid – howsoever cautious and slow that labour be – a secret way from thy house here beneath the rocks of this hill unto the vale below. Now this way must not lead toward the Way of Escape, for my heart bids me trust it not, but even to that far distant pass, the Cleft of Eagles in the southern mountains; and the further this delving reach thitherward beneath the plain so much the better would I esteem it – yet let all this labour be kept dark save from a few."

Now there are none such delvers of earth or rock as the Noldoli (and this Melko knows), but in those places is the earth of a great hardness; and Tuor said: "The rocks of the hill of Amon Gwareth are as iron, and only with much travail may they be cloven; yet if this be done in secret then must great time and patience be added; but the stone of the floor of the Vale of Tumladin is as forgéd steel, nor may it be hewn without the knowledge of the Gondothlim save in moons and years."

Idril said then: "Sooth this may be, but such is my rede, and there is yet time to spare." Then Tuor said that he might not see all its purport, "but 'better is any plan than a lack of counsel', and I will do even as thou sayest".

Now it so chanced that not long after Meglin went to the hills for the getting of ore, and straying in the mountains alone was taken by some of the Orcs prowling there, and they would do him evil and terrible hurt, knowing him to be a man of the Gondothlim. This was however unknown of Tuor's watchers. But evil came into the heart of Meglin, and he said to his captors: "Know then that I am Meglin son of Eöl who had to wife Isfin sister of Turgon king of the Gondothlim." But they said: "What is that to us?" And Meglin answered: "Much is it to you; for if you slay me, be it speedy or slow, ye will lose great tidings concerning the city of Gondolin that your master would rejoice to hear." Then the Orcs stayed their hands, and said they would give him life if the matters he opened to them seemed to merit that; and Meglin told them of all the fashion of that plain and city, of its walls and their height and thickness, and the valour of its gates; of the host of men at arms who now obeyed Turgon he spake, and the countless hoard of weapons gathered for their equipment, of the engines of war and the venomous fires.

Then the Orcs were wroth, and having heard these matters were yet for slaying him there and then as one who impudently enlarged the power of his miserable folk to the mockery of the great might and puissance of Melko; but Meglin catching at a straw said: "Think ye not that ye would rather pleasure your master if ye bore to his feet so noble a captive, that he might hear my tidings of himself and judge of their verity?"

Now this seemed good to the Orcs, and they returned from the mountains about Gondolin to the Hills of Iron and the dark halls of Melko; thither they haled Meglin with them, and now was he in a sore dread. But when he knelt before the black throne of Melko in terror of the grimness of the shapes about him, of the wolves that sat beneath that chair and of the adders that twined about its legs, Melko bade him speak. Then told he those tidings, and Melko hearkening spake very fair to him, that the insolence of his heart in great measure returned.

Now the end of this was that Melko aided by the cunning of Meglin devised a plan for the overthrow of Gondolin. For this Meglin's reward was to be a great captaincy among the Orcs – yet Melko purposed not in his heart to fulfil such a promise – but Tuor and Eärendel should Melko burn, and Idril be given to Meglin's arms – and such promises was that evil one fain to redeem. Yet as meed of treachery did Melko threaten Meglin with the torment of the Balrogs. Now these were demons with whips of flame and claws of steel by whom he tormented those of the Noldoli who durst withstand him in anything – and the Eldar have called them Malkarauki. But the rede that Meglin gave to Melko was that not all the host of the Orcs nor the Balrogs in their fierceness might by assault or siege hope ever to overthrow the walls and gates of Gondolin even if they availed to win unto the plain without. Therefore he counselled Melko to devise out of his sorceries a succour for his warriors in their endeavour. From the greatness of his wealth of metals and his powers of fire he bid him make beasts like snakes and dragons of irresistible might that should overcreep the Encircling Hills and lap that plain and its fair city in flame and death.

Then Meglin was bidden fare home lest at his absence men suspect somewhat; but Melko wove about him the spell of bottomless dread, and he had thereafter neither joy nor quiet in his heart. Nonetheless he wore a fair mask of good liking and gaiety, so that men said: "Meglin is softened", and he was held in less disfavour; yet Idril feared him the more. Now Meglin said: "I have laboured much and am minded to rest, and to join in the dance and the song and the merrymakings of the folk", and he went no more quarrying stone or ore in the hills: yet in sooth he sought herein to drown his fear and disquiet. A dread possessed him that Melko was ever at hand, and this came of the spell; and he durst never again wander amid the mines lest he again fall in with the Orcs and be bidden once more to the terrors of the halls of darkness.

Now the years fare by, and egged by Idril Tuor keepeth ever at his secret delving; but seeing that the leaguer of spies hath grown thinner Turgon dwelleth more at ease and in less fear. Yet these years are filled by Melko in the utmost ferment of labour, and all the thrall-folk of the Noldoli must dig unceasingly for metals while Melko sitteth and deviseth fires and calleth flames and smokes to come from the lower heats, nor doth he suffer any of the Noldoli to stray ever a foot from their places of bondage. Then on a time Melko assembled all his most cunning smiths and sorcerers, and of iron and flame they wrought a host of monsters such as have only at that time been seen and shall not again be till the Great End. Some were all of iron so cunningly linked that they might flow like slow rivers of metal or coil themselves around and above all obstacles before them, and these were filled in their innermost depths with the grimmest of the Orcs with scimitars and spears; others of bronze and copper were given hearts and spirits of blazing fire, and they blasted all that stood before them with the terror of their snorting or trampled whatso escaped the ardour of their breath; yet others were creatures of pure flame that writhed like ropes of molten metal, and they brought to ruin whatever fabric they came nigh, and iron and stone melted before them and became as water, and upon them rode the Balrogs in hundreds; and these were the most dire of all those monsters which Melko devised against Gondolin.

Now when the seventh summer had gone since the treason of Meglin, and Eärendel was yet of very tender years though a valorous child, Melko withdrew all his spies, for every path and corner of the mountains was now known to him; yet the Gondothlim thought in their unwariness that Melko would no longer seek against them, perceiving their might and the impregnable strength of their dwelling.

But Idril fell into a dark mood and the light of her face was clouded, and many wondered thereat; yet Turgon reduced the watch and ward to its ancient numbers, and to somewhat less, and as autumn came and the gathering of fruits was over folk turned with glad hearts to the feasts of winter: but Tuor stood upon the battlements and gazed upon the Encircling Hills.

Now behold, Idril stood beside him, and the wind was in her hair, and Tuor thought that she was exceeding beautiful, and stooped to kiss her; but her face was sad, and she said: "Now come the days when thou must make choice," and Tuor knew not what she said. Then drawing him within their halls she said to him how her heart misgave her for fear concerning Eärendel her son, and for boding that some great evil was nigh, and that Melko would be at the bottom of it. Then Tuor would comfort her, but might not, and she questioned him concerning the secret delving, and he said how it now led a league into the plain, and at that was her heart somewhat lightened. But still she counselled that the delving be pressed on, and that henceforth should speed weigh more than secrecy, "because now is the time very near". And another rede she gave him, and this he took also, that certain of the bravest and most true among the lords and warriors of the Gondothlim be chosen with care and told of that secret way and its issue. These she counselled him to make into a stout guard and to give them his emblem to wear that they become his folk, and to do thus under pretext of the right and dignity of a great lord, kinsman to the king. "Moreover," said she, "I will get my father's favour to that." In secret too she whispered to folk that if the city came to its last stand or Turgon be slain that they rally about Tuor and her son, and to this they laughed a yea, saying however that Gondolin would stand as long as Taniquetil or the Mountains of Valinor.

Yet to Turgon she spoke not openly, nor suffered Tuor to do so, as he desired, despite their love and reverence for him – a great and a noble and a glorious king he was – seeing that he trusted in Meglin and held with blind obstinacy his belief in the impregnable might of the city and that Melko sought no more against it, perceiving no hope therein. Now in this he was ever strengthened by the cunning sayings of Meglin. Behold, the guile of that Gnome was very great, for he wrought much in the dark, so that folk said: "He doth well to bear the sign of a sable mole"; and by reason of the folly of certain of the quarrymen, and yet more by reason of the loose words of certain among his kin to whom word was somewhat unwarily spoken by Tuor, he gathered a knowledge of the secret work and laid against that a plan of his own.

So winter deepened, and it was very cold for those regions, so that frost fared about the plain of Tumladin and ice lay on its pools; yet the fountains played ever on Amon Gwareth and the two trees blossomed, and folk made merry till the day of terror that was hidden in the heart of Melko.

In these ways that bitter winter passed, and the snows lay deeper than ever before on the Encircling Hills; yet in its time a spring of wondrous glory melted the skirts of those white mantles and the valley drank the waters and burst into flowers. So came and passed with revelry of children the festival of Nost-na-Lothion or the Birth of Flowers, and the hearts of the Gondothlim were uplifted for the good promise of the year; and now at length is that great feast Tarnin Austa or the Gates of Summer near at hand. For know that on a night it was their custom to begin a solemn ceremony at midnight, continuing it even till the dawn of Tarnin Austa broke, and no voice was uttered in the city from midnight till the break of day, but the dawn they hailed with ancient songs. For years uncounted had the coming of summer thus been greeted with music of choirs, standing upon their gleaming eastern wall; and now comes even the night of vigil and the city is filled with silver lamps, while in the groves upon the new-leaved trees lights of jewelled colours swing, and low musics go along the ways, but no voice sings until the dawn.

The sun has sunk beyond the hills and folk array them for the festival very gladly and eagerly – glancing in expectation to the East. Lo! even when she had gone and all was dark, a new light suddenly began, and a glow there was, but it was beyond the northward heights,[26] and men marvelled, and there was a thronging of the walls and battlements. Then wonder grew to doubt as that light waxed and became yet redder, and doubt to dread as men saw the snow upon the mountains dyed as it were with blood. And thus it was that the fire-serpents of Melko came upon Gondolin.

Then came over the plain riders who bore breathless tidings from those who kept vigil on the peaks; and they told of the fiery hosts and the shapes like dragons, and said: "Melko is upon us." Great was the fear and anguish within that beauteous city, and the streets and byeways were filled with the weeping of women and the wailing of children, and the squares with the mustering of soldiers and the ring of arms. There were the gleaming banners of all the great houses and kindreds of the Gondothlim. Mighty was the array of the house of the king and their colours were white and gold and red, and their emblems the moon and the sun and the scarlet heart.[27] Now in the midmost of these stood Tuor above all heads, and his mail of silver gleamed; and about him was a press of the stoutest of the folk. Lo! all these wore wings as it were of swans or gulls upon their helms, and the emblem of the White Wing was upon their shields. But the folk of Meglin were drawn up in the same place, and sable was their harness, and they bore no sign or emblem, but their round caps of steel were covered with moleskin, and they fought with axes two-headed like mattocks. There Meglin prince of Gondobar gathered many warriors of dark countenance and lowering gaze about him, and a ruddy glow shone upon their faces and gleamed about the polished surfaces of their accoutrement. Behold, all the hills to the north were ablaze, and it was as if rivers of fire ran down the slopes that led to the plain of Tumladin, and folk might already feel the heat thereof.

And many other kindreds were there, the folk of the Swallow and the Heavenly Arch, and from these folk came the greatest number and the best of the bowmen, and they were arrayed upon the broad places of the walls. Now the folk of the Swallow bore a fan of feathers on their helms, and they were arrayed in white and dark blue and in purple and black and showed an arrowhead on their shields. Their lord was Duilin, swiftest of all men to run and leap and surest of archers at a mark. But they of the Heavenly Arch being a folk of uncounted wealth were arrayed in a glory of colours, and their arms were set with jewels that flamed in the light now over the sky. Every shield of that battalion was of the blue of the heavens and its boss a jewel built of seven gems, rubies and amethysts and sapphires, emeralds, chrysoprase, topaz, and amber, but an opal of great size was set in their helms. Egalmoth was their chieftain, and wore a blue mantle upon which the stars were broidered in crystal, and his sword was bent – now none else of the Noldoli bore curved swords – yet he trusted rather to the bow, and shot therewith further than any among that host.

There too were the folk of the Pillar and of the Tower of Snow, and both these kindreds were marshalled by Penlod, tallest of Gnomes. There were those of the Tree, and they were a great house, and their raiment was green. They fought with iron-studded clubs or with slings, and their lord Galdor was held the most valiant of all the Gondothlim save Turgon alone. There stood the house of the Golden Flower who bare a rayed sun upon their shield, and their chief Glorfindel bare a mantle so broidered in threads of gold that it was diapered with celandine as a field in spring; and his arms were damascened with cunning gold.

Then came there from the south of the city the people of the Fountain, and Ecthelion was their lord, and silver and diamonds were their delight; and swords very long and bright and pale did they wield, and they went into battle to the music of flutes. Behind them came the host of the Harp, and this was a battalion of brave warriors; but their leader Salgant was a craven, and he fawned upon Meglin. They were dight with tassels of silver and tassels of gold, and a harp of silver shone in their blazonry upon a field of black; but Salgant bore one of gold, and he alone rode into battle of all the sons of the Gondothlim, and he was heavy and squat.

Now the last of the battalions was furnished by the folk of the Hammer of Wrath, and of these came many of the best smiths and craftsmen, and all that kindred reverenced Aulë the Smith more than all other Ainur. They fought with great maces like hammers, and their shields were heavy, for their arms were very strong. In older days they had been much recruited by Noldoli who escaped from the mines of Melko, and the hatred of this house for the works of that evil one and the Balrogs his demons was exceeding great. Now their leader was Rog, strongest of the Gnomes, scarce second in valour to that Galdor of the Tree. The sign of this people was the Stricken Anvil, and a hammer that smiteth sparks about it was set on their shields, and red gold and black iron was their delight. Very numerous was that battalion, nor had any amongst them a faint heart, and they won the greatest glory of all those fair houses in that struggle against doom; yet were they ill-fated, and none ever fared away from that field, but fell about Rog and vanished from the Earth; and with them much craftsmanship and skill has been lost for ever.[28]

This was the fashion and the array of the eleven houses of the Gondothlim with their signs and emblems, and the bodyguard of Tuor, the folk of the Wing, was accounted the twelfth. Now is the face of that chieftain grim and he looks not to live long – and there in his house upon the walls Idril arrays herself in mail, and seeks Eärendel. And that child was in tears for the strange lights of red that played about the walls of the chamber where he slept; and tales that his nurse Meleth had woven him concerning fiery Melko at times of his waywardness came to him and troubled him. But his mother coming set about him a tiny coat of mail that she had let fashion in secret, and at that time he was glad and exceeding proud, and he shouted for pleasure. Yet Idril wept, for much had she cherished in her heart the fair city and her goodly house, and the love of Tuor and herself that had dwelt therein; but now she saw its destroying nigh at hand, and feared that her contriving would fail against this overwhelming might of the terror of the serpents.

It was now four hours still from middle night, and the sky was red in the north and in the east and west; and those serpents of iron had reached the levels of Tumladin, and those fiery ones were among the lowest slopes of the hills, so that the guards were taken and set in evil torment by the Balrogs that scoured all about, saving only to the furthest south where was Cristhorn the Cleft of Eagles.

Then did King Turgon call a council, and thither fared Tuor and Meglin as royal princes; and Duilin came with Egalmoth and Penlod the tall, and Rog strode thither with Galdor of the Tree and golden Glorfindel and Ecthelion of the voice of music. Thither too fared Salgant atremble at the tidings, and other nobles beside of less blood but better heart.

Then spake Tuor and this was his rede, that a mighty sally be made forthwith, ere the light and heat grew too great in the plain; and many backed him, being but of different minds as to whether the sally should be made by the entire host with the maids and wives and children amidmost, or by diverse bands seeking out in many directions; and to this last Tuor leaned.

But Meglin and Salgant alone held other counsel and were for holding to the city and seeking to guard those treasures that lay within. Out of guile did Meglin speak thus, fearing lest any of the Noldoli escape the doom that he had brought upon them for the saving of his skin, and he dreaded lest his treason become known and somehow vengeance find him in after days. But Salgant spake both echoing Meglin and being grievously afraid of issuing from the city, for he was fain rather to do battle from an impregnable fortress than to risk hard blows upon the field.

Then the lord of the house of the Mole played upon the one weakness of Turgon, saying: "Lo! O King, the city of Gondolin contains a wealth of jewels and metals and stuffs and of things wrought by the hands of the Gnomes to surpassing beauty, and all these thy lords – more brave meseems than wise – would abandon to the Foe. Even should victory be thine upon the plain thy city will be sacked and the Balrogs get hence with a measureless booty"; and Turgon groaned, for Meglin had known his great love for the wealth and loveliness of that burg[29] upon Amon Gwareth. Again said Meglin, putting fire in his voice: "Lo! Hast thou for nought laboured through years uncounted at the building of walls of impregnable thickness and in the making of gates whose valour may not be overthrown; is the power of the hill Amon Gwareth become as lowly as the deep vale, or the hoard of weapons that lie upon it and its unnumbered arrows of so little worth that in the hour of peril thou wouldst cast all aside and go naked into the open against enemies of steel and fire, whose trampling shakes the earth and the Encircling Mountains ring with the clamour of their footsteps?"

And Salgant quaked to think of it and spake noisily, saying: "Meglin speaks well, O King, hear thou him." Then the king took the counsel of those twain though all the lords said otherwise, nay rather the more for that: therefore at his bidding does all that folk abide now the assault upon their walls. But Tuor wept and left the king's hall, and gathering the men of the Wing went through the streets seeking his home; and by that hour was the light great and lurid and there was stifling heat and a black smoke and stench arose about the pathways to the city.

And now came the Monsters across the valley and the white towers of Gondolin reddened before them; but the stoutest were in dread seeing those dragons of fire and those serpents of bronze and iron that fare already about the hill of the city; and they shot unavailing arrows at them. Then is there a cry of hope, for behold, the snakes of fire may not climb the hill for its steepness and for its glassiness, and by reason of the quenching waters that fall upon its sides; yet they lie about its feet and a vast steam arises where the streams of Amon Gwareth and the flames of the serpents drive together. Then grew there such a heat that women became faint and men sweated to weariness beneath their mail, and all the springs of the city, save only the fountain of the king, grew hot and smoked.

But now Gothmog lord of Balrogs, captain of the hosts of Melko, took counsel and gathered all his things of iron that could coil themselves around and above all obstacles before them. These he bade pile themselves before the northern gate; and behold, their great spires reached even to its threshold and thrust at the towers and bastions about it, and by reason of the exceeding heaviness of their bodies those gates fell, and great was the noise thereof: yet the most of the walls around them still stood firm. Then the engines and the catapults of the king poured darts and boulders and molten metals on those ruthless beasts, and their hollow bellies clanged beneath the buffeting, yet it availed not for they might not be broken, and the fires rolled off them. Then were the topmost opened about their middles, and an innumerable host of the Orcs, the goblins of hatred, poured therefrom into the breach; and who shall tell of the gleam of their scimitars or the flash of the broad-bladed spears with which they stabbed?

Then did Rog shout in a mighty voice, and all the people of the Hammer of Wrath and the kindred of the Tree with Galdor the valiant leapt at the foe. There the blows of their great hammers and the dint of their clubs rang to the Encircling Mountains and the Orcs fell like leaves; and those of the Swallow and the Arch poured arrows like the dark rains of autumn upon them, and both

Orcs and Gondothlim fell thereunder for the smoke and the confusion. Great was that battle, yet for all their valour the Gondothlim by reason of the might of ever increasing numbers were borne slowly backwards till the goblins held part of the northernmost city.

At this time is Tuor at the head of the folk of the Wing struggling in the turmoil of the streets, and now he wins through to his house and finds that Meglin is before him. Trusting in the battle now begun about the northern gate and in the uproar in the city, Meglin had looked to this hour for the consummation of his designs. Learning much of the secret delving of Tuor (yet only at the last moment had he got this knowledge and he could not discover all) he said nought to the king or any other, for it was his thought that of a surety that tunnel would go in the end toward the Way of Escape, this being the most nigh to the city, and he had a mind to use this to his good, and to the ill of the Noldoli. Messengers by great stealth he despatched to Melko to set a guard about the outer issue of that Way when the assault was made; but he himself thought now to take Eärendel and cast him into the fire beneath the walls, and seizing Idril he would constrain her to guide him to the secrets of the passage, that he might win out of this terror of fire and slaughter and drag her withal along with him to the lands of Melko. Now Meglin was afeared that even the secret token which Melko had given him would fail in that direful sack, and was minded to help that Ainu to the fulfilment of his promises of safety. No doubt had he however of the death of Tuor in that great burning, for to Salgant he had confided the task of delaying him in the king's halls and egging him straight thence into the deadliest of the fight – but lo! Salgant fell into a terror unto death, and he rode home and lay there now aquake on his bed; but Tuor fared home with the folk of the Wing.

Now Tuor did this, though his valour leapt to the noise of war, that he might take farewell of Idril and Eärendel, and speed them with a bodyguard down the secret way ere he returned himself to the battle throng to die if must be: but he found a press of the Mole-folk about his door, and these were the grimmest and least good-hearted of folk that Meglin might get in that city. Yet were they free Noldoli and under no spell of Melko's like their master, wherefore though for the lordship of Meglin they aided not Idril, no more would they touch of his purpose despite all his curses.

Now then Meglin had Idril by the hair and sought to drag her to the battlements out of cruelty of heart, that she might see the fall of Eärendel to the flames; but he was cumbered by that child, and she fought, alone as she was, like a tigress for all her beauty and slenderness. There he now struggles and delays amid oaths while that folk of the Wing draw nigh – and lo! Tuor gives a shout so great that the Orcs hear it afar and waver at the sound of it. Like a crash of tempest the guard of the Wing were amid the men of the Mole, and these were stricken asunder. When Meglin saw this he would stab Eärendel with a short knife he had; but that child bit his left hand, that his teeth sank in, and he staggered, and stabbed weakly, and the mail of the small coat turned the blade aside; and thereupon Tuor was upon him and his wrath was terrible to see. He seized Meglin by that hand that held the knife and broke the arm with the wrench, and then taking him by the middle leapt with him upon the walls, and flung him far out. Great was the fall of his body, and it smote Amon Gwareth three times ere it pitched in the midmost of the flames; and the name of Meglin has gone out in shame from among Eldar and Noldoli.

Then the warriors of the Mole being more numerous than those few of the Wing, and loyal to their lord, came at Tuor, and there were great blows, but no man might stand before the wrath of Tuor, and they were smitten and driven to fly into what dark holes they might, or flung from the walls. Then Tuor and his men must get them to the battle of the Gate, for the noise of it has grown very great, and Tuor has it still in his heart that the city may stand; yet with Idril he left there Voronwë against his will and some other swordsmen to be a guard for her till he returned or might send tidings from the fray.

Now was the battle at that gate very evil indeed, and Duilin of the Swallow as he shot from the walls was smitten by a fiery bolt of the Balrogs who leapt about the base of Amon Gwareth; and he fell from the battlements and perished. Then the Balrogs continued to shoot darts of fire and flaming arrows like small snakes into the sky, and these fell upon the roofs and gardens of Gondolin till all the trees were scorched, and the flowers and grass burned up, and the whiteness of those walls and colonnades was blackened and seared: yet a worse matter was it that a company of those demons climbed upon the coils of the serpents of iron and thence loosed unceasingly from their bows and slings till a fire began to burn in the city to the back of the main army of the defenders.

Then said Rog in a great voice: "Who now shall fear the Balrogs for all their terror? See before us the accursed ones who for ages have tormented the children of the Noldoli, and who now set a fire

at our backs with their shooting. Come ye of the Hammer of
Wrath and we will smite them for their evil." Thereupon he lifted
his mace, and its handle was long; and he made a way before him
by the wrath of his onset even unto the fallen gate: but all the
people of the Stricken Anvil ran behind like a wedge, and sparks
came from their eyes for the fury of their rage. A great deed was
that sally, as the Noldoli sing yet, and many of the Orcs were
borne backward into the fires below; but the men of Rog leapt
even upon the coils of the serpents and came at those Balrogs and
smote them grievously, for all they had whips of flame and claws of
steel, and were in stature very great. They battered them into
nought, or catching at their whips wielded these against them,
that they tore them even as they had aforetime torn the Gnomes;
and the number of Balrogs that perished was a marvel and dread to
the hosts of Melko, for ere that day never had any of the Balrogs
been slain by the hand of Elves or Men.

Then Gothmog Lord of Balrogs gathered all his demons that
were about the city and ordered them thus: a number made for the
folk of the Hammer and gave before them, but the greater company rushing upon the flank contrived to get to their backs, higher
upon the coils of the drakes and nearer to the gates, so that Rog
might not win back save with great slaughter among his folk. But
Rog seeing this essayed not to win back, as was hoped, but with all
his folk fell on those whose part was to give before him; and they
fled before him now of dire need rather than of craft. Down into
the plain were they harried, and their shrieks rent the airs of
Tumladin. Then that house of the Hammer fared about smiting
and hewing the astonied bands of Melko till they were hemmed at
the last by an overwhelming force of the Orcs and the Balrogs, and
a fire-drake was loosed upon them. There did they perish about
Rog hewing to the last till iron and flame overcame them, and it is
yet sung that each man of the Hammer of Wrath took the lives of
seven foemen to pay for his own. Then did dread fall more heavily
still upon the Gondothlim at the death of Rog and the loss of his
battalion, and they gave back further yet into the city, and Penlod
perished there in a lane with his back to the wall, and about him
many of the men of the Pillar and many of the Tower of Snow.

Now therefore Melko's goblins held all the gate and a great part
of the walls on either side, whence numbers of the Swallow and
those of the Rainbow were thrust to doom; but within the city they
had won a great space reaching nigh to the centre, even to the
Place of the Well that adjoined the Square of the Palace. Yet about

those ways and around the gate their dead were piled in uncounted heaps, and they halted therefore and took counsel, seeing that for the valour of the Gondothlim they had lost many more than they had hoped and far more than those defenders. Fearful too they were for that slaughter Rog had done amid the Balrogs, because of those demons they had great courage and confidence of heart.

Now then the plan that they made was to hold what they had won, while those serpents of bronze and with great feet for trampling climbed slowly over those of iron, and reaching the walls there opened a breach wherethrough the Balrogs might ride upon the dragons of flame: yet they knew this must be done with speed, for the heats of those drakes lasted not for ever, and might only be plenished from the wells of fire that Melko had made in the fastness of his own land.

But even as their messengers were sped they heard a sweet music that was played amid the host of the Gondothlim and they feared what it might mean; and lo! there came Ecthelion and the people of the Fountain whom Turgon till now had held in reserve, for he watched the most of that affray from the heights of his tower. Now marched these folk to a great playing of their flutes, and the crystal and silver of their array was most lovely to see amid the red light of the fires and the blackness of the ruins.

Then on a sudden their music ceased and Ecthelion of the fair voice shouted for the drawing of swords, and before the Orcs might foresee his onslaught the flashing of those pale blades was amongst them. 'Tis said that Ecthelion's folk there slew more of the goblins than fell ever in all the battles of the Eldalië with that race, and that his name is a terror among them to this latest day, and a warcry to the Eldar.

Now it is that Tuor and the men of the Wing fare into the fight and range themselves beside Ecthelion and those of the Fountain, and the twain strike mighty blows and ward each many a thrust from the other, and harry the Orcs so that they win back almost to the gate. But there behold a quaking and a trampling, for the dragons labour mightily at beating a path up Amon Gwareth and at casting down the walls of the city; and already there is a gap therein and a confusion of masonry where the ward-towers have fallen in ruin. Bands of the Swallow and of the Arch of Heaven there fight bitterly amid the wreck or contest the walls to east and west with the foe; but even as Tuor comes nigh driving the Orcs, one of those brazen snakes heaves against the western wall and a great mass of it shakes and falls, and behind comes a creature of fire and Balrogs upon it. Flames gust from the jaws of that worm and folk wither before it, and the wings of the helm of Tuor are blackened, but he stands and gathers about him his guard and all of the Arch and Swallow he can find, whereas on his right Ecthelion rallies the men of the Fountain of the South.

Now the Orcs again take heart from the coming of the drakes, and they mingle with the Balrogs that pour about the breach, and they assail the Gondothlim grievously. There Tuor slew Othrod a lord of the Orcs cleaving his helm, and Balcmeg he hewed asunder, and Lug he smote with his axe that his limbs were cut from beneath him at the knee, but Ecthelion shore through two captains of the goblins at a sweep and cleft the head of Orcobal· their chiefest champion to his teeth; and by reason of the great doughtiness of those two lords they came even unto the Balrogs. Of those demons of power Ecthelion slew three, for the brightness of his sword cleft the iron of them and did hurt to their fire, and they writhed; yet of the leap of that axe Dramborleg that was swung by the hand of Tuor were they still more afraid, for it sang like the rush of eagle's wings in the air and took death as it fell, and five of them went down before it.

But so it is that few cannot fight always against the many, and Ecthelion's left arm got a sore rent from a whip of the Balrog's and his shield fell to earth even as that dragon of fire drew nigh amid the ruin of the walls. Then Ecthelion must lean on Tuor, and Tuor might not leave him, though the very feet of the trampling beast were upon them, and they were like to be overborne: but Tuor hewed at a foot of the creature so that flame spouted forth, and that serpent screamed, lashing with its tail; and many of both Orcs and Noldoli got their death therefrom. Now Tuor gathered his might and lifted Ecthelion, and amid a remnant of the folk got thereunder and escaped the drake; yet dire was the killing of men that beast had wrought, and the Gondothlim were sorely shaken.

Thus it was that Tuor son of Peleg gave before the foe, fighting as he yielded ground, and bore from that battle Ecthelion of the Fountain, but the drakes and the foemen held half the city and all the north of it. Thence marauding bands fared about the streets and did much ransacking, or slew in the dark men and women and children, and many, if occasion let, they bound and led back and flung in the iron chambers amid the dragons of iron, that they might drag them afterward to be thralls of Melko.

Now Tuor reached the Square of the Folkwell by a way entering from the north, and found there Galdor denying the western entry by the Arch of Inwë to a horde of the goblins, but about him was now but a few of those men of the Tree. There did Galdor become the salvation of Tuor, for he fell behind his men stumbling beneath Ecthelion over a body that lay in the dark, and the Orcs had taken them both but for the sudden rush of that champion and the dint of his club.

There were the scatterlings of the guard of the Wing and of the houses of the Tree and the Fountain, and of the Swallow and the Arch, welded to a good battalion, and by the counsel of Tuor they gave way out of that Place of the Well, seeing that the Square of the King that lay next was the more defensible. Now that place had aforetime contained many beautiful trees, both oak and poplar, around a great well of vast depth and great purity of water; yet at that hour it was full of the riot and ugliness of those hideous people of Melko, and those waters were polluted with their carcases.

Thus comes the last stout gathering of those defenders in the Square of the Palace of Turgon. Among them are many wounded and fainting, and Tuor is weary for the labours of the night and the weight of Ecthelion who is in a deadly swoon. Even as he led that battalion in by the Road of Arches from the north-west (and they had much ado to prevent any foe getting behind their backs) a noise arose at the eastward of the square, and lo! Glorfindel is driven in with the last of the men of the Golden Flower.

Now these had sustained a terrible conflict in the Great Market to the east of the city, where a force of Orcs led by Balrogs came on them at unawares as they marched by a circuitous way to the fight about the gate. This they did to surprise the foe upon his left flank, but were themselves ambuscaded; there fought they bitterly for hours till a fire-drake new-come from the breach overwhelmed them, and Glorfindel cut his way out very hardly and with few men; but that place with its stores and its goodly things of fine workmanship was a waste of flames.

The story tells that Turgon had sent the men of the Harp to their aid because of the urgency of messengers from Glorfindel, but Salgant concealed this bidding from them, saying they were to garrison the square of the Lesser Market to the south where he dwelt, and they fretted thereat. Now however they brake from Salgant and were come before the king's hall; and that was very timely, for a triumphant press of foemen was at Glorfindel's heels. On these the men of the Harp unbidden fell with great eagerness and utterly redeemed the cravenhood of their lord, driving the

enemy back into the market, and being leaderless fared even over
wrathfully, so that many of them were trapped in the flames or
sank before the breath of the serpent that revelled there.

Tuor now drank of the great fountain and was refreshed, and
loosening Ecthelion's helm gave him to drink, splashing his face
that his swoon left him. Now those lords Tuor and Glorfindel
clear the square and withdraw all the men they may from the
entrances and bar them with barriers, save as yet on the south.
Even from that region comes now Egalmoth. He had had charge of
the engines on the wall; but long since deeming matters to call
rather for handstrokes about the streets than shooting upon the
battlements he gathered some of the Arch and of the Swallow
about him, and cast away his bow. Then did they fare about the
city dealing good blows whenever they fell in with bands of the
enemy. Thereby he rescued many bands of captives and gathered
no few wandering and driven men, and so got to the King's Square
with hard fighting; and men were fain to greet him for they had
feared him dead. Now are all the women and children that had
gathered there or been brought in by Egalmoth stowed in the
king's halls, and the ranks of the houses made ready for the last. In
that host of survivors are some, be it however few, of all the
kindreds save of the Hammer of Wrath alone; and the king's house
is as yet untouched. Nor is this any shame, for their part was ever
to bide fresh to the last and defend the king.

But now the men of Melko have assembled their forces, and
seven dragons of fire are come with Orcs about them and Balrogs
upon them down all the ways from north, east, and west, seeking
the Square of the King. Then there was carnage at the barriers,
and Egalmoth and Tuor went from place to place of the defence,
but Ecthelion lay by the fountain; and that stand was the most
stubborn-valiant that is remembered in all the songs or in any tale.
Yet at long last a drake bursts the barrier to the north – and there
had once been the issue of the Alley of Roses and a fair place to see
or to walk in, but now there is but a lane of blackness and it is filled
with noise.

Tuor stood then in the way of that beast, but was sundered from
Egalmoth, and they pressed him backward even to the centre of
the square nigh the fountain. There he became weary from the
strangling heat and was beaten down by a great demon, even
Gothmog lord of Balrogs, son of Melko. But lo! Ecthelion, whose
face was of the pallor of grey steel and whose shield-arm hung limp
at his side, strode above him as he fell; and that Gnome drave at

the demon, yet did not give him his death, getting rather a wound to his sword-arm that his weapon left his grasp. Then leapt Ecthelion lord of the Fountain, fairest of the Noldoli, full at Gothmog even as he raised his whip, and his helm that had a spike upon it he drave into that evil breast, and he twined his legs about his foeman's thighs; and the Balrog yelled and fell forward; but those two dropped into the basin of the king's fountain which was very deep. There found that creature his bane; and Ecthelion sank steel-laden into the depths, and so perished the lord of the Fountain after fiery battle in cool waters.[30]

Now Tuor had arisen when the assault of Ecthelion gave him space, and seeing that great deed he wept for his love of that fair Gnome of the Fountain, but being wrapped in battle he scarce cut his way to the folk about the palace. There seeing the wavering of the enemy by reason of the dread of the fall of Gothmog the marshal of the hosts, the royal house laid on and the king came down in splendour among them and hewed with them, that they swept again much of the square, and of the Balrogs slew even two score, which is a very great prowess indeed: but greater still did they do, for they hemmed in one of the Fire-drakes for all his flaming, and forced him into the very waters of the fountain that he perished therein. Now this was the end of that fair water; and its pools turned to steam and its spring was dried up, and it shot no more into the heaven, but rather a vast column of vapour arose to the sky and the cloud therefrom floated over all the land.

Then dread fell on all for the doom of the fountain, and the square was filled with mists of scalding heat and blinding fogs, and the people of the royal house were killed therein by heat and by the foe and by the serpents and by one another: but a body of them saved the king, and there was a rally of men beneath Glingol and Bansil.

Then said the king: "Great is the fall of Gondolin", and men shuddered, for such were the words of Amnon the prophet of old;[31] but Tuor speaking wildly for ruth and love of the king cried: "Gondolin stands yet, and Ulmo will not suffer it to perish!" Now were they at that time standing, Tuor by the Trees and the king upon the Stairs, as they had stood aforetime when Tuor spake the embassy of Ulmo. But Turgon said: "Evil have I brought upon the Flower of the Plain in despite of Ulmo, and now he leaveth it to wither in the fire. Lo! hope is no more in my heart for my city of loveliness, but the children of the Noldoli shall not be worsted for ever."

Then did the Gondothlim clash their weapons, for many stood

nigh, but Turgon said: "Fight not against doom, O my children! Seek ye who may safety in flight, if perhaps there be time yet: but let Tuor have your lealty." But Tuor said: "Thou art king"; and Turgon made answer: "Yet no blow will I strike more", and he cast his crown at the roots of Glingol. Then did Galdor who stood there pick it up, but Turgon accepted it not, and bare of head climbed to the topmost pinnacle of that white tower that stood nigh his palace. There he shouted in a voice like a horn blown among the mountains, and all that were gathered beneath the Trees and the foemen in the mists of the square heard him: "Great is the victory of the Noldoli!" And 'tis said that it was then middle night, and that the Orcs yelled in derision.

Then did men speak of a sally, and were of two minds. Many held that it were impossible to burst through, nor might they even so get over the plain or through the hills, and that it were better therefore to die about the king. But Tuor might not think well of the death of so many fair women and children, were it at the hands of their own folk in the last resort, or by the weapons of the enemy, and he spake of the delving and of the secret way. Therefore did he counsel that they beg Turgon to have other mind, and coming among them lead that remnant southward to the walls and the entry of that passage; but he himself burnt with desire to fare thither and know how Idril and Eärendel might be, or to get tidings hence to them and bid them begone speedily, for Gondolin was taken. Now Tuor's plan seemed to the lords desperate indeed – seeing the narrowness of the tunnel and the greatness of the company that must pass it – yet would they fain take this rede in their straits. But Turgon hearkened not, and bid them fare now ere it was too late, and "Let Tuor," said he, "be your guide and your chieftain. But I Turgon will not leave my city, and will burn with it." Then sped they messengers again to the tower, saying: "Sire, who are the Gondothlim if thou perish? Lead us!" But he said: "Lo! I abide here"; and a third time, and he said: "If I am king, obey my behests, and dare not to parley further with my commands." After that they sent no more and made ready for the forlorn attempt. But the folk of the royal house that yet lived would not budge a foot, but gathered thickly about the base of the king's tower. "Here," said they, "we will stay if Turgon goes not forth"; and they might not be persuaded.

Now was Tuor torn sorely between his reverence for the king and the love for Idril and his child, wherewith his heart was sick; yet already serpents fare about the square trampling upon dead and dying, and the foe gathers in the mists for the last onslaught; and the choice must be made. Then because of the wailing of the women in the halls of the palace and the greatness of his pity for that sad remainder of the peoples of Gondolin, he gathered all that rueful company, maids, children and mothers, and setting them amidmost marshalled as well as he might his men around them. Deepest he set them at flank and at rear, for he purposed falling back southward fighting as best he might with the rearguard as he went; and thus if it might so be to win down the Road of Pomps to the Place of the Gods ere any great force be sent to circumvent him. Thence was it his thought to go by the Way of Running Waters past the Fountains of the South to the walls and to his home; but the passage of the secret tunnel he doubted much. Thereupon espying his movement the foe made forthwith a great onslaught upon his left flank and his rear – from east and north – even as he began to withdraw; but his right was covered by the king's hall and the head of that column drew already into the Road of Pomps.

Then some of the hugest of the drakes came on and glared in the fog, and he must perforce bid the company to go at a run, fighting on the left at haphazard; but Glorfindel held the rear manfully and many more of the Golden Flower fell there. So it was that they passed the Road of Pomps and reached Gar Ainion, the Place of the Gods; and this was very open and at its middle the highest ground of all the city. Here Tuor looks for an evil stand and it is scarce in his hope to get much further; but behold, the foe seems already to slacken and scarce any follow them, and this is a wonder. Now comes Tuor at their head to the Place of Wedding, and lo! there stands Idril before him with her hair unbraided as on that day of their marriage before; and great is his amaze. By her stood Voronwë and none other, but Idril saw not even Tuor, for her gaze was set back upon the Place of the King that now lay somewhat below them. Then all that host halted and looked back whither her eyes gazed and their hearts stood still; for now they saw why the foe pressed them so little and the reason of their salvation. Lo! a drake was coiled even on the very steps of the palace and defiled their whiteness; but swarms of the Orcs ransacked within and dragged forth forgotten women and children or slew men that fought alone. Glingol was withered to the stock and Bansil was blackened utterly, and the king's tower was beset. High up could they descry the form of the king, but about the base a serpent of iron spouting flame lashed and rowed with his tail, and

Balrogs were round him; and there was the king's house in great anguish, and dread cries carried up to the watchers. So was it that the sack of the halls of Turgon and that most valiant stand of the royal house held the mind of the foe, so that Tuor got thence with his company, and stood now in tears upon the Place of the Gods.

Then said Idril: "Woe is me whose father awaiteth doom even upon his topmost pinnacle; but seven times woe whose lord hath gone down before Melko and will stride home no more!" – for she was distraught with the agony of that night.

Then said Tuor: "Lo! Idril, it is I, and I live; yet now will I get thy father hence, be it from the Hells of Melko!" With that he would make down the hill alone, maddened by the grief of his wife; but she coming to her wits in a storm of weeping clasped his knees saying: "My lord! My lord!" and delayed him. Yet even as they spake a great noise and a yelling rose from that place of anguish. Behold, the tower leapt into a flame and in a stab of fire it fell, for the dragons crushed the base of it and all who stood there. Great was the clangour of that terrible fall, and therein passed Turgon King of the Gondothlim, and for that hour the victory was to Melko.

Then said Idril heavily: "Sad is the blindness of the wise"; but Tuor said: "Sad too is the stubbornness of those we love – yet 'twas a valiant fault," then stooping he lifted and kissed her, for she was more to him than all the Gondothlim; but she wept bitterly for her father. Then turned Tuor to the captains, saying: "Lo, we must get hence with all speed, lest we be surrounded"; and forthwith they moved onward as swiftly as they might and got them far from thence ere the Orcs tired of sacking the palace and rejoicing at the fall of the tower of Turgon.

Now are they in the southward city and meet but scattered bands of plunderers who fly before them; yet do they find fire and burning everywhere for the ruthlessness of that enemy. Women do they meet, some with babes and some laden with chattels, but Tuor would not let them bear away aught save a little food. Coming now at length to a greater quiet Tuor asked Voronwë for tidings, in that Idril spake not and was well-nigh in a swoon; and Voronwë told him of how she and he had waited before the doors of the house while the noise of those battles grew and shook their hearts; and Idril wept for lack of tidings from Tuor. At length she had sped the most part of her guard down the secret way with Eärendel, constraining them to depart with imperious words, yet was her grief great at that sundering. She herself would bide, said she, nor seek to live after her lord; and then she fared about gathering womenfolk and wanderers and speeding them down the tunnel, and smiting marauders with her small band; nor might they dissuade her from bearing a sword.

At length they had fallen in with a band somewhat too numerous, and Voronwë had dragged her thence but by the luck of the Gods, for all else with them perished, and their foe burned Tuor's house; yet found not the secret way. "Therewith," said Voronwë, "thy lady became distraught of weariness and grief, and fared into the city wildly to my great fear – nor might I get her to sally from the burning."

About the saying of these words were they come to the southern walls and nigh to Tuor's house, and lo! it was cast down and the wreckage was asmoke; and thereat was Tuor bitterly wroth. But there was a noise that boded the approach of Orcs, and Tuor despatched that company as swiftly as might be down that secret way.

Now is there great sorrow upon that staircase as those exiles bid farewell to Gondolin; yet are they without much hope of further life beyond the hills, for how shall any slip from the hand of Melko?

Glad is Tuor when all have passed the entrance and his fear lightens; indeed by the luck of the Valar only can all those folk have got therein unspied of the Orcs. Some now are left who casting aside their arms labour with picks from within and block up the entry of the passage, faring then after the host as they might; but when that folk had descended the stairway to a level with the valley the heat grew to a torment for the fire of the dragons that were about the city; and they were indeed nigh, for the delving was there at no great depth in the earth. Boulders were loosened by the tremors of the ground and falling crushed many, and fumes were in the air so that their torches and lanterns went out. Here they fell over bodies of some that had gone before and perished, and Tuor was in fear for Eärendel; and they pressed on in great darkness and anguish. Nigh two hours were they in that tunnel of the earth, and towards its end it was scarce finished, but rugged at the sides and low.[32]

Then came they at the last lessened by wellnigh a tithe to the tunnel's opening, and it debouched cunningly in a large basin where once water had lain, but it was now full of thick bushes. Here were gathered no small press of mingled folk whom Idril and Voronwë sped down the hidden way before them, and they were weeping softly in weariness and sorrow, but Eärendel was not there. Thereat were Tuor and Idril in anguish of heart.[33] Lamentation was there too among all those others, for amidmost of the plain about them loomed afar the hill of Amon Gwareth crowned with flames, where had stood the gleaming city of their home. Fire-drakes are about it and monsters of iron fare in and out of its gates, and great is that sack of the Balrogs and Orcs. Somewhat of comfort has this nonetheless for the leaders, for they judge the plain to be nigh empty of Melko's folk save hard by the city, for thither have fared all his evil ones to revel in that destruction.

"Now," therefore said Galdor, "we must get as far hence toward the Encircling Mountains as may be ere dawn come upon us, and that giveth no great space of time, for summer is at hand."[34] Thereat rose a dissension, for a number said that it were folly to make for Cristhorn as Tuor purposed. "The sun," say they, "will be up long ere we win the foothills, and we shall be whelmed in the plain by those drakes and those demons. Let us fare to Bad Uthwen, the Way of Escape, for that is but half the journeying, and our weary and our wounded may hope to win so far if no further."

Yet Idril spake against this, and persuaded the lords that they trust not to the magic of that way that had aforetime shielded it from discovery: "for what magic stands if Gondolin be fallen?" Nonetheless a large body of men and women sundered from Tuor and fared to Bad Uthwen, and there into the jaws of a monster who by the guile of Melko at Meglin's rede sat at the outer issue that none came through. But the others, led by one Legolas Greenleaf of the house of the Tree, who knew all that plain by day or by dark, and was night-sighted, made much speed over the vale for all their weariness, and halted only after a great march. Then was all the Earth spread with the grey light of that sad dawn which looked no more on the beauty of Gondolin; but the plain was full of mists – and that was a marvel, for no mist or fog came there ever before, and this perchance had to do with the doom of the fountain of the king. Again they rose, and covered by the vapours fared long past dawn in safety, till they were already too far away for any to descry them in those misty airs from the hill or from the ruined walls.

Now the Mountains or rather their lowest hills were on that side seven leagues save a mile from Gondolin, and Cristhorn the Cleft of Eagles two leagues of upward going from the beginning of the Mountains, for it was at a great height; wherefore they had yet two leagues and part of a third to traverse amid the spurs and foothills, and they were very weary.[35] By now the sun hung well above a saddle in the eastern hills, and she was very red and great; and the mists nigh them were lifted, but the ruins of Gondolin were utterly hidden as in a cloud. Behold then at the clearing of the airs they saw, but a few furlongs off, a knot of men that fled on foot, and these were pursued by a strange cavalry, for on great wolves rode Orcs, as they thought, brandishing spears. Then said Tuor: "Lo! there is Eärendel my son; behold, his face shineth as a star in the waste,[36] and my men of the Wing are about him, and they are in sore straits." Forthwith he chose fifty of the men that were least weary, and leaving the main company to follow he fared over the plain with that troop as swiftly as they had strength left. Coming now to carry of voice Tuor shouted to the men about Eärendel to stand and flee not, for the wolfriders were scattering them and slaying them piecemeal, and the child was upon the shoulders of one Hendor, a house-carle of Idril's, and he seemed like to be left with his burden. Then they stood back to back and Hendor and Eärendel amidmost; but Tuor soon came up, though all his troop were breathless.

Of the wolfriders there were a score, and of the men that were about Eärendel but six living; therefore had Tuor opened his men into a crescent of but one rank, and hoped so to envelop the riders, lest any escaping bring tidings to the main foe and draw ruin upon the exiles. In this he succeeded, so that only two escaped, and therewithal wounded and without their beasts, wherefore were their tidings brought too late to the city.

Glad was Eärendel to greet Tuor, and Tuor most fain of his child; but said Eärendel: "I am thirsty, father, for I have run far – nor had Hendor need to bear me." Thereto his father said nought, having no water, and thinking of the need of all that company that he guided; but Eärendel said again: "'Twas good to see Meglin die so, for he would set arms about my mother – and I liked him not; but I would travel in no tunnels for all Melko's wolfriders." Then Tuor smiled and set him upon his shoulders. Soon after this the main company came up, and Tuor gave Eärendel to his mother who was in a great joy; but Eärendel would not be borne in her arms, for he said: "Mother Idril, thou art weary, and warriors in mail ride not among the Gondothlim, save it be old Salgant!" and his mother laughed amid her sorrow; but Eärendel said: "Nay, where is Salgant?" – for Salgant had told him quaint tales or played drolleries with him at times, and Eärendel had much laughter of the old Gnome in those days when he came many a day to the house of Tuor, loving the good wine and fair repast he there received. But none could say where Salgant was, nor can they now. Mayhap he was whelmed by fire upon his bed; yet some have it that he was taken captive to the halls of Melko and made his buffoon – and this is an ill fate for a noble of the good race of the Gnomes. Then was Eärendel sad at that, and walked beside his mother in silence.

Now came they to the foothills and it was full morning but still grey, and there nigh to the beginning of the upward road folk stretched them and rested in a little dale fringed with trees and with hazel-bushes, and many slept despite their peril, for they were utterly spent. Yet Tuor set a strict watch, and himself slept not. Here they made one meal of scanty food and broken meats; and Eärendel quenched his thirst and played beside a little brook. Then said he to his mother: "Mother Idril, I would we had good Ecthelion of the Fountain here to play to me on his flute, or make me willow-whistles! Perchance he has gone on ahead?" But Idril said nay, and told what she had heard of his end. Then said Eärendel that he cared not ever to see the streets of Gondolin again, and he wept bitterly; but Tuor said that he would not again see those streets, "for Gondolin is no more".

Thereafter nigh to the hour of sundown behind the hills Tuor bade the company arise, and they pressed on by rugged paths. Soon now the grass faded and gave way to mossy stones, and trees fell away, and even the pines and firs grew sparse. About the set of the sun the way so wound behind a shoulder of the hills that they might not again look toward Gondolin. There all that company turned, and lo! the plain is clear and smiling in the last light as of old; but afar off as they gazed a great flare shot up against the darkened north – and that was the fall of the last tower of Gondolin, even that which had stood hard by the southern gate, and whose shadow fell oft across the walls of Tuor's house. Then sank the sun, and they saw Gondolin no more.

Now the pass of Cristhorn, that is the Eagles' Cleft, is one of dangerous going, and that host had not ventured it by dark, lanternless and without torches, and very weary and cumbered with women and children and sick and stricken men, had it not been for their great fear of Melko's scouts, for it was a great company and might not fare very secretly. Darkness gathered rapidly as they approached that high place, and they must string out into a long and straggling line. Galdor and a band of men spear-armed went ahead, and Legolas was with them, whose eyes were like cats' for the dark, yet could they see further. Thereafter followed the least weary of the women supporting the sick and the wounded that could go on foot. Idril was with these, and Eärendel who bore up well, but Tuor was in the midmost behind them with all his men of the Wing, and they bare some who were grievously hurt, and Egalmoth was with him, but he had got a hurt in that sally from the square. Behind again came many women with babes, and girls, and lamed men, yet was the going slow enough for them. At the rearmost went the largest band of men battle-whole, and there was Glorfindel of the golden hair.

Thus were they come to Cristhorn, which is an ill place by reason of its height, for this is so great that spring nor summer come ever there, and it is very cold. Indeed while the valley dances in the sun, there all the year snow dwells in those bleak places, and even as they came there the wind howled, coming from the north behind them, and it bit sorely. Snow fell and whirled in wind-eddies and got into their eyes, and this was not good, for there the path is narrow, and of the right or westerly hand a sheer wall rises nigh seven chains from the way, ere it bursts atop into jagged pinnacles where are many eyries. There dwells Thorndor King of Eagles, Lord of the Thornhoth, whom the Eldar named Sorontur. But of the other hand is a fall not right sheer yet dreadly steep, and it has long teeth of rock up-pointing so that one may climb down – or fall maybe – but by no means up. And from that deep is no escape at either end any more than by the sides, and Thorn Sir runs at bottom. He falls therein from the south over a great precipice but with a slender water, for he is a thin stream in those heights, and he issues to the north after flowing but a rocky mile above ground down a narrow passage that goes into the mountain, and scarce a fish could squeeze through with him.

Galdor and his men were come now to the end nigh to where Thorn Sir falls into the abyss, and the others straggled, for all Tuor's efforts, back over most of the mile of the perilous way between chasm and cliff, so that Glorfindel's folk were scarce come to its beginning, when there was a yell in the night that echoed in that grim region. Behold, Galdor's men were beset in the dark suddenly by shapes leaping from behind rocks where they had lain hidden even from the glance of Legolas. It was Tuor's thought that they had fallen in with one of Melko's ranging companies, and he feared no more than a sharp brush in the dark, yet he sent the women and sick around him rearward and joined his men to Galdor's, and there was an affray upon the perilous path. But now rocks fell from above, and things looked ill, for they did grievous hurt; but matters seemed to Tuor yet worse when the noise of arms came from the rear, and tidings were said to him by a man of the Swallow that Glorfindel was ill bested by men from behind, and that a Balrog was with them.

Then was he sore afraid of a trap, and this was even what had in truth befallen; for watchers had been set by Melko all about the encircling hills. Yet so many did the valour of the Gondothlim draw off to the assault ere the city could be taken that these were but thinly spread, and were at the least here in the south. Nonetheless one of these had espied the company as they started the upward going from the dale of hazels, and as many bands were got together against them as might be, and devised to fall upon the exiles to front and rear even upon the perilous way of Cristhorn. Now Galdor and Glorfindel held their own despite the surprise of assault, and many of the Orcs were struck into the abyss; but the falling of the rocks was like to end all their valour, and the flight from Gondolin to come to ruin. The moon about that hour rose above the pass, and the gloom somewhat lifted, for his pale light filtered into dark places; yet it lit not the path for the height of the walls. Then arose Thorndor, King of Eagles, and he loved not Melko, for Melko had caught many of his kindred and chained them against sharp rocks to squeeze from them the magic words whereby he might learn to fly (for he dreamed of contending even against Manwë in the air); and when they would not tell he cut off their wings and sought to fashion therefrom a mighty pair for his use, but it availed not.

Now when the clamour from the pass rose to his great eyrie he said: "Wherefore are these foul things, these Orcs of the hills, climbed near to my throne; and why do the sons of the Noldoli cry out in the low places for fear of the children of Melko the accursed? Arise O Thornhoth, whose beaks are of steel and whose talons swords!"

Thereupon there was a rushing like a great wind in rocky places, and the Thornhoth, the people of the Eagles, fell on those Orcs who had scaled above the path, and tore their faces and their hands and flung them to the rocks of Thorn Sir far below. Then were the Gondothlim glad, and they made in after days the Eagle a sign of their kindred in token of their joy, and Idril bore it, but Eärendel loved rather the Swan-wing of his father. Now unhampered Galdor's men bore back those that opposed them, for they were not very many and the onset of the Thornhoth affrighted them much; and the company fared forward again, though Glorfindel had fighting enough in the rear. Already the half had passed the perilous way and the falls of Thorn Sir, when that Balrog that was with the rearward foe leapt with great might on certain lofty rocks that stood into the path on the left side upon the lip of the chasm, and thence with a leap of fury he was past Glorfindel's men and among the women and the sick in front, lashing with his whip of flame. Then Glorfindel leapt forward upon him and his golden armour gleamed strangely in the moon, and he hewed at that demon that it leapt again upon a great boulder and Glorfindel after. Now there was a deadly combat upon that high rock above the folk; and these, pressed behind and hindered ahead, were grown so close that well nigh all could see, yet was it over ere Glorfindel's men could leap to his side. The ardour of Glorfindel drave that Balrog from point to point, and his mail fended him from its whip and claw. Now had he beaten a heavy swinge upon its iron helm, now hewn off the creature's whip-arm at the elbow. Then sprang the Balrog in the torment of his pain and fear full at Glorfindel, who stabbed like a dart of a snake; but he found only a shoulder, and was grappled, and they swayed to a fall upon the crag-top. Then Glorfindel's left hand sought a dirk, and this he thrust up that it pierced the Balrog's belly nigh his own face (for that demon was double his stature); and it shrieked, and fell backwards from the rock, and falling clutched Glorfindel's yellow locks beneath his cap, and those twain fell into the abyss.

Now was this a very grievous thing, for Glorfindel was most dearly beloved — and lo! the dint of their fall echoed about the hills, and the abyss of Thorn Sir rang. Then at the death-cry of the Balrog the Orcs before and behind wavered and were slain or fled far away, and Thorndor himself, a mighty bird, descended to the abyss and brought up the body of Glorfindel; but the Balrog lay, and the water of Thorn Sir ran black for many a day far below in Tumladin.

Still do the Eldar say when they see good fighting at great odds of power against a fury of evil: "Alas! 'Tis Glorfindel and the Balrog", and their hearts are still sore for that fair one of the Noldoli. Because of their love, despite the haste and their fear of the advent of new foes, Tuor let raise a great stone-cairn over Glorfindel just there beyond the perilous way by the precipice of Eagle-stream, and Thorndor has let not yet any harm come thereto, but yellow flowers have fared thither and blow ever now

about that mound in those unkindly places; but the folk of the
Golden Flower wept at its building and might not dry their tears.

Now who shall tell of the wanderings of Tuor and the exiles of
Gondolin in the wastes that lie beyond the mountains to the south
of the vale of Tumladin? Miseries were theirs and death, colds and
hungers, and ceaseless watches. That they won ever through those
regions infested by Melko's evil came from the great slaughter and
damage done to his power in that assault, and from the speed and
wariness with which Tuor led them; for of a certain Melko knew of
that escape and was furious thereat. Ulmo had heard tidings in the
far oceans of the deeds that were done, but he could not yet aid
them for they were far from waters and rivers – and indeed they
thirsted sorely, and they knew not the way.

But after a year and more of wandering, in which many a time
they journeyed long tangled in the magic of those wastes only to
come again upon their own tracks, once more the summer came,
and nigh to its height[37] they came at last upon a stream, and
following this came to better lands and were a little comforted.
Here did Voronwë guide them, for he had caught a whisper of
Ulmo's in that stream one late summer's night – and he got ever
much wisdom from the sound of waters. Now he led them even till
they came down to Sirion which that stream fed, and then both
Tuor and Voronwë saw that they were not far from the outer issue
of old of the Way of Escape, and were once more in that deep
dale of alders. Here were all the bushes trampled and the trees
burnt, and the dale-wall scarred with flame, and they wept, for
they thought they knew the fate of those who sundered aforetime
from them at the tunnel-mouth.

Now they journeyed down that river but were again in fear from
Melko, and fought affrays with his Orc-bands and were in peril
from the wolfriders, but his firedrakes sought not at them, both
for the great exhaustion of their fires in the taking of Gondolin,
and the increasing power of Ulmo as the river grew. So came they
after many days – for they went slowly and got their sustenance
very hardly – to those great heaths and morasses above the Land of
Willows, and Voronwë knew not those regions. Now here goes
Sirion a very great way under earth, diving at the great cavern of
the Tumultuous Winds, but running clear again above the Pools
of Twilight, even where Tulkas[38] after fought with Melko's self.
Tuor had fared over these regions by night and dusk after Ulmo
came to him amid the reeds, and he remembered not the ways. In

places that land is full of deceits and very marshy; and here the
host had long delay and was vexed by sore flies, for it was autumn
still, and agues and fevers fared amongst them, and they cursed
Melko.

Yet came they at last to the great pools and the edges of that
most tender Land of Willows; and the very breath of the winds
thereof brought rest and peace to them, and for the comfort of that
place the grief was assuaged of those who mourned the dead in that
great fall. There women and maids grew fair again and their sick
were healed, and old wounds ceased to pain; yet they alone who of
reason feared their folk living still in bitter thraldom in the Hells of
Iron sang not, nor did they smile.

Here they abode very long indeed, and Eärendel was a grown
boy ere the voice of Ulmo's conches drew the heart of Tuor, that
his sea-longing returned with a thirst the deeper for years of
stifling; and all that host arose at his bidding, and got them down
Sirion to the Sea.

Now the folk that had passed into the Eagles' Cleft and who saw
the fall of Glorfindel had been nigh eight hundreds — a large
wayfaring, yet was it a sad remnant of so fair and numerous
a city. But they who arose from the grasses of the Land of
Willows in years after and fared away to sea, when spring set
celandine in the meads and they had held sad festival in memorial
of Glorfindel, these numbered but three hundreds and a score of
men and man-children, and two hundreds and three score of
women and maid-children. Now the number of women was few
because of their hiding or being stowed by their kinsfolk in secret
places in the city. There they were burned or slain or taken and
enthralled, and the rescue-parties found them too seldom; and it is
the greatest ruth to think of this, for the maids and women of the
Gondothlim were as fair as the sun and as lovely as the moon and
brighter than the stars. Glory dwelt in that city of Gondolin of the
Seven Names, and its ruin was the most dread of all the sacks of
cities upon the face of Earth. Nor Bablon, nor Ninwi, nor the
towers of Trui, nor all the many takings of Rûm that is greatest
among Men, saw such terror as fell that day upon Amon Gwareth
in the kindred of the Gnomes; and this is esteemed the worst work
that Melko has yet thought of in the world.

Yet now those exiles of Gondolin dwelt at the mouth of Sirion
by the waves of the Great Sea. There they take the name of
Lothlim, the people of the flower, for Gondothlim is a name too
sore to their hearts; and fair among the Lothlim Eärendel grows in

the house of his father,[39] and the great tale of Tuor is come to its waning.'

Then said Littleheart son of Bronweg: 'Alas for Gondolin.'

And no one in all the Room of Logs spake or moved for a great while.

## NOTES

1   Not of course the great journey to the Sea from the Waters of Awakening, but the expedition of the Elves of Kôr for the rescue of the Gnomes (see I. 26).

2   A *korin* is defined in *The Cottage of Lost Play* (I.16) as 'a great circular hedge, be it of stone or of thorn or even of trees, that encloses a green sward'; Meril-i-Turinqi dwelt 'in a great *korin* of elms'.

3   *Tôn a Gwedrin* is the Tale-fire.

4   There is here a direction: 'See hereafter the Nauglafring', but this is struck out.

5   On Heorrenda see pp. 290ff, 323. A small space is left after the words 'it is thus' to mark the place of the poem in Old English that was to be inserted, but there is no indication of what it was to be.

> (*In the following notes 'the original reading' refers to the text of* Tuor A, *and of* Tuor B *before the emendation in question. It does not imply that the reading of* Tuor A *was, or was not, found in the original pencilled text (in the great majority of cases this cannot be said).*)

6   This passage, beginning with the words 'And Tuor entered that cavern . . .' on p. 149, is a late replacement written on a slip (see p. 147). The original passage was largely similar in meaning, but contained the following:

> Now in delving that riverway beneath the hills the Noldoli worked unknown to Melko who in those deep days held them yet hidden and thralls beneath his will. Rather were they prompted by Ulmo who strove ever against Melko; and through Tuor he hoped to devise for the Gnomes release from the terror of the evil of Melko.

7   'three days': 'three years' all texts, but 'days?' pencilled above 'years' in *Tuor B*.

8   The 'evolution' of sea-birds through Ossë is described in the tale of *The Coming of the Elves*, I.123; but the sentence here derives from the original pencilled text of *Tuor A*.

9   In the typescript *Tuor C* a blank was left here (see p. 147) and subsequently filled in with 'Ulmo', not 'Ainur'.

10    The original reading was: 'Thou Tuor of the lonely heart the Valar will not to dwell for ever in fair places of birds and flowers; nor would they lead thee through this pleasant land . . .'

11    *Tuor C* adds here: 'with Ulmo's aid'.

12    The reference to the Battle of Unnumbered Tears is a later addition to *Tuor B*. The original reading was: 'who alone escaped Melko's power when he caught their folk . . .'

13    In *Tuor A* and *B Voronwë* is used throughout, but this phrase, with the form *Bronweg*, is an addition to *Tuor B* (replacing the original 'Now after many days these twain found a deep dale').

14    The typescript *Tuor C* has here:

> . . . that none, were they not of the blood of the Noldoli, might light on it, neither by chance nor agelong search. Thus was it secure from all ill hap save treachery alone, and never would Tûr have won thereto but for the steadfastness of that Gnome Voronwë.

In the next sentence *Tuor C* has 'yet even so no few of the bolder of the Gnomes enthralled would slip down the river Sirion from the fell mountains'.

15    The original reading was: 'his speech they comprehended, though somewhat different was the tongue of the free Noldoli by those days to that of the sad thralls of Melko.' The typescript *Tuor C* has: 'they comprehended him for they were Noldoli. Then spake Tûr also in the same tongue . . .'

16    The original reading was: 'It was early morn when they drew near the gates and many eyes gazed . . .' But when Tuor and Voronwë first saw Gondolin it was 'in the new light of the morning' (p. 158), and it was 'a day's light march' across the plain; hence the change made later to *Tuor B*.

17    'Evil One': original reading 'Ainu'.

18    This passage, from 'Rugged was his aspect . . .', is a replacement on a separate slip; the original text was:

> Tuor was goodly in countenance but rugged and unkempt of locks and clad in the skins of bears, yet his stature was not overgreat among his own folk, but the Gondothlim, though not bent as were no few of their kin who laboured at ceaseless delving and hammering for Melko, were small and slender and lithe.

In the original passage Men are declared to be of their nature taller than the Elves of Gondolin. See pp. 142, 220.

19    'come hither': 'escaped from Melko' *Tuor C*.

20    'folk': original reading 'men'. This is the only place where 'men' in reference to Elves is changed. The use is constant in *The Fall of Gondolin*, and even occurs once in an odd-sounding reference to

the hosts of Melko: 'But now the men of Melko have assembled their
forces' (p. 183).

21    The passage ending here and beginning with the words 'Then
Tuor's heart was heavy . . .' on p. 162 was bracketed by my father in
*Tuor B*, and on a loose slip referring to this bracketed passage he
wrote:

> (If nec[essary]): Then is told how Idril daughter of the king
> added her words to the king's wisdom so that Turgon bid Tuor
> rest himself awhile in Gondolin, and being forewise prevailed on
> him [to] abide there in the end. How he came to love the daughter
> of the king, Idril of the Silver Feet, and how he was taught deeply
> in the lore of that great folk and learned of its history and the
> history of the Elves. How Tuor grew in wisdom and mighty in the
> counsels of the Gondothlim.

The only narrative difference here from the actual text lies in
the introduction of the king's daughter Idril as an influence on
Tuor's decision to remain in Gondolin. The passage is otherwise an
extremely abbreviated summary of the account of Tuor's instruction in Gondolin, with omission of what is said in the text about the
preparations of the Gondothlim against attack; but I do not think
that this was a proposal for shortening the written tale. Rather, the
words 'If necessary' suggest strongly that my father had in mind
only a reduction for oral delivery – and that was when it was read to
the Exeter College Essay Club in the spring of 1920; see p. 147.
Another proposed shortening is given in note 32.

22    This passage, beginning 'Great love too had Idril for Tuor . . .', was
written on a separate slip and replaced the original text as follows:

> The king hearing of this, and finding that his child Idril, whom
> the Eldar speak of as Irildë, loved Tuor in return, he consented to
> their being wed, seeing that he had no son, and Tuor was like to
> make a kinsman of strength and consolation. There were Idril and
> Tuor wed before the folk in that Place of the Gods, Gar Ainion,
> nigh the king's palace; and that was a day of mirth to the city of
> Gondolin, but of (&c.)

The replacement states that the marriage of Tuor and Idril was the
first but not the last of the unions of Man and Elf, whereas it is said
in the Name-list to *The Fall of Gondolin* that Eärendel was 'the
only being that is half of the kindred of the Eldalië and half of Men'
(see p. 215).

23    The phrase 'and that tale of Isfin and Eöl may not here be told' was
added to *Tuor B*. See p. 220.

24    Original reading: 'a name wrought of the tongue of the Gondothlim'.

25    The sapphires given to Manwë by the Noldoli are referred to in the

tale of *The Coming of the Elves*, I.128. The original pencilled text of *Tuor A* can be read here: 'bluer than the sapphires of Súlimo'.

26  The passage ending here and beginning with 'In these ways that bitter winter passed . . .' is inserted on a separate sheet in *Tuor B* (but is not part of the latest layer of emendation); it replaces a much shorter passage going back to the primary text of *Tuor A*:

> Now on midwinter's day at early even the sun sank betimes beyond the mountains, and lo! when she had gone a light arose beyond the hills to the north, and men marvelled (&c.)

See notes 34 and 37.

27  The Scarlet Heart: the heart of Finwë Nólemë, Turgon's father, was cut out by Orcs in the Battle of Unnumbered Tears, but it was regained by Turgon and became his emblem; see I.241 and note 11.

28  This passage describing the array and the emblems of the houses of the Gondothlim was relatively very little affected by the later revision of *Tuor A*; the greater part of it is in the original pencilled text, which was allowed to stand, and all the names appear to be original.

29  The word 'burg' is used in the Old English sense of a walled and fortified town.

30  The death of Ecthelion in the primary text of *Tuor A* is legible; the revision introduced a few changes of wording, but no more.

31  This sentence, from 'and men shuddered', was added to *Tuor B*. On the prophecy see I.172.

32  *Tuor B* is bracketed from 'Now comes Tuor at their head to the Place of Wedding' on p. 186 to this point, and an inserted slip relating to this bracketing reads:

> How Tuor and his folk came upon Idril wandering distraught in the Place of the Gods. How Tuor and Idril from that high place saw the sack of the King's Hall and the ruin of the King's Tower and the passing of the king, for which reason the foe followed not after. How Tuor heard tidings of Voronwë that Idril had sent Eärendel and her guard down the hidden way, and fared into the city in search of her husband; how in peril from the enemy they had rescued many that fled and sent them down the secret way. How Tuor led his host with the luck of the Gods to the mouth of that passage, and how all descended into the plain, sealing the entrance utterly behind them. How the sorrowful company issued into a dell in the vale of Tumladin.

This is simply a summary of the text as it stands; I suppose it was a cut proposed for the recitation of the tale if that seemed to be taking too long (see note 21).

33  This passage, from 'Here were gathered . . .', replaced in *Tuor B* the original reading: 'Here they are fain to rest, but finding no signs of

Eärendel and his escort Tuor is downcast, and Idril weeps.' This was rewritten partly for narrative reasons, but also to put it into the past tense. In the next sentence the text was emended from 'Lamentation is there . . .' and 'about them looms . . .' But the sentence following ('Fire-drakes are about it . . .') was left untouched; and I think that it was my father's intention, only casually indicated and never carried through, to reduce the amount of 'historical present' in the narrative.

34   'for summer is at hand': the original reading was 'albeit it is winter'. See notes 26 and 37.

35   The original reading was:

> Now the Mountains were on that side seven leagues save a mile from Gondolin, and Cristhorn the Cleft of Eagles another league of upward going from the beginning of the Mountains; wherefore they were now yet two leagues and part of a third from the pass, and very weary thereto.

36   'Behold, his face shineth as a star in the waste' was added to *Tuor B*.

37   This passage, from 'But after a year and more of wandering . . .', replaced the original reading 'But after a half-year's wandering, nigh midsummer'. This emendation depends on the changing of the time of the attack on Gondolin from midwinter to the 'Gates of Summer' (see notes 26 and 34). Thus in the revised version summer is retained as the season when the exiles came to the lands about Sirion, but they spent a whole year and more, rather than a half-year, to reach them.

38   'even where Tulkas': original reading: 'even where Noldorin and Tulkas'. See pp. 278–9.

39   The original pencilled text of *Tuor A* had 'Fair among the Lothlim grows Eärendel in Sornontur the house of Tuor'. The fourth letter of this name could as well be read as a *u*.

### Changes made to names in
*The Fall of Gondolin*

*Ilfiniol* < *Elfriniol* in the first three occurrences of the name in the initial linking passage, *Ilfiniol* so written at the fourth.

(In *The Cottage of Lost Play* (I.15) the Gong-warden of Mar Vanwa Tyaliéva is named only *Littleheart*; in the *Link* to *The Music of the Ainur* his Elvish name is *Ilverin* < *Elwenildo* (I.46, 52); and in the *Link* to the *Tale of Tinúviel* he is *Ilfiniol* < *Elfriniol* as here, while the typescript has *Ilfrin* (p. 7).

In the head-note to the Name-list to *The Fall of Gondolin* he is *Elfrith* < *Elfriniel*, and this is the only place where the meaning of the name 'Littleheart' is explained (p. 148); the Name-list has an

entry *'Elf* meaneth "heart" (as Elfin *Elben*): *Elfrith* is Littleheart'
(see I.255, entry *Ilverin*). In another projected list of names,
abandoned after only a couple of entries had been made, we meet
again the form *Elfrith*, and also *Elbenil* > *Elwenil*.
This constant changing of name is to be understood in relation to
swiftly changing phonological ideas and formulations, but even so is
rather extraordinary.)

> *In the following notes it is to be understood, for brevity's*
> *sake, that names in* Tuor B *(before emendation) are found*
> *in the same form in* Tuor A; *e.g.* 'Mithrim < Asgon *in* Tuor B'
> *implies that* Tuor A *has* Asgon *(unchanged).*

*Tuor*    Although sometimes emended to *Tûr* in *Tuor B*, and invariably
written *Tûr* in the typescript *Tuor C*, I give *Tuor* throughout; see
p. 148.

*Dor Lómin*    This name was so written from the first in *Tuor B*. *Tuor A*
has, at the first three occurrences, *Aryador* > *Mathusdor*; at the
fourth, *Aryador* > *Mathusdor* > *Dor Lómin*.

*Mithrim*    < *Asgon* throughout *Tuor B*; *Tuor C* has *Asgon* unchanged.

*Glorfalc or Cris Ilbranteloth* (p. 150)    *Tuor A* has *Glorfalc or Teld*
*Quing Ilon*; *Tuor B* as written had no Elvish names, *Glorfalc or*
*Cris Ilbranteloth* being a later addition.

*Ainur*    As in the first draft of *The Music of the Ainur* (I.61) the
original text of *Tuor A* had *Ainu* plural.

*Falasquil*    At both occurrences (p. 152) in *Tuor A* this replaces the
original name now illegible but beginning with *Q*; in *Tuor B* my
mother left blanks and added the name later in pencil; in *Tuor C*
blanks are left in the typescript and not filled in.

*Arlisgion*    This name was added later to *Tuor B*.

*Orcs*    *Tuor A* and *B* had *Orqui* throughout; my father emended this in
*Tuor B* to *Orcs*, but not consistently, and in the later part of the
tale not at all. In one place only (p. 193, in Thorndor's speech)
both texts have *Orcs* (also *Orc-bands* p. 195). As with the name
*Tuor/Tûr* I give throughout the form that was to prevail.
    At the only occurrence of the singular the word is written with a *k*
in both *Tuor A* and *B* ('Ork's blood', p. 165).

*Gar Thurion*    < *Gar Furion* in *Tuor B* (*Gar Furion* in *Tuor C*).

*Loth*    < *Lôs* in *Tuor B* (*Lôs* in *Tuor C*).

*Lothengriol*    < *Lósengriol* in *Tuor B* (*Lósengriol* in *Tuor C*).

*Taniquetil*    At the occurrence on p. 161 there was added in the original
text of *Tuor A*: (*Danigwiel*), but this was struck out.

*Kôr*    Against this name (p. 161) is pencilled in *Tuor B*: *Tûn*. See I.222,
II.292.

*Gar Ainion*    < *Gar Ainon* in *Tuor B* (p. 164; at the occurrence on
p. 186 not emended, but I read *Gar Ainion* in both places).

*Nost-na-Lothion*    < *Nost-na-Lossion* in *Tuor B*.

*Duilin*   At the first occurrence (p. 173) < *Duliglin* in the original text of
   *Tuor A*.

*Rog*   In *Tuor A* spelt *Rôg* in the earlier occurrences, *Rog* in the later; in
   *Tuor B* spelt *Rôg* throughout but mostly emended later to *Rog*.

*Dramborleg*   At the occurrence on p. 181 < *Drambor* in the original
   text of *Tuor A*.

*Bansil*   At the occurrence on p. 184 only, *Bansil* > *Banthil* in *Tuor B*.

*Cristhorn*   From the first occurrence on p. 189 written *Cristhorn* (not
   *Cris Thorn*) in *Tuor A*; *Cris Thorn Tuor B* throughout.

*Bad Uthwen*   < *Bad Uswen* in *Tuor B*. The original reading in *Tuor A*
   was (apparently) *Bad Usbran*.

*Sorontur*   < *Ramandur* in *Tuor B*.

*Bablon, Ninwi, Trui, Rûm*   The original text of *Tuor A* had *Babylon*,
   *Nineveh*, *Troy*, and (probably) *Rome*. These were changed to the
   forms given in the text, except *Nineveh* > *Ninwë*, changed to
   *Ninwi* in *Tuor B*.

## Commentary on
## The Fall of Gondolin

### §1.   The primary narrative

As with the *Tale of Turambar* I break my commentary on this tale into
sections. I refer frequently to the much later version (which extends only
to the coming of Tuor and Voronwë to sight of Gondolin across the
plain) printed in *Unfinished Tales* pp. 17–51 ('Of Tuor and his Coming
to Gondolin'); this I shall call here 'the later *Tuor*'.

### (i)   Tuor's journey to the Sea and the visitation
of Ulmo (pp. 149–56)

In places the later *Tuor* (the abandonment of which is one of the saddest
facts in the whole history of incompletion) is so close in wording to *The
Fall of Gondolin*, written more than thirty years before, as to make it
almost certain that my father had it in front of him, or at least had
recently reread it. Striking examples from the late version (pp. 23–4)
are: 'The sun rose behind his back and set before his face, and where the
water foamed among the boulders or rushed over sudden falls, at morning
and evening rainbows were woven across the stream'; 'Now he said: "It is
a fay-voice," now: "Nay, it is a small beast that is wailing in the waste"';
'[Tuor] wandered still for some days in a rugged country bare of trees;
and it was swept by a wind from the sea, and all that grew there, herb or
bush, leaned ever to the dawn because of the prevalence of that wind
from the West' – which are very closely similar to or almost identical with

passages in the tale (pp. 150–1). But the differences in the narrative are profound.

Tuor's origin is left vague in the old story. There is a reference in the *Tale of Turambar* (p. 88) to 'those kindreds about the waters of Asgon whence after arose Tuor son of Peleg', but here it is said that Tuor did not dwell with his people (who 'wandered the forests and fells') but 'lived alone about that lake called Mithrim [< Asgon]', on which he journeyed in a small boat with a prow made like the neck of a swan. There is indeed scarcely any linking reference to other events, and of course no trace of the Grey-elves of Hithlum who in the later story fostered him, or of his outlawry and hunting by the Easterlings; but there are 'wandering Noldoli' in Dor Lómin (Hisilómë, Hithlum) – on whom see p. 65 – from whom Tuor learnt much, including their tongue, and it was they who guided him down the dark river-passage under the mountains. There is in this a premonition of Gelmir and Arminas, the Noldorin Elves who guided Tuor through the Gate of the Noldor (later *Tuor* pp. 21–2), and the story that the Noldoli 'made that hidden way at the prompting of Ulmo' survived in the much richer historical context of the later legend, where 'the Gate of the Noldor . . . was made by the skill of that people, long ago in the days of Turgon' (later *Tuor* p. 18).

The later *Tuor* becomes very close to the old story for a time when Tuor emerges out of the tunnel into the ravine (later called Cirith Ninniach, but still a name of Tuor's own devising); many features recur, such as the stars shining in the 'dark lane of sky above him', the echoes of his harping (in the tale of course without the literary echoes of Morgoth's cry and the voices of Fëanor's host that landed there), his doubt concerning the mournful calling of the gulls, the narrowing of the ravine where the incoming tide (fierce because of the west wind) met the water of the river, and Tuor's escape by climbing to the cliff-top (but in the tale the connection between Tuor's curiosity concerning the gulls and the saving of his life is not made: he climbed the cliff in response to the prompting of the Ainur). Notable is the retention of the idea that Tuor was the first of Men to reach the Sea, standing on the cliff-top with outspread arms, and of his 'sea-longing' (later *Tuor* p. 25). But the story of his dwelling in the cove of Falasquil and his adornment of it with carvings (and of course the floating of timber down the river to him by the Noldoli of Dor Lómin) was abandoned; in the later legend Tuor finds on the coast ruins of the ancient harbour-works of the Noldor from the days of Turgon's lordship in Nevrast, and of Turgon's former dwelling in these regions before he went to Gondolin there is in the old story no trace. Thus the entire Vinyamar episode is absent from it, and despite the frequent reminder that Ulmo was guiding Tuor as the instrument of his designs, the essential element in the later legend of the arms left for him by Turgon on Ulmo's instruction (*The Silmarillion* pp. 126, 238–9) is lacking.

The southward-flying swans (seven, not three, in the later *Tuor*) play essentially the same part in both narratives, drawing Tuor to continue his journey; but the emblem of the Swan was afterwards given a different origin, as 'the token of Annael and his foster-folk', the Grey-elves of Mithrim (later *Tuor* p. 25).

Both in the route taken (for the geography see p. 217) and in the seasons of the year my father afterwards departed largely from the original story of Tuor's journey to Gondolin. In the later *Tuor* it was the Fell Winter after the fall of Nargothrond, the winter of Túrin's return to Hithlum, when he and Voronwë journeyed in snow and bitter cold eastwards beneath the Mountains of Shadow. Here the journey takes far longer: he left Falasquil in 'the latest days of summer' (as still in the later *Tuor*) but he went down all the coast of Beleriand to the mouths of Sirion, and it was the summer of the following year when he lingered in the Land of Willows. (Doubtless the geography was less definite than it afterwards became, but its general resemblance to the later map seems assured by the description (p. 153) of the coast's trending after a time eastwards rather than southwards.)

Only in its place in the narrative structure is there resemblance between Ulmo's visitation of Tuor in the Land of Willows in a summer twilight and his tremendous epiphany out of the rising storm on the coast at Vinyamar. It is however most remarkable that the old vision of the Land of Willows and its drowsy beauty of river-flowers and butterflies was not lost, though afterwards it was Voronwë, not Tuor, who wandered there, devising names, and who stood enchanted 'knee-deep in the grass' (p. 155; later *Tuor* p. 35), until his fate, or Ulmo Lord of Waters, carried him down to the Sea. Possibly there is a faint reminiscence of the old story in Ulmo's words (later *Tuor* p. 28): 'Haste thou must learn, and *the pleasant road that I designed for thee* must be changed.'

In the tale, Ulmo's speech to Tuor (or at least that part of it that is reported) is far more simple and brief, and there is no suggestion there of Ulmo's 'opposing the will of his brethren, the Lords of the West'; but two essential elements of his later message are present, that Tuor will find the words to speak when he stands before Turgon, and the reference to Tuor's unborn son (in the later *Tuor* much less explicit: 'But it is not for thy valour only that I send thee, but to bring into the world a hope beyond thy sight, and a light that shall pierce the darkness').

(ii) *The journey of Tuor and Voronwë to Gondolin* (pp. 156–8)

Of Tuor's journey to Gondolin, apart from his sojourn in the Land of Willows, little is told in the tale, and Voronwë only appears late in its course as the one Noldo who was not too fearful to accompany him further; of Voronwë's history as afterwards related there is no word, and he is not an Elf of Gondolin.

It is notable that the Noldoli who guided Tuor northwards from the Land of Willows call themselves thralls of Melko. On this matter the *Tales* present a consistent picture. It is said in the *Tale of Tinúviel* (p. 9) that

> all the Eldar both those who remained in the dark or who had been lost upon the march from Palisor and those Noldoli too who fared back into the world after [Melko] seeking their stolen treasury fell beneath his power as thralls.

In *The Fall of Gondolin* it is said that the Noldoli did their service to Ulmo in secret, and 'out of fear of Melko wavered much' (p. 154), and Voronwë spoke to Tuor of 'the weariness of thraldom' (pp. 156-7); Melko sent out his army of spies 'to search out the dwelling of the Noldoli that had escaped his thraldom' (p. 166). These 'thrall-Noldoli' are represented as moving as it were freely about the lands, even to the mouths of Sirion, but they 'wandered as in a dream of fear, doing [Melko's] ill bidding, for the spell of bottomless dread was on them and they felt the eyes of Melko burn them from afar' (*Tale of Turambar*, p. 77). This expression is often used: Voronwë rejoiced in Gondolin that he no longer dreaded Melko with 'a binding terror' – 'and of a sooth that spell which Melko held over the Noldoli was one of bottomless dread, so that he seemed ever nigh them even were they far from the Hells of Iron, and their hearts quaked and they fled not even when they could' (p. 159). The spell of bottomless dread was laid too on Meglin (p. 169).

There is little in all this that cannot be brought more or less into harmony with the later narratives, and indeed one may hear an echo in the words of *The Silmarillion* (p. 156):

> But ever the Noldor feared most the treachery of those of their own kin, who had been thralls in Angband; for Morgoth used some of these for his evil purposes, and feigning to give them liberty sent them abroad, but their wills were chained to his, and they strayed only to come back to him again.

Nonetheless one gains the impression that at that time my father pictured the power of Melko when at its height as operating more diffusedly and intangibly, and perhaps also more universally, in the Great Lands. Whereas in *The Silmarillion* the Noldor who are not free are prisoners in Angband (whence a few may escape, and others with enslaved wills may be sent out), here all save the Gondothlim are 'thralls', controlled by Melko from afar, and Melko asserts that the Noldoli are all, by their very existence in the Great Lands, his slaves by right. It is a difference difficult to define, but that there is a difference may be seen in the improbability, for the later story, of Tuor being guided on his way to Gondolin by Noldor who were in any sense slaves of Morgoth.

The entrance to Gondolin has some general similarity to the far fuller and more precisely visualised account in the later *Tuor*: a deep river-gorge, tangled bushes, a cave-mouth – but the river is certainly Sirion (see the passage at the end of the tale, p. 195, where the exiles come back to the entrance), and the entrance to the secret way is in one of the steep river banks, quite unlike the description of the Dry River whose ancient bed was itself the secret way (later *Tuor* pp. 43–4). The long tunnel which Tuor and Voronwë traverse in the tale leads them at length not only to the Guard but also to sunlight, and they are 'at the foot of steep hills' and can see the city: in other words there is a simple conception of a plain, a ring-wall of mountains, and a tunnel through them leading to the outer world. In the later *Tuor* the approach to the city is much stranger: for the tunnel of the Guard leads to the ravine of Orfalch Echor, a great rift from top to bottom of the Encircling Mountains ('sheer as if axe-cloven', p. 46), up which the road climbed through the successive gates until it came to the Seventh Gate, barring the rift at the top. Only when this last gate was opened and Tuor passed through was he able to see Gondolin; and we must suppose (though the narrative does not reach this point) that the travellers had to descend again from the Seventh Gate in order to reach the plain.

It is notable that Tuor and Voronwë are received by the Guard without any of the suspicion and menace that greeted them in the later story (p. 45).

### (iii)   *Tuor in Gondolin* (pp. 159–64)

With this section of the narrative compare *The Silmarillion*, p. 126:

> Behind the circle of the mountains the people of Turgon grew and throve, and they put forth their skill in labour unceasing, so that Gondolin upon Amon Gwareth became fair indeed and fit to compare even with Elven Tirion beyond the sea. High and white were its walls, and smooth its stairs, and tall and strong was the Tower of the King. There shining fountains played, and in the courts of Turgon stood images of the Trees of old, which Turgon himself wrought with elven-craft; and the Tree which he made of gold was named Glingal, and the Tree whose flowers he made of silver was named Belthil.

The image of Gondolin was enduring, and it reappears in the glimpses given in notes for the continuation of the later *Tuor* (*Unfinished Tales* p. 56): 'the stairs up to its high platform, and its great gate . . . the Place of the Fountain, the King's tower on a pillared arcade, the King's house . . .' Indeed the only real difference that emerges from the original account concerns the Trees of Gondolin, which in the former were unfading, 'shoots of old from the glorious Trees of Valinor', but in *The Silmarillion* were images made of the precious metals. On the Trees of Gondolin see the entries *Bansil* and *Glingol* from the Name-list, given below pp. 214–16. The gift by the Gods of these 'shoots' (which 'blossomed eternally without abating') to Inwë and Nólemë at the time of the building of Kôr, each being given a shoot of either Tree, is mentioned in *The Coming of the Elves* (I.123), and in *The Hiding of Valinor* there is a reference to the uprooting of those given to Nólemë, which 'were gone no one knew whither, and more had there never been' (I.213).

But a deep underlying shift in the history of Gondolin separates the earlier and later accounts: for whereas in the *Lost Tales* (and later) Gondolin was only discovered *after* the Battle of Unnumbered Tears when the host of Turgon retreated southwards down Sirion, in *The Silmarillion* it had been found by Turgon of Nevrast more than four hundred years before (442 years before Tuor came to Gondolin in the Fell Winter after the fall of Nargothrond in the year 495 of the Sun). In the tale my father imagined a great age passing *between* the Battle of Unnumbered Tears and the destruction of the city ('unstaying labour *through ages of years* had not sufficed to its building and adornment whereat folk travailed yet', p. 163); afterwards, with radical changes in the chronology of the First Age after the rising of the Sun and Moon, this period was reduced to no more than (in the last extant version of 'The Tale of Years' of the First Age) thirty-eight years. But the old conception can still be felt in the passage on p. 240 of *The Silmarillion* describing the withdrawal of the people of Gondolin from all concern with the world outside after the Nirnaeth Arnoediad, with its air of long years passing.*

In *The Silmarillion* it is explicit that Turgon devised the city to be 'a memorial of Tirion upon Túna' (p. 125), and it became 'as beautiful as a memory of Elven Tirion' (p. 240). This is not said in the old story, and indeed in the *Lost Tales* Turgon himself had never known Kôr (he was born in the Great Lands after the return of the Noldoli from Valinor, I.167, 238, 240); one may feel nonetheless that the tower of the King, the fountains and stairs, the white marbles of Gondolin embody a recollection of Kôr as it is described in *The Coming of the Elves and the Making of Kôr* (I.122–3).

I have said above that 'despite the frequent reminder that Ulmo was guiding Tuor as the instrument of his designs, the essential element in the later legend of the arms left for him by Turgon on Ulmo's instruction is lacking'. Now however we seem to see the germ of this conception in Turgon's words to Tuor (p. 161): 'Thy coming was set in our books of wisdom, and it has been written that there would come to pass many great things in the homes of the Gondothlim whenso thou faredst hither.' Yet it is clear from Tuor's reply that as yet the establishment of Gondolin was no part of Ulmo's design, since 'there have come to the ears of Ulmo whispers of your dwelling and your hill of vigilance against the evil of Melko, and he is glad'.

* Of the story of Gondolin from Tuor's coming to its destruction my father wrote nothing after the version of 'The Silmarillion' made (very probably) in 1930; and in this the old conception of its history was still present. This was the basis for much of Chapter 23 in the published work.

In the tale, Ulmo foresaw that Turgon would be unwilling to take up arms against Melko, and he fell back, through the mouth of Tuor, on a second counsel: that Turgon send Elves from Gondolin down Sirion to the coasts, there to build ships to carry messages to Valinor. To this Turgon replied, decisively and unanswerably, that he had sent messengers down the great river with this very purpose 'for years untold', and since all had been unavailing he would now do so no more. Now this clearly relates to a passage in *The Silmarillion* (p. 159) where it is said that Turgon, after the Dagor Bragollach and the breaking of the Siege of Angband,

> sent companies of the Gondolindrim in secret to the mouths of Sirion and the Isle of Balar. There they built ships, and set sail into the uttermost West upon Turgon's errand, seeking for Valinor, to ask for pardon and aid of the Valar; and they besought the birds of the sea to guide them. But the seas were wild and wide, and shadow and enchantment lay upon them; and Valinor was hidden. Therefore none of the messengers of Turgon came into the West, and many were lost and few returned.

Turgon did indeed do so once more, after the Battle of Unnumbered Tears (*The Silmarillion* p. 196), and the only survivor of that last expedition into the West was Voronwë of Gondolin. Thus, despite profound changes in chronology and a great development in the narrative of the last centuries of the First Age, the idea of the desperate attempts of Turgon to get a message through to Valinor goes back to the beginning.

Another aboriginal feature is that Turgon had no son; but (curiously) no mention whatsoever is made in the tale of his wife, the mother of Idril. In *The Silmarillion* (p. 90) his wife Elenwë was lost in the crossing of the Helcaraxë, but obviously this story belongs to a later period, when Turgon was born in Valinor.

The tale of Tuor's sojourn in Gondolin survived into the brief words of *The Silmarillion* (p. 241):

> And Tuor remained in Gondolin, for its bliss and its beauty and the wisdom of its people held him enthralled; and he became mighty in stature and in mind, and learned deeply of the lore of the exiled Elves.

In the present tale he 'heard tell of Ilúvatar, the Lord for Always, who dwelleth beyond the world', and of the Music of the Ainur. Knowledge of the very existence of Ilúvatar was, it seems, a prerogative of the Elves; long afterwards in the garden of Mar Vanwa Tyaliéva (I. 49) Eriol asked Rúmil: 'Who was Ilúvatar? Was he of the Gods?' and Rúmil answered: 'Nay, that he was not; for he made them. Ilúvatar is the Lord for Always, who dwells beyond the world.'

(iv)    *The encirclement of Gondolin;*
*the treachery of Meglin* (pp. 164–71)

The king's daughter was from the first named 'Idril of the Silver Feet'
(Irildë in the language of the 'Eldar', note 22); Meglin (later Maeglin)
was his nephew, though the name of his mother (Turgon's sister) Isfin
was later changed.

In this section of the narrative the story in *The Silmarillion*
(pp. 241–2) preserved all the essentials of the original version, with one
major exception. The wedding of Tuor and Idril took place with the
consent and full favour of the king, and there was great joy in Gondolin
among all save Maeglin (whose love of Idril is told earlier in *The
Silmarillion*, p. 139, where the barrier of his being close kin to her, not
mentioned in the tale, is emphasised). Idril's power of foreseeing and
her foreboding of evil to come; the secret way of her devising (but in the
tale this led south from the city, and the Eagles' Cleft was in the
southern mountains); the loss of Meglin in the hills while seeking for
ore; his capture by Orcs, his treacherous purchase of life, and his return
to Gondolin to avert suspicion (with the detail of his changed mood
thereafter and 'smiling face') – all this remained. Much is of course
absent (whether rejected or merely passed over) in the succinct account
devised for *The Silmarillion* – where there is no mention, for example, of
Idril's dream concerning Meglin, the watch set on him when he went to
the hills, the formation on Idril's advice of a guard bearing Tuor's
emblem, the refusal of Turgon to doubt the invulnerability of the city
and his trust in Meglin, Meglin's discovery of the secret way,* or the
remarkable story that it was Meglin himself who conceived the idea of the
monsters of fire and iron and communicated it to Melko – a valuable
defector indeed!

The great difference between the versions lies of course in the nature
of Melko/Morgoth's knowledge of Gondolin. In the tale, he had by
means of a vast army of spies† already discovered it before ever Meglin
was captured, and creatures of Melko had found the 'Way of Escape'
and looked down on Gondolin from the surrounding heights. Meglin's
treachery in the old story lay in his giving an exact account of the
structure of the city and the preparations made for its defence – and in his
advice to Melko concerning the monsters of flame. In *The Silmarillion*,
on the other hand, there is the element, devised much later, of the
unconscious betrayal by Húrin to Morgoth's spies of the general region in
which Gondolin must be sought, in 'the mountainous land between

---

* This is in fact specifically denied in *The Silmarillion*: 'she contrived it that the work was
known but to few, and no whisper of it came to Maeglin's ears.'

† It seems that the 'creatures of blood' (said to be disliked by the people of Gondolin,
p. 166), snakes, wolves, weasels, owls, falcons, are here regarded as the natural servants
and allies of Melko.

Anach and the upper waters of Sirion, whither [Morgoth's] servants had never passed' (p. 241); but 'still no spy or creature out of Angband could come there because of the vigilance of the eagles' – and of this rôle of the eagles of the Encircling Mountains (though hostile to Melko, p. 193) there is in the original story no suggestion.

Thus in *The Silmarillion* Morgoth remained in ignorance until Maeglin's capture of the precise location of Gòndolin, and Maeglin's information was of correspondingly greater value to him, as it was also of greater damage to the city. The history of the last years of Gondolin has thus a somewhat different atmosphere in the tale, for the Gondothlim are informed of the fact that Melko has 'encompassed the vale of Tumladin around' (p. 167), and Turgon makes preparations for war and strengthens the watch on the hills. The withdrawal of all Melko's spies shortly before the attack on Gondolin did indeed bring about a renewal of optimism among the Gondothlim, and in Turgon not least, so that when the attack came the people were unprepared; but in the later story the shock of the sudden assault is much greater, for there has never been any reason to suppose that the city is in immediate danger, and Idril's foreboding is peculiar to herself and more mysterious.

### (v)    *The array of the Gondothlim* (pp. 171–4)

Though the central image of this part of the story – the people of Gondolin looking out from their walls to hail the rising sun on the feast of the Gates of Summer, but seeing a red light rising in the north and not in the east – survived, of all the heraldry in this passage scarcely anything is found in later writings. Doubtless, if my father had continued the later *Tuor*, much would have re-emerged, however changed, if we judge by the rich 'heraldic' descriptions of the great gates and their guards in the Orfalch Echor (pp. 46–50). But in the concise account in *The Silmarillion* the only vestiges are the titles Ecthelion 'of the Fountain'* and Glorfindel 'chief of the House of the Golden Flower of Gondolin'. Ecthelion and Glorfindel are named also in *The Silmarillion* (p. 194) as Turgon's captains who guarded the flanks of the host of Gondolin in their retreat down Sirion from the Nirnaeth Arnoediad, but of other captains named in the tale there is no mention afterwards† – though it is significant that the eighteenth Ruling Steward of Gondor was named Egalmoth, as the

---

* In the later *Tuor* (p. 50) he is 'Lord of the Fountains', plural (the reading in the manuscript is certain).

† In the version of 'The Silmarillion' made in 1930 (see footnote on p. 208), the last account of the Fall of Gondolin to be written and the basis for that in chapter 23 of the published work, the text actually reads: '. . . much is told in *The Fall of Gondolin*: of the death of Rog without the walls, and of the battle of Ecthelion of the Fountain ', &c. I removed the reference to Rog (*The Silmarillion* p. 242) on the grounds that it was absolutely certain that my father would not have retained this name as that of a lord of Gondolin.

seventeenth and twenty-fifth were named Ecthelion (*The Lord of the Rings*, Appendix A (I,ii)).*

Glorfindel 'of the golden hair' (p. 192) remains 'yellow-haired Glorfindel' in *The Silmarillion*, and this was from the beginning the meaning of his name.

(vi)    The battle of Gondolin (pp. 174–88)

Virtually the entire history of the fighting in Gondolin is unique in the tale of *The Fall of Gondolin*; the whole story is summarised in *The Silmarillion* (p. 242) in a few lines:

> Of the deeds of desperate valour there done, by the chieftains of the noble houses and their warriors, and not least by Tuor, much is told in *The Fall of Gondolin*: of the battle of Ecthelion of the Fountain with Gothmog Lord of Balrogs in the very square of the King, where each slew the other, and of the defence of the tower of Turgon by the people of his household, until the tower was overthrown: and mighty was its fall and the fall of Turgon in its ruin.
>
> Tuor sought to rescue Idril from the sack of the city, but Maeglin had laid hands on her, and on Eärendil; and Tuor fought with Maeglin on the walls, and cast him far out, and his body as it fell smote the rocky slopes of Amon Gwareth thrice ere it pitched into the flames below. Then Tuor and Idril led such remnants of the people of Gondolin as they could gather in the confusion of the burning down the secret way which Idril had prepared.

(In this highly compressed account the detail that Maeglin's body struck the slopes of Amon Gwareth three times before it 'pitched' into the flames was retained.) It would seem from *The Silmarillion* account that Maeglin's attempt on Idril and Eärendil took place much later in the fighting, and indeed shortly before the escape of the fugitives down the tunnel; but I think that this is far more likely to be the result of compression than of a change in the narrative of the battle.

In the tale Gondolin is very clearly visualised as a city, with its markets and its great squares, of which there are only vestiges in later writing (see above, p. 207); and there is nothing vague in the description of the fighting. The early conception of the Balrogs makes them less terrible, and certainly more destructible, than they afterwards became: they

---

* In a very late note written on one of the texts that constitute chapter 16 of *The Silmarillion* ('Of Maeglin') my father was thinking of making the 'three lords of his household' whom Turgon appointed to ride with Aredhel from Gondolin (p. 131) Glorfindel, Ecthelion, and Egalmoth. He notes that Ecthelion and Egalmoth 'are derived from the primitive F[all of]G[ondolin]', but that they 'are well-sounding and have been in print' (with reference to the names of the Stewards of Gondor). Subsequently he decided against naming Aredhel's escort.

existed in 'hundreds' (p. 170),* and were slain by Tuor and the
Gondothlim in large numbers: thus five fell before Tuor's great axe
Dramborleg, three before Ecthelion's sword, and two score were slain by
the warriors of the king's house. The Balrogs are 'demons of power'
(p. 181); they are capable of pain and fear (p. 194); they are attired in
iron armour (pp. 181, 194), and they have whips of flame (a character
they never lost) and claws of steel (pp. 169, 179).

In *The Silmarillion* the dragons that came against Gondolin were 'of
the brood of Glaurung', which 'were become now many and terrible';
whereas in the tale the language employed (p. 170) suggests that some at
least of the 'Monsters' were inanimate 'devices', the construction of
smiths in the forges of Angband. But even the 'things of iron' that
'opened about their middles' to disgorge bands of Orcs are called
'ruthless beasts', and Gothmog 'bade' them 'pile themselves' (p. 176);
those made of bronze or copper 'were given hearts and spirits of blazing
fire'; while the 'fire-drake' that Tuor hewed screamed and lashed with its
tail (p. 181).

A small detail of the narrative is curious: what 'messengers' did Meglin
send to Melko to warn him to guard the outer entrance of the Way of
Escape (where he guessed that the secret tunnel must lead in the end)?
Whom could Meglin trust sufficiently? And who would dare to go?

(vii)   *The escape of the fugitives
and the battle in Cristhorn* (pp. 188–95)

The story as told in *The Silmarillion* (p. 243) is somewhat fuller in its
account of the escape of the fugitives from the city and the ambush in the
Eagles' Cleft (there called Cirith Thoronath) than in that of the assault
and sack itself, but only in one point are the two narratives actually at
variance – as already noticed, the Eagles' Cleft was afterwards moved
from the southern parts of the Encircling Mountains to the northern, and
Idril's tunnel led north from the city (the comment is made that it was not
thought 'that any fugitives would take a path towards the north and the
highest parts of the mountains and the nighest to Angband'). The tale
provides a richness of detail and an immediacy that is lacking in the short
version, where such things as the tripping over dead bodies in the hot and
reeking underground passage have disappeared; and there is no mention
of the Gondothlim who against the counsel of Idril and Tuor went to the
Way of Escape and were there destroyed by the dragon lying in wait,† or
of the fight to rescue Eärendel.

* The idea that Morgoth disposed of a 'host' of Balrogs endured long, but in a late note my
father said that only very few ever existed – 'at most seven'.

† This element in the story was in fact still present in the 1930 'Silmarillion' (see
footnote on p. 208), but I excluded it from the published work on account of evidence in a
much later text that the old entrance to Gondolin had by this time been blocked up – a fact
which was then written into the text in chapter 23 of *The Silmarillion*.

In the tale appears the keen-sighted Elf Legolas Greenleaf, first of the names of the Fellowship of the Ring to appear in my father's writings (see p. 217 on this earlier Legolas), followed by Gimli (an Elf) in the *Tale of Tinúviel*.

In one point the story of the ambush in Cristhorn seems difficult to follow: this is the statement on p. 193 that the moon 'lit not the path for the height of the walls'. The fugitives were moving southwards through the Encircling Mountains, and the sheer rockwall above the path in the Eagles' Cleft was 'of the right or westerly hand', while on the left there was 'a fall . . . dreadly steep'. Surely then the moon rising in the east would illuminate the path?

The name *Cristhorn* appears in my father's drawing of 'Gondolin and the Vale of Tumladin from Cristhorn', September 1928 (*Pictures by J. R. R. Tolkien*, 1979, no. 35).

### (viii)   *The wanderings of the Exiles of Gondolin* (pp. 195–7)

In *The Silmarillion* (p. 243) it is said that 'led by Tuor son of Huor the remnant of Gondolin passed over the mountains, and came down into the Vale of Sirion'. One would suppose that they came down into Dimbar, and so 'fleeing southward by weary and dangerous marches they came at length to Nan-tathren, the Land of Willows'. It seems strange in the tale that the exiles were wandering in the wilderness for more than a year, and yet achieved only to the outer entrance of the Way of Escape; but the geography of this region may have been vaguer when *The Fall of Gondolin* was written.

In *The Silmarillion* when Tuor and Idril went down from Nan-tathren to the mouths of Sirion they 'joined their people to the company of Elwing, Dior's daughter, that had fled thither but a little while before'. Of this there is no mention here; but I postpone consideration of this part of the narrative.

### §2   *Entries in the Name-list to The Fall of Gondolin*

On this list see p. 148, where the head-note to it is given. Specifically linguistic information from the list, including meanings, is incorporated in the Appendix on Names, but I collect here some statements of other kind (arranged in alphabetical order) that are contained in it.

*Bablon* 'was a city of Men, and more rightly *Babylon*, but such is the Gnomes' name as they now shape it, and they got it from Men aforetime.'

*Bansil* 'Now this name had the Gondothlim for that tree before their king's door which bore silver blossom and faded not − and its name had Elfriniel from his father Voronwë; and it meaneth "Fairgleam". Now that tree of which it was a shoot (brought in the deep ages out of Valinor by the Noldoli) had like properties, but greater, seeing that for half the twenty-four hours it lit all Valinor with silver light. This the Eldar still tell of as *Silpion* or "Cherry-moon", for its blossom was like that of a cherry in spring – but of that tree in Gondolin they know no name, and the Noldoli tell of it alone.'

*Dor Lómin* 'or the "Land of Shadows" was that region named of the Eldar Hisilómë (and this means Shadowy Twilights) where Melko shut Men, and it is so called by reason of the scanty sun which peeps little over the Iron Mountains to the east and south of it – there dwell now the Shadow Folk. Thence came Tuor to Gondolin.'

*Eärendel* 'was the son of Tuor and Idril and 'tis said the only being that is half of the kindred of the Eldalië and half of Men. He was the greatest and first of all mariners among Men, and saw regions that Men have not yet found nor gazed upon for all the multitude of their boats. He rideth now with Voronwë upon the winds of the firmament nor comes ever further back than Kôr, else would he die like other Men, so much of the mortal is in him.'

(For these last statements about Eärendel see pp. 264–5. The statement that Eärendel was 'the only being that is half of the kindred of the Eldalië and half of Men' is very notable. Presumably this was written when Beren was an Elf, not a Man (see p. 139); Dior son of Beren and Tinúviel appears in the *Tale of the Nauglafring*, but there Beren is an Elf, and Dior is not Half-elven. In the tale of *The Fall of Gondolin* itself it is said, but in a later replacement passage (p. 164 and note 22), that Tuor was the first but not the last to wed 'a daughter of Elfinesse'. On the extraordinary statement in the *Tale of Turambar* that Tamar Lamefoot was Half-elven see p. 130.)

*Ecthelion* 'was that lord of the house of the Fountain, who had the fairest voice and was most skilled in musics of all the Gondothlim. He won renown for ever by his slaying of Gothmog son of Melko, whereby Tuor was saved from death but Ecthelion was drowned with his foe in the king's fountain.'

*Egalmoth* was 'lord of the house of the Heavenly Arch, and got even out of the burning of Gondolin, and dwelt after at the mouth of Sirion, but was slain in a dire battle there when Melko seized Elwing'.
(See p. 258.)

*Galdor* 'was that valiant Gnome who led the men of the Tree in many a charge and yet won out of Gondolin and even the onslaught of Melko upon the dwellers at Sirion's mouth and went back to the ruins with Eärendel. He dwelleth yet in Tol Eressëa (said Elfriniel), and still do some of his folk name themselves *Nos Galdon*, for *Galdon* is a tree, and thereto Galdor's name akin.' The last phrase was emended to read: '*Nos nan Alwen*, for *Alwen* is a Tree.'

(For Galdor's return to the ruins of Gondolin with Eärendel see
p. 258.)

*Glingol* 'meaneth "singing-gold" ('tis said), and this name was that
which the Gondothlim had for that other of the two unfading trees
in the king's square which bore golden bloom. It also was a shoot
from the trees of Valinor (see rather where Elfrith has spoken of
Bansil), but of Lindeloktë (which is "singing-cluster") or Laurelin
[*emended from* Lindelaurë] (which is "singing-gold") which lit all
Valinor with golden light for half the 24 hours.'
  (For the name *Lindeloktë* see I. 22, 258 (entry *Lindelos*).)

*Glorfindel* 'led the Golden Flower and was the best beloved of the
Gondothlim, save it be Ecthelion, but who shall choose. Yet he was
hapless and fell slaying a Balrog in the great fight in Cristhorn. His
name meaneth Goldtress for his hair was golden, and the name of
his house in Noldorissa *Los 'lóriol'* (emended from *Los Glóriol*).

*Gondolin* 'meaneth stone of song (whereby figuratively the Gnomes
meant stone that was carven and wrought to great beauty), and this
was the name most usual of the Seven Names they gave to their city
of secret refuge from Melko in those days before the release.'

*Gothmog* 'was a son of Melko and the ogress Fluithuin and his name is
Strife-and-hatred, and he was Captain of the Balrogs and lord of
Melko's hosts ere fair Ecthelion slew him at the taking of Gondolin.
The Eldar named him *Kosmoko* or *Kosomok(o)*, but 'tis a name
that fitteth their tongue no way and has an ill sound even in our own
rougher speech, said Elfrith [*emended from* Elfriniel].'
  (In a list of names of the Valar associated with the tale of *The
Coming of the Valar* (I.93) it is said that Melko had a son 'by
Ulbandi' called *Kosomot*; the early 'Qenya' dictionary gives
*Kosomoko* = Gnomish *Gothmog*, I.258. In the tale Gothmog is
called the 'marshal' of the hosts of Melko (p. 184).)
  In the later development of the legends Gothmog was the slayer
of Fëanor, and in the Battle of Unnumbered Tears it was he who
slew Fingon and captured Húrin (*The Silmarillion* pp. 107, 193,
195). He is not of course called later 'son of Melkor'; the 'Children of
the Valar' was a feature of the earlier mythology that my father
discarded.
  In the Third Age *Gothmog* was the name of the lieutenant of
Minas Morgul (*The Return of the King* V.6).)

*Hendor* 'was a house-carle of Idril's and was aged, but bore Eärendel
down the secret passage.'

*Idril* 'was that most fair daughter of the king of Gondolin whom Tuor
loved when she was but a little maid, and who bare him Eärendel.
Her the Elves name *Irildë*; and we speak of as *Idril Tal-Celeb* or
Idril of the Silver Feet, but they *Irildë Taltelepta*.'
  See the Appendix on Names, entry *Idril*.

*Indor* 'was the name of the father of Tuor's father, wherefore did the Gnomes name Eärendel *Gon Indor* and the Elves *Indorildo* or *Indorion*.'

*Legolas* 'or Green-leaf was a man of the Tree, who led the exiles over Tumladin in the dark, being night-sighted, and he liveth still in Tol Eressëa named by the Eldar there *Laiqalassë*; but the book of Rúmil saith further hereon.'
(See I. 267, entry *Tári-Laisi*.)

## §3 Miscellaneous Matters

### (i) The geography of The Fall of Gondolin

I have noticed above (p. 205) that in Tuor's journey all along the coast of what was afterwards Beleriand to the mouths of Sirion there is an unquestionable resemblance to the later map, in the trend of the coast from north-south to east-west. It is also said that after he left Falasquil 'the distant hills marched ever nearer to the margin of the sea', and that the spurs of the Iron Mountains 'run even to the sea' (pp. 152–3). These statements can likewise be readily enough related to the map, where the long western extension of the Mountains of Shadow (Ered Wethrin), forming the southern border of Nevrast, reached the sea at Vinyamar (for the equation of the Mountains of Iron and the Mountains of Shadow see I. 111–12).

Arlisgion, 'the place of reeds' (p. 153) above the mouths of Sirion, survived in Lisgardh 'the land of reeds at the Mouths of Sirion' in the later *Tuor* (p. 34); and the feature that the great river passed underground for a part of its course goes back to the earliest period, as does that of the Meres of Twilight, Aelin-uial ('the Pools of Twilight', p. 195). There is here however a substantial difference in the tale from *The Silmarillion* (p. 122), where Aelin-uial was the region of great pools and marshes where 'the flood of Sirion was stayed'; *south of the Meres* the river 'fell from the north in a mighty fall . . . and then he plunged suddenly underground into great tunnels that the weight of his falling waters delved'. Here on the other hand the Pools of Twilight are clearly *below* the 'cavern of the Tumultuous Winds' (never mentioned later) where Sirion dives underground. But the Land of Willows, below the region of Sirion's underground passage, is placed as it was to remain.

Thus the view I expressed (p. 141) of the geographical indications in the *Tale of Turambar* can be asserted also of those of *The Fall of Gondolin*.

### (ii) Ulmo and the other Valar in The Fall of Gondolin

In the speech of Tuor inspired by Ulmo that he uttered at his first meeting with Turgon (p. 161) he said: 'the hearts of the Valar are angered . . . seeing the sorrow of the thraldom of the Noldoli and the wanderings of Men.' This is greatly at variance with what is told in *The Hiding of Valinor*, especially the following (I. 208–9):*

> The most of the Valar moreover were fain of their ancient ease and desired only peace, wishing neither rumour of Melko and his violence nor murmur of the restless Gnomes to come ever again among them to disturb their happiness; and for such reasons they also clamoured for the concealment of the land. Not the least among these were Vána and Nessa, albeit most even of the great Gods were of one mind. In vain did Ulmo of his foreknowing plead before them for pity and pardon on the Noldoli . . .

Subsequently Tuor said (p. 161): 'the Gods sit in Valinor, though their mirth is minished for sorrow and fear of Melko, and they hide their land and weave about it inaccessible magic that no evil come to its shores.' Turgon in his reply ironically echoed and altered the words: 'they that sit within [*i.e. in Valinor*] reck little of the dread of Melko or the sorrow of the world, but hide their land and weave about it inaccessible magic, that no tidings of evil come ever to their ears.'

How is this to be understood? Was this Ulmo's 'diplomacy'? Certainly Turgon's understanding of the motives of the Valar chimes better with what is said of them in *The Hiding of Valinor*.

But the Gnomes of Gondolin reverenced the Valar. There were 'pomps of the Ainur' (p. 165); a great square of the city and its highest point was Gar Ainion, the Place of the Gods, where weddings were celebrated (pp. 164, 186); and the people of the Hammer of Wrath 'reverenced Aulë the Smith more than all other Ainur' (p. 174).

Of particular interest is the passage (p. 165) in which a reason is given for Ulmo's choice of a Man as the agent of his designs: 'Now Melko was not much afraid of the race of Men in those days of his great power, and for this reason did Ulmo work through one of this kindred for the better deceiving of Melko, seeing that no Valar and scarce any of the Eldar or Noldoli might stir unmarked of his vigilance.' This is the only place where a reason is expressly offered, save for an isolated early note, where two reasons are given:

(1) 'the wrath of the Gods' (i.e. against the Gnomes);

(2) 'Melko did not fear Men – had he thought that any messengers were getting to Valinor he would have redoubled his vigilance and evil and hidden the Gnomes away utterly.'

---

* It also seems to be at variance with the story that all Men were shut in Hithlum by Melko's decree after the Battle of Unnumbered Tears; but 'wanderings' is a strange word in the context, since the next words are 'for Melko ringeth them in the Land of Shadows'.

But this is too oblique to be helpful.

The conception of 'the luck of the Gods' occurs again in this tale (pp. 188, 200 note 32), as it does in the *Tale of Turambar*: see p. 141. The Ainur 'put it into Tuor's heart' to climb the cliff out of the ravine of Golden Cleft for the saving of his life (p. 151).

Very strange is the passage concerning the birth of Eärendel (p. 165): 'In these days came to pass the fulfilment of the time of the desire of the Valar and the hope of the Eldalië, for in great love Idril bore to Tuor a son and he was called Eärendel.' Is it to be understood that the union of Elf and mortal Man, and the birth of their offspring, was 'the desire of the Valar' – that the Valar foresaw it, or hoped for it, as the fulfilment of a design of Ilúvatar from which great good should come? There is no hint or suggestion of such an idea elsewhere.

## (iii)   *Orcs*

There is a noteworthy remark in the tale (p. 159) concerning the origin of the Orcs (or *Orqui* as they were called in *Tuor A*, and in *Tuor B* as first written): 'all that race were bred of the subterranean heats and slime.' There is no trace yet of the later view that 'naught that had life of its own, nor the semblance of life, could ever Melkor make since his rebellion in the Ainulindalë before the Beginning', or that the Orcs were derived from enslaved Quendi after the Awakening (*The Silmarillion* p. 50). Conceivably there is a first hint of this idea of their origin in the words of the tale in the same passage: 'unless it be that certain of the Noldoli were twisted to the evil of Melko and mingled among these Orcs', although of course this is as it stands quite distinct from the idea that the Orcs were actually bred from Elves.

Here also occurs the name *Glamhoth* of the Orcs, a name that reappears in the later *Tuor* (pp. 39 and 54 note 18).

On Balrogs and Dragons in *The Fall of Gondolin* see pp. 212–13.

## (iv)   *Noldorin in the Land of Willows*

'Did not even after the days of Tuor Noldorin and his Eldar come there seeking for Dor Lómin and the hidden river and the caverns of the Gnomes' imprisonment; yet thus nigh to their quest's end were like to abandon it? Indeed sleeping and dancing here . . . they were whelmed by the goblins sped by Melko from the Hills of Iron and Noldorin made bare escape thence' (p. 154). This was the Battle of Tasarinan, mentioned in the *Tale of Turambar* (pp. 70, 140), at the time of the great expedition of the Elves from Kôr. Cf. Lindo's remark in *The Cottage of Lost Play* (I.16) that his father Valwë 'went with Noldorin to find the Gnomes'.

Noldorin (Salmar, companion of Ulmo) is also said in the tale to have fought beside Tulkas at the Pools of Twilight against Melko himself, though his name was struck out (p. 195 and note 38); this was after the Battle of Tasarinan. On these battles see pp. 278 ff.

### (v)    *The stature of Elves and Men*

The passage concerning Tuor's stature on p. 159, before it was rewritten (see note 18), can only mean that while Tuor was not himself unusually tall for a Man he was nonetheless taller than the Elves of Gondolin, and thus agrees with statements made in the *Tale of Turambar* (see p. 142). As emended, however, the meaning is rather that Men and Elves were not greatly distinct in stature.

### (vi)    *Isfin and Eöl*

The earliest version of this tale is found in the little *Lost Tales* notebook (see I. 171), as follows:

### Isfin and Eöl

Isfin daughter of Fingolma loved from afar by Eöl (Arval) of the Mole-kin of the Gnomes. He is strong and in favour with Fingolma and with the Sons of Fëanor (to whom he is akin) because he is a leader of the Miners and searches after hidden jewels, but he is illfavoured and Isfin loathes him.

(Fingolma as a name for Finwë Nólemë appears in outlines for *Gilfanon's Tale*, I. 238–9.) We have here an illfavoured miner named Eöl 'of the Mole' who loves Isfin but is rejected by her with loathing; and this is obviously closely parallel to the illfavoured miner Meglin with the sign of the sable mole seeking the hand of Idril, who rejects him, in *The Fall of Gondolin*. It is difficult to know how to interpret this. The simplest explanation is that the story adumbrated in the little notebook is actually earlier than that in *The Fall of Gondolin*; that Meglin did not yet exist; and that subsequently the image of the 'ugly miner – unsuccessful suitor' became that of the son, the object of desire becoming Idril (niece of Isfin), while a new story was developed for the father, Eöl the dark Elf of the forest who ensnared Isfin. But it is by no means clear where Eöl the miner was when he 'loved from afar' Isfin daughter of Fingolma. There seems to be no reason to think that he was associated with Gondolin; more probably the idea of the miner bearing the sign of the Mole entered Gondolin with Meglin.

# IV

# THE NAUGLAFRING

We come now to the last of the original *Lost Tales* to be given consecutive narrative form. This is contained in a separate notebook, and it bears the title *The Nauglafring: The Necklace of the Dwarves*.

The beginning of this tale is somewhat puzzling. Before the telling of *The Fall of Gondolin* Lindo told Littleheart that 'it is the desire of all that you tell us the tales of Tuor and of Eärendel as soon as may be' (p. 144), and Littleheart replied: 'It is a mighty tale, and seven times shall folk fare to the Tale-fire ere it be rightly told; and so twined is it with those stories of the Nauglafring and of the Elf-march that I would fain have aid in that telling of Ailios here . . .' Thus Littleheart's surrender of the chair of the tale-teller to Ailios at the beginning of the present text, so that Ailios should tell of the Nauglafring, fits the general context well; but we should not expect the new tale to be introduced with the words 'But after a while silence fell', since *The Fall of Gondolin* ends 'And no one in all the Room of Logs spake or moved for a great while.' In any case, after the very long *Fall of Gondolin* the next tale would surely have waited till the following evening.

This tale is once again a manuscript in ink over a wholly erased original in pencil, but only so far as the words 'sate his greed' on page 230. From this point to the end there is only a primary manuscript in pencil in the first stage of composition, written in haste – in places hurled on to the page, with a good many words not certainly decipherable; and a part of this was extensively rewritten while the tale was still in progress (see note 13).

## The Nauglafring
### The Necklace of the Dwarves

But after a while silence fell, and folk murmured 'Eärendel', but others said 'Nay – what of the Nauglafring, the Necklace of the Dwarves.' Therefore said Ilfiniol, leaving the chair of the tale-teller: 'Yea, better would the tale be told if Ailios would relate the matters concerning that necklace,' and Ailios being nowise unwilling thus began, looking upon the company.

'Remember ye all how Úrin the Steadfast cast the gold of Glorund before the feet of Tinwelint, and after would not touch it

again, but went in sorrow back to Hisilómë, and there died?' And
all said that that tale was still fresh in their hearts.

'Behold then,' said Ailios, 'in great grief gazed the king upon
Úrin as he left the hall, and he was weary for the evil of Melko that
thus deceived all hearts; yet tells the tale that so potent were the
spells that Mîm the fatherless had woven about that hoard that,
even as it lay upon the floor of the king's halls shining strangely in
the light of the torches that burnt there, already were all who
looked upon it touched by its subtle evil.

Now therefore did those of Úrin's band murmur, and one said
to the king: "Lo, lord, our captain Úrin, an old man and mad, has
departed, but we have no mind to forego our gain."

Then said Tinwelint, for neither was he untouched by the
golden spell: "Nay then, know ye not that this gold belongs to the
kindred of the Elves in common, for the Rodothlim who won it
from the earth long time ago are no more, and no one has especial
claim[1] to so much as a handful save only Úrin by reason of his son
Túrin, who slew the Worm, the robber of the Elves; yet Túrin is
dead and Úrin will have none of it; and Túrin was my man."

At those words the outlaws fell into great wrath, until the king
said: "Get ye now gone, and seek not O foolish ones to quarrel
with the Elves of the forest, lest death or the dread enchantments
of Valinor find you in the woods. Neither revile ye the name of
Tinwelint their king, for I will reward you richly enough for your
travail and the bringing of the gold. Let each one now approach
and take what he may grasp with either hand, and then depart in
peace."

Now were the Elves of the wood in turn displeased, who long
had stood nigh gazing on the gold; but the wild folk did as they
were bid, and yet more, for some went into the hoard twice and
thrice, and angry cries were raised in that hall. Then would
the woodland Elves hinder them of their thieving, and a great
dissension arose, so that though the king would stay them none
heeded him. Then did those outlaws being fierce and fearless folk
draw swords and deal blows about them, so that soon there was a
great fight even upon the steps of the high-seat of the king.
Doughty were those outlaws and great wielders of sword and axe
from their warfare with Orcs,[2] so that many were slain ere the
king, seeing that peace and pardon might no longer be, summoned
a host of his warriors, and those outlaws being wildered with the
stronger magics of the king[3] and confused in the dark ways of
the halls of Tinwelint were all slain fighting bitterly; but the

king's hall ran with gore, and the gold that lay before his throne, scattered and spurned by trampling feet, was drenched with blood. Thus did the curse of Mîm the Dwarf begin its course; and yet another sorrow sown by the Noldoli of old in Valinor was come to fruit.[4]

Then were the bodies of the outlaws cast forth, but the woodland Elves that were slain Tinwelint let bury nigh to the knoll of Tinúviel, and 'tis said that the great mound stands there still in Artanor, and for long the fairies called it Cûm an-Idrisaith, the Mound of Avarice.

Now came Gwenniel to Tinwelint and said: "Touch not this gold, for my heart tells me it is trebly cursed. Cursed indeed by the dragon's breath, and cursed by thy lieges' blood that moistens it, and the death of those[5] they slew; but some more bitter and more binding ill methinks hangs over it that I may not see."

Then, remembering the wisdom of Gwenniel his wife, the king was minded to hearken to her, and he bade gather it up and cast it into the stream before the gates. Yet even so he might not shake off its spell, and he said to himself: "First will I gaze my last upon its loveliness ere I fling it from me for ever." Therefore he let wash it clean of its stains of blood in clear waters, and display it before him. Now such mighty heaps of gold have never since been gathered in one place; and some thereof was wrought to cups, to basons, and to dishes, and hilts there were for swords, and scabbards, and sheaths for daggers; but the most part was of red gold unwrought lying in masses and in bars. The value of that hoard no man could count, for amid the gold lay many gems, and these were very beautiful to look upon, for the fathers of the Rodothlim had brought them out of Valinor, a portion of that boundless treasury the Noldoli had there possessed.

Now as he gazed Tinwelint said: "How glorious is this treasure! And I have not a tithe thereof, and of the gems of Valinor none save that Silmaril that Beren won from Angamandi." But Gwenniel who stood by said: "And that were worth all that here lies, were it thrice as great."

Then arose one from among the company, and that was Ufedhin, a Gnome; but more had he wandered about the world than any of the king's folk, and long had he dwelt with the Nauglath and the Indrafangs their kin. The Nauglath are a strange race and none know surely whence they be; and they serve not Melko nor Manwë and reck not for Elf or Man, and some say that they have not heard of Ilúvatar, or hearing disbelieve.

Howbeit in crafts and sciences and in the knowledge of the virtues of all things that are in the earth[6] or under the water none excel them; yet they dwell beneath the ground in caves and tunnelled towns, and aforetime Nogrod was the mightiest of these. Old are they, and never comes a child among them, nor do they laugh. They are squat in stature, and yet are strong, and their beards reach even to their toes, but the beards of the Indrafangs are the longest of all, and are forked, and they bind them about their middles when they walk abroad. All these creatures have Men called 'Dwarves', and say that their crafts and cunning surpass that of the Gnomes in marvellous contrivance, but of a truth there is little beauty in their works of themselves, for in those things of loveliness that they have wrought in ages past such renegade Gnomes as was Ufedhin have ever had a hand. Now long had that Gnome forsaken his folk, becoming leagued with the Dwarves of Nogrod, and was at that time come to the realms of Tinwelint with certain other Noldoli of like mind bearing swords and coats of mail and other smithyings of exquisite skill in which the Nauglath in those days did great traffic with the free Noldoli, and, 'tis said, with the Orcs and soldiers of Melko also.

As he stood in that place the spell of the gold had pierced the heart of Ufedhin more deeply than the heart of any there, and he could not endure that it should all be cast away, and these were his words: "An evil deed is this that Tinwelint the king intends; or who hereafter shall say that the kindreds of the Eldalië love things of beauty if a king of the Eldar cast so great a store of loveliness into the dark woodland waters where none but the fishes may after behold it? Rather than this should be, I beg of thee, O King, to suffer the craftsmen of the Dwarves to try their skill upon this unwrought gold, that the name of the golden treasury of Tinwelint become heard in all lands and places. This will they do, I promise thee, for small guerdon, might they but save the hoard from ruin."

Then looked the king upon the gold and he looked upon Ufedhin, and that Gnome was clad very richly, having a tunic of golden web and a belt of gold set with tiny gems; and his sword was damasked in strange wise,[7] but a collar of gold and silver interlaced most intricate was round his neck, and Tinwelint's raiment could in no wise compare with that of the wayfarer in his halls. Again looked Tinwelint upon the gold, and it shone yet more alluring fair, nor ever had the sparkle of the gems seemed so brilliant, and Ufedhin said again: "Or in what manner, O King, dost thou guard that Silmaril of which all the world hath heard?"

Now Gwenniel warded it in a casket of wood bound with iron, and Ufedhin said it was shame so to set a jewel that should not touch aught less worthy than the purest gold. Then was Tinwelint abashed, and yielded, and this was the agreement that he made with Ufedhin. Half the gold should the king measure and give to the hands of Ufedhin and his company, and they should bear it away to Nogrod and the dwellings of the Dwarves. Now those were a very long journey southward beyond the wide forest on the borders of great heaths nigh Umboth-muilin the Pools of Twilight, on the marches of Tasarinan. Yet after but seven full moons back would the Nauglath fare bearing the king's loan all wrought to works of greatest cunning, yet in no wise would the weight and purity of the gold be minished. Then would they speak to Tinwelint, and an he liked not the handiwork then would they return and say no more; yet if it seemed good to him then of that which remained would they fashion such marvellous things for his adornment and for Gwenniel the Queen as never had Gnome or Dwarf made yet.

"For," said Ufedhin, "the cunning of the Nauglath have I learnt, and the beauty of design that only can the Noldoli compass do I know – yet shall the wages of our labour be small indeed, and we will name it before thee when all is done."

Then by reason of the glamour of the gold the king repented his agreement with Ufedhin, and he liked not altogether his words, and he would not suffer so great a store of gold to be borne without surety out of his sight for seven moons to the distant dwellings of the Dwarves; yet was he minded nonetheless to profit by their skill. Therefore suddenly he let seize Ufedhin, and his folk, and he said unto them: "Here shall ye remain as hostages in my halls until I see again my treasury." Now Tinwelint thought in his heart that Ufedhin and his Gnomes were of the utmost service to the Dwarves, and no covetice would be strong enough to bring them to forsake him; but that Gnome was very wroth, saying: "The Nauglath are no thieves, O King, nor yet their friends"; but Tinwelint said: "Yet the light of overmuch gold has made many thieves, who were not so before," and Ufedhin perforce consented, yet he forgave not Tinwelint in his heart.

Therefore was the gold now borne to Nogrod by folk of the king guided by one only of Ufedhin's companions, and the agreement of Ufedhin and Tinwelint spoken to Naugladur, the king of those places.

Now during the time of waiting Ufedhin was kindly entreated

in the courts of Tinwelint, yet was he idle perforce, and he fretted inwardly. In his leisure he pondered ever what manner of lovely thing of gold and jewels he would after fashion for Tinwelint, but this was only for the greater ensnaring of the king, for already he began to weave dark plots most deep of avarice and revenge.

On the very day of the fullness of the seventh moon thereafter the watchers on the king's bridge cried: "Lo! there comes a great company through the wood, and all it seems are aged men, and they bear very heavy burdens on their backs." But the king hearing said: "It is the Nauglath, who keep their tryst: now mayst thou go free, Ufedhin, and take my greeting to them, and lead them straightway to my hall"; and Ufedhin sallied forth gladly, but his heart forgot not its resentment. Therefore having speech privily with the Nauglath he prevailed upon them to demand at the end a very great reward, and one thereto that the king might not grant unhumbled; and more of his designs also did he unfold, whereby that gold might fare in the end to Nogrod for ever.

Now come the Dwarves nonetheless over the bridge and before the chair of Tinwelint, and behold, the things of their workman-ship they had conveyed thither in silken cloths, and boxes of rare woods carven cunningly. In other wise had Úrin haled the treasure thither, and half thereof lay yet in his rude sacks and clumsy chests; yet when the gold was once more revealed, then did a cry of wonder arise, for the things the Nauglath had made were more wondrous far than the scanty vessels and the ornaments that the Rodothlim wrought of old. Cups and goblets did the king behold, and some had double bowls or curious handles interlaced, and horns there were of strange shape, dishes and trenchers, flagons and ewers, and all appurtenances of a kingly feast. Candlesticks there were and sconces for the torches, and none might count the rings and armlets, the bracelets and collars, and the coronets of gold; and all these were so subtly made and so cunningly adorned that Tinwelint was glad beyond the hope of Ufedhin.

But as yet the designs of Ufedhin came to nought, for in no wise would Tinwelint suffer or him or those of the Nauglath to depart to Nogrod with or without that portion of the unwrought gold that yet remained, and he said: "How shall it be thought that after the weariness of your burdened journeys hither I should let you so soon be gone, to noise the lack of courtesy of Tinwelint abroad in Nogrod? Stay now awhile and rest and feast, and afterward shall ye have the gold that remains to work your pleasure on; nor shall aught of help that I or my folk may afford be wanting in your labour, and a reward rich and more than just awaits you at the end."

But they knew nonetheless that they were prisoners, and trying the exits privily found them strongly warded. Being therefore without counsel they bowed before the king, and the faces of the Dwarf-folk show seldom what they think. Now after a time of rest was that last smithying begun in a deep place of Tinwelint's abode which he caused to be set apart for their uses, and what their hearts lacked therein fear supplied, and in all that work Ufedhin had a mighty part.

A golden crown they made for Tinwelint, who yet had worn nought but a wreath of scarlet leaves, and a helm too most glorious they fashioned; and a sword of dwarven steel brought from afar was hilted with bright gold and damascened in gold and silver with strange figurings wherein was pictured clear the wolf-hunt of Karkaras Knife-fang, father of wolves. That was a more wonderful sword than any Tinwelint had seen before, and outshone the sword in Ufedhin's belt the king had coveted. These things were of Ufedhin's cunning, but the Dwarves made a coat of linked mail of steel and gold for Tinwelint, and a belt of gold. Then was the king's heart gladdened, but they said: "All is not finished," and Ufedhin made a silver crown for Gwenniel, and aided by the Dwarves contrived slippers of silver crusted with diamonds, and the silver thereof was fashioned in delicate scales, so that it yielded as soft leather to the foot, and a girdle he made too of silver blended with pale gold. Yet were those things but a tithe of their works, and no tale tells a full count of them.

Now when all was done and their smithcraft given to the king, then said Ufedhin: "O Tinwelint, richest of kings, dost thou think these things fair?" And he said: "Yea"; but Ufedhin said: "Know then that great store of thy best and purest gold remaineth still, for we have husbanded it, having a boon to ask of thee, and it is this: we would make thee a carcanet and to its making lay all the skill and cunning that we have, and we desire that this should be the most marvellous ornament that the Earth has seen, and the greatest of the works of Elves and Dwarves. Therefore we beg of thee to let us have that Silmaril that thou treasurest, that it may shine wondrously amid the Nauglafring, the Necklace of the Dwarves."

Then again did Tinwelint doubt Ufedhin's purpose, yet did he yield the boon, an they would suffer him to be present at that smithying.

None are that yet live,' quoth Ailios,[8] 'who have seen that most glorious thing, save only[9] Littleheart son of Bronweg, yet are many things told thereof. Not only was it wrought with the greatest skill and subtlety in the world but it had a magic power, and there was no throat so great or so slender whereon it sat not with grace and loveliness. Albeit a weight beyond belief of gold was used in the making, lightly it hung upon its wearer as a strand of flax; and all such as clasped it about their necks seemed, as it hung upon their breasts, to be of goodly countenance, and women seemed most fair. Gems uncounted were there in that carcanet of gold, yet only as a setting that did prepare for its great central glory, and led the eye thereto, for amidmost hung like a little lamp of limpid fire the Silmaril of Fëanor, jewel of the Gods. Yet alas, even had that gold of the Rodothlim held no evil spell still had that carcanet been a thing of little luck, for the Dwarves were full of bitterness, and all its links were twined with baleful thoughts. Now however did they bear it before the king in its new-gleaming splendour; and then was the joy of Tinwelint king of the woodland Elves come to its crowning, and he cast the Nauglafring about his throat, and straightway the curse of Mîm fell upon him. Then said Ufedhin: "Now, O Lord, that thou art pleased beyond thy hope, perchance thou wilt grant the craftsmen thy kingly reward, and suffer them to depart also in joy to their own lands."

But Tinwelint, bewildered by the golden spell and the curse of Mîm, liked not the memory of his tryst; yet dissembling he bid the craftsmen come before him, and he praised their handiwork with royal words. At length said he: "'Twas said to me by one Ufedhin that at the end such reward as ye wished ye would name before me, yet would it be small enough, seeing that the labour was of love and of Ufedhin's desire that the golden hoard be not cast away and lost. What then do ye wish that I may grant?"

Then said Ufedhin scornfully: "For myself, nothing, O Lord; indeed the guestkindliness of thy halls for seven moons and three is more than I desire." But the Dwarves said: "This do we ask. For our labours during seven moons each seven jewels of Valinor, and seven robes of magic that only Gwendelin[10] can weave, and each a sack of gold; but for our great labour during three moons in thy halls unwilling, we ask each three sacks of silver, and each a cup of gold wherein to pledge thy health, O King, and each a fair maiden of the woodland Elves to fare away with us to our homes."

Then was King Tinwelint wroth indeed, for what the Dwarves had asked was of itself a goodly treasury, seeing that their company was very great; and he had no mind thus to devour the dragon's hoard, but never could he deliver maidens of the Elves unto illshapen Dwarves without undying shame.

Now that demand they had made only by the design of Ufedhin, yet seeing the anger of the king's face they said: "Nay, but this is not all, for in payment of Ufedhin's captivity for seven moons seven stout Elves must come with us and abide seven times seven years among us as bondsmen and menials in our labour."

Thereat arose Tinwelint from his seat, and calling summoned his weaponed thanes and warriors, that these surrounded the Nauglath and those Gnomes. Then said he: "For your insolence each three stripes with stinging withes shall ye receive, and Ufedhin seven, and afterwards will we speak of recompense."

When this was done, and a flame of bitter vengeance lit in those deep hearts, he said: "Lo, for your labour of seven months six pieces of gold and one of silver each shall have, and for your labours in my halls each three pieces of gold and some small gem that I can spare. For your journey hither a great feast shall ye eat and depart with good store against your return, and ere ye go ye shall drink to Tinwelint in elfin wine; yet, mark ye, for the sustenance of Ufedhin seven idle months about my halls shall ye each pay a piece of gold, and of silver two, for he has not aught himself and shall not receive since he desires it not, yet methinks he is at the bottom of your arrogance."

Then were the Dwarves paid their reward like common smiths of bronze and iron, and constrained to yield once more therefrom payment for Ufedhin – "else," said the king, "never shall ye get him hence." Then sat they to a great feast and dissembled their mood; yet at the end the time of their going came, and they drank to Tinwelint in elfin wine, but they cursed him in their beards, and Ufedhin swallowed not and spat the wine from his mouth upon the threshold.

Now tells the tale that the Nauglath fared home again, and if their greed had been kindled when first the gold was brought to Nogrod now was it a fierce flame of desire, and moreover they burnt under the insults of the king. Indeed all that folk love gold and silver more dearly than aught else on Earth, while that treasury was haunted by a spell and by no means were they armed against it. Now one there had been, Fangluin* the aged, who had counselled them from the first never to return the king's loan, for

* In the margin of the manuscript is written: *Fangluin: Bluebeard.*

said he: "Ufedhin we may later seek by guile to release, if it seem good," but at that time this seemed not policy to Naugladur their lord, who desired not warfare with the Elves.Yet now did Fangluin jeer at them mightily on their return, saying they had flung away their labour for a botcher's wage and a draught of wine and gotten dishonour thereto, and he played upon their lust, and Ufedhin joined his bitter words thereto. Therefore did Naugladur hold a secret council of the Dwarves of Nogrod, and sought how he might both be avenged upon Tinwelint, and sate his greed.[11]

Yet after long pondering he saw not how he might achieve his purpose save by force, and there was little hope therein, both by reason of the great strength of numbers of the Elves of Artanor in those days, and of the woven magic of Gwenniel that guarded all those regions, so that men of hostile heart were lost and came not to those woods; nor indeed could any such come thither unaided by treachery from within.

Now even as those aged ones sat in their dark halls and gnawed their beards, behold a sound of horns, and messengers were come from Bodruith of the Indrafangs, a kindred of the Dwarves that dwelt in other realms. Now these brought tidings of the death of Mîm the fatherless at the hand of Úrin and the rape of Glorund's gold, which tale had but new come to Bodruith's ears. Now hitherto the Dwarves knew not the full tale concerning that hoard, nor more than Ufedhin might tell hearing the speech in Tinwelint's halls, and Úrin had not spoken the full count thereof ere he departed. Hearing therefore these tidings new wrath was added to their lust and a clamour arose among them, and Naugladur vowed to rest not ere Mîm was thrice avenged — "and more," said he, "meseems the gold belongs of right to the people of the Dwarves."

This then was the design; and by his deeds have the Dwarves been severed in feud for ever since those days with the Elves, and drawn more nigh in friendship to the kin of Melko. Secretly he let send to the Indrafangs that they prepare their host against a day that he would name, whenso the time should be ripe; and a hidden forging of bitter steel then was in Belegost the dwelling of the Indrafangs. Moreover he gathered about him a great host of the Orcs, and wandering goblins, promising them a good wage, and the pleasure of their Master moreover, and a rich booty at the end; and all these he armed with his own weapons. Now came unto Naugladur an Elf, and he was one of Tinwelint's folk, and he offered to lead that host through the magics of Gwendelin, for he was bitten by the gold-lust of Glorund's hoard, and so did the curse of Mîm come upon Tinwelint and treachery first arose among the Elves of Artanor. Then did Naugladur [?smile] bitterly, for he knew that the time was ripe and Tinwelint delivered to him. Now each year about the time of the great wolf-hunt of Beren Tinwelint was wont to keep the memory of that day by a hunt in the woods, and it was a very mighty chase and thronged with very many folk, and nights of merriment and feasting were there in the forest. Now Naugladur learnt of that Elf Narthseg, whose name is bitter to the Eldar yet, that the king would fare a-hunting at the next high moon but one, and straight-way he sent the trysted sign, a bloodstained knife, to Bodruith at Belegost. Now all that host assembled on the confines of the woods, and no word came yet unto the king.

Now tells the tale that one came unto Tinwelint, and Tinwelint knew him not for the wild growth of his hair – and lo! it was Mablung, and he said: "Lo, even in the depths of the forest have we heard that this year you will celebrate the death of Karkaras with a high-tide greater than even before, O King – and behold I have returned to bear you company." And the king was full of mirth and fain to greet Mablung the brave; and at the words of Mablung that Huan captain of Dogs was come also into Artanor was he glad indeed.

Behold now Tinwelint the king rode forth a-hunting, and more glorious was his array than ever aforetime, and the helm of gold was above his flowing locks, and with gold were the trappings of his steed adorned; and the sunlight amid the trees fell upon his face, and it seemed to those that beheld it like to the glorious face of the sun at morning; for about his throat was clasped the Nauglafring, the Necklace of the Dwarves. Beside him rode Mablung the Heavyhand in the place of honour by reason of his deeds at that great hunt aforetime – but Huan of the Dogs was ahead of the hunters, and men thought that great dog bore him strangely, but mayhap there was something in the wind that day he liked not.

Now is the king far in the woods with all his company, and the horns grow faint in the deep forest, but Gwendelin sits in her bower and foreboding is in her heart and eyes. Then said an Elfmaid, Nielthi: "Wherefore, O Lady, art thou sorrowful at the hightide of the king?" And Gwendelin said: "Evil seeks our land, and my heart misgives me that my days in Artanor are speeding to their end, yet if I should lose Tinwelint then would I wish never to have wandered forth from Valinor." But Nielthi said: "Nay, O Lady Gwendelin, hast thou not woven great magic all about us, so that we fear not?" But the queen made answer: "Yet meseems there is a rat that gnaws the threads and all the web has come unwoven." Even at that word there was a cry about the doors, and suddenly it grew to a fierce noise . . . by the clash of steel. Then went Gwendelin unafraid forth from her bower, and behold, a sudden multitude of Orcs and Indrafangs held the bridge, and there was war within the cavernous gates; but that place ran with blood, and a great heap of slain lay there, for the onset had been secret and all unknown.

Then did Gwendelin know well that her foreboding was true, and that treachery had found her realm at last, yet did she hearten those few guards that remained to her and had fared not to the hunt, and valiantly they warded the palace of the king until the tide of numbers bore them back [and] fire and blood found all the halls and deep ways of that great fortress of the Elves.

Then did those Orcs and Dwarves ransack all the chambers seeking for treasure, and lo! one came and sate him in the high seat of the king laughing loud, and Gwendelin saw that it was Ufedhin, and mocking he bid her be seated in her ancient seat beside the king's. Then Gwendelin gazed upon him so that his glance fell, and she said: "Wherefore, O renegade, dost thou defile my lord's seat? Little had I thought to see any of the Elves sit there, a robber, stained with murder, a league-fellow of the truceless enemies of his kin. Or thinkest thou it is a glorious deed to assail an ill-armed house what time its lord is far away?" But Ufedhin said nought, shunning the bright eyes of Gwendelin, wherefore said she anew: "Get thee now gone with thy foul Orcs, lest Tinwelint coming repay thee bitterly."

Then at last did Ufedhin answer, and he laughed, but ill at ease, and he looked not at the queen, but he said listening to a sound without: "Nay, but already is he come." And behold, Naugladur entered now and a host of the Dwarves were about him, but he bore the head of Tinwelint crowned and helmed in gold; but the necklace of all wonder was clasped about the throat of Naugladur. Then did Gwendelin see in her heart all that had befallen, and how the curse of the gold had fallen on the realm of Artanor, and never has she danced or sung since that dark hour; but Naugladur bid gather all things of gold or silver or of precious stones and bear them to Nogrod – "and whatso remains of goods or folk may the

Orcs keep, or slay, as they desire. Yet the Lady Gwendelin Queen of Artanor shall fare with me."

Then said Gwendelin: "Thief and murderer, child of Melko, yet art thou a fool, for thou canst not see what hangs over thine own head." By reason of the anguish of her heart was her sight grown very clear, and she read by her fay-wisdon the curse of Mîm and much of what would yet betide.

Then did Naugladur in his triumph laugh till his beard shook, and bid seize her: but none might do so, for as they came towards her they groped as if in sudden dark, or stumbled and fell tripping each the other, and Gwendelin went forth from the places of her abode, and her bitter weeping filled the forest. Now did a great darkness fall upon her mind and her counsel and lore forsook her, that she wandered she knew not whither for a great while; and this was by reason of her love for Tinwelint the king, for whom she had chosen never to fare back to Valinor and the beauty of the Gods, dwelling always in the wild forests of the North; and now did there seem to her neither beauty nor joy be it in Valinor or in the Lands Without. Many of the scattered Elves in her wayward journeyings she met, and they took pity on her, but she heeded them not. Tales had they told her, but she hearkened not over much since Tinwelint was dead; nonetheless must ye know how even in the hour that Ufedhin's host brake the palace and despoiled it, and other companies as great and as terrible of the Orcs and Indrafangs fell with death and fire upon all the realm of Tinwelint, behold the brave hunt of the king were resting amid mirth and laughter, but Huan stalked apart. Then suddenly were the woods filled with noise and Huan bayed aloud; but the king and his company were all encircled with armed foes. Long they fought bitterly there among the trees, and the Nauglath – for such were their foes – had great scathe of them or ever they were slain. Yet in the end were they all fordone, and Mablung and the king fell side by side – but Naugladur it was who swept off the head of Tinwelint after he was dead, for living he dared not so near to his bright sword or the axe of Mablung.[12]

Now doth the tale know no more to tell of Huan, save that even while the swords still sang that great dog was speeding through the land, and his way led him as the [?wind] to the land of i·Guilwarthon, the living-dead, where reigned Beren and Tinúviel the daughter of Tinwelint. Not in any settled abode did those twain dwell, nor had their realm boundaries well-marked – and indeed no other messenger save Huan alone to whom all ways were known had ever found Beren and obtained his aid so soon.[13] Indeed the tale tells that even as that host of the Orcs were burning all the land of Tinwelint and the Nauglath and the Indrafangin were wending homeward burdened utterly with spoils of gold and precious things, came Huan to Beren's lodge, and it was dusk. Lo, Beren sat upon a tree root and Tinúviel danced on a green sward in the gloaming as he gazed upon her, when suddenly stood Huan before them, and Beren gave a cry of joy and wonder, for it was long since he and Huan had hunted together. But Tinúviel looking upon Huan saw that he bled, and there was a tale to read in his great eyes. And she said suddenly: "What evil then has fallen upon Artanor?" and Huan said: "Fire and death and the terror of Orcs; but Tinwelint is slain."

Then did both Beren and Tinúviel weep bitter tears; nor did the full tale of Huan dry their eyes. When then it was told to the end leapt Beren to his feet in white wrath, and seizing a horn that hung at his belt he blew a clear blast thereon that rang round all the neighbouring hills, and an elfin folk all clad in green and brown sprang as it were by magic towards him from every glade and coppice, stream and fell.

Now not even Beren knew the tale of those myriad folk that followed his horn in the woods of Hisilómë, and or ever the moon was high above the hills the host assembled in the glade of his abiding was very great, yet were they lightly armed and the most bore only knives and bows. "Yet," said Beren, "speed is that which now we need the most"; and certain Elves at his bidding fared like deer before him, seeking news of the march of the Dwarves and Indrafangs, but at dawn he followed at the head of the green Elves, and Tinúviel abode in the glade and wept unto herself for the death of Tinwelint, and Gwendelin also she mourned as dead.

Now is to tell that the laden host of the Dwarves fared from the place of their ransacking, and Naugladur was at their head, and beside him Ufedhin and Bodruith; and ever as he rode Ufedhin sought to put the dread eyes of Gwendelin from his mind and could not, and all happiness was fled from his heart that shrivelled under the memory of that glance; nor was this the only disquiet that tortured him, for if ever he raised his eyes lo! they lighted on the Necklace of the Dwarves shining about the aged neck of Naugladur, and then all other thoughts save bottomless desire of its beauty were banished.

Thus did those three fare and with them all their host, but so great became the torment of Ufedhin's mind that in the end he might not endure it more, but at night when a halt was called he crept stealthily to the place where Naugladur slept, and coming upon that aged one wrapt in slumbers would slay that Dwarf and lay hands upon the wondrous Nauglafring. Now even as he sought to do so, behold one seized his throat suddenly from behind, and it was Bodruith, who filled with the same lust sought also to make that lovely thing his own; but coming upon Ufedhin would slay him by reason of his kinship to Naugladur. Then did Ufedhin stab suddenly backward at hazard in the dark with a keen knife long and slender that he had with him for the bane of Naugladur, and that knife pierced the vitals of Bodruith Lord of Belegost so that he fell dying upon Naugladur, and the throat of Naugladur and the magic carcanet were drenched anew with blood.

Thereat did Naugladur awake with a great cry, but Ufedhin fled gasping from that place, for the long fingers of the Indrafang had well-nigh choked him. Now when some bore torches swiftly to that place Naugladur thought that Bodruith alone had sought to rob him of the jewel, and marvelled how he had thus been timely slain, and he proclaimed a rich reward to the slayer of Bodruith if that man would come forward telling all that he had seen. Thus was it that none perceived the flight of Ufedhin for a while, and wrath awoke between the Dwarves of Nogrod and the Indrafangs, and many were slain ere the Indrafangs being in less number were scattered and got them as best they might to Belegost, bearing scant treasury with them. Of this came the agelong feud between those kindreds of the Dwarves that has spread to many lands and caused many a tale, whereof the Elves know little tidings and Men have seldom heard. Yet may it be seen how the curse of Mîm came early home to rest among his own kin, and would indeed it had gone no further and had visited the Eldar never more.

Lo, when the flight of Ufedhin came also to light then was Naugladur in wrath, and he let kill all the Gnomes that remained in the host. Then said he: "Now are we rid of Indrafangs and Gnomes and all traitors, and nought more do I fear at all."

But Ufedhin ranged the wild lands in great fear and anguish, for him seemed that he had become a traitor to his kin, blood-guilty to the Elves, and haunted with the [?burning] eyes of Gwendelin the queen, for nought but exile and misery, and no smallest part nor share had he in the gold of Glorund, for all his heart was afire with lust; yet few have pitied him.

Now tells the tale that he fell in with the rangers of Beren's folk, and these gaining from him sure knowledge of all the host and

array of Naugladur and the ways he purposed to follow, they sped
back like wind among the trees unto their lord; but Ufedhin
revealed not to them who he was, feigning to be an Elf of Artanor
escaped from bondage in their host. Now therefore they entreated
him well, and he was sent back to Beren that their captain might
. . . . . . . . . . . his words, and albeit Beren marvelled at his
[?cowardly] . . . . . .[14] and downward glance it seemed to him that
he brought safe word, and he set a trap for Naugladur.

No longer did he march hotly on the trail of the Dwarves, but
knowing that they would essay the passage of the river Aros at a
certain time he turned aside, faring swiftly with his light-footed
Elves by straighter paths that he might reach Sarnathrod the
Stony Ford before them. Now the Aros is a fierce stream – and is it
not that very water that more near its spring runs swiftly past the
aged doors of the Rodothlim's caves and the dark lairs of Glorund[15]
– and in those lower regions by no means can be crossed by a great
host of laden men save at this ford, nor is it overeasy here. Never
would Naugladur have taken that way had he knowledge of Beren
– yet blinded by the spell and the dazzling gold he feared nought
either within or without his host, and he was in haste to reach
Nogrod and its dark caverns, for the Dwarves list not long to abide
in the bright light of day.

Now came all that host to the banks of Aros, and their array was
thus: first a number of unladen Dwarves most fully armed, and
amidmost the great company of those that bore the treasury of
Glorund, and many a fair thing beside that they had haled from
Tinwelint's halls; and behind these was Naugladur, and he bestrode
Tinwelint's horse, and a strange figure did he seem, for the legs of
the Dwarves are short and crooked, but two Dwarves led that
horse for it went not willingly and it was laden with spoil. But
behind these came again a mass of armed men but little laden; and
in this array they sought to cross Sarnathrod on their day of doom.

Morn was it when they reached the hither bank and high noon
saw them yet passing in long-strung lines and wading slowly the
shallow places of the swift-running stream. Here doth it widen out
and fare down narrow channels filled with boulders atween long
spits of shingle and stones less great. Now did Naugladur slip
from his burdened horse and prepare to get him over, for the
armed host of the vanguard had climbed already the further bank,
and it was great and sheer and thick with trees, and the bearers of
the gold were some already stepped thereon and some amidmost
of the stream, but the armed men of the rear were resting awhile.

Suddenly is all that place filled with the sound of elfin horns, and one . . . . .[16] with a clearer blast above the rest, and it is the horn of Beren, the huntsman of the woods. Then is the air thick with the slender arrows of the Eldar that err not neither doth the wind bear them aside, and lo, from every tree and boulder do the brown Elves and the green spring suddenly and loose unceasingly from full quivers. Then was there a panic and a noise in the host of Naugladur, and those that waded in the ford cast their golden burdens in the waters and sought affrighted to either bank, but many were stricken with those pitiless darts and fell with their gold into the currents of the Aros, staining its clear waters with their dark blood.

Now were the warriors on the far bank [?wrapped] in battle and rallying sought to come at their foes, but these fled nimbly before them, while [?others] poured still the hail of arrows upon them, and thus got the Eldar few hurts and the Dwarf-folk fell dead unceasingly. Now was that great fight of the Stony Ford . . . . . . nigh to Naugladur, for even though Naugladur and his captains led their bands stoutly never might they grip their foe, and death fell like rain upon their ranks until the most part broke and fled, and a noise of clear laughter echoed from the Elves thereat, and they forebore to shoot more, for the illshapen figures of the Dwarves as they fled, their white beards torn by the wind, filled them [with] mirth. But now stood Naugladur and few were about him, and he remembered the words of Gwendelin, for behold, Beren came towards him and he cast aside his bow, and drew a bright sword; and Beren was of great stature among the Eldar, albeit not of the girth and breadth of Naugladur of the Dwarves.

Then said Beren: "Ward thy life an thou canst, O crook-legged murderer, else will I take it," and Naugladur bid him even the Nauglafring, the necklace of wonder, that he be suffered to go unharmed; but Beren said: "Nay, that may I still take when thou art slain," and thereat he made alone upon Naugladur and his companions, and having slain the foremost of these the others fled away amid elfin laughter, and so Beren came upon Naugladur, slayer of Tinwelint. Then did that aged one defend himself doughtily, and 'twas a bitter fight, and many of the Elves that watched for love and fear of their captain fingered their bow-strings, but Beren called even as he fought that all should stay their hands.

Now little doth the tale tell of wounds and blows of that affray, save that Beren got many hurts therein, and many of his shrewdest blows did little harm to Naugladur by reason of the [?skill] and magic of his dwarfen mail; and it is said that three hours they fought and Beren's arms grew weary, but not those of Naugladur accustomed to wield his mighty hammer at the forge, and it is more than like that otherwise would the issue have been but for the curse of Mîm; for marking how Beren grew faint Naugladur pressed him ever more nearly, and the arrogance that was of that grievous spell came into his heart, and he thought: "I will slay this Elf, and his folk will flee in fear before me," and grasping his sword he dealt a mighty blow and cried: "Take here thy bane, O stripling of the woods," and in that moment his foot found a jagged stone and he stumbled forward, but Beren slipped aside from that blow and catching at his beard his hand found the carcanet of gold, and therewith he swung Naugladur suddenly off his feet upon his face: and Naugladur's sword was shaken from his grasp, but Beren seized it and slew him therewith, for he said: "I will not sully my bright blade with thy dark blood, since there is no need." But the body of Naugladur was cast into the Aros.

Then did he unloose the necklace, and he gazed in wonder at it – and beheld the Silmaril, even the jewel he won from Angband and gained undying glory by his deed; and he said: "Never have mine eyes beheld thee O Lamp of Faëry burn one half so fair as now thou dost, set in gold and gems and the magic of the Dwarves"; and that necklace he caused to be washed of its stains, and he cast it not away, knowing nought of its power, but bore it with him back into the woods of Hithlum.

But the waters of Aros flowed on for ever above the drowned hoard of Glorund, and so do still, for in after days Dwarves came from Nogrod and sought for it, and for the body of Naugladur; but a flood arose from the mountains and therein the seekers perished; and so great now is the gloom and dread of that Stony Ford that none seek the treasure that it guards nor dare ever to cross the magic stream at that enchanted place.

But in the vales of Hithlum was there gladness at the home-coming of the Elves, and great was the joy of Tinúviel to see her lord once more returning amidst his companies, but little did it ease her grief for the death of Tinwelint that Naugladur was slain and many Dwarves beside. Then did Beren seek to comfort her, and taking her in his arms he set the glorious Nauglafring about her neck, and all were blinded by the greatness of her beauty; and Beren said: "Behold the Lamp of Fëanor that thou

and I did win from Hell," and Tinúviel smiled, remembering the
first days of their love and those days of travail in the wild.

Now is it to be said that Beren sent for Ufedhin and well
rewarded him for his words of true guidance whereof the Dwarves
had been overcome, and he bid him dwell in . . . . among his folk,
and Ufedhin was little loth; yet on a time, no great space thereafter, did that thing betide which he least desired. For came there
a sound of very sorrowful singing in the woods, and behold, it was
Gwendelin wandering distraught, and her feet bore her to the
midmost of a glade where sat Beren and Tinúviel; and at that hour
it was new morning, but at the sound all nigh ceased their speaking
and were very still. Then did Beren gaze in awe upon Gwendelin,
but Tinúviel cried suddenly in sorrow mixed with joy: "O mother
Gwendelin, whither do thy feet bear thee, for methought thee
dead"; but the greeting of those twain upon the greensward was
very sweet. And Ufedhin fled from among the Elves, for he could
not endure to look upon the eyes of Gwendelin, and madness took
him, and none may say what was his unhappy weird thereafter;
and little but a tortured heart got he from the Gold of Glorund.

Now hearing the cries of Ufedhin Gwendelin looked in wonder
after him, and stayed her tender words; and memory came back
into her eyes so that she cried as in amaze beholding the Necklace
of the Dwarves that hung about the white throat of Tinúviel.
Then wrathfully she asked of Beren what it might portend, and
wherefore he suffered the accursed thing to touch Tinúviel; and
told Beren[17] all that tale such as Huan had told him, in deed or
guess, and of the pursuit and fighting at the ford he told also,
saying at the end: "Nor indeed do I see who, now that Lord
Tinwelint is fared to Valinor, should so fittingly wear that jewel of
the Gods as Tinúviel." But Gwendelin told of the dragon's ban
upon the gold and the [?staining] of blood in the king's halls, "and
yet another and more potent curse, whose arising I know not, is
woven therewith," said she, "nor methinks was the labour of the
Dwarves free from spells of the most enduring malice." But Beren
laughed, saying that the glory of the Silmaril and its holiness
might overcome all such evils, even as it burnt the [?foul] flesh of
Karkaras. "Nor," said he, "have I seen ever my Tinúviel so fair as
now she is, clasped in the loveliness of this thing of gold"; but
Gwendelin said: "Yet the Silmaril abode in the Crown of Melko,
and that is the work of baleful smiths indeed."

Then said Tinúviel that she desired not things of worth
or precious stones but the elfin gladness of the forest, and to

pleasure Gwendelin she cast it from her neck; but Beren was little pleased and he would not suffer it to be flung away, but warded it in his . . . . . . . .[18]

Thereafter did Gwendelin abide a while in the woods among them and was healed; and in the end she fared wistfully back to the land of Lórien and came never again into the tales of the dwellers of Earth; but upon Beren and Tinúviel fell swiftly that doom of mortality that Mandos had spoken when he sped them from his halls – and in this perhaps did the curse of Mîm have [?potency] in that it came more soon upon them; nor this time did those twain fare the road together, but when yet was the child of those twain, Dior[19] the Fair, a little one, did Tinúviel slowly fade, even as the Elves of later days have done throughout the world, and she vanished in the woods, and none have seen her dancing ever there again. But Beren searched all the lands of Hithlum and of Artanor ranging after her; and never has any of the Elves had more loneliness than his, or ever he too faded from life, and Dior his son was left ruler of the brown Elves and the green, and Lord of the Nauglafring.

Mayhap what all Elves say is true, that those twain hunt now in the forest of Oromë in Valinor, and Tinúviel dances on the green swards of Nessa and of Vána daughters of the Gods for ever more; yet great was the grief of the Elves when the Guilwarthon went from among them, and being leaderless and lessened of magic their numbers minished; and many fared away to Gondolin, the rumour of whose growing power and glory ran in secret whispers among all the Elves.

Still did Dior when come to manhood rule a numerous folk, and he loved the woods even as Beren had done; and songs name him mostly Ausir the Wealthy for his possession of that wondrous gem set in the Necklace of the Dwarves. Now the tales of Beren and Tinúviel grew dim in his heart, and he took to wearing it about his neck and to love its loveliness most dearly; and the fame of that jewel spread like fire through all the regions of the North, and the Elves said one to another: "A Silmaril of Fëanor burns in the woods of Hisilómë."

Now fare the long days of Elfinesse unto that time when Tuor dwelt in Gondolin; and children then had Dior the Elf,[20] Auredhir and Elwing, and Auredhir was most like to his forefather Beren, and all loved him, yet none so dearly as did Dior; but Elwing the fairy have all poesies named as beautiful as Tinúviel if that indeed may be, yet hard is it to say seeing the great loveliness of the elfin folk of yore. Now those were days of happiness in the vales of Hithlum, for there was peace with Melko and the Dwarves who had but one thought as they plotted against Gondolin, and Angband was full of labour; yet is it to tell that bitterness entered into the hearts of the seven sons of Fëanor, remembering their oath. Now Maidros, whom Melko maimed, was their leader; and he called to his brethren Maglor and Dinithel, and to Damrod, and to Celegorm, to Cranthor and to Curufin the Crafty, and he said to them how it was now known to him that a Silmaril of those their father Fëanor had made was now the pride and glory of Dior of the southern vales, "and Elwing his daughter bears it whitherso she goes – but do you not forget," said he, "that we swore to have no peace with Melko nor any of his folk, nor with any other of Earth-dwellers that held the Silmarils of Fëanor from us. For what," said Maidros, "do we suffer exile and wandering and rule over a scant and forgotten folk, if others gather to their hoard the heirlooms that are ours?"

Thus was it that they sent Curufin the Crafty to Dior, and told him of their oath, and bid him give that fair jewel back unto those whose right it was; but Dior gazing on the loveliness of Elwing would not do so, and he said that he could not endure that the Nauglafring, fairest of earthly craft, be so despoiled. "Then," said Curufin, "must the Nauglafring unbroken be given to the sons of Fëanor," and Dior waxed wroth, bidding him be gone, nor dare to claim what his sire Beren the Onehanded won with his hand from the [?jaws] of Melko – "other twain are there in the selfsame place," said he, "an your hearts be bold enow."

Then went Curufin unto his brethren, and because of their unbreakable oath and of their [?thirst] for that Silmaril (nor indeed was the spell of Mîm and of the dragon wanting) they planned war upon Dior – and the Eldar cry shame upon them for that deed, the first premeditated war of elfin folk upon elfin folk, whose name otherwise were glorious among the Eldalië for their sufferings. Little good came thereby to them; for they fell unawares upon Dior, and Dior and Auredhir were slain, yet behold, Evranin the nurse of Elwing, and Gereth a Gnome, took her unwilling in a flight swift and sudden from those lands, and they bore with them the Nauglafring, so that the sons of Fëanor saw it not; but a host of Dior's folk, coming with all speed yet late unto the fray, fell suddenly on their rear, and there was a great battle, and Maglor was slain with swords, and Mai . . . .[21] died of wounds in the wild, and Celegorm was pierced with a hundred

arrows, and Cranthor beside him. Yet in the end were the sons of
Fëanor masters of the field of slain, and the brown Elves and the
green were scattered over all the lands unhappy, for they would
not hearken to Maidros the maimed, nor to Curufin and Damrod
who had slain their lord; and it is said that even on the day of
that battle of the Elves Melko sought against Gondolin, and the
fortunes of the Elves came to their uttermost waning.

Now was naught left of the seed of Beren Ermabwed son of
Egnor save Elwing the Lovely, and she wandered in the woods,
and of the brown Elves and the green a few gathered to her, and
they departed for ever from the glades of Hithlum and got them to
the south towards Sirion's deep waters, and the pleasant lands.

And thus did all the fates of the fairies weave then to one strand,
and that strand is the great tale of Eärendel; and to that tale's true
beginning are we now come.'

Then said Ailios: 'And methinks that is tale enow for this time
of telling.'

## NOTES

1   This sentence is a rewriting of the text, which had originally:

> "Nay then, know ye not that this gold belongs to the kindred of
> the Elves, who won it from the earth long time ago, and no one
> among Men has claim . . ."

The remainder of this scene, ending with the slaughter of Úrin's
band, was rewritten at many points, with the same object as in the
passage just cited – to convert Úrin's band from Men to Elves, as
was done also at the end of Eltas' tale (see p. 118 note 33). Thus
original 'Elves' was changed to 'Elves of the wood, woodland Elves',
and original 'Men' to 'folk, outlaws'; and see notes 2, 3, 5.

2   The original sentence here was:

> Doughty were those Men and great wielders of sword and axe,
> and still in those unfaded days might mortal weapons wound the
> bodies of the elfin-folk.

See note 1.

3   The original sentence here was: 'and those Men being wildered with
magics'. See note 1.

4   This sentence, from 'and yet another sorrow . . .', was added to the
text later.

5   'those': the text has 'the Men', obviously left unchanged through
oversight. See note 1.

6 'in the earth' is an emendation of the original reading 'on the earth'.

7 'damasked in strange wise', i.e. 'damascened', ornamentally inlaid with designs in gold and silver. The word 'damascened' is used of the sword of Tinwelint made by the Dwarves, on which were seen images of the wolf-hunt (p. 227), and of Glorfindel's arms (p. 173).

8 The text has 'Eltas', but with 'Ailios' written above in pencil. Since Ailios appears as the teller at the beginning of the tale, and not as the result of emendation, 'Eltas' here was probably no more than a slip.

9 'save only' is a later emendation of the original 'not even'. See p. 256.

10 It is odd that *Gwendelin* appears here, not *Gwenniel* as hitherto in this tale. Since the first part of the tale is in ink over an erased pencil text, the obvious explanation is that the erased text had *Gwendelin* and that my father changed this to *Gwenniel* as he went along, overlooking it in this one instance. But the matter is probably more complex – one of those small puzzles with which the texts of the *Lost Tales* abound – for after the manuscript in ink ceases the form *Gwenniel* occurs, though once only, and *Gwendelin* is then used for all the rest of the tale. See *Changes made to Names*, p. 244.

11 Here the manuscript in ink ends; see p. 221.

12 Against this sentence my father wrote a direction that the story was to be that the Nauglafring caught in the bushes and held the king.

13 A rejected passage in the manuscript here gives an earlier version of the events, according to which it was Gwendelin, not Huan, who brought the news to Beren:

> . . . and her bitter weeping filled the forest. Now there did Gwendeling [*sic*] gather to her many of the scattered woodland Elves and of them did she hear how matters had fared even as she had guessed: how the hunting party had been surrounded and o'erwhelmed by the Nauglath while the Indrafangs and Orcs fell suddenly with death and fire upon all the realm of Tinwelint, and not the least host was that of Ufedhin that slew the guardians of the bridge; and it was said that Naugladur had slain Tinwelint when he was borne down by numbers, and folk thought Narthseg a wild Elf had led the foemen hither, and he had been slain in the fighting.
>
> Then seeing no hope Gwendelin and her companions fared with the utmost speed out of that land of sorrow, even to the kingdom of i·Guilwarthon in Hisilómë, where reigned Beren and Tinúviel her daughter. Now Beren and Tinúviel lived not in any settled abode, nor had their realm boundaries well-marked, and no other messenger save Gwendelin daughter of the Vali had of a surety found those twain the living-dead so soon.

It is clear from the manuscript that the return of Mablung and Huan to Artanor and their presence at the hunt (referred to in general terms at the end of the *Tale of Tinúviel*, p. 41) was added to the tale, and with this new element went the change in Gwendelin's movements immediately after the disaster. But though the textual history is here extremely hard to interpet, what with erasures and additions on loose pages, I think it is almost certain that this reshaping was done while the original composition of the tale was still in progress.

14    The first of these lacunae that I have left in the text contains two words, the first possibly 'believe' and the second probably 'best'. In the second lacuna the word might conceivably be 'pallor'.

15    This sentence, from 'and is it not that very water . . .', is struck through and bracketed, and in the margin my father scribbled: 'No [?that] is Narog.'

16    The illegible word might be 'brays': the word 'clearer' is an emendation from 'hoarser'.

17    'and told Beren': i.e., 'and Beren told'. The text as first written had 'Then told Beren . . .'

18    The illegible word might just possibly be 'treasury', but I do not think that it is.

19    *Dior* replaced the name *Ausir*, which however occurs below as another name for Dior.

20    'Dior the Elf' is an emendation from 'Dior then an aged Elf'.

21    The latter part of this name is quite unclear: it might be read as *Maithog*, or as *Mailweg*. See *Changes made to Names* under *Dinithel*.

Changes made to names in
*The Tale of the Nauglafring*

*Ilfiniol* (p. 221) here so written from the first: see p. 201.

*Gwenniel* is used throughout the revised section of the tale except at the last occurrence (p. 228), where the form is *Gwendelin*; in the pencilled part of the tale at the first occurrence of the queen's name it is again *Gwenniel* (p. 230), but thereafter always *Gwendelin* (see note 10).

The name of the queen in the *Lost Tales* is as variable as that of Littleheart. In *The Chaining of Melko* and *The Coming of the Elves* she is *Tindriel* > *Wendelin*. In the *Tale of Tinúviel* she is *Wendelin* > *Gwendeling* (see p. 50); in the type-script text of *Tinúviel Gwenethlin* > *Melian*; in the *Tale of Turambar Gwendeling* > *Gwedheling*; in the present tale *Gwendelin/Gwenniel* (the form *Gwendeling* occurs in the rejected passage given in note 13); and in the Gnomish dictionary *Gwendeling* > *Gwedhiling*.

*Belegost*    At the first occurrence (p. 230) the manuscript has *Ost Belegost*, with *Ost* circled as if for rejection, and *Belegost* is the reading subsequently.

(*i*·)*Guilwarthon* In the *Tale of Tinúviel*, p. 41, the form is
*i·Cuilwarthon*. At the occurrence on p. 240 the ending of the
name does not look like *-on*, but as I cannot say what it is I give
*Guilwarthon* in the text.
*Dinithel* could also be read as *Durithel* (p. 241). This name was written
in later in ink over an earlier name in pencil now scarcely legible,
though clearly the same as that beginning *Mai* . . . . which appears
for this son of Fëanor subsequently (see note 21).


Commentary on
*The Tale of the Nauglafring*

In this commentary I shall not compare in detail the *Tale of the
Nauglafring* with the story told in *The Silmarillion* (Chapter 22, *Of the
Ruin of Doriath*). The stories are profoundly different in essential
features – above all, in the reduction of the treasure brought by Húrin
from Nargothrond to a single object, the Necklace of the Dwarves, which
had long been in existence (though not, of course, containing the
Silmaril); while the whole history of the relation between Thingol and
the Dwarves is changed. My father never again wrote any part of this
story on a remotely comparable scale, and the formation of the published
text was here of the utmost difficulty; I hope later to give an account of it.

While it is often difficult to differentiate what my father omitted in his
more concise versions (in order to keep them concise) from what he
rejected, it seems clear that a large part of the elaborate narrative of the
*Tale of the Nauglafring* was early abandoned. In subsequent writing
the story of the fighting between Úrin's band and Tinwelint's Elves
disappeared, and there is no trace afterwards of Ufedhin or the other
Gnomes that lived among the Dwarves, of the story that the Dwarves
took half the unwrought gold ('the king's loan') away to Nogrod to
make precious objects from it, of the keeping of Ufedhin hostage, of
Tinwelint's refusal to let the Dwarves depart, of their outrageous
demands, of their scourging and their insulting payment.

We meet here again the strong emphasis on Tinwelint's love of treasure
and lack of it, in contrast to the later conception of his vast wealth (see my
remarks, pp. 128–9). The Silmaril is kept in a wooden casket (p. 225),
Tinwelint has no crown but a wreath of scarlet leaves (p. 227), and he
is far less richly clad and accoutred than 'the wayfarer in his halls'
(Ufedhin). This is very well in itself – the Woodland Elf corrupted by
the lure of golden splendour, but it need not be remarked again how
strangely at variance is this picture with that of Thingol Lord of
Beleriand, who had a vast treasury in his marvellous underground realm
of Menegroth, the Thousand Caves – itself largely contrived by the
Dwarves of Belegost in the distant past (*The Silmarillion* pp. 92–3), and
who most certainly did not need the aid of Dwarves at this time to make

him a crown and a fine sword, or vessels to adorn his banquets. Thingol in the later conception is proud, and stern; he is also wise, and powerful, and greatly increased in stature and in knowledge through his union with a Maia. Could such a king have sunk to the level of miserly swindling that is portrayed in the *Tale of the Nauglafring*?

Great stress is indeed placed on the enormous size of the hoard – 'such mighty heaps of gold have never since been gathered in one place', p. 223 – which is made so vast that it becomes hard to believe that a band of wandering outlaws could have brought it to the halls of the woodland Elves, even granting that 'some was lost upon the way' (p. 114). There is perhaps some difference here from the account of the Rodothlim and their works in the *Tale of Turambar* (p. 81), where there is certainly no suggestion that the Rodothlim possessed treasures coming out of Valinor – though this idea remained through all the vicissitudes of this part of the story: it is said of the Lord of Nargothrond in *The Silmarillion* (p. 114) that 'Finrod had brought more treasures out of Tirion than any other of the princes of the Noldor'.

More important, the elements of 'spell' and 'curse' are dominant in this tale, to such a degree that they might almost be said to be the chief actors in it. The curse of Mîm on the gold is felt at every turn of the narrative. Vengeance for him is one motive in Naugladur's decision to attack the Elves of Artanor (p. 230). His curse is fulfilled in the 'agelong feud' between the kindreds of the Dwarves (p. 235) – of which all trace was afterwards effaced, with the loss of the entire story of Ufedhin's intent to steal the Necklace from Naugladur sleeping, the killing of Bodruith Lord of Belegost, and the fighting between the two clans of Dwarves. Naugladur was 'blinded by the spell' in taking so imprudent a course out of Artanor (p. 236); and the curse of Mîm is made the 'cause' of his stumbling on a stone in his fight with Beren (p. 238). It is even, and most surprisingly, suggested as a reason for the short second lives of Beren and Tinúviel (p. 240); and finally 'the spell of Mîm' is an element in the attack on Dior by the Fëanorians (p. 241). An important element also in the tale is the baleful nature of the Nauglafring, for the Dwarves made it with bitterness; and into the complex of curses and spells is introduced also 'the dragon's ban upon the gold' (p. 239) or 'the spell of the dragon' (p. 241). It is not said in the *Tale of Turambar* that Glorund had cursed the gold or enspelled it; but Mîm said to Úrin (p. 114): 'Has not Glorund lain long years upon it, and the evil of the drakes of Melko is on it, and no good can it bring to Man or Elf.' Most notably, Gwendelin implies, against Beren's assertion that 'its holiness might overcome all such evils', that the Silmaril itself is unhallowed, since it 'abode in the Crown of Melko' (p. 239). In the later of the two 'schemes' for the *Lost Tales* (see I. 107 note 3) it is said that the Nauglafring 'brought sickness to Tinúviel'.*

* It is said in the Gnomish dictionary that the curse of Mîm was 'appeased' when the Nauglafring was lost in the sea; see the Appendix on Names, entry *Nauglafring*.

But however much the chief actors in this tale are 'enspelled' or blindly carrying forward the mysterious dictates of a curse, there is no question but that the Dwarves in the original conception were altogether more ignoble than they afterwards became, more prone to evil to gain their ends, and more exclusively impelled by greed; that Doriath should be laid waste by mercenary Orcs under Dwarvish paymasters (p. 230) was to become incredible and impossible later. It is even said that by the deeds of Naugladur 'have the Dwarves been severed in feud for ever since those days with the Elves, and drawn more nigh in friendship to the kin of Melko' (p. 230); and in the outlines for *Gilfanon's Tale* the Nauglath are an evil people, associates of goblins (I. 236–7). In a rejected outline for the *Tale of the Nauglafring* (p. 136) the Necklace was made 'by certain Úvanimor (Nautar or Nauglath)', Úvanimor being defined elsewhere as 'monsters, giants, and ogres'. With all this compare *The Lord of the Rings*, Appendix F (I): 'They [the Dwarves] are not evil by nature, and few ever served the Enemy of free will, whatever the tales of Men may have alleged.'

The account of the Dwarves in this tale is of exceptional interest in other respects. 'The beards of the Indrafangs' have been named in Tinúviel's 'lengthening spell' (pp. 19, 46); but this is the first description of the Dwarves in my father's writings – already with the spelling that he maintained against the unceasing opposition of proof-readers – and they are eminently recognisable in their dour and hidden natures, in their 'unloveliness' (*The Silmarillion* p. 113), and in their 'marvellous skill with metals' (*ibid.* p. 92). The strange statement that 'never comes a child among them' is perhaps to be related to 'the foolish opinion among Men' referred to in *The Lord of the Rings*, Appendix A (III), 'that there are no Dwarf-women, and that the Dwarves "grow out of stone".' In the same place it is said that 'it is because of the fewness of women among them that the kind of the Dwarves increases slowly'.

It is also said in the tale that it is thought by some that the Dwarves 'have not heard of Ilúvatar'; on knowledge of Ilúvatar among Men see p. 209.

According to the Gnomish dictionary *Indrafang* was 'a special name of the Longbeards or Dwarves', but in the tale it is made quite plain that the Longbeards were on the contrary the Dwarves of Belegost; the Dwarves of Nogrod were the Nauglath, with their king Naugladur. It must be admitted however that the use of the terms is sometimes confusing, or confused: thus the description of the Nauglath on pp. 223–4 seems to be a description of all Dwarves, and to include the Indrafangs, though this cannot have been intended. The reference to 'the march of the Dwarves and Indrafangs' (p. 234) must be taken as an ellipse, i.e. 'the Dwarves of Nogrod and the Indrafangs'. Naugladur of Nogrod and Bodruith of Belegost are said to have been akin (p. 235), though this perhaps only means that they were both Dwarves whereas Ufedhin was an Elf.

The Dwarf-city of Nogrod is said in the tale to lie 'a very long journey southward beyond the wide forest on the borders of those great heaths nigh Umboth-muilin the Pools of Twilight, on the marches of Tasarinan' (p. 225). This could be interpreted to mean that Nogrod was itself 'on the borders of those great heaths nigh Umboth-muilin'; but I think that this is out of the question. It would be a most improbable place for Dwarves, who 'dwell beneath the earth in caves and tunnelled towns, and aforetime Nogrod was the mightiest of these' (p. 224). Though mountains are not specifically mentioned here in connection with Dwarves, I think it extremely likely that my father at this time conceived their cities to be in the mountains, as they were afterwards. Further, there seems nothing to contradict the view that the configuration of the lands in the *Lost Tales* was essentially similar to that of the earliest and later 'Silmarillion' maps; and on them, 'a very long journey southward' is totally inappropriate to. that between the Thousand Caves and the Pools of Twilight.

The meaning must therefore be, simply, 'a very long journey southward beyond the wide forest', and what follows places the wide forest, not Nogrod; the forest being, in fact, the Forest of Artanor.

The Pools of Twilight are described in *The Fall of Gondolin*, but the Elvish name does not there appear (see pp. 195–6, 217).

Whether Belegost was near to or far from Nogrod is not made plain; it is said in this passage that the gold should be borne away 'to Nogrod and the dwellings of the Dwarves', but later (p. 230) the Indrafangs are 'a kindred of the Dwarves that dwelt in other realms'.

In his association with the Dwarves Ufedhin is reminiscent of Eöl, Maeglin's father, of whom it is said in *The Silmarillion* (p. 133) that 'for the Dwarves he had more liking than any other of the Elvenfolk of old'; cf. *ibid.* p. 92: 'Few of the Eldar went ever to Nogrod or Belegost, save Eöl of Nan Elmoth and Maeglin his son.' In the early forms of the story of Eöl and Isfin (referred to in *The Fall of Gondolin*, p. 165) Eöl has no association with Dwarves. In the present tale there is mention (p. 224) of 'great traffic' carried on by the Dwarves 'with the free Noldoli' (with Melko's servants also) in those days: we may wonder who these free Noldoli were, since the Rodothlim had been destroyed, and Gondolin was hidden. Perhaps the sons of Fëanor are meant, or Egnor Beren's father (see p. 65).

The idea that it was the Dwarves of Nogrod who were primarily involved survived into the later narrative, but they became exclusively so, and those of Belegost specifically denied all aid to them (*The Silmarillion* p. 233).

Turning now to the Elves, Beren is here of course still an Elf (see p. 139), and in his second span of life he is the ruler, in Hithlum–Hisilómë, of an Elvish people so numerous that 'not even Beren knew the tale of those myriad folk' (p. 234); they are called 'the green Elves' and 'the brown Elves and the green', for they were 'clad in green and brown',

and Dior ruled them in Hithlum after the final departure of Beren and
Tinúviel. Who were they? It is far from clear how they are to be set into
the conception of the Elves of the Great Lands as it appears in other
Tales. We may compare the passage in *The Coming of the Elves*
(I. 118–19):

> Long after the joy of Valinor had washed its memory faint [i.e., the
> memory of the journey through Hisilómë] the Elves sang still sadly of
> it, and told tales of many of their folk whom they said and say were lost
> in those old forests and ever wandered there in sorrow. Still were they
> there long after when Men were shut in Hisilómë by Melko, and still
> do they dance there when Men have wandered far over the lighter
> places of the Earth. Hisilómë did Men name Aryador, and the Lost
> Elves did they call the Shadow Folk, and feared them.

But in that tale the conception still was that Tinwelint ruled 'the
scattered Elves of Hisilomë', and in the outlines for *Gilfanon's Tale* the
'Shadow Folk' of Hisilómë had ceased to be Elves (see p. 64). In any case,
the expression 'green Elves', coupled with the fact that it was the Green-
elves of Ossiriand whom Beren led to the ambush of the Dwarves at Sarn
Athrad in the later story (*The Silmarillion* p. 235), shows which Elvish
people they were to become, even though there is as yet no trace of
Ossiriand beyond the river Gelion and the story of the origin of the
Laiquendi (*ibid.* pp. 94, 96).

It was inevitable that 'the land of the dead that live' should cease to be
in Hisilómë (which seems to have been in danger of having too many
inhabitants), and a note on the manuscript of the *Tale of the Nauglafring*
says: 'Beren must be in "Doriath beyond Sirion" on a . . . . . not
in Hithlum.' Doriath beyond Sirion was the region called in *The Silmarillion* (p. 122) Nivrim, the West March, the woods on the west bank
of the river between the confluence of Teiglin and Sirion and Aelin-uial,
the Meres of Twilight. In the *Tale of Tinúviel* Beren and Tinúviel,
called i·Cuilwarthon, 'became mighty fairies in the lands about the north
of Sirion' (p. 41).

Gwendelin/Gwenniel appears a somewhat faint and ineffective figure
by comparison with the Melian of *The Silmarillion*. Conceivably, an
aspect of this is the far slighter protection afforded to the realm of
Artanor by her magic than that of the impenetrable wall and deluding
mazes of the Girdle of Melian (see p. 63). But the nature of the protection
in the old conception is very unclear. In the *Tale of the Nauglafring* the
coming of the Dwarves from Nogrod is only known when they approach
the bridge before Tinwelint's caves (p. 226); on the other hand, it is said
(p. 230) that the 'woven magic' of the queen was a defence against 'men of
hostile heart', who could never make their way through the woods unless
aided by treachery from within. Perhaps this provides an explanation of
a sort of how the Dwarves bringing treasure from Nogrod were able to

penetrate to the halls of Tinwelint without hindrance and apparently undetected (cf. also the coming of Úrin's band in the *Tale of Turambar*, p. 114). In the event, the protective magic was easily – too easily – overthrown by the simple device of a single treacherous Elf of Artanor who 'offered to lead the host through the magics of Gwendelin'. This was evidently unsatisfactory; but I shall not enter further into this question here. Extraordinary difficulties of narrative structure were caused by this element of the inviolability of Doriath, as I hope to describe at a future date.

It might be thought that the story of the drowning of the treasure at the Stony Ford (falling into the waters of the river with the Dwarves who bore it) was evolved from that in the rejected conclusion of the *Tale of Turambar* (p. 136) – Tinwelint 'hearing that curse [set on the treasure by Úrin] caused the gold to be cast into a deep pool of the river before his doors'. In the *Tale of the Nauglafring*, however, Tinwelint, influenced by the queen's foreboding words, still has the intention of doing this, but does not fulfil his intention (p. 223).

The account of the second departure of Beren and Tinúviel (p. 240) raises again the extremely difficult question of the peculiar fate that was decreed for them by the edict of Mandos, which I have discussed on pp. 59–60. There I have suggested that

> the peculiar dispensation of Mandos in the case of Beren and Tinúviel as here conceived is therefore that their whole 'natural' destiny as Elves was changed: having died as Elves might die (from wounds or from grief) they were not reborn as new beings, but returned in their own persons – yet now 'mortal even as Men'.

Here however Tinúviel 'faded', and vanished in the woods; and Beren searched all Hithlum and Artanor for her, until he too 'faded from life'. Since this fading is here quite explicitly the mode in which 'that doom of mortality that Mandos had spoken' came upon them (p. 240), it is very notable that it is likened to, and even it seems identified with, the fading of 'the Elves of later days throughout the world' – as though in the original idea Elvish fading was a form of mortality. This is in fact made explicit in a later version.

The seven Sons of Fëanor, their oath (sworn not in Valinor but after the coming of the Noldoli to the Great Lands), and the maiming of Maidros appear in the outlines for *Gilfanon's Tale*; and in the latest of these outlines the Fëanorians are placed in Dor Lómin (= Hisilómë, Hithlum), see I. 238, 240, 243. Here, in the *Tale of the Nauglafring*, appear for the first time the names of the Sons of Fëanor, five of them (Maidros, Maglor, Celegorm, Cranthor, Curufin) in the forms, or almost the forms, they were to retain, and Curufin already with his sobriquet 'the Crafty'. The names Amrod and Amras in *The Silmarillion* were a late change; for long these two sons of Fëanor were Damrod (as here) and Díriel (here Dinithel or Durithel, see *Changes made to Names*, p. 245).

Here also appear Dior the Fair, also called Ausir the Wealthy, and his daughter Elwing; his son Auredhir early disappeared in the development of the legends. But Dior ruled in 'the southern vales' (p. 241) of Hisilómë, not in Artanor, and there is no suggestion of any renewal of Tinwelint's kingdom after his death, in contrast to what was told later (*The Silmarillion* p. 236); moreover the Fëanorians, as noted above, dwelt also in Hisilómë – and how all this is to be related to what is said elsewhere of the inhabitants of that region I am unable to say: cf. the *Tale of Tinúviel*, p. 10: 'Hisilómë where dwelt Men, and thrall-Noldoli laboured, and few free-Eldar went.'

A very curious statement is made in this concluding part of the tale, that 'those were days of happiness in the vales of Hithlum, for there was peace with Melko and the Dwarves who had but one thought as they plotted against Gondolin' (p. 241). Presumably 'peace with Melko' means no more than that Melko had averted his attention from those lands; but nowhere else is there any reference to the Dwarves' plotting against Gondolin.

In the typescript version of the *Tale of Tinúviel* (p. 43) it is said that if Turgon King of Gondolin was the most glorious of the kings of the Elves who defied Melko, 'for a while the most mighty *and the longest free* was Thingol of the Woods'. The most natural interpretation of this expression is surely that Gondolin fell before Artanor; whereas in *The Silmarillion* (p. 240) 'Tidings were brought by Thorondor Lord of Eagles of the fall of Nargothrond, and after of the slaying of Thingol and of Dior his heir, and of the ruin of Doriath; but Turgon shut his ear to word of the woes without.' In the present tale we see the same chronology, in that many of the Elves who followed Beren went after his departure to Gondolin, 'the rumour of whose growing power and glory ran in secret whispers among all the Elves' (p. 240), though here the destruction of Gondolin is said to have taken place on the very day that Dior was attacked by the Sons of Fëanor (p. 242). To evade the discrepancy therefore we must interpret the passage in the *Tale of Tinúviel* to mean that Thingol remained free for a longer period of years than did Turgon, irrespective of the dates of their downfalls.

Lastly, the statements that Cûm an-Idrisaith, the Mound of Avarice, 'stands there still in Artanor' (p. 223), and that the waters of Aros still flow above the drowned hoard (p. 238), are noteworthy as indications that nothing analogous to the Drowning of Beleriand was present in the original conception.

# V

# THE TALE OF EÄRENDEL

The 'true beginning' of the *Tale of Eärendel* was to be the dwelling at Sirion's mouth of the Lothlim (the point at which *The Fall of Gondolin* ends: 'and fair among the Lothlim Eärendel grows in the house of his father', pp. 196–7) and the coming there of Elwing (the point at which the *Tale of the Nauglafring* ends: 'they departed for ever from the glades of Hithlum and got them to the south towards Sirion's deep waters, and the pleasant lands. And thus did all the fates of the fairies weave then to one strand, and that strand is the great tale of Eärendel; and to that tale's true beginning are we now come', p. 242). The matter is complicated, however, as will be seen in a moment, by my father's also making the *Nauglafring* the first part of the *Tale of Eärendel*.

But the great tale was never written; and for the story as he then conceived it we are wholly dependent on highly condensed and often contradictory outlines. There are also many isolated notes; and there are the very early Eärendel poems. While the poems can be precisely dated, the notes and outlines can not; and it does not seem possible to arrange them in order so as to provide a clear line of development.

One of the outlines for the *Tale of Eärendel* is the earlier of the two 'schemes' for the *Lost Tales* which are the chief materials for *Gilfanon's Tale*; and I will repeat here what I said of this in the first part (I.233):

> There is no doubt that [the earlier of the two schemes] was composed when the *Lost Tales* had reached their furthest point of development, as represented by the latest texts and arrangements given in this book. Now when this outline comes to the matter of *Gilfanon's Tale* it becomes at once very much fuller, but then contracts again to cursory references for the tales of Tinúviel, Túrin, Tuor, and the Necklace of the Dwarves, and once more becomes fuller for the tale of Eärendel.

This scheme B (as I will continue to call it) provides a coherent if very rough narrative plan, and divides the story into seven parts, of which the first (marked 'Told') is 'The Nauglafring down to the flight of Elwing'. This sevenfold division is referred to by Littleheart at the beginning of *The Fall of Gondolin* (p. 144):

> It is a mighty tale, and seven times shall folk fare to the Tale-fire ere it be rightly told; and so twined is it with those stories of the Nauglafring and of the Elf-march that I would fain have aid in that telling . . .

If the six parts following the *Tale of the Nauglafring* were each to be of comparable length, the whole *Tale of Eärendel* would have been somewhere near half the length of all the tales that were in fact written; but my father never afterwards returned to it on any ample scale. I give now the concluding part of Scheme B.

Tale of Eärendel begins, with which is interwoven the Nauglafring and the March of the Elves. For further details see Notebook C.*

*First part.* The tale of the Nauglafring down to the flight of Elwing.

*Second part.* The dwelling at Sirion. Coming thither of Elwing, and the love of her and Eärendel as girl and boy. Ageing of Tuor – his secret sailing after the conches of Ulmo in Swanwing.
Eärendel sets sail to the North to find Tuor, and if needs be Mandos. Sails in Eärámë. Wrecked. Ulmo appears. Saves him, bidding him sail to Kôr – 'for for this hast thou been brought out of the Wrack of Gondolin'.

*Third part.* Second attempt of Eärendel to Mandos. Wreck of Falasquil and rescue by the Oarni.[1] He sights the Isle of Seabirds 'whither do all the birds of all waters come at whiles'. Goes back by land to Sirion.
Idril has vanished (she set sail at night). The conches of Ulmo call Eärendel. Last farewell of Elwing. Building of Wingilot.

*Fourth part.* Eärendel sails for Valinor. His many wanderings, occupying several years.

*Fifth part.* Coming of the birds of Gondolin to Kôr with tidings. Uproar of the Elves. Councils of the Gods. March of the Inwir (death of Inwë), Teleri, and Solosimpi.
Raid upon Sirion and captivity of Elwing.
Sorrow and wrath of Gods, and a veil dropped between Valmar and Kôr, for the Gods will not destroy it but cannot bear to look upon it.
Coming of the Eldar. Binding of Melko. Faring to Lonely Isle. Curse of the Nauglafring and death of Elwing.

*Sixth part.* Eärendel reaches Kôr and finds it empty. Fares home in sorrow (and sights Tol Eressëa and the fleet of the Elves, but a great wind and darkness carries him away, and he misses his way and has a voyage eastward).
Arriving at length at Sirion finds it empty. Goes to the ruins of Gondolin. Hears of tidings. Sails to Tol Eressëa. Sails to the Isle of Seabirds.

*Seventh part.* His voyage to the firmament.

* For 'Notebook C' see p. 254.

Written at the end of the text is: 'Rem[ainder] of Scheme in Notebook C'. These references in Scheme B to 'Notebook C' are to the little pocket-book which goes back to 1916–17 but was used for notes and suggestions throughout the period of the *Lost Tales* (see I.171). At the beginning of it there is an outline (here called 'C') headed 'Eärendel's Tale, Tuor's son', which is in fair harmony with Scheme B:

> Eärendel dwells with Tuor and Irildë[2] at Sirion's mouth by the sea (on the Isles of Sirion). Elwing of the Gnomes of Artanor[3] flees to them with the Nauglafring. Eärendel and Elwing love one another as boy and girl.
>
> Great love of Eärendel and Tuor. Tuor ages, and Ulmo's conches far out west over the sea call him louder and louder, till one evening he sets sail in his twilit boat with purple sails, Swanwing, Alqarámë.[4] Idril sees him too late. Her song on the beach of Sirion.
>
> When he does not return grief of Eärendel and Idril. Eärendel (urged also by Idril who is immortal) desires to set sail and search even to Mandos. [*Marginal addition*:] Curse of Nauglafring rests on his voyages. Ossë his enemy.
>
> Fiord of the Mermaid. Wreck. Ulmo appears at wreck and saves them, telling them he must go to Kôr and is saved for that.
>
> Elwing's grief when she learns Ulmo's bidding. 'For no man may tread the streets of Kôr or look upon the places of the Gods and dwell in the Outer Lands in peace again.'
>
> Eärendel departs all the same and is wrecked by the treachery of Ossë and saved only by the Oarni (who love him) with Voronwë and dragged to Falasquil.
>
> Eärendel makes his way back by land with Voronwë. Finds that Idril has vanished.[5] His grief. Prays to Ulmo and hears the conches. Ulmo bids him build a new and wonderful ship of the wood of Tuor from Falasquil. Building of Wingilot.

There are four items headed 'Additions' on this page of the notebook:

> Building of Eärámë (Eaglepinion).
> Noldoli add their pleading to Ulmo's bidding.
> Eärendel surveys the first dwelling of Tuor at Falasquil.
> The voyage to Mandos and the Icy Seas.

The outline continues:

> Voronwë and Eärendel set sail in Wingilot. Driven south. Dark regions. Fire mountains. Tree-men. Pygmies. Sarqindi or cannibal-ogres.
>
> Driven west. Ungweliantë. Magic Isles. Twilit Isle [*sic*]. Little-heart's gong awakes the Sleeper in the Tower of Pearl.[6]

Kôr is found. Empty. Eärendel reads tales and prophecies in the waters. Desolation of Kôr. Eärendel's shoes and self powdered with diamond dust so that they shine brightly.

Homeward adventures. Driven east – the deserts and red palaces where dwells the Sun.[7]

Arrives at Sirion, only to find it sacked and empty. Eärendel distraught wanders with Voronwë and comes to the ruins of Gondolin. Men are encamped there miserably. Also Gnomes searching still for lost gems (or some Gnomes gone back to Gondolin).

Of the binding of Melko.[8] The wars with Men and the departure to Tol Eressëa (the Eldar unable to endure the strife of the world). Eärendel sails to Tol Eressëa and learns of the sinking of Elwing and the Nauglafring. Elwing became a seabird. His grief is very great. His garments and body shine like diamonds and his face is in silver flame for the grief and . . . . . . . . . .

He sets sail with Voronwë and dwells on the Isle of Seabirds in the northern waters (not far from Falasquil) – and there hopes that Elwing will return among the seabirds, but she is seeking him wailing along all the shores and especially among wreckage.

After three times seven years he sails again for halls of Mandos with Voronwë – he gets there because [?only] those who still . . . . . . . . . . and had suffered may do so – Tuor is gone to Valinor and nought is known of Idril or of Elwing.

Reaches bar at margin of the world and sets sail on oceans of the firmament in order to gaze over the Earth. The Moon mariner chases him for his brightness and he dives through the Door of Night. How he cannot now return to the world or he will die.

He will find Elwing at the Faring Forth.

Tuor and Idril some say sail now in Swanwing and may be seen going swift down the wind at dawn and dusk.

### The Co-events to Eärendel's Tale

Raid upon Sirion by Melko's Orcs and the captivity of Elwing.

Birds tell Elves of the Fall of Gondolin and the horrors of the fate of the Gnomes. Counsels of the Gods and uproar of the Elves. March of the Inwir and Teleri. The Solosimpi go forth also but fare along all the beaches of the world, for they are loth to fare far from the sound of the sea – and only consent to go with the Teleri under these conditions – for the Noldoli slew some of their kin at Kópas.

This outline then goes on to the events after the coming of the Elves of Valinor into the Great Lands, which will be considered in the next chapter.

Though very much fuller, there seems to be little in C that is certainly contradictory to what is said in B, and there are elements in the latter that are absent from the former. In discussing these outlines I follow the divisions of the tale made in B.

*Second part.* A little more is told in C of Tuor's departure from Sirion (in B there is no mention of Idril); and there appears the motive of Ossë's hostility to Eärendel and the curse of the Nauglafring as instrumental in his shipwrecks. The place of the first wreck is called the Fiord of the Mermaid. The word 'them' rather than 'him' in 'Ulmo saves them, telling them he must go to Kôr' is certain in the manuscript, which possibly suggests that Idril or Elwing (or both) were with Eärendel.

*Third part.* In B Eärendel's second voyage, like the first, is explicitly an attempt to reach Mandos (seeking his father), whereas in C it seems that the second is undertaken rather in order to fulfil Ulmo's bidding that he sail to Kôr (to Elwing's grief). In C Voronwë is named as Eärendel's companion on the second voyage which ended at Falasquil; but the Isle of Seabirds is not mentioned at this point. In C Wingilot is built 'of the wood of Tuor from Falasquil'; in *The Fall of Gondolin* Tuor's wood was hewed for him by the Noldoli in the forests of Dor Lómin and floated down the hidden river (p. 152).

*Fourth part.* Whereas B merely refers to Eärendel's 'many wanderings, occupying several years' in his quest for Valinor, C gives some glimpses of what they were to be, as Wingilot was driven to the south and then into the west. The encounter with Ungweliantë on the western voyage is curious; it is said in *The Tale of the Sun and Moon* that 'Melko held the North and Ungweliant the South' (see I.182, 200).

In C we meet again the Sleeper in the Tower of Pearl (said to be Idril, though this was struck out, note 6) awakened by Littleheart's gong; cf. the account of Littleheart in *The Cottage of Lost Play* (I.15):

> He sailed in Wingilot with Eärendel in that last voyage wherein they sought for Kôr. It was the ringing of this Gong on the Shadowy Seas that awoke the Sleeper in the Tower of Pearl that stands far out to west in the Twilit Isles.

In *The Coming of the Valar* it is said that the Twilit Isles 'float' on the Shadowy Seas 'and the Tower of Pearl rises pale upon their most western cape' (I.68; cf. I.125). But there is no other mention in C of Littleheart, Voronwë's son, as a companion of Eärendel, though he was named earlier in the outline, in a rejected phrase, as present at the Mouths of Sirion (see note 5), and in the *Tale of the Nauglafring* (p. 228) Ailios says that none still living have seen the Nauglafring 'save only Littleheart son of Bronweg' (where 'save only' is an emendation from 'not even').

*Fifth and sixth parts.* In C we meet the image of Eärendel's shoes shining from the dust of diamonds in Kôr, an image that was to survive (*The Silmarillion* p. 248):

> He walked in the deserted ways of Tirion, and the dust upon his raiment and his shoes was a dust of diamonds, and he shone and glistened as he climbed the long white stairs.

But in *The Silmarillion* Tirion was deserted because it was 'a time of festival, and wellnigh all the Elvenfolk were gone to Valimar, or were gathered in the halls of Manwë upon Taniquetil'; here on the other hand it seems at least strongly implied, in both B and C, that Kôr was empty because the Elves of Valinor had departed into the Great Lands, as a result of the tidings brought by the birds of Gondolin. In these very early narrative schemes there is no mention of Eärendel's speaking to the Valar, as the ambassador of Elves and Men (*The Silmarillion* p. 249), and we can only conclude, extraordinary as the conclusion is, that Eärendel's great western voyage, though he attained his goal, was fruitless, that he was not the agent of the aid that did indeed come out of Valinor to the Elves of the Great Lands, and (most curious of all) that Ulmo's designs for Tuor had no issue. In fact, my father actually wrote in the 1930 version of 'The Silmarillion':

> Thus it was that the many emissaries of the Gnomes in after days came never back to Valinor – save one: and he came too late.

The words 'and he came too late' were changed to 'the mightiest mariner of song', and this is the phrase that is found in *The Silmarillion*, p. 102. It is unfortunately never made clear in the earliest writings what was Ulmo's purpose in bidding Eärendel sail to Kôr, for which he had been saved from the ruin of Gondolin. What would he have achieved, had he come to Kôr 'in time', more than in the event did take place after the coming of tidings from Gondolin – the March of the Elves into the Great Lands? In a curious note in C, not associated with the present outline, my father asked: 'How did King Turgon's messengers get to Valinor or gain the Gods' consent?' and answered: 'His messengers never got there. Ulmo [*sic*] but the birds brought tidings to the Elves of the fate of Gondolin (the doves and pigeons of Turgon) and they [?arm and march away].'
    The coming of the message was followed by 'the councils (counsels C) of the Gods and the uproar of the Elves', but in C nothing is said of 'the sorrow and wrath of the Gods' or 'the veil dropped between Valmar and Kôr' referred to in B: where the meaning can surely only be that the March of the Elves from Valinor was undertaken in direct opposition to the will of the Valar, that the Valar were bitterly opposed to the intervention of the Elves of Valinor in the affairs of the Great Lands. There may well be a connection here with Vairë's words (I. 19): 'When the fairies left

Kôr that lane [i.e. Olórë Mallë that led past the Cottage of Lost Play]
*was blocked for ever with great impassable rocks'*. Elsewhere there
is only one other reference to the effect of the message from across the
sea, and that is in the words of Lindo to Eriol in *The Cottage of Lost
Play* (I. 16):

> Inwë, whom the Gnomes call Inwithiel . . . . . was King of all the Eldar
> when they dwelt in Kôr. That was in the days before hearing the
> lament of the world [i.e. the Great Lands] Inwë led them forth to the
> lands of Men.

Later, Meril-i-Turinqi told Eriol (I. 129) that Inwë, her grandsire's sire,
'perished in that march into the world', but Ingil his son 'went long ago
back to Valinor and is with Manwë'; and there is a reference to Inwë's
death in B.

In C the Solosimpi only agreed to accompany the expedition on
condition that they remain by the sea, and the reluctance of the Third
Kindred, on account of the Kinslaying at Swanhaven, survived (*The
Silmarillion* p. 251). But there is no suggestion that the Elves of Valinor
were transported by ship, indeed the reverse, for the Solosimpi 'fare
along all the beaches of the world', and the expedition is a 'March';
though there is no indication of how they came to the Great Lands.

Both outlines refer to Eärendel being driven eastwards on his homeward voyage from Kôr, and to his finding the dwellings at Sirion's mouth
ravaged when he finally returned there; but B does not say who carried
out the sack and captured Elwing. In C it was a raid by Orcs of Melko; cf.
the entry in the Name-list to *The Fall of Gondolin* (p. 215): '*Egalmoth*
. . . got even out of the burning of Gondolin, and dwelt after at the mouth
of Sirion, but was slain in a dire battle there when Melko seized Elwing'.

Neither outline refers to Elwing's escape from captivity. Both mention
Eärendel's going back to the ruins of Gondolin – in C he returns there
with Voronwë and finds Men and Gnomes; another entry in the Name-
list to *The Fall of Gondolin* (p. 215) bears on this: '*Galdor* . . . won out
of Gondolin and even the onslaught of Melko upon the dwellers at
Sirion's mouth and went back to the ruins with Eärendel.'

Both outlines mention the departure of the Elves from the Great
Lands, after the binding of Melko, to Tol Eressëa, C adding a reference
to 'wars with Men' and to the Eldar being 'unable to endure the strife
of the world', and both refer to Eärendel's going there subsequently, but
the order of events seems to be different: in B Eärendel on his way back
from Kôr 'sights Tol Eressëa and the fleet of the Elves' (presumably the
fleet returning from the Great Lands), whereas in C the departure of the
Elves is not mentioned until after Eärendel's return to Sirion. But the
nature of these outlines is not conveyed in print: they were written at
great speed, catching fugitive thoughts, and cannot be pressed hard.
However, with the fate of Elwing B and C seem clearly to part company:

in B there is a simple reference to her death, apparently associated with
the curse of the Nauglafring, and from the order in which the events are
set down it may be surmised that her death took place on the journey to
Tol Eressëa; C specifically refers to the 'sinking' of Elwing and the
Nauglafring – but says that Elwing became a seabird, an idea that
survived (*The Silmarillion* p. 247). This perhaps gives more point to
Eärendel's going to the Isle of Seabirds, mentioned in both B and C: in
the latter he 'hopes that Elwing will return among the seabirds'.

*Seventh part.* In B the concluding part of the tale is merely summarised in the words 'His voyage to the firmament', with a reference to
the other outline C, and in the latter we get some glimpses of a narrative.
It seems to be suggested that the brightness of Eärendel (quite unconnected with the Silmaril) arose from the 'diamond dust' of Kôr, but also
in some sense from the exaltation of his grief. An isolated jotting elsewhere in C asks: 'What became of the Silmarils after the capture of
Melko?' My father at this time gave no answer to the question; but the
question is itself a testimony to the relatively minor importance of
the jewels of Fëanor, if also, perhaps, a sign of his awareness that they
would not always remain so, that in them lay a central meaning of the
mythology, yet to be discovered.

It seems too that Eärendel sailed into the sky in continuing search for
Elwing ('he sets sail on the oceans of the firmament in order to gaze over
the Earth'); and that his passing through the Door of Night (the entrance
made by the Gods in the Wall of Things in the West, see I.215–16) did
not come about through any devising, but because he was hunted by the
Moon. With this last idea, cf. I.193, where Ilinsor, steersman of
the Moon, is said to 'hunt the stars'.

The later of the two schemes for the *Lost Tales*, which gives a quite
substantial outline for *Gilfanon's Tale*, where I have called it 'D' (see
I.234), here fails us, for the concluding passage is very condensed, in
part erased, and ends abruptly early in the *Tale of Eärendel*. I give it
here, beginning at a slightly earlier point in the narrative:

Of the death of Tinwelint and the flight of Gwenethlin [see p. 51].
How Beren avenged Tinwelint and how the Necklace became his.
How it brought sickness to Tinúviel [see p. 246], and how Beren and
Tinúviel faded from the Earth. How their sons [*sic*] dwelt after them
and how the sons of Fëanor came up against them with a host because
of the Silmaril. How all were slain but Elwing daughter of Daimord
[see p. 139] son of Beren fled with the Necklace.
Of Tuor's vessel with white sails.

How folk of the Lothlim dwelt at Sirion's Mouth. Eärendel grew
fairest of all Men that were or are. How the mermaids (Oarni) loved

him. How Elwing came to the Lothlim and of the love of Elwing and Eärendel. How Tuor fell into age, and how Ulmo beckoned to him at eve, and he set forth on the waters and was lost. How Idril swam after him.

(In the following passage my father seems at first to have written: 'Eärendel . . . . . . . Oarni builded Wingilot and set forth in search of . . . . leaving Voronwë with Elwing', where the first lacuna perhaps said 'with the aid of', though nothing is now visible; but then he wrote 'Eärendel built Swanwing', and then partly erased the passage: it is impossible to see now what his intention was.)

Elwing's lament. How Ulmo forbade his quest but Eärendel would yet sail to find a passage to Mandos. How Wingilot was wrecked at Falasquil and how Eärendel found the carven house of Tuor there.

Here Scheme D ends. There is also a reference at an earlier point in it to 'the messengers sent from Gondolin. The doves of Gondolin fly to Valinor at the fall of that town.'

This outline seems to show a move to reduce the complexity of the narrative, with Wingilot being the ship in which Eärendel attempted to sail to Mandos and in which he was wrecked at Falasquil; but the outline is too brief and stops too soon to allow any certain conclusions to be drawn.

A fourth outline, which I will call 'E', is found on a detached sheet; in this Tuor is called Tûr (see p. 148).

Fall of Gondolin. The feast of Glorfindel. The dwelling by the waters of Sirion's mouth. The mermaids come to Eärendel.

Tûr groweth sea-hungry — his song to Eärendel. One evening he calls Eärendel and they go to the shore. There is a skiff. Tûr bids farewell to Eärendel and bids him thrust it off — the skiff fares away into the West. Eärendel hears a great song swelling from the sea as Tûr's skiff dips over the world's rim. His passion of tears upon the shore. The lament of Idril.

The building of Earum.[9] The coming of Elwing. Eärendel's reluctance. The whetting of Idril. The voyage and foundering of Earum in the North, and the vanishing of Idril. How the seamaids rescued Eärendel, and brought him to Tûr's bay. His coastwise journey.

The rape of Elwing. Eärendel discovers the ravaging of Sirion's mouth.

The building of Wingelot. He searches for Elwing and is blown far to the South. Wirilómë. He escapes eastward. He goes back westward; he descries the Bay of Faëry. The Tower of Pearl, the magic isles, the great shadows. He finds Kôr empty; he sails back, crusted with dust and his face afire. He learns of Elwing's foundering. He sitteth on the Isle of Seabirds. Elwing as a seamew comes to him. He sets sail over the margent of the world.

Apart from the fuller account of Tuor's departure from the mouths of Sirion, not much can be learned from this – it is too condensed. But even allowing for speed and compression, there seem to be essential differences from B and C. Thus in this outline (E) Elwing, as it appears, comes to Sirion at a later point in the story, after the departure of Tuor; but the raid and capture of Elwing seems to take place at an earlier point, while Eärendel is on his way back to Sirion from his shipwreck in the North (not, as in B and C, while he is on the great voyage in Wingilot that took him to Kôr). Here, it seems, there was to be only one northward journey, ending in the shipwreck of Earámë/Earum near Falasquil. Though it cannot be demonstrated, I incline to think that E was subsequent to B and C: partly because the reduction of two northward voyages ending in shipwreck to one seems more likely than the other way about, and partly because of the form *Tûr*, which, though it did not survive, replaced *Tuor* for a time (p. 148).

One or two other points may be noticed in this outline. The great spider, called *Ungweliantë* in C but here *Wirilómë* ('Gloomweaver', see I.152), is here encountered by Eärendel in the far South, not as in C on his westward voyage: see p. 256. Elwing in this version comes to Eärendel as a seabird (as she does in *The Silmarillion*, p. 247), which is not said in C and even seems to be denied.

Another isolated page (associated with the poem 'The Bidding of the Minstrel', see pp. 269–70 below) gives a very curious account of Eärendel's great voyage:

> Eärendel's boat goes through North. Iceland. [*Added in margin*: back of North Wind.] Greenland, and the wild islands: a mighty wind and crest of great wave carry him to hotter climes, to back of West Wind. Land of strange men, land of magic. The home of Night. The Spider. He escapes from the meshes of Night with a few comrades, sees a great mountain island and a golden city [*added in margin*: Kôr] – wind blows him southward. Tree-men, Sun-dwellers, spices, fire-mountains, red sea: Mediterranean (loses his boat (travels afoot through wilds of Europe?)) or Atlantic.* Home. Waxes aged. Has a new boat builded. Bids adieu to his north land. Sails west again to the lip of the world, just as the Sun is diving into the sea. He sets sail upon the sky and returns no more to earth.

> The golden city was Kôr and he had caught the music of the Solosimpë, and returns to find it, only to find that the fairies have departed from Eldamar. See little book. Dusted with diamond dust climbing the deserted streets of Kôr.

---

\* The words in this passage ('Tree-men, Sun-dwellers . . .') are clear but the punctuation is not, and the arrangement here may not be that intended.

One would certainly suppose this account to be earlier than anything so far considered (both from the fact that Eärendel's history after his return from the great voyage seems to bear no relation to that in B and C, and from his voyage being set in the lands and oceans of the known world), were it not for the reference to the 'little book', which must mean 'Notebook C', from which the outline C above is taken (see p. 254). But I think it very probable (and the appearance of the MS rather supports this) that the last paragraph ('The golden city. was Kôr . . .') was added later, and that the rest of the outline belongs with the earliest writing of the poem, in the winter of 1914.

It is notable that only here in the earliest writings is it made clear that the 'diamond dust' that coated Eärendel came from the streets of Kôr (cf. the passage from *The Silmarillion* cited on p. 257).

Another of the early Eärendel poems, 'The Shores of Faëry', has a short prose preface, which if not as old as the first composition of the poem itself (July 1915, see p. 271) is certainly not much later:

Eärendel the Wanderer who beat about the Oceans of the World in his white ship Wingelot sat long while in his old age upon the Isle of Seabirds in the Northern Waters ere he set forth upon a last voyage.

He passed Taniquetil and even Valinor, and drew his bark over the bar at the margin of the world, and launched it on the Oceans of the Firmament. Of his ventures there no man has told, save that hunted by the orbed Moon he fled back to Valinor, and mounting the towers of Kôr upon the rocks of Eglamar he gazed back upon the Oceans of the World. To Eglamar he comes ever at plenilune when the Moon sails a-harrying beyond Taniquetil and Valinor.*

Both here and in the outline associated with 'The Bidding of the Minstrel' Eärendel was conceived to be an old man when he journeyed into the firmament.

No other 'connected' account of the *Tale of Eärendel* exists from the earliest period. There are however a number of separate notes, mostly in the form of single sentences, some found in the little notebook C, others jotted down on slips. I collect these references here more or less in the sequence of the tale.

(i) 'Dwelling in the Isle of Sirion in a house of snow-white stone.' – In C (p. 254) it is said that Eärendel dwelt with Tuor and Idril at Sirion's mouth by the sea 'on the Isles of Sirion'.

---

* This preface is found in all the texts of the poem save the earliest, and the versions of it differ only in name-forms: *Wingelot/Vingelot* and *Eglamar/Eldamar* (varying in the same ways as in the accompanying versions of the poem, see textual notes p. 272), and *Kôr* > *Tûn* in the third text, *Tûn* in the fourth. For *Egla* = *Elda* see I. 251 and II. 338, and for *Tûn* see p. 292.

(ii) 'The Oarni give to Eärendel a wonderful shining silver coat that wets not. They love Eärendel, in Ossë's despite, and teach him the lore of boat-building and of swimming, as he plays with them about the shores of Sirion.' – In the outlines are found references to the love of the Oarni for Eärendel (D, p. 259), the coming of the mermaids to him (E, p. 260), and to Ossë's enmity (C, p. 254).

(iii) Eärendel was smaller than most men but nimble-footed and a swift swimmer (but Voronwë could not swim).

(iv) 'Idril and Eärendel see Tuor's boat dropping into the twilight and a sound of song.' – In B Tuor's sailing is 'secret' (p. 253), in C 'Idril sees him too late' (p. 254), and in E Eärendel is present at Tuor's departure and thrusts the boat out: 'he hears a great song swelling from the sea' (p. 260).

(v) 'Death of Idril? – follows secretly after Tuor.' – That Idril died is denied in C: 'Tuor and Idril some say sail now in Swanwing . . .' (p. 255); in D Idril swam after him (p. 260).

(vi) 'Tuor has sailed back to Falasquil and so back up Ilbranteloth to Asgon where he sits playing on his lonely harp on the islanded rock.' – This is marked with a query and an 'X' implying rejection of the idea. There are curious references to the 'islanded rock' in Asgon in the outlines for Gilfanon's Tale (see I. 238).

(vii) 'The fiord of the Mermaid: enchantment of his sailors. Mermaids are not Oarni (but are earthlings, or fays? – or both).' – In D (p. 259) Mermaids and Oarni are equated.

(viii) The ship Wingilot was built of wood from Falasquil with 'aid of the Oarni'. – This was probably said also in D: see p. 260.

(ix) Wingilot was 'shaped as a swan of pearls'.

(x) 'The doves and pigeons of Turgon's courtyard bring message to Valinor – only to Elves.' – Other references to the birds that flew from Gondolin also say that they came to the Elves, or to Kôr (pp. 253, 255, 257).

(xi) 'During his voyages Eärendel sights the white walls of Kôr gleaming afar off, but is carried away by Ossë's adverse winds and waves.' – The same is said in B (p. 253) of Eärendel's sighting of Tol Eressëa on his homeward voyage from Kôr.

(xii) 'The Sleeper in the Tower of Pearl awakened by Littleheart's gong: a messenger that was despatched years ago by Turgon and enmeshed in magics. Even now he cannot leave the Tower and warns them of the magic.' – In C there is a statement, rejected, that the Sleeper in the Tower of Pearl was Idril herself (see note 6).

(xiii) 'Ulmo's protection removed from Sirion in wrath at Eärendel's second attempt to Mandos, and hence Melko overwhelmed it.' – This note is struck through, with an 'X' written against it; but in D (p. 260) it is said that 'Ulmo forbade his quest but Eärendel would yet sail to find a passage to Mandos'. The meaning of this must be that it was contrary to Ulmo's purpose that Eärendel should seek to Mandos for his father, but must rather attempt to reach Kôr.

(xiv) 'Eärendel weds Elwing before he sets sail. When he hears of her
loss he says that his children shall be "all such men hereafter as dare the
great seas in ships".' – With this cf. *The Cottage of Lost Play* (I.13):
'even such a son of Eärendel as was this wayfarer', and (I.18): 'a man of
great and excellent travel, a son meseems of Eärendel'. In an outline of
Eriol's life (I.24) it is said that he was a son of Eärendel, born under his
beam, and that if a beam from Eärendel fall on a child newborn he
becomes 'a child of Eärendel' and a wanderer. In the early dictionary of
Qenya there is an entry: *Eärendilyon* 'son of Eärendel (used of any
mariner)' (I.251).

(xv) 'Eärendel goes even to the empty Halls of Iron seeking Elwing.' –
Eärendel must have gone to Angamandi (empty after the defeat of
Melko) at the same time as he went to the ruins of Gondolin (pp. 253,
255).

(xvi) The loss of the ship carrying Elwing and the Nauglafring took
place on the voyage to Tol Eressëa with the exodus of the Elves from the
Great Lands. – See my remarks, pp. 258–9. For the 'appeasing' of Mîm's
curse by the drowning of the Nauglafring see the Appendix on Names,
entry *Nauglafring*. The departure of the Elves to Tol Eressëa is discussed in the next chapter (p. 280).

(xvii) 'Eärendel and the northern tower on the Isle of Seabirds.' – In C
(p. 255) Eärendel 'sets sail with Voronwë and dwells on the Isle of
Seabirds in the northern waters (not far from Falasquil) – and there
hopes that Elwing will return among the seabirds'; in B (p. 253) 'he
sights the Isle of Seabirds "whither do all the birds of all waters come at
whiles".' There is a memory of this in *The Silmarillion*, p. 250: 'Therefore there was built for [Elwing] a white tower northward upon the
borders of the Sundering Seas; and thither at times all the seabirds of
the earth repaired.'

(xviii) When Eärendel comes to Mandos he finds that Tuor is '*not* in
Valinor, nor Erumáni, and neither Elves nor Ainu know where he is. (He
is with Ulmo.)' – In C (p. 255) Eärendel, reaching the Halls of Mandos,
learns that Tuor 'is gone to Valinor'. For the possibility that Tuor might
be in Erumáni or Valinor see I.91 ff.

(xix) Eärendel 'returns from the firmament ever and anon with
Voronwë to Kôr to see if the Magic Sun has been lit and the fairies have
come back – but the Moon drives him back'. – On Eärendel's return from
the firmament see (xxi) below; on the Rekindling of the Magic Sun see
p. 286.

Two statements about Eärendel cited previously may be added here:
(xx) In the tale of *The Theft of Melko* (I.141) it is said that 'on the
walls of Kôr were many dark tales written in pictured symbols, and runes
of great beauty were drawn there too or carved upon stones, and Eärendel
read many a wondrous tale there long ago'.

(xxi) The Name-list to *The Fall of Gondolin* has the following entry
(cited on p. 215): '*Eärendel* was the son of Tuor and Idril and 'tis said

the only being that is half of the kindred of the Eldalië and half of Men. He was the greatest and first of all mariners among Men, and saw regions that Men have not yet found nor gazed upon for all the multitude of their boats. He rideth now with Voronwë upon the winds of the firmament nor comes ever further back than Kôr, else would he die like other Men, so much of the mortal is in him.' – In the outline associated with the poem 'The Bidding of the Minstrel' Eärendel 'sets sail upon the sky and returns no more to earth' (p. 261); in the prose preface to 'The Shores of Faëry' 'to Eglamar he comes ever at plenilune when the Moon sails a-harrying beyond Taniquetil and Valinor' (p. 262); in outline C 'he cannot now return to the world or he will die' (p. 255); and in citation (xix) above he 'returns from the firmament ever and anon with Voronwë to Kôr'.

In *The Silmarillion* (p. 249) Manwë's judgement was that Eärendel and Elwing 'shall not walk ever again among Elves or Men in the Outer Lands'; but it is also said that Eärendel returned to Valinor from his 'voyages beyond the confines of the world' (*ibid.* p. 250), just as it is said in the Name-list to *The Fall of Gondolin* that he does not come ever further back than Kôr. The further statement in the Name-list, that if he did he would die like other Men, 'so much of the mortal is in him', was in some sense echoed long after in a letter of my father's written in 1967: '*Eärendil*, being in part descended from Men, was not allowed to set foot on Earth again, and became a star shining with the light of the Silmaril' (*The Letters of J. R. R. Tolkien* no. 297).

This brings to an end all the 'prose' materials that bear on the earliest form of the *Tale of Eärendel* (apart from a few other references to him that appear in the next chapter). With these outlines and notes we are at a very early stage of composition, when the conceptions were fluid and had not been given even preliminary narrative form: the myth was present in certain images that were to endure, but these images had not been articulated.

I have already noticed (p. 257) the remarkable fact that there is no hint of the idea that it was Eärendel who by his intercession brought aid out of the West; equally there is no suggestion that the Valar hallowed his ship and set him in the sky, nor that his light was that of the Silmaril. Nonetheless there were already present the coming of Eärendel to Kôr (Tirion) and finding it deserted, the dust of diamonds on his shoes, the changing of Elwing into a seabird, the passing of his ship through the Door of Night, and the sanction against his return to the lands east of the Sea. The raid on the Havens of Sirion appears in the early outlines, though that was an act of Melko's, not of the Fëanorians; and Tuor's departure also, but without Idril, whom he left behind. His ship was *Alqarámë*, Swanwing: afterwards it bore the name *Eärrámë*, with the meaning 'Sea-wing' (*The Silmarillion* p. 245), which retained, in form but not in meaning, the name of Eärendel's first ship *Eärámë* 'Eaglepinion' (pp. 253–4, and see note 9).

It is interesting to read my father's statement, made some half-century later (in the letter of 1967 referred to above), concerning the origins of Eärendil:

This name is in fact (as is obvious) derived from Anglo-Saxon *éarendel*. When first studying Anglo-Saxon professionally (1913–   ) – I had done so as a boyish hobby when supposed to be learning Greek and Latin – I was struck by the great beauty of this word (or name), entirely coherent with the normal style of Anglo-Saxon, but euphonic to a peculiar degree in that pleasing but not 'delectable' language. Also its form strongly suggests that it is in origin a proper name and not a common noun. This is borne out by the obviously related forms in other Germanic languages; from which amid the confusions and debasements of late traditions it at least seems certain that it belonged to astronomical-myth, and was the name of a star or star-group. To my mind the Anglo-Saxon uses seem plainly to indicate that it was a star presaging the dawn (at any rate in English tradition): that is what we now call *Venus*: the morning star as it may be seen shining brilliantly in the dawn, before the actual rising of the Sun. That is at any rate how I took it. Before 1914 I wrote a 'poem' upon Eärendel who launched his ship like a bright spark from the havens of the Sun. I adopted him into my mythology – in which he became a prime figure as a mariner, and eventually as a herald star, and a sign of hope to men. *Aiya Eärendil Elenion Ancalima* ([The Lord of the Rings] II.329) 'hail Eärendil brightest of Stars' is derived at long remove from *Éalá Éarendel engla beorhtast*.* But the name could not be adopted just like that: it had to be accommodated to the Elvish linguistic situation, at the same time as a place for this person was made in legend. From this, far back in the history of 'Elvish', which was beginning, after many tentative starts in boyhood, to take definite shape at the time of the name's adoption, arose eventually (a) the C[ommon]E[lvish] stem *AYAR 'sea', primarily applied to the Great Sea of the West, lying between Middle-earth and Aman the Blessed Realm of the Valar; and (b) the element, or verbal base (N)DIL, 'to love, be devoted to' – describing the attitude of one to a person, thing, cause, or occupation to which one is devoted for its own sake. Eärendil became a character in the earliest written (1916–17) of the major legends: *The Fall of Gondolin*, the greatest of the *Pereldar* 'Half-elven', son of *Tuor* of the most renowned House of the Edain, and *Idril* daughter of the King of Gondolin.

My father did not indeed here say that his *Eärendel* contained from the beginning elements that in combination give a meaning like 'Sea-lover'; but it is in any case clear that at the time of the earliest extant writings on

---

* From the Old English poem *Crist*: *éalá! éarendel engla beorhtast ofer mid-dangeard monnum sended*.

the subject the name was associated with an Elvish word *ea* 'eagle' – see p. 265 on the name of Eärendel's first ship *Eärámë* 'Eaglepinion'. In the Name-list to *The Fall of Gondolin* this is made explicit: '*Earendl* [*sic*] though belike it hath some kinship to the Elfin *ea* and *earen* "eagle" and "eyrie" (wherefore cometh to mind the passage of Cristhorn and the use of the sign of the Eagle by Idril [see p. 193]) is thought to be woven of that secret tongue of the Gondothlim [see p. 165].'

★

I give lastly four early poems of my father's in which Eärendel appears.

## I

### *Éalá Éarendel Engla Beorhtast*

There can be little doubt that, as Humphrey Carpenter supposes (*Biography* p. 71), this was the first poem on the subject of Eärendel that my father composed, and that it was written at Phoenix Farm, Gedling, Nottinghamshire, in September 1914.[10] It was to this poem that he was referring in the letter of 1967 just cited – 'I wrote a "poem" upon Eärendel who launched his ship like a bright spark': cf. line 5 'He launched his bark like a silver spark . . .'

There are some five different versions, each one incorporating emendations made in the predecessor, though only the first verse was substantially rewritten. The title was originally 'The Voyage of Éarendel the Evening Star', together with (as customarily) an Old English version of this: *Scipfæreld Éarendeles Æfensteorran*; this was changed in a later copy to *Éalá Éarendel Engla Beorhtast* 'The Last Voyage of Eärendel', and in still later copies the modern English name was removed. I give it here in the last version, the date of which cannot be determined, though the handwriting shows it to be substantially later than the original composition; together with all the divergent readings of the earliest extant version in footnotes.

> Éarendel arose where the shadow flows
>      At Ocean's silent brim;
> Through the mouth of night as a ray of light
>      Where the shores are sheer and dim                    4
> He launched his bark like a silver spark
>      From the last and lonely sand;
> Then on sunlit breath of day's fiery death
>      He sailed from Westerland.                             8

He threaded his path o'er the aftermath
  Of the splendour of the Sun,
And wandered far past many a star
  In his gleaming galleon.                                      12
On the gathering tide of darkness ride
  The argosies of the sky,
And spangle the night with their sails of light
  As the streaming star goes by.                               16

Unheeding he dips past these twinkling ships,
  By his wayward spirit whirled
On an endless quest through the darkling West
  O'er the margin of the world;                                20
And he fares in haste o'er the jewelled waste
  And the dusk from whence he came
With his heart afire with bright desire
  And his face in silver flame.                                24

The Ship of the Moon from the East comes soon
  From the Haven of the Sun,
Whose white gates gleam in the coming beam
  Of the mighty silver one.                                    28
Lo! with bellying clouds as his vessel's shrouds
  He weighs anchor down the dark,
And on shimmering oars leaves the blazing shores
  In his argent-timbered bark.                                 32

*Readings of the earliest version:*
1–8   Éarendel sprang up from the Ocean's cup
        In the gloom of the mid-world's rim;
      From the door of Night as a ray of light
        Leapt over the twilight brim,
      And launching his bark like a silver spark
        From the golden-fading sand
      Down the sunlit breath of Day's fiery Death
        He sped from Westerland.

10    splendour] glory
11    wandered] went wandering
16    streaming] Evening
17    Unheeding] But unheeding
18    wayward] wandering
19    endless] magic      darkling] darkening
20    O'er the margin] Toward the margent
22    And the dusk] To the dusk
25    The Ship] For the Ship
31    blazing] skiey
32    timbered] orbéd

Then Éarendel fled from that Shipman dread
  Beyond the dark earth's pale,
Back under the rim of the Ocean dim,
  And behind the world set sail;                          36
And he heard the mirth of the folk of earth
  And the falling of their tears,
As the world dropped back in a cloudy wrack
  On its journey down the years.                          40

Then he glimmering passed to the starless vast
  As an isléd lamp at sea,
And beyond the ken of mortal men
  Set his lonely errantry,                                44
Tracking the Sun in his galleon
  Through the pathless firmament,
Till his light grew old in abysses cold
  And his eager flame was spent.                          48

There seems every reason to think that this poem preceded all the
outlines and notes given in this chapter, and that verbal similarities to
the poem found in these are echoes (e.g. 'his face is in silver flame',
outline C, p. 255; 'the margent of the world', outline E, p. 260).

In the fourth verse of the poem the Ship of the Moon comes forth from
the Haven of the Sun; in the tale of *The Hiding of Valinor* (I. 215) Aulë
and Ulmo built two havens in the east, that of the Sun (which was 'wide
and golden') and that of the Moon (which was 'white, having gates of
silver and of pearl') – but they were both 'within the same harbourage'.
As in the poem, in the *Tale of the Sun and Moon* the Moon is urged on
by 'shimmering oars' (I. 195).

## II

### The Bidding of the Minstrel

This poem, according to a note that my father scribbled on one of the
copies, was written at St. John's Street, Oxford (see I. 27) in the winter
of 1914; there is no other evidence for its date. In this case the earliest
workings are extant, and on the back of one of the sheets is the outline

33  Then] And
38  And the falling of] And hearkened to

46–8  And voyaging the skies
    Till his splendour was shorn by the birth of Morn
    And he died with the Dawn in his eyes.

account of Eärendel's great voyage given on p. 261. The poem was then much longer than it became, but the workings are exceedingly rough; they have no title. To the earliest finished text a title was added hastily later: this apparently reads 'The Minstrel renounces the song'. The title then became 'The Lay of Eärendel', changed in the latest text to 'The Bidding of the Minstrel, from the Lay of Eärendel'.

There are four versions following the original rough draft, but the changes made in them were slight, and I give the poem here in the latest form, noting only that originally the minstrel seems to have responded to the 'bidding' much earlier – at line 5, which read 'Then harken – a tale of immortal sea-yearning'; and that 'Eldar' in line 6 and 'Elven' in line 23 are emendations, made on the latest text, of 'fairies', 'fairy'.

> 'Sing us yet more of Eärendel the wandering,
> Chant us a lay of his white-oared ship,
> More marvellous-cunning than mortal man's pondering,
> Foamily musical out on the deep.
> Sing us a tale of immortal sea-yearning                          5
> The Eldar once made ere the change of the light,
> Weaving a winelike spell, and a burning
> Wonder of spray and the odours of night;
> Of murmurous gloamings out on far oceans;
> Of his tossing at anchor off islets forlorn                      10
> To the unsleeping waves' never-ending sea-motions;
> Of bellying sails when a wind was born,
> And the gurgling bubble of tropical water
> Tinkled from under the ringéd stem,
> And thousands of miles was his ship from those wrought her       15
> A petrel, a sea-bird, a white-wingéd gem,
> Gallantly bent on measureless faring
> Ere she came homing in sea-laden flight,
> Circuitous, lingering, restlessly daring,
> Coming to haven unlooked for, at night.'                         20
>
> 'But the music is broken, the words half-forgotten,
> The sunlight has faded, the moon is grown old,
> The Elven ships foundered or weed-swathed and rotten,
> The fire and the wonder of hearts is acold.
> Who now can tell, and what harp can accompany                    25
> With melodies strange enough, rich enough tunes,
> Pale with the magic of cavernous harmony,
> Loud with shore-music of beaches and dunes,
> How slender his boat; of what glimmering timber;
> How her sails were all silvern and taper her mast,               30
> And silver her throat with foam and her limber
> Flanks as she swanlike floated past!

The song I can sing is but shreds one remembers
Of golden imaginings fashioned in sleep,
A whispered tale told by the withering embers                35
Of old things far off that but few hearts keep.'


## III

### The Shores of Faëry

This poem is given in its earliest form by Humphrey Carpenter, *Biography*, pp. 76–7.[11] It exists in four versions each as usual incorporating slight changes; my father wrote the date of its composition on three of the copies, viz. 'July 8–9, 1915'; 'Moseley and Edgbaston, Birmingham July 1915 (walking and on bus). Retouched often since – esp. 1924'; and 'First poem of my mythology, Valinor . . . . . . . . . . 1910'. This last cannot have been intended for the date of composition, and the illegible words preceding it may possibly be read as 'thought of about'. But it does not in any case appear to have been 'the first poem of the mythology': that, I believe, was *Éalá Éarendel Engla Beorhtast* – and my father's mention of this poem in his letter of 1967 (see p. 266) seems to suggest this also.

The Old English title was *Ielfalandes Strand* (The Shores of Elfland). It is preceded by a short prose preface which has been given above, p. 262. I give it here in the latest version (undateable), with all readings from the earliest in footnotes.

East of the Moon, west of the Sun
There stands a lonely hill;
Its feet are in the pale green sea,
Its towers are white and still,
Beyond Taniquetil                                     5
In Valinor.
Comes never there but one lone star
That fled before the moon;
And there the Two Trees naked are
That bore Night's silver bloom,                        10
That bore the globéd fruit of Noon
In Valinor.
There are the shores of Faëry

---

*Readings of the earliest version:*

1   East . . . . . west] West . . . . . East
7   No stars come there but one alone
8   fled before] hunted with
9   For there the Two Trees naked grow
10  bore] bear     11   bore] bear

With their moonlit pebbled strand
Whose foam is silver music                    15
On the opalescent floor
Beyond the great sea-shadows
On the marches of the sand
That stretches on for ever
To the dragonheaded door,                     20
The gateway of the Moon,
Beyond Taniquetil
In Valinor.
West of the Sun, east of the Moon
Lies the haven of the star,                    25
The white town of the Wanderer
And the rocks of Eglamar.
There Wingelot is harboured,
While Eärendel looks afar
O'er the darkness of the waters                30
Between here and Eglamar —
Out, out, beyond Taniquetil
In Valinor afar.

There are some interesting connections between this poem and the tale
of *The Coming of the Elves and the Making of Kôr*. The 'lonely hill'
of line 2 is the hill of Kôr (cf. the tale, I. 122: 'at the head of this long creek
there stands a lonely hill which gazes at the loftier mountains'), while 'the
golden feet of Kôr' (a line replaced in the later versions of the poem) and
very probably 'the sand That stretches on for ever' are explained by the
passage that follows in the tale:

> Thither [i.e. to Kôr] did Aulë bring all the dust of magic metals that
> his great works had made and gathered, and he piled it about the foot
> of that hill, and most of this dust was of gold, and a sand of gold
> stretched away from the feet of Kôr out into the distance where the
> Two Trees blossomed.

18      marches] margent
20–21   To the dragonheaded door, The gateway of the Moon] From the golden feet of Kôr
24      West of the Sun, east of the Moon] O! West of the Moon, East of the Sun
27      rocks] rock
28      Wingelot] *Earliest text* Wingelot > Vingelot; *second text* Vingelot; *third text*
        Vingelot > Wingelot; *last text* Wingelot
30      O'er the darkness of the waters] On the magic and the wonder
31      Between] 'Tween

In the latest text *Elvenland* is lightly written over *Faëry* in line 13, and *Eldamar* against
*Eglamar* in line 27 (only); *Eglamar > Eldamar* in the second text.

With the 'dragonheaded door' (line 20) cf. the description of the Door of
Night in *The Hiding of Valinor* (I. 215–16):

> Its pillars are of the mightiest basalt and its lintel likewise, but great
> dragons of black stone are carved thereon, and shadowy smoke pours
> slowly from their jaws.

In that description the Door of Night is not however 'the gateway of the
Moon', for it is the Sun that passes through it into the outer dark,
whereas 'the Moon dares not the utter loneliness of the outer dark by
reason of his lesser light and majesty, and he journeys still beneath the
world [i.e. through the waters of Vai]'.

## IV

### The Happy Mariners

I give lastly this poem whose subject is the Tower of Pearl in the Twilit
Isles. It was written in July 1915,[12] and there are six texts preceding the
version which was published (together with 'Why the Man in the Moon
came down too soon') at Leeds in 1923* and which is the first of the two
given here.

### (1)

I know a window in a western tower
That opens on celestial seas,
And wind that has been blowing round the stars
Comes to nestle in its tossing draperies.
It is a white tower builded in the Twilight Isles,                     5
Where Evening sits for ever in the shade;
It glimmers like a spike of lonely pearl
That mirrors beams forlorn and lights that fade;
And sea goes washing round the dark rock where it stands,
And fairy boats go by to gloaming lands                              10
All piled and twinkling in the gloom
With hoarded sparks of orient fire

---

* *A Northern Venture:* see I.204, footnote. Mr Douglas A. Anderson has kindly
supplied me with a copy of the poem in this version, which had been very slightly altered
from that published in *The Stapeldon Magazine* (Exeter College, Oxford), June 1920
(Carpenter, p. 268). – *Twilight* in line 5 of the Leeds version is almost certainly an error,
for *Twilit*, the reading of all the original texts.

That divers won in waters of the unknown Sun –
And, maybe, 'tis a throbbing silver lyre,
Or voices of grey sailors echo up                                      15
Afloat among the shadows of the world
In oarless shallop and with canvas furled;
For often seems there ring of feet and song
Or twilit twinkle of a trembling gong.

O! happy mariners upon a journey long                                  20
To those great portals on the Western shores
Where far away constellate fountains leap,
And dashed against Night's dragon-headed doors,
In foam of stars fall sparkling in the deep.
While I alone look out behind the Moon                                 25
From in my white and windy tower,
Ye bide no moment and await no hour,
But chanting snatches of a mystic tune
Go through the shadows and the dangerous seas
Past sunless lands to fairy leas                                       30
Where stars upon the jacinth wall of space
Do tangle burst and interlace.
Ye follow Earendel through the West,
The shining mariner, to Islands blest;
While only from beyond that sombre rim                                 35
A wind returns to stir these crystal panes
And murmur magically of golden rains
That fall for ever in those spaces dim.

In *The Hiding of Valinor* (I. 215) it is told that when the Sun was first
made the Valar purposed to draw it beneath the Earth, but that

> it was too frail and lissom; and much precious radiance was spilled in
> their attempts about the deepest waters, and escaped to linger as secret
> sparks in many an unknown ocean cavern. These have many elfin
> divers, and divers of the fays, long time sought beyond the outmost
> East, even as is sung in the song of the Sleeper in the Tower of Pearl.

That 'The Happy Mariners' was in fact 'the song of the Sleeper in the
Tower of Pearl' seems assured by lines 10–13 of the poem.
   For 'Night's dragon-headed doors' see p. 273. The meaning of *jacinth*
in 'the jacinth wall of space' (line 31) is 'blue'; cf. 'the deep-blue walls' in
*The Hiding of Valinor* (I. 215).

Many years later my father rewrote the poem, and I give this version
here. Still later he turned to it again and made a few further alterations
(here recorded in footnotes); at this time he noted that the revised
version dated from '1940?'.

(2)

I know a window in a Western tower
that opens on celestial seas,
and there from wells of dark behind the stars
blows ever cold a keen unearthly breeze.
It is a white tower builded on the Twilit Isles,                    5
and springing from their everlasting shade
it glimmers like a house of lonely pearl,
where lights forlorn take harbour ere they fade.

Its feet are washed by waves that never rest.
There silent boats go by into the West                    10
all piled and twinkling in the dark
with orient fire in many a hoarded spark
that divers won
in waters of the rumoured Sun.
There sometimes throbs below a silver harp,                    15
touching the heart with sudden music sharp;
or far beneath the mountains high and sheer
the voices of grey sailors echo clear,
afloat among the shadows of the world
in oarless ships and with their canvas furled,                    20
chanting a farewell and a solemn song:
for wide the sea is, and the journey long.

O happy mariners upon a journey far,
beyond the grey islands and past Gondobar,
to those great portals on the final shores                    25
where far away constellate fountains leap,
and dashed against Night's dragon-headed doors
in foam of stars fall sparkling in the deep!
While I, alone, look out behind the moon
from in my white and windy tower,                    30
ye bide no moment and await no hour,
but go with solemn song and harpers' tune
through the dark shadows and the shadowy seas
to the last land of the Two Trees,
whose fruit and flower are moon and sun,                    35
where light of earth is ended and begun.

*Last revisions:*
3    and there *omitted*
4    blows ever cold] there ever blows
17   mountains] mountain
22   the journey] their journey
29   While I look out alone          30   imprisoned in the white and windy tower
31   ye] you          33–6 *struck through*

Ye follow Eärendel without rest,
the shining mariner, beyond the West,
who passed the mouth of night and launched his bark
upon the outer seas of everlasting dark.                              40
Here only comes at whiles a wind to blow
returning darkly down the way ye go,
with perfume laden of unearthly trees.
Here only long afar through window-pane
I glimpse the flicker of the golden rain                              45
that falls for ever on the outer seas.

I cannot explain the reference (in the revised version only, line 24) to
the journey of the mariners 'beyond the grey islands and past Gondobar'.
*Gondobar* ('City of Stone') was one of the seven names of Gondolin
(p. 158).


# NOTES

1   Falasquil was the name of Tuor's dwelling on the coast (p. 152); the
    Oarni, with the Falmaríni and the Wingildi, are called 'the spirits of
    the foam and the surf of ocean' (I.66).

2   *Irildë*: the 'Elvish' name corresponding to Gnomish *Idril*. See the
    Appendix on Names, entry *Idril*.

3   'Elwing of the *Gnomes* of Artanor' is perhaps a mere slip.

4   For the Swan-wing as the emblem of Tuor see pp. 152, 164, 172,
    193.

5   The words 'Idril has vanished' replace an earlier reading: 'Sirion has
    been sacked and only Littleheart (Ilfrith) remained who tells the
    tale.' *Ilfrith* is yet another version of Littleheart's Elvish name (see
    pp. 201–2).

6   Struck out here: 'The Sleeper is Idril but he does not know.'

7   Cf. *Kortirion among the Trees* (I.36, lines 129–30): 'I need not
    know the desert or red palaces Where dwells the sun'; lines retained
    slightly changed in the second (1937) version (I.39).

8   This passage, from 'Eärendel distraught . . .', replaced the following:
    '[*illegible name, possibly* Orlon] is [?biding] there and tells him of
    the sack of Sirion and the captivity of Elwing. The faring of the
    Koreldar and the binding of Melko.' Perhaps the words 'The faring
    of the Koreldar' were struck out by mistake (cf. Outline B).

9   *Earum* is emended (at the first occurrence only) from *Earam*; and
    following it stood the name *Earnhama*, but this was struck out.
    *Earnhama* is Old English, 'Eagle-coat', 'Eagle-dress'.

37  Ye] You       40  outer *omitted*
41–3  *struck through*        46  the] those
*Line added at end:* beyond the country of the shining Trees.

10  The two earliest extant texts date it thus, one of them with the addition 'Ex[eter] Coll[ege] Essay Club Dec. 1914', and on a third is written 'Gedling, Notts., Sept. 1913 [error for 1914] and later'. My father referred to having read 'Eärendel' to the Essay Club in a letter to my mother of 27 November 1914.

11  But *rocks* in line 27 (26) should read *rock*.

12  According to one note it was written at 'Barnt Green [see *Biography* p. 36] July 1915 and Bedford and later', and another note dates it 'July 24 [1915], rewritten Sept. 9'. The original workings are on the back of an unsent letter dated from Moseley (Birmingham) July 11, 1915; my father began military training at Bedford on July 19.

# VI

# THE HISTORY OF ERIOL OR
# ÆLFWINE AND THE END OF THE
# TALES

In this final chapter we come to the most difficult (though not, as I hope to show, altogether insoluble) part of the earliest form of the mythology: its end, with which is intertwined the story of Eriol/Ælfwine – and with that, the history and original significance of Tol Eressëa. For its eluci- dation we have some short pieces of connected narrative, but are largely dependent on the same materials as those that constitute *Gilfanon's Tale* and the story of Eärendel: scribbled plot-outlines, endlessly varying, written on separate slips of paper or in the pages of the little notebook 'C' (see p. 254). In this chapter there is much material to consider, and for convenience of reference within the chapter I number the various citations consecutively. But it must be said that no device of presentation can much diminish the inherent complexity and obscurity of the matter.

The fullest account (bald as it is) of the March of the Elves of Kôr and the events that followed is contained in notebook C, continuing on from the point where I left that outline on p. 255, after the coming of the birds from Gondolin, the 'counsels of the Gods and uproar of the Elves', and the 'March of the Inwir and Teleri', with the Solosimpi only agreeing to accompany the expedition on condition that they remain by the sea. The outline continues:

(1)     Coming of the Eldar. Encampment in the Land of Willows of
        first host. Overwhelming of Noldorin and Valwë. Wanderings
        of Noldorin with his harp.
        Tulkas overthrows Melko in the battle of the Silent Pools. Bound
        in Lumbi and guarded by Gorgumoth the hound of Mandos.
        Release of the Noldoli. War with Men as soon as Tulkas and
        Noldorin have fared back to Valinor.
        Noldoli led to Valinor by Egalmoth and Galdor.

There have been previous references in the *Lost Tales* to a battle in Tasarinan, the Land of Willows: in the *Tale of Turambar* (pp. 70, 140), and, most notably, in *The Fall of Gondolin* (p. 154), where when Tuor's sojourn in that land is described there is mention of events that would take place there in the future:

Did not even after the days of Tuor Noldorin and his Eldar come there seeking for Dor Lómin and the hidden river and the caverns of the Gnomes' imprisonment; yet thus nigh to their quest's end were like to abandon it? Indeed sleeping and dancing here . . . they were whelmed by the goblins sped by Melko from the Hills of Iron and Noldorin made bare escape thence.

Valwë has been mentioned once before, by Lindo, on Eriol's first evening in Mar Vanwa Tyaliéva (I. 16): 'My father Valwë who went with Noldorin to find the Gnomes.' Of Noldorin we know also that he was the Vala Salmar, the twin-brother of Ómar-Amillo; that he entered the world with Ulmo, and that in Valinor he played the harp and lyre and loved the Noldoli (I. 66, 75, 93, 126).

An isolated note states:

(2) Noldorin escapes from the defeat of the Land of Willows and takes his harp and goes seeking in the Iron Mountains for Valwë and the Gnomes until he finds their place of imprisonment. Tulkas follows. Melko comes to meet him.

The only one of the great Valar who is mentioned in these notes as taking part in the expedition to the Great Lands is Tulkas; but whatever story underlay his presence, despite the anger and sorrow of the Valar at the March of the Elves (see p. 257), is quite irrecoverable. (A very faint hint concerning it is found in two isolated notes: 'Tulkas gives – or the Elves take *limpë* with them', and '*Limpë* given by the Gods (Oromë? Tulkas?) when Elves left Valinor'; cf. *The Flight of the Noldoli* (I. 166): 'no *limpë* had they [the Noldoli] as yet to bring away, for that was not given to the fairies until long after, when the March of Liberation was undertaken'.) According to (1) above Tulkas fought with and overthrew Melko 'in the battle of the Silent Pools'; and the Silent Pools are the Pools of Twilight, 'where Tulkas after fought with Melko's self' (*The Fall of Gondolin*, p. 195; the original reading here was 'Noldorin and Tulkas').

The name *Lumbi* is found elsewhere (in a list of names associated with the tale of *The Coming of the Valar*, I. 93), where it is said to be Melko's third dwelling; and a jotting in notebook C, sufficiently mysterious, reads: 'Lumfad. Melko's dwelling after release. Castle of Lumbi.' But this story also is lost.

That the Noldoli were led back to Valinor by Egalmoth and Galdor, as stated in (1), is notable. This is contradicted in detail by a statement in the Name-list to *The Fall of Gondolin*, which says (p. 215) that Egalmoth was slain in the raid on the dwelling at the mouth of Sirion when Elwing was taken; and contradicted in general by the next citation to be given, which denies that the Elves were permitted to dwell in Valinor.

The only other statement concerning these events is found in the first of the four outlines that constitute *Gilfanon's Tale*, which I there called 'A' (I. 234). This reads:

(3)   March of the Elves out into the world.
The capture of Noldorin.
The camp in the Land of Willows.
Army of Tulkas at the Pools of Twilight . . . . . . and [?many]
Gnomes, but Men fall on them out of Hisilómë.
Defeat of Melko.
Breaking of Angamandi and release of captives.
Hostility of Men. The Gnomes collect some of the jewels.
Elwing and most of the Elves go back to dwell in Tol Eressëa. The
Gods will not let them dwell in Valinor.

This seems to differ from (1) in the capture of Noldorin and in the attack of Men from Hisilómë before the defeat of Melko; but the most notable statement is that concerning the refusal of the Gods to allow the Elves to dwell in Valinor. There is no reason to think that this ban rested only, or chiefly, on the Noldoli. The text, (3), does not refer specifically to the Gnomes in this connection; and the ban is surely to be related to 'the sorrow and wrath of the Gods' at the time of the March of the Elves (p. 253). Further, it is said in *The Cottage of Lost Play* (I. 16) that Ingil son of Inwë returned to Tol Eressëa with 'most of the fairest and the wisest, most of the merriest and the kindest, of all the Eldar', and that the town that he built there was named 'Koromas or "the Resting of the Exiles of Kôr".' This is quite clearly to be connected with the statement in (3) that 'Most of the Elves go back to dwell in Tol Eressëa', and with that given on p. 255: 'The wars with Men and the departure to Tol Eressëa (the Eldar unable to endure the strife of the world)'. These indications taken together leave no doubt, I think, that my father's original conception was of the Eldar of Valinor undertaking the expedition into the Great Lands against the will of the Valar; together with the rescued Noldoli they returned over the Ocean, but being refused re-entry into Valinor they settled in Tol Eressëa, as 'the Exiles of Kôr'. That some did return in the end to Valinor may be concluded from the words of Meril-i-Turinqi (I. 129) that Ingil, who built Kortirion, 'went long ago back to Valinor and is with Manwë'. But Tol Eressëa remained the land of the fairies in the early conception, the Exiles of Kôr, Eldar and Gnomes, speaking both *Eldarissa* and *Noldorissa*.

It seems that there is nothing else to be found or said concerning the original story of the coming of aid out of the West and the renewed assault on Melko.

★

The conclusion of the whole story as originally envisaged was to be rejected in its entirety. For it we are very largely dependent on the outline in notebook C, continuing on from citation (1) above; this is extremely rough and disjointed, and is given here in a very slightly edited form.


(4)   After the departure of Eärendel and the coming of the Elves to Tol Eressëa (and most of this belongs to the history of Men) great ages elapse; Men spread and thrive, and the Elves of the Great Lands fade. As Men's stature grows theirs diminishes. Men and Elves were formerly of a size, though Men always larger.[1]

Melko again breaks away, by the aid of Tevildo (who in long ages gnaws his bonds); the Gods are in dissension about Men and Elves, some favouring the one and some the other. Melko goes to Tol Eressëa and tries to stir up dissension among the Elves (between Gnomes and Solosimpi), who are in consternation and send to Valinor. No help comes, but Tulkas sends privily Telimektar (Taimonto) his son.[2]

Telimektar of the silver sword and Ingil surprise Melko and wound him, and he flees and climbs up the great Pine of Tavrobel. Before the Inwir left Valinor Belaurin (Palúrien)[3] gave them a seed, and said that it must be guarded, for great tidings would one day come of its growth. But it was forgotten, and cast in the garden of Gilfanon, and a mighty pine arose that reached to Ilwë and the stars.[4]

Telimektar and Ingil pursue him, and they remain now in the sky to ward it, and Melko stalks high above the air seeking ever to do a hurt to the Sun and Moon and stars (eclipses, meteors). He is continually frustrated, but on his first attempt – saying that the Gods stole his fire for its making – he upset the Sun, so that Urwendi fell into the Sea, and the Ship fell near the ground, scorching regions of the Earth. The clarity of the Sun's radiance has not been so great since, and something of magic has gone from it. Hence it is, and long has been, that the fairies dance and sing more sweetly and can the better be seen by the light of the Moon – because of the death of Urwendi.

The 'Rekindling of the Magic Sun' refers in part to the Trees and in part to Urwendi.

Fionwë's rage and grief. In the end he will slay Melko.

'Orion' is only the image of Telimektar in the sky? [sic] Varda gave him stars, and he bears them aloft that the Gods may know he watches; he has diamonds on his sword-sheath, and this will go red when he draws his sword at the Great End.

But now Telimektar, and Gil[5] who follows him like a Blue Bee, ward off evil, and Varda immediately replaces any stars that Melko loosens and casts down.

Although grieved at the Gods' behest, the Pine is cut down; and

Melko is thus now out of the world – but one day he will find a way back, and the last great uproars will begin before the Great End.

The evils that still happen come about in this wise. The Gods can cause things to enter the hearts of Men, but not of Elves (hence their difficult dealings in the old days of the Exile of the Gnomes) – and though Melko sits without, gnawing his fingers and gazing in anger on the world, he can suggest evil to Men so inclined – but the lies he planted of old still grow and spread.

Hence Melko can now work hurt and damage and evil in the world only through Men, and he has more power and subtlety with Men than Manwë or any of the Gods, because of his long sojourn in the world and among Men.

In these early chartings we are in a primitive mythology, with Melko reduced to a grotesque figure chased up a great pine-tree, which is thereupon cut down to keep him out of the world, where he 'stalks high above the air' or 'sits without, gnawing his fingers', and upsets the Sun-ship so that Urwendi falls into the Sea – and, most strangely, meets her death.

That Ingil (Gil) who with Telimektar pursues Melko is to be identified with Ingil son of Inwë who built Kortirion is certain and appears from several notes; see the Appendix on Names to Vol. I, entries *Ingil, Telimektar*. This is the fullest statement of the Orion-myth, which is referred to in the *Tale of the Sun and Moon* (see I.182, 200):

of Nielluin [Sirius] too, who is the Bee of Azure, Niclluin whom still may all men see in autumn or winter burning nigh the foot of Telimektar son of Tulkas whose tale is yet to tell.

In the Gnomish dictionary it is said (I.256) that Gil rose into the heavens and 'in the likeness of a great bee bearing honey of flame' followed Telimektar. This presumably represents a distinct conception from that referred to above, where Ingil 'went long ago back to Valinor and is with Manwë' (I.129).

With the reference to Fionwë's slaying of Melko 'in the end' cf. the end of *The Hiding of Valinor* (I.219):

Fionwë Úrion, son of Manwë, of love for Urwendi shall in the end be Melko's bane, and shall destroy the world to destroy his foe, and so shall all things then be rolled away.

Cf. also the *Tale of Turambar*, p. 116, where it is said that Turambar 'shall stand beside Fionwë in the Great Wrack'.

For the prophecies and hopes of the Elves concerning the Rekindling of the Magic Sun see pp. 285–6.

The outline in C continues and concludes thus (again with some very slight and insignificant editing):

**(5)** Longer ages elapse. Gilfanon is now the oldest and wisest Elf in Tol Eressëa, but is not of the Inwir – hence Meril-i-Turinqi is Lady of the Isle.
Eriol comes to Tol Eressëa. Sojourns at Kortirion. Goes to Tavrobel to see Gilfanon, and sojourns in the house of a hundred chimneys – for this is the last condition of his drinking *limpë*. Gilfanon bids him write down all he has heard before he drinks. Eriol drinks *limpë*. Gilfanon tells him of things to be; that in his mind (although the fairies hope not) he believes that Tol Eressëa will become a dwelling of Men. Gilfanon also prophesies concerning the Great End, and of the Wrack of Things, and of Fionwë, Tulkas, and Melko and the last fight on the Plains of Valinor.
Eriol ends his life at Tavrobel but in his last days is consumed with longing for the black cliffs of his shores, even as Meril said.
The book lay untouched in the house of Gilfanon during many ages of Men.
The compiler of the Golden Book takes up the Tale: one of the children of the fathers of the fathers of Men. [*Against this is written:*] It may perhaps be much better to let Eriol himself see the last things and finish the book.
Rising of the Lost Elves against the Orcs and Nautar.[6] The time is not ready for the Faring Forth, but the fairies judge it to be necessary. They obtain through Ulmo the help of Uin,[7] and Tol Eressëa is uprooted and dragged near to the Great Lands, nigh to the promontory of Rôs. A magic bridge is cast across the intervening sound. Ossë is wroth at the breaking of the roots of the isle he set so long ago – and many of his rare sea-treasures grow about it – that he tries to wrench it back; and the western half breaks off, and is now the Isle of Íverin.
The Battle of Rôs: the Island-elves and the Lost Elves against Nautar, Gongs,[8] Orcs, and a few evil Men. Defeat of the Elves. The fading Elves retire to Tol Eressëa and hide in the woods.
Men come to Tol Eressëa and also Orcs, Dwarves, Gongs, Trolls, etc. After the Battle of Rôs the Elves faded with sorrow. They cannot live in air breathed by a number of Men equal to their own or greater; and ever as Men wax more powerful and numerous so the fairies fade and grow small and tenuous, filmy and transparent, but Men larger and more dense and gross. At last Men, or almost all, can no longer see the fairies.
The Gods now dwell in Valinor, and come scarcely ever to the world, being content with the restraining of the elements from utterly destroying Men. They grieve much at what they see; *but Ilúvatar is over all.*

On the page opposite the passage about the Battle of Rôs is written:

A great battle between Men at the Heath of the Sky-roof (now the Withered Heath), about a league from Tavrobel. The Elves and the Children flee over the Gruir and the Afros.
'Even now do they approach and our great tale comes to its ending.'
The book found in the ruins of the house of a hundred chimneys.

That Gilfanon was the oldest of the Elves of Tol Eressëa, though Meril held the title of Lady of the Isle, is said also in the *Tale of the Sun and Moon* (I.175): but what is most notable is that Gilfanon (not Ailios, teller of the *Tale of the Nauglafring*, whom Gilfanon replaced, see I.197 note 19 and 229ff.) appears in this outline, which must therefore be late in the period of the composition of the *Lost Tales*.

Also noteworthy are the references to Eriol's drinking *limpë* at Gilfanon's 'house of a hundred chimneys'. In *The Cottage of Lost Play* (I.17) Lindo told Eriol that he could not give him *limpë* to drink:

Turinqi only may give it to those not of the Eldar race, and those that drink must dwell always with the Eldar of the Island until such time as they fare forth to find the lost families of the kindred.

Meril-i-Turinqi herself, when Eriol besought her for a drink of *limpë*, was severe (I.98):

If you drink this drink . . . even at the Faring Forth, should Eldar and Men fall into war at the last, still must you stand by us against the children of your kith and kin, but until then never may you fare away home though longings gnaw you . . .

In the text described in I.229ff. Eriol bemoans to Lindo the refusal to grant him his desire, and Lindo, while warning him against 'thinking to overpass the bounds that Ilúvatar hath set', tells him that Meril has not irrevocably refused him. In a note to this text my father wrote: '. . . Eriol fares to Tavrobel – after Tavrobel he drinks of *limpë*.'

The statement in this passage of outline C that Eriol 'in his last days is consumed with longing for the black cliffs of his shores, even as Meril said' clearly refers to the passage in *The Chaining of Melko* from which I have cited above:

On a day of autumn will come the winds and a driven gull, maybe, will wail overhead, and lo! you will be filled with desire, remembering the black coasts of your home. (I.96).

Lindo's reference, in the passage from *The Cottage of Lost Play* cited above, to the faring forth of the Eldar of Tol Eressëa 'to find the lost families of the kindred' must likewise relate to the mentions in (5) of the Faring Forth (though the time was not ripe), of the 'rising of the Lost Elves against the Orcs and Nautar', and of 'the Island-elves and the Lost Elves' at the Battle of Rôs. Precisely who are to be understood by the 'Lost Elves' is not clear; but in *Gilfanon's Tale* (I. 231) all Elves of the Great Lands 'that never saw the light at Kôr' (Ilkorins), whether or not they left the Waters of Awakening, are called 'the lost fairies of the world', and this seems likely to be the meaning here. It must then be supposed that there dwelt on Tol Eressëa only the Eldar of Kôr (the 'Exiles') and the Noldoli released from thraldom under Melko; the Faring Forth was to be the great expedition from Tol Eressëa for the rescue of those who had never departed from the Great Lands.

In (5) we meet the conception of the dragging of Tol Eressëa back eastwards across the Ocean to the geographical position of England – it becomes England (see I. 26); that the part which was torn off by Ossë, the Isle of Íverin, is Ireland is explicitly stated in the Qenya dictionary. The promontory of Rôs is perhaps Brittany.

Here also there is a clear definition of the 'fading' of the Elves, their physical diminution and increasing tenuity and transparency, so that they become invisible (and finally incredible) to gross Mankind. This is a central concept of the early mythology: the 'fairies', as now conceived by Men (in so far as they are rightly conceived), have *become* so. They were not always so. And perhaps most remarkable in this remarkable passage, there is the final and virtually complete withdrawal of the Gods (to whom the Eldar are 'most like in nature', I. 57) from the concerns of 'the world', the Great Lands across the Sea. They watch, it seems, since they grieve, and are therefore not wholly indifferent to what passes in the lands of Men; but they are henceforward utterly remote, hidden in the West.

Other features of (5), the Golden Book of Tavrobel, and the Battle of the Heath of the Sky-roof, will be explained shortly. I give next a separate passage found in the notebook C under the heading 'Rekindling of the Magic Sun. Faring Forth.'

(6)  The Elves' prophecy is that one day they will fare forth from Tol Eressëa and on arriving in the world will gather all their fading kindred who still live in the world and march towards Valinor – through the southern lands. This they will only do with the help of Men. If Men aid them, the fairies will take Men to Valinor – those that wish to go – fight a great battle with Melko in Erumáni and open Valinor.[9] Laurelin and Silpion will be rekindled, and the mountain wall being destroyed then soft radiance will spread over all the world, and the Sun and Moon will be recalled. If Men oppose them and aid Melko the Wrack of the Gods and the ending of the fairies will result – and maybe the Great End.

On the opposite page is written:

> Were the Trees relit all the paths to Valinor would become clear to
> follow – and the Shadowy Seas open clear and free – Men as well as
> Elves would taste the blessedness of the Gods, and Mandos be emptied.

This prophecy is clearly behind Vairë's words to Eriol (I. 19–20): '. . .
the Faring Forth, when if all goes well the roads through Arvalin to
Valinor shall be thronged with the sons and daughters of Men.'
     Since 'the Sun and Moon will be recalled' when the Two Trees give
light again, it seems that here 'the Rekindling of the Magic Sun' (to which
the toast was drunk in Mar Vanwa Tyaliéva, I. 17, 65) refers to the
relighting of the Trees. But in citation (4) above it is said that 'the
"Rekindling of the Magic Sun" refers in part to the Trees and in part to
Urwendi', while in the *Tale of the Sun and Moon* (I. 179) Yavanna
seems to distinguish the two ideas:

> 'Many things shall be done and come to pass, and the Gods grow old,
> and the Elves come nigh to fading, ere ye shall see the rekindling of
> these trees or the Magic Sun relit', and the Gods knew not what she
> meant, speaking of the Magic Sun, nor did for a long while after.

Citation (xix) on p. 264 does not make the reference clear: Eärendel
'returns from the firmament ever and anon with Voronwë to Kôr to see if
the Magic Sun has been lit and the fairies have come back'; but in the
following isolated note the Rekindling of the Magic Sun explicitly means
the re-arising of Urwendi:

(7)     Urwendi imprisoned by Móru (upset out of the boat by Melko and
          only the Moon has been magic since). The Faring Forth and the
          Battle of Erumáni would release her and rekindle the Magic Sun.

     This 'upsetting' of the Sun-ship by Melko and the loss of the Sun's
'magic' is referred to also in (4), where it is added that Urwendi fell into
the sea and met her 'death'. In the tale of *The Theft of Melko* it is said
(I. 151) that the cavern in which Melko met Ungweliant was the place
where the Sun and Moon were imprisoned afterwards, for 'the primeval
spirit Móru' was indeed Ungweliant (see I. 261). The Battle of Erumáni
is referred to also in (6), and is possibly to be identified with 'the last fight
on the plains of Valinor' prophesied by Gilfanon in (5). But the last part
of (5) shows that the Faring Forth came to nothing, and the prophecies
were not fulfilled.

     There are no other references to the dragging of Tol Eressëa across the
Ocean by Uin the great whale, to the Isle of Íverin, or to the Battle
of Rôs; but a remarkable writing survives concerning the aftermath of

the 'great battle between Men at the Heath of the Sky-roof (now the Withered Heath), about a league from Tavrobel' (end of citation (5)). This is a very hastily pencilled and exceedingly difficult text titled *Epilogue*. It begins with a short prefatory note:

(8)    Eriol flees with the fading Elves from the Battle of the High Heath (Ladwen-na-Dhaideloth) and crosses the Gruir and the Afros.
         The last words of the book of Tales. Written by Eriol at Tavrobel before he sealed the book.

This represents the development mentioned as desirable in (5), that Eriol should 'himself see the last things and finish the book'; but an isolated note in C shows my father still uncertain about this even after the *Epilogue* was in being: 'Prologue by the writer of Tavrobel [*i.e., such a Prologue is needed*] telling how he found Eriol's writings and put them together. His epilogue after the battle of Ladwen Daideloth is written.'
     The rivers Gruir and Afros appear also in the passage about the battle at the end of (5). Since it is said there that the Heath was about a league from Tavrobel, the two rivers are clearly those referred to in the *Tale of the Sun and Moon*: 'the Tower of Tavrobel beside the rivers' (I.174, and see I.196 note 2). In scattered notes the battle is also called 'the Battle of the Heaven Roof' and 'the Battle of Dor-na-Dhaideloth'.[10]
     I give now the text of the *Epilogue*:

     And now is the end of the fair times come very nigh, and behold, all the beauty that yet was on earth – fragments of the unimagined loveliness of Valinor whence came the folk of the Elves long long ago – now goeth it all up in smoke. Here be a few tales, memories ill-told, of all that magic and that wonder twixt here and Eldamar of which I have become acquaint more than any mortal man since first my wandering footsteps came to this sad isle.
     Of that last battle of the upland heath whose roof is the wide sky – nor was there any other place beneath the blue folds of Manwë's robe so nigh the heavens or so broadly and so well encanopied – what grievous things I saw I have told.
     Already fade the Elves in sorrow and the Faring Forth has come to ruin, and Ilúvatar knoweth alone if ever now the Trees shall be relit while the world may last. Behold, I stole by evening from the ruined heath, and my way fled winding down the valley of the Brook of Glass, but the setting of the Sun was blackened with the reek of fires, and the waters of the stream were fouled with the war of men and grime of strife. Then was my heart bitter to see the bones of the good earth laid bare with winds where the destroying hands of men had torn the heather and the fern and burnt them to make sacrifice to Melko and to lust of ruin; and the thronging places of the bees that all day hummed among the whins and whortlebushes long ago bearing rich honey down

to Tavrobel – these were now become fosses and [?mounds] of stark red earth, and nought sang there nor danced but unwholesome airs and flies of pestilence.

Now the Sun died and behold, I came to that most magic wood where once the ageless oaks stood firm amid the later growths of beech and slender trees of birch, but all were fallen beneath the ruthless axes of unthinking men. Ah me, here was the path beaten with spells, trodden with musics and enchantment that wound therethrough, and this way were the Elves wont to ride a-hunting. Many a time there have I seen them and Gilfanon has been there, and they rode like kings unto the chase, and the beauty of their faces in the sun was as the new morning, and the wind in their golden hair like to the glory of bright flowers shaken at dawn, and the strong music of their voices like the sea and like trumpets and like the noise of very many viols and of golden harps unnumbered. And yet again have I seen the people of Tavrobel beneath the Moon, and they would ride or dance across the valley of the two rivers where the grey bridge leaps the joining waters; and they would fare swiftly as clad in dreams, spangled with gems like to the grey dews amid the grass, and their white robes caught the long radiance of the Moon . . . . . . . . . . . . . and their spears shivered with silver flames.

And now sorrow and . . . . . has come upon the Elves, empty is Tavrobel and all are fled, [?fearing] the enemy that sitteth on the ruined heath, who is not a league away; whose hands are red with the blood of Elves and stained with the lives of his own kin, who has made himself an ally to Melko and the Lord of Hate, who has fought for the Orcs and Gongs and the unwholesome monsters of the world – blind, and a fool, and destruction alone is his knowledge. The paths of the fairies he has made to dusty roads where thirst [?lags wearily] and no man greeteth another in the way, but passes by in sullenness.

So fade the Elves and it shall come to be that because of the encompassing waters of this isle and yet more because of their unquenchable love for it that few shall flee, but as men wax there and grow fat and yet more blind ever shall they fade more and grow less; and those of the after days shall scoff, saying Who are the fairies – lies told to the children by women or foolish men – who are these fairies? And some few shall answer: Memories faded dim, a wraith of vanishing loveliness in the trees, a rustle of the grass, a glint of dew, some subtle intonation of the wind; and others yet fewer shall say . . . . . 'Very small and delicate are the fairies now, yet we have eyes to see and ears to hear, and Tavrobel and Kortirion are filled yet with [?this] sweet folk. Spring knows them and Summer too and in Winter still are they among us, but in Autumn most of all do they come out, for Autumn is their season, fallen as they are upon the Autumn of their days. What shall the dreamers of the earth be like when their winter come.

Hark O my brothers, they shall say, the little trumpets blow; we hear a sound of instruments unimagined small. Like strands of wind, like mystic half-transparencies, Gilfanon Lord of Tavrobel rides out tonight amid his folk, and hunts the elfin deer beneath the paling sky. A music of forgotten feet, a gleam of leaves, a sudden bending of the grass,[11] and wistful voices murmuring on the bridge, and they are gone.

But behold, Tavrobel shall not know its name, and all the land be changed, and even these written words of mine belike will all be lost; and so I lay down the pen, and so of the fairies cease to tell.

Another text that bears on these matters is the prose preface to *Kortirion among the Trees* (1915), which has been given in Part I 25–6, but which I repeat here:

**(9)**   Now on a time the fairies dwelt in the Lonely Isle after the great wars with Melko and the ruin of Gondolin; and they builded a fair city amidmost of that island, and it was girt with trees. Now this city they called Kortirion, both in memory of their ancient dwelling of Kôr in Valinor, and because this city stood also upon a hill and had a great tower tall and grey that Ingil son of Inwë their lord let raise.

Very beautiful was Kortirion and the fairies loved it, and it became rich in song and poesy and the light of laughter; but on a time the great Faring Forth was made, and the fairies had rekindled once more the Magic Sun of Valinor but for the treason and faint hearts of Men. But so it is that the Magic Sun is dead and the Lonely Isle drawn back unto the confines of the Great Lands, and the fairies are scattered through all the wide unfriendly pathways of the world; and now Men dwell even on this faded isle, and care nought or know nought of its ancient days. Yet still there be some of the Eldar and the Noldoli of old who linger in the island, and their songs are heard about the shores of the land that once was the fairest dwelling of the immortal folk.

And it seems to the fairies and it seems to me who know that town and have often trodden its disfigured ways that autumn and the falling of the leaf is the season of the year when maybe here or there a heart among Men may be open, and an eye perceive how is the world's estate fallen from the laughter and the loveliness of old. Think on Kortirion and be sad – yet is there not hope?

★

At this point we may turn to the history of Eriol himself. My father's early conceptions of the mariner who came to Tol Eressëa are here again no more than allusive outlines in the pages of the little notebook C, and some of this material cannot be usefully reproduced. Perhaps the earliest is a collection of notes headed 'Story of Eriol's Life', which I gave in Vol.

I.23–4 but with the omission of some features that were not there relevant. I repeat it here, with the addition of the statements previously omitted.

**(10)**   Eriol's original name was Ottor, but he called himself *Wǽfre* (Old English: 'restless, wandering') and lived a life on the waters. His father was named Eoh (Old English: 'horse'); and Eoh was slain by his brother Beorn, either 'in the siege' or 'in a great battle'. Ottor Wǽfre settled on the island of Heligoland in the North Sea, and wedded a woman named Cwén; they had two sons named Hengest and Horsa 'to avenge Eoh'.

Then sea-longing gripped Ottor Wǽfre (he was 'a son of Eärendel', born under his beam), and after the death of Cwén he left his young children. Hengest and Horsa avenged Eoh and became great chieftains; but Ottor Wǽfre set out to seek, and find, Tol Eressëa (*se uncúpa holm*, 'the unknown island').

In Tol Eressëa he wedded, being made young by *limpë* (here also called by the Old English word *líp*), Naimi (Éadgifu), niece of Vairë, and they had a son named Heorrenda.

It is then said, somewhat inconsequentially (though the matter is in itself of much interest, and recurs nowhere else), that Eriol told the fairies of *Wóden, Þunor, Tíw*, etc. (these being the Old English names of the Germanic gods who in Old Scandinavian form are *Óðinn, Þórr, Týr*), and they identified them with Manweg, Tulkas, and a third whose name is illegible but is not like that of any of the great Valar. Eriol adopted the name of *Angol*.

Thus it is that through Eriol and his sons the *Engle* (i.e. the English) have the true tradition of the fairies, of whom the *Íras* and the *Wéalas* (the Irish and Welsh) tell garbled things.

Thus a specifically English fairy-lore is born, and one more true than anything to be found in Celtic lands.

The wedding of Eriol in Tol Eressëa is never referred to elsewhere; but his son Heorrenda is mentioned (though not called Eriol's son) in the initial link to *The Fall of Gondolin* (p. 145) as one who 'afterwards' turned a song of Meril's maidens into the language of his people. A little more light will be shed on Heorrenda in the course of this chapter.

Associated with these notes is a title-page and a prologue that breaks off after a few lines:

**(11)**                        The Golden Book of Heorrenda
                        being the book of the
                        Tales of Tavrobel

                        ————————

                        Heorrenda of Hægwudu

This book have I written using those writings that my father
Wǽfre (whom the Gnomes named after the regions of his home
Angol) did make in his sojourn in the holy isle in the days of the
Elves; and much else have I added of those things which his eyes
saw not afterward; yet are such things not yet to tell.

For know

Here then the Golden Book was compiled from Eriol's writings by his
son Heorrenda – in contrast to (5), where it was compiled by someone
unnamed, and in contrast also to the *Epilogue* (8), where Eriol himself
concluded and 'sealed the book'.

As I have said earlier (I.24) *Angol* refers to the ancient homeland
of the 'English' before their migration across the North Sea (for the
etymology of *Angol*/*Eriol* 'ironcliffs' see I.24,252).

(12)    There is also a genealogical table accompanying the outline (10)
and altogether agreeing with it. The table is written out in two forms that
are identical save in one point: for Beorn, brother of Eoh, in the one,
there stands in the other *Hasen of Isenóra* (Old English: 'iron shore').
But at the end of the table is introduced the cardinal fact of all these
earliest materials concerning Eriol and Tol Eressëa: Hengest and Horsa,
Eriol's sons by Cwén in Heligoland, and Heorrenda, his son by Naimi in
Tol Eressëa, are bracketed together, and beneath their names is written:

conquered Íeg
('seo unwemmede Íeg')
now called Englaland
and there dwell the Angolcynn or Engle.

*Íeg* is Old English, 'isle'; *seo unwemmede Íeg* 'the unstained isle'. I
have mentioned before (I.25, footnote) a poem of my father's written at
Étaples in June 1916 and called 'The Lonely Isle', addressed to England:
this poem bears the Old English title *seo Unwemmede Íeg*.

(13)    There follow in the notebook C some jottings that make precise
identifications of places in Tol Eressëa with places in England.
First the name *Kortirion* is explained. The element *Kôr* is derived
from an earlier *Qorǎ*, yet earlier *Guorǎ*; but from *Guorǎ* was also
derived (i.e. in Gnomish) the form *Gwâr*. (This formulation agrees with
that in the Gnomish dictionary, see I.257). Thus *Kôr* = *Gwâr*,
and *Kortirion* = *\*Gwarmindon* (the asterisk implying a hypothetical,
unrecorded form). The name that was actually used in Gnomish had the
elements reversed, *Mindon-Gwar*. (*Mindon*, like *Tirion*, meant, and
continued always to mean, 'tower'. The meaning of *Kôr*/*Gwâr* is not
given here, but both in the tale of *The Coming of the Elves* (I.122) and
in the Gnomish dictionary (I.257) the name is explained as referring to
the *roundness* of the hill of Kôr.)

The note continues (using Old English forms): 'In Wíelisc *Caergwâr*, in Englisc *Warwíc*.' Thus the element *War-* in *Warwick* is derived from the same Elvish source as *Kor-* in *Kortirion* and *Gwar* in *Mindon-Gwar*.[12] Lastly, it is said that 'Hengest's capital was Warwick'.

Next, Horsa (Hengest's brother) is associated with *Oxenaford* (Old English: Oxford), which is given the equivalents Q[enya] *Taruktarna* and Gnomish *Taruithorn (see the Appendix on Names, p. 347).

The third of Eriol's sons, Heorrenda, is said to have had his 'capital' at Great Haywood (the Staffordshire village where my parents lived in 1916–17, see I. 25); and this is given the Qenya equivalents *Tavaros(së)* and *Taurossë*, and the Gnomish *Tavrobel* and *Tavrost*; also 'Englisc [i.e. Old English] *Hægwudu se gréata, Gréata Hægwudu*'.[13]

These notes conclude with the statement that 'Heorrenda called Kôr or Gwâr "Tûn".' In the context of these conceptions, this is obviously the Old English word *tûn*, an enclosed dwelling, from which has developed the modern word *town* and the place-name ending *-ton*. *Tûn* has appeared several times in the *Lost Tales* as a later correction, or alternative to *Kôr*, changes no doubt dating from or anticipating the later situation where the city was *Tûn* and the name *Kôr* was restricted to the hill on which it stood. Later still *Tûn* became *Túna*, and then when the city of the Elves was named *Tirion* the hill became *Túna*, as it is in *The Silmarillion*; by then it had ceased to have any connotation of 'dwelling-place' and had cut free from all connection with its actual origin, as we see it here, in Old English *tûn*, Heorrenda's 'town'.

Can all these materials be brought together to form a coherent narrative? I believe that they can (granting that there are certain irreconcilable differences concerning Eriol's life), and would reconstruct it thus:

- The Eldar and the rescued Noldoli departed from the Great Lands and came to Tol Eressëa.

- In Tol Eressëa they built many towns and villages, and in Alalminórë, the central region of the island, Ingil son of Inwë built the town of Koromas, 'the Resting of the Exiles of Kôr' ('Exiles', because they could not return to Valinor); and the great tower of Ingil gave the town its name *Kortirion*. (See I. 16.)

- Ottor Wǽfre came from Heligoland to Tol Eressëa and dwelt in the Cottage of Lost Play in Kortirion; the Elves named him *Eriol* or *Angol* after the 'iron cliffs' of his home.

- After a time, and greatly instructed in the ancient history of Gods, Elves, and Men, Eriol went to visit Gilfanon in the village of Tavrobel, and there he wrote down what he had learnt; there also he at last drank *limpë*.

- In Tol Eressëa Eriol was wedded and had a son named Heorrenda (Half-elven!). (According to (5) Eriol died at Tavrobel, consumed with longing for 'the black cliffs of his shores'; but according to (8), certainly later, he lived to see the Battle of the Heath of the Sky-roof.)

- The Lost Elves of the Great Lands rose against the dominion of the servants of Melko; and the untimely Faring Forth took place, at which time Tol Eressëa was drawn east back across the Ocean and anchored off the coasts of the Great Lands. The western half broke off when Ossë tried to drag the island back, and it became the Isle of Íverin (= Ireland).

- Tol Eressëa was now in the geographical position of England.

- The great battle of Rôs ended in the defeat of the Elves, who retreated into hiding in Tol Eressëa.

- Evil men entered Tol Eressëa, accompanied by Orcs and other hostile beings.

- The Battle of the Heath of the Sky-roof took place not far from Tavrobel, and (according to (8)) was witnessed by Eriol, who completed the Golden Book.

- The Elves faded and became invisible to the eyes of almost all Men.

- The sons of Eriol, Hengest, Horsa, and Heorrenda, conquered the island and it became 'England'. They were not hostile to the Elves, and from them the English have 'the true tradition of the fairies'.

- Kortirion, ancient dwelling of the fairies, came to be known in the tongue of the English as Warwick; Hengest dwelt there, while Horsa dwelt at Taruithorn (Oxford) and Heorrenda at Tavrobel (Great Haywood). (According to (11) Heorrenda completed the Golden Book.)

This reconstruction may not be 'correct' in all its parts: indeed, it may be that any such attempt is artificial, treating all the notes and jottings as of equal weight and all the ideas as strictly contemporaneous and relatable to each other. Nonetheless I believe that it shows rightly in essentials how my father was thinking of ordering the narrative in which the *Lost Tales* were to be set; and I believe also that this was the conception that still underlay the *Tales* as they are extant and have been given in these books.

For convenience later I shall refer to this narrative as 'the *Eriol* story'. Its most remarkable features, in contrast to the later story, are the transformation of Tol Eressëa into England, and the early appearance of the mariner (in relation to the whole history) and his importance.

In fact, my father was exploring (before he decided on a radical transformation of the whole conception) ideas whereby his importance would be greatly increased.

**(14)**   From very rough jottings it can be made out that Eriol was to be so tormented with home longing that he set sail from Tol Eressëa with his son Heorrenda, against the command of Meril-i-Turinqi (see the passage cited on p. 284 from *The Chaining of Melko*); but his purpose in doing so was also 'to hasten the Faring Forth', which he 'preached' in the lands of the East. Tol Eressëa was drawn back to the confines of the Great Lands, but at once hostile peoples named the *Guiðlin* and the *Brithonin* (and in one of these notes also the *Rúmhoth*, Romans) invaded the island. Eriol died, but his sons Hengest and Horsa conquered the Guiðlin. But because of Eriol's disobedience to the command of Meril, in going back before the time for the Faring Forth was ripe, 'all was cursed'; and the Elves faded before the noise and evil of war. An isolated sentence refers to 'a strange prophecy that a man of good will, yet through longing after the things of Men, may bring the Faring Forth to nought'.

Thus the part of Eriol was to become cardinal in the history of the Elves; but there is no sign that these ideas ever got beyond this exploratory stage.

★

I have said that I think that the reconstruction given above ('the *Eriol* story') is in essentials the conception underlying the framework of the *Lost Tales*. This is both for positive and negative reasons: positive, because he is there still named *Eriol* (see p. 300), and also because Gilfanon, who enters (replacing Ailios) late in the development of the *Tales*, appears also in citation (5) above, which is one of the main contributors to this reconstruction; negative, because there is really nothing to contradict what is much the easiest assumption. There is no explicit statement anywhere in the *Lost Tales* that Eriol came from England. At the beginning (I.13) he is only 'a traveller from far countries'; and the fact that the story he told to Vëannë of his earlier life (pp. 4–7) agrees well with other accounts where his home is explicitly in England does no more than show that the story remained while the geography altered — just as the 'black coasts' of his home survived in later writing to become the western coasts of Britain, whereas the earliest reference to them is the etymology of *Angol* 'iron cliffs' (his own name, = *Eriol*, from the land 'between the seas', Angeln in the Danish peninsula, whence he came: see I.252). There is in fact a very early, rejected, sketch of Eriol's life in which essential features of the same story are outlined — the attack on his father's dwelling (in this case the destruction of Eoh's castle by his brother Beorn, see citation (10)), Eriol's captivity and escape — and in this note it is said that Eriol afterwards 'wandered over the wilds of the Central Lands to the Inland Sea, *Wendelsæ* [Old English, the Mediterranean], and hence to the shores of the Western Sea', whence his father had originally come. The mention in the typescript text of the *Link* to the *Tale of Tinúviel* (p. 6) of wild men out of the Mountains of the East, *which the duke could see from his tower*, seems likewise to imply that at this time Eriol's original home was placed in some 'continental' region.

The only suggestion, so far as I can see, that this view might not be correct is found in an early poem with a complex history, texts of which I give here.

The earliest rough drafts of this poem are extant; the original title was 'The Wanderer's Allegiance', and it is not clear that it was at first conceived as a poem in three parts. My father subsequently wrote in subtitles on these drafts, dividing the poem into three: *Prelude*, *The Inland City*, and *The Sorrowful City*, with (apparently) an overall title *The Sorrowful City*; and added a date, March 16–18, 1916. In the only later copy of the whole poem that is extant the overall title is *The Town of Dreams and the City of Present Sorrow*, with the three parts titled: *Prelude* (Old English *Foresang*), *The Town of Dreams* (Old English *Þæt Slæpende Tún*), and *The City of Present Sorrow* (Old English *Seo Wépende Burg*). This text gives the dates 'March 1916, Oxford and Warwick; rewritten Birmingham November 1916'. 'The Town of Dreams' is Warwick, on the River Avon, and 'The City of Present Sorrow' is Oxford, on the Thames, during the First War; there is no evident association of any kind with Eriol or the *Lost Tales*.


### Prelude

In unknown days my fathers' sires
Came, and from son to son took root
Among the orchards and the river-meads
And the long grasses of the fragrant plain:
Many a summer saw they kindle yellow fires
Of iris in the bowing reeds,
And many a sea of blossom turn to golden fruit
In wallèd gardens of the great champain.

★

There daffodils among the ordered trees
Did nod in spring, and men laughed deep and long
Singing as they laboured happy lays
And lighting even with a drinking-song.
There sleep came easy for the drone of bees
Thronging about cottage gardens heaped with flowers;
In love of sunlit goodliness of days
There richly flowed their lives in settled hours –
But that was long ago,

And now no more they sing, nor reap, nor sow,
And I perforce in many a town about this isle
Unsettled wanderer have dwelt awhile.

### The Town of Dreams

Here many days once gently past me crept
In this dear town of old forgetfulness;
Here all entwined in dreams once long I slept
And heard no echo of the world's distress
Come through the rustle of the elms' rich leaves,
While Avon gurgling over shallows wove
Unending melody, and morns and eves
Slipped down her waters till the Autumn came,
(Like the gold leaves that drip and flutter then,
Till the dark river gleams with jets of flame
That slowly float far down beyond our ken.)

For here the castle and the mighty tower,
More lofty than the tiered elms,
More grey than long November rain,
Sleep, and nor sunlit moment nor triumphal hour,
Nor passing of the seasons or the Sun
Wakes their old lords too long in slumber lain.

No watchfulness disturbs their splendid dream,
Though laughing radiance dance down the stream;
And be they clad in snow or lashed by windy rains,
Or may March whirl the dust about the winding lanes,
The Elm robe and disrobe her of a million leaves
Like moments clustered in a crowded year,
Still their old heart unmoved nor weeps nor grieves,
Uncomprehending of this evil tide,
Today's great sadness, or Tomorrow's fear:
Faint echoes fade within their drowsy halls
Like ghosts; the daylight creeps across their walls.

### *The City of Present Sorrow*

There is a city that far distant lies
And a vale outcarven in forgotten days –
There wider was the grass, and lofty elms more rare;
The river-sense was heavy in the lowland air.
There many willows changed the aspect of the earth and skies
Where feeding brooks wound in by sluggish ways,
And down the margin of the sailing Thames
Around his broad old bosom their old stems
Were bowed, and subtle shades lay on his streams
Where their grey leaves adroop o'er silver pools
Did knit a coverlet like shimmering jewels
Of blue and misty green and filtering gleams.

★

O agéd city of an all too brief sojourn,
I see thy clustered windows each one burn
With lamps and candles of departed men.
The misty stars thy crown, the night thy dress,
Most peerless-magical thou dost possess
My heart, and old days come to life again;
Old mornings dawn, or darkened evenings bring
The same old twilight noises from the town.
Thou hast the very core of longing and delight,
To thee my spirit dances oft in sleep
Along thy great grey streets, or down
A little lamplit alley-way at night –
Thinking no more of other cities it has known,
Forgetting for a while the tree-girt keep,
And town of dreams, where men no longer sing.
For thy heart knows, and thou shedst many tears
For all the sorrow of these evil years.
Thy thousand pinnacles and fretted spires
Are lit with echoes and the lambent fires
Of many companies of bells that ring
Rousing pale visions of majestic days
The windy years have strewn down distant ways;
And in thy halls still doth thy spirit sing
Songs of old memory amid thy present tears,
Or hope of days to come half-sad with many fears.
Lo! though along thy paths no laughter runs
While war untimely takes thy many sons,
No tide of evil can thy glory drown
Robed in sad majesty, the stars thy crown.

★

In addition, there are two texts in which a part of *The City of Present Sorrow* is treated as a separate entity. This begins with 'O agéd city of an all too brief sojourn', and is briefer: after the line 'Thinking no more of other cities it has known' it ends:

> Forgetting for a while that all men weep
> It strays there happy and to thee it sings
> 'No tide of evil can thy glory drown,
> Robed in sad majesty, the stars thy crown!'

This was first called *The Sorrowful City*, but the title was then changed to *Wínsele wéste, windge reste réte berofene* (*Beowulf* lines 2456–7, very slightly adapted: 'the hall of feasting empty, the resting places swept by the wind, robbed of laughter').

There are also two manuscripts in which *The Town of Dreams* is treated as a separate poem, with a subtitle *An old town revisited*; in one of these the primary title was later changed to *The Town of Dead Days*.

Lastly, there is a poem in two parts called *The Song of Eriol*. This is found in three manuscripts, the later ones incorporating minor changes made to the predecessor (but the third has only the second part of the poem).

### The Song of Eriol

Eriol made a song in the Room of the Tale-fire telling how his feet were set to wandering, so that in the end he found the Lonely Isle and that fairest town Kortirion.

I

> In unknown days my fathers' sires
> Came, and from son to son took root
> Among the orchards and the river-meads
> And the long grasses of the fragrant plain:
>
> Many a summer saw they kindle yellow fires
> Of flaglilies among the bowing reeds,
> And many a sea of blossom turn to golden fruit
> In walléd gardens of the great champain.
>
> There daffodils among the ordered trees
> Did nod in spring, and men laughed deep and long
> Singing as they laboured happy lays
> And lighting even with a drinking-song.

There sleep came easy for the drone of bees
Thronging about cottage gardens heaped with flowers;
In love of sunlit goodliness of days
There richly flowed their lives in settled hours –
       But that was long ago,
     And now no more they sing, nor reap, nor sow;
     And I perforce in many a town about this isle
     Unsettled wanderer have dwelt awhile.


                          2

Wars of great kings and clash of armouries,
Whose swords no man could tell, whose spears
Were numerous as a wheatfield's ears,
Rolled over all the Great Lands; and the Seas

Were loud with navies; their devouring fires
Behind the armies burned both fields and towns;
And sacked and crumbled or to flaming pyres
Were cities made, where treasuries and crowns,

Kings and their folk, their wives and tender maids
Were all consumed. Now silent are those courts,
Ruined the towers, whose old shape slowly fades,
And no feet pass beneath their broken ports.

                          ★


There fell my father on a field of blood,
And in a hungry siege my mother died,
And I, a captive, heard the great seas' flood
Calling and calling, that my spirit cried

For the dark western shores whence long ago had come
Sires of my mother, and I broke my bonds,
Faring o'er wasted valleys and dead lands
Until my feet were moistened by the western sea,
Until my ears were deafened by the hum,
The splash, and roaring of the western sea –
       But that was long ago
     And now the dark bays and unknown waves I know,
     The twilight capes, the misty archipelago,
     And all the perilous sounds and salt wastes 'tween this isle
     Of magic and the coasts I knew awhile.

                          ★

One of the manuscripts of *The Song of Eriol* bears a later note: 'Easington 1917–18' (Easington on the estuary of the Humber, see Humphrey Carpenter, *Biography*, p. 97). It may be that the second part of *The Song of Eriol* was written at Easington and added to the first part (formerly the *Prelude*) already in existence.

Little can be derived from this poem of a strictly narrative nature, save the lineaments of the same tale: Eriol's father fell 'on a field of blood', when 'wars of great kings . . . rolled over all the Great Lands', and his mother died 'in a hungry siege' (the same phrase is used in the *Link* to the *Tale of Tinúviel*, pp. 5–6); he himself was made a captive, but escaped, and came at last to the shores of the Western Sea (whence his mother's people had come).

The fact that the first part of *The Song of Eriol* is also found as the Prelude to a poem of which the subjects are Warwick and Oxford might make one suspect that the castle with a great tower overhanging a river in the story told by Eriol to Vëannë was once again Warwick. But I do not think that this is so. There remains in any case the objection that it would be difficult to accommodate the attack on it by men out of the Mountains of the East which the duke could see from his tower; but also I think it is plain that the original tripartite poem had been disseuered, and the *Prelude* given a new bearing: my father's 'fathers' sires' became Eriol's 'fathers' sires'. At the same time, certain powerful images were at once dominant and fluid, and the great tower of Eriol's home was indeed to become the tower of Kortirion or Warwick, when (as will be seen shortly) the structure of the story of the mariner was radically changed. And nothing could show more clearly than does the evolution of this poem the complex root from which the story rose.

Humphrey Carpenter, writing in his *Biography* of my father's life after he returned to Oxford in 1925, says (p. 169):

He made numerous revisions and recastings of the principal stories in the cycle, deciding to abandon the original sea-voyager 'Eriol' to whom the stories were told, and instead renaming him 'Ælfwine' or 'elf-friend'.

That *Eriol* was (for a time) displaced by *Ælfwine* is certain. But while it may well be that at the time of the texts now to be considered the name *Eriol* had actually been rejected, in the first version of 'The Silmarillion' proper, written in 1926, *Eriol* reappears, while in the earliest *Annals of Valinor*, written in the 1930s, it is said that they were translated in Tol Eressëa 'by Eriol of Leithien, that is Ælfwine of the Angelcynn'. On the other hand, at this earlier period it seems entirely justifiable on the evidence to treat the two names as indicative of different narrative projections – 'the *Eriol* story' and 'the *Ælfwine* story'.

'Ælfwine', then, is associated with a new conception, *subsequent to* the writing of the *Lost Tales*. The mariner is Ælfwine, not Eriol, in the second 'Scheme' for the *Tales*, which I have called 'an unrealised project for the revision of the whole work' (see I. 234). The essential difference may be made clear now, before citing the difficult evidence: *Tol Eressëa is now in no way identified with England*, and the story of the drawing back of the Lonely Island across the sea has been abandoned. England is indeed still at the heart of this later conception, and is named *Luthany*.[14] The mariner, Ælfwine, is an Englishman sailing westward from the coast of Britain; and his role is diminished. For whereas in the writings studied thus far he comes to Tol Eressëa *before* the dénouement and disaster of the Faring Forth, and either he himself or his descendants witness the devastation of Tol Eressëa by the invasion of Men and their evil allies (in one line of development he was even to be responsible for it, p. 294), in the later narrative outlines he does not arrive until all the grievous history is done. His part is only to learn and to record.[15]

I turn now to a number of short and very oblique passages, written on separate slips, but found together and clearly dating from much the same time.

(15)  Ælfwine of England dwelt in the South-west; he was of the kin of Ing, King of Luthany. His mother and father were slain by the sea-pirates and he was made captive.
    He had always loved the fairies: his father had told him many things (of the tradition of Ing). He escapes. He beats about the northern and western waters. He meets the Ancient Mariner – and seeks for Tol Eressëa (*seo unwemmede íeg*), whither most of the unfaded Elves have retired from the noise, war, and clamour of Men.
    The Elves greet him, and the more so when they learn of him who he is. They call him *Lúthien* the man of Luthany. He finds his own tongue, the ancient English tongue, is spoken in the isle.

The 'Ancient Mariner' has appeared in the story that Eriol told to Vëannë (pp. 5, 7), and much more will be told of him subsequently.

(16)  Ælfwine of Englaland, [*added later*: driven by the Normans,] arrives in Tol Eressëa, whither most of the fading Elves have withdrawn from the world, and there fade now no more.
    Description of the harbour of the southern shore. The fairies greet him well hearing he is from Englaland. He is surprised to hear them speak the speech of Ælfred of Wessex, though to one another they spoke a sweet and unknown tongue.
    The Elves name him Lúthien for he is come from Luthany, as they call it ('friend' and 'friendship'). Eldaros or Ælfhâm. He is

sped to Rôs their capital. There he finds the Cottage of Lost Play, and Lindo and Vairë.

He tells who he is and whence, and why he has long sought for the isle (by reason of traditions in the kin of Ing), and he begs the Elves to come back to Englaland.

Here begins (as an explanation of why they cannot) the series of stories called the Book of Lost Tales.

In this passage (16) Ælfwine becomes more firmly rooted in English history: he is apparently a man of eleventh-century Wessex – but as in (15) he is of 'the kin of Ing'. The capital of the Elves of Tol Eressëa is not Kortirion but Rôs, a name now used in a quite different application from that in citation (5), where it was a promontory of the Great Lands.

I have been unable to find any trace of the process whereby the name *Lúthien* came to be so differently applied afterwards (*Lúthien Tinúviel*). Another note of this period explains the name quite otherwise: 'Lúthien or Lúsion was son of Telumaith (Telumektar). Ælfwine loved the sign of Orion, and made the sign, hence the fairies called him Lúthien (Wanderer).' There is no other mention of Ælfwine's peculiar association with Orion nor of this interpretation of the name Lúthien; and this seems to be a development that my father did not pursue.

It is convenient to give here the opening passage from the second Scheme for the *Lost Tales*, referred to above; this plainly belongs to the same time as the rest of these 'Ælfwine'.notes, when the *Tales* had been written so far as they ever went within their first framework.

(17)    Ælfwine awakens upon a sandy beach. He listens to the sea, which is far out. The tide is low and has left him.

Ælfwine meets the Elves of Rôs; finds they speak the speech of the English, beside their own sweet tongue. Why they do so – the dwelling of Elves in Luthany and their faring thence and back. They clothe him and feed him, and he sets forth to walk along the island's flowery ways.

The scheme goes on to say that on a summer evening Ælfwine came to Kortirion, and thus differs from (16), where he goes to 'Rôs their capital', in which he finds the Cottage of Lost Play. The name Rôs seems to be used here in yet another sense – possibly a name for Tol Eressëa.

(18)    He is sped to Ælfhâm (Elfhome) Eldos where Lindo and Vairë tell him many things: of the making and ancient fashion of the world: of the Gods: of the Elves of Valinor: of Lost Elves and Men: of the Travail of the Gnomes: of Eärendel: of the Faring Forth and the Loss of Valinor: of the disaster of the Faring Forth and the war with evil Men. The retreat to Luthany where Ingwë was king.

Of the home-thirst of the Elves and how the greater number sought back to Valinor. The loss of Elwing. How a new home was made by the Solosimpi and others in Tol Eressëa. How the Elves continually sadly leave the world and fare thither.

For the interpretation of this passage it is essential to realise (the key indeed to the understanding of this projected history) that 'the Faring Forth' does *not* here refer to the Faring Forth in the sense in which it has been used hitherto – that from Tol Eressëa for the Rekindling of the Magic Sun, which ended in ruin, but to the March of the Elves of Kôr and the 'Loss of Valinor' that the March incurred (see pp. 253, 257, 280). It is not indeed clear why it is here called a 'disaster': but this is evidently to be associated with 'the war with evil Men', and war between Elves and Men at the time of the March from Kôr is referred to in citations (1) and (3).

In 'the *Eriol* story' it is explicit that after the March from Kôr the Elves departed from the Great Lands to Tol Eressëa; here on the other hand 'the war with evil Men' is followed by 'the retreat to Luthany where Ingwë was king'. The (partial) departure to Tol Eressëa is from Luthany; the loss of Elwing seems to take place on one of these voyages. As will be seen, the 'Faring Forth' of 'the *Eriol* story' has disappeared as an event of Elvish history, and is only mentioned as a prophecy and a hope.

Schematically the essential divergence of the two narrative structures can be shown thus:

| (*Eriol* story) | (*Ælfwine* story) |
|---|---|
| March of the Elves of Kôr to the Great Lands | March of the Elves of Kôr to the Great Lands (called 'the Faring Forth') |
| War with Men in the Great Lands | War with Men in the Great Lands |
| Retreat of the Elves to Tol Eressëa (loss of Elwing) | Retreat of the Elves to Luthany (> England) ruled by Ingwë |
| | Departure of many Elves to Tol Eressëa (loss of Elwing) |
| Eriol sails from the East (North Sea region) to Tol Eressëa | Ælfwine sails from England to Tol Eressëa |
| The Faring Forth, drawing of Tol Eressëa to the Great Lands; ultimately Tol Eressëa > England | |

This is of course by no means a full statement of the *Ælfwine* story, and is merely set out to indicate the radical difference of structure. Lacking from it is the history of Luthany, which emerges from the passages that now follow.

**(19)** *Luthany* means 'friendship', *Lúthien* 'friend'. Luthany the only land where Men and Elves once dwelt an age in peace and love.

How for a while after the coming of the sons of Ing the Elves throve again and ceased to fare away to Tol Eressëa.

How Old English became the sole mortal language which an Elf will speak to a mortal that knows no Elfin.

**(20)** Ælfwine of England (whose father and mother were slain by the fierce Men of the Sea who knew not the Elves) was a great lover of the Elves, especially of the shoreland Elves that lingered in the land. He seeks for Tol Eressëa whither the fairies are said to have retired.

He reaches it. The fairies call him Lúthien. He learns of the making of the world, . . . . . . . of Gods and Elves, of Elves and Men, down to the departure to Tol Eressëa.

How the Faring Forth came to nought, and the fairies took refuge in Albion or Luthany (the Isle of Friendship).

Seven invasions.

Of the coming of Men to Luthany, how each race quarrelled, and the fairies faded, until [?the most] set sail, after the coming of the Rúmhoth, for the West. Why the Men of the seventh invasion, the Ingwaiwar, are more friendly.

Ingwë and Eärendel who dwelt in Luthany before it was an isle and was [*sic*] driven east by Ossë to found the Ingwaiwar.

**(21)** All the descendants of Ing were well disposed to Elves; hence the remaining Elves of Luthany spoke to [?them] in the ancient tongue of the English, and since some have fared . . . . . to Tol Eressëa that tongue is there understood, and all who wish to speak to the Elves, if they know not and have no means of learning Elfin speeches, must converse in the ancient tongue of the English.

In (20) the term 'Faring Forth' must again be used as it is in (18), of the March from Kôr. There it was called a 'disaster' (see p. 303), and here it is said that it 'came to nought': it must be admitted that it is hard to see how that can be said, if it led to the binding of Melko and the release of the enslaved Noldoli (see (1) and (3)).

Also in (20) is the first appearance of the idea of the Seven Invasions of Luthany. One of these was that of the Rúmhoth (mentioned also in (14)) or Romans; and the seventh was that of the Ingwaiwar, who were not hostile to the Elves.

Here something must be said of the name *Ing* (*Ingwë*, *Ingwaiar*) in these passages. As with the introduction of Hengest and Horsa, the association of the mythology with ancient English legend is manifest. But it would serve no purpose, I believe, to enter here into the obscure and speculative scholarship of English and Scandinavian origins: the

Roman writers' term *Inguaeones* for the Baltic maritime peoples from whom the English came; the name *Ingwine* (interpretable either as *Ing-wine* 'the friends of Ing' or as containing the same *Ingw-* seen in *Inguaeones*); or the mysterious personage *Ing* who appears in the Old English *Runic Poem*:

> Ing wæs ærest   mid East-Denum
> gesewen secgum   oþ he siþþan east
> ofer wæg gewat;   wæn æfter ran

– which may be translated: 'Ing was first seen by men among the East Danes, until he departed eastwards over the waves; his car sped after him.' It would serve no purpose, because although the connection of my father's *Ing*, *Ingwë* with the shadowy *Ing* (*Ingw-*) of northern historical legend is certain and indeed obvious he seems to have been intending no more than an *association* of his mythology with known traditions (though the words of the *Runic Poem* were clearly influential). The matter is made particularly obscure by the fact that in these notes the names *Ing* and *Ingwë* intertwine with each other, but are never expressly differentiated or identified.

Thus Ælfwine was 'of the kin of Ing, King of Luthany' (15, 16), but the Elves retreated 'to Luthany where Ingwë was king' (18). The Elves of Luthany throve again 'after the coming of the sons of Ing' (19), and the Ingwaiwar, seventh of the invaders of Luthany, were more friendly to the Elves (20), while Ingwë 'founded' the Ingwaiwar (20). This name is certainly to be equated with Inguaeones (see above), and the invasion of the Ingwaiwar (or 'sons of Ing') equally certainly represents the 'Anglo-Saxon' invasion of Britain. Can *Ing*, *Ingwë* be equated? So far as this present material is concerned, I hardly see how they can not be. Whether this ancestor-founder is to be equated with *Inwë* (whose son was *Ingil*) of the *Lost Tales* is another question. It is hard to believe that there is no connection (especially since *Inwë* in *The Cottage of Lost Play* is emended from *Ing*, I.22), yet it is equally difficult to see what that connection could be, since Inwë of the *Lost Tales* is an Elda of Kôr (Ingwë Lord of the Vanyar in *The Silmarillion*) while Ing(wë) of 'the *Ælfwine* story' is a Man, the King of Luthany and Ælfwine's ancestor. (In outlines for *Gilfanon's Tale* it is said that Ing King of Luthany was descended from Ermon, or from Ermon and Elmir (the first Men, I.236–7).)

The following outlines tell some more concerning Ing(wë) and the Ingwaiwar:

(22)   How Ing sailed away at eld [i.e. in old age] into the twilight, and Men say he came to the Gods, but he dwells on Tol Eressëa, and will guide the fairies one day back to Luthany when the Faring Forth takes place.*

* The term 'Faring Forth' is used here in a prophetic sense, not as it is in (18) and (20).

How he prophesied that his kin should fare back again and possess Luthany until the days of the coming of the Elves.

How the land of Luthany was seven times invaded by Men, until at the seventh the children of the children of Ing came back to their own.

How at each new war and invasion the Elves faded, and each loved the Elves less, until the Rúmhoth came – and they did not even believe they existed, and the Elves all fled, so that save for a few the isle was empty of the Elves for three hundred years.

**(23)**  How Ingwë drank *limpë* at the hands of the Elves and reigned ages in Luthany.

How Eärendel came to Luthany to find the Elves gone.

How Ingwë aided him, but was not suffered to go with him. Eärendel blessed all his progeny as the mightiest sea-rovers of the world.[16]

How Ossë made war upon Ingwë because of Eärendel, and Ing longing for the Elves set sail, and all were wrecked after being driven far east.

How Ing the immortal came among the Dani OroDáni Urdainoth East Danes.

How he became the half-divine king of the Ingwaiwar, and taught them many things of Elves and Gods, so that some true knowledge of the Gods and Elves lingered in that folk alone.

Part of another outline that does not belong with the foregoing passages but covers the same part of the narrative as (23) may be given here:

**(24)**  Eärendel takes refuge with [Ingwë] from the wrath of Ossë, and gives him a draught of *limpë* (enough to assure immortality). He gives him news of the Elves and the dwelling on Tol Eressëa.

Ingwë and a host of his folk set sail to find Tol Eressëa, but Ossë blows them back east. They are utterly wrecked. Only Ingwë rescued on a raft. He becomes king of the Angali, Euti, Saksani, and Firisandi,* who adopt the title of Ingwaiwar. He teaches them much magic and first sets men's hearts to seafaring westward. . . . . .

After a great [?age of rule] Ingwë sets sail in a little boat and is heard of no more.

It is clear that the intrusion of Luthany, and Ing(wë), into the conception has caused a movement in the story of Eärendel: whereas in the older version he went to Tol Eressëa after the departure of the Eldar and Noldoli from the Great Lands (pp. 253, 255), now he goes to

---

* Angles, Saxons, Jutes, and Frisians.

Luthany; and the idea of Ossë's enmity towards Eärendel (pp. 254, 263) is retained but brought into association with the origin of the Ingwaiwar.
   It is clear that the narrative structure is:

- Ing(wë) King of Luthany.
- Eärendel seeks refuge with him (after [many of] the Elves have departed to Tol Eressëa).
- Ing(wë) seeks Tol Eressëa but is driven into the East.
- Seven invasions of Luthany.
- The people of Ing(wë) are the Ingwaiwar, and they 'come back to their own' when they invade Luthany from across the North Sea.

(25)   Luthany was where the tribes first embarked in the Lonely Isle for Valinor, and whence they landed for the Faring Forth,* whence [also] many sailed with Elwing to find Tol Eressëa.

That Luthany was where the Elves, at the end of the great journey from Palisor, embarked on the Lonely Isle for the Ferrying to Valinor, is probably to be connected with the statement in (20) that 'Ingwë and Eärendel dwelt in Luthany before it was an isle'.

(26)   There are other references to the channel separating Luthany from the Great Lands: in rough jottings in notebook C there is mention of an isthmus being cut by the Elves, 'fearing Men now that Ingwë has gone', and 'to the white cliffs where the silver spades of the Teleri worked'; also in the next citation.

(27)   The Elves tell Ælfwine of the ancient manner of Luthany, of Kortirion or Gwarthyryn (Caer Gwâr),[17] of Tavrobel.
   How the fairies dwelt there a hundred ages before Men had the skill to build boats to cross the channel – so that magic lingers yet mightily in its woods and hills.
   How they renamed many a place in Tol Eressëa after their home in Luthany. Of the Second Faring Forth and the fairies' hope to reign in Luthany and replant there the magic trees – and it depends most on the temper of the Men of Luthany (since they first must come there) whether all goes well.

Notable here is the reference to 'the Second Faring Forth', which strongly supports my interpretation of the expression 'Faring Forth' in (18), (20), and (25); but the prophecy or hope of the Elves concerning

* In the sense of the March of the Elves from Kôr, as in (18) and (20).

the Faring Forth has been greatly changed from its nature in citation (6):
here, the Trees are to be replanted in Luthany.

**(28)**  How Ælfwine lands in Tol Eressëa and it seems to him like his own
land made . . . . . . . clad in the beauty of a happy dream. How the
folk comprehended [his speech] and learn whence he is come by
the favour of Ulmo. How he is sped to Kortirion.

With these two passages it is interesting to compare (9), the prose preface
to *Kortirion among the Trees*, according to which Kortirion was a city
built by the Elves in Tol Eressëa; and when Tol Eressëa was brought
across the sea, becoming England, Kortirion was renamed in the tongue
of the English *Warwick* (13). In the new story, Kortirion is likewise an
ancient dwelling of the Elves, but with the change in the fundamental
conception it is in Luthany; and the Kortirion to which Ælfwine comes
in Tol Eressëa is the second of the name (being called 'after their home in
Luthany'). There has thus been a very curious transference, which may
be rendered schematically thus:

> (I)   Kortirion, Elvish dwelling in Tol Eressëa.
> Tol Eressëa ———→ England.
> Kortirion = Warwick.

> (II)  Kortirion, Elvish dwelling in Luthany (> England).
> Elves ———→ Tol Eressëa.
> Kortirion (2) in Tol Eressëa named after Kortirion (1)
> in Luthany.

On the basis of the foregoing passages, (15) to (28), we may attempt to
construct a narrative taking account of all the essential features:

–   March of the Elves of Kôr (called 'the Faring Forth', or (by implication in 27) 'the First Faring Forth') into the Great Lands, landing in
Luthany (25), and the Loss of Valinor (18).

–   War with evil Men in the Great Lands (18).

–   The Elves retreated to Luthany (not yet an island) where Ing(wë)
was king (18, 20).

–   Many [but by no means all] of the Elves of Luthany sought back west
over the sea and settled in Tol Eressëa; but Elwing was lost (18, 25).

–   Places in Tol Eressëa were named after places in Luthany (27).

–   Eärendel came to Luthany, taking refuge with Ing(wë) from the
hostility of Ossë (20, 23, 24).

–   Eärendel gave Ing(wë) *limpë* to drink (24), *or* Ing(wë) received
*limpë* from the Elves before Eärendel came (23).

- Eärendel blessed the progeny of Ing(wë) before his departure (23).
- Ossë's hostility to Eärendel pursued Ing(wë) also (23, 24).
- Ing(wë) set sail (with many of his people, 24) to find Tol Eressëa (23, 24).
- Ing(wë)'s voyage, through the enmity of Ossë, ended in shipwreck, but Ing(wë) survived, and far to the East [i.e. after being driven across the North Sea] he became King of the Ingwaiwar the ancestors of the Anglo-Saxon invaders of Britain (23, 24).
- Ing(wë) instructed the Ingwaiwar in true knowledge of the Gods and Elves (23) and turned their hearts to seafaring westwards (24). He prophesied that his kin should one day return again to Luthany (22).
- Ing(wë) at length departed in a boat (22, 24), and was heard of no more (24), or came to Tol Eressëa (22).
- After Ing(wë)'s departure from Luthany a channel was made so that Luthany became an isle (26); but Men crossed the channel in boats (27).
- Seven successive invasions took place, including that of the Rúmhoth or Romans, and at each new war more of the remaining Elves of Luthany fled over the sea (20, 22).
- The seventh invasion, that of the Ingwaiwar, was however not hostile to the Elves (20, 21); and these invaders were 'coming back to their own' (22), since they were the people of Ing(wë).
- The Elves of Luthany (now England) throve again and ceased to leave Luthany for Tol Eressëa (19), and they spoke to the Ingwaiwar in their own language, Old English (21).
- Ælfwine was an Englishman of the Anglo-Saxon period, a descendant of Ing(wë), who had derived a knowledge of and love of the Elves from the tradition of his family (15, 16).
- Ælfwine came to Tol Eressëa, found that Old English was spoken there, and was called by the Elves Lúthien 'friend', the Man of Luthany (the Isle of Friendship) (15, 16, 19).

I claim no more for this than that it seems to me to be the only way in which these *disjecta membra* can be set together into a comprehensive narrative scheme. It must be admitted even so that it requires some forcing of the evidence to secure apparent agreement. For example, there seem to be different views of the relation of the Ingwaiwar to Ing(wë): they are 'the sons of Ing' (19), 'his kin' (22), 'the children of the children of Ing' (22), yet he seems to have become the king and teacher of North Sea peoples who had no connection with Luthany or the Elves (23, 24). (Over whom did he rule when the Elves first retreated to Luthany (18, 23)?) Again, it is very difficult to fit the 'hundred ages' during which the

Elves dwelt in Luthany before the invasions of Men began (27) to the rest of the scheme. Doubtless in these jottings my father was thinking with his pen, exploring independent narrative paths; one gets the impression of a ferment of ideas and possibilities rapidly displacing one another, from which no one stable narrative core can be extracted. A complete 'solution' is therefore in all probability an unreal aim, and this reconstruction no doubt as artificial as that attempted earlier for 'the *Eriol* story' (see p. 293). But here as there I believe that this outline shows as well as can be the direction of my father's thought at that time.

There is very little to indicate the further course of 'the *Ælfwine* story' after his sojourn in Tol Eressëa (as I have remarked, p. 301, the part of the mariner is only to learn and record tales out of the past); and virtually all that can be learned from these notes is found on a slip that reads:

(29)  How Ælfwine drank of *limpë* but thirsted for his home, and went back to Luthany; and thirsted then unquenchably for the Elves, and went back to Tavrobel the Old and dwelt in the House of the Hundred Chimneys (where grows still the child of the child of the Pine of Belawryn) and wrote the Golden Book.

Associated with this is a title-page:

(30)               The Book of Lost Tales
              and the History of the Elves of Luthany
                           [?being]
              The Golden Book of Tavrobel
the same that Ælfwine wrote and laid in the House of a Hundred Chimneys at Tavrobel, where it lieth still to read for such as may.

These are very curious. Tavrobel the Old must be the original Tavrobel in Luthany (after which Tavrobel in Tol Eressëa was named, just as Kortirion in Tol Eressëa was named after Kortirion = Warwick in Luthany); and the House of the Hundred Chimneys (as also the Pine of Belawryn, on which see p. 281 and note 4) was to be displaced from Tol Eressëa to Luthany. Presumably my father intended to rewrite those passages in the 'framework' of the *Lost Tales* where the House of a Hundred Chimneys in Tavrobel is referred to; unless there was to be another House of a Hundred Chimneys in Tavrobel the New in Tol Eressëa.

Lastly, an interesting entry in the Qenya dictionary may be mentioned here: *Parma Kuluinen* 'the Golden Book – the collected book of legends, especially of Ing and Eärendel'.

★

In the event, of all these projections my father only developed the story of Ælfwine's youth and his voyage to Tol Eressëa to a full and polished form, and to this work I now turn; but first it is convenient to collect the passages previously considered that bear on it.

In the opening *Link* to the *Tale of Tinúviel* Eriol said that 'many years agone', when he was a child, his home was 'in an old town of Men girt with a wall now crumbled and broken, and a river ran thereby over which a castle with a great tower hung'.

> My father came of a coastward folk, and the love of the sea that I had never seen was in my bones, and my father whetted my desire, for he told me tales that his father had told him before. Now my mother died in a cruel and hungry siege of that old town, and my father was slain in bitter fight about the walls, and in the end I Eriol escaped to the shoreland of the Western Sea.

Eriol told then of

> his wanderings about the western havens, . . . of how he was wrecked upon far western islands until at last upon one lonely one he came upon an ancient sailor who gave him shelter, and over a fire within his lonely cabin told him strange tales of things beyond the Western Seas, of the Magic Isles and that most lonely one that lay beyond. . . .
> 'Ever after,' said Eriol, 'did I sail more curiously about the western isles seeking more stories of the kind, and thus it is indeed that after many great voyages I came myself by the blessing of the Gods to Tol Eressëa in the end . . .'

In the typescript version of this *Link* it is further told that in the town where Eriol's parents lived and died

> there dwelt a mighty duke, and did he gaze from the topmost battlements never might he see the bounds of his wide domain, save where far to east the blue shapes of the great mountains lay – yet was that tower held the most lofty that stood in the lands of Men.

The siege and sack of the town were the work of 'the wild men from the Mountains of the East'.

At the end of the typescript version the boy Ausir assured Eriol that 'that ancient mariner beside the lonely sea was none other than Ulmo's self, who appeareth not seldom thus to those voyagers whom he loves'; but Eriol did not believe him.

I have given above (pp. 294–5) reasons for thinking that in 'the *Eriol* story' this tale of his youth was not set in England.

Turning to the passages concerned with the later, *Ælfwine* story, we learn from (15) that Ælfwine dwelt in the South-west of England and

that his mother and father were slain by 'the sea-pirates', and from (20)
that they were slain by 'the fierce Men of the Sea'; from (16) that he was
'driven by the Normans'. In (15) there is a mention of his meeting with
'the Ancient Mariner' during his voyages. In (16) he comes to 'the
harbour of the southern shore' of Tol Eressëa; and in (17) he 'awakens
upon a sandy beach' at low tide.

   I come now to the narrative that finally emerged. It will be observed,
perhaps with relief, that Ing, Ingwë, and the Ingwaiwar have totally
disappeared.

## ÆLFWINE OF ENGLAND

There are three versions of this short work. One is a plot-outline of
less than 500 words, which for convenience of reference I shall call
*Ælfwine A*; but the second is a much more substantial narrative bearing
the title *Ælfwine of England*. This was written in 1920 or later: demon-
strably not earlier, for my father used for it scraps of paper pinned
together, and some of these are letters to him, all dated in February
1920.[18] The third text no doubt began as a fair copy in ink of the second,
to which it is indeed very close at first, but became as it proceeded a complete rewriting at several points, with the introduction of much new
matter, and it was further emended after it had been completed. It bears
no title in the manuscript, but must obviously be called *Ælfwine of
England* likewise.
   For convenience I shall refer to the first fully-written version as
*Ælfwine I* and to its rewriting as *Ælfwine II*. The relation of *Ælfwine A*
to these is hard to determine, since it agrees in some respects with
the one and in some with the other. It is obvious that my father had
*Ælfwine I* in front of him when he wrote *Ælfwine II*, but it seems likely
that he drew on *Ælfwine A* at the same time.
   I give here the full text of *Ælfwine II* in its final form, with all noteworthy emendations and all important differences from the other texts in
the notes (differences in names, and changes to names, are listed
separately).

   There was a land called England, and it was an island of the
West, and before it was broken in the warfare of the Gods it was
westernmost of all the Northern lands, and looked upon the
Great Sea that Men of old called Garsecg;[19] but that part that
was broken was called Ireland and many names besides, and its
dwellers come not into these tales.
   All that land the Elves named Lúthien[20] and do so yet. In
Lúthien alone dwelt still the most part of the Fading Companies,
the Holy Fairies that have not yet sailed away from the world,

beyond the horizon of Men's knowledge, to the Lonely Island, or even to the Hill of Tûn[21] upon the Bay of Faëry that washes the western shores of the kingdom of the Gods. Therefore is Lúthien even yet a holy land, and a magic that is not otherwise lingers still in many places of that isle.

Now amidmost of that island is there still a town that is aged among Men, but its age among the Elves is greater far; and, for this is a book of the Lost Tales of Elfinesse, it shall be named in their tongue Kortirion, which the Gnomes call Mindon Gwar.[22] Upon the hill of Gwar dwelt in the days of the English a man and his name was Déor, and he came thither from afar, from the south of the island and from the forests and from the enchanted West, where albeit he was of the English folk he had long time wandered. Now the Prince of Gwar was in those days a lover of songs and no enemy of the Elves, and they lingered yet most of all the isle in those regions about Kortirion (which places they called Alalminórë, the Land of Elms), and thither came Déor the singer to seek the Prince of Gwar and to seek the companies of the Fading Elves, for he was an Elf-friend. Though Déor was of English blood, it is told that he wedded to wife a maiden from the West, from Lionesse as some have named it since, or Evadrien 'Coast of Iron' as the Elves still say. Déor found her in the lost land beyond Belerion whence the Elves at times set sail.

Mirth had Déor long time in Mindon Gwar, but the Men of the North, whom the fairies of the island called Forodwaith, but whom Men called other names, came against Gwar in those days when they ravaged wellnigh all the land of Lúthien. Its walls availed not and its towers might not withstand them for ever, though the siege was long and bitter.

There Éadgifu (for so did Déor name the maiden of the West, though it was not her name aforetime)[23] died in those evil hungry days; but Déor fell before the walls even as he sang a song of ancient valour for the raising of men's hearts. That was a desperate sally, and the son of Déor was Ælfwine, and he was then but a boy left fatherless. The sack of that town thereafter was very cruel, and whispers of its ancient days alone remained, and the Elves that had grown to love the English of the isle fled or hid themselves for a long time, and none of Elves or Men were left in his old halls to lament the fall of Óswine Prince of Gwar.

Then Ælfwine, even he whom the unfaded Elves beyond the waters of Garsecg did after name Eldairon of Lúthien (which is

Ælfwine of England), was made a thrall to the fierce lords of the
Forodwaith, and his boyhood knew evil days. But behold a
wonder, for Ælfwine knew not and had never seen the sea, yet
he heard its great voice speaking deeply in his heart, and its
murmurous choirs sang ever in his secret ear between wake and
sleep, that he was filled with longing. This was of the magic of
Éadgifu, maiden of the West, his mother, and this longing
unquenchable had been hers all the days that she dwelt in the
quiet inland places among the elms of Mindon Gwar – and
amidmost of her longing was Ælfwine her child born, and the
Foamriders, the Elves of the Sea-marge, whom she had known
of old in Lionesse, sent messengers to his birth. But now
Éadgifu was gone beyond the Rim of Earth, and her fair form
lay unhonoured in Mindon Gwar, and Déor's harp was silent,
but Ælfwine laboured in thraldom until the threshold of manhood, dreaming dreams and filled with longing, and at rare
times holding converse with the hidden Elves.

At last his longing for the sea bit him so sorely that he
contrived to break his bonds, and daring great perils and suffering many grievous toils he escaped to lands where the Lords of
the Forodwaith had not come, far from the places of Déor's
abiding in Mindon Gwar. Ever he wandered southward and to
the west, for that way his feet unbidden led him. Now Ælfwine
had in a certain measure the gift of elfin-sight (which was not
given to all Men in those days of the fading of the Elves and still
less is it granted now), and the folk of Lúthien were less faded
too in those days, so that many a host of their fair companies he
saw upon his wandering road. Some there were dwelt yet and
danced yet about that land as of old, but many more there were
that wandered slowly and sadly westward; for behind them all
the land was full of burnings and of war, and its dwellings ran
with tears and with blood for the little love of Men for Men – nor
was that the last of the takings of Lúthien by Men from Men,
which have been seven, and others mayhap still shall be. Men of
the East and of the West and of the South and of the North have
coveted that land and dispossessed those who held it before
them, because of its beauty and goodliness and of the glamour
of the fading ages of the Elves that lingered still among its trees
beyond its high white shores.[24]

Yet at each taking of that isle have many more of the most
ancient of all dwellers therein, the folk of Lúthien, turned
westward; and they have got them in ships at Belerion in the

West and sailed thence away for ever over the horizon of Men's knowledge, leaving the island the poorer for their going and its leaves less green; yet still it abides the richest among Men in the presence of the Elves. And it is said that, save only when the fierce fathers of Men, foes of the Elves, being new come under the yoke of Evil,[25] entered first that land, never else did so great a concourse of elfin ships and white-winged galleons sail to the setting sun as in those days when the ancient Men of the South set first their mighty feet upon the soil of Lúthien – the Men whose lords sat in the city of power that Elves and Men have called Rûm (but the Elves alone do know as Magbar).[26]

Now is it the dull hearts of later days rather than the red deeds of cruel hands that set the minds of the little folk to fare away; and ever and anon a little ship[27] weighs anchor from Belerion at eve and its sweet sad song is lost for ever on the waves. Yet even in the days of Ælfwine there was many a laden ship under elfin sails that left those shores for ever, and many a comrade he had, seen or half-unseen, upon his westward road. And so he came at last to Belerion, and there he laved his weary feet in the grey waters of the Western Sea, whose great roaring drowned his ears. There the dim shapes of Elvish[28] boats sailed by him in the gloaming, and many aboard called to him farewell. But he might not embark on those frail craft, and they refused his prayer – for they were not willing that even one beloved among Men should pass with them beyond the edge of the West, or learn what lies far out on Garsecg the great and measureless sea. Now the men who dwelt thinly about those places nigh Belerion were fishermen, and Ælfwine abode long time amongst them, and being of nature shaped inly thereto he learned all that a man may of the craft of ships and of the sea. He recked little of his life, and he set his ocean-paths wider than most of those men, good mariners though they were; and there were few in the end who dared to go with him, save Ælfheah the fatherless who was with him in all ventures until his last voyage.[29]

Now on a time journeying far out into the open sea, being first becalmed in a thick mist, and after driven helpless by a mighty wind from the East, he espied some islands lying in the dawn, but he won not ever thereto for the winds changing swept him again far away, and only his strong fate saved him to see the black coasts of his abiding once again. Little content was he with his good fortune, and purposed in his heart to sail some time again yet further into the West, thinking unwitting it was the Magic Isles of the songs of Men that he had seen from afar. Few companions could he get for this adventure. Not all men love to sail a quest for the red sun or to tempt the dangerous seas in thirst for undiscovered things. Seven such found he in the end, the greatest mariners that were then in England, and Ulmo Lord of the Sea afterward took them to himself and their names are now forgotten, save Ælfheah only.[30] A great storm fell upon their ship even as they had sighted the isles of Ælfwine's desire, and a great sea swept over her; but Ælfwine was lost in the waves, and coming to himself saw no sign of ship or comrades, and he lay upon a bed of sand in a deep-walled cove. Dark and very empty was the isle, and he knew then that these were not those Magic Isles of which he had heard often tell.[31]

There wandering long, 'tis said, he came upon many hulls of wrecks rotting on the long gloomy beaches, and some were wrecks of many mighty ships of old, and some were treasure-laden. A lonely cabin looking westward he found at last upon the further shore, and it was made of the upturned hull of a small ship. An ancient man dwelt there, and Ælfwine feared him, for the eyes of the man were as deep as the unfathomable sea, and his long beard was blue and grey; great was his stature, and his shoes were of stone,[32] but he was all clad in tangled rags, sitting beside a small fire of drifted wood.

In that strange hut beside an empty sea did Ælfwine long abide for lack of other shelter or of other counsel, thinking his ship lost and his comrades drowned. But the ancient man grew kindly toward him, and questioned Ælfwine concerning his coming and his goings and whither he had desired to sail before the storm took him. And many things before unheard did Ælfwine hear tell of him beside that smoky fire at eve, and strange tales of wind-harried ships and harbourless tempests in the forbidden waters. Thus heard Ælfwine how the Magic Isles were yet a great voyage before him keeping a dark and secret ward upon the edge of Earth, beyond whom the waters of Garsecg grow less troublous and there lies the twilight of the latter days of Fairyland. Beyond and on the confines of the Shadows lies the Lonely Island looking East to the Magic Archipelago and to the lands of Men beyond it, and West into the Shadows beyond which afar off is glimpsed the Outer Land, the kingdom of the Gods – even the aged Bay of Faëry whose glory has grown dim. Thence slopes the world steeply beyond the Rim of Things to Valinor, that is God-home, and to the

Wall and to the edge of Nothingness whereon are sown the stars. But the Lonely Isle is neither of the Great Lands or of the Outer Land, and no isle lies near it.

In his tales that aged man named himself the Man of the Sea, and he spoke of his last voyage ere he was cast in wreck upon this outer isle, telling how ere the West wind took him he had glimpsed afar off bosomed in the deep the twinkling lanterns of the Lonely Isle. Then did Ælfwine's heart leap within him, but he said to that aged one that he might not hope to get him a brave ship or comrades more. But that Man of the Sea said: 'Lo, this is one of the ring of Harbourless Isles that draw all ships towards their hidden rocks and quaking sands, lest Men fare over far upon Garsecg and see things that are not for them to see. And these isles were set here at the Hiding of Valinor, and little wood for ship or raft does there grow on them, as may be thought;[33] but I may aid thee yet in thy desire to depart from these greedy shores.'

Thereafter on a day Ælfwine fared along the eastward strands gazing at the many unhappy wrecks there lying. He sought, as often he had done before, if he might see perchance any sign or relic of his good ship from Belerion. There had been that night a storm of great violence and dread, and lo! the number of wrecks was increased by one, and Ælfwine saw it had been a large and well-built ship of cunning lines such as the Forodwaith then loved. Cast far up on the treacherous sands it stood, and its great beak carven as a dragon's head still glared unbroken at the land. Then went the Man of the Sea out when the tide began to creep in slow and shallow over the long flats. He bore as a staff a timber great as a young tree, and he fared as if he had no need to fear tide or quicksand until he came far out where his shoulders were scarce above the yellow waters of the incoming flood to that carven prow, that now alone was seen above the water. Then Ælfwine marvelled watching from afar, to see him heave by his single strength the whole great ship up from the clutches of the sucking sand that gripped its sunken stern; and when it floated he thrust it before him, swimming now with mighty strokes in the deepening water. At that sight Ælfwine's fear of the aged one was renewed, and he wondered what manner of being he might be; but now the ship was thrust far up on the firmer sands, and the swimmer strode ashore, and his mighty beard was full of strands of sea-weed, and sea-weed was in his hair.

When that tide again forsook the Hungry Sands the Man of
the Sea bade Ælfwine go look at that new-come wreck, and
going he saw it was not hurt; but there were within nine dead
men who had not long ago been yet alive. They lay abottom
gazing at the sky, and behold, one whose garb and mien still
proclaimed a chieftain of Men lay there, but though his locks
were white with age and his face was pale in death, still a proud
man and a fierce he looked. 'Men of the North, Forodwaith, are
they,' said the Man of the Sea, 'but hunger and thirst was their
death, and their ship was flung by last night's storm where she
stuck in the Hungry Sands, slowly to be engulfed, had not fate
thought otherwise.'

'Truly do you say of them, O Man of the Sea; and him I know
well with those white locks, for he slew my father; and long was
I his thrall, and Orm men called him, and little did I love him.'

'And his ship shall it be that bears you from this Harbourless
Isle,' said he; 'and a gallant ship it was of a brave man, for few
folk have now so great a heart for the adventures of the sea as
have these Forodwaith, who press ever into the mists of the
West, though few live to take back tale of all they see.'

Thus it was that Ælfwine escaped beyond hope from that
island, but the Man of the Sea was his pilot and steersman, and
so they came after few days to a land but little known.[34] And the
folk that dwell there are a strange folk, and none know how they
came thither in the West, yet are they accounted among the
kindreds of Men, albeit their land is on the outer borders of the
regions of Mankind, lying yet further toward the Setting Sun
beyond the Harbourless Isles and further to the North than is
that isle whereon Ælfwine was cast away. Marvellously skilled
are these people in the building of ships and boats of every kind
and in the sailing of them; yet do they fare seldom or never to
the lands of other folk, and little do they busy themselves with
commerce or with war. Their ships they build for love of that
labour and for the joy they have only to ride the waves in them.
And a great part of that people are ever aboard their ships, and
all the water about the island of their home is ever white with
their sails in calm or storm. Their delight is to vie in rivalry with
one another with their boats of surpassing swiftness, driven by
the winds or by the ranks of their long-shafted oars. Other
rivalries have they with ships of great seaworthiness, for with
these will they contest who will weather the fiercest storms (and
these are fierce indeed about that isle, and it is iron-coasted save

for one cool harbour in the North). Thereby is the craft of their shipwrights proven; and these people are called by Men the Ythlings,[35] the Children of the Waves, but the Elves call the island Eneadur, and its folk the Shipmen of the West.[36]

Well did these receive Ælfwine and his pilot at the thronging quays of their harbour in the North, and it seemed to Ælfwine that the Man of the Sea was not unknown to them, and that they held him in the greatest awe and reverence, hearkening to his requests as though they were a king's commands. Yet greater was his amaze when he met amid the throngs of that place two of his comrades that he had thought lost in the sea; and learnt that those seven mariners of England were alive in that land, but the ship had been broken utterly on the black shores to the south, not long after the night when the great sea had taken Ælfwine overboard.

Now at the bidding of the Man of the Sea do those islanders with great speed fashion a new ship for Ælfwine and his fellows, since he would fare no further in Orm's ship; and its timbers were cut, as the ancient sailor had asked, from a grove of magic oaks far inland that grew about a high place of the Gods, sacred to Ulmo Lord of the Sea, and seldom were any of them felled. 'A ship that is wrought of this wood,' said the Man of the Sea, 'may be lost, but those that sail in it shall not in that voyage lose their lives; yet may they perhaps be cast where they little think to come.'

But when that ship was made ready that ancient sailor bid them climb aboard, and this they did, but with them went also Bior of the Ythlings, a man of mighty sea-craft for their aid, and one who above any of that strange folk was minded to sail at times far from the land of Eneadur to West or North or South. There stood many men of the Ythlings upon the shore beside that vessel; for they had builded her in a cove of the steep shore that looked to the West, and a bar of rock with but a narrow opening made here a sheltered pool and mooring place, and few like it were to be found in that island of sheer cliffs. Then the ancient one laid his hand upon her prow and spoke words of magic, giving her power to cleave uncloven waters and enter unentered harbours, and ride untrodden beaches. Twin rudder-paddles, one on either side, had she after the fashion of the Ythlings, and each of these he blessed, giving them skill to steer when the hands that held them failed, and to find lost courses, and to follow stars that were hid. Then he strode away,

and the press of men parted before him, until climbing he came
to a high pinnacle of the cliffs. Then leapt he far out and down
and vanished with a mighty flurry of foam where the great
breakers gathered to assault the towering shores.

Ælfwine saw him no more, and he said in grief and amaze:
'Why was he thus weary of life? My heart grieves that he is
dead,' but the Ythlings smiled, so that he questioned some that
stood nigh, saying: 'Who was that mighty man, for meseems ye
know him well,' and they answered him nothing. Then thrust
they forth that vessel valiant-timbered[37] out into the sea, for no
longer would Ælfwine abide, though the sun was sinking to the
Mountains of Valinor beyond the Western Walls. Soon was her
white sail seen far away filled with a wind from off the land, and
red-stained in the light of the half-sunken sun; and those aboard
her sang old songs of the English folk that faded on the sailless
waves of the Western Seas, and now no longer came any sound
of them to the watchers on the shore. Then night shut down and
none on Eneadur saw that strong ship ever more.[38]

So began those mariners that long and strange and perilous
voyage whose full tale has never yet been told. Nought of their
adventures in the archipelagoes of the West, and the wonders
and the dangers that they found in the Magic Isles and in seas
and sound unknown, are here to tell, but of the ending of their
voyage, how after a time of years sea-weary and sick of heart
they found a grey and cheerless day. Little wind was there, and
the clouds hung low overhead; while a grey rain fell, and nought
could any of them descry before their vessel's beak that moved
now slow and uncertain over the long dead waves. That day had
they trysted to be the last ere they turned their vessel homeward
(if they might), save only if some wonder should betide or any
sign of hope. For their heart was gone. Behind them lay the
Magic Isles where three of their number slept upon dim strands
in deadly sleep, and their heads were pillowed on white sand
and they were clad in foam, wrapped about in the agelong spells
of Eglavain. Fruitless had been all their journeys since, for ever
the winds had cast them back without sight of the shores of the
Island of the Elves.[39] Then said Ælfheah[40] who held the helm:
'Now, O Ælfwine, is the trysted time! Let us do as the Gods and
their winds have long desired — cease from our heart-weary
quest for nothingness, a fable in the void, and get us back if the
Gods will it seeking the hearths of our home.' And Ælfwine

yielded. Then fell the wind and no breath came from East or West, and night came slowly over the sea.

Behold, at length a gentle breeze sprang up, and it came softly from the West; and even as they would fill their sails therewith for home, one of those shipmen on a sudden said: 'Nay, but this is a strange air, and full of scented memories,' and standing still they all breathed deep. The mists gave before that gentle wind, and a thin moon they might see riding in its tattered shreds, until behind it soon a thousand cool stars peered forth in the dark. 'The night-flowers are opening in Faëry,' said Ælfwine; 'and behold,' said Bior,[41] 'the Elves are kindling candles in their silver dusk,' and all looked whither his long hand pointed over their dark stern. Then none spoke for wonder and amaze, seeing deep in the gloaming of the West a blue shadow, and in the blue shadow many glittering lights, and ever more and more of them came twinkling out, until ten thousand points of flickering radiance were splintered far away as if a dust of the jewels self-luminous that Fëanor made were scattered on the lap of the Ocean.

'Then is that the Harbour of the Lights of Many Hues,' said Ælfheah, 'that many a little-heeded tale has told of in our homes.' Then saying no more they shot out their oars and swung about their ship in haste, and pulled towards the never-dying shore. Near had they come to abandoning it when hardly won. Little did they make of that long pull, as they thrust the water strongly by them, and the long night of Faërie held on, and the horned moon of Elfinesse rode over them.

Then came there music very gently over the waters and it was laden with unimagined longing, that Ælfwine and his comrades leant upon their oars and wept softly each for his heart's half-remembered hurts, and memory of fair things long lost, and each for the thirst that is in every child of Men for the flawless loveliness they seek and do not find. And one said: 'It is the harps that are thrumming, and the songs they are singing of fair things; and the windows that look upon the sea are full of light.' And another said: 'Their stringéd violins complain the ancient woes of the immortal folk of Earth, but there is a joy therein.' 'Ah me,' said Ælfwine, 'I hear the horns of the Fairies shimmering in magic woods – such music as I once dimly guessed long years ago beneath the elms of Mindon Gwar.'

And lo! as they spoke thus musing the moon hid himself, and the stars were clouded, and the mists of time veiled the shore, and nothing could they see and nought more hear, save the sound of the surf of the seas in the far-off pebbles of the Lonely Isle; and soon the wind blew even that faint rustle far away. But Ælfwine stood forward with wide-open eyes unspeaking, and suddenly with a great cry he sprang forward into the dark sea, and the waters that filled him were warm, and a kindly death it seemed enveloped him. Then it seemed to the others that they awakened at his voice as from a dream; but the wind now suddenly grown fierce filled all their sails, and they saw him never again, but were driven back with hearts all broken with regret and longing. Pale elfin boats awhile they would see beating home, maybe, to the Haven of Many Hues, and they hailed them; but only faint echoes afar off were borne to their ears, and none led them ever to the land of their desire; who after a great time wound back all the mazy clue of their long tangled ways, until they cast anchor at last in the haven of Belerion, aged and wayworn men. And the things they had seen and heard seemed after to them a mirage, and a phantasy, born of hunger and sea-spells, save only to Bior of Eneadur of the Ship-folk of the West.

Yet among the seed of these men has there been many a restless and wistful spirit thereafter, since they were dead and passed beyond the Rim of Earth without need of boat or sail. But never while life lasted did they leave their sea-faring, and their bodies are all covered by the sea.[42]

The narrative ends here. There is no trace of any further continuation, though it seems likely that *Ælfwine of England* was to be the beginning of a complete rewriting of the *Lost Tales*. It would be interesting to know for certain when *Ælfwine II* was written. The handwriting of the manuscript is certainly changed from that of the rest of the *Lost Tales*; yet I am inclined to think that it followed *Ælfwine I* at no great interval, and the first version is unlikely to be much later than 1920 (see p. 312).

At the end of *Ælfwine II* my father jotted down two suggestions: (1) that Ælfwine should be made 'an early pagan Englishman who fled to the West'; and (2) that 'the Isle of the Old Man' should be cut out and all should be shipwrecked on Eneadur, the Isle of the Ythlings. The latter would (astonishingly) have entailed the abandonment of the foundered ship, with the Man of the Sea thrusting it to shore on the incoming tide, and the dead Vikings 'lying abottom gazing at the sky'.

In this narrative – in which the 'magic' of the early Elves is most intensely conveyed, in the seamen's vision of the Lonely Isle beneath 'the horned moon of Elfinesse' – Ælfwine is still placed in the context of the figures of ancient English legend: his father is Déor the Minstrel. In the great Anglo-Saxon manuscript known as the Exeter Book there is a little poem of 42 lines to which the title of *Déor* is now given. It is an utterance of the minstrel Déor, who, as he tells, has lost his place and been supplanted in his lord's favour by another bard, named Heorrenda; in the body of the poem Déor draws examples from among the great misfortunes recounted in the heroic legends, and is comforted by them, concluding each allusion with the fixed refrain *þæs ofereode; þisses swa mæg*, which has been variously translated; my father held that it meant 'Time has passed since then, this too can pass'.[43]

From this poem came both Déor and Heorrenda. In 'the *Eriol* story' Heorrenda was Eriol's son born in Tol Eressëa of his wife Naimi (p. 290), and was associated with Hengest and Horsa in the conquest of the Lonely Isle (p. 291); his dwelling in England was at Tavrobel (p. 292). I do not think that my father's Déor the Minstrel of Kortirion and Heorrenda of Tavrobel can be linked more closely to the Anglo-Saxon poem than in the names alone – though he did not take the names at random. He was moved by the glimpsed tale (even if, in the words of one of the poem's editors, 'the autobiographical element is purely fictitious, serving only as a pretext for the enumeration of the heroic stories'); and when lecturing on *Beowulf* at Oxford he sometimes gave the unknown poet a name, calling him *Heorrenda*.

Nor, as I believe, can any more be made of the other Old English names in the narrative: Óswine prince of Gwar, Éadgifu, Ælfheah (though the names are doubtless in themselves 'significant': thus *Óswine* contains *ós* 'god' and *wine* 'friend', and *Éadgifu éad* 'blessedness' and *gifu* 'gift'). The Forodwaith are of course Viking invaders from Norway or Denmark; the name Orm of the dead ship's captain is well-known in Norse. But all this is a mise-en-scène that is historical only in its bearings, not in its structure.

The idea of the seven invasions of Lúthien (Luthany) remained (p. 314), and that of the fading and westward flight of the Elves (which indeed was never finally lost),[44] but whereas in the outlines the invasion of the Ingwaiwar (i.e. the Anglo-Saxons) was the seventh (see citations (20) and (22)), here the Viking invasions are portrayed as coming upon the English – 'nor was that the last of the takings of Lúthien by Men from Men' (p. 314), obviously a reference to the Normans.

There is much of interest in the 'geographical' references in the story. At the very beginning there is a curious statement about the breaking off of Ireland 'in the warfare of the Gods'. Seeing that 'the *Ælfwine* story' does not include the idea of the drawing back of Tol Eressëa eastwards across the sea, this must refer to something quite other than the story in (5), p. 283, where the Isle of Íverin was broken off when Ossë tried to wrench back Tol Eressëa. What this was I do not know; but it seems conceivable that this is the first trace or hint of the great cataclysm at the end of the Elder Days, when Beleriand was drowned. (I have found no trace of any connection between the harbour of *Belerion* and the region of *Beleriand*.)

Kortirion (Mindon Gwar) is in this tale of course 'Kortirion the Old', the original Elvish dwelling in Lúthien, after which Kortirion in Tol Eressëa was named (see pp. 308, 310); in the same way we must suppose that the name Alalmínórë (p. 313) for the region about it ('Warwickshire') was given anew to the midmost region of Tol Eressëa.

Turning to the question of the islands and archipelagoes in the Great Sea, what is said in *Ælfwine of England* may first be compared with the passages of geographical description in *The Coming of the Valar* (I.68) and *The Coming of the Elves* (I.125), which are closely similar the one to the other. From these passages we learn that there are many lands and islands in the Great Sea before the Magic Isles are reached; beyond the Magic Isles is Tol Eressëa; and beyond Tol Eressëa are the Shadowy Seas, 'whereon there float the Twilit Isles', the first of the Outer Lands. Tol Eressëa itself 'is held neither of the Outer Lands or of the Great Lands' (I.125); it is far out in mid-ocean, and 'no land may be seen for many leagues' sail from its cliffs' (I.121). With this account *Ælfwine of England* agrees closely; but to it is added now the archipelago of the Harbourless Isles.

As I have noted before (I.137), this progression from East to West of Harbourless Isles, Magic Isles, the Lonely Isle, and then the Shadowy Seas in which were the Twilit Isles, was afterwards changed, and it is said in *The Silmarillion* (p. 102) that at the time of the Hiding of Valinor

> the Enchanted Isles were set, and all the seas about them were filled with shadows and bewilderment. And these isles were strung as a net in the Shadowy Seas from the north to the south, before Tol Eressëa, the Lonely Isle, is reached by one sailing west. Hardly might any vessel pass between them, for in the dangerous sounds the waves sighed for ever upon dark rocks shrouded in mist. And in the twilight a great weariness came upon mariners and a loathing of the sea; but all that ever set foot upon the islands were there entrapped, and slept until the Change of the World.

As a conception, the Enchanted Isles are derived primarily from the old Magic Isles, set at the time of the Hiding of Valinor and described in that Tale (I.211): 'Ossë set them in a great ring about the western limits of the mighty sea, so that they guarded the Bay of Faëry', and

> all such as stepped thereon came never thence again, but being woven in the nets of Oinen's hair the Lady of the Sea, and whelmed in agelong slumber that Lórien set there, lay upon the margin of the waves, as those do who being drowned are cast up once more by the movements

of the sea; yet rather did these hapless ones sleep unfathomably and
the dark waters laved their limbs . . .

Here three of Ælfwine's companions

> slept upon dim strands in deadly sleep, and their heads were pillowed
> on white sand and they were clad in foam, wrapped about in the
> agelong spells of Eglavain (p. 320).

(I do not know the meaning of the name *Eglavain*, but since it clearly
contains *Egla* (Gnomish, = *Elda*, see I.251) it perhaps meant
'Elfinesse'.) But the Enchanted Isles derive also perhaps from the Twilit
Isles, since the Enchanted Isles were likewise in twilight and were set in
the Shadowy Seas (cf. I.224); and from the Harbourless Isles as well,
which, as Ælfwine was told by the Man of the Sea (p. 317), were set at the
time of the Hiding of Valinor – and indeed served the same purpose as
did the Magic Isles, though lying far further to the East.

Eneadur, the isle of the Ythlings (Old English *ýð* 'wave'), whose life
is so fully described in *Ælfwine of England*, seems never to have been
mentioned again. Is there in Eneadur and the Shipmen of the West
perhaps some faint foreshadowing of the early Númenóreans in their
cliff-girt isle?

The following passage (pp. 316–17) is not easy to interpret:

> Thence [i.e. from the Bay of Faëry] slopes the world steeply beyond
> the Rim of Things to Valinor, that is God-home, and to the Wall and
> to the edge of Nothingness whereon are sown the stars.

In the *Ambarkanta* or 'Shape of the World' of the 1930s a map of the
world shows the surface of the Outer Land sloping steeply westwards
from the Mountains of Valinor. Conceivably it is to this slope that my
father was referring here, and the Rim of Things is the great mountain-
wall; but this seems very improbable. There are also references in
*Ælfwine of England* to 'the Rim of Earth', beyond which the dead pass
(pp. 314, 322); and in an outline for the *Tale of Eärendel* (p. 260)
Tuor's boat 'dips over the world's rim'. More likely, I think, the
expression refers to the rim of the horizon ('the horizon of Men's
knowledge', p. 313).

The expression 'the sun was sinking to the Mountains of Valinor
beyond the Western Walls' (p. 320) I am at a loss to explain according to
what has been told in the *Lost Tales*. A possible, though scarcely
convincing, interpretation is that the sun was sinking towards Valinor,
*whence it would pass* 'beyond the Western Walls' (i.e. through the
Door of Night, see I.215–16).

Lastly, the suggestion (p. 313) is notable that the Elves sailing west from Lúthien might go beyond the Lonely Isle and reach even back to Valinor; on this matter see p. 280.

★

Before ending, there remains to discuss briefly a matter of a general nature that has many times been mentioned in the texts, and especially in these last chapters: that of the 'diminutiveness' of the Elves.

It is said several times in the *Lost Tales* that the Elves of the ancient days were of greater bodily stature than they afterwards became. Thus in *The Fall of Gondolin* (p. 159): 'The fathers of the fathers of Men were of less stature than Men now are, and the children of Elfinesse of greater growth'; in an outline for the abandoned tale of Gilfanon (I.235) very similarly: 'Men were almost of a stature at first with Elves, the fairies being far greater and Men smaller than now'; and in citation (4) in the present chapter: 'Men and Elves were formerly of a size, though Men always larger.' Other passages suggest that the ancient Elves were of their nature of at any rate somewhat slighter build (see pp. 142, 220).

The diminishing in the stature of the Elves of later times is very explicitly related to the coming of Men. Thus in (4) above: 'Men spread and thrive, and the Elves of the Great Lands fade. As Men's stature grows theirs diminishes'; and in (5): 'ever as Men wax more powerful and numerous so the fairies fade and grow small and tenuous, filmy and transparent, but Men larger and more dense and gross. At last Men, or almost all, can no longer see the fairies.' The clearest picture that survives of the Elves when they have 'faded' altogether is given in the *Epilogue* (p. 289):

> Like strands of wind, like mystic half-transparencies, Gilfanon Lord of Tavrobel rides out tonight amid his folk, and hunts the elfin deer beneath the paling sky. A music of forgotten feet, a gleam of leaves, a sudden bending of the grass, and wistful voices murmuring on the bridge, and they are gone.

But according to the passages bearing on the later '*Ælfwine*' version, the Elves of Tol Eressëa who had left Luthany were unfaded, or had ceased to fade. Thus in (15): 'Tol Eressëa, whither most of the unfaded Elves have retired from the noise, war, and clamour of Men'; and (16): 'Tol Eressëa, whither most of the fading Elves have withdrawn from the world, and there fade now no more'; also in *Ælfwine of England* (p. 313): 'the unfaded Elves beyond the waters of Garsecg'.

On the other hand, when Eriol came to the Cottage of Lost Play the doorward said to him (I.14):

> Small is the dwelling, but smaller still are they that dwell here – for all who enter must be very small indeed, or of their own good wish become as very little folk even as they stand upon the threshold.

I have commented earlier (I. 32) on the oddity of the idea that the Cottage and its inhabitants were peculiarly small, in an island entirely inhabited by Elves. But my father, if he had ever rewritten *The Cottage of Lost Play*, would doubtless have abandoned this; and it may well be that he was in any case turning away already at the time of *Ælfwine II* from the idea that the 'faded' Elves were diminutive, as is suggested by his rejection of the word 'little' in 'little folk', 'little ships' (see note 27).

Ultimately, of course, the Elves shed all associations and qualities that would be now commonly considered 'fairylike', and those who remained in the Great Lands in Ages of the world at this time unconceived were to grow greatly in stature and in power: there was nothing filmy or transparent about the heroic or majestic Eldar of the Third Age of Middle-earth. Long afterwards my father would write, in a wrathful comment on a 'pretty' or 'ladylike' pictorial rendering of Legolas:

> He was tall as a young tree, lithe, immensely strong, able swiftly to draw a great war-bow and shoot down a Nazgûl, endowed with the tremendous vitality of Elvish bodies, so hard and resistant to hurt that he went only in light shoes over rock or through snow, the most tireless of all the Fellowship.

★

This brings to an end my rendering and analysis of the early writings bearing on the story of the mariner who came to the Lonely Isle and learned there the true history of the Elves. I have shown, convincingly as I hope, the curious and complex way in which my father's vision of the significance of Tol Eressëa changed. When he jotted down the synopsis (10), the idea of the mariner's voyage to the Island of the Elves was of course already present; but he journeyed out of the East and the Lonely Isle of his seeking was – England (though not yet the land of the English and not yet lying in the seas where England lies). When later the entire concept was shifted, England, as 'Luthany' or 'Lúthien', remained preeminently the Elvish land; and Tol Eressëa, with its meads and coppices, its rooks' nests in the elm-trees of Alalminórë, seemed to the English mariner to be remade in the likeness of his own land, which the Elves had lost at the coming of Men: for it was indeed a re-embodiment of Elvish Luthany far over the sea.

All this was to fall away afterwards from the developing mythology; but Ælfwine left many marks on its pages before he too finally disappeared.

Much in this chapter is necessarily inconclusive and uncertain; but I believe that these very early notes and projections are rightly disinterred. Although, as 'plots', abandoned and doubtless forgotten, they bear witness to truths of my father's heart and mind that he never abandoned. But these notes were scribbled down in his youth, when for him Elvish magic 'lingered yet mightily in the woods and hills of Luthany'; in his old age all was gone West-over-sea, and an end was indeed come for the Eldar of story and of song.

# NOTES

1 On this statement about the stature of Elves and Men see pp. 326–7.

2 For the form *Taimonto* (*Taimondo*) see I. 268, entry *Telimektar*.

3 *Belaurin* is the Gnomish equivalent of *Palúrien* (see I. 264).

4 A side-note here suggests that perhaps the Pine should not be in Tol Eressëa. – For *Ilwë*, the middle air, that is 'blue and clear and flows among the stars', see I. 65, 73.

5 *Gil* = *Ingil*. At the first occurrence of *Ingil* in this passage the name was written *Ingil* (*Gil*), but (*Gil*) was struck out.

6 The word *Nautar* occurs in a rejected outline for the *Tale of the Nauglafring* (p. 136), where it is equated with *Nauglath* (Dwarves).

7 *Uin*: 'the mightiest and most ancient of whales', chief among those whales and fishes that drew the 'island-car' (afterwards Tol Eressëa) on which Ulmo ferried the Elves to Valinor (I. 118–20).

8 *Gongs*: these are evil beings obscurely related to Orcs: see I. 245 note 10, and the rejected outlines for the *Tale of the Nauglafring* given on pp. 136–7.

9 A large query is written against this passage.

10 The likeness of this name to *Dor Daedeloth* is striking, but that is the name of the realm of Morgoth in *The Silmarillion*, and is interpreted 'Land of the Shadow of Horror'; the old name (whose elements are *dai* 'sky' and *teloth* 'roof') has nothing in common with the later except its form.

11 Cf. *Kortirion among the Trees* (I. 34, 37, 41): *A wave of bowing grass*.

12 The origin of *Warwick* according to conventional etymology is uncertain. The element *wic*, extremely common in English place-names, meant essentially a dwelling or group of dwellings. The earliest recorded form of the name is *Wæring wic*, and *Wæring* has been thought to be an Old English word meaning a dam, a derivative from *wer*, Modern English *weir*: thus 'dwellings by the weir'.

13 Cf. the title-page given in citation (11): *Heorrenda of Hægwudu*. – No forms of the name of this Staffordshire village are actually recorded from before the Norman Conquest, but the Old English form was undoubtedly *hæg-wudu* 'enclosed wood' (cf. the *High Hay*, the great hedge that protected Buckland from the Old Forest in *The Lord of the Rings*).

14 The name Luthany, of a country, occurs five times in Francis

Thompson's poem *The Mistress of Vision*. As noted previously (I. 29) my father acquired the Collected Poems of Francis Thompson in 1913–14; and in that copy he made a marginal note against one of the verses that contains the name *Luthany* – though the note is not concerned with the name. But whence Thompson derived *Luthany* I have no idea. He himself described the poem as 'a fantasy' (Everard Meynell, *The Life of Francis Thompson*, 1913, p. 237).

This provides no more than the origin of the name as a series of sounds, as with *Kôr* from Rider Haggard's *She,** or *Rohan* and *Moria* mentioned in my father's letter of 1967 on this subject (*The Letters of J. R. R. Tolkien*, pp. 383–4), in which he said:

> This leads to the matter of 'external history': the actual way in which I came to light on or choose certain sequences of sound to use as names, *before* they were given a place inside the story. I think, as I said, this is unimportant: the labour involved in my setting out what I know and remember of the process, or in the guess-work of others, would be far greater than the worth of the results. The spoken forms would simply be mere audible forms, and when transferred to the prepared linguistic situation in my story would receive meaning and significance according to that situation, and to the nature of the story told. It would be entirely delusory to refer to the sources of the sound-combination to discover any meanings overt or hidden.

15  The position is complicated by the existence of some narrative outlines of extreme roughness and near-illegibility in which the mariner is named Ælfwine and yet essential elements of 'the *Eriol* story' are present. These I take to represent an intermediate stage. They are very obscure, and would require a great deal of space to present and discuss; therefore I pass them by.

16  Cf. p. 264 (xiv).

17  *Caer Gwâr*: see p. 292.

18  It may be mentioned here that when my father read *The Fall of Gondolin* to the Exeter College Essay Club in the spring of 1920 the mariner was still *Eriol*, as appears from the notes for his preliminary remarks on that occasion (see *Unfinished Tales* p. 5). He said here, very strangely, that 'Eriol lights by accident on the Lonely Island'.

19  *Garsecg* (pronounced *Garsedge*, and so written in *Ælfwine* A) was one of the many Old English names of the sea.

20  In *Ælfwine I* the land is likewise named *Lúthien*, not *Luthany*. In *Ælfwine* A, on the other hand, the same distinction is made as in the outlines: 'Ælfwine of England (whom the fairies after named

___

* There is no external evidence for this, but it can hardly be doubted. In this case it might be thought that since the African Kôr was a city built on the top of a great mountain standing in isolation the relationship was more than purely 'phonetic'.

Lúthien (friend) of Luthany (friendship)).' – At this first occurrence (only) of *Lúthien* in *Ælfwine II* the form *Leithian* is
pencilled above, but *Lúthien* is not struck out. *The Lay of Leithian*
was afterwards the title of the long poem of Beren and Lúthien
Tinúviel.

21    The *Hill of Tûn*, i.e. the hill on which the city of Tûn was built: see
p. 292.

22    *Mindon Gwar*: see p. 291.

23    *Éadgifu*: in 'the *Eriol* story' this Old English name (see p. 323) was
given as an equivalent to Naimi, Eriol's wife whom he wedded in
Tol Eressëa (p. 290).

24    In *Ælfwine I* the text here reads: 'by reason of her beauty and
goodliness, even as that king of the Franks that was upon a time
most mighty among men hath said . . .' [*sic*]. In *Ælfwine II* the
manuscript in ink stops at 'high white shores', but after these words
my father pencilled in: 'even as that king of the Franks that was
in those days the mightiest of earthly kings hath said . . .' [*sic*]. The
only clue in *Ælfwine of England* to the period of Ælfwine's life is
the invasion of the Forodwaith (Vikings); the mighty king of the
Franks may therefore be Charlemagne, but I have been unable
to trace any such reference.

25    *Evil* is emended from *Melko*. *Ælfwine I* does not have the phrase.

26    *Ælfwine I* has: 'when the ancient Men of the South from
Micelgeard the Heartless Town set their mighty feet upon the soil
of Lúthien.' This text does not have the reference to Rûm and
Magbar. The name *Micelgeard* is struck through, but *Mickleyard*
is written at the head of the page. *Micelgeard* is Old English (and
*Mickleyard* a modernisation of this in spelling), though it does
not occur in extant Old English writings and is modelled on Old
Norse *Mikligarðr* (Constantinople). – The peculiar hostility of
the Romans to the Elves of Luthany is mentioned by implication in
citation (20), and their disbelief in their existence in (22).

27    The application, frequent in *Ælwine I*, of 'little' to the fairies
(Elves) of Lúthien and their ships was retained in *Ælfwine II* as
first written, but afterwards struck out. Here the word is twice
retained, perhaps unintentionally.

28    *Elvish* is a later emendation of *fairy*.

29    This sentence, from 'save Ælfheah . . .', was added later in
*Ælfwine II*; it is not in *Ælfwine I*. – The whole text to this point
in *Ælfwine I* and *II* is compressed into the following in *Ælfwine A*:

> Ælfwine of England (whom the fairies after named Lúthien
> (friend) of Luthany (friendship)) born of Déor and Éadgifu.
> Their city burned and Déor slain and Éadgifu dies. Ælfwine a
> thrall of the Winged Helms. He escapes to the Western Sea
> and takes ship from Belerion and makes great voyages. He is

seeking for the islands of the West of which Éadgifu had told him in his childhood.

30  *Ælfwine I* has here: 'But three men could he find as his companions; and Ossë took them unto him.' *Ossë* was emended to *Neorth*; and then the sentence was struck through and rewritten: 'Such found he only three; and those three Neorth after took unto him and their names are not known.' Neorth = Ulmo; see note 39.

31  *Ælfwine A* reads: 'He espies some islands lying in the dawn but is swept thence by great winds. He returns hardly to Belerion. He gathers the seven greatest mariners of England; they sail in spring. They are wrecked upon the isles of Ælfwine's desire and find them desert and lonely and filled with gloomy whispering trees.' This is at variance with *Ælfwine I* and *II* where Ælfwine is cast on to the island alone; but agrees with *II* in giving Ælfwine seven companions, not three.

32  A clue that this was Ulmo: cf. *The Fall of Gondolin* (p. 155): 'he was shod with mighty shoes of stone.'

33  In *Ælfwine A* they were 'filled with gloomy whispering trees' (note 31).

34  From the point where the Man of the Sea said: 'Lo, this is one of the ring of Harbourless Isles . . .' (p. 317) to here (i.e. the whole episode of the foundered Viking ship and its captain Orm, slayer of Ælfwine's father) there is nothing corresponding in *Ælfwine I*, which has only: 'but that Man of the Sea aided him in building a little craft, and together, guided by the solitary mariner, they fared away and came to a land but little known.' For the narrative in *Ælfwine A* see note 39.

35  At one occurrence of the name *Ythlings* (Old English *ýð* 'wave') in Ælfwine I it is written *Ythlingas*, with the Old English plural ending.

36  *The Shipmen of the West*: emendation from *Eneathrim*.

37  Cf. in the passage of alliterative verse in my father's *On Translating Beowulf* (*The Monsters and the Critics and Other Essays*, 1983, p. 63): *then away thrust her to voyage gladly valiant-timbered*.

38  The whole section of the narrative concerning the island of the Ythlings is more briefly told in *Ælfwine I* (though, so far as it goes, in very much the same words) with several features of the later story absent (notably the cutting of timber in the grove sacred to Ulmo, and the blessing of the ship by the Man of the Sea). The only actual difference of structure, however, is that whereas in *Ælfwine II* Ælfwine finds again his seven companions in the land of the Ythlings, and sails west with them, together with Bior of the Ythlings, in *Ælfwine I* they were indeed drowned, and he got seven companions from among the Ythlings (among whom Bior is not named).

39    The plot-outline *Ælfwine A* tells the story from the point where
Ælfwine and his seven companions were cast on the Isle of the Man
of the Sea (thus differing from *Ælfwine I* and *II*, where he came
there alone) thus:

> They wander about the island upon which they have been cast
> and come upon many decaying wrecks – often of mighty ships,
> some treasure-laden. They find a solitary cabin beside a lonely
> sea, built of old ship-wood, where dwells a solitary and strange
> old mariner of dread aspect. He tells them these are the Harbour-
> less Isles whose enchanted rocks draw all ships thither, lest men
> fare over far upon Garsedge [*see note 19*] – and they were
> devised at the Hiding of Valinor. Here, he says, the trees are
> magical. They learn many strange things about the western world
> of him and their desire is whetted for adventure. He aids them to
> cut holy trees in the island groves and to build a wonderful
> vessel, and shows them how to provision it against a long voyage
> (that water that drieth not save when heart fails, &c.). This he
> blesses with a spell of adventure and discovery, and then dives
> from a cliff-top. They suspect it was Neorth Lord of Waters.
>
> They journey many years among strange western islands hear-
> ing often many strange reports – of the belt of Magic Isles which
> few have passed; of the trackless sea beyond where the wind
> bloweth almost always from the West; of the edge of the twilight
> and the far-glimpsed isle there standing, and its glimmering
> haven. They reach the magic island [*read* islands?] and three
> are enchanted and fall asleep on the shore.
>
> The others beat about the waters beyond and are in despair –
> for as often as they make headway west the wind changes and
> bears them back. At last they tryst to return on the morrow if
> nought other happens. The day breaks chill and dull, and they
> lie becalmed looking in vain through the pouring rain.

This narrative differs from both *Ælfwine I* and *II* in that here
there is no mention of the Ythlings; and Ælfwine and his seven
companions depart on their long western voyage from the Harbourless Isle of the ancient mariner. It agrees with *Ælfwine I* in the
name Neorth; but it foreshadows *II* in the cutting of sacred trees
to build a ship.

40    In *Ælfwine I* Ælfheah does not appear, and his two speeches in
this passage are there given to one *Gelimer*. Gelimer (Geilamir) was
the name of a king of the Vandals in the sixth century.

41    In *Ælfwine I* Bior's speech is given to Gelimer (see note 40).

42    *Ælfwine I* ends in almost the same words as *Ælfwine II*, but with a
most extraordinary difference; Ælfwine does not leap overboard,
but returns with his companions to Belerion, and so never comes to

Tol Eressëa! 'Very empty thereafter were the places of Men for
Ælfwine and his mariners, and of their seed have been many
restless and wistful folk since they were dead . . .' Moreover my
father seems clearly to have been going to say the same in *Ælfwine
II*, but stopped, struck out what he had written, and introduced the
sentence in which Ælfwine leapt into the sea. I cannot see any way
to explain this.

*Ælfwine A* ends in much the same way as *Ælfwine II*:

As night comes on a little breath springs up and the clouds lift.
They hoist sail to return – when suddenly low down in the dusk
they see the many lights of the Haven of Many Hues twinkle
forth. They row thither, and hear sweet music. Then the mist
wraps all away and the others rousing themselves say it is a mirage
born of hunger, and with heavy hearts prepare to go back, but
Ælfwine plunges overboard and swims into the dark until he is
overcome in the waters, and him seems death envelops him. The
others sail away home and are out of the tale.

43   Literally, as he maintained: 'From that (grief) one moved on; from
     this in the same way one can move on.'
44   There are long roots beneath the words of *The Fellowship of the
     Ring* (I. 2): 'Elves . . . could now be seen passing westward through
     the woods in the evening, passing and not returning; but they
     were leaving Middle-earth and were no longer concerned with its
     troubles.' '"That isn't anything new, if you believe the old tales,"'
     said Ted Sandyman, when Sam Gamgee spoke of the matter.

I append here a synopsis of the structural differences between the
three versions of *Ælfwine of England*.

| A | I | II |
|---|---|---|
| Æ. sails from Belerion and sees 'islands in the dawn'. | As in A | As in A, but his companion Ælfheah is named. |
| Æ. sails again with 7 mariners of England. They are shipwrecked on the isle of the Man of the Sea but all survive. | Æ. has only 3 companions, and he alone survives the shipwreck. | Æ. has 7 companions, and is alone on the isle of the Man of the Sea, believing them drowned. |
| The Man of the Sea helps them to build a ship but does not go with them. | The Man of the Sea helps Æ. to build a boat and goes with him. | Æ. and the Man of the Sea find a stranded Viking ship and sail away in it together. |

| A | I | II |
|---|---|---|
| The Man of the Sea dives into the sea from a cliff-top of his isle. | They come to the Isle of the Ythlings. The Man of the Sea dives from a cliff-top. Æ. gets 7 companions from the Ythlings. | As in I, but Æ. finds his 7 companions from England, who were not drowned; to them is added Bior of the Ythlings. |
| On their voyages 3 of Æ.'s companions are enchanted in the Magic Isles. | As in A, but in this case they are Ythlings. | As in A |
| They are blown away from Tol Eressëa after sighting it; Æ. leaps overboard, and the others return home. | They are blown away from Tol Eressëa, and all, including Æ., return home. | As in A |

### Changes made to names, and differences in names, in the texts of *Ælfwine of England*

*Lúthien*    The name of the land in I and II; in A *Luthany* (see note 20).
*Déor*    At the first occurrence only in I *Déor* < *Heorrenda*, subsequently *Déor*; A *Déor*.
*Evadrien*    In I < *Erenol*. *Erenol* = 'Iron Cliff'; see I. 252, entry *Eriol*.
*Forodwaith*    II has *Forodwaith* < *Forwaith* < *Gwasgonin*; I has *Gwasgonin or the Winged Helms*; A has *the Winged Helms*.
*Outer Land*    < *Outer Lands* at both occurrences in II (pp. 316–17).
*Ælfheah*    I has *Gelimer* (at the first occurrence only < *Helgor*).
*Shipmen of the West*    In II < *Eneathrim*.

# APPENDIX
## NAMES IN THE *LOST TALES* – PART II

This appendix is designed only as an adjunct and extension to that in Part One. Names that have already been studied in Part One are not given entries in the following notes, if there are entries under that name in Part One, e.g. *Melko*, *Valinor*; but if, as is often the case, the etymological information in Part One is contained in an entry under some other name, this is shown, e.g. '*Gilim* See I.260 (*Melko*)'.

Linguistic information from the Name-list to *The Fall of Gondolin* (see p. 148) incorporated in these notes is referred to 'NFG'. 'GL' and 'QL' refer to the Gnomish and Qenya dictionaries (see I.246ff.). *Qenya* is the term used in both these books and is strictly the name of the language spoken in Tol Eressëa; it does not appear elsewhere in the early writings, where the distinction is between 'Gnomish' on the one hand and 'Elfin', 'Eldar', or 'Eldarissa' on the other.

★

**Alqaramë**  For the first element Qenya *alqa* 'swan' see I.249 (*Alqaluntë*). Under root RAHA QL gives *râ* 'arm', *rakta* 'stretch out, reach', *ráma* 'wing', *rámavoitë* 'having wings'; GL has *ram* 'wing, pinion', and it is noted that Qenya *ráma* is a confusion of this and a word *róma* 'shoulder'.

**Amon Gwareth**  Under root AM(U) 'up(wards)' QL gives *amu* 'up(wards)', *amu-* 'raise', *amuntë* 'sunrise', *amun(d)* 'hill'; GL has *am* 'up(wards)', *amon* 'hill, mount', adverb 'uphill'.

GL gives the name as *Amon 'Wareth* 'Hill of Ward', also *gwareth* 'watch, guard, ward', from the stem *gwar-* 'watch' seen also in the name of *Tinfang Warble* (*Gwarbilin* 'Birdward', I.268). See *Glamhoth, Gwarestrin*.

**Angorodin**  See I.249 (*Angamandi*) and I.256 (*Kalormë*).

**Arlisgion**  GL gives *Garlisgion* (see I.265 (*Sirion*)), as also does NFG, which has entries '*Garlisgion* was our name, saith Elfrith, for the Place of Reeds which is its interpretation', and '*lisg* is a reed (*liskë*)'. GL has *lisg, lisc* 'reed, sedge', and QL *liskë* with the same meaning. For *gar* see I.251 (*Dor Faidwen*).

**Artanor**  GL has *athra* 'across, athwart', *athron* adverb 'further, beyond', *athrod* 'crossing, ford' (changed later to *adr(a), adron, adros*). With *athra, adr(a)* is compared Qenya *arta*. Cf. also the name *Dor Athro* (p. 41). It is clear that both *Artanor* and *Dor Athro* meant 'the Land Beyond'. Cf. *Sarnathrod*.

**Asgon**   An entry in NFG says: *'Asgon* A lake in the "Land of Shadows" Dor Lómin, by the Elves named *Aksan.'*

**Ausir**   GL gives *avos* 'fortune, wealth, prosperity,' *avosir, Ausir* 'the same (personified)'; also *ausin* 'rich', *aus(s)aith* or *avosaith* 'avarice'. Under root AWA in QL are *autë* 'prosperity, wealth; rich', *ausië* 'wealth'.

**Bablon**   See p. 214.

**Bad Uthwen**   Gnomish *uthwen* 'way out, exit, escape', see I. 251 *(Dor Faidwen)*. The entry in NFG says: *'Bad Uthwen* [emended from *Uswen*] meaneth but "way of escape" and is in Eldarissa *Uswevandë.'* For *vandë* see I. 264 *(Qalvanda)*.

**Balcmeg**   In NFG it is said that Balcmeg 'was a great fighter among the Orclim *(Orqui* say the Elves) who fell to the axe of Tuor – 'tis in meaning "heart of evil".' (For *-lim* in *Orclim* see *Gondothlim.*) The entry for *Balrog* in NFG says: *'Bal* meaneth evilness, and *Balc* evil, and *Balrog* meaneth evil demon.' GL has *balc* 'cruel': see I. 250 *(Balrog)*.

**Bansil**   For the entry in NFG, where this name is translated 'Fairgleam', see p. 214; and for the elements of the name see I. 272 *(Vána)* and I. 265 *(Sil)*.

**Belaurin**   See I. 264 *(Palúrien)*.

**Belcha**   See I. 260 *(Melko)*. NFG has an entry: *'Belca* Though here [i.e. in the Tale] of overwhelming custom did Bronweg use the elfin names, this was the name aforetime of that evil Ainu.'

**Beleg**   See I. 254 *(Haloisi Velikë)*.

**Belegost**   For the first element see *Beleg*. GL gives *ost* 'enclosure, yard – town', also *oss* 'outer wall, town wall', *osta-* 'surround with walls, fortify', *ostor* 'enclosure, circuit of walls'. QL under root OSO has *os(t)* 'house, cottage', *osta* 'homestead', *ostar* 'township', *ossa* 'wall and moat'.

**bo-**   A late entry in GL: *'bo (bon)* (cf. Qenya *vô, vondo* "son") as patronymic prefix, *bo- bon-* "son of"'; as an example is given *Tuor bo-Beleg*. There is also a word *bôr* 'descendant'. See *go-, Indorion*.

**Bodruith**   In association with *bod-* 'back, again' GL has the words *bodruith* 'revenge', *bodruithol* 'vengeful (by nature)', *bodruithog* 'thirsting for vengeance', but these were struck out. There is also *gruith* 'deed of horror, violent act, vengeance'. – It may be that Bodruith Lord of Belegost was supposed to have received his name from the events of the *Tale of the Nauglafring*.

**Cópas Alqalunten**   See I. 257 *(Kópas)* and I. 249 *(Alqaluntë)*.

**Cris Ilbranteloth**   GL gives the group *crisc* 'sharp', *criss* 'cleft, gash, gully', *crist* 'knife', *crista-* 'slash, cut, slice'; NFG: *'Cris* meaneth much as doth *falc*, a cleft, ravine, or narrow way of waters with high walls'. QL under root KIRI 'cut, split' has *kiris* 'cleft, crack' and other words. For *ilbrant* 'rainbow' see I.256 (*Ilweran*). The final element is *teloth* 'roofing, canopy': see I.267–8 (*Teleri*).

**Cristhorn**  For *Cris* see *Cris Ilbranteloth*, and for *thorn* see I.266 (*Sorontur*). In NFG is the entry: '*Cris Thorn* is Eagles' Cleft or *Sornekiris*.'

**Cuilwarthon**  For *cuil* see I.257 (*Koivië-néni*); the second element is not explained.

**Cûm an-Idrisaith**  For *cûm* 'mound' see I.250 (*Cûm a Gumlaith*). *Idrisaith* is thus defined in GL: 'cf. *avosaith*, but that means avarice, money-greed, but *idrisaith* = excessive love of gold and gems and beautiful and costly things' (for *avosaith* see *Ausir*). Related words are *idra* 'dear, precious', *idra* 'to value, prize', *idri* (*id*) 'a treasure, a jewel', *idril* 'sweetheart' (see *Idril*).

**Curufin**  presumably contains *curu* 'magic'; see I.269 (*Tolli Kuruvar*).

**Dairon**  GL includes this name but without etymological explanation: '*Dairon* the fluter (Qenya *Sairon*).' See *Mar Vanwa Tyaliéva* below.

**Danigwiel**  In GL the Gnomish form is *Danigwethil*; see I.266 (*Taniquetil*). NFG has an entry: '*Danigwethil* do the Gnomes call *Taniquetil*; but seek for tales concerning that mountain rather in the elfin name.'

**(bo-)Dhrauthodavros**  '(Son of) the weary forest'. Gnomish *drauth* 'weary, toilworn', *drauthos* 'toil, weariness', *drautha-* 'to be weary'; for the second element *tavros* see I.267 (*Tavari*).

**Dor Athro**  See *Artanor, Sarnathrod*.

**Dor-na-Dhaideloth**  For Gnomish *dai* 'sky' see I.268 (*Telimektar*), and for *teloth* 'roofing, canopy' see *ibid*. (*Teleri*); cf. *Cris Ilbranteloth*.

**Dramborleg**  NFG has the following entry: '*Dramborleg* (or as it may be named *Drambor*) meaneth in its full form Thudder-sharp, and was the axe of Tuor that smote both a heavy dint as of a club and cleft as a sword; and the Eldar say *Tarambor* or *Tarambolaika*.' QL gives *Tarambor, Tarambolaike* 'Tuor's axe' under root TARA, TARAMA 'batter, thud, beat', with *taran, tarambo* 'buffet', and *taru* 'horn' (included here with a query: see *Taruithorn*). No Gnomish equivalents are cited in GL.

The second element is Gnomish *leg, lêg* 'keen, piercing', Qenya *laika*; cf. *Legolast* 'keen-sight', I.267 (*Tári-Laisi*).

**Duilin**  NFG has the following entry: '*Duilin* whose name meaneth Swallow was the lord of that house of the Gondothlim whose sign was the swallow and was surest of the archers of the Eldalië, but fell in the fall of Gondolin. Now the names of those champions appear but in Noldorissa, seeing that Gnomes they were, but his name would be in Eldarissa *Tuilindo*, and that of his house (which the Gnomes called *Nos Duilin*) *Nossë Tuilinda*.' *Tuilindo* '(spring-singer), swallow' is given in QL, see I.269 (*Tuilérë*); GL has *duilin(g)* 'swallow', with *duil, duilir* 'Spring', but these last were struck through and in another part of the book appear *tuil, tuilir* 'Spring' (see I.269).

For *nossë* 'kin, people' see I.272 (*Valinor*); GL does not give *nos* in this sense, but has *nosta-* 'be born', *nost* 'birth; blood, high birth; birthday', and *noss* (changed to *nôs*) 'birthday'. Cf. *Nost-na-Lothion* 'the Birth of Flowers', *Nos Galdon, Nos nan Alwen*.

**Eärámë** For *ea* 'eagle' see I.251 (*Eärendel*), and for *rámë* see *Alqarámë*. GL has an entry *Iorothram, -um* '= Qenya *Eärámë* or Eaglepinion, a name of one of Eärendel's boats'. For Gnomish *ior, ioroth* 'eagle' see I.251 (*Eärendel*), and cf. the forms *Earam, Earum* as the name of the ship (pp. 260, 276).

**Eärendel** See pp. 266–7 and I.251.

**Eärendilyon** See I.251 (*Eärendel*), and *Indorion*.

**Ecthelion** Both GL and NFG derive this name from *ecthel* 'fountain', to which corresponds Qenya *ektelë*. (This latter survived: cf. the entry *kel-* in the Appendix to *The Silmarillion*: 'from *et-kelë* "issue of water, spring" was derived, with transposition of the consonants, Quenya *ehtelë*, Sindarin *eithel*'. A later entry in GL gives *aithil* (< *ektl*) 'a spring'.) – A form *kektelë* is also found in Qenya from root KELE, KELU: see I.257 (*Kelusindi*).

**Egalmoth** NFG has the following entry: '*Egalmoth* is a great name, yet none know clearly its meaning – some have said its bearer was so named in that he was worth a thousand Elves (but Rúmil says nay) and others that it signifies the mighty shoulders of that Gnome, and so saith Rúmil, but perchance it was woven of a secret tongue of the Gondothlim' (for the remainder of this entry see p. 215). For Gnomish *moth* '1000' see I.270 (*Uin*).

GL interprets the name as Rúmil did, deriving it from *alm* (< *alðam-*)'the broad of the back from shoulder to shoulder, back, shoulders', hence *Egalmoth* = 'Broadshoulder'; the name in Qenya is said to be *Aikaldamor*, and an entry in QL of the same date gives *aika* 'broad, vast', comparing Gnomish *eg, egrin*. These in turn GL glosses as 'far away, wide, distant' and 'wide, vast, broad; far' (as in *Egla*; see I.251 (*Eldar*)).

**Eglamar** See I.251 (*Eldamar*). NFG has the following entry: '*Egla* said the son of Bronweg was the Gnome name of the Eldar (now but seldom used) who dwelt in Kôr, and they were called *Eglothrim* [emended from *Eglothlim*] (that is *Eldalië*), and their tongue *Lam Eglathon* or *Egladrin*. Rúmil said these names *Egla* and *Elda* were akin, but Elfrith cared not overmuch for such lore and they seem not over alike.' With this cf. I. 251 (*Eldar*). GL gives *lam* 'tongue', and *lambë* is found in QL: a word that survived into later Quenya. In QL it is given as a derivative of root LAVA 'lick', and defined 'tongue (of body, but also of land, or even = "speech")'.

**Eldarissa**  appears in QL ('the language of the Eldar') but without explanation of the final element. Possibly it was derived from the root ISI: *ista* 'know', *issë* 'knowledge, lore', *iswa, isqa* 'wise', etc.

**Elfrith**  See pp. 201–2, and I. 255 (*Ilverin*).

**Elmavoitë**  'One-handed' (Beren). See *Ermabwed*.

**Elwing**  GL has the following entry: '*Ailwing* older spelling of *Elwing* = "lake foam". As a noun = "white water-lily". The name of the maiden loved by Ioringli' (*Ioringli = Eärendel*, see I. 251). The first element appears in the words *ail* 'lake, pool', *ailion* 'lake', Qenya *ailo, ailin* – cf. later *Aelin-uial*. The second element is *gwing* 'foam': see I. 273 (*Wingilot*).

**Erenol**  See I. 252 (*Eriol*).

**Ermabwed**  'One-handed' (Beren). GL gives *mab* 'hand', *amabwed, mabwed* 'having hands', *mabwedri* 'dexterity', *mabol* 'skilful', *mablios* 'cunning', *mablad, mablod* 'palm of hand', *mabrin(d)* 'wrist'. A related word in Qenya was said in GL to be *mapa* (root MAPA) 'seize', but this statement was struck out. QL has also a root MAHA with many derivatives, notably *mā* (= *maha*) 'hand', *mavoitë* 'having hands' (cf. *Elmavoitë*).

**Faiglindra**  'Long-tressed' (Airin). Gnomish *faigli* 'hair, long tresses (especially used of women)'; *faiglion* 'having long hair', and *faiglim* of the same meaning, 'especially as a proper name', *Faiglim, Aurfaiglim* 'the Sun at noon'. With this is bracketed the word *faiglin(d)ra*.

**Failivrin**  Together with *fail* 'pale, pallid', *failthi* 'pallor', and *Failin* a name of the Moon, GL gives *Failivrin*: '(1) a maid beloved by Silmo; (2) a name among the Gnomes of many maidens of great beauty, especially Failivrin of the Rothwarin in the Tale of Turumart.' (In the Tale *Rothwarin* was replaced by *Rodothlim*.) The second element is *brin*, Qenya *vírin*, 'a magic glassy substance of great lucency used in fashioning the Moon. Used of things of great and pure transparency.' For *vírin* see I. 192–3.

**Falasquil**  Three entries in NFG refer to this name (for *falas* see also I. 253 (*Falman*)):

'*Falas* meaneth (even as *falas* or *falassë* in Eldar) a beach.'

'*Falas-a-Gwilb* the "beach of peace" was *Falasquil* in Elfin where Tuor at first dwelt in a sheltered cove by the Great Sea.' *-a-Gwilb* is struck through and above is written, apparently, '*Wilb or Wilma*.

'*Gwilb* meaneth "full of peace", which is *gwilm*.'

GL gives *gwîl, gwilm, gwilthi* 'peace', and *gwilb* 'quiet, peaceful'.

**Fangluin** 'Bluebeard'. See *Indrafang*. For *luin* 'blue' see I.262 (*Nielluin*).

**Foalókë**  Under a root FOHO 'hide, hoard, store up' QL gives *foa* 'hoard, treasure', *foina* 'hidden', *fölë* 'secrecy, a secret', *fôlima* 'secretive', and *foalókë* 'name of a serpent that guarded a treasure'. *lókë* 'snake' is derived from a root LOKO 'twine, twist, curl'.

GL originally had entries *fû, fûl, fûn* 'hoard', *fûlug* 'a dragon (who guards treasure)', and *ulug* 'wolf'. By later changes this construction was altered to *fuis* 'hoard', *fuithlug, -og* (the form that appears in the text, p. 70), *ulug* 'dragon' (cf. Qenya *lókë*). An entry in NFG reads: '*Lûg* is *lókë* of the Eldar, and meaneth "drake".'

**Fôs'Almir**  (Earlier name of *Faskala-númen*; translated in the text (p. 115) 'the bath of flame'.) For *fôs* 'bath' see I.253 (*Faskala-númen*). GL gives three names: '*Fôs Aura, Fôs'Almir,* and *Fôs na Ngalmir*, i.e. Sun's bath = the Western Sea.' For *Galmir, Aur,* names of the Sun, see I.254 and I.271 (*Úr*).

**Fuithlug**  See *Foalókë.*

**Galdor**  For the entry in NFG concerning Galdor see p. 215; as first written *galdon* was there said to mean 'tree', and Galdor's people to be named *Nos Galdon. Galdon* is not in GL. Subsequently *galdon* > *alwen*, and *alwen* does appear in GL, as a word of poetic vocabulary: *alwen* '= *orn*'. – Cf. Qenya *alda* 'tree' (see I.249 (*Aldaron*)), and the later relationship Quenya *alda*, Sindarin *galadh.*

**Gar Thurion**  NFG has the earlier form *Gar Furion* (p. 202), and GL has *furn, furion* 'secret, concealed', also *fûr* 'a lie' (Qenya *furu*) and *fur-* 'to conceal; to lie'. QL has *furin* and *hurin* 'hidden, concealed' (root FURU or HURU). With *Thurion* cf. *Thuringwethil* 'Woman of Secret Shadow', and *Thurin* 'the Secret', Finduilas' name for Túrin (*Unfinished Tales* pp. 157, 159).

**Gil**  See I.256 (*Ingil*).

**Gilim**  See I.260 (*Melko*).

**Gimli**  GL has *gimli* '(sense of) hearing', with *gim-* 'hear', *gimriol* 'attentive' (changed to 'audible'), *gimri* 'hearkening, attention'. The hearing of Gimli, the captive Gnome in the dungeons of Tevildo, 'was the keenest that has been in the world' (p. 29).

**Glamhoth**  GL defines this as 'name given by the Goldothrim to the Orcin: People of Dreadful Hate' (cf. 'folk of dreadful hate', p. 160). For *Goldothrim* see I.262 (*Noldoli*). The first element is *glâm* 'hatred, loathing'; other words are *glamri* 'bitter feud', *glamog* 'loathsome'. An entry in NFG says: '*Glam* meaneth "fierce hate" and even as *Gwar* has no kindred words in Eldar.'

For *hoth* 'folk' see I.264 (*orchoth* in entry *Orc*), and cf. *Goldothrim, Gondothlim, Rúmhoth, Thornhoth.* Under root HOSO QL gives *hos* 'folk', *hossë* 'army, band, troop', *hostar* 'tribe', *horma* 'horde, host'; also *Sankossi* 'the Goblins', equivalent of Gnomish *Glamhoth*, and evidently compounded of *sankë* 'hateful' (root SṆKṆ 'rend, tear') and *hossë*.

**Glend**  Perhaps connected with Gnomish *glenn* 'thin, fine', *glendrin* 'slender', *glendrinios* 'slenderness', *glent, glentweth* 'thinness'; Qenya root LENE 'long', which developed its meaning in different directions: 'slow, tedious, trailing', and 'stretch, thin': *lenka* 'slow', *lenwa* 'long and thin, straight, narrow', *lenu-* 'stretch', etc.

**Glingol**  For the entry in NFG, where the name is translated 'singing-gold', see p. 216; and see I.258 (*Lindelos*). The second element is *culu* 'gold', for which see I.255 (*Ilsaluntë*); another entry in NFG reads: '*Culu* or *Culon* is a name we have in poesy for *Glor* (and. Rúmil saith that it is the Elfin *Kulu*, and -*gol* in our *Glingol*).'

**Glorfalc**  For *glor* see I.258 (*Laurelin*). NFG has an entry: '*Glor* is gold and is that word that cometh in verse of the Kôr-Eldar *laurë* (so saith Rúmil).'

*Falc* is glossed in GL '(1) cleft, gash; (2) cleft, ravine, cliffs' (also given is *falcon* 'a great two-handed sword, twibill', which was changed to *falchon*, and so close to English *falchion* 'broadsword'). NFG has: '*Falc* is cleft and is much as *Cris*; being Elfin *Falqa*'; and under root FḶKḶ in QL are *falqa* 'cleft, mountain pass, ravine' and *falqan* 'large sword'. GL has a further entry: *Glorfalc* 'a great ravine leading out of Garioth'. *Garioth* is here used of Hisilómë; see I.252 (*Eruman*). Cf. later *Orfalch Echor*.

**Glorfindel**  For the entry in NFG, where the name is rendered 'Goldtress', see p. 216. For *glor* see I.258 (*Laurelin*), and *Glorfalc*. GL had an entry *findel* 'lock of hair', together with *fith* (*fidhin*) 'a single hair', *fidhra* 'hairy', but *findel* was struck out; later entries are *finn* 'lock of hair' (see *fin-* in the Appendix to *The Silmarillion*) and *fingl* or *finnil* 'tress'. NFG: '*Findel* is "tress", and is the Elfin *Findil*.' Under root FIRI QL gives *findl* 'lock of hair' and *firin* 'ray of the sun'.

In another place in GL the name *Glorfindel* was given, and translated 'Goldlocks', but it was changed later to *Glorfinn*, with a variant *Glorfingl*.

**Glorund**  For *glor* see I.258 (*Laurelin*), and *Glorfalc*. GL gives *Glorunn* 'the great drake slain by Turumart'. Neither of the Qenya forms *Laurundo, Undolaurë* (p. 84) appear in QL, which gives an earlier name for 'the great worm', *Fentor*, together with *fent* 'serpent', *fenumë* 'dragon'. As this entry was first written it read 'the great worm slain by Ingilmo'; to this was added 'or Turambar'.

**Golosbrindi**  (Earlier name of Hirilorn, rendered in the text (p. 51) 'Queen of the Forest'.) A word *goloth* 'forest' is given in GL, derived from *\*gwōloth*, which is itself composed of *aloth* (*alos*), a verse word meaning 'forest' (= *taur*), and the prefix *\*ngua* > *gwa*, unaccented *go*, 'together, in one', 'often used merely intensively'.

The corresponding word in Qenya is said to be *málos*, which does not appear in QL.

**Gondobar**  See *Gondolin*, and for *-bar* see I.251 (*Eldamar*). In GL the form *Gondobar* was later changed to *Gonthobar*.

**Gondolin**  To the entries cited in I.254 may be added that in NFG: '*Gond* meaneth a stone, or stone, as doth Elfin *on* and *ondo*.' For the statement about Gondolin (where the name is rendered 'stone of song') in NFG see p. 216; and for the latest formulation of the etymology of *Gondolin* see the Appendix to *The Silmarillion*, entry *gond*.

**Gondothlim**  GL has the following entry concerning the word *lim* 'many', Qenya *limbë* (not in QL): 'It is frequently suffixed and so becomes a second plural inflexion. In the singular it = English "many a", as *golda-lim*. It is however most often suffixed to the plural in those nouns making their plural in *-th*. It then changes to *-rim* after *-l*. Hence great confusion with *grim* "host" and *thlim* "race", as in *Goldothrim* ("the people of the Gnomes").' NFG has an entry: '*Gondothlim* meaneth "folk of stone" and (saith Rúmil) is *Gond* "stone", whereto be added *Hoth* "folk" and that *-lim* we Gnomes add after to signify "the many".' Cf. *Lothlim*, *Rodothlim*, and *Orclim* in entry *Balcmeg*; for *hoth* see *Glamhoth*.

**Gondothlimbar**  See *Gondolin*, *Gondothlim*, and for *-bar* see I.251 (*Eldamar*). In GL the form *Gondothlimbar* was later changed to '*Gonthoflimar or Gonnothlimar*'.

**go-**  An original entry in GL, later struck out, was: *gon- go-* 'son of, patronymic prefix (cf. suffix *ios/ion/io* and Qenya *yô, yondo*)'. The replacement for this is given above under *bo-*. See *Indorion*.

**Gon Indor**  See *go-*, *Indorion*.

**Gothmog**  See pp. 67, 216, and I.258 (*Kosomot*). GL has *mog-* 'detest, hate', *mogri* 'detestation', *mogrin* 'hateful'; Qenya root MOKO 'hate'. In addition to *goth* 'war, strife' (Qenya root KOSO 'strive') may be noted *gothwen* 'battle', *gothweg* 'warrior', *gothwin* 'Amazon', *gothriol* 'warlike', *gothfeng* 'war-arrow', *gothwilm* 'armistice'.

**Gurtholfin**  GL: *Gurtholfin* 'Urdolwen, a sword of Turambar's, Wand of Death'. Also given is *gurthu* 'death' (Qenya *urdu*; not in QL). The second element of the name is *olfin(g)* (also *olf*) 'branch, wand, stick' (Qenya *olwen(n)*).

It may be noted that in QL Turambar's sword is given as *Sangahyando* 'cleaver of throngs', from roots SANGA 'pack tight, press' (*sanga* 'throng') and HYARA 'plough through' (*hyar* 'plough', *hyanda* 'blade, share'). *Sangahyando* 'Throng-cleaver' survived to become the name of a man in Gondor (see the Appendix to *The Silmarillion*, entry *thang*).

**Gwar**  See I.257 (*Kôr, korin*).

**Gwarestrin**  Rendered in the Tale (p. 158) as 'Tower of Guard', and so also in NFG; GL glosses it 'watchtower (especially as a name of Gondolin)'. A late entry in GL gives *estirin, estirion, estrin* 'pinnacle', beside *esc* 'sharp point, sharp edge'. The second element of this word is *tiri(o)n*; see I.258 (*Kortirion*). For *gwar* see *Amon Gwareth*.

**Gwedheling** See I.273 (*Wendelin*).

**Heborodin** 'The Encircling Hills.' Gnomish preposition *heb* 'round about, around'; *hebrim* 'boundary', *hebwirol* 'circumspect'. For *orod* see I.256 (*Kalormë*).

**Hirilorn** GL gives *hiril* 'queen (a poetic use), princess; feminine of *bridhon*'. For *bridhon* see *Tevildo*. The second element is *orn* 'tree'. (It may be mentioned here that the word *neldor* 'beech' is found in QL; see the Appendix to *The Silmarillion*, entry *neldor*).

**Idril** For Gnomish *idril* 'sweetheart' see *Cûm an-Idrisaith*. There is another entry in GL as follows: *Idhril* 'a girl's name often confused with *Idril*. *Idril* = "beloved" but *Idhril* = "mortal maiden". Both appear to have been the names of the daughter of Turgon – or apparently *Idril* was the older and the Kor-eldar called her *Irildë* (= *Idhril*) because she married Tuor.' Elsewhere in GL appear *idhrin* 'men, earth-dwellers; especially used as a folk-name contrasted with *Eglath* etc.; cf. Qenya *indi*', and *Idhru, Idhrubar* 'the world, all the regions inhabited by Men; cf. Qenya *irmin*'. In QL these words *indi* and *irmin* are given under root IRI 'dwell?', with *irin* 'town', *indo* 'house', *indor* 'master of house' (see *Indor*), etc.; but *Irildë* does not appear. Similar words are found in Gnomish: *ind, indos* 'house, hall', *indor* 'master (of house), lord'.

After the entry in NFG on *Idril* which has been cited (p.216) a further note was added: 'and her name meaneth "Beloved", but often do Elves say *Idhril* which more rightly compares with *Irildë* and that meaneth "mortal maiden", and perchance signifies her wedding with Tuor son of Men.' An isolated note (written in fact on a page of the *Tale of the Nauglafring*) says: 'Alter name of *Idril* to *Idhril*. The two were confused: *Idril* = "beloved", *Idhril* = "maiden of mortals". The Elves thought this her name and called her *Irildë* (because she married Tuor Pelecthon).'

**Ilbranteloth** See *Cris Ilbranteloth*.

**Ilfiniol, Ilfrith** See I.255 (*Ilverin*).

**Ilúvatar** An entry in NFG may be noticed here: '*En* do the mystic sayings of the Noldoli also name *Ilathon* [emended from *Âd Ilon*], who is Ilúvatar – and this is like the Eldar *Enu*.' QL gives *Enu*, the Almighty Creator who dwells without the world. For *Ilathon* see I.255–6 (*Ilwë*).

**Indor** (Father of Tuor's father Peleg). This is perhaps the word *indor* 'master (of house), lord' (see *Idril*) used as a proper name.

**Indorion**   See *go-*. QL gives *yô, yond-* as poetic words for 'son', adding: 'but very common as *-ion* in patronymics (and hence practically = "descendant")'; also *yondo* 'male descendant, usually (great) grandson' (cf. Eärendel's name *Gon Indor*). Cf. *Eärendilyon*.

**Indrafang**   GL has *indra* 'long (also used of time)', *indraluin* 'long ago'; also *indravang* 'a special name of the *nauglath* or dwarves', on which see p. 247. These forms were changed later to *in(d)ra, in(d)rafang, in(d)raluin/idhraluin*.

An original entry in GL was *bang* 'beard' = Qenya *vanga*, but this was struck out; and another word with the same meaning as *Indravang* was originally entered as *Bangasur* but changed to *Fangasur*. The second element of this is *sûr* 'long, trailing', Qenya *sóra*, and a later addition here is *Surfang* 'a long-beard, a *naugla* or *inrafang*'. Cf. *Fangluin*, and later *Fangorn* 'Treebeard'.

**Irildë**   See *Idril*.

**Isfin**   NFG has this entry: '*Isfin* was the sister of Turgon Lord of Gondolin, whom Eöl at length wedded; and it meaneth either "snow-locks" or "exceeding-cunning".' Long afterwards my father, noting that *Isfin* was 'derived from the earliest (1916) form of *The Fall of Gondolin*', said that the name was 'meaningless'; but with the second element cf. *finn* 'lock of hair' (see *Glorfindel*) or *fim* 'clever', *finthi* 'idea, notion', etc. (see I. 253 (*Finwë*)).

**Ivárë**   GL gives *Ior* 'the famous "piper of the sea"', Qenya *Ivárë*.'

**Íverin**   A late entry in GL gives *Aivrin or Aivrien* 'an island off the west coast of Tol Eressëa, Qenya *Íwerin* or *Iverindor*.' QL has *Íverind-* 'Ireland'.

**Karkaras**   In GL this is mentioned as the Qenya form; the Gnomish name of 'the great wolf-warden of Belca's door' was *Carcaloth* or *Carcamoth*, changed to *Carchaloth, Carchamoth*. The first element is *carc* 'jag, point, fang'; QL under root KṚKṚ has *karka* 'fang, tooth, tusk', *karkassë, karkaras* 'row of spikes or teeth'.

**Kosmoko**   See *Gothmog*.

**Kurûki**   See I. 269 (*Tolli Kuruvar*).

**Ladwen-na-Dhaideloth**   'Heath of the Sky-roof'. See *Dor-na-Dhaideloth*. GL gives *ladwen* '(1) levelness, flatness; (2) a plain, heath; (3) a plane; (4) surface.' Other words are *ladin* 'level, smooth; fair, equable' (cf. *Tumladin*), *lad* 'a level' (cf. *mablad* 'palm of hand' mentioned under *Ermabwed*), *lada-* 'to smooth out, stroke, soothe, beguile', and *ladwinios* 'equity'. There are also words *bladwen* 'a plain' (see I. 264 (*Palúrien*)), and *fladwen* 'meadow' (with *flad* 'sward' and *Fladweth Amrod (Amrog)* 'Nomad's Green', 'a place in *Tol Erethrin* where Eriol sojourned a while; nigh to Tavrobel.' *Amrog, amrod* = 'wanderer', 'wandering', from *amra-* 'go up and down, live in the mountains, wander'; see *Amon Gwareth*).

**Laiqalassë**   See I. 267 (*Tári-laisi*), I. 254 (*Gar Lossion*).

**Laurundo**   See *Glorund*.

**Legolas**   See *Laiqalassë*.

**Lindeloktë**   See I. 258 (*Lindelos*).

**Linwë Tinto**   See I. 269 (*Tinwë Linto*).

**Lókë**   See *Foalókë*.

**Lôs**   See I. 254 (*Gar Lossion*). The later form *loth* does not appear in GL (which has however *lothwing* 'foamflower'). NFG has '*Lôs* is a flower and in Eldarissa *lossë* which is a rose' (all after the word 'flower' struck out).

**Lósengriol**   As with *lôs*, the later form *lothengriol* does not appear in GL. *Losengriol* is translated 'lily of the valley' in GL, which gives the Gnomish words *eng* 'smooth, level', *enga* 'plain, vale', *engri* 'a level', *engriol* 'vale-like; of the vale'. NFG says '*Eng* is a plain or vale and *Engriol* that which liveth or dwelleth therein', and translates *Lósengriol* 'flower of the vale or lily of the valley'.

**Los 'lóriol**   (changed from *Los Glóriol*; the Golden Flower of Gondolin). See I. 254 (*Gar Lossion*), and for *glóriol* 'golden' see I. 258 (*Laurelin*).

**Loth, Lothengriol**   See *Lôs, Lósengriol*.

**Lothlim**   See *Lôs* and *Gondothlim*. The entry in NFG reads: '*Lothlim* being for *Loslim* meaneth folk of the flower, and is that name taken by the Exiles of Gondolin (which city they had called *Lôs* aforetime).'

**Mablung**   For *mab* 'hand' see *Ermabwed*. The second element is *lung* 'heavy; grave, serious'; related words are *lungra-* 'weigh, hang heavy', *luntha* 'balance, weigh', *lunthang* 'scales'.

**Malkarauki**   See I. 250 (*Balrog*).

**Mar Vanwa Tyaliéva**   See I. 260 and add: a late entry in GL gives the Gnomish name, *Bara Dhair Haithin*, the Cottage of Lost Play; also *daira-* 'play' (with *dairwen* 'mirth', etc.), and *haim or haithin* 'gone, departed, lost' (with *haitha-* 'go, walk', etc.). Cf. *Dairon*.

**Mathusdor**   (Aryador, Hisilómë). In GL are given *math* 'dusk', *mathrin* 'dusky', *mathusgi* 'twilight', *mathwen* 'evening'. See *Umboth-muilin*.

**Mavwin**   A noun *mavwin* 'wish' in GL was struck out, but related words allowed to stand: *mav-* 'like', *mavra* 'eager after', *mavri* 'appetite', *mavrin* 'delightful, desirable', *mavros* 'desire', *maus* 'pleasure; pleasant'. Mavwin's name in Qenya, *Mavoinë*, is not in QL, unless it is to be equated with *maivoinë* 'great longing'.

**Meleth**   A noun *meleth* 'love' is found in GL; see I. 262 (*Nessa*).

**Melian, Melinon, Melinir**   None of these names occur in the glossaries, but probably all are derivatives of the stem *mel-* 'love'; see I. 262 (*Nessa*). The later etymology of *Melian* derived the name from *mel-* 'love' (*Melyanna* 'dear gift').

**Meoita, Miaugion, Miaulë**   See *Tevildo*.

**Mindon-Gwar**   For *mindon* 'tower' see I. 260 (*Minethlos*); and for *Gwar* see p. 291 and I. 257 (*Kôr, korin*).

**Morgoth**   See p. 67 and *Gothmog*. For the element *mor-* see I. 261 (*Mornië*).

**Mormagli, Mormakil**   See I. 261 (*Mornië*) and I. 259 (*Makar*).

**Nan Dumgorthin**   See p. 62. For *nan* see I. 261 (*Nandini*).

**Nantathrin**   This name does not occur in the *Lost Tales*, where the Land of Willows is called *Tasarinan*, but GL gives it (see I. 265 (*Sirion*)) and NFG has an entry: '*Dor-tathrin* was that Land of Willows of which this and many a tale tells.' GL has *tathrin* 'willow', and QL *tasarin* of the same meaning.

**Nauglafring**   GL has the following entry: '*Nauglafring = Fring na Nauglithon*, the Necklace of the Dwarves. Made for Ellu by the Dwarves from the gold of Glorund that Mîm the fatherless cursed and that brought ruin on Beren Ermabwed and Damrod his son and was not appeased till it sank with Elwing beloved of Eärendel to the bottom of the sea.' For Damrod (Daimord) son of Beren see pp. 139, 259, and for the loss of Elwing and the Nauglafring see pp. 255, 264. This is the only reference to the 'appeasing' of Mîm's curse. – Gnomish *fring* means 'carcanet, necklace' (Qenya *firinga*).

**Níniel**   Cf. Gnomish *nîn* 'tear', *ninios* 'lamentation', *ninna-* 'weep'; see I. 262 (*Nienna*).

**Nínin-Udathriol**   ('Unnumbered Tears'). See *Níniel*. GL gives *tathn* 'number', *tathra-* 'number, count', *udathnarol, udathriol* 'innumerable'. *Û-* is a 'negative prefix with any part of speech'. (QL casts no light on *Nieriltasinwa*, p. 84, apart from the initial element *nie* 'tear', see I. 262 (*Nienna*).)

**Noldorissa**   See *Eldarissa*.

**Nos Galdon, Nos nan Alwen**   See *Duilin, Galdor*.

**Nost-na-Lothion**   See *Duilin*.

**Parma Kuluinen**   The Golden Book, see p. 310. This entry is given in QL under root PARA: *parma* 'skin, bark; parchment; book, writings'. This word survived in later Quenya (*The Lord of the Rings* III. 401). For *Kuluinen* see *Glingol*.

**Peleg**   (Father of Tuor). GL has a common noun *peleg* 'axe', verb *pelectha-* 'hew' (QL *pelekko* 'axe', *pelekta-* 'hew'). Cf. Tuor's name *Pelecthon* in the note cited under *Idril*.

**Ramandur**   See I. 259 (*Makar*).

**Rog**   GL gives an adjective *rôg, rog* 'doughty, strong'. But with the Orcs' name for Egnor Beren's father, Rog the Fleet, cf. *arog* 'swift, rushing', and *raug* of the same meaning; Qenya *arauka*.

**Rôs**   GL gives yet another meaning of this name: 'the Sea' (Qenya *Rása*).

**Rodothlim**   See *Rothwarin* (earlier form replaced by *Rodothlim*).

**Rothwarin**   GL has this name in the forms *Rothbarin, Rosbarin*: '(literally "cavern-dwellers") name of a folk of secret Gnomes and also of the regions about their cavernous homes on the banks of the river.' Gnomish words derived from the root ROTO 'hollow' are *rod* 'tube, stem', *ross* 'pipe', *roth* 'cave, grot', *rothrin* 'hollow', *rodos* 'cavern'; QL gives *rotsë* 'pipe', *róta* 'tube', *ronta, rotwa* 'hollow', *rotelë* 'cave'.

**Rúmhoth**   See *Glamhoth*.

**Rúsitaurion**   GL gives a noun *rûs* (*rôs*) 'endurance, longsuffering, patience', together with adjective *rô* 'enduring, longsuffering; quiet, gentle', and verb *rô-* 'remain, stay; endure'. For *taurion* see I.267 (*Tavari*).

**Sarnathrod**   Gnomish *sarn* 'a stone'; for *athrod* 'ford' see *Artanor*.

**Sarqindi**   ('Cannibal-ogres'). This must derive from the root SṚKṚ given in QL, with derivatives *sarko* 'flesh', *sarqa* 'fleshy', *sarkuva* 'corporeal, bodily'.

**Silpion**   An entry in NFG (p. 215) translates the name as 'Cherry-moon'. In QL is a word *pio* 'plum, cherry' (with *piukka* 'black-berry', *piosenna* 'holly', etc.), and also *Valpio* 'the holy cherry of Valinor'. GL gives *Piosil* and *Silpios*, without translation, as names of the Silver Tree, and also a word *piog* 'berry'.

**Taimonto**   See I.268 (*Telimektar*).

**Talceleb, Taltelepta**   (Name of *Idril*/*Irildë*, 'of the Silver Feet'.) The first element is Gnomish *tâl* 'foot (of people and animals)'; related words are *taltha* 'foot (of things), base, pedestal, pediment', *talrind, taldrin* 'ankle', *taleg, taloth* 'path' – another name for the Way of Escape into Gondolin was *Taleg Uthwen* (see *Bad Uthwen*). QL under root TALA 'support' gives *tala* 'foot', *talwi* (dual) 'the feet', *talas* 'sole', etc. For the second element see I.268 (*Telimpë*). QL gives the form *telepta* but without translation.

**Tarnin Austa**   For *tarn* 'gate' see I.261 (*Moritarnon*). GL gives *aust* 'summer'; cf. *Aur* 'the Sun', I.271 (*Ûr*).

**Taruithorn, Taruktarna**   (Oxford). GL gives *târ* 'horn' and *tarog* 'ox' (Qenya *taruku-*), *Taruithron* older *Taruitharn* 'Oxford'. Immediately following these words are *tarn* 'gate' and *taru* '(1) cross (2) crossing'. QL has *taru* 'horn' (see *Dramborleg*), *tarukka* 'horned', *tarukko, tarunko* 'bull', *Taruktarna* 'Oxford', and under root TARA *tara-* 'cross, go athwart', *tarna* 'crossing, passage'.

**Tasarinan**   See *Nantathrin*.

**Taurfuin**   See I. 267 (*Tavari*) and I. 253 (*Fui*).

**Teld Quing Ilon**   NFG has an entry: '*Cris a Teld Quing Ilon* signifieth Gully of the Rainbow Roof, and is in the Eldar speech *Kiris Iluqingatelda*'; a *Teld Quing Ilon* was struck out and replaced by *Ilbranteloth*. Another entry reads: '*Ilon* is the sky'; in GL *Ilon* (= Qenya *Ilu*) is the name of *Ilúvatar* (see I. 255 (*Ilwë*)). *Teld* does not appear in GL, but related words as *telm* 'roof' are given (see I. 267–8 (*Teleri*)); and *cwing* = 'a bow'. QL has *iluqinga* 'rainbow' (see I. 256 (*Ilweran*)) and *telda* 'having a roof' (see I. 268 (*Telimektar*)). For *Cris, Kiris* see *Cris Ilbranteloth*.

**Tevildo, Tifil**   For the etymology see I. 268, to which can be added that the earlier Gnomish form *Tifil* (later *Tiberth*) is associated in GL with a noun *tif* 'resentment, ill-feeling, bitterness'.

   *Vardo Meoita* 'Prince of Cats': for *Vardo* see I. 273 (*Varda*). QL gives *meoi* 'cat'.

   *Bridhon Miaugion* 'Prince of Cats': *bridhon* 'king, prince', cf. *Bridhil*, Gnomish name of Varda (I. 273). Nouns *miaug, miog* 'tomcat' and *miauli* 'she-cat' (changed to *miaulin*) are given in GL, where the Prince of Cats is called *Tifil Miothon or Miaugion*. *Miaulë* was the name of Tevildo's cook (p. 28).

**Thorndor**   See I. 266 (*Sorontur*).

**Thornhoth**   See *Glamhoth*.

**Thorn Sir**   See I. 265 (*Sirion*).

**Tifanto**   This name is clearly to be associated with the Gnomish words (*tif-, tifin*) given in I. 268 (*Tinfang*).

**Tifil**   See *Tevildo*.

**Tirin**   See I. 258 (*Kortirion*).

**Tôn a Gwedrin**   *Tôn* is a Gnomish word meaning 'fire (on a hearth)', related to *tan* and other words given under *Tanyasalpë* (I. 266–7); *Tôn a Gwedrin* 'the Tale-fire' in *Mar Vanwa Tyaliéva*. Cf. *Tôn Sovriel* 'the fire lake of Valinor' (*sovriel* 'purification', *sovri* 'cleansing'; *sôn* 'pure, clean', *soth* 'bath', *sô-* 'wash, clean, bathe').

   *Gwedrin* belongs with *cwed-* (preterite *cwenthi*) 'say, tell', *cweth* 'word', *cwent* 'tale, saying', *cwess* 'saying, proverb', *cwedri* 'telling (of tales)', *ugwedriol* 'unspeakable, ineffable'. In QL under root QETE are *qet- (qentë)* 'speak, talk', *quent* 'word', *qentelë* 'sentence', *Eldaqet = Eldarissa*, etc. Cf. the Appendix to *The Silmarillion*, entry *quen- (quet-)*.

**Tumladin**   For the first element, Gnomish *tûm* 'valley', see I. 269 (*Tombo*), and for the second, *ladin* 'level, smooth' see *Ladwen na Dhaideloth*.

**Turambar**   For the first element see I. 260 (*Meril-i-Turinqi*). QL gives *amarto, ambar* 'Fate', and also (root MŖTŖ) *mart* 'a piece of luck', *marto* 'fortune, fate, lot', *mart-* 'it happens' (impersonal). GL has *mart* 'fate', *martion* 'fated, doomed, fey'; also *umrod* and *umbart* 'fate'.

**Turumart**   See *Turambar*.

**Ufedhin**   Possible connections of this name are Gnomish *uf* 'out of, forth from', or *fedhin* 'bound by agreement, ally, friend'.

**Ulbandi**   See I.260 (*Melko*).

**Ulmonan**   The Gnomish name was *Ingulma(n)* (*Gulma* = *Ulmo*), with the prefix *in-* (*ind-, im-*) 'house of' (*ind* 'house', see *Idril*). Other examples of this formation are *Imbelca, Imbelcon* 'Hell (house of Melko)', *inthorn* 'eyrie', *Intavros* 'forest' (properly 'the forest palace of Tavros').

**Umboth-muilin**   Gnomish *umboth, umbath* 'nightfall'; *Umbathor* is a name of Garioth (see I.252 (*Eruman*)). This word is derived from *\*mbaþ-*, related to *\*maþ-* seen in *math* 'dusk': see *Mathusdor*. The second element is *muil* 'tarn', Qenya *moilë*.

**Undolaurë**   See *Glorund*.

**Valar**   NFG has the following entry: '*Banin* [emended from *Banion*] or *Bandrim* [emended from *Banlim*]. Now these dwell, say the Noldoli, in *Gwalien* [emended from *Banien*] but they are spoken of ever by Elfrith and the others in their Elfin names as the *Valar* (or *Vali*), and that glorious region of their abode is *Valinor*.' See I.272 (*Valar*).

# SHORT GLOSSARY OF OBSOLETE, ARCHAIC, AND RARE WORDS

Words that have been given in the similar glossary to Part I (such as *an* 'if', *fain*, *lief*, *meed*, *rede*, *ruth*) are not as a rule repeated here. Some words of current English used in obsolete senses are included.

**acquaint**   old past participle, superseded by *acquainted*, 287
**ardour**   burning heat, 38, 170 (modern sense 194)
**bested**   beset, 193
**bravely**   splendidly, showily, 75
**broidure**   embroidery, 163. Not recorded, but *broid-* varied with *broud-* etc. in Middle English, and *broudure* 'embroidery' is found.
**burg**   walled and fortified town, 175
**byrnie**   body-armour, corslet, coat-of-mail, 163
**carcanet**   ornamental collar or necklace, 227–8, 235, 238
**carle**   (probably) serving-man, 85; **house-carle** 190
**chain**   linear measure (a chain's length), sixty-six feet, 192
**champain**   level, open country, 295, 298
**clue**   thread, 322
**cot**   small cottage, 95, 141
**damasked**   224, **damascened** 173, 227, ornamentally inlaid with designs in gold and silver.
**diapered**   covered with a small pattern, 173
**dight**   arrayed, fitted out, 173
**drake**   dragon, 41, 46, 85–7, etc. (*Drake* is the original English word, Old English *draca*, derived from Latin; *dragon* was from French).
**drolleries**   comic plays or entertainments, 190
**enow**   enough, 241–2
**enthralled**   enslaved, 97, 163, 196, 198
**entreat**   treat, 26, 77, 87, 236 (modern sense 38)
**errant**   wandering, 42
**estate**   situation, 97
**ewer**   pitcher for water, 226
**eyot**   small island, 7
**fathom**   linear measure (six feet), formerly not used only of water, 78
**fell in dread**   fell into dread, 106
**force**   waterfall, 105 (Northern English, from Scandinavian).
**fordone**   overcome, 233
**fosses**   pits, 288
**fretted**   adorned with elaborate carving, 297

**glamour**   enchantment, spell, 314
**greaves**   armour for the lower leg, 163
**guestkindliness**   hospitality, 228. Apparently not recorded; used in I.175.
**haply**   perhaps, 13, 94, 99
**hie**   hasten; **hie thee**, hasten, 75
**high-tide**   festival, 231
**house-carle**   190, see **carle**.
**inly**   inwardly, 315
**jacinth**   blue, 274
**kempt**   combed, 75; **unkempt**, uncombed, 159
**kirtle**   long coat or tunic, 154
**knave**   male child, boy, 96 (the original sense of the word, long since lost).
**lair**   in **the dragon's lair**, 105, the place where the dragon was lying (i.e. happened at that time to be lying).
**lambent**   (of flame) playing lightly on a surface without burning, 297
**league**   about three miles, 171, 189, 201
**lealty**   loyalty, 185
**let**   desisted, 166; allowed, 181; **had let fashion**, had had fashioned, 174, **let seize**, had (him) seized, 225, **let kill**, had (them) killed, 235
**like**   please, 41; **good liking**, good will, friendly disposition, 169
**list**   wish, 85, 101; like, 236
**or ever**   before ever, 5–6, 38, 80, 110, 233–4, 240
**or ... or**   either ... or, 226
**pale**   boundary, 269
**ports**   gateways, 299
**prate**   chatter, speak to no purpose, 75
**puissance**   power, 168
**repair**   make one's way, go, 162
**runagate**   deserter, 15, 44 (the same word in origin as **renegade**, 15, 44, 224, 232)
**scathe**   hurt, harm, 99, 233
**scatterlings**   wanderers, stragglers, 182
**sconces**   brackets fastened on a wall, to carry candle or torch, 226
**scullion**   menial kitchen-servant, drudge, 17, 45
**shallop**   274. See I.275; but here the boat is defined as oarless.
**silvern**   silver, 270 (the original Old English adjective).
**slot**   track of an animal, 38, 96 (=**spoor** 38).
**stead**   farm, 89
**stricken**   in **the Stricken Anvil**, struck, beaten, 174, 179
**swinge**   stroke, blow, 194
**thews**   strength, bodily power, 33
**tilth**   cultivated (tilled) land, 4, 88, 101
**tithe**   tenth part, 188, 223, 227

**travail**   hardship, suffering, 77, 82, 239; toil, 168; **travailed**, toiled, 163; **travailing**, enduring hardship, 75
**trencher**   large dish or platter, 226
**uncouth**   85 perhaps has the old meaning 'strange', but elsewhere (13, 75, 115) has the modern sense.
**vambrace**   armour for the fore-arm, 163
**weird**   fate, 85–6, 111, 155, 239
**whin**   gorse, 287
**whortle**   whortleberry, bilberry; **whortlebush** 287
**withe**   withy, flexible branch of willow, 229
**worm**   serpent, dragon, 85–8, etc.
**wrack**   downfall, ruin, 116, 253, 283, 285

# INDEX

This index is made on the same basis as that to Part I, but selected references are given in rather more cases, and the individual *Lost Tales* are not included. In view of the large number of names that appear in Part II fairly full cross-references are provided to associated names (earlier and later forms, equivalents in different languages, etc.). As in the index to Part I, the more important names occurring in *The Silmarillion* are not given explanatory definitions; and references sometimes include passages where the person or place is not actually named.

especially 61, and see *Doriath, Land(s) Beyond*. References to the
protection of Artanor by the magic of the Queen: 9, 35–6, 43, 47–8,
63, 76, 122, 132, 137, 230–2, 249–50
*Arval*   An early name of Eöl. 220
*Arvalin*   286
*Aryador*   'Land of Shadow', name of Hisilómë among Men. 15, 42, 44,
    50–1, 61, 70, 202, 249. See *Dor Lómin, Hisilómë, Hithlum, Land
    of Shadow(s), Mathusdor*.
*Asgon*   Earlier name of (Lake) Mithrim. 70, 88, 202, 204, 263. See
    *Mithrim*.
*Atlantic Ocean*   261
*Aulë*   19, 46, 174, 218, 269, 272
*Auredhir*   Son of Dior. 240–1, 251
*Ausir*   (1) 'The Wealthy', name of Dior. 240, 244, 251. (2) A boy of Mar
    Vanwa Tyaliéva. 5, 7–8, 40–2, 50, 59, 311
*Avari*   64
*Avon, River*   295–6


*Bablon*   Gnomish form of *Babylon*. 196, 203, 214; *Babylon* 203, 214
*Bad Uthwen*   The Way of Escape into the plain of Gondolin. 189, 203;
    earlier *Bad Uswen, Bad Usbran* 203. See *Way of Escape*.
*Balar, Isle of*   209
*Balcmeg*   Orc slain by Tuor in Gondolin. 181
*Balrog(s)*   15, 34, 44, 67, 85, 156, 169–70, 174–6, 178–84, 186, 189,
    193–4, 212–13, 216. Numbers of, 170, 179, 184, 213; des-
    cribed, 169, 181, 194, 212–13. See *Malkarauki*.
*Bansil*   'Fair-gleam', the Tree of Gondolin with silver blossom. 160,
    184, 186, 203, 207, 214, 216; later form *Banthil* 203. See *Belthil*.
*Barad-dûr*   67
*Baragund*   Father of Morwen. 139
*Barahir*   Father of Beren. 43, 51. (Replaced *Egnor*.)
*Battle of Unnumbered Tears*   Called also *the Battle of Tears, of
    Uncounted Tears, of Lamentation*, and *the great battle*. 9–10,
    17, 43–5, 65–6, 70, 73, 77, 83–4, 88, 91, 101, 120–1, 140, 142, 157,
    198, 200, 208–9, 216, 218. See *Nieriltasinwa, Nínin-Udathriol*.
*Bay of Faëry*   See *Faëry*.
*Bee of Azure*   Sirius. 282; *Blue Bee* 281. See *Nielluin*.
*Belaurin*   Gnomish form of *Palúrien*. 281, 328; *Belawryn* 310
*Belcha*   Gnomish name of Melko. *Belcha Morgoth* 44, 67
*Beleg*   21, 47, 59, 62, 73, 76–83, 102, 118, 121–4, 141–2. Called
    'wood-ranger', 'hunter', 'huntsman' 73, 76–7, 81, 123; a Noldo 78,
    122–3; later surname *Cúthalion* 'Strongbow' 59, 62, 124
*Belegost*   City of the Indrafang Dwarves. 230–1, 235, 244–8; *Ost
    Belegost* 244
*Beleriand*   64, 128, 205, 217, 245, 324; Drowning of Beleriand 251,
    324

*Guarded Plain of Nargothrond*   See *Talath Dirnen*.
*Guilwarthon*   See *I·Guilwarthon*.
*Guiðlin*   Invaders of Tol Eressëa. 294
*Gully of the Rainbow Roof*   See *Cris Ilbranteloth, Teld Quing Ilon*.
*Gumlin*   The elder of Túrin's guardians on the journey to Artanor. 74, 76, 92–3, 127. See *Grithnir*.
*Gumniow*   Apparently an alternative name for Tevildo's doorkeeper (see *Umuiyan*). 24
*Gurtholfin*   'Wand of Death', Túrin's sword (later *Gurthang*). 83, 85, 90, 99, 107–8, 112, 119; earlier form *Gortholfin* 119
*Gwar, Gwâr* = *Mindon Gwar* (Kortirion). 291, 313; *hill of Gwar* 313; *Prince of Gwar* 313, 323. *Gwarthyryn* 307. See *Caergwâr*.
*Gwarestrin*   'Tower of Guard', one of the Seven Names of Gondolin. 158
*Gwasgonin*   'Winged Helms', earlier name for the Forodwaith. 334
*Gwedheling*   Queen of Artanor; name replacing *Gwendeling* in the *Tale of Turambar*. 73, 76, 94–6, 119, 244; *Gwedhiling* (replacing *Gwendeling* in the Gnomish dictionary) 50, 119, 244. See *Artanor*.
*Gwendelin*   Queen of Artanor; name replaced by *Gwenniel* in the *Tale of the Nauglafring*. 228, 231–5, 237, 239–40, 243–4, 246, 249–50. See *Artanor*.
*Gwendeling*   Queen of Artanor; name replacing *Wendelin* in the *Tale of Tinúviel*. 8–10, 12, 14–15, 17–19, 22–3, 30, 33, 35–7, 49–51, 63–4, 66, 119, 243–4. See *Artanor*.
*Gwenethlin*   Queen of Artanor; name replaced by *Melian* in the typescript text of the *Tale of Tinúviel*. 51, 244, 259
*Gwenniel*   Queen of Artanor; name replacing *Gwendelin* in the *Tale of the Nauglafring*. 223, 225, 227, 230, 243–4, 249. See *Artanor*.
*Gwindor*   Elf of Nargothrond, companion of Túrin (earlier *Flinding*). 62, 123–4. See *Flinding*.

*Hador, House of*   120, 126
*Hægwudu*   See *Great Haywood, Heorrenda*.
*Half-elven*   130, 215, 265–6, 293
*Hall of Play Regained*   In Mar Vanwa Tyaliéva. 4
*Hall(s) of Iron*   Angamandi. 166, 264; *halls of darkness* 169
*Hammer of Wrath*   Name of one of the kindreds of the Gondothlim. 174, 176, 179, 183, 218. See *Rog* (2), *Stricken Anvil*.
*Happy Mariners, The*   (poem) 273–6
*Harbourless Isle(s)*   317–18, 324–5, 331–2; *Isle of the Old Man* 322; other references to the Isles 5, 7, 311, 315–16, 333
*Harbour of the Lights of Many Hues*   In Tol Eressëa. 321; *Haven of Many Hues* 322, 333
*Harp, The*   Name of one of the kindreds of the Gondothlim. 173, 182. See *Salgant*.

*Ingwaiwar*  People deriving their origin from Ing(wë) as their founder-ruler, Anglo-Saxons. 304–7, 309, 312, 323

*Ingwë*  (1) See *Ing* (1). (2) Lord of the Vanyar. 305. See *Inwë*.

*Ingwine*  See 305.

*Inland Sea*  The Mediterranean. 294.

*Inwë*  King of the Eldar of Kôr (later Ingwë Lord of the Vanyar). 208, 253, 258, 280, 282, 289, 292, 305; *the Arch of Inwë* in Gondolin 182

*Inwir*  The royal clan of the Teleri (= the later Vanyar), kindred of Inwë. 4, 253, 255, 278, 281, 283

*Inwithiel*  Gnomish name of Inwë. 258

*Íras*  (Old English) The Irish. 290

*Ireland*  285, 293, 312, 323. See *Íverin*.

*Irildë*  Name of Idril in Eldarissa. 199, 210, 216, 254, 276; *Irildë Taltelepta, Irildë of the Silver Feet* 216. See *Idril*.

*Iron Crown*  See *Melko*.

*Iron Mountains* 10–11, 14, 43, 61, 70, 77, 140, 153, 215, 217, 279; *Mountains of Iron* 13, 156, 217; *Hills of Iron* 87, 154, 161, 169, 219, 279; *Bitter Hills* 12, 22, 29, 61. See *Angorodin*.

*Isfin*  Sister of Turgon, mother of Meglin. 165, 168, 199, 210, 220, 248. See *Aredhel*.

*Island-elves*  Elves of Tol Eressëa. 283, 285

*Isle of Seabirds*  253, 255–6, 259–60, 262, 264; tower on 264

*Isle of Werewolves*  53. See *Tol-in-Gaurhoth*.

*Ivárë*  Minstrel of the Elves, 'who plays beside the sea'. 10, 59

*Íverin, Isle of*  Ireland. 283, 285–6, 293, 323. See *Ireland*.

*Ivrin*  See *Eithel Ivrin*.

*Jutes*  306. See *Euti*.

*Kapalen*  Name preceding Tifanto (Dairon). 49–50

*Karkaras*  'Knife-fang', 'father of wolves'. 19, 21, 31, 33–4, 36, 38–9, 56, 58–9, 68, 227, 231, 239; *Carcaras* 46, 68; *Hell-wolf* 38. See *Knife-fang; Carcharoth*.

*King's hall, palace, tower, fountain, square*  In Gondolin. See *Square of the Palace*.

*King's House, Royal House*  Of the Gondothlim. 172, 183–5, 187, 213

*Kinslaying at Swanhaven*  258

*Knife-fang*  21, 31, 33, 68, 227. See *Karkaras*.

*Kôr*  City of the Elves in Eldamar and the hill on which it was built. 8–9, 42, 64, 71, 77, 115, 119, 123, 141, 145, 148–9, 161, 197, 202, 208, 215, 219, 253–65, 271–2, 278, 280, 285–6, 289, 291–2, 303–5, 307–8, 329; see especially 291–2, and see *Tûn, Túna, Tirion*.

*Kópas*  Haven (of the Swanships). 255. See *Cópas Alqalunten*.

*Koreldar*  Elves of Kôr. 276

name among the Gnomes, though *makil* is an 'Eldar' form (I.259).
84, 86, 94, 112, 116, 118, 125, 128. See *Mormagli, Mormegil*.
*Mormegil*  'Black Sword', Túrin (later form of the name). 125, 128
*Morning Star*  266
*Móru*  The 'Primeval Night' personified in the Great Spider. 286
*Morwen*  120–1, 126–8, 135, 139. (Replaced *Mavwin*.)
*Mound of Avarice*  See *Cûm an-Idrisaith*.
*Mountain of the World*  See *Taniquetil*.
*Mountains of Darkness*  = *Mountains of Iron*. 162
*Mountains of Iron*  See *Iron Mountains*.
*Mountains of Night*  The mountains on which grew Taurfuin, the
    Forest of Night. 20, 46, 62
*Mountains of Shadow*  61–2, 122, 205, 217. See *Ered Wethrin*.
*Mountains of Terror*  See *Ered Gorgoroth*.
*Mountains of the East*  6, 295, 300, 311
*Mountains of Valinor*  161, 171, 285, 320, 325
*Music of the Ainur*  (not including references to the Tale) 146, 163,
    209. See *Ainulindalë*.


*Naimi*  Ælfwine's wife, Elf of Tol Eressëa. 290–1, 323, 330. See *Éadgifu*
    (1).
*Nan*  A Giant. 19, 46, 67–8
*Nandorin*  122
*Nan Dumgorthin*  'The Land of the Dark Idols'. 35, 62, 68; *Nan
    Dungorthin* 62
*Nan Dungortheb*  'The Valley of Dreadful Death'. 62–3
*Nan Elmoth*  248
*Nan-tathren*  140, 214. See *Land of Willows, Tasarinan*.
*Nargothrond*  53–4, 56, 61, 123–6, 128–9, 131, 135, 137, 140–1, 205,
    208, 245–6, 251; see especially 123–4
*Narn i Hîn Húrin*  119–22, 124, 126–35, 142
*Narog*  123, 132, 135, 141, 244. See *Aros*.
*Narthseg*  The Elf who betrayed Artanor to the Dwarves. 231, 243
*Naugladur*  Lord of the Dwarves of Nogrod. 225, 230–8, 243, 246–7
    (called *king* 225).
*Nauglafring*  The Necklace of the Dwarves (references include both
    names). 41, 59, 72, 136–7, 144, 221, 227–8, 231–2, 234–5, 237–41,
    243, 245–7, 252–6, 259, 264; see especially 228
*Nauglath*  The Dwarves of Nogrod. 68, 136–7, 223–6, 229, 233–4,
    243, 247, 328; see especially 247
*Nautar*  Apparently = *Nauglath*. 136, 247, 283, 285, 328
*Nazgûl*  327
*Necklace of the Dwarves*  See *Nauglafring*.
*Necromancer, The*  53–5
*Nellas*  Elf of Doriath who bore witness at the trial of Túrin. 121

*Oarni*  Spirits of the Sea (identified with 'mermaids' 259, identity denied 263). 253–4, 259–60, 263, 276. See *Mermaids*.

*Oikeroi*  A cat, thane of Tevildo, slain by Huan. 27–8, 30–2, 55–8

*Oinen*  See *Uinen*.

*Old English*  (including citations, words, titles of poems) 197, 200, 266–7, 271, 276, 290–2, 294–5, 298, 301, 304–5, 309, 323, 325, 328–31. Old English spoken by the Elves of Tol Eressëa 301–2, 304, 309

*Old Forest*  328

*Olórë Mallë*  'The Path of Dreams'. 48, 70, 119, 258. See *Way of Dreams*.

*Olwë*  Lord of the Solosimpi in Thingol's place. 50. See *Ellu* (2).

*Ómar*  Youngest of the great Valar, called also *Amillo*. 279

*Ónen*  Earlier name of Uinen. 51

*Orcobal*  Champion of the Orcs, slain by Ecthelion in Gondolin. 181

*Orcs*  Selected references: origin of 14, 159, 219; *children of Melko* 193; described 99, 159–60; sight and hearing of 78–9, 165–6; wolfriders 44, 67, 84, 190, 195; Orcs' blood in Meglin 165; *sons of the Orcs* 165; mercenaries of the Dwarves 230, 247. Singular *Ork* 202, plural *Orqui* 136, 202, 219. See *Goblins*.

*Orfalch Echor*  The great rift in the Encircling Mountains by which Gondolin was approached. 207, 211

*Orgof*  Elf of Artanor, slain by Túrin. 74–6, 122, 142

*Orion*  281–2, 302. See *Telimektar*.

*Orlin*  Man of Hisilómë, slain in Brodda's hall by Turambar. 90

*Orm*  Sea-captain of the Forodwaith, slayer of Déor Ælfwine's father. 318–19, 323, 331

*Orodreth*  Lord of the Rodothlim. 82–4, 98, 117, 123–4

*Oromë*  8, 42, 240, 279

*Orqui*  Earlier plural of *Orc* (*Ork*). See *Orcs*.

*Ossë*  150, 197, 254, 256, 263, 283, 285, 293, 304, 306–9, 323–4, 331

*Ossiriand*  249

*Ost Belegost*  See *Belegost*.

*Óswine*  Prince of Gwar (Kortirion). 313, 323

*Óðinn*  290. See *Wóden*.

*Othrod*  A lord of the Orcs, slain by Tuor in Gondolin. 181

*Ottor Wæfre*  Eriol. 290, 292; Wæfre 291

*Outer Dark*  273, 276

*Outer Land(s)*  (1) The Great Lands (Middle-earth). 254, 265. See *Lands Without*. (2) The lands West of the Great Sea. 316–17, 324–5, 334

*Outer Oceans, Outer Sea(s)*  154, 160, 276. See *Vai*.

*Oxford*  146, 269, 292–3, 295, 300, 323; (Old English) *Oxenaford* 292; poem *The City of Present Sorrow* 295–8. See *Taruithorn*, *Taruktarna*.

*Oxford English Dictionary*  69, 147

9

2 I VENE KEMEN

NÚME

VAITYA

YLWE

VILNA

ORONTO

PALISOR

KUVIENEN

I NORI LANDAR

VILNA

UR

LUVIER

SIL

J. TOLLI KURUVAR

TOL ERESSEA *

TOL KIMPELEAR

JAROS VALATARIVA

HALOSI VÉLIKE

TANIQUETIL

VALINOR

ULMONAN

UIN

HARMALIN

I SILDE

VAI- (NENI ERUMÉAR)

# THE BOOK OF LOST TALES

## PART I

# THE HISTORY OF MIDDLE-EARTH

J. R. R. TOLKIEN

# The
# Book of Lost Tales

## PART I

Christopher Tolkien

HarperCollins*Publishers*

HarperCollins*Publishers* Ltd
1 London Bridge Street
London SE1 9GF

HarperCollins*Publishers*
Macken House, 39/40 Mayor Street Upper
Dublin 1, D01 C9W8, Ireland

www.tolkien.co.uk
www.tolkienestate.com

This hardback edition 2023
1

First published in Great Britain by
George Allen & Unwin (Publishers) Ltd 1983,
and by HarperCollins*Publishers* 1991

Copyright © The Tolkien Estate Limited and C.R. Tolkien 1983

A CIP catalogue record for this book is available
from the British Library

ISBN 978-0-00-866314-8

Printed and bound in the UK using 100% Renewable Electricity
by CPI Group (UK) Ltd

# CONTENTS

# FOREWORD

*The Book of Lost Tales*, written between sixty and seventy years ago, was the first substantial work of imaginative literature by J. R. R. Tolkien, and the first emergence in narrative of the Valar, of the Children of Ilúvatar, Elves and Men, of the Dwarves and the Orcs, and of the lands in which their history is set, Valinor beyond the western ocean, and Middle-earth, the 'Great Lands' between the seas of east and west. Some fifty-seven years after my father ceased to work on the *Lost Tales*, *The Silmaril-lion*,* profoundly transformed from its distant forerunner, was published; and six years have passed since then. This Foreword seems a suitable opportunity to remark on some aspects of both works.

*The Silmarillion* is commonly said to be a 'difficult' book, needing explanation and guidance on how to 'approach' it; and in this it is con-trasted to *The Lord of the Rings*. In Chapter 7 of his book *The Road to Middle-earth* Professor T. A. Shippey accepts that this is so ('*The Silmarillion* could never be anything but hard to read', p. 201), and expounds his view of why it should be. A complex discussion is not treated justly when it is extracted, but in his view the reasons are essentially two (p. 185). In the first place, there is in *The Silmarillion* no 'mediation' of the kind provided by the hobbits (so, in *The Hobbit*, 'Bilbo acts as the link between modern times and the archaic world of dwarves and dragons'). My father was himself well aware that the absence of hobbits would be felt as a lack, were 'The Silmarillion' to be published – and not only by readers with a particular liking for them. In a letter written in 1956 (*The Letters of J. R. R. Tolkien*, p. 238), soon after the publication of *The Lord of the Rings*, he said:

> I do not think it would have the appeal of the L.R. – no hobbits! Full of mythology, and elvishness, and all that 'heigh stile' (as Chaucer might say), which has been so little to the taste of many reviewers.

In 'The Silmarillion' the draught is pure and unmixed; and the reader is worlds away from such 'mediation', such a deliberate collison (far more than a matter of styles) as that produced in the meeting between King Théoden and Pippin and Merry in the ruins of Isengard:

> 'Farewell, my hobbits! May we meet again in my house! There you shall sit beside me and tell me all that your hearts desire: the deeds of

---

* When the name is printed in italics, I refer to the work as published; when in inverted commas, to the work in a more general way, in any or all of its forms.

your grandsires, as far as you can reckon them . . .'
The hobbits bowed low. 'So that is the King of Rohan!' said Pippin
in an undertone. 'A fine old fellow. Very polite.'

In the second place,

> Where *The Silmarillion* differs from Tolkien's earlier works is in its
> refusal to accept novelistic convention. Most novels (including *The
> Hobbit* and *The Lord of the Rings*) pick a character to put in the fore-
> ground, like Frodo and Bilbo, and then tell the story as it happens to
> him. The novelist of course is inventing the story, and so retains
> omniscience: he can explain, or show, what is 'really' happening and
> contrast it with the limited perception of his character.

There is, then, and very evidently, a question of literary 'taste' (or
literary 'habituation') involved; and also a question of literary 'disappointment' – the '(mistaken) disappointment in those who wanted a second
*Lord of the Rings*' to which Professor Shippey refers. This has even produced a sense of outrage – in one case formulated to me in the words
'It's like *the Old Testament*!': a dire condemnation against which, clearly,
there can be no appeal (though this reader cannot have got very far
before being overcome by the comparison). Of course, 'The Silmarillion'
was intended to move the heart and the imagination, directly, and without
peculiar effort or the possession of unusual faculties; but its mode is
inherent, and it may be doubted whether any 'approach' to it can greatly
aid those who find it unapproachable.
There is a third consideration (which Professor Shippey does not indeed
advance in the same context):

> One quality which [*The Lord of the Rings*] has in abundance is the
> Beowulfian 'impression of depth', created just as in the old epic by
> songs and digressions like Aragorn's lay of Tinúviel, Sam Gamgee's
> allusions to the Silmaril and the Iron Crown, Elrond's account of
> Celebrimbor, and dozens more. This, however, is a quality of *The
> Lord of the Rings*, not of the inset stories. To tell these in their own right
> and expect them to retain the charm they got from their larger setting
> would be a terrible error, an error to which Tolkien would be more
> sensitive than any man alive. As he wrote in a revealing letter dated
> 20 September 1963:

>> I am doubtful myself about the undertaking [to write *The Silmarillion*].
>> Part of the attraction of The L.R. is, I think, due to the glimpses of
>> a large history in the background: an attraction like that of viewing
>> far off an unvisited island, or seeing the towers of a distant city
>> gleaming in a sunlit mist. To go there is to destroy the magic, unless
>> new unattainable vistas are again revealed. (*Letters*, p. 333)

*To go there is to destroy the magic.* As for the revealing of 'new un-attainable vistas', the problem there – as Tolkien must have thought many times – was that in *The Lord of the Rings* Middle-earth was already old, with a vast weight of history behind it. *The Silmarillion*, though, in its longer form, was bound to begin at the beginning. How could 'depth' be created when you had nothing to reach further back to?

The letter quoted here certainly shows that my father felt this, or perhaps rather one should say, at times felt this, to be a problem. Nor was it a new thought: while he was writing *The Lord of the Rings*, in 1945, he said in a letter to me (*Letters*, p. 110):

A story must be told or there'll be no story, yet it is the untold stories that are most moving. I think you are moved by *Celebrimbor* because it conveys a sudden sense of endless *untold* stories: mountains seen far away, never to be climbed, distant trees (like Niggle's) never to be approached – or if so only to become 'near trees' . . .

This matter is perfectly illustrated for me by Gimli's song in Moria, where great names out of the ancient world appear utterly remote:

> The world was fair, the mountains tall,
> In Elder Days before the fall
> Of mighty kings in Nargothrond
> And Gondolin, who now beyond
> The Western Seas have passed away . . .

'I like that!' said Sam. 'I should like to learn it. *In Moria, in Khazad-dûm.* But it makes the darkness seem heavier, thinking of all those lamps.' By his enthusiastic 'I like that!' Sam not only 'mediates' (and engagingly 'Gamgifies') the 'high', the mighty kings of Nargothrond and Gondolin, Durin on his carven throne, but places them at once at an even remoter distance, a magical distance that it might well seem (*at that moment*) destructive to traverse.

Professor Shippey says that 'to tell [the stories that are only alluded to in *The Lord of the Rings*] in their own right and expect them to retain the charm they got from their larger setting would be a terrible error'. The 'error' presumably lies in the holding of such an expectation, if the stories were told, not in the telling of the stories at all; and it is apparent that Professor Shippey sees my father as wondering, in 1963, whether he should or should not put pen to paper, for he expands the words of the letter, 'I am doubtful myself about the undertaking', to mean 'the undertaking to write *The Silmarillion*'. But when my father said this he was not – most emphatically not – referring to the work itself, which was in any case already written, and much of it many times over (the allusions in *The Lord of the Rings* are not illusory): what was in question for him, as he said earlier in this same letter, was its *presentation*, in a publication, *after* the appearance of *The Lord of the Rings*, when, as he thought, the right time to make it known was already gone.

I am afraid all the same that the presentation will need a lot of work, and I work so slowly. The legends have to be worked over (they were written at different times, some many years ago) and made consistent; and they have to be integrated with The L.R.; and they have to be given some progressive shape. No simple device, like a journey and a quest, is available.

I am doubtful myself about the undertaking . . .

When after his death the question arose of publishing 'The Silmarillion' in some form, I attached no importance to this doubt. The effect that 'the glimpses of a large history in the background' have in *The Lord of the Rings* is incontestable and of the utmost importance, but I did not think that the 'glimpses' used there with such art should preclude all further knowledge of the 'large history'.

The literary 'impression of depth . . . created by songs and digressions' cannot be made a criterion by which a work in a wholly different mode is measured: this would be to treat the history of the Elder Days as of value primarily or even solely in the artistic use made of it in *The Lord of the Rings*. Nor should the device of a backward movement in imagined time to dimly apprehended events, whose attraction lies in their very dimness, be understood mechanically, as if a fuller account of the mighty kings of Nargothrond and Gondolin would imply a dangerously near approach to the bottom of the well, while an account of the Creation would signify the striking of the bottom and a definitive running-out of 'depth' – 'nothing to reach further back to'.

This, surely, is not how things work, or at least not how they need work. 'Depth' in this sense implies a relation between different temporal layers or levels within the same world. Provided that the reader has a place, a point of vantage, *in the imagined time* from which to look back, the extreme oldness of the extremely old can be made apparent and made to be felt continuously. And the very fact that *The Lord of the Rings* establishes such a powerful sense of a real time-structure (far more powerful than can be done by mere chronological assertion, tables of dates) provides this necessary vantage-point. To read *The Silmarillion* one must place oneself imaginatively at the time of the ending of the Third Age – within Middle-earth, looking back: at the temporal point of Sam Gamgee's 'I like that!' – adding, 'I should like to know more about it'. Moreover the compendious or epitomising form and manner of *The Silmarillion*, with its suggestion of ages of poetry and 'lore' behind it, strongly evokes a sense of 'untold tales', even in the telling of them; 'distance' is never lost. There is no narrative urgency, the pressure and fear of the immediate and unknown event. We do not actually see the Silmarils as we see the Ring. The maker of 'The Silmarillion', as he himself said of the author of *Beowulf*, 'was telling of things already old and weighted with regret, and he expended his art in making keen that touch upon the heart which sorrows have that are both poignant and remote'.

As has now been fully recorded, my father greatly desired to publish 'The Silmarillion' together with *The Lord of the Rings*. I say nothing of its practicability at the time, nor do I make any guesses at the subsequent fate of such a much longer combined work, quadrilogy or tetralogy, or at the different courses that my father might then have taken – for the further development of 'The Silmarillion' itself, the history of the Elder Days, would have been arrested. But by its posthumous publication nearly a quarter of a century later the natural order of presentation of the whole 'Matter of Middle-earth' was inverted; and it is certainly debatable whether it was wise to publish in 1977 a version of the primary 'legendarium' standing on its own and claiming, as it were, to be self-explanatory. The published work has no 'framework', no suggestion of what it is and how (within the imagined world) it came to be. This I now think to have been an error.

The letter of 1963 quoted above shows my father pondering the mode in which the legends of the Elder Days might be presented. The original mode, that of *The Book of Lost Tales*, in which a Man, Eriol, comes after a great voyage over the ocean to the island where the Elves dwell and learns their history from their own lips, had (by degrees) fallen away. When my father died in 1973 'The Silmarillion' was in a characteristic state of disarray: the earlier parts much revised or largely rewritten, the concluding parts still as he had left them some twenty years before; but in the latest writing there is no trace or suggestion of any 'device' or 'framework' in which it was to be set. I think that in the end he concluded that nothing would serve, and no more would be said beyond an explanation of how (within the imagined world) it came to be recorded.

In the original edition of *The Lord of the Rings* Bilbo gave to Frodo at Rivendell as his parting gift 'some books of lore that he had made at various times, written in his spidery hand, and labelled on their red backs: *Translations from the Elvish, by B.B.*' In the second edition (1966) 'some books' was changed to 'three books', and in the *Note on the Shire Records* added to the Prologue in that edition my father said that the content of 'the three large volumes bound in red leather' was preserved in that copy of the Red Book of Westmarch which was made in Gondor by the King's Writer Findegil in the year 172 of the Fourth Age; and also that

These three volumes were found to be a work of great skill and learning in which ... [Bilbo] had used all the sources available to him in Rivendell, both living and written. But since they were little used by Frodo, being almost entirely concerned with the Elder Days, no more is said of them here.

In *The Complete Guide to Middle-earth* Robert Foster says: *'Quenta Silmarillion* was no doubt one of Bilbo's *Translations from the Elvish* preserved in the Red Book of Westmarch.' So also I have assumed: the 'books of lore' that Bilbo gave to Frodo provided in the end the solution: they were 'The Silmarillion'. But apart from the evidence cited here, there is, so far as I know, no other statement on this matter anywhere in my father's writings; and (wrongly, as I think now) I was reluctant to step into the breach and make definite what I only surmised.

The choice before me, in respect of 'The Silmarillion', was threefold. I could withhold it indefinitely from publication, on the ground that the work was incomplete and incoherent between its parts. I could accept the nature of the work as it stood, and, to quote my Foreword to the book, 'attempt to present the diversity of the materials – to show "The Silmarillion" as in truth a continuing and evolving creation extending over more than half a century'; and that, as I have said in *Unfinished Tales* (p. 1), would have entailed 'a complex of divergent texts interlinked by commentary' – a far larger undertaking than those words suggest. In the event, I chose the third course, 'to work out a single text, selecting and arranging in such a way as seemed to me to produce the most coherent and internally self-consistent narrative'. Having come, at length, to that decision, all the editorial labour of myself and of Guy Kay who assisted me was directed to the end that my father had stated in the letter of 1963: 'The legends have to be worked over . . . and made consistent; and they have to be integrated with the L.R.' Since the object was to present 'The Silmarillion' as 'a completed and cohesive entity' (though that could not in the nature of the case be entirely successful), it followed that there would be in the published book no exposition of the complexities of its history.

Whatever may be thought of this matter, the result, which I by no means foresaw, has been to add a further dimension of obscurity to 'The Silmarillion', in that uncertainty about the age of the work, whether it is to be regarded as 'early' or 'late' or in what proportions, and about the degree of editorial intrusion and manipulation (or even invention), is a stumbling-block and a source of much misapprehension. Professor Randel Helms, in *Tolkien and the Silmarils* (p. 93), has stated the question thus:

> Anyone interested, as I am, in the growth of *The Silmarillion* will want to study *Unfinished Tales*, not only for its intrinsic value but also because its relationship to the former provides what will become a classic example of a long-standing problem in literary criticism: what, really, *is* a literary work? Is it what the author intended (or may have intended) it to be, or is it what a later editor makes of it? The problem becomes especially intense for the practising critic when, as happened with *The Silmarillion*, a writer dies before finishing his work and leaves more than one version of some of its parts, which then find publication elsewhere. Which version will the critic approach as the 'real' story?

But he also says: 'Christopher Tolkien has helped us in this instance by honestly pointing out that *The Silmarillion* in the shape that we have it is the invention of the son not the father'; and this is a serious misapprehension to which my words have given rise.

Again, Professor Shippey, while accepting (p. 169) my assurance that a 'very high proportion' of the 1937 'Silmarillion' text remained into the published version, is nonetheless elsewhere clearly reluctant to see it as other than a 'late' work, even the latest work of its author. And in an article entitled 'The Text of *The Hobbit*: Putting Tolkien's Notes in Order' (English Studies in Canada, VII, 2, Summer 1981) Constance B. Hieatt concludes that 'it is very clear indeed that we shall never be able to see the progressive steps of authorial thinking behind *The Silmarillion*'.

But beyond the difficulties and the obscurities, what is certain and very evident is that for the begetter of Middle-earth and Valinor there was a deep coherence and vital interrelation between all its times, places, and beings, whatever the literary modes, and however protean some parts of the conception might seem when viewed over a long lifetime. He himself understood very well that many who read *The Lord of the Rings* with enjoyment would never wish to regard Middle-earth as more than the mise-en-scène of the story, and would delight in the sensation of 'depth' without wishing to explore the deep places. But the 'depth' is not of course an illusion, like a line of imitation book-backs with no books inside them; and Quenya and Sindarin are comprehensive structures. There are explorations to be conducted in this world with perfect right quite irrespective of literary-critical considerations; and it is proper to attempt to comprehend its structure in its largest extent, from the myth of its Creation. Every person, every feature of the imagined world that seemed significant to its author is then worthy of attention in its own right, Manwë or Fëanor no less than Gandalf or Galadriel, the Silmarils no less than the Rings; the Great Music, the divine hierarchies, the abodes of the Valar, the fates of the Children of Ilúvatar, are essential elements in the perception of the whole. Such enquiries are in no way illegitimate in principle; they arise from an acceptance of the imagined world as an object of contemplation or study valid as many other objects of contemplation or study in the all too unimaginary world. It was in this opinion and in the knowledge that others shared it that I made the collection called *Unfinished Tales*.

But the author's vision of his own vision underwent a continual slow shifting, shedding and enlarging: only in *The Hobbit* and *The Lord of the Rings* did parts of it emerge to become fixed in print, in his own lifetime. The study of Middle-earth and Valinor is thus complex; for the object of the study was not stable, but exists, as it were 'longitudinally' in time (the author's lifetime), and not only 'transversely' in time, as a printed book that undergoes no essential further change. By the publication of 'The Silmarillion' the 'longitudinal' was cut 'transversely', and a kind of finality imposed.

★

This rather rambling discussion is an attempt to explain my primary motives in offering *The Book of Lost Tales* for publication. It is the first step in presenting the 'longitudinal' view of Middle-earth and Valinor: when the huge geographical expansion, swelling out from the centre and (as it were) thrusting Beleriand into the west, was far off in the future; when there were no 'Elder Days' ending in the drowning of Beleriand, for there were as yet no other Ages of the World; when the Elves were still 'fairies', and even Rúmil the learned Noldo was far removed from the magisterial 'loremasters' of my father's later years. In *The Book of Lost Tales* the princes of the Noldor have scarcely emerged, nor the Grey-elves of Beleriand; Beren is an Elf, not a Man, and his captor, the ultimate precursor of Sauron in that rôle, is a monstrous cat inhabited by a fiend; the Dwarves are an evil people; and the historical relations of Quenya and Sindarin were quite differently conceived. These are a few especially notable features, but such a list could be greatly prolonged. On the other hand, there was already a firm underlying structure that would endure. Moreover in the history of the history of Middle-earth the development was seldom by outright rejection – far more often it was by subtle transformation in stages, so that the growth of the legends (the process, for instance, by which the Nargothrond story made contact with that of Beren and Lúthien, a contact not even hinted at in the *Lost Tales*, though both elements were present) can seem like the growth of legends among peoples, the product of many minds and generations.

The Book of Lost Tales* was begun by my father in 1916–17 during the First War, when he was 25 years old, and left incomplete several years later. It is the starting-point, at least in fully-formed narrative, of the history of Valinor and Middle-earth; but before the *Tales* were complete he turned to the composition of long poems, the *Lay of Leithian* in rhyming couplets (the story of Beren and Lúthien), and *The Children of Húrin* in alliterative verse. The prose form of the 'mythology' began again from a new starting-point* in a quite brief synopsis, or 'Sketch' as he called it, written in 1926 and expressly intended to provide the necessary background of knowledge for the understanding of the alliterative poem. The further written development of the prose form proceeded from that 'Sketch' in a direct line to the version of 'The Silmarillion' which was nearing completion towards the end of 1937, when my father broke off to send it as it stood to Allen and Unwin in November of that year; but there were also important side-branches and subordinate texts composed in the 1930s, as the *Annals of Valinor* and the *Annals of Beleriand* (fragments of which are extant also in the Old English translations made by Ælfwine (Eriol)), the cosmological account called *Ambarkanta*, the

---

* Only in the case of *The Music of the Ainur* was there a direct development, manuscript to manuscript, from *The Book of Lost Tales* to the later forms; for *The Music of the Ainur* became separated off and continued as an independent work.

Shape of the World, by Rúmil, and the *Lhammas* or 'Account of Tongues', by Pengolod of Gondolin. Thereafter the history of the First Age was laid aside for many years, until *The Lord of the Rings* was completed, but in the years preceding its actual publication my father returned to 'The Silmarillion' and associated works with great vigour.

This edition of the *Lost Tales* in two parts is to be, as I hope, the beginning of a series that will carry the history further through these later writings, in verse and prose; and in this hope I have applied to this present book an 'overriding' title intended to cover also those that may follow it, though I fear that 'The History of Middle-earth' may turn out to have been over-ambitious. In any case this title does not imply a 'History' in the conventional sense: my intention is to give complete or largely complete texts, so that the books will be more like a series of editions. I do not set myself as a primary object the unravelling of many single and separate threads, but rather the making available of works that can and should be read as wholes.

The tracing of this long evolution is to me of deep interest, and I hope that it may prove so to others who have a taste for this kind of enquiry: whether the major transformations of plot or cosmological theory, or such a detail as the premonitory appearance of Legolas Greenleaf the keen-sighted in the tale of *The Fall of Gondolin*. But these old manuscripts are by no means of interest only for the study of origins. Much is to be found there that my father never (so far as one can tell) expressly rejected, and it is to be remembered that 'The Silmarillion', from the 1926 'Sketch' onwards, was written as an abridgement or epitome, giving the substance of much longer works (whether existing in fact, or not) in a smaller compass. The highly archaic manner devised for his purpose was no fustian: it had range and great vigour, peculiarly apt to convey the magical and eerie nature of the early Elves, but as readily turned to the sarcastic, sneering Melko or the affairs of Ulmo and Ossë. These last approach at times a comic conception, and are delivered in a rapid and lively language that did not survive in the gravity of my father's later 'Silmarillion' prose (so Ossë 'fares about in a foam of business' as he anchors the islands to the sea-bed, the cliffs of Tol Eressëa new-filled with the first sea-birds 'are full of a chattering and a smell of fish, and great conclaves are held upon its ledges', and when the Shoreland Elves are at last drawn over the sea to Valinor Ulmo marvellously 'fares at the rear in his fishy car and trumpets loudly for the discomfiture of Ossë').

The *Lost Tales* never reached or even approached a form in which my father could have considered their publication before he abandoned them; they were experimental and provisional, and the tattered notebooks in which they were written were bundled away and left unlooked at as the years passed. To present them in a printed book has raised many thorny editorial problems. In the first place, the manuscripts are intrinsically very difficult: partly because much of the text was written rapidly in pencil and is now in places extremely hard to read, requiring a magnifying glass and much patience, not always rewarded. But also in some of the *Tales* my father erased the original pencilled text and wrote a revised version over it in ink – and since at this period he used bound notebooks rather than loose sheets, he was liable to find himself short of space: so detached portions of tales were written in the middle of other tales, and in places a fearsome textual jigsaw puzzle was produced.

Secondly, the *Lost Tales* were not all written progressively one after the other in the sequence of the narrative; and (inevitably) my father began a new arrangement and revision of the *Tales* while the work was still in progress. *The Fall of Gondolin* was the first of the tales told to Eriol to be composed, and the *Tale of Tinúviel* the second, but the events of those tales take place towards the end of the history; on the other hand the extant texts are later revisions. In some cases nothing earlier than the revised form can now be read; in some both forms are extant for all, or a part, of their length; in some there is only a preliminary draft; and in some there is no formed narrative at all, but only notes and projections. After much experimentation I have found that no method of presentation is feasible but to set out the *Tales* in the sequence of the narrative.

And finally, as the writing of the *Tales* progressed, relations were changed, new conceptions entered, and the development of the languages *pari passu* with the narrative led to continual revision of names.

An edition that takes account of such complexities, as this does, rather than attempt to smooth them artificially away, is liable to be an intricate and crabbed thing, in which the reader is never left alone for a moment. I have attempted to make the *Tales* themselves accessible and uncluttered while providing a fairly full account, for those who want it, of the actual textual evidences. To achieve this I have drastically reduced the quantity of annotation to the texts in these ways: the many changes made to names are all recorded, but they are lumped together at the end of each tale, not recorded individually at each occurrence (the places where the names occur can be found from the Index); almost all annotation concerned with content is taken up into, or boiled down into, a commentary or short essay following each tale; and almost all linguistic comment (primarily the etymology of names) is collected in an Appendix on Names at the end of the book, where will be found a great deal of information relating to the earliest stages of the 'Elvish' languages. In this way the numbered notes are very largely restricted to variants and divergences found in other texts, and the reader who does not wish to trouble with these can read the *Tales* knowing that that is almost all that he is missing.

The commentaries are limited in their scope, being mostly concerned to discuss the implications of what is said within the context of the *Tales* themselves, and to compare them with the published *Silmarillion*. I have eschewed parallels, sources, influences; and have mostly avoided the complexities of the development between the *Lost Tales* and the published work (since to indicate these even cursorily would, I think, be distracting), treating the matter in a simplified way, as between two fixed points. I do not suppose for one moment that my analyses will prove either altogether just or altogether accurate, and there must be clues to the solution of puzzling features in the *Tales* which I have failed to observe. There is also included a short glossary of words occurring in the *Tales* and poems that are obsolete, archaic, or rare.

The texts are given in a form very close to that of the original manuscripts. Only the most minor and obvious slips have been silently corrected; where sentences fall awkwardly, or where there is a lack of grammatical cohesion, as is sometimes the case in the parts of the *Tales* that never got beyond a first rapid draft, I have let them stand. I have allowed myself greater freedom in providing punctuation, for my father when writing at speed often punctuated erratically or not at all; and I have gone further than he did in consistency of capitalisation. I have adopted, though hesitantly, a consistent system of accentuation for Elvish names. My father wrote, for instance: *Palúrien, Palúrien, Palurien*; *Ōnen, Onen*; *Kôr, Kor*. I have used the acute accent for macron, circumflex, and acute (and occasional grave) accents of the original texts, but the circumflex on monosyllables – thus *Palúrien, Ónen, Kôr*: the same system, at least to the eye, as in later Sindarin.

Lastly, the division of this edition into two parts is entirely due to the length of the *Tales*. The edition is conceived as a whole, and I hope that the second part will appear within a year of the first; but each part has its own Index and Appendix on Names. The second part contains what are in many respects the most interesting of the *Tales*: *Tinúviel, Turambar* (Túrin), *The Fall of Gondolin*, and the *Tale of the Nauglafring* (the Necklace of the Dwarves); outlines for the *Tale of Eärendel* and the conclusion of the work; and *Ælfwine of England*.

# I

# THE COTTAGE OF LOST PLAY

On the cover of one of the now very battered 'High School Exercise Books'
in which some of the *Lost Tales* were composed my father wrote: *The
Cottage of Lost Play, which introduceth [the] Book of Lost Tales*; and on
the cover is also written, in my mother's hand, her initials, E.M.T., and
a date, Feb. 12th 1917. In this book the tale was written out by my mother;
and it is a fair copy of a very rough pencilled manuscript of my father's
on loose sheets, which were placed inside the cover. Thus the date of the
actual composition of this tale could have been, but probably was not,
earlier than the winter of 1916–17. The fair copy follows the original text
precisely; some further changes, mostly slight (other than in the matter
of names), were then made to the fair copy. The text follows here in
its final form.

Now it happened on a certain time that a traveller from far
countries, a man of great curiosity, was by desire of strange lands
and the ways and dwellings of unaccustomed folk brought in a ship
as far west even as the Lonely Island, Tol Eressëa in the fairy speech,
but which the Gnomes[1] call Dor Faidwen, the Land of Release, and
a great tale hangs thereto.

Now one day after much journeying he came as the lights of evening
were being kindled in many a window to the feet of a hill in a broad
and woody plain. He was now near the centre of this great island and
for many days had wandered its roads, stopping each night at what
dwelling of folk he might chance upon, were it hamlet or good town,
about the hour of eve at the kindling of candles. Now at that time
the desire of new sights is least, even in one whose heart is that of
an explorer; and then even such a son of Eärendel as was this wayfarer turns his thoughts rather to supper and to rest and the telling
of tales before the time of bed and sleep is come.

Now as he stood at the foot of the little hill there came a faint
breeze and then a flight of rooks above his head in the clear even
light. The sun had some time sunk beyond the boughs of the elms
that stood as far as eye could look about the plain, and some time
had its last gold faded through the leaves and slipped across the
glades to sleep beneath the roots and dream till dawn.

Now these rooks gave voice of home-coming above him, and with a swift turn came to their dwelling in the tops of some high elms at the summit of this hill. Then thought Eriol (for thus did the people of the island after call him, and its purport is 'One who dreams alone', but of his former names the story nowhere tells): 'The hour of rest is at hand, and though I know not even the name of this fair-seeming town upon a little hill here I will seek rest and lodging and go no further till the morrow, nor go even then perchance, for the place seems fair and its breezes of a good savour. To me it has the air of holding many secrets of old and wonderful and beautiful things in its treasuries and noble places and in the hearts of those that dwell within its walls.'

Now Eriol was coming from the south and a straight road ran before him bordered at one side with a great wall of grey stone topped with many flowers, or in places overhung with great dark yews. Through them as he climbed the road he could see the first stars shine forth, even as he afterwards sang in the song which he made to that fair city.

Now was he at the summit of the hill amidst its houses, and stepping as if by chance he turned aside down a winding lane, till, a little down the western slope of the hill, his eye was arrested by a tiny dwelling whose many small windows were curtained snugly, yet only so that a most warm and delicious light, as of hearts content within, looked forth. Then his heart yearned for kind company, and the desire for wayfaring died in him – and impelled by a great longing he turned aside at this cottage door, and knocking asked one who came and opened what might be the name of this house and who dwelt therein. And it was said to him that this was Mar Vanwa Tyaliéva, or the Cottage of Lost Play, and at that name he wondered greatly. There dwelt within, 'twas said, Lindo and Vairë who had built it many years ago, and with them were no few of their folk and friends and children. And at this he wondered more than before, seeing the size of the cottage; but he that opened to him, perceiving his mind, said: 'Small is the dwelling, but smaller still are they that dwell here – for all who enter must be very small indeed, or of their own good wish become as very little folk even as they stand upon the threshold.'

Then said Eriol that he would dearly desire to come therein and seek of Vairë and Lindo a night's guest-kindliness, if so they would, and if he might of his own good wish become small enough there upon the threshold. Then said the other, 'Enter', and Eriol stepped in, and behold, it seemed a house of great spaciousness and very great delight, and the lord of it, Lindo, and his wife, Vairë, came forth to greet him; and his heart was more glad within him than it had yet been in all his wanderings, albeit since his landing in the Lonely Isle his joy had been great enough.

And when Vairë had spoken the words of welcome, and Lindo had asked of him his name and whence he came and whither he might be seeking, and he had named himself the Stranger and said that he came from the Great Lands,[2] and that he was seeking whitherso his desire for travel led him, then was the evening meal set out in the great hall and Eriol bidden thereto. Now in this hall despite the summertide were three great fires – one at the far end and one on either side of the table, and save for their light as Eriol entered all was in a warm gloom. But at that moment many folk came in bearing candles of all sizes and many shapes in sticks of strange pattern: many were of carven wood and others of beaten metal, and these were set at hazard about the centre table and upon those at the sides.

At that same moment a great gong sounded far off in the house with a sweet noise, and a sound followed as of the laughter of many voices mingled with a great pattering of feet. Then Vairë said to Eriol, seeing his face filled with a happy wonderment: 'That is the voice of Tombo, the Gong of the Children, which stands outside the Hall of Play Regained, and it rings once to summon them to this hall at the times for eating and drinking, and three times to summon them to the Room of the Log Fire for the telling of tales,' and added Lindo: 'If at his ringing once there be laughter in the corridors and a sound of feet, then do the walls shake with mirth and stamping at the three strokes in an evening. And the sounding of the three strokes is the happiest moment in the day of Littleheart the Gong-warden, as he himself declares who has known happiness enough of old; and ancient indeed is he beyond count in spite of his merriness of soul. He sailed in Wingilot with Eärendel in that last voyage wherein they sought for Kôr. It was the ringing of this Gong on the Shadowy Seas that awoke the Sleeper in the Tower of Pearl that stands far out to west in the Twilit Isles.'

To these words did Eriol's mind so lean, for it seemed to him that a new world and very fair was opening to him, that he heard naught else till he was bidden by Vairë to be seated. Then he looked up, and lo, the hall and all its benches and chairs were filled with children of every aspect, kind, and size, while sprinkled among them were folk of all manners and ages. In one thing only were all alike, that a look of great happiness lit with a merry expectation of further mirth and joy lay on every face. The soft light of candles too was upon them all; it shone on bright tresses and gleamed about dark hair, or here and there set a pale fire in locks gone grey. Even as he gazed all arose and with one voice sang the song of the Bringing in of the Meats. Then was the food brought in and set before them, and thereafter the bearers and those that served and those that waited, host and hostess, children and guest, sat down: but Lindo first blessed both food and company. As they ate Eriol fell into speech with Lindo and his wife, telling them tales of his old days and of his adventures, especially those he had encountered upon the journey that had brought him to the Lonely Isle, and asking in return many things concerning the fair land, and most of all of that fair city wherein he now found himself.

Lindo said to him: 'Know then that today, or more like 'twas yesterday, you crossed the borders of that region that is called Alalminórë or the "Land of Elms", which the Gnomes call Gar Lossion, or the "Place of Flowers". Now this region is accounted the centre of the island, and its fairest realm; but above all the towns and villages of Alalminórë is held Koromas, or as some call it, Kortirion, and this city is the one wherein you now find yourself. Both because it stands at the heart of the island, and from the height of its mighty tower, do those that speak of it with love call it the Citadel of the Island, or of the World itself. More reason is there thereto than even great love, for all the island looks to the dwellers here for wisdom and leadership, for song and lore; and here in a great *korin* of elms dwells Meril-i-Turinqi. (Now a *korin* is a great circular hedge, be it of stone or of thorn or even of trees, that encloses a green sward.) Meril comes of the blood of Inwë, whom the Gnomes call Inwithiel, he that was King of all the Eldar when they dwelt in Kôr. That was in the days before hearing the lament of the world Inwë led them forth to the lands of Men: but those great and sad things and how the Eldar came to this fair and lonely island, maybe I will tell them another time.

'But after many days Ingil son of Inwë, seeing this place to be very fair, rested here and about him gathered most of the fairest and the wisest, most of the merriest and the kindest, of all the Eldar.[3] Here among those many came my father Valwë who went with Noldorin to find the Gnomes, and the father of Vairë my wife, Tulkastor. He was of Aulë's kindred, but had dwelt long with the Shoreland Pipers, the Solosimpi, and so came among the earliest to the island.

'Then Ingil builded the great tower[4] and called the town Koromas, or "the Resting of the Exiles of Kôr", but by reason of that tower it is now mostly called Kortirion.'

Now about this time they drew nigh the end of the meal; then did Lindo fill his cup and after him Vairë and all those in the hall, but to Eriol he said: 'Now this which we put into our cups is *limpë*, the drink of the Eldar both young and old, and drinking, our hearts keep youth and our mouths grow full of song, but this drink I may not administer: Turinqi only may give it to those not of the Eldar race, and those that drink must dwell always with the Eldar of the Island until such time as they fare forth to find the lost families of the kindred.' Then he filled Eriol's cup, but filled it with golden wine from ancient casks of the Gnomes; and then all rose and drank 'to the Faring Forth and the Rekindling of the Magic Sun'. Then sounded the Gong of the Children thrice, and a glad clamour arose in the hall, and some swung back big oaken doors at the hall's end – at that end which had no hearth. Then many seized those candles that were set in tall wooden sticks and held them aloft while others laughed and chattered, but all made a lane midmost of the company down which went Lindo and Vairë and Eriol, and as they passed the doors the throng followed them.

Eriol saw now that they were in a short broad corridor whose walls half-way up were arrassed; and on those tapestries were many stories pictured whereof he knew not at that time the purport. Above the tapestries it seemed there were paintings, but he could not see for gloom, for the candle-bearers were behind, and before him the only light came from an open door through which poured a red glow as of a big fire. 'That,' said Vairë, 'is the Tale-fire blazing in the Room of Logs; there does it burn all through the year, for 'tis a magic fire, and greatly aids the teller in his tale – but thither we now go,' and Eriol said that that seemed better to him than aught else.

Then all that company came laughing and talking into the room whence came the red glow. A fair room it was as might be felt even by the fire-flicker which danced upon the walls and low ceiling, while deep shadows lay in the nooks and corners. Round the great hearth was a multitude of soft rugs and yielding cushions strewn; and a little to one side was a deep chair with carven arms and feet. And so it was that Eriol felt at that time and at all others whereon he entered there at the hour of tale-telling, that whatso the number of the folk and children the room felt ever just great enough but not large, small enough but not overthronged.

Then all sat them down where they would, old and young, but Lindo in the deep chair and Vairë upon a cushion at his feet, and Eriol rejoicing in the red blaze for all that it was summer stretched nigh the hearthstone.

Then said Lindo: 'Of what shall the tales be tonight? Shall they be of the Great Lands, and of the dwellings of Men; of the Valar and Valinor; of the West and its mysteries, of the East and its glory, of the South and its untrodden wilds, of the North and its power and strength; or of this island and its folk; or of the old days of Kôr where our folk once dwelt? For that this night we entertain a guest, a man of great and excellent travel, a son meseems of Eärendel, shall it be of voyaging, of beating about in a boat, of winds and the sea?'[5]

But to this questioning some answered one thing and some another, till Eriol said: 'I pray you, if it be to the mind of the others, for this time tell me of this island, and of all this island most eagerly would I learn of this goodly house and this fair company of maids and boys, for of all houses this seems to me the most lovely and of all gatherings the sweetest I have gazed upon.'

Then said Vairë: 'Know then that aforetime, in the days of[6] Inwë (and farther back it is hard to go in the history of the Eldar), there was a place of fair gardens in Valinor beside a silver sea. Now this place was near the confines of the realm but not far from Kôr, yet by reason of its distance from the sun-tree Lindelos there was a light there as of summer evening, save only when the silver lamps were kindled on the hill at dusk, and then little lights of white would dance and quiver on the paths, chasing black shadow-dapples under the trees. This was a time of joy to the children, for it was mostly at this hour that a new comrade would come down the lane called Olórë Mallë or the Path of Dreams. It has been said to me, though the truth I know not, that that lane ran by devious routes to the homes of Men, but that way we never trod when we fared thither ourselves. It was a lane of deep banks and great overhanging hedges, beyond which stood many tall trees wherein a perpetual whisper seemed to live; but not seldom great glow-worms crept about its grassy borders.

'Now in this place of gardens a high gate of lattice-work that shone golden in the dusk opened upon the lane of dreams, and from there led winding paths of high box to the fairest of all the gardens, and amidmost of the garden stood a white cottage. Of what it was built, nor when, no one knew, nor now knows, but it was said to me that it shone with a pale light, as it was of pearl, and its roof was a thatch, but a thatch of gold.

'Now on one side of the cot stood a thicket of white lilac and at the other end a mighty yew, from whose shoots the children fashioned bows or clambered by his branches upon the roof. But in the lilacs every bird that ever sang sweetly gathered and sang. Now the walls of the cottage were bent with age and its many small lattice windows were twisted into strange shapes. No one, 'tis said, dwelt in the cottage, which was however guarded secretly and jealously by the Eldar so that no harm came nigh it, and that yet might the children playing therein in freedom know of no guardianship. This was the Cottage of the Children, or of the Play of Sleep, and not of Lost Play, as has wrongly been said in song among Men – for no play was lost then, and here alas only and now is the Cottage of Lost Play.

'These too were the earliest children – the children of the fathers of the fathers of Men that came there; and for pity the Eldar sought to guide all who came down that lane into the cottage and the garden, lest they strayed into Kôr and became enamoured of the glory of Valinor; for then would they either stay there for ever, and great grief fall on their parents, or would they wander back and long for ever vainly, and become strange and wild among the children of Men. Nay, some even who wandered on to the edge of the rocks of Eldamar and there strayed, dazzled by the fair shells and the fishes of many colours, the blue pools and the silver foam, they drew back to the cottage, alluring them gently with the odour of many flowers. Yet even so there were a few who heard on that beach the sweet piping of the Solosimpi afar off and who played not with the other children but climbed to the upper windows and gazed out, straining to see the far glimpses of the sea and the magic shores beyond the shadows and the trees.

'Now for the most part the children did not often go into the house, but danced and played in the garden, gathering flowers or chasing the golden bees and butterflies with embroidered wings that the Eldar set within the garden for their joy. And many children have there become comrades, who after met and loved in the lands of Men, but of such things perchance Men know more than I can tell you. Yet some there were who, as I have told, heard the Solosimpi piping afar off, or others who straying again beyond the garden caught a sound of the singing of the Telelli on the hill, and even some who reaching Kôr afterwards returned home, and their minds and hearts were full of wonder. Of the misty aftermemories of these, of their broken tales and snatches of song, came many strange legends that delighted Men for long, and still do, it may be; for of such were the poets of the Great Lands.[7]

'Now when the fairies left Kôr that lane was blocked for ever with great impassable rocks, and there stands of a surety the cottage empty and the garden bare to this day, and will do until long after the Faring Forth, when if all goes well the roads through Arvalin to Valinor shall be thronged with the sons and daughters of Men. But seeing that no children came there for refreshment and delight, sorrow and greyness spread amongst them and Men ceased almost to believe in, or think of, the beauty of the Eldar and the glory of the Valar, till one came from the Great Lands and besought us to relieve the darkness.

'Now there is alas no safe way for children from the Great Lands hither, but Meril-i-Turinqi hearkened to his boon and chose Lindo my husband to devise some plan of good. Now Lindo and I, Vairë, had taken under our care the children – the remainder of those who found Kôr and remained with the Eldar for ever: and so here we builded of good magic this Cottage of Lost Play: and here old tales, old songs, and elfin music are treasured and rehearsed. Ever and anon our children fare forth again to find the Great Lands, and go about among the lonely children and whisper to them at dusk in early bed by night-light and candle-flame, or comfort those that weep. Some I am told listen to the complaints of those that are punished or chidden, and hear their tales and feign to take their part, and this seems to me a quaint and merry service.

'Yet all whom we send return not and that is great grief to us, for it is by no means out of small love that the Eldar held children from Kôr, but rather of thought for the homes of Men; yet in the Great Lands, as you know well, there are fair places and lovely regions of much allurement, wherefore it is only for the great necessity that we adventure any of the children that are with us. Yet the most come back hither and tell us many stories and many sad things of their journeys – and now I have told most of what is to tell of the Cottage of Lost Play.'

Then Eriol said: 'Now these are tidings sad and yet good to hear, and I remember me of certain words that my father spake in my early boyhood. It had long, said he, been a tradition in our kindred that one of our father's fathers would speak of a fair house and magic gardens, of a wondrous town, and of a music full of all beauty and longing – and these things he said he had seen and heard as a child, though how and where was not told. Now all his life was he restless, as if a longing half-expressed for unknown things dwelt within him; and 'tis said that he died among rocks on a lonely coast on a night of storm – and moreover that most of his children and their children since have been of a restless mind – and methinks I know now the truth of the matter.'

And Vairë said that 'twas like to be that one of his kindred had found the rocks of Eldamar in those old days.

## NOTES

1 *Gnomes*: the Second Kindred, the *Noldoli* (later *Noldor*). For the use of the word *Gnomes* see p. 43; and for the linguistic distinction made here see pp. 50–1.

2 The 'Great Lands' are the lands East of the Great Sea. The term 'Middle-earth' is never used in the *Lost Tales*, and in fact does not appear until writings of the 1930s.

3 In both MSS the words 'of all the Eldar' are followed by: 'for of most noble there were none, seeing that to be of the blood of the Eldar is equal and sufficient'; but this was struck out in the second MS.

4 The original reading was 'the great Tirion', changed to 'the great tower'.

5 This sentence, from 'a son meseems . . .', replaced in the original MS an earlier reading: 'shall it be of Eärendel the wanderer, who alone of the sons of Men has had great traffic with the Valar and Elves, who alone of their kindred has seen beyond Taniquetil, even he who sails for ever in the firmament?'

6 The original reading was 'before the days of', changed to 'in the first days of', and then to the reading given.

7 This last phrase was an addition to the second MS.


## Changes made to names in
## *The Cottage of Lost Play*

The names were at this time in a very fluid state, reflecting in part the rapid development of the languages that was then taking place. Changes were made to the original text, and further changes, at different times, to the second text, but it seems unnecessary in the following notes to go into the detail of when and where the changes were made. The names are given in the order of their occurrence in the tale. The signs 〉 and 〈 are used to mean 'changed to' and 'changed from'.

*Dor Faidwen*   The Gnomish name of Tol Eressëa was changed many times: *Gar Eglos* 〉 *Dor Edloth* 〉 *Dor Usgwen* 〉 *Dor Uswen* 〉 *Dor Faidwen*.

*Mar Vanwa Tyaliéva*   In the original text a space was left for the Elvish name, subsequently filled in as *Mar Vanwa Taliéva*.

*Great Lands*   Throughout the tale *Great Lands* is an emendation of *Outer Lands*, when the latter was given a different meaning (lands West of the Great Sea).

*Wingilot* 〈 *Wingelot*.

*Gar Lossion* 〈 *Losgar*.

*Koromas* ⟨ *Kormas*.

*Meril-i-Turinqi*   The first text has only *Turinqi*, with in one place a space left for a personal name.

*Inwë*   ⟨ *Ing* at each occurrence.

*Inwithiel*   ⟨ *Gim Githil*, which was in turn ⟨ *Githil*.

*Ingil*   ⟨ *Ingilmo*.

*Valwë*   ⟨ *Manwë*. It seems possible that *Manwë* as the name of Lindo's father was a mere slip.

*Noldorin*   The original reading was *Noldorin whom the Gnomes name Goldriel*; *Goldriel* was changed to *Golthadriel*, and then the reference to the Gnomish name was struck out, leaving only *Noldorin*.

*Tulkastor*   ⟨ *Tulkassë* ⟨ *Turenbor*.

*Solosimpi*   ⟨ *Solosimpë* at each occurrence.

*Lindelos*   ⟨ *Lindeloksë* ⟨ *Lindeloktë Singing Cluster* (*Glingol*).

*Telelli*   ⟨ *Telellë*.

*Arvalin*   ⟨ *Harmalin* ⟨ *Harwalin*.


## Commentary on
### The Cottage of Lost Play

The story of Eriol the mariner was central to my father's original conception of the mythology. In those days, as he recounted long after in a letter to his friend Milton Waldman,* the primary intention of his work was to satisfy his desire for a specifically and recognizably *English* literature of 'faerie':

> I was from early days grieved by the poverty of my own beloved country: it had no stories of its own (bound up with its tongue and soil), not of the quality that I sought, and found (as an ingredient) in legends of other lands. There was Greek, and Celtic, and Romance, Germanic, Scandinavian, and Finnish (which greatly affected me); but nothing English, save impoverished chap-book stuff.

In his earliest writings the mythology was anchored in the ancient legendary history of England; and more than that, it was peculiarly associated with certain places in England.

Eriol, himself close kin of famous figures in the legends of North-western Europe, came at last on a voyage westward over the ocean to Tol Eressëa, the Lonely Isle, where Elves dwelt; and from them he learned 'The Lost Tales of Elfinesse'. But his rôle was at first to be more important in the structure of the work than (what it afterwards became) simply that of a man of later days who came to 'the land of the Fairies' and there acquired

---

* *The Letters of J. R. R. Tolkien*, ed. Humphrey Carpenter, 1981, p. 144. The letter was almost certainly written in 1951.

lost or hidden knowledge, which he afterwards reported in his own tongue: at first, Eriol was to be an important element in the fairy-history itself – the witness of the ruin of Elvish Tol Eressëa. The element of ancient English history or 'historical legend' was at first not merely a framework, isolated from the great tales that afterwards constituted 'The Silmarillion', but an integral part of their ending. The elucidation of all this (so far as elucidation is possible) must necessarily be postponed to the end of the *Tales*; but here something at least must be said of the history of Eriol up to the time of his coming to Tol Eressëa, and of the original significance of the Lonely Isle.

The 'Eriol-story' is in fact among the knottiest and most obscure matters in the whole history of Middle-earth and Aman. My father abandoned the writing of the *Lost Tales* before he reached their end, and when he abandoned them he had also abandoned his original ideas for their conclusion. Those ideas can indeed be discerned from his notes; but the notes were for the most part pencilled at furious speed, the writing now rubbed and faint and in places after long study scarcely decipherable, on little slips of paper, disordered and dateless, or in a little notebook in which, during the years when he was composing the *Lost Tales*, he jotted down thoughts and suggestions (see p. 171). The common form of these notes on the 'Eriol' or 'English' element is that of short outlines, in which salient narrative features, often without clear connection between them, are set down in the manner of a list; and they vary constantly among themselves.

In what must be, at any rate, among the very earliest of these outlines, found in this little pocket-book, and headed 'Story of Eriol's Life', the mariner who came to Tol Eressëa is brought into relation with the tradition of the invasion of Britain by Hengest and Horsa in the fifth century A.D. This was a matter to which my father gave much time and thought; he lectured on it at Oxford and developed certain original theories, especially in connection with the appearance of Hengest in *Beowulf*.*

From these jottings we learn that Eriol's original name was *Ottor*, but that he called himself *Wǽfre* (an Old English word meaning 'restless, wandering') and lived a life on the waters. His father was named *Eoh* (a word of the Old English poetic vocabulary meaning 'horse'); and Eoh was slain by his brother *Beorn* (in Old English 'warrior', but originally meaning 'bear', as does the cognate word *björn* in Old Norse; cf. Beorn the shape-changer in *The Hobbit*). Eoh and Beorn were the sons of *Heden* 'the leather and fur clad', and Heden (like many heroes of Northern legend) traced his ancestry to the god Wóden. In other notes there are other connections and combinations, and since none of this story was written as a coherent narrative these names are only of significance as showing the direction of my father's thought at that time.

Ottor Wǽfre settled on the island of Heligoland in the North Sea, and

* J. R. R. Tolkien, *Finn and Hengest*, ed. Alan Bliss, 1982.

he wedded a woman named *Cwén* (Old English: 'woman', 'wife'); they had two sons named 'after his father' *Hengest* and *Horsa* 'to avenge Eoh' (*hengest* is another Old English word for 'horse').

Then sea-longing gripped Ottor Wǽfre: he was a son of *Eärendel*, born under his beam. If a beam from Eärendel fall on a child new-born he becomes 'a child of Eärendel' and a wanderer. (So also in *The Cottage of Lost Play* Eriol is called both by the author and by Lindo a 'son of Eärendel'.) After the death of Cwén Ottor left his young children. Hengest and Horsa avenged Eoh and became great chieftains; but Ottor Wǽfre set out to seek, and find, Tol Eressëa, here called in Old English *se uncúþa holm*, 'the unknown island'.

Various things are told in these notes about Eriol's sojourn in Tol Eressëa which do not appear in *The Book of Lost Tales*, but of these I need here only refer to the statements that 'Eriol adopted the name of *Angol*' and that he was named by the Gnomes (the later Noldor, see below p. 43) *Angol* 'after the regions of his home'. This certainly refers to the ancient homeland of the 'English' before their migration across the North Sea to Britain: Old English *Angel, Angul*, modern German *Angeln*, the region of the Danish peninsula between the Flensburg fjord and the river Schlei, south of the modern Danish frontier. From the west coast of the peninsula it is no very great distance to the island of Heligoland.

In another place *Angol* is given as the Gnomish equivalent of *Eriollo*, which names are said to be those of 'the region of the northern part of the Great Lands, "between the seas", whence Eriol came'. (On these names see further under *Eriol* in the Appendix on Names.)

It is not to be thought that these notes represent in all respects the story of Eriol as my father conceived it when he wrote *The Cottage of Lost Play* – in any case, it is said expressly there that *Eriol* means 'One who dreams alone', and that 'of his former names the story nowhere tells' (p. 14). But what is important is that (according to the view that I have formed of the earliest conceptions, apparently the best explanation of the very difficult evidence) this was still the leading idea when it was written: *Eriol came to Tol Eressëa from the lands to the East of the North Sea.* He belongs to the period preceding the Anglo-Saxon invasions of Britain (as my father, for his purposes, wished to represent it).

Later, his name changed to *Ælfwine* ('Elf-friend'), the mariner became an Englishman of the 'Anglo-Saxon period' of English history, who sailed west over sea to Tol Eressëa – he sailed from England out into the Atlantic Ocean; and from this later conception comes the very remarkable story of *Ælfwine of England*, which will be given at the end of the *Lost Tales*. But in the earliest conception he was not an Englishman of England: England in the sense of the land of the English did not yet exist; for the cardinal fact (made quite explicit in extant notes) of this conception is that *the Elvish isle to which Eriol came was England* – that is to say, Tol Eressëa would become England, the land of the English, at the end of the story. Koromas or Kortirion, the town in the centre of Tol Eressëa to which Eriol comes in *The Cottage of Lost Play*, would become in after days Warwick (and the elements *Kor-* and *War-* were etymologically connected);* Alalminórë, the Land of Elms, would be Warwickshire; and Tavrobel, where Eriol sojourned for a while in Tol Eressëa, would afterwards be the Staffordshire village of Great Haywood.

None of this is explicit in the written *Tales*, and is only found in notes independent of them; but it seems certain that it was still present when *The Cottage of Lost Play* was written (and indeed, as I shall try to show later, underlies all the *Tales*). The fair copy that my mother made of it was dated February 1917. From 1913 until her marriage in March 1916 she lived in Warwick and my father visited her there from Oxford; after their marriage she lived for a while at Great Haywood (east of Stafford), since it was near the camp where my father was stationed, and after his return from France he was at Great Haywood in the winter of 1916–17. Thus the identification of Tol Eressëan Tavrobel with Great Haywood cannot be earlier than 1916, and the fair copy of *The Cottage of Lost Play* (and quite possibly the original composition of it) was actually done there.

In November 1915 my father wrote a poem entitled *Kortirion among the Trees* which was dedicated to Warwick.† To the first fair copy of the poem there is appended a prose introduction, as follows:

Now on a time the fairies dwelt in the Lonely Isle after the great wars with Melko and the ruin of Gondolin; and they builded a fair city amidmost of that island, and it was girt with trees. Now this city they called Kortirion, both in memory of their ancient dwelling of Kôr in Valinor, and because this city stood also upon a hill and had a great tower tall and grey that Ingil son of Inwë their lord let raise.

Very beautiful was Kortirion and the fairies loved it, and it became rich in song and poesy and the light of laughter; but on a time the great Faring Forth was made, and the fairies had rekindled once more the Magic Sun of Valinor but for the treason and faint hearts of Men. But so it is that the Magic Sun is dead and the Lonely Isle drawn back unto the confines of the Great Lands, and the fairies are scattered through all the wide unfriendly pathways of the world; and now Men dwell even on this faded isle, and care nought or know nought of its ancient days. Yet still there be some of the Eldar and the Noldoli‡ of old who linger in the island, and their songs are heard about the shores of the land that once was the fairest dwelling of the immortal folk.

* The great tower or *tirion* that Ingil son of Inwe built (p. 16) and the great tower of Warwick Castle are not identified, but at least it is certain that Koromas had a great tower because Warwick has one.

† This poem is given, in three different texts, on pp. 33–43. – A poem written at Étaples in the Pas de Calais in June 1916 and entitled 'The Lonely Isle' is explicitly addressed to England. See *Letters*, p. 437, note 4 to letter 43.

‡ For the distinction between *Eldar* and *Noldoli* see pp. 50–1.

And it seems to the fairies and it seems to me who know that town and have often trodden its disfigured ways that autumn and the falling of the leaf is the season of the year when maybe here or there a heart among Men may be open, and an eye perceive how is the world's estate fallen from the laughter and the loveliness of old. Think on Kortirion and be sad - yet is there not hope?

Both here and in *The Cottage of Lost Play* there are allusions to events still in the future when Eriol came to Tol Eressëa; and though the full exposition and discussion of them must wait until the end of the *Tales* it needs to be explained here that 'the Faring Forth' was a great expedition made from Tol Eressëa for the rescue of the Elves who were still wandering in the Great Lands - cf. Lindo's words (p. 17): 'until such time as they fare forth to find the lost families of the kindred'. At that time Tol Eressëa was uprooted, by the aid of Ulmo, from the sea-bottom and dragged near to the western shores of the Great Lands. In the battle that followed the Elves were defeated, and fled into hiding in Tol Eressëa; Men entered the isle, and the fading of the Elves began. The subsequent history of Tol Eressëa is the history of England; and Warwick is 'disfigured Kortirion', itself a memory of ancient Kôr (the later Tirion upon Túna, city of the Elves in Aman; in the *Lost Tales* the name Kôr is used both of the city and the hill).

Inwë, referred to in *The Cottage of Lost Play* as 'King of all the Eldar when they dwelt in Kôr', is the forerunner of Ingwë King of the Vanyar Elves in *The Silmarillion*. In a story told later to Eriol in Tol Eressëa Inwë reappears as one of the three Elves who went first to Valinor after the Awakening, as was Ingwë in *The Silmarillion*; his kindred and descendants were the *Inwir*, of whom came Meril-i-Turinqi, the Lady of Tol Eressëa (see p. 50). Lindo's references to Inwë's hearing 'the lament of the world' (i.e. of the Great Lands) and to his leading the Eldar forth to the lands of Men (p. 16) are the germ of the story of the coming of the Hosts of the West to the assault on Thangorodrim: 'The host of the Valar prepared for battle; and beneath their white banners marched the Vanyar, the people of Ingwë . . .' (*The Silmarillion*, p. 251). Later in the *Tales* it is said to Eriol by Meril-i-Turinqi that 'Inwë was the eldest of the Elves, and had lived yet in majesty had he not perished in that march into the world; but Ingil his son went long ago back to Valinor and is with Manwë'. In *The Silmarillion*, on the other hand, it is said of Ingwë that 'he entered into Valinor [in the beginning of the days of the Elves] and sits at the feet of the Powers, and all Elves revere his name; but he came never back, nor looked again upon Middle-earth' (p. 53).

Lindo's words about the sojourn of Ingil in Tol Eressëa 'after many days', and the interpretation of the name of his town Koromas as 'the Resting of the Exiles of Kôr', refer to the return of the Eldar from the Great Lands after the war on Melko (Melkor, Morgoth) for the deliverance of the enslaved Noldoli. His words about his father Valwë 'who went with

Noldorin to find the Gnomes' refer to an element in this story of the expedition from Kôr.*

It is important to see, then, that (if my general interpretation is correct) in *The Cottage of Lost Play* Eriol comes to Tol Eressëa *in the time after* the Fall of Gondolin and the march of the Elves of Kôr into the Great Lands for the defeat of Melko, when the Elves who had taken part in it had returned over the sea to dwell in Tol Eressëa; but *before the time* of the 'Faring Forth' and the removal of Tol Eressëa to the geographical position of England. This latter element was soon lost in its entirety from the developing mythology.

★

Of the 'Cottage' itself it must be said at once that very little light can be cast on it from other writings of my father's; for the entire conception of the Children who went to Valinor was to be abandoned almost without further trace. Later in the *Lost Tales*, however, there are again references to Olórë Mallë. After the description of the Hiding of Valinor, it is told that at the bidding of Manwë (who looked on the event with sorrow) the Valar Oromë and Lórien devised strange paths from the Great Lands to Valinor, and the way of Lórien's devising was Olórë Mallë the Path of Dreams; by this road, when 'Men were yet but new-wakened on the earth', 'the children of the fathers of the fathers of Men' came to Valinor in their sleep (pp. 211, 213). There are two further mentions in tales to be given in Part II: the teller of the *Tale of Tinúviel* (a child of Mar Vanwa Tyaliéva) says that she saw Tinúviel and her mother with her own eyes 'when journeying by the Way of Dreams in long past days', and the teller of the *Tale of Turambar* says that he 'trod Olórë Mallë in the days before the fall of Gondolin'.

There is also a poem on the subject of the Cottage of Lost Play, which has many of the details of the description in the prose text. This poem, according to my father's notes, was composed at 59 St John's Street, Oxford, his undergraduate lodgings, on 27–28 April 1915 (when he was 23). It exists (as is constantly the case with the poems) in several versions, each modified in detail from the preceding one, and the end of the poem was twice entirely rewritten. I give it here first in the earliest form, with changes made to this in notes at the foot of the page, and then in the final version, the date of which cannot be certainly determined. I suspect that it was very much later – and may indeed have been one of the revisions made to old poems when the collection *The Adventures of Tom Bombadil* (1962) was being prepared, though it is not mentioned in my father's correspondence on that subject.

The original title was: *You and Me | and the Cottage of Lost Play* (with

* A little light on Lindo's references to the ringing of the Gong on the Shadowy Seas and the Sleeper in the Tower of Pearl will be shed when the story of Eärendel is reached at the end of the *Tales*.

an Old English rendering *þæt húsincel ǽrran gamenes*), which was changed
to *Mar Vanwa Tyaliéva, The Cottage of Lost Play*; in the final version it
is *The Little House of Lost Play: Mar Vanwa Tyaliéva*. The verse-lines
are indented as in the original texts.

You & Me
and the Cottage of Lost Play

You and me – we know that land
   And often have been there
In the long old days, old nursery days,
   A dark child and a fair.
5    Was it down the paths of firelight dreams
   In winter cold and white,
Or in the blue-spun twilit hours
Of little early tucked-up beds
   In drowsy summer night,
10   That You and I got lost in Sleep
   And met each other there –
Your dark hair on your white nightgown,
   And mine was tangled fair?

We wandered shyly hand in hand,
15    Or rollicked in the fairy sand
And gathered pearls and shells in pails,
   While all about the nightingales
   Were singing in the trees.
We dug for silver with our spades
20    By little inland sparkling seas,
Then ran ashore through sleepy glades
   And down a warm and winding lane
We never never found again
   Between high whispering trees.

25   The air was neither night or day,
   But faintly dark with softest light,
When first there glimmered into sight
   The Cottage of Lost Play.
'Twas builded very very old
30    White, and thatched with straws of gold,
   And pierced with peeping lattices
   That looked toward the sea;

  1  You and I
  3  In the long old days, the shining days,
15  in the golden sand
23  That now we cannot find again
25  night nor day
29  New-built it was, yet very old,

And our own children's garden-plots
Were there – our own forgetmenots,
35    Red daisies, cress and mustard,
        And blue nemophilë.
O! all the borders trimmed with box
Were full of favourite flowers – of phlox,
Of larkspur, pinks, and hollyhocks
40    Beneath a red may-tree:
And all the paths were full of shapes,
Of tumbling happy white-clad shapes,
        And with them You and Me.
And some had silver watering-cans
45    And watered all their gowns,
Or sprayed each other; some laid plans
    To build them houses, fairy towns,
        Or dwellings in the trees;
And some were clambering on the roof;
50    Some crooning lonely and aloof;
And some were dancing fairy-rings
    And weaving pearly daisy-strings,
        Or chasing golden bees;
But here and there a little pair
55    With rosy cheeks and tangled hair
        Debated quaint old childish things – *
        And we were one of these.


37  And all the borders
43  That laughed with You and Me.
47  little towns
56  Debated ancient childish things

Lines 58–65 (p. 30) were subsequently rewritten:

But why it was there came a time
When we could take the road no more,
    Though long we looked, and high would climb,
    Or gaze from many a seaward shore
To find the path between sea and sky
    To those old gardens of delight;
And how it goes now in that land,
    If there the house and gardens stand,
        Still filled with children clad in white –
        We know not, You and I.

---

* This seems to echo the lines of Francis Thompson's poem *Daisy*:

Two children did we stray and talk
Wise, idle, childish things.

My father acquired the Works of Francis Thompson in 1913 and 1914.

And why it was Tomorrow came
And with his grey hand led us back;
60          And why we never found the same
Old cottage, or the magic track
That leads between a silver sea
And those old shores and gardens fair
Where all things are, that ever were –
65                  We know not, You and Me.

This is the final version of the poem:

### The Little House of Lost Play
#### Mar Vanwa Tyaliéva

We knew that land once, You and I,
and once we wandered there
in the long days now long gone by,
a dark child and a fair.
5          Was it on the paths of firelight thought
in winter cold and white,
or in the blue-spun twilit hours
of little early tucked-up beds
in drowsy summer night,
10          that you and I in Sleep went down
to meet each other there,
your dark hair on your white nightgown
and mine was tangled fair?

We wandered shyly hand in hand,
15          small footprints in the golden sand,
and gathered pearls and shells in pails,
while all about the nightingales
were singing in the trees.
We dug for silver with our spades,
20          and caught the sparkle of the seas,
then ran ashore to greenlit glades,
and found the warm and winding lane
that now we cannot find again,
between tall whispering trees.

25          The air was neither night nor day,
an ever-eve of gloaming light,
when first there glimmered into sight
the Little House of Play.
New-built it was, yet very old,

62   That leads between the sea and sky
63   To those old shores
65   We know not, You and I.

30          white, and thatched with straws of gold,
             and pierced with peeping lattices
                that looked toward the sea;
          and our own children's garden-plots
          were there: our own forgetmenots,
35          red daisies, cress and mustard,
             and radishes for tea.
          There all the borders, trimmed with box,
          were filled with favourite flowers, with phlox,
          with lupins, pinks, and hollyhocks,
40             beneath a red may-tree;
          and all the gardens full of folk
          that their own little language spoke,
             but not to You and Me.

          For some had silver watering-cans
45             and watered all their gowns,
          or sprayed each other; some laid plans
          to build their houses, little towns
             and dwellings in the trees.
          And some were clambering on the roof;
50          some crooning lonely and aloof;
          some dancing round the fairy-rings
          all garlanded in daisy-strings,
             while some upon their knees
          before a little white-robed king
55          crowned with marigold would sing
             their rhymes of long ago.
          But side by side a little pair
          with heads together, mingled hair,
             went walking to and fro
60          still hand in hand; and what they said,
          ere Waking far apart them led,
             that only we now know.

It is notable that the poem was called *The Cottage*, or *The Little House of Lost Play*, whereas what is described is the Cottage of the Children in Valinor, near the city of Kôr; but this, according to Vairë (p. 19), 'the Cottage of the Play of Sleep', was 'not of Lost Play, as has wrongly been said in song among Men'.

I shall not attempt any analysis or offer any elucidation of the ideas embodied in the 'Cottages of the Children'. The reader, however he interprets them, will in any case not need to be assisted in his perception of the personal and particular emotions in which all was still anchored.

As I have said, the conception of the coming of mortal children in sleep to the gardens of Valinor was soon to be abandoned in its entirety, and in the developed mythology there would be no place for it – still less for the idea that in some possible future day 'the roads through Arvalin to Valinor shall be thronged with the sons and daughters of Men'.

Likewise, all the 'elfin' diminutiveness soon disappeared. The idea of the Cottage of the Children was already in being in 1915, as the poem *You and Me* shows; and it was in the same year, indeed on the same days of April, that *Goblin Feet* (or *Cumaþ þá Nihtielfas*) was written, concerning which my father said in 1971: 'I wish the unhappy little thing, representing all that I came (so soon after) to fervently dislike, could be buried for ever.'* Yet it is to be observed that in early notes Elves and Men are said to have been 'of a size' in former days, and the smallness (and filminess and transparency) of the 'fairies' is an aspect of their 'fading', and directly related to the domination of Men in the Great Lands. To this matter I shall return later. In this connection, the diminutiveness of the Cottage is very strange, since it seems to be a diminutiveness peculiar to itself: Eriol, who has travelled for many days through Tol Eressëa, is astonished that the dwelling can hold so many, and he is told that all who enter it must be, or must become, very small. But Tol Eressëa is an island inhabited by Elves.

I give now three texts of the poem *Kortirion among the Trees* (later *The Trees of Kortirion*). The very earliest workings (November 1915) of this poem are extant,† and there are many subsequent texts. The prose introduction to the early form has been cited on pp. 25–6. A major revision was made in 1937, and another much later; by this time it was almost a different poem. Since my father sent it to Rayner Unwin in February 1962 as a possible candidate for inclusion in *The Adventures of Tom Bombadil*, it seems virtually certain that the final version dates from that time.‡

I give the poem first in its pre-1937 form, when only slight changes had yet been made. In one of the earliest copies it bears a title in Old English: *Cor Tirion þæra béama on middes*, and is 'dedicated to Warwick'; but in another the second title is in Elvish (the second word is not perfectly legible): *Narquelion la . . tu y aldalin Kortirionwen* (i.e. 'Autumn (among) the trees of Kortirion').

---

* He had been asked for his permission to include the poem in an anthology, as it had been several times previously. See Humphrey Carpenter, *Biography*, p. 74, where (a part only) of the poem is printed, and also his bibliography *ibid.* (year 1915).

† According to my father's notes, the original composition dates from November 21–28, 1915, and was written in Warwick on 'a week's leave from camp'. This is not precisely accurate, since letters to my mother survive that were written from the camp on November 25 and 26, in the second of which he says that he has 'written out a pencil copy of "Kortirion"'.

‡ In his letter my father said: '*The Trees* is too long and too ambitious, and even if considered good enough would probably upset the boat.'

*Kortirion among the Trees*

*The First Verses*

  O fading town upon a little hill,
   Old memory is waning in thine ancient gates,
  The robe gone gray, thine old heart almost still;
   The castle only, frowning, ever waits
5  And ponders how among the towering elms
  The Gliding Water leaves these inland realms
   And slips between long meadows to the western sea –
  Still bearing downward over murmurous falls
   One year and then another to the sea;
10  And slowly thither have a many gone
  Since first the fairies built Kortirion.

  O spiry town upon a windy hill
   With sudden-winding alleys shady-walled
  (Where even now the peacocks pace a stately drill,
15   Majestic, sapphirine, and emerald),
  Behold thy girdle of a wide champain
  Sunlit, and watered with a silver rain,
   And richly wooded with a thousand whispering trees
  That cast long shadows in many a bygone noon,
20   And murmured many centuries in the breeze.
  Thou art the city of the Land of Elms,
  Alalminórë in the Faery Realms.

  Sing of thy trees, old, old Kortirion!
  Thine oaks, and maples with their tassels on,
25  Thy singing poplars; and the splendid yews
  That crown thine agéd walls and muse
   Of sombre grandeur all the day –
  Until the twinkle of the early stars
  Is tangled palely in their sable bars;
30  Until the seven lampads of the Silver Bear
  Swing slowly in their shrouded hair
   And diadem the fallen day.
  O tower and citadel of the world!
  When bannered summer is unfurled
35  Most full of music are thine elms –
  A gathered sound that overwhelms
   The voices of all other trees.
  Sing then of elms, belov'd Kortirion,
  How summer crowds their full sails on,
40  Like clothéd masts of verdurous ships,
  A fleet of galleons that proudly slips
   Across long sunlit seas.

*The Second Verses*

Thou art the inmost province of the fading isle
Where linger yet the Lonely Companies.
45 Still, undespairing, do they sometimes slowly file
Along thy paths with plaintive harmonies:
The holy fairies and immortal elves
That dance among the trees and sing themselves
A wistful song of things that were, and could be yet.
50 They pass and vanish in a sudden breeze,
A wave of bowing grass – and we forget
Their tender voices like wind-shaken bells
Of flowers, their gleaming hair like golden asphodels.

Spring still hath joy: thy spring is ever fair
55 Among the trees; but drowsy summer by thy streams
Already stoops to hear the secret player
Pipe out beyond the tangle of her forest dreams
The long thin tune that still do sing
The elvish harebells nodding in a jacinth ring
60 Upon the castle walls;
Already stoops to listen to the clear cold spell
Come up her sunny aisles and perfumed halls:
A sad and haunting magic note,
A strand of silver glass remote.

65 Then all thy trees, old town upon a windy bent,
Do loose a long sad whisper and lament;
For going are the rich-hued hours, th'enchanted nights
When flitting ghost-moths dance like satellites
Round tapers in the moveless air;
70 And doomed already are the radiant dawns,
The fingered sunlight dripping on long lawns;
The odour and the slumbrous noise of meads,
When all the sorrel, flowers, and pluméd weeds
Go down before the scyther's share.
75 Strange sad October robes her dewy furze
In netted sheen of gold-shot gossamers,
And then the wide-umbraged elm begins to fail;
Her mourning multitudes of leaves go pale
Seeing afar the icy shears
80 Of Winter, and his blue-tipped spears
Marching unconquerable upon the sun
Of bright All-Hallows. Then their hour is done,
And wanly borne on wings of amber pale
They beat the wide airs of the fading vale
85 And fly like birds across the misty meres.

*The Third Verses*

Yet is this season dearest to my heart,
    Most fitting to the little faded town
With sense of splendid pomps that now depart
    In mellow sounds of sadness echoing down
90      The paths of stranded mists. O! gentle time
When the late mornings are bejewelled with rime,
    And the blue shadows gather on the distant woods.
The fairies know thy early crystal dusk
    And put in secret on their twilit hoods
95      Of grey and filmy purple, and long bands
Of frosted starlight sewn by silver hands.

They know the season of the brilliant night,
    When naked elms entwine in cloudy lace
The Pleiades, and long-armed poplars bar the light
100      Of golden-rondured moons with glorious face.
O fading fairies and most lonely elves
Then sing ye, sing ye to yourselves
    A woven song of stars and gleaming leaves;
Then whirl ye with the sapphire-wingéd winds;
105      Then do ye pipe and call with heart that grieves
To sombre men: 'Remember what is gone –
The magic sun that lit Kortirion!'

Now are thy trees, old, old Kortirion,
    Seen rising up through pallid mists and wan,
110      Like vessels floating vague and long afar
    Down opal seas beyond the shadowy bar
        Of cloudy ports forlorn:
They leave behind for ever havens throng'd
Wherein their crews a while held feasting long
115      And gorgeous ease, who now like windy ghosts
Are wafted by slow airs to empty coasts;
    There are they sadly glimmering borne
    Across the plumbless ocean of oblivion.
Bare are thy trees become, Kortirion,
120      And all their summer glory swiftly gone.
The seven lampads of the Silver Bear
    Are waxen to a wondrous flare
        That flames above the fallen year.
Though cold thy windy squares and empty streets;
125      Though elves dance seldom in thy pale retreats
(Save on some rare and moonlit night,
A flash, a whispering glint of white),
    Yet would I never need depart from here.

*The Last Verse*

I need not know the desert or red palaces
130        Where dwells the sun, the great seas or the magic isles,
The pinewoods piled on mountain-terraces;
        And calling faintly down the windy miles
Touches my heart no distant bell that rings
In populous cities of the Earthly Kings.
135        Here do I find a haunting ever-near content
Set midmost of the Land of withered Elms
(Alalminórë of the Faery Realms);
        Here circling slowly in a sweet lament
Linger the holy fairies and immortal elves
140  Singing a song of faded longing to themselves.

★

I give next the text of the poem as my father rewrote it in 1937, in the
later of slightly variant forms.

*Kortirion among the Trees*

I

O fading town upon an inland hill,
        Old shadows linger in thine ancient gate,
Thy robe is grey, thine old heart now is still;
        Thy towers silent in the mist await
5        Their crumbling end, while through the storeyed elms
The Gliding Water leaves these inland realms,
        And slips between long meadows to the Sea,
Still bearing downward over murmurous falls
        One day and then another to the Sea;
10  And slowly thither many years have gone,
Since first the Elves here built Kortirion.

O climbing town upon thy windy hill
        With winding streets, and alleys shady-walled
Where now untamed the peacocks pace in drill
15        Majestic, sapphirine, and emerald;
Amid the girdle of this sleeping land,
Where silver falls the rain and gleaming stand
        The whispering host of old deep-rooted trees
That cast long shadows in many a bygone noon,
20        And murmured many centuries in the breeze;
Thou art the city of the Land of Elms,
Alalminórë in the Faery Realms.

Sing of thy trees, Kortirion, again:
The beech on hill, the willow in the fen,
25    The rainy poplars, and the frowning yews
Within thine agéd courts that muse
    In sombre splendour all the day;
Until the twinkle of the early stars
Comes glinting through their sable bars,
30    And the white moon climbing up the sky
Looks down upon the ghosts of trees that die
    Slowly and silently from day to day.
O Lonely Isle, here was thy citadel,
Ere bannered summer from his fortress fell.
35    Then full of music were thine elms:
Green was their armour, green their helms,
    The Lords and Kings of all thy trees.
Sing, then, of elms, renowned Kortirion,
That under summer crowd their full sail on,
40    And shrouded stand like masts of verdurous ships,
A fleet of galleons that proudly slips
    Across long sunlit seas.


## II

Thou art the inmost province of the fading isle,
    Where linger yet the Lonely Companies;
45    Still, undespairing, here they slowly file
    Along thy paths with solemn harmonies:
The holy people of an elder day,
Immortal Elves, that singing fair and fey
    Of vanished things that were, and could be yet,
50    Pass like a wind among the rustling trees,
    A wave of bowing grass, and we forget
Their tender voices like wind-shaken bells
Of flowers, their gleaming hair like golden asphodels.

Once Spring was here with joy, and all was fair
55    Among the trees; but Summer drowsing by the stream
Heard trembling in her heart the secret player
    Pipe, out beyond the tangle of her forest dream,
The long-drawn tune that elvish voices made
Foreseeing Winter through the leafy glade;
60    The late flowers nodding on the ruined walls
Then stooping heard afar that haunting flute
    Beyond the sunny aisles and tree-propped halls;
For thin and clear and cold the note,
As strand of silver glass remote.

65      Then all thy trees, Kortirion, were bent,
        And shook with sudden whispering lament:
        For passing were the days, and doomed the nights
        When flitting ghost-moths danced as satellites
            Round tapers in the moveless air;
70      And doomed already were the radiant dawns,
        The fingered sunlight drawn across the lawns;
        The odour and the slumbrous noise of meads,
        Where all the sorrel, flowers, and pluméd weeds
            Go down before the scyther's share.
75      When cool October robed her dewy furze
        In netted sheen of gold-shot gossamers,
        Then the wide-umbraged elms began to fail;
        Their mourning multitude of leaves grew pale,
            Seeing afar the icy spears
80      Of Winter marching blue behind the sun
        Of bright All-Hallows. Then their hour was done,
        And wanly borne on wings of amber pale
        They beat the wide airs of the fading vale,
        And flew like birds across the misty meres.


                            III

85      This is the season dearest to the heart,
            And time most fitting to the ancient town,
        With waning musics sweet that slow depart
            Winding with echoed sadness faintly down
        The paths of stranded mist. O gentle time,
90      When the late mornings are begemmed with rime,
            And early shadows fold the distant woods!
        The Elves go silent by, their shining hair
            They cloak in twilight under secret hoods
        Of grey, and filmy purple, and long bands
95      Of frosted starlight sewn by silver hands.

        And oft they dance beneath the roofless sky,
            When naked elms entwine in branching lace
        The Seven Stars, and through the boughs the eye.
            Stares golden-beaming in the round moon's face.
100     O holy Elves and fair immortal Folk,
            You sing then ancient songs that once awoke
            Under primeval stars before the Dawn;
        You whirl then dancing with the eddying wind,
            As once you danced upon the shimmering lawn
105     In Elvenhome, before we were, before
        You crossed wide seas unto this mortal shore.

Now are thy trees, old grey Kortirion,
Through pallid mists seen rising tall and wan,
Like vessels floating vague, and drifting far
110    Down opal seas beyond the shadowy bar
     Of cloudy ports forlorn;
Leaving behind for ever havens loud,
Wherein their crews a while held feasting proud
And lordly ease, they now like windy ghosts
115    Are wafted by slow airs to windy coasts,
     And glimmering sadly down the tide are borne.
Bare are thy trees become, Kortirion;
The rotted raiment from their bones is gone.
The seven candles of the Silver Wain,
120    Like lighted tapers in a darkened fane,
     Now flare above the fallen year.
Though court and street now cold and empty lie,
And Elves dance seldom neath the barren sky,
Yet under the white moon there is a sound
125    Of buried music still beneath the ground.
     When winter comes, I would meet winter here.

I would not seek the desert, or red palaces
    Where reigns the sun, nor sail to magic isles,
Nor climb the hoary mountains' stony terraces;
130    And tolling faintly over windy miles
To my heart calls no distant bell that rings
In crowded cities of the Earthly Kings.
    For here is heartsease still, and deep content,
Though sadness haunt the Land of withered Elms
135    (Alalminórë in the Faery Realms);
     And making music still in sweet lament
The Elves here holy and immortal dwell,
And on the stones and trees there lies a spell.

★

I give lastly the final poem, in the second of two slightly different versions; composed (as I believe) nearly half a century after the first.

### The Trees of Kortirion

#### I

##### Alalminórë

O ancient city on a leaguered hill!
Old shadows linger in your broken gate,

Your stones are grey, your old halls now are still,
   Your towers silent in the mist await
5   Their crumbling end, while through the storeyed elms
The River Gliding leaves these inland realms
   And slips between long meadows to the Sea,
Still bearing down by weir and murmuring fall
   One day and then another to the Sea;
10   And slowly thither many days have gone
Since first the Edain built Kortirion.

Kortirion! Upon your island hill
   With winding streets, and alleys shadow-walled
Where even now the peacocks pace in drill
15   Majestic, sapphirine and emerald,
Once long ago amid this sleeping land
Of silver rain, where still year-laden stand
   In unforgetful earth the rooted trees
That cast long shadows in the bygone noon,
20   And whispered in the swiftly passing breeze,
Once long ago, Queen of the Land of Elms,
High City were you of the Inland Realms.

Your trees in summer you remember still:
The willow by the spring, the beech on hill;
25   The rainy poplars, and the frowning yews
Within your aged courts that muse
   In sombre splendour all the day,
Until the firstling star comes glimmering,
And flittermice go by on silent wing;
30   Until the white moon slowly climbing sees
In shadow-fields the sleep-enchanted trees
   Night-mantled all in silver-grey.
Alalminor! Here was your citadel,
Ere bannered summer from his fortress fell;
35   About you stood arrayed your host of elms:
Green was their armour, tall and green their helms,
   High lords and captains of the trees.
But summer wanes. Behold, Kortirion!
The elms their full sail now have crowded on
40   Ready to the winds, like masts amid the vale
Of mighty ships too soon, too soon, to sail
   To other days beyond these sunlit seas.

## II

### *Narquelion**

Alalminórë! Green heart of this Isle
Where linger yet the Faithful Companies!
45   Still undespairing here they slowly file
Down lonely paths with solemn harmonies:
The Fair, the first-born in an elder day,
Immortal Elves, who singing on their way
  Of bliss of old and grief, though men forget,
50   Pass like a wind among the rustling trees,
  A wave of bowing grass, and men forget
Their voices calling from a time we do not know,
Their gleaming hair like sunlight long ago.

A wind in the grass! The turning of the year.
55   A shiver in the reeds beside the stream,
A whisper in the trees – afar they hear,
  Piercing the heart of summer's tangled dream,
Chill music that a herald piper plays
Foreseeing winter and the leafless days.
60   The late flowers trembling on the ruined walls
Already stoop to hear that elven-flute.
  Through the wood's sunny aisles and tree-propped halls
Winding amid the green with clear cold note
Like a thin strand of silver glass remote.

65   The high-tide ebbs, the year will soon be spent;
And all your trees, Kortirion, lament.
At morn the whetstone rang upon the blade,
At eve the grass and golden flowers were laid
  To wither, and the meadows bare.
70   Now dimmed already comes the tardier dawn,
Paler the sunlight fingers creep across the lawn.
The days are passing. Gone like moths the nights
When white wings fluttering danced like satellites
  Round tapers in the windless air.
75   Lammas is gone. The Harvest-moon has waned.
Summer is dying that so briefly reigned.
Now the proud elms at last begin to quail,
Their leaves uncounted tremble and grow pale,
  Seeing afar the icy spears

* With the name *Narquelion* (which appears also in the title in Elvish of
the original poem, see p. 32) cf. *Narquelië* 'Sun-fading', name of the tenth
month in Quenya (*The Lord of the Rings*, Appendix D).

80      Of winter march to battle with the sun.
        When bright All-Hallows fades, their day is done,
        And borne on wings of amber wan they fly
        In heedless winds beneath the sullen sky,
            And fall like dying birds upon the meres.

### III

*Hrívion**

85      Alas! Kortirion, Queen of Elms, alas!
            This season best befits your ancient town
        With echoing voices sad that slowly pass,
            Winding with waning music faintly down
        The paths of stranded mist. O fading time,
90      When morning rises late all hoar with rime,
            And early shadows veil the distant woods!
        Unseen the Elves go by, their shining hair
            They cloak in twilight under secret hoods
        Of grey, their dusk-blue mantles gird with bands
95      Of frosted starlight sewn by silver hands.

        At night they dance beneath the roofless sky,
            When naked elms entwine in branching lace
        The Seven Stars, and through the boughs the eye
            Stares down cold-gleaming in the high moon's face.
100     O Elder Kindred, fair immortal folk!
        You sing now ancient songs that once awoke
            Under primeval stars before the Dawn;
        You dance like shimmering shadows in the wind,
            As once you danced upon the shining lawn
105     Of Elvenhome, before we were, before
        You crossed wide seas unto this mortal shore.

        Now are your trees, old grey Kortirion,
        Through pallid mists seen rising tall and wan,
        Like vessels vague that slowly drift afar
110     Out, out to empty seas beyond the bar
            Of cloudy ports forlorn;
        Leaving behind for ever havens loud,
        Wherein their crews a while held feasting proud
        In lordly ease, they now like windy ghosts
115     Are wafted by cold airs to friendless coasts,
            And silent down the tide are borne.
        Bare has your realm become, Kortirion,

* Cf. *hrívë* 'winter', *The Lord of the Rings*, Appendix D.

Stripped of its raiment, and its splendour gone.
Like lighted tapers in a darkened fane
120  The funeral candles of the Silver Wain
Now flare above the fallen year.
Winter is come. Beneath the barren sky
The Elves are silent. But they do not die!
Here waiting they endure the winter fell
125  And silence. Here I too will dwell;
Kortirion, I will meet the winter here.

IV

*Mettanyë**

I would not find the burning domes and sands
Where reigns the sun, nor dare the deadly snows,
Nor seek in mountains dark the hidden lands
130  Of men long lost to whom no pathway goes;
I heed no call of clamant bell that rings
Iron-tongued in the towers of earthly kings.
Here on the stones and trees there lies a spell
Of unforgotten loss, of memory more blest
135  Than mortal wealth. Here undefeated dwell
The Folk Immortal under withered elms,
Alalminórë once in ancient realms.

★

I conclude this commentary with a note on my father's use of the word *Gnomes* for the *Noldor*, who in the *Lost Tales* are called *Noldoli*. He continued to use it for many years, and it still appeared in earlier editions of *The Hobbit*.†

In a draft for the final paragraph of Appendix F to *The Lord of the Rings* he wrote:

I have sometimes (not in this book) used 'Gnomes' for *Noldor* and 'Gnomish' for *Noldorin*. This I did, for whatever Paracelsus may have thought (if indeed he invented the name) to some 'Gnome' will still

* *Mettanyë* contains *metta* 'ending', as in *Ambar-metta*, the ending of the world (*The Return of the King*, VI.5).
† In Chapter 3, *A Short Rest*, 'swords of the High Elves of the West' replaced 'swords of the elves that are now called Gnomes'; and in Chapter 8, *Flies and Spiders*, the phrase 'There the Light-elves and the Deep-elves and the Sea-elves went and lived for ages' replaced 'There the Light-elves and the Deep-elves (or Gnomes) and the Sea-elves lived for ages'.

suggest knowledge.* Now the High-elven name of this people, Noldor, signifies Those who Know; for of the three kindreds of the Eldar from their beginning the Noldor were ever distinguished both by their knowledge of things that are and were in this world, and by their desire to know more. Yet they in no way resembled the Gnomes either of learned theory or popular fancy; and I have now abandoned this rendering as too misleading. For the Noldor belonged to a race high and beautiful, the elder Children of the world, who now are gone. Tall they were, fair-skinned and grey-eyed, and their locks were dark, save in the golden house of Finrod . . .

In the last paragraph of Appendix F *as published* the reference to 'Gnomes' was removed, and replaced by a passage explaining the use of the word *Elves* to translate *Quendi* and *Eldar* despite the diminishing of the English word. This passage – referring to the Quendi as a whole – continues however with the same words as in the draft: 'They were a race high and beautiful, and among them the Eldar were as kings, who now are gone: the People of the Great Journey, the People of the Stars. They were tall, fair of skin and grey-eyed, though their locks were dark, save in the golden house of Finrod . . .' Thus these words describing characters of face and hair were actually written of the Noldor only, and *not* of all the Eldar: indeed the Vanyar had golden hair, and it was from Finarfin's Vanyarin mother Indis that he, and Finrod Felagund and Galadriel his children, had their golden hair that marked them out among the princes of the Noldor. But I am unable to determine how this extraordinary perversion of meaning arose.†

* Two words are in question: (1) Greek *gnōmē* 'thought, intelligence' (and in the plural 'maxims, sayings', whence the English word *gnome*, a maxim or aphorism, and adjective *gnomic*); and (2) the word *gnome* used by the 16th-century writer Paracelsus as a synonym of *pygmaeus*. Paracelsus 'says that the beings so called have the earth as their element . . . through which they move unobstructed as fish do through water, or birds and land animals through air' (*Oxford English Dictionary* s.v. *Gnome²*). The O.E.D. suggests that whether Paracelsus invented the word himself or not it was intended to mean 'earth-dweller', and discounts any connection with the other word *Gnome*. (This note is repeated from that in *The Letters of J. R. R. Tolkien*, p. 449; see the letter (no. 239) to which it refers.)

† The name *Finrod* in the passage at the end of Appendix F is now in error: Finarfin was Finrod, and Finrod was Inglor, until the second edition of *The Lord of the Rings*, and in this instance the change was overlooked.

# II

# THE MUSIC OF THE AINUR

In another notebook identical to that in which *The Cottage of Lost Play*
was written out by my mother, there is a text in ink in my father's hand
(and all the other texts of the *Lost Tales* are in his hand, save for a fair
copy of *The Fall of Gondolin**) entitled: *Link between Cottage of Lost Play
and (Tale 2) Music of Ainur*. This follows on directly from Vairë's last
words to Eriol on p. 20, and in turn links on directly to *The Music of the
Ainur* (in a third notebook identical to the other two). The only indication
of date for the *Link* and the *Music* (which were, I think, written at the
same time) is a letter of my father's of July 1964 (*Letters* p. 345), in which
he said that while in Oxford 'employed on the staff of the then still incomplete great Dictionary' he 'wrote a cosmogonical myth, "The Music
of the Ainur" '. He took up the post on the Oxford Dictionary in November
1918 and relinquished it in the spring of 1920 (*Biography* pp. 99, 102).
If his recollection was correct, and there is no evidence to set against it,
some two years or more elapsed between *The Cottage of Lost Play* and
*The Music of the Ainur*.

The *Link* between the two exists in only one version, for the text in
ink was written over a draft in pencil that was wholly erased. In this case
I follow the *Link* with a brief commentary, before giving *The Music of the
Ainur*.

'But,' said Eriol, 'still are there many things that remain dark to
me. Indeed I would fain know who be these Valar; are they the
Gods?'

'So be they,' said Lindo, 'though concerning them Men tell many
strange and garbled tales that are far from the truth, and many
strange names they call them that you will not hear here'; but Vairë
said: 'Nay then, Lindo, be not drawn into more tale-telling tonight,
for the hour of rest is at hand, and for all his eagerness our guest is
way-worn. Send now for the candles of sleep, and more tales to his
head's filling and his heart's satisfying the wanderer shall have on
the morrow.' But to Eriol she said: 'Think not that you must leave
our house tomorrow of need; for none do so – nay, all may remain
while a tale remains to tell which they desire to hear.'

Then said Eriol that all desire of faring abroad had left his heart

* The actual title of this tale is *Tuor and the Exiles of Gondolin*, but my
father referred to it as *The Fall of Gondolin* and I do likewise.

and that to be a guest there a while seemed to him fairest of all things. Thereupon came in those that bore the candles of sleep, and each of that company took one, and two of the folk of the house bade Eriol follow them. One of these was the door-ward who had opened to his knocking before. He was old in appearance and grey of locks, and few of that folk were so; but the other had a weather-worn face and blue eyes of great merriment, and was very slender and small, nor might one say if he were fifty or ten thousand. Now that was Ilverin or Littleheart. These two guided him down the corridor of broidered stories to a great stair of oak, and up this he followed them. It wound up and round until it brought them to a passage lit by small pendent lamps of coloured glass, whose swaying cast a spatter of bright hues upon the floors and hangings.

In this passage the guides turned round a sudden corner, then going down a few dark steps flung open a door before him. Now bowing they wished him good sleep, and said Littleheart: 'dreams of fair winds and good voyages in the great seas', and then they left him; and he found that he stood in a chamber that was small, and had a bed of fairest linen and deep pillows set nigh the window – and here the night seemed warm and fragrant, although he had but now come from rejoicing in the blaze of the Tale-fire logs. Here was all the furniture of dark wood, and as his great candle flickered its soft rays worked a magic with the room, till it seemed to him that sleep was the best of all delights, but that fair chamber the best of all for sleep. Ere he laid him down however Eriol opened the window and scent of flowers gusted in therethrough, and a glimpse he caught of a shadow-filled garden that was full of trees, but its spaces were barred with silver lights and black shadows by reason of the moon; yet his window seemed very high indeed above those lawns below, and a nightingale sang suddenly in a tree nearby.

Then slept Eriol, and through his dreams there came a music thinner and more pure than any he heard before, and it was full of longing. Indeed it was as if pipes of silver or flutes of shape most slender-delicate uttered crystal notes and threadlike harmonies beneath the moon upon the lawns; and Eriol longed in his sleep for he knew not what.

When he awoke the sun was rising and there was no music save that of a myriad of birds about his window. The light struck through the panes and shivered into merry glints, and that room with its fragrance and its pleasant draperies seemed even sweeter than before; but Eriol arose, and robing himself in fair garments laid ready for him that he might shed his raiment stained with travel went forth and strayed about the passages of the house, until he chanced upon a little stairway, and going down this he came to a porch and a sunny court. Therein was a lattice-gate that opened to his hand and led into that garden whose lawns were spread beneath the window of his room. There he wandered breathing the airs and watching the sun rise above the strange roofs of that town, when behold the aged door-ward was before him, coming along a lane of hazel-bushes. He saw not Eriol, for he held his head as ever bent towards the earth, and muttered swiftly to himself; but Eriol spake bidding him good morrow, and thereat he started.

Then said he: 'Your pardon, sir! I marked you not, for I was listening to the birds. Indeed sir you find me in a sour temper; for lo! here I have a black-winged rogue fat with impudence who singeth songs before unknown to me, and in a tongue that is strange! It irks me sir, it irks me, for methought at least I knew the simple speeches of all birds. I have a mind to send him down to Mandos for his pertness!' At this Eriol laughed heartily, but said the door-ward: 'Nay sir, may Tevildo Prince of Cats harry him for daring to perch in a garden that is in the care of Rúmil. Know you that the Noldoli grow old astounding slow, and yet have I grey hairs in the study of all the tongues of Valar and of Eldar. Long ere the fall of Gondolin, good sir, I lightened my thraldom under Melko in learning the speech of all monsters and goblins – have I not conned even the speeches of beasts, disdaining not the thin voices of the voles and mice? – have I not cadged a stupid tune or two to hum of the speechless beetles? Nay, I have worried at whiles even over the tongues of Men, but Melko take them! they shift and change, change and shift, and when you have them are but a hard stuff whereof to labour songs or tales. Wherefore is it that this morn I felt as Ómar the Vala who knows all tongues, as I hearkened to the blending of the voices of the birds comprehending each, recognising each well-loved tune, when *tiripti lirilla* here comes a bird, an imp of Melko – but I weary you sir, with babbling of songs and words.'

'Nay, not so,' quoth Eriol, 'but I beg of you be not disheartened by one fat imp of an ousel. If my eyes deceive not, for a good age of years you have cared for this garden. Then must you know store of songs and tongues sufficient to comfort the heart of the greatest of all sages, if indeed this be the first voice that you have heard therein, and lacked its interpretation. Is it not said that the birds of every district, nay almost of every nest, speak unalike?'

''Tis said so, and said truly,' quoth Rúmil, 'and all the songs of Tol Eressëa are to be heard at times within this garden.'

'More than heart-content am I,' said Eriol, 'to have learned that one fair tongue which the Eldar speak about this isle of Tol Eressëa – but I marvelled to hear you speak as if there were many speeches of the Eldar: are there so?'

'Aye,' said Rúmil, 'for there is that tongue to which the Noldoli cling yet – and aforetime the Teleri, the Solosimpi, and the Inwir had all their differences. Yet these were slighter and are now merged in that tongue of the island Elves which you have learnt. Still are there the lost bands too that dwell wandering sadly in the Great Lands, and maybe they speak very strangely now, for it was ages gone that that march was made from Kôr, and as I hold 'twas but the long wandering of the Noldoli about the Earth and the black ages of their thraldom while their kin dwelt yet in Valinor that caused the deep sundering of their speech. Akin nonetheless be assuredly Gnome-speech and Elfin of the Eldar, as my lore teacheth me – but lo! I weary you again. Never have I found another ear yet in the world that grew not tired ere long of such discourse. "Tongues and speeches," they will say, "one is enough for me" – and thus said Littleheart the Gong-warden once upon a time: "Gnome-speech," said he, "is enough for me – did not that one Eärendel and Tuor and Bronweg my father (that mincingly ye miscall Voronwë) speak it and no other?" Yet he had to learn the Elfin in the end, or be doomed either to silence or to leave Mar Vanwa Tyaliéva – and neither fate would his heart suffer. Lo! now he is chirping Eldar like a lady of the Inwir, even Meril-i-Turinqi our queen herself – Manwë care for her. But even these be not all – there is beside the secret tongue in which the Eldar wrote many poesies and books of wisdom and histories of old and earliest things, and yet speak not. This tongue do only the Valar use in their high counsels, and not many of the Eldar of these days may read it or solve its characters. Much of it I learnt in Kôr, a lifetime gone, of the goodness of Aulë, and thereby I know many matters: very many matters.'

'Then,' quoth Eriol, 'maybe you can tell me of things that I greatly desire to know since the words by the Tale-fire yester-eve. Who be the Valar – Manwë, Aulë, and the ones ye name – and wherefore came ye Eldar from that home of loveliness in Valinor?'

Now came those two to a green arbour and the sun was up and warm, and the birds sang mightily, but the lawns were spread with gold. Then Rúmil sat upon a seat there of carven stone grown with moss, and said he: 'Very mighty are the things that you ask, and their true answer delves beyond the uttermost confines of the wastes of time, whither even the sight of Rúmil the aged of the Noldoli may not see; and all the tales of the Valar and the Elves are so knit together that one may scarce expound any one without needing to set forth the whole of their great history.'

'Yet', said Eriol, 'tell me, Rúmil, I beg, some of what you know even of the first beginnings, that I may begin to understand those things that are told me in this isle.'

But Rúmil said: 'Ilúvatar was the first beginning, and beyond that no wisdom of the Valar or of Eldar or of Men can go.'

'Who was Ilúvatar?' said Eriol. 'Was he of the Gods?'

'Nay,' said Rúmil, 'that he was not, for he made them. Ilúvatar is the Lord for Always who dwells beyond the world; who made it and is not of it or in it, but loves it.'

'This have I never heard elsewhere,' said Eriol.

'That may be,' said Rúmil, 'for 'tis early days in the world of Men as yet, nor is the Music of the Ainur much spoken of.'

'Tell me,' said Eriol, 'for I long to learn, what was the Music of the Ainur?'

*Commentary on the Link between The Cottage of Lost Play and The Music of the Ainur*

Thus it was that the *Ainulindalë* was first to be heard by mortal ears, as Eriol sat in a sunlit garden in Tol Eressëa. Even after Eriol (or Ælfwine) had fallen away, Rúmil remained, the great Noldorin sage of Tirion 'who first achieved fitting signs for the recording of speech and song' (*The Silmarillion* p. 63), and *The Music of the Ainur* continued to be ascribed to him, though invested with the gravity of a remote time he moved far away from the garrulous and whimsical philologist of Kortirion. It is to be noted that in this account Rúmil had been a slave under Melko.

Here the Exile of the Noldor from Valinor appears, for it is to this that Rúmil's words about the march from Kôr undoubtedly refer, rather than to Inwë's 'march into the world' (pp. 16, 26); and something is said also of the languages, and of those who spoke them.

In this link-passage Rúmil asserts:

(1) that the *Teleri, Solosimpi,* and *Inwir* had linguistic differences in the past;

(2) but that these dialects are now merged in the 'tongue of the island Elves';

(3) that the tongue of the *Noldoli* (Gnomes) was deeply sundered through their departure into the Great Lands and their captivity under Melko;

(4) that those Noldoli who now dwell in Tol Eressëa have learnt the tongue of the island Elves; but others remain in the Great Lands. (When Rúmil spoke of 'the lost bands that dwell wandering sadly in the Great

Lands' who 'maybe speak very strangely now' he seems to have been referring to remnants of the Noldorin exiles from Kôr who had not come to Tol Eressëa (as he himself had done), rather than to Elves who never went to Valinor.)*

In the *Lost Tales* the name given to the Sea-elves afterwards called the *Teleri* − the third of the three 'tribes' − is *Solosimpi* ('Shoreland Pipers'). It must now be explained that, confusingly enough, the first of the tribes, that led by King Inwë, were called the *Teleri* (the *Vanyar* of *The Silmarillion*). Who then were the *Inwir*? Eriol was told later by Meril-i-Turinqi (p. 115) that the Teleri were those that followed Inwë, 'but his kindred and descendants are that royal folk the Inwir of whose blood I am.' The Inwir were then a 'royal' clan *within the Teleri*; and the relation between the old conception and that of *The Silmarillion* can be shown thus:

|      | Lost Tales              |              | The Silmarillion |
|------|-------------------------|--------------|------------------|
| I    | Teleri                  | .. .. .. ..  | Vanyar           |
|      | (including Inwir)       |              |                  |
| II   | Noldoli                 | .. .. .. ..  | Noldor           |
|      | (Gnomes)                |              |                  |
| III  | Solosimpi               | .. .. .. ..  | Teleri           |

In this link-passage Rúmil seems to say that the 'Eldar' are distinct from the 'Gnomes' − 'akin nonetheless be assuredly Gnome-speech and Elfin of the Eldar'; and 'Eldar' and 'Noldoli' are opposed in the prose preamble to *Kortirion among the Trees* (p. 25). Elsewhere 'Elfin', as a language, is used in opposition to 'Gnomish', and 'Eldar' is used of a word of form in contradistinction to 'Gnomish'. It is in fact made quite explicit in the *Lost Tales* that the Gnomes were themselves Eldar − for instance, 'the Noldoli, who were the sages of the Eldar' (p. 58); but on the other hand we read that after the Flight of the Noldoli from Valinor Aulë 'gave still his love to those few faithful Gnomes who remained still about his halls, yet did he name them thereafter "Eldar"' (p. 176). This is not so purely contradictory as appears at first sight. It seems that (on the one hand) the opposition of 'Eldar' or 'Elfin' to 'Gnomish' arose because Gnomish had become a language apart; and while the Gnomes were certainly themselves Eldar, their language was not. But (on the other hand) the Gnomes had long ago left Kôr, and thus came to be seen as not 'Koreldar', and therefore not 'Eldar'. The word *Eldar* had thus narrowed its meaning, but might at any moment be expanded again to the older sense in which the Noldoli were 'Eldar'.

If this is so, the narrowed sense of *Eldar* reflects the situation in after days in Tol Eressëa; and indeed, in the tales that follow, where the

* On the other hand it is possible that by 'the lost bands' he did in fact mean the Elves who were lost on the journey from the Waters of Awakening (see p. 118); i.e. the implication is: 'if the sundering of the speech of the Noldoli from that of the Eldar who remained in Valinor is very deep, how much more so must be the speech of those who never crossed the sea'.

narrative is concerned with the time before the rebellion of the Noldoli
and their departure from Valinor, they are firmly 'Eldar'. *After* the
rebellion, in the passage cited above, Aulë would not call the Noldoli
who remained in Valinor by that name – and, by implication, he would
not call those who had departed 'Eldar'.

The same ambiguity is present in the words *Elves* and *Elfin*. Rúmil
here calls the language of the Eldar 'Elfin' in opposition to 'Gnomish';
the teller of the *Tale of Tinúviel* says: 'This is my tale, and 'tis a tale of
the Gnomes, wherefore I beg that thou fill not Eriol's ear with thy Elfin
names', and in the same passage 'Elves' are specifically opposed to
'Gnomes'. But, again, in the tales that follow in this book, *Elves* and
*Eldar* and *Eldalië* are used interchangeably of the Three Kindreds (see
for instance the account of the debate of the Valar concerning the summoning of the Elves to Valinor, pp. 116–18). And finally, an apparently
similar variation is seen in the word 'fairy'; thus Tol Eressëa is the name
'in the fairy speech', while 'the Gnomes call it Dor Faidwen' (p. 13), but
on the other hand Gilfanon, a Gnome, is called 'one of the oldest of the
fairies' (p. 175).

It will be seen from Rúmil's remarks that the 'deep sundering' of the
speech of the Elves into two branches was at this time given an historical
basis wholly different from that which afterwards caused the division.
Here, Rúmil ascribes it to 'the long wandering of the Noldoli about the
Earth and the black ages of their thraldom while their kin dwelt yet in
Valinor' – in later terms, 'the Exile of the Noldor'. In *The Silmarillion*
(see especially pp. 113, 129) the Noldor brought the Valinórean tongue to
Middle-earth but abandoned it (save among themselves), and adopted
instead the language of Beleriand, *Sindarin* of the Grey-elves, who had
never been to Valinor: Quenya and Sindarin were of common origin,
but their 'deep sundering' had been brought about through vast ages of
separation. In the *Lost Tales*, on the other hand, the Noldor still brought
the Elvish speech of Valinor to the Great Lands, but they retained it,
and there it itself changed and became wholly different. In other words,
in the original conception the 'second tongue' only split off from the
parent speech through the departure of the Gnomes from Valinor into the
Great Lands; whereas afterwards the 'second tongue' separated from the
'first tongue' near the very beginning of Elvish existence in the world.
Nonetheless, Gnomish *is* Sindarin, in the sense that Gnomish is *the actual
language* that ultimately, as the whole conception evolved, became that
of the Grey-elves of Beleriand.

With Rúmil's remarks about the secret tongue which the Valar use and
in which the Eldar once wrote poetry and books of wisdom, but few of
them now know it, cf. the following note found in the little *Lost Tales*
pocket-book referred to on p. 23:

The Gods understood the language of the Elves but used it not among
themselves. The wiser of the Elves learned much of the speech of the

Gods and long treasured that knowledge among both Teleri and Noldoli, but by the time of the coming to Tol Eressëa none knew it save the Inwir, and now that knowledge is dead save in Meril's house.

Some new persons appear in this passage. Ómar the Vala 'who knows all tongues' did not survive the *Lost Tales*; a little more is heard of him subsequently, but he is a divinity without much substance. Tuor and Bronweg appear from the tale of *The Fall of Gondolin*, which was already written; *Bronweg* is the Gnomish form of *Voronwë*, that same Voronwë who accompanied Tuor from Vinyamar to Gondolin in the later legend. Tevildo Prince of Cats was a demonic servant of Melko and the remote forerunner of Sauron; he is a principal actor in the original story of Beren and Tinúviel, which was also already written (the *Tale of Tinúviel*).

Littleheart the Gong-warden, son of Bronweg, now receives an Elvish name, *Ilverin* (an emendation from *Elwenildo*).

### The Music of the Ainur

The original hastily pencilled and much emended draft text of *The Music of the Ainur* is still extant, on loose sheets placed inside the cover of the notebook that contains a fuller and much more finished text written in ink. This second version was however closely based on the first, and changed it chiefly by additions. The text given here is the second, but some passages where the two differ notably are annotated (few of the differences between the two texts are in my opinion of much significance). It will be seen from passages of the first draft given in the notes that the plural was originally *Ainu*, not *Ainur*, and that *Ilúvatar* was originally *Ilu* (but *Ilúvatar* also occurs in the draft).

Then said Rúmil:

'Hear now things that have not been heard among Men, and the Elves speak seldom of them; yet did Manwë Súlimo, Lord of Elves and Men, whisper them to the fathers of my father in the deeps of time.[1] Behold, Ilúvatar dwelt alone. Before all things he sang into being the Ainur first, and greatest is their power and glory of all his creatures within the world and without. Thereafter he fashioned them dwellings in the void, and dwelt among them, teaching them all manner of things, and the greatest of these was music.

Now he would speak propounding to them themes of song and joyous hymn, revealing many of the great and wonderful things that he devised ever in his mind and heart, and now they would make music unto him, and the voices of their instruments rise in splendour about his throne.

Upon a time Ilúvatar propounded a mighty design of his heart to the Ainur, unfolding a history whose vastness and majesty had never been equalled by aught that he had related before, and the glory of its beginning and the splendour of its end amazed the Ainur, so that they bowed before Ilúvatar and were speechless.

Then said Ilúvatar: "The story that I have laid before you, and that great region of beauty that I have described unto you as the place where all that history might be unfolded and enacted, is related only as it were in outline. I have not filled all the empty spaces, neither have I recounted to you all the adornments and things of loveliness and delicacy whereof my mind is full. It is my desire now that ye make a great and glorious music and a singing of this theme; and (seeing that I have taught you much and set brightly the Secret Fire within you)[2] that ye exercise your minds and powers in adorning the theme to your own thoughts and devising. But I will sit and hearken and be glad that through you I have made much beauty to come to Song."

Then the harpists, and the lutanists, the flautists and pipers, the organs and the countless choirs of the Ainur began to fashion the theme of Ilúvatar into great music; and a sound arose of mighty melodies changing and interchanging, mingling and dissolving amid the thunder of harmonies greater than the roar of the great seas, till the places of the dwelling of Ilúvatar and the regions of the Ainur were filled to overflowing with music, and the echo of music, and the echo of the echoes of music which flowed even into the dark and empty spaces far off. Never was there before, nor has there been since, such a music of immeasurable vastness of splendour; though it is said that a mightier far shall be woven before the seat of Ilúvatar by the choirs of both Ainur and the sons of Men after the Great End. Then shall Ilúvatar's mightiest themes be played aright; for then Ainur and Men will know his mind and heart as well as may be, and all his intent.

But now Ilúvatar sat and hearkened, and for a great while it seemed very good to him, for the flaws in that music were few, and it seemed to him the Ainur had learnt much and well. But as the great theme progressed it came into the heart of Melko to interweave matters of his own vain imagining that were not fitting to that great theme of Ilúvatar. Now Melko had among the Ainur been given some of the greatest gifts of power and wisdom and knowledge by Ilúvatar; and he fared often alone into the dark places and the voids seeking the Secret Fire that giveth Life and Reality (for he had a very hot desire to bring things into being of his own); yet he found it not, for it dwelleth with Ilúvatar, and that he knew not till afterward.[3]

There had he nonetheless fallen to thinking deep cunning thoughts of his own, all of which he showed not even to Ilúvatar. Some of these devisings and imaginings he now wove into his music, and straightway harshness and discordancy rose about him, and many of those that played nigh him grew despondent and their music feeble, and their thoughts unfinished and unclear, while many others fell to attuning their music to his rather than to the great theme wherein they began.

In this way the mischief of Melko spread darkening the music, for those thoughts of his came from the outer blackness whither Ilúvatar had not yet turned the light of his face; and because his secret thoughts had no kinship with the beauty of Ilúvatar's design its harmonies were broken and destroyed. Yet sat Ilúvatar and hearkened till the music reached a depth of gloom and ugliness unimaginable; then did he smile sadly and raised his left hand, and immediately, though none clearly knew how, a new theme began among the clash, like and yet unlike the first, and it gathered power and sweetness. But the discord and noise that Melko had aroused started into uproar against it, and there was a war of sounds, and a clangour arose in which little could be distinguished.

Then Ilúvatar raised his right hand, and he no longer smiled but wept; and behold a third theme, and it was in no way like the others, grew amid the turmoil, till at the last it seemed there were two musics progressing at one time about the feet of Ilúvatar, and these were utterly at variance. One was very great and deep and beautiful, but it was mingled with an unquenchable sorrow, while the other was now grown to unity and a system of its own, but was loud and vain and arrogant, braying triumphantly against the other as it thought to drown it, yet ever, as it essayed to clash most fearsomely, finding itself but in some manner supplementing or harmonising with its rival.

At the midmost of this echoing struggle, whereat the halls of Ilúvatar shook and a tremor ran through the dark places, Ilúvatar raised up both his hands, and in one unfathomed chord, deeper then the firmament, more glorious than the sun, and piercing as the light of Ilúvatar's glance, that music crashed and ceased.

Then said Ilúvatar: "Mighty are the Ainur, and glorious, and among them is Melko the most powerful in knowledge; but that he may know, and all the Ainur, that I am Ilúvatar, those things that ye have sung and played, lo! I have caused to be - not in the musics that ye make in the heavenly regions, as a joy to me and a play unto yourselves, alone, but rather to have shape and reality even as have ye Ainur, whom I have made to share in the reality of Ilúvatar myself. Maybe I shall love these things that come of my song even as I love the Ainur who are of my thought,[4] and maybe more. Thou Melko shalt see that no theme can be played save it come in the end of Ilúvatar's self, nor can any alter the music in Ilúvatar's despite. He that attempts this finds himself in the end but aiding me in devising a thing of still greater grandeur and more complex wonder: – for lo! through Melko have terror as fire, and sorrow like dark waters, wrath like thunder, and evil as far from my light as the depths of the uttermost of the dark places, come into the design that I laid before you. Through him has pain and misery been made in the clash of overwhelming musics; and with confusion of sound have cruelty, and ravening, and darkness, loathly mire and all putrescence of thought or thing, foul mists and violent flame, cold without mercy, been born, and death without hope. Yet is this through him and not by him; and he shall see, and ye all likewise, and even shall those beings, who must now dwell among his evil and endure through Melko misery and sorrow, terror and wickedness, declare in the end that it redoundeth only to my great glory, and doth but make the theme more worth the hearing, Life more worth the living, and the World so much the more wonderful and marvellous, that of all the deeds of Ilúvatar it shall be called his mightiest and his loveliest."

Then the Ainur feared and comprehended not all that was said, and Melko was filled with shame and the anger of shame; but Ilúvatar seeing their amaze arose in glory and went forth from his dwellings, past those fair regions he had fashioned for the Ainur, out into the dark places; and he bade the Ainur follow him.

Now when they reached the midmost void they beheld a sight of surpassing beauty and wonder where before had been emptiness; but Ilúvatar said: "Behold your choiring and your music! Even as ye played so of my will your music took shape, and lo! even now the world unfolds and its history begins as did my theme in your hands. Each one herein will find contained within the design that is mine the adornments and embellishments that he himself devised; nay, even Melko will discover those things there which he thought to contrive of his own heart, out of harmony with my mind, and he will find them but a part of the whole and tributary to its glory. One thing only have I added, the fire that giveth Life and Reality" – and behold, the Secret Fire burnt at the heart of the world.

Then the Ainur marvelled to see how the world was globed amid the void and yet separated from it; and they rejoiced to see light, and found it was both white and golden, and they laughed for the pleasure of colours, and for the great roaring of the ocean they were filled with longing. Their hearts were glad because of air and the winds, and the matters whereof the Earth was made – iron and stone and silver and gold and many substances: but of all these water was held the fairest and most goodly and most greatly praised. Indeed there liveth still in water a deeper echo of the Music of the Ainur than in any substance else that is in the world, and at this latest day many of the Sons of Men will hearken unsatedly to the voice of the Sea and long for they know not what.

Know then that water was for the most part the dream and invention of Ulmo, an Ainu whom Ilúvatar had instructed deeper than all others in the depths of music; while the air and winds and the ethers of the firmament had Manwë Súlimo devised, greatest and most noble of the Ainur. The earth and most of its goodly substances did Aulë contrive, whom Ilúvatar had taught many things of wisdom scarce less than Melko, yet was there much therein that was nought of his.[5]

Now Ilúvatar spake to Ulmo and said: "Seest thou not how Melko hath bethought him of biting colds without moderation, yet hath not destroyed the beauty of thy crystal waters nor of all thy limpid pools. Even where he has thought to conquer utterly, behold snow has been made, and frost has wrought his exquisite works; ice has reared his castles in grandeur."

Again said Ilúvatar: "Melko hath devised undue heats, and fires without restraint, and yet hath not dried up thy desire nor utterly quelled the music of thy seas. Rather behold now the height and glory of the clouds and the magic that dwells in mist and vapours; listen to the whisper of rains upon the earth."

Then said Ulmo: "Yea truly is water fairer now than was my best devising before. Snow is of a loveliness beyond my most secret thoughts, and if there is little music therein, yet rain is beautiful indeed and hath a music that filleth my heart, so glad am I that my ears have found it, though its sadness is among the saddest of all things. Lo! I will go seek Súlimo of the air and winds, that he and I play melodies for ever and ever to thy glory and rejoicing."

Now Ulmo and Manwë have been great friends and allies in almost all matters since then.[6]

Now even as Ilúvatar spake to Ulmo, the Ainur beheld how the world unfolded, and that history which Ilúvatar had propounded to them as a great music was already being carried out. It is of their gathered memories of the speech of Ilúvatar and the knowledge, incomplete it may be, that each has of their music, that the Ainur know so much of the future that few things are unforeseen by them – yet are there some that be hidden even from these.[7] So the Ainur gazed; until long before the coming of Men – nay, who does not know that it was countless ages before even the Eldar arose and sang their first song and made the first of all the gems, and were seen by both Ilúvatar and the Ainur to be of exceeding loveliness – there grew a contention among them, so enamoured did they become of the glory of the world as they gazed upon it, and so enthralled by the history enacted therein to which the beauty of the world was but the background and the scene.

Now this was the end, that some abode still with Ilúvatar beyond the world – and these were mostly those who had been engrossed in their playing with thoughts of Ilúvatar's plan and design, and cared only to set it forth without aught of their own devising to adorn it; but some others, and among them many of the most beautiful and wisest of the Ainur, craved leave of Ilúvatar to dwell within the world. For said they: "We would have the guarding of those fair things of our dreams, which of thy might have now attained to reality and surpassing beauty; and we would instruct both Eldar and Men in their wonder and uses whenso the times come that those appear upon Earth by your intent, first the Eldar and at length the fathers of the fathers of Men." And Melko feigned that he desired to control the violence of the heats and turmoils he had set in the Earth, but of a truth purposed deep in his heart to usurp the power of the other Ainur and make war upon Eldar and Men, for he was wroth at those great gifts which Ilúvatar had purposed to give to these races.[8]

Now Eldar and Men were of Ilúvatar's devising only, nor, for they comprehended not fully when Ilúvatar first propounded their being, did any of the Ainur dare in their music to add anything to their fashion; and these races are for that reason named rightly the Children of Ilúvatar. This maybe is the cause wherefore many others of the Ainur, beside Melko, have ever been for meddling with both Elves and Men, be it of good or evil intent; yet seeing that Ilúvatar made the Eldar most like in nature if not in power and stature to the Ainur, while to Men he gave strange gifts, their dealings have been chiefly with the Elves.[9]

Knowing all their hearts, still did Ilúvatar grant the desire of the Ainur, nor is it said he was grieved thereat. So entered these great

ones into the world, and these are they whom we now call the Valar
(or the Vali, it matters not).[10] They dwelt in Valinor, or in the firmament; and some on earth or in the deeps of the Sea. There Melko
ruled both fires and the cruellest frost, both the uttermost colds and
the deepest furnaces beneath the hills of flame; and whatso is violent
or excessive, sudden or cruel, in the world is laid to his charge, and
for the most part with justice. But Ulmo dwells in the outer ocean
and controls the flowing of all waters and the courses of rivers, the
replenishment of springs and the distilling of rains and dews throughout the world. At the bottom of the sea he bethinks him of music
deep and strange yet full ever of a sorrow: and therein he has aid
from Manwë Súlimo.

The Solosimpi, what time the Elves came and dwelt in Kôr,
learnt much of him, whence cometh the wistful allurement of their
piping and their love to dwell ever by the shore. Salmar there was
with him, and Ossë and Ónen to whom he gave the control of the
waves and lesser seas, and many another.

But Aulë dwelt in Valinor and fashioned many things; tools and
instruments he devised and was busied as much in the making of
webs as in the beating of metals; tillage too and husbandry was his
delight as much as tongues and alphabets, or broideries and painting.
Of him did the Noldoli, who were the sages of the Eldar and thirsted
ever after new lore and fresh knowledge, learn uncounted wealth of
crafts, and magics and sciences unfathomed. From his teaching,
whereto the Eldar brought ever their own great beauty of mind and
heart and imagining, did they attain to the invention and making of
gems; and these were not in the world before the Eldar, and the
finest of all gems were Silmarilli, and they are lost.

Yet was the greatest and chief of those four great ones Manwë
Súlimo; and he dwelt in Valinor and sate in a glorious abode upon
a throne of wonder on the topmost pinnacle of Taniquetil that
towers up upon the world's edge. Hawks flew ever to and fro about
that abode, whose eyes could see to the deeps of the sea or penetrate
the most hidden caverns and profoundest darkness of the world.
These brought him news from everywhere of everything, and little
escaped him – yet did some matters lie hid even from the Lord of
the Gods. With him was Varda the Beautiful, and she became his
spouse and is Queen of the Stars, and their children were Fionwë-
Úrion and Erinti most lovely. About them dwell a great host of fair
spirits, and their happiness is great; and men love Manwë even more
than mighty Ulmo, for he hath never of intent done ill to them nor
is he so fain of honour or so jealous of his power as that ancient one

of Vai. The Teleri whom Inwë ruled were especially beloved of him, and got of him poesy and song; for if Ulmo hath a power of musics and of voices of instruments Manwë hath a splendour of poesy and song beyond compare.

Lo, Manwë Súlimo clad in sapphires, ruler of the airs and wind, is held lord of Gods and Elves and Men, and the greatest bulwark against the evil of Melko.'[11]

Then said Rúmil again:

'Lo! After the departure of these Ainur and their vassalage all was quiet for a great age while Ilúvatar watched. Then on a sudden he said: "Behold I love the world, and it is a hall of play for Eldar and Men who are my beloved. But when the Eldar come they will be the fairest and the most lovely of all things by far; and deeper in the knowledge of beauty, and happier than Men. But to Men I will give a new gift, and a greater." Therefore he devised that Men should have a free virtue whereby within the limits of the powers and substances and chances of the world they might fashion and design their life beyond even the original Music of the Ainur that is as fate to all things else. This he did that of their operations everything should in shape and deed be completed, and the world fulfilled unto the last and smallest.[12] Lo! Even we Eldar have found to our sorrow that Men have a strange power for good or ill and for turning things despite Gods and Fairies to their mood in the world; so that we say: "Fate may not conquer the Children of Men, but yet are they strangely blind, whereas their joy should be great."

Now Ilúvatar knew that Men set amid the turmoils of the Ainur would not be ever of a mind to use that gift in harmony with his intent, but thereto he said: "These too in their time shall find that all they have done, even the ugliest of deeds or works, redounds at the end only to my glory, and is tributary to the beauty of my world." Yet the Ainur say that the thought of Men is at times a grief even to Ilúvatar; wherefore if the giving of that gift of freedom was their envy and amazement, the patience of Ilúvatar at its misuse is a matter of the greatest marvelling to both Gods and Fairies. It is however of one with this gift of power that the Children of Men dwell only a short time in the world alive, yet do not perish utterly for ever, whereas the Eldar dwell till the Great End[13] unless they be slain or waste in grief (for to both of these deaths are they subject), nor doth eld subdue their strength, except it may be in ten thousand centuries; and dying they are reborn in their children, so that their number minishes not, nor grows. Yet while the Sons of Men will

after the passing of things of a certainty join in the Second Music
of the Ainur, what Ilúvatar has devised for the Eldar beyond the
world's end he has not revealed even to the Valar, and Melko has
not discovered it.'

## NOTES

1   This opening sentence is lacking in the draft.
2   The reference to the setting of the Secret Fire within the Ainur is
    lacking in the draft.
3   This passage, from 'Now Melko had among the Ainur ...', is developed
    from one much briefer in the draft: 'Melko had among the Ainu fared
    most often alone into the dark places and the voids [*added afterwards*:
    seeking the secret fires].'
4   The words 'my song' and 'my thought' were in the text as written in
    reversed positions, and were emended afterwards in pencil to the
    reading given. At the beginning of the text occurs the phrase:
    'Before all things he sang into being the Ainur first.' Cf. the opening
    of the *Ainulindalë* in *The Silmarillion*: 'The Ainur . . . that were the
    offspring of his thought.'
5   There is no reference here in the draft to Manwë or Aulë.
6   This sentence concerning the friendship and alliance of Manwë and
    Ulmo is lacking in the draft.
7   This passage was quite different in the draft text:
    And even as Ilu was speaking to Ulmo the Ainu beheld how the
    great history which Ilu had propounded to them to their amaze-
    ment and whereto all his glory was but the hall of its enactment –
    how it was unfolding in myriad complexities even as had been the
    music they played about the feet of Ilu, how beauty was whelmed
    in uproar and tumult and again new beauty arose therefrom, how the
    earth changed and stars went out and stars were kindled, and the
    air swept about the firmament, and the sun and moon were
    loosened on their courses and had life.
8   This sentence concerning Melko is lacking in the draft.
9   In the draft this paragraph reads:
    Now Eldar and Men were of Ilu's devising alone, nor had any of
    the Ainu nor even Melko aught to do with their fashioning, though
    in truth his music of old and his deeds in the world mightily
    affected their history thereafter. For this reason maybe, Melko and
    many of the Ainu out of good or evil mind would ever be for
    meddling with them, but seeing that Ilu had made the Eldar too
    alike in nature if not in stature to the Ainu their dealings have been
    chiefly with Men.
    The conclusion of this passage seems to be the only place where the
    second text is in direct contradiction of the draft.

10  The draft has: 'and these are they whom ye and we now call the Valur and Valir.'

11  The entire passage following the mention of the Solosimpi and 'their love to dwell ever by the shore' is lacking in the draft.

12  For this passage the draft has:

"... but to Men I will appoint a task and give a great gift." And he devised that they should have free will and the power of fashioning and designing beyond the original music of the Ainu, that by reason of their operations all things shall in shape and deed be fulfilled, and the world that comes of the music of the Ainu be completed unto the last and smallest.

13  'whereas the Eldar dwell for ever' draft text.

## Changes made to names in
*The Music of the Ainur*

*Ainur*  Always *Ainu* in the draft text.

*Ilúvatar*  Usually *Ilu* in the draft text, but also *Ilúvatar*.

*Ulmo*  In the draft text Ulmo is thus named but also *Linqil* (corrected to *Ulmo*).

*Solosimpi* ⟨ *Solosimpë*.

*Valar or Vali*  Draft text *Valur and Valir* (these appear to be masculine and feminine forms).

*Ónen* ⟨*Ówen*.

*Vai* ⟨*Ulmonan*.

## Commentary on
*The Music of the Ainur*

A linking passage continues the text of *The Music of the Ainur* and leads into the story of *The Building of Valinor* without any break in the narrative; but I postpone this link until the next chapter. The actual written text is likewise continuous between the two tales, and there is no suggestion or indication that the composition of *The Building of Valinor* did not follow that of *The Music of the Ainur*.

In later years the Creation myth was revised and rewritten over and over again; but it is notable that in this case only and in contrast to the development of the rest of the mythology there is a direct tradition, manuscript to manuscript, from the earliest draft to the final version: each text is directly based on the one preceding.* Moreover, and most

---

\* For comparison with the published text in *The Silmarillion* it should be noted that some of the matter of the early version does not appear in the *Ainulindalë* itself but at the end of Chapter 1, *Of the Beginning of Days* (pp. 39–42).

remarkably, the earliest version, written when my father was 27 or 28 and embedded still in the context of the Cottage of Lost Play, was so evolved in its conception that it underwent little change of an essential kind. There were indeed very many changes, which can be followed stage by stage through the successive texts, and much new matter came in; but the fall of the original sentences can continually be recognized in the last version of the *Ainulindalë*, written more than thirty years later, and even many phrases survived.

It will be seen that the great theme that Ilúvatar propounded to the Ainur was originally made somewhat more explicit ('The story that I have laid before you,' p. 53), and that the words of Ilúvatar to the Ainur at the end of the Music contained a long declaration of what Melko had brought about, of what he had introduced into the world's history (p. 55). But by far the most important difference is that in the early form the Ainur's first sight of the World was in its actuality ('even now the world unfolds and its history begins', p. 55), not as a Vision that was taken away from them and only given existence in the words of Ilúvatar: *Eä! Let these things Be!* (*The Silmarillion* p. 20).

Yet when all differences have been observed, they are much less remarkable than the solidity and completeness with which the myth of the Creation emerged at its first beginning.

In this 'Tale', also, many specific features of less general import make their appearance; and many of them were to survive. Manwë, called 'lord of Gods and Elves and Men', is surnamed *Súlimo*, 'ruler of the airs and wind'; he is clad in sapphires, and hawks of penetrating sight fly from his dwelling on Taniquetil (*The Silmarillion* p. 40); he loves especially the Teleri (the later Vanyar), and from him they received their gifts of poetry and song; and his spouse is Varda, Queen of the Stars.

Manwë, Melko, Ulmo, and Aulë are marked out as 'the four great ones'; ultimately the great Valar, the *Aratar*, came to be numbered nine, but there was much shifting in the membership of the hierarchy before this was reached. The characteristic concerns of Aulë, and his particular association with the Noldoli, emerge here as they were to remain, though there is attributed to him a delight in 'tongues and alphabets', whereas in *The Silmarillion* (p. 39), while this is not denied, it seems to be implied that this was rather the peculiar endowment and skill of the Noldorin Elves; later in the *Lost Tales* (p. 141) it is said that Aulë himself 'aided by the Gnomes contrived alphabets and scripts'. Ulmo, specially associated with the Solosimpi (the later Teleri), is here presented as more 'fain of his honour and jealous of his power' than Manwë; and he dwells in Vai. Vai is an emendation of Ulmonan; but this is not simply a replacement of one name by another: Ulmonan was the name of Ulmo's halls, which were in Vai, the Outer Ocean. The significance of Vai, an important element in the original cosmology, will emerge in the next chapter.

Other divine beings now appear. Manwë and Varda have offspring, Fionwë-Úrion and Erinti. Erinti later became Ilmarë 'handmaid of Varda'

(*The Silmarillion* p. 30), but nothing was ever told of her (see p. 202). Fionwë, his name long afterwards changed to Eönwë, endured to become the Herald of Manwë, when the idea of 'the Children of the Valar' was abandoned. Beings subordinate to Ulmo, Salmar, Ossë, and Ónen (later Uinen) appear; though these all survived in the pantheon, the conception of Maiar did not emerge for many years, and Ossë was long numbered among the Valar. The Valar are here referred to as 'Gods' (indeed when Eriol asked 'are they the Gods?' Lindo replied that they were, p. 45), and this usage survived until far on in the development of the mythology.

The idea of Elvish rebirth in their own children is here formally stated, and the different fates of Elves and Men. In this connection, the following curious matter may be mentioned. Early in the text just given (p. 53) occurs the sentence: 'It is said that a mightier [music] far shall be woven before the seat of Ilúvatar by the choirs of both Ainur *and the sons of Men* after the Great End'; and in the concluding sentence of the text: 'Yet while *the sons of Men* will after the passing of things of a certainty join in the Second Music of the Ainur, what Ilúvatar has devised for the Eldar beyond the world's end he has not revealed even to the Valar, and Melko has not discovered it.' Now in the first revision of the *Ainulindalë* (which dates from the 1930s) the first of these sentences was changed to read: '. . . by the choirs of the Ainur *and the Children of Ilúvatar* after the end of days'; whereas the second remained, in this essential, unchanged. This remained the case right through to the final version. It is possible that the change in the first passage was unintentional, the substitution of another common phrase, and that this was never subsequently picked up. However, in the published work (pp. 15, 42) I left the two passages as they stand.

# III

# THE COMING OF THE VALAR
# AND THE BUILDING OF VALINOR

As I have already noticed, the next tale is linked to *The Music of the Ainur* without narrative break; and it has no title in the text. It is contained in three separate books (the *Lost Tales* were written in the most bewildering fashion, with sections from different tales interleaved with each other); and on the cover of the book that has the opening section, following on *The Music of the Ainur*, is written: 'containeth also the Coming of the Valar and beginneth the Building of Valinor'. The text is in ink, written over an erased pencil manuscript.

Then when Rúmil finished and fell silent Eriol said after a pause: 'Great are these tidings and very new and strange in my ears, yet doth it seem that most whereof you have yet told happened outside this world, whereas if I know now wherefrom comes its life and motion and the ultimate devising of its history, I would still hear many things of the earliest deeds within its borders; of the labours of the Valar I would know, and the great beings of most ancient days. Whereof, tell me, are the Sun or the Moon or the Stars, and how came their courses and their stations? Nay more – whence are the continents of the earth, the Outer Lands, the great seas, and the Magic Isles? Even of the Eldar and their arising and of the coming of Men I would listen to your tales of wisdom and wonder.'

Then answered Rúmil: 'Nay, but your questions are nigh as long and wordy as my tales – and the thirst of your curiosity would dry a well deeper than even my lore, an I let you drink and come again unstinted to your liking. Indeed you know not what you ask nor the length and complexity of the stories you would hear. Behold, the sun is well above the roofs and this is no hour of the day for the telling of tales. Rather is it time already, and something more, for the breaking of the fast.' With these words Rúmil went down that lane of hazels, and passing a space of sunlight entered the house at great speed, for all that he looked ever before his toes as he went.

But Eriol sat musing in that arbour, pondering what he had heard, and many questions came into his mind that he desired to ask, until he forgot that he fasted still. But now comes Littleheart and another bearing covers and fair linen, and they say to him: 'It is the words of

Rúmil the Sage that you are fainting in the Arbour of the Thrushes
for hunger and for weariness of his garrulous tongue – and thinking
that very like to be, we are come to aid thee.'

Then Eriol thanked them, and breaking his fast spent the remainder of that fair day hidden in the quiet alleys of that garden deep in
thought; nor did he have lack of pleasance, for although it seemed
enclosed within great stone walls covered with fruit-trees or with
climbing plants whose golden and red blossoms shone beneath the
sun, yet were the nooks and corners of the garden, its coppices and
lawns, its shady ways and flowering fields, without end, and exploration discovered always something new. Nonetheless even greater was
his joy when that night again the toast was drunk to the 'Rekindling
of the Magic Sun' and the candles held aloft and the throng went
once more to the room where the Tale-fire burnt.

There said Lindo: 'Is it to be tales, as of custom, again this night,
or shall it be musics and the singing of songs?' And the most said
songs and music, and thereat skilled ones arose who sang old melodies
or maybe roused dead minstrelsy of Valinor to life amid the flicker
of that firelit room. Some too spake poesies concerning Kôr, and
Eldamar, short snatches of the wealth of old; but soon the song and
music died down and there was a quiet, while those there thought of
the departed beauty and longed eagerly for the Rekindling of the
Magic Sun.

Now at length spake Eriol to Lindo, saying: 'One Rúmil the door-
ward, and, methought, a great sage, did this morning in the garden
relate to me the beginning of the world and the coming of the Valar.
Now fain would I hear of Valinor!'

Then said Rúmil, for he sat upon a stool in a deep-shadowed nook:
'Then with the leave of Lindo and of Vairë I will begin the tale, else
will you go on asking for ever; and may the company have pardon if
they hear old tales again.' But Vairë said that those words concerning
the oldest things were far from stale yet in the ears of the Eldar.

Then said Rúmil:

'Behold, Manwë Súlimo and Varda the Beautiful arose. Varda it
was who at the playing of the Music had thought much of light that
was of white and silver, and of stars. Those twain gathered now
wings of power to themselves and fared swiftly through the three
airs. Vaitya is that which is wrapped dark and sluggish about the
world and without it, but Ilwë is blue and clear and flows among the
stars, and last came they to Vilna that is grey and therein may the
birds fly safely.

With them came many of those lesser Vali who loved them and

had played nigh them and attuned their music to theirs, and these are the Mánir and the Súruli, the sylphs of the airs and of the winds. Now swiftly as they fared Melko was there before them, having rushed headlong flaming through the airs in the impetuosity of his speed, and there was a tumult of the sea where he had dived and the mountains above him spouted flames and the earth gaped and rocked; but Manwë beholding this was wroth.

Thereafter came Ulmo and Aulë, and with Ulmo were none, save Salmar only who was after known as Noldorin, for good though the heart of that mighty one he thought ever deep thoughts alone, and was silent and aloof and haughty even to the Ainur; but with Aulë was that great lady Palúrien whose delights were richness and fruits of the earth, for which reason has she long been called Yavanna among the Eldar. About them fared a great host who are the sprites of trees and woods, of dale and forest and mountain-side, or those that sing amid the grass at morning and chant among the standing corn at eve. These are the Nermir and the Tavari, Nandini and Orossi, brownies, fays, pixies, leprawns, and what else are they not called, for their number is very great: yet must they not be confused with the Eldar, for they were born before the world and are older than its oldest, and are not of it, but laugh at it much, for had they not somewhat to do with its making, so that it is for the most part a play for them; but the Eldar are of the world and love it with a great and burning love, and are wistful in all their happiness for that reason.

Now behind those greatest chieftains came Falman-Ossë of the waves of the sea and Ónen his consort, and with them the troops of the Oarni and Falmaríni and the long-tressed Wingildi, and these are the spirits of the foam and the surf of ocean. Now Ossë was a vassal and subordinate to Ulmo, and was so for fear and reverence and not for love. Behind him there came Tulkas Poldórëa rejoicing in his strength, and those brethren the Fánturi, Fantur of Dreams who is Lórien Olofántur, and Fantur of Death who is Vefántur Mandos, and those twain also who are named Tári for they are ladies of great worship, queens of the Valar. The one was the spouse of Mandos, and is known to all as Fui Nienna by reason of her glooms, and she is fain of mourning and tears. Many other names has she that are spoken seldom and all are grievous, for she is Núri who sighs and Heskil who breedeth winter, and all must bow before her as Qalmë-Tári the mistress of death. But lo, the other was the spouse of Oromë the hunter who is named Aldaron king of forests, who shouts for joy upon mountain-tops and is nigh as lusty as that perpetual youth Tulkas. Oromë is the son of Aulë and Palúrien, and that Tári who is his wife is known to all as Vána the fair and loveth mirth and youth and beauty, and is happiest of all beings, for she is Tuilérë or as the Valar said Vána Tuivána who bringeth spring, and all sing her praises as Tári-Laisi mistress of life.

Yet even when all these had crossed the confines of the world and Vilna was in uproar with their passing, there came still hurrying late Makar and his fierce sister Meássë; and it had been better had they not found the world but remained for ever with the Ainur beyond Vaitya and the stars, for both were spirits of quarrelsome mood, and with some other lesser ones who came now with them had been the first and chief to join in the discords of Melko and to aid in the spreading of his music.

Last of all came Ómar who is called Amillo, youngest of the great Valar, and he sang songs as he came.

Then when all these great spirits were gathered together within the confines of the world Manwë spake to them, saying: "Lo now! How may the Valar abide in this fair place or be happy and rejoice in its goodness, if Melko be suffered to destroy it, and make fire and turmoil, so that we have not where to sit in peace, nor may the earth blossom or the designs of Ilúvatar come to being?"

Then all the Valar were angered with Melko, and Makar alone spoke against Manwë; but the rest chose certain of their number to seek out the wrongdoer, and these were Mandos and Tulkas, Mandos for that of his dread aspect was Melko more in fear than of aught else save it were the strength of Tulkas' arm, and Tulkas was the other.

Now those two sought him out and constrained him to come before Manwë, and Tulkas whose heart misliked the crooked guile of Melko gave him a blow with his fist, and he abode that then but did not forget. Yet did he speak the Gods fair, and said how he did scant harm, revelling only a while in the newness of the world; nor, said he, would he ever seek to do aught against the lordship of Manwë or the dignity of those chiefs Aulë and Ulmo, nor indeed to the hurt of any beside. Rather was it his counsel that each of the Valar should now depart and dwell amid those things that he loved upon Earth, nor should any seek to extend his sway beyond its just boundaries. In this there was some covert reflection upon Manwë and Ulmo, but of the Gods some took his words in faith and would use his advice, but others distrusted; and in the midst of their debate Ulmo arose and went to the Outermost Seas that were set beyond the Outer Lands. He loved not high words nor concourse of folk, and in those deep waters moveless and empty he purposed to dwell, leaving the governance of the Great and lesser seas to Ossë and Ónen his vassals. Yet ever of his magic deep in his outermost sea-halls of Ulmonan he controlled the faint stirrings of the Shadowy Seas, and ruled the lakes and springs and rivers of the world.

Now this was the manner of the Earth in those days, nor has it since changed save by the labours of the Valar of old. Mightiest of regions are the Great Lands where Men do dwell and wander now, and the Lost Elves sing and dance upon the hills; but beyond their westernmost limits lie the Great Seas, and in that vast water of the West are many smaller lands and isles, ere the lonely seas are found whose waves whisper about the Magic Isles. Farther even than this, and few are the boats of mortal men that have dared so far, are set the Shadowy Seas whereon there float the Twilit Isles and the Tower of Pearl rises pale upon their most western cape; but as yet it was not built, and the Shadowy Seas stretched dark away till their uttermost shore in Eruman.

Now the Twilit Isles are reckoned the first of the Outer Lands, which are these and Eruman and Valinor. Eruman or Arvalin is to the southward, but the Shadowy Seas run even to the edges of Eldamar to the north; yet must ships sail farther to reach these silver strands, for beyond Eruman stand the Mountains of Valinor in a great ring curving westward, and the Shadowy Seas to north of Eruman bend a vast bay inward, so that waves beat even upon the feet of the great cliffs and the Mountains stand beside the sea. There is Taniquetil glorious to behold, loftiest of all mountains, clad in purest snow, and he looks from the bay's head southward across Eruman and northward across the Bay of Faëry; indeed all the Shadowy Seas, even the sails of ships upon the sunlit waters of the great ocean and the throngs about westward havens in the lands of Men could afterward be seen therefrom, albeit that distance is counted out in unimagined leagues. But as yet the Sun had not risen and the Mountains of Valinor had not been raised, and the vale of Valinor lay wide and cold. Beyond Valinor I have never seen or heard, save that of a surety there are the dark waters of the Outer Seas, that have no tides, and they are very cool and thin, that no boat can sail upon their bosom or fish swim within their depths, save the enchanted fish of Ulmo and his magic car.

Thither is he now gone, but the Gods hold council concerning the words of Melko. It was the rede of Aulë and of his wife Palúrien, for they were the most grieved by the mischief of Melko's turmoils and trusted his promises not at all, that the Gods should not separate as

he bid, lest he take it into his heart perchance to attack them singly
or do hurt to their possessions. "Is he not," said they, "more powerful
than any one of us save Manwë only? Rather let us build a dwelling
wherein we may abide in joy together, faring only at need to the
care and survey of our goods and fiefs. There even such as be of
other mind may dwell at times, and find rest and pleasance after
labours in the world." Now Aulë's mind and fingers itched already
to be making things, and he urged this matter the more for that;
and to most of the Gods it seemed a good counsel, and they fared
about the world seeking a place to dwell in. Those were the days of
Gloaming (Lomendánar), for light there was, silver and golden, but
it was not gathered together but flowed and quivered in uneven
streams about the airs, or at times fell gently to the earth in glittering
rain and ran like water on the ground; and at that time Varda in her
playing had set but a few stars within the sky.

In this dimness the Gods stalked North and South and could see
little; indeed in the deepest of these regions they found great cold
and solitude and the rule of Melko already fortified in strength; but
Melko and his servants were delving in the North, fashioning the
grim halls of Utumna, for he had no thought to dwell amongst the
others, howso he might feign peace and friendship for the time.

Now because of the darkness Aulë suaded Melko to build two
towers to the North and South, for he purposed to set upon them
mighty lamps one upon each. These did Aulë himself fashion of gold
and silver, and the pillars were raised by Melko and were very tall,
and shone like pale blue crystal; and when Aulë smote them with
his hand they rang like metal. They sprang up through the lower air
even to Ilwë and the stars, and Melko said they were of an imperishable substance of great strength that he had devised; and he lied,
for he knew that they were of ice. That one of the North he named
Ringil and of the South Helkar, and the lamps were made ready and
set upon them, being filled with gathered light, silver to the North
and golden to the South. This light had Manwë and Varda gathered
lavishly from the sky, that the Gods might the better explore the
regions of the world, and choose the fairest for their home.

Now in that flaming light did they fare East and West, and East
was a waste of tumbled lands and West great seas of darkness, for
indeed they were gathered now upon those Twilit Isles and stood
there gazing westward, when lo! the lamps to North and South
flickered and fell, and as they fell the waters rose about the isles.
Now these things they did not then understand, but it so happened
that the blaze of those lights had melted the treacherous ice of the

pillars of Melko, Ringil and Helkar, and great floods of water had poured from them into the Shadowy Seas. So great was their thaw that whereas those seas were at first of no great size but clear and warm, now were they black and wide and vapours lay upon them and deep shades, for the great cold rivers that poured into them. Thus were the mighty lamps unseated from on high and the clangour of their fall shook the stars, and some of their light was spilled again into the air, but much flowed upon the earth and made fires and deserts for its great volume ere it gathered into lakes and pools.

Then was the time of first night and it was very long; but the Valar were sorely wroth at the treachery of Melko and were like to be whelmed in the shadowy seas that now arose and sucked about their feet, covering many of the islands in their waves.

Then Ossë, for Ulmo was not there, gathered to him the Oarni, and putting forth their might they dragged that island whereon stood the Valar westward from the waters till they came to Eruman, whose high shores held the angry flood – and that was the first tide.

Then said Manwë: "Now will we make a dwelling speedily and a bulwark against evil." So they fared over Arvalin and saw a wide open space beyond, reaching for unknown leagues even to the Outer Seas. There, said Aulë, would be a place well suited to great building and to a fashioning of realms of delight; wherefore the Valar and all their folk first gathered the most mighty rocks and stones from Arvalin and reared therewith huge mountains between it and that plain which now they name Valinor, or the land of the Gods. Aulë indeed it was himself who laboured for seven ages at Manwë's bidding in the piling of Taniquetil, and the world rumbled in the gloom and Melko heard the noises of their labour. By reason of their great masonry is Erumáni now very broad and bare and of a marvellous level, for they removed all the stone and rock that was there; but the Mountains of Valinor are rugged and of impregnable height. Seeing at length that these towered mightily between Valinor and the world the Gods drew breath; but Aulë and Tulkas fared abroad with many of their folk and brought back all they might of marbles and good stones, of iron and gold and silver and bronze and all manner of substances. These they heaped amid the plain, and straightway Aulë began to labour mightily.

At last he says: "It is ill working in this gloom, and 'twas an evil deed of Melko's that brought to ruin those fair lamps." But Varda answering said: "Still is there much light remaining both in the airs and that which floweth spilled upon the earth", and she wished to gather new store and set a beacon on Taniquetil. But Manwë suffered not more radiance to be gleaned from heaven, for that the dark was already that of night, but at his asking Ulmo rose from his deeps and fared to the blazing lakes and the pools of brilliance. Therefrom he drew rivers of light into vast vessels, pouring back waters in their place, and with these he got him back to Valinor. There was all the light poured into two great cauldrons that Aulë fashioned in the gloom against his return, and those are called Kulullin and Silindrin.

Now in the midmost vale they digged two great pits, and those are leagues asunder yet nigh together beside the vastness of that plain. In the one did Ulmo set seven rocks of gold brought from the most silent deeps of the sea, and a fragment was cast thereafter of the lamp that had burned awhile upon Helkar in the South. Then was the pit covered with rich earths that Palúrien devised, and Vána came who loveth life and sunlight and at whose song the flowers arise and open, and the murmur of her maidens round her was like to the merry noise of folk that stir abroad for the first time on a bright morning. There sang she the song of spring upon the mound, and danced about it, and watered it with great streams of that golden light that Ulmo had brought from the spilled lakes – yet was Kulullin almost o'erflowing at the end.

But in the other pit they cast three huge pearls that Ossë found in the Great Sea, and a small star Varda cast after them, and they covered it with foams and white mists and thereafter sprinkled lightly earth upon it, but Lórien who loveth twilights and flittering shadows, and sweet scents borne upon evening winds, who is the lord of dreams and imaginings, sat nigh and whispered swift noise-less words, while his sprites played half-heard tunes beside him like music stealing out into the dark from distant dwellings; and the Gods poured upon that place rivers of the white radiance and silver light which Silindrin held even to the brim – and after their pouring was Silindrin yet well nigh full.

Then came Palúrien, even Kémi the Earth-lady, wife of Aulë, mother of the lord of forests, and she wove spells about those two places, deep enchantments of life and growth and putting forth of leaf, blossoming and yielding of fruit – but she mingled no word of fading in her song. There having sung she brooded for a great while, and the Valar sat in a circle about, and the plain of Valinor was dark. Then after a time there came at last a bright gleam of gold amid the gloom, and a cry of joy and praise was sent up by the Valar and all their companies. Behold from that place that had been watered from Kulullin rose a slender shoot, and from its bark pale gold effulgence poured; yet did that plant grow apace so that in seven hours there was a tree of mighty stature, and all the Valar and their folk might sit beneath its branches. Of a great shapeliness and goodly growth was that stock, and nought was there to break its smooth rind, which glowed faintly with a yellow light, for a vast height above the earth. Then did fair boughs thrust overhead in all directions, and golden buds swelled from all the twigs and lesser branches, and from these burst leaves of a rich green whose edges shone. Already was the light that that tree gave wide and fair, but as the Valar gazed it put forth blossom in exceeding great profusion, so that all its boughs were hidden by long swaying clusters of gold flowers like a myriad hanging lamps of flame, and light spilled from the tips of these and splashed upon the ground with a sweet noise.

Then did the Gods praise Vána and Palúrien and rejoice in the light, saying to them: "Lo, this is a very fair tree indeed, and must have a name unto itself," and Kémi said: "Let it be called Laurelin, for the brightness of its blossom and the music of its dew," but Vána would call it Lindeloksë, and both names remain.

Now was it twelve hours since Lindeloksë had first sprouted, and at that hour did a glint of silver pierce the yellow blaze, and behold the Valar saw a shoot arise in that place whereto the pools of Silindrin had been poured. It had a bark of tender white that gleamed like pearls and it grew even as swiftly as had Laurelin, and as it grew the glory of Laurelin abated and its blossom shone less, till that tree glowed only gently as in sleep: but, behold, the other waxed now to a stature even as lofty as Laurelin, and its stock was yet more shapely and more slender, and its rind like silk, but its boughs above were thicker and more tangled and its twigs denser, and they put forth masses of bluish green leaves like spearheads.

Then did the Valar stare in wonder, but Palúrien said: "Not yet has this tree ceased its growing", and behold as she spake it blossomed, and its blossoms did not hang in clusters but were like separate flowers growing each on fine stems that swung together, and were as silver and pearls and glittering stars and burnt with a white light; and it seemed as if the tree's heart throbbed, and its radiance wavered thereto waxing and waning. Light like liquid silver distilled from its bole and dripped to earth, and it shed a very great illumination about the plain, yet was that not as wide as the light of the tree of gold, and by reason also of its great leaves and of the throb of its inward life it cast a continual flutter of shadows among the pools of its brightness, very clear and black; whereat Lórien could not contain his joy, and even Mandos smiled. But Lórien said: "Lo! I will give this tree a name and call it Silpion", and that has ever been its name since. Then Palúrien arose and said to the Gods: "Gather ye now all the light that drips in liquid shape from this fair tree and store it in Silindrin, and let it fare thence but very sparingly. Behold, this tree, when the twelve hours of its fullest light are past, will wane again, and thereat will Laurelin blaze forth once more; but that it may not be exhausted water it ever gently from the cauldron of Kulullin at the hour when Silpion grows dim, but to Silpion do ye in the same manner, pouring back the gathered light from deep Silindrin at every waning of the tree of gold. Light is the sap of these trees and their sap is light!"

And in these words did she signify that albeit these trees must needs be watered with light to have sap and live, yet of their growth and being did they ever make light in great abundance still over and beyond that which their roots sucked in; but the Gods hearkened to her bidding, and Vána caused one of her own maidens, even Urwen, to care ever for this task of watering Laurelin, while Lórien bade Silmo, a youth he loved, to be ever mindful of the refreshing of Silpion. Wherefore is it said that at either watering of the trees there was a wondrous gloaming of gold and silver and mingled lights great beauty ere one tree quite faded or the other came to its full glory.

Now because of the bright trees had Aulë light in plenty for his works, and he set about many tasks, and Tulkas aided him much, and Palúrien mother of magic was at his side. First upon Taniquetil was a great abode raised up for Manwë and a watchtower set. Thence did he speed his darting hawks and receive them on his return, and thither fared often in later days Sorontur King of Eagles whom Manwë gave much might and wisdom.

That house was builded of marbles white and blue and stood amid the fields of snow, and its roofs were made of a web of that blue air called *ilwë* that is above the white and grey. This web did Aulë and his wife contrive, but Varda spangled it with stars, and Manwë dwelt thereunder; but in the plain in the full radiance of the trees was a cluster of dwellings built like a fair and smiling town, and that town was named Valmar. No metal and no stone, nor any wood of mighty trees was spared to their raising. Their roofs were of gold and their floors silver and their doors of polished bronze; they were lifted with spells and their stones were bound with magic. Separate from these and bordering upon the open vale was a great court, and this was Aulë's house, and it was filled with magic webs woven of the light of Laurelin and the sheen of Silpion and the glint of stars; but others there were made of threads of gold and silver and iron and bronze beaten to the thinness of a spider's filament, and all were woven with beauty to stories of the musics of the Ainur, picturing those things that were and shall be, or such as have only been in the glory of the mind of Ilúvatar.

In this court were some of all the trees that after grew upon the earth, and a pool of blue water lay among them. There fruits fell throughout the day, thudding richly to the earth upon the grass of its margin, and were gathered by Palúrien's maids for her feasting and her lord's.

Ossë too had a great house, and dwelt therein whenso a conclave of the Valar was held or did he grow weary of the noise of the waves upon his seas. Ónen and the Oarni brought thousands of pearls for its building, and its floors were of sea-water, and its tapestries like the glint of the silver skins of fishes, and it was roofed with foam. Ulmo dwelt not in Valmar and fared back after its building to the Outer Seas, and did he have need ever of sojourn in Valinor he would go as guest to the halls of Manwë; – but this was not often. Lórien too dwelt far away, and his hall was great and dimly lit and had wide gardens. The place of his dwelling he called Murmuran, which Aulë made of mists gathered beyond Arvalin upon the Shadowy Seas. 'Twas set in the South by the feet of the Mountains of Valinor upon the confines of the realm, but its gardens wandered marvellously about, winding nigh to the feet of Silpion whose shining lit them strangely. They were full of labyrinths and mazes, for Palúrien had given Lórien great wealth of yewtrees and cedars, and of pines that exuded drowsy odours in the dusk; and these hung over deep pools. Glowworms crept about their borders and Varda had set stars within their depths for the pleasure of Lórien, but his sprites sang wonderfully in these gardens and the scent of nightflowers and the songs of sleepy nightingales filled them with great loveliness. There too grew the poppies glowing redly in the dusk, and those the Gods called *fumellar* the flowers of sleep – and Lórien used them much in his enchantments. Amidmost of those pleasances was set within a ring of shadowy cypress towering high that deep vat Silindrin. There it lay in a bed of pearls, and its surface unbroken was shot with silver flickerings, and the shadows of the trees lay on it, and the Mountains of Valinor could see their faces mirrored there. Lórien gazing upon it saw many visions of mystery pass across its face, and that he suffered never to be stirred from its sleep save when Silmo came noiselessly with a silver urn to draw a draught of its shimmering cools, and fared softly thence to water the roots of Silpion ere the tree of gold grew hot.

Otherwise was the mind of Tulkas, and he dwelt amidmost of Valmar. Most youthful is he and strong of limb and lusty, and for that is he named Poldórëa who loveth games and twanging of bows and boxing, wrestling, running, and leaping, and songs that go with a swing and a toss of a well-filled cup. Nonetheless is he no wrangler or striker of blows unprovoked as is Makar, albeit there are none of Valar or Úvanimor (who are monsters, giants, and ogres) that do not fear the sinews of his arm and the buffet of his iron-clad fist, when he has cause for wrath. His was a house of mirth and revelry; and it sprang high into the air with many storeys, and had a tower of bronze and pillars of copper in a wide arcade. In its court men played and rivalled one another in doughty feats, and there at times would that fair maiden Nessa wife of Tulkas bear goblets of the goodliest wine and cooling drinks among the players. But most she loved to retire unto a place of fair lawns whose turf Oromë her brother had culled from the richest of all his forest glades, and Palúrien had planted it with spells that it was always green and smooth. There danced she among her maidens as long as Laurelin was in bloom, for is she not greater in the dance than Vána herself?

In Valmar too dwelt Noldorin known long ago as Salmar, playing now upon his harps and lyres, now sitting beneath Laurelin and raising sweet music with an instrument of the bow. There sang Amillo joyously to his playing, Amillo who is named Ómar, whose voice is the best of all voices, who knoweth all songs in all speeches; but whiles if he sang not to his brother's harp then would he be trilling in the gardens of Oromë when after a time Nielíqui, little maiden, danced about its woods.

Now Oromë had a vast domain and it was beloved by him, and no less by Palúrien his mother. Behold, the groves of trees they planted upon the plain of Valinor and even upon the foothills of the mountains have no compare on Earth. Beasts revelled there, deer among the trees, and herds of kine among its spaces and wide grass-lands; bison there were, and horses roaming unharnessed, but these strayed never into the gardens of the Gods, yet were they in peace and had no fear, for beasts of prey dwelt not among them, nor did Oromë fare to hunting in Valinor. Much indeed as he loves those realms yet is he very often in the world without; more often even than Ossë and as often as Palúrien, and then does he become the greatest of all huntsmen. But in Valmar his halls are wide and low, and skins and fells of great richness and price are strewn there without end upon the floor or hung upon the walls, and spears and bows and knives thereto. In the midst of each room and hall a living tree grows and holds up the roof, and its bole is hung with trophies and with antlers. Here is all Oromë's folk in green and brown and there is a noise of boisterous mirth, and the lord of forests makes lusty cheer; but Vána his wife so often as she may steals thence. Far away from the echoing courts of that house lie her gardens, fenced stoutly from the wilder lands with whitethorn of great size that blossoms like everlasting snow. Its innermost solitude is walled with roses, and this is the place best beloved of that fair lady of the Spring. Amidmost of this place of odorous air did Aulë set long ago that cauldron, gold Kulullin, filled ever with the radiance of Laurelin like shining water, and thereof he contrived a fountain so that all the garden was full of the health and happiness of its pure light. Birds sang there all the year with the full throat of spring, and flowers grew in a riot of blossom and of glorious life. Yet was none ever of that splendour spilled from the vat of gold save when Vána's maidens led by Urwen left that garden at the waxing of Silpion to water the roots of the tree of flame; but by the fountain it was always light with the amber light of day, as bees made busy about the roses, and there trod Vána lissomly while larks sang above her golden head.

So fair were these abodes and so great the brilliance of the trees of Valinor that Vefántur and Fui his wife of tears might not endure to stay there long, but fared away far to the northward of those regions, where beneath the roots of the most cold and northerly of the Mountains of Valinor, that rise here again almost to their height nigh Arvalin, they begged Aulë to delve them a hall. Wherefore, that all the Gods might be housed to their liking, he did so, and they and all their shadowy folk aided him. Very vast were those caverns that they made stretching even down under the Shadowy Seas, and they are full of gloom and filled with echoes, and all that deep abode is known to Gods and Elves as Mandos. There in a sable hall sat Vefántur, and he called that hall with his own name Vê. It was lit only with a single vessel placed in the centre, wherein there lay some gleaming drops of the pale dew of Silpion: it was draped with dark vapours and its floors and columns were of jet. Thither in after days fared the Elves of all the clans who were by illhap slain with weapons or did die of grief for those that were slain – and only so might the Eldar die, and then it was only for a while. There Mandos spake their doom, and there they waited in the darkness, dreaming of their past deeds, until such time as he appointed when they might again be born into their children, and go forth to laugh and sing again. To Vê Fui came not much, for she laboured rather at the distilling of salt humours whereof are tears, and black clouds she wove and floated up that they were caught in the winds and went about the world, and their lightless webs settled ever and anon upon those that dwelt therein. Now these tissues were despairs and hopeless mourning, sorrows and blind grief. The hall that she loved best was one yet wider and more dark than Vê, and she too named it with her own name, calling it Fui. Therein before her black chair burnt a brazier with a single flickering coal, and the roof was of bats' wings, and the pillars that upheld it and the walls about were made of basalt. Thither came the sons of Men to hear their doom, and thither are they brought by all the multitude of ills that Melko's evil music set within the world. Slaughters and fires, hungers and mishaps, diseases and blows dealt in the dark, cruelty and bitter cold and anguish and their own folly bring them here; and Fui reads their hearts. Some then she keeps in Mandos beneath the mountains and some she drives forth beyond the hills and Melko seizes them and bears them to Angamandi, or the Hells of Iron, where they have evil days. Some too, and these are the many, she sends aboard the black ship Mornië, who lieth ever and anon in a dark harbour of the North awaiting those times when the sad pomp winds to the beach down slow rugged paths from Mandos.

Then, when she is laden, of her own accord she spreads her sable sails and before a slow wind coasts down those shores. Then do all aboard as they come South cast looks of utter longing and regret to that low place amid the hills where Valinor may just be glimpsed upon the far off plain; and that opening is nigh Taniquetil where is the strand of Eldamar. No more do they ever see of that bright place, but borne away dwell after on the wide plains of Arvalin. There do they wander in the dusk, camping as they may, yet are they not utterly without song, and they can see the stars, and wait in patience till the Great End come.

Few are they and happy indeed for whom at a season doth Nornorë the herald of the Gods set out. Then ride they with him in chariots or upon good horses down into the vale of Valinor and feast in the halls of Valmar, dwelling in the houses of the Gods until the Great End come. Far away are they from the black mountains of the North or the misty plains of Arvalin, and music and fair light is theirs, and joy.

And lo! Now have I recounted the manner of the dwellings of all the great Gods which Aulë of his craftsmanship raised in Valinor, but Makar and his fierce sister Meássë built them a dwelling of themselves, aided only by their own folk, and a grim hall it was.

Upon the confines of the Outer Lands did it stand, nor was it very far from Mandos. Of iron was it made, and unadorned. There fought the vassals of Makar clad in armour, and a clash there was and a shouting and a braying of trumps, but Meássë fared among the warriors and egged them to more blows, or revived the fainting with strong wine that they might battle still; and her arms were reddened to the elbow dabbling in that welter. None of the Gods fared ever there, save Tulkas, and did they seek to visit Mandos they went thither by circuitous paths to avoid passing nigh to that clamorous hall; but Tulkas would at times wrestle there with Makar or deal sledge-blows among the fighters, and this he did that he might not grow soft in his fair living, for he loved not that company nor in sooth did they love him and his great unangered strength. Now the battle of the courts of Makar was waged unceasingly save when men gathered in the halls for feasting, or at those times when Makar and Meássë were far abroad hunting together in the black mountains wolves and bears. But that house was full of weapons of battle in great array, and shields of great size and brightness of polish were on the walls. It was lit with torches, and fierce songs of victory, of sack and harrying, were there sung, and the torches' red light was reflected in the blades of naked swords. There sit often Makar and his sister listening to the songs, and Makar has a huge bill across his knees and Meássë holds a spear. But in those days ere the closing of Valinor did these twain fare mostly about the Earth and were often far from the land, for they loved the unbridled turmoils which Melko roused throughout the world.

Therefore is Valinor now built, and there is great peace there, and the Gods in joy, for those quarrelsome spirits dwell not much among them, and Melko comes not nigh.'

Then said a child among the company, a great drinker-in of both tales and poesies: 'And would that he had never come there since, and would that I might have seen that land still gleaming new as Aulë left it.' Now she had heard Rúmil tell his tale before and was much in thought of it, but to the most of the company it was new, even as it was to Eriol, and they sat amazed. Then said Eriol: 'Very mighty and glorious are the Valar, and I would fain hear yet more of those oldest days, did I not see the glimmer of the Candles of Sleep that fare now hither'; but another child spoke from a cushion nigh Lindo's chair and said: 'Nay, 'tis in the halls of Makar I would fain be, and get perchance a sword or knife to wear; yet in Valmar methinks 'twould be good to be a guest of Oromë', and Lindo laughing said: ''Twould be good indeed,' and thereat he arose, and the tale-telling was over for that night.

NOTES

Changes made to names in
*The Coming of the Valar and the Building of Valinor*

*Ónen* ⟨ *Ówen* (at the first occurrence only; subsequently *Ónen* is the
name as first written).

*Eruman* and *Arvalin* The names of this region were originally written
*Habbanan* and *Harmalin*, but were emended throughout the tale
(except in two cases where *Habbanan* was overlooked) to *Eruman*
(once *Erumáni*, p. 70) and *Arvalin*. (In the last three occurrences
*Habbanan* ⟩ *Arvalin*, whereas in the earlier ones *Habbanan* ⟩ *Eruman*;
but the difference is presumably without significance, since the names
*Habbanan* / *Harmalin* and later *Eruman* / *Arvalin* were interchange-
able.) In *The Cottage of Lost Play* the changes were *Harwalin* ⟩
*Harmalin* ⟩ *Arvalin* (p. 22).

*Lomendánar* ⟨ *Lome Danar*.

*Silindrin* ⟨ *Telimpë* (*Silindrin*) (at the first occurrence only; subsequently
*Silindrin* is the name as first written).

*Lindeloksë* ⟨ *Lindelótë* (cf. p. 22).

Commentary on
*The Coming of the Valar and the Building of Valinor*

The abundant instruction provided by Rúmil on this occasion is best
discussed in sections, and I begin with:

(i) The Coming of the Valar and their encounter with Melko
(pp. 65–7)

The description of the entry of the Valar into the world was not retained,
though the account of them in this passage is the ultimate origin of that
in the *Valaquenta* (*The Silmarillion* pp. 25–9): not, however, by continuous
manuscript progression. The passage is of much interest, for here appear
all at once many figures of the mythology who were to endure, beside
others who were not. It is remarkable how many of the names of the
Valar in the earliest writings were never afterwards displaced or reshaped:
*Yavanna*, *Tulkas*, *Lórien*, *Nienna*, *Oromë*, *Aldaron*, *Vána*, *Nessa*, first
appearing in this tale, and *Manwë*, *Súlimo*, *Varda*, *Ulmo*, *Aulë*, *Mandos*,
*Ossë*, *Salmar*, who have appeared previously. Some were retained in a
modified form: *Melkor* for *Melko*, *Uinen* (which appears already later in
the *Lost Tales*) for *Ónen*, *Fëanturi* for *Fánturi*; while yet others, as Yavanna
*Palúrien* and Tulkas *Poldórëa*, survived long in the 'Silmarillion' tradition
before being displaced by *Kementári* (but cf. *Kémi* 'Earth-lady' in this

tale) and *Astaldo*. But some of these early Valar had disappeared by the next stage or phase after the *Lost Tales*: Ómar-Amillo, and the barbaric war-gods Makar and Meássë.

Here appear also certain relations that survived to the latest form. Thus Lórien and Mandos were from the beginning 'brethren', each with his special association, of 'dreams' and 'death'; and Nienna stood from the beginning in a close relationship with them, here as 'the spouse of Mandos', though afterwards as the sister of the Fëanturi. The original conception of Nienna was indeed darker and more fearful, a death-goddess in close association with Mandos, than it afterwards became. Ossë's uncertain relations with Ulmo are seen to go back to the beginnings; but Ulmo's haughtiness and aloofness subsequently disappeared, at least as a feature of his divine 'character' explicitly described. Vána was already the spouse of Oromë, but Oromë was the son of Aulë and (Yavanna) Palúrien; in the later evolution of the myths Vána sank down in relation to Nienna, whereas Oromë rose, becoming finally one of the great Valar, the *Aratar*.

Particularly interesting is the passage concerning the host of lesser spirits who accompanied Aulë and Palúrien, from which one sees how old is the conception of the Eldar as quite dissimilar in essential nature from 'brownies, fays, pixies, leprawns', since the Eldar are 'of the world' and bound to it, whereas those others are beings from before the world's making. In the later work there is no trace of any such explanation of the 'pixie' element in the world's population: the Maiar are little referred to, and certainly not said to include such beings as 'sing amid the grass at morning and chant among the standing corn at eve'.*

Salmar, companion of Ulmo, who has appeared in *The Music of the Ainur* (p. 58), is now identified with Noldorin, who was mentioned by Vairë in *The Cottage of Lost Play* (p. 16); such of his story as can be discerned will appear later. Subsequent writings say nothing of him save that he came with Ulmo and made his horns (*The Silmarillion* p. 40).

In the later development of this narrative there is no mention of Tulkas (or Mandos!) going off to round up Melkor at the very outset of the history of the Valar in Arda. In *The Silmarillion* we learn rather of the great war between the Valar and Melkor 'before Arda was full-shaped', and how it was the coming of Tulkas from 'the far heaven' that routed him, so that he fled from Arda and 'brooded in the outer darkness'.

---

* Cf. *The Silmarillion* p. 30: 'With the Valar came other spirits whose being also began before the world, of the same order as the Valar but of less degree. These are the Maiar, the people of the Valar, and their servants and helpers. Their number is not known to the Elves, and few have names in any of the tongues of the Children of Ilúvatar.' An earlier version of this passage reads: 'Many lesser spirits they [the Valar] brought in their train, both great and small, and some of these Men have confused with the Eldar or Elves; but wrongly, for they were before the world, but Elves and Men awoke first in the world after the coming of the Valar.'

(ii) The earliest conception of the Western Lands, and the Oceans

In *The Cottage of Lost Play* the expression 'Outer Lands' was used of the lands to the east of the Great Sea, later Middle-earth; this was then changed to 'Great Lands' (p. 21). The 'Outer Lands' are now defined as

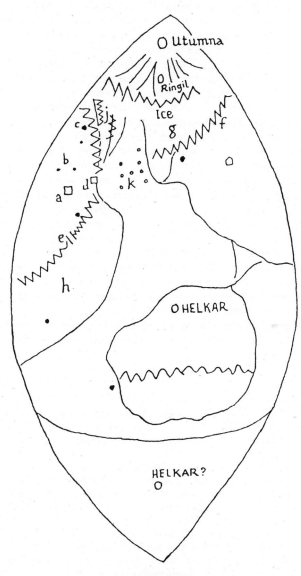

The earliest map

the Twilit Isles, Eruman (or Arvalin), and Valinor (p. 68). A curious
usage, which often appears in the *Lost Tales*, is the equation of 'the world'
with the Great Lands, or with the whole surface of the earth east of the
Outer Lands; so the mountains 'towered mightily between Valinor and
the world' (p. 70), and King Inwë heard 'the lament of the world' (p. 16).
It is convenient to reproduce here a map (p. 81), which actually appears
in the text of a later tale (that of *The Theft of Melko and the Darkening
of Valinor*). This map, drawn on a manuscript page with the text written
round it, is no more than a quick scribble, in soft pencil, now rubbed and
faded, and in many features difficult or impossible to interpret. The redrawing is as accurate as I can make it, the only feature lost being some
indecipherable letters (beginning with M) preceding the word *Ice*. I
have added the letters *a*, *b*, *c*, etc. to make the discussion easier to follow.

Utumna (later Utumno) is placed in the extreme North, north of the
lamp-pillar Ringil; the position of the southern pillar seems from this
map to have been still undecided. The square marked *a* is obviously
Valmar, and I take the two dots marked *b* to be the Two Trees, which are
stated later to have been to the north of the city of the Gods. The dot
marked *c* is fairly clearly the domain of Mandos (cf. p. 76, where it is
said that Vefántur Mandos and Fui Nienna begged Aulë to delve them a
hall 'beneath the roots of the most cold and northerly of the Mountains
of Valinor');* the dot to the south of this can hardly represent the hall
of Makar and Meássë, since it is said (pp. 77–8) that though it was not very
far from Mandos it stood 'upon the confines of the Outer Lands'.

The area which I have marked *h* is Eruman / Arvalin (which ultimately
came to be named Avathar), earlier *Habbanan* / *Harmalin* (*Harwalin*),
which are simple alternatives (see p. 79).

Later, in a map of the world made in the 1930s, the western shore of
the Great Sea bends in a gentle and regular curve westward from north
to south, while the Mountains of Valinor bend in virtually the reverse of
the same curve eastward, )(; where the two curves come together at their
midpoints are Túna, and Taniquetil. Two areas of land in the shape of
elongated Vs thus extend northward and southward from the midpoint,
between the Mountains and the Sea, which draw steadily away from each

---

* In *The Silmarillion* (p. 28) the halls of Mandos stood 'westward in
Valinor'. The final text of the *Valaquenta* actually has 'northward', but I
changed this to 'westward' in the published work (and similarly 'north' to
'west' on p. 52) on the basis of the statement in the same passage that Nienna's
halls are 'west of West, upon the borders of the world', but are near to
those of Mandos. In other passages it is clear that Mandos' halls were
conceived as standing on the shores of the Outer Sea; cf. *The Silmarillion*
p. 186: 'For the spirit of Beren at her bidding tarried in the halls of Mandos,
until Lúthien came to say her last farewell upon the dim shores of the
Outer Sea, whence Men that die set out never to return'. The conceptions
of 'northward in Valinor' and 'on the shores of the Outer Sea' are not however contradictory, and I regret this piece of unwarranted editorial meddling.

other; and these are named Eruman (to the northward) and Arvalin (to the southward).

In the little primitive map the line of the mountains is already thus, and it is described in the text as 'a great ring curving westward' (the curve is westward if the extremities are considered rather than the central portion) But the curve of the coast is different. Unhappily the little map is here very obscure, for there are several lines (marked *j*) extending northwards from Kôr (marked *d*), and it is impossible to make out whether marks on them are directions for erasure or whether they represent parallel mountain-chains. But I think that in fact these lines merely represent variant ideas for the curve of the Mountains of Valinor in the north; and I have little doubt that at this time my father had no conception of a region of 'waste' north of Kôr and east of the mountains. This interpretation of the map agrees well with what is said in the tale (p. 68): 'the Shadowy Seas to north of Eruman bend a vast bay inwards, so that waves beat even upon the feet of the great cliffs, and the Mountains stand beside the sea', and 'Taniquetil looks from the bay's head southward across Eruman and northward across the Bay of Faëry'. On this view the name *Eruman* (later *Araman*), at first an alternative to *Arvalin*, was taken over for the northern waste when the plan of the coastal regions became more symmetrical.

It is said in the tale (p. 68) that 'in that vast water of the West are many smaller lands and isles, ere the lonely seas are found whose waves whisper about the Magic Isles'. The little circles on the map (marked *k*) are evidently a schematic representation of these archipelagoes (of the Magic Isles more will be told later). The Shadowy Seas, as will emerge more clearly later, were a region of the Great Sea west of Tol Eressëa. The other letters on the map refer to features that have not yet entered the narrative.

In this tale we meet the important cosmological idea of the Three Airs, Vaitya, Ilwë, and Vilna, and of the Outer Ocean, tideless, cold, and 'thin'. It has been said in *The Music of the Ainur* (p. 58) that Ulmo dwells in the Outer Ocean and that he gave to Ossë and Onen 'control of the waves and lesser seas'; he is there called 'the ancient one of Vai' (emended from Ulmonan). It is now seen that *Ulmonan* is the name of his halls in the Outer Ocean, and also that the 'lesser seas' controlled by Ossë and Onen include the Great Sea (p. 68).

There exists a very early and very remarkable drawing, in which the world is seen in section, and is presented as a huge 'Viking' ship, with mast arising from the highest point of the Great Lands, single sail on which are the Sun and Moon, sailropes fastened to Taniquetil and to a great mountain in the extreme East, and curved prow (the black marks on the sail are an ink-blot). This drawing was done fairly rapidly in soft pencil on a small sheet; and it is closely associated with the cosmology of the *Lost Tales*.

I give here a list of the names and words written on the drawing with,

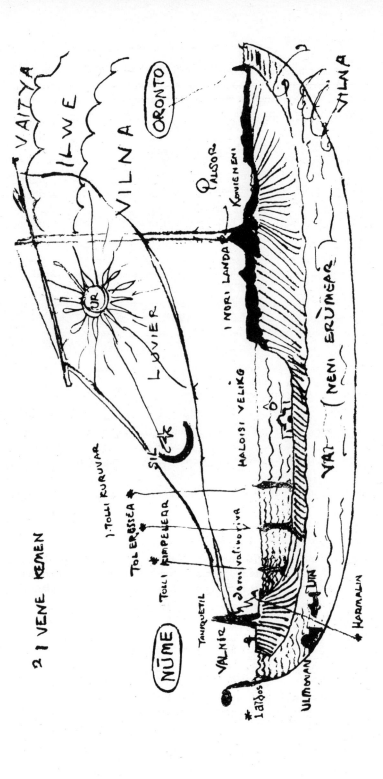

2 I VENE KEMEN

VAITYA

ILWE

VILNA

ORONTO

VILNA

PALSOR

KOVIENEN

I NÓRI LANDA

UR

LOVIER

SIL

HALOISI VELIKO

VAI · (NENI ERÚMEAR)

I·TOLLI KURUVAR

TOL ERESSËA

I·TOLLI RIMPELEAR

DOROI VALINÓRIVA

TANIQUETIL

NÚME

VALMIR

UIN

HARMALIN

ULMONAN

I·ALÐOS

so far as possible, their meanings (but without any etymological detail, for which see the Appendix on Names, where names and words occurring only on this drawing are given separate entries).

*I Vene Kemen*   This is clearly the title of the drawing; it might mean 'The Shape of the Earth' or 'The Vessel of the Earth' (see the Appendix on Names, entry *Glorvent*).

*Nūme* 'West'.

*Valinor*; *Taniquetil*   (The vast height of Taniquetil, even granting the formalisation of this drawing, is noteworthy: it is described in the tale as being so high that 'the throngs about westward havens in the lands of Men could be seen therefrom' (p. 68). Its fantastic height is conveyed in my father's painting, dating from 1927–8 (*Pictures by J. R. R. Tolkien*, no. 31).)

*Harmalin*   Earlier name of *Arvalin* (see p. 79).

*i aldas*   'The Trees' (standing to the west of Taniquetil).

*Toros valinoriva*   *Toros* is obscure, but in any case the first letter of the first word, if it is a T, is a very uncharacteristic one. The reference seems to be to the Mountains of Valinor.

*Tolli Kimpelear*   These must be the Twilit Isles, but I have found no other occurrence of *Kimpelear* or anything similar.

*Tol Eressëa*   'The Lonely Isle'.

*I Tolli Kuruvar*   'The Magic Isles'.

*Haloisi Velike*   'The Great Sea'.

*Ō*   'The Sea'. (What is the structure at the sea-bottom shown below the name *Ō*? It must surely be the dwelling of Ossë beneath the Great Sea that is referred to in the next tale (p. 106).)

*I Nori Landar*   Probably means 'The Great Lands'.

*Koivienéni*   The precursor of *Cuiviénen*, the Waters of Awakening.

*Palisor*   The land where the Elves awoke.

*Sil* 'Moon'.

*Ūr* 'Sun'.

*Luvier* 'Clouds'.

*Oronto* 'East'.

*Vaitya*, *Ilwë*, and *Vilna* appear in the three layers described in the tale (p. 65), and *Vilna* reappears in the bottom right-hand corner of the drawing. There is nothing said in the *Lost Tales* to explain this last feature, nor is it at all evident what is represented by the curled lines in the same place (see p. 86).

*Ulmonan*   The halls of Ulmo.

*Uin*   The Great Whale, who appears later in the *Tales*.

*Vai*   The Outer Ocean.

*Neni Erùmear*   'Outermost Waters' = *Vai*.

It is seen from the drawing that the world floats in and upon Vai. This is indeed how Ulmo himself describes it to the Valar in a later tale (p. 214):

Lo, there is but one Ocean, and that is Vai, for those that Ossë esteemeth
as oceans are but seas, waters that lie in the hollows of the rock . . . In
this vast water floateth the wide Earth upheld by the word of Ilúvatar . . .

In the same passage Ulmo speaks of the islands in the seas, and says that
('save some few that swim still unfettered') they 'stand now like pinnacles
from their weedy depths', as is also well seen in the drawing.

It might seem a plausible idea that there was some connection (physical
as well as etymological) between *Vai* and *Vaitya*, the outermost of the
Three Airs, 'wrapped dark and sluggish about the world and without it'
(at a later point in the *Tales*, p. 181, there is a reference to 'the dark
and tenuous realm of Vaitya that is outside all'). In the next 'phase' of
the mythical cosmology (dating from the 1930s, and very clearly and fully
documented and illustrated in a work called *Ambarkanta*, The Shape of
the World) the whole world is contained within *Vaiya*, a word meaning
'fold, envelope'; Vaiya 'is more like to sea below the Earth and more
like to air above the Earth' (which chimes with the description of the
waters of Vai (p. 68) as very 'thin', so that no boat can sail on them nor
fish swim in them, save the enchanted fish of Ulmo and his car); and in
Vaiya below the Earth dwells Ulmo. Thus Vaiya is partly a development
of Vaitya and partly of Vai.

Now since in the earliest word-list of the Qenya tongue (see the
Appendix on Names) both *Vaitya* ('the outermost air beyond the world')
and *Vai* ('the outer ocean') are derived from a root *vaya-* 'enfold', and
since Vaitya in the present tale is said to be 'wrapped about the world
and without it', one might think that Vaitya-Vai already in the early
cosmology was a continuous enfolding substance, and that the later
cosmology, in this point, only makes explicit what was present but un-
expressed in the *Lost Tales*. But there is certainly no actual suggestion of
this idea in any early writing; and when we look again at the drawing it
seems untenable. For Vai is obviously *not* continuous with Vaitya; and
if the appearance of Vilna in the bottom of the drawing is taken to mean
that the Earth, *and* the ocean Vai in and on which it floats, were contained
within the Three Airs, of which we see the reappearance of the innermost
(Vilna) below the earth and Vai, then the suggestion that Vaitya–Vai were
continuous is still more emphatically confounded.

There remains the baffling question of the representation of the world
as a ship. In only one place is there a suggestion that my father conceived
the world in such a way: the passage that I have cited above, in which
Ulmo addresses the Valar on the subject of Vai, concludes:

O Valar, ye know not all wonders, and many secret things are there
*beneath the Earth's dark keel*, even where I have my mighty halls of
Ulmonan, that ye have never dreamed on.

But in the drawing Ulmonan is not beneath the ship's keel, it is within the ship's hull; and I am inclined to think that Ulmo's words 'beneath the Earth's dark keel' refer to the shape of the Earth itself, which is certainly ship-like. Moreover, close examination of the original drawing strongly suggests to me that the mast and sail, and still more clearly the curved prow, *were added afterwards*. Can it be that the shape of the Earth and of Vai as he had drawn them – with the appearance of a ship's hull – prompted my father to add mast, sail, and prow as a *jeu d'esprit*, without deeper significance? That seems uncharacteristic and unlikely, but I have no other explanation to offer.*

### (iii) The Lamps (pp. 69–70)

In this part of the narrative the tale differs remarkably from the later versions. Here there is no mention of the dwelling of the Valar on the Isle of Almaren after the making of the Lamps (*The Silmarillion* p. 35), nor of course of the return of Melko from 'outside' – because here Melko not only did not leave the world after entering it, but actually himself made the pillars of the Lamps. In this story, though Melko was distrusted by some, his guileful co-operation (even to the extent of contributing names for the pillars) was accepted, whereas in the later story his hostility and malice were known and manifest to the Valar, even though they did not know of his return to Arda and the building of Utumno until too late. In the present tale there is a trickiness, a low cunning, in Melko's behaviour that could not survive (yet the story of his deceitful making of the pillars out of ice survived into the versions of the 1930s).

Later, it was the Lamps themselves that were named (ultimately, after intervening forms had been devised and discarded, *Illuin* the northern Lamp and *Ormal* the southern). In *The Silmarillion* Ringil (containing *ring* 'cold') survived only as the name of Fingolfin's sword, but Helcar is that of the Inland Sea which 'stood where aforetime the roots of the mountain of Illuin had been' (p. 49). In the present tale Helkar was the name of the southern, not the northern, pillar. Now *helkar* meant 'utter cold' (see the Appendix on Names), which shows that Helkar was originally in the extreme south (as it is in one of the two positions given for it on the little map, p. 81), just as Ringil was in the extreme north. In the tale there is no mention of the formation of Inland Seas at the fall of the Lamps; this idea appeared later, but it seems virtually certain that it arose from the story of the melting pillars of ice.

There is no later reference to the building of the Mountains of Valinor from great rocks gathered in Eruman / Arvalin, so that the region became flat and stoneless.

* If this is so, and if *I Vene Kemen* means 'The Earth-Ship', then this title must have been added to the drawing at the same time as the mast, sail, and prow. – In the little notebook referred to on p. 23 there is an isolated note: 'Map of the Ship of the World.'

### (iv) The Two Trees (pp. 71–3)

This earliest account of the uprising of the Two Trees illuminates some elements of later versions more concentrated in expression. The enduring feature that the ground beneath Silpion (Telperion) was 'dappled with the shadows of his fluttering leaves' (*The Silmarillion* p. 38) is seen to have had its origin in the 'throbbing of the tree's heart'. The conception of light as a liquid substance that 'splashed upon the ground', that ran in rivers and was poured in cauldrons, though not lost in the published work (pp. 38–9), is here more strongly and physically expressed. Some features were never changed, as the clustered flowers of Laurelin and the shining edges of its leaves.

On the other hand there are notable differences between this and the later accounts: above all perhaps that Laurelin was in origin the Eldar Tree. The Two Trees had here periods of twelve hours, not as later seven;* and the preparations of the Valar for the birth of the Trees, with all their detail of physical 'magic', were afterwards abandoned. The two great 'cauldrons' Kulullin and Silindrin survived in the 'great vats like shining lakes' in which Varda hoarded 'the dews of Telperion and the rain that fell from Laurelin' (*ibid.* p. 39), though the names disappeared, as did the need to 'water' the Trees with the light gathered in the vats or cauldrons – or at any rate it is not mentioned later. Urwen ('Sun-maiden') was the forebear of Arien, Maia of the Sun; and Tilion, steersman of the Moon in *The Silmarillion*, who 'lay in dreams by the pools of Estë [Lórien's wife], in Telperion's flickering beams', perhaps owes something to the figure of Silmo, whom Lórien loved.

As I noted earlier, 'in the later evolution of the myths Vána sank down in relation to Nienna', and here it is Vána and (Yavanna) Palúrien who are the midwives of the birth of the Trees, not as afterwards Yavanna and Nienna.

As regards the names of the Trees, *Silpion* was for long the name of the White Tree; *Telperion* did not appear till long after, and even then *Silpion* was retained and is mentioned in *The Silmarillion* (p. 38) as one of its names. *Laurelin* goes back to the beginning and was never changed, but its other name in the *Lost Tales*, *Lindelokse* and other similar forms, was not retained.

### (v) The Dwellings of the Valar (pp. 73 ff.)

This account of the mansions of the Valar was very largely lost in the subsequent versions. In the published work nothing is told of Manwë's dwelling, save the bare fact that his halls were 'above the everlasting snow, upon Oiolossë, the uttermost tower of Taniquetil' (p. 26). Here

---

* Palúrien's words (p. 73) 'This tree, *when the twelve hours of its fullest light are past*, will wane again' seem to imply a longer space than twelve hours; but probably the period of waning was not allowed for. In an annotated list of names to the tale of *The Fall of Gondolin* it is said that Silpion lit all Valinor with silver light 'for half the twenty-four hours'.

now appears Sorontur King of Eagles, a visitor to Manwë's halls (cf. *The Silmarillion* p. 110: 'For Manwë to whom all birds are dear, and to whom they bring news upon Taniquetil from Middle-earth, had sent forth the race of Eagles'); he had in fact appeared already in the tale of *The Fall of Gondolin*, as 'Thorndor [the Gnomish name] King of Eagles whom the Eldar name Ramandur', Ramandur being subsequently emended to Sorontur.

Of Valmar and the dwellings of the Valar in the city scarcely anything survived in later writing, and there remain only phrases here and there (the 'golden streets' and 'silver domes' of Valmar, 'Valmar of many bells') to suggest the solidity of the original description, where Tulkas' house of many storeys had a tower of bronze and Oromë's halls were upheld by living trees with trophies and antlers hung upon their trunks. This is not to say that all such imagining was definitively abandoned: as I have said in the Foreword, the *Lost Tales* were followed by a version so compressed as to be no more than a résumé (as was its purpose), and the later development of the mythology proceeded from that – a process of re-expansion. Many things never referred to again after the *Lost Tales* may have continued to exist in a state of suspension, as it were. Valmar certainly remained a city, with gates, streets, and dwellings. But in the context of the later work one could hardly conceive of the tempestuous Ossë being possessed of a house in Valmar, even if its floor were of seawater and its roof of foam; and of course the hall of Makar and Meássë (where the life described owes something to the myths of the Unending Battle in ancient Scandinavia) disappeared with the disappearance of those divinities – a 'Melko-faction' in Valinor that was bound to prove an embarrassment.

Several features of the original descriptions endured: the rarity of Ulmo's visits to Valmar (cf. *The Silmarillion* p. 40), the frequency with which Palúrien and Oromë visit 'the world without' (*ibid.* pp. 29, 41, 47), the association of the gardens of Lórien with Silpion and of the gardens of Vána with Laurelin (*ibid.* p. 99); and much that is said here of the divine 'characters' can be seen to have remained, even if differently expressed. Here also appears Nessa, already as the wife of Tulkas and the sister of Oromë, excelling in the dance; and Ómar-Amillo is now named the brother of Noldorin-Salmar. It appears elsewhere (see p. 93) that Nielíqui was the daughter of Oromë and Vána.

(vi) The Gods of Death and the Fates of Elves and Men
(pp. 76–7)

This section of the tale contains its most surprising and difficult elements. Mandos and his wife Nienna appear in the account of the coming of the Valar into the world at the beginning of the tale (p. 66), where they are named 'Fantur of Death, Vefántur Mandos' and 'Fui Nienna', 'mistress of death'. In the present passage it is said that Vefántur named his dwelling Vê by his own name, whereas afterwards (*The Silmarillion* p. 28) he was called by the name of his dwelling; but in the early writing there is a distinction between the region (Mandos) and the halls (Vê and Fui) within the region. There is here no trace of Mandos as the 'Doomsman of the Valar', who 'pronounces his dooms and his judgements only at the bidding of Manwë', one of the most notable aspects of the later conception of this Vala; nor, since Nienna is the wife of Mandos, has Vairë the Weaver, his wife in the later story, appeared, with her tapestries that portray 'all things that have ever been in Time' and clothe the halls of Mandos 'that ever widen as the ages pass' – in the *Lost Tales* the name Vairë is given to an Elf of Tol Eressëa. Tapestries 'picturing those things that were and shall be' are found here in the halls of Aulë (p. 74).

Most important in the passage concerning Mandos is the clear statement about the fate of Elves who die: that they wait in the halls of Mandos until Vefántur decrees their release, to be reborn in their own children. This latter idea has already appeared in the tale of *The Music of the Ainur* (p. 59), and it remained my father's unchanged conception of Elvish 'immortality' for many years; indeed the idea that the Elves might die only from the wounds of weapons or from grief was never changed – it also has appeared in *The Music of the Ainur* (*ibid.*): 'the Eldar dwell till the Great End unless they be slain or waste in grief', a passage that survived with little alteration in *The Silmarillion* (p. 42).

With the account of Fui Nienna, however, we come upon ideas in deep contradiction to the central thought of the later mythology (and in this passage, also, there is a strain of another kind of mythic conception, in the 'conceits' of 'the distilling of salt humours whereof are tears', and the black clouds woven by Nienna which settle on the world as 'despairs and hopeless mourning, sorrows and blind grief'). Here we learn that Nienna is the judge of Men in her halls named *Fui* after her own name; and some she keeps in the region of Mandos (where is her hall), while the greater number board the black ship Mornië – which does no more than ferry these dead down the coast to Arvalin, where they wander in the dusk until the end of the world. But yet others are driven forth to be seized by Melko and taken to endure 'evil days' in Angamandi (in what sense are they dead, or mortal?); and (most extraordinary of all) there are a very few who go to dwell among the Gods in Valinor. We are far away here from the Gift of Ilúvatar, whereby Men are not bound to the world, but leave it, none know where;* and this is the true meaning of Death (for

---

* Cf. *The Silmarillion* p. 104: 'Some say that they [Men] too go to the halls of Mandos; but their place of waiting there is not that of the Elves, and Mandos under Ilúvatar alone save Manwë knows whither they go after the time of recollection in those silent halls beside the Outer Sea.' Also *ibid.* p. 186: 'For the spirit of Beren at her bidding tarried in the halls of Mandos, unwilling to leave the world, until Lúthien came to say her last farewell upon the dim shores of the Outer Sea, whence Men that die set out never to return.'

the death of the Elves is a 'seeming death', *The Silmarillion* p. 42): the final and inescapable exit.

But a little illumination, if of a very misty kind, can be shed on the idea of Men, after death, wandering in the dusk of Arvalin, where they 'camp as they may' and 'wait in patience till the Great End'. I must refer here to the details of the changed names of this region, which have been given on p. 79. It is clear from the early word-lists or dictionaries of the two languages (for which see the Appendix on Names) that the meaning of *Harwalin* and *Arvalin* (and probably *Habbanan* also) was 'nigh Valinor' or 'nigh the Valar'. From the Gnomish dictionary it emerges that the meaning of *Eruman* was 'beyond the abode of the Mánir' (i.e. south of Taniquetil, where dwelt Manwë's spirits of the air), and this dictionary also makes it clear that the word *Mánir* was related to Gnomish *manos*, defined as 'a spirit that has gone to the Valar or to Erumáni', and *mani* 'good, holy'. The significance of these etymological connections is very unclear.

But there is also a very early poem on the subject of this region. This, according to my father's notes, was written at Brocton Camp, Staffordshire, in December 1915 or at Étaples in June 1916; and it is entitled *Habbanan beneath the Stars*. In one of the three texts (in which there are no variants) there is a title in Old English: *þā gebletsode* ['blessed'] *felda under þām steorrum*, and in two of them *Habbanan* in the title was emended to *Eruman*; in the third *Eruman* stood from the first. The poem is preceded by a short prose preamble.

### Habbanan beneath the Stars

Now Habbanan is that region where one draws nigh to the places that are not of Men. There is the air very sweet and the sky very great by reason of the broadness of the Earth.

> In Habbanan beneath the skies
> Where all roads end however long
> There is a sound of faint guitars
> And distant echoes of a song,
> For there men gather into rings
> Round their red fires while one voice sings –
> And all about is night.

★

> Not night as ours, unhappy folk,
> Where nigh the Earth in hazy bars,
> A mist about the springing of the stars,
> There trails a thin and wandering smoke
> Obscuring with its veil half-seen
> The great abysmal still Serene.

★

A globe of dark glass faceted with light
Wherein the splendid winds have dusky flight;
Untrodden spaces of an odorous plain
That watches for the moon that long has lain
And caught the meteors' fiery rain –
Such there is night.

★

There on a sudden did my heart perceive
That they who sang about the Eve,
Who answered the bright-shining stars
With gleaming music of their strange guitars,
These were His wandering happy sons
Encamped upon those aëry leas
Where God's unsullied garment runs
In glory down His mighty knees.

★

A final evidence comes from the early Qenya word-list. The original
layer of entries in this list dates (as I believe, see the Appendix on Names)
from 1915, and among these original entries, under a root *mana* (from
which *Manwë* is derived), is given a word *manimo* which means a soul who
is in *manimuine* 'Purgatory'.

This poem, and this entry in the word-list, offer a rare and very sug-
gestive glimpse of the mythic conception in its earliest phase; for here
ideas that are drawn from Christian theology are explicitly present. It is
disconcerting to perceive that they are still present in this tale. For in the
tale there is an account of the fates of dead Men after judgement in the
black hall of Fui Nienna. Some ('and these are the many') are ferried by
the death-ship to (Habbanan) Eruman, where they wander in the dusk
and wait in patience till the Great End; some are seized by Melko and
tormented in Angamandi 'the Hells of Iron'; and some few go to dwell
with the Gods in Valinor. Taken with the poem and the evidence of the
early 'dictionaries', can this be other than a reflection of Purgatory, Hell,
and Heaven?

This becomes all the more extraordinary if we refer to the concluding
passage of the tale of *The Music of the Ainur* (p. 59), where Ilúvatar said:
'To Men I will give a new gift and a greater', the gift that they might
'fashion and design their life beyond even the original Music of the Ainur
that is as fate to all things else', and where it is said that 'it is one with
this gift of power that the Children of Men dwell only for a short time in
the world alive, yet do not perish utterly for ever . . .' In the final form
given in *The Silmarillion* pp. 41–2 this passage was not very greatly
changed. The early version does not, it is true, have the sentences:

But the sons of Men die indeed, and leave the world; wherefore they are called the Guests, or the Strangers. Death is their fate, the gift of Ilúvatar, which as Time wears even the Powers shall envy.

Even so, it seems clear that this central idea, the Gift of Death, was already present. This matter I must leave, as a conundrum that I cannot solve. The most obvious explanation of the conflict of ideas within these tales would be to suppose *The Music of the Ainur* later than *The Coming of the Valar and the Building of Valinor*; but as I have said (p. 61) all the appearances are to the contrary.

Lastly may be noticed the characteristic linguistic irony whereby *Eruman* ultimately became *Araman*. For *Arvalin* meant simply 'near Valinor', and it was the other name *Eruman* that had associations with spirits of the dead; but *Araman* almost certainly simply means 'beside Aman'. And yet the same element *man-* 'good' remains, for *Aman* was derived from it ('the Unmarred State').

Two minor matters in the conclusion of the tale remain to be noticed. Here Nornorë is the Herald of the Gods; afterwards this was Fionwë (later Eonwë), see p. 63. And in the reference to 'that low place amid the hills where Valinor may just be glimpsed', near to Taniquetil, we have the first mention of the gap in the Mountains of Valinor where was the hill of the city of the Elves.

On blank pages near the end of the text of this tale my father wrote a list of secondary names of the Valar (as Manwë *Súlimo*, etc.). Some of these names appear in the text of the *Tales*; those that do not are given in the Appendix on Names under the primary names. It emerges from this list that Ómar-Amillo is the twin of Salmar-Noldorin (they are named as brothers in the tale, p. 75); that Nielíqui (p. 75) is the daughter of Oromë and Vána; and that Melko has a son ('by Ulbandi') called Kosomot: this, it will emerge later, was Gothmog Lord of Balrogs, whom Ecthelion slew in Gondolin.

# IV

## THE CHAINING OF MELKO

Following the end of Rúmil's tale of *The Coming of the Valar and the Building of Valinor* there is a long interlude before the next one, though the manuscript continues without even interrupting the paragraph. But on the cover of the notebook *The Chaining of Melko* is given as a separate title, and I have adopted this. The text continues in ink over an erased pencil manuscript.

That night Eriol heard again in his sleep the music that had so moved him on the first night; and the next morning he went again into the gardens early. There he met Vairë, and she called him *Eriol*: 'that was the first making and uttering of that name'. Eriol told Vairë of the 'dream-musics' he had heard, and she said that it was no dream-music, but rather the flute of Timpinen, 'whom those Gnomes Rúmil and Littleheart and others of my house call Tinfang'. She told him that the children called him Tinfang Warble; and that he played and danced in summer dusks for joy of the first stars: 'at every note a new one sparkles forth and glisters. The Noldoli say that they come out too soon if Tinfang Warble plays, and they love him, and the children will watch often from the windows lest he tread the shadowy lawns unseen.' She told Eriol that he was 'shier than a fawn – swift to hide and dart away as any vole: a footstep on a twig and he is away, and his fluting will come mocking from afar'.

'And a marvel of wizardry liveth in that fluting,' said Eriol, 'if that it be indeed which I have heard now for two nights here.'

'There be none,' said Vairë, 'not even of the Solosimpi, who can rival him therein, albeit those same pipers claim him as their kin; yet 'tis said everywhere that this quaint spirit is neither wholly of the Valar nor of the Eldar, but is half a fay of the woods and dells, one of the great companies of the children of Palúrien, and half a Gnome or a Shoreland Piper.[1] Howso that be he is a wondrous wise and strange creature, and he fared hither away with the Eldar long ago, marching nor resting among them but going always ahead piping strangely or whiles sitting aloof. Now does he play about the gardens of the land; but Alalminórë he loves the best, and this garden best of all. Ever and again we miss his piping for long months, and we say: "Tinfang Warble has gone heart-breaking in the Great Lands, and many a one in those far regions will hear his piping in the dusk outside tonight." But on a sudden will his flute be heard again at an hour of gentle gloaming, or will he play beneath a goodly moon and the stars go bright and blue.'

'Aye,' said Eriol, 'and the hearts of those that hear him go beating with a quickened longing. Meseemed 'twas my desire to open the window and leap forth, so sweet was the air that came to me from without, nor might I drink deep enough, but as I listened I wished to follow I know not whom, I know not whither, out into the magic of the world beneath the stars.'

'Then of a sooth 'twas Timpinen who played to you,' said Vairë, 'and honoured are you, for this garden has been empty of his melody many a night. Now, however, for such is the eeriness of that sprite, you will ever love the evenings of summer and the nights of stars, and their magic will cause your heart to ache unquenchably.'

'But have you not all heard him many times and often, that dwell here,' said Eriol, 'yet do not seem to me like those who live with a longing that is half understood and may not be fulfilled.'

'Nor do we so, for we have *limpë*,' said she, '*limpë* that alone can cure, and a draught of it giveth a heart to fathom all music and song.'

'Then,' said Eriol, 'would I might drain a goblet of that good .drink'; but Vairë told him that that might only be if he sought out Meril the queen.

Of this converse of Eriol and Vairë upon the lawn that fair day-tide came it that Eriol set out not many days thereafter – and Tinfang Warble had played to him many times by dusk, by starry light and moongleam, till his heart was full. In that was Littleheart his guide, and he sought the dwellings of Meril-i-Turinqui in her *korin* of elms.

Now the house of that fair lady was in that very city, for at the foot of the great tower which Ingil had built was a wide grove of the most ancient and beautiful elms that all that Land of Elms possessed. High to heaven they rose in three lessening storeys of bright foliage, and the sunlight that filtered through was very cool – a golden green. Amidst of these was a great green sward of grass smooth as a web of stuffs, and about it those trees stood in a circle, so that shades were heavy at its edge but the gaze of the sun fell all day on its middle. There stood a beautiful house, and it was builded all of white and of a whiteness that shone, but its roof was so o'ergrown with mosses and with houseleek and many curious clinging plants that of what it was once fashioned might not be seen for the glorious maze of colours, golds and red-russets, scarlets and greens.

Innumerable birds chattered in its eaves; and some sang upon the housetops, while doves and pigeons circled in flights about the *korin*'s borders or swooped to settle and sun upon the sward. Now all that dwelling was footed in flowers. Blossomy clusters were about it, ropes and tangles, spikes and tassels all in bloom, flowers in panicles and umbels or with great wide faces gazing at the sun. There did they loose upon the faintly stirring airs their several odours blended to a great fragrance of exceeding marvellous enchantment, but their hues and colours were scattered and gathered seemingly as chance and the happiness of their growth directed them. All day long there went a hum of bees among those flowers: bees fared about the roof and all the scented beds and ways; even about the cool porches of the house. Now Littleheart and Eriol climbed the hill and it was late afternoon, and the sun shone brazen upon the western side of Ingil's tower. Soon came they to a mighty wall of hewn stone blocks, and this leaned outward, but grasses grew atop of it, and harebells, and yellow daisies.

A wicket they found in the wall, and beyond was a glade beneath the elms, and there ran a pathway bordered of one side with bushes while of the other flowed a little running water whispering over a brown bed of leafy mould. This led even to the sward's edge, and coming thither said Littleheart pointing to that white house: 'Behold the dwelling of Meril-i-Turinqui, and as I have no errand with so great a lady I will get me back again.' Then Eriol went over the sunny lawn alone until he was nigh shoulder-high in the tall flowers that grew before the porches of the door; and as he drew near a sound of music came to him, and a fair lady amid many maidens stepped forth as it were to meet him. Then said she smiling: 'Welcome, O mariner of many seas – wherefore do you seek the pleasure of my quiet gardens and their gentle noise, when the salt breezes of the sea and the snuff of winds and a swaying boat should rather be your joy?'

For a while Eriol might say nought thereto, being tongue-tied by the beauty of that lady and the loveliness of that place of flowers; yet at length he muttered that he had known sea enough, but of this most gracious land he might never be sated. 'Nay,' said she, 'on a day of autumn will come the winds and a driven gull, maybe, will wail overhead, and lo! you will be filled with desire, remembering the black coasts of your home.'[2] 'Nay, lady,' said Eriol, and now he spoke with eager voice, 'nay, not so, for the spirit that flutes upon twilit lawns has filled my heart with music, and I thirst for a draught of *limpë*!'

Then straightway did the smiling face of Meril grow grave, and bidding her maidens depart she prayed Eriol follow her to a space nigh to the house, and this was of cool grass but not very short. Fruit-trees grew there, and about the roots of one, an apple-tree of great girth and age, the soil was piled so that there was now a broad seat around its bole, soft and grass-covered. There sat Meril and she gazed upon Eriol and said: 'Know you then what it is that you ask?' and he said: 'I know nought save that I desire to know the soul of every song and of all music and to dwell always in fellowship and kinship with this wondrous people of the Eldar of the Isle, and to be free of unquenchable longing even till the Faring Forth, even till the Great End!'

But Meril said: 'Fellowship is possible, maybe, but kinship not so, for Man is Man and Elda Elda, and what Ilúvatar has made unalike may not become alike while the world remains. Even didst thou dwell here till the Great End and for the health of *limpë* found no death, yet then must thou die and leave us, for Man must die once. And hearken, O Eriol, think not to escape unquenchable longing with a draught of *limpë* – for only wouldst thou thus exchange desires, replacing thy old ones with new and deeper and more keen. Desire unsatisfied dwells in the hearts of both those races that are called the Children of Ilúvatar, but with the Eldar most, for their hearts are filled with a vision of beauty in great glory.' 'Yet, O Queen,' said Eriol thereto, 'let me but taste of this drink and become an agelong fellow of your people: O queen of the Eldalië, that I may be as the happy children of Mar Vanwa Tyaliéva.' 'Nay, not yet can I do that,' said Meril, 'for 'tis a graver matter far to give this drink to one who has known life and days already in the lands of Men than for a child to drink who knows but little else; yet even these did we keep a long while ere we gave them the wine of song, teaching them first much lore and testing their hearts and souls. Therefore I bid you now bide still longer and learn all that you may in this our isle. Lo, what do you know of the world, or of the ancient days of Men, or of the roots which those things that now are have far back in time, or what of the Eldalië and all their wisdom, that you should claim our cup of youth and poesy?'

'The tongue of Tol Eressëa do I know, and of the Valar have I heard, and the great world's beginning, and the building of Valinor; to musics have I hearkened and to poesy and the laughter of the Elves, and all I have found true and good, and my heart knows and it saith to me that these shall I always henceforth love, and love alone' – thus answered Eriol, and his heart was sore for the refusal of the Queen.

'Yet nothing do you know of the coming of the Elves, of the fates wherein they move, nor their nature and the place that Ilúvatar has given to them. Little do you reck of that great splendour of their home in Eldamar upon the hill of Kôr, nor all the sorrow of our parting. What know you of our travail down all the dark ways of the world, and the anguish we have known because of Melko; of the sorrows we have suffered, and do yet, because of Men, of all the fears that darken our hopes because of Men? Know you the wastes of tears that lie between our life in Tol Eressëa and that time of laughter that we knew in Valinor? O child of Men who wouldst be sharer of the fates of the Eldalië, what of our high desires and all those things we look for still to be – for lo! if you drink this drink all these must you know and love, having one heart with us – nay, even at the Faring Forth, should Eldar and Men fall into war at the last, still must you stand by us against the children of your kith and kin, but until then never may you fare away home though longings gnaw you – and the desires that at whiles consume a full-grown man who drinketh *limpë* are a fire of unimagined torture – knew you these things, O Eriol, when you fared hither with your request?'

'Nay, I knew them not,' said Eriol sadly, 'though often have I questioned folk thereof.'

'Then lo!' said Meril, 'I will begin a tale, and tell you some of it ere the long afternoon grows dim – but then must you fare hence again in patience'; and Eriol bowed his head.

'Then,' said Meril, 'now I will tell you of a time of peace the world once knew, and it is known as "Melko's Chains".[3] Of the Earth I will tell you as the Eldar found it and of the manner of their awakening into it.

Behold, Valinor is built, and the Gods dwell in peace, for Melko is far in the world delving deep and fortifying himself in iron and cold, but Makar and Meássë ride upon the gales and rejoice in earthquakes and the overmastering furies of the ancient seas. Light and beautiful is Valinor, but there is a deep twilight upon the world, for the Gods have gathered so much of that light that had before flowed about the airs. Seldom now falls the shimmering rain as it was used, and there reigns a gloom lit with pale streaks or shot with red where Melko spouts to heaven from a fire-torn hill.

Then Palúrien Yavanna fared forth from her fruitful gardens to survey the wide lands of her domain, and wandered the dark continents sowing seed and brooding upon hill and dale. Alone in that agelong gloaming she sang songs of the utmost enchantment, and of such deep magic were they that they floated about the rocky places and their echoes lingered for years of time in hill and empty plain, and all the good magics of all later days are whispers of the memories of her echoing song.

Then things began to grow there, fungus and strange growths heaved in damp places and lichens and mosses crept stealthily across the rocks and ate their faces, and they crumbled and made dust, and the creeping plants died in the dust, and there was mould, and ferns and warted plants grew in it silently, and strange creatures thrust their heads from crannies and crept over the stones. But Yavanna wept, for this was not the fair vigour that she had thought of – and thereupon Oromë came to her leaping in the dusk, but Tuivána would not leave the radiance of Kulullin nor Nessa the green swards of her dancing.

Then Oromë and Palúrien put forth all their might, and Oromë blew great blasts upon his horn as though he would awake the grey rocks to life and lustihead. Behold, at these blasts the great forest reared and moaned about the hills, and all the trees of dark leaf came to being, and the world was shaggy with a growth of pines and odorous with resinous trees, and firs and cedars hung their blue and olive draperies about the slopes, and yews began the centuries of their growth. Now was Oromë less gloomy and Palúrien was comforted, seeing the beauty of the first stars of Varda gleaming in the pale heavens through the shadows of the first trees' boughs, and hearing the murmur of the dusky forests and the creaking of the branches when Manwë stirred the airs.

At that time did many strange spirits fare into the world, for there were pleasant places dark and quiet for them to dwell in. Some came from Mandos, aged spirits that journeyed from Ilúvatar with him who are older than the world and very gloomy and secret, and some from the fortresses of the North where Melko then dwelt in the deep dungeons of Utumna. Full of evil and unwholesome were they; luring and restlessness and horror they brought, turning the dark into an ill and fearful thing, which it was not before. But some few danced thither with gentle feet exuding evening scents, and these came from the gardens of Lórien.

Still is the world full of these in the days of light, lingering alone in shadowy hearts of primeval forests, calling secret things across a starry waste, and haunting caverns in the hills that few have found: – but the pinewoods are yet too full of these old unelfin and inhuman spirits for the quietude of Eldar or of Men.

When this great deed was done then Palúrien would fain rest from her long labours and return to taste the sweet fruits of Valinor, and be refreshed beneath the tree of Laurelin whose dew is light, and Oromë was for beechwoods on the plains of the great Gods; but Melko who long time had delved in fear because of the wrath of the

Valar at his treacherous dealing with their lamps burst forth now into a great violence, for he had thought the world abandoned by the Gods to him and his. Beneath the very floors of Ossë he caused the Earth to quake and split and his lower fires to mingle with the sea. Vaporous storms and a great roaring of uncontrolled sea-motions burst upon the world, and the forests groaned and snapped. The sea leapt upon the land and tore it, and wide regions sank beneath its rage or were hewn into scattered islets, and the coast was dug into caverns. The mountains rocked and their hearts melted, and stone poured like liquid fire down their ashen sides and flowed even to the sea, and the noise of the great battles of the fiery beaches came roaring even through the Mountains of Valinor and drowned the singing of the Gods. Then rose Kémi Palúrien, even Yavanna that giveth fruits, and Aulë who loveth all her works and the substances of the earth, and they climbed to the halls of Manwë and spake to him, saying that all that goodliness was going utterly to wreck for the fiery evil of Melko's untempered heart, and Yavanna pleaded that all her agelong labour in the twilight be not drowned and buried. Thither, as they spake, came Ossë raging like a tide among the cliffs, for he was wroth at the upheaval of his realm and feared the displeasure of Ulmo his overlord. Then arose Manwë Súlimo, Lord of Gods and Elves, and Varda Tinwetári was beside him, and he spake in a voice of thunder from Taniquetil, and the Gods in Valmar heard it, and Vefántur knew the voice in Mandos, and Lórien was aroused in Murmuran.

Then was a great council held between the Two Trees at the mingling of the lights, and Ulmo came thither from the outer deeps; and of the redes there spoken the Gods devised a plan of wisdom, and the thought of Ulmo was therein and much of the craft of Aulë and the wide knowledge of Manwë.

Behold, Aulë now gathered six metals, copper, silver, tin, lead, iron, and gold, and taking a portion of each made with his magic a seventh which he named therefore *tilkal*,* and this had all the properties of the six and many of its own. Its colour was bright green or red in varying lights and it could not be broken, and Aulë alone could forge it. Thereafter he forged a mighty chain, making it of all seven metals welded with spells to a substance of uttermost hardness and brightness and smoothness, but of *tilkal* he had not sufficient to add more than a little to each link. Nonetheless he made two manacles of *tilkal* only and four fetters likewise. Now the chain was

* Footnote in the manuscript: '*T*(*ambë*) *I*(*lsa*) *L*(*atúken*) *K*(*anu*) *A*(*nga*) *L*(*aurë*). *ilsa* and *laurë* are the 'magic' names of ordinary *telpë* and *kulu*.'

named *Angaino*, the oppressor, and the manacles *Vorotemnar* that bind for ever, but the fetters *Ilterendi* for they might not be filed or cleft. But the desire of the Gods was to seek out Melko with great power – and to entreat him, if it might be, to better deeds; yet did they purpose, if naught else availed, to overcome him by force or guile, and set him in a bondage from which there should be no escape.

Now as Aulë smithied the Gods arrayed themselves in armour, which they had of Makar, and he was fain to see them putting on weapons and going as to war, howso their wrath be directed against Melko. But when the great Gods and all their folk were armed, then Manwë climbed into his blue chariot whose three horses were the whitest that roamed in Oromë's domain, and his hand bore a great white bow that would shoot an arrow like a gust of wind across the widest seas. Fionwë his son stood behind him and Nornorë who was his herald ran before; but Oromë rode alone upon a chestnut horse and had a spear, and Tulkas strode mightily beside his stirrup, having a tunic of hide and a brazen belt and no weapon save a gauntlet upon his right hand, iron-bound. Telimektar his son but just war-high was by his shoulder with a long sword girt about his waist by a silver girdle. There rode the Fánturi upon a car of black, and there was a black horse upon the side of Mandos and a dappled grey upon the side of Lórien, and Salmar and Ómar came behind running speedily, but Aulë who was late tarrying overlong at his smithy came last, and he was not armed, but caught up his long-handled hammer as he left his forge and fared hastily to the borders of the Shadowy Sea, and the fathoms of his chain were borne behind by four of his smithy-folk.

Upon those shores Falman-Ossë met them and drew them across on a mighty raft whereon he himself sat in shimmering mail; but Ulmo Vailimo was far ahead roaring in his deep-sea car and trumpeting in wrath upon a horn of conches. Thus was it that the Gods got them over the sea and through the isles, and set foot upon the wide lands, and marched in great power and anger ever more to the North. Thus they passed the Mountains of Iron and Hisilómë that lies dim beyond, and came to the rivers and hills of ice. There Melko shook the earth beneath them, and he made snow-capped heights to belch forth flame, yet for the greatness of their array his vassals who infested all their ways availed nothing to hinder them on their journey. There in the deepest North beyond even the shattered pillar Ringil they came upon the huge gates of deep Utumna, and Melko shut them with great clangour before their faces.

Then Tulkas angered smote them thunderously with his great fist, and they rang and stirred not, but Oromë alighting grasped his horn and blew such a blast thereon that they fled open instantly, and Manwë raised his immeasurable voice and bade Melko come forth.

But though deep down within those halls Melko heard him and was in doubt, he would not come, but sent Langon his servant and said by him that "Behold, he was rejoiced and in wonder to see the Gods before his gates. Now would he gladly welcome them, yet for the poverty of his abode not more than two of them could he fitly entertain; and he begged that neither Manwë nor Tulkas be of the two, for the one merited and the other demanded hospitality of great cost and richness. Should this not be to their mind then would he fain hearken to Manwë's herald and learn what it were the Gods so greatly desired that they must leave their soft couches and indolence of Valinor for the bleak places where Melko laboured humbly and did his toilsome work."

Then Manwë and Ulmo and all the Gods were exceeding wroth at the subtlety and fawning insolence of his words, and Tulkas would have started straightway raging down the narrow stairs that descended out of sight beyond the gates, but the others withheld him, and Aulë gave counsel that it was clear from Melko's words that he was awake and wary in this matter, and it could most plainly be seen which of the Gods he was most in fear of and desired least to see standing in his halls – "therefore," said he, "let us devise how these twain may come upon him unawares and how fear may perchance drive him into betterment of ways." To this Manwë assented, saying that all their force might scarce dig Melko from his stronghold, whereas that deceit must be very cunningly woven that would ensnare the master of guile. "Only by his pride is Melko assailable," quoth Manwë, "or by such a struggle as would rend the earth and bring evil upon us all," and Manwë sought to avoid all strife twixt Ainur and Ainur. When therefore the Gods had concerted a plan to catch Melko in his overweening pride they wove cunning words purporting to come from Manwë himself, and these they put in the mouth of Nornorë, who descended and spoke them before the seat of Melko. "Behold," said he, "the Gods be come to ask the pardon of Melko, for seeing his great anger and the rending of the world beneath his rage they have said one to another: 'Lo! wherefore is Melko displeased?' and one to another have answered beholding the tumults of his power: 'Is he not then the greatest among us – why dwells not the mightiest of the Valar in Valinor? Of a surety he has cause for indignation. Let us get us to Utumna and beseech him to dwell in

Valinor that Valmar be not empty of his presence.' To this," said he, "Tulkas alone would not assent, but Manwë bowed to the common voice (this the Gods said knowing the rancour that Melko had for Poldórëa) and now have they come constraining Tulkas with violence to beg thee to pardon them each one and to fare home with them and complete their glory, dwelling, if it be thy pleasure, in the halls of Makar, until such time as Aulë can build thee a great house; and its towers shall overtop Taniquetil." To this did Melko answer eagerly, for already his boundless pride surged up and drowned his cunning.

"At last do the Gods speak fair words and just, but ere I grant their boon my heart must be appeased for old affronts. Therefore must they come putting aside their weapons at the gate, and do homage to me in these my deep halls of Utumna: – but lo! Tulkas I will not see, and if I come to Valinor then will I thrust him out." These things did Nornorë report, and Tulkas smote his hands in wrath, but Manwë returned answer that the Gods would do as Melko's heart desired, yet would Tulkas come and that in chains and be given to Melko's power and pleasure; and this was Melko eager to grant for the humiliation of the Valar, and the chaining of Tulkas gave him great mirth.

Then the Valar laid aside their weapons at the gates, setting however folk to guard them, and placed the chain Angaino about the neck and arms of Tulkas, and even he might scarce support its great weight alone; and now they follow Manwë and his herald into the caverns of the North. There sat Melko in his chair, and that chamber was lit with flaming braziers and full of evil magic, and strange shapes moved with feverish movement in and out, but snakes of great size curled and uncurled without rest about the pillars that upheld that lofty roof. Then said Manwë: "Behold, we have come and salute you here in your own halls; come now and be in Valinor."

But Melko might not thus easily forgo his sport. "Nay first," said he, "wilt thou come Manwë and kneel before me, and after you all the Valar; but last shall come Tulkas and kiss my foot, for I have in mind something for which I owe Poldórëa no great love." Now he purposed to spurn Tulkas in the mouth in payment of that buffet long ago, but the Valar had foreseen something of this and did but make play of humiliation that Melko might thereby be lured from his stronghold of Utumna. In sooth Manwë hoped even to the end for peace and amity, and the Gods would at his bidding indeed have received Melko into Valinor under truce and pledges of friendship, had not his pride been insatiate and his obstinacy in evil unconquerable. Now however was scant mercy left for him within their hearts, seeing that he abode in his demand that Manwë should do homage and Tulkas bend to those ruthless feet; nonetheless the Lord of Gods and Elves approaches now the chair of Melko and makes to kneel, for such was their plan the more to ensnare that evil one; but lo, so fiercely did wrath blaze up in the hearts of Tulkas and Aulë at that sight that Tulkas leapt across the hall at a bound despite Angaino, and Aulë was behind him and Oromë followed his father and the hall was full of tumult. Then Melko sprang to his feet shouting in a loud voice and his folk came through all those dismal passages to his aid. Then lashed he at Manwë with an iron flail he bore, but Manwë breathed gently upon it and its iron tassels were blown backward, and thereupon Tulkas smote Melko full in his teeth with his fist of iron, and he and Aulë grappled with him, and straight he was wrapped thirty times in the fathoms of Angaino.

Then said Oromë: "Would that he might be slain" – and it would have been well indeed, but the great Gods may not yet be slain.[4] Now is Melko held in dire bondage and beaten to his knees, and he is constrained to command all his vassalage that they molest not the Valar – and indeed the most of these, affrighted at the binding of their lord, fled away to the darkest places.

Tulkas indeed dragged Melko out before the gates, and there Aulë set upon each wrist one of the Vorotemnar and upon each ankle twain of the Ilterendi, and *tilkal* went red at the touch of Melko, and those bands have never since been loosened from his hands and feet. Then the chain is smithied to each of these and Melko borne thus helpless away, while Tulkas and Ulmo break the gates of Utumna and pile hills of stone upon them. And the saps and cavernous places beneath the surface of the earth are full yet of the dark spirits that were prisoned that day when Melko was taken, and yet many are the ways whereby they find the outer world from time to time – from fissures where they shriek with the voices of the tide on rocky coasts, down dark water-ways that wind unseen for many leagues, or out of the blue arches where the glaciers of Melko find their end.

After these things did the Gods return to Valmar by long ways and dark, guarding Melko every moment, and he gnawed his consuming rage. His lip was split and his face has had a strange leer upon it since that buffet dealt him by Tulkas, who even of policy could not endure to see the majesty of Manwë bow before the accursed one.

Now is a court set upon the slopes of Taniquetil and Melko arraigned before all the Vali[5] great and small, lying bound before the silver chair of Manwë. Against him speaketh Ossë, and Oromë, and Ulmo in deep ire, and Vána in abhorrence, proclaiming his deeds of cruelty and violence; yet Makar still spake for him, although not warmly, for said he: "'Twere an ill thing if peace were for always: already no blow echoes ever in the eternal quietude of Valinor, wherefore, if one might neither see deed of battle nor riotous joy even in the world without, then 'twould be irksome indeed, and I for one long not for such times!" Thereat arose Palúrien in sorrow and tears, and told of the plight of Earth and of the great beauty of her designs and of those things she desired dearly to bring forth; of all the wealth of flower and herbage, of tree and fruit and grain that the world might bear if it had but peace. "Take heed, O Valar, that both Elves and Men be not devoid of all solace whenso the times come for them to find the Earth"; but Melko writhed in rage at the name of Eldar and of Men and at his own impotence.

Now Aulë mightily backed her in this and after him many else of the Gods, yet Mandos and Lórien held their peace, nor do they ever speak much at the councils of the Valar or indeed at other times, but Tulkas arose angrily from the midst of the assembly and went from among them, for he could not endure parleying where he thought the guilt to be clear. Liever would he have unchained Melko and fought him then and there alone upon the plain of Valinor, giving him many a sore buffet in meed of his illdoings, rather than making high debate of them. Howbeit Manwë sate and listened and was moved by the speech of Palúrien, yet was it his thought that Melko was an Ainu and powerful beyond measure for the future good or evil of the world; wherefore he put away harshness and his doom was this. For three ages during the displeasure of the Gods should Melko be chained in a vault of Mandos by that chain Angaino, and thereafter should he fare into the light of the Two Trees, but only so that he might for four ages yet dwell as a servant in the house of Tulkas, and obey him in requital of his ancient malice. "Thus," said Manwë, "and yet but hardly, mayst thou win favour again sufficient that the Gods suffer thee to abide thereafter in an house of thine own and to have some slight estate among them as befitteth a Vala and a lord of the Ainur."

Such was the doom of Manwë, and even to Makar and Meássë it seemed good, albeit Tulkas and Palúrien thought it merciful to peril. Now doth Valinor enter upon its greatest time of peace, and all the earth beside, while Melko bideth in the deepest vaults of Mandos and his heart grows black within him.

Behold the tumults of the sea abate slowly, and the fires beneath the mountains die; the earth quakes no more and the fierceness of

the cold and the stubbornness of the hills and rivers of ice is melted
to the uttermost North and to the deepest South, even to the regions
about Ringil and Helkar. Then Palúrien goes once more out over the
Earth, and the forests multiply and spread, and often is Oromë's
horn heard behind her in the dimness: now do nightshade and
bryony begin to creep about the brakes, and holly and ilex are seen
upon the earth. Even the faces of the cliffs are grown with ivies and
trailing plants for the calm of the winds and the quietude of the sea,
and all the caverns and the shores are festooned with weeds, and great
sea-growths come to life swaying gently when Ossë moves the waters.

Now came that Vala and sat upon a headland of the Great Lands,
having leisure in the stillness of his realm, and he saw how Palúrien
was filling the quiet dusk of the Earth with flitting shapes. Bats
and owls whom Vefántur set free from Mandos swooped about the
sky, and nightingales sent by Lórien from Valinor trilled beside still
waters. Far away a nightjar croaked, and in dark places snakes that
slipped from Utumna when Melko was bound moved noiselessly
about; a frog croaked upon a bare pool's border.

Then he sent word to Ulmo of the new things that were done, and
Ulmo desired not that the waters of the inner seas be longer unpeopled, but came forth seeking Palúrien, and she gave him spells,
and the seas began to gleam with fish or strange creatures crawled at
bottom; yet the shellfish and the oysters no-one of Valar or of Elves
knows whence they are, for already they gaped in the silent waters
or ever Melko plunged therein from on high, and pearls there were
before the Eldar thought or dreamed of any gem.

Three great fish luminous in the dark of the sunless days went
ever with Ulmo, and the roof of Ossë's dwelling beneath the Great
Sea shone with phosphorescent scales. Behold that was a time of
great peace and quiet, and life struck deep roots into the new-made
soils of Earth, and seeds were sown that waited only for the light to
come, and it is known and praised as the age of "Melko's Chains".'

## NOTES

1    The following passage was added here, apparently very soon after the
     writing of the text, but was later firmly struck through:

     The truth is that he is a son of Linwë Tinto King of the Pipers who
     was lost of old upon the great march from Palisor, and wandering in
     Hisilómë found the lonely twilight spirit (Tindriel) Wendelin
     dancing in a glade of beeches. Loving her he was content to leave

his folk and dance for ever in the shadows, but his children Timpinen and Tinúviel long after joined the Eldar again, and tales there are concerning them both, though they are seldom told.

The name *Tindriel* stood alone in the manuscript as written, but it was then bracketed and *Wendelin* added in the margin. These are the first references in the consecutive narrative to Thingol (Linwë Tinto), Hithlum (Hisilómë), Melian (Tindriel, Wendelin), and Lúthien Tinúviel; but I postpone discussion of these allusions.

2 Cf. the explanation of the names *Eriol* and *Angol* as 'ironcliffs' referred to in the Appendix on Names (entry *Eriol*).

3 Associated with the story of the sojourn of Eriol (Ælfwine) in Tol Eressëa, and the 'Lost Tales' that he heard there, are two 'schemes' or synopses setting out the plan of the work. One of these is, for much of its length, a résumé of the *Tales* as they are extant; the other, certainly the later, is divergent. In this second scheme, in which the voyager is called Ælfwine, the tale on the second night by the Tale-fire is given to 'Evromord the Door-ward', though the narrative-content was to be the same (The Coming of the Gods; the World-fashioning and the Building of Valinor; the Planting of the Two Trees). After this is written (a later addition): 'Ælfwine goes to beg *limpë* of Meril; she sends him back.' The third night by the Tale-fire is thus described:

> The Door-ward continues of the Primeval Twilight. The Furies of Melko. Melko's Chains and the awakening of the Elves. (How Fankil and many dark shapes escape into the world.) [Given to Meril but to be placed as here and much abridged.]

It seems certain that this was a revision in intention only, never achieved. It is notable that in the actual text, as also in the first of these two 'schemes', Rúmil's function in the house is that of doorward – and Rúmil, not Evromord, was the name that was preserved long after as the recounter of The Music of the Ainur.

4 The text as originally written read: 'but the great Gods may not be slain, though their children may and all those lesser people of the Vali, albeit only at the hands of some one of the Valar.'

5 *Vali* is an emendation from *Valar*. Cf. Rúmil's words (p. 58): 'they whom we now call the Valar (or Vali, it matters not).'

## Commentary on
### *The Chaining of Melko*

In the interlude between this tale and the last we encounter the figure of Timpinen or Tinfang. This being had existed in my father's mind for some years, and there are two poems about him. The first is entitled *Tinfang Warble*; it is very brief, but exists in three versions. According to a note by my father the original was written at Oxford in 1914, and it was

rewritten at Leeds in '1920–23'. It was finally published in 1927 in a
further altered form, which I give here.*

### Tinfang Warble

O the hoot! O the hoot!
How he trillups on his flute!
O the hoot of Tinfang Warble!

Dancing all alone,
Hopping on a stone,
Flitting like a fawn,
In the twilight on the lawn,
And his name is Tinfang Warble!

The first star has shown
And its lamp is blown
to a flame of flickering blue.
He pipes not to me,
He pipes not to thee,
He whistles for none of you.
His music is his own,
The tunes of Tinfang Warble!

In the earliest version Tinfang is called a 'leprawn', and in the early
glossary of the Gnomish speech he is a 'fay'.

The second poem is entitled *Over Old Hills and Far Away*. This exists
in five texts, of which the earliest bears an Old English title as well
(of the same meaning): *Ʒeond fyrne beorgas ʒ heonan feor*. Notes by my
father state that it was written at Brocton Camp in Staffordshire between
December 1915 and February 1916, and rewritten at Oxford in 1927.
The final version given here differs in many details of wording and in
places whole lines from earlier versions, from which I note at the end a
few interesting readings.

### Over Old Hills and Far Away

It was early and still in the night of June,
And few were the stars, and far was the moon,
The drowsy trees drooping, and silently creeping
Shadows woke under them while they were sleeping.

5    I stole to the window with stealthy tread
Leaving my white and unpressed bed;
And something alluring, aloof and queer,
Like perfume of flowers from the shores of the mere

* Publication was in a periodical referred to in the cutting preserved from
it as 'I.U.M[agazine]').

That in Elvenhome lies, and in starlit rains
10    Twinkles and flashes, came up to the panes
Of my high lattice-window. Or was it a sound?
I listened and marvelled with eyes on the ground.
For there came from afar a filtered note
Enchanting sweet, now clear, now remote,
15    As clear as a star in a pool by the reeds,
As faint as the glimmer of dew on the weeds.

Then I left the window and followed the call
Down the creaking stairs and across the hall
Out through a door that swung tall and grey,
20    And over the lawn, and away, away!

It was Tinfang Warble that was dancing there,
Fluting and tossing his old white hair,
Till it sparkled like frost in a winter moon;
And the stars were about him, and blinked to his tune
25    Shimmering blue like sparks in a haze,
As always they shimmer and shake when he plays.

My feet only made there the ghost of a sound
On the shining white pebbles that ringed him round,
Where his little feet flashed on a circle of sand,
30    And the fingers were white on his flickering hand.
In the wink of a star he had leapt in the air
With his fluttering cap and his glistening hair;
And had cast his long flute right over his back,
Where it hung by a ribbon of silver and black.

35    His slim little body went fine as a shade,
And he slipped through the reeds like a mist in the glade;
And he laughed like thin silver, and piped a thin note,
As he flapped in the shadows his shadowy coat.
O! the toes of his slippers were twisted and curled,
40    But he danced like a wind out into the world.

He is gone, and the valley is empty and bare
Where lonely I stand and lonely I stare.
Then suddenly out in the meadows beyond,
Then back in the reeds by the shimmering pond,
45    Then afar from a copse where the mosses are thick
A few little notes came trillaping quick.

I leapt o'er the stream and I sped from the glade,
For Tinfang Warble it was that played;
I must follow the hoot of his twilight flute

50          Over reed, over rush, under branch, over root,
            And over dim fields, and through rustling grasses
            That murmur and nod as the old elf passes,
            Over old hills and far away
            Where the harps of the Elvenfolk softly play.

*Earlier readings:*

1–2        'Twas a very quiet evening once in June –
            And I thought that stars had grown bright too soon –
            Cf. the prose text, p. 94: 'The Noldoli say that [the stars] come
            out too soon if Tinfang Warble plays'.

8          from the shores of the mere] by the fairies' mere

9          Elvenhome] emendation made on the text of the final version,
            replacing 'Fairyland'.

24         Till the stars came out, as it seemed, too soon.
            Cf. the note to line 2.

25–6       They always come out when he warbles and plays,
            And they shine bright blue as long as he stays.
            Cf. the prose text, p. 95: 'or will he play beneath a goodly moon
            and the stars go bright and blue.'

54         Elvenfolk] emendation made on the text of the final version,
            replacing 'fairies'.

★

The first part of this story of *The Chaining of Melko* came to have a very
different form in later versions, where (*The Silmarillion* p. 35) it was
during the sojourn of the Valar on the Isle of Almaren, under the light of
the Two Lamps, that 'the seeds that Yavanna had sown began swiftly to
sprout and to burgeon, and there arose a multitude of growing things
great and small, mosses and grasses and great ferns, and trees whose tops
were crowned with cloud'; and that 'beasts came forth and dwelt in the
grassy plains, or in the rivers and the lakes, or walked in the shadows of
the woods'. This was the Spring of Arda; but after the coming of Melkor
and the delving of Utumno 'green things fell sick and rotted, and rivers
were choked with weeds and slime, and fens were made, rank and poisonous, the breeding place of flies; and forests grew dark and perilous,
the haunts of fear; and beasts became monsters of horn and ivory and
dyed the earth with blood'. Then came the fall of the Lamps, and 'thus
ended the Spring of Arda' (p. 37). After the building of Valinor and the
arising of the Two Trees 'Middle-earth lay in a twilight beneath the
stars' (p. 39), and Yavanna and Oromë alone of the Valar returned there
at times: 'Yavanna would walk there in the shadows, grieving because the
growth and promise of the Spring of Arda was stayed. And she set a sleep
upon many things that had arisen in the Spring, so that they should not

age, but should wait for a time of awakening that yet should be' (p. 47).
'But already the oldest living things had arisen: in the seas the great weeds,
and on earth the shadow of great trees; and in the valleys of the night-clad
hills there were dark creatures old and strong.'

In this earliest narrative, on the other hand, there is no mention of the
beginning of growth during the time when the Lamps shone (see p. 69),
and the first trees and low plants appeared under Yavanna's spells in the
twilight after their overthrow. Moreover in the last sentence of this tale
'seeds were sown', in that time of 'quiet dusk' while Melko was chained,
'that waited only for the light to come'. Thus in the early story Yavanna
sows in the dark with a view (it seems) to growth and flowering in later
days of sunlight, whereas in all the subsequent versions the goddess in
the time of darkness sows no more, but rather lays a sleep on many things
that had arisen beneath the light of the Lamps in the Spring of Arda.
But both in the early tale and in *The Silmarillion* there is a suggestion that
Yavanna foresees that light will come in the end to the Great Lands, to
Middle-earth.

The conception of a flowing, liquid light in the airs of Earth is again
very marked, and it seems that in the original idea the twilight ages of the
world east of the sea were still illumined by the traces of this light
('Seldom now falls the shimmering rain as it was used, and there reigns a
gloom lit with pale streaks', p. 98) as well as by the stars of Varda, even
though 'the Gods have gathered so much of that light that had before
flowed about the airs' (*ibid.*).

The renewed cosmic violence is conceivably the precursor of the great
Battle of the Powers in the later mythology (*The Silmarillion* p. 51); but
in this earliest tale Melko's upheavals are the cause of the Valar's visitation,
whereas the Battle of the Powers, in which the shape of Middle-earth was
changed, resulted from it. In *The Silmarillion* it was the discovery of the
newly-awakened Elves by Oromë that led the Valar to the assault on
Utumno.

In its rich narrative detail, as in its 'primitive' air, the tale told by
Meril-i-Turinqi of the capture of Melko bears little relation to the later
narrative; while the tone of the encounter at Utumna, and the treacherous
shifts of the Valar to ensnare him, is foreign to it likewise. But some
elements survived: the chain Angainor forged by Aulë (if not the marvellous metal *tilkal* with its most uncharacteristically derived name), the
wrestling of Tulkas with Melko, his imprisonment in Mandos for 'three
ages', and the idea that his fortress was not destroyed to its foundations.
It emerges too that the clement and trustful character of Manwë was
early defined; while the reference to Mandos' seldom speaking is possibly
a foreshadowing of his pronouncing his judgements only at the bidding
of Manwë (see p. 90). The origin of nightingales in the domain of Lórien
in Valinor is already present.

Lastly, it may seem from the account of the journey of the Valar in
this tale that Hisilómë (which survived without any further change as the

Quenya name of Hithlum) was here a quite distinct region from the later Hithlum, since it is placed *beyond* the Mountains of Iron: in *The Silmarillion* the Mountains of Iron are said to have been reared by Melkor 'as a fence to his citadel of Utumno': 'they stood upon the borders of the regions of everlasting cold, in a great curve from east to west' (p. 118). But in fact the 'Mountains of Iron' here correspond to the later 'Mountains of Shadow' (*Ered Wethrin*). In an annotated list of names accompanying the tale of *The Fall of Gondolin* the name *Dor Lómin* is thus defined:

> *Dor Lómin* or the 'Land of Shadow' was that region named of the Eldar *Hisilómë* (and this means 'Shadowy Twilights') . . . and it is so called by reason of the scanty sun which peeps little over the Iron Mountains to the east and south of it.

On the little map given on p. 81 the line of peaks which I have marked *f* almost certainly represents these mountains, and the region to the north of them, marked *g*, is then Hisilómë.

The manuscript continues, from the point where I have ended the text in this chapter, with no break; but this point is the end of a section in the mythological narrative (with a brief interruption by Eriol), and the remainder of Meril-i-Turinqi's tale is reserved to the next chapter. Thus I make two tales of one.

# V

# THE COMING OF THE ELVES
# AND THE MAKING OF KÔR

I take this title from the cover of the book (which adds also 'How the
Elves did fashion Gems'), for as I have already remarked the narrative
continues without a new heading.

Then said Eriol: 'Sad was the unchaining of Melko, methinks, even
did it seem merciful and just – but how came the Gods to do this
thing?'

Then Meril[1] continuing said:

'Upon a time thereafter was the third period of Melko's prison-
ment beneath the halls of Mandos come nearly to its ending. Manwë
sat upon the top of the mountain and gazed with his piercing eyes
into the shades beyond Valinor, and hawks flew to him and from him
bearing many great tidings, but Varda was singing a song and looking
upon the plain of Valinor. Silpion was at that time glimmering and
the roofs of Valmar below were black and silver beneath its rays;
and Varda was joyous, but on a sudden Manwë spake, saying:
"Behold, there is a gleam of gold beneath the pine-trees, and the
deepest gloaming of the world is full of a patter of feet. The Eldar
have come, O Taniquetil!" Then Varda arose swiftly and stretched
her arms out North and South, and unbraided her long hair, and
lifted up the Song of the Valar, and Ilwë was filled with the loveliness
of her voice.

Then did she descend to Valmar and to the abode of Aulë; and
he was making vessels of silver for Lórien. A bason filled with the
radiance of Telimpë[2] was by his side, and this he used cunningly in
his craft, but now Varda stood before him and said: "The Eldar have
come!" and Aulë flung down his hammer saying: "Then Ilúvatar
hath sent them at last," and the hammer striking some ingots of
silver upon the floor did of its magic smite silver sparks to life, that
flashed from his windows out into the heavens. Varda seeing this
took of that radiance in the bason and mingled it with molten silver
to make it more stable, and fared upon her wings of speed, and set
stars about the firmament in very great profusion, so that the skies
grew marvellously fair and their glory was doubled; and those stars

that she then fashioned have a power of slumbers, for the silver of their bodies came of the treasury of Lórien and their radiance had lain in Telimpë long time in his garden.

Some have said that the Seven Stars were set at that time by Varda to commemorate the coming of the Eldar, and that Morwinyon who blazes above the world's edge in the west was dropped by her as she fared in great haste back to Valinor. Now this is indeed the true beginning of Morwinyon and his beauty, yet the Seven Stars were not set by Varda, being indeed the sparks from Aulë's forge whose brightness in the ancient heavens urged Varda to make their rivals; yet this did she never achieve.

But now even as Varda is engaged in this great work, behold, Oromë pricks over the plain, and drawing rein he shouts aloud so that all the ears in Valmar may hear him: "*Tulielto! Tulielto!* They have come - they have come!" Then he stands midway between the Two Trees and winds his horn, and the gates of Valmar are opened, and the Vali troop into the plain, for they guess that tidings of wonder have come into the world. Then spake Oromë: "Behold the woods of the Great Lands, even in Palisor the midmost region where the pinewoods murmur unceasingly, are full of a strange noise. There did I wander, and lo! 'twas as if folk arose betimes beneath the latest stars. There was a stir among the distant trees and words were spoken suddenly, and feet went to and fro. Then did I say what is this deed that Palúrien my mother has wrought in secret, and I sought her out and questioned her, and she answered: 'This is no work of mine, but the hand of one far greater did this. Ilúvatar hath awakened his children at the last - ride home to Valinor and tell the Gods that the Eldar have come indeed!' "

Then shouted all the people of Valinor: "*I·Eldar tulier* - the Eldar have come" - and it was not until that hour that the Gods knew that their joy had contained a flaw, or that they had waited in hunger for its completion, but now they knew that the world had been an empty place beset with loneliness having no children for her own.

Now once more is council set and Manwë sitteth before the Gods there amid the Two Trees - and those had now borne light for four ages. Every one of the Vali fare thither, even Ulmo Vailimo in great haste from the Outer Seas, and his face is eager and glad.

On that day Manwë released Melko from Angaino before the full time of his doom, but the manacles and the fetters of *tilkal* were not unloosed, and he bore them yet upon wrist and ankle. Great joy blindeth even the forewisdom of the Gods. Last of all came Palúrien Yavanna hasting from Palisor, and the Valar debated concerning the

Eldar; but Melko sat at the feet of Tulkas and feigned a glad and humble cheer. At length it is the word of the Gods that some of the new-come Eldar be bidden to Valinor, there to speak to Manwë and his people, telling of their coming into the world and of the desires that it awakened in them.

Then does Nornorë, whose feet flash invisibly for the greatness of their speed, hurtle from Valinor bearing the embassy of Manwë, and he goes unstaying over both land and sea to Palisor. There he finds a place deep in a vale surrounded by pine-clad slopes; its floor is a pool of wide water and its roof the twilight set with Varda's stars. There had Oromë heard the awaking of the Eldar, and all songs name that place Koivië-néni or the Waters of Awakening.

Now all the slopes of that valley and the bare margin of the lake, even the rugged fringes of the hills beyond, are filled with a concourse of folk who gaze in wonder at the stars, and some sing already with voices that are very beautiful. But Nornorë stood upon a hill and was amazed for the beauty of that folk, and because he was a Vala they seemed to him marvellously small and delicate and their faces wistful and tender. Then did he speak in the great voice of the Valar and all those shining faces turned towards his voice.

"Behold O Eldalië, desired are ye for all the age of twilight, and sought for throughout the ages of peace, and I come even from Manwë Súlimo Lord of the Gods who abides upon Taniquetil in peace and wisdom to you who are the Children of Ilúvatar, and these are the words he put into my mouth to speak: Let now some few of you come back with me – for am I not Nornorë herald of the Valar – and enter Valinor and speak with him, that he may learn of your coming and of all your desires."

Great was the stir and wonder now about the waters of Koivië, and its end was that three of the Eldar came forward daring to go with Nornorë, and these he bore now back to Valinor, and their names as the Elves of Kôr have handed them on were Isil Inwë, and Finwë Nólemë who was Turondo's father, and Tinwë Lintö father of Tinúviel – but the Noldoli call them Inwithiel, Golfinweg, and Tinwelint. Afterward they became very great among the Eldar, and the Teleri were those who followed Isil, but his kindred and descendants are that royal folk the Inwir of whose blood I am. Nolemë was lord of the Noldoli, and of his son Turondo (or Turgon as they called him) are great tales told, but Tinwë[3] abode not long with his people, and yet 'tis said lives still lord of the scattered Elves of Hisilómë, dancing in its twilight places with Wendelin his spouse, a sprite come long long ago from the quiet gardens of Lórien; yet greatest of all the Elves did Isil Inwë become, and folk reverence his mighty name to this day.

Behold now brought by Nornorë the three Elves stood before the Gods, and it was at that time the changing of the lights, and Silpion was waning but Laurelin was awakening to his greatest glory, even as Silmo emptied the urn of silver about the roots of the other Tree. Then those Elves were utterly dazed and astonied by the splendour of the light, whose eyes knew only the dusk and had yet seen no brighter things than Varda's stars, but the beauty and majestic strength of the Gods in conclave filled them with awe, and the roofs of Valmar blazing afar upon the plain made them tremble, and they bowed in reverence – but Manwë said to them: "Rise, O Children of Ilúvatar, for very glad are the Gods of your coming! Tell us how ye came; how found ye the world; what seemeth it to you who are its first offspring, or with what desires doth it fill you."

But Nólemë answering said: "Lo! Most mighty one, whence indeed come we! For meseems I awoke but now from a sleep eternally profound, whose vast dreams already are forgotten." And Tinwë said thereto that his heart told him that he was new-come from illimitable regions, yet he might not recollect by what dark and strange paths he had been brought; and last spake Inwë, who had been gazing upon Laurelin while the others spake, and he said: "Knowing neither whence I come nor by what ways nor yet whither I go, the world that we are in is but one great wonderment to me, and methinks I love it wholly, yet it fills me altogether with a desire for light."

Then Manwë saw that Ilúvatar had wiped from the minds of the Eldar all knowledge of the manner of their coming, and that the Gods might not discover it; and he was filled with deep astonishment; but Yavanna who hearkened also caught her breath for the stab of the words of Inwë, saying that he desired light. Then she looked upon Laurelin and her heart thought of the fruitful orchards in Valmar, and she whispered to Tuivána who sat beside her, gazing upon the tender grace of those Eldar; then those twain said to Manwë: "Lo! the Earth and its shadows are no place for creatures so fair, whom only the heart and mind of Ilúvatar have conceived. Fair are the pine-forests and the thickets, but they are full of unelfin spirits and Mandos' children walk abroad and vassals of Melko lurk in strange places – and we ourselves would not be without the sight of this sweet folk. Their distant laughter has filtered to our ears from Palisor, and we would have it echo always about us in our halls and pleasaunces in Valmar. Let the Eldar dwell among us, and the well of our joy be filled from new springs that may not dry up."

Then arose a clamour among the Gods and the most spake for Palúrien and Vána, whereas Makar said that Valinor was builded for the Valar – "and already is it a rose-garden of fair ladies rather than an abode of men. Wherefore do ye desire to fill it with the children of the world?" In this Meássë backed him, and Mandos and Fui were cold to the Eldar as to all else; yet was Varda vehement in support of Yavanna and Tuivána, and indeed her love for the Eldar has ever been the greatest of all the folk of Valinor; and Aulë and Lórien, Oromë and Nessa and Ulmo most mightily proclaimed their desire for the bidding of the Eldar to dwell among the Gods. Wherefore, albeit Ossë spake cautiously against it – belike out of that ever-smouldering jealousy and rebellion he felt against Ulmo – it was the voice of the council that the Eldar should be bidden, and the Gods awaited but the judgement of Manwë. Behold even Melko seeing where was the majority insinuated his guileful voice into the pleading, and has nonetheless since those days maligned the Valar, saying they did but summon the Eldar as to a prison out of covetice and jealousy of their beauty. Thus often did he lie to the Noldoli afterwards when he would stir their restlessness, adding beside all truth that he alone had withstood the general voice and spoken for the freedom of the Elves.

Maybe indeed had the Gods decided otherwise the world had been a fairer place now and the Eldar a happier folk, but never would they have achieved such glory, knowledge, and beauty as they did of old, and still less would any of Melko's redes have benefited them.

Now having hearkened to all that was said Manwë gave judgement and was glad, for indeed his heart leaned of itself to the leading of the Eldar from the dusky world to the light of Valinor. Turning to the three Eldar he said: "Go ye back now to your kindreds and Nornorë shall bring you swiftly there, even to Koivië-néni in Palisor. Behold, this is the word of Manwë Súlimo, and the voice of the Valar's desire, that the people of the Eldalië, the Children of Ilúvatar, fare to Valinor, and there dwell in the splendour of Laurelin and the radiance of Silpion and know the happiness of the Gods. An abode of surpassing beauty shall they possess, and the Gods will aid them in its building."

Thereto answered Inwë: "Fain are we indeed of thy bidding, and who of the Eldalië that have already longed for the beauty of the stars will stay or rest till his eyes have feasted on the blessed light of Valinor!" Thereafter Nornorë guided those Elves back to the bare margins of Koivië-néni, and standing upon a boulder Inwë spake the embassy to all those hosts of the Eldalië that Ilúvatar waked first upon the Earth, and all such as heard his words were filled with desire to see the faces of the Gods.

When Nornorë returning told the Valar that the Elves were indeed coming and that Ilúvatar had set already a great multitude upon the Earth, the Gods made mighty preparation. Behold Aulë gathers his tools and stuffs and Yavanna and Tuivána wander about the plain even to the foothills of the mountains and the bare coasts of the Shadowy Seas, seeking them a home and an abiding-place; but Oromë goeth straightway out of Valinor into the forests whose every darkling glade he knew and every dim path had traversed, for he purposed to guide the troops of the Eldar from Palisor over all the wide lands west till they came to the confines of the Great Sea.

To those dark shores fared Ulmo, and strange was the roaring of the unlit sea in those most ancient days upon that rocky coast that bore still the scars of the tumultuous wrath of Melko. Falman-Ossë was little pleased to see Ulmo in the Great Seas, for Ulmo had taken that island whereon Ossë himself had drawn the Gods to Arvalin, saving them from the rising waters when Ringil and Helkar thawed beneath their blazing lamps. That was many ages past in the days when the Gods were new-come strangers in the world, and during all that time the island had floated darkly in the Shadowy Seas, desolate save when Ossë climbed its beaches on his journeys in the deeps; but now Ulmo had come upon his secret island and harnessed thereto a host of the greatest fish, and amidmost was Uin the mightiest and most ancient of whales; and he bid these put forth their strength, and they drew the island mightily to the very shores of the Great Lands, even to the coast of Hisilómë northward of the Iron Mountains whither all the deepest shades withdrew when the Sun first arose.

Now Ulmo stands there and there comes a glint in the woods that marched even down to the sea-foam in those quiet days, and behold! he hears the footsteps of the Teleri crackle in the forest, and Inwë is at their head beside the stirrup of Oromë. Grievous had been their march, and dark and difficult the way through Hisilómë the land of shade, despite the skill and power of Oromë. Indeed long after the joy of Valinor had washed its memory faint the Elves sang still sadly of it, and told tales of many of their folk whom they said and say were lost in those old forests and ever wandered there in sorrow. Still were they there long after when Men were shut in Hisilómë by Melko, and still do they dance there when

Men have wandered far over the lighter places of the Earth. Hisilómë did Men name Aryador, and the Lost Elves did they call the Shadow Folk, and feared them.

Nonetheless the most of the great companies of the Teleri came now to the beaches and climbed therefrom upon the island that Ulmo had brought. Ulmo counselled them that they wait not for the other kindreds, and though at first they will not yield, weeping at the thought, at last are they persuaded, and straightway are drawn with utmost speed beyond the Shadowy Seas and the wide bay of Arvalin to the strands of Valinor. There does the distant beauty of the trees shining down the opening in the hills enchant their hearts, and yet do they stand gazing back across the waters they have passed, for they know not where those other kindreds of their folk may be, and not even the loveliness of Valinor do they desire without them.

Then leaving them silent and wondering on the shore Ulmo draws back that great island-car to the rocks of Hisilómë, and behold, warmed by the distant gleam of Laurelin that lit upon its western edge as it lay in the Bay of Faëry, new and more tender trees begin to grow upon it, and the green of herbage is seen upon its slopes.

Now Ossë raises his head above the waves in wrath, deeming himself slighted that his aid was not sought in the ferrying of the Elves, but his own island taken unasked. Fast does he follow in Ulmo's wake and yet is left far behind, for Ulmo set the might of the Valar in Uin and the whales. Upon the cliffs there stand already the Noldoli in anguish, thinking themselves deserted in the gloom, and Nóleme Finwë who had led them thither hard upon the rear of the Teleri went among them enheartening them. Full of travail their journey too had been, for the world is wide and nigh half across it had they come from most distant Palisor, and in those days neither sun shone nor moon gleamed, and pathways were there none be it of Elves or of Men. Oromë too was far ahead riding before the Teleri upon the march and was now gone back into the lands. There the Solosimpi were astray in the forests stretching deep behind, and his horn wound faintly in the ears of those upon the shore, from whence that Vala sought them up and down the dark vales of Hisilómë.

Therefore now coming Ulmo thinks to draw the Noldoli swiftly to the strand of Valinor, returning once again for those others when Oromë shall have led them to the coast. This does he, and Falman beholds that second ferrying from afar and spumes in rage, but great is the joy of the Teleri and Noldoli upon that shore where the lights are those of late summer afternoons for the distant glow of Lindelöksë. There may I leave them for a while and tell of the strange happenings that befell the Solosimpi by reason of Ossë's wrath, and of the first dwelling upon Tol Eressëa.

Fear falls upon them in that old darkness, and beguiled by the fair music of the fay Wendelin, as other tales set forth more fully elsewhere, their leader Tinwë Linto was lost, and long they sought him, but it was in vain, and he came never again among them.⁴ When therefore they heard the horn of Oromë ringing in the forest great was their joy, and gathering to its sound soon are they led to the cliffs, and hear the murmur of the sunless sea. Long time they waited there, for Ossë cast storms and shadows about the return of Ulmo, so that he drove by devious ways, and his great fish faltered in their going; yet at the last do they too climb upon that island and are drawn towards Valinor; and one Ellu they chose in place of Tinwë, and he has ever since been named the Lord of the Solosimpi.⁵

Behold now less than half the distance have they traversed, and the Twilit Isles float still far aloof, when Ossë and Ónen waylay them in the western waters of the Great Sea ere yet the mists of the Shadowy Seas are reached. Then Ossë seizes that island in his great hand, and all the great strength of Uin may scarcely drag it onward, for at swimming and in deeds of bodily strength in the water none of the Valar, not even Ulmo's self, is Ossë's match, and indeed Ulmo was not at hand, for he was far ahead piloting the great craft in the glooms that Ossë had gathered, leading it onward with the music of his conches. Now ere he can return Ossë with Ónen's aid had brought the isle to a stand, and was anchoring it even to the sea-bottom with giant ropes of those leather-weeds and polyps that in those dark days had grown already in slow centuries to unimagined girth about the pillars of his deep-sea house. Thereto as Ulmo urges the whales to put forth all their strength and himself aids with all his godlike power, Ossë piles rocks and boulders of huge mass that Melko's ancient wrath had strewn about the seafloor, and builds these as a column beneath the island.

Vainly doth Ulmo trumpet and Uin with the flukes of his un-measured tail lash the seas to wrath, for thither Ossë now brings every kind of deep sea creature that buildeth itself a house and dwelling of stony shell; and these he planted about the base of the island: corals there were of every kind and barnacles and sponges like stone. Nonetheless for a very great while did that struggle endure, until at length Ulmo returned to Valmar in wrath and dismay. There did he warn the other Valar that the Solosimpi may not yet be brought thither, for that the isle has grown fast in the most lonely waters of the world.

There stands that island yet – indeed thou knowest it, for it is called "the Lonely Isle" – and no land may be seen for many leagues' sail from its cliffs, for the Twilit Isles upon the bosom of the Shadowy Seas are deep in the dim West, and the Magic Isles lie backward in the East.

Now therefore do the Gods bid the Elves build a dwelling, and Aulë aided them in that, but Ulmo fares back to the Lonely Island, and lo! it stands now upon a pillar of rock upon the seas' floor, and Ossë fares about it in a foam of business anchoring all the scattered islands of his domain fast to the ocean-bed. Hence came the first dwelling of the Solosimpi on the Lonely Island, and the deeper sundering of that folk from the others both in speech and customs; for know that all these great deeds of the past that make but a small tale now were not lightly achieved and in a moment of time, but rather would very many men have grown and died betwixt the binding of the Islands and the making of the Ships.

Twice now had that isle of their dwelling caught the gleam of the glorious Trees of Valinor, and so was it already fairer and more fertile and more full of sweet plants and grasses than the other places of all the world beside where great light had not been seen; indeed the Solosimpi say that birches grew there already, and many reeds, and turf there was upon the western slopes. There too were many caverns, and there was a stretching shoreland of white sand about the feet of black and purple cliffs, and here was the dwelling even in those deepest days of the Solosimpi.

There Ulmo sate upon a headland and spake to them words of comfort and of the deepest wisdom; and all sea-lore he told them, and they hearkened; and music he taught them, and they made slender pipes of shells. By reason of that labour of Ossë there are no strands so strewn with marvellous shells as were the white beaches and the sheltered coves of Tol Eressëa, and the Solosimpi dwelt much in caves, and adorned them with those sea-treasures, and the sound of their wistful piping might be heard for many a long day come faintly down the winds.

Then Falman-Ossë's heart melted towards them and he would have released them, save for the new joy and pride he had that their beauty dwelt thus amidmost of his realm, so that their pipes gave perpetual pleasure to his ear, and Uinen[6] and the Oarni and all the spirits of the waves were enamoured of them.

So danced the Solosimpi upon the waves' brink, and the love of the sea and rocky coasts entered in their hearts, even though they gazed in longing towards the happy shores whither long ago the Teleri and Noldoli had been borne.

Now these after a season took hope and their sorrow grew less bitter, learning how their kindred dwelt in no unkindly land, and Ulmo had them under his care and guardianship. Wherefore they heeded now the Gods' desire and turned to the building of their home; and Aulë taught them very much lore and skill, and Manwë also. Now Manwë loved more the Teleri, and from him and from Ómar did they learn deeper of the craft of song and poesy than all the Elves beside; but the Noldoli were beloved most by Aulë, and they learned much of his science, till their hearts became unquiet for the lust of more knowing, but they grew to great wisdom and to great subtlety of skill.

Behold there is a low place in that ring of mountains that guards Valinor, and there the shining of the Trees steals through from the plain beyond and gilds the dark waters of the bay of Arvalin,[7] but a great beach of finest sand, golden in the blaze of Laurelin, white in the light of Silpion, runs inland there, where in the trouble of the ancient seas a shadowy arm of water had groped in toward Valinor, but now there is only a slender water fringed with white. At the head of this long creek there stands a lonely hill which gazes at the loftier mountains. Now all the walls of that inlet of the seas are luxuriant with a marvellous vigour of fair trees, but the hill is covered only with a deep turf, and harebells grow atop of it ringing softly in the gentle breath of Súlimo.

Here was the place that those fair Elves bethought them to dwell, and the Gods named that hill Kôr by reason of its roundness and its smoothness. Thither did Aulë bring all the dust of magic metals that his great works had made and gathered, and he piled it about the foot of that hill, and most of this dust was of gold, and a sand of gold stretched away from the feet of Kôr out into the distance where the Two Trees blossomed. Upon the hill-top the Elves built fair abodes of shining white – of marbles and stones quarried from the Mountains of Valinor that glistened wondrously,[8] silver and gold and a substance of great hardness and white lucency that they contrived of shells melted in the dew of Silpion, and white streets there were bordered with dark trees that wound with graceful turns or climbed with flights of delicate stairs up from the plain of Valinor to topmost Kôr; and all those shining houses clomb each shoulder higher than the others till the house of Inwë was reached that was the uppermost, and had a slender silver tower shooting skyward like a needle, and a white lamp of piercing ray was set therein that shone upon the shadows of the bay, but every window of the city on the hill of Kôr looked out toward the sea.

Fountains there were of great beauty and frailty and roofs and pinnacles of bright glass and amber that was made by Palúrien and Ulmo, and trees stood thick on the white walls and terraces, and their golden fruit shone richly.

Now at the building of Kôr the Gods gave to Inwë and to Nólemë a shoot each of either of those glorious trees, and they grew to very small and slender elfin trees, but blossomed both eternally without abating, and those of the courts of Inwë were the fairest, and about them the Teleri sang songs of happiness, but others singing also fared up and down the marble flights and the wistful voices of the Noldoli were heard about the courts and chambers; but yet the Solosimpi dwelt far off amid the sea and made windy music on their pipes of shell.

Now is Ossë very fain of those Solosimpi, the shoreland pipers, and if Ulmo be not nigh he sits upon a reef at sea and many of the Oarni are by him, and hearkens to their voice and watches their flitting dances on this shore, but to Valmar he dare not fare again for the power of Ulmo in the councils of the Valar and . . . . . . . . . the wrath of that mighty one at the anchoring of the islands.

Indeed war had been but held off by the Gods, who desired peace and would not suffer Ulmo to gather the folk of the Valar and assail Ossë and rend the islands from their new roots. Therefore does Ossë sometimes ride the foams out into the bay of Arvalin[9] and gaze upon the glory on the hills, and he longs for the light and happiness upon the plain, but most for the song of birds and the swift movement of their wings into the clear air, grown weary of his silver and dark fish silent and strange amid the deep waters.

But on a day some birds came flying high from the gardens of Yavanna, and some were white and some black and some both black and white; and being dazed among the shadows they had not where to settle, and Ossë coaxed them, and they settled about his mighty shoulders, and he taught them to swim and gave them great strength of wing, for of such strength of shoulder he had more than any [?other] being and was the greatest of swimmers; and he poured fishy oils upon their feathers that they might bear the waters, and he fed them on small fish.

Then did he turn away to his own seas, and they swam about him or fared above him on low wing crying and piping; and he showed them dwellings on the Twilit Isles and even about the cliffs of Tol Eressëa, and the manner of diving and of spearing fish they learned there, and their voices became harsh for the rugged places of their life far from the soft regions of Valinor or wailing for the music of

the Solosimpi and sighing of the sea. And now have all that great
folk of gulls and seamews and petrels come into their kingdom; and
puffins are there, and eider-duck, and cormorants, and gannets, and
rock-doves, and the cliffs are full of a chattering and a smell of fish,
and great conclaves are held upon their ledges, or among spits and
reefs among the waters. But the proudest of all these birds were the
swans, and these Ossë let dwell in Tol Eressëa, [?flying] along its
coasts or paddling inland up its streams; and he set them there as a
gift and joy to the Solosimpi. But when Ulmo heard of these new
deeds he was ill-pleased for the havoc wrought amid the fishes wherewith he had filled the waters with the aid of Palúrien.

Now do the Solosimpi take great joy of [?their] birds, new creatures
to them, and of swans, and behold upon the lakes of Tol Eressëa
already they fare on rafts of fallen timber, and some harness thereto
swans and speed across the waters; but the more hardy dare out
upon the sea and the gulls draw them, and when Ulmo saw that he
was very glad. For lo! the Teleri and Noldoli complain much to
Manwë of the separation of the Solosimpi, and the Gods desire them
to be drawn to Valinor; but Ulmo cannot yet think of any device
save by help of Ossë and the Oarni, and will not be humbled to this.
But now does he fare home in haste to Aulë, and those twain got
them speedily to Tol Eressëa, and Oromë was with them, and there
is the first hewing of trees that was done in the world outside Valinor.
Now does Aulë of the sawn wood of pine and oak make great vessels
like to the bodies of swans, and these he covers with the bark of
silver birches, or . . . . . with gathered feathers of the oily plumage
of Ossë's birds, and they are nailed and [?sturdily] riveted and fastened
with silver, and he carves prows for them like the upheld necks of
swans, but they are hollow and have no feet; and by cords of great
strength and slimness are gulls and petrels harnessed to them, for
they were tame to the hands of the Solosimpi, because their hearts
were so turned by Ossë.

Now are the beaches upon the western shores of Tol Eressëa,
even at Falassë Númëa (Western Surf), thronged with that people
of the Elves, and drawn up there is a very great host indeed of those
swanships, and the cry of the gulls above them is unceasing. But the
Solosimpi arise in great numbers and climb into the hollow bodies
of these new things of Aulë's skill, and more of their kin fare ever
to the shores, marching to the sound of innumerable pipes and flutes.

Now all are embarked and the gulls fare mightily into the twilit
sky, but Aulë and Oromë are in the foremost galley and the mightiest,
and seven hundred gulls are harnessed thereto and it gleams with

silver and white feathers, and has a beak of gold and eyes of jet and amber. But Ulmo fares at the rear in his fishy car and trumpets loudly for the discomfiture of Ossë and the rescue of the Shoreland Elves.

But Ossë seeing how these birds have been to his undoing is very downcast, yet for the presence of those three Gods and indeed for his love of the Solosimpi that had grown by now very great he molested not their white fleet, and they came thus over the grey leagues of the ocean, through the dim sounds, and the mists of the Shadowy Seas, even to the first dark waters of the bay of Arvalin.

Know then that the Lonely Island is upon the confines of the Great Sea. Now that Great Sea or the Western Water is beyond the western-most limits of the Great Lands, and in it are many lands and islands ere beyond their anchorage you reach the Magic Isles, and beyond these still lies Tol Eressëa. But beyond Tol Eressëa is the misty wall and those great sea glooms beneath which lie the Shadowy Seas, and thereon float the Twilit Isles whither only pierced at clearest times the faintest twinkle of the far gleam of Silpion. But in the western-most of these stood the Tower of Pearl built in after days and much sung in song; but the Twilit Isles are held the first of the Outer Lands, which are these and Arvalin and Valinor, and Tol Eressëa is held neither of the Outer Lands or of the Great Lands where Men after roamed. But the farthest shore of those Shadowy Seas is Arvalin or Erumáni to the far south, but more northerly do they lap the very coasts of Eldamar, and here are they broader to one faring west. Beyond Arvalin tower those huge Mountains of Valinor which are in a great ring bending slowly west, but the Shadowy Seas make a vast bay to the north of Arvalin running right up to the black feet of the mountains, so that here they border upon the waters and not upon the lands, and there at the bay's innermost stands Taniquetil, glorious to behold, loftiest of all mountains clad in purest snow, looking across Arvalin half south and half north across that mighty Bay of Faëry, and so beyond the Shadowy Seas themselves, even so that all the sails upon the sunlit waters of the Great Sea in after days (when the Gods had made that lamp) and all the throngs about the western havens of the Lands of Men could be seen from its summit; and yet is that distance counted only in unimagined leagues.

But now comes that strange fleet nigh these regions and eager eyes look out. There stands Taniquetil and he is purple and dark of one side with gloom of Arvalin and of the Shadowy Seas, and lit in glory of the other by reason of the light of the Trees of Valinor. Now where the seas lapped those shores of old their waves long ere their breaking were suddenly lit by Laurelin were it day or by Silpion were it night, and the shadows of the world ceased almost abruptly and the waves laughed. But an opening in the mountains on those shores let through a glimpse of Valinor, and there stood the hill of Kôr, and the white sand runs up the creek to meet it, but its feet are in green water, and behind the sand of gold fares away farther than eye can guess, and indeed beyond Valinor who has heard or seen anything save Ulmo, yet of a certainty here spread the dark waters of the Outer Seas: tideless are they and very cool, and so thin that no boat can float upon their bosom, and few fish swim beneath their depths.

But now upon the hill of Kôr is a running and a joyous concourse, and all the people of the Teleri and Noldoli fare out of the gates and wait to welcome the coming of the fleet upon the shore. And now those ships leave the shadows and now are caught in the bright gleam about the inner bay, and now are they beached high and the Solosimpi dance and pipe, and mingle with the singing of the Teleri and the Noldoli's faint music.

Far behind lay Tol Eressëa in silence and its woods and shores were still, for nearly all that host of sea-birds had flown after the Eldar and wailed now about the shores of Eldamar: but Ossë dwelt in despondency and his silver halls in Valmar abode long empty, for he came no nearer to them for a great while than the shadow's edge, whither came the wailing of his sea-birds far away.

Now the Solosimpi abode not much in Kôr but had strange dwellings among the shoreland rocks, and Ulmo came and sat among them as aforetime in Tol Eressëa, and that was his time of greatest mirth and gentleness, and all his lore and love of music he poured out to them, and they drank it eagerly. Musics did they make and weave catching threads of sound whispered by waters in caverns or by wave-tops brushed by gentle winds; and these they twined with the wail of gulls and the echoes of their own sweet voices in the places of their home. But the Teleri and Inwir gathered [?harvest] of poesy and song, and were oftenest among the Gods, dancing in the skiey halls of Manwë for the joy of Varda of the Stars, or filling the streets and courts of Valmar with the strange loveliness of their pomps and revelry; for Oromë and for Nessa they danced upon green swards, and the glades of Valinor knew them as they flitted among the gold-lit trees, and Palúrien was very merry for the sight of them. Often were the Noldoli with them and made much music for the multitude of their harps and viols was very sweet, and Salmar loved them; but their greatest delight was in the courts of Aulë, or in their own dear homes in Kôr, fashioning many beautiful things and weaving many stories. With paintings and broidered hangings and carvings of great delicacy they filled all their city, and even did Valmar grow more fair beneath their skilful hands.

Now is to tell how the Solosimpi fared often about the near seas in their swanships, or drawn by the birds, or paddling themselves with great oars that they had made to the likeness of the webs of swan or duck; and they dredged the sea-beds and won wealth of the slim shells of those magic waters and uncounted store of pearls of a most pure and starry lustre: and these were both their glory and delight and the envy of the other Eldar who longed for them to shine in the adornment of the city of Kôr.

But those of the Noldoli whom Aulë had most deeply taught laboured in secret unceasingly, and of Aulë they had wealth of metals and of stones and marbles, and of the leave of the Valar much store too was granted to them of the radiance of Kulullin and of Telimpë held in hidden bowls. Starlight they had of Varda and strands of the bluest *ilwë* Manwë gave them; water of the most limpid pools in that creek of Kôr, and crystal drops from all the sparkling founts in the courts of Valmar. Dews did they gather in the woods of Oromë, and flower-petals of all hues and honeys in Yavanna's gardens, and they chased the beams of Laurelin and Silpion amongst the leaves. But when all this wealth of fair and radiant things was gathered, they got of the Solosimpi many shells white and pink, and purest foam, and lastly some few pearls. These pearls were their model, and the lore of Aulë and the magic of the Valar were their tools, and all the most lovely things of the substance of the Earth the matters of their craft – and therefrom did the Noldoli with great labour invent and fashion the first gems. Crystals did they make of the waters of the springs shot with the lights of Silpion; amber and chrysoprase and topaz glowed beneath their hands, and garnets and rubies they wrought, making their glassy substance as Aulë had taught them but dyeing them with the juices of roses and red flowers, and to each they gave a heart of fire. Emeralds some made of the water of the creek of Kôr and glints among the grassy glades of Valinor, and sapphires did they fashion in great profusion, [?tingeing] them with the airs of Manwë; amethysts there were and moonstones, beryls and onyx, agates of blended marbles and many lesser stones, and their hearts were very glad, nor were they content with a few, but made them jewels in immeasurable number till all the fair substances were well nigh exhausted and the great piles of those gems might not be concealed but blazed in the light like beds of brilliant flowers. Then took they those pearls that had and some of wellnigh all their jewels and made a new gem of a milky pallor shot with gleams like echoes of all other stones, and this they thought very fair, and they were opals; but still some laboured on, and of starlight and the purest water-drops, of the dew of Silpion, and the thinnest air, they made diamonds, and challenged any to make fairer.

Then arose Fëanor of the Noldoli and fared to the Solosimpi and begged a great pearl, and he got moreover an urn full of the most luminous phosphor-light gathered of foam in dark places, and with these he came home, and he took all the other gems and did gather their glint by the light of white lamps and silver candles, and he took the sheen of pearls and the faint half-colours of opals, and he [?bathed] them in phosphorescence and the radiant dew of Silpion, and but a single tiny drop of the light of Laurelin did he let fall therein, and giving all those magic lights a body to dwell in of such perfect glass as he alone could make nor even Aulë compass, so great was the slender dexterity of the fingers of Fëanor, he made a jewel — and it shone of its own . . . . . . . .[10] radiance in the uttermost dark; and he set it therein and sat a very long while and gazed at its beauty. Then he made two more, and had no more stuffs: and he fetched the others to behold his handiwork, and they were utterly amazed, and those jewels he called Silmarilli, or as we say the name in the speech of the Noldoli today Silubrilthin.[11] Wherefore though the Solosimpi held ever that none of the gems of the Noldoli, not even that majestic shimmer of diamonds, overpassed their tender pearls, yet have all held who ever saw them that the Silmarils of Fëanor were the most beautiful jewels that ever shone or [?glowed].

Now Kôr is lit with this wealth of gems and sparkles most marvellously, and all the kindred of the Eldalië are made rich in their loveliness by the generosity of the Noldoli, and the Gods' desire of their beauty is sated to the full. Sapphires in great [?wonder] were given to Manwë and his raiment was crusted with them, and Oromë had a belt of emeralds, but Yavanna loved all the gems, and Aulë's delight was in diamonds and amethysts. Melko alone was given none of them, for that he had not expiated his many crimes, and he lusted after them exceedingly, yet said nought, feigning to hold them of lesser worth than metals.

But now all the kindred of the Eldalië has found its greatest bliss, and the majesty and glory of the Gods and their home is augmented to the greatest splendour that the world has seen, and the Trees shone on Valinor, and Valinor gave back their light in a thousand scintillations of splintered colours; but the Great Lands were still and dark and very lonesome, and Ossë sat without the precincts and saw the moongleam of Silpion twinkle on the pebbles of diamonds and of crystals which the Gnomes cast in prodigality about the margin of the seas, and the glassy fragments splintered in their labouring glittered about the seaward face of Kôr; but the pools amid the dark rocks were filled with jewels, and the Solosimpi whose robes were sewn with pearls danced about them, and that was the fairest of all shores, and the music of the waters about those silver strands was beyond all sounds enchanting.

These were the rocks of Eldamar, and I saw them long ago, for Inwë was my grandsire's sire[12]; and [?even] he was the eldest of the Elves and had lived yet in majesty had he not perished in that march into the world, but Ingil his son went long ago back to Valinor and is with Manwë. And I am also akin to the shoreland dancers, and these things that I tell you I know they are true; and the magic and the wonder of the Bay of Faëry is such that none who have seen it as it was then can speak without a catch of the breath and a sinking of the voice.'

Then Meril the Queen ceased her long tale, but Eriol said nought, gazing at the long radiance of the westering sun gleaming through the apple boles, and dreaming of Faëry. At length said Meril: 'Fare now home, for the afternoon has waned, and the telling of the tale has set a weight of desire in my heart and in thine. But be in patience and bide yet ere ye seek fellowship with that sad kindred of the Island Elves.'

But Eriol said: 'Even now I know not and it passes my heart to guess how all that loveliness came to fading, or the Elves might be prevailed to depart from Eldamar.'

But Meril said: 'Nay, I have lengthened the tale too much for love of those days, and many great things lie between the making of the gems and the coming back to Tol Eressëa: but these things many know as well as I, and Lindo or Rúmil of Mar Vanwa Tyaliéva would tell them more skilfully than I.' Then did she and Eriol fare back to the house of flowers, and Eriol took his leave ere the western face of Ingil's tower was yet grown grey with dusk.

## NOTES

1  The manuscript has *Vairë*, but this can only be a slip.
2  The occurrence of the name *Telimpë* here, and again later in the tale, as also in that of *The Sun and Moon*, is curious; in the tale of *The*

*Coming of the Valar and the Building of Valinor* the name was changed at its first appearance from *Telimpë* (*Silindrin*) to *Silindrin*, and at subsequent occurrences *Silindrin* was written from the first (p. 79).

3  The manuscript has *Linwë* here, and again below; see under *Tinwë Linto* in 'Changes made to names' at the end of these notes.

4  This sentence, from 'and beguiled . . .', was added after, though not to all appearance much after, the writing of the text.

5  This sentence, from 'and one Ellu . . .', was added at the same time as that referred to in note 4.

6  The first occurrence of the form *Uinen*, and so written at the time of composition (i.e. not corrected from *Ónen*).

7  *Arvalin*: thus written at the time of composition, not emended from *Habbanan* or *Harmalin* as previously.

8  When my father wrote these texts, he wrote first in pencil, and then subsequently wrote over the top of it in ink, erasing the pencilled text – of which bits can be read here and there, and from which one can see that he altered the pencilled original somewhat as he went along. At the words 'glistened wondrously', however, he abandoned the writing of the new text in ink, and from this point we have only the original pencilled manuscript, which is in places exceedingly difficult to read, being more hasty, and also soft and smudged in the course of time. In deciphering this text I have been in places defeated, and I use brackets and question-marks to indicate uncertain readings, and rows of dots to show roughly the length of illegible words.

It is to be emphasized therefore that from here on there is only a *first draft*, and one written very rapidly, dashed onto the page.

9  *Arvalin:* here and subsequently emended from *Habbanan*; see note 7. The explanation is clearly that the name *Arvalin* came in at or before the time of the rewriting in ink over the pencilled text; though further on in the narrative we are here at an earlier stage of composition.

10  The word might be read as 'wizardous'.

11  Other forms (beginning *Sigm-*) preceded *Silubrilthin* which cannot be read with certainty. Meril speaks as if the Gnomish name was the form used in Tol Eressëa, but it is not clear why.

12  'my grandsire's sire': the original reading was 'my grandsire'.


Changes made to names in
*The Coming of the Elves and the Making of Kôr*


*Tinwë Linto* ⟨ *Linwë Tinto* (this latter is the form of the name in an interpolated passage in the preceding tale, see p. 106 note 1). At two subsequent occurrences of *Linwë* (see note 3 above) the name was

not changed, clearly through oversight; in the two added passages
where the name occurs (see notes 4 and 5 above) the form is *Tinwë*
(*Linto*).
*Inwithiel* 〈 *Gim-githil* (the same change in *The Cottage of Lost Play*, see
p. 22).
*Tinwelint* 〈 *Tintoglin.*
*Wendelin* 〈 *Tindriel* (cf. the interpolated passage in the previous tale,
p. 106 note 1).
*Arvalin* 〈 *Habbanan* throughout the tale except once, where the name
was written *Arvalin* from the first; see notes 7 and 9 above.
*Lindeloksë* 〈 *Lindelótë* (the same change in *The Coming of the Valar and
the Building of Valinor*, see p. 79).
*Erumáni* 〈 *Harwalin.*


Commentary on
*The Coming of the Elves and the Making of Kôr*


I have already (p. 111) touched on the great difference in the structure of
the narrative at the beginning of this tale, namely that here the Elves
awoke *during* Melko's captivity in Valinor, whereas in the later story it
was the very fact of the Awakening that brought the Valar to make war
on Melkor, which led to his imprisonment in Mandos. Thus the ultimately
very important matter of the capture of the Elves about Cuiviénen by
Melkor (*The Silmarillion* pp. 49–50) is necessarily entirely absent. The
release of Melko from Mandos here takes place far earlier, before the
coming of the Elvish 'ambassadors' to Valinor, and Melko plays a part in
the debate concerning the summons.
    The story of Oromë's coming upon the newly-awakened Elves is seen
to go back to the beginnings (though here Yavanna Palúrien was also
present, as it appears), but its singular beauty and force is the less for the
fact of their coming being known independently to Manwë, so that the
great Valar did not need to be told of it by Oromë. The name *Eldar* was
already in existence in Valinor before the Awakening, and the story of
its being given by Oromë ('the People of the Stars') had not arisen – as
will be seen from the Appendix on Names, *Eldar* had a quite different
etymology at this time. The later distinction between the *Eldar* who
followed Oromë on the westward journey to the ocean and the *Avari*,
the Unwilling, who would not heed the summons of the Valar, is not
present, and indeed in this tale there is no suggestion that any Elves who
heard the summons refused it; there were however, according to another
(later) tale, Elves who never left Palisor (pp. 231, 234).
    Here it is Nornorë, Herald of the Gods, not Oromë, who brought the
three Elves to Valinor and afterwards returned them to the Waters of
Awakening (and it is notable that even in this earliest version, given more

than the later to 'explanations', there is no hint of how they passed from the distant parts of the Earth to Valinor, when afterwards the Great March was only achieved with such difficulty). The story of the questioning of the three Elves by Manwë concerning the nature of their coming into the world, and their loss of all memory of what preceded their awakening, did not survive the *Lost Tales*. A further important shift in the structure is seen in Ulmo's eager support of the party favouring the summoning of the Elves to Valinor; in *The Silmarillion* (p. 52) Ulmo was the chief of those who 'held that the Quendi should be left free to walk as they would in Middle-earth'.

I set out here the early history of the names of the chief Eldar.

*Elu Thingol* (Quenya *Elwë Singollo*) began as *Linwë Tinto* (also simply *Linwë*); this was changed to *Tinwë Linto* (*Tinwë*). His Gnomish name was at first *Tintoglin*, then *Tinwelint*. He was the leader of the Solosimpi (the later Teleri) on the Great Journey, but he was beguiled in Hisilómë by the 'fay' (*Tindriel* >) *Wendelin* (later *Melian*), who came from the gardens of Lórien in Valinor; he became lord of the Elves of Hisilómë, and their daughter was *Tinúviel*. The leader of the Solosimpi in his place was, confusingly, *Ellu* (afterwards *Olwë*, brother of Elwë).

The lord of the Noldoli was *Finwë Nólemë* (also *Nólemë Finwë*, and most commonly simply *Nólemë*); the name *Finwë* remained throughout the history. In the Gnomish speech he was *Golfinweg*. His son was *Turondo*, in Gnomish *Turgon* (later Turgon became Finwë's grandson, being the son of Finwë's son Fingolfin).

The lord of the Teleri (afterwards the Vanyar) was (*Ing* >) *Inwë*, here called *Isil Inwë*, named in Gnomish (*Gim-githil* >) *Inwithiel*. His son, who built the great tower of Kortirion, was (*Ingilmo* >) *Ingil*. The 'royal clan' of the Teleri were the Inwir. Thus:

| *Lost Tales* (later forms of names) | *The Silmarillion* |
|---|---|
| Isil Inwë (Gnomish Inwithiel) lord of the Teleri  .. .. .. .. | Ingwë lord of the Vanyar |
| (his son Ingil) | |
| Finwë Nólemë (Gnomish Golfinweg) lord of the Noldoli  .. .. .. | Finwë lord of the Noldor |
| (his son Turondo, Gnomish Turgon) | (his grandson Turgon) |
| Tinwë Linto (Gnomish Tinwelint) lord of the Solosimpi, later lord of the Elves of Hisilómë | Elwë Singollo (Sindarin Elu Thingol) lord of the Teleri, later lord of the Grey-elves of Beleriand |
| Wendelin  .. .. .. .. .. | Melian |
| (their daughter Tinúviel)  .. .. .. | (their daughter Lúthien Tinúviel) |

Ellu, lord of the Solosimpi after      Olwë, lord of the Teleri
   the loss of Tinwë Linto         after the loss of his
                               brother Elwë Singollo

★

In *The Silmarillion* (p. 48) is described the second star-making of Varda
before and in preparation for the coming of the Elves:

> Then Varda went forth from the council, and she looked out from the
> height of Taniquetil, and beheld the darkness of Middle-earth beneath
> the innumerable stars, faint and far. Then she began a great labour,
> greatest of all the works of the Valar since their coming into Arda.
> She took the silver dews from the vats of Telperion, and therewith she
> made new stars and brighter against the coming of the First-born . . .

In the earliest version we see the conception already present that the stars
were created in two separate acts – that a new star-making by Varda
celebrated the coming of the Elves, even though here the Elves were
already awakened; and that the new stars were derived from the liquid
light fallen from the Moon-tree, Silpion. The passage just cited from
*The Silmarillion* goes on to tell that it was at the time of the second star-
making that Varda 'high in the north as a challenge to Melkor set the
crown of seven mighty stars to swing, Valacirca, the Sickle of the Valar
and sign of doom'; but here this is denied, and a special origin is claimed
for the Great Bear, whose stars were not of Varda's contriving but were
sparks that escaped from Aulë's forge. In the little notebook mentioned
on p. 23, which is full of disjointed jottings and hastily noted projects, a
different form of this myth appears:

> The Silver Sickle
> The seven butterflies
> Aulë was making a silver sickle. Melko interrupted his work telling him
> a lie concerning the lady Palúrien. Aulë so wroth that he broke the
> sickle with a blow. Seven sparks leapt up and winged into the heavens.
> Varda caught them and gave them a place in the heavens as a sign of
> Palúrien's honour. They fly now ever in the shape of a sickle round and
> round the pole.

There can be no doubt, I think, that this note is earlier than the present
text.

    The star Morwinyon, 'who blazes above the world's edge in the west',
is Arcturus; see the Appendix on Names. It is nowhere explained why
Morwinyon-Arcturus is mythically conceived to be always in the west.

Turning now to the Great March and the crossing of the ocean, the origin of Tol Eressëa in the island on which Ossë drew the Gods to the western lands at the time of the fall of the Lamps (see p. 70) was necessarily lost afterwards with the loss of that story, and Ossë ceased to have any proprietary right upon it. The idea that the Eldar came to the shores of the Great Lands in three large and separated companies (in the order Teleri – Noldori – Solosimpi, as later Vanyar – Noldor – Teleri) goes back to the beginning; but here the first people and the second people each crossed the ocean alone, whereas afterwards they crossed together.

In *The Silmarillion* (p. 58) 'many years' elapsed before Ulmo returned for the last of the three kindreds, the Teleri, so long a time that they came to love the coasts of Middle-earth, and Ossë was able to persuade some of them to remain (Círdan the Shipwright and the Elves of the Falas, with their havens at Brithombar and Eglarest). Of this there is no trace in the earliest account, though the germ of the idea of the long wait of the lastcomers for Ulmo's return is present. In the published version the cause of Ossë's rage against the transportation of the Eldar on the floating island has disappeared, and his motive for anchoring the island in the ocean is wholly different: indeed he did this at the bidding of Ulmo (*ibid.* p. 59), who was opposed to the summoning of the Eldar to Valinor in any case. But the anchoring of Tol Eressëa as a rebellious act of Ossë's long remained an element in the story. It is not made clear what other 'scattered islands of his domain' (p. 121) Ossë anchored to the sea-bottom; but since on the drawing of the World-Ship the Lonely Isle, the Magic Isles, and the Twilit Isles are all shown in the same way as 'standing like pinnacles from the weedy depths' (see pp. 84–6) it was probably these that Ossë now established (though Rúmil and Meril still speak of the Twilit Isles as 'floating' on the Shadowy Seas, pp. 68, 125).

In the old story it is made very clear that Tol Eressëa was made fast far out in the mid-ocean, and 'no land may be seen for many leagues' sail from its cliffs'. That was indeed the reason for its name, which was diminished when the Lonely Isle came to be set in the Bay of Eldamar. But the words used of Tol Eressëa, 'the Lonely Isle, that looks both west and east', in the last chapter of *The Silmarillion* (relatively very little worked on and revised), undoubtedly derive from the old story; in the tale of *Ælfwine of England* is seen the origin of this phrase: 'the Lonely Island looking East to the Magic Archipelago and to the lands of Men beyond it, and West into the Shadows beyond which afar off is glimpsed the Outer Land, the kingdom of the Gods'. The deep sundering of the speech of the Solosimpi from that of the other kindreds, referred to in this tale (p. 121), is preserved in *The Silmarillion*, but the idea arose in the days when Tol Eressëa was far further removed from Valinor.

As is very often to be observed in the evolution of these myths, an early idea survived in a wholly altered context: here, the growth of trees and plants on the westward slopes of the floating island began with its twice lying in the Bay of Faëry and catching the light of the Trees when the Teleri and Noldoli disembarked, and its greater beauty and fertility remained from those times after it was anchored far away from Valinor in the midst of the ocean; afterwards, this idea survived in the context of the light of the Trees passing through the Calacirya and falling on Tol Eressëa near at hand in the Bay of Eldamar. Similarly, it seems that Ulmo's instruction of the Solosimpi in music and sea-lore while sitting 'upon a headland' of Tol Eressëa after its binding to the sea-bottom was shifted to Ossë's instruction of the Teleri 'in all manner of sea-lore and sea-music' sitting on a rock off the coast of Middle-earth (*The Silmarillion* p. 58).

Very noteworthy is the account given here of the gap in the Mountains of Valinor. In *The Silmarillion* the Valar made this gap, the Calacirya or Pass of Light, only after the coming of the Eldar to Aman, for 'even among the radiant flowers of the Tree-lit gardens of Valinor they [the Vanyar and Noldor] longed still at times to see the stars' (p. 59); whereas in this tale it was a 'natural' feature, associated with a long creek thrust in from the sea.

From the account of the coming of the Elves to the shores of the Great Lands it is seen (p. 118) that Hisilómë was a region bordering the Great Sea, agreeing with its identification as the region marked *g* on the earliest map, see pp. 81, 112; and most remarkably we meet here the idea that Men were shut in Hisilómë by Melko, an idea that survived right through to the final form in which the Easterling Men were rewarded after the Nirnaeth Arnoediad for their treacherous service to Morgoth by being confined in Hithlum (*The Silmarillion* p. 195).

In the description of the hill and city of Kôr appear several features that were never lost in the later accounts of Tirion upon Túna. Cf. *The Silmarillion* p. 59:

> Upon the crown of Túna the city of the Elves was built, the white walls and terraces of Tirion; and the highest of the towers of that city was the Tower of Ingwë, Mindon Eldaliéva, whose silver lamp shone far out into the mists of the sea.

The dust of gold and 'magic metals' that Aulë piled about the feet of Kôr powdered the shoes and clothing of Eärendil when he climbed the 'long white stairs' of Tirion (*ibid.* p. 248).

It is not said here whether the shoots of Laurelin and Silpion that the Gods gave to Inwë and Nólemë, which 'blossomed both eternally without abating', were also givers of light, but later in the *Lost Tales* (p. 213), after the Flight of the Noldoli, the Trees of Kôr are again referred to, and there the trees given to Inwë 'shone still', while the trees given to Nólemë had been uprooted and 'were gone no one knew whither.' In *The Silmaril-lion* it is said that Yavanna made for the Vanyar and the Noldor 'a tree like to a lesser image of Telperion, save that it did not give light of its own being'; it was 'planted in the courts beneath the Mindon and there flourished, and its seedlings were many in Eldamar'. Thence came the Tree of Tol Eressëa.

In connection with this description of the city of the Elves in Valinor I give here a poem entitled *Kôr*. It was written on April 30th, 1915 (two days after *Goblin Feet* and *You and Me*, see pp. 27, 32), and two texts of it are extant: the first, in manuscript, has a subtitle 'In a City Lost and Dead'. The second, a typescript, was apparently first entitled *Kôr*, but this was changed to *The City of the Gods*, and the subtitle erased; and with this title the poem was published at Leeds in 1923.* No changes were made to the text except that in the penultimate line 'no bird sings' was altered already in the manuscript to 'no voice stirs'. It seems possible, especially in view of the original subtitle, that the poem described Kôr after the Elves had left it.

### Kôr

#### In a City Lost and Dead

A sable hill, gigantic, rampart-crowned
Stands gazing out across an azure sea
Under an azure sky, on whose dark ground
Impearled as 'gainst a floor of porphyry
Gleam marble temples white, and dazzling halls;
And tawny shadows fingered long are made
In fretted bars upon their ivory walls
By massy trees rock-rooted in the shade
Like stony chiselled pillars of the vault
With shaft and capital of black basalt.
There slow forgotten days for ever reap
The silent shadows counting out rich hours;
And no voice stirs; and all the marble towers
White, hot and soundless, ever burn and sleep.

★

The story of the evolution of sea-birds by Ossë, and of how the Solosimpi went at last to Valinor in ships of swan-shape drawn by gulls, to the chagrin of Ossë, is greatly at variance with the account in *The Silmarillion* (p. 61):

Through a long age they [the Teleri] dwelt in Tol Eressëa; but slowly their hearts were changed, and were drawn towards the light that flowed out over the sea to the Lonely Isle. They were torn between the love of the music of the waves upon their shores, and the desire to see

* Publication was in a magazine called *The Microcosm*, edited by Dorothy Ratcliffe, Volume VIII no. 1, Spring 1923.

again their kindred and to look upon the splendour of Valinor; but in the end desire of the light was the stronger. Therefore Ulmo, submitting to the will of the Valar, sent to them Ossë, their friend, and he though grieving taught them the craft of ship-building; and when their ships were built he brought them as his parting gift many strong-winged swans. Then the swans drew the white ships of the Teleri over the windless sea; and thus at last and latest they came to Aman and the shores of Eldamar.

But the swans remained as a gift of Ossë to the Elves of Tol Eressëa, and the ships of the Teleri retained the form of the ships built by Aulë for the Solosimpi: they 'were made in the likeness of swans, with beaks of gold and eyes of gold and jet' (*ibid.*).

The passage of geographical description that follows (p. 125) is curious; for it is extremely similar to (and even in some phrases identical with) that in the tale of *The Coming of the Valar and the Building of Valinor*, p. 68. An explanation of this repetition is suggested below. This second version gives in fact little new information, its chief difference of substance being the mention of Tol Eressëa. It is now made clear that the Shadowy Seas were a region of the Great Sea west of Tol Eressëa. In *The Silmarillion* (p. 102) the conception had changed, with the change in the anchorage of Tol Eressëa: at the time of the Hiding of Valinor

the Enchanted Isles were set, and all the seas about them were filled with shadows and bewilderment. And these isles were strung as a net in the Shadowy Seas from the north to the south, before Tol Eressëa, the Lonely Isle, is reached by one sailing west.

There is a further element of repetition in the account of the gap in the Mountains of Valinor and the hill of Kôr at the head of the creek (p. 126), which have already been described earlier in this same tale (p. 122). The explanation of this repetition is almost certainly to be found in the two layers of composition in this tale (see note 8 above); for the first of these passages is in the revised portion and the second in the original, pencilled text. My father in his revision had, I think, simply taken in earlier the passage concerning the gap in the Mountains, the hill and the creek, and if he had continued the revision of the tale to its end the second passage would have been excised. This explanation may be suggested also for the repetition of the passage concerning the islands in the Great Sea and the coast of Valinor from the tale of *The Coming of the Valar and the Building of Valinor*; but in that case the implication must be that the revision in ink over the original pencilled manuscript was carried out when the latter was already far ahead in the narrative.

In *The Silmarillion* the entire account of the making of gem-stones by the Noldoli has become compressed into these words (p. 60):

> And it came to pass that the masons of the house of Finwë, quarrying in the hills after stone (for they delighted in the building of high towers), first discovered the earth-gems, and brought them forth in countless myriads; and they devised tools for the cutting and shaping of gems, and carved them in many forms. They hoarded them not, but gave them freely, and by their labour enriched all Valinor.

Thus the rhapsodic account at the end of this tale of the making of gems out of 'magic' materials – starlight, and *ilwë*, dews and petals, glassy substances dyed with the juice of flowers – was abandoned, and the Noldor became miners, skilful indeed, but mining only what was there to be found in the rocks of Valinor. On the other hand, in an earlier passage in *The Silmarillion* (p. 39), the old idea is retained: 'The Noldor also it was who first achieved the making of gems.' It need not be said that everything was to be gained by the discretion of the later writing; in this early narrative the Silmarils are not strongly marked out from the accumulated wonder of all the rest of the gems of the Noldoli's making.

Features that remained are the generosity of the Noldor in the giving of their gems and the scattering of them on the shores (cf. *The Silmarillion* p. 61: 'Many jewels the Noldor gave them [the Teleri], opals and diamonds and pale crystals, which they strewed upon the shores and scattered in the pools'); the pearls that the Teleri got from the sea (*ibid.*); the sapphires that the Noldor gave to Manwë ('His sceptre was of sapphire, which the Noldor wrought for him', *ibid.* p. 40); and, of course, Fëanor as the maker of the Silmarils – although, as will be seen in the next tale, Fëanor was not yet the son of Finwë (Nólemë).

★

I conclude this commentary with another early poem that bears upon the matter of this tale. It is said in the tale (p. 119) that Men in Hisilómë feared the Lost Elves, calling them the Shadow Folk, and that their name for the land was *Aryador*. The meaning of this is given in the early Gnomish word-list as 'land or place of shadow' (cf. the meanings of *Hisilómë* and *Dor Lómin*, p. 112).

The poem is called *A Song of Aryador*, and is extant in two copies; according to notes on these it was written in an army camp near Lichfield on September 12th, 1915. It was never, to my knowledge, printed. The first copy, in manuscript, has the title also in Old English: *An léoþ Éargedores*; the second, in typescript, has virtually no differences in the text, but it may be noted that the first word of the third verse, 'She', is an emendation from 'He' in both copies.

*A Song of Aryador*

In the vales of Aryador
By the wooded inland shore
Green the lakeward bents and meads
Sloping down to murmurous reeds
That whisper in the dusk o'er Aryador:

'Do you hear the many bells
Of the goats upon the fells
Where the valley tumbles downward from the pines?
Do you hear the blue woods moan
When the Sun has gone alone
To hunt the mountain-shadows in the pines?

She is lost among the hills
And the upland slowly fills
With the shadow-folk that murmur in the fern;
And still there are the bells
And the voices on the fells
While Eastward a few stars begin to burn.

Men are kindling tiny gleams
Far below by mountain-streams
Where they dwell among the beechwoods near the shore,
But the great woods on the height
Watch the waning western light
And whisper to the wind of things of yore,

When the valley was unknown,
And the waters roared alone,
And the shadow-folk danced downward all the night,
When the Sun had fared abroad
Through great forests unexplored
And the woods were full of wandering beams of light.

Then were voices on the fells
And a sound of ghostly bells
And a march of shadow-people o'er the height.
In the mountains by the shore
In forgotten Aryador
There was dancing and was ringing;
There were shadow-people singing
Ancient songs of olden gods in Aryador.'

# VI
# THE THEFT OF MELKO
# AND THE DARKENING OF VALINOR

This title is again taken from the cover of the book containing the text; the narrative, still written rapidly in pencil (see note 8 to the last chapter), with some emendations from the same time or later, continues without a break.

Now came Eriol home to the Cottage of Lost Play, and his love for all the things that he saw about him and his desire to understand them all became more deep. Continually did he thirst to know yet more of the history of the Eldar; nor did he ever fail to be among those who fared each evening to the Room of the Tale-fire; and so on a time when he had already sojourned some while as a guest of Vairë and Lindo it so passed that Lindo at his entreaty spake thus from his deep chair:

'Listen then, O Eriol, if thou wouldst [know] how it so came that the loveliness of Valinor was abated, or the Elves might ever be constrained to leave the shores of Eldamar. It may well be that you know already that Melko dwelt in Valmar as a servant in the house of Tulkas in those days of the joy of the Eldalië; there did he nurse his hatred of the Gods, and his consuming jealousy of the Eldar, but it was his lust for the beauty of the gems for all his feigned indifference that in the end overbore his patience and caused him to design deep and evilly.

Now the Noldoli alone at those times had the art of fashioning these beautiful things, and despite their rich gifts to all whom they loved the treasure they possessed of them was beyond count the greatest, wherefore Melko whenever he may consorteth with them, speaking cunning words. In this way for long he sought to beg gifts of jewels for himself, and maybe also catching the unwary to learn something of their hidden art, but when none of these devices succeeded he sought to sow evil desires and discords among the Gnomes, telling them that lie concerning the Council when the Eldar were first bidden to Valinor.[1] "Slaves are ye," he would say, "or children, an you will, bidden play with toys and seek not to stray or know too much. Good days mayhap the Valar give you, as

ye say; seek but to cross their walls and ye shall know the hardness
of their hearts. Lo, they use your skill, and to your beauty they hold
fast as an adornment of their realms. This is not love, but selfish
desire – make test of it. Ask for your inheritance that Ilúvatar designed
for you – the whole wide world to roam, with all its mysteries to
explore, and all its substances to be material of such mighty crafts
as never can be realised in these narrow gardens penned by the
mountains, hemmed in by the impassable sea."

Hearing these things, despite the true knowledge which Nólemë
had and spread abroad, there were many who hearkened with half
their hearts to Melko, and restlessness grew amongst them, and
Melko poured oil on their smouldering desires. From him they
learnt many things it were not good for any but the great Valar to
know, for being half-comprehended such deep and hidden things
slay happiness; and besides many of the sayings of Melko were
cunning lies or were but partly true, and the Noldoli ceased to sing,
and their viols fell silent upon the hill of Kôr, for their hearts grew
somewhat older as their lore grew deeper and their desires more
swollen, and the books of their wisdom were multiplied as the leaves
of the forest. For know that in those days Aulë aided by the Gnomes
contrived alphabets and scripts, and on the walls of Kôr were many
dark tales written in pictured symbols, and runes of great beauty
were drawn there too or carved upon stones, and Eärendel read
many a wondrous tale there long ago, and mayhap still is many a
one still there to read, if it be not corrupted into dust. The other
Elves heeded these things not over much, and were at times sad and
fearful at the lessened gladness of their kinsmen. Great mirth had
Melko at this and wrought in patience biding his time, yet no nearer
did he get to his end, for despite all his labours the glory of the
Trees and the beauty of the gems and the memory of the dark ways
from Palisor held back the Noldoli – and ever Nólemë spake against
Melko, calming their restlessness and discontents.

At length so great became his care that he took counsel with
Fëanor, and even with Inwë and Ellu Melemno (who then led the
Solosimpi), and took their rede that Manwë himself be told of the
dark ways of Melko.

And Melko knowing this was in great anger against the Gnomes,
and going first before Manwë bowed very low, and said how the
Noldoli dared murmur to his ears against Manwë's lordship, claiming
that in skill and beauty they (whom Ilúvatar had destined to possess
all the earth) far surpassed the Valar, for whom they must labour
unrecompensed. Heavy was Manwë's heart at these words, for he

had feared long that that great amity of the Valar and Eldar be ever perchance broken, knowing that the Elves were children of the world and must one day return to her bosom. Nay, who shall say but that all these deeds, even the seeming needless evil of Melko, were but a portion of the destiny of old? Yet cold was the Lord of the Gods to the informer, and lo! even as he questioned him further the embassy of Nólemë came thither, and being granted leave spake the truth before him. By reason of the presence of Melko perchance they spoke somewhat less skilfully in their own cause than they might, and perchance even the heart of Manwë Súlimo was tainted with the poison of Melko's words, for that venom of Melko's malice is very strong and subtle indeed.

Howbeit, both Melko and the Noldoli were chidden and dismissed. Melko indeed was bidden get him back to Mandos and there dwell awhile in penitence, nor dare to walk in Valmar for many moons, not until the great festival that now approached had come and gone; but Manwë fearing lest the pollution of their discontent spread among the other kindreds commanded Aulë to find other places and thither lead the Noldoli, and build them a new town where they might dwell.

Great was the sorrow upon the hill of Kôr when those tidings were brought thither, and though all were wroth with the treachery of Melko, yet was there now a new bitterness against the Gods, and the murmuring louder than before.

A little stream, and its name was *Híri*, ran down from the hills, northward of the opening to the coast where Kôr was built, and it wandered thence across the plain no one knew whither. Maybe it found the Outer Seas, for north of the roots of Silpion it dived into the earth and there was a rugged place and a rock-ringed dale; and here the Noldoli purposed to abide, or rather to await the passing of wrath from Manwë's heart, for in no way as yet would they accept the thought of leaving Kôr for ever.

Caves they made in the walls of that dale, and thither they bore their wealth of gems, of gold and silver and fair things; but their ancient homes in Kôr were empty of their voices, filled only with their paintings and their books of lore, and the streets of Kôr and all the ways of Valmar shone still with [?gems] and carven marbles telling of the days of the happiness of the Gnomes that cometh now upon its waning.

Now Melko gets him gone to Mandos, and far from Valinor he plans rebellion and vengeance upon both Gnomes and Gods. Indeed, dwelling for nigh three ages in the vaults of Mandos Melko had made

friends to himself of certain gloomy spirits there and perverted them
to ill, promising them great lands and regions on the Earth for their
[?having] if they aided him when he called on them in need; and
now he gathers them to him in the dark ravines of the mountains
about Mandos. Thence sends he spies, invisible as fleeting shades
when Silpion is in bloom, and learns of those doings of the Noldoli
and of all that passes in the plain. Now soon after it chanced indeed
that the Valar and Eldar held a great feast, even that one that Manwë
had spoken of, bidding Melko rid Valmar of his presence at that time;
for know that they made merry on one day every seventh year to
celebrate the coming of the Eldar into Valinor, and every third year
a lesser feast to commemorate the coming of the white fleet of the
Solosimpi to the shores of Eldamar; but at every twenty-first year
when both these feasts fell together they held one of the greatest
magnificence, and it endured for seven days, and for this cause such
years were called "Years of Double Mirth";* and these feasts all
the Koreldar wherever they now may be in the wide world still do
celebrate. Now that feast that approacheth is one of Double Mirth,
and all the hosts of the Gods and Elves made ready to celebrate it
most gloriously. Pomps there were and long processions of the
Elves, dancing and singing, that wound from Kôr to Valmar's gates.
A road had been laid against this festival from the westward gate of
Kôr even to the turrets of the mighty arch which opened in the walls
of Valmar northward towards the Trees. Of white marble it was and
many a gentle stream flowing from the far mountains crossed its
path. Here it would leap into slender bridges marvellously fenced
with delicate balustrades that shone like pearls; scarcely did these
clear the water, so that lilies of great beauty growing upon the bosom
of the streams that fared but gently in the plain thrust their wide
blossoms about its borders and iris marched along its flanks; for
by cunning delving runnels of clearest water were made to flow from
stream to stream bordering that whole long way with the cool noise
of rippling water. At places mighty trees grew on either side, or at
places the road would open to a glade and fountains spring by magic
high into the air for the refreshment of all who sped that way.

Now came the Teleri led by the white-robed people of the Inwir,
and the throbbing of their congregated harps beat the air most
sweetly; and after them went the Noldoli mingling once more with
their own dear folk by Manwë's clemency, that his festival might be
duly kept, but the music that their viols and instruments awoke was
now more sweetly sad than ever before. And last came the people

* Added in the margin here: *Samírien.*

of the shores, and their piping blent with voices brought the sense
of tides and murmurous waves and the wailing cry of the coast-
loving birds thus inland deep upon the plain.

Then was all that host marshalled before the gate of Valmar, and
at the word and sign from Inwë as one voice they burst in unison into
the Song of Light. This had Lirillo² written and taught them, and it
told of the longing of the Elves for light, of their dread journey
through the dark world led by the desire of the Two Trees, and sang
of their utmost joy beholding the faces of the Gods and their renewed
desire once more to enter Valmar and tread the Valar's blessed
courts. Then did the gates of Valmar open and Nornorë bid them
enter, and all that bright company passed through. There Varda
met them, standing amid the companies of the Mánir and the Súruli,
and all the Gods made them welcome, and feasts there were in all
the great halls thereafter.

Now their custom was on the third day to robe themselves all in
white and blue and ascend to the heights of Taniquetil, and there
would Manwë speak to them as he thought fit of the Music of the
Ainur and the glory of Ilúvatar, and of things to be and that had been.
And on that day would Kôr and Valmar be silent and still, but the
roof of the world and the slope of Taniquetil shine with the gleaming
raiment of the Gods and Elves, and all the mountains echo with
their speech – but afterward on the last day of merriment the Gods
would come to Kôr and sit upon the slopes of its bright hill, gazing in
love upon that slender town, and thereafter blessing it in the name
of Ilúvatar would depart ere Silpion came to bloom; and so would
end the days of Double Mirth.

But in this fateful year Melko dared of his blasphemous heart
to choose that very day of Manwë's speech upon Taniquetil for the
carrying out of his designs; for then would Kôr and Valmar and the
rock-ringed dale of Sirnúmen be unguarded: for against whom
indeed had Elf or Vala need to guard in those old days?

Creeping then down with his dark people on the third day of
Samírien, as that feast was named, he passed the dark halls of
Makar's abode (for even that wild Vala had gone to Valmar to honour
the time, and indeed all of the Gods went there saving Fui and
Vefántur only, and Ossë even was there, dissembling for those seven
days his feud and jealousy with Ulmo). Here does a thought come to
Melko's heart, and he arms himself and his band stealthily with
swords very sharp and cruel, and this was well for them: for now
do they all steal into the vale of Sirnúmen where the Noldoli had
their present dwelling, and behold the Gnomes by reason of the

workings in their hearts of Melko's own teaching had become wary and suspicious beyond the wont of the Eldar of those days. Guards of some strength were set over the treasures there that went not to the feast, albeit this was contrary to the customs and ordinances of the Gods. Now is there suddenly bitter war awake in the heart of Valinor and those guards are slain, even while the peace and gladness upon Taniquetil afar is very great – indeed for that reason none heard their cries. Now Melko knew that it was indeed war for ever between himself and all those other folk of Valinor, for he had slain the Noldoli – guests of the Valar – before the doors of their own homes. With his own hand indeed he slew Bruithwir father of Fëanor,[3] and bursting into that rocky house that he defended laid hands upon those most glorious gems, even the Silmarils, shut in a casket of ivory. Now all that great treasury of gems he despoiled, and lading himself and all his companions to the utmost he seeks how he may escape.

Know then that Oromë had great stables and a breeding ground of good horses not so far from this spot, where a wild forest land had grown up. Thither Melko steals, and a herd of black horses he captures, cowing them with the terror that he could wield. Astride those his whole company of thieves rides far away, after destroying what things of lesser value they deemed it impossible to carry thence. Making a wide circuit and faring with the speed of hurricanes such as only the divine horses of Oromë ridden by the children of the Gods could compass they pass far to the west of Valmar in the un-tracked regions where the light of the Trees was thin. Long ere the folk had come down from Taniquetil and long ere the end of the feast or ever the Noldoli fared back to find their homes despoiled, Melko and his [?thieves] were ridden to the deep south, and finding there a low place in the hills they passed into the plains of Eruman. Well might Aulë and Tulkas bemoan their carelessness in leaving that low place long ago when they reared those hills to fend all evil from the plain – for that was the place where they were accustomed to enter Valinor after their quarryings in the fields of Arvalin.[4] It is said indeed that this riding in a half-circle, laborious and perilous as it was, was at first no part of Melko's design, for rather had he purposed to get to northward over the passes nigh to Mandos; but this he was warned might not be done, for Mandos and Fui never left those realms, and all the ravines and chasms of the northward mountains were infested with their folk, nor for all his gloom was Mandos any rebel against Manwë or an abetter of evil deeds.

Far to the north if one may endure the colds as Melko could it is said in ancient lore that the Great Seas narrow to a little thing, and without aid of ships Melko and his company might thus have got into the world safely; but this was not done, and the sad tale took its appointed course, or the Two Trees might yet have shone and the Elves sung still in Valinor.

At length that daytide of festival is over and the Gods are turned back towards Valmar, treading the white road from Kôr. The lights twinkle in the city of the Elves and peace dwells there, but the Noldoli fare over the plain to Sirnúmen sadly. Silpion is gleaming in that hour, and ere it wanes the first lament for the dead that was heard in Valinor rises from that rocky vale, for Fëanor laments the death of Bruithwir; and many of the Gnomes beside find that the spirits of their dead have winged their way to Vê. Then messengers ride hastily to Valmar bearing tidings of the deeds, and there they find Manwë, for he has not yet left that town for his abode upon Taniquetil.

"Alas, O Manwë Súlimo," they cry, "evil has pierced the Mountains of Valinor and fallen upon Sirnúmen of the Plain. There lies Bruithwir sire of Fëanor[5] dead and many of the Noldoli beside, and all our treasury of gems and fair things and the loving travail of our hands and hearts through many years is stolen away. Whither O Manwë whose eyes see all things? Who has done this evil, for the Noldoli cry for vengeance, O most [?just] one!"

Then said Manwë to them: "Behold O Children of the Noldoli, my heart is sad towards you, for the poison of Melko has already changed you, and covetice has entered your hearts. Lo! had ye not thought your gems and fabrics[6] of better worth than the festival of the folk or the ordinances of Manwë your lord, this had not been, and Bruithwir go-Maidros and those other hapless ones still had lived, and your jewels been in no greater peril. Nay, my wisdom teaches me that because of the death of Bruithwir and his comrades shall the greatest evils fall on Gods and Elves, and Men to be. Without the Gods who brought you to the light and gave you all the materials of your craft, teaching your first ignorance, none of these fair things you love now so well ever would have been; what has been done may again be done, for the power of the Valar does not change; but of more worth than all the glory of Valinor and all the grace and beauty of Kôr is peace and happiness and wisdom, and these once lost are harder to recapture. Cease then to murmur and to speak against the Valar, or to set yourselves in your hearts as equals to their majesty; rather depart now in penitence knowing full well that Melko has wrought this evil against you, and that your secret trafficking with him has brought you all this loss and sorrow. Trust him not again therefore, nor any others that whisper secret words of discontent among you, for its fruit is humiliation and dismay."

And the embassy was abashed and afraid and went back unto Sirnúmen utterly cast down; yet was Manwë's heart heavier than theirs, for things had gone ill indeed, and yet he foresaw that worse would be; and so did the destinies of the Gods work out, for lo! to the Noldoli Manwë's words seemed cold and heartless, and they knew not his sorrow and his tenderness; and Manwë thought them strangely changed and turned to covetice, who longed but for comfort, being like children very full of the loss of their fair things.

Now Melko findeth himself in the wastes of Arvalin and knoweth not how he may escape, for the gloom there is very great, and he knoweth not those regions that stretch there unto the utmost south. Therefore he sent a messenger claiming the inviolable right of a herald (albeit this was a renegade servant of Mandos whom Melko had perverted) over the pass to Valinor, and there standing before the gates of Valmar[7] he demanded audience of the Gods; and it was asked of him whence he came, and he said from Ainu Melko, and Tulkas would have hurled stones at him from the walls and slain him, but the others as yet suffered him not to be mishandled, but despite their anger and loathing they admitted him to the great square of gold that was before Aulë's courts. And at the same hour riders were sent to Kôr and to Sirnúmen summoning the Elves, for it was guessed that this matter touched them near. When all was made ready the messenger took stand beside the needle of pure gold whereon Aulë had written the story of the kindling of the Tree of gold (in Lórien's courts stood one of silver with another tale), and on a sudden Manwë said: "Speak!" and his voice was as a clap of wrathful thunder, and the courts rang, but the envoy unabashed uttered his message, saying:

"The Lord Melko, ruler of the world from the darkest east to the outer slopes of the Mountains of Valinor unto his kinsmen the Ainur. Behold, in compensation for divers grievous affronts and for long times of unjust imprisonment despite his noble estate and blood that he has at your hands suffered, now has he taken, as is due to him, certain small treasures held by the Noldoli, your slaves. Great grief is it to him that of these he has slain some, in that they would do him hurt in the evil of their hearts; yet their blasphemous intent will he now put from memory, and all the past injuries that ye the

Gods have wrought him will he so far forget as once again to show
his presence in that place that is called Valmar, if ye will hearken to
his conditions and fulfil them. For know that the Noldoli shall be
his servants and shall adorn him a house; moreover of right he does
demand —" but hereon even as the herald lifted up his voice yet
louder swelling with his words of insolence, so great became the
wrath of the Valar that Tulkas and several of his house leapt down
and seizing him stopped his mouth, and the place of council was in
uproar. Indeed Melko had not thought to gain aught but time and
the confusion of the Valar by this embassage of insolence.

Then Manwë bid him unhand the herald, but the Gods arose
crying with one voice: "This is no herald, but a rebel, a thief, and
a murderer." "He hath defiled the sanctity of Valinor," shouted
Tulkas, "and cast his insolence in our teeth." Now the mind of all
the Elves was as one in this matter. Hope they had none of the
recovery of the jewels save by the capture of Melko, which was now
a matter beyond hope, but they would have no parley with Melko
whatsoever and would treat him as an outlaw and all his folk. (And
this was the meaning of Manwë, saying that the death of Bruithwir
would be the root of the greatest evil, for it was that slaying that most
inflamed both Gods and Elves.)[8]

To this end they spoke in the ears of Varda and Aulë, and Varda
befriended their cause before Manwë, and Aulë yet more stoutly, for
his heart was sore too for the theft of so many things of exquisite
craft and workmanship; but Tulkas Poldórëa needed no pleading,
being hot with ire. Now these great advocates moved the council
with their words, so that in the end it is Manwë's doom that word
he sent back to Melko rejecting him and his words and outlawing
him and all his followers from Valinor for ever. These words would
he now speak to the envoy, bidding him begone to his master with
them, but the folk of the Vali and the Elves would have none of it,
and led by Tulkas they took that renegade to the topmost peak of
Taniquetil, and there declaring him no herald and taking the mountain and the stars to witness of the same they cast him to the boulders
of Arvalien so that he was slain, and Mandos received him into his
deepest caves.

Then Manwë seeing in this rebellion and their violent deed the
seed of bitterness cast down his sceptre and wept; but the others
spake unto Sorontur King of Eagles upon Taniquetil and by him
were the words of Manwë sent to Melko: "Begone for ever, O
accursed, nor dare to parley more with Gods or Elves. Neither shall
thy foot nor that of any who serve thee tread the soil of Valinor again

while the world endures." And Sorontur sought out Melko and said as he was bidden, and of the death of his envoy he told [?too]. Then Melko would have slain Sorontur, being mad with anger at the death of his messenger; and verily this deed was not in accord with the strict justice of the Gods, yet was the anger of those at Valmar sorely tempted; but Melko has ever cast it against the Gods most bitterly, twisting it into a black tale of wrong; and between that evil one and Sorontur has there ever since been hate and war, and that was most bitter when Sorontur and his folk fared to the Iron Mountains and there abode, watching all that Melko did.

Now Aulë goeth to Manwë and speaketh enheartening words, saying how Valmar still stands and the Mountains are high and a sure bulwark against evil. "Lo! if Melko sets once more turmoils in the world, was he not bound in chains aforetime, and so may be again: – but behold, soon will I and Tulkas fill that pass that leads to Erumáni and the seas, that Melko come not ever that way hither again."

But Manwë and Aulë plan to set guards about all those mountains until such time as Melko's deeds and places of abode without become known.

Then does Aulë fall to speech with Manwë concerning the Noldoli, and he pleads much for them, saying that Manwë wrought with anxiety has done hardly by them, for that of Melko in sooth alone is the evil come, whereas the Eldar are not slaves nor servants but beings of a wondrous sweetness and beauty – that they were guests for ever of the Gods. Therefore does Manwë bid them now, an they will, go back to Kôr, and, if they so desire, busy themselves in fashioning gems and fabrics anew, and all things of beauty and cost that they may need in their labour shall be given to them even more lavishly than before.

But when Fëanor heard this saying, he said: "Yea, but who shall give us back the joyous heart without which works of loveliness and magic cannot be? – and Bruithwir is dead, and my heart also." Many nonetheless went then back to Kôr, and some semblance of old joy is then restored, though for the lessened happiness of their hearts their labours do not bring forth gems of the old lustre and glory. But Fëanor dwelt in sorrow with a few folk in Sirnúmen, and though he sought day and night to do so he could in no wise make other jewels like to the Silmarils of old, that Melko snatched away; nor indeed has any craftsman ever done so since. At length does he abandon the attempt, sitting rather beside the tomb of Bruithwir, that is called the Mound of the First Sorrow,* and is well named for

* In the margin are written Gnomish names: 'Cùm a Gumlaith or Cùm a Thegranaithos'.

all the woe that came from the death of him who was laid there. There brooded Fëanor bitter thoughts, till his brain grew dazed by the black vapours of his heart, and he arose and went to Kôr. There did he speak to the Gnomes, dwelling on their wrongs and sorrows and their minished wealth and glory – bidding them leave this prison-house and get them into the world. "As cowards have the Valar become; but the hearts of the Eldar are not weak, and we will see what is our own, and if we may not get it by stealth we will do so by violence. There shall be war between the Children of Ilúvatar and Ainu Melko. What if we perish in our quest? The dark halls of Vê be little worse than this bright prison . . . ."9 And he prevailed thus upon some to go before Manwë with himself and demand that the Noldoli be suffered to leave Valinor in peace and set safely by the Gods upon the shores of the world whence they had of old been ferried.

Then Manwë was grieved by their request and forbade the Gnomes to utter such words in Kôr if they desired still to dwell there among the other Elves; but then changing from harshness he told them many things concerning the world and its fashion and the dangers that were already there, and the worse that might soon come to be by reason of Melko's return. "My heart feels, and my wisdom tells me," said he, "that no great age of time will now elapse ere those other Children of Ilúvatar, the fathers of the fathers of Men, do come into the world – and behold it is of the unalterable Music of the Ainur that the world come in the end for a great while under the sway of Men; yet whether it shall be for happiness or sorrow Ilúvatar has not revealed, and I would not have strife or fear or anger come ever between the different Children of Ilúvatar, and fain would I for many an age yet leave the world empty of beings who might strive against the new-come Men and do hurt to them ere their clans be grown to strength, while the nations and peoples of the Earth are yet infants." To this he added many words concerning Men and their nature and the things that would befall them, and the Noldoli were amazed, for they had not heard the Valar speak of Men, save very seldom; and had not then heeded overmuch, deeming these creatures weak and blind and clumsy and beset with death, nor in any ways likely to match the glory of the Eldalië. Now therefore, although Manwë had unburdened his heart in this way hoping that the Noldoli, seeing that he did not labour without a purpose or a reason, would grow calmer and more trustful of his love, rather were they astonished to discover that the Ainur made the thought of Men so great a matter, and Manwë's words achieved the opposite of his wish; for Fëanor in his misery twisted them into an evil semblance, when standing again before the throng of Kôr he spake these words:

"Lo, now do we know the reason of our transportation hither as it were cargoes of fair slaves! Now at length are we told to what end we are guarded here, robbed of our heritage in the world, ruling not the wide lands, lest perchance we yield them not to a race unborn. To these foresooth – a sad folk, beset with swift mortality, a race of burrowers in the dark, clumsy of hand, untuned to songs or musics, who shall dully labour at the soil with their rude tools, to these whom still he says are of Ilúvatar would Manwë Súlimo lordling of the Ainur give the world and all the wonders of its land, all its hidden substances – give it to these, that is our inheritance. Or what is this talk of the dangers of the world? A trick to deceive us; a mask of words! O all ye children of the Noldoli, whomso will no longer be house-thralls of the Gods however softly held, arise I bid ye and get you from Valinor, for now is the hour come and the world awaits."

In sooth it is a matter for great wonder, the subtle cunning of Melko – for in those wild words who shall say that there lurked not a sting of the minutest truth, nor fail to marvel seeing the very words of Melko pouring from Fëanor his foe, who knew not nor remembered whence was the fountain of these thoughts; yet perchance the [?outmost] origin of these sad things was before Melko himself, and such things must be – and the mystery of the jealousy of Elves and Men is an unsolved riddle, one of the sorrows at the world's dim roots.

Howso these deep things be, the fierce words of Fëanor got him instantly a mighty following, for a veil there seemed before the hearts of the Gnomes – and mayhap even this was not without the know-ledge of Ilúvatar. Yet would Melko have been rejoiced to hear it, seeing his evil giving fruit beyond his hopes. Now however that evil one wanders the dark plains of Eruman, and farther south than any-one had yet penetrated he found a region of the deepest gloom, and it seemed to him a good place wherein for the time to hide his stolen treasure.

Therefore he seeks until he finds a dark cavern in the hills, and webs of darkness lie about so that the black air might be felt heavy and choking about one's face and hands. Very deep and winding were those ways having a subterranean outlet on the sea as the ancient books say, and here on a time were the Moon and Sun imprisoned afterward;[10] for here dwelt the primeval spirit Móru whom even the Valar know not whence or when she came, and the folk of Earth have given her many names. Mayhap she was bred of mists and darkness on the confines of the Shadowy Seas, in that utter dark that came between the overthrow of the Lamps and the kindling of the Trees, but more like she has always been; and she it is who loveth still to dwell in that black place taking the guise of an unlovely spider, spinning a clinging gossamer of gloom that catches in its mesh stars and moons and all bright things that sail the airs. Indeed it was because of her labours that so little of that overflowing light of the Two Trees flowed ever into the world, for she sucked light greedily, and it fed her, but she brought forth only that darkness that is a denial of all light. Ungwë Lianti the great spider who enmeshes did the Eldar call her, naming her also Wirilómë or Gloom-weaver, whence still do the Noldoli speak of her as Ungoliont the spider or as Gwerlum the Black.

Now between Melko and Ungwë Lianti was there friendship from the first, when she found him and his comrades straying in her caves, but Gloomweaver was ahungered of the brightness of that hoard of jewels so soon as she saw them.

Now Melko having despoiled the Noldoli and brought sorrow and confusion into the realm of Valinor through less of that hoard than aforetime, having now conceived a darker and deeper plan of aggrandisement; therefore seeing the lust of Ungwë's eyes he offers her all that hoard, saving only the three Silmarils, if she will abet him in his new design. This she granteth readily, and so came all that treasury of most lovely gems fairer than any others that the world has seen into the foul keeping of Wirilómë, and was wound in webs of darkness and hidden deep in the caverns of the eastern slopes of the great hills that are the southern boundary of Eruman.

Deeming that now is the time to strike while Valinor is yet in uproar nor waiting for Aulë and Tulkas to block the passage in the hills, Melko and Wirilómë crept into Valinor and lay hidden in a valley of the foothills until Silpion was in bloom; but all the while was Gloomweaver spinning her most lightless webs and ill-enchanted shades. These she lets float down so that in place of the fair silver light of Silpion all about the western plain of Valinor there creeps now a dim uncertain darkness and faint lights waver in it. Then does she throw a black cloak of invisibility about Melko and herself and they steal across the plain, and the Gods are in wonder and the Elves in Kôr are afraid; nonetheless they do not as yet suspect the hand of Melko in this, thinking rather it is some work of Ossë's, who at times with his storms caused great mists and darkness to be wafted off the Shadowy Seas, encroaching even the bright airs of Valinor;

though in this he met the anger both of Ulmo and of Manwë. Then Manwë sent forth a sweet westerly breath wherewith he was accustomed at such times to blow all sea-humours back eastward over the waters, but such gentle breathing availed nothing against the woven night heavy and clinging that Wirilómë had spread far abroad. Thus was it that unmarked Melko and the Spider of Night reached the roots of Laurelin, and Melko summoning all his godlike might thrust a sword into its beauteous stock, and the fiery radiance that spouted forth assuredly had consumed him even as it did his sword, had not Gloomweaver cast herself down and lapped it thirstily, plying even her lips to the wound in the tree's bark and sucking away its life and strength.

By accursed fortune this deed was not straightway marked, for it was the time of Laurelin's accustomed deepest repose; and now behold, never more would it wake to glory, scattering beauty and joy upon the faces of the Gods. Because of that great draught of light suddenly pride surged in Gwerlum's heart, and she heeded not Melko's warnings, but sate herself now nigh to the roots of Silpion and spouted forth evil fumes of night that flowed like rivers of blackness even to the gates of Valmar. Now Melko takes the weapon that remains to him, a knife, and will injure the bole of Silpion as much as time will allow; but a Gnome called Daurin (Tórin) wandering from Sirnúmen in great boding of ill sees him and makes for him, crying aloud. So great was the onrush of that impetuous Gnome that ere Melko is aware he has hewn at Wirilómë where in the likeness of a spider she sprawls upon the ground. Now the slender blade that Daurin wielded came from the forge of Aulë and was steeped in *miruvor*, or never had he done harm to that secret [?being], but now he cleaves one of her great legs, and his blade is stained with her black gore, a poison to all [?things] whose life is light. Then Wirilómë writhing throws a thread about him and he may not get free, and Melko ruthless stabs him. Then wresting that bright slender blade from his dying grasp he thrusts it deep into Silpion's trunk, and the poison of Gwerlum black upon it dried the very sap and essence of the tree, and its light died suddenly to a dismal glow lost in impenetrable dusk.

Then did Melko and Wirilómë turn in flight, nor is it too soon, for some that were behind Daurin seeing his fate fled in terror both to Kôr and Valmar, stumbling madly in the darkness, but indeed already the Valar are riding forth upon the plain speeding as fast as may be yet too late to defend the Trees which they now know to be in danger.

Now do those Noldoli confirm their fears, saying how Melko is indeed the author of the mischief, and they have but one desire and that is to lay hands upon him and his accomplices ere they can escape beyond the mountains.

Tulkas is in the van of that great hunt leaping surefooted in the dimness, and Oromë may not keep up with him, for even his divine steed cannot rush as headlong in the gathering night as does Poldórëa in the fire of his wrath. Ulmo hears the shouting in his house in Vai, and Ossë [?thrusteth] his head above the Shadowy Seas and seeing no longer any light come down the valley of Kôr he leaps upon the beach of Eldamar and runs in haste to join the Ainur in their hunt. Now is the only light place left in Valinor that garden where the golden fountain sprang from Kulullin, and then were Vána and Nessa and Urwen and many maids and ladies of the Valar in tears, but Palúrien girds her lord as he stands impatiently, and Varda has ridden forth from Taniquetil by her lord's side bearing a blazing star before him as a torch.

Telimektar son of Tulkas is with those noble ones, and his face and weapons gleam as silver in the dark, but now all the Gods and all their folk ride this way and that, and some have [?hasty] torches in their hands, so that the plain is full of pale wandering lights and the sound of voices hallooing in the dusk.

Even as Melko speeds away a vanguard of the chase sweeps by the Trees, and well nigh the Vali faint for anguish at the ruin they see there; but now Melko and certain of his comrades, aforetime children of Mandos, are separated from Ungwë, who wrapped in night gets her gone southward and over the mountains to her home, nor does that chase ever draw nigh to her; but the others flee northward with great speed, for Melko's comrades have knowledge of the mountains there, and hope to get [?him] through. There came a place at length where the shadow-veils were thin and they were viewed by a scattered band of the Vali, and Tulkas was amongst them; who now with a great roar leaps at them. Indeed it might have come to battle upon the plain betwixt Tulkas and Melko had not the distance been overgreat, so that even as Tulkas gained to within spearcast of Melko a belt of mist took the fugitives again and the mocking laugh of Melko seems to come first from one side and then from the other, now from his elbow almost, now from far ahead, and Tulkas turns wildly about and Melko slips away.

Then Makar and Meássë rode in all haste north with their folk, arousing Mandos and ordering the guarding of the mountain paths, but either Makar was too late or Melko's cunning defeated him –

and the mind of Makar was not oversubtle, for no glimpse of that Ainu did they see, though assuredly he did escape that way, and worked much evil after in the world, yet none are there whom I have heard tell ever of the manner of his perilous flight back to the ice-kingdoms of the North.'

## NOTES

1 See p. 117.
2 *Lirillo* appears in the list of secondary names of the Valar referred to on p. 93 as a name of Salmar-Noldorin.
3 'father of Fëanor' is the final reading after a prolonged hesitation between 'son of Fëanor' and 'brother of Fëanor'.
4 For the story of the taking of rock and stone from Arvalin (Eruman) for the raising of the Mountains of Valinor see p. 70.
5 'sire of Fëanor' is an emendation from 'son of Fëanor'; see note 3.
6 After the word 'fabrics' there stood the following sentence, which was struck through: 'which the Gods could an they listed have created in an hour' – a sentence notable in itself and also for its excision.
7 The MS page beginning with the words 'before the gates of Valmar' and ending with 'unabashed uttered his message, saying' is written round the little world-map reproduced and described on pp. 81 ff.
8 In this part of the tale the manuscript consists of detached passages, with directions from one to another; the place of this sentence is not perfectly clear, but seems most probably to belong here.
9 The dots are in the original.
10 'afterward' is an emendation from 'of old'. A question mark is written in the margin against this sentence.

## Changes made to names in
### The Theft of Melko and the Darkening of Valinor

*Ellu Melemno* ⟨ *Melemno* (in Chapter V, p. 120, in an added sentence, the leader of the Solosimpi is *Ellu*).
*Sirnúmen* ⟨ *Numessir* (at the first two occurrences; subsequently *Sirnúmen* was the form first written).
*Eruman* ⟨ *Harmalin* (pp. 145, 152), ⟨ *Habbanan* (p. 151).
*Arvalin* ⟨ *Harvalien* ⟨ *Habbanan* (p. 145), ⟨ *Harvalien* ⟨ *Harmalin* (p. 147); *Arvalien* thus first written p. 148.
*Bruithwir* replaces an earlier name, probably *Maron*.
*Bruithwir go-Maidros* ⟨ *Bruithwir go-Fëanor*. *go-* is a patronymic, 'son of'. See notes 3 and 5 above.

*Móru*   This name could equally well be read, as also at its occasional occurrences elsewhere, as *Morn* (see the Appendix on Names). It replaces here another name, probably *Mordi*.

*Ungoliont* ⟨ *Gungliont.*

*Daurin* (*Tórin*)   The original reading at the first occurence was *Fëanor*, changed to (?)*Daurlas* . . . . . . . . *akin to Fëanor*, and then to *a Gnome called Daurin* (*Tórin*). The subsequent occurrences of *Daurin* are emendations of *Fëanor*.


Commentary on
## The Theft of Melko and the Darkening of Valinor

The story of the corruption of the Noldoli by Melko was ultimately told quite differently; for there entered the matter of the strife between Finwë's sons Fëanor and Fingolfin (*The Silmarillion* p. 69), of which in the tale there is no trace, and where in any case Fëanor is not the son of Finwë Nólemë but of one Bruithwir. The primary motive in the later story of Melkor's desire for the Silmarils (*ibid.* p. 67) is here represented only by a lust for the gems of the Noldoli in general: it is indeed a remarkable feature of the original mythology that though the Silmarils were present they were of such relatively small importance. There is essential agreement with the later story in its being the Noldoli at whom Melko aimed his attack, and there is a quite close, if limited, similarity in the arguments he used: the confinement of the Elves in Valinor by the Valar, and the broad realms in the East that were rightly theirs – but notably absent from Melko's words is any reference to the coming of Men: this element is in the tale introduced later and quite differently, by Manwë himself (p. 150). Moreover the particular association of the Noldoli with the evil Vala arises from his desire for their gems: in *The Silmarillion* (p. 66) the Noldor turned to him for the instruction he could give, while the other kindreds held aloof.

From this point the narratives diverge altogether; for the secret evil of Melkor was in *The Silmarillion* laid bare as a result of the enquiry held into the quarrel of the Noldorin princes, whereas here its revelation came about more simply from the anxiety of Finwë Nólemë about the unrest of his people. The later story is of course far superior, in that Melkor was sought by the Valar as a known enemy as soon as his machinations were uncovered (though he escaped), whereas in the tale, despite there being now every evidence that he was by no means reformed, he was merely told to go and think things over in Mandos. The germ of the story in *The Silmarillion* of Fëanor's banishment to Formenos, where he was accompanied by Finwë, is present, though here the entire people of the Noldoli are ordered to leave Kôr for the rugged dale northwards where the stream Híri plunged underground, and the command to do so seems to have been less a punishment meted out to them by Manwë than a precaution and a safeguard.

In connection with the place of the banishment of the Noldoli, here called *Sirnúmen* ('Western Stream'), it may be mentioned that in an isolated note found in the little book referred to on p. 23 it is stated: 'The river of the second rocky dwelling of the Gnomes in Valinor was *kelusindi* and the spring at its source *kapalinda*.'

Very remarkable is the passage (p. 142) where Manwë is said to know that 'the Elves were children of the world and must one day return to her bosom'. As I have noticed earlier (p. 82) 'the world' is often equated with the Great Lands, and this usage occurs repeatedly in the present tale, but it is not clear to me whether this sense is intended here. I incline to think that the meaning of the phrase is that at 'the Great End' the Eldar, being bound to the Earth, cannot return with the Valar and spirits that were 'before the world' (p. 66) to the regions whence they came (cf. the conclusion of the original *Music of the Ainur*, p. 60).

Coming to the account of the theft of the jewels, the structure of the narrative is again radically different from the later story, in that there Melkor's attack on the Noldor of Formenos, the theft of the Silmarils and the slaying of Finwë, was accomplished *after* his meeting with Ungoliant in the South and the destruction of the Two Trees; Ungoliant was with him at Formenos. Nor in the earliest version is there any mention of Melko's previous visit to Formenos (*The Silmarillion* pp. 71–2), after which he passed through the Calacirya and went northwards up the coast, returning later in secret to Avathar (Arvalin, Eruman) to seek out Ungoliant.

On the other hand the great festival was already the occasion for Melko's theft of the Silmarils from the dwelling of the Noldoli, though the festival was wholly different in having a purely commemorative purpose (see *The Silmarillion* pp. 74–5), and it was a necessary part of that purpose that the Solosimpi should be present (in *The Silmarillion* 'Only the Teleri beyond the mountains still sang upon the shores of the sea; for they recked little of seasons or times . . .').

Of Melko's dark accomplices out of Mandos (some of them said to be 'aforetime children of Mandos', p. 154) there is no trace later, nor of his theft of Oromë's horses; and while Melko is here said to have wished to leave Valinor by passes over the northern mountains, but to have thought better of it (leading to a reflection on what might have been the fate of Valinor had he not), in the later story his movement northwards was a feint. But it is interesting to observe the germ of the one in the other, the underlying idea never lost of a northward and then a southward movement, even though it takes place at a different point in the narrative and has a different motivation.

Interesting also is the emergence of the idea that a close kinsman of Fëanor's – only after much hesitation between brother and son becoming fixed on the father — was slain by Melkor in the dwelling of the Noldoli, Sirnúmen, precursor of Formenos; but the father had yet to be identified with the lord of the Noldoli.

In this passage there are some slight further geographical indications. The Two Trees stood to the north of the city of Valmar (p. 143), as they are shown on the map (see pp. 81–2); and, again in agreement with the map, the Great Lands and the Outer Lands came very close together in the far North (p. 146). Most notably, the gap in the Mountains of Valinor shown on the map and which I marked with the letter *e* is now explained: 'the low place in the hills' by which Melko and his following passed out of Valinor into Arvalin-Eruman, a gap left by Tulkas and Aulë for their own entry into Valinor at the time of the raising of the mountains (p. 145).

Of the next part of this tale (pp. 146–9) almost nothing survived. Manwë's lecture to the Noldoli disappeared (but some of its content is briefly expressed at another place in the narrative of *The Silmarillion*, p. 68: 'The Noldor began to murmur against [the Valar], and many became filled with pride, forgetting how much of what they had and knew came to them in gift from the Valar'). Manwë's naming of Fëanor's father Bruithwir by the patronymic *go-Maidros* is notable: though the name *Maidros* was subsequently to be that of Fëanor's eldest son, not of his grandfather, it was from the outset associated with the 'Fëanorians'. There is no trace later of the strange story of the renegade servant of Mandos, who brought Melko's outrageous message to the Valar, and who was hurled to his death from Taniquetil by the irrepressible Tulkas in direct disobedience to Manwë; nor of the sending of Sorontur to Melko as the messenger of the Gods (it is not explained how Sorontur knew where to find him). It is said here that afterwards 'Sorontur and his folk fared to the Iron Mountains and there abode, watching all that Melko did'. I have noticed in commenting (pp. 111–12) on *The Chaining of Melko* that the Iron Mountains, said to be south of Hisilómë (pp. 101, 118), there correspond to the later Mountains of Shadow (*Ered Wethrin*). On the other hand, in the *Tale of the Sun and Moon* (p. 176) Melko after his escape from Valinor makes himself 'new dwellings in that region of the North where stand the Iron Mountains very high and terrible to see'; and in the original *Tale of Turambar** it is said that Angband lay beneath the roots of the northernmost fastnesses of the Iron Mountains, and that these mountains were so named from 'the Hells of Iron' beneath them. The statement in the present tale that Sorontur 'watched all that Melko did' from his abode in the Iron Mountains obviously implies likewise that Angband was beneath them; and the story that Sorontur (Thorondor) had his eyries on Thangorodrim before he removed them to Gondolin survived long in the 'Silmarillion' tradition (see *Unfinished Tales* p. 43 and note 25). There is thus, apparently, a contradictory usage of the term

* The actual title of this tale is *The Tale of Turambar and the Foalókë*, the *Foalókë* being the Dragon.

'Iron Mountains' within the *Lost Tales*; unless it can be supposed that these mountains were conceived as a continuous range, the southerly extension (the later Mountains of Shadow) forming the southern fence of Hisilómë, while the northern peaks, being above Angband, gave the range its name. Evidence that this is so will appear later.

In the original story the Noldoli of Sirnúmen were given permission (through the intercession of Aulë) to return to Kôr, but Fëanor remained there in bitterness with a few others; and thus the situation of the later narrative – the Noldor in Tirion, but Fëanor at Formenos – is achieved, with the element absent of Fëanor's banishment and unlawful return to the city of the Elves. An underlying difference to be noted is that in *The Silmarillion* (pp. 61–2) the Vanyar had long since departed from Tirion and gone to dwell on Taniquetil or in Valinor: of this there is no suggestion in the old tale; and of course there is the central structural difference between the early and late narratives – when Fëanor raises his standard of rebellion the Trees are still shining in Valinor.

In the tale, a good while seems to elapse after the loss of the treasures of the Noldoli, during which they set to work again with lessened joy and Fëanor sought in vain to remake the Silmarils: this element must of course disappear in the later, much tauter structure, where Fëanor (refusing to hand over the Silmarils to the Valar for the healing of the Trees and not yet knowing that Melko has taken them) knows without attempting it that he cannot remake them any more than Yavanna can remake the Trees.

The embassage of Fëanor and other Noldoli to Manwë, demanding that the Gods ferry them back to the Great Lands, was excised, and with it Manwë's remarkable instruction to them concerning the coming of Men – and his expressed reluctance to have the Eldar return to 'the world' while Men were still in their infancy. No such idea is represented in *The Silmarillion* as being in Manwë's mind (nor is there any suggestion that Manwë's knowledge was so great); and indeed, where in the old story it was Manwë's very description of Men and account of his policy with regard to them that gave rise to Fëanor's rhetoric against them, and which gave strong colour to his assertion of the Valar's true motive for bringing the Eldar to Valinor, in *The Silmarillion* (p. 68) these ideas are a part of the lies of Melkor (I have noticed above that in Melko's persuasions of the Noldoli in the tale there is no reference to the coming of Men).

An otherwise unknown element in the Music of the Ainur is revealed in Manwë's words: that the world shall come in the end for a great while under the sway of Men. In the original version there are several suggestions in reflective asides that all was fated: so here 'the jealousy of Elves and Men' is seen as perhaps a necessary part of the unfolding of the history of the world, and earlier in the tale (p. 142) it is asked: 'Who shall say but that all these deeds, even the seeming needless evil of Melko, were but a portion of the destiny of old?'

But for all the radical changes in the narrative the characteristic note of Fëanor's rhetoric remained; his speech to the Noldoli of Kôr rises in the same rhythms as his speech by torchlight to the Noldor of Tirion (*The Silmarillion* pp. 82–3).

In the story of Melko and Ungoliont it is seen that essential elements were present *ab initio*: the doubt as to her origin, her dwelling in the desolate regions in the south of the Outer Lands, her sucking in of light to bring forth webs of darkness; her alliance with Melko, his rewarding her with the gems stolen from the Noldoli (though this was differently treated later), the piercing of the Trees by Melko and Ungoliont's sucking up the light; and the great hunt mounted by the Valar, which failed of its object through darkness and mist, allowing Melko to escape out of Valinor by the northward ways.

Within this structure there are as almost always a great many points of difference between the first story and the later versions. In *The Silmarillion* (p. 73) Melkor went to Avathar because he knew of Ungoliant's dwelling there, whereas in the tale she found him wandering there seeking a way of escape. In the tale her origin is unknown, and though this element may be said to have remained in *The Silmarillion* ('The Eldar know not whence she came', *ibid.*), by the device of 'Some have said . . .' a clear explanation is in fact given: she was a being from 'before the world', perverted by Melkor, who had been her lord, though she denied him. The original idea of 'the primeval spirit Móru' (p. 151) is made explicit in an entry in the early word-list of the Gnomish language, where the name *Muru* is defined as 'a name of the Primeval Night personified as Gwerlum or Gungliont'.*

The old story markedly lacks the quality of the description in *The Silmarillion* of the descent of Melkor and Ungoliant from Mount Hyarmentir into the plain of Valinor; and there too the great festival of the Valar and Eldar was in progress at the time: here it is long since over. In *The Silmarillion* the assault on the Trees came at the time of the mingling of the lights (p. 75), while here Silpion was in full bloom; and the detail of the account of the destruction of the Trees is rendered quite different through the presence of the Gnome Daurin, afterwards abandoned without trace. Thus in the old story it is not actually said that Ungoliont drank the light of Silpion, but only that the tree died from her poison on Daurin's blade, with which Melko stabbed its trunk; and in *The Silmarillion* Ungoliant went to 'the Wells of Varda' and drank them dry also. It is puzzling that the Gnome was first named Fëanor, since he was slain by Melko. It would seem that my father was at least momentarily entertaining the idea that Fëanor would play no part in the story of the Noldoli in the Great Lands; but in outlines for a later tale (pp. 238–9) he died in Mithrim. In this passage is the first appearance of *miruvor*, defined in the early Qenya word-list as 'nectar, drink of the Valar'; with this cf. *The Road Goes Ever On*, p. 61, where my father stated that it was the name given by the Valar to the drink poured at their festivals,

---

* In the tale (see p. 156) the name *Gungliont* was originally written, but was emended to *Ungoliont*.

and compared it to the nectar of the Olympian Gods (in the translation of *Namárië* he rendered *miruvórë* 'nectar', *ibid.* p. 58).

Most important of the differences in the tale is the immediate return of Ungoliont to her lair in the south, so that all the story in *The Silmarillion* (pp. 80–1) of 'the Thieves' Quarrel', the rescue of Melkor by the Balrogs, and Ungoliant's coming into Nan Dungortheb, is absent from the narrative in the *Lost Tales*; the surrender of the gems of the Noldoli to Ungoliont takes place in the early version at the time of her first meeting with Melko – in *The Silmarillion* he did not then possess them, for the attack on Formenos had not yet taken place.

# VII

# THE FLIGHT OF THE NOLDOLI

There is no break in Lindo's narrative, which continues on in the same hastily-pencilled form (and near this point passes to another similar note-book, clearly with no break in composition), but I have thought it convenient to introduce a new chapter, or a new 'Tale', here, again taking the title from the cover of the book.

'Nonetheless the Gods did not give up hope, but many a time would meet beneath the ruined tree of Laurelin and thence break and scour the land of Valinor once more unwearingly, desiring fiercely to avenge the hurts done to their fair realm; and now the Eldar at their summons aided in the chase that labours not only in the plain but toils both up and down the slopes of the mountains, for there is no escape from Valinor to west, where lie the cold waters of the Outer Seas.

But Fëanor standing in the square about Inwë's house in topmost Kôr will not be silenced, and cries out that all the Noldoli shall gather about him and hearken, and many thousands of them come to hear his words bearing slender torches, so that that place is filled with a lurid light such as has never before shone on those white walls. Now when they are gathered there and Fëanor sees that far the most of the company is of the kin of the Noldor[1] he exhorts them to seize now this darkness and confusion and the weariness of the Gods to cast off the yoke – for thus demented he called the days of bliss in Valinor – and get them hence carrying with them what they might or listed. "If all your hearts be too faint to follow, behold I Fëanor go now alone into the wide and magic world to seek the gems that are my own, and perchance many great and strange adventures will there befall me more worthy of a child of Ilúvatar than a servant of the Gods."[2]

Then is there a great rush of those who will follow him at once, and though wise Nólemë speaks against this rashness they will not hear him, and ever the tumult groweth wilder. Again Nólemë pleads that at least they send an embassy to Manwë to take due farewell and maybe get his goodwill and counsel for their journeying, but Fëanor persuades them to cast away even such moderate wisdom, saying that to do so were but to court refusal, and that Manwë would forbid them and prevent them: "What is Valinor to us," say they, "now that its light is come to little – as lief and liever would we have the untrammeled world." Now then they arm themselves as best they may – for nor Elves nor Gods in those days bethought themselves overmuch of weapons – and store of jewels they took and stuffs of raiment; but all their books of their lore they left behind, and indeed there was not much therein that the wise men among them could not match from memory. But Nólemë seeing that his counsel prevailed not would not be separated from his folk, and went with them and aided them in all their preparations. Then did they get them down the hill of Kôr lit by the flame of torches, and so faring in haste along the creek and the shores of that arm of the Shadowy Sea that encroached here upon the hills they found the seaward dwellings of the Solosimpi.

The next short section of the text was struck through afterwards, the words 'Insert the Battle of Kópas Alqalunten' written across it, and replaced by a rider. The rejected section reads:

The most of that folk were gone a-hunting with the Gods, but some of those that remained they suaded to cast in their lot with them, as already had some of the Teleri, but of the Inwir none would hearken to their words. Now having nigh as many maids and women as of men and boys (albeit many especially of the youngest children were left in Kôr and Sirnúmen) they were at a loss, and in this extremity, being distraught with sorrows and wildered in mind, the Noldoli did those deeds which afterwards they most bitterly rued – for by them was the displeasure laid heavily on all their folk and the hearts even of their kindred were turned against them for a while.

   Coming upon Cópas where was a haven of great quiet beloved of the Solosimpi they seized all the ships of that people and embarked thereon their womenfolk and children and some few [?others] wherewith were those of the Solosimpi who had joined them, for these had a skill in navigation. In this way marching endlessly along the beach that grew wilder and more evil going as it trended to the North, while the fleet coasted beside them not far out to sea, it has been said to me that the Noldoli got them from Valinor; however I know not the matter deeply, and maybe there are tales known to none of the Gnome-kin that relate more clearly the sad happenings of that time. Moreover have I heard say

The rider that replaces this passage was written carefully and very legibly in ink on separate sheets, at how great an interval of time I cannot say.

## The Kinslaughter
### (Battle of Kópas Alqalunten)

The most of that folk were gone a-hunting with the Gods, but many
there were gathered about the beaches before their dwellings and
dismay was abroad among them, yet still were no few busy about the
places of their ships, and the chief of these was that one they named
Kópas, or more fully Kópas Alqaluntë, the Haven of the Swanships.*
Now Swanhaven was like a bason of quiet waters, save that towards
the eastward and the seas the ring of rocks that enclosed it sank
somewhat, and there did the sea pierce through, so that there was
a mighty arch of living stone. So great was this that save of the
mightiest ships two might pass therethrough, one going out maybe
and another seeking inward to the quiet blue waters of the haven,
nor would the mast-tops come nigh to grazing on the rock. Not
much of the light of the Trees came thither aforetime by reason of
the wall, wherefore was it lit ever with a ring of lamps of gold, and
lanterns there were too of many colours tokening the wharves and
landings of the different houses; but through the arch the pale
waters of the Shadowy Seas might distantly be glimpsed, lit faintly
with the shining of the Trees. Very beautiful was that harbour to
gaze upon, what time the white fleets came shimmering home and
the troubled waters broke the mirrored radiance of the lamps into
rippling lights, weaving strange patterns of many twinkling lines.
But now were all those vessels lying still, and a deep gloom was
settled on the place at the fading of the Trees.

Of the Solosimpi none would hearken to the wild words of the
Noldoli, save a few that might be counted on two hands; and so did
that folk wander unhappily northward along the shores of Eldamar,
even till they came to the cliff-tops that gazed down upon Swanhaven,
and therefrom had the Solosimpi of old cut winding stairs in the
rock leading down to the harbour's edge. Now northward thence the
way was very rugged and evil, and the Noldoli had with them nigh
as many maids and women as of men and boys (albeit many especially
of the youngest children were left in Kôr and in Sirnúmen and many
tears were shed thereat); wherefore were they now at a loss, and in
this extremity, distraught with sorrows and wildered in mind, they
here wrought those deeds which afterwards they have most bitterly

---

* In the margin is written *Ielfethẏþ*. This is Old English, representing the
interpretation of the Elvish name made by Eriol in his own language: the
first element meaning 'swan' (*ielfetu*), and the second (later 'hithe') meaning
'haven, landing-place'.

repented – for by them was for a while the displeasure of the Gods laid heavily upon all their folk and the hearts even of the Eldalië were turned against them.

Behold, the counsel of Fëanor is that by no means can that host hope to win swiftly along the coast save by the aid of ships; "and these," said he, "an the shore-elves will not give them, we must take". Wherefore going down to the harbour they essayed to go upon those ships that there lay, but the Solosimpi said them nay, yet for the great host of the Gnome-folk they did not as yet resist; but a new wrath awoke there between Eldar and Eldar. So did the Noldoli embark all their womenfolk and children and a great host beside upon those ships, and casting them loose they oared them with a great multitude of oars towards the seas. Then did a great anger blaze in the hearts of the Shoreland Pipers, seeing the theft of those vessels that their cunning and long labours had fashioned, and some there were that the Gods had made of old on Tol Eressëa as has been recounted, wondrous and magic boats, the first that ever were. So sprang up suddenly a voice among them: "Never shall these thieves leave the Haven in our ships", and all those of the Solosimpi that were there ran swiftly atop of the cliff-wall to where the archway was wherethrough that fleet must pass, and standing there they shouted to the Gnomes to return; but these heeded them not and held ever on their course, and the Solosimpi threatened them with rocks and strung their elfin bows.

Seeing this and believing war already to be kindled came now those of the Gnomes who might not fare aboard the ships but whose part it was to march along the shores, and they sped behind the Solosimpi, until coming suddenly upon them nigh the Haven's gate they slew them bitterly or cast them in the sea; and so first perished the Eldar neath the weapons of their kin, and that was a deed of horror. Now the number of the Solosimpi that fell was very many, and of the Gnomes not a few, for they had to fight hard to win their way back from those narrow cliff-top paths, and many of the shore-land folk hearing the affray were gathered in their rear.

At length however it is done, and all those ships have passed out to the wide seas, and the Noldoli fared far away, but the little lamps are broken and the Haven is dark and very still, save for the faint sound of tears. Of like kind were all the works of Melko in this world.

Now tells the tale that as the Solosimpi wept and the Gods scoured all the plain of Valinor or sat despondent neath the ruined Trees a great age passed and it was one of gloom, and during that time the Gnome-folk suffered the very greatest evils and all the unkindliness of the world beset them. For some marched endlessly along that shore until Eldamar was dim and forgotten far behind, and wilder grew the ways and more impassable as it trended to the North, but the fleet coasted beside them not far out to sea and the shore-farers might often see them dimly in the gloom, for they fared but slowly in those sluggish waves.

Yet of all the sorrows that walked those ways I know not the full tale, nor have any told it, for it would be an ill tale, and though the Gnomes relate many things concerning those days more clearly than I can, yet do they in no wise love to dwell upon the sad happenings of that time and will not often awake its memory. Nonetheless have I heard it said

The inserted rider ends here and we return to the original roughly-pencilled text:

that never would they have made the dreadful passage of the Qerkaringa³ had they or yet been subject to weariness, sickness, and the many weaknesses that after became their lot dwelling far from Valinor. Still was the blessed food of the Gods and their drink rich in their veins and they were half-divine – but no *limpë* had they as yet to bring away, for that was not given to the fairies until long after, when the March of Liberation was undertaken, and the evils of the world which Melko poisoned with his presence soon fell upon them.'

'Nay, if thou wilt forgive me bursting in upon thy tale,' quoth Eriol, 'what meaneth thy saying "the dread passage of the Qerkaringa"?'

'Know then,' said Lindo, 'that the trend of the coasts of Eldamar and those coasts that continue that strand northward beyond the wide haven of Kópas is ever to the East, so that after uncounted miles, more northward even than the Mountains of Iron and upon the confines of the Icy Realms, the Great Seas aided by a westerly bend of the shores of the Great Lands dwindle to a narrow sound. Now the passage of that water is of impassable peril, for it is full of evil currents and eddies of desperate strength, and islands of floating ice swim therein, grinding and crashing together with a dread noise and destroying both great fish and vessels, do any ever dare to venture there. In those days however a narrow neck, which the Gods after destroyed, ran out from the western land almost to the eastern shores, yet it was of ice and snow [?pillared] and torn into gaps and cliffs and was all but untraversable, and that was the

Helkaraksë or Icefang,[4] and it was a remnant of the old and terrible ices that crept throughout those regions ere Melko was chained and the North became clement for a while, and it maintained itself there by reason of the narrowness of the seas and the [?jamming] of the ice-isles floating down from the deepest North whither winter had withdrawn. Now that strip of water that flowed still between Icefang's tip and the Great Lands was called Qerkaringa or Chill Gulf.[5]

Had Melko indeed known of the Gnomes' wild attempt to cross it he might have overwhelmed them all in that ill place or done whatso he willed, but many months had gone since he himself had fled perchance by that very way, and he was now far afield. Say I not well, Rúmil, with regard to these things?'

'Thou hast told the true tale,' said Rúmil, 'yet hast thou not said how ere they came to Helkaraksë the host passed by that place where Mornië is wont to be beached, for there a steep and rugged path winds down from Mandos deep in the mountains that the souls whom Fui sends to Arvalin must tread.[6] There did a servant of Vefántur spy them and asking what might that wayfaring mean pled with them to return, but they answered him scornfully, so that standing upon a high rock he spoke to them aloud and his voice came even to the fleet upon the waves; and he foretold to them many of the evil adventures that after came to them, warning them against Melko, and at last he said: "Great is the fall of Gondolin", and none there understood, for Turondo son of Nólemë[7] was not yet upon the Earth. But the wise men stored his sayings, for Mandos and all his people have a power of prophecy, and these words were treasured long among them as the Prophecies of Amnos, for thus was the place where they were spoken called at that time, which now is Hanstová-nen[8] or the beaching place of Mornië.

After that the Noldoli journeyed slowly, and when the awful isthmus of Helkaraksë was before them some were for ferrying all the host, part at a time, across the sea, venturing rather over the perilous waters than seeking to find passage over the gulfs and treacherous crevasses of the isthmus of ice. This they tried, and a great ship was lost with all aboard by reason of a certain fearsome eddy that was in the bay nigh where Helkaraksë jutted from the western mainland; and that eddy at times spins around like a vast top and shrieks with a loud wailing noise most terrible to hear, and such things as approach are sucked down to its monstrous deep and crushed there upon jags of ice and rock; and the name of the eddy is Wiruin. Wherefore are the Noldoli in great anguish and perplexity, for even could they find a way through the terrors of the Helkaraksë,

behold they cannot even so reach the inner world, for still there lies
that gap at the far end, and though but narrow the screech of water
rushing therethrough can be heard thus far away, and the boom of
ice splitting from the cape came to them, and the crash and buffet
of the ice-isles that thrust down from the North through that dreadful
strait.

Now the presence of those floating isles of ice no doubt was due
to the presence of Melko once more in the far North, for winter
had retreated to the uttermost North and South, so that almost it
had no foothold in the world remaining in those days of peace that
are called Melko's Chains; but nonetheless it was this very activity
of Melko that in the end proved the salvation of the Noldoli, for
behold they now are constrained to lead all their womenfolk and the
mariners of their host out of the ships, and there on those bleak
shores they beach them and set now a miserable encampment.

Songs name that dwelling[9] the Tents of Murmuring, for there
arose much lamentation and regret, and many blamed Fëanor bitterly,
as indeed was just, yet few deserted the host for they suspected that
there was no welcome ever again for them back to Valinor – and this
some few who sought to return indeed found, though this entereth
not into this tale.

When their woes are now at the blackest and scarce any look for
return of any joy again, behold winter unfurls her banners again and
marches slowly south clad in ice with spears of frost and lashes of
hail. Yet so great is the cold that the floating ice packs and jams
and piles like hills between the end of Helkaraksë[10] and the Eastern
land, and in the end does it become so strong that the current moves
it not. Then abandoning their stolen ships they leave their sorrowful
encampment and strive to cross the terrors of the Qerkaringa. Who
shall tell of their misery in that march or of those numbers who were
lost, falling into great pits of ice where far below hidden water boiled,
or losing their way until cold overcame them – for evil as it was so
many and desperate things befell them after in the Great Lands
that it was lessened in their minds to a thing of less worth, and in
sooth tales that told of the leaving of Valinor were never sweet in
the ears of the Noldoli after, were they thralls or citizens of Gondolin.
Yet even so such things may not slay the Gnome-kin, and of those
there lost still 'tis said some wander sadly there among the icehills,
unknowing of all things that have befallen their folk, and some
essayed to get them back to Valinor, and Mandos has them, and some
following after found in long days their unhappy kin again. Howso
it be, a gaunt and lessened band indeed did in the end reach the

rocky soil of the Eastern lands, and there stood looking backward over the ice of Helkaraksë and of Qerkaringa at the spurs of hills beyond the sea, for far away in the gathering southward mists rose those most glorious heights of Valinor, fencing them for ever from their kindred and their homes.

Thus came the Noldoli into the world.'

And with those words of Rúmil's the story of the darkening of Valinor was at an end.

'Great was the power of Melko for ill,' saith Eriol, 'if he could indeed destroy with his cunning the happiness and glory of the Gods and of the Elves, darkening the light of their hearts no less than of their dwelling, and bringing all their love to naught! This must surely be the worst deed that ever he has done.'

'Of a truth never has such evil again been done in Valinor,' said Lindo, 'but Melko's hand has laboured at worse things in the world, and the seeds of his evil have waxen since those days to a great and terrible growth.'

'Nay,' said Eriol, 'yet can my heart not think of other griefs, for sorrow at the destruction of those most fair Trees and the darkness of the world.'

## NOTES

1   The manuscript seems certainly to have the form *Noldor* here. – It is to be remembered that in the old story the Teleri (i.e. the later Vanyar) had not departed from Kôr; see p. 159.

2   At the top of the manuscript page and fairly clearly referring to Fëanor's words my father wrote: 'Increase the element of the desire for Silmarils'. Another note refers to the section of the narrative that begins here and says that it 'wants a lot of revision: the [?thirst ?lust] for jewels – especially for the sacred Silmarils – wants emphasizing. And the all-important battle of Cópas Alqaluntë where the Gnomes slew the Solosimpi must be inserted.' This note was then struck through and marked 'done', but only the latter direction was in fact followed: this is the rider on the Kinslaughter given on pp. 164–6.

3   Against this my father wrote in the margin: '*Helkaraksë* Icefang *Qerkaringa* the water'; see note 5.

4   *Helkaraksë or Icefang*: earlier reading *Qerkaringa*; see note 5.

5   This passage, from ' "Know then," said Lindo . . .', replaces an earlier version which I do not give, for it contains almost nothing that is not in the replacement; and the last sentence of the replacement is a later addition still. It is to be noted however that in the first version the neck of land is called *Qerkaringa* (as also in the replacement passage at first, see note 4), with the remark that 'the name has also

been given to the sound beyond'. This then was the earlier idea: *Qerkaringa* the name primarily of the neck of land, but extended also to the sound (presumably at that stage *querka* did not mean 'gulf'). My father than decided that *Qerkaringa* was the name of the sound and introduced the name *Helkaraksë* for the neck of land; hence the marginal annotation given in note 3 above. At this point he added the last sentence of the replacement passage, 'Now that strip of water that flowed still between Icefang's tip and the Great Lands was called Qerkaringa or Chill Gulf', and emended *Qerkaringa* in the body of the passage (note 4) to *Helkaraksë or Icefang*, carrying this change through the rest of the tale (on p. 169 *of Qerkaringa* > *of Helkaraksë and of Qerkaringa*).

6   For the path down from Mandos, the black ship Mornië, and its journey down the coast to Arvalin, see pp. 77, 90 ff.

7   Turondo or Turgon, son of Nólemë, has been named previously, p. 115.

8   The reading *Hanstovánen* is slightly uncertain, and another name 'or . . . . . *Mornien*' follows it. See under 'Changes made to names' below.

9   After the word 'dwelling' there is a space left for the insertion of an Elvish name.

10  MS *Qerkaringa* unemended, but clearly the western promontory (the Icefang) is referred to, and I therefore read *Helkaraksë* in the text (see note 5).

## Changes made to names in
### The Flight of the Noldoli

*Helkaraksë* < *Qerkaringa* (for the details of, and the explanation of this change see note 5 above).

*Arvalin* < *Habbanan*.

*Amnos* < *Emnon* < *Morniento*.

*Hanstovánen*   The name of 'the beaching place of Mornië' was first written *Mornielta* (last letters uncertain), then *Vane* (or *Vone*) *Hansto*; this latter was not struck out, but the form in the text (which may also be read as *Hanstavánen*) seems to be the final one. After *Hanstovánen* follows 'or . . . . . *Mornien*'.

## Commentary on
### The Flight of the Noldoli

In this 'tale' (in reality the conclusion of the long tale of 'The Theft of Melko and the Darkening of Valinor' told by Lindo and finished by

Rúmil) is found the oldest account of the departure of the Gnomes out of Valinor. Here the Gods continue the vain pursuit and search long after Melko has escaped, and moreover are aided in it by the Eldar (including the Solosimpi, who as the later Teleri portrayed in *The Silmarillion* would hardly have left their shores and their ships). Fëanor's return to Kôr and his haranguing of the Noldoli (and, in this account, others) by the light of their torches is seen to be an original feature; but his sons have not yet appeared, nor indeed any of the Noldorin princes descended from Finwë save Turondo (Turgon), of whom it is specifically stated (p. 167) that he was 'not yet upon the Earth'. There is no Oath of Fëanor, and the later story of the divided counsels of the Noldor appears only in the attempt of Nólemë (Finwë) to calm the people – Nólemë thus playing the later part of Finarfin (*The Silmarillion* p. 83). In *The Silmarillion*, after the Kinslaying at Alqualondë and the Prophecy of the North, Finarfin and many of his people returned to Valinor and were pardoned by the Valar (p. 88); but here those few who went back found there was no welcome for them, or else 'Mandos has them' (p. 168).

In the rejected section given on p. 163, which was replaced by the account of the battle of Kópas Alqualunten, the reference to 'those deeds which afterwards the Noldoli most bitterly rued' must be simply to the theft of the ships of the Solosimpi, since there is no suggestion of any worse actions (in the replacement passage almost the same words are used of the Kinslaying). The actual emergence of the idea that the Noldoli were guilty of worse than theft at Kópas is seen in a note in the little book (see p. 23) that my father used to jot down thoughts and suggestions – many of these being no more than single sentences, or mere isolated names, serving as reminders of work to be done, stories to be told, or changes to be made. This note reads:

The wrath of the Gods and Elves very great – even let some Noldoli slay some Solosimpi at Kópas – and let Ulmo plead for them (? if Ulmo so fond of the Solosimpi).

This was struck through and marked 'done', and the recommendation here that Ulmo should plead for the Noldoli is found in the tale of *The Hiding of Valinor* (p. 209).

In the description of Kópas the 'mighty arch of living stone' survived into the 'arch of living rock sea-carved' in the much briefer description of Alqualondë in *The Silmarillion* (p. 61); and we see here the reason for the Haven's being 'lit with many lamps' (*ibid.*) – because little light came there from the Two Trees on account of the rock-wall around it (though the darkness of Alqualondë is implied by the statement in *The Silmarillion* that it 'lay upon the confines of Eldamar, north of the Calacirya, where the light of the stars was bright and clear').

The events at the Haven were differently conceived in detail from the later story, but still with much general agreement; and though the storm raised by Uinen (*ibid.* p. 87) does not appear in the original version, the picture of the Noldoli journeying northward some along the shore and some in the vessels remained.

There are interesting indications of the geography of the northern regions. There is no suggestion of a great wasteland (later Araman) between the northern Mountains of Valinor and the sea, a conclusion reached earlier (p. 83), and supported incidentally by the accounts of the steep path from Mandos in the mountains down to the beaching place of the black ship Mornië (pp. 77, 167). The name *Helkaraksë*, 'Icefang', first appearing in emendations to the text and given to the neck or promontory running out from the western land, was afterwards re-applied to what is here called *Qerkaringa*, the strait filled with ice-floes that 'grind and crash together'; but this was when the *Helcaraxë*, 'the Grinding Ice', had come to have a quite different geographical significance in the much more sophisticated world-picture that my father evolved during the next 'phase' of the mythology.

In *The Silmarillion* (p. 87) there is a suggestion that the speaker of the Prophecy of the North was Mandos himself 'and no lesser herald of Manwë', and its gravity, indeed its centrality in the mythology, is far greater; here there is no suggestion of a 'doom' or 'curse', but only a foretelling. This foretelling included the dark words 'Great is the fall of Gondolin'. In the tale of *The Fall of Gondolin* (but in an interpolated sentence very possibly later than the present tale) Turgon, standing upon the stairs of his palace amid the destruction of the city, uttered these same words, 'and men shuddered, for such were the words of Amnon the prophet of old'. Here *Amnon* (rather than *Amnos* as in the present text, itself an emendation from *Emnon*) is not a place but a person (the servant of Vefántur who uttered the prophecy?). In the little notebook referred to above occurs the following jotting:

Prophecy of Amnon. Great is the fall of Gondolin. Lo Turgon shall not fade till the lily of the valley fadeth.

In some other notes for the *Lost Tales* this takes the form:

Prophecy of Amnon. 'Great is the fall of Gondolin' and 'When the lily of the valley withers then shall Turgon fade'.

In these notes *Amnon* might be either place or person. The 'lily of the valley' is Gondolin itself, one of whose Seven Names was *Losengriol*, later *Lothengriol*, which is translated 'flower of the vale or lily of the valley'.

There is an interesting statement in the old story (p. 166) that the Noldoli would never have passed the ice if they had yet been subject to the 'weariness, sickness, and the many weaknesses that after became their lot dwelling far from Valinor', but 'still was the blessed food of the Gods and their drink rich in their veins and they were half-divine'. This is echoed in the words of *The Silmarillion* (p. 90) that the Noldor were 'but new-come from the Blessed Realm, and not yet weary with the weariness of Earth'. On the other hand it was specifically said in the Prophecy of the North (*ibid.* p. 88) that 'though Eru appointed you to die not in Eä, *and no sickness may assail you*, yet slain ye may be, and slain ye shall be,' &c.

Of the treachery of the Fëanorians, sailing away in the ships and leaving the host of Fingolfin on the shores of Araman, there is of course in the old story no trace; but the blaming of Fëanor was already present ('the Tents of Murmuring', p. 168). It is a remarkable aspect of the earliest version of the mythology that while so much of the narrative structure was firm and was to endure, the later 'genealogical' structure had scarcely emerged. Turgon existed as the son of (Finwë) Nólemë, but there is no suggestion that Fëanor was close akin to the lord of the Noldoli, and the other princes, Fingolfin, Finarfin, Fingon, Felagund, do not appear at all, in any form, or by any name.

# VIII

# THE TALE OF THE SUN AND MOON

The *Tale of the Sun and Moon* is introduced by an 'Interlude' (as it is called in the manuscript) in which there appears, as a guest at Mar Vanwa Tyaliéva, one Gilfanon of Tavrobel. This interlude exists also in a rejected earlier version.

The tale itself is for most of its length a manuscript in ink over an erased pencilled original, but towards its end (see note 19) it becomes a primary manuscript in ink with the pencilled draft extant in another book.

The *Tale of the Sun and Moon* is very long, and I have shortened it in places in brief paraphrase, without omitting any detail of interest. (A note of my father's refers to this tale as 'in need of great revision, cutting-down, and [?reshaping]'.)

## Gilfanon a·Davrobel

Now it is not to be thought that as Eriol hearkened to many tales which spake of divers sorrows of the Elves that the thirst for *limpë* grew less within him, for it was not so, and ever as the throng sat about the Tale-fire he was an eager questioner, seeking to learn all the history of the folk even down to those days that then were, when the elfin people dwelt again together in the isle.

Knowing now therefore something of the glorious fashion of their ancient home and of the splendour of the Gods, he pondered often on the coming of the days of Sunlight and of Moonsheen, and of the doings of the Elves in the world without, and of their adventures there with Men ere Melko compassed their estrangement; wherefore one night he said, sitting before the Tale-fire: 'Whence be the Sun and Moon, O Lindo? For as yet have I heard only of the Two Trees and their sad fading, but of the coming of Men, or of the deeds of the Elves beyond Valinor has no one told me.'

Now there happened that night to be present a guest both at their board and at their tale-telling, and his name was Gilfanon, and all named him beside Gilfanon a·Davrobel,[1] for he came from that region of the isle where stands the Tower of Tavrobel beside the rivers,[2] and about it dwelt the Gnome-folk still as one people, naming the places in their own tongue. That region was Gilfanon wont to

name the fairest of all the isle, and the Gnome-kin its best folk,
albeit ere the coming of the folk thither long had he dwelt away from
the Noldoli, faring with Ilkorins in Hisilómë and Artanor,[3] and
thereto had he become as few Elves did a great friend and companion
of the Children of Men of those days. To their legends and their
memories he added his own knowledge, for he had been deep-versed
in many lores and tongues once in the far days of Kôr, and experience
had he beside of many very ancient deeds, being indeed one of the
oldest of the fairies[4] and the most aged that now dwelt in the isle,
albeit Meril held the title of Lady of the Isle by reason of her blood.

Therefore said Lindo now, answering Eriol: 'Behold, Gilfanon
here can tell thee much of such matters, and it were well if you
fared hence away with him to sojourn awhile in Tavrobel. – Nay,
look not thus,' he laughed, seeing Eriol's face, 'for we do not banish
thee yet – but of a sooth he who would drink of *limpë* were wise first
to seek the guestkindliness of Gilfanon, in whose ancient house – the
House of the Hundred Chimneys, that stands nigh the bridge of
Tavrobel[5] – may many things be heard of both past and that are to
come.'

'Methinks,' said Gilfanon to Eriol, 'that Lindo seeks to rid himself
of two guests at once; howso he may not do so yet, for I purpose to
stay in Kortirion a sennight yet, and moreover to feast at his good
board meanwhile, and stretch me by the Tale-fire too – thereafter
maybe thou and I will fare away and thou shalt see the full loveliness
of the fairies' isle – but now let Lindo raise up his voice and tell us
yet more of the splendour of the Gods and their works, a theme that
never wearies him!'

At that was Lindo well-pleased, for of a truth he loved to tell
such tales and sought often an occasion for recalling them, and said
he: 'Then will I tell the story of the Sun and Moon and of the Stars,
that Eriol may hearken to his desire,' and Eriol was well pleased,
but Gilfanon said: 'Speak on, my Lindo – yet lengthen not the tale
for ever.'

Then did Lindo lift up his voice,[6] and it was the most pleasant to
hearken to of all tale-tellers, and he said:*

'A tale I tell of that time of the first flight of the Gnomes, and
behold they are but newly fled. Now came that grievous news to
the Gods and the other Elves, and at first none believed. Nonetheless
the tidings came still unto them, and by many different messengers.
Some were of the Teleri, who had heard the speech of Fëanor in
the square of Kôr and had seen the Noldoli depart thence with all

* Written in the margin: 'Beginning of The Sun and Moon'.

the goods they might convey; others were of the Solosimpi, and these brought the dire tidings of the swanships' rape and the dread kinslaughter of the Haven, and the blood that lay on the white shores of Alqaluntë.

Lastly came some hotfoot from Mandos who had gazed upon that sad throng nigh the strands of Amnor, and the Gods knew that the Gnomes were far abroad, and Varda and all the Elves wept, for now seemed the darkness black indeed and that more than the outward light of the fair Trees was slain.

Strange is to tell that albeit Aulë had loved the Noldoli above all the Elves and had taught them all they knew and given them great stores of wealth, now was his heart most turned against them, for he deemed them ingrate in that they had bidden him no farewell, and for their ill deeds among the Solosimpi he was grieved to the heart. "Speak not," said he, "the name of the Noldoli ever again unto me," and albeit he gave still his love to those few faithful Gnomes who remained still about his halls, yet did he name them thereafter "Eldar".

But the Teleri and the Solosimpi having wept at first, when the onslaught of the Haven became known to all dried their tears and horror and anguish held their hearts, and they too spake seldom of the Noldoli, save sadly or in whispers behind closed doors; and those few of the Noldoli that remained behind were named the Aulenossë or kindred of Aulë, or were taken into the other kindreds, and the Gnome-folk has no place or name remaining now in all Valinor.

Now is it to tell that after a great while it seemed to Manwë that the hunt of the Gods availed nothing, and that surely Melko is now escaped out of Valinor; wherefore he sent Sorontur into the world, and Sorontur came not back for long, and still Tulkas and many others ranged the land, but Manwë stood beside the darkened Trees and his heart was very heavy as he pondered deep and gloomily, but at that time could he see little light of hope. Suddenly there is a sound of wings in that place, for Sorontur King of Eagles is come again on strong wings through the dusk, and behold alighting on the boughs of darkened Silpion he tells how Melko is now broken into the world and many evil spirits are gathered to him: "but," quoth he, "methinks never more will Utumna open unto him, and already is he busy making himself new dwellings in that region of the North where stand the Iron Mountains very high and terrible to see. Yet O Manwë Lord of the Air, other tidings have I also for thy ear, for lo! as I winged my way homeward hither over the black seas and over the unkindly lands a sight I saw of greatest wonder and amaze:

a fleet of white ships that drifted empty in the gales, and some were
burning with bright fires, and as I marvelled behold I saw a great
concourse of folk upon the shores of the Great Lands, and they
gazed all westward, but some were still wandering in the ice – for
know, this was at that place where are the crags of Helkarakse and
the murderous waters of Qerkaringa flowed of old, which now are
stopped with ice. Swooping methought I heard the sound of wailing
and of sad words spoken in the Eldar tongue; and this tale do I
bring to thee for thy unravelling."

But Manwë knew thereby that the Noldoli were gone for ever
and their ships burned or abandoned, and Melko too was in the
world, and the hunt of no avail; and belike it is in memory of those
deeds that it has ever been a saying in the mouths of Elves and Men
that those burn their boats who put all hope from them of change of
mind or counsel. Therefore now Manwë lifted up his unmeasurable
voice calling to the Gods, and all those about the wide lands of
Valinor hearkened and returned.

There first came Tulkas weary and dust-covered, for none had
leapt about that plain as he. Seven times had he encompassed all its
width and thrice had he scaled the mountain-wall, and all those
measureless slopes and pastures, meads and forests, he had traversed,
burnt by his desire to punish the spoiler of Valinor. There came
Lórien and leaned against the withered bole of Silpion, and wept the
wrack of his quiet gardens by the trampling hunt; there too was
Meássë and with her Makar, and his hand was red for he had come
upon twain of Melko's comrades as they fled, and he slew them as they
ran, and he alone had aught of joy in those ill times. Ossë was there
and his beard of green was torn and his eyes were dim, and he gasped
leaning on a staff and was very much athirst, for mighty as he was
about the seas and tireless, such desperate travail on the bosom of
Earth spent his vigour utterly.

Salmar and Ómar stood by and their instruments of music made
no sound and they were heavy of heart, yet not so bitterly as was
Aulë, lover of the earth and of all things made or gained by good
labour therefrom, for of all the Gods he had loved Valmar most
wholly and Kôr and all their treasures, and the smile of the fair
plains without, and its ruin cut his heart. With him was Yavanna,
Earth-queen, and she had hunted with the Gods and was spent; but
Vána and Nessa wept as maidens still beside the founts of gold
Kulullin.

Ulmo alone came not to the Trees, but went down to the beach
of Eldamar, and there he stood gazing into the gloom far out to

sea, and he called often with his most mighty voice as though he would draw back those truants to the bosom of the Gods, and whiles he played deep longing music on his magic conches, and to him alone, lest it be⁷ Varda lady of the stars, was the going of the Gnomes a greater grief than even the ruin of the Trees. Aforetime had Ulmo loved the Solosimpi very dearly, yet when he heard of their slaughter by the Gnomes he grieved indeed but anger hardened not his heart, for Ulmo was foreknowing more than all the Gods, even than great Manwë, and perchance he saw many of the things that should spring from that flight and the dread pains of the unhappy Noldoli in the world, and the anguish wherewith they would expiate the blood of Kópas, and he would that it need not be.

Now when all were thus come together, then spake Manwë to them and told the tidings of Sorontur and how the chase had failed, but at that time the Gods were wildered in the gloom and had little counsel, and sought each one his home and places of old delight now dead, and there sat in silence and dark pondering. Yet some fared ever and anon out upon the plain and gazed wistfully at the faded Trees as though those withered boughs would one day burgeon with new light: this came not to pass, and Valinor was full of shadows and of gloom, and the Elves wept and could not be comforted, and the Noldoli had bitter sorrow in the northern lands.

Thereafter in a great time it pierced the grief and the weariness of the Gods that light is gone from Valinor for ever, and that never again will those Trees bloom again at their appointed times. Only the light of the stars remained, save where a glow lay about the fountain of Kulullin playing still or a pale gleam lingered nigh deep Telimpë,⁸ vat of dreams. Yet even these were dimmed and tarnished, for the Trees bore dew no more for their replenishment.

Wherefore does Vána arise and seek Lórien, and with them go Urwendi and Silmo⁹ and many of both Vali and the Elves; and they gather much light of gold and silver in great vessels and fare sadly to the ruined Trees. There singeth Lórien most wistful songs of magic and enchantment about the stock of Silpion, and he bid water his roots with the radiance of Telimpë; and this was lavishly done, albeit small store thereof remained now in the dwellings of the Gods. In like manner doth Vána, and she sings old golden songs of the happier days, and bids her maidens dance their bright dances even such as they were used to dance upon the sward of the rose-gardens nigh Kulullin, and as they danced she flooded the roots of Laurelin with streams from out her golden jars.

Yet all their singing and enchantment is of little worth, and though the roots of the Trees seem to drink all that they may pour yet can they see no stir of life renewed nor faintest gleam of light; nor withered leaf glows with sap nor blossom lifts its drooping stem. Indeed in the frenzy of their grief they had poured out all the last remaining stores of brightness that the Gods retained, had not of a fortune Manwë and Aulë come upon them in that hour, being drawn thither by their singing in the gloom, and stayed them, saying: "Lo, O Vána, and thou O Lórien, what is this rashness? And wherefore did ye not first take counsel of your brethren? For know ye not that that which ye spill unthinking upon the earth is become more precious than all the things the world contains; and when it is gone perchance not all the wisdom of the Gods may get us more."

Then Vána said: "Pardon, O Manwë Súlimo, and let my sorrow and my tears be my excuse; yet aforetime did this draught fail never to refresh the heart of Laurelin, and she bare ever in return a fruit of light more plentiful than we gave; and methought the Gods sat darkly in their halls and for the weight of their grief essayed no remedy of their ills. But behold now have Lórien and I put forth our spells and nought may they avail," and Vána wept.

Now was it the thought of many that those twain Lórien and Vána might not avail to heal the wounds of Laurelin and Silpion, in that no word of the Earth-lady, mother of magics, was mingled in their spells. Therefore many said: "Let us seek Palúrien, for of her magic maybe these Trees shall again know some portion of their ancient glory – and then if light be renewed Aulë and his craftsmen may repair the hurts of our fair realm, and happiness will be once more twixt Erumáni and the Sea"[10] – but of the darkness and ill days that had long been without the hills few recked or thought.

Now therefore they called for Yavanna, and she came and asked them what they would, and hearing she wept and spake before them, saying: "Know ye, O Valar, and ye sons and daughters of the Eldar, Children of Ilúvatar, first offspring of the forests of the Earth, that never may these Two Trees bloom again, and others like them may not be brought to life for many many ages of the world. Many things shall be done and come to pass, and the Gods grow old, and the Elves come nigh to fading, ere ye shall see the rekindling of these Trees or the Magic Sun relit," and the Gods knew not what she meant, speaking of the Magic Sun, nor did for a long while after. But Tulkas hearing said: "Why speakest thou these words, O Kémi Palúrien, for foretelling is not thy wont, and that of evil least of all?" And others there were who said: "Ay, and never before has Kémi the Earth-lady been hard of counsel or lacked a spell of deepest virtue," and they besought her to put forth her power. But Yavanna said: " 'Tis of fate and the Music of the Ainur. Such marvels as those Trees of gold and silver may even the Gods make but once, and that in the youth of the world; nor may all my spells avail to do what ye now ask."

Then said Vána: "How then sayest thou, Aulë, mighty contriver, who art called *i·Talka Marda* – Smith of the World – for the might of thy works, how are we to obtain light that is needful to our joy? For what is Valinor without light, or what art thou an thou losest thy skill, as, meseems, in this hour thy spouse has done?"

"Nay," said Aulë, "light may not be fashioned by smithcraft, O Vána-Laisi, nor can any even of the Gods devise it, if the sap of the Trees of wonder be dried for ever." But Palúrien answering also said: "Lo, O Tuivána, and ye beside of the Vali and of the Elves, think ye only and always of Valinor, forgetting the world without? – for my heart saith to me that already were it time for the Gods to take up once more the battle for the world and expel therefrom the powers of Melko ere they be waxen to o'erwhelming strength." But Vána comprehended not Palúrien's mind, thinking only of her Tree of gold, and she abode ill-content; but Manwë and Varda, and with them Aulë and Yavanna, fared thence, and in secret conclave they took deep and searching counsel one of another, and at the last they bethought them of a rede of hope. Then did Manwë call together all the folk of Valinor once more; and that great throng was gathered even in Vána's bower amidst her roses, where Kulullin's fountains were, for the plain without lay now all cold and dark. There came even the leaders of the Elves and sat at the feet of the Gods, nor had that before been done; but when all were come together Aulë arose and said: "Hearken ye all. A rede has Manwë Súlimo Valatúru* to declare, and the mind of the Earth-lady and of the Queen of the Stars is therein, nor yet is my counsel absent."

Then was there a great silence that Manwë might speak, and he said: "Behold O my people, a time of darkness has come upon us, and yet I have it in mind that this is not without the desire of Ilúvatar. For the Gods had well-nigh forgot the world that lies without expectant of better days, and of Men, Ilúvatar's younger sons that soon must come. Now therefore are the Trees withered that so filled our land with loveliness and our hearts with mirth that wider desires came not into them, and so behold, we must turn now

---

* In margin: 'also *Valahíru*'.

our thoughts to new devices whereby light may be shed upon both the world without and Valinor within."

Then told he them concerning those stores of radiance they still possessed; for of silver light they had no great store save only that that yet lay in Telimpë, and a lesser measure that Aulë had in basons in his smithy. Some indeed had the Eldar lovingly saved in tiny vessels as it flowed and wasted in the soils about the stricken bole, but it was little enough.

Now the smallness of their store of white light was due to many causes, in that Varda had used greatly of it when she kindled mighty stars about the heavens, both at the coming of the Eldar and at other times. Moreover that Tree Silpion bore dew of light less richly far than Laurelin had been wont to do, and nonetheless, for it was less hot and fiery-subtle, did the Gods and Elves have need of it always in their magic crafts, and had mingled it with all manner of things that they devised, and in this were the Noldoli the chief.

Now golden light not even the Gods could tame much to their uses, and had suffered it to gather in the great vat Kulullin to the great increase of its fountains, or in other bright basons and wide pools about their courts, for the health and glory of its radiance was very great. 'Tis said indeed that those first makers of jewels, of whom Fëanor has the greatest fame, alone of the Eldar knew the secret of subtly taming golden light to their uses, and they dared use their knowledge but very sparingly, and now is that perished with them out of the Earth. Yet even of this golden radiance was there no unfailing source, now that Laurelin dripped her sweet dew no more. Of this necessity did Manwë shape his plan, and it was caught from that very sowing of the stars that Varda did of yore; for to each of the stars had she given a heart of silver flame set in vessels of crystals and pale glass and unimagined substances of faintest colours: and these vessels were some made like to boats, and buoyed by their hearts of light they fared ever about Ilwë, yet could they not soar into the dark and tenuous realm of Vaitya that is outside all. Now winged spirits of the utmost purity and beauty – even the most ethereal of those bright choirs of the Mánir and the Súruli who fare about the halls of Manwë on Taniquetil or traverse all the airs that move upon the world – sate in those starry boats and guided them on mazy courses high above the Earth, and Varda gave them names, but few of these are known.

Others there were whose vessels were like translucent lamps set quivering above the world, in Ilwë or on the very confines of Vilna and the airs we breathe, and they flickered and waned for the stirring of the upper winds, yet abode where they hung and moved not; and of these some were very great and beautiful and the Gods and Elves among all their riches loved them; and thence indeed the jewel-makers catch their inspiration. Not least did they love Morwinyon of the west, whose name meaneth the glint at dusk, and of his setting in the heavens much has been told; and of Nielluin too, who is the Bee of Azure, Nielluin whom still may all men see in autumn or in winter burning nigh the foot of Telimektar son of Tulkas whose tale is yet to tell.

But lo! (said Lindo) the beauty of the stars hath drawn me far afield, and yet I doubt not in that great speech, the mightiest Manwë ever spake before the Gods, mention he made of them yet more loving than was mine. For behold, he desired in this manner to bring the hearts of the Gods to consider his design, and having spoken of the stars he shaped thus his final words: "Behold," said Manwë, "this is now the third essay of the Gods to bring light into dark places, and both the Lamps of the North and South, and the Trees of the plain, Melko hath brought to ruin. Now in the air only hath Melko no power for ill, wherefore it is my rede that we build a great vessel brimming with golden light and the hoarded dews of Laurelin, and this do set afloat like a mighty ship high above the dark realms of the Earth. There shall it thread far courses through the airs and pour its light on all the world twixt Valinórë and the Eastern shores."

Now Manwë designed the course of the ship of light to be between the East and West, for Melko held the North and Ungweliant the South, whereas in the West was Valinor and the blessed realms, and in the East great regions of dark lands that craved for light.

Now it is said (quoth Lindo) that, whereas certain of the Gods of their divine being might, an they wished, fare with a great sudden-ness of speed through Vilna and the low airs, yet might none even of the Valar, not Melko himself, nor any other save Manwë and Varda and their folk alone avail to pass beyond: for this was the word of Ilúvatar when he sped them to the world at their desire, that they should dwell for ever within the world if once they entered it, nor should leave it, until its Great End came, being woven about it in the threads of its fate and becoming part thereof. Yet more, to Manwë alone, knowing the purity and glory of his heart, did Ilúvatar grant the power of visiting the uttermost heights; and breathing the great clear Serene which lies so far above the world that no finest dust of it, nor thinnest odour of its lives, nor faintest echo of its song or sorrow comes there; but far below it gleams palely beneath the stars and the shadows of the Sun and Moon faring back and forth from Valinor flutter upon its face. There walks Manwë Súlimo often far out beyond the stars and watches it with love, and he is very near the heart of Ilúvatar.

But this has ever been and is yet the greatest bitterness to Melko, for in no wise of himself could he now forsake the bosom of the Earth, and belike ye shall yet hear how mightily his envy was increased when the great vessels of radiance set sail; but now is it to tell that so moving were the words and so great their wisdom that[11] the most part of the Gods thought his purpose good, and they said: "Let Aulë busy himself then with all his folk in the fashioning of this ship of light", and few said otherwise, though 'tis told that Lórien was little pleased, fearing lest shadow and quiet and secret places ceased to be, and of a surety Vána might think of little else for the greatness of her vain desire to see the rekindling of the Trees.

Then said Aulë: "The task ye set me is of the utmost difficulty, yet will I do all that I may therein," and he begged the aid of Varda the starfashioner, and those twain departed and were lost in the gloom a great while.

The narrative continues with an account of the failure of Aulë and Varda to devise any substance that was not 'too gross to swim the airs or too frail to bear the radiance of Kulullin'; and when this was made known Vána and Lórien asked that, since Manwë's design had failed, he should command Yavanna to attempt the healing of the Trees.

At length therefore did Manwë bid Yavanna to put forth her power, and she was loath, but the clamour of the folk constrained her, and she begged for some of the radiance of white and gold; but of this would Manwë and Aulë spare only two small phials, saying that if the draught of old had power to heal the Trees already had they been blooming, for Vána and Lórien had poured it unstintingly upon their roots. Then sorrowfully Yavanna stood upon the plain and her form trembled and her face was very pale for the greatness of the effort that her being put forth, striving against fate. The phial of gold she held in her right hand and the silver in her left, and standing between the Trees she lifted them on high, and flames of red and of white arose from each like flowers, and the ground shook, and the earth opened, and a growth of flowers and plants leapt up therefrom about her feet, white and blue about her left side and red and gold about her right, and the Gods sat still and in amaze. Then going she cast each phial upon its proper Tree and sang the songs of unfading growth and a song of resurrection after death and withering; and suddenly she sang no more. Midway she stood between the

Trees and utter silence fell, then there was a great noise heard and none knew what passed, but Palúrien lay swooning on the Earth; but many leapt beside her and raised her from the ground, and she trembled and was afraid.

"Vain, O children of the Gods," she cried, "is all my strength. Lo, at your desire I have poured my power upon the Earth like water, and like water the Earth has sucked it from me – it is gone and I can do no more." And the Trees stood still gaunt and stark, and all the companies wept beholding her, but Manwë said: "Weep not, O children of the Gods, the irreparable harm, for many fair deeds may be yet to do, and beauty hath not perished on the earth nor all the counsels of the Gods been turned to nought"; but nonetheless folk left that place in sorrow, save Vána only, and she clung to the bole of Laurelin and wept.

Now was the time of faintest hope and darkness most profound fallen on Valinor that was ever yet; and still did Vána weep, and she twined her golden hair about the bole of Laurelin and her tears dropped softly at its roots; and even as the dew of her gentle love touched that tree, behold, a sudden pale gleam was born in those dark places. Then gazed Vána in wonder, and even where her first tears fell a shoot sprang from Laurelin, and it budded, and the buds were all of gold, and there came light therefrom like a ray of sunlight beneath a cloud.

Then sped Vána a little way out upon the plain, and she lifted up her sweet voice with all her power and it came trembling faintly to the gates of Valmar, and all the Valar heard. Then said Ómar: "'Tis the voice of Vána's lamentation," but Salmar said: "Nay, listen more, for rather is there joy in that sound," and all that stood by hearkened, and the words they heard were *I·kal'antúlien*, Light hath returned.

Loud then was the murmur about the streets of Valmar, and folk sped thronging over the plain, and when they beheld Vána beneath the Tree and the new shoot of gold then suddenly did a song of very mighty praise and joy burst forth on every tongue; and Tulkas said: "Lo, mightier have the spells of Yavanna proved than her foretelling!" But Yavanna gazing upon Vána's face said: "Alas, 'tis not so, for in this have my spells played but a lesser part, and more potent has the gentle love of Vána been and her falling tears a dew more healing and more tender than all the radiance of old: yet as for my foretelling, soon wilt thou see, O Tulkas, if thou dost but watch."

Then did all the folk gaze on Laurelin, and behold, those buds opened and put forth leaves, and these were of finest gold and of other kind to those of old, and even as they watched the branch bore golden blossom, and it was thronged with flowers. Now as swiftly as its blossoms opened full it seemed a gust of wind came suddenly and shook them from their slender stems, blowing them about the heads of those that watched like jets of fire, and folk thought there was evil in that; but many of the Eldar chased those shining petals far and wide and gathered them in baskets, yet save such as were of golden threads or of other metals these might not contain those ardent blooms and were all consumed and burnt, that the petals were lost again.

One flower there was however greater than the others, more shining, and more richly golden, and it swayed to the winds but fell not; and it grew, and as it grew of its own radiant warmth it fructified. Then as its petals fell and were treasured a fruit there was of great beauty hanging from that bough of Laurelin, but the leaves of the bough grew sere and they shrivelled and shone no more. Even as they dropped to earth the fruit waxed wonderfully, for all the sap and radiance of the dying Tree were in it, and the juices of that fruit were like quivering flames of amber and of red and its pips like shining gold, but its rind was of a perfect lucency smooth as a glass whose nature is transfused with gold and therethrough the moving of its juices could be seen within like throbbing furnace-fires. So great became the light and richness of that growth and the weight of its fruitfulness that the bough bent thereunder, and it hung as a globe of fires before their eyes.

Then said Yavanna to Aulë: "Bear thou up the branch, my lord, lest it snap and the fruit of wonder be dashed rudely to the ground; and the greatest ruth would that be, for know ye all that this is the last flame of life that Laurelin shall show." But Aulë had stood by as one lost in sudden thought since first that fruit came to ripening, and he answered now saying: "Very long indeed did Varda and I seek through the desolate homes and gardens for materials of our craft. Now do I know that Ilúvatar has brought my desire into my hand." Then calling to Tulkas to aid him he severed the stem of that fruit, and they that behold gasped and were astonied at his ruthlessness.

Loudly they murmured, and some cried: "Woe to him that ravishes anew our Tree," and Vána was in great ire. Yet did none dare to draw nigh, for those twain Aulë and Tulkas might scarcely bear up even upon their godlike shoulders that great globe of flame and were tottering beneath it. Hearing their anger indeed Aulë stayed, saying: "Cease ye of little wisdom and have a patience," but even with those words his foot went astray and he stumbled, and even Tulkas might not bear that fruit alone, so that it fell, and striking stony ground burst asunder. Straightway such a blinding radiance leapt forth as even the full bloom of Laurelin had not yielded of old, and the darkened eyes of the Vali were dazzled so that they fell back stunned; but a pillar of light rose from that place smiting the heavens that the stars paled above it and the face of Taniquetil went red afar off, and Aulë alone of all those there was unmoved by sorrow. Then said Aulë: "Of this can I make a ship of light – surpassing even the desire of Manwë," and now Varda and many others, even Vána, understood his purpose and were glad. But they made a mighty corbel of twisted gold, and strewing it with ardent petals of its own bloom they laid therein the halves of the fruit of noon and uplifting it with many hands bore it away with much singing and great hope. Then coming to the courts of Aulë they set it down, and thereupon began the great smithying of the Sun; and this was the most cunning-marvellous of all the works of Aulë Talkamarda, whose works are legion. Of that perfect rind a vessel did he make, diaphanous and shining, yet of a tempered strength, for with spells of his own he overcame its brittleness, nor in any way was its subtle delicacy thereby diminished.

Now the most ardent radiance poured therein neither spilled nor dimmed, nor did that vessel receive any injury therefrom, yet would it swim the airs more lightly than a bird; and Aulë was overjoyed, and he fashioned that vessel like a great ship broad of beam, laying one half of the rind within the other so that its strength might not be broken.

There follows an account of how Vána, repenting of her past murmurings, cut short her golden hair and gave it to the Gods, and from her hair they wove sails and ropes 'more strong than any mariner hath seen, yet of the slenderness of gossamer'. The masts and spars of the ship were all of gold.

Then that the Ship of the Heavens might be made ready unto the last, the unfading petals of the latest flower of Laurelin were gathered like a star at her prow, and tassels and streamers of glancing light were hung about her bulwarks, and a flash of lightning was caught in her mast to be a pennant; but all that vessel was filled to the brim with the blazing radiance of gold Kulullin and mingled therein drops of the juices of the fruit of noon, and these were very hot, and thereafter scarcely might the bosom of the Earth withhold her, and she leapt at her cords like a captive bird that listeth for the airs.

Then did the Gods name that ship, and they called her Sári which is the Sun, but the Elves Úr which is fire;[12] but many other names does she bear in legend and in poesy. The Lamp of Vána is she named among the Gods in memory of Vána's tears and her sweet tresses that she gave; and the Gnomes call her Galmir the gold-gleamer[13] and Glorvent the ship of gold, and Bráglorin the blazing vessel, and many a name beside; and her names among Men no man has counted them.

Behold now it is to be told how while that galleon was a-building others nigh to where the Two Trees once grew fashioned a great bason and folk laboured mightily at it. Its floor they made of gold and its walls of polished bronze, and an arcade of golden pillars topped with fires engirdled it, save only on the East; but Yavanna set a great and nameless spell around it, so that therein was poured the most of the waters of the fruit of noon and it became a bath of fire. Indeed is it not called Tanyasalpë, the bowl of fire, even Faskalanúmen, the Bath of the Setting Sun, for here when Urwendi after returned from the East and the first sunset came on Valinor the ship was drawn down and its radiance refreshed against new voyagings on the morrow while the Moon held High Heaven.

Now the making of this place of fire is more wondrous than seems, for so subtle were those radiances that set in the air they spilled not nor sank, nay rather they rose and floated away far above Vilna, being of the utmost buoyancy and lightness; yet now did nought escape from Faskalan which burnt amid the plain, and light came to Valinor therefrom, yet by reason of the deepness of the bason it fared not far abroad and the ring of shadows stood close in.

Then said Manwë, looking upon the glory of that ship as it strained to be away: "Who shall steer us this boat and guide its course above the realms of Earth, for even the holy bodies of the Valar, meseems, may not for long endure to bathe in this great light."

But a great thought came into the heart of Urwendi, and she said that she was not adread, and begged leave to become the mistress of the Sun and to make herself ready for that office as Ilúvatar set it in her heart to do. Then did she bid a many of her maidens follow her, even of those who had aforetime watered the roots of Laurelin with light, and casting aside their raiment they went down into that pool Faskalan as bathers into the sea, and its golden foams went over their bodies, and the Gods saw them not and were afraid. But after a while they came again to the brazen shores and were not as before, for their bodies were grown lucent and shone as with an ardour within, and light flashed from their limbs as they moved, nor might any raiment endure to cover their glorious bodies any more. Like air were they, and they trod as lightly as does sunlight on the earth, and saying no word they climbed upon the ship, and that vessel heaved against its great cords and all the folk of Valinor might scarce restrain it.

Now at last by Manwë's command do they climb the long slopes of Taniquetil and draw i·Kalaventë the Ship of Light along with them, nor is that any great task; and now do they stand on the wide space before great Manwë's doors, and the ship is on the western slope of the mountain trembling and tugging at its bonds, and already so great is its glory become that sunbeams pour out over the shoulders of Taniquetil and a new light is in the sky, and the waters of the Shadowy Seas beyond are touched with such fire as they never yet had seen. In that hour 'tis said that all creatures that wandered in the world stood still and wondered, even as Manwë going spake to Urwendi and said: "Go now, most wondrous maiden washed in fire, and steer the ship of divine light above the world, that joy may search out its narrowest crannies and all the things that sleep within its bosom may awake";[14] but Urwendi answered not, looking only eagerly to the East, and Manwë bade cast the ropes that held her, and straightway the Ship of the Morning arose above Taniquetil and the bosom of the air received it.

Ever as it rose it burned the brighter and the purer till all Valinor was filled with radiance, and the vales of Erúmáni and the Shadowy Seas were bathed in light, and sunshine was spilled on the dark plain of Arvalin, save only where Ungweliantë's clinging webs and darkest fumes still lay too thick for any radiance to filter through.

Then all looking up saw that heaven was blue, and very bright and beautiful, but the stars fled as that great dawn came upon the world; and a gentle wind blew from the cold lands to meet the vessel and filled its gleaming sails, and white vapours mounted from off the misty seas below toward her, that her prow seemed to cleave a white and airy foam. Yet did she waver not, for the Mánir that fared about her drew her by golden cords, and higher and higher the Sun's great galleon arose, until even to the sight of Manwë it was but a disc of fire wreathed in veils of splendour that slowly and majestically wandered from the West.

Now ever as it drew further on its way so grew the light in Valinor more mellow, and the shadows of the houses of the Gods grew long, slanting away towards the waters of the Outer Seas, but Taniquetil threw a great westering shadow that waxed ever longer and deeper, and it was afternoon in Valinor.'

Then said Gilfanon laughing: 'Nay, but, good sir, you lengthen the tale mightily, for methinks you love to dwell upon the works and deeds of the great Gods, but an you set not a measure to your words our stranger here will live not to hear of those things that happened in the world when at length the Gods gave to it the light they so long had withholden – and such tales, methinks, were a variety pleasing to hear.'

But Eriol had of a sooth been listening very eagerly to the sweet voice of Lindo, and he said: 'But a little while agone, a day perchance the Eldar would esteem it, did I come hither, yet no longer do I love the name of stranger, neither will Lindo ever lengthen the tale beyond my liking, whatsoever he tells, but behold this history is all to my heart.'

But Lindo said: 'Nay, nay, I have indeed more to tell; yet, O Eriol, the things that Gilfanon hath upon his lips are well worth the hearing – indeed never have I nor any here heard a full count of these matters. As soon therefore as may be will I wind up my tale and make an end, but three nights hence let us have another tale-telling, and it shall be one of greater ceremony, and musics there shall be, and all the children of the House of Lost Play shall here be gathered together at his feet to hear Gilfanon relate the travail of the Noldoli and the coming of Mankind.'

Now these words mightily pleased Gilfanon and Eriol, and many beside were glad, but now doth Lindo proceed:

'Know then that to such vast heights did the Sunship climb, and climbing blazed ever hotter and brighter, that ere long its glory was wider than ever the Gods conceived of when that vessel was still harboured in their midst. Everywhere did its great light pierce and all the vales and darkling woods, the bleak slopes and rocky streams, lay dazzled by it, and the Gods were amazed. Great was the magic and wonder of the Sun in those days of bright Urwendi, yet not so tender and so delicately fair as had the sweet Tree Laurelin once been; and thus whisper of new discontent awoke in Valinor, and words ran among the children of the Gods, for Mandos and Fui were wroth, saying that Aulë and Varda would for ever be meddling with the due order of the world, making it a place where no quiet or peaceful shadow could remain; but Lórien sat and wept in a grove of trees beneath the shade of Taniquetil and looked upon his gardens stretching beneath, still disordered by the great hunt of the Gods, for he had not had the heart for their mending. There the nightingales were silent for the heat danced above the trees, and his poppies were withered, and his evening flowers drooped and gave no scent; and Silmo stood sadly by Telimpë that gleamed wanly as still waters rather than the shining dew of Silpion, so overmastering was the

great light of day. Then Lórien arose and said to Manwë: "Call back
your glittering ship, O Lord of the Heavens, for the eyes of us ache
by reason of its flaming, and beauty and soft sleep is driven far away.
Rather the darkness and our memories than this, for this is not the
old loveliness of Laurelin, and Silpion is no more." Nor were any
of the Gods utterly content, knowing in their hearts that they had
done a greater thing than they at first knew, and never again would
Valinor see such ages as had passed; and Vána said that Kulullin's
fount was dulled and her garden wilted in the heat, and her roses
lost their hues and fragrance, for the Sun then sailed nearer to the
Earth than it now does.

Then Manwë chid them for their fickleness and discontent, but
they were not appeased; and suddenly spake Ulmo, coming from
outer Vai: "Lord Manwë, neither are their counsels nor thine to be
despised. Have ye then not yet understood, O Valar, wherein lay
much of the great beauty of the Trees of old? – In change, and in
slow alternation of fair things, the passing blending sweetly with that
which was to come."

But Lórien said suddenly: "O Valatúru, the Lord of Vai speaketh
words wiser than ever before, and they fill me with a great longing,"
and he left them thereupon and went out upon the plain, and it was
then three daytimes, which is the length of three blossomings of
Laurelin of old, since the Ship of Morning was unmoored. Then for
four daytimes more sate Lórien beside the stock of Silpion and the
shadows gathered shyly round him, for the Sun was far to the East,
beating about the heavens where it listed, since Manwë had not as
yet ruled its course and Urwendi was bidden fare as seemed good to
her. Yet even so Lórien is not appeased, not though the darkness
of the mountains creep across the plain, and a mist bloweth in from
off the sea and a vague and flitting twilight gathers once more in
Valinor, but long he sits pondering why the spells of Yavanna wrought
only upon Laurelin.

Then Lórien sang to Silpion, saying that the Valar were lost 'in a wilderness of gold and heat, or else in shadows full of death and unkindly
glooms,' and he touched the wound in the bole of the Tree.

Lo, even as he touched that cruel hurt, a light glowed faintly
there as if radiant sap still stirred within, but a low branch above
Lórien's bowed head burgeoned suddenly, and leaves of a very dark
green, long and oval, budded and unfolded upon it, yet was all the
Tree beside bare and dead and has ever been so since. Now it was at

that time seven times seven days since the fruit of noon was born upon Laurelin, and many of the Eldar and of the sprites and of the Gods were drawn nigh, listening to Lórien's song; but he heeded them not, gazing upon the Tree.

Lo, its new leaves were crusted with a silver moisture, and their undersides were white and set with pale gleaming filaments. Buds there were of flowers also upon the bough, and they opened, but a dark mist of the sea gathered about the tree, and the air grew bitterly cold as it never before had been in Valinor, and those blossoms faded and fell and none heeded them. One only was there at the branch's end that opening shone of its own light and no mist or cold harmed it, but indeed waxing it seemed to suck the very vapours and transform them subtly to the silver substance of its body; and it grew to be a very pale and wondrous glistering flower, nor did even the purest snow upon Taniquetil gleaming in the light of Silpion outrival it, and its heart was of white flame and it throbbed, waxing and waning marvellously. Then said Lórien for the joy of his heart: "Behold the Rose of Silpion", and that rose grew till the fruit of Laurelin had been but little greater, and ten thousand crystal petals were in that flower, and it was drenched in a fragrant dew like honey and this dew was light. Now Lórien would suffer none to draw near, and this will he rue for ever: for the branch upon which the Rose hung yielded all its sap and withered, nor even yet would he suffer that blossom to be plucked gently down, being enamoured of its loveliness and lusting to see it grow mightier than the fruit of noon, more glorious than the Sun.

Then snapped the withered bough and the Rose of Silpion fell, and some of its dewy light was roughly shaken from it, and here and there a petal was crushed and tarnished, and Lórien cried aloud and sought to lift it gently up, but it was too great. Therefore did the Gods let send to Aulë's halls, for there was a great silver charger, like to a table of the giants, and they set the latest bloom of Silpion upon it, and despite its hurts its glory and fragrance and pale magic were very great indeed.

Now when Lórien had mastered his grief and ruth he spake the counsel that Ulmo's words had called to his heart: that the Gods build another vessel to match the galleon of the Sun, "and it shall be made from the Rose of Silpion," said he, "and in memory of the waxing and waning of these Trees for twelve hours shall the Sunship sail the heavens and leave Valinor, and for twelve shall Silpion's pale bark mount the skies, and there shall be rest for tired eyes and weary hearts."

This then was the manner of the shaping of the Moon, for Aulë
would not dismember the loveliness of the Rose of Silver, and he
called rather to him certain of those Eldar of his household who
were of the Noldoli of old[15] and had consorted with the jewel-
makers. Now these revealed to him much store of crystals and delicate
glasses that Fëanor and his sons[16] had laid up in secret places in
Sirnúmen, and with the aid of those Elves and of Varda of the stars,
who gave even of the light of those frail boats of hers to give limpid
clearness to their fashioning, he brought to being a substance thin
as a petal of a rose, clear as the most transparent elfin glass, and
very smooth, yet might Aulë of his skill bend it and fashion it, and
naming it he called it *virin*. Of *virin* now he built a marvellous vessel,
and often have men spoken of the Ship of the Moon, yet is it scarce
like to any bark that sailed or sea or air. Rather was it like an island
of pure glass, albeit not very great, and tiny lakes there were bordered
with snowy flowers that shone, for the water of those pools that
gave them sap was the radiance of Telimpë. Midmost of that shimmering isle was wrought a cup of that crystalline stuff that Aulë
made and therein the magic Rose was set, and the glassy body of
the vessel sparkled wonderfully as it gleamed therein. Rods there
were and perchance they were of ice, and they rose upon it like aëry
masts, and sails were caught to them by slender threads, and Uinen
wove them of white mists and foam, and some were sprent with
glinting scales of silver fish, some threaded with tiniest stars like
points of light — sparks caught in snow when Nielluin was shining.

Thus was the Ship of the Moon, the crystal island of the Rose,
and the Gods named it Rána, the Moon, but the fairies Sil, the
Rose,[17] and many a sweet name beside. Ilsaluntë or the silver shallop
has it been called, and thereto the Gnomes have called it Minethlos
or the argent isle and Crithosceleg the disc of glass.

Now Silmo begged to sail upon the oceans of the firmament
therein, but he might not, for neither was he of the children of the
air nor might he find a way to cleanse his being of its earthwardness
as had Urwendi[18] done, and little would it have availed to enter
Faskalan had he dared essay it, for then would Rána have shrivelled
before him. Manwë bade therefore Ilinsor, a spirit of the Súruli
who loved the snows and the starlight and aided Varda in many of
her works, to pilot this strange-gleaming boat, and with him went
many another spirit of the air arrayed in robes of silver and white,
or else of palest gold; but an aged Elf with hoary locks stepped
upon the Moon unseen and hid him in the Rose, and there dwells
he ever since and tends that flower, and a little white turret has he

builded on the Moon where often he climbs and watches the heavens,
or the world beneath, and that is Uolë Kúvion who sleepeth never.
Some indeed have named him the Man in the Moon, but Ilinsor is
it rather who hunts the stars.

Now is to tell how the plan that Lórien devised was changed, for
the white radiance of Silpion is by no means so buoyant and ethereal
as is the flame of Laurelin, nor *virin* so little weighty as the rind of
the bright fruit of noon; and when the Gods laded the white ship
with light and would launch it upon the heavens, behold, it would
not rise above their heads. Moreover, behold, that living Rose
continued to give forth a honey as of light that distills upon the isle
of glass, and a dew of moonbeams glistens there, yet rather does this
weigh the vessel than buoy it as did the increase of the Sunship's
flames. So is it that Ilinsor must return at times, and that overflowing
radiance of the Rose is stored in Valinor against dark days – and it is
to tell that such days come ever and anon, for then the white flower of
the isle wanes and scarcely shines, and then must it be refreshed and
watered with its silver dew, much as Silpion was wont of old to be.

Hence was it that a pool was builded hard by the dark southern
wall of Valmar, and of silver and white marbles were its walls, but
dark yews shut it in, being planted in a maze most intricate about it.
There Lórien hoarded the pale dewy light of that fair Rose, and he
named it the Lake Irtinsa.

So comes it that for fourteen nights men may see Rána's bark
float upon the airs, and for other fourteen the heavens know it not;
while even on those fair nights when Rána fares abroad it showeth
not ever the same aspect as doth Sári the glorious, for whereas that
bright galleon voyageth even above Ilwë and beyond the stars and
cleaveth a dazzling way blinding the heavens, highest of all things
recking little of winds or motions of the airs, yet Ilinsor's bark is
heavier and less filled with magic and with power, and fareth never
above the skies but saileth in the lower folds of Ilwë threading a
white swathe among the stars. For this reason the high winds trouble
it at times, tugging at its misty shrouds; and often are these torn and
scattered, and the Gods renew them. At times too are the petals of
the Rose ruffled, and its white flames blown hither and thither like
a silver candle guttering in the wind. Then doth Rána heave and toss
about the air, as often you may see him, and mark the slender curve
of his bright keel, his prow now dipping, now his stern; and whiles
again he sails serenely to the West, and up through the pure lucency
of his frame the wide Rose of Silpion is seen, and some say the aged
form of Uolë Kúvion beside.

Then indeed is the Ship of the Moon very fair to look upon, and
the Earth is filled with slender lights and deep quick-moving shadows,
and radiant dreams go with cool wings about the world, but Lórien
has ruth amid his gladness, because his flower bears yet, and will for
ever, the faint marks of its bruising and its fall; and all men can see
them clearly.

But[19] lo,' saith Lindo, 'I run on ahead, for yet have I only told
that the silver ship is newly built, and Ilinsor yet but first stepped
aboard – and now do the Gods draw that vessel once again up the
steep sides of old Taniquetil singing as they go songs of Lórien's
folk that long have been dumb in Valinor. Slower was that wayfaring than the lifting of the Ship of Morn, and all the folk strain
lustily at the ropes, until Oromë coming harnesses thereto a herd of
wild white horses, and thus comes the vessel to the topmost place.

Then behold, the galleon of the Sun is seen afar beating golden
from the East, and the Valar marvel to descry the glowing peaks of
many a mountain far away, and isles glimmering green in seas once
dark. Then cried Ossë: "Look, O Manwë, but the sea is blue, as
blue wellnigh as Ilwë that thou lovest!" and "Nay," said Manwë,
"envy we not Ilwë, for the sea is not blue alone, but grey and green
and purple, and most beauteous-flowered with foaming white. Nor
jade nor amethyst nor porphyry set with diamonds and with pearls
outrival the waters of the Great and little seas when the sunlight
drenches them."

So saying Manwë sent Fionwë his son, swiftest of all to move
about the airs, and bade him say to Urwendi that the bark of the Sun
come back awhile to Valinor, for the Gods have counsels for her ear;
and Fionwë fled most readily, for he had conceived a great love for
that bright maiden long ago, and her loveliness now, when bathed
in fire she sate as the radiant mistress of the Sun, set him aflame with
the eagerness of the Gods. So was it that Urwendi brought her ship
unwilling above Valinor, and Oromë cast a noose of gold abouṭ it,
and it was drawn slowly down upon the Earth, and behold, the woods
upon Taniquetil glowed once more in the mingled light of silver and
of gold, and all were minded of the ancient blending of the Trees;
but Ilsaluntë paled before the galleon of the Sun till almost it seemed
to burn no more. So ended the first day upon the world, and it was
very long and full of many marvellous deeds that Gilfanon may tell;
but now the Gods beheld the evening deepen over the world as the
Sunship was drawn down and the glow upon the mountains faded,
and the sparkle of the seas went out. Then the primeval darkness
crept out again once more from many stealthy lairs, but Varda was

glad to see the steady shining of the stars. Far upon the plain was
Sári drawn, and when she was gone Ilsaluntë was haled upon the
topmost peak so that his white lucency fell out thence over the wide
world and the first night was come. Indeed in these days darkness
is no more within the borders of the world, but only night, and night
is another and a different thing, by reason of the Rose of Silpion.

Now however does Aulë fill the brimming vessel of that flower
with white radiance, and many of the Súruli white-winged glide
beneath and bear it slowly up and set it among the company of the
stars. There does it swim slowly, a pale and glorious thing, and
Ilinsor and his comrades sit them upon its rim and with shimmering
oars urge it bravely through the sky; and Manwë breathed upon its
bellying sails till it was wafted far away, and the beat of the unseen
oars against the winds of night faded and grew faint.

Of this manner was the first rising of the Moon above Taniquetil,
and Lórien rejoiced, but Ilinsor was jealous of the supremacy of the
Sun, and he bade the starry mariners flee before him and the constellate lamps go out, but many would not, and often he set sail in
chase of them, and the little ships of Varda fled before the huntsman
of the firmament, and were not caught: – and that, said Lindo, 'is
all, methinks, I know to tell of the building of those marvellous
ships and their launching on the air.'[20]

'But,' said Eriol, 'nay, surely that is not so, for at the tale's beginning methought you promised us words concerning the present
courses of the Sun and Moon and their rising in the East, and I for
one, by the leave of the others here present am not minded to release
you of your word.'

Then quoth Lindo laughing, 'Nay, I remember not the promise,
and did I make it then it was rash indeed, for the things you ask are
nowise easy to relate, and many matters concerning the deeds in
those days in Valinor are hidden from all save only the Valar. Now
however am I fain rather to listen, and thou Vairë perchance will
take up the burden of the tale.'

Thereat did all rejoice, and the children clapped their hands, for
dearly did they love those times when Vairë was the teller of the
tale; but Vairë said:

'Lo, tales I tell of the deep days, and the first is called *The Hiding
of Valinor*.'

## NOTES

1 The manuscript has here *Gilfan a·Davrobel*, but in the rejected

earlier version of this passage the reading is *Gilfanon a·Davrobel*, suggesting that *Gilfan* was not intentional.

2  See pp. 24–5 on the relation of Tavrobel to the Staffordshire village of Great Haywood. At Great Haywood the river Sow joins the Trent.

3  In the rejected version of this 'interlude' Gilfanon's history is differently recounted: 'he was long before an Ilkorin and had dwelt ages back in Hisilómë'; 'he came to Tol Eressëa after the great march [i.e. Inwë's 'march into the world', the great expedition from Kôr, see p. 26], for he had adopted blood-kinship with the Noldoli.' − This is the first occurrence of the term *Ilkorin*, which refers to Elves who were 'not of Kôr' (cf. the later term *Úmanyar*, Elves 'not of Aman'). *Artanor* is the precursor of Doriath.

4  Gilfanon, a Gnome, is here called the oldest of the *fairies*; see p. 51.

5  No explanation of 'the House of the Hundred Chimneys', near the bridge of Tavrobel, is known to me, but I have never visited Great Haywood, and it may be that there was (or is) a house there that gave rise to it.

6  The rejected form of the 'interlude' is quite different in its latter part:

> Therefore said Lindo in answer to Eriol: 'Behold, Gilfanon here can tell you much of such matters, but first of all must you be told of the deeds that were done in Valinor when Melko slew the Trees and the Gnomes marched away into the darkness. 'Tis a long tale but well worth the hearkening.' For Lindo loved to tell such tales and sought often an occasion for recalling them; but Gilfanon said: 'Speak on, my Lindo, but methinks the tale will not be told tonight or for many a night after, and I shall have fared long back to Tavrobel.' 'Nay,' said Lindo, 'I will not make the tale overlong, and tomorrow shall be all your own.' And so saying Gilfanon sighed, but Lindo lifted up his voice . . .

7  'lest it be': this curious expression is clear in the manuscript; the usage seems wholly unrecorded, but the meaning intended must be 'unless it be', i.e. 'to him alone, unless also to Varda . . .'

8  On *Telimpë* as the name of the 'Moon-cauldron', rather than *Silindrin*, see pp. 79 and 129 note 2.

9  See pp. 73, 88. At previous occurrences the name is *Urwen*, not *Urwendi*.

10  'twixt Erumáni and the Sea': i.e., the Outer Sea, Vai, the western bound of Valinor.

11  The passage beginning 'For behold, he desired in this manner . . .' on p. 182 and continuing to this point was added on a detached sheet and replaced a very much shorter passage in which Manwë briefly declared his plan, and nothing was said about the powers of the Valar. But I do not think that the replacement was composed significantly later than the body of the text.

12  The earlier reading here was: 'Then did the Gods name that ship, and they called her Ûr which is the Sun', etc.

13  The earlier reading here was: 'and the Gnomes call her Aur the Sun, and Galmir the goldgleamer', etc.

14 An isolated note refers to the coming forth of more wholesome creatures when the Sun arose (i.e. over the Great Lands), and says that 'all the birds sang in the first dawn'.

15 The Aulenossë: see p. 176.

16 This is the first appearance of the Sons of Fëanor.

17 Earlier reading: 'the silver rose'.

18 *Urwendi*: manuscript *Urwandi*, but I think that this was probably unintended.

19 From this point the text of the *Tale of the Sun and Moon* ceases to be written over an erased pencilled original, and from the same point the original text is extant in another book. In fact, to the end of the *Tale of the Sun and Moon* the differences are slight, no more than alterations of wording; but the original text does explain the fact that at the first occurrence of the name *Gilfanon* on p. 189 the original reading was *Ailios*. One would guess in any case that this was a slip, a reversion to an earlier name, and that this is so is shown by the first version, which has, for 'many marvellous deeds that Gilfanon may tell' (p. 194), 'many marvellous deeds as Ailios shall tell'.

20 From this point the second version diverges sharply from the first. The first reads as follows:

> And that is all, methinks,' said Lindo, 'that I know to tell of those fairest works of the Gods'; but Ailios said: 'Little doth it cost thee to spin the tale, an it be of Valinor; it is a while since ye offered us a . . . . . tale concerning the rising of the Sun and Moon in the East, and a flow of speech has poured from thee since then, but now art thou minded to [?tease], and no word of that promise.' Of a truth Ailios beneath his roughness liked the words of Lindo as well as any, and he was eager to learn of the matter.
>
> 'That is easy told,' said Lindo . . .

What follows in the original version relates to the matter of the next chapter (see p. 220 note 2).

Ailios here claims that a promise made by Lindo has not been fulfilled, just as does Eriol, more politely, in the second version. The beginning of the tale in the first version is not extant, and perhaps as it was originally written Lindo did make this promise; but in the second he says no such thing (indeed Eriol's question was 'Whence be the Sun and Moon?'), and at the end of his tale denies that he had done so, when Eriol asserts it.

Changes made to names in
*The Tale of the Sun and Moon*

*Amnor* ⟨ *Amnos* (*Amnos* is the form in *The Flight of the Noldoli*, ⟨ *Emnon*; the form *Amnon* also occurs, see p. 172).

For changes in the passage on the names of the Sun see notes 12 and 13.
*Gilfanon* ⟨ *Ailios* (p. 189, at the first occurrence only, see note 19).
*Minethlos* ⟨ *Mainlos.*
*Uolë Kúvion* ⟨ *Uolë Mikúmi*, only at the second occurrence on p. 193;
    at the first occurrence, *Uolë Mikúmi* was left unchanged, though
    I have given *Uolë Kúvion* in the text.
*Ship of Morning* ⟨ *Kalaventë* (p. 190; *i·Kalaventë* 'the Ship of Light'
    occurs unemended in the text on p. 188).
*the Sunship's flames* ⟨ *the flames of Kalaventë* (p. 193).
*Sári* ⟨ *Kalavénë* (pp. 193, 195. *Kalavénë* is the form in the original
    version, see note 19).


Commentary on
*The Tale of the Sun and Moon*


The effect of the opening of this tale is undoubtedly to emphasize more
strongly than in the later accounts the horror aroused by the deeds of
the Noldoli (notable is Aulë's bitterness against them, of which nothing
is said afterwards), and also the finality and absoluteness of their exclusion
from Valinor. But the idea that some Gnomes remained in Valinor (the
Aulenossë, p. 176) survived; cf. *The Silmarillion* p. 84:

> And of all the Noldor in Valinor, who were grown now to a great
> people, but one tithe refused to take the road: some for the love that
> they bore to the Valar (and to Aulë not least), some for the love of
> Tirion and the many things that they had made; none for fear of peril
> by the way.

Sorontur's mission and the tidings that he brought back were to be
abandoned. Very striking is his account of the empty ships drifting, of
which 'some were burning with bright fires': the origin of Fëanor's burning
of the ships of the Teleri at Losgar in *The Silmarillion* (p. 90), where
however there is a more evident reason for doing so. That Melko's second
dwelling-place in the Great Lands was distinct from Utumna is here
expressly stated, as also that it was in the Iron Mountains (cf. pp. 149,
158); the name *Angamandi* 'Hells of Iron' has occurred once in the *Lost
Tales*, in the very strange account of the fate of Men after death (p. 77).
In later accounts Angband was built on the site of Utumno, but finally
they were separated again, and in *The Silmarillion* Angband had existed
from ancient days before the captivity of Melkor (p. 47). It is not explained
in the present tale why 'never more will Utumna open to him' (p. 176),
but doubtless it was because Tulkas and Ulmo broke its gates and piled
hills of stone upon them (p. 104).
    In the next part of the tale (pp. 177 ff.) much light is cast on my father's
early conception of the powers and limitations of the great Valar. Thus

Yavanna and Manwë (brought to this realization by Yavanna?) are shown to believe that the Valar have done ill, or at least failed to achieve the wider designs of Ilúvatar ('I have it in mind that this [time of darkness] is not without the desire of Ilúvatar'): the idea of 'selfish', inward-looking Gods is plainly expressed, Gods content to tend their gardens and devise their devisings behind their mountains, leaving 'the world' to shape itself as it may. And this realization is an essential element in their conceiving the making of the Sun and Moon, which are to be such bodies as may light not only 'the blessed realms' (an expression which occurs here for the first time, p. 182) but all the rest of the dark Earth. Of all this there is only a trace in *The Silmarillion* (p. 99):

> These things the Valar did, recalling in their twilight the darkness of the lands of Arda; and they resolved now to illumine Middle-earth and with light to hinder the deeds of Melkor.

Of much interest also is the 'theological' statement in the early narrative concerning the binding of the Valar to the World as the condition of their entering it (p. 182); cf. *The Silmarillion* p. 20:

> But this condition Ilúvatar made, or it is the necessity of their love, that their power should thenceforward be contained and bounded in the World, to be within it for ever, until it is complete, so that they are its life and it is theirs.

In the tale this condition is an express physical limitation: none of the Valar, save Manwë and Varda and their attendant spirits, could pass into the higher airs above Vilna, though they could move at great speed within the lowest air.

From the passage on p. 178, where it is said that Ulmo, despite his love for the Solosimpi and grief at the Kinslaying, was yet not filled with anger against the Noldoli, for he 'was foreknowing more than all the Gods, even than great Manwë', it is seen that Ulmo's peculiar concern for the exiled Eldar – which plays such an important if mysterious part in the development of the story – was there from the beginning; as also was Yavanna's thought, expressed in *The Silmarillion* p. 78:

> Even for those who are mightiest under Ilúvatar there is some work that they may accomplish once, and once only. The Light of the Trees I brought into being, and within Eä I can do so never again.

Yavanna's reference to the Magic Sun and its relighting (which has appeared in the toast drunk in the evening in the Cottage of Lost Play, pp. 17, 65) is obviously intended to be obscure at this stage.

There is no later reference to the story of the wastage of light by Lórien and Vána, pouring it over the roots of the Trees unavailingly.

Turning to Lindo's account of the stars (pp. 181–2), *Morwinyon* has appeared in an earlier tale (p. 114), with the story that Varda dropped it 'as she fared in great haste back to Valinor', and that it 'blazes above the world's edge in the west'; in the present tale Morwinyon (which according to both the Qenya and Gnomish word-lists is Arcturus) is again strangely represented as being a luminary always of the western sky. It is said here that while some of the stars were guided by the Mánir and the Súruli 'on mazy courses', others, including Morwinyon and Nielluin, 'abode where they hung and moved not'. Is the explanation of this that in the ancient myths of the Elves there was a time when the regular apparent movement of all the heavenly bodies from East to West had not yet begun? This movement is nowhere explained mythically in my father's cosmology.

Nielluin ('Blue Bee') is Sirius (in *The Silmarillion* called *Helluin*), and this star had a place in the legend of Telimektar son of Tulkas, though the story of his conversion into the constellation of Orion was never clearly told (cf. *Telumehtar* 'Orion' in *The Lord of the Rings* Appendix E, I). Nielluin was Inwë's son Ingil, who followed Telimektar 'in the likeness of a great bee bearing honey of flame' (see the Appendix on Names under *Ingil* and *Telimektar*).

The course of the Sun and Moon between East and West (rather than in some other direction) is here given a rationale, and the reason for avoiding the South is Ungweliant's presence there. This seems to give Ungweliant a great importance and also a vast area subject to her power of absorbing light. It is not made clear in the tale of *The Darkening of Valinor* where her dwelling was. It is said (p. 151) that Melko wandered 'the dark plains of Eruman, and farther south than anyone yet had penetrated he found a region of the deepest gloom' – the region where he found the cavern of Ungweliant, which had 'a subterranean outlet on the sea'; and after the destruction of the Trees Ungweliant 'gets her gone southward and over the mountains to her home' (p. 154). It is impossible to tell from the vague lines on the little map (p. 81) what was at this time the configuration of the southern lands and seas.

In comparison with the last part of the tale, concerning the last fruit of Laurelin and the last flower of Silpion, the making from them of the Sun and Moon, and the launching of their vessels (pp. 183–95), Chapter XI of *The Silmarillion* (constituted from two later versions not greatly dissimilar the one from the other) is extremely brief. Despite many differences the later versions read in places almost as summaries of the early story, but it is often hard to say whether the shortening depends rather on my father's feeling (certainly present, see p. 174) that the description was too long, was taking too large a place in the total structure, or an actual rejection of some of the ideas it contains, and a desire to diminish the extreme 'concreteness' of its images. Certainly there is here a revelling in materials of 'magic' property, gold, silver, crystal, glass, and above all light conceived as a liquid element, or as dew, as honey, an element that can be bathed in and gathered into vessels, that has quite largely disappeared from *The Silmarillion* (although, of course, the idea of light as liquid, dripping down, poured and hoarded, sucked up by Ungoliant, remained essential to the conception of the Trees, this idea becomes in the later writing less palpable and the divine operations are given less 'physical' explanation and justification).

As a result of this fullness and intensity of description, the origin of the Sun and Moon in the last fruit and last flower of the Trees has less of mystery than in the succinct and beautiful language of *The Silmarillion*; but also much is said here to emphasize the great size of the 'Fruit of Noon', and the increase in the heat and brilliance of the Sunship after its launching, so that the reflection rises less readily that if the Sun that brilliantly illumines the whole Earth was but one fruit of Laurelin then Valinor must have been painfully bright and hot in the days of the Trees. In the early story the last outpourings of life from the dying Trees are utterly strange and 'enormous', those of Laurelin portentous, even ominous; the Sun is astoundingly bright and hot even to the Valar, who are awestruck and disquieted by what has been done (the Gods knew 'that they had done a greater thing than they at first knew', p. 190); and the anger and distress of certain of the Valar at the burning light of the Sun enforces the feeling that in the last fruit of Laurelin a terrible and unforeseen power has been released. This distress does indeed survive in *The Silmarillion* (p. 100), in the reference to 'the prayers of Lórien and Estë, who said that sleep and rest had been banished from the Earth, and the stars were hidden'; but in the tale the blasting power of the new Sun is intensely conveyed in the images of 'the heat dancing above the trees' in the gardens of Lórien, the silent nightingales, the withered poppies and the drooping evening flowers.

In the old story there is a mythical explanation of the Moon's phases (though not of eclipses), and of the markings on its face through the story of the breaking of the withered bough of Silpion and the fall of the Moonflower – a story altogether at variance with the explanation given in *The Silmarillion* (*ibid.*). In the tale the fruit of Laurelin also fell to the ground, when Aulë stumbled and its weight was too great for Tulkas to bear alone: the significance of this event is not made perfectly clear, but it seems that, had the Fruit of Noon not burst asunder, Aulë would not have understood its structure and conceived that of the Sunship.

To whatever extent the great differences between the versions in this part of the Mythology may be due to later compression, there remain a good many actual contradictions, of which I note here only some of the more important, in addition to that concerning the markings on the Moon already mentioned. Thus in *The Silmarillion* the Moon rose first, 'and was the elder of the new lights as was Telperion of the Trees' (*ibid.*); in the old story the reverse is true both of the Trees and of the new lights. Again, in *The Silmarillion* it is Varda who decides their motions, and she changes these from her first plan at the plea of Lórien and Estë, whereas here it is Lórien's very distress at the coming of Sunlight that leads to the last blossoming of Silpion and the making of the Moon. The Valar indeed play different roles throughout; and here far greater importance attaches to the acts of Vána and Lórien, whose relations with the Sun and Moon are at once deeper and more explicit than they afterwards became, as they had been with the Trees (see p. 71); in *The Silmarillion* it was Nienna who watered the Trees with her tears (p. 98). In *The Silmarillion* the Sun and Moon move nearer to Arda than 'the ancient stars' (p. 99), but here they move at quite different levels in the firmament.

But a feature in which later compression can be certainly discerned is the elaborate description in the tale of the Moon as 'an island of pure glass', 'a shimmering isle', with little lakes of the light from Telimpë bordered with shining flowers and a crystalline cup amidmost in which was set the Moonflower; only from this is explicable the reference in *The Silmarillion* to Tilion's steering 'the island of the Moon'. The aged Elf Uolë Kúvion (whom 'some indeed have named the Man in the Moon') seems almost to have strayed in from another conception; his presence gives difficulty in any case, since we have just been told (p. 192) that Silmo could not sail in the Moonship because he was not of the children of the air and could not 'cleanse his being of its earthwardness'. – An isolated heading 'Uolë and Erinti' in the little pocket-book used among things for suggestions of stories to be told (see p. 171) no doubt implies that a tale was preparing on the subject of Uolë; cf. the Tale of Qorinómi concerning Urwendi and Erinti's brother Fionwë (p. 215). No traces of these tales are to be found and they were presumably never written. Another note in the pocket-book calls Uolë Mikúmi (the earlier name of Uolë Kúvion, see p. 198) 'King of the Moon'; and a third refers to a poem 'The Man in the Moon' which is to be sung by Eriol, 'who says he will sing them a song of a legend touching Uolë Mikúmi as Men have it'. My father wrote a poem about the Man in the Moon in March 1915, but if it was this that he was thinking of including it would have startled the company of Mar Vanwa Tyaliéva – and he would have had to change its references to places in England which were not yet in existence. Although it is very probable that he had something quite different in mind, I think it may be of interest to give this poem in an early form (see p. 204).

As the mythology evolved and changed, the Making of the Sun and Moon became the element of greatest difficulty; and in the published *Silmarillion* this chapter does not seem of a piece with much of the rest of the work, and could not be made to be so. Towards the end of his life my father was indeed prepared to dismantle much of what he had built, in the attempt to solve what he undoubtedly felt to be a fundamental problem.

### *Note on the order of the Tales*

The development of the *Lost Tales* is here in fact extremely complex. After the concluding words of *The Flight of the Noldoli*, 'the story of the darkening of Valinor was at an end' (p. 169), my father wrote: 'See on beyond in other books', but in fact he added subsequently the short dialogue between Lindo and Eriol ('Great was the power of Melko for ill . . .') which is given at the end of *The Flight of the Noldoli*.

The page-numbering of the notebooks shows that the next tale was to be the *Tale of Tinúviel*, which is written in another book. This long story (to be given in Part II), the oldest extant version of 'Beren and Lúthien', begins with a long *Link* passage; and the curious thing is that this *Link* begins with the very dialogue between Lindo and Eriol just referred to, in almost identical wording, and this can be seen to be its original place; but here it was struck through.

I have mentioned earlier (p. 45) that in a letter written by my father in 1964 he said that he wrote *The Music of the Ainur* while working in Oxford on the staff of the Dictionary, a post that he took up in November 1918 and relinquished in the spring of 1920. In the same letter he said that he wrote ' "The Fall of Gondolin" during sick-leave from the army in 1917', and 'the original version of the "Tale of Lúthien Tinúviel and Beren" later in the same year'. There is nothing in the manuscripts to suggest that the tales that follow *The Music of the Ainur* to the point we have now reached were not written consecutively and continuously from *The Music*, while my father was still in Oxford.

At first sight, then, there is a hopeless contradiction in the evidence: for the *Link* in question refers explicitly to the Darkening of Valinor, a tale written *after* his appointment in Oxford at the end of 1918, but is a link to the *Tale of Tinúviel*, which he said that he wrote in 1917. But the *Tale of Tinúviel* (and the *Link* that precedes it) is in fact a text in ink written over an erased pencilled original. It is, I think, certain that this *rewriting* of *Tinúviel* was considerably later. It was linked to *The Flight of the Noldoli* by the speeches of Lindo and Eriol (the link-passage is integral and continuous with the *Tale of Tinúviel* that follows it, and was not added afterwards). At this stage my father must have felt that the *Tales* need not necessarily be told in the actual sequence of the narrative (for *Tinúviel* belongs of course to the time after the making of the Sun and Moon).

The rewritten *Tinúviel* was followed with no break by a first form of the 'interlude' introducing Gilfanon of Tavrobel as a guest in the house, and this led into the *Tale of the Sun and Moon*. But subsequently my father changed his mind, and so struck out the dialogue of Lindo and Eriol from the beginning of the *Link* to *Tinúviel*, which was not now to follow *The Flight of the Noldoli*, and wrote it out again in the other book at the end of that tale. At the same time he rewrote the Gilfanon 'interlude' in an extended form, and placed it at the end of *The Flight of the Noldoli*. Thus:

| Flight of the Noldoli | Flight of the Noldoli |
| Words of Lindo and Eriol | Words of Lindo and Eriol |

| | |
|---|---|
| Tale of Tinúviel | Gilfanon 'interlude' (rewritten) |
| Gilfanon 'interlude' | Tale of the Sun and Moon and |
| Tale of the Sun and Moon and | the Hiding of Valinor |
| the Hiding of Valinor | |

That the rewriting of *Tinúviel* was one of the latest elements in the composition of the *Lost Tales* seems clear from the fact that it is followed by the first form of the Gilfanon 'interlude', written at the same time: for Gilfanon replaced Ailios, and Ailios, not Gilfanon, is the guest in the house in the earlier versions of the *Tale of the Sun and Moon* and *The Hiding of Valinor*, and is the teller of the *Tale of the Nauglafring*.

The poem about the Man in the Moon exists in many texts, and was published at Leeds in 1923;* long after and much changed it was included in *The Adventures of Tom Bombadil* (1962). I give it here in a form close to the earlier published version, but with a few (mostly very minor) alterations made subsequently. The 1923 version was only a little retouched from the earliest workings – where it has the title 'Why the Man in the Moon came down too soon: an East Anglian phantasy'; in the first finished text the title is 'A Faërie: Why the Man in the Moon came down too soon', together with one in Old English: *Se Móncyning*.

### Why the Man in the Moon
### came down too soon

The Man in the Moon had silver shoon
 And his beard was of silver thread;
He was girt with pale gold and inaureoled
 With gold about his head.     4
Clad in silken robe in his great white globe
 He opened an ivory door
With a crystal key, and in secrecy
 He stole o'er a shadowy floor;    8

Down a filigree stair of spidery hair
 He slipped in gleaming haste,
And laughing with glee to be merry and free
 He swiftly earthward raced.    12
He was tired of his pearls and diamond twirls;
 Of his pallid minaret
Dizzy and white at its lunar height
 In a world of silver set;    16

* '*A Northern Venture:* verses by members of the Leeds University English School Association' (Leeds, at the Swan Press, 1923). I have not seen this publication and take these details from Humphrey Carpenter, *Biography*, p. 269.

And adventured this peril for ruby and beryl
  And emerald and sapphire,
And all lustrous gems for new diadems,
  Or to blazon his pale attire.           20
He was lonely too with nothing to do
  But to stare at the golden world,
Or strain for the hum that would distantly come
  As it gaily past him whirled;        24

And at plenilune in his argent moon
  He had wearily longed for Fire –
Not the limpid lights of wan selenites,
  But a red terrestrial pyre        28
With impurpurate glows of crimson and rose
  And leaping orange tongue;
For great seas of blues and the passionate hues
  When a dancing dawn is young;      32

For the meadowy ways like chrysoprase
  By winding Yare and Nen.
How he longed for the mirth of the populous Earth
  And the sanguine blood of men;      36
And coveted song and laughter long
  And viands hot and wine,
Eating pearly cakes of light snowflakes
  And drinking thin moonshine.      40

He twinkled his feet as he thought of the meat,
  Of the punch and the peppery brew,
Till he tripped unaware on his slanting stair,
  And fell like meteors do;      44
As the whickering sparks in splashing arcs
  Of stars blown down like rain
From his laddery path took a foaming bath
  In the Ocean of Almain;      48

And began to think, lest he melt and stink,
  What in the moon to do,
When a Yarmouth boat found him far afloat,
  To the mazement of the crew      52
Caught in their net all shimmering wet
  In a phosphorescent sheen
Of bluey whites and opal lights
  And delicate liquid green.      56

With the morning fish − 'twas his regal wish −
  They packed him to Norwich town,
To get warm on gin in a Norfolk inn,
  And dry his watery gown.                              60
Though Saint Peter's knell waked many a bell
  In the city's ringing towers
To shout the news of his lunatic cruise
  In the early morning hours,                           64

No hearths were laid, not a breakfast made,
  And no one would sell him gems;
He found ashes for fire, and his gay desire
  For chorus and brave anthems                          68
Met snores instead with all Norfolk abed,
  And his round heart nearly broke,
More empty and cold than above of old,
  Till he bartered his fairy cloak          -           72

With a half-waked cook for a kitchen nook,
  And his belt of gold for a smile,
And a priceless jewel for a bowl of gruel,
  A sample cold and vile                                76
Of the proud plum-porridge of Anglian Norwich −
  He arrived so much too soon
For unusual guests on adventurous quests
  From the Mountains of the Moon.                       80

It seems very possible that the 'pallid minaret' reappears in the 'little
white turret' which Uolë Kúvion built on the Moon, 'where often he
climbs and watches the heavens, or the world beneath'. The minaret of
the Man in the Moon survives in the final version.

The Ocean of Almain is the North Sea (*Almain* or *Almany* was a name
of Germany in earlier English); the Yare is a Norfolk river which falls
into the sea at Yarmouth, and the Nene (pronounced also with a short
vowel) flows into the Wash.

# IX

# THE HIDING OF VALINOR

The link to this tale, which is told by Vairë, has been given at the end of the last (p. 195). The manuscript continues as in the latter part of *The Tale of the Sun and Moon* (see p. 197 note 19), with an earlier draft also extant, to which reference is made in the notes.

'Lo, tales I tell of the deep days, and the first is called *The Hiding of Valinor*.

Already have ye heard,' said she, 'of the setting forth of the Sun and Moon upon their wayward journeyings, and many things are there to tell concerning the awakening of the Earth beneath their light; but hear now of the thoughts and deeds of the dwellers in Valinor in those mighty days.

Now is it to tell that so wide were the wanderings of those boats of light that the Gods found it no easy thing to govern all their comings and their goings as they had purposed at the first, and Ilinsor was loath to yield the heaven to Urwendi, and Urwendi set sail often before Ilinsor's due return, being eager and hot of mood. Wherefore were both vessels often far afloat at one and the same time, and the glory of them sailing most nigh to the very bosom of the Earth, as often they did at that time, was very great and very terrible to see.

Then did a vague uneasiness begin to stir anew in Valinor, and the hearts of the Gods were troubled, and the Eldar spake one to another, and this was their thought.

"Lo, all the world is grown clear as the courtyards of the Gods, straight to walk upon as are the avenues of Vansamírin or the terraces of Kôr; and Valinor no longer is safe, for Melko hates us without ceasing, and he holds the world without and many and wild are his allies there" – and herein in their hearts they[1] numbered even the Noldoli, and wronged them in their thought unwittingly, nor did they forget Men, against whom Melko had lied of old. Indeed in the joy of the last burgeoning of the Trees and the great and glad labour of that fashioning of ships the fear of Melko had been laid aside, and the bitterness of those last evil days and of the Gnome-folk's flight was fallen into slumber – but now when Valinor had peace once more and its lands and gardens were mended of their hurts memory awoke their anger and their grief again.

Indeed if the Gods forgot not the folly of the Noldoli and hardened their hearts, yet more wroth were the Elves, and the Solosimpi were full of bitterness against their kin, desiring never more to see their faces in the pathways of their home. Of these the chief were those whose kin had perished at the Haven of the Swans, and their leader was one Ainairos who had escaped from that fray leaving his brother dead; and he sought unceasingly with his words to persuade the Elves to greater bitterness of heart.

Now this was a grief to Manwë, yet did he see that as yet his design was not complete, and that the wisdom of the Valar must needs be bent once more to the more perfect government of the Sun and Moon. Wherefore he summoned the Gods and Elves in conclave, that their counsel might better his design, and moreover he hoped with soft words of wisdom to calm their anger and uneasiness ere evil came of it. For clearly he saw herein the poison of Melko's lies that live and multiply wherever he may cast them more fruitfully than any seed that is sown upon the Earth; and already it was reported to him that the ancient murmuring of the Elves was begun anew concerning their freedom, and that pride made some full of folly, so that they might not endure the thought of the coming of Mankind.

Now then sat Manwë in heavy mood before Kulullin and looked searchingly upon the Valar gathered nigh and upon the Eldar about his knees, but he opened not his full mind, saying to them only that he had called them in council once more to determine the courses of the Sun and Moon and devise an order and wisdom in their paths. Then straightway spake Ainairos before him saying that other matters were deeper in their hearts than this, and he laid before the Gods the mind of the Elves concerning the Noldoli and of the nakedness of the land of Valinor toward the world beyond. Thereat arose much tumult and many of the Valar and their folk supported him loudly, and some others of the Eldar cried out that Manwë and Varda had caused their kindred to dwell in Valinor promising them unfailing joy therein – now let the Gods see to it that their gladness was not minished to a little thing, seeing that Melko held the world and they dared not fare forth to the places of their awakening even an they would. The most of the Valar moreover were fain of their ancient ease and desired only peace, wishing neither rumour of Melko and his violence nor murmur of the restless Gnomes to come ever again among them to disturb their happiness; and for such reasons they also clamoured for the concealment of the land. Not the least among these were Vána and Nessa, albeit most even of the great Gods were of one mind. In vain did Ulmo of his foreknowing plead before them for pity and pardon on the Noldoli, or Manwë unfold the secrets of the Music of the Ainur and the purpose of the world; and long and very full of that noise was that council, and more filled with bitterness and burning words than any that had been; wherefore did Manwë Súlimo depart at length from among them, saying that no walls or bulwarks might now fend Melko's evil from them which lived already among them and clouded all their minds.

So came it that the enemies of the Gnomes carried the council of the Gods and the blood of Kópas began already its fell work; for now began that which is named the Hiding of Valinor, and Manwë and Varda and Ulmo of the Seas had no part therein, but none others of the Valar or the Elves held aloof therefrom, albeit Yavanna and Oromë her son were uneasy in their hearts.

Now Lórien and Vána led the Gods and Aulë lent his skill and Tulkas his strength, and the Valar went not at that time forth to conquer Melko, and the greatest ruth was that to them thereafter, and yet is; for the great glory of the Valar by reason of that error came not to its fullness in many ages of the Earth, and still doth the world await it.²

In those days however they were unwitting of these things, and they set them to new and mighty labours such as had not been seen among them since the days of the first building of Valinor. The encircling mountains did they make more utterly impassable of their eastern side than ever were they before, and such earth-magics did Kémi weave about their precipices and inaccessible peaks that of all the dread and terrible places in the mighty Earth was that rampart of the Gods that looked upon Eruman the most dire and perilous, and not Utumna nor the places of Melko in the Hills of Iron were so filled with insuperable fear. Moreover even upon the plains about their eastward . . .³ were heaped those impenetrable webs of clinging dark that Ungweliantë sloughed in Valinor at the Trees' destroying. Now did the Gods cast them forth from their bright land, that they might entangle utterly the steps of all who fared that way, and they flowed and spread both far and wide, lying even upon the bosom of the Shadowy Seas until the Bay of Faëry grew dim and no radiance of Valinor filtered there, and the twinkling of the lamps of Kôr died or ever it passed the jewelled shores. From North to South marched the enchantments and inaccessible magic of the Gods, yet were they

not content; and they said: Behold, we will cause all the paths that
fare to Valinor both known and secret to fade utterly from the world,
or wander treacherously into blind confusion.

This then they did, and no channel in the seas was left that was
not beset with perilous eddies or with streams of overmastering
strength for the confusion of all ships. And spirits of sudden storms
and winds unlooked-for brooded there by Ossë's will, and others of
inextricable mist. Neither did they forget even the long circuitous
ways that messengers of the Gods had known and followed through
the dark wildernesses of the North and the deepest South; and when
all was done to their mind Lórien said: "Now doth Valinor stand
alone, and we have peace," and Vána sang once more about her
garden in the lightness of her heart.

Alone among all did the hearts of the Solosimpi misgive them, and
they stood upon the coasts nigh to their ancient homes and laughter
came not easily again amongst them, and they looked upon the Sea
and despite its peril and its gloom they feared it lest it still might
bring evil into the land. Then did some of them going speak to
Aulë and to Tulkas who stood nigh, saying: "O great ones of the
Valar, full well and wondrously have the Gods laboured, yet do we
think in our hearts that something is yet lacking; for we have not
heard that the way of the escape of the Noldoli, even the dread
passage of Helkaraksë's cliffs, is destroyed. Yet where the children
of the Eldar have trodden so may the sons of Melko return, despite
all your enchantments and deceits; neither are we in peace at heart
by reason of the undefended sea."

Thereat did Tulkas laugh, saying that naught might come now
to Valinor save only by the topmost airs, "and Melko hath no power
there; neither have ye, O little ones of the Earth". Nonetheless at
Aulë's bidding he fared with that Vala to the bitter places of the
sorrow of the Gnomes, and Aulë with the mighty hammer of his
forge smote that wall of jagged ice, and when it was cloven even to
the chill waters Tulkas rent it asunder with his great hands and the
seas roared in between, and the land of the Gods was sundered
utterly from the realms of Earth.[4]

This did they at the Shoreland Elves' behest, yet by no means
would the Gods suffer that low place in the hills beneath Taniquetil
that lets upon the Bay of Faëry to be piled with rocks as the Solosimpi
desired, for there had Oromë many pleasant woods and places of
delight, and the Teleri[5] would not endure that Kôr should be destroyed or pressed too nearly by the gloomy mountain walls.

Then spake the Solosimpi to Ulmo, and he would not listen to them, saying that never had they learnt such bitterness of heart of his music, and that rather had they been listening to whispers of Melko the accursed. And going from Ulmo some were abashed, but others went and sought out Ossë, and he aided them in Ulmo's despite; and of Ossë's labour in those days are come the Magic Isles; for Ossë set them in a great ring about the western limits of the mighty sea, so that they guarded the Bay of Faëry, and albeit in those days the huge glooms of that far water overreached all the Shadowy Seas and stretched forth tongues of darkness towards them, still were they themselves surpassing fair to look upon. And such ships as fare that way must needs espy them or ever they reach the last waters that wash the elfin shores, and so alluring were they that few had power to pass them by, and did any essay to then sudden storms drove them perforce against those beaches whose pebbles shone like silver and like gold. Yet all such as stepped thereon came never thence again, but being woven in the nets of Oinen's[6] hair the Lady of the Sea, and whelmed in agelong slumber that Lórien set there, lay upon the margin of the waves, as those do who being drowned are cast up once more by the movements of the sea; yet rather did these hapless ones sleep unfathomably and the dark waters laved their limbs, but their ships rotted, swathed in weeds, on those enchanted sands, and sailed never more before the winds of the dim West.[7]

Now when Manwë gazing in sorrow from high Taniquetil saw all these things done he sent for Lórien and for Oromë, thinking them less stubborn of heart than the others, and when they were come he spoke earnestly with them; yet he would not that the labour of the Gods be undone, for he thought it not altogether ill, but he prevailed on those twain to do his bidding in certain matters. And in this manner did they so; for Lórien wove a way of delicate magic, and it fared by winding roads most secret from the Eastern lands and all the great wildernesses of the world even to the walls of Kôr, and it ran past the Cottage of the Children of the Earth[8] and thence down the "lane of whispering elms" until it reached the sea.

But the gloomy seas and all the straits it bridged with slender bridges resting on the air and greyly gleaming as it were of silken mists lit by a thin moon, or of pearly vapours; yet beside the Valar and the Elves have no Man's eyes beheld it save in sweet slumbers in their heart's youth. Longest of all ways is it and few are there ever reach its end, so many lands and marvellous places of allurement and of loveliness doth it pass ere it comes to Elfinesse, yet smooth is it to the feet and none tire ever who fare that way.

Such,' then said Vairë, 'was and still is the manner of Olórë
Mallë, the Path of Dreams; but of far other sort was the work of
Oromë, who hearing the words of Manwë went speedily to Vána his
wife, and begged of her a tress of her long golden hair. Now the hair
of Vána the fair had become more long and radiant still since the
days of her offering to Aulë, and she gave to Oromë of its golden
threads. Then did he dip these in the radiance of Kulullín, but
Vána wove them cunningly to a leash immeasurable, and therewith
Oromë strode swiftly to the gatherings of Manwë on the mountain.

Then calling loudly that Manwë and Varda and all their folk
come forth he held before their eyes his thong of gold, and they
knew not his purpose; but Oromë bid them cast their eyes on that
Hill that is called Kalormë standing hugely in the lands most distant from Valinor, and is held most lofty save Taniquetil, yet
seemeth therefrom a dim thing fading afar off. Even as they watched
Oromë stepped back, and putting all his cunning and his strength
thereto he made a mighty cast, and that golden cord sped in a curve
through the sky until its noose caught Kalormë's topmost pinnacle.
Then by the magic of its making and the cunning of Oromë's hand
it stayed a bright golden curve and neither drooped nor sagged; but
Oromë fastened its hither end to a pillar in Manwë's courts, and
turning to those who gazed upon him said: "Who then listeth to
wander in the Great Lands, let him follow me," and thereat he set
foot upon the thong and sped like the wind out over the gulf even to
Kalormë, while all upon Taniquetil were silent in amaze. Now did
Oromë loosen the thong from Kalormë's peak and run as swiftly
back, ravelling it as he came, until once more he stood before Manwë.
Then said he: "Lo, O Súlimo Lord of the Airs, a way I have devised
whereby any of the Valar of good heart may fare whithersoever they
list in the Great Lands; for whither they wish I will cast my slender
bridge, and its hither end wilt thou securely guard."

And of this work of Oromë's came that mighty wonder of the
heavens that all men look upon and marvel at, and some fear much,
pondering what it may portend. Yet doth that bridge wear a different
aspect at different times and in various regions of the Earth, and
seldom is it visible to Men and Elves. Now because it glistens most
marvellously in the slanting rays of the Sun, and when the rains of
heaven moisten it it shines most magically therein and the gold light
breaks upon its dripping cords to many hues of purple, green, and
red, so do men most often name it the Rainbow, but many other
names have they fashioned also, and the fairies call it Ilweran the
Bridge of Heaven.

Now living Men may not tread the swaying threads of Ilweran and few of the Eldar have the heart, yet other paths for Elves and Men to fare to Valinor are there none since those days save one alone, and it is very dark; yet is it very short, the shortest and swiftest of all roads, and very rough, for Mandos made it and Fui set it in its place. Qalvanda is it called, the Road of Death, and it leads only to the halls of Mandos and Fui. Twofold is it, and one way tread the Elves and the other the souls of Men, and never do they mingle.[9]

'Thus,' said Vairë, 'was the Hiding of Valinor achieved, and the Valar let slip the chance of a glory more splendid and enduring even than that great glory which was theirs and still is. Nonetheless are there still very mighty tidings of those days to tell, of which per-chance I may now recount to you a few; and one I will name *The Haven of the Sun*.

Behold, now are the hearts of all set at rest by the truce[10] of Manwë and the Valar, and while the Gods feast in Valmar and the heaven is full of the ungoverned glory of the Ships of Light the Elves go back at last to rebuild the happiness of Kôr; and there they seek to forget all the sorrows and all the labours that had come among them since the Release of Melko. Now does Kôr become the fairest and most delicate-lovely of all the realms of Valinor, for in the courtyard of Inwë those two elfin trees shone still tenderly; and they were shoots of the glorious Trees now dead given by the Gods to Inwë in the first days of that town's building. Others too had been given to Nólemë, but these were uprooted and were gone no one knew whither, and more had there never been.[11]

Yet even though the Elves trusted the Valar to shield the land and weave protection about them, and though the days of sorrow faring into the past grew dim, still could they not yet utterly shake away the memory of their unhappiness; nor did they ever so, until after the magic way of Lórien was complete and the children of the fathers of the fathers of Men first were suffered to come there in sweet sleep; then did a new joy burn very brightly in their hearts, but these things were not yet come to pass and Men were yet but new-wakened on the Earth.

But Manwë and Ulmo knowing their hour was come held high councils for their protection. Many designs they made therein, and they were weighed down by the thought of Melko and the wandering of the Gnomes; yet did the other folk of Valinor trouble themselves little with such matters yet. Nonetheless Manwë ventured to speak once more to the Valar, albeit he uttered no word of Men, and he

reminded them that in their labours for the concealment of their
land they had let slip from thought the waywardness of the Sun
and Moon. Now it was the fear of Manwë lest the Earth become
unbearable by reason of the great light and heat of those bright
things, and Yavanna's heart was in accord with him in that, but the
most of the Valar and the Elves saw good in his design because in
the lifting of the Sun and Moon to higher paths they thought to set
a final end to all their labours, removing those piercing beams more
far, that all those hills and regions of their abode be not too bright
illumined, and that none might ever again espy them afar off.

Wherefore said some: "Let us send now messengers to discover
the fashion of the world in the uttermost East beyond even the
sight of Manwë from the Mountain of the World." Then arose
Oromë: "That I can tell you, for I have seen. In the East beyond the
tumbled lands there is a silent beach and a dark and empty sea."
And the Gods marvelled at these tidings, yet never before had any
save Oromë listed to see or hear such things, not even Yavanna the
Earth-lady. Nought do I say of Ulmo Vailimo, Lord of Vai, for of
a truth all such matters he knew from the beginning of the Earth.
Now therefore did that ancient one follow Oromë, expounding to the
Valar what was the secret nature of the Earth, and he said:

"Lo, there is but one Ocean, and that is Vai, for those that Ossë
esteemeth as oceans are but seas, waters that lie in the hollows of
the rock; but Vai runneth from the Wall of Things unto the Wall
of Things whithersoever you may fare. Now to the North is it so
cold that even its pale waters are frozen to a depth beyond thought
or sounding, and to the South is such utter darkness and deceit by
reason of Ungoliont[12] that none save I alone may find a way. In
this vast water floateth the wide Earth upheld by the word of Ilúvatar,
for nought else or fish or bark will swim therein to whom I have not
spoken the great word that Ilúvatar said to me and bound them
with the spell; but of the wide Earth is even Valinor a part, and the
substance of the Earth is stone and metal, and the seas are pools in
its hollows, and the islands save some few that swim still unfettered
stand now like pinnacles from their weedy depths. Know then that
somewhat nearer stands Valinor to the great Wall of Things wherein
Ilúvatar hath enclosed us than doth that furthest Eastern shore:
and this do I know, for diving beneath the world often have I
visited those unharboured beaches; for lo, O Valar, ye know not all
wonders, and many secret things are there beneath the Earth's dark
keel, even where I have my mighty halls of Ulmonan, that ye have
never dreamed on."

But said Manwë: "True is that, O Ulmo Vailimo; but what is it to our present purpose?" And Ulmo answered: "Lo, I will take Aulë the Smith with me and convey him safe and swift beneath the waters of Vai in my deep-sea car, even to the Eastern shores, and there will he and I build havens for the Ships, and from the East hereafter shall they arise and give their fullest light and glory to Men who need them, and to the unhappy Noldoli, following one the other over the sky, and coming home to Valinor. Here, when their hearts wax faint by reason of their journeyings, shall they rest awhile upon the Outer Seas and Urwendi bathe in Faskalan and Ilinsor drink of the quiet waters of the Lake Irtinsa, ere ever they return again."

Now this speech had Manwë and Ulmo designed in collusion, and the Valar and Eldar hearkened for divers reasons as before; wherefore was Aulë sped now with Ulmo, and they builded great havens in the East beside the soundless sea; and the haven of the Sun was wide and golden, but the haven of the Moon was set within the same harbourage, and it was white, having gates of silver and of pearl that shone faintly so soon as the Sun sank from the heavens into Valinor; at that hour do those gates open of themselves before the issuing Moon, but none of the Eldar have seen these things save Uolë Kúvion, and he has told no tale.

Now at first the Valar purposed to draw the Sun and Moon beneath the Earth, hallowing them with Ulmo's spell that Vai harm them not, each at its appointed time; yet in the end they found that Sári[13] might not, even so, safely come beneath the world, for it was too frail and lissom; and much precious radiance was spilled in their attempts about the deepest waters, and escaped to linger as secret sparks in many an unknown ocean cavern. These have many elfin divers, and divers of the fays, long time sought beyond the outmost East, even as is sung in the song of the Sleeper in the Tower of Pearl.[14]

Indeed for a while mishap fell even upon bright Urwendi, that she wandered the dark grots and endless passages of Ulmo's realm until Fionwë found her and brought her back to Valinor – but the full tale is called the Tale of Qorinómi and may not here be told.[15]

Thus came it that the Gods dared a very great deed, the most mighty of all their works; for making a fleet of magic rafts and boats with Ulmo's aid – and otherwise had none of these endured to sail upon the waters of Vai – they drew to the Wall of Things, and there they made the Door of Night (Moritarnon or Tarn Fui as the Eldar name it in their tongues). There it still stands, utterly black and huge against the deep-blue walls. Its pillars are of the mightiest basalt and its lintel likewise, but great dragons of black stone are carved thereon, and shadowy smoke pours slowly from their jaws. Gates it has unbreakable, and none know how they were made or set, for the Eldar were not suffered to be in that dread building, and it is the last secret of the Gods; and not the onset of the world will force that door, which opens to a mystic word alone. That word Urwendi only knows and Manwë who spake it to her; for beyond the Door of Night is the outer dark, and he who passes therethrough may escape the world and death and hear things not yet for the ears of Earth-dwellers, and this may not be.

In the East however was the work of the Gods of other sort, for there was a great arch made, and, 'tis said, 'tis all of shining gold and barred with silver gates, yet few have beheld it even of the Gods for the wealth of glowing vapours that are often swathed about it. Now the Gates of Morn open also before Urwendi only, and the word she speaks is the same that she utters at the Door of Night, but it is reversed.

So comes it that ever now, as the Ship of the Moon leaves his haven in the East and his gates of pearl, Ulmo draws the galleon of the Sun before the Door of Night. Then speaks Urwendi the mystic word, and they open outward before her, and a gust of darkness sweeps in but perishes before her blazing light; and the galleon of the Sun goes out into the limitless dark, and coming behind the world finds the East again. There doth Sári filled with the lightness of the morning ride through the gates and Urwendi and her maidens make a sound of golden horns, and dawn is spilt upon the eyes of Men.[16]

Yet many a time and oft a tiny star-ship of Varda that has dipped into the Outer Seas, as often they will, is sucked through that Door of Night behind the Sun; and some track her galleon through the starless vast back unto the Eastern Wall, and some are lost for ever, and some glimmer beyond the Door until the Sunship issues forth again.[17] Then do these leap back and rush up into the sky again, or flee across its spaces; and this is a very beautiful thing to see — the Fountains of the Stars.

Behold, the Moon dares not the utter loneliness of the outer dark by reason of his lesser light and majesty, and he journeys still beneath the world and many are the chances of that way; wherefore is it that he is often less timely than the Sun and is more fickle. Sometimes he comes not after Sári at all, and other times is late and maketh but a little voyage or even dares the heavens while Urwendi still is there. Then smile the Gods wistfully and say: "It is the mingling of the lights once more."[18]

Long was this indeed the manner of the ships' guidance, and long was it after those days that the Gods grew afraid once more for the Sun and Moon because of certain tidings of those days, which perchance may after be told; and because of their fear a new and strange thing befell. Now the manner of this mayhap I may tell before I make an end; and it is called *The Weaving of the Days and Months and of the Years.*

For know that even as the great Gods sat in conclave pondering how they might fetter the lamps of heaven ever to their hand and guide their goings even as a charioteer doth guide his galloping horses, behold three aged men stood before them and saluted Manwë.

But Manwë asked them who they were, "for well I know," quoth he, "that ye are not of the glad folk that dwell in Valmar or the gardens of the Gods," and the Valar marvelled how they came unaided to their land. Now those men were of strange aspect, seeming aged beyond count albeit of strength untamed. And one that stood at the left was exceeding small and short, and another amidmost of middle stature, and the third was long and tall; and the first had short hair and a small beard, and the other's was neither long nor short, but the beard of the third swept the earth before his feet as he walked. Now after a while he that was short and small spake in answer to Manwë, and he said: "Brothers are we; and men of exceeding subtle craft"; and the other answered: "Lo, Danuin, Ranuin, and Fanuin are we called,* and I am Ranuin, and Danuin has spoken." Then said Fanuin: "And we will offer thee our skill in your perplexity – yet who we are and whence we come or whither we go that we will tell to you only if ye accept our rede and after we have wrought as we desire."

Then some of the Gods said them nay, fearing a trick (even perhaps of Melko), and others would grant their request, and such was the counsel that in the end prevailed because of the great perplexity of the time. Then did those three Danuin and Ranuin and Fanuin beg that a room might be set apart for them; and this was done in Aulë's house. There did they spin and weave in secret, and after a space of twice twelve hours Danuin came forth and spake to Manwë, saying: "Behold my handicraft!"; and none knew his intent, for his hands were empty. But when the Ship of the Sun returned then went Danuin to her stern, and laying his hand thereon he bid Ulmo draw her, as was his wont, over the waters to the Door of Night; and when Ulmo was gone a little way from the further

* In the margin is written *Dōgor Mōnaþ 7 Missére*, Old English words meaning 'Day, Month, and Year'.

shore of Valinor Danuin stepped back, and behold Ulmo might not draw the Sunship further, not though he put forth all his strength. Then were Manwë and Ulmo and all that beheld afraid, but Danuin after released the Sun and went from among them, and they might not find him; but after twenty nights and eight came forth Ranuin and he said also: "Behold my handicraft!" and yet no more could be seen in his outstretched hands than before in those of Danuin. Now Ranuin waited until Ilinsor brought the Rose of Silpion unto Valinor, and then going he set his hands against a jag of glass upon that isle, and thereafter might no man stir Ilinsor's bark far from Ranuin against his will; but again Ranuin spake no word and went from among them; then Rána was released, but Ranuin no man could find.

Now the Gods pondered long what this might portend, but nought more betid until thirteen times had Rána waxed and waned. Then came forth Fanuin, and he bid the Gods detain Ilinsor that at Sári's coming both ships might stand in Valinor at once. But when this was done he begged aid of the Gods, "for," said he, "I have fashioned somewhat of great weight that I would fain show to you, yet cannot of my own strength hale it forth." And seven of the stoutest from the halls of Tulkas went to the place of Fanuin's labouring and could not see aught therein; but he bid them stoop, and them seemed they laid hands upon a mighty cable and staggered beneath it as they laid it upon their shoulders, yet could they not see it.

Then going unto Sári and to Rána in turn Fanuin moved his hands as though he were making fast a great rope to each of those vessels; but when all was done he said to Manwë: "Lo, O Súlimo Lord of the Gods, the work is wrought and the ships of light are set in the unbreakable fetters of time, which neither ye, nor they, may ever break, nor may they escape therefrom, albeit these fetters are invisible to all beings that Ilúvatar has made; for nonetheless are they the strongest of things."

Then suddenly behold Danuin and Ranuin stood beside him, and Danuin going to Manwë placed in his hand a slender cord, but Manwë saw it not. "Herewith," said Danuin, "O Manwë Súlimo, canst thou govern the goings and comings of the Sun, and never may she be brought beyond the guidance of your hand, and such is the virtue of this cord that the goings and returnings of the Sun shall be accounted the most timely and inevitable of all things on Earth." Thereafter did Ranuin in like manner, and behold Manwë felt a stout rope within his palm invisible. "Herewith," said Ranuin, "shalt thou hold and steer the wayward Moon, as well as may be, and so great is the virtue of the 'thong of Ranuin' that even the fickle and untimely Moon shall be a measure of time to Elves and Men.'' Lastly did Fanuin bid bear his mighty cable's end to Manwë, and Manwë touched it, and it was made fast to a great rock upon Taniquetil (that is called therefore Gonlath), and Fanuin said: "Now doth this mightiest cable hold both the Moon and Sun in tow; and herewith mayest thou coordinate their motions and inter-weave their fates; for the rope of Fanuin is the Rope of Years, and Urwendi issuing through the Door of Night shall wind it all tangled with the daycord's slender meshes, round and about the Earth until the Great End come – and so shall all the world and the dwellers within it, both Gods and Elves and Men, and all the creatures that go and the things that have roots thereon, be bound about in the bonds of Time."

Then were all the Gods afraid, seeing what was come, and knowing that hereafter even they should in counted time be subject to slow eld and their bright days to waning, until Ilúvatar at the Great End calls them back. But Fanuin said: "Nay, it is but the Music of the Ainur: for behold, who are we, Danuin, Ranuin, and Fanuin, Day and Month and Year, but the children of Aluin, of Time, who is the oldest of the Ainur, and is beyond, and subject to Ilúvatar; and thence came we, and thither go we now." Then did those three vanish from Valinor; but of such is the framing of the moveless courses of the Sun and Moon, and the subjection of all things within the world to time and change.

But as for the Ships of Light themselves, behold! O Gilfanon and all that hearken, I will end the tale of Lindo and Vairë concerning the building of the Sun and Moon with that great foreboding that was spoken among the Gods when first the Door of Night was opened. For 'tis said that ere the Great End come Melko shall in some wise contrive a quarrel between Moon and Sun, and Ilinsor shall seek to follow Urwendi through the Gates, and when they are gone the Gates of both East and West will be destroyed, and Urwendi and Ilinsor shall be lost. So shall it be that Fionwë Úrion, son of Manwë, of love for Urwendi shall in the end be Melko's bane, and shall destroy the world to destroy his foe, and so shall all things then be rolled away.'[19]

And thus ended Vairë, and the great tale fell silent in the room.

## NOTES

1   'they': original reading 'the Solosimpi'.

2    The rejected draft text of the tale to this point is remarkably brief, and reads as follows (following on from Ailios' remarks given on p. 197, note 20):

> 'That is easy told,' said Lindo; 'for the murmurings that I have spoken of grew ever louder, and came to speech at that council which was now summoned to fix the courses of the Sun and Moon; and all the ancient grievance that had flamed before at Melko's instigation concerning the freedom of the Elves – even that strife that ended in the Exile of the Noldoli – grew sore again. Yet were few now in pity of the Gnomes, and such of the Eldar whom the newlit world allured dared not for the power of Melko break from Valinor; wherefore in the end the enemies of the Gnomes, despite all that Ulmo might say or plead, and despite the clemency of Manwë, carried the counsels of the Gods – and so came that which stories name the [Closing >] Hiding of Valinor. And the Gods went not at that time forth to fight Melko, and their greatest opportunity for glory and eternal honour was let slip, [even as the Music of Ilúvatar had foreboded – and they little understood it – and who knows if the salvation of the world and the freeing of Men and Elves shall ever come from them again? Some there are who whisper that it is not so, and hope dwelleth only in a far land of Men, but how so that may be I do not know.]

The concluding passage is thus bracketed in the manuscript, with a question-mark against it.

3    The word looks like 'east'. The word 'eastward' was added to the text, and it may be that my father intended to change 'east' to 'eastward edge' or something similar.

4    Here 'Earth' is clearly used, if strangely so, in the same way as is 'the world', to mean the Great Lands as distinguished from the Outer Lands of the West.

5    The Teleri (i.e. the later Vanyar) had not in the old story departed from Kôr (see p. 159).

6    Originally Ówen and then Ónen, the name of Ossë's wife has already appeared in the final form Uinen (pp. 121, 192); but Oinen here is clear, and clearly intended.

7    In the draft text the account of the Hiding of Valinor is very brief, and moves on quickly to the Path of Dreams. The webs of darkness laid on the eastward slopes of the mountains were not those 'sloughed in Valinor' by Ungweliantë, but are merely compared to 'the most clinging that ever Ungweliantë wove'. Helkaraksë and the Magic Isles are only mentioned in a marginal direction that they are to be included.

8    'Earth' is again used in the sense of the Great Lands (see note 4). The draft has here 'Children of the World'.

9    While there are no differences of any substance in the account of the Olórë Mallë in the two texts, in the first there is no mention of Oromë's

Path of the Rainbow. – An isolated note, obviously written before the present Tale, says: 'When the Gods close Valinor . . . Lórien leaves a path across the mountains called Olórë Mallë, and Manwë the Rainbow where he walks to survey the world. It is only visible after rain, for then it is wet.'

10 'truce': earlier reading 'compromise'. It is notable how Manwë is portrayed as *primus inter pares* rather than as ruler over the other Valar.

11 On the Trees of Kôr see pp. 123, 135.

12 See p. 200.

13 *Sári* is here (and subsequently) the name as written, not an emendation from *Kalavénë*, the name in the draft texts of *The Sun and Moon* and *The Hiding of Valinor* (see p. 198). The reading of the draft in this place is 'the Sunship', itself an alteration from 'the ships', for my father first wrote that neither ship could safely be drawn beneath the Earth.

14 The Sleeper in the Tower of Pearl is named in *The Cottage of Lost Play*, p. 15. The song of the sleeper is virtually certainly the poem *The Happy Mariners*, originally written in 1915 and published in 1923 (see Humphrey Carpenter, *Biography*, Appendix C, p. 269); this will be given in two versions in connection with the materials for the *Tale of Eärendel* in the second part of the *Lost Tales*. The poem contains a reference to the boats that pass the Tower of Pearl, piled 'with hoarded sparks of orient fire / that divers won in waters of the unknown Sun'.

15 The original draft has here: 'but that is the tale of Qorinómi and I dare not tell it here, for friend Ailios is watching me' (see p. 197, notes 19 and 20).

16 The draft text had here at first: 'and the galleon of the Sun goes out into the dark, and coming behind the world finds the East again, but there there is no door and the Wall of Things is lower; and filled with the lightness of the morning Kalavénë rides above it and dawn is split upon the Eastern hills and falls upon the eyes of Men.' Part of this, from 'but there there is no door', was bracketed, and the passage about the great arch in the East and the Gates of Morn introduced. In the following sentence, the draft had 'back over the Eastern Wall', changed to the reading of the second text, 'back unto the Eastern Wall'. For the name *Kalavénë* see p. 198.

17 I.e., until the Sunship issues forth, through the Door of Night, into the outer dark; as the Sunship leaves, the shooting stars pass back into the sky.

18 The second version of this part of Vairë's tale, 'The Haven of the Sun', follows the original draft (as emended) fairly closely, with no differences of any substance; but the part of her tale that now follows, 'The Weaving of the Days and Months and Years', is wholly absent from the draft text.

19  This concluding passage differs in several points from the original
    version. In that, Ailios appears again, for Gilfanon; the 'great fore-
    boding' was spoken among the Gods 'when they designed first to
    build the Door of Night'; and when Ilinsor has followed Urwendi
    through the Gates 'Melko will destroy the Gates and raise the Eastern
    Wall beyond the [?skies] and Urwendi and Ilinsor shall be lost'.


### Changes made to names in
### The Hiding of Valinor


*Vansamirin* < *Samírien's road* (*Samírien* occurs as the name of the Feast
    of Double Mirth, pp. 143-4).
*Kôr* < *Kortirion* (p. 207). Afterwards, though *Kôr* was not struck out,
    my father wrote above it *Tûn*, with a query, and the same at the
    occurrence of *Kôr* on p. 210. This is the first appearance in the
    text of the *Lost Tales* of this name, which ultimately gave rise to
    *Túna* (the hill on which Tirion was built).
*Ainairos* < *Oivárin*.
*Moritarnon, Tarn Fui*  The original draft of the tale has '*Móritar* or
    *Tarna Fui*'.
*Sári*  The original draft has *Kalavéně* (see p. 198 and note 13 above).
At the first occurrence of the names of the three Sons of Time the sequence
    of forms was:
    *Danuin* < *Danos* < an illegible form *Dan..*
    *Ranuin* < *Ranos* < *Ranoth* < *Rôn*
    *Fanuin* < *Lathos* < *Lathweg*
    Throughout the remainder of the passage: *Danuin* < *Dana; Ranuin* <
    *Ranoth; Fanuin* < *Lathweg*.
*Aluin* < *Lúmin*.


### Commentary on
### The Hiding of Valinor


The account of the Council of the Valar and Eldar in the opening of this
tale (greatly developed from the preliminary draft given in note 2) is
remarkable and important in the history of my father's ideas concerning
the Valar and their motives. In *The Silmarillion* (p. 102) the Hiding of
Valinor sprang from the assault of Melkor on the steersman of the Moon:

> But seeing the assault upon Tilion the Valar were in doubt, fearing
> what the malice and cunning of Morgoth might yet contrive against
> them. Being unwilling to make war upon him in Middle-earth, they
> remembered nonetheless the ruin of Almaren; and they resolved that
> the like should not befall Valinor.

A little earlier in *The Silmarillion* (p. 99) reasons are given for the unwillingness of the Valar to make war:

> It is said indeed that, even as the Valar made war upon Melkor for the sake of the Quendi, so now for that time they forbore for the sake of the Hildor, the Aftercomers, the younger Children of Ilúvatar. For so grievous had been the hurts of Middle-earth in the war upon Utumno that the Valar feared lest even worse should now befall; whereas the Hildor should be mortal, and weaker than the Quendi to withstand fear and tumult. Moreover it was not revealed to Manwë where the beginning of Men should be, north, south, or east. Therefore the Valar sent forth light, but made strong the land of their dwelling.

In *The Silmarillion* there is no vestige of the tumultuous council, no suggestion of a disagreement among the Valar, with Manwë, Varda and Ulmo actively disapproving the work and holding aloof from it; no mention, equally, of any pleading for pity on the Noldor by Ulmo, nor of Manwë's disgust. In the old story it was the hostility of some of the Eldar towards the Noldoli, led by an Elf of Kópas (Alqualondë) – who likewise disappeared utterly: in the later account there is never a word about the feelings of the Elves of Valinor for the exiled Noldor – that was the starting-point of the Hiding of Valinor; and it is most curious to observe that the action of the Valar here sprang essentially from indolence mixed with fear. Nowhere does my father's early conception of the *fainéant* Gods appear more clearly. He held moreover quite explicitly that their failure to make war upon Melko then and there was a deep error, diminishing themselves, and (as it appears) irreparable. In his later writing the Hiding of Valinor remained indeed, but only as a great fact of mythological antiquity; there is no whisper of its condemnation.

The blocking-up and utter isolation of Valinor from the world without is perhaps even more strongly emphasized in the early narrative. The cast-off webs of Ungweliant and the use to which the Valar put them disappeared in the later story. Most notable is the different explanation of the fact that the gap in the encircling heights (later named the Calacirya) was not blocked up. In *The Silmarillion* (p. 102) it is said that the pass was not closed

> because of the Eldar that were faithful, and in the city of Tirion upon the green hill Finarfin yet ruled the remnant of the Noldor in the deep cleft of the mountains. For all those of elven-race, even the Vanyar and Ingwë their lord, must breathe at times the outer air and the wind that comes over the sea from the lands of their birth; and the Valar would not sunder the Teleri wholly from their kin.

The old motive of the Solosimpi (> Teleri) wishing this to be done (sufficiently strange, for did the Shoreland Pipers wish to abandon the shores?) disappeared in the general excision of their bitter resentment against the Noldoli, as did Ulmo's refusal to aid them, and Ossë's willingness to do so in Ulmo's despite. The passage concerning the Magic Isles, made by Ossë, is the origin of the conclusion of Chapter XI of *The Silmarillion*:

> And in that time, which songs call *Nurtalë Valinoréva*, the Hiding of Valinor, the Enchanted Isles were set, and all the seas about them were filled with shadows and bewilderment. And these isles were strung as a net in the Shadowy Seas from the north to the south, before Tol Eressëa, the Lonely Isle, is reached by one sailing west. Hardly might any vessel pass between them, for in the dangerous sounds the waves sighed for ever upon dark rocks shrouded in mist. And in the twilight a great weariness came upon mariners and a loathing of the sea; but all that ever set foot upon the islands were there entrapped, and slept until the Change of the World.

It is clear from this passage in the tale that the Magic Isles were set to the east of the Shadowy Seas, though 'the huge glooms . . . . stretched forth tongues of darkness towards them'; while in an earlier passage (p. 125) it is said that beyond Tol Eressëa (which was itself beyond the Magic Isles) 'is the misty wall and those great sea-glooms beneath which lie the Shadowy Seas'. The later 'Enchanted Isles' certainly owe much as a conception to the Magic Isles, but in the passage just cited from *The Silmarillion* they were set in the Shadowy Seas and were in twilight. It is possible therefore that the Enchanted Isles derive also from the Twilit Isles (pp. 68, 125).

The account of the works of Tulkas and Aulë in the northern regions (p. 210) does not read as perfectly in accord with what has been said previously, though a real contradiction is unlikely. On pp. 166-7 it is plainly stated that there was a strip of water (Qerkaringa, the Chill Gulf) between the tip of the 'Icefang' (Helkaraksë) and the Great Lands at the time of the crossing of the Noldoli. In this same passage the Icefang is referred to as 'a narrow neck, which the Gods after destroyed'. The Noldoli were able to cross over to the Great Lands despite 'that gap at the far end' (p. 168) because in the great cold the sound had become filled with unmoving ice. The meaning of the present passage may be, however, that by the destruction of the Icefang a much wider gap was made, so that there was now no possibility of any crossing by that route.

Of the three 'roads' made by Lórien, Oromë, and Mandos there is no vestige in my father's later writing. The Rainbow is never mentioned, nor is there ever any hint of an explanation of how Men and Elves pass to the halls of Mandos. But it is difficult to interpret this conception of the 'roads' - to know to what extent there was a purely figurative content in the idea.

For the road of Lórien, Olóre Mallë the Path of Dreams, which is described by Vairë in *The Cottage of Lost Play*, see pp. 18, 27 ff. There Vairë told that Olóre Mallë came from the lands of Men, that it was 'a lane of deep banks and great overhanging hedges, beyond which stood many tall trees wherein a perpetual whisper seemed to live', and that from this lane a high gate led to the Cottage of the Children or of the Play of Sleep. This was not far from Kôr, and to it came 'the children of the fathers of the fathers of Men'; the Eldar guided them into the Cottage and its garden if they could, 'lest they strayed into Kôr and became enamoured of the glory of Valinor'. The accounts in the two tales seem to be in general agreement, though it is difficult to understand the words in the present passage 'it ran past the Cottage of the Children of the Earth and *thence* down the "lane of whispering elms" *until it reached* the sea'. It is very notable that still at this stage in the development of the mythology, when so much more had been written since the coming of Eriol to Tol Eressëa, the conception of the children of Men coming in sleep by a mysterious 'road' to a cottage in Valinor had by no means fallen away.

In the account of Oromë's making of the Rainbow-bridge, the noose that he cast caught on the summit of the great mountain Kalormë ('Sun-rising-hill') in the remotest East. This mountain is seen on the 'World-Ship' drawing, p. 84.

The story that Vairë named 'The Haven of the Sun' (pp. 213 ff.) provides the fullest picture of the structure of the world that is to be found in the earliest phase of the mythology. The Valar, to be sure, seem strangely ignorant on this subject – the nature of the world that came into being so largely from their own devising, if they needed Ulmo to acquaint them with such fundamental truths. A possible explanation of this ignorance may be found in the radical difference in the treatment of the Creation of the World between the early and later forms of *The Music of the Ainur*. I have remarked earlier (p. 62) that originally the Ainur's first sight of the world was already in its actuality, and Ilúvatar said to them: 'even now the world unfolds and its history begins'; whereas in the developed form it was a vision that was taken away from them, and only given existence in the word of Ilúvatar: *Eä! Let these things Be!* It is said in *The Silmarillion* (p. 20) that

when the Valar entered into Eä they were at first astounded and at a loss, for it was as if naught was yet made which they had seen in vision, and all was but on point to begin and yet unshaped . . .

and there follows (pp. 21–2) an account of the vast labours of the Valar in the actual 'construction' of the world:

They built lands and Melkor destroyed them; valleys they delved and Melkor raised them up; mountains they carved and Melkor threw them down; seas they hollowed and Melkor spilled them . . .

In the old version there is none of this, and one gains the impression (though nothing is explicit) that the Valar came into a world that was already 'made', and unknown to them ('the Gods stalked north and south and could see little; indeed in the deepest of these regions they found great cold and solitude . . .', p. 69). Although the conception of the world was indeed derived in large measure from their own playing in the Music, its reality came from the creative act of Ilúvatar ('We would have the guarding of those fair things of our dreams, which of thy might have now attained to reality', p. 57); and the knowledge possessed by the Valar of the actual properties and dimensions of their habitation was correspondingly smaller (so we may perhaps assume) than it was afterwards conceived to be.

But this is to lean rather heavily on the matter. More probably, the ignorance of the Valar is to be attributed to their curious collective isolation and indifference to the world beyond their mountains that is so much emphasized in this tale.

However this may be, Ulmo at this time informed the Valar that the whole world is an Ocean, Vai, on which the Earth floats, 'upheld by the word of Ilúvatar'; and all the seas of the Earth, even that which divides Valinor from the Great Lands, are hollows in the Earth's surface, and are thus distinct from Vai, which is of another nature. All this we have already seen (pp. 84 ff.); and in an earlier tale something has been said (p. 68) of the nature of the upholding waters:

> Beyond Valinor I have never seen or heard, save that of a surety there are the dark waters of the Outer Seas, that have no tides, and they are very cool and thin, that no boat can sail upon their bosom or fish swim within their depths, save the enchanted fish of Ulmo and his magic car.

So here Ulmo says that neither fish nor boat will swim in its waters 'to whom I have not spoken the great word that Ilúvatar said to me and bound them with the spell'.

At the outer edge of Vai stands the Wall of Things, which is described as 'deep-blue' (p. 215). Valinor is nearer to the Wall of Things than is the eastern shore of the Great Lands, which must mean that Vai is narrower in the West than in the East. In the Wall of Things the Gods at this time made two entrances, in the West the Door of Night and in the East the Gates of Morn; and what lies beyond these entrances in the Wall is called 'the starless vast' and 'the outer dark'. It is not made clear how the outer air ('the dark and tenuous realm of Vaitya that is outside all', p. 181) is to be related to the conception of the Wall of Things or the Outer Dark. In the rejected preliminary text of this tale my father wrote at first (see note 16 above) that in the East 'the Wall of Things is lower', so that when the Sun returns from the Outer Dark it does not enter the eastern sky by a door but 'rides above' the Wall. This was then changed, and the idea of the Door in the Eastern Wall, the Gates of Morn, introduced; but the implication seems clear that the Walls were originally conceived like the walls of terrestrial cities, or gardens – walls with a top: a 'ring-fence'. In the cosmological essay of the 1930s, the *Ambarkanta*, the Walls are quite other:

> About the World are the *Ilurambar*, or Walls of the World. They are as ice and glass and steel, being above all imagination of the Children of Earth cold, transparent, and hard. They cannot be seen, nor can they be passed, save by the Door of Night.
> Within these walls the Earth is globed: above, below, and upon all sides is *Vaiya*, the Enfolding Ocean. But this is more like to sea below the Earth and more like to air above the Earth.

See further p. 86.

The Tale of Qorinómi (p. 215) was never in fact told – in the first version of the present tale (see note 15 above) it seems that Vairë would have liked to tell it, but felt the beady eye of the captious Ailios upon her. In the early Qenya word-list *Qorinómi* is defined as 'the name of the Sun', literally 'Drowned in the Sea', the name being a derivative from a root meaning 'choke, suffocate, drown', with this explanation: 'The Sun, after fleeing from the Moon, dived into the sea and wandered in the caverns of the Oaritsi.' *Oaritsi* is not given in the word-list, but *oaris* = 'mermaid'. Nothing is said in the *Lost Tales* of the Moon giving chase to the Sun; it was the stars of Varda that Ilinsor, 'huntsman of the firmament', pursued, and he was 'jealous of the supremacy of the Sun' (p. 195).

The conclusion of Vairë's tale, 'The Weaving of Days, Months, and Years', shows (as it seems to me) my father exploring a mode of mythical imagining that was for him a dead end. In its formal and explicit symbolism it stands quite apart from the general direction of his thought, and he excised it without trace. It raises, also, a strange question. In what possible sense were the Valar 'outside Time' before the weavings of Danuin, Ranuin, and Fanuin? In *The Music of the Ainur* (p. 55) Ilúvatar said: 'even now the world unfolds *and its history begins*'; in the final version (*The Silmarillion* p. 20) it is said that

> The Great Music had been but the growth and flowering of thought in the Timeless Halls, and the Vision only a foreshowing; but now they had entered in at the beginning of Time . . .

(It is also said in *The Silmarillion* (p. 39) that when the Two Trees of Valinor began to shine there began the Count of Time; this refers to the beginning of the measurement of Time from the waxing and the waning of the Trees.)

In the present tale the works of Danuin, Ranuin, and Fanuin are said to be the cause of 'the subjection of all things within the world to time and change'. But the very notion of a history, a consecutive story, self-evidently implies time and change; how then can Valinor be said only now to come under the necessity of change, with the ordering of the motions of the Sun and Moon, when it has undergone vast changes in the course of the story of the *Lost Tales?* Moreover the Gods now know 'that *hereafter* even they should in counted time be subject to slow eld and their bright days to waning'. But the very statement (for instance) that Ómar-Amillo was 'the youngest of the great Valar' who entered the world (p. 67) is an assertion that the other Valar, older than he, were 'subject to eld'. 'Age' has of course for mortal beings two aspects, which draw always closer: time passes, and the body decays. But of the 'natural' immortality of the Eldar it is said (p. 59): 'nor doth eld subdue their strength, unless it may be in ten thousand centuries'. Thus they 'age' (so Gilfanon is 'the most aged that now dwelt in the isle' and is 'one of the oldest of the fairies', p. 175), but they do not 'age' (do not become enfeebled). Why then do the Gods know that 'hereafter' they will be 'subject to slow eld' – which can only mean ageing in the latter sense? It may well be that there is a deeper thought here than I can fathom; but certainly I cannot explain it.

Finally, at the end of all the early writing concerning it, it may be remarked how major a place was taken in my father's original conception by the creation of the Sun and the Moon and the government of their motions: the astronomical myth is central to the whole. Afterwards it was steadily diminished, until in the end, perhaps, it would have disappeared altogether.

# X

## GILFANON'S TALE: THE TRAVAIL OF THE NOLDOLI AND THE COMING OF MANKIND

The rejected draft text of *The Hiding of Valinor* continues a little way beyond the end of Vairë's tale, thus:

> Now after the telling of this tale no more was there of speaking for that night, but Lindo begged Ailios to consent to a tale-telling of ceremony to be held the next night or as soon as might be; but Ailios would not agree, pleading matters that he must needs journey to a distant village to settle. So was it that the tale-telling was fixed ere the candles of sleep were lit for a sevennight from that time – and that was the day of Turuhalmë[1] or the Logdrawing. "Twill be a fitting day,' saith Lindo, 'for the sports of the morning in the snow and the gathering of the logs from the woods and the songs and drinking of Turuhalmë will leave us of right mood to listen to old tales beside this fire.'

As I have noticed earlier (p. 204), the original form of the *Tale of the Sun and Moon* and *The Hiding of Valinor* belonged to the phase before the entry of Gilfanon of Tavrobel, replacing Ailios.

Immediately following this rejected draft text, on the same manuscript page, the text in ink of the *Tale of Turambar* (Túrin) begins, with these words:

> When then Ailios had spoken his fill the time for the lighting of candles was at hand, and so came the first day of Turuhalmë to an end; but on the second night Ailios was not there, and being asked by Lindo one Eltas began a tale . . .

What was Ailios' tale to have been? (for I think it certain that it was never written). The answer becomes clear from a separate short text, very rough, which continues on from the discussion at the end of *The Hiding of Valinor*, given above. This tells that at length the day of Turuhalmë was come, and the company from Mar Vanwa Tyaliéva went into the snowy woods to bring back firewood on sleighs. Never was the Tale-fire allowed to go out or to die into grey ash, but on the eve of Turuhalmë it sank always to a smaller blaze until Turuhalmë itself, when great logs were brought into the Room of the Tale-fire and being blessed by Lindo with ancient magic roared and flared anew upon the hearth. Vairë blessed the door and lintel

of the hall and gave the key to Rúmil, making him once again the Door-
ward, and to Littleheart was given the hammer of his gong. Then Lindo
said, as he said each year:

> 'Lift up your voices, O Pipers of the Shore, and ye Elves of Kôr sing
> aloud; and all ye Noldoli and hidden fairies of the world dance ye and
> sing, sing and dance O little children of Men that the House of Memory
> resound with your voices . . .'

Then was sung a song of ancient days that the Eldar made when they
dwelt beneath the wing of Manwë and sang on the great road from Kôr
to the city of the Gods (see pp. 143-4).

It was now six months since Eriol went to visit Meril-i-Turinqi beseech-
ing a draught of *limpë* (see pp. 96–8), and that desire had for a time
fallen from him; but on this night he said to Lindo: 'Would I might drink
with thee!' To this Lindo replied that Eriol should not 'think to overpass
the bounds that Ilúvatar hath set', but also that he should consider that
'not yet hath Meril denied thee thy desire for ever'. Then Eriol was sad,
for he guessed in his deepest heart that 'the savour of *limpë* and the blessedness of the Elves might not be his for ever'.

The text ends with Ailios preparing to tell a tale:

'I tell but as I may those things I have seen and known of very ancient
days within the world when the Sun rose first, and there was travail and
much sorrow, for Melko reigned unhampered and the power and strength
that went forth from Angamandi reached almost to the ends of the great
Earth.'

It is clear that no more was written. If it had been completed it would
have led into the opening of *Turambar* cited above ('When then Ailios
had spoken his fill . . .'); and it would have been central to the history
of the Great Lands, telling of the coming of the Noldoli from Valinor,
the Awakening of Men, and the Battle of Unnumbered Tears.

The text just described, linking *The Hiding of Valinor* to Ailios' un-
written tale, was not struck out, and my father later wrote on it: 'To
come after the Tale of Eärendel and before Eriol fares to Tavrobel – after
Tavrobel he drinks of *limpë*.' This is puzzling, since he cannot have
intended the story of the Coming of Men to follow that of Eärendel; but
it may be that he intended only to use the substance of this short text,
describing the Turuhalmë ceremonies, without its ending.

However this may be, he devised a new framework for the telling of
these tales, though he did not carry it through, and the revised account
of the arranging of the next tale-telling has appeared in the *Tale of the
Sun and Moon*, where after Gilfanon's interruption (p. 189) it was agreed
that three nights after that on which *The Sun and Moon* and *The Hiding
of Valinor* were told by Lindo and Vairë there should be a more ceremonial
occasion, on which Gilfanon should relate 'the travail of the Noldoli and
the coming of Mankind'.

Gilfanon's tale follows on, with consecutive page-numbers, from the second version of Vairë's tale of *The Hiding of Valinor*; but Gilfanon here tells it on the night following, not three days later. Unhappily Gilfanon was scarcely better served than Ailios had been, for if Ailios scarcely got started Gilfanon stops abruptly after a very few pages. What there is of his tale is very hastily written in pencil, and it is quite clear that it ends where it does because my father wrote no more of it. It was here that my father abandoned the *Lost Tales* – or, more accurately, abandoned those that still waited to be written; and the effects of this withdrawal never ceased to be felt throughout the history of 'The Silmarillion'. The major stories to follow Gilfanon's, those of Beren and Tinúviel, Túrin Turambar, the Fall of Gondolin, and the Necklace of the Dwarves, had been written and (in the first three cases) rewritten; and the last of these was to lead on to 'the great tale of Eärendel'. But that was not even begun. Thus the *Lost Tales* lack their middle, and their end.

I give here the text of Gilfanon's Tale so far as it goes.

Now when Vairë made an end, said Gilfanon: 'Complain not if on the morrow I weave a long tale, for the things I tell of cover many years of time, and I have waited long to tell them,' and Lindo laughed, saying he might tell to his heart's desire all that he knew.

But on the morrow Gilfanon sat in the chair and in this wise he began:

'Now many of the most ancient things of the Earth are forgotten, for they were lost in the darkness that was before the Sun, and no lore may recover them; yet mayhap this is new to the ears of many here that when the Teleri, the Noldoli, and the Solosimpi fared after Oromë and afterward found Valinor, yet was that not all of the race of the Eldalië that marched from Palisor, and those who remained behind are they whom many call the Qendi, the lost fairies of the world, but ye Elves of Kôr name Ilkorins, the Elves that never saw the light of Kôr. Of these some fell out upon the way, or were lost in the trackless glooms of those days, being wildered and but newly awakened on the Earth, but the most were those who left not Palisor at all, and a long time they dwelt in the pine-woods of Palisor, or sat in silence gazing at the mirrored stars in the pale still Waters of Awakening. Such great ages fared over them that the coming of Nornorë among them faded to a distant legend, and they said one to another that their brethren had gone westward to the Shining Isles. There, said they, do the Gods dwell, and they called them the Great Folk of the West, and thought they dwelt on firelit islands in the sea; but many had not even seen the great waves of that mighty water.

Now the Eldar or Qendi had the gift of speech direct from Ilúvatar, and it is but the sunderance of their fates that has altered them and made them unlike; yet is none so little changed as the tongue of the Dark Elves of Palisor.[2]

Now the tale tells of a certain fay, and names him Tû the wizard, for he was more skilled in magics than any that have dwelt ever yet beyond the land of Valinor; and wandering about the world he found the . . .[3] Elves and he drew them to him and taught them many deep things, and he became as a mighty king among them, and their tales name him the Lord of Gloaming and all the fairies of his realm Hisildi or the twilight people. Now the places about Koivië-néni the Waters of Awakening are rugged and full of mighty rocks, and the stream that feeds that water falls therein down a deep cleft . . . . a pale and slender thread, but the issue of the dark lake was beneath the earth into many endless caverns falling ever more deeply into the bosom of the world. There was the dwelling of Tû the wizard, and fathomless hollow are those places, but their doors have long been sealed and none know now the entry.

There was . . . . a pallid light of blue and silver flickering ever, and many strange spirits fared in and out beside the [?numbers] of the Elves. Now of those Elves there was one Nuin, and he was very wise, and he loved much to wander far abroad, for the eyes of the Hisildi were become exceeding keen, and they might follow very faint paths in those dim days. On a time did Nuin wander far to the east of Palisor, and few of his folk went with him, nor did Tû send them ever to those regions on his business, and strange tales were told concerning them; but now[4] curiosity overcame Nuin, and journeying far he came to a strange and wonderful place the like of which he had not seen before. A mountainous wall rose up before him, and long time he sought a way thereover, till he came upon a passage, and it was very dark and narrow, piercing the great cliff and winding ever down. Now daring greatly he followed this slender way, until suddenly the walls dropped upon either hand and he saw that he had found entrance to a great bowl set in a ring of unbroken hills whose compass he could not determine in the gloom.

Suddenly about him there gushed the sweetest odours of the Earth - nor were more lovely fragrances ever upon the airs of Valinor, and he stood drinking in the scents with deep delight, and amid the fragrance of [?evening] flowers came the deep odours that many pines loosen upon the midnight airs.

Suddenly afar off down in the dark woods that lay above the valley's bottom a nightingale sang, and others answered palely afar off, and Nuin well-nigh swooned at the loveliness of that dreaming place, and he knew that he had trespassed upon Murmenalda or the "Vale of Sleep", where it is ever the time of first quiet dark beneath young stars, and no wind blows.

Now did Nuin descend deeper into the vale, treading softly by reason of some unknown wonder that possessed him, and lo, beneath the trees he saw the warm dusk full of sleeping forms, and some were twined each in the other's arms, and some lay sleeping gently all alone, and Nuin stood and marvelled, scarce breathing.

Then seized with a sudden fear he turned and stole from that hallowed place, and coming again by the passage through the mountain he sped back to the abode of Tû; and coming before that oldest of wizards he said unto him that he was new come from the Eastward Lands, and Tû was little pleased thereat; nor any the more when Nuin made an end of his tale, telling of all he there saw – "and methought," said he, "that all who slumbered there were children, yet was their stature that of the greatest of the Elves."

Then did Tû fall into fear of Manwë, nay even of Ilúvatar the Lord of All, and he said to Nuin:

Here *Gilfanon's Tale* breaks off. The wizard Tû and the Dark Elf Nuin disappeared from the mythology and never appear again, together with the marvellous story of Nuin's coming upon the forms of the Fathers of Mankind still asleep in the Vale of Murmenalda – though from the nature of the work and the different degrees of attention that my father later gave to its different parts one cannot always distinguish between elements definitively abandoned and elements held in 'indefinite abeyance'. And unhappy though it is that this tale should have been abandoned, we are nonetheless by no means entirely in the dark as to how the narrative would have proceeded.

I have referred earlier (p. 107, note 3) to the existence of two 'schemes' or outlines setting out the plan of the *Lost Tales*; and I have said that one of these is a résumé of the *Tales* as they are extant, while the other is divergent, a project for a revision that was never undertaken. There is no doubt that the former of these, which for the purposes of this chapter I will call 'B', was composed when the *Lost Tales* had reached their furthest point of development, as represented by the latest texts and arrangements given in this book. Now when this outline comes to the matter of *Gilfanon's Tale* it becomes at once very much fuller, but then contracts again to cursory references for the tales of Tinúviel, Túrin, Tuor, and the Necklace of the Dwarves, and once more becomes fuller for the tale of Eärendel. It is clear, therefore, that B is the preliminary form, according to the method that my father regularly used in those days, of *Gilfanon's Tale*, and indeed the part of the tale that was written as a proper narrative is obviously following the outline quite closely, while substantially expanding it.

There is also an extremely rough, though full, outline of the matter of *Gilfanon's Tale* which though close to B has things that B does not, and vice versa; this is virtually certainly the predecessor of B, and in this chapter will be called 'A'.

The second outline referred to above, an unrealized project for the revision of the whole work, introduces features that need not be discussed here; it is sufficient to say that the mariner was now Ælfwine, not Eriol, and that his previous history was changed, but that the general plan of the *Tales* themselves was largely intact (with several notes to the effect that they needed abridging or recasting). This outline I shall call 'D'. How much time elapsed between B and D cannot be said, but I think probably not much. It seems possible that this new scheme was associated with the sudden breaking-off of *Gilfanon's Tale*. As with B, D suddenly expands to a much fuller account when this point is reached.

Lastly, a much briefer and more cursory outline, which however adds one or two interesting points, also has Ælfwine instead of Eriol; this followed B and preceded D, and is here called 'C'.

I shall not give all these outlines *in extenso*, which is unnecessary in view of the amount of overlap between them; on the other hand to combine them all into one would be both inaccurate and confusing. But since A and B are very close they can be readily combined into one; and I follow this account by that of D, with C in so far as it adds anything of note. And since in the matter of *Gilfanon's Tale* the outlines are clearly divided into two parts, the Awakening of Men and the history of the Gnomes in the Great Lands, I treat the narrative in each case in these two parts, separately.

There is no need to give the material of the outlines in the opening passage of *Gilfanon's Tale* that was actually written, but there are some points of difference between the outlines and the tale to be noted.

A and B call the wizard-king Túvo, not Tù; in C he is not named, and in D he is Tù 'the fay', as in the tale. Evil associations of this being appear in A: 'Melko meets with Túvo in the halls of Mandos during his enchainment. He teaches Túvo much black magic.' This was struck out, and nothing else is said of the matter; but both A and B say that it was after the escape of Melko and the ruin of the Trees that Túvo entered the world and 'set up a wizard kingship in the middle lands'.

In A, only, the Elves who remained behind in Palisor are said to have been of the people of the Teleri (the later Vanyar). This passage of *Gilfanon's Tale* is the first indication we have had that there were any such Elves (see p. 131); and I incline to think that the conception of the Dark Elves (the later Avari) who never undertook the journey from the Waters of Awakening only emerged in the course of the composition of the *Lost Tales*. But the name *Qendi*, which here first appears in the early narratives, is used somewhat ambiguously. In the fragment of the written tale, the words 'those who remained behind are they whom many call the Qendi, the lost fairies of the world,[5] but ye Elves of Kôr name Ilkorins' seem an altogether explicit statement that Qendi=Dark Elves; but a little later Gilfanon speaks of 'the Eldar or Qendi', and in the outline B it is said that 'a number of the original folk called Qendi (the name Eldar being given by the Gods) remained in Palisor'. These latter statements seem to show equally clearly that *Qendi* was intended as a term for all Elves.

The contradiction is however only apparent. *Qendi* was indeed the original name of all the Elves, and *Eldar* the name given by the Gods and adopted by the Elves of Valinor; those who remained behind preserved the old name *Qendi*. The early word-list of the Gnomish tongue states explicitly that the name *Elda* was given to the 'fairies' by the Valar and was 'adopted largely by them; the Ilkorins still preserved the old name *Qendi*, and this was adopted as the name of the reunited clans in Tol Eressëa'.[6]

In both A and B it is added that 'the Gods spoke not among themselves the tongues of the Eldalië, but could do so, and they comprehended all tongues. The wiser of the Elves learned the secret speech of the Gods and long treasured it, but after the coming to Tol Eressëa none remembered it save the Inwir, and now that knowledge has died save in the house of Meril.' With this compare Rúmil's remarks to Eriol, p. 48: 'There is beside the secret tongue in which the Eldar wrote many poesies and books of wisdom and histories of old and earliest things, and yet speak not. This tongue do only the Valar use in their high counsels, and not many of the Eldar of these days may read it or solve its characters.'

Nuin's words to Tù on the stature of the sleepers in the Vale of Murmenalda are curious. In A is added: 'Men were almost of a stature at first with Elves, the fairies being far greater and Men smaller than now. As the power of Men has grown the fairies have dwindled and Men waxed somewhat.' Other early statements indicate that Men and Elves were originally of very similar stature, and that the diminishing in that of the Elves was closely related to the coming of, and the dominance of, Men. Nuin's words are therefore puzzling, especially since in A they immediately precede the comment on the original similarity of size; for he can surely only mean that the sleepers in Murmenalda were very large by comparison with the Elves. That the sleepers were in fact children, not merely likened in some way to children, is made clear in D: 'Nuin finds the Slumbrous Dale (Murmenalda) where countless sleeping children lie.'

We come now to the point where the narrative is carried forward only in the outlines.

## The Awakening of Men
### according to the earlier outlines

The wizard Túvo told Nuin that the sleepers he had found were the new Children of Ilúvatar, and that they were waiting for light. He forbade any of the Elves to wake them or to visit those places, being frightened of the wrath of Ilúvatar; but despite this Nuin went there often and watched, sitting on a rock. Once he stumbled against a sleeper, who stirred but did not wake. At last, overcome by curiosity, he awakened two, named Ermon and Elmir; they were dumb and very much afraid, but he taught them much of the Ilkorin tongue, for which reason he is called Nuin Father of Speech. Then came the First Dawn; and Ermon and Elmir alone of Men saw the first Sun rise in the West and come over to the Eastward Haven. Now Men came forth from Murmenalda as 'a host of sleepy children'.

(In the tale of *The Hiding of Valinor* it was long after the first rising of the Sunship from Valinor that its Haven in the East was built; see pp. 214–15. It is interesting that the first Men, Ermon and Elmir, were woken by Nuin before the first rising of the Sun, and although it was known to Túvo that Men were 'waiting for light' no connection is made between Nuin's act and the Sunrise. But of course one cannot judge the inner tenor of the narrative from such summaries. It is notable also that whereas the tongue of the Elves, in origin one and the same, was a direct gift of Ilúvatar (p. 232), Men were born into the world without language and received it from the instruction of an Ilkorin. Cf. *The Silmarillion*, p. 141: 'It is said also that these Men [the people of Bëor] had long had dealings with the Dark Elves east of the mountains, and from them had learned much of their speech; and since all the languages of the Quendi were of one origin, the language of Bëor and his folk resembled the Elven-tongue in many words and devices.')

At this point in the story the agents of Melko appear, the Úvanimor, 'bred in the earth' by him (Úvanimor, 'who are monsters, giants, and ogres', have been mentioned in an earlier tale, p. 75); and Túvo protected Men and Elves from them and from 'evil fays'. A makes mention of Orcs besides.

A servant of Melko named 'Fúkil or Fangli' entered the world, and coming among Men perverted them, so that they fell treacherously upon the Ilkorins; there followed the Battle of Palisor, in which the people of Ermon fought beside Nuin. According to A 'the fays and those Men that aided them were defeated', but B calls it an 'undecided battle'; and the Men corrupted by Fangli fled away and became 'wild and savage tribes', worshipping Fangli and Melko. Thereafter (in A only) Palisor was possessed by 'Fangli and his hosts of Nauglath (or Dwarves)'. (In the early writings the Dwarves are always portrayed as an evil people.)

From this outline it is seen that the corruption of certain Men in the beginning of their days by the agency of Melko was a feature of the earliest phase of the mythology; but of all the story here sketched there is no more than a hint or suggestion, at most, in *The Silmarillion* (p. 141): ' "A darkness lies behind us," Bëor said; "and we have turned our backs upon it, and we do not desire to return thither even in thought." '[7]

The Awakening of Men
according to the later outline

Here it is told at the beginning of the narrative that Melko's Úvanimor had escaped when the Gods broke the Fortress of the North, and were wandering in the forests; Fankil servant of Melko dwelt uncaptured in the world. (Fankil=Fangli / Fúkil of A and B. In C he is called 'child of Melko'. Fankil has been mentioned at an earlier point in D, when at the time of the Awakening of the Elves 'Fankil and many dark shapes escaped into the world'; see p. 107, note 3.)

Nuin 'Father of Speech', who went again and again to Murmenalda despite the warnings of Tû (which are not here specified), woke Ermon and Elmir, and taught them speech and many things else. Ermon and Elmir alone of Mankind saw the Sun arising in the West, and the seeds of Palúrien bursting forth into leaf and bud. The hosts of Men came forth as sleepy children, raising a dumb clamour at the Sun; they followed it westward when it returned, and were grievously afraid of the first Night. Nuin and Ermon and Elmir taught them speech.

Men grew in stature, and gathered knowledge of the Dark Elves,[8] but Tû faded before the Sun and hid in the bottomless caverns. Men dwelt in the centre of the world and spread thence in all directions; and a very great age passed.

Fankil with the Dwarves and Goblins went among Men, and bred estrangement between them and the Elves; and many Men aided the Dwarves. The folk of Ermon alone stood by the fairies in the first war of Goblins and Elves (Goblins is here an emendation from Dwarves, and that from Men), which is called the War of Palisor. Nuin died at the hands of the Goblins through the treachery of Men. Many kindreds of Men were driven to the eastern deserts and the southern forests, whence came dark and savage peoples.

The hosts of Tareg the Ikorin marched North-west hearing a rumour of the Gnomes; and many of the lost kindreds joined him.

The History of the Exiled Gnomes
according to the earlier outlines

The Gnomes, after the passage of Helkaraksë, spread into Hisilómë, where they had 'trouble' with the ancient Shadow Folk in that land – in A called 'fay-people', in B 'Úvalear fays'. (We have met the Shadow Folk of Hisilómë before, in the tale of The Coming of the Elves, p. 119, but there this is a name given by Men, after they were shut in Hisilómë by Melko, to the Lost Elves who remained there after straying on the march from Palisor. It will be seen in the later outlines that these Shadow Folk were an unknown people wholly distinct from Elves; and it seems therefore that the name was preserved while given a new interpretation.)

The Gnomes found the Waters of Asgon* and encamped there; then took place the Counting of the Folk, the birth of Turgon with 'prophecies', and the death of Fëanor. On this last matter the outlines are divergent. In A it was Nólemë, called also Fingolma, who died: 'his bark vanishes down a hidden way – said to be the way that Tuor after escaped by. He sailed to offer sacrifice in the islanded rock in Asgon.' (To whom was he sacrificing?) In B, as first written, it was likewise 'Fingolma (Nólemë)' who died, but this was emended to Fëanor; 'his bark vanished down a hidden [way] – said to be that opening that the Noldoli after enlarged and fashioned to a path, so that Tuor escaped that way. He sailed to the Islanded Rock in Asgon because he saw something brightly glitter there and sought his jewels.'

Leaving Asgon the Gnomes passed the Bitter Hills and fought their first battle with Orcs in the foothills of the Iron Mountains. (For the Iron Mountains as the southern border of Hisilómë see pp. 111–12, 158–9.) In the *Tale of Tinúviel* Beren came from Hisilómë, from 'beyond the Bitter Hills', and 'through the terrors of the Iron Mountains', and it thus seems clear that the Bitter Hills and the Iron Mountains may be equated.)

The next camp of the Gnomes was 'by Sirion' (which here first appears); and here the Gnomes first met the Ilkorins – A adding that these Ilkorins were originally of the Noldoli, and had been lost on the march from Palisor. The Gnomes learned from them of the coming of Men and of the Battle of Palisor; and they told the Ilkorins of the tidings in Valinor, and of their search for the jewels.

Now appears for the first time Maidros son of Fëanor (previously, in the tale of *The Theft of Melko*, the name was given to Fëanor's grandfather, pp. 146, 158). Maidros, guided by Ilkorins, led a host into the hills, either 'to seek for the jewels' (A), or 'to search the dwellings of Melko' (B – this should perhaps read 'search for the dwellings of Melko', the reading of C), but they were driven back with slaughter from the doors of Angamandi; and Maidros himself was taken alive, tortured – because he would not reveal the secret arts of the Noldoli in the making of jewels – and sent back to the Gnomes maimed. (In A, which still had Nólemë rather than Fëanor die in the Waters of Asgon, it was Fëanor himself who led the host against Melko, and it was Fëanor who was captured, tortured, and maimed.)

Then the Seven Sons of Fëanor swore an oath of enmity for ever against any that should hold the Silmarils. (This is the first appearance of the Seven Sons, and of the Oath, though that Fëanor had sons is mentioned in the *Tale of the Sun and Moon*, p. 192.)

The hosts of Melko now approached the camp of the Gnomes by Sirion, and they fled south, and dwelt then at Gorfalon, where they made the acquaintance of Men, both good and bad, but especially those of Ermon's folk; and an embassy was sent to Túvo, to Tinwelint (i.e. Thingol,

* later Lake Mithrim.

see p. 132), and to Ermon.[9] A great host was arrayed of Gnomes, Ilkorins, and Men, and Fingolma (Nólemë) marshalled it in the Valley of the Fountains, afterwards called the Vale of Weeping Waters. But Melko himself went into the tents of Men and beguiled them, and some of them fell treacherously on the rear of the Gnomes even as Melko's host attacked them; others Melko persuaded to abandon their friends, and these, together with others that he led astray with mists and wizardries, he beguiled into the Land of Shadows. (With this cf. the reference in the tale of *The Coming of the Elves* to the shutting of Men in Hisilómë by Melko, p. 118.)

Then took place 'the terrible Battle of Unnumbered Tears'. The Children of Úrin* (Sons of Úrin, A) alone of Men fought to the last, and none (save two messengers) came out of the fray; Turgon and a great regiment, seeing the day lost, turned and cut their way out, and rescued a part of the women and children. Turgon was pursued, and there is a reference to 'Mablon the Ilkorin's sacrifice to save the host'; Maidros and the other sons of Fëanor quarrelled with Turgon – because they wanted the leadership, A – and departed into the south. The remainder of the survivors and fugitives were surrounded, and swore allegiance to Melko; and he was wrathful, because he could not discover whither Turgon had fled.

After a reference to 'the Mines of Melko' and 'the Spell of Bottomless Dread' (the spell that Melko cast upon his slaves), the story concludes with 'the Building of Gondolin' and 'the estrangement of Men and Elves in Hisilómë, owing to the Battle of Unnumbered Tears': Melko fostered distrust and kept them spying on each other, so that they should not combine against him; and he fashioned the false-fairies or Kaukareldar in their likeness, and these deceived and betrayed Men.[10]

Since the outlines at this point return to mere headings for the tales of Tinúviel, Túrin, etc., it is clear that *Gilfanon's Tale* would have ended here.


## The History of the Exiled Gnomes
### according to the later outline


The Gnomes sojourned in the Land of Shadows (i.e. Hisilómë), and had dealings with the Shadow Folk. These were fays (C); no one knows whence they came: they are not of the Valar nor of Melko, but it is thought that they came from the outer void and primeval dark when the world was first fashioned. The Gnomes found 'the Waters of Mithrim (Asgon)', and here Fëanor died, drowned in the Waters of Mithrim. The Gnomes devised weapons for the first time, and quarried the dark hills. (This is curious, for it has been said in the account of the Kinslaughter at Alqaluntë that 'so first perished the Eldar neath the weapons of their kin', p. 165.

* later Húrin.

The first acquisition of weapons by the Eldar remained a point of uncertainty for a long time.)

The Gnomes now fought for the first time with the Orcs and captured
the pass of the Bitter Hills; thus they escaped out of the Land of Shadows,
to Melko's fear and amazement. They entered the Forest of Artanor (later
Doriath) and the Region of the Great Plains (perhaps the forerunner of
the later Talath Dirnen, the Guarded Plain of Nargothrond); and the
host of Nólemë grew to a vast size. They practised many arts, but would
dwell no longer in settled abodes. The chief camp of Nólemë was about
the waters of Sirion; and the Gnomes drove the Orcs to the foothills of
the Iron Mountains. Melko gathered his power in secret wrath.

Turgon was born to Nólemë.

Maidros, 'chief son of Fëanor', led a host against Angband, but was
driven back with fire from its gates, and he was taken alive and tortured –
according to C, repeating the story of the earlier outline, because he would
not reveal the secret arts of jewel-making. (It is not said here that Maidros
was freed and returned, but it is implied in the Oath of the Seven Sons
that follows.)

The Seven Sons of Fëanor swore their terrible oath of hatred for ever
against all, Gods or Elves or Men, who should hold the Silmarils; and
the Children of Fëanor left the host of Nólemë and went back into Dor
Lómin, where they became a mighty and a fierce race.

The hosts of Tareg the Ilkorin (see p. 237) found the Gnomes at the
Feast of Reunion; and the Men of Ermon first saw the Gnomes. Then
Nólemë's host, swollen by that of Tareg and by the sons of Ermon, pre-
pared for battle; and messengers were sent out North, South, East, and
West. Tinwelint alone refused the summons, and he said: 'Go not into
the hills.' Úrin and Egnor* marched with countless battalions.

Melko withdrew all his forces and Nólemë believed that he was afraid.
The hosts of Elfinesse drew into the Tumbled Lands and encamped in
the Vale of Fountains (Gorfalong), or as it was afterwards called the
Valley of Weeping Waters.

(The outline D differs in its account of the events before the Battle of
Unnumbered Tears from that in the earlier ones, here including C. In
the earlier, the Gnomes fled from the camp by Sirion when Melko's hosts
approached, and retreated to Gorfalon, where the great host of Gnomes,
Ilkorins, and Men was gathered, and arrayed in the Valley of the Fountains.
In D, there is no mention of any retreat by Nólemë's hosts: rather, it
seems, they advanced from the camp by Sirion into the Vale of Fountains
(Gorfalong). But from the nature of these outlines they cannot be too
closely pressed. The outline C, which ends here, says that when the
Gnomes first encountered Men at Gorfalon the Gnomes taught them
crafts – and this was one of the starting-points, no doubt, of the later
Elf-friends of Beleriand.)

* The father of Beren.

Certain Men suborned by Melko went among the camp as minstrels and betrayed it. Melko fell upon them at early dawn in a grey rain, and the terrible Battle of Unnumbered Tears followed, of which no full tale is told, for no Gnome will ever speak of it. (In the margin here my father wrote: 'Melko himself was there?' In the earlier outline Melko himself entered the camp of his enemies.)

In the battle Nólemë was isolated and slain, and the Orcs cut out his heart; but Turgon rescued his body and his heart, and it became his emblem.[11] Nearly half of all the Gnomes and Men who fought there were slain.

Men fled, and the sons of Úrin alone stood fast until they were slain; but Úrin was taken. Turgon was terrible in his wrath, and his great battalion hewed its way out of the fight by sheer prowess.

Melko sent his host of Balrogs after them, and Mablon the Ilkorin died to save them when pursued. Turgon fled south along Sirion, gathering women and children from the camps, and aided by the magic of the stream escaped into a secret place and was lost to Melko.

The Sons of Fëanor came up too late and found a stricken field: they slew the spoilers who were left, and burying Nólemë they built the greatest cairn in the world over him and the [?Gnomes]. It was called the Hill of Death.

There followed the Thraldom of the Noldoli. The Gnomes were filled with bitterness at the treachery of Men, and the ease with which Melko beguiled them. The outline concludes with references to 'the Mines of Melko' and 'the Spell of Bottomless Dread', and the statement that all the Men of the North were shut in Hisilómë.

The outline D then turns to the story of Beren and Tinúviel, with a natural connection from the tale just sketched: 'Beren son of Egnor wandered out of Dor Lómin* into Artanor . . .' This is to be the next story told by the Tale-fire (as also in outline B); in D the matter of *Gilfanon's Tale* is to take four nights.

★

If certain features are selected from these outlines, and expressed in such a way as to emphasize agreement rather than disagreement, the likeness to the narrative structure of *The Silmarillion* is readily apparent. Thus:

- The Noldoli cross the Helkaraksë and spread into Hisilómë, making their encampment by Asgon (Mithrim);
- They meet Ilkorin Elves (=Úmanyar);
- Fëanor dies;
- First battle with Orcs;
- A Gnomish army goes to Angband;

* i.e. Hisilómë; see p. 112.

- Maidros captured, tortured, and maimed;
- The Sons of Fëanor depart from the host of the Elves (in D only);
- A mighty battle called the Battle of Unnumbered Tears is fought between Elves and Men and the hosts of Melko;
- Treachery of Men, corrupted by Melko, at that battle;
- But the people of Úrin (Húrin) are faithful, and do not survive it;
- The leader of the Gnomes is isolated and slain (in D only);
- Turgon and his host cut their way out, and go to Gondolin;
- Melko is wrathful because he cannot discover where Turgon has gone;
- The Fëanorians come late to the battle (in D only);
- A great cairn is piled (in D only).

These are essential features of the story that were to survive. But the unlikenesses are many and great. Most striking of all is that the entire later history of the long years of the Siege of Angband, ending with the Battle of Sudden Flame (Dagor Bragollach), of the passage of Men over the Mountains into Beleriand and their taking service with the Noldorin Kings, had yet to emerge; indeed these outlines give the effect of only a brief time elapsing between the coming of the Noldoli from Kôr and their great defeat. This effect may be to some extent the result of the compressed nature of these outlines, and indeed the reference in the last of them, D, to the practice of many arts by the Noldoli (p. 240) somewhat counteracts the impression — in any case, Turgon, born when the Gnomes were in Hisilómë or (according to D) when they were encamped by Sirion, is full grown at the Battle of Unnumbered Tears.[12] Even so, the picture in *The Silmarillion* of a period of centuries elapsing while Morgoth was straitly confined in Angband and 'behind the guard of their armies in the north the Noldor built their dwellings and their towers' is emphatically not present. In later 'phases' of the history my father steadily expanded the period between the rising of the Sun and Moon and the Battle of Unnumbered Tears. It is essential, also, to the old conception that Melko's victory was so complete and overwhelming: vast numbers of the Noldoli became his thralls, and wherever they went lived in the slavery of his spell; in Gondolin alone were they free — so in the old tale of *The Fall of Gondolin* it is said that the people of Gondolin 'were that kin of the Noldoli who alone escaped Melko's power, when at the Battle of Unnumbered Tears he slew and enslaved their folk and wove spells about them and caused them to dwell in the Hells of Iron, faring thence at his will and bidding only'. Moreover Gondolin was not founded until *after* the Battle of Unnumbered Tears.[13]

Of Fëanor's death in the early conception we can discern little; but at least it is clear that it bore no relation to the story of his death in *The Silmarillion* (p. 107). In these early outlines the Noldoli, leaving Hisilómë, had their first affray with the Orcs in the foothills of the Iron Mountains or in the pass of the Bitter Hills, and these heights pretty clearly correspond to the later Mountains of Shadow, Ered Wethrin (see pp. 158, 238);

but in *The Silmarillion* (p. 106) the first encounter of the Noldor with the Orcs was in Mithrim.

The meeting of Gnomes and Ilkorins survived in the meeting of the new-come Noldor with the Grey-elves of Mithrim (*ibid.* p. 108); but the Noldor heard rather of the power of King Thingol of Doriath than of the Battle of Palisor.

Whereas in these outlines Maidros son of Fëanor led an attack on Angband which was repulsed with slaughter and his own capture, in *The Silmarillion* it was Fingolfin who appeared before Angband, and being met with silence prudently withdrew to Mithrim (p. 109). Maidros (Maedhros) had been already taken at a meeting with an embassage of Morgoth's that was supposed to be a parley, and he heard the sound of Fingolfin's trumpets from his place of torment on Thangorodrim – where Morgoth set him until, as he said, the Noldor forsook their war and departed. Of the divided hosts of the Noldor there is of course no trace in the old story; and the rescue of Maedhros by Fingon, who cut off his hand in order to save him, does not appear in any form: rather is he set free by Melko, though maimed, and without explanation given. But it is very characteristic that the maiming of Maidros – an important 'moment' in the legends – should never itself be lost, though it came to be given a wholly different setting and agency.

The Oath of the Sons of Fëanor was here sworn after the coming of the Gnomes from Valinor, and after the death of their father; and in the later outline D they then left the host of (Finwë) Nólemë, Lord of the Noldoli, and returned to Dor Lómin (Hisilómë). In this and in other features that appear only in D the story is moved nearer to its later form. In the return to Dor Lómin is the germ of the departure of the Fëanorians from Mithrim to the eastern parts of Beleriand (*The Silmarillion* p. 112); in the Feast of Reunion that of Mereth Aderthad, the Feast of Reuniting, held by Fingolfin for the Elves of Beleriand (*ibid.* p. 113), though the participants are necessarily greatly different; in the latecoming of the Fëanorians to the stricken field of Unnumbered Tears that of the delayed arrival of the host of Maedhros (*ibid.* pp. 190–2); in the cutting-off and death of (Finwë) Nólemë in the battle that of the slaying of Fingon (*ibid.* p. 193 – when Finwë came to be Fëanor's father, and thus stepped into the place of Bruithwir, killed by Melko in Valinor, his position as leader of the hosts in the Battle of Unnumbered Tears was taken by Fingon); and in the great cairn called the Hill of Death, raised by the Sons of Fëanor, that of the Haudh-en-Ndengin or Hill of Slain, piled by Orcs in Anfauglith (*ibid.* p. 197). Whether the embassy to Túvo, Tinwelint, and Ermon (which in D becomes the sending of messengers) remotely anticipates the Union of Maedhros (*ibid.* pp. 188–9) is not clear, though Tinwelint's refusal to join forces with Nólemë survived in Thingol's rejection of Maedhros' approaches (p. 189). I cannot certainly explain Tinwelint's words 'Go not into the hills', but I suspect that 'the hills' are the Mountains of Iron (in *The Hiding of Valinor*, p. 209, called 'the Hills of Iron') above

Angband, and that he warned against an attack on Melko; in the old *Tale of Turambar* Tinwelint said: 'Of the wisdom of my heart and the fate of the Valar did I not go with my folk to the Battle of Unnumbered Tears.'

Other elements in the story of the battle that survived – the steadfastness of the folk of Úrin (Húrin), the escape of Turgon – already existed at this time in a tale that had been written (that of Túrin).

The geographical indications are slight, and there is no map of the Great Lands for the earliest period of the legends; in any case these questions are best left until the tales that take place in those lands. The Vale (or Valley) of the Fountains, afterwards the Valley (or Vale) of Weeping Waters, is in D explicitly equated with Gorfalong, which in the earlier outlines is given as Gorfalon, and seems to be distinct; but in any case neither these, nor 'the Tumbled Lands', can be brought into relation with any places or names in the later geography – unless (especially since in D Turgon is said to have fled 'south down Sirion') it may be supposed that something like the later picture of the Pass of Sirion was already in being, and that the Vale of the Fountains, or of Weeping Waters, was a name for it.

## NOTES

1   Above *Turuhalmë* are written *Duruchalm* (struck out) and *Halmadhurwion*.
2   This paragraph is marked with queries.
3   The word may be read equally well as 'dim' or 'dun'.
4   The original reading here was: 'and few of his folk went with him, and this Tû forbade to his folk, fearing the wrath of Ilúvatar and Manwë; yet did' (sc. curiosity overcome Nuin, etc.).
5   Earlier in the *Tales*, 'the Lost Elves' are those who were lost from the great journey and wandered in Hisilómë (see p. 118).
6   In the tale the 'fairies' of Tû's dominion (i.e. the Dark Elves) are given the name *Hisildi*, the twilight people; in outlines A and B, in addition to *Hisildi*, other names are given: *Humarni, Kaliondi, Lómëarni*.
7   Cf. also Sador's words to Túrin in his boyhood (*Unfinished Tales* p. 61): 'A darkness lies behind us, and out of it few tales have come. The fathers of our fathers may have had things to tell, but they did not tell them. Even their names are forgotten. The Mountains stand between us and the life that they came from, flying from no man now knows what.'
8   Cf. *The Silmarillion* p. 104: 'It is told that ere long they met Dark Elves in many places, and were befriended by them; and Men became the companions and disciples in their childhood of these ancient folk, wanderers of the Elven-race who never set out upon the paths to Valinor, and knew of the Valar only as a rumour and a distant name.'

9  Above *Ermon* is written, to all appearance, the Old English word *Æsc* ('ash'). It seems conceivable that this is an anglicizing of Old Norse *Askr* ('ash'), in the northern mythology the name of the first man, who with the first woman (*Embla*) were made by the Gods out of two trees that they found on the seashore (Völuspá strophe 17; *Snorra Edda, Gylfaginning* §8).

10  The text has here the bracketed word '(Gongs)'. This might be thought to be a name for the *Kaukareldar* or 'false-fairies', but in the Gnomish word-list *Gong* is defined as 'one of a tribe of the Orcs, a goblin'.

11  The cutting out of Nólemë's heart by the Orcs, and its recapture by Turgon his son, is referred to in an isolated early note, which says also that Turgon encased it in gold; and the emblem of the King's Folk in Gondolin, the Scarlet Heart, is mentioned in the tale of *The Fall of Gondolin*.

12  Cf. p. 167: 'Turondo son of Nólemë was not yet upon the Earth.' *Turgon* was the Gnomish name of *Turondo* (p. 115). In the later story Turgon was a leader of the Noldor from Valinor.

13  After the story was changed, and the founding of Gondolin was placed far earlier, the concluding part of *The Silmarillion* was never brought into harmony; and this was a main source of difficulty in the preparation of the published work.

# APPENDIX
## NAMES IN THE *LOST TALES* – PART I

There exist two small books, contemporary with the *Lost Tales*, which contain the first 'lexicons' of the Elvish languages; and both of them are very difficult documents.

One is concerned with the language called, in the book, *Qenya*, and I shall refer to this book as 'QL' (Qenya Lexicon). A good proportion of the entries in the first half of the alphabet were made at one time, when the work was first begun; these were very carefully written, though the pencil is now faint. Among these original entries is this group:

> *Lemin* 'five'
> *Lempe* 'ten'
> *Leminkainen* '23'

The choice of '23' suggests that this was my father's age at the time, and that the book was begun therefore in 1915. This is supported by some of the statements made in the first layer of entries about certain figures of the mythology, statements that are at odds with everything that is said elsewhere, and which give glimpses of a stage even earlier than the *Lost Tales*.

The book naturally continued in use, and many entries (virtually all of those in the second part of the alphabet) are later than this first layer, though nothing more definite can be said than that all entries belong to the period of (or not long preceding) the *Lost Tales*.

The words in QL are arranged according to 'roots', and a note at the beginning states:

> Roots are in capitals, and are not words in use at all, but serve as an elucidation of the words grouped together and a connection between them.

There is a good deal of uncertainty, expressed by queries, in the formulation of the roots, and in the ascription of words to one root or another, as my father moved among different etymological ideas; and in some cases it seems clear that the word was 'there', so to speak, but its etymology remained to be certainly defined, and not vice versa. The roots themselves are often difficult to represent, since certain consonants carry diacritic marks that are not defined. The notes on names that follow inevitably give a slightly more positive impression than does the book itself.

The other book is a dictionary of the Gnomish language, *Goldogrin*, and I shall refer to this as 'GL' (Goldogrin, or Gnomish, Lexicon). This is not arranged historically, by roots (though occasionally roots are given), but rather, in plan at least, as a conventional dictionary; and it contains a remarkable number of words. The book is entitled *i·Lam na·Ngoldathon* (i.e. 'the tongue of the Gnomes'): *Goldogrin*, with a date: 1917. Written beneath the title is *Eriol Sarothron* (i.e. 'Eriol the Voyager'), *who else is called Angol but in his own folk Ottor Wǽfre* (see p. 23).*

The great difficulty in this case is the intensity with which my father used this diminutive book, emending, rejecting, adding, in layer upon layer, so that in places it has become very hard to interpret. Moreover later changes to the forms in one entry were not necessarily made in related entries; thus the stages of a rapidly expanding linguistic conception are very confused in their representation. These little books were working materials, by no means the setting-out of finished ideas (it is indeed quite clear that GL in particular closely accompanied the actual composition of the *Tales*). Further, the languages changed even while the first 'layer' was being entered in GL; for example, the word *mô* 'sheep' was changed later to *moth*, but later in the dictionary *uimoth* 'sheep of the waves' was the form first written.

It is immediately obvious that an already extremely sophisticated and phonetically intricate historical structure lies behind the languages at this stage; but it seems that (unhappily and frustratingly) very little indeed in the way of phonological or grammatical description now survives from those days. I have found nothing, for instance, that sets out even in the sketchiest way the phonological relations between the two languages. Some early phonological description does exist for Qenya, but this became through later alterations and substitutions such a baffling muddle (while the material is in any case intrinsically extremely complex) that I have been unable to make use of it.

To attempt to use later materials for the elucidation of the linguistic ideas of the earliest period would in this book be quite impractical. But the perusal of these two vocabularies shows in the clearest possible way how deeply involved were the developments in the mythology and in the languages, and it would be seriously misleading to publish the *Lost Tales* without some attempt to show the etymological connections of the names that appear in them. I give therefore as much information, derived from these books, as is possible, but without any speculation beyond them. It is evident, for instance, that a prime element in the etymological constructions was slight variation in ancient 'roots' (caused especially by differences in the formation of consonants) that in the course of ages yielded very complex semantic situations; or again, that an old vocalic 'ablaut' (variation, in length or quality, of vowels in series) was present;

---

* The note concerning *Angol* and *Eriollo* referred to on p. 24 is written inside the cover of GL.

but I have thought it best merely to try to present the content of the dictionaries as clearly as I can.

It is noteworthy that my father introduced a kind of 'historical punning' here and there: so for instance the root SAHA 'be hot' yields (beside *saiwa* 'hot' or *sára* 'fiery') *Sahóra* 'the South', and from NENE 'flow' come *nen* 'river', *nénu* 'yellow water-lily', and *nénuvar* 'pool of lilies' – cf. *nenuphar* 'water-lily', modern French *nénufar*. There are also several resemblances to early English that are obviously not fortuitous, as *hôr* 'old', HERE 'rule', *rûm* 'secret (whisper)'.

It will be seen that a great many elements in the later languages, Qenya and Sindarin, as they are known from the published works, go back to the beginning; the languages, like the legends, were a continuous evolution, expansion, and refinement. But the historical status and relationship of the two languages as they were conceived at this time was radically changed later on: see p. 51.

The arrangement of the material has proved difficult, and indeed without a better understanding of relationships and their shifting formulations could scarcely be made satisfactory. The system I have adopted is to give etymologically-connected groups of words, in both Qenya and Gnomish, under an important name that contains one of them; to this entry other occurrences of a word in the group are referred (e.g. *glor-* in *Glorvent*, *Bráglorin* is referred to the entry *Laurelin*, where the etymological associations of Qenya *laurë* 'gold' are given).* Every name in the *Lost Tales* of this volume is given – that is, if any contemporary etymological information is to be found concerning it: any name not found in the following list is either quite opaque to me, or at least cannot be identified with any certainty. Rejected names are also included, on the same basis, but are given under the names that replaced them (e.g. *Dor Uswen* under *Dor Faidwen*).

The list of secondary names of the Valar which is written out on blank facing pages in the tale of *The Coming of the Valar* (see p. 93) is referred to as 'the Valar name-list'. The sign ⟨ is used only where it is used in the Gnomish dictionary, as *alfa* ⟨ *alchwa*, meaning that the one was historically derived from the other: it is not used in this Appendix to refer to alterations made by my father in the dictionaries themselves.

★

**Ainur**    Among the original entries in QL are *ainu* 'a pagan god' and *aini* 'a pagan goddess', together with *áye* 'hail!' and *Ainatar* 'Ilúvatar, God'. (Of course no one *within* the context of the mythology can call

---

* Later Quenya and Sindarin forms are only exceptionally mentioned. For such words see the vocabularies given in *An Introduction to Elvish*, ed. J. Allan, Bran's Head Books, 1978; also the Appendix to *The Silmarillion*.

the Ainur 'pagan'.) GL has *Ain*: 'also with distinctive masc. and fem. forms *Ainos* and *Ainil*, a God, i.e. one of the Great Valar'.

**Alalminórë** See *Aldaron*, *Valinor*. In QL *Alalminórë* is glossed 'Land of Elms, one of the provinces of Inwinórë in which is situated Kortirion (Warwickshire)'; i.e. *Alalminórë*=Warwickshire (see p. 25). Gnomish words are *lalm* or *larm*, also *lalmir*, 'elm'.

**Aldaron** In QL is a root ALA 'spread', with derivatives *alda* 'tree', *aldëa* 'tree-shadowed', *aldëon* 'avenue of trees', and *alalmë* 'elm' (see *Alalminórë*). In GL this name of Oromë appears as *Aldor* and *Ormaldor* (*Oromë* is *Orma* in Gnomish); *ald* 'wood (material)', later altered to *âl*.

**Alqaluntë** QL *alqa* 'swan'; GL *alcwi*, with the corresponding word in Qenya here given as *alqë*, *alcwi* changed later to *alfa* < *alchwa*.

QL *luntë* 'ship' from root LUTU, with other derivatives *lúto* 'flood' and verb *lutta-*, *lutu-* 'flow, float' (cf. *Ilsaluntë*). GL has correspondingly *lunta* 'ship', *lud-* 'flow, stream, float'.

**Aluin** See *Lúmin*.

**Amillo** This appears in QL but with no indication of meaning; *Amillion* is Amillo's month, February (one of the most 'primitive' entries).

**Angaino** Together with *angayassë* 'misery', *angaitya* 'torment', *Angaino* is given in QL separately from the 'iron' words (see *Angamandi*) and was first defined as 'a giant', emended to 'the great chain'. In GL Melko has a name *Angainos*, with a note: 'Do not confuse Gnomish *Angainos* with Qenya *Angaino* (Gnomish *Gainu*), the great chain of *tilkal*.' Under *Gainu* there is a later note: 'popularly connected with *ang* "iron" but really = "tormentor".'

**Angamandi** QL has *anga* 'iron' (which is the *a* of *tilkal*, p. 100), *angaina* 'of iron', *Angaron(ti)* 'Mountains of Iron', and *Angamandu* or *Eremandu* 'Hells of Iron' (added later: 'or *Angamandi*, plural'). The Gnomish forms are *ang* 'iron' (as in *Angol*, see under *Eriol*), *angrin* 'of iron', *Angband* – which, strangely, is said in GL to be 'Melko's great fortress after the battle of Countless Lamentation down to the battle of the Twilit Pool' (when Tulkas finally overthrew Melko). See *Mandos*.

**Angol** See *Eriol*.

**Arvalin** See *Eruman*.

**Aryador** This is said (p. 119) to be the name among Men of Hisilómë; but according to GL it was a word of Ilkorin origin, meaning 'land or place of shadow'; QL *Arëandor*, *Arëanor* 'name of a mountainous district, the abode of the Shadow Folk' (see p. 237). See *Eruman*.

**Asgon** GL has *Asgon* 'name of a lake in Dor Lómin (Hisilómë), Q. *Aksanda*'; QL has *aksa* 'waterfall', of which the Gnomish equivalent is given as *acha* of the same meaning. (No light is cast on the later name *Mithrim* in the dictionaries.)

**Aulë** A word *aulë* 'shaggy' is given in QL as a derivative from a root owo (whence also *oa* 'wool', *uë* 'fleece'), but without any indication that this is to be connected with the name of the Vala. The Gnomish form of his name is *Óla*, changed to *Óli*, without further information. In the Valar name-list Aulë is called also *Tamar* or *Tamildo*. These are given in QL without translation under root TAMA 'smelt, forge', with *tambë* 'copper' (the *t* of *tilkal*, p. 100), *tambina* 'of copper', *tamin* 'forge'; Gnomish words are *tam* 'copper', *tambin* 'of copper', *tambos* 'cauldron'. For other names of Aulë see *Talka Marda*.

**Aulenossë**   For *nossë* 'kin, people' see *Valinor*.

**Aur**   Gnomish name of the Sun; see *Úr*.

**Balrog**   GL defines *Balrog* as 'a kind of fire-demon; creatures and servants of Melko'. With the article the form is *i'Malrog*, plural *i'Malraugin*. Separate entries give *bal* 'anguish' (original initial consonant *mb-*), *balc* 'cruel'; and *graug* 'demon'. Qenya forms are mentioned: *araukë* and *Malkaraukë*. In QL *Malkaraukë* with other words such as *malkanë* 'torture' are given under a root MALA (MBALA) '(crush), hurt, damage', but the relation of this to MALA 'crush, squeeze' (see *Olórë Mallë*) was apparently not decided. There are also *Valkaraukë* and *valkanë* 'torture', but again the relationship is left obscure.

**Bráglorin**   Defined in the text (p. 187) as 'the blazing vessel', but translated in GL as 'Golden Wain, a name of the Sun', with a note: 'also in analytical form *i·Vreda 'Loriol'*; *brada* 'waggon, wain'. For *-glorin* see *Laurelin*.

**Bronweg**   GL has *Bronweg* '(the constant one), name of a famous Gnome', with related words as *brod*, *bronn* 'steadfast', *bronweth* 'constancy'. In QL *Voronwë* (see p. 48) 'the faithful' is derived from the root VORO, with *vor*, *voro* 'ever', *voronda* 'faithful', *vorima* 'everlasting', etc. Cf. *Vorotemnar*.

   The common ending *-weg* is not given in GL, but cf. *gweg* 'man', plural *gwaith*.

**Cûm a Gumlaith**   'The Mound of the First Sorrow', tomb of Bruithwir, p. 149. GL *cûm* 'mound, especially burial-mound' (also *cum-* 'lie', *cumli* 'couch'); *gumlaith* 'weariness of spirit, grief' (*blaith* 'spirit').

**Cûm a Thegranaithos**   See preceding entry. GL *thegra* 'first, foremost', *thegor* 'chief'; *naitha-* 'lament, weep, wail for', *naithol* 'miserable'.

**Danuin**   GL has *dana* 'day (24 hours)', with reference to Qenya *sana* (not in QL); *Dana* was an earlier reading for *Danuin* (p. 222). The same element appears in *Lomendánar* 'Days of Gloaming'.

**Dor Faidwen**   Gnomish *dôr* (< *ndor-*) '(inhabited) land, country, people of the land'; see *Valinor*.

   *Dor Faidwen* is translated in the text 'Land of Release' (p. 13); GL has *faidwen* 'freedom' and many related words, as *fair* 'free', *faith* 'liberty', etc. In QL under root FAYA appear *fairë* 'free', *fairië* 'freedom', *fainu-* 'release'.

*Dor Faidwen* was the final Gnomish name of Tol Eressëa after many changes (p. 21), but little light can be cast on the earlier forms. *Gar* in *Gar Eglos* is a Gnomish word meaning 'place, district'. *Dor Us(g)wen*: GL gives the stem *us-* 'leave, depart' (also *uthwen* 'way out, exit'), and QL under root USU 'escape' has *uswë* 'issue, escape' and *usin* 'he escapes'.

**Dor Lómin** See *Valinor, Hisilómë.*

**Eärendel** In an annotated list of names accompanying *The Fall of Gondolin* there is a suggestion, attributed to Littleheart son of Voronwë, that *Eärendel* had 'some kinship to the Elfin *ea* and *earen* "eagle" and "eyrie" ', and in QL these words (both given the meaning 'eagle') are placed with *Eärendel*, though not explicitly connected. In the tale itself it is said that 'there are many interpretations both among Elves and Men' of the name *Eärendel*, with a suggestion that it was a word of 'some secret tongue' spoken by the people of Gondolin.

GL has an entry: *Ioringli* 'true Gnomish form of Eärendel's name, though the Eldar-form has been also adopted and often is met in transition state as *Iarendel, Iorendel*' (on the distinction between 'Gnomish' and 'Eldar' see p. 50). Gnomish words for 'eagle' are *ior, ioroth*.

In QL is an entry *Eärendilyon* 'son of Eärendel (used of any mariner)'; cf. p. 13.

**Eldamar** For the first element see *Eldar.* – In QL the following words are given in a group: *mar* (*mas-*) 'dwelling of men, the Earth, -land', *mardo* 'dweller', *masto* 'village', and *-mas* equivalent to English *-ton*, *-by* in place-names (cf. *Mar Vanwa Tyaliéva*; *Koromas*; *i·Talka Marda* 'Smith of the World', Aulë). In GL are *bar* 'home' (< *mbar-*), and derivatives, as *baros* 'hamlet', also *-bar* as suffix 'dweller', or 'home, -ham'.

The Gnomish equivalent of *Eldamar* was *Eglobar* (Gnomish *Egla* = Qenya *Elda*): '*Eglobar* "Elfinesse" = Q. *Eldamar*, i.e. Elfhome; the land on the edge of Valinor where the fairies dwelt and built Côr. Also in forms *Eglabar, Eglamar, Eglomar.*' In QL *Eldamar* is said, in a very early entry, to be 'the rocky beach in western Inwinórë (Faëry)'; 'upon this rock was the white town built called Kôr'.

**Eldar** In QL *Elda* is given separately, without etymological connections, and defined as 'a beach-fay or *Solosimpë* (shore-piper)'. This is a glimpse of an earlier conception than that found in the *Lost Tales*: the *Eldar* were originally the Sea-elves. GL has the entry *Egla* ' "a being from outside", name of the fairies given by the Valar and largely adopted by them, =Q. *Elda*' (see p. 235); also *eg, êg* 'far away, distant'. The association of *Eldar* with the stars does not go back to the beginning.

**Erinti** She appears in QL in an isolated, early entry (afterwards struck through). Nothing is ever told of Erinti in the *Lost Tales*, but in this note she is called the Vala of love, music, and beauty, also named *Lotessë* and *Akairis* ('bride'), sister of Noldorin and Amillo. These three alone (i.e. of the Valar) have left Valinor, and dwell in Inwenórë (Tol Eressëa); she herself dwells in Alalminórë in a *korin* of elms guarded by the fairies. The second half of the month of *avestalis* (January) is called *Erintion*.

There is no trace of this elsewhere; but clearly, when Erinti became the daughter of Manwë and Varda her dwelling in Alalminórë was taken over by Meril-i-Turinqi, the Lady of Tol Eressëa.

In the Valar name-list Erinti is called also *Kalainis*; this word appears in QL with the meaning 'May', one of many derivatives from the root KALA (see *Galmir*).

**Eriol**   In *The Cottage of Lost Play* (p. 14) *Eriol* is translated 'One who dreams alone'. In QL the elements of this interpretation are given under the roots ERE 'remain alone' (see *Tol Eressëa*) and LORO 'slumber' (see *Lórien*). In GL appears the note cited on p. 24 that Gnomish *Angol* and Qenya *Eriollo* were the names of the region 'between the seas' whence Eriol came (=Angeln in the Danish peninsula); and in an isolated note elsewhere *Angol* is derived from *ang* 'iron' and *ól* 'cliff', while Eriol is said to mean the same – 'this being the name of the fairies for the parts [*sic*] of his home (ironcliffs)'. Meril refers to 'the black coasts of your home' (p. 96). In this note the interpretation 'One who dreams alone' is said to be a pun on Lindo's part.

For *ang* 'iron' see *Angamandi*. GL has *ol*, *óla* 'cliff, seaward precipice', with Qenya forms *ollo*, *oldō*. *ere(n)* 'iron or steel' is given in QL, and this element appears also in the alternative name *Eremandu* for *Angamandu*, 'Hells of Iron'.

**Eruman**   The names of this region are as difficult as the original conception of the region itself (see pp. 91 ff.). The form *Erumáni* (which occurs in the *Tales* as well as *Eruman*) appears in QL under ERE 'out' (cf. *Neni Erúmëar*) without further information. GL has a long entry under *Edhofon*, which=Q. *Erumáni*: it is a 'dark land outside Valinor and to the south of the Bay of Faëry, that ran right up to the bases of the western side of the Mountains of Valinor; its farthest northern point touched upon the roots of Taniquetil, hence *Edhofon* 〈 *Eðusmānī-*, i.e. beyond the abode of the Mánir. Hence also the Q. title *Afalinan* or *Arvalion*, i.e. nigh Valinor.' The implication of this seems to be that Taniquetil was 'the abode of the Mánir', as is comprehensible, since the Mánir were particularly associated with Manwë (the Gnomish words *móna*, *móni* are defined as 'spirits of the air, children of Manwë'), and therefore Eruman was beyond (south of) their abode. See *Mánir*.

GL also states that Edhofon was called *Garioth*; and *Garioth* is 'the true Gnome form' of the name *Aryador* (a word of Ilkorin origin) 'land of shadow', though applied not to Hisilómë but to Edhofon / Eruman.

According to QL *Harwalin* 'near the Valar' contains *har(e)* 'near'; the entries in GL are too confusing to cite, for the forms of *Harwalin* / *Arvalin* were changed over and over again. A late entry in GL gives a prefix *ar-* 'beside, along with'. For *Habbanan* see *Valar*.

**Falassë Númëa**  Translated in the text (p. 124) as 'Western Surf'; see *Falman, Númë*.

**Falman**  In QL the root FALA has derivatives *falma* 'foam', *falmar* 'wave as it breaks', *falas(s)* 'shore, beach', *Falman*=Ossë; cf. *Falassë Númea, Falmarini*. GL has *falm* 'breaker, wave', *falos* 'sea-marge, surf', *Falmon* or *Falathron* 'names of Otha [Ossë], =Q. *Falman* and *Falassar*'.

**Falmaríni**  See *Falman*.

**Fanturi**  In QL *fantur*, without translation but with reference to Lórien and Mandos, is given under root FANA, with several derivatives all referring to visions, dreams, falling asleep. In GL (a late entry) the form is *Fanthor*, plural *i·Fanthaurin* 'the name of each of the two brothers, of sleep, of death'.

**Fanuin**  GL has *fann* 'a year'. For the rejected names *Lathos, Lathweg* (p. 222) see *Gonlath*.

**Faskala-númen, Faskalan**  Translated in the text (p. 187) as 'Bath of the Setting Sun'. GL has *fas-* 'wash', *fasc* 'clean', *fasca-* 'splash, sprinkle', *fós* 'bath'. For *-númen* see *Númë*.

**Fëanor**  The only evidence for the meaning of this name is given under *Fionwë-Úrion*.

**Fingolma**  See *Nólemë*.

**Finwë**  As a proper name this is not in the dictionaries, but GL gives a common noun *finweg* 'craftsman, man of skill' (with *fim* 'clever; right hand' and other related words); for *-weg* see *Bronweg*. In QL derivatives of root FINI are *finwa* 'sagacious', *finië, findë* 'cunning'. See *Nólemë*.

**Fionwë-Úrion**  *Fion* 'son' is given separately in QL (a hurried later addition), with the note 'especially Fion(wë) the Vala'. In Gnomish he is '*Auros Fionweg*, or *Fionaur Fionor*'. In a later entry in GL '*Fionaur (Fionor)*=Q. *Fëanor* (goblet-smith)', and among the original entries is *fion* 'bowl, goblet'. There is no indication that this refers to Fëanor the Gnome.

For the second element (*Úrion, Auros*) see *Úr*. In the Valar name-list Fionwë is called *Kalmo*; see *Galmir*.

**Fui**  In QL are *hui* 'fog, dark, murk, night' and *huiva* 'murky', and also '*Fui* (=*hui*) wife of Vê'. In Gnomish she is *Fuil* 'Queen of the Dark', and related words are *fui* 'night', *fuin* 'secret, dark'.

**fumellar**  The 'flowers of sleep' (poppies) in Lórien's gardens (p. 74). QL under root FUMU 'sleep' has *fúmë* 'sleep' (noun), *fúmella, fúmellot* 'poppy'.

**Galmir**   Translated in the text (p. 187) as 'the goldgleamer' (a name of the Sun). This is a derivative of Gnomish *gal-* 'shine', which in Qenya is KALA 'shine golden', and of which a great many derivatives are given in QL, as *kala-* 'shine', *kálë* 'morning', *kalma* 'daylight', *Kalainis* 'May' (see *Erinti*), *kalwa* 'beautiful', etc. Cf. *Kalormë*, *Kalaventë*, and *i·kal'antúlien* 'Light hath returned' (p. 184).

**Gar Lossion**   Translated in the text (p. 16) as 'Place of Flowers' (Gnomish name of Alalminórë). For *Gar* see *Dor Faidwen*. GL gives *lost* 'blossom' and *lôs* 'flower', but it is noted that they are probably unconnected and that *lôs* is more likely to be related to *lass* 'leaf', also used to mean 'petal'. (QL has *lassë* 'leaf', *lasselanta* 'the Fall, Autumn'.) See *Lindelos*.

**Glorvent**   For the element *Glor-* see *Laurelin*. – GL had *Glorben(d)* 'ship of gold', changed later to *Glorvent* 'boat of gold'; *benn* 'shape, cut, fashion', *benc*, *bent* 'small boat'. QL has the root VENE 'shape, cut out, scoop', with derivatives *venië*, *venwë* 'shape, cut' and *venë* 'small boat, vessel, dish'. Cf. the title of the 'World-Ship' drawing, *I Vene Kemen* (see p. 85), and the Sun's name *i·Kalaventë* (*Kalavénë*).

**Golfinweg**   See *Nólemë*, *Finwë*.

**Gondolin**   QL does not give this name, but *ondo* 'stone' appears under root ONO 'hard'. In GL *Gondolin* is said to=Qenya *Ondolin* (changed to *Ondolinda*) 'singing stone'. There is also an entry *gond* 'great stone, rock'; later this was changed to *gonn*, and a note added that *Gondolin*= *Gonn Dolin*, together with an entry *dólin* 'song'. See *Lindelos*.

**Gong**   GL gives no other information beyond that cited on p. 245, note 10, but compares *sithagong* 'dragonfly' (*sitha* 'fly', *Sithaloth* or *Sithaloctha* ('fly-cluster'), the Pleiades).

**Gonlath**   This is the name of the great rock on Taniquetil to which Fanuin's cable was tied (p. 219); the second element must therefore be Gnomish *lath* 'a year', which appears also in the rejected names for Fanuin, *Lathos* and *Lathweg* (p. 222). For *Gon-* see *Gondolin*.

**Gwerlum**   This is given in GL with the translation 'Gloomweaver'; *gwer-* 'wind, turn, bend', but also used in the sense of the root *gwidh-* 'plait, weave'. QL has a root GWERE 'whirl, twirl, twist', but the name *Wirilómë* of the great Spider is placed under the root GWIÐI, whence also *windelë* 'loom', *winda* 'woof', *wistë* 'weft'. The name of the great eddy *Wiruin* (p. 167), not in the dictionaries, must belong here. For the element *-lómë*, *-lum* see *Hisilómë*.

**Haloisi Velikë**   (On the 'World-Ship' drawing, p. 84.) In QL *haloisi* 'the sea (in storm)' is given under a root HALA, with other derivatives *haloitë* 'leaping', *halta-* 'to leap'.

    To Qenya *velikë* 'great' corresponds Gnomish *beleg* 'mighty, great' (as in Beleg the Bowman in the tale of Túrin).

**Helkar**   QL under root HELE has *helkë* 'ice', *helka* 'ice-cold', *hilkin* 'it freezes', *halkin* 'frozen'. GL has *helc*, *heleg* 'ice', *hel-* 'freeze', *heloth* 'frost', etc., and *helcor* 'arctic cold, utter frost'; this last was changed to read *helchor* 'antarctic cold, utter frost of the South (the pillar of the Southern Lamp). Q. *Helkar*.'

**Helkaraksë**  See *Helkar*; *Helkaraksë* is not in either dictionary and the second element is obscure, unless it is to be connected with Q. *aksa* 'waterfall' (see *Asgon*).

**Heskil**  The root HESE 'winter' in QL has derivatives *Heskil* 'winter one', *Hesin* 'winter', *hessa* 'dead, withered', *hesta-* 'wither'. In GL are *Hess* 'winter, especially as name of Fuil', and *hesc* 'withered, dead; chill'. For another name of Fui Nienna see *Vailimo*.

**Hisildi**  See *Hisilómë*.

**Hisilómë**  Under the root HISI QL gives *hísë*, *histë* 'dusk', *Hisinan* 'Land of Twilight'. For the translation of *Hisilómë* as 'Shadowy Twilights' see p. 112.

The root LOMO has many derivatives, as *lómë* 'dusk, gloom, darkness', *lómëar* 'child of gloom' (cf. *Lómëarni*), *lómin* 'shade, shadow', *lomir* 'I hide', *lomba* 'secret'. Cf. *Wirilómë*. Gnomish words are *lôm* 'gloom, shade', *lómin* 'shadowy, gloomy' and noun 'gloom': so *Dor Lómin*. The same element occurs in *Lomendánar* 'Days of Gloaming'.

**Ilinsor**  A late entry in GL gives *Glinthos*=Qenya *Ilinsor*, Helmsman of the Moon. The first element is probably *glint* 'crystal'. *Ilinsor* does not appear in QL.

**Ilkorin**  A negative prefix *il-* is given in both dictionaries; in GL it is said that *il-* 'denotes the opposite, the reversal, i.e. more than the mere negation'. See *Kôr*.

**Ilsaluntë**  (Name of the Moon.) *Ilsa* is given in QL as 'the mystic name of silver, as *laurë* of gold'; it is the *i* of *tilkal*, p. 100. For *luntë* 'ship' see *Alqaluntë*. The Gnomish name is *Gilthalont*; *giltha* 'white metal' is said to be properly the same as *celeb* 'silver' (Q. *telpë*), but now including *gais* 'steel', *ladog* 'tin', etc., as opposed to *culu* 'gold'; and *culu* is said to be a poetic word for 'gold' but 'also used mythically as a class name of all red and yellow metals, as *giltha* of white and grey'. See *Telimpë*.

**Ilterendi**  In the text the fetters are called *Ilterendi* 'for they might not be filed or cleft' (p. 101); but root TERE in QL has derivatives with a sense of 'boring' (*tereva* 'piercing', *teret* 'auger, gimlet').

**Ilúvatar**  There can be no doubt that the original meaning of *Ilúvatar* was 'Sky-father' (in QL is found *atar* 'father'); see *Ilwë*.

**Ilverin**  Elvish name of Littleheart son of Bronweg. The rejected name *Elwenildo* (p. 52) contains the word *elwen* 'heart' given in QL; GL gives the word *ilf* 'heart (especially used of feelings)', and several names (*Ilfin(g)*, *Ilfiniol*, *Ilfrith*) corresponding to Qenya *Ilwerin*.

**Ilwë**  In QL the word *ilu* is glossed 'ether, the slender airs among the stars', while in GL the Gnomish name *Ilon* of Illúvatar is said to= Qenya *Ilu*. In QL *ilwë* was first glossed 'sky, heavens', with a later

addition 'the blue air that is about the stars, the middle layers';
to this in Gnomish corresponds *ilwint* - concerning which it is
explained in GL that the true form *ilwi* or *ilwin* was perverted to
*ilwint* through association with *gwint* 'face', as if it meant 'face of
God'. Other words found in Gnomish are *Ilbar*, *Ilbaroth* 'heaven,
the uttermost region beyond the world'; *Ilador*, *Ilathon* = *Ilúvatar*;
*ilbrant* 'rainbow' (see *Ilweran*).

**Ilweran**   QL gives *Ilweran*, *Ilweranta* 'rainbow' (another word for the
rainbow in Qenya is *Iluqinga*, in which *qinga* means 'bow'; *qingi-*
'twang, of strings, harp'). In Gnomish the corresponding forms are
*Ilbrant* or *Ilvrant*, which are said in GL to be falsely associated with
*brant* 'bow (for shooting)'; the second element is related rather to
*rantha* 'arch, bridge', as Q. *Ilweran(ta)* shows.

**Ingil**   In GL the Gnomish names of Inwë's son are *Gilweth* and *Githilma*;
*Gil* is the star Sirius, and is said to be the name of Gilweth after he
rose into the heavens and 'in the likeness of a great bee bearing honey
of flame followed Daimord [Telimektar, Orion]'; see entries *Nielluin*,
*Telimektar*. No explanation of these names is given, but *Gil(weth)*
is clearly connected with *gil-* 'gleam', *gilm* 'moonlight', *giltha* 'white
metal' (see *Ilsaluntë*). For *Githilma* see *Isil*.

**Inwë**   In QL this, the name of 'the ancient king of the fairies who led
them to the world', is a derivative of a root INI 'small', whence also
the adjective *inya* and the names *Inwilis*, *Inwinórë* 'Faëry' and
'England' (the latter struck out). Tol Eressëa was here said to have
been named *Inwinórë* after Inwë, but this was changed to say that
it was named *Ingilnórë* after his son Ingil. These entries relate to a
very early conception (see *Alalminórë*, *Eldamar*). For other names
of Inwë see *Inwithiel*, *Isil*.

**Inwir**   See *Inwë*. In GL the 'noble clan of the Tilthin' (Teleri) are called
*Imrim*, singular *Im* (see *Inwithiel*).

**Inwithiel**   In the texts *Inwithiel*, Gnomish name of King Inwë, is an
emendation from *(Gim)Githil* (pp. 22, 131). In GL these names
*Inwithiel*, *Githil* are given as additional to his proper names *Inweg*
or *Im*. See *Isil*.

**Isil**   In the tale of *The Coming of the Elves* (p. 115) Inwë is called
*Isil Inwë*, and in GL the Gnomish form corresponding to *Isil* is
*Githil* (to the name of his son *Githilma* corresponds Qenya *Isilmo*).
In QL is a root ISI (*iska* 'pale', *is* 'light snow'), of which the Gnomish
equivalent is given as *ith-* or *gith-*; GL has a word *ith* 'fine snow'.

**Kalaventë**   See *Galmir*, *Glorvent*.

**Kalormë**   This appears in QL among the derivatives of root KALA (see
*Galmir*), with the meaning 'hill-crest over which the Sun rises'.
*ormë* = 'summit, crest', from a root ORO with apparently a base
sense of 'rise': *or* 'on', *oro* 'hill', *oro-* 'rise', *orto-* 'raise', *oronta* 'steep',
*orosta* 'ascension', etc.; Gnomish *or* 'on, onto, on top', *orod*, *ort*

'mountain', *orm* 'hill-top', *oros, orost-* 'rising'. Cf. *Oromë, Orossi, Tavrobel.*

**Kapalinda** (The source of the river in the place of the banishment of the Noldoli in Valinor, p. 157.) QL has *kapalinda* 'spring of water' among derivatives of root KAPA 'leap, spring'; *linda* is obscure.

**Kaukareldar** Under the root KAWA 'stoop' in QL are derivations *kauka* 'crooked, bent, humped', *kauko* 'humpback', *kawin* 'I bow', *kaurë* 'fear', *kaurëa* 'timid'.

**Kelusindi** (The river in the place of the banishment of the Noldoli in Valinor, p. 157; in the text called *Sirnúmen.*) In QL under root KELE, KELU 'flow, trickle, ooze' are given many derivatives including *kelusindi* 'a river', also *kelu, kelumë* 'stream', *kektelë* 'fountain' (also in the form *ektelë*), etc. For *-sindi* see *Sirion.*

**Kémi** QL gives *kemi* 'earth, soil, land' and *kemen* 'soil', from root KEME. The Gnomish name is *Címir*, which=Q. *Kémi* 'Mother Earth'. There is also a Gnomish word *grosgen* 'soil' in which *-gen* is said to= Q. *kémi.*

**Koivië-néni** 'Waters of Awakening.' In QL under root KOYO 'have life' are derivatives *koi, koirë* 'life', *koitë* 'living being', *koina, koirëa* 'alive', *koiva* 'awake', *koivië* 'awakening'. In GL are *cuil* 'life', *cuith* 'life, living body', etc.; *cwiv-* 'be awake', *cwivra-* 'awaken', *cuivros* 'awakening': *Nenin a Gwivros* 'Waters of Awakening'. For *-néni, Nenin* see *Neni Erúmëar.*

**Kópas** QL has *kópa* 'harbour', the only word given under root KOPO 'keep, guard'. GL has *gobos* 'haven', with a reference to Q. *kópa, kópas*; also *gob* 'hollow of hand', *gobli* 'dell'.

**Kôr** In QL this name is given under the root KORO 'revere?', with the note 'the ancient town built above the rocks of Eldamar, whence the fairies marched into the world'; also placed here are *korda* 'temple', *kordon* 'idol'. The Gnomish form is here given as *Côr*, but in GL *Côr* ('the hill of the fairies and the town thereon near the shores of the Bay of Faëry') was replaced by *Gwâr, Goros* '=Q. *Kôr* the town on the round hill'. This interpretation of the name *Kôr* clearly replaces that in QL, which belongs with the earliest layer of entries. See further under *korin.*

**korin** See *Kôr.* In QL there is a second root KORO (i.e. distinct from that which gave *Kôr*); this has the meaning 'be round, roll', and has such derivatives as *korima* 'round', *kornë* 'loaf', also *korin* 'a circular enclosure, especially on a hill-top'. At the same time as *Côr* was replaced by *Gwâr, Goros* in GL the word *gorin* (*gwarin*) 'circle of trees, =Q. *korin*' was entered, and all these forms derive from the same root (*gwas-* or *gor-* ⟨ *guor*=Q. *kor-*), which would seem to signify 'roundness'; so in the tale of *The Coming of the Elves* 'the Gods named that hill Kôr by reason of its roundness and its smoothness' (p. 122).

**Koromas** A separate and early entry in QL defines *Kormas* (the form in the text before emendation to *Koromas*, p. 22) thus: 'the new capital of the fairies after their retreat from the hostile world to Tol Eressëa, now Inwinórë. It was named in memory of Kôr and because of its great tower was called also *Kortirion*.' For -*mas* see *Eldamar*.

**Kortirion**  The word *tirion* 'a mighty tower, a city on a hill' is given in QL under root TIRI 'stick up', with *tinda* 'spike', *tirin* 'tall tower', *tirios* 'a town with walls and towers'. There is also another root TIRI, differing in the nature of the medial consonant, with meaning 'watch, guard, keep; look at, observe', whence *tiris* 'watch, vigil', etc. In GL are *tir-* 'look out for, await', *tirin* (poetic form *tirion*) 'watch-tower, turret', *Tirimbrithla* 'the Tower of Pearl' (see *Silmarilli*).

**Kosomot**  Son of Melko (see p. 93). With a different second element, *Kosomoko*, this name is found in QL under root MOKO 'hate' (*mokir* 'I hate'), and the corresponding Gnomish form is there said to be *Gothmog*. The first element is from root KOSO 'strive', in Gnomish *goth* 'war, strife', with many derivative words.

**Kulullin**  This name is not among the derivatives of KULU 'gold' in QL, nor does it appear with the Gnomish words (mostly names of the Sun) containing *culu* in GL. For the meaning of *culu* in Gnomish see *Ilsaluntë*.

**Laisi**  See *Tári-Laisi*.

**Laurelin**  QL has *laurë* 'gold (much the same as *kulu*)', *laurina* 'golden'. *laurë* is the final *l* of *tilkal* (p. 100, where it is said to be the 'magic' name of gold, as *ilsa* of silver). The Gnomish words are *glôr* 'gold', *glôrin*, *glôriol* 'golden', but GL gives no names of the Golden Tree. Cf. *Bráglorin*, *Glorvent*.

**limpë**  *limpë* 'drink of the fairies' is given in QL under root LIPI, with *lipte-* 'to drip', *liptë* 'a little drop', *lipil* 'little glass'. Corresponding forms in GL are *limp* or *limpelis* 'the drink of the fairies', *lib-* 'to drip', *lib* 'a drop', *libli* 'small glass'.

**Lindeloksë**  At one occurrence in the texts an emendation from *Lindoktë* and itself emended to *Lindelos* (p. 22), at others an emendation from *Lindelótë* and itself allowed to stand (pp. 79, 131). See *Lindelos*.

**Lindelos**  *Linde-* is one of many derivatives from the root LIRI 'sing', as *lin* 'melody', *lindelë* 'song, music', *lindelëa* 'melodious', *lirit* 'poem', *lirilla* 'lay, song' (cf. Rúmil's *tiripti lirilla*, p. 47), and the name of the Vala *Lirillo*. GL has *lir-* 'sing' and *glîr* 'song, poem'. *Lindelos* is not given in QL, which has the name rejected in the text *Lindeloktë* (p. 22), here translated 'singing cluster, laburnum'.

*Loktë* 'blossom (of flowers in bunches or clusters)' is derived from a root LOHO, with *lokta-* 'sprout, put forth leaves or flowers'. This is said to be an extended form of root OLO 'tip', whence *olë* 'three', *olma* 'nine', *ólemë* 'elbow'. Another extended form of this root is LO'O, from which are derived *lóte* 'a flower' (and *-lot* 'the common form in compounds') and many other words; cf. *Lindelóte*, another rejected name of the Golden Tree (pp. 79, 131), *Wingilot*. For Gnomish words see *Gar Lossion*. No Gnomish name of the Golden Tree is found in GL, but it was in fact *Glingol* (which originally appeared in the text, see p. 22); GL has *glin* 'sound, voice, utterance' (also *lin* 'sound'), with the note that *-glin, -grin* is a suffix in the names of languages, as *Goldogrin* Gnomish.

**Lirillo** (A name of Salmar-Noldorin, p. 144.) See *Lindelos*.

**Lómëarni** (A name of the Dark Elves, p. 244 note 6.) See *Hisilómë*.

**Lomendánar** 'Days of Gloaming' (p. 69). See *Hisilómë, Danuin*.

**Lórien** A derivative of the root LORO 'slumber', with *lor-* 'to slumber', *lorda* 'drowsy, slumbrous'; also *olor, olórë* 'dream', *olórëa* 'dreamy'. (For much later formulation of words from this root, including *Olórin* (Gandalf), see *Unfinished Tales* p. 396.) In GL are given *lûr* 'slumber', *Lúriel* changed to *Lúrin*=Qenya *Lórien*, and also *olm, oloth, olor* 'dream, apparition, vision', *oltha* 'appear as an apparition'. Cf. *Eriol, Olofantur, Olórë Mallë*.

**Lúmin** (Rejected name for Aluin 'Time', p. 222.) GL has *lûm* 'time', *luin* 'gone, past', *lu* 'occasion, time', *lûtha* 'pass (of time), come to pass'. *Aluin* perhaps belongs here also.

**Luvier** I have translated this word on the 'World-Ship' drawing as 'Clouds' (p. 85) on the basis of words in QL derived from the root LUVU: *luvu-* 'lower, brood', *lumbo* 'dark lowering cloud', *lúrë* 'dark weather', *lúrëa* 'dark, overcast'. GL has *lum* 'cloud', *lumbri* 'foul weather', *lumbrin, lumba* 'overcast', *lur-* 'hang, lower, of clouds'.

**Makar** Given in QL ('God of battle') under root MAKA, with *mak-* 'slay', *makil* 'sword'. His Gnomish name is *Magron* or *Magorn*, with related words *mactha-* 'slay', *macha* 'slaughter, battle', *magli* 'a great sword'. See *Meássë*.

In the Valar name-list Makar is called also *Ramandor*. This was the original name of the King of the Eagles in *The Fall of Gondolin*, replaced by *Sorontur*. In QL under root RAMA (*rama-* 'to shout', *rambë* 'a shout', *ran* 'noise') *Ramandor* is translated 'the Shouter, =Makar'.

**Mandos** This name is defined in QL as 'the halls of Vê and Fui (hell)', and a comparison made with *-mandu* in *Angamandu* 'Hells of Iron'. In GL is the following entry: '*Bandoth* [later changed to *Bannoth*] (cf. *Angband*)=Mandos (1) the region of the waiting souls of the dead (2) the God who judged the dead Elves and Gnomes (3) improperly used exclusively of his hall, properly called *Gwê* [changed to *Gwî*] or *Ingwi*'. For this distinction between the region *Mandos*, in which dwelt the death-gods, and their halls *Vê* and *Fui*, see pp. 76, 89-90.

**Mánir** Not in QL; but GL has '*móna* or *móni*: the spirits of the air,

children of Manweg'. Further relations are indicated in the following
entry: *'manos* (plural *manossin*): a spirit that has gone to the Valar
or to Erumáni (Edhofon). Cf. *móna*, Q. *máne.*' See *Eruman* and pp.
91 ff. Other words are *mani* 'good (of men and character only), holy'
(QL *mane* 'good (moral)'), *mandra* 'noble', and *Manweg* (Q. *Manwë*).

**Manwë**   See *Mánir*. The Gnomish names are *Man* and *Manweg* (for
-*weg* see *Bronweg*).

**Mar Vanwa Tyaliéva**   For *Mar* see *Eldamar*, and for *Vanwa* see
*Qalvanda*. *Tyalië* 'play, game' is an isolated entry in QL under root
TYALA.

**Meássë**   A late, hasty entry in QL adds *Meássë* 'sister of Makar, Amazon
with bloody arms' to the root MEHE 'ooze?', whence *mear* 'gore'. In
GL she is *Mechos* and *Mechothli* (*mechor* 'gore'), and is also called
*Magrintha* 'the red-handed' (*magru=macha* 'slaughter, battle',
*magrusaig* 'bloodthirsty'). In the Valar name-list she is called *Rávë*
or *Ravenni*; in QL the root RAVA has many derivatives, as *rauta-*
'to hunt', *raust* 'hunting, preying', *Raustar* a name of Oromë, *rau*
(plural *rávi*) 'lion', *ravennë* 'she-lion', *Rávi* a name of Meássë. Very
similar forms are given in GL: *rau* 'lion', *rausta* 'to hunt', *raust*
'hunt'.

**Melko**   The name is entered in QL but without etymological affinity.
In GL the corresponding name is *Belca*, changed to *Belcha*, with a
note referring to Qenya *velka* 'flame'. In the Valar name-list he is
called *Yelur* (root DYELE, whence Qenya *yelwa* 'cold', *Yelin* 'winter');
the Gnomish form is *Geluim*, *Gieluim*, 'name of Belcha when exer-
cising his opposite functions of extreme cold, Q. *Yeloimu*', cf. *Gilim*
'winter'. Melko is also called in the name-list *Ulban(d)*, which is
found in QL glossed 'monster', under the negative prefix UL-;
his son Kosomot (Gothmog) was 'by Ulbandi' (p. 93). Other names
for him in Gnomish are *Uduvrin* (see *Utumna*) and *Angainos* (see
*Angaino*).

**Meril-i-Turinqi**   *Meril* is not in QL, but *turinqi* 'queen' is given with
a great many other derivatives of the root TURU 'be strong', including
*Turambar* (*Turumarto*), and *tur* 'king'. In GL are *tur-* 'can, have
power to', *tûr* 'king', *turwin* 'queen', *turm* 'authority, rule; strength'.
*turinthi* 'princess, especially title of Gwidhil'. Cf. *Sorontur*, *Valatúru*.
*Tuor*.

There are also these later additions in GL: '*Gwidhil-i-Durinthi*=
*Meril-i-Turinqi* Queen of Flowers'; *gwethra* 'bloom, flourish'; and
the stem *gwedh-* is here compared to Qenya *mer-*, which is not in QL.

**Minethlos**   GL *min* 'one, single', *mindon* 'tower, properly an isolated
turret or peak', *mineth* 'island', *Minethlos* 'Argent Isle (Moon)' – the
same translation is given in the text, p. 192. Under root MĪ QL has
*mir* 'one', *minqë* 'eleven'; and under root MINI *mindon* 'turret'. The
second element of *Minethlos* must in fact be *lôs* 'flower' (see *Gar
Lossion*).

**Miruvor**   QL *miruvórë* 'nectar, drink of the Valar' (see p. 161), with *miru* 'wine'; GL *mirofor* (or *gurmir*) 'drink of the Gods', *mir*, *miros* 'wine'.

**Moritarnon**   'Door of Night' (see *Mornië*). GL gives *tarn* 'gate', *tarnon* 'porter'. Cf. *Tarn Fui*.

**Mornië**   Not in QL, but one of the many derivatives of root MORO, as *moru-* 'to hide', *mori* 'night', *morna*, *morqa* 'black', *morion* 'son of the dark'. (A curious item is *Morwen* 'daughter of the dark', Jupiter. In the original tale of Túrin his mother was not named Morwen.) The Gnomish name of the death-ship is *Mornir*, a later addition to original entries *morn* 'dark, black', *morth* 'darkness', *mortha* 'dim', with the note 'the black ship that plies between Mandos and Erumáni, Q. *Mornië* (Black Grief)'. The second element is therefore *nir* 'grief' (⟨ *niēr-*), to which Qenya *nyérë* is said to correspond. Cf. *Moritarnon*, *Móru*, *Morwinyon*.

**Móru**   GL in a later addition gives *Muru* 'a name of the Primeval Night personified as Gwerlum or Gungliont', hence my reading in the text *Móru* rather than *Morn* (p. 156). Among the original entries in GL is *múri* 'darkness, night'. See *Mornië*.

**Morwinyon**   This name of the star Arcturus is translated in the text (p. 182) as 'the glint at dusk', and QL, giving it under root MORO (see *Mornië*), renders it 'glint in the dark'. QL has a root GWINI with derivative word *wintil* 'a glint'.
The Gnomish name is *Morwinthi*; presumably connected are *gwim*, *gwinc* 'spark, flash', *gwimla* 'wink, twinkle'.

**Murmenalda**   Translated in the text as 'Vale of Sleep', 'the Slumbrous Dale' (pp. 233, 235). QL under root MURU gives *muru-* 'to slumber', *murmë* 'slumber', *murmëa* 'slumbrous'. The second element is from a root NLDL, of which the derivatives in QL are *nal(lë)* 'dale, dell' and *nalda* 'valley' used as an adjective. In Gnomish occur *nal* 'dale, vale', *nal* 'down, downwards', *nalos* 'sinking, setting, slope', *Nalosaura* 'sunset', etc. Cf. *Murmuran*.

**Murmuran**   See *Murmenalda*. GL gives the Gnomish form corresponding to Qenya *Murmuran* as *Mormaurien* 'abode of Lúriel', but this seems to be of different etymology: cf. *Malmaurien*=*Olórë Mallë*, the Path of Dreams, *maur* 'dream, vision'.

**Nandini**   On an isolated paper that gives a list of the different clans of 'fays' the *Nandini* are 'fays of the valleys'. QL gives a root NARA with derivatives *nan(d)* 'woodland', *nandin* 'dryad'; GL has *nandir* 'fay of the country, Q. *nandin*', together with *nand* 'field, acre' (plural *nandin* 'country'), *nandor* 'farmer', etc.

**Nauglath**   GL gives the following words: *naug* and *naugli* 'dwarf', *naugla* 'of the dwarves', *nauglafel* 'dwarf-natured, i.e. mean, avaricious' (see p. 236). QL has nothing corresponding, but in GL the Qenya equivalent of *naug* is said to be *nauka*.

**Neni Erúmëar**  (On the 'World-Ship' drawing, where I have translated it 'Outermost Waters', p. 85.) QL under root NENE 'flow' has *nen* 'river, water', and the same form occurs in Gnomish. *Erúmëa* 'outer, outermost' is given in QL as a derivative of ERE 'out', as in *Eruman*. Cf. *Koivië-néni*.

**Nermir**  In the list of fays referred to under *Nandini* the *Nermir* are 'fays of the meads'. QL has an isolated entry *Nermi* 'a field-spirit', and GL has *Nermil* 'a fay that haunts meadows and river-banks'.

**Nessa**  This name does not appear in the dictionaries. – In the Valar name-list she is called *Helinyetillë* and *Melesta*. In QL, among the very early entries, *helin* is the name of the violet or pansy, and *Helinyetillë* is glossed 'Eyes of Heartsease' (that being a name of the pansy); cf. *yéta* 'look at'. But in QL this is a name of Erinti. There was clearly much early shifting among the goddesses of Spring, the ascription of names and rôles (see *Erinti*). *Melesta* is doubtless from root MELE 'love' (*meles(së)* 'love', *melwa* 'lovely', etc.; Gnomish *mel-* 'to love', *meleth* 'love', *melon, meltha* 'beloved', etc.).

**Nielíqui**  In QL this name (*Nieliqi*, also *Nielikki, Nyelikki*) is derived from the root NYEHE 'weep' (see *Nienna*). Where her tears fell snow-drops (*nieninqë*, literally 'white tear') sprang. See the poem *Nieninqë* in J. R. R. Tolkien, *The Monsters and the Critics and Other Essays*, 1983, p. 215. For *ninqë* see *Taniquetil*.

The second element of *Nielíqui* is presumably from the root LIQI, whence *linqë* 'water', *liqin* 'wet', *liqis* 'transparence', etc. (see *Ulmo*).

**Nielluin**  This name of the star Sirius is translated in the text (p. 182) as 'the Bee of Azure' (see *Ingil*). The first element is from the root NEHE, whence *nektë* 'honey', *nier* (< *neier* < *neχier*) 'honey-bee', *nierwes* 'hive'. The name of Sirius is given in QL as *Niellúnë* or *Nierninwa*; both *ninwa* and *lúnë* are Qenya words meaning 'blue'. In Gnomish the name of the star is *Niothluimi*, =Qenya *Nielluin*: *nio, nios* 'bee' and many related words, *luim* 'blue'.

**Nienna**  In QL *Nyenna* the goddess is given under a root NYE(NE) 'bleat', whence *nyéni* 'she-goat', *nyéna-* 'lament', etc.; but there is a note 'or all to root NYEHE'. This means 'weep': *nië* 'tear' (cf. *Nielíqui*), *nyenyë* 'weeping'. In GL the forms of the name are *Nenni(r)*, *Nenir*, *Ninir*, without etymological connections given, but cf. *nín* 'tear'.

**Noldoli**  The root NOL 'know' in QL has derivatives *Noldo* 'Gnome' and *Noldorinwa* adjective, *Noldomar* 'Gnomeland', and *Noldorin* 'who dwelt awhile in Noldomar and brought the Gnomes back to Inwenórë'. It seems that *Noldomar* means the Great Lands. But it is very curious that in these entries, which are among the earliest, 'Gnome' is an emendation of 'Goblin'; cf. the poem *Goblin Feet* (1915), and its Old English title *Cumaþ þá Nihtielfas* (p. 32).

In Gnomish 'Gnome' is *Golda* ('i.e. wise one'); *Goldothrim* 'the people of the Gnomes', *Goldogrin* their tongue, *Goldobar, Goldomar* 'Gnomeland'. The equivalent of *Noldorin* in GL is *Goldriel*, which was the form antecedent to *Golthadriel* in the text before both were struck out (p. 22). See *Nólemë*.

**Noldorin**   See *Noldoli*.

**Nólemë**   This is given in QL as a common noun, 'deep lore, wisdom' (see *Noldoli*). The Gnomish name of Finwë Nólemë, *Golfinweg* (p. 115), contains the same element, as must also the name *Fingolma* given to him in outlines for *Gilfanon's Tale* (pp. 238-9).

**I Nori Landar**   (On the 'World-Ship' drawing, probably meaning 'the Great Lands', pp. 84-5.) For *nori* see *Valinor*. Nothing similar to *landar* appears in QL; GL gives a word *land* (*lann*) 'broad'.

**Nornorë**   In QL this name has the form *Nornoros* 'herald of the Gods', and with the verb *nornoro-* 'run on, run smoothly' is derived from a root NORO 'run, ride, spin, etc.'. GL has similar words, *nor-* run', roll', *norn* 'wheel', *nûr* 'smooth, rolling free'. The name corresponding to Qenya *Nornorë* is here *Drondor* 'messenger of the Gods' (*drond* 'race, course, track' and *drô* 'wheel-track, rut'); *Drondor* was later changed to *Dronúrin* (< *Noronōr-*) and *drond* to *dronn*.

**Númë**   (On the 'World-Ship' drawing.) In QL *númë* 'West' is derived from root NUHU 'bow, bend down, stoop, sink'; other words are *núta-* 'stoop, sink', *númeta-*, *numenda-* 'get low (of the Sun)', *númëa* 'in the West'. Gnomish *num-* 'sink, descend', *númin* 'in the West', *Auranúmin* 'sunset', *numbros* 'incline, slope', *nunthi* 'downward'. Cf. *Falassë Númëa*, *Faskala-númen*, *Sirnúmen*.

**Núri**   Name of Fui Nienna: 'Núri who sighs', p. 66. This is given without translation in QL under root NURU, with *núru-* 'growl (of dogs), grumble', *nur* 'growl, complaint'. In Gnomish she is *Nurnil*, with associated words *nur-* 'growl, grumble', *nurn* 'lament', *nurna-* 'bewail, lament'.

**Ô**   (On the 'World-Ship' drawing: 'the Sea', pp. 84-5.) See *Ónen*.

**Oarni**   See *Ónen*.

**Olofantur**   See *Lórien, Fanturi*.

**Olórë Mallë**   For *Olórë* see *Lórien*. *mallë* 'street' appears in QL under root MALA 'crush' (see *Balrog*); the Gnomish form is *mal* 'paved way, road', and the equivalent of *Olórë Mallë* is *Malmaurien* (see *Murmuran*).

**Ónen**   The root 'o'o in QL has derivatives *Ô*, a poetic word, 'the sea', *oar* 'child of the sea, merchild', *oaris* (*-ts*), *oarwen* 'mermaid', and *Ossë*; the name *Ówen* (antecedent of *Ónen* in the text, pp. 61, 79) also appears, and evidently means the same as *oarwen* (for *-wen* see *Urwen*). The later form *Uinen* in the Tales is apparently Gnomish; GL *Únen* 'Lady of the Sea', changed later to *Uinen*. A form *Oinen* also occurs (p. 211).

In the Valar name-list Ónen is called also *Solórë* (see *Solosimpi*) and *Ui Oarista*. This latter appears in QL, with the definition 'Queen of the Mermaids', together with *Uin* 'the primeval whale'; but how these relate to the other names is obscure.

**Orc**  QL *ork* (*orq-*) 'monster, demon'. GL *orc* 'goblin', plural *orcin*, *orchoth* (*hoth* 'folk, people', *hothri* 'army', *hothron* 'captain').

**Oromë**  In QL *Oromë* 'son of Aulë' is placed under a root ORO that is distinct (apparently because of the nature of the consonant) from ORO (with meaning of 'steepness, rising') given under *Kalormë*; but these roots are said to be 'much confused'. This second root yields *órë* 'the dawn, Sunrise, East', *órëa* 'of the dawn, Eastern', *orontë*, *oronto* 'Sunrise', *osto* 'the gates of the Sun', and *Ostor* 'the East, the Sun when she issues from her white gates'. It is noted that *Oromë* should perhaps be placed under the other root, but there is no indication of the connections of the name. In *The Hiding of Valinor* (p. 214) Oromë has a particular knowledge of the East of the world. His name in Gnomish is *Orma*; and in the Valar name-list he is also called *Raustar*, for which see *Meássë*.

**Oronto**  (On the 'World-Ship' drawing, 'East'.) See *Oromë*.

**Orossi**  In the list of fays referred to under *Nandini* the *Orossi* are 'fays of the mountains', and this name is thus a derivative from the root ORO seen in *Kalormë*.

**Ossë**  See *Ónen*. His Gnomish name is *Otha* or *Oth*.

**Palisor**  See *Palúrien*.

**Palúrien**  An early entry in QL gives *Palurin* 'the wide world' under a root PALA, whose derivatives have a common general sense of 'flatness', among them *palis* 'sward, lawn', whence no doubt *Palisor*. In GL the corresponding name is *Belaurin*, *B(a)laurin*; but she is also called *Bladorwen* 'the wide earth, the world and its plants and fruits, Mother Earth' (related words are *blant* 'flat, open, expansive, candid', *blath* 'floor', *bladwen* 'a plain'). See *Yavanna*.

**Poldórëa**  Not in QL, but GL gives several corresponding forms: *Polodweg*=Tulcus (*polod* 'power, might, authority'); *polodrin* 'mighty', also in poetic form *Poldurin* or *Poldorin* which is especially used as epithet of Tulcus; Q. *Poldórëa*'.

**Qalmë-Tári**  The root is QALA 'die', whence *qalmë* 'death', *qalin* 'dead', and other words of the same meaning. *Tári* is from TAHA: *tâ* 'high', *tára* 'lofty', *tári* 'queen', etc.; Gnomish *dâ* 'high', *dara* 'lofty', *daroth* 'summit, peak'. Cf. *Taniquetil*.

**Qalvanda**  'The Road of Death' (p. 213). See *Qalmë-Tári*. The second element is from root VAHA: whence *vâ* past tense 'went', *vand-* 'way, path', *vandl* 'staff', *vanwa* 'gone on the road, past, over, lost' (as in *Mar Vanwa Tyaliéva*). Cf. *Vansamírin*.

**Qerkaringa**  The first element is obscure; for -*ringa* see *Ringil*.

**Qorinómi**  See p. 227. The root is QORO/QOSO, whence *qoro-* 'choke, suffocate', *qorin* 'drowned, choked', etc.

**Rána**  Not in QL, but GL has *Rân* 'the Moon (Q. *Rána*)' and *ranoth* 'month' (*Ranoth* was a rejected name preceding *Ranuin*, p. 222).

In the text (p. 192) it is said that the Gods named the Moon *Rána*.

**Ranuin** See *Rána*.

**Ringil** QL gives *ringa* 'damp, cold, chilly', *ringwë* 'rime, frost', *rin* 'dew'; GL *rî* 'coolness', *ring* 'cool, cold, a sudden breeze or cold breath', and (a later addition) *Ringli* 'the arctic colds, the North Pole (see the tale of the Coming of the Ainur)'. Cf. *Qerkaringa*.

**Rúmil** This name is not found in either dictionary, but seems likely to be connected with words given in GL: *rû* and *rûm* 'secret, mystery', *ruim* 'secret, mysterious', *rui* 'whisper', *ruitha* 'to whisper'.

**Salmar** This name must belong with derivatives of the root SALA: *salma* 'lyre', *salmë* 'harp-playing', etc.

**Samírien** ('The Feast of Double Mirth', p. 143.) Presumably derived from the root MIRI 'smile'; *sa-* is referred to in QL as an 'intensive prefix'. Cf. *Vansamírin*.

**Sári** Not in either dictionary, but in QL the root SAHA/SAHYA yields *sâ* 'fire', *saiwa* 'hot', *Sahóra* 'the South'; GL has *sâ* 'fire' (poetic form *sai*), *sairin* 'fiery', *saiwen* 'summer', and other words.

**Sil** Under the root SILI QL gives a long list of words beginning with *Sil* 'Moon' and all with meanings of whiteness or white light, but neither *Silpion* nor *Silmaril* occurs in it. In GL *Sil* 'properly = "Rose of Silpion", see Tale of the Making of the Sun and Moon, but often used poetically = Whole Moon or Rân'. In this tale (p. 192) it is said that the fairies named the Moon 'Sil, the Rose' (earlier reading 'the silver rose').

**Silindrin** The 'Moon-cauldron' does not appear in either dictionary; the nearest form is *Silindo* in QL, which is a name of Jupiter. See *Sil*.

**Silmarilli** See *Sil*. In GL the equivalent of 'Q. *Silmaril*' is *silubrill-* (*silum(b)aril-*), plural *silubrilthin* (which occurs in the text, p. 128); a later addition compares *brithla* 'pearl', Qenya *marilla* (not in QL). The Tower of Pearl was named in Gnomish *Tirimbrithla*.

**Silmo** See *Sil*. In QL *Silmo* is translated 'the Moon', and in GL *Silma* is given as the Gnomish equivalent of Qenya *Silmo*.

**Silpion** See *Sil*. The Gnomish names are *Silpios* or *Piosil*, but no meaning is given.

**Silubrilthin** See *Silmarilli*.

**Sirion** QL root SIRI 'flow', with derivatives *sindi* 'river' (cf. *Kelusindi*), *sírë* 'stream', *sirima* 'liquid, flowing'. In GL are given *sîr* 'river', *siriol* 'flowing', and *Sirion* (poetic word) 'river, properly name of the famous magic river that flowed through Garlisgion and Nantathrin' (*Garlisgion* 'the Place of Reeds' survived in *Lisgardh* 'the land of reeds at the Mouths of Sirion', *Unfinished Tales* p. 34). Cf. *Sirnúmen*, and the name it replaced, *Numessir*.

**Sirnúmen** See *Sirion*, *Númë*.

**Solosimpi** QL gives *Solosimpë* 'the Shoreland Pipers', of which the first element is from root SOLO: *solmë* 'wave', *solor, solossë* 'surf, surge' (cf. *Solórë*, name of Ónen), and the second from SIPI 'whistle, pipe': *simpa, simpina* 'pipe, flute', *simpisë* 'piping', *simpetar* 'piper'. In GL the Gnomish name of the Solosimpi is *Thlossibin* or *Thlossibrim*, from *thloss* 'breaker', with a variant *Flossibrim*. The word *floss* is said to have been formed from *thloss* by influence of *flass* 'seamarge, surf; margin, fringe'.

**Sorontur** Derived from a root SORO 'eagle': *sor, sornë* 'eagle', *sornion* 'eyrie', *Sorontur* 'King of Eagles'. For *-tur* see *Meril-i-Turinqi*. The Gnomish forms are *thorn* 'eagle', *thrond* '(eyrie), pinnacle', *Thorndor* and *Throndor* 'King of Eagles'.

**Súlimo** In QL under the three root-forms SUHYU, SUHU, SUFU 'air, breathe, exhale, puff' are given *sû* 'noise of wind', *súlimë* 'wind', and *Súlimi, -o* 'Vali of Wind=Manwë and Varda'. This probably means that Manwë was *Súlimo* and Varda *Súlimi*, since Varda is called *Súlimi* in the Valar name-list; but in GL it is said that Manwë and Varda were together called *i·Súlimi*. GL has *sû* 'noise of wind', *súltha* 'blow (of wind)', but Manwë's wind-name is *Saulmoth* (*saul* 'a great wind'), which is said to be an older form of later *Solmoth*; and this '=Q. *Súlimo*'.

In Gnomish he is also called *Gwanweg* (*gwâ* 'wind', *gwam* 'gust of wind'), often combined with *Man* (see *Manwë*) as *Man 'Wanweg*=Q. *Manwë Súlimo.* The root GWĀ appears in QL: *wâ* 'wind', *wanwa* 'great gale', *wanwavoitë* 'windy'; and in the Valar name-list Manwë and Varda are together called *Wanwavoisi*.

**Súruli** See *Súlimo*. *Súruli* is not in QL, but GL has *Sulus* (plurals *Sulussin* and *Suluthrim*) 'one of Manwë's two clans of air-spirits, Q. *Súru* plural *Súruli*'.

**Talka Marda** This title of Aulë, translated in the text (p. 180) as 'Smith of the World', is not found in QL, but GL gives '*Martaglos*, correctly *Maltagros*, title of Óla, Smith of the World' as the equivalent of Qenya *Talka Marwa*; also *tagros, taglos* 'smith'. He is also called *Óla Mar*; and in the Valar name-list *Aulë Mar*. (Long afterwards this title of Aulë reappeared. In a very late note he is given the name *mbartanō* 'world-artificer' > Quenya *Martamo*, Sindarin *Barthan*.)

**Taniquetil** Under the root TAHA (see *Qalmë-Tári*) *Taniqetil* is given in QL with the meaning 'lofty snowcap'. The second element is from root NIQI (*ninqë* 'white', *niqis* 'snow', *niqetil* 'snowcap'; cf. *nieninqë* 'white tear' (snowdrop) in entry *Níeliqui*).

The Gnomish form is *Danigwethil* (*dâ* 'high'), but the second element seems to be different, since GL gives a word *nigweth* 'storm (properly of snow, but that sense has evaporated)'.

**Tanyasalpë** Translated in the text 'the bowl of fire' (p. 187). *salpa* 'bowl' is given in QL under a root SḶPḶ, with *sulp-* 'lick', *salpa* 'take a sup of', *sulpa* 'soup'. *Tanya* is not in QL; GL has *tan* 'firewood', *tantha-* 'kindle', *tang* 'flame, flash', and *Tanfa* 'the lowest of all airs, the hot air of the deep places'.

**Tári-Laisi** For *Tári* see *Qalmë-Tári*. In QL the root LAYA 'be alive, flourish' has derivatives *lairë* 'meadow', *laiqa* 'green', *laito* and *laisi* both meaning 'youth, vigour, new life'. The Gnomish words are *laib* (also *glaib*) 'green', *laigos* 'greenness', =Q. *laiqassë*', *lair* (also *glair*) 'meadow'. The following note is of great interest: 'Note *Laigolas*=green-leaf [see *Gar Lossion*], becoming archaic because of final form becoming *laib*, gave *Legolast* i.e. keen-sight [*last* 'look, glance', *leg*, *lêg* 'keen, piercing']. But perhaps both were his names, as the Gnomes delighted to give two similar-sounding names of dissimilar meaning, as *Laigolas Legolast, Túrin Turambar*, etc. *Legolas* the ordinary form is a confusion of the two.' (Legolas Green-leaf appears in the tale of *The Fall of Gondolin*; he was an Elf of Gondolin, and being night-sighted he led the fugitives from the city over the plain in the dark. A note associated with the tale says that 'he liveth still in Tol Eressëa named by the Eldar there *Laiqalassë*'.)

**Tarn Fui** See *Moritarnon, Fui*.

**Tavari** In the list of fays referred to under *Nandini* the *Tavari* are 'fays of the woods'. In QL *tavar* (*tavarni*) 'dale-sprites' is derived from a root TAVA, whence also *tauno* 'forest', *taulë* 'great tree', *tavas* 'woodland'. GL has *tavor* 'a wood-fay', *taur, tavros* 'forest' (*Tavros* also a proper name, 'chief wood-fay, the Blue Spirit of the Woods'. Later, *Tavros* became a name of Oromë, leading through *Tauros* to the form *Tauron* in *The Silmarillion*).

**Tavrobel** This is given in GL with the translation 'wood-home' (see *Tavari*). The element *pel* is said to be 'usual only in such place-names as *Tavrobel*', and means 'village, hamlet, -ham'. In a separate note elsewhere an additional Gnomish name *Tavrost* is given, and Qenya names *Tavaros(së), Taurossë*. *Tavrost* evidently contains *rost* 'slope, hillside, ascent', with associated words *rosta* 'ascent' (*Rost'aura* 'Sunrise'), *ront* 'high, steep', ascribed to a stem *rō-, oro-*. These are etymological variants of words given under *Kalormë*.

**Telelli** This term, which occurs once only in the Tales (p. 19), is obscure. In QL, in early entries, a complex of words is given all of which mean 'little elf': these include *Teler* and *Telellë*, and the adjectives *telerëa* and *telella*. There is no suggestion of any distinction between them. An isolated note states that young Elves of all clans who dwelt in Kôr to perfect their arts of singing and poetry were called *Telelli*; but in another place *Telellin*, a dialect, appears to be used instead of *Telerin*. See *Teleri*.

**Teleri** See *Telelli*. In GL appears *Tilith* 'an elf, a member of the first of the three tribes of the fairies or Eldar; plural *Tilthin*'. The later meaning of *Teleri*, when it became the name of the Third Tribe, was already potentially present: QL gives a root TEL + U with derivatives *telu-* 'to finish, end', *telu* (noun), *telwa* 'last, late', with the suggestion that this was perhaps an extension of root TELE 'cover in' (see *Telimek-*

*tar*). In GL these meanings 'cover in – close – finish' are expressly assigned to the root TEL-: *telm* 'roof, sky', *teloth* 'roofing, canopy, shelter', *telu-* 'to close, end, finish', *telu* 'end'.

**Telimektar**   In QL *Telimektar*, *Telimbektar* is glossed 'Orion, literally Swordsman of Heaven', and is given under the root TELE 'cover in', together with *tel* 'roof', *telda* 'having a roof', *telimbo* 'canopy; sky', etc. *-mektar* probably derives from the root MAKA, see *Makar*. The Gnomish form is *Telumaithar*.

In the Valar name-list he is called also *Taimondo*. There are substantial notes on this name in both dictionaries, which appear to have been entered at the same time. In QL *Taimondo* and *Taimordo*, names of Telimektar, together with *Taimë*, *Taimië* 'the sky', were entered under the root TAHA (see *Qalmë-Tári*). The Gnomish equivalent is *Daimord* (*dai*, *daimoth* 'sky, heaven'), who appears also in the GL entry concerning Inwë's son Ingil (Gil, Sirius): he rose into the heavens in the likeness of a great bee and 'followed Daimord' (see *Ingil*). But the word *mordo* 'warrior, hero' in Qenya was actually a borrowing from Gnomish *mord*, and the true Quenya equivalent of *mord* was *mavar* 'shepherd' – this being the original meaning of the Gnomish word also, which developed that of 'man, warrior' through its use in poetry after it had become obsolete in prose and speech. Thus *Daimord* originally meant 'Shepherd of the Sky', as did the original Qenya name *Taimavar*, altered under the influence of the Gnomish name to *Taimondo*, *Taimordo*.

**Telimpë**   Not in QL under root TELPE, which has however *telempë*= *telpë* 'silver'. Gnomish words are *celeb* 'silver', *celebrin* 'of silver', *Celebron*, *Celioth* names of the Moon. See *Ilsaluntë*.

**Tevildo**   Given in QL under root TEFE (with derivatives *teve-* 'to hate', *tevin*, *tevië* 'hatred') and explained as 'the Lord of Cats' (see p. 47). The Gnomish form is *Tifil*, 'Prince of Cats'.

**Tilkal**   A name made up of the initial sounds of six names of metals (see p. 100 and footnote). For *tambë* 'copper' see *Aulë*, and for *ilsa* 'silver' see *Ilsaluntë*. *Latúken* 'tin' is given as a separate entry in QL, with *latukenda* 'of tin'; the Gnomish form is *ladog*. *Kanu* 'lead', *kanuva* 'leaden' are placed under a root KANA in QL. For *anga* 'iron' see *Angamandi*, and for *laurë* 'gold' see *Laurelin*.

**Timpinen**   The name stands in QL as the only derivative of a root TIFI, but under root TIPI are given *timpë* 'fine rain', *timpinë* 'spray', etc. See *Tinfang*.

**Tinfang**   The entry in GL is: '*Tinfing* or *Tinfang* the fluter (surnamed *Gwarbilin* or Birdward), a fay; cf. Q. *timpinen* a fluter (*Timpando*, *Varavilindo*)'. Other Gnomish words are *tif-* 'whistle', *timpa-* 'ring, jingle', *timpi* 'little bell', *timp* 'hoot, note of a flute', *tifin* 'small flute'. The first element in *Gwarbilin* is seen also in *Amon Gwareth* 'Hill of Watch', which occurs in the tale of *The Fall of Gondolin*; the second is *bilin(c)* 'sparrow, small bird'.

**Tinwë Linto, Tinwelint**` GL has: '*Tinweg* (also *Lintinweg*) and more
usually *Tinwelint*, =Q. *Tinwë Linto*; originally leader of the Solosimpi (after led by Ellu), but became King of the Lost Elves of
Artanor'. The first element of the name is derived from TIN-, with
such derivatives as *tim* 'spark, gleam, (star)', *tintiltha-* 'twinkle',
*tinwithli* 'star-cluster, constellation'. The second element is possibly
Gnomish *lint* 'quick, nimble, light' – which my father referred to in
his essay 'A Secret Vice' (*The Monsters and the Critics and Other
Essays*, 1983, p. 205) as a word he remembered from a very early
stage of his linguistic constructions. The name is not in QL either
in the earlier form (*Linwë Tinto*, p. 130) or the later, but under root
TINI are *tinwë* 'star', *tint* '(silver) spark', etc., and also *lintitinwë*
'having many stars', the first element of this being a multiplicative
prefix *li-, lin-*. Cf. *Tinwetári*.

**Tinwetári** 'Queen of Stars'. For the elements of this name see *Tinwë
Linto, Qalmë-Tári*. The corresponding Gnomish name is *Tinturwin*
with a different second element (see *Meril-i-Turinqi*). Varda is also
called *Timbridhil, Timfiril*, with the same first element (*Bridhil*
being the Gnomish name of Varda), and *Gailbridh(n)ir*, which contains *gail* 'star' (corresponding to Qenya *ilë* in *Ílivarda*, not found in
QL).

**Tol Eressëa** Under root TOLO QL has derivatives *tol* 'island; any rise
standing alone in water, plain of green, etc.', *tolmen* 'boss (of shield),
isolated round hill, etc.', *tolos* 'knob, lump', *tólë* 'centre', and other
words. GL gives *tol* 'an isle with high steep coasts'.

*Eressëa* is given in QL under root ERE (distinct from that seen in
*Eruman*) 'remain alone': *er* 'only, but, still', *eressë* 'singly, only,
alone', *eressëa* 'lonely', *erda* 'solitary, deserted', *erin* 'remains'. In
Gnomish the Lonely Isle is *Tol Erethrin* (*er* 'one', *ereth* 'solitude',
*erethrin* 'solitary, lonely', etc.)

**Tolli Kuruvar** (On the 'World-Ship' drawing, 'the Magic Isles', pp.
84–5.) For *Tolli* see *Tol Eressëa*. QL has a group *kuru* 'magic,
wizardry', *kuruvar* 'wizard', *kuruni* 'witch', with a note: 'of the good
magic'. GL has *curu* 'magic', *curug* 'wizard', *curus* 'witch'.

**Tombo** *Tombo* 'gong' is derived in QL from a root TUMU 'swell (with
idea of hollowness)', together with *tumbë* 'trumpet', *tumbo* 'dark
vale', *tumna* 'deep, profound, dark or hidden' (see *Utumna*). Words
in Gnomish are *tûm* 'valley', *tum* 'hollow', *tumli* 'dale', *tumbol* 'valley-
like, hollow', *tumla-* 'hollow out'.

**Tuilérë** QL root TUYU: *tuilë* 'Spring, literally a budding – also collec-
tively: buds, new shoots, fresh green', *Tuilérë* 'Spring', and several
other words, as *tuilindo* '(spring-singer), swallow'. Gnomish forms
are *tuil, tuilir* 'Spring' (with the note that *Tuilir*=Vána); but Vána
is also called *Hairen* 'Spring', presumably connected with *hair*
'punctual, timely', *hai* 'punctually', *haidri* 'forenoon'.

**Tuivána** See *Tuilérë, Vána*.

**tulielto, &c.**   *Tulielto* is translated 'they have come' (p. 114), and *I·Eldar tulier* 'the Eldar have come' (*ibid.*); *I·kal'antúlien* is translated 'Light hath returned' (p. 184). QL under root TULU 'fetch, bring, bear; move, come' has the verb *tulu-* of the same meaning, also *tulwë* 'pillar, standard, pole', *tulma* 'bier'. GL has *tul-* 'bring; come', *tultha-* 'lift, carry'.

**Tulkas**   QL gives the name under root TULUK, with *tulunka* 'steady, firm', *tulka-* 'fix, set up, establish'. The Gnomish form is *Tulcus* (-*os*), with related words *tulug* 'steady, firm', *tulga-* 'make firm, settle, steady, comfort'.

**Tulkastor**   The name does not appear in the dictionaries (nor the precedent forms, *Tulkassë*, *Turenbor*, p. 22); see *Tulkas*, *Meril-i-Turinqi.*

**Tuor**   *Tuor* is not given in the dictionaries, but it is probably derived (since the name is also written *Túr*) from the root TURU 'be strong'; see *Meril-i-Turinqi.*

**Turgon**   Neither *Turondo* nor Gnomish *Turgon* are given in the dictionaries, and beyond the likelihood that the first element is from the root TURU (see *Meril-i-Turinqi*) these names cannot be explained.

**Turuhalmë**   'The Logdrawing' (p. 229). A second root TURU (TUSO) 'kindle' in QL (differing in the medial consonant from TURU 'be strong') has many derivatives: *turu-*, *tunda-* 'kindle', *turu* 'properly= firewood, but used of wood in general', *turúva* 'wooden', *tusturë* 'tinder', etc. In GL are *duru* 'wood: pole, beam, or log', *durog* 'wooden'.

The second element is in Gnomish *halm* 'drawing, draught (of fishes etc.)'. The name of the festival is *Duruchalmo(s)=Halm nadhuruthon* (*Duruchalm* was written in the text and struck out, p. 244), translated 'Yule'; this was changed later to *Durufui* 'Yule (night), i.e. Log-night' (see *Fui*).

**Uin**   See *Ónen.* In GL *uin* is a common noun, 'whale', named after *Uin* 'Gulma's great whale' (*Gulma=Ulmo*); but apparently (though this entry is rather obscure) the original meaning of *uin*, preserved in poetry, was 'wave'. Another Gnomish word for 'whale' is *uimoth* 'sheep of the waves' (*moth* 'sheep', also '1000', probably originally 'flock'; *mothweg* 'shepherd').

**Uinen**   See *Ónen.*

**Ulmo**   *Ulmo* is given in QL under the root ULU 'pour, flow fast', together with *ulu-* and *ulto-* 'pour', in transitive and intransitive senses. His name in Gnomish is *Gulma*, with corresponding verbs *gul-* and *gulta-*. In the draft text of *The Music of the Ainur* he is also called *Linqil*: see *Nieliqui.* For other names see *Vailimo.*

**Ulmonan**   See *Ulmo*; the second element of this name is not explained.

**Ungoliont**   See *Ungwë Lianti.*

**Ungwë Lianti, Ungweliant(ë)**   Under a queried root GUNGU QL gives *ungwë* 'spider, especially *Ungwë* the Gloomweaver, usually *Ungwelianti*'. The second element is from root LI+*ya* 'entwine', with derivatives *lia* 'twine', *liantë* 'tendril', *liantassë* 'vine'. In GL the name as originally entered was *Gungliont*, as also first written in the text (p. 156); later this was changed to '*Ungweliont* or *Ungoliont*'. The second element is assigned to root *li̅-* (*lind* 'twine').

**Uolë Kúvion**   *Kúvion* was changed from *Mikúmi* (p. 198). The name is not in QL under the root KUVU 'bend, bow', which has derivatives *kú* 'crescent Moon', *kúnë* 'crescent, bow'. GL gives *cú* 'bow, crescent; the waxing or waning Moon', and also '*Cuvonweg: Úl Cuvonweg* (=Q. *Ólë Kúmion*), the Moonking'. Under *Úl* the Qenya equivalent is however *Uolë*, and here it is said that the name *Úl* is usually in the phrase *Úl·a·Rinthilios*; while *Rinthilios* is glossed 'the orbed Moon, name of the Moon-elf' (*rinc* 'circular', noun 'disc'; *rin-* 'revolve, return').

**Úr**   The root URU/USU in QL has derivatives *uru* 'fire', *úrin* 'blazing hot', *uruvoitë* 'fiery', *urúva* 'like fire', *urwa* 'on fire', *Úr* 'the Sun' (with other forms *Úri, Úrinki, Urwen*), *Úrion* 'a name of Fionwë', *urna* 'oven', *usta-*, *urya-* 'burn' (transitive and intransitive). The Gnomish form is *Aur* (*aurost* 'dawn'), and also a poetic word *Uril*. See *Fionwë-Úrion, Urwen*.

**Urwen, Urwendi**   In the earlier tales in this book the form is *Urwen*, becoming *Urwendi* in the *Tale of the Sun and Moon*. The original entry in GL was '*Urwendi* and *Urwin* (Q. *Urwen*) the maiden of the Sun-ship', but this was later changed to read '*Urwedhin* and *Urwin* (Q. *Urwendi*)'. In QL (see *Úr*) *Urwen* appears as a name of the Sun. In the Valar name-list the Sun-maiden is also called *Úrinki*, and this also appears in QL as a name of the Sun.

   The element *-wen* is given in QL under root GWENE: *wen* and *wendi* 'maid, girl', *-wen* feminine patronymic, like masculine *-ion*, *wendelë* 'maidenhood' (see *Wendelin*). In GL the forms were much changed and confused. The words given have stems in *gwin-*, *gwen-*, *gweth*, with meanings 'woman', 'girl', etc.; the root seems to have been changed from *gweni-* to *gwedhe-*, with reference both to Qenya *meril* (see *Meril-i-Turinqi*) and Qenya *wendi*.

**Utumna**   In QL the root of *Utumna* ('lower regions of gloom and darkness in the North, Melko's first dwelling') is not given, but cf. the word *tumna* 'deep, profound, dark or hidden' cited under *Tombo*. In Gnomish the forms are *Udum* and *Uduvna*; Belcha (Melko) is called *Uduvrin*.

**Úvanimor**   See *Vána*.

**Vai**   The root VAYA 'enfold' in QL yields *Vai* 'the Outer Ocean', *Vaimo* or *Vailimo* 'Ulmo as Ruler of Vai', *vaima* 'robe', *vainë* 'sheath', *vainolë* 'quiver', *vaita-* 'to wrap', *Vaitya* 'the outermost airs beyond the world', etc. In Gnomish the form is *Bai*, with related words

*Baithon* 'the outer airs', *baith* 'garment', *baidha* 'to clothe', *bain* 'clad (Q. *vaina*)'.

**Vailimo**   See *Vai*. In Gnomish the form is *Belmoth* (< *Bailmoth*); there is also a poetic name *Bairos*. Ulmo is also called in Gnomish *i Chorweg a·Vai*, i.e. 'the old one of Vai' (*hôr* 'old, ancient (only of things still existing)', *hortha-* 'grow old', *horoth* 'old age', *Hôs* 'old age', a name of Fuil). For *-weg* see *Bronweg*.

**Vaitya**   See *Vai*.

**Valahíru**   (Marginal addition in the text against *Valatúru*, p. 180.) Not in the dictionaries, but probably to be associated with QL root HERE 'rule, have power': *heru-* 'to rule', *heru* 'lord', *heri* 'lady', *hérë* 'lordship'.

**Valar**   In QL '*Valar* or *Vali*' is derived from root VALA, with masc. singular *Valon* or *Valmo* and fem. singular *Valis* or *Valdë*; other words are *valin*, *valimo* 'happy', *vald-* 'blessedness, happiness'.

The Gnomish words are complicated and curious. As first written, there was *Ban* 'a god, one of the great Valar', plural *Banin*, and '*Dor'Vanion*=*Dor Banion*=*Gwalien* (or *Valinor*)'. All this was struck out. Elsewhere in GL is given the root GWAL 'fortune, happiness': *Gwala* 'one of the gods, including their divine folk and children, hence often used of one of the lesser folk as opposed to *Ban*'; *Gwalon* and *Gwalthi* corresponding to Qenya *Valon*, *Valsi*; *gwalt* 'good luck – any providential occurrence or thought: "the luck of the Valar", *i·walt ne Vanion* (Q. *valto*)'; and other abstract words, as *gwalweth* 'fortune, happiness'. Of the later interpretation of *Valar* there is thus no suggestion. See further under *Vána*.

**Valatúru**   See *Valar*, *Meril-i-Turinqi*.

**Valinor**   In QL two forms are given, *Valinor* and *Valinórë* (the latter also occurs in the text, p. 182), both glossed 'Asgard' (i.e. the City of the Gods in Norse mythology). For the Gnomish names (*Gwalien*, etc.) see *Valar*.

*nórë* is found in QL under the root NŌ 'become, be born', and is glossed 'native land, nation, family, country', also *-nor*, 'the form in compounds'. Other words are *nosta-* 'give birth', *nosta* 'birth, birthday', *nostalë* 'species, kind', *nossë* 'kin, people' (as in *Aulenossë*). The Gnomish form is *dôr*: see *Dor Faidwen*.

**Valmar**   See *Valar*, *Eldamar*.

**Vána**   A derivative of QL root VANA, together with *vanë* 'fair', *vanessë* 'beauty', *vanima* 'proper, right, fair', *úvanimo* 'monster' (*ú-*='not'), etc. Here also are given *Vanar* and *Vani*=*Valar*, *Vali*, with the note: 'cf. Gnomish *Ban-*'. See *Valar*.

Vána's name in Gnomish was *Gwân* or *Gwani* (changed later to *Gwann* or *Gwannuin*); *gwant*, *gwandra* 'beautiful', *gwanthi* 'beauty'.

**Vána-Laisi**   See Vána, Tári-Laisi.

**Vansamírin**   This name replaced *Samírien's road* in the text (p. 222). See *Qalvanda*, *Samírien*.

**Varda**  In QL the name is given with *vard-* 'rule, govern', *vardar* 'king', *varni* 'queen'. In Gnomish *Varda* was called *Bridhil* (and *Timbridhil*, see *Tinwetári*), which is cognate with Qenya *vard-*.

**Vê**  QL gives *Vê* 'name of Fantur' under root VEHE, but without meaning ascribed or other derivatives. The form in GL is *Gwê*, changed to *Gwi*: 'name of the hall of Bandoth, Q. *Vê*'. See *Mandos*, *Vefántur*.

**Vefántur**  In GL the Vala himself is called *Bandoth Gwê* (changed to *Bannoth Gwî*), *Gwefantur* (changed to *Gwifanthor*), and *Gwivannoth*.

**Vene Kemen**  See *Glorvent*, *Kémi*.

**Vilna**  In QL the root VILI (without meaning given) has derivatives *Vilna* (changed later to *Vilya*) '(lower) air', *Vilmar* 'dwelling of Manwë – the upper airs (but not *ilu*)', *vilin* 'airy, breezy', *vilë* 'gentle breeze'. The words 'but not *ilu*' refer to the definition of *ilu* in the sense of *ilwë*, the middle air among the stars (see *ilwë*). Manwë's dwelling *Vilmar* is not named elsewhere.

The Gnomish names for the lowest air were *Gwilfa* or *Fâ*; the latter is said to be of unknown etymology. The corresponding Qenya names are given in GL as *Fâ* and *Favilna*, and these appear in QL under a root FAGA without translation, merely as equivalents of *Vilna*. Other Gnomish words are *gwil-* 'sail, float, fly', *gwilith* 'breeze', *gwilbrin* 'butterfly': these correspond to words in QL under a root GWILI, *wili-* 'sail, float, fly', *wilin* 'bird', *wilwarin* 'butterfly'. Another name of Manweg as Lord of the Winds, *Famfir*, is given in GL.

**Voronwë**  See *Bronweg*.

**Vorotemnar**  For *voro* 'ever' see *Bronweg*. *Temnar* must be from root TEME 'tie', of which no derivative words are listed in QL.

**Wendelin**  This is not in QL, but GL gives *Gwendeling* (changed later to *Gwedhiling*) as the Gnomish name corresponding to Qenya *Wendelin*; 'Queen of the Woodland Elves, mother of Tinúviel' (the only occurrence of the name *Tinúviel* in the dictionaries). The name must be related to Qenya *wen* 'maid, girl' and the Gnomish forms given under *Urwen*.

**Wingildi**  See *Wingilot*.

**Wingilot**  Under the root GWINGI/GWIGI in QL are *wingë* 'foam, spindrift', *wingilot* 'foamflower, Eärendel's boat', and *wingild-* 'nymph' (cf. *Wingildi*). For the element *-lot* see *Lindelos*.

GL has the entry: '*Gwingalos* or *Gwingli*=*Lothwinga* or Foamflower, the name of Eärendel's (Ioringli's) boat'; also *lothwing* 'foamflower', *gwing* 'wavecrest, foam', and *gwingil* 'foam-maiden (mermaid, one of the attendants of Uinen)'.

**Wirilómë**  See *Gwerlum*.

**Wiruin**  See *Gwerlum*.

**Yavanna**  In QL this name is given under the root YAVA, together with *yavin* 'bears fruit', *yáva* 'fruit', *yávan* 'harvest, autumn'. The Gnomish form is *Ifon*, *Ivon*, 'especially in the combinations *Ivon Belaurin*, *Ivon Cimir*, *Ivon i·Vladorwen*'; see *Kémi*, *Palúrien*.

# SHORT GLOSSARY OF OBSOLETE, ARCHAIC, AND RARE WORDS

**an**   if, 64, 140, 149, 155, 165, 180, 182, 189, 197, 208

**arrassed**   covered with arras (rich figured tapestry), 17

**astonied**   stunned, astonished, 116, 185

**bason**   formerly a common spelling of *basin*, 164 etc.

**bent**   open place covered with grass, 34

**brakes**   thickets, 106

**charger**   large dish, 191

**clamant**   clamorous, noisy, 43

**clomb**   old past tense of *climb*, 122

**constellate**   formed into a constellation, 195

**cools**   coolnesses, 74

**corbel**   basket, 186

**covetice**   (inordinate) desire, 117; covetousness, 146–7

**eld**   old age, 59, 219, 228

**fain**   gladly, 45, 150; disposed, desirous, 195; **fain of** well-pleased with, 117, 208

**fane**   temple, 39, 43

**fey**   37. The old senses were 'fated, approaching death; presaging death'. It seems very unlikely that the later sense 'possessing or displaying magical, fairylike, or unearthly qualities' (O.E.D. Supplement) was intended.

**flittermice**   bats, 40

**go**   move, in the phrase *all the creatures that go* 219

**houseleek**   a fleshy plant that grows on the walls and roofs of houses, 95

**inaureoled**   surrounded with a halo, 204 (the word is only recorded in the O.E.D. in a poem by Francis Thompson, 1897).

**jacinth**   blue, 34

**lampads**   35. The word is only recorded in the O.E.D. (first used by Coleridge) of the seven lamps of fire burning before the throne of God in the Book of Revelation, iv.5.

**lets upon**   gives on to, opens on to, 210

**lief**   gladly, willingly, 163; **liever** more gladly, more willingly, rather, 105, 163

**lustihead**   vigour, 99

**meed**   requital, 105

**minished**   reduced, diminished, 150, 208

**or ... or**   either ... or, 127, 192, 214

**or yet**   apparently means 'already', 166

**ousel**   blackbird, 47 (now spelt *ouzel*, in *Ring-ouzel* and other bird-names).

**pleasance**   'A pleasure-ground, usually attached to a mansion; sometimes a secluded part of a garden, but more often a separate enclosure
laid out with shady walks, trees and shrubs . . .' (O.E.D.) This sense is
present in *pleasa(u)nces* 74, 116, but in *rest and pleasance* 69 the sense
is 'enjoyment, pleasure'; in *nor did he have lack of pleasance* 65 either
meaning may be intended, but I think probably the former.

**pled**   old past tense of *plead*, 167

**plenilune**   the time of full moon, 205 (see *Letters* p. 310).

**pricks**   (spurs his horse), rides fast, 114. *Oromë pricks over the plain*
echoes the first line of *The Faerie Queene*, *A Gentle Knight was
pricking on the plaine.*

**recked**   troubled, cared, 179

**rede**   counsel, advice, 141, 182, 217; plan, 180; **redes** counsels, 117

**rondured** (in **golden-rondured**)   35. *Rondure* 'circle, rounded form';
*rondured* is not recorded.

**ruth**   matter of sorrow, calamity, 185; distress, grief, 191; remorse, 194;
in *the greatest ruth was that to* [*the Valar*] *thereafter* 209 the sense is
unclear: 'matter of sorrow or regret', or possibly 'harm, ill'.

**saps**   deep diggings, 104

**sate**   old past tense of *sit*, 58, 105, 153, 181, 190, 194

**seamews**   seagulls, 124

**selenites**   inhabitants of the Moon, 205

**shallop**   192. This word had precise applications to particular kinds of
boat, but here apparently means 'open boat propelled by oars and sail'.

**share**   34, 38. *share*=ploughshare, but used here of the blade of a scythe.

**sledge-blows**   blows as of a *sledge*, a large heavy hammer, 78

**sprent**   past participle of the lost verb *sprenge* 'sprinkle, scatter', 192

**sprite(s)**   spirit(s), 71, 74, 95, 115, 191

**suaded**   persuaded, 69, 163

**trillups**   108, **trillaping** 109. This word is not recorded in any dictionary
available to me.

**umbraged** (in **wide-umbraged**)   34, 38. *Umbraged* 'shaded, shadowed',
but here in the sense 'shadowing', 'casting a shade'.

**web(s)**   woven fabric, 58, 73, 95 (also used in senses 'webbed feet' 127,
'cobwebs' 77, etc.)

**whickering**   205 (*whickering sparks*). The verb *whicker* meant to laugh or
titter, or of a horse to whinny, but the O.E.D. cites a line from
Masefield *the wall-top grasses whickered in the breeze*, and the 1920
Supplement to the Dictionary gives a meaning 'to make a hurtling
sound', with a single citation where the word is used of a thunderbolt
*whickering* through the sky. In the 1962 version of *The Man in the
Moon* the word *flickering* occurs in this verse.

**whitethorn**   hawthorn, 76

**wildered**   perplexed, bewildered, 163–4, 178, 231

**wrack**   devastation, ruin, 177 (cf. (*w*)*rack and ruin*).

# INDEX

This index provides (in intention) complete page-references to all entries with the exception of *Eldar/Elves*, *Gods/Valar*, and *Valinor*; the entries include the rejected name-forms given in the Notes, but the Appendix on Names is not covered. Occasionally references are given to pages where a person or place is not actually named, as 'the door-ward' p. 46 under *Rúmil*. References are given to mentions of Tales that will appear in Part II, but not to mentions of those in this book. The explanatory statements are kept very brief, and names defined in the Index to *The Silmarillion* are not as a rule explained here.

*Fingon* 173, 243

*Finrod Felagund* 44, 173. See *Inglor*.

*Finwë* Lord of the Noldoli; called also *Nólemë, Nólemë Finwë, Finwë Nólemë* (all references are collected here). 115–16, 119, 123, 132, 135, 138, 141–2, 156–7, 162–3, 167, 170–1, 173, 213, 238–41, 243, 245. See *Fingolma, Golfinweg.*

*Fionwë, Fionwë-Úrion* Son of Manwë and Varda. 58, 62–3, 93, 101, 194, 202, 215, 219

*Formenos* 156–9, 161

*Fruit of Noon* 186–7, 191, 193, 201

*Fui* Death-goddess, called also *Nienna, Fui Nienna* (all references are collected here). 66, 76–7, 79–80, 82, 88–90, 92, 117, 144–5, 167, 189, 202, 213; *Fui* as name of her abode 77, 90. See *Heskil, Núri, Qalmë-Tári.*

*Fúkil* Earlier name of Fankil. 236–7. See *Fangli.*

*Fumellar* Poppies in the gardens of Lórien. 74

*Galadriel* 44

*Galmir* 'Goldgleamer', a name of the Sun (Gnomish). 187, 196

*Gar Eglos* Original Gnomish name of Tol Eressëa (replaced by *Dor Edloth* etc.) 21

*Gar Lossion* 'Place of Flowers', Gnomish name of Alalminórë. 16, 21. (Replaced *Losgar.*)

*Gates of Morn* 216, 221, 226; *Gates of East and West* (i.e. the Gates of Morn and the Door of Night) 219

*Gilfanon* (*Gilfanon a·Davrobel, Gilfanon of Tavrobel*) 51, 174–5, 188–9, 194–8, 203–4, 219, 222, 228–31, 235. (Replaced *Ailios.*)

*Gim-Githil* Gnomish name of Inwë. 22, 131–2. (Replaced *Githil,* replaced by *Inwithiel.*)

*Githil* 22. See *Gim-Githil.*

*Glingol* Gnomish name of the Golden Tree of Valinor. 22

*Gloomweaver* Translation of *Wirilómë, Gwerlum,* the great Spider. 152–3

*Glorvent* 'Ship of Gold', a name of the Sun (Gnomish). 187

*Gnomes* (including *Gnome-folk, Gnome-kin*) 13, 16–17, 21–2, 24, 27, 43–4, 49–51, 62, 94, 129, 140–2, 144, 146, 150–1, 153, 156–7, 160, 163, 165–9, 171, 174–6, 178, 187, 192, 196, 198, 207–10, 213, 220, 234, 237–43. See especially 43–4, 50–1, and see *Noldoli.*

*Gnomish, Gnome-speech, tongue of the Gnomes* 21–2, 24, 43, 48, 50–2, 89, 91, 108, 130, 132, 138, 160, 200, 235, 245

*Goblin Feet* (poem) 32, 136; on the meaning of *Goblin* here see the Appendix, entry *Noldoli,* p. 262.

*Goblins* 47, 237, 245

*Gods* *Passim*; on the nature and character of the Gods (*Valar,* see 63) and their relation to Manwë see especially 103–4, 111, 149, 182, 189–90, 199, 209, 213, 219–20, 222–3, 225–6, 228; language of the Gods 47–8, 51–2, 235. See *Children of the Gods.*

*go-Fëanor, go-Maidros* 'son of Fëanor, of Maidros'. 155; 146, 155, 158

156–9, 162, 172, 176–84, 186–8, 190, 192, 194–6, 199, 208–9, 211–21, 223, 230, 233, 244; called *Lord of the Air* 176, *of the Heavens* 190, *of Gods and Elves and Men, of the Gods, of Gods and Elves, of Elves and Men* 52, 58–9, 62, 100, 104, 115, 142, 218. See *Súlimo, Valahíru, Valatúru; Valwë.*

*March of Liberation*  The great expedition from Kôr. 166; *march into the world* 26, 129, 196

*Mar Vanwa Tyaliéva*  The Cottage of Lost Play in Kortirion. 14, 21 (also *Taliéva*), 27–8, 30, 48, 97, 129, 174, 202, 229; in title of poem 28, 30

*Meássë*  Warrior goddess. 67, 77–8, 80, 82, 89, 98, 105, 117, 154, 177

*Melemno, Ellu Melemno*  See *Ellu.*

*Melian*  107, 132–3. See *Tindriel, Wendelin.*

*Melko*  25–7, 47, 49, 52–60, 62–3, 66–70, 77–9, 87, 89–90, 92–3, 98–107, 111, 113–18, 120, 128, 131, 133, 135, 140–54, 156–60, 165–9, 171, 174, 176–7, 180, 182–3, 196, 198, 200, 203, 207–11, 213, 217, 219–20, 222–3, 230, 234, 236–44; *son(s) of Melko* 93, 210, *child of Melko* 237; *Melko's Chains* 98, 107, 168; *Mines of Melko* 239, 241. See *Melkor, Morgoth.*

*Melkor*  26, 79–80, 110, 112, 131, 133, 156–61, 198–9, 222–3, 225

*Men, Mankind*  16, 18–20, 25–7, 31–2, 45, 47, 49, 52–3, 56–7, 59–61, 63–4, 68, 77, 80, 82, 90–3, 97–9, 105, 118–19, 125, 134–5, 138–9, 146, 150, 156, 159, 174–5, 177, 180, 187, 189, 198, 207–8, 211–13, 215–16, 219–21, 223–5, 230, 233–42, 244. On the nature and fate of Men see especially 59–61, 77, 90–3, 150–1

*Mereth Aderthad*  The Feast of Reuniting. 243

*Meril-i-Turinqi*  The Lady of Tol Eressëa; also *Meril, Turinqi.* 16–17, 20, 22, 26, 48, 50, 52, 95–8, 107, 111–13, 129–30, 134, 175, 230, 235; *Lady of the Isle* 175

*Mettanyë*  The last part of the poem *The Trees of Kortirion.* 43

*Middle-earth*  21, 23, 26, 51, 81, 89, 110–11, 132–5, 199, 222–3

*Middle lands*  234

*Mindon Eldaliéva*  135

*Minethlos*  A name of the Moon (Gnomish). 192, 198. (Replaced *Mainlos.*)

*Miruvor*  153, 160; *miruvórë* 161

*Mithrim*  (lake and region) 160, 238–9, 241, 243. See *Asgon.*

*Moon, The*  60, 64, 83, 85, 88, 119, 151, 174–5, 182, 187, 192–3, 195, 197, 199–203, 206–8, 214–20, 227–8, 242; *Ship of the Moon* 192, 194, 216; *Man in the Moon* 193, 202; *King of the Moon* 202; *Harvest Moon* 41. See *Haven of the Moon*; and for other names of the Moon see 192.

*Morgoth*  26, 135, 222, 242–3

*Moritarnon*  'The Door of Night'. 215, 222; *Móritar* 222. See *Door of Night, Tarn Fui.*

*Mornië*  The black ship that ferries the dead from Mandos. 77, 90, 92, 167, 170, 172

*Samírien* Feast of Double Mirth in Valinor. 143–4, 222; *Samírien's road* 222 (see *Vansamírin*).

*Sári* Name of the Sun given by the Gods. 186, 193, 195, 198, 215–16, 218, 221–2

*Sauron* 52

*Scarlet Heart, The* Emblem of the King's Folk in Gondolin. 245

*Second Kindred* The Gnomes or Noldoli. 21

*Secret Fire* 53, 55, 60

*Sea-elves* 43, 50

*Seven Stars* 38, 42 (perhaps referring to the Pleiades); 114 (referring to the Great Bear); *Seven Butterflies* 133. See *Great Bear, Valacirca*.

*Shadow Folk* (1) Name among Men of the Lost Elves of Hisilómë. 119, 138–9, 237. (2) Fays of unknown origin encountered by the Noldoli in Hisilómë. 237, 239

*Shadowy Seas* Region of the Great Sea west of Tol Eressëa (see especially 68, 125). 15, 27, 68, 70, 74, 76, 83, 118–21, 125, 134, 137, 152, 154, 164, 188, 209, 211, 224; *Shadowy Sea* 101, 163, *the Shadows* 134

*Shining Isles* Dwelling of the Gods and the Eldar of Valinor, as imagined by the Ilkorins. 231

*Ship of the Heavens, Ship of (the) Morn(ing)* See *Sun.*

*Ship of the Moon* See Moon

*Ship of the World* 83–7, 134, 225

*Shoreland Elves* See *Shoreland Pipers.*

*Shoreland Pipers* The Solosimpi (afterwards called Teleri). 16, 50, 94, 123, 165, 223; *Pipers of the Shore* 230; *the Pipers* 106; *shoreland dancers* 129; *Shoreland Elves, shoreland folk* 125, 165, 210, *shore-elves* 165

*Sickle of the Valar* See *Valacirca*; *the Silver Sickle* 133

*Sil* Name of the Moon. 85, 192

*Silindrin* The cauldron of silver light in Valinor; name varying with *Telimpë*. 71–4, 79, 88, 130, 196

*Silmarilli* The Silmarils. 58, 128. See *Silubrilthin*.

*Silmarils* 128, 138, 145, 149, 152, 156–7, 159, 162, 169, 238, 240

*Silmarillion, The* 23, 26, 49–51, 60–3, 79–80, 82, 87–92, 110–12, 131–8, 156–61, 171–3, 198–202, 222–5, 227, 231, 236, 241–5

*Silmo* The guardian of the tree Silpion. 73–4, 88, 116, 178, 189, 192, 202

*Silpion* The silver tree of Valinor. 73–4, 76, 88–9, 113, 116–17, 122, 125–9, 133, 135, 142–4, 146, 152–3, 160, 176–9, 181, 189–91, 193, 200–2. See *Rose of Silpion.*

*Silubrilthin* Gnomish name of the Silmarils. 128, 130

*Sindarin* 51, 132

*Singollo* See *Elwë.*

*Sirion* 238, 240–2, 244; *Pass of Sirion* 244

*Sirius* 200. See *Helluin, Nielluin.*

*Sirnúmen* The dale in Valinor where the Noldoli dwelt after their banishment from Kôr. (142), 144, 146 (*Sirnúmen of the Plain*), 147, 149, 153, 155, 157–9, 163–4, 192. (Replaced *Numessir*.)

*Tavari*  Fays of the woods. 66
*Tavrobel*  A place in Tol Eressëa. 25, 175, 196, 230; *Bridge of Tavrobel*
175, 196; *Tower of Tavrobel* 174; *Gilfanon a·Davrobel, Gilfanon of
Tavrobel* 174, 195-6, 203, 229
*Telelli*  Name of certain Elves (see Appendix, p. 267). 19, 22; earlier
*Telellë* 22
*Teleri*  (1) The first kindred of the Elves (afterwards called Vanyar). 48-50,
52, 59, 62, 115, 118-19, 121-4, 126, 132, 134, 143, 163, 169, 175-6,
210, 220, 231, 234. (2) In later sense, =Solosimpi of the *Lost Tales*.
50, 62, 132-8, 157, 171, 198, 223
*Telimektar*  Son of Tulkas. 101, 154, 182, 200. See *Telumehtar*.
*Telimpë*  The cauldron of silver light in Valinor; name varying with
*Silindrin*. 79, 113-14, 127, 129-30, 178, 181, 189, 192, 196, 202
*Telperion*  88, 133, 135, 201
*Telumehtar*  Orion. 200. See *Telimektar*.
*Tents of Murmuring*  Dwelling of the Noldoli by the Helkaraksë. 168, 173
*Tevildo Prince of Cats*  47, 52
*Thangorodrim*  26, 158, 243
*Thingol*  107, 238, 243; *Elu Thingol* 132. See *Tinwë Linto, Tinwelint*.
*Thompson, Francis*  29
*Thorndor*  Gnomish name of Sorontur, King of Eagles. 89; later form
*Thorondor* 158
*Three Kindreds*  51
*Tilion*  Steersman of the Moon. 88, 202, 222
*Tilkal*  Metal devised by Aulë for the chaining of Melko. 100, 104, 111, 114
*Time*  See especially 218-19, 227-8
*Timpinen*  Name of Tinfang in the tongue of the Eldar. 94-5, 107
*Tindriel*  Early name of Melian. 106-7, 131-2. (Replaced by *Wendelin*.)
*Tinfang*  Gnomish name of Timpinen the piper; called *Tinfang Warble*
(see the Appendix, p. 268). 94-5, 107-10; poems *Tinfang Warble,
Over Old Hills and Far Away* 107-10
*Tintoglin*  Earlier name of Tinwelint. 131-2
*Tinúviel*  Daughter of Tinwelint (afterwards Lúthien (Tinúviel) daughter
of Thingol). 27, 107, 115, 132; the *Tale of Tinúviel* 27, 51-2, 203-4,
231, 233, 238-9, 241. See *Lúthien*.
*Tinwelint*  Gnomish name of Tinwë Linto (afterwards Thingol). 115,
131-2, 238, 240, 243-4. (Replaced *Tintoglin*.)
*Tinwë Linto, Tinwë*  Lord of the Solosimpi, who was lost on the Great
Journey and became Lord of the Elves of Hisilómë; afterwards
*Thingol*. 115-16, 120, 130-3. (Replaced *Linwë Tinto*.)
*Tinwetári*  'Queen of Stars', name of Varda. 100
*Tirion*  26, 49, 135, 159-60, 198, 222-3
*Tol Eressëa*  13, 21-7, 32, 47-50, 52, 83, 85, 90, 97-8, 107, 120-1, 123-6,
129-30, 134-7, 165, 196, 224-5, 235. See *Lonely Island*.
*Tombo*  The 'Gong of the Children' in Mar Vanwa Tyaliéva. 15. See *Gong
of the Children, Littleheart*.

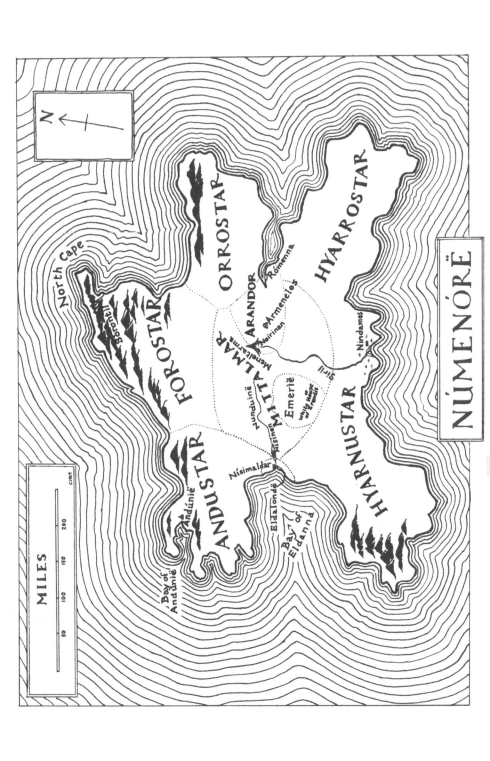

NÚMENÓRË

# UNFINISHED TALES

*[Tengwar script inscription at top of page]*

*[Tengwar script inscription at bottom of page]*

TOLKIEN

# UNFINISHED TALES
## of Númenor and Middle-earth

by

## J. R. R. TOLKIEN

*edited with introduction, commentary, index and maps by*

CHRISTOPHER TOLKIEN

HarperCollins*Publishers*

HarperCollins*Publishers* Ltd
1 London Bridge Street
London SE1 9GF

HarperCollins*Publishers*
Macken House, 39/40 Mayor Street Upper
Dublin 1, D01 C9W8, Ireland

www.tolkien.co.uk
www.tolkienestate.com

This hardback edition 2023
1

First published in Great Britain by
George Allen & Unwin (Publishers) Ltd 1980,
and by HarperCollins*Publishers* 1992

A CIP catalogue record for this book is available
from the British Library

ISBN 978-0-00-866313-1

Printed and bound in the UK using 100% Renewable Electricity
by CPI Group (UK) Ltd

# CONTENTS

## PART THREE: THE THIRD AGE

# NOTE

It has been necessary to distinguish author and editor in different ways in different parts of this book, since the incidence of commentary is very various. The author appears in larger type in the primary texts throughout; if the editor intrudes into one of these texts he is in smaller type indented from the margin (e.g. p. 294). In *The History of Galadriel and Celeborn*, however, where the editorial text is predominant, the reverse indentation is employed. In the Appendices (and also in *The Further Course of the Narrative* of 'Aldarion and Erendis', pp. 205 ff.) both author and editor are in the smaller type, with citations from the author indented (e.g. p. 154).

Notes to texts in the Appendices are given as footnotes rather than as numbered references; and the author's own annotation of a text at a particular point is indicated throughout by the words '[Author's note]'.

# INTRODUCTION

The problems that confront one given responsibility for the writings of a dead author are hard to resolve. Some persons in this position may elect to make no material whatsoever available for publication, save perhaps for work that was in a virtually finished state at the time of the author's death. In the case of the unpublished writings of J. R. R. Tolkien this might seem at first sight the proper course; since he himself, peculiarly critical and exacting of his own work, would not have dreamt of allowing even the more completed narratives in this book to appear without much further refinement.

On the other hand, the nature and scope of his invention seems to me to place even his abandoned stories in a peculiar position. That *The Silmarillion* should remain unknown was for me out of the question, despite its disordered state, and despite my father's known if very largely unfulfilled intentions for its transformation; and in that case I presumed, after long hesitation, to present the work not in the form of an historical study, a complex of divergent texts interlinked by commentary, but as a completed and cohesive entity. The narratives in this book are indeed on an altogether different footing: taken together they constitute no whole, and the book is no more than a collection of writings, disparate in form, intent, finish, and date of composition (and in my own treatment of them), concerned with Númenor and Middle-earth. But the argument for their publication is not different in its nature, though it is of lesser force, from that which I held to justify the publication of *The Silmarillion*. Those who would not have forgone the images of Melkor with Ungoliant looking down from the summit of Hyarmentir upon 'the fields and pastures of Yavanna, gold beneath the tall wheat of the gods'; of the shadows of Fingolfin's host cast by the first moonrise in the West; of Beren lurking in wolf's shape beneath the throne of Morgoth; or of the light of the Silmaril suddenly revealed in the darkness of the Forest of Neldoreth – they will find, I believe, that imperfections of form in these tales are much outweighed by the voice (heard now for the last time) of Gandalf, teasing the lordly Saruman at the meeting of the White Council in the year 2851, or describing in Minas Tirith after the end of the War of the Ring how it was that he came to send the Dwarves to the celebrated party at Bag-End; by the arising of Ulmo Lord of Waters out of the sea at Vinyamar; by Mablung of Doriath hiding 'like a vole' beneath the ruins of the bridge at Nargothrond; or by the death of Isildur as he floundered up out of the mud of Anduin.

Many of the pieces in this collection are elaborations of matters told more briefly, or at least referred to, elsewhere; and it must be said at once that much in the book will be found unrewarding by readers of *The Lord of the Rings* who, holding that the historical structure of Middle-earth is a means and not an end, the mode of the narrative and not its purpose, feel small desire of further exploration for its own sake, do not wish to know how the Riders of the Mark of Rohan were organised, and would leave the Wild Men of the Drúadan Forest firmly where they found them. My father would certainly not have thought them wrong. He said in a letter written in March 1955, before the publication of the third volume of *The Lord of the Rings*:

> I now wish that no appendices had been promised! For I think their appearance in truncated and compressed form will satisfy nobody: certainly not me; clearly from the (appalling mass of) letters I receive not those people who like that kind of thing – astonishingly many; while those who enjoy the book as an 'heroic romance' only, and find 'unexplained vistas' part of the literary effect, will neglect the appendices, very properly.
>
> I am not now at all sure that the tendency to treat the whole thing as a kind of vast game is really good – certainly not for me who find that kind of thing only too fatally attractive. It is, I suppose, a tribute to the curious effect that a story has, when based on very elaborate and detailed workings, of geography, chronology, and language, that so many should clamour for sheer 'information', or 'lore'.

In a letter of the following year he wrote:

> . . . while many like you demand maps, others wish for geological indications rather than places; many want Elvish grammars, phonologies, and specimens; some want metrics and prosodies. . . . Musicians want tunes, and musical notation; archaeologists want ceramics and metallurgy; botanists want a more accurate description of the *mallorn*, of *elanor, niphredil, alfirin, mallos,* and *symbelmynë*; historians want more details about the social and political structure of Gondor; general enquirers want information about the Wainriders, the Harad, Dwarvish origins, the Dead Men, the Beornings, and the missing two wizards (out of five).

But whatever view may be taken of this question, for some, as for myself, there is a value greater than the mere uncovering of curious detail in learning that Vëantur the Númenórean brought his ship Entulessë, the 'Return', into the Grey Havens on the spring winds of the six hundredth year of the Second Age, that the tomb of Elendil the Tall was set by Isildur his son on the summit of the beacon-hill Halifirien, that the Black Rider whom the Hobbits saw in the foggy darkness on the far side of Bucklebury Ferry was Khamûl, chief of the Ringwraiths of Dol Guldur – or even that the childlessness of Tarannon twelfth King of Gondor (a fact recorded in an Appendix to *The Lord of the Rings*) was associated with the hitherto wholly mysterious cats of Queen Berúthiel.

The construction of the book has been difficult, and in the result is somewhat complex. The narratives are all 'unfinished', but to a greater or lesser degree, and in different senses of the word, and have required different treatment; I shall say something below about each one in turn, and here only call attention to some general features.

The most important is the question of 'consistency', best illustrated from the section entitled 'The History of Galadriel and Celeborn'. This is an 'Unfinished Tale' in a larger sense: not a narrative that comes to an abrupt halt, as in 'Of Tuor and his Coming to Gondolin', nor a series of fragments, as in 'Cirion and Eorl', but a primary strand in the history of Middle-earth that never received a settled definition, let alone a final written form. The inclusion of the unpublished narratives and sketches of narrative on this subject therefore entails at once the acceptance of the history not as a fixed, independently-existing reality which the author 'reports' (in his 'persona' as translator and redactor), but as a growing and shifting conception in his mind. When the author has ceased to publish his works himself, after subjecting them to his own detailed criticism and comparison, the further knowledge of Middle-earth to be found in his unpublished writings will often conflict with what is already 'known'; and new elements set into the existing edifice will in such cases tend to contribute less to the history of the invented world itself than to the history of its invention. In this book I have accepted from the outset that this must be so; and except in minor details such as shifts in nomenclature (where retention of the manuscript form would lead to disproportionate confusion or disproportionate space in elucidation) I have made no alterations for the sake of consistency with published works, but rather drawn attention throughout to conflicts and variations. In this respect therefore 'Unfinished Tales' is essentially different from *The Silmarillion*, where a primary though not exclusive objective in the editing was to achieve cohesion both internal and external; and except in a few specified cases I have indeed treated the published form of *The Silmarillion* as a fixed point of reference of the same order as the writings published by my father himself, without taking into account the innumerable 'unauthorised' decisions between variants and rival versions that went into its making.

In content the book is entirely narrative (or descriptive): I have excluded all writings about Middle-earth and Aman that are of a primarily philosophic or speculative nature, and where such matters from time to time arise I have not pursued them. I have imposed a simple structure of convenience by dividing the texts into Parts corresponding to the first Three Ages of the World, there being in this inevitably some overlap, as with the legend of Amroth and its discussion in 'The History of Galadriel and Celeborn'. The fourth part is an appendage, and may require some excuse in a book called 'Unfinished Tales', since the pieces it contains are generalised and discursive essays with little or no element of 'story'. The section on the Drúedain did indeed owe its original inclusion to the story of 'The Faithful Stone' which forms a small part of it; and this section led me to introduce those on the Istari and the Palantíri, since they (especially the former) are matters about which many people have expressed curiosity, and this book seemed a convenient place to expound what there is to tell.

The notes may seem to be in some places rather thick on the ground, but it will be seen that where clustered most densely (as in 'The Disaster of the Gladden Fields') they are due less to the editor than to the author, who in his later work tended to compose in this way, driving several subjects abreast by means of interlaced notes. I have throughout tried to make it clear what is editorial and what is not. And because of this abundance of original material appearing in the notes and appendices I have thought it best not to restrict the page-references in the Index to the texts themselves but to cover all parts of the book except the Introduction.

I have throughout assumed on the reader's part a fair knowledge of the published works of my father (more especially *The Lord of the Rings*), for to have done otherwise would have greatly enlarged the editorial element, which may well be thought quite sufficient already. I have, however, included short defining statements with almost all the primary entries in the Index, in the hope of saving the reader from constant reference elsewhere. If I have been inadequate in explanation or unintentionally obscure, Mr Robert Foster's *Complete Guide to Middle-earth* supplies, as I have found through frequent use, an admirable work of reference.

Page-references to *The Silmarillion* are to the hardback edition; to *The Lord of the Rings* by title of the volume, book, and chapter.

There follow now primarily bibliographical notes on the individual pieces.

★ ★ ★

PART ONE

I

*Of Tuor and his Coming to Gondolin*

My father said more than once that 'The Fall of Gondolin' was the first of the tales of the First Age to be composed, and there is no evidence to set against his recollection. In a letter of 1964 he declared that he wrote it ' "out of my head" during sick-leave from the army in 1917', and at other times he gave the date as 1916 or 1916–17. In a letter to me written in 1944 he said: 'I first began to write [The Silmarillion] in army huts, crowded, filled with the noise of gramophones': and indeed some lines of verse in which appear the Seven Names of Gondolin are scribbled on the back of a piece of paper setting out 'the chain of responsibility in a battalion'. The earliest manuscript is still in existence, filling two small school exercise-books; it was written rapidly in pencil, and then, for much of its course, overlaid with writing in ink, and heavily emended. On the basis of this text my mother, apparently in 1917, wrote out a fair copy; but this in turn was further substantially emended, at some time that I cannot determine, but probably in 1919–20, when my father was in Oxford on the staff of the then still uncompleted Dictionary. In the spring of 1920 he was invited to read a paper to the Essay Club of his college (Exeter); and he read 'The Fall of Gondolin'. The notes of what he intended to say by way of introduction to his 'essay' still survive. In these he apologised for not having been able to produce a critical paper, and went on: 'Therefore I must read something already written, and in desperation I have fallen back on this Tale. It has of course never seen the light before. . . . A complete cycle of events in an Elfinesse of my own imagining has for some time past grown up (rather, has been constructed) in my mind. Some of the episodes have been scribbled down. . . . This tale is not the best of them, but it is the only one that has so far been revised at all and that, insufficient as that revision has been, I dare read aloud.'

The tale of Tuor and the Exiles of Gondolin (as 'The Fall of Gondolin' is entitled in the early MSS) remained untouched for many years, though my father at some stage, probably between 1926 and 1930, wrote a brief, compressed version of the story to stand as part of *The Silmarillion* (a title which, incidentally, first appeared in his letter to *The Observer* of 20 February 1938); and this was changed subsequently to bring it into harmony with altered conceptions in other parts of the book. Much later he began work on an entirely refashioned account, entitled 'Of Tuor and the Fall of Gondolin'. It seems very likely that this was written in 1951, when *The Lord of the Rings* was finished but its publication doubtful. Deeply changed in style and bearings, yet retaining many of the essentials of the story written in his youth, 'Of Tuor and the Fall of Gondolin' would have given in fine detail the whole legend that constitutes the brief 23rd chapter of the published *Silmarillion*; but, grievously, he went no further than the coming of Tuor and Voronwë to the last gate and Tuor's sight of Gondolin across the plain of Tumladen. To his reasons for abandoning it there is no clue.

This is the text that is given here. To avoid confusion I have retitled it 'Of Tuor and his Coming to Gondolin', since it tells nothing of the fall of the city. As always with my father's writings there are variant readings, and in one short section (the approach to and passage of the river Sirion by Tuor and Voronwë) several competing forms; some minor editorial work has therefore been necessary.

It is thus the remarkable fact that the only full account that my father ever wrote of the story of Tuor's sojourn in Gondolin, his union with Idril Celebrindal, the birth of Eärendil, the treachery of Maeglin, the sack of the city, and the escape of the fugitives – a story that was a central element in his imagination of the First Age – was the narrative composed in his youth. There is no question, however, that that (most remarkable) narrative is not suitable for inclusion in this book. It is written in the extreme archaistic style that my father employed at that time, and it inevitably embodies conceptions out of keeping with the world of *The Lord of the Rings* and *The Silmarillion* in its published form. It belongs with the rest of the earliest phase of the mythology, 'the Book of Lost Tales': itself a very substantial work, of the utmost interest to one concerned with the origins of Middle-earth, but requiring to be presented in a lengthy and complex study if at all.

## II

### The Tale of the Children of Húrin

The development of the legend of Túrin Turambar is in some respects the most tangled and complex of all the narrative elements in the story of the First Age. Like the tale of Tuor and the Fall of Gondolin it goes back to the very beginnings, and is extant in an early prose narrative (one of the 'Lost Tales') and in a long, unfinished poem in alliterative verse. But whereas the later 'long version' of *Tuor* never proceeded very far, my father carried the later 'long version' of *Túrin* much nearer completion. This is called *Narn i Hîn Húrin*; and this is the narrative that is given in the present book.

There are however great differences in the course of the long *Narn* in the degree to which the narrative approaches a perfected or final form. The concluding section (from The Return of Túrin to Dor-lómin to The Death of Túrin) has undergone only marginal editorial alteration; while the first section (to the end of Túrin in Doriath) required a good deal of revision and selection, and in some places some slight compression, the original texts being scrappy and disconnected. But the central section of the narrative (Túrin among the outlaws, Mîm the Petty-dwarf, the land of Dor-Cúarthol, the death of Beleg at Túrin's hand, and Túrin's life in Nargothrond) constituted a much more difficult editorial problem. The *Narn* is here at its least finished, and in places diminishes to outlines of possible turns in the story. My father was still evolving this part when he ceased to work on it; and the shorter version for *The Silmarillion* was to wait on the final development of the *Narn*. In preparing the text of *The Silmarillion* for publication I derived, by necessity, much of this section of the tale of Túrin from these very materials, which are of quite extraordinary complexity in their variety and interrelations.

For the first part of this central section, as far as the beginning of Túrin's sojourn in Mîm's dwelling on Amon Rûdh, I have contrived a narrative, in scale commensurate with other parts of the *Narn*, out of the existing materials (with one gap, see p. 96 and note 12); but from that point onwards (see p. 104) until Túrin's coming to Ivrin after the fall of Nargothrond I have found it unprofitable to attempt it. The gaps in the *Narn* are here too large, and could only be filled from the published text of *The Silmarillion*; but in an Appendix (pp. 150 ff.) I have cited isolated fragments from this part of the projected larger narrative.

In the third section of the *Narn* (beginning with The Return of Túrin to Dor-lómin) a comparison with *The Silmarillion* (pp. 215–26) will show many close correspondences, and even identities of wording; while in the first section there are two extended passages that I have excluded from the present text (see p. 58 and note 1, and p. 66 and note 2), since they are close variants of passages that appear elsewhere and are included in the published *Silmarillion*. This overlapping and interrelation between one work and another may be explained in different ways, from different points of view. My father delighted in re-telling on different scales; but some parts did not call for more extended treatment in a larger version, and there was no need to rephrase for the sake of it. Again, when all was still fluid and the final organisation of the distinct narratives still a long way off, the same passage might be experimentally placed in either. But an explanation can be found at a different level. Legends like that of Túrin Turambar had been given a particular poetic form long ago – in this case, the *Narn i Hîn Húrin* of the poet Dírhavel – and phrases, or even whole passages, from it (especially at moments of great rhetorical intensity, such as Túrin's address to his sword before his death) would be preserved intact by those who afterwards made condensations of the history of the Elder Days (as *The Silmarillion* is conceived to be).

# PART TWO

## I

### *A Description of the Island of Númenor*

Although descriptive rather than narrative, I have included selections from my father's account of Númenor, more especially as it concerns the physical nature of the Island, since it clarifies and naturally accompanies the tale of Aldarion and Erendis. This account was certainly in existence by 1965, and was probably written not long before that.

I have redrawn the map from a little rapid sketch, the only one, as it appears, that my father ever made of Númenor. Only names or features found on the original have been entered on the redrawing. In addition, the original shows another haven on the Bay of Andúnië, not far to the westward of Andúnië itself; the name is hard to read, but is almost certainly *Almaida*. This does not, so far as I am aware, occur elsewhere.

## II

### *Aldarion and Erendis*

This story was left in the least developed state of all the pieces in this collection, and has in places required a degree of editorial rehandling

that made me doubt the propriety of including it. However, its very great
interest as the single story (as opposed to records and annals) that survived
at all from the long ages of Númenor before the narrative of its end (the
*Akallabêth*), and as a story unique in its content among my father's
writings, persuaded me that it would be wrong to omit it from this collection of 'Unfinished Tales'.

To appreciate the necessity for such editorial treatment it must be
explained that my father made much use, in the composition of narrative,
of 'plot-outlines', paying meticulous attention to the dating of events, so
that these outlines have something of the appearance of annal-entries in
a chronicle. In the present case there are no less than five of these schemes,
varying constantly in their relative fullness at different points and not
infrequently disagreeing with each other at large and in detail. But these
schemes always had a tendency to move into pure narrative, especially
by the introduction of short passages of direct speech; and in the fifth
and latest of the outlines for the story of Aldarion and Erendis the narrative
element is so pronounced that the text runs to some sixty manuscript
pages.

This movement away from a staccato annalistic style in the present
tense into fullblown narrative was however very gradual, as the writing
of the outline progressed; and in the earlier part of the story I have rewritten much of the material in the attempt to give some degree of
stylistic homogeneity throughout its course. This rewriting is entirely a
matter of wording, and never alters meaning or introduces unauthentic
elements.

The latest 'scheme', the text primarily followed, is entitled *The Shadow
of the Shadow: the Tale of the Mariner's Wife; and the Tale of the Queen
Shepherdess*. The manuscript ends abruptly, and I can offer no certain
explanation of why my father abandoned it. A typescript made to this
point was completed in January 1965. There exists also a typescript of
two pages that I judge to be the latest of all these materials; it is evidently
the beginning of what was to be a finished version of the whole story, and
provides the text on pp. 173–5 in this book (where the plot-outlines are
at their most scanty). It is entitled *Indis i · Kiryamo 'The Mariner's Wife':
a tale of ancient Númenórë, which tells of the first rumour of the Shadow*.

At the end of this narrative (p. 205) I have set out such scanty indications
as can be given of the further course of the story.


III

*The Line of Elros: Kings of Númenor*

Though in form purely a dynastic record, I have included this because
it is an important document for the history of the Second Age, and a great
part of the extant material concerning that Age finds a place in the texts

and commentary in this book. It is a fine manuscript in which the dates of the Kings and Queens of Númenor and of their reigns have been copiously and sometimes obscurely emended: I have endeavoured to give the latest formulation. The text introduces several minor chronological puzzles, but also allows clarification of some apparent errors in the Appendices to *The Lord of the Rings*.

The genealogical table of the earlier generations of the Line of Elros is taken from several closely-related tables that derive from the same period as the discussion of the laws of succession in Númenor (pp. 208–9). There are some slight variations in minor names: thus *Vardilmë* appears also as *Vardilyë*, and *Yávien* as *Yávië*. The forms given in my table I believe to be later.

## IV

### The History of Galadriel and Celeborn

This section of the book differs from the others (save those in Part Four) in that there is here no single text but rather an essay incorporating citations. This treatment was enforced by the nature of the materials; as is made clear in the course of the essay, a history of Galadriel can only be a history of my father's changing conceptions, and the 'unfinished' nature of the tale is not in this case that of a particular piece of writing. I have restricted myself to the presentation of his unpublished writings on the subject, and forgone any discussion of the larger questions that underlie the development; for that would entail consideration of the entire relation between the Valar and the Elves, from the initial decision (described in *The Silmarillion*) to summon the Eldar to Valinor, and many other matters besides, concerning which my father wrote much that falls outside the scope of this book.

The history of Galadriel and Celeborn is so interwoven with other legends and histories – of Lothlórien and the Silvan Elves, of Amroth and Nimrodel, of Celebrimbor and the making of the Rings of Power, of the war against Sauron and the Númenórean intervention – that it cannot be treated in isolation, and thus this section of the book, together with its five Appendices, brings together virtually all the unpublished materials for the history of the Second Age in Middle-earth (and the discussion in places inevitably extends into the Third). It is said in the Tale of Years given in Appendix B to *The Lord of the Rings*: 'Those were the dark years for Men of Middle-earth, but the years of the glory of Númenor. Of events in Middle-earth the records are few and brief, and their dates are often uncertain.' But even that little surviving from the 'dark years' changed as my father's contemplation of it grew and changed; and I have made no attempt to smooth away inconsistency, but rather exhibited it and drawn attention to it.

Divergent versions need not indeed always be treated solely as a question of settling the priority of composition; and my father as 'author' or 'inventor' cannot always in these matters be distinguished from the 'recorder' of ancient traditions handed down in diverse forms among different peoples through long ages (when Frodo met Galadriel in Lórien, more than sixty centuries had passed since she went east over the Blue Mountains from the ruin of Beleriand). 'Of this two things are said, though which is true only those Wise could say who now are gone.'

In his last years my father wrote much concerning the etymology of names in Middle-earth. In these highly discursive essays there is a good deal of history and legend embedded; but being ancillary to the main philological purpose, and introduced as it were in passing, it has required extraction. It is for this reason that this part of the book is largely made up of short citations, with further material of the same kind placed in the Appendices.

# PART THREE

## I

### *The Disaster of the Gladden Fields*

This is a 'late' narrative – by which I mean no more, in the absence of any indication of precise date, than that it belongs in the final period of my father's writing on Middle-earth, together with 'Cirion and Eorl', 'The Battles of the Fords of Isen', 'the Drúedain', and the philological essays excerpted in 'The History of Galadriel and Celeborn', rather than to the time of the publication of *The Lord of the Rings* and the years following it. There are two versions: a rough typescript of the whole (clearly the first stage of composition), and a good typescript incorporating many changes that breaks off at the point where Elendur urged Isildur to flee (p. 274). The editorial hand has here had little to do.

## II

### *Cirion and Eorl and the Friendship of Gondor and Rohan*

I judge these fragments to belong to the same period as 'The Disaster of the Gladden Fields', when my father was greatly interested in the earlier history of Gondor and Rohan; they were doubtless intended to form parts of a substantial history, developing in detail the summary accounts given in Appendix A to *The Lord of the Rings*. The material is in the first stage of composition, very disordered, full of variants, breaking off into rapid jottings that are in part illegible.

## III

### *The Quest of Erebor*

In a letter written in 1964 my father said:

> There are, of course, quite a lot of links between *The Hobbit* and *The Lord of the Rings* that are not clearly set out. They were mostly written or sketched out, but cut out to lighten the boat: such as Gandalf's exploratory journeys, his relations with Aragorn and Gondor; all the movements of Gollum, until he took refuge in Moria, and so on. I actually wrote in full an account of what really happened before Gandalf's visit to Bilbo and the subsequent 'Unexpected Party', as seen by Gandalf himself. It was to have come in during a looking-back conversation in Minas Tirith; but it had to go, and is only represented in brief in Appendix A pp. 358–60, though the difficulties that Gandalf had with Thorin are omitted.

This account of Gandalf's is given here. The complex textual situation is described in the Appendix to the narrative, where I have given substantial extracts from an earlier version.

## IV

### *The Hunt for the Ring*

There is much writing bearing on the events of the year 3018 of the Third Age, which are otherwise known from the Tale of Years and the reports of Gandalf and others to the Council of Elrond; and these writings are clearly those referred to as 'sketched out' in the letter just cited. I have given them the title 'The Hunt for the Ring'. The manuscripts themselves, in great though hardly exceptional confusion, are sufficiently described on p. 342; but the question of their date (for I believe them all, and also those of 'Concerning Gandalf, Saruman, and the Shire', given as the third element in this section, to derive from the same time) may be mentioned here. They were writtten after the publication of *The Lord of the Rings*, for there are references to the pagination of the printed text; but they differ in the dates they give for certain events from those in the Tale of Years in Appendix B. The explanation is clearly that they were written after the publication of the first volume but before that of the third, containing the Appendices.

## V

### *The Battle of the Fords of Isen*

This, together with the account of the military organisation of the Rohirrim and the history of Isengard given in an Appendix to the text, belongs with other late pieces of severe historical analysis; it presented relatively little difficulty of a textual kind, and is only unfinished in the most obvious sense.

# PART FOUR

## I

### The Drúedain

Towards the end of his life my father revealed a good deal more about the Wild Men of the Drúadan Forest in Anórien and the statues of the Púkel-men on the road up to Dunharrow. The account given here, telling of the Drúedain in Beleriand in the First Age, and containing the story of 'The Faithful Stone', is drawn from a long, discursive, and unfinished essay concerned primarily with the interrelations of the languages of Middle-earth. As will be seen, the Drúedain were to be drawn back into the history of the earlier Ages; but of this there is necessarily no trace in the published *Silmarillion*.

## II

### The Istari

It was proposed soon after the acceptance of *The Lord of the Rings* for publication that there should be an index at the end of the third volume, and it seems that my father began to work on it in the summer of 1954, after the first two volumes had gone to press. He wrote of the matter in a letter of 1956: 'An index of names was to be produced, which by etymological interpretation would provide quite a large Elvish vocabulary. . . . I worked at it for months, and indexed the first two volumes (it was the chief cause of the delay of Volume III), until it became clear that size and cost were ruinous.'

In the event there was no index to *The Lord of the Rings* until the second edition of 1966, but my father's original rough draft has been preserved. From it I derived the plan of my index to *The Silmarillion*, with translation of names and brief explanatory statements, and also, both there and in the index to this book, some of the translations and the wording of some of the 'definitions'. From it comes also the 'essay on the Istari' with which this section of the book opens – an entry wholly uncharacteristic of the original index in its length, if characteristic of the way in which my father often worked.

For the other citations in this section I have given in the text itself such indications of date as can be provided.

# III

## The Palantíri

For the second edition of *The Lord of the Rings* (1966) my father made substantial emendations to a passage in *The Two Towers*, III 11 'The Palantír' (three-volume hardback edition p. 203), and some others in the same connection in *The Return of the King*, V 7 'The Pyre of Denethor' (edition cited p. 132), though these emendations were not incorporated in the text until the second impression of the revised edition (1967). This section of the present book is derived from writings on the *palantíri* associated with this revision; I have done no more than assemble them into a continuous essay.

★ ★ ★

## The Map of Middle-earth

My first intention was to include in this book the map that accompanies *The Lord of the Rings* with the addition to it of further names; but it seemed to me on reflection that it would be better to copy my original map and take the opportunity to remedy some of its minor defects (to remedy the major ones being beyond my powers). I have therefore re-drawn it fairly exactly, on a scale half as large again (that is to say, the new map as drawn is half as large again as the old map in its published dimensions). The area shown is smaller, but the only features lost are the Havens of Umbar and the Cape of Forochel.* This has allowed of a different and larger mode of lettering, and a great gain in clarity.

All the more important place-names that occur in this book but not in *The Lord of the Rings* are included, such as *Lond Daer, Drúwaith Iaur, Edhellond, the Undeeps, Greylin*; and a few others that might have been, or should have been, shown on the original map, such as the rivers *Harnen* and *Carnen, Annúminas, Eastfold, Westfold*, the *Mountains of Angmar*. The mistaken inclusion of *Rhudaur* alone has been corrected by the addition of *Cardolan* and *Arthedain*, and I have shown the little island of *Himling* off the far north-western coast, which appears on one of my father's sketch-maps and on my own first draft. *Himling* was the earlier form of *Himring* (the great hill on which Maedhros son of Fëanor

---

* I have little doubt now that the water marked on my original map as 'The Icebay of Forochel' was in fact only a small part of the Bay (referred to in *The Lord of the Rings*, Appendix A I iii, as 'immense'), which extended much further to the north-east: its northern and western shores being formed by the great Cape of Forochel, of which the tip, unnamed, appears on my original map. In one of my father's map-sketches the northern coast of Middle-earth is shown stretching in a great curve east-north-east from the Cape, the most northerly point being some 700 miles north of Carn Dûm.

had his fortress in *The Silmarillion*), and though the fact is nowhere referred to it is clear that Himring's top rose above the waters that covered drowned Beleriand. Some way to the west of it was a larger island named *Tol Fuin*, which must be the highest part of *Taur-nu-Fuin*. In general, but not in all cases, I have preferred the Sindarin name (if known), but I have usually given the translated name as well when that is much used. It may be noted that 'The Northern Waste', marked at the head of my original map, seems in fact certainly to have been intended as an equivalent to *Forodwaith*.*

I have thought it desirable to mark in the entire length of the Great Road linking Arnor and Gondor, although its course between Edoras and the Fords of Isen is conjectural (as also is the precise placing of Lond Daer and Edhellond).

Lastly, I would emphasize that the exact preservation of the style and detail (other than nomenclature and lettering) of the map that I made in haste twenty-five years ago does not argue any belief in the excellence of its conception or execution. I have long regretted that my father never replaced it by one of his own making. However, as things turned out it became, for all its defects and oddities, 'the Map', and my father himself always used it as a basis afterwards (while frequently noticing its inadequacies). The various sketch-maps that he made, and from which mine was derived, are now a part of the history of the writing of *The Lord of the Rings*. I have thought it best therefore, so far as my own contribution to these matters extends, to let my original design stand, since it does at least represent the structure of my father's conceptions with tolerable faithfulness.

*\*Forodwaith* only occurs once in *The Lord of the Rings* (Appendix A I iii) and there refers to ancient inhabitants of the Northlands, of whom the Snowmen of Forochel were a remnant; but the Sindarin word (*g*)*waith* was used both of regions and of the peoples inhabiting them (cf. *Enedwaith*). In one of my father's sketch-maps *Forodwaith* seems to be explicitly equated with 'The Northern Waste', and in another is translated 'Northerland'.

# PART ONE

---

# THE FIRST AGE

# I

## OF TUOR AND HIS
## COMING TO GONDOLIN

Rían, wife of Huor, dwelt with the people of the House of Hador; but when rumour came to Dor-lómin of the Nirnaeth Arnoediad, and yet she could hear no news of her lord, she became distraught and wandered forth into the wild alone. There she would have perished, but the Grey-elves came to her aid. For there was a dwelling of this people in the mountains westward of Lake Mithrim; and thither they led her, and she was there delivered of a son before the end of the Year of Lamentation.

And Rían said to the Elves: 'Let him be called *Tuor*, for that name his father chose, ere war came between us. And I beg of you to foster him, and to keep him hidden in your care; for I forebode that great good, for Elves and Men, shall come from him. But I must go in search of Huor, my lord.'

Then the Elves pitied her; but one Annael, who alone of all that went to war from that people had returned from the Nirnaeth, said to her: 'Alas, lady, it is known now that Huor fell at the side of Húrin his brother; and he lies, I deem, in the great hill of slain that the Orcs have raised upon the field of battle.'

Therefore Rían arose and left the dwelling of the Elves, and she passed through the land of Mithrim and came at last to the Haudh-en-Ndengin in the waste of Anfauglith, and there she laid her down and died. But the Elves cared for the infant son of Huor, and Tuor grew up among them; and he was fair of face, and golden-haired after the manner of his father's kin, and he became strong and tall and valiant, and being fostered by the Elves he had lore and skill no less than the princes of the Edain, ere ruin came upon the North.

But with the passing of the years the life of the former folk of Hithlum, such as still remained, Elves or Men, became ever harder and more perilous. For as is elsewhere told, Morgoth broke his pledges to the Easterlings that had served him, and he denied to them the rich lands of Beleriand which they had coveted, and he drove away these evil folk into Hithlum, and there commanded them to dwell. And though they loved Morgoth no longer, they served him still in fear, and hated all the Elven-folk; and they despised the remnant of the House of Hador (the aged and women and children, for the most part), and they oppressed them, and wedded their women by force, and took their lands and goods, and enslaved their children. Orcs came and went about the land as they would, pursuing the lingering Elves into the fastnesses of the mountains, and taking many captive to the mines of Angband to labour as the thralls of Morgoth.

Therefore Annael led his small people to the caves of Androth, and there they lived a hard and wary life, until Tuor was sixteen years of age and was become strong and able to wield arms, the axe and bow of the Grey-elves; and his heart grew hot within him at the tale of the griefs of his people, and he wished to go forth and avenge them on the Orcs and Easterlings. But Annael forbade this.

'Far hence, I deem, your doom lies, Tuor son of Huor,' he said. 'And this land shall not be freed from the shadow of Morgoth until Thangorodrim itself be overthrown. Therefore we are resolved at last to forsake it, and to depart into the South; and with us you shall go.'

'But how shall we escape the net of our enemies?' said Tuor. 'For the marching of so many together will surely be marked.'

'We shall not march through the land openly,' said Annael; 'and if our fortune is good we shall come to the secret way which we call Annon-in-Gelydh, the Gate of the Noldor; for it was made by the skill of that people, long ago in the days of Turgon.'

At that name Tuor was stirred, though he knew not why; and he questioned Annael concerning Turgon. 'He is a son of Fingolfin,' said Annael, 'and is now accounted High King of the Noldor, since the fall of Fingon. For he lives yet, most feared of the foes of Morgoth, and he escaped from the ruin of the Nirnaeth, when Húrin of Dor-lómin and Huor your father held the passes of Sirion behind him.'

'Then I will go and seek Turgon,' said Tuor; 'for surely he will lend me aid for my father's sake?'

'That you cannot,' said Annael. 'For his stronghold is hidden from the eyes of Elves and Men, and we know not where it stands. Of the Noldor some, maybe, know the way thither, but they will speak of it to none. Yet if you would have speech with them, then come with me, as I bid you; for in the far havens of the South you may meet with wanderers from the Hidden Kingdom.'

Thus it came to pass that the Elves forsook the caves of Androth, and Tuor went with them. But their enemies kept watch upon their dwellings, and were soon aware of their march; and they had not gone far from the hills into the plain before they were assailed by a great force of Orcs and Easterlings, and they were scattered far and wide, fleeing into the gathering night. But Tuor's heart was kindled with the fire of battle, and he would not flee, but boy as he was he wielded the axe as his father before him, and for long he stood his ground and slew many that assailed him; but at the last he was overwhelmed and taken captive and led before Lorgan the Easterling. Now this Lorgan was held the chieftain of the Easterlings and claimed to rule all Dor-lómin as a fief under Morgoth; and he took Tuor to be his slave. Hard and bitter then was his life; for it pleased Lorgan to treat Tuor the more evilly as he was of the kin of the former lords, and he sought to break, if he could, the pride of the House of Hador. But Tuor saw wisdom, and endured all pains and taunts with watchful patience; so that in time his lot was somewhat lightened, and at the least he was not starved, as were many of Lorgan's unhappy thralls. For he was strong and skilful, and Lorgan fed his beasts of burden well, while they were young and could work.

But after three years of thraldom Tuor saw at last a chance of escape. He was come now almost to his full stature, taller and swifter than any of the Easterlings; and being sent with other thralls on an errand of labour into the woods he turned suddenly on the guards and slew them with an axe, and fled into the hills. The Easterlings hunted him with dogs, but without avail; for wellnigh all the hounds of Lorgan were his friends, and if they came up with him they would fawn upon him, and then run homeward at his command. Thus he came back at last to the caves of Androth and dwelt there alone. And for four years he was an outlaw in the land of his fathers, grim and solitary; and his name was feared, for he went often abroad, and slew many of the Easterlings that he came upon. Then they set a great price upon his head; but they did not dare to come to his hiding-place, even with strength of men, for they feared the Elven-folk, and shunned the caves where they had dwelt. Yet it is said that Tuor's journeys were not made for the purpose of vengeance; rather he sought ever for the Gate of the Noldor, of which Annael had spoken. But he found it not, for he knew not where to look, and such few of the Elves as lingered still in the mountains had not heard of it.

Now Tuor knew that, though fortune still favoured him, yet in the end the days of an outlaw are numbered, and are ever few and without hope. Nor was he willing to live thus for ever a wild man in the houseless hills, and his heart urged him ever to great deeds. Herein, it is said, the power of Ulmo was shown. For he gathered tidings of all that passed in Beleriand, and every stream that flowed from Middle-earth to the Great Sea was to him a messenger, both to and fro; and he remained also in friendship, as of old, with Círdan and the Shipwrights at the Mouths of Sirion.[1] And at this time most of all Ulmo gave heed to the fates of the House of Hador, for in his deep counsels he purposed that they should play great part in his designs for the succour of the Exiles; and he knew well of the plight of Tuor, for Annael and many of his folk had indeed escaped from Dor-lómin and come at last to Círdan in the far South.

Thus it came to pass that on a day in the beginning of the year (twenty and three since the Nirnaeth) Tuor sat by a spring that trickled forth near to the door of the cave where he dwelt; and he looked out westward towards the cloudy sunset. Then suddenly it came into his heart that he would wait no longer, but would arise and go. 'I will leave now the grey land of my kin that are no more,' he cried, 'and I will go in search of my doom! But whither shall I turn? Long have I sought the Gate and found it not.'

Then he took up the harp which he bore ever with him, being skilled in playing upon its strings, and heedless of the peril of his clear voice alone in the waste he sang an elven-song of the North for the uplifting of hearts. And even as he sang the well at his feet began to boil with great increase of water, and it overflowed, and a rill ran noisily down the rocky hillside before him. And Tuor took this as a sign, and he arose at once and followed after it. Thus he came down from the tall hills of Mithrim and passed out into the northward plain of Dor-lómin; and ever the stream grew as he followed it westward, until after three days he could descry in the west the long grey ridges of Ered Lómin that in those regions marched north and south, fencing off the far coastlands of the Western Shores. To those hills in all his journeys Tuor had never come.

Now the land became more broken and stony again, as it approached the hills, and soon it began to rise before Tuor's feet, and the stream went down into a cloven bed. But even as dim dusk came on the third day of his journey, Tuor found before him a wall of rock, and there was an opening therein like a great arch; and the stream passed in and was lost. Then Tuor was dismayed, and he said: 'So my hope has cheated me! The sign in the hills has led me only to a dark end in the midst of the land of my enemies.' And grey at heart he sat among the rocks on the high bank of the stream, keeping watch through a bitter fireless night; for it was yet but the month of Súlimë, and no stir of spring had come to that far northern land, and a shrill wind blew from the East.

But even as the light of the coming sun shone pale in the far mists of Mithrim, Tuor heard voices, and looking down he saw in amazement two Elves that waded in the shallow water; and as they climbed up steps hewn in the bank, Tuor stood up and called to them. At once they drew their bright swords and sprang towards him. Then he saw that they were grey-cloaked but mail-clad under; and he marvelled, for they were fairer and more fell to look upon, because of the light of their eyes, than any of the Elven-folk that he yet had known. He stood to his full height and awaited them; but when they saw that he drew no weapon, but stood alone and greeted them in the Elven-tongue, they sheathed their swords and spoke courteously to him. And one said: 'Gelmir and Arminas we are, of Finarfin's people. Are you not one of the Edain of old that dwelt in these lands ere the Nirnaeth? And indeed of the kindred of Hador and Húrin I deem you; for so the gold of your head declares you.'

And Tuor answered: 'Yea, I am Tuor, son of Huor, son of Galdor, son of Hador; but now at last I desire to leave this land where I am outlawed and kinless.'

'Then,' said Gelmir, 'if you would escape and find the havens in the South, already your feet have been guided on the right road.'

'So I thought,' said Tuor. 'For I followed a sudden spring of water in the hills, until it joined this treacherous stream. But now I know not whither to turn, for it has gone into darkness.'

'Through darkness one may come to the light,' said Gelmir.

'Yet one will walk under the Sun while one may,' said Tuor. 'But since you are of that people, tell me if you can where lies the Gate of the Noldor. For I have sought it long, ever since Annael my foster-father of the Grey-elves spoke of it to me.'

Then the Elves laughed, and said: 'Your search is ended; for we have ourselves just passed that Gate. There it stands before you!' And they pointed to the arch into which the water flowed. 'Come now! Through darkness you shall come to the light. We will set your feet on the road, but we cannot guide you far; for we are sent back to the lands whence we fled upon an urgent errand.' 'But fear not,' said Gelmir: 'a great doom is written upon your brow, and it shall lead you far from these lands, far indeed from Middle-earth, as I guess.'

Then Tuor followed the Noldor down the steps and waded in the cold water, until they passed into the shadow beyond the arch of

stone. And then Gelmir brought forth one of those lamps for which
the Noldor were renowned; for they were made of old in Valinor,
and neither wind nor water could quench them, and when they were
unhooded they sent forth a clear blue light from a flame imprisoned
in white crystal.[2] Now by the light that Gelmir held above his head
Tuor saw that the river began to go suddenly down a smooth slope
into a great tunnel, but beside its rock-hewn course there ran long
flights of steps leading on and downward into a deep gloom beyond
the beam of the lamp.

When they had come to the foot of the rapids they stood under a
great dome of rock, and there the river rushed over a steep fall with
a great noise that echoed in the vault, and it passed then on again
beneath another arch into a further tunnel. Beside the falls the Noldor
halted, and bade Tuor farewell.

'Now we must return and go our ways with all speed,' said Gelmir;
'for matters of great peril are moving in Beleriand.'

'Is then the hour come when Turgon shall come forth?' said Tuor.

Then the Elves looked at him in amazement. 'That is a matter
which concerns the Noldor rather than the sons of Men,' said
Arminas. 'What know you of Turgon?'

'Little,' said Tuor; 'save that my father aided his escape from
the Nirnaeth, and that in his hidden stronghold dwells the hope of
the Noldor. Yet, though I know not why, ever his name stirs in my
heart, and comes to my lips. And had I my will, I would go in search
of him, rather than tread this dark way of dread. Unless, perhaps,
this secret road is the way to his dwelling?'

'Who shall say?' answered the Elf. 'For since the dwelling of
Turgon is hidden, so also are the ways thither. I know them not,
though I have sought them long. Yet if I knew them, I would not
reveal them to you, nor to any among Men.'

But Gelmir said: 'Yet I have heard that your House has the favour
of the Lord of Waters. And if his counsels lead you to Turgon, then
surely shall you come to him, withersoever you turn. Follow now the
road to which the water has brought you from the hills, and fear not!
You shall not walk long in darkness. Farewell! And think not that
our meeting was by chance; for the Dweller in the Deep moves
many things in this land still. *Anar kaluva tielyanna!*'[3]

With that the Noldor turned and went back up the long stairs;
but Tuor stood still, until the light of their lamp was lost, and he was
alone in a darkness deeper than night amid the roaring of the falls.
Then summoning his courage he set his left hand to the rock-wall,
and felt his way forward, slowly at first, and then more quickly, as

he became more used to the darkness and found nothing to hinder him. And after a great while, as it seemed to him, when he was weary and yet unwilling to rest in the black tunnel, he saw far before him a light; and hastening on he came to a tall and narrow cleft, and followed the noisy stream between its leaning walls out into a golden evening. For he was come into a deep ravine with tall sheer sides, and it ran straight towards the West; and before him the setting sun, going down through a clear sky, shone into the ravine and kindled its walls with yellow fire, and the waters of the river glittered like gold as they broke and foamed upon many gleaming stones.

In that deep place Tuor went on now in great hope and delight, finding a path beneath the southern wall, where there lay a long and narrow strand. And when night came, and the river rushed on unseen, save for a glint of high stars mirrored in dark pools, then he rested, and slept; for he felt no fear beside that water, in which the power of Ulmo ran.

With the coming of day he went on again without haste. The sun rose behind his back and set before his face, and where the water foamed among the boulders or rushed over sudden falls, at morning and evening rainbows were woven across the stream. Wherefore he named that ravine Cirith Ninniach.

Thus Tuor journeyed slowly for three days, drinking the cold water but desiring no food, though there were many fish that shone as gold and silver, or gleamed with colours like to the rainbows in the spray above. And on the fourth day the channel grew wider, and its walls lower and less sheer; but the river ran deeper and more strongly, for high hills now marched on either side, and fresh waters spilled from them into Cirith Ninniach over shimmering falls. There long while Tuor sat, watching the swirling of the stream and listening to its endless voice, until night came again and stars shone cold and white in the dark lane of sky above him. Then he lifted up his voice, and plucked the strings of his harp, and above the noise of the water the sound of his song and the sweet thrilling of the harp were echoed in the stone and multiplied, and went forth and rang in the night-clad hills, until all the empty land was filled with music beneath the stars. For though he knew it not, Tuor was now come to the Echoing Mountains of Lammoth about the Firth of Drengist. There once long ago Fëanor had landed from the sea, and the voices of his host were swelled to a mighty clamour upon the coasts of the North ere the rising of the Moon.[4]

Then Tuor was filled with wonder and stayed his song, and slowly the music died in the hills, and there was silence. And then amid

the silence he heard in the air above him a strange cry; and he knew
not of what creature that cry came. Now he said: 'It is a fay-voice,'
now: 'Nay, it is a small beast that is wailing in the waste'; and then,
hearing it again, he said: 'Surely, it is the cry of some nightfaring
bird that I know not.' And it seemed to him a mournful sound, and
yet he desired nonetheless to hear it and follow it, for it called him,
he knew not whither.

The next morning he heard the same voice above his head, and
looking up he saw three great white birds beating down the ravine
against the westerly wind, and their strong wings shone in the new-
risen sun, and as they passed over him they wailed aloud. Thus for
the first time he beheld the great gulls, beloved of the Teleri. Then
Tuor arose to follow them, and so that he might better mark whither
they flew he climbed the cliff upon his left hand, and stood upon the
top, and felt a great wind out of the West rush against his face; and
his hair streamed from his head. And he drank deep of that new air,
and said: 'This uplifts the heart like the drinking of cool wine!'
But he knew not that the wind came fresh from the Great Sea.

Now Tuor went on once more, seeking the gulls, high above the
river; and as he went the sides of the ravine drew together again, and
he came to a narrow channel, and it was filled with a great noise of
water. And looking down Tuor saw a great marvel, as it seemed to
him; for a wild flood came up the narrows and strove with the river
that would still press on, and a wave like a wall rose up almost to the
cliff-top, crowned with foam-crests flying in the wind. Then the
river was thrust back, and the incoming flood swept roaring up the
channel, drowning it in deep water, and the rolling of the boulders
was like thunder as it passed. Thus Tuor was saved by the call of
the sea-birds from death in the rising tide; and that was very great
because of the season of the year and of the high wind from the sea.

But now Tuor was dismayed by the fury of the strange waters, and
he turned aside and went away southward, and so came not to the
long shores of the Firth of Drengist, but wandered still for some days
in a rugged country bare of trees; and it was swept by a wind from
the sea, and all that grew there, herb or bush, leaned ever to the dawn
because of the prevalence of that wind from the West. In this way
Tuor passed into the borders of Nevrast, where once Turgon had
dwelt; and at last at unawares (for the cliff-tops at the margin of the
land were higher than the slopes behind) he came suddenly to the
black brink of Middle-earth, and saw the Great Sea, Belegaer the
Shoreless. And at that hour the sun went down beyond the rim of

the world, as a mighty fire; and Tuor stood alone upon the cliff with outspread arms, and a great yearning filled his heart. It is said that he was the first of Men to reach the Great Sea, and that none, save the Eldar, have ever felt more deeply the longing that it brings.

Tuor tarried many days in Nevrast, and it seemed good to him, for that land, being fenced by mountains from the North and East and nigh to the sea, was milder and more kindly than the plains of Hithlum. He was long used to dwell alone as a hunter in the wild, and he found no lack of food; for spring was busy in Nevrast, and the air was filled with the noise of birds, both those that dwelt in multitudes upon the shores and those that teemed in the marshes of Linaewen in the midst of the hollow land; but in those days no voice of Elves or Men was heard in all the solitude.

To the borders of the great mere Tuor came, but its waters were beyond his reach, because of the wide mires and the pathless forests of reeds that lay all about; and soon he turned away, and went back to the coast, for the Sea drew him, and he was not willing to dwell long where he could not hear the sound of its waves. And in the shorelands Tuor first found traces of the Noldor of old. For among the tall and sea-hewn cliffs south of Drengist there were many coves and sheltered inlets, with beaches of white sand among the black gleaming rocks, and leading down to such places Tuor found often winding stairs cut in the living stone; and by the water-edge were ruined quays, built of great blocks hewn from the cliffs, where elven-ships had once been moored. In those regions Tuor long remained, watching the ever-changing sea, while through spring and summer the slow year wore on, and darkness deepened in Beleriand, and the autumn of the doom of Nargothrond drew near.

And, maybe, birds saw from afar the fell winter that was to come;[5] for those that were wont to go south gathered early to depart, and others that used to dwell in the North came from their homes to Nevrast. And one day, as Tuor sat upon the shore, he heard the rush and whine of great wings, and he looked up and saw seven white swans flying in a swift wedge southward. But as they came above him they wheeled and flew suddenly down, and alighted with a great plash and churning of water.

Now Tuor loved swans, which he knew on the grey pools of Mithrim; and the swan moreover had been the token of Annael and his foster-folk. He rose therefore to greet the birds, and called to them, marvelling to behold that they were greater and prouder than any of their kind that he had seen before; but they beat their wings and uttered harsh cries, as if they were wroth with him and would drive him from the shore. Then with a great noise they rose again from the water and flew above his head, so that the rush of their wings blew upon him as a whistling wind; and wheeling in a wide circle they ascended into the high air and went away south.

Then Tuor cried aloud: 'Here now comes another sign that I have tarried too long!' And straightway he climbed to the cliff-top, and there he beheld the swans still wheeling on high; but when he turned southward and set out to follow them, they flew swiftly away.

Now Tuor journeyed south along the coast for full seven days, and each morning he was aroused by the rush of wings above him in the dawn, and each day the swans flew on as he followed after. And as he went the great cliffs became lower, and their tops were clothed deep with flowering turf; and away eastward there were woods turning yellow in the waning of the year. But before him, drawing ever nearer, he saw a line of great hills that barred his way, marching westward until they ended in a tall mountain: a dark and cloud-helmed tower reared upon mighty shoulders above a great green cape thrust out into the sea.

Those grey hills were indeed the western outliers of Ered Wethrin, the north-fence of Beleriand, and the mountain was Mount Taras, westernmost of all the towers of that land, whose head a mariner would first descry across the miles of the sea, as he drew near to the mortal shores. Beneath its long slopes in bygone days Turgon had dwelt in the halls of Vinyamar, eldest of all the works of stone that the Noldor built in the lands of their exile. There it still stood, desolate but enduring, high upon great terraces that looked towards the sea. The years had not shaken it, and the servants of Morgoth had passed it by; but wind and rain and frost had graven it, and upon the coping of its walls and the great shingles of its roof there was a deep growth of grey-green plants that, living upon the salt air, throve even in the cracks of barren stone.

Now Tuor came to the ruins of a lost road, and he passed amid green mounds and leaning stones, and so came as the day was waning to the old hall and its high and windy courts. No shadow of fear or evil lurked there, but an awe fell upon him, thinking of those that had dwelt there and had gone, none knew whither: the proud people, deathless but doomed, from far beyond the Sea. And he turned and looked, as often their eyes had looked, out across the glitter of the unquiet waters to the end of sight. Then he turned back again, and saw that the swans had alighted on the highest terrace, and stood before the west-door of the hall; and they beat their wings, and it seemed to him that they beckoned him to enter. Then Tuor went up the wide stairs, now half-hidden in thrift and campion, and he passed under the mighty lintel and entered the shadows of the house of Turgon; and he came at last to a high-pillared hall. If great it had appeared from without, now vast and wonderful it seemed to Tuor from within, and for awe he wished not to awake the echoes in its emptiness. Nothing could he see there, save at the eastern end a high seat upon a dais, and softly as he might he paced towards it; but the sound of his feet rang upon the paved floor as the steps of doom, and echoes ran before him along the pillared aisles.

As he stood before the great chair in the gloom, and saw that it was hewn of a single stone and written with strange signs, the sinking sun drew level with a high window under the westward gable, and a shaft of light smote the wall before him, and glittered as it were upon burnished metal. Then Tuor marvelling saw that on the wall behind the throne there hung a shield and a great hauberk, and a helm and a long sword in a sheath. The hauberk shone as it were wrought of silver untarnished, and the sunbeam gilded it with sparks of gold. But the shield was of a shape strange to Tuor's eyes, for it was long and tapering; and its field was blue, in the midst of which was wrought an emblem of a white swan's wing. Then Tuor spoke, and his voice rang as a challenge in the roof: 'By this token I will take these arms unto myself, and upon myself whatsoever doom they bear.'[6] And he lifted down the shield and found it light and wieldy beyond his guess; for it was wrought, it seemed, of wood, but overlaid by the craft of elven-smiths with plates of metal, strong yet thin as foil, whereby it had been preserved from worm and weather.

Then Tuor arrayed himself in the hauberk, and set the helm upon his head, and he girt himself with the sword; black were sheath and belt with clasps of silver. Thus armed he went forth from Turgon's hall, and stood upon the high terraces of Taras in the red light of the sun. None were there to see him, as he gazed westward, gleaming in silver and gold, and he knew not that in that hour he appeared as one of the Mighty of the West, and fit to be the father of the kings of the Kings of Men beyond the Sea, as it was indeed his doom to be;[7] but in the taking of those arms a change came upon Tuor son of Huor, and his heart grew great within him. And as he stepped down from the doors the swans did him reverence, and plucking each a great feather from their wings they proffered them to him, laying their long necks upon the stone before his feet; and he took

the seven feathers and set them in the crest of his helm, and straightway the swans arose and flew north in the sunset, and Tuor saw
them no more.

Now Tuor felt his feet drawn to the sea-strand, and he went down
by long stairs to a wide shore upon the north side of Taras-ness;
and as he went he saw that the sun was sinking low into a great
black cloud that came up over the rim of the darkening sea; and it
grew cold, and there was a stirring and murmur as of a storm to come.
And Tuor stood upon the shore, and the sun was like a smoky fire
behind the menace of the sky; and it seemed to him that a great
wave rose far off and rolled towards the land, but wonder held him,
and he remained there unmoved. And the wave came towards him,
and upon it lay a mist of shadow. Then suddenly as it drew near it
curled, and broke, and rushed forward in long arms of foam; but
where it had broken there stood dark against the rising storm a
living shape of great height and majesty.
     Then Tuor bowed in reverence, for it seemed to him that he beheld
a mighty king. A tall crown he wore like silver, from which his long
hair fell down as foam glimmering in the dusk; and as he cast back
the grey mantle that hung about him like a mist, behold! he was clad
in a gleaming coat, close-fitted as the mail of a mighty fish, and in a
kirtle of deep green that flashed and flickered with sea-fire as he
strode slowly towards the land. In this manner the Dweller of the
Deep, whom the Noldor name Ulmo, Lord of Waters, showed
himself to Tuor son of Huor of the House of Hador beneath Vinyamar.
     He set no foot upon the shore, but standing knee-deep in the
shadowy sea he spoke to Tuor, and then for the light of his eyes and
for the sound of his deep voice that came as it seemed from the
foundations of the world, fear fell upon Tuor and he cast himself
down upon the sand.
     'Arise, Tuor, son of Huor!' said Ulmo. 'Fear not my wrath,
though long have I called to thee unheard; and setting out at last
thou hast tarried on thy journey hither. In the Spring thou shouldst
have stood here; but now a fell winter cometh soon from the land
of the Enemy. Haste thou must learn, and the pleasant road that I
designed for thee must be changed. For my counsels have been
scorned,[8] and a great evil creeps upon the Valley of Sirion, and
already a host of foes is come between thee and thy goal.'
     'What then is my goal, Lord?' said Tuor.
     'That which thy heart hath ever sought,' answered Ulmo: 'to find
Turgon, and look upon the hidden city. For thou art arrayed thus

to be my messenger, even in the arms which long ago I decreed for thee. Yet now thou must under shadow pass through peril. Wrap thyself therefore in this cloak, and cast it never aside, until thou come to thy journey's end.'

Then it seemed to Tuor that Ulmo parted his grey mantle, and cast to him a lappet, and as it fell about him it was for him a great cloak wherein he might wrap himself over all, from head to foot.

'Thus thou shalt walk under my shadow,' said Ulmo. 'But tarry no more; for in the lands of Anar and in the fires of Melkor it will not endure. Wilt thou take up my errand?'

'I will, Lord,' said Tuor.

'Then I will set words in thy mouth to say unto Turgon,' said Ulmo. 'But first I will teach thee, and some things thou shalt hear which no Man else hath heard, nay, not even the mighty among the Eldar.' And Ulmo spoke to Tuor of Valinor and its darkening, and the Exile of the Noldor, and the Doom of Mandos, and the hiding of the Blessed Realm. 'But behold!' said he, 'in the armour of Fate (as the Children of Earth name it) there is ever a rift, and in the walls of Doom a breach, until the full-making, which ye call the End. So it shall be while I endure, a secret voice that gainsayeth, and a light where darkness was decreed. Therefore, though in the days of this darkness I seem to oppose the will of my brethren, the Lords of the West, that is my part among them, to which I was appointed ere the making of the World. Yet Doom is strong, and the shadow of the Enemy lengthens; and I am diminished, until in Middle-earth I am become now no more than a secret whisper. The waters that run westward wither, and their springs are poisoned, and my power withdraws from the land; for Elves and Men grow blind and deaf to me because of the might of Melkor. And now the Curse of Mandos hastens to its fulfilment, and all the works of the Noldor shall perish, and every hope which they build shall crumble. The last hope alone is left, the hope that they have not looked for and have not prepared. And that hope lieth in thee; for so I have chosen.'

'Then shall Turgon not stand against Morgoth, as all the Eldar yet hope?' said Tuor. 'And what wouldst thou of me, Lord, if I come now to Turgon? For though I am indeed willing to do as my father and stand by that king in his need, yet of little avail shall I be, a mortal man alone, among so many and so valiant of the High Folk of the West.'

'If I choose to send thee, Tuor son of Huor, then believe not that thy one sword is not worth the sending. For the valour of the Edain the Elves shall ever remember as the ages lengthen, marvelling that they gave life so freely of which they had on earth so little. But it is not for thy valour only that I send thee, but to bring into the world a hope beyond thy sight, and a light that shall pierce the darkness.'

And as Ulmo said these things the mutter of the storm rose to a great cry, and the wind mounted, and the sky grew black; and the mantle of the Lord of Waters streamed out like a flying cloud. 'Go now,' said Ulmo, 'lest the Sea devour thee! For Ossë obeys the will of Mandos, and he is wroth, being a servant of the Doom.'

'As thou commandest,' said Tuor. 'But if I escape the Doom, what words shall I say unto Turgon?'

'If thou come to him,' answered Ulmo, 'then the words shall arise in thy mind, and thy mouth shall speak as I would. Speak and fear not! And thereafter do as thy heart and valour lead thee. Hold fast to my mantle, for thus shalt thou be guarded. And I will send one to thee out of the wrath of Ossë, and thus shalt thou be guided: yea, the last mariner of the last ship that shall seek into the West until the rising of the Star. Go now back to the land!'

Then there was a noise of thunder, and lightning flared over the sea; and Tuor beheld Ulmo standing among the waves as a tower of silver flickering with darting flames; and he cried against the wind:

'I go, Lord! Yet now my heart yearneth rather to the Sea.'

And thereupon Ulmo lifted up a mighty horn, and blew upon it a single great note, to which the roaring of the storm was but a wind-flaw upon a lake. And as he heard that note, and was encompassed by it, and filled with it, it seemed to Tuor that the coasts of Middle-earth vanished, and he surveyed all the waters of the world in a great vision: from the veins of the lands to the mouths of the rivers, and from the strands and estuaries out into the deep. The Great Sea he saw through its unquiet regions teeming with strange forms, even to its lightless depths, in which amid the everlasting darkness there echoed voices terrible to mortal ears. Its measureless plains he surveyed with the swift sight of the Valar, lying windless under the eye of Anar, or glittering under the horned Moon, or lifted in hills of wrath that broke upon the Shadowy Isles,[9] until remote upon the edge of sight, and beyond the count of leagues, he glimpsed a mountain, rising beyond his mind's reach into a shining cloud, and at its feet a long surf glimmering. And even as he strained to hear the sound of those far waves, and to see clearer that distant light, the note ended, and he stood beneath the thunder of the storm, and lightning many-branched rent asunder the heavens above him. And Ulmo was gone, and the sea was in tumult, as the wild waves of Ossë rode against the walls of Nevrast.

Then Tuor fled from the fury of the sea, and with labour he won his way back to the high terraces; for the wind drove him against the cliff, and when he came out upon the top it bent him to his knees. Therefore he entered again the dark and empty hall for shelter, and he sat nightlong in the stone seat of Turgon. The very pillars trembled for the violence of the storm, and it seemed to Tuor that the wind was full of wailing and wild cries. Yet being weary he slept at times, and his sleep was troubled with many dreams, of which naught remained in waking memory save one: a vision of an isle, and in the midst of it was a steep mountain, and behind it the sun went down, and shadows sprang into the sky; but above it there shone a single dazzling star.

After this dream Tuor fell into a deep sleep, for before the night was over the tempest passed, driving the black clouds into the East of the world. He awoke at length in the grey light, and arose, and left the high seat, and as he went down the dim hall he saw that it was filled with sea-birds driven in by the storm; and he went out as the last stars were fading in the West before the coming day. Then he saw that the great waves in the night had ridden high upon the land, and had cast their crests above the cliff-tops, and weed and shingle-drift were flung even upon the terraces before the doors. And Tuor looked down from the lowest terrace and saw, leaning against its wall among the stones and the sea-wrack, an Elf, clad in a grey cloak sodden with the sea. Silent he sat, gazing beyond the ruin of the beaches out over the long ridges of the waves. All was still, and there was no sound save the roaring of the surf below.

As Tuor stood and looked at the silent grey figure he remembered the words of Ulmo, and a name untaught came to his lips, and he called aloud: 'Welcome, Voronwë! I await you.'[10]

Then the Elf turned and looked up, and Tuor met the piercing glance of his sea-grey eyes, and knew that he was of the high folk of the Noldor. But fear and wonder grew in his gaze as he saw Tuor standing high upon the wall above him, clad in his great cloak like a shadow out of which the elven-mail gleamed upon his breast.

A moment thus they stayed, each searching the face of the other, and then the Elf stood up and bowed low before Tuor's feet. 'Who are you, lord?' he said. 'Long have I laboured in the unrelenting sea. Tell me: have great tidings befallen since I walked the land? Is the Shadow overthrown? Have the Hidden People come forth?'

'Nay,' Tuor answered. 'The Shadow lengthens, and the Hidden remain hid.'

Then Voronwë looked at him long in silence. 'But who are you?'

he asked again. 'For many years ago my people left this land, and none have dwelt here since. And now I perceive that despite your raiment you are not of them, as I thought, but are of the kindred of Men.'

'I am,' said Tuor. 'And are you not the last mariner of the last ship that sought the West from the Havens of Círdan?'

'I am,' said the Elf. 'Voronwë son of Aranwë am I. But how you know my name and fate I understand not.'

'I know, for the Lord of Waters spoke to me yestereve,' answered Tuor, 'and he said that he would save you from the wrath of Ossë, and send you hither to be my guide.'

Then in fear and wonder Voronwë cried: 'You have spoken with Ulmo the Mighty? Then great indeed must be your worth and doom! But whither should I guide you, lord? For surely a king of Men you must be, and many must wait upon your word.'

'Nay, I am an escaped thrall,' said Tuor, 'and I am an outlaw alone in an empty land. But I have an errand to Turgon the Hidden King. Know you by what road I may find him?'

'Many are outlaw and thrall in these evil days who were not born so,' answered Voronwë. 'A lord of Men by right you are, I deem. But were you the highest of all your folk, no right would you have to seek Turgon, and vain would be your quest. For even were I to lead you to his gates, you could not enter in.'

'I do not bid you to lead me further than the gate,' said Tuor. 'There Doom shall strive with the Counsel of Ulmo. And if Turgon will not receive me, then my errand will be ended, and Doom shall prevail. But as for my right to seek Turgon: I am Tuor son of Huor and kin to Húrin, whose names Turgon will not forget. And I seek also by the command of Ulmo. Will Turgon forget that which he spoke to him of old: *Remember that the last hope of the Noldor cometh from the Sea*? Or again: *When peril is nigh one shall come from Nevrast to warn thee*?[11] I am he that should come, and I am arrayed thus in the gear that was prepared for me.'

Tuor marvelled to hear himself speak so, for the words of Ulmo to Turgon at his going from Nevrast were not known to him before, nor to any save the Hidden People. Therefore the more amazed was Voronwë; but he turned away, and looked toward the Sea, and he sighed.

'Alas!' he said. 'I wish never again to return. And often have I vowed in the deeps of the sea that, if ever I set foot on land again, I would dwell at rest far from the Shadow in the North, or by the Havens of Círdan, or maybe in the fair fields of Nan-tathren, where the spring is sweeter than heart's desire. But if evil has grown while I have wandered, and the last peril approaches them, then I must go to my people.' He turned back to Tuor. 'I will lead you to the hidden gates,' he said; 'for the wise will not gainsay the counsels of Ulmo.'

'Then we will go together, as we are counselled,' said Tuor. 'But mourn not, Voronwë! For my heart says to you that far from the Shadow your long road shall lead you, and your hope shall return to the Sea.'[12]

'And yours also,' said Voronwë. 'But now we must leave it, and go in haste.'

'Yea,' said Tuor. 'But whither will you lead me, and how far? Shall we not first take thought how we may fare in the wild, or if the way be long, how pass the harbourless winter?'

But Voronwë would answer nothing clearly concerning the road. 'You know the strength of Men,' he said. 'As for me, I am of the Noldor, and long must be the hunger and cold the winter that shall slay the kin of those who passed the Grinding Ice. Yet how think you that we could labour countless days in the salt wastes of the sea? Or have you not heard of the waybread of the Elves? And I keep still that which all mariners hold until the last.' Then he showed beneath his cloak a sealed wallet clasped upon his belt. 'No water nor weather will harm it while it is sealed. But we must husband it until great need; and doubtless an outlaw and hunter may find other food ere the year worsens.'

'Maybe,' said Tuor. 'But not in all lands is it safe to hunt, be the game never so plentiful. And hunters tarry on the road.'

Now Tuor and Voronwë made ready to depart. Tuor took with him the small bow and arrows that he had brought, beside the gear that he had taken from the hall; but his spear, upon which his name was written in the elven-runes of the North, he set upon the wall in token that he had passed. No arms had Voronwë save a short sword only.

Before the day was broad they left the ancient dwelling of Turgon, and Voronwë led Tuor about, westward of the steep slopes of Taras, and across the great cape. There once the road from Nevrast to Brithombar had passed, that now was but a green track between old turf-clad dikes. So they came into Beleriand, and the north region of the Falas; and turning eastward they sought the dark eaves of Ered Wethrin, and there they lay hid and rested until day had waned to dusk. For though the ancient dwellings of the Falathrim, Brithombar and Eglarest, were still far distant, Orcs now dwelt there and all the land was infested by the spies of Morgoth: he feared the ships of Círdan that would come at times raiding to the shores, and join with the forays sent forth from Nargothrond.

Now as they sat shrouded in their cloaks as shadows under the hills, Tuor and Voronwë spoke much together. And Tuor questioned Voronwë concerning Turgon, but Voronwë would tell little of such matters, and spoke rather of the dwellings upon the Isle of Balar, and of the Lisgardh, the land of reeds at the Mouths of Sirion.

'There now the numbers of the Eldar increase,' he said, 'for ever more flee thither of either kin from the fear of Morgoth, weary of war. But I forsook not my people of my own choice. For after the Bragollach and the breaking of the Siege of Angband doubt first came into Turgon's heart that Morgoth might prove too strong. In that year he sent out the first of his folk that passed his gates from within: a few only, upon a secret errand. They went down Sirion to the shores about the Mouths, and there built ships. But it availed them nothing, save to come to the great Isle of Balar and there establish lonely dwellings, far from the reach of Morgoth. For the Noldor have not the art of building ships that will long endure the waves of Belegaer the Great.[13]

'But when later Turgon heard of the ravaging of the Falas and the sack of the ancient Havens of the Shipwrights that lie away there before us, and it was told that Círdan had saved a remnant of his people and sailed away south to the Bay of Balar, then he sent out messengers anew. That was but a little while ago, yet it seems in memory the longest portion of my life. For I was one of those that he sent, being young in years among the Eldar. I was born here in Middle-earth in the land of Nevrast. My mother was of the Grey-elves of the Falas, and akin to Círdan himself – there was much mingling of the peoples in Nevrast in the first days of Turgon's kingship – and I have the sea-heart of my mother's people. Therefore I was among the chosen, since our errand was to Círdan, to seek his aid in our shipbuilding, that some message and prayer for aid might come to the Lords of the West ere all was lost. But I tarried on the way. For I had seen little of the lands of Middle-earth, and we came to Nan-tathren in the spring of the year. Lovely to heart's enchantment is that land, Tuor, as you shall find, if ever your feet go upon the southward roads down Sirion. There is the cure of all sea-longing, save for those whom Doom will not release. There Ulmo is but the servant of Yavanna, and the earth has brought to life a wealth of fair things that is beyond the thought of hearts in the hard hills of the North. In that land Narog joins Sirion, and they haste no more, but flow broad and quiet through living meads; and all about the shining river are flaglilies like a blossoming forest, and the grass is filled with flowers, like gems, like bells, like flames of red and gold, like a waste of many-coloured stars in a firmament of green. Yet fairest of all are the willows of Nan-tathren, pale green, or silver in the wind, and the rustle of their innumerable leaves is a spell of music: day and night would flicker by uncounted, while still I stood knee-deep in grass and listened. There I was enchanted, and forgot the Sea in my heart. There I wandered, naming new flowers, or lay adream amid the singing of the birds, and the humming of bees and flies; and there I might still dwell in delight, forsaking all my kin, whether the ships of the Teleri or the swords of the Noldor, but my doom would not so. Or the Lord of Waters himself, maybe; for he was strong in that land.

'Thus it came into my heart to make a raft of willow-boughs and move upon the bright bosom of Sirion; and so I did, and so I was taken. For on a day, as I was in the midst of the river, a sudden wind came and caught me, and bore me away out of the Land of Willows down to the Sea. Thus I came last of the messengers to Círdan; and of the seven ships that he built at Turgon's asking all but one were then full-wrought. And one by one they set sail into the West, and none yet has ever returned, nor has any news of them been heard.

'But the salt air of the sea now stirred anew the heart of my mother's kin within me, and I rejoiced in the waves, learning all ship-lore, as were it already stored in the mind. So when the last ship, and the greatest, was made ready, I was eager to be gone, saying within my thought: "If the words of the Noldor be true, then in the West there are meads with which the Land of Willows cannot compare. There is no withering nor any end of Spring. And perhaps even I, Voronwë, may come thither. And at the worst to wander on the waters is better far than the Shadow in the North." And I feared not, for the ships of the Teleri no water may drown.

'But the Great Sea is terrible, Tuor son of Huor; and it hates the Noldor, for it works the Doom of the Valar. Worse things it holds than to sink into the abyss and so perish: loathing, and loneliness, and madness; terror of wind and tumult, and silence, and shadows where all hope is lost and all living shapes pass away. And many shores evil and strange it washes, and many islands of danger and fear infest it. I will not darken your heart, son of Middle-earth, with the tale of my labour seven years in the Great Sea from the North even into the South, but never to the West. For that is shut against us.

'At the last, in black despair, weary of all the world, we turned and fled from the doom that so long had spared us, only to strike us the more cruelly. For even as we descried a mountain from afar, and I cried: "Lo! There is Taras, and the land of my birth," the wind awoke, and great clouds thunder-laden came up from the West. Then the waves hunted us like living things filled with malice, and the lightnings smote us; and when we were broken down to a helpless hull the seas leaped upon us in fury. But as you see, I was spared; for it seemed to me that there came a wave, greater and yet calmer than all the others, and it took me and lifted me from the ship, and bore me high upon its shoulders, and rolling to the land it cast me upon the turf, and then drained away, pouring back over the cliff in a great waterfall. There but one hour had I sat when you came upon me, still dazed by the sea. And still I feel the fear of it, and the bitter loss of all my friends that went with me so long and so far, beyond the sight of mortal lands.'

Voronwë sighed, and spoke then softly as if to himself. 'But very bright were the stars upon the margin of the world, when at times the clouds about the West were drawn aside. Yet whether we saw only clouds still more remote, or glimpsed indeed, as some held, the Mountains of the Pelóri about the lost strands of our long home, I know not. Far, far away they stand, and none from mortal lands shall come there ever again, I deem.' Then Voronwë fell silent; for night had come, and the stars shone white and cold.

Soon after Tuor and Voronwë arose and turned their backs toward the sea, and set out upon their long journey in the dark; of which there is little to tell, for the shadow of Ulmo was upon Tuor, and none saw them pass, by wood or stone, by field or fen, between the setting and the rising of the sun. But ever warily they went, shunning the night-eyed hunters of Morgoth, and forsaking the trodden ways of Elves and Men. Voronwë chose their path and Tuor followed. He asked no vain questions, but noted well that they went ever eastward along the march of the rising mountains, and turned never southward: at which he wondered, for he believed, as did well nigh all Elves and Men, that Turgon dwelt far from the battles of the North.

Slow was their going by twilight or by night in the pathless wilds, and the fell winter came down swiftly from the realm of Morgoth. Despite the shelter of the hills the winds were strong and bitter, and soon the snow lay deep upon the heights, or whirled through the passes, and fell upon the woods of Núath ere the full-shedding of their withered leaves.[14] Thus though they set out before the middle of

Narquelië, the Hísimë came in with biting frost even as they drew nigh to the Sources of Narog.

There at the end of a weary night in the grey of dawn they halted; and Voronwë was dismayed, looking about him in grief and fear. Where once the fair pool of Ivrin had lain in its great stone basin carved by falling waters, and all about it had been a tree-clad hollow under the hills, now he saw a land defiled and desolate. The trees were burned or uprooted; and the stone-marges of the pool were broken, so that the waters of Ivrin strayed and wrought a great barren marsh amid the ruin. All now was but a welter of frozen mire, and a reek of decay lay like a foul mist upon the ground.

'Alas! Has the evil come even here?' Voronwë cried. 'Once far from the threat of Angband was this place; but ever the fingers of Morgoth grope further.'

'It is even as Ulmo spoke to me,' said Tuor: '*The springs are poisoned, and my power withdraws from the waters of the land.*'

'Yet,' said Voronwë, 'a malice has been here with strength greater than that of Orcs. Fear lingers in this place.' And he searched about the edges of the mire, until suddenly he stood still and cried again: 'Yea, a great evil!' And he beckoned to Tuor, and Tuor coming saw a slot like a huge furrow that passed away southward, and at either side, now blurred, now sealed hard and clear by frost, the marks of great clawed feet. 'See!' said Voronwë, and his face was pale with dread and loathing. 'Here not long since was the Great Worm of Angband, most fell of all the creatures of the Enemy! Late already is our errand to Turgon. There is need of haste.'

Even as he spoke thus, they heard a cry in the woods, and they stood still as grey stones, listening. But the voice was a fair voice, though filled with grief, and it seemed that it called ever upon a name, as one that searches for another who is lost. And as they waited one came through the trees, and they saw that he was a tall Man, armed, clad in black, with a long sword drawn; and they wondered, for the blade of the sword also was black, but the edges shone bright and cold. Woe was graven in his face, and when he beheld the ruin of Ivrin he cried aloud in grief, saying: 'Ivrin, Faelivrin! Gwindor and Beleg! Here once I was healed. But now never shall I drink the draught of peace again.'

Then he went swiftly away towards the North, as one in pursuit, or on an errand of great haste, and they heard him cry *Faelivrin, Finduilas!* until his voice died away in the woods.[15] But they knew not that Nargothrond had fallen, and this was Túrin son of Húrin, the Blacksword. Thus only for a moment, and never again, did the paths of those kinsmen, Túrin and Tuor, draw together.

When the Blacksword had passed, Tuor and Voronwë held on their way for a while, though day had come; for the memory of his grief was heavy upon them, and they could not endure to remain beside the defilement of Ivrin. But before long they sought a hiding-place, for all the land was filled now with a foreboding of evil. They slept little and uneasily, and as the day wore it grew dark and a great snow fell, and with the night came a grinding frost. Thereafter the snow and ice relented not at all, and for five months the Fell Winter, long remembered, held the North in bonds. Now Tuor and Voronwë were tormented by the cold, and feared to be revealed by the snow to hunting enemies, or to fall into hidden dangers treacherously cloaked. Nine days they held on, ever slower and more painfully, and Voronwë turned somewhat north, until they crossed the three well-streams of Teiglin; and then he bore eastward again, leaving the mountains, and went warily, until they passed Glithui and came to the stream of Malduin, and it was frozen black.[16]

Then Tuor said to Voronwë: 'Fell is this frost, and death draws near to me, if not to you.' For they were now in evil case: it was long since they had found any food in the wild, and the waybread was dwindling; and they were cold and weary. 'Ill is it to be trapped between the Doom of the Valar and the Malice of the Enemy,' said Voronwë. 'Have I escaped the mouths of the sea but to lie under the snow?'

But Tuor said: 'How far is now to go? For at last, Voronwë, you must forgo your secrecy with me. Do you lead me straight, and whither? For if I must spend my last strength, I would know to what that may avail.'

'I have led you as straight as I safely might,' answered Voronwë. 'Know then now that Turgon dwells still in the north of the land of the Eldar, though that is believed by few. Already we draw nigh to him. Yet there are many leagues still to go, even as a bird might fly; and for us Sirion is yet to cross, and great evil, maybe, lies between. For we must come soon to the Highway that ran of old down from the Minas of King Finrod to Nargothrond.[17] There the servants of the Enemy will walk and watch.'

'I counted myself the hardiest of Men,' said Tuor, 'and I have endured many winters' woe in the mountains; but I had a cave at my back and fire then, and I doubt now my strength to go much further thus hungry through the fell weather. But let us go on as far as we may before hope fails.'

'No other choice have we,' said Voronwë, 'unless it be to lay us down here and seek the snow-sleep.'

Therefore all through that bitter day they toiled on, deeming the peril of foes less than the winter; but ever as they went they found less snow, for they were now going southward again down into the Vale of Sirion, and the Mountains of Dor-lómin were left far behind. In the deepening dusk they came to the Highway at the bottom of a tall wooded bank. Suddenly they were aware of voices, and looking out warily from the trees they saw a red light below. A company of Orcs was encamped in the midst of the road, huddled about a large wood-fire.

'*Gurth an Glamhoth!*' Tuor muttered.[18] 'Now the sword shall come from under the cloak. I will risk death for mastery of that fire, and even the meat of Orcs would be a prize.'

'Nay!' said Voronwë. 'On this quest only the cloak will serve. You must forgo the fire, or else forgo Turgon. This band is not alone in the wild: cannot your mortal sight see the far flame of other posts to the north and to the south? A tumult will bring a host upon us. Hearken to me, Tuor! It is against the law of the Hidden Kingdom that any should approach the gates with foes at their heels; and that law I will not break, neither for Ulmo's bidding, nor for death. Rouse the Orcs, and I leave you.'

'Then let them be,' said Tuor. 'But may I live yet to see the day when I need not sneak aside from a handful of Orcs like a cowed dog.'

'Come then!' said Voronwë. 'Debate no more, or they will scent us. Follow me!'

He crept then away through the trees, southward down the wind, until they were midway between that Orc-fire and the next upon the road. There he stood still a long while listening.

'I hear none moving on the road,' he said, 'but we know not what may be lurking in the shadows.' He peered forward into the gloom and shuddered. 'The air is evil,' he muttered. 'Alas! Yonder lies the land of our quest and hope of life, but death walks between.'

'Death is all about us,' said Tuor. 'But I have strength left only for the shortest road. Here I must cross, or perish. I will trust to the mantle of Ulmo, and you also it shall cover. Now I will lead!'

So saying he stole to the border of the road. Then clasping Voronwë close he cast about them both the folds of the grey cloak of the Lord of Waters, and stepped forth.

All was still. The cold wind sighed as it swept down the ancient road. Then suddenly it too fell silent. In the pause Tuor felt a

change in the air, as if the breath from the land of Morgoth had
failed a while, and faint as a memory of the Sea came a breeze from
the West. As a grey mist on the wind they passed over the stony
street and entered a thicket on its eastern brink.

All at once from near at hand there came a wild cry, and many
others along the borders of the road answered it. A harsh horn blared,
and there was the sound of running feet. But Tuor held on. He had
learned enough of the tongue of the Orcs in his captivity to know the
meaning of those cries: the watchers had scented them and heard
them, but they were not seen. The hunt was out. Desperately he
stumbled and crept forward with Voronwë at his side, up a long slope
deep in whin and whortleberry among knots of rowan and low birch.
At the top of the ridge they halted, listening to the shouts behind and
the crashing of the Orcs in the undergrowth below.

Beside them was a boulder that reared its head out of a tangle of
heath and brambles, and beneath it was such a lair as a hunted beast
might seek and hope there to escape pursuit, or at the least with its
back to stone to sell its life dearly. Down into the dark shadow Tuor
drew Voronwë, and side by side under the grey cloak they lay and
panted like tired foxes. No word they spoke; all their heed was in
their ears.

The cries of the hunters grew fainter; for the Orcs thrust never
deep into the wild lands at either hand, but swept rather down and
up the road. They recked little of stray fugitives, but spies they
feared and the scouts of armed foes; for Morgoth had set a guard on
the highway, not to ensnare Tuor and Voronwë (of whom as yet he
knew nothing) nor any coming from the West, but to watch for the
Blacksword, lest he should escape and pursue the captives of
Nargothrond, bringing help, it might be, out of Doriath.

The night passed, and the brooding silence lay again upon the
empty lands. Weary and spent Tuor slept beneath Ulmo's cloak; but
Voronwë crept forth and stood like a stone silent, unmoving, piercing
the shadows with his Elvish eyes. At the break of day he woke Tuor,
and he creeping out saw that the weather had indeed for a time
relented, and the black clouds were rolled aside. There was a red
dawn, and he could see far before him the tops of strange mountains
glinting against the eastern fire.

Then Voronwë said in a low voice: '*Alae! Ered en Echoriath, ered
e·mbar nin!*'[19] For he knew that he looked on the Encircling Mountains and the walls of the realm of Turgon. Below them, eastward, in
a deep and shadowy vale lay Sirion the fair, renowned in song; and
beyond, wrapped in mist, a grey land climbed from the river to the

broken hills at the mountains' feet. 'Yonder lies Dimbar,' said Voronwë. 'Would we were there! For there our foes seldom dare to walk. Or so it was, while the power of Ulmo was strong in Sirion. But all may now be changed[20] – save the peril of the river: it is already deep and swift, and even for the Eldar dangerous to cross. But I have led you well; for there gleams the Ford of Brithiach, yet a little southward, where the East Road that of old ran all the way from Taras in the West made the passage of the river. None now dare to use it save in desperate need, neither Elf nor Man nor Orc, since that road leads to Dungortheb and the land of dread between the Gorgoroth and the Girdle of Melian; and long since has it faded into the wild, or dwindled to a track among weeds and trailing thorns.'[21]

Then Tuor looked as Voronwë pointed, and far away he caught the glimmer as of open waters under the brief light of dawn; but beyond loomed a darkness, where the great forest of Brethil climbed away southward into a distant highland. Now warily they made their way down the valley-side, until at last they came to the ancient road descending from the waymeet on the borders of Brethil, where it crossed the highway from Nargothrond. Then Tuor saw that they were come close to Sirion. The banks of its deep channel fell away in that place, and its waters, choked by a great waste of stones,[22] were spread out into broad shallows, full of the murmur of fretting streams. Then after a little the river gathered together again, and delving a new bed flowed away towards the forest, and far off vanished into a deep mist that his eye could not pierce; for there lay, though he knew it not, the north march of Doriath within the shadow of the Girdle of Melian.

At once Tuor would hasten to the ford, but Voronwë restrained him, saying: 'Over the Brithiach we may not go in open day, nor while any doubt of pursuit remains.'

'Then shall we sit here and rot?' said Tuor. 'For such doubt will remain while the realm of Morgoth endures. Come! Under the shadow of the cloak of Ulmo we must go forward.'

Still Voronwë hesitated, and looked back westward; but the track behind was deserted, and all about was quiet save for the rush of the waters. He looked up, and the sky was grey and empty, for not even a bird was moving. Then suddenly his face brightened with joy, and he cried aloud: 'It is well! The Brithiach is guarded still by the enemies of the Enemy. The Orcs will not follow us here; and under the cloak we may pass now without more doubt.'

'What new thing have you seen?' said Tuor.

'Short is the sight of Mortal Men!' said Voronwë. 'I see the Eagles of the Crissaegrim; and they are coming hither. Watch a while!'

Then Tuor stood at gaze; and soon high in the air he saw three shapes beating on strong wings down from the distant mountain-peaks now wreathed again in cloud. Slowly they descended in great circles, and then stooped suddenly upon the wayfarers; but before Voronwë could call to them they turned with a wide sweep and rush, and flew northward along the line of the river.

'Now let us go,' said Voronwë. 'If there be any Orc nearby, he will lie cowering nose to ground, until the eagles have gone far away.'

Swiftly down a long slope they hastened, and passed over the Brithiach, walking often dryfoot upon shelves of shingle, or wading in the shoals no more than knee-deep. The water was clear and very cold, and there was ice upon the shallow pools, where the wandering streams had lost their way among the stones; but never, not even in the Fell Winter of the Fall of Nargothrond, could the deadly breath of the North freeze the main flood of Sirion.[23]

On the far side of the ford they came to a gully, as it were the bed of an old stream, in which no water now flowed; yet once, it seemed, a torrent had cloven its deep channel, coming down from the north out of the mountains of the Echoriath, and bearing thence all the stones of the Brithiach down into Sirion.

'At last beyond hope we find it!' cried Voronwë. 'See! Here is the mouth of the Dry River, and that is the road we must take.'[24] Then they passed into the gully, and as it turned north and the slopes of the land went steeply up, so its sides rose upon either hand, and Tuor stumbled in the dim light among the stones with which its rough bed was strewn. 'If this is a road,' he said, 'it is an evil one for the weary.'

'Yet it is the road to Turgon,' said Voronwë.

'Then the more do I marvel,' said Tuor, 'that its entrance lies open and unguarded. I had looked to find a great gate, and strength of guard.'

'That you shall yet see,' said Voronwë. 'This is but the approach. A road I named it; yet upon it none have passed for more than three hundred years, save messengers few and secret, and all the craft of the Noldor has been expended to conceal it, since the Hidden People entered in. Does it lie open? Would you have known it, if you had not had one of the Hidden Kingdom for a guide? Or would you have guessed it to be but the work of the weathers and the waters of the wilderness? And are there not the Eagles, as you have seen? They are the folk of Thorondor, who dwelt once even on Thangorodrim ere Morgoth grew so mighty, and dwell now in the Mountains of Turgon since the fall of Fingolfin.[25] They alone save the Noldor know the Hidden Kingdom and guard the skies above it, though as yet no servant of the Enemy has dared to fly into the high airs; and they bring much news to the King of all that moves in the lands without. Had we been Orcs, doubt not that we should have been seized, and cast from a great height upon the pitiless rocks.'

'I doubt it not,' said Tuor. 'But it comes into my mind to wonder also whether news will not now come to Turgon of our approach swifter than we. And if that be good or ill, you alone can say.'

'Neither good nor ill,' said Voronwë. 'For we cannot pass the Guarded Gate unmarked, be we looked for or no; and if we come there the Guards will need no report that we are not Orcs. But to pass we shall need a greater plea than that. For you do not guess, Tuor, the peril that we then shall face. Blame me not, as one un-warned, for what may then betide; may the power of the Lord of Waters be shown indeed! For in that hope alone have I been willing to guide you, and if it fails then more surely shall we die than by all the perils of wild and winter.'

But Tuor said: 'Forebode no more. Death in the wild is certain; and death at the Gate is yet in doubt to me, for all your words. Lead me still on!'

Many miles they toiled on in the stones of the Dry River, until they could go no further, and the evening brought darkness into the deep cleft; they climbed out then on to the east bank, and they had now come into the tumbled hills that lay at the feet of the mountains. And looking up Tuor saw that they towered up in a fashion other than that of any mountains that he had seen; for their sides were like sheer walls, piled each one above and behind the lower, as were they great towers of many-storeyed precipices. But the day had waned, and all the lands were grey and misty, and the Vale of Sirion was shrouded in shadow. Then Voronwë led him to a shallow cave in a hillside that looked out over the lonely slopes of Dimbar, and they crept within, and there they lay hid; and they ate their last crumbs of food, and were cold, and weary, but slept not. Thus did Tuor and Voronwë come in the dusk of the eighteenth day of Hísimë, the thirty-seventh of their journey, to the towers of the Echoriath and the threshold of Turgon, and by the power of Ulmo escaped both the Doom and the Malice.

When the first glimmer of day filtered grey amid the mists of Dimbar they crept back into the Dry River, and soon after its course turned eastward, winding up to the very walls of the mountains; and straight before them there loomed a great precipice, rising sheer and sudden from a steep slope upon which grew a tangled thicket of thorn-trees. Into this thicket the stony channel entered, and there it was still dark as night; and they halted, for the thorns grew far down the sides of the gully, and their lacing branches were a dense roof above it, so low that often Tuor and Voronwë must crawl under like beasts stealing back to their lair.

But at last, as with great labour they came to the very foot of the cliff, they found an opening, as it were the mouth of a tunnel worn in the hard rock by waters flowing from the heart of the mountains. They entered, and within there was no light, but Voronwë went steadily forward, while Tuor followed with his hand upon his shoulder, bending a little, for the roof was low. Thus for a time they went on blindly, step by step, until presently they felt the ground beneath their feet had become level and free from loose stones. Then they halted and breathed deeply, as they stood listening. The air seemed fresh and wholesome, and they were aware of a great space around and above them; but all was silent, and not even the drip of water could be heard. It seemed to Tuor that Voronwë was troubled and in doubt, and he whispered: 'Where then is the Guarded Gate? Or have we indeed now passed it?'

'Nay,' said Voronwë. 'Yet I wonder, for it is strange that any incomer should creep thus far unchallenged. I fear some stroke in the dark.'

But their whispers aroused the sleeping echoes, and they were enlarged and multiplied, and ran in the roof and the unseen walls, hissing and murmuring as the sound of many stealthy voices. And even as the echoes died in the stone, Tuor heard out of the heart of the darkness a voice speak in the Elven-tongues: first in the High Speech of the Noldor, which he knew not; and then in the tongue of Beleriand, though in a manner somewhat strange to his ears, as of a people long sundered from their kin.[26]

'Stand!' it said. 'Stir not! Or you will die, be you foes or friends.'

'We are friends,' said Voronwë.

'Then do as we bid,' said the voice.

The echo of their voices rolled into silence. Voronwë and Tuor stood still, and it seemed to Tuor that many slow minutes passed, and a fear was in his heart such as no other peril of his road had brought. Then there came the beat of feet, growing to a tramping loud as the march of trolls in that hollow place. Suddenly an elven-lantern was unhooded, and its bright ray was turned upon Voronwë before him, but nothing else could Tuor see save a dazzling star in the darkness; and he knew that while that beam was upon him he could not move, neither to flee nor to run forward.

For a moment they were held thus in the eye of the light, and then the voice spoke again, saying: 'Show your faces!' And Voronwë cast back his hood, and his face shone in the ray, hard and clear, as if graven in stone; and Tuor marvelled to see its beauty. Then he spoke proudly, saying: 'Know you not whom you see? I am Voronwë son of Aranwë of the House of Fingolfin. Or am I forgotten in my own land after a few years? Far beyond the thought of Middle-earth I have wandered, yet I remember your voice, Elemmakil.'

'Then Voronwë will remember also the laws of his land,' said the voice. 'Since by command he went forth, he has the right to return. But not to lead hither any stranger. By that deed his right is void, and he must be led as a prisoner to the king's judgement. As for the stranger, he shall be slain or held captive at the judgement of the Guard. Lead him hither that I may judge.'

Then Voronwë led Tuor towards the light, and as they drew near many Noldor, mail-clad and armed, stepped forward out of the darkness and surrounded them with drawn swords. And Elemmakil, captain of the Guard, who bore the bright lamp, looked long and closely at them.

'This is strange in you, Voronwë,' he said. 'We were long friends. Why then would you set me thus cruelly between the law and my friendship? If you had led hither unbidden one of the other houses of the Noldor, that were enough. But you have brought to knowledge of the Way a mortal Man – for by his eyes I perceive his kin. Yet free can he never again go, knowing the secret; and as one of alien kin that has dared to enter, I should slay him – even though he be your friend and dear to you.'

'In the wide lands without, Elemmakil, many strange things may befall one, and tasks unlooked for be laid on one,' Voronwë answered. 'Other shall the wanderer return than as he set forth. What I have done, I have done under command greater than the law of the Guard. The King alone should judge me, and him that comes with me.'

Then Tuor spoke, and feared no longer. 'I come with Voronwë son of Aranwë, because he was appointed to be my guide by the Lord of Waters. To this end was he delivered from the wrath of the Sea and the Doom of the Valar. For I bear from Ulmo an errand to the son of Fingolfin, and to him will I speak it.'

Thereat Elemmakil looked in wonder upon Tuor. 'Who then are you?' he said. 'And whence come you?'

'I am Tuor son of Huor of the House of Hador and the kindred of Húrin, and these names, I am told, are not unknown in the Hidden Kingdom. From Nevrast I have come through many perils to seek it.'

'From Nevrast?' said Elemmakil. 'It is said that none dwell there, since our people departed.'

'It is said truly,' answered Tuor. 'Empty and cold stand the courts of Vinyamar. Yet thence I come. Bring me now to him that built those halls of old.'

'In matters so great judgement is not mine,' said Elemmakil. 'Therefore I will lead you to the light where more may be revealed, and I will deliver you to the Warden of the Great Gate.'

Then he spoke in command, and Tuor and Voronwë were set between tall guards, two before and three behind them; and their captain led them from the cavern of the Outer Guard, and they passed, as it seemed, into a straight passage, and there walked long upon a level floor, until a pale light gleamed ahead. Thus they came at length to a wide arch with tall pillars upon either hand, hewn in the rock, and between hung a great portcullis of crossed wooden bars, marvellously carved and studded with nails of iron.

Elemmakil touched it, and it rose silently, and they passed through; and Tuor saw that they stood at the end of a ravine, the like of which he had never before beheld or imagined in his thought, long though he had walked in the wild mountains of the North; for beside the Orfalch Echor Cirith Ninniach was but a groove in the rock. Here the hands of the Valar themselves, in ancient wars of the world's beginning, had wrested the great mountains asunder, and the sides of the rift were sheer as if axe-cloven, and they towered up to heights unguessable. There far aloft ran a ribbon of sky, and against its deep blue stood black peaks and jagged pinnacles, remote but hard, cruel as spears. Too high were those mighty walls for the winter sun to overlook, and though it was now full morning faint stars glimmered above the mountain-tops, and down below all was dim, but for the pale light of lamps set beside the climbing road. For the floor of the ravine sloped steeply up, eastward, and upon the left hand Tuor saw beside the stream-bed a wide way, laid and paved with stone, winding upward till it vanished into shadow.

'You have passed the First Gate, the Gate of Wood,' said Elemmakil. 'There lies the way. We must hasten.'

How far that deep road ran Tuor could not guess, and as he stared onward a great weariness came upon him like a cloud. A chill wind hissed over the faces of the stones, and he drew his cloak close about him. 'Cold blows the wind from the Hidden Kingdom!' he said.

'Yea, indeed,' said Voronwë; 'to a stranger it might seem that pride has made the servants of Turgon pitiless. Long and hard seem the leagues of the Seven Gates to the hungry and wayworn.'

'If our law were less stern, long ago guile and hatred would have entered and destroyed us. That you know well,' said Elemmakil. 'But we are not pitiless. Here there is no food, and the stranger may not go back through a gate that he has passed. Endure then a little, and at the Second Gate you shall be eased.'

'It is well,' said Tuor, and he went forward as he was bidden. After a little he turned, and saw that Elemmakil alone followed with Voronwë. 'There is no need more of guards,' said Elemmakil, reading his thought. 'From the Orfalch there is no escape for Elf or Man, and no returning.'

Thus they went on up the steep way, sometimes by long stairs, sometimes by winding slopes, under the daunting shadow of the cliff, until some half-league from the Wooden Gate Tuor saw that the way was barred by a great wall built across the ravine from side to side, with stout towers of stone at either hand. In the wall was a great archway above the road, but it seemed that masons had blocked it with a single mighty stone. As they drew near its dark and polished face gleamed in the light of a white lamp that hung above the midst of the arch.

'Here stands the Second Gate, the Gate of Stone,' said Elemmakil; and going up to it he thrust lightly upon it. It turned upon an unseen pivot, until its edge was towards them, and the way was open upon either side; and they passed through, into a court where stood many armed guards clad in grey. No word was spoken, but Elemmakil led his charges to a chamber beneath the northern tower; and there food and wine was brought to them, and they were permitted to rest a while.

'Scant may the fare seem,' said Elemmakil to Tuor. 'But if your claim be proved, hereafter it shall richly be amended.'

'It is enough,' said Tuor. 'Faint were the heart that needed better healing.' And indeed such refreshment did he find in the drink and food of the Noldor that soon he was eager to go on.

After a little space they came to a wall yet higher and stronger than before, and in it was set the Third Gate, the Gate of Bronze: a great twofold door hung with shields and plates of bronze, wherein were wrought many figures and strange signs. Upon the wall above its lintel were three square towers, roofed and clad with copper that by some device of smith-craft were ever bright and gleamed as fire in the rays of the red lamps ranged like torches along the wall. Again silently they passed the gate, and saw in the court beyond a yet greater company of guards in mail that glowed like dull fire; and the blades of their axes were red. Of the kindred of the Sindar of Nevrast for the most part were those that held this gate.

Now they came to the most toilsome road, for in the midst of the Orfalch the slope was at the steepest, and as they climbed Tuor saw the mightiest of the walls looming dark above him. Thus at last they drew near the Fourth Gate, the Gate of Writhen Iron. High and black was the wall, and lit with no lamps. Four towers of iron stood upon it, and between the two inner towers was set an image of a great eagle wrought in iron, even the likeness of King Thorondor himself, as he would alight upon a mountain from the high airs. But as Tuor stood before the gate it seemed to his wonder that he was looking through boughs and stems of imperishable trees into a pale glade of the Moon. For a light came through the traceries of the gate, which were wrought and hammered into the shapes of trees with writhing roots and woven branches laden with leaves and flowers. And as he passed through he saw how this could be; for the wall was of great thickness, and there was not one grill but three in line, so set that to one who approached in the middle of the way each formed part of the device; but the light beyond was the light of day.

For they had climbed now to a great height above the lowlands where they began, and beyond the Iron Gate the road ran almost level. Moreover, they had passed the crown and heart of the Echoriath, and the mountain-towers now fell swiftly down towards the inner hills, and the ravine opened wider, and its sides became less sheer. Its long shoulders were mantled with white snow, and the light of the sky snow-mirrored came white as moonlight through a glimmering mist that filled the air.

Now they passed through the lines of the Iron Guards that stood behind the Gate; black were their mantles and their mail and long shields, and their faces were masked with vizors bearing each an eagle's beak. Then Elemmakil went before them and they followed him into the pale light; and Tuor saw beside the way a sward of grass, where like stars bloomed the white flowers of *uilos*, the Ever-mind that knows no season and withers not;[27] and thus in wonder and lightening of heart he was brought to the Gate of Silver.

The wall of the Fifth Gate was built of white marble, and was low

and broad, and its parapet was a trellis of silver between five great
globes of marble; and there stood many archers robed in white.
The gate was in shape as three parts of a circle, and wrought of
silver and pearl of Nevrast in likenesses of the Moon; but above the
Gate upon the midmost globe stood an image of the White Tree
Telperion, wrought of silver and malachite, with flowers made of
great pearls of Balar.[28] And beyond the Gate in a wide court paved
with marble, green and white, stood archers in silver mail and white-
crested helms, a hundred upon either hand. Then Elemmakil led
Tuor and Voronwë through their silent ranks, and they entered
upon a long white road, that ran straight towards the Sixth Gate;
and as they went the grass-sward became wider, and among the
white stars of *uilos* there opened many small flowers like eyes of
gold.

So they came to the Golden Gate, the last of the ancient gates of
Turgon that were wrought before the Nirnaeth; and it was much
like the Gate of Silver, save that the wall was built of yellow marble,
and the globes and parapet were of red gold; and there were six
globes, and in the midst upon a golden pyramid was set an image of
Laurelin, the Tree of the Sun, with flowers wrought of topaz in long
clusters upon chains of gold. And the Gate itself was adorned with
discs of gold, many-rayed, in likenesses of the Sun, set amid devices
of garnet and topaz and yellow diamonds. In the court beyond were
arrayed three hundred archers with long bows, and their mail was
gilded, and tall golden plumes rose from their helmets; and their
great round shields were red as flame.

Now sunlight fell upon the further road, for the walls of the hills
were low on either side, and green, but for the snows upon their
tops; and Elemmakil hastened forward, for the way was short to the
Seventh Gate, named the Great, the Gate of Steel that Maeglin
wrought after the return from the Nirnaeth, across the wide entrance
to the Orfalch Echor.

No wall stood there, but on either hand were two round towers
of great height, many-windowed, tapering in seven storeys to a turret
of bright steel, and between the towers there stood a mighty fence of
steel that rusted not, but glittered cold and white. Seven great
pillars of steel there were, tall with the height and girth of strong
young trees, but ending in a bitter spike that rose to the sharpness
of a needle; and between the pillars were seven cross-bars of steel,
and in each space seven times seven rods of steel upright, with heads
like the broad blades of spears. But in the centre, above the midmost
pillar and the greatest, was raised a mighty image of the king-helm

of Turgon, the Crown of the Hidden Kingdom, set about with diamonds.

No gate or door could Tuor see in this mighty hedge of steel, but as he drew near through the spaces between its bars there came, as it seemed to him, a dazzling light, and he shaded his eyes, and stood still in dread and wonder. But Elemmakil went forward, and no gate opened to his touch; but he struck upon a bar, and the fence rang like a harp of many strings, giving forth clear notes in harmony that ran from tower to tower.

Straightway there issued riders from the towers, but before those of the north tower came one upon a white horse; and he dismounted and strode towards them. And high and noble as was Elemmakil, greater and more lordly was Ecthelion, Lord of the Fountains, at that time Warden of the Great Gate.[29] All in silver was he clad, and upon his shining helm there was set a spike of steel pointed with a diamond; and as his esquire took his shield it shimmered as if it were bedewed with drops of rain, that were indeed a thousand studs of crystal.

Elemmakil saluted him and said: 'Here have I brought Voronwë Aranwion, returning from Balar; and here is the stranger that he has led hither, who demands to see the King.'

Then Ecthelion turned to Tuor, but he drew his cloak about him and stood silent, facing him; and it seemed to Voronwë that a mist mantled Tuor and his stature was increased, so that the peak of his high hood over-topped the helm of the Elf-lord, as it were the crest of a grey sea-wave riding to the land. But Ecthelion bent his bright glance upon Tuor, and after a silence he spoke gravely, saying:[30] 'You have come to the Last Gate. Know then that no stranger who passes it shall ever go out again, save by the door of death.'

'Speak not ill-boding! If the messenger of the Lord of Waters go by that door, then all those who dwell here will follow him. Lord of the Fountains, hinder not the messenger of the Lord of Waters!'

Then Voronwë and all those who stood near looked again in wonder at Tuor, marvelling at his words and voice. And to Voronwë it seemed as if he heard a great voice, but as of one who called from afar off. But to Tuor it seemed that he listened to himself speaking, as if another spoke with his mouth.

For a while Ecthelion stood silent, looking at Tuor, and slowly awe filled his face, as if in the grey shadow of Tuor's cloak he saw visions from far away. Then he bowed, and went to the fence and laid hands upon it, and gates opened inward on either side of the pillar of the Crown. Then Tuor passed through, and coming to a high sward that looked out over the valley beyond, he beheld a vision of Gondolin amid the white snow. And so entranced was he that for long he could look at nothing else; for he saw before him at last the vision of his desire out of dreams of longing.

Thus he stood and spoke no word. Silent upon either hand stood a host of the army of Gondolin; all of the seven kinds of the Seven Gates were there represented; but their captains and chieftains were upon horses, white and grey. Then even as they gazed on Tuor in wonder, his cloak fell down, and he stood there before them in the mighty livery of Nevrast. And many were there who had seen Turgon himself set these things upon the wall behind the High Seat of Vinyamar.

Then Ecthelion said at last: 'Now no further proof is needed; and even the name he claims as son of Huor matters less than this clear truth, that he comes from Ulmo himself.'[31]

## NOTES

1   In *The Silmarillion* p. 196 it is said that when the Havens of Brithombar and Eglarest were destroyed in the year after the Nirnaeth Arnoediad those of the Elves of the Falas that escaped went with Círdan to the Isle of Balar, 'and they made a refuge for all that could come thither; for they kept a foothold also at the Mouths of Sirion, and there many light and swift ships lay hid in the creeks and waters where the reeds were dense as a forest'.

2   The blue-shining lamps of the Noldorin Elves are referred to else-where, though they do not appear in the published text of *The Silmarillion*. In earlier versions of the tale of Túrin Gwindor, the Elf of Nargothrond who escaped from Angband and was found by Beleg in the forest of Taur-nu-Fuin, possessed one of these lamps (it can be seen in my father's painting of that meeting, see *Pictures by J. R. R. Tolkien*, 1979, no. 37); and it was the overturning and uncovering of Gwindor's lamp so that its light shone out that showed Túrin the face of Beleg whom he had killed. In a note on the story of Gwindor they are called 'Fëanorian lamps', of which the Noldor themselves did not know the secret; and they are there described as 'crystals hung in a fine chain net, the crystals being ever shining with an inner blue radiance'.

3   'The sun shall shine upon your path.' – In the very much briefer story told in *The Silmarillion*, there is no account of how Tuor found the Gate of the Noldor, nor any mention of the Elves Gelmir and Arminas. They appear however in the tale of Túrin (*The Silmarillion* p. 212) as the messengers who brought Ulmo's warning to Nargoth-

rond; and there they are said to be of the people of Finarfin's son
Angrod, who after the Dagor Bragollach dwelt in the south with
Círdan the Shipwright. In a longer version of the story of their
coming to Nargothrond, Arminas, comparing Túrin unfavourably
with his kinsman, speaks of having met Tuor 'in the wastes of
Dor-lómin'; see p. 161.

4   In *The Silmarillion* pp. 80–1 it is told that when Morgoth and
Ungoliant struggled in this region for possession of the Silmarils
'Morgoth sent forth a terrible cry, that echoed in the mountains.
Therefore that region was called Lammoth; for the echoes of his
voice dwelt there ever after, so that any who cried aloud in that land
awoke them, and all the waste between the hills and the sea was
filled with a clamour as of voices in anguish.' Here, on the other hand,
the conception is rather that any sound uttered there was magnified
in its own nature; and this idea is clearly also present at the beginning
of ch. 13 of *The Silmarillion*, where (in a passage very similar to the
present) 'even as the Noldor set foot upon the strand their cries were
taken up into the hills and multiplied, so that a clamour as of countless mighty voices filled all the coasts of the North'. It seems that
according to the one 'tradition' Lammoth and Ered Lómin (Echoing
Mountains) were so named from their retaining the echoes of
Morgoth's dreadful cry in the toils of Ungoliant; while according to
the other the names are simply descriptive of the nature of sounds
in that region.

5   Cf. *The Silmarillion* p. 215: 'And Túrin hastened along the ways to
the north, through the lands now desolate between Narog and Teiglin,
and the Fell Winter came down to meet him; for in that year snow
fell ere autumn was passed, and spring came late and cold.'

6   In *The Silmarillion* p. 126 it is told that when Ulmo appeared to
Turgon at Vinyamar and bade him go to Gondolin, he said: 'Thus
it may come to pass that the curse of the Noldor shall find thee too
ere the end, and treason awake within thy walls. Then they shall be
in peril of fire. But if this peril draweth nigh indeed, then even from
Nevrast one shall come to warn thee, and from him beyond ruin
and fire hope shall be born for Elves and Men. Leave therefore in
this house arms and a sword, that in years to come he may find them,
and thus shalt thou know him, and not be deceived.' And Ulmo
declared to Turgon of what kind and stature should be the helm
and mail and sword that he left behind.

7   Tuor was the father of Eärendil, who was the father of Elros Tar-
Minyatur, the first King of Númenor.

8   This must refer to the warning of Ulmo brought to Nargothrond by
Gelmir and Arminas; see pp. 159 ff.

9   The Shadowy Isles are very probably the Enchanted Isles described
at the end of *The Silmarillion* ch. 11, which were 'strung as a net

in the Shadowy Seas from the north to the south' at the time of the Hiding of Valinor.

10 Cf. *The Silmarillion* p. 196: 'At the bidding of Turgon [after the Nirnaeth Arnoediad] Círdan built seven swift ships, and they sailed out into the West; but no tidings of them came ever back to Balar, save of one, and the last. The mariners of that ship toiled long in the sea, and returning at last in despair they foundered in a great storm within sight of the coasts of Middle-earth; but one of them was saved by Ulmo from the wrath of Ossë, and the waves bore him up, and cast him ashore in Nevrast. His name was Voronwë; and he was one of those that Turgon sent forth as messengers from Gondolin.' Cf. also *The Silmarillion* p. 239.

11 The words of Ulmo to Turgon appear in *The Silmarillion* ch. 15 in the form: 'Remember that the true hope of the Noldor lieth in the West and cometh from the Sea,' and 'But if this peril draweth nigh indeed, then even from Nevrast one shall come to warn thee.'

12 Nothing is told in *The Silmarillion* of the further fate of Voronwë after his return to Gondolin with Tuor; but in the original story ('Of Tuor and the Exiles of Gondolin') he was one of those who escaped from the sack of the city – as is implied by the words of Tuor here.

13 Cf. *The Silmarillion* p. 159: '[Turgon] believed also that the ending of the Siege was the beginning of the downfall of the Noldor, unless aid should come; and he sent companies of the Gondolindrim in secret to the mouths of Sirion and the Isle of Balar. There they built ships, and set sail into the uttermost West upon Turgon's errand, seeking for Valinor, to ask for pardon and aid of the Valar; and they besought the birds of the sea to guide them. But the seas were wild and wide, and shadow and enchantment lay upon them; and Valinor was hidden. Therefore none of the messengers of Turgon came into the West, and many were lost and few returned.'

In one of the 'constituent texts' of *The Silmarillion* it is said that although the Noldor 'had not the art of shipbuilding, and all the craft that they built foundered or were driven back by the winds', yet after the Dagor Bragollach 'Turgon ever maintained a secret refuge upon the Isle of Balar', and when after the Nirnaeth Arnoediad Círdan and the remnant of his people fled from Brithombar and Eglarest to Balar 'they mingled with Turgon's outpost there'. But this element in the story was rejected, and thus in the published text of *The Silmarillion* there is no reference to the establishment of dwellings on Balar by Elves from Gondolin.

14 The woods of Núath are not mentioned in *The Silmarillion* and are not marked on the map that accompanies it. They extended westward from the upper waters of the Narog towards the source of the river Nenning.

15  Cf. *The Silmarillion* pp. 209–10: 'Finduilas daughter of Orodreth the
    King knew [Gwindor] and welcomed him, for she had loved him
    before the Nirnaeth, and so greatly did Gwindor love her beauty that
    he named her Faelivrin, which is the gleam of the sun on the pools
    of Ivrin.'

16  The river Glithui is not mentioned in *The Silmarillion* and is not
    named on the map, though it is shown: a tributary of the Teiglin
    joining that river some way north of the inflowing of the Malduin.

17  This road is referred to in *The Silmarillion*, p. 205: 'The ancient
    road . . . that led through the long defile of Sirion, past the isle where
    Minas Tirith of Finrod had stood, and so through the land between
    Malduin and Sirion, and on through the eaves of Brethil to the
    Crossings of Teiglin.'

18  'Death to the *Glamhoth*!' This name, though it does not occur in
    *The Silmarillion* or in *The Lord of the Rings*, was a general term in
    the Sindarin language for Orcs. The meaning is 'din-horde', 'host of
    tumult'; cf. Gandalf's sword *Glamdring*, and *Tol-in-Gaurhoth*, the Isle
    of (the host of) Werewolves.

19  *Echoriath*: the Encircling Mountains about the plain of Gondolin.
    *ered e·mbar nin*: the mountains of my home.

20  In *The Silmarillion*, pp. 200–1, Beleg of Doriath said to Túrin (at a
    time some years before that of the present narrative) that Orcs had
    made a road through the Pass of Anach, 'and Dimbar which used
    to be at peace is falling under the Black Hand'.

21  By this road Maeglin and Aredhel fled to Gondolin pursued by Eöl
    (*The Silmarillion* ch. 16); and afterwards Celegorm and Curufin took
    it when they were expelled from Nargothrond (*ibid.* p. 176). Only in
    the present text is there any mention of its westward extension to
    Turgon's ancient home at Vinyamar under Mount Taras; and its
    course is not marked on the map from its junction with the old
    south road to Nargothrond at the north-western edge of Brethil.

22  The name *Brithiach* contains the element *brith* 'gravel', as also in
    the river *Brithon* and the haven of *Brithombar*.

23  In a parallel version of the text at this point, almost certainly rejected
    in favour of the one printed, the travellers did not cross the Sirion
    by the Ford of Brithiach, but reached the river several leagues to the
    north of it. 'They trod a toilsome path to the brink of the river, and
    there Voronwë cried: "See a wonder! Both good and ill does it
    forebode. Sirion is frozen, though no tale tells of the like since the
    coming of the Eldar out of the East. Thus we may pass and save
    many weary miles, too long for our strength. Yet thus also others
    may have passed, or may follow." ' They crossed the river on the ice
    unhindered, and 'thus did the counsels of Ulmo turn the malice of
    the Enemy to avail, for the way was shortened, and at the end of

their hope and strength Tuor and Voronwë came at last to the Dry
River at its issuing from the skirts of the mountains'.

24   Cf. *The Silmarillion* p. 125: 'But there was a deep way under the
mountains delved in the darkness of the world by waters that flowed
out to join the streams of Sirion; and this way Turgon found, and so
came to the green plain amid the mountains, and saw the island-hill
that stood there of hard smooth stone; for the vale had been a great
lake in ancient days.'

25   It is not said in *The Silmarillion* that the great eagles ever dwelt on
Thangorodrim. In ch. 13 (p. 110) Manwë 'sent forth the race of
Eagles, commanding them to dwell in the crags of the North, and to
keep watch upon Morgoth'; while in ch. 18 (p. 154) Thorondor 'came
hasting from his eyrie among the peaks of the Crissaegrim' for the
rescue of Fingolfin's body before the gates of Angband. Cf. also *The
Return of the King* VI 4: 'Old Thorondor, who built his eyries in the
inaccessible peaks of the Encircling Mountains when Middle-earth
was young.' In all probability the conception of Thorondor's dwelling
at first upon Thangorodrim, which is found also in an early Silmarillion text, was later abandoned.

26   In *The Silmarillion* nothing is said specifically concerning the speech
of the Elves of Gondolin; but this passage suggests that for some of
them the High Speech (Quenya) was in ordinary use. It is stated in
a late linguistic essay that Quenya was in daily use in Turgon's house,
and was the childhood speech of Eärendil; but that 'for most of the
people of Gondolin it had become a language of books, and as the
other Noldor they used Sindarin in daily speech'. Cf. *The Silmarillion*
p. 129: after the edict of Thingol 'the Exiles took the Sindarin tongue
in all their daily uses, and the High Speech of the West was spoken
only by the lords of the Noldor among themselves. Yet that speech
lived ever as a language of lore, wherever any of that people dwelt.'

27   These were the flowers that bloomed abundantly on the burial mounds
of the Kings of Rohan below Edoras, and which Gandalf named in
the language of the Rohirrim (as translated into Old English) *simbelmynë*, that is 'Evermind', 'for they blossom in all the seasons of the
year, and grow where dead men rest'. (*The Two Towers* III 6.) The
Elvish name *uilos* is only given in this passage, but the word is found
also in *Amon Uilos*, as the Quenya name *Oiolossë* ('Ever-snow-white',
the Mountain of Manwë) was rendered into Sindarin. In 'Cirion and
Eorl' the flower is given another Elvish name, *alfirin* (p. 303).

28   In *The Silmarillion* p. 92 it is said that Thingol rewarded the Dwarves
of Belegost with many pearls: 'These Círdan gave to him, for they
were got in great number in the shallow waters about the Isle of
Balar.'

29   Ecthelion of the Fountain is mentioned in *The Silmarillion* as one
of Turgon's captains who guarded the flanks of the host of Gondolin

in their retreat down Sirion from the Nirnaeth Arnoediad, and as the slayer of Gothmog Lord of Balrogs, by whom he himself was slain, in the assault on the city.

30　From this point the carefully-written, though much-emended, manuscript ceases, and the remainder of the narrative is hastily scribbled on a scrap of paper.

31　Here the narrative finally comes to an end, and there remain only some hasty jottings indicating the course of the story:

Tuor asked the name of the City, and was told its seven names. (It is notable, and no doubt intentional, that the name Gondolin is never once used in the narrative until the very end (p. 51): always it is called the Hidden Kingdom or the Hidden City). Ecthelion gave orders for the sounding of the signal, and trumpets were blown on the towers of the Great Gate, echoing in the hills. After a hush, they heard far off answering trumpets blown upon the city walls. Horses were brought (a grey horse for Tuor); and they rode to Gondolin.

A description of Gondolin was to follow, of the stairs up to its high platform, and its great gate; of the mounds (this word is uncertain) of mallorns, birches, and evergreen trees; of the Place of the Fountain, the King's tower on a pillared arcade, the King's house, and the banner of Fingolfin. Now Turgon himself would appear, 'tallest of all the Children of the World, save Thingol', with a white and gold sword in a ruel-bone (ivory) sheath, and welcome Tuor. Maeglin would be seen standing on the right of the throne, and Idril the King's daughter seated on the left; and Tuor would speak the message of Ulmo either 'in the hearing of all' or 'in the council-chamber'.

Other disjointed notes indicate that there was to be a description of Gondolin as seen by Tuor from far off; that Ulmo's cloak would vanish when Tuor spoke the message of Turgon; that it would be explained why there was no Queen of Gondolin; and that it was to be emphasized, either when Tuor first set eyes upon Idril or at some earlier point, that he had known or even seen few women in his life. Most of the women and all the children of Annael's company in Mithrim were sent away south; and as a thrall Tuor had seen only the proud and barbaric women of the Easterlings, who treated him as a beast, or the unhappy slaves forced to labour from childhood, for whom he had only pity.

It may be noted that later mentions of mallorns in Númenor, Lindon, and Lothlórien do not suggest, though they do not deny, that those trees flourished in Gondolin in the Elder Days (see pp. 167–8), and that the wife of Turgon, Elenwë, was lost long before in the crossing of the Helcaraxë by the host of Fingolfin (*The Silmarillion* p. 90).

# II

# NARN I HÎN HÚRIN

*The Tale of the Children of Húrin*

### The Childhood of Túrin

Hador Goldenhead was a lord of the Edain and well-beloved by the Eldar. He dwelt while his days lasted under the lordship of Fingolfin, who gave to him wide lands in that region of Hithlum which was called Dor-lómin. His daughter Glóredhel wedded Haldir son of Halmir, lord of the Men of Brethil; and at the same feast his son Galdor the Tall wedded Hareth, the daughter of Halmir.

Galdor and Hareth had two sons, Húrin and Huor. Húrin was by three years the elder, but he was shorter in stature than other men of his kin; in this he took after his mother's people, but in all else he was like Hador his grandfather, fair of face and golden-haired, strong in body and fiery of mood. But the fire in him burned steadily, and he had great endurance of will. Of all Men of the North he knew most of the counsels of the Noldor. Huor his brother was tall, the tallest of all the Edain save his own son Tuor only, and a swift runner; but if the race were long and hard Húrin would be the first home, for he ran as strongly at the end of the course as at the beginning. There was great love between the brothers, and they were seldom apart in their youth.

Húrin wedded Morwen, the daughter of Baragund son of Bregolas of the House of Bëor; and she was thus of close kin to Beren One-hand. Morwen was dark-haired and tall, and for the light of her glance and the beauty of her face men called her Eledhwen, the elven-fair; but she was somewhat stern of mood and proud. The sorrows of the House of Bëor saddened her heart; for she came as an exile to Dor-lómin from Dorthonion after the ruin of the Bragollach.

Túrin was the name of the eldest child of Húrin and Morwen, and he was born in that year in which Beren came to Doriath and found Lúthien Tinúviel, Thingol's daughter. Morwen bore a daughter also to Húrin, and she was named Urwen; but she was called Lalaith, which is Laughter, by all that knew her in her short life.

Huor wedded Rían, the cousin of Morwen; she was the daughter of

Belegund son of Bregolas. By hard fate was she born into such days, for she was gentle of heart and loved neither hunting nor war. Her love was given to trees and to the flowers of the wild, and she was a singer and a maker of songs. Two months only had she been wedded to Huor when he went with his brother to the Nirnaeth Arnoediad, and she never saw him again.[1]

In the years after the Dagor Bragollach and the fall of Fingolfin the shadow of the fear of Morgoth lengthened. But in the four hundred and sixty-ninth year after the return of the Noldor to Middle-earth there was a stirring of hope among Elves and Men; for the rumour ran among them of the deeds of Beren and Lúthien, and the putting to shame of Morgoth even upon his throne in Angband, and some said that Beren and Lúthien yet lived, or had returned from the Dead. In that year also the great counsels of Maedhros were almost complete, and with the reviving strength of the Eldar and the Edain the advance of Morgoth was stayed, and the Orcs were driven back from Beleriand. Then some began to speak of victories to come, and of redressing the Battle of the Bragollach, when Maedhros should lead forth the united hosts, and drive Morgoth underground, and seal the Doors of Angband.

But the wiser were uneasy still, fearing that Maedhros revealed his growing strength too soon, and that Morgoth would be given time enough to take counsel against him. 'Ever will some new evil be hatched in Angband beyond the guess of Elves and Men,' they said. And in the autumn of that year, to point their words, there came an ill wind from the North under leaden skies. The Evil Breath it was called, for it was pestilent; and many sickened and died in the fall of the year in the northern lands that bordered on the Anfauglith, and they were for the most part the children or the rising youth in the houses of Men.

In that year Túrin son of Húrin was yet only five years old, and Urwen his sister was three in the beginning of spring. Her hair was like the yellow lilies in the grass as she ran in the fields, and her laughter was like the sound of the merry stream that came singing out of the hills past the walls of her father's house. Nen Lalaith it was named, and after it all the people of the household called the child Lalaith, and their hearts were glad while she was among them.

But Túrin was loved less than she. He was dark-haired as his mother, and promised to be like her in mood also; for he was not merry, and spoke little, though he learned to speak early and ever seemed older than his years. Túrin was slow to forget injustice or mockery; but the fire of his father was also in him, and he could be sudden and fierce. Yet he was quick to pity, and the hurts or sadness of living things might move him to tears; and he was like his father in this also, for Morwen was stern with others as with herself. He loved his mother, for her speech to him was forthright and plain; but his father he saw little, for Húrin was often long away from home with the host of Fingon that guarded Hithlum's eastern borders, and when he returned his quick speech, full of strange words and jests and half-meanings, bewildered Túrin and made him uneasy. At that time all the warmth of his heart was for Lalaith his sister; but he played with her seldom, and liked better to guard her unseen and to watch her going upon grass or under tree, as she sang such songs as the children of the Edain made long ago when the tongue of the Elves was still fresh upon their lips.

'Fair as an Elf-child is Lalaith,' said Húrin to Morwen; 'but briefer, alas! And so fairer, maybe, or dearer.' And Túrin hearing these words pondered them, but could not understand them. For he had seen no Elf-children. None of the Eldar at that time dwelt in his father's lands, and once only had he seen them, when King Fingon and many of his lords had ridden through Dor-lómin and passed over the bridge of Nen Lalaith, glittering in silver and white.

But before the year was out the truth of his father's words was shown; for the Evil Breath came to Dor-lómin, and Túrin took sick, and lay long in a fever and dark dream. And when he was healed, for such was his fate and the strength of life that was in him, he asked for Lalaith. But his nurse answered: 'Speak no more of Lalaith, son of Húrin; but of your sister Urwen you must ask tidings of your mother.'

And when Morwen came to him, Túrin said to her: 'I am no longer sick, and I wish to see Urwen; but why must I not say Lalaith any more?'

'Because Urwen is dead, and laughter is stilled in this house,' she answered. 'But you live, son of Morwen; and so does the Enemy who has done this to us.'

She did not seek to comfort him any more than herself; for she met her grief in silence and coldness of heart. But Húrin mourned openly, and he took up his harp and would make a song of lamentation; but he could not, and he broke his harp, and going out he lifted up his hand towards the North, crying: 'Marrer of Middle-earth, would that I might see thee face to face, and mar thee as my lord Fingolfin did!'

But Túrin wept bitterly at night alone, though to Morwen he

never again spoke the name of his sister. To one friend only he turned at that time, and to him he spoke of his sorrow and the emptiness of the house. This friend was named Sador, a house-man in the service of Húrin; he was lame, and of small account. He had been a woodman, and by ill-luck or the mishandling of his axe he had hewn his right foot, and the footless leg had shrunken; and Túrin called him Labadal, which is 'Hopafoot', though the name did not displease Sador, for it was given in pity and not in scorn. Sador worked in the outbuildings, to make or mend things of little worth that were needed in the house, for he had some skill in the working of wood; and Túrin would fetch him what he lacked, to spare his leg, and sometimes he would carry off secretly some tool or piece of timber that he found unwatched, if he thought his friend might use it. Then Sador smiled, but bade him return the gifts to their places; 'Give with a free hand, but give only your own,' he said. He rewarded as he could the kindness of the child, and carved for him the figures of men and beasts; but Túrin delighted most in Sador's tales, for he had been a young man in the days of the Bragollach, and loved now to dwell upon the short days of his full manhood before his maiming.

'That was a great battle, they say, son of Húrin. I was called from my tasks in the wood in the need of that year; but I was not in the Bragollach, or I might have got my hurt with more honour. For we came too late, save to bear back the bier of the old lord, Hador, who fell in the guard of King Fingolfin. I went for a soldier after that, and I was in Eithel Sirion, the great fort of the Elf-kings, for many years; or so it seems now, and the dull years since have little to mark them. In Eithel Sirion I was when the Black King assailed it, and Galdor your father's father was the captain there in the King's stead. He was slain in that assault; and I saw your father take up his lordship and his command, though but new-come to manhood. There was a fire in him that made the sword hot in his hand, they said. Behind him we drove the Orcs into the sand; and they have not dared to come within sight of the walls since that day. But alas! my love of battle was sated, for I had seen spilled blood and wounds enough; and I got leave to come back to the woods that I yearned for. And there I got my hurt; for a man that flies from his fear may find that he has only taken a short cut to meet it.'

In this way Sador would speak to Túrin as he grew older; and Túrin began to ask many questions that Sador found hard to answer, thinking that others nearer akin should have had the teaching. And one day Túrin said to him: 'Was Lalaith indeed like an Elf-child, as my father said? And what did he mean, when he said that she was briefer?'

'Very like,' said Sador; 'for in their first youth the children of Men and Elves seem close akin. But the children of Men grow more swiftly, and their youth passes soon; such is our fate.'

Then Túrin asked him: 'What is fate?'

'As to the fate of Men,' said Sador, 'you must ask those that are wiser than Labadal. But as all can see, we weary soon and die; and by mischance many meet death even sooner. But the Elves do not weary, and they do not die save by great hurt. From wounds and griefs that would slay Men they may be healed; and even when their bodies are marred they return again, some say. It is not so with us.'

'Then Lalaith will not come back?' said Túrin. 'Where has she gone?'

'She will not come back,' said Sador. 'But where she has gone no man knows; or I do not.'

'Has it always been so? Or do we suffer some curse of the wicked King, perhaps, like the Evil Breath?'

'I do not know. A darkness lies behind us, and out of it few tales have come. The fathers of our fathers may have had things to tell, but they did not tell them. Even their names are forgotten. The Mountains stand between us and the life that they came from, flying from no man now knows what.'

'Were they afraid?' said Túrin.

'It may be,' said Sador. 'It may be that we fled from the fear of the Dark, only to find it here before us, and nowhere else to fly to but the Sea.'

'We are not afraid any longer,' said Túrin, 'not all of us. My father is not afraid, and I will not be; or at least, as my mother, I will be afraid and not show it.'

It seemed then to Sador that Túrin's eyes were not like the eyes of a child, and he thought: 'Grief is a hone to a hard mind.' But aloud he said: 'Son of Húrin and Morwen, how it will be with your heart Labadal cannot guess; but seldom and to few will you show what is in it.'

Then Túrin said: 'Perhaps it is better not to tell what you wish, if you cannot have it. But I wish, Labadal, that I were one of the Eldar. Then Lalaith might come back, and I should still be here, even if she were long away. I shall go as a soldier with an Elf-king as soon as I am able, as you did, Labadal.'

'You may learn much of them,' said Sador, and he sighed. 'They are a fair folk and wonderful, and they have a power over the hearts

of Men. And yet I think sometimes that it might have been better
if we had never met them, but had walked in lowlier ways. For already
they are ancient in knowledge; and they are proud and enduring.
In their light we are dimmed, or we burn with too quick a flame,
and the weight of our doom lies the heavier on us.'

'But my father loves them,' said Túrin, 'and he is not happy without them. He says that we have learned nearly all that we know from
them, and have been made a nobler people; and he says that the Men
that have lately come over the Mountains are hardly better than Orcs.'

'That is true,' answered Sador; 'true at least of some of us. But
the up-climbing is painful, and from high places it is easy to fall low.'

At this time Túrin was almost eight years old, in the month of
Gwaeron in the reckoning of the Edain, in the year that cannot be
forgotten. Already there were rumours among his elders of a great
mustering and gathering of arms, of which Túrin heard nothing; and
Húrin, knowing her courage and her guarded tongue, often spoke
with Morwen of the designs of the Elven-kings, and of what might
befall, if they went well or ill. His heart was high with hope, and he
had little fear for the outcome of the battle; for it did not seem to
him that any strength in Middle-earth could overthrow the might
and splendour of the Eldar. 'They have seen the Light in the West,'
he said, 'and in the end Darkness must flee from their faces.' Morwen
did not gainsay him; for in Húrin's company the hopeful ever
seemed the more likely. But there was knowledge of Elven-lore in
her kindred also, and to herself she said: 'And yet did they not leave
the Light, and are they not now shut out from it? It may be that the
Lords of the West have put them out of their thought; and how then
can even the Elder Children overcome one of the Powers?'

No shadow of such doubt seemed to lie upon Húrin Thalion; yet
one morning in the spring of that year he awoke as after unquiet
sleep, and a cloud lay on his brightness that day; and in the evening
he said suddenly: 'When I am summoned, Morwen Eledhwen, I
shall leave in your keeping the heir of the House of Hador. The
lives of Men are short, and in them there are many ill chances, even
in time of peace.'

'That has ever been so,' she answered. 'But what lies under your
words?'

'Prudence, not doubt,' said Húrin; yet he looked troubled. 'But
one who looks forward must see this: that things will not remain as
they were. This will be a great throw, and one side must fall lower
than it now stands. If it be the Elven-kings that fall, then it must

go evilly with the Edain; and we dwell nearest to the Enemy. But if things do go ill, I will not say to you: *Do not be afraid!* For you fear what should be feared, and that only; and fear does not dismay you. But I say: *Do not wait!* I shall return to you as I may, but do not wait! Go south as swiftly as you can; and I shall follow, and I shall find you, though I have to search through all Beleriand.'

'Beleriand is wide, and houseless for exiles,' said Morwen. 'Whither should I flee, with few or with many?'

Then Húrin thought for a while in silence. 'There is my mother's kin in Brethil,' he said. 'That is some thirty leagues, as the eagle flies.'

'If such an evil time should indeed come, what help would there be in Men?' said Morwen. 'The House of Bëor has fallen. If the great House of Hador falls, in what holes shall the little Folk of Haleth creep?'

'They are few and unlearned, but do not doubt their valour,' said Húrin. 'Where else is hope?'

'You do not speak of Gondolin,' said Morwen.

'No, for that name has never passed my lips,' said Húrin. 'Yet the word is true that you have heard: I have been there. But I tell you now truly, as I have told no other, and will not: I do not know where it stands.'

'But you guess, and guess near, I think,' said Morwen.

'It may be so,' said Húrin. 'But unless Turgon himself released me from my oath, I could not tell that guess, even to you; and therefore your search would be vain. But were I to speak, to my shame, you would at best but come at a shut gate; for unless Turgon comes out to war (and of that no word has been heard, and it is not hoped) no one will come in.'

'Then if your kin are not hopeful, and your friends deny you,' said Morwen, 'I must take counsel for myself; and to me now comes the thought of Doriath. Last of all defences will the Girdle of Melian be broken, I think; and the House of Bëor will not be despised in Doriath. Am I not now kin of the king? For Beren son of Barahir was grandson of Bregor, as was my father also.'

'My heart does not lean to Thingol,' said Húrin. 'No help will come from him to King Fingon; and I know not what shadow falls on my spirit when Doriath is named.'

'At the name of Brethil my heart also is darkened,' said Morwen.

Then suddenly Húrin laughed, and he said: 'Here we sit debating things beyond our reach, and shadows that come out of dream. Things will not go so ill; but if they do, then to your courage and counsel all is committed. Do then what your heart bids you; but do it swiftly. And if we gain our ends, then the Elven-kings are resolved to restore all the fiefs of Bëor's house to his heirs; and a high inheritance will come to our son.'

That night Túrin half-woke, and it seemed to him that his father and mother stood beside his bed, and looked down on him in the light of the candles that they held; but he could not see their faces.

On the morning of Túrin's birthday Húrin gave his son a gift, an Elf-wrought knife, and the hilt and the sheath were silver and black; and he said: 'Heir of the House of Hador, here is a gift for the day. But have a care! It is a bitter blade, and steel serves only those that can wield it. It will cut your hand as willingly as aught else.' And setting Túrin on a table he kissed his son, and said: 'You overtop me already, son of Morwen; soon you will be as high on your own feet. In that day many may fear your blade.'

Then Túrin ran from the room and went away alone, and in his heart there was a warmth like the warmth of the sun upon the cold earth that sets growth astir. He repeated to himself his father's words, Heir of the House of Hador; but other words came also to his mind: Give with a free hand, but give of your own. And he went to Sador and cried: 'Labadal, it is my birthday, the birthday of the heir of the House of Hador! And I have brought you a gift to mark the day. Here is a knife, just such as you need; it will cut anything that you wish, as fine as a hair.'

Then Sador was troubled, for he knew well that Túrin had himself received the knife that day; but men held it a grievous thing to refuse a free-given gift from any hand. He spoke then to him gravely: 'You come of a generous kin, Túrin son of Húrin. I have done nothing to equal your gift, and I cannot hope to do better in the days that are left to me; but what I can do, I will.' And when Sador drew the knife from the sheath he said: 'This is a gift indeed: a blade of elven steel. Long have I missed the feel of it.'

Húrin soon marked that Túrin did not wear the knife, and he asked him whether his warning had made him fear it. Then Túrin answered: 'No; but I gave the knife to Sador the woodwright.'

'Do you then scorn your father's gift?' said Morwen; and again Túrin answered: 'No; but I love Sador, and I feel pity for him.'

Then Húrin said: 'All three gifts were your own to give, Túrin: love, pity, and the knife the least.'

'Yet I doubt if Sador deserves them,' said Morwen. 'He is self-maimed by his own want of skill, and he is slow with his tasks, for he spends much time on trifles unbidden.'

'Give him pity nonetheless,' said Húrin. 'An honest hand and a true heart may hew amiss; and the harm may be harder to bear than the work of a foe.'

'But you must wait now for another blade,' said Morwen. 'Thus the gift shall be a true gift and at your own cost.'

Nonetheless Túrin saw that Sador was treated more kindly thereafter, and was set now to the making of a great chair for the lord to sit on in his hall.

There came a bright morning in the month of Lothron when Túrin was roused by sudden trumpets; and running to the doors he saw in the court a great press of men on foot and on horse, and all fully armed as for war. There also stood Húrin, and he spoke to the men and gave commands; and Túrin learned that they were setting out that day for Barad Eithel. These were Húrin's guards and household men; but all the men of his land were summoned. Some had gone already with Huor his father's brother; and many others would join the Lord of Dor-lómin on the road, and go behind his banner to the great muster of the King.

Then Morwen bade farewell to Húrin without tears; and she said: 'I will guard what you leave in my keeping, both what is and what shall be.'

And Húrin answered her: 'Farewell, Lady of Dor-lómin; we ride now with greater hope than ever we have known before. Let us think that at this midwinter the feast shall be merrier than in all our years yet, with a fearless spring to follow after!' Then he lifted Túrin to his shoulder, and cried to his men: 'Let the heir of the House of Hador see the light of your swords!' And the sun glittered on fifty blades as they leaped forth, and the court rang with the battle-cry of the Edain of the North: *Lacho calad! Drego morn!* Flame Light! Flee Night!

Then at last Húrin sprang into his saddle, and his golden banner was unfurled, and the trumpets sang again in the morning; and thus Húrin Thalion rode away to the Nirnaeth Arnoediad.

But Morwen and Túrin stood still by the doors, until far away they heard the faint call of a single horn on the wind: Húrin had passed over the shoulder of the hill, beyond which he could see his house no more.

## The Words of Húrin and Morgoth

Many songs are sung and many tales are told by the Elves of the Nirnaeth Arnoediad, the Battle of Unnumbered Tears, in which

Fingon fell and the flower of the Eldar withered. If all were retold
a man's life would not suffice for the hearing;[2] but now is to be told
only of what befell Húrin son of Galdor, Lord of Dor-lómin, when
beside the stream of Rivil he was taken at last alive by the command
of Morgoth, and carried off to Angband.

Húrin was brought before Morgoth, for Morgoth knew by his arts
and his spies that Húrin had the friendship of the King of Gondolin;
and he sought to daunt him with his eyes. But Húrin could not yet
be daunted, and he defied Morgoth. Therefore Morgoth had him
chained and set in slow torment; but after a while he came to him,
and offered him his choice to go free whither he would, or to receive
power and rank as the greatest of Morgoth's captains, if he would
but reveal where Turgon had his stronghold, and aught else that he
knew of the King's counsels. But Húrin the Steadfast mocked him,
saying: 'Blind you are Morgoth Bauglir, and blind shall ever be,
seeing only the dark. You know not what rules the hearts of Men,
and if you knew you could not give it. But a fool is he who accepts
what Morgoth offers. You will take first the price and then withhold the promise; and I should get only death, if I told you what
you ask.'

Then Morgoth laughed, and he said: 'Death you may yet crave
from me as a boon.' Then he took Húrin to the Haudh-en-Nirnaeth,
and it was then new-built and the reek of death was upon it; and
Morgoth set Húrin upon its top and bade him look west towards
Hithlum, and think of his wife and his son and other kin. 'For they
dwell now in my realm,' said Morgoth, 'and they are at my mercy.'

'You have none,' answered Húrin. 'But you will not come at
Turgon through them; for they do not know his secrets.'

Then wrath mastered Morgoth, and he said: 'Yet I may come at
you, and all your accursed house; and you shall be broken on my
will, though you all were made of steel.' And he took up a long sword
that lay there and broke it before the eyes of Húrin, and a splinter
wounded his face; but Húrin did not blench. Then Morgoth stretching
out his long arm towards Dor-lómin cursed Húrin and Morwen and
their offspring, saying: 'Behold! The shadow of my thought shall
lie upon them wherever they go, and my hate shall pursue them to
the ends of the world.'

But Húrin said: 'You speak in vain. For you cannot see them, nor
govern them from afar: not while you keep this shape, and desire
still to be a King visible upon earth.'

Then Morgoth turned upon Húrin, and he said: 'Fool, little

among Men, and they are the least of all that speak! Have you seen
the Valar, or measured the power of Manwë and Varda? Do you know
the reach of their thought? Or do you think, perhaps, that their
thought is upon you, and that they may shield you from afar?'

'I know not,' said Húrin. 'Yet so it might be, if they willed. For
the Elder King shall not be dethroned while Arda endures.'

'You say it,' said Morgoth. 'I am the Elder King: Melkor, first
and mightiest of all the Valar, who was before the world, and made it.
The shadow of my purpose lies upon Arda, and all that is in it bends
slowly and surely to my will. But upon all whom you love my thought
shall weigh as a cloud of Doom, and it shall bring them down into
darkness and despair. Wherever they go, evil shall arise. Whenever
they speak, their words shall bring ill counsel. Whatsoever they do
shall turn against them. They shall die without hope, cursing both
life and death.'

But Húrin answered: 'Do you forget to whom you speak? Such
things you spoke long ago to our fathers; but we escaped from your
shadow. And now we have knowledge of you, for we have looked on
the faces that have seen the Light, and heard the voices that have
spoken with Manwë. Before Arda you were, but others also; and you
did not make it. Neither are you the most mighty; for you have
spent your strength upon yourself and wasted it in your own emptiness. No more are you now than an escaped thrall of the Valar, and
their chain still awaits you.'

'You have learned the lessons of your masters by rote,' said
Morgoth. 'But such childish lore will not help you, now they are all
fled away.'

'This last then I will say to you, thrall Morgoth,' said Húrin, 'and
it comes not from the lore of the Eldar, but is put into my heart in
this hour. You are not the Lord of Men, and shall not be, though all
Arda and Menel fall in your dominion. Beyond the Circles of the
World you shall not pursue those who refuse you.'

'Beyond the Circles of the World I will not pursue them,' said
Morgoth. 'For beyond the Circles of the World there is Nothing.
But within them they shall not escape me, until they enter into
Nothing.'

'You lie,' said Húrin.

'You shall see and you shall confess that I do not lie,' said Morgoth.
And taking Húrin back to Angband he set him in a chair of stone
upon a high place of Thangorodrim, from which he could see afar
the land of Hithlum in the west and the lands of Beleriand in the
south. There he was bound by the power of Morgoth; and Morgoth

standing beside him cursed him again and set his power upon him, so that he could not move from that place, nor die, until Morgoth should release him.

'Sit now there,' said Morgoth, 'and look out upon the lands where evil and despair shall come upon those whom you have delivered to me. For you have dared to mock me, and have questioned the power of Melkor, Master of the fates of Arda. Therefore with my eyes you shall see, and with my ears you shall hear, and nothing shall be hidden from you.'

### The Departure of Túrin

To Brethil three men only found their way back at last through Taur-nu-Fuin, an evil road; and when Glóredhel Hador's daughter learned of the fall of Haldir she grieved and died.

To Dor-lómin no tidings came. Rían wife of Huor fled into the wild distraught; but she was aided by the Grey-elves of the hills of Mithrim, and when her child, Tuor, was born they fostered him. But Rían went to the Haudh-en-Nirnaeth, and laid herself down there, and died.

Morwen Eledhwen remained in Hithlum, silent in grief. Her son Túrin was only in his ninth year, and she was again with child. Her days were evil. The Easterlings came into the land in great numbers, and they dealt cruelly with the people of Hador, and robbed them of all that they possessed and enslaved them. All the people of Húrin's homelands that could work or serve any purpose they took away, even young girls and boys, and the old they killed or drove out to starve. But they dared not yet lay hands on the Lady of Dor-lómin, or thrust her from her house; for the word ran among them that she was perilous, and a witch who had dealings with the white-fiends: for so they named the Elves, hating them, but fearing them more.[3] For this reason they also feared and avoided the mountains, in which many of the Eldar had taken refuge, especially in the south of the land; and after plundering and harrying the Easterlings drew back northwards. For Húrin's house stood in the south-east of Dor-lómin, and the mountains were near; Nen Lalaith indeed came down from a spring under the shadow of Amon Darthir, over whose shoulder there was a steep pass. By this the hardy could cross Ered Wethrin and come down by the wells of Glithui into Beleriand. But this was not known to the Easterlings, nor to Morgoth yet; for all that country, while the House of Fingolfin stood, was secure from him, and none of his servants had ever come there. He trusted that Ered Wethrin was a wall insurmountable, both against escape from the north and against assault from the south; and there was indeed no other pass, for the unwinged, between Serech and far westward where Dor-lómin marched with Nevrast.

Thus it came to pass that after the first inroads Morwen was let be, though there were men that lurked in the woods about, and it was perilous to stir far abroad. There still remained under Morwen's shelter Sador the woodwright and a few old men and women, and Túrin, whom she kept close within the garth. But the homestead of Húrin soon fell into decay, and though Morwen laboured hard she was poor, and would have gone hungry but for the help that was sent to her secretly by Aerin, Húrin's kinswoman; for a certain Brodda, one of the Easterlings, had taken her by force to be his wife. Alms were bitter to Morwen; but she took this aid for the sake of Túrin and her unborn child, and because, as she said, it came of her own. For it was this Brodda who had seized the people, the goods, and the cattle of Húrin's homelands, and carried them off to his own dwellings. He was a bold man, but of small account among his own people before they came to Hithlum; and so, seeking wealth, he was ready to hold lands that others of his sort did not covet. Morwen he had seen once, when he rode to her house on a foray; but a great dread of her had seized him. He thought that he had looked in the fell eyes of a white-fiend, and he was filled with a mortal fear lest some evil should overtake him; and he did not ransack her house, nor discover Túrin, else the life of the heir of the true lord would have been short.

Brodda made thralls of the Strawheads, as he named the people of Hador, and set them to build him a wooden hall in the land to the northward of Húrin's house; and within a stockade his slaves were herded like cattle in a byre, but ill guarded. Among them some could still be found uncowed and ready to help the Lady of Dor-lómin, even at their peril; and from them came secretly tidings of the land to Morwen, though there was little hope in the news they brought. But Brodda took Aerin as a wife and not a slave, for there were few women amongst his own following, and none to compare with the daughters of the Edain; and he hoped to make himself a lordship in that country, and have an heir to hold it after him.

Of what had happened and of what might happen in the days to come Morwen said little to Túrin; and he feared to break her silence with questions. When the Easterlings first came into Dor-lómin he said to his mother: 'When will my father come back, to cast out these ugly thieves? Why does he not come?'

Morwen answered: 'I do not know. It may be that he was slain, or that he is held captive; or again it may be that he was driven far away, and cannot yet return through the foes that surround us.'

'Then I think that he is dead,' said Túrin, and before his mother he restrained his tears; 'for no one could keep him from coming back to help us, if he were alive.'

'I do not think that either of those things are true, my son,' said Morwen.

As the time lengthened the heart of Morwen grew darker with fear for her son Túrin, heir of Dor-lómin and Ladros; for she could see no hope for him better than to become a slave of the Easterling men, before he was much older. Therefore she remembered her words with Húrin, and her thought turned again to Doriath; and she resolved at last to send Túrin away in secret, if she could, and to beg King Thingol to harbour him. And as she sat and pondered how this might be done, she heard clearly in her thought the voice of Húrin saying to her: *Go swiftly! Do not wait for me!* But the birth of her child was drawing near, and the road would be hard and perilous; the more that went the less hope of escape. And her heart still cheated her with hope unadmitted; her inmost thought foreboded that Húrin was not dead, and she listened for his footfall in the sleepless watches of the night, or would wake thinking that she had heard in the courtyard the neigh of Arroch his horse. Moreover, though she was willing that her son should be fostered in the halls of another, after the manner of that time, she would not yet humble her pride to be an alms-guest, not even of a king. Therefore the voice of Húrin, or the memory of his voice, was denied, and the first strand of the fate of Túrin was woven.

Autumn of the Year of Lamentation was drawing on before Morwen came to this resolve, and then she was in haste; for the time for journeying was short, but she dreaded that Túrin would be taken, if she waited over winter. Easterlings were prowling round the garth and spying on the house. Therefore she said suddenly to Túrin: 'Your father does not come. So you must go, and go soon. It is as he would wish.'

'Go?' cried Túrin. 'Whither shall we go? Over the Mountains?'

'Yes,' said Morwen, 'over the Mountains, away south. South – that way some hope may lie. But I did not say *we*, my son. You must go, but I must stay.'

'I cannot go alone!' said Túrin. 'I will not leave you. Why should we not go together?'

'I cannot go,' said Morwen. 'But you will not go alone. I shall send Gethron with you, and Grithnir too, perhaps.'

'Will you not send Labadal?' said Túrin.

'No, for Sador is lame,' said Morwen, 'and it will be a hard road. And since you are my son and the days are grim, I will not speak softly: you may die on that road. The year is getting late. But if you stay, you will come to a worse end: to be a thrall. If you wish to be a man, when you come to a man's age, you will do as I bid, bravely.'

'But I shall leave you only with Sador, and blind Ragnir, and the old women,' said Túrin. 'Did not my father say that I am the heir of Hador? The heir should stay in Hador's house to defend it. Now I wish that I still had my knife!'

'The heir should stay, but he cannot,' said Morwen. 'But he may return one day. Now take heart! I will follow you, if things grow worse; if I can.'

'But how will you find me, lost in the wild?' said Túrin; and suddenly his heart failed him, and he wept openly.

'If you wail, other things will find you first,' said Morwen. 'But I know whither you are going, and if you come there, and if you remain there, there I will find you, if I can. For I am sending you to King Thingol in Doriath. Would you not rather be a king's guest than a thrall?'

'I do not know,' said Túrin. 'I do not know what a thrall is.'

'I am sending you away so that you need not learn it,' Morwen answered. Then she set Túrin before her and looked into his eyes, as if she were trying to read some riddle there. 'It is hard, Túrin, my son,' she said at length. 'Not hard for you only. It is heavy on me in evil days to judge what is best to do. But I do as I think right; for why else should I part with the thing most dear that is left to me?'

They spoke no more of this together, and Túrin was grieved and bewildered. In the morning he went to find Sador, who had been hewing sticks for firing, of which they had little, for they dared not stray out in the woods; and now he leant on his crutch and looked at the great chair of Húrin, which had been thrust unfinished in a corner. 'It must go,' he said, 'for only bare needs can be served in these days.'

'Do not break it yet,' said Túrin. 'Maybe he will come home, and then it will please him to see what you have done for him while he was away.'

'False hopes are more dangerous than fears,' said Sador, 'and they will not keep us warm this winter.' He fingered the carving on the chair, and sighed. 'I wasted my time,' he said, 'though the hours seemed pleasant. But all such things are short-lived; and the joy in the making is their only true end, I guess. And now I might as well give you back your gift.'

Túrin put out his hand, and quickly withdrew it. 'A man does not take back his gifts,' he said.

'But if it is my own, may I not give it as I will?' said Sador.

'Yes,' said Túrin, 'to any man but me. But why should you wish to give it?'

'I have no hope of using it for worthy tasks,' Sador said. 'There will be no work for Labadal in days to come but thrall-work.'

'What is a thrall?' said Túrin.

'A man who was a man but is treated as a beast,' Sador answered. 'Fed only to keep alive, kept alive only to toil, toiling only for fear of pain or death. And from these robbers he may get pain or death just for their sport. I hear that they pick some of the fleet-footed and hunt them with hounds. They have learned quicker from the Orcs than we learnt from the Fair Folk.'

'Now I understand things better,' said Túrin.

'It is a shame that you should have to understand such things so soon,' said Sador; then seeing the strange look on Túrin's face: 'What do you understand now?'

'Why my mother is sending me away,' said Túrin, and tears filled his eyes.

'Ah!' said Sador, and he muttered to himself: 'But why so long delayed?' Then turning to Túrin he said: 'That does not seem news for tears to me. But you should not speak your mother's counsels aloud to Labadal, or to any one. All walls and fences have ears these days, ears that do not grow on fair heads.'

'But I must speak with someone!' said Túrin. 'I have always told things to you. I do not want to leave you, Labadal. I do not want to leave this house or my mother.'

'But if you do not,' said Sador, 'soon there will be an end of the House of Hador for ever, as you must understand now. Labadal does not want you to go; but Sador servant of Húrin will be happier when Húrin's son is out of the reach of the Easterlings. Well, well, it cannot be helped: we must say farewell. Now will you not take my knife as a parting gift?'

'No!' said Túrin. 'I am going to the Elves, to the King of Doriath, my mother says. There I may get other things like it. But I shall

not be able to send you any gifts, Labadal. I shall be far away and
all alone.' Then Túrin wept; but Sador said to him: 'Hey now!
Where is Húrin's son? For I heard him say, not long ago: *I shall go
as a soldier with an Elf-king, as soon as I am able.*'

Then Túrin stayed his tears, and he said: 'Very well: if those
were the words of the son of Húrin, he must keep them, and go. But
whenever I say that I will do this or that, it looks very different
when the time comes. Now I am unwilling. I must take care not to
say such things again.'

'It would be best indeed,' said Sador. 'So most men teach, and
few men learn. Let the unseen days be. Today is more than enough.'

Now Túrin was made ready for the journey, and he bade farewell
to his mother, and departed in secret with his two companions. But
when they bade Túrin turn and look back upon the house of his
father, then the anguish of parting smote him like a sword, and he
cried: 'Morwen, Morwen, when shall I see you again?' But Morwen
standing on her threshold heard the echo of that cry in the wooded
hills, and she clutched the post of the door so that her fingers were
torn. This was the first of the sorrows of Túrin.

Early in the year after Túrin was gone Morwen gave birth to her
child, and she named her Nienor, which is Mourning; but Túrin
was already far away when she was born. Long and evil was his road,
for the power of Morgoth was ranging far abroad; but he had as
guides Gethron and Grithnir, who had been young in the days of
Hador, and though they were now aged they were valiant, and they
knew well the lands, for they had journeyed often through Beleriand
in former times. Thus by fate and courage they passed over the
Shadowy Mountains, and coming down into the Vale of Sirion they
passed into the Forest of Brethil; and at last, weary and haggard,
they reached the confines of Doriath. But there they became bewildered, and were enmeshed in the mazes of the Queen, and
wandered lost amid the pathless trees, until all their food was spent.
There they came near to death, for winter came cold from the
North; but not so light was Túrin's doom. Even as they lay in despair
they heard a horn sounded. Beleg the Strongbow was hunting in
that region, for he dwelt ever upon the marches of Doriath, and he
was the greatest woodsman of those days. He heard their cries and
came to them, and when he had given them food and drink he
learned their names and whence they came, and he was filled with
wonder and pity. And he looked with liking upon Túrin, for he had

the beauty of his mother and the eyes of his father, and he was sturdy and strong.

'What boon would you have of King Thingol?' said Beleg to the boy.

'I would be one of his knights, to ride against Morgoth, and avenge my father,' said Túrin.

'That may well be, when the years have increased you,' said Beleg. 'For though you are yet small you have the makings of a valiant man, worthy to be a son of Húrin the Steadfast, if that were possible.' For the name of Húrin was held in honour in all the lands of the Elves. Therefore Beleg gladly became the guide of the wanderers, and he led them to a lodge where he dwelt at that time with other hunters, and there they were housed while a messenger went to Menegroth. And when word came back that Thingol and Melian would receive the son of Húrin and his guardians, Beleg led them by secret ways into the Hidden Kingdom.

Thus Túrin came to the great bridge over the Esgalduin, and passed the gates of Thingol's halls; and as a child he gazed upon the marvels of Menegroth, which no mortal Man before had seen, save Beren only. Then Gethron spoke the message of Morwen before Thingol and Melian; and Thingol received them kindly, and set Túrin upon his knee in honour of Húrin, mightiest of Men, and of Beren his kinsman. And those that saw this marvelled, for it was a sign that Thingol took Túrin as his foster-son; and that was not at that time done by kings, nor ever again by Elf-lord to a Man. Then Thingol said to him: 'Here, son of Húrin, shall your home be; and in all your life you shall be held as my son, Man though you be. Wisdom shall be given you beyond the measure of mortal Men, and the weapons of the Elves shall be set in your hands. Perhaps the time may come when you shall regain the lands of your father in Hithlum; but dwell now here in love.'

Thus began the sojourn of Túrin in Doriath. With him for a while remained Gethron and Grithnir his guardians, though they yearned to return again to their lady in Dor-lómin. Then age and sickness came upon Grithnir, and he stayed beside Túrin until he died; but Gethron departed, and Thingol sent with him an escort to guide him and guard him, and they brought words from Thingol to Morwen. They came at last to Húrin's house, and when Morwen learned that Túrin was received with honour in the halls of Thingol her grief was lightened; and the Elves brought also rich gifts from Melian, and a message bidding her return with Thingol's folk to

Doriath. For Melian was wise and foresighted, and she hoped thus to avert the evil that was prepared in the thought of Morgoth. But Morwen would not depart from her house, for her heart was yet unchanged and her pride still high; moreover Nienor was a babe in arms. Therefore she dismissed the Elves of Doriath with her thanks, and gave them in gift the last small things of gold that remained to her, concealing her poverty; and she bade them take back to Thingol the Helm of Hador. But Túrin watched ever for the return of Thingol's messengers; and when they came back alone he fled into the woods and wept, for he knew of Melian's bidding and he had hoped that Morwen would come. This was the second sorrow of Túrin.

When the messengers spoke Morwen's answer, Melian was moved with pity, perceiving her mind; and she saw that the fate which she foreboded could not lightly be set aside.

The Helm of Hador was given into Thingol's hands. That helm was made of grey steel adorned with gold, and on it were graven runes of victory. A power was in it that guarded any who wore it from wound or death, for the sword that hewed it was broken, and the dart that smote it sprang aside. It was wrought by Telchar, the smith of Nogrod, whose works were renowned. It had a visor (after the manner of those that the Dwarves used in their forges for the shielding of their eyes), and the face of one that wore it struck fear into the hearts of all beholders, but was itself guarded from dart and fire. Upon its crest was set in defiance a gilded image of the head of Glaurung the dragon; for it had been made soon after he first issued from the gates of Morgoth. Often Hador, and Galdor after him, had borne it in war; and the hearts of the host of Hithlum were uplifted when they saw it towering high amid the battle, and they cried: 'Of more worth is the Dragon of Dor-lómin than the gold-worm of Angband!'

But in truth this helm had not been made for Men, but for Azaghâl Lord of Belegost, he who was slain by Glaurung in the Year of Lamentation.[4] It was given by Azaghâl to Maedhros, as guerdon for the saving of his life and treasure, when Azaghâl was waylaid by Orcs upon the Dwarf-road in East Beleriand.[5] Maedhros afterwards sent it as a gift to Fingon, with whom he often exchanged tokens of friendship, remembering how Fingon had driven Glaurung back to Angband. But in all Hithlum no head and shoulders were found stout enough to bear the dwarf-helm with ease, save those of Hador and his son Galdor. Fingon therefore gave it to Hador, when he received the lordship of Dor-lómin. By ill-fortune Galdor did not wear it when he defended Eithel Sirion, for the assault was sudden, and he ran barehead to the walls, and an orc-arrow pierced his eye. But Húrin did not wear the Dragon-helm with ease, and in any case he would not use it, for he said: 'I would rather look on my foes with my true face.' Nonetheless he accounted the helm among the greatest heirlooms of his house.

Now Thingol had in Menegroth deep armouries filled with great wealth of weapons: metal wrought like fishes' mail and shining like water in the moon; swords and axes, shields and helms, wrought by Telchar himself or by his master Gamil Zirak the old, or by elven-wrights more skilful still. For some things he had received in gift that came out of Valinor and were wrought by Fëanor in his mastery, than whom no craftsman was greater in all the days of the world. Yet Thingol handled the Helm of Hador as though his hoard were scanty, and he spoke courteous words, saying: 'Proud were the head that bore this helm, which the sires of Húrin bore.'

Then a thought came to him, and he summoned Túrin, and told him that Morwen had sent to her son a mighty thing, the heirloom of his fathers. 'Take now the Dragonhead of the North,' he said, 'and when the time comes wear it well.' But Túrin was yet too young to lift the helm, and he heeded it not because of the sorrow of his heart.

### Túrin in Doriath

In the years of his childhood in the kingdom of Doriath Túrin was watched over by Melian, though he saw her seldom. But there was a maiden named Nellas, who lived in the woods; and at Melian's bidding she would follow Túrin if he strayed in the forest, and often she met him there, as it were by chance. From Nellas Túrin learned much concerning the ways and the wild things of Doriath, and she taught him to speak the Sindarin tongue after the manner of the ancient realm, older, and more courteous, and richer in beautiful words.[6] Thus for a little while his mood was lightened, until he fell again under shadow, and that friendship passed like a morning of spring. For Nellas did not go to Menegroth, and was unwilling ever to walk under roofs of stone; so that as Túrin's boyhood passed and he turned his thoughts to the deeds of men, he saw her less and less often, and at last called for her no more. But she watched over him still, though now she remained hidden.[7]

Nine years Túrin dwelt in the halls of Menegroth. His heart and thought turned ever to his own kin, and at times he had tidings of them for his comfort. For Thingol sent messengers to Morwen as often as he might, and she sent back words for her son; thus Túrin heard that his sister Nienor grew in beauty, a flower in the grey North, and that Morwen's plight was eased. And Túrin grew in stature until he became tall among Men, and his strength and hardihood were renowned in the realm of Thingol. In those years he learned much lore, hearing eagerly the histories of ancient days; and he became thoughtful, and sparing in speech. Often Beleg Strongbow came to Menegroth to seek him, and led him far afield, teaching him woodcraft and archery and (which he loved best) the handling of swords; but in crafts of making he had less skill, for he was slow to learn his own strength, and often marred what he made with some sudden stroke. In other matters also it seemed that fortune was unfriendly to him, so that often what he designed went awry, and what he desired he did not gain; neither did he win friendship easily, for he was not merry, and laughed seldom, and a shadow lay on his youth. Nonetheless he was held in love and esteem by those who knew him well, and he had honour as the fosterling of the King.

Yet there was one that begrudged him this, and ever the more as Túrin drew nearer to manhood: Saeros, son of Ithilbor, was his name. He was of the Nandor, being one of those who took refuge in Doriath after the fall of their lord Denethor upon Amon Ereb, in the first battle of Beleriand. These Elves dwelt for the most part in Arthórien, between Aros and Celon in the east of Doriath, wandering at times over Celon into the wild lands beyond; and they were no friends to the Edain since their passage through Ossiriand and settlement in Estolad. But Saeros dwelt mostly in Menegroth, and won the esteem of the king; and he was proud, dealing haughtily with those whom he deemed of lesser state and worth than himself. He became a friend of Daeron the minstrel,[8] for he also was skilled in song; and he had no love for Men, and least of all for any kinsman of Beren Erchamion. 'Is it not strange,' said he, 'that this land should be opened to yet another of this unhappy race? Did not the other do harm enough in Doriath?' Therefore he looked askance on Túrin and on all that he did, saying what ill he could of it; but his words were cunning and his malice veiled. If he met with Túrin alone, he spoke haughtily to him and showed plain his contempt; and Túrin grew weary of him, though for long he returned ill words with silence, for Saeros was great among the people of Doriath and a counsellor of the King. But the silence of Túrin displeased Saeros as much as his words.

In the year that Túrin was seventeen years old, his grief was renewed; for all tidings from his home ceased at that time. The power of Morgoth had grown yearly, and all Hithlum was now under his shadow. Doubtless he knew much of the doings of Húrin's kin, and had not molested them for a while, so that his design might be fulfilled; but now in pursuit of this purpose he set a close watch upon all the passes of the Shadowy Mountains, so that none might come out of Hithlum nor enter it, save at great peril, and the Orcs swarmed about the sources of Narog and Teiglin and the upper waters of Sirion. Thus there came a time when the messengers of Thingol did not return, and he would send no more. He was ever loath to let any stray beyond the guarded borders, and in nothing had he shown greater good will to Húrin and his kin than in sending his people on the dangerous roads to Morwen in Dor-lómin.

Now Túrin grew heavy-hearted, not knowing what new evil was afoot, and fearing that an ill fate had befallen Morwen and Nienor; and for many days he sat silent, brooding on the downfall of the House of Hador and the Men of the North. Then he rose up and went to seek Thingol; and he found him sitting with Melian under Hírilorn, the great beech of Menegroth.

Thingol looked on Túrin in wonder, seeing suddenly before him in the place of his fosterling a Man and a stranger, tall, dark-haired, looking at him with deep eyes in a white face. Then Túrin asked Thingol for mail, sword, and shield, and he reclaimed now the Dragon-helm of Dor-lómin; and the king granted him what he sought, saying: 'I will appoint you a place among my knights of the sword; for the sword will ever be your weapon. With them you may make trial of war upon the marches, if that is your desire.'

But Túrin said: 'Beyond the marches of Doriath my heart urges me; I long rather for assault upon the Enemy, than for defence of the borderlands.'

'Then you must go alone,' said Thingol. 'The part of my people in the war with Angband I rule according to my wisdom, Túrin son of Húrin. No force of the arms of Doriath will I send out at this time; nor in any time that I can yet foresee.'

'Yet you are free to go as you will, son of Morwen,' said Melian. 'The Girdle of Melian does not hinder the going of those that passed in with our leave.'

'Unless wise counsel will restrain you,' said Thingol.

'What is your counsel, lord?' said Túrin.

'A Man you seem in stature,' Thingol answered, 'but nonetheless you have not come to the fullness of your manhood that shall be. When that time comes, then, maybe, you can remember your kin; but there is little hope that one Man alone can do more against the

Dark Lord than to aid the Elf-lords in their defence, as long as that may last.'

Then Túrin said: 'Beren my kinsman did more.'

'Beren, and Lúthien,' said Melian. 'But you are over-bold to speak so to the father of Lúthien. Not so high is your destiny, I think, Túrin son of Morwen, though your fate is twined with that of the Elven-folk, for good or for ill. Beware of yourself, lest it be ill.' Then after a silence she spoke to him again, saying: 'Go now, fosterson; and heed the counsel of the king. Yet I do not think that you will long abide with us in Doriath after the coming of manhood. If in days to come you remember the words of Melian, it will be for your good: fear both the heat and the cold of your heart.'

Then Túrin bowed before them, and took his leave. And soon after he put on the Dragon-helm, and took arms, and went away to the north-marches, and was joined to the elven-warriors who there waged unceasing war upon the Orcs and all servants and creatures of Morgoth. Thus while yet scarcely out of his boyhood his strength and courage were proved; and remembering the wrongs of his kin he was ever forward in deeds of daring, and he received many wounds by spear or arrow or the crooked blades of the Orcs. But his doom delivered him from death; and word ran through the woods, and was heard far beyond Doriath, that the Dragon-helm of Dor-lómin was seen again. Then many wondered, saying: 'Can the spirit of Hador or of Galdor the Tall return from death; or has Húrin of Hithlum escaped indeed from the pits of Angband?'

One only was mightier in arms among the march-wardens of Thingol at that time than Túrin, and that was Beleg Cúthalion; and Beleg and Túrin were companions in every peril, and walked far and wide in the wild woods together.

Thus three years passed, and in that time Túrin came seldom to Thingol's halls; and he cared no longer for his looks or his attire, but his hair was unkempt, and his mail covered with a grey cloak stained with the weather. But it chanced in the third summer, when Túrin was twenty years old, that desiring rest and needing smith-work for the repair of his arms he came unlooked for to Menegroth in the evening; and he went into the hall. Thingol was not there, for he was abroad in the greenwood with Melian, as was his delight at times in the high summer. Túrin went to a seat without heed, for he was wayworn, and filled with thought; and by ill-luck he set himself at a board among the elders of the realm, and in that very place where Saeros was accustomed to sit. Saeros, entering late, was

angered, believing that Túrin had done this in pride, and with intent
to affront him; and his anger was not lessened to find that Túrin was
not rebuked by those that sat there, but welcomed among them.

For a while therefore Saeros feigned to be of like mind, and took
another seat, facing Túrin across the board. 'Seldom does the march-
warden favour us with his company,' he said; 'and I gladly yield
my accustomed seat for the chance of speech with him.' And much
else he said to Túrin, questioning him concerning the news from
the borders, and his deeds in the wild; but though his words seemed
fair, the mockery in his voice could not be mistaken. Then Túrin
became weary, and he looked about him, and knew the bitterness of
exile; and for all the light and laughter of the Elven-halls his thought
turned to Beleg and their life in the woods, and thence far away,
to Morwen in Dor-lómin in the house of his father; and he frowned,
because of the darkness of his thoughts, and made no answer to
Saeros. At this, believing the frown aimed at himself, Saeros restrained his anger no longer; and he took out a golden comb, and cast
it on the board before Túrin, saying: 'Doubtless, Man of Hithlum,
you came in haste to this table, and may be excused your ragged
cloak; but you have no need to leave your head untended as a thicket
of brambles. And perhaps if your ears were uncovered you would
hear better what is said to you.'

Túrin said nothing, but turned his eyes upon Saeros, and there
was a glint in their darkness. But Saeros did not heed the warning,
and returned the gaze with scorn, saying for all to hear: 'If the Men
of Hithlum are so wild and fell, of what sort are the women of that
land? Do they run like deer clad only in their hair?'

Then Túrin took up a drinking-vessel and cast it in Saeros' face,
and he fell backward with great hurt; and Túrin drew his sword and
would have run at him, but Mablung the Hunter, who sat at his side,
restrained him. Then Saeros rising spat blood upon the board, and
spoke from a broken mouth: 'How long shall we harbour this woodwose?[9] Who rules here tonight? The king's law is heavy upon those
who hurt his lieges in the hall; and for those who draw blades there
outlawry is the least doom. Outside the hall I could answer you,
Woodwose!'

But when Túrin saw the blood upon the table his mood became
cold; and releasing himself from Mablung's grasp he left the hall
without a word.

Then Mablung said to Saeros: 'What ails you tonight? For this
evil I hold you to blame; and it may be that the King's law will judge
a broken mouth a just return for your taunting.'

'If the cub has a grievance, let him bring it to the King's judgement,' answered Saeros. 'But the drawing of swords here is not to be excused for any such cause. Outside the hall, if the woodwose draws on me, I shall kill him.'

'That seems to me less certain,' said Mablung; 'but if either be slain it will be an evil deed, more fit for Angband than Doriath, and more evil will come of it. Indeed I think that some shadow of the North has reached out to touch us tonight. Take heed, Saeros son of Ithilbor, lest you do the will of Morgoth in your pride, and remember that you are of the Eldar.'

'I do not forget it,' said Saeros; but he did not abate his wrath, and through the night his malice grew, nursing his injury.

In the morning, when Túrin left Menegroth to return to the north-marches, Saeros waylaid him, running out upon him from behind with drawn sword and shield on arm. But Túrin, trained in the wild to wariness, saw him from the corner of his eye, and leaping aside he drew swiftly and turned upon his foe. 'Morwen!' he cried, 'now your mocker shall pay for his scorn!' And he clove Saeros' shield, and then they fought together with swift blades. But Túrin had been long in a hard school, and had grown as agile as any Elf, but stronger. He soon had the mastery, and wounding Saeros' sword-arm he had him at his mercy. Then he set his foot on the sword that Saeros had let fall. 'Saeros,' he said, 'there is a long race before you, and clothes will be a hindrance; hair must suffice.' And suddenly throwing him to the ground he stripped him, and Saeros felt Túrin's great strength, and was afraid. But Túrin let him up, and then 'Run!' he cried. 'Run! And unless you go as swift as the deer I shall prick you on from behind.' And Saeros fled into the wood, crying wildly for help; but Túrin came after him like a hound, and however he ran, or swerved, still the sword was behind him to egg him on.

The cries of Saeros brought many others to the chase, and they followed after, but only the swiftest could keep up with the runners. Mablung was in the forefront of these, and he was troubled in mind, for though the taunting had seemed evil to him, 'malice that wakes in the morning is the mirth of Morgoth ere night'; and it was held moreover a grievous thing to put any of the Elven-folk to shame, self-willed, without the matter being brought to judgement. None knew at that time that Túrin had been assailed first by Saeros, who would have slain him.

'Hold, hold, Túrin!' he cried. 'This is Orc-work in the woods!' But Túrin called back: 'Orc-work in the woods for Orc-words in the hall!' and sprang again after Saeros; and he, despairing of aid and thinking his death close behind, ran wildly on, until he came suddenly to a brink where a stream that fed Esgalduin flowed in a deep cleft through high rocks, and it was wide for a deer-leap. There Saeros in his great fear attempted the leap; but he failed of his footing on the far side and fell back with a cry, and was broken on a great stone in the water. So he ended his life in Doriath; and long would Mandos hold him.

Túrin looked down on his body lying in the stream, and he thought: 'Unhappy fool! From here I would have let him walk back to Menegroth. Now he has laid a guilt upon me undeserved.' And he turned and looked darkly on Mablung and his companions, who now came up and stood near him on the brink. Then after a silence Mablung said: 'Alas! But come back now with us, Túrin, for the King must judge these deeds.'

But Túrin said: 'If the King were just, he would judge me guiltless. But was not this one of his counsellors? Why should a just king choose a heart of malice for his friend? I abjure his law and his judgement.'

'Your words are unwise,' said Mablung, though in his heart he felt pity for Túrin. 'You shall not turn runagate. I bid you return with me, as a friend. And there are other witnesses. When the King learns the truth you may hope for his pardon.'

But Túrin was weary of the Elven-halls, and he feared lest he be held captive; and he said to Mablung: 'I refuse your bidding. I will not seek King Thingol's pardon for nothing; and I will go now where his doom cannot find me. You have but two choices: to let me go free, or to slay me, if that would fit your law. For you are too few to take me alive.'

They saw in his eyes that this was true, and they let him pass; and Mablung said: 'One death is enough.'

'I did not will it, but I do not mourn it,' said Túrin. 'May Mandos judge him justly; and if ever he return to the lands of the living, may he prove wiser. Farewell!'

'Fare free!' said Mablung; 'for that is your wish. But well I do not hope for, if you go in this way. A shadow is on your heart. When we meet again, may it be no darker.'

To that Túrin made no answer, but left them, and went swiftly away, none knew whither.

It is told that when Túrin did not return to the north-marches of Doriath and no tidings could be heard of him, Beleg Strongbow came himself to Menegroth to seek him; and with heavy heart he gathered news of Túrin's deeds and flight. Soon afterwards Thingol and Melian came back to their halls, for the summer was waning; and when the King heard report of what had passed he sat upon his throne in the great hall of Menegroth, and about him were all the lords and counsellors of Doriath.

Then all was searched and told, even to the parting words of Túrin; and at the last Thingol sighed, and he said: 'Alas! How has this shadow stolen into my realm? Saeros I accounted faithful and wise; but if he lived he would feel my anger, for his taunting was evil, and I hold him to blame for all that chanced in the hall. So far Túrin has my pardon. But the shaming of Saeros and the hounding of him to his death were wrongs greater than the offence, and these deeds I cannot pass over. They show a hard heart, and proud.' Then Thingol fell silent, but at last he spoke again in sadness. 'This is an ungrateful fosterson, and a Man too proud for his state. How shall I harbour one who scorns me and my law, or pardon one who will not repent? Therefore I will banish Túrin son of Húrin from the kingdom of Doriath. If he seeks entry he shall be brought to judgement before me; and until he sues for pardon at my feet he is my son no longer. If any here accounts this unjust, let him speak.'

Then there was silence in the hall, and Thingol lifted up his hand to pronounce his doom. But at that moment Beleg entered in haste, and cried: 'Lord, may I yet speak?'

'You come late,' said Thingol. 'Were you not bidden with the others?'

'Truly, lord,' answered Beleg, 'but I was delayed; I sought for one whom I knew. Now I bring at last a witness who should be heard, ere your doom falls.'

'All were summoned who had aught to tell,' said the King. 'What can he tell now of more weight than those to whom I have listened?'

'You shall judge when you have heard,' said Beleg. 'Grant this to me, if I have ever deserved your grace.'

'To you I grant it,' said Thingol. Then Beleg went out, and led in by the hand the maiden Nellas, who dwelt in the woods, and came never into Menegroth; and she was afraid, both for the great pillared hall and the roof of stone, and for the company of many eyes that watched her. And when Thingol bade her speak, she said: 'Lord, I was sitting in a tree'; but then she faltered in awe of the King, and could say no more.

At that the King smiled, and said: 'Others have done this also, but have felt no need to tell me of it.'

'Others indeed,' said she, taking courage from his smile. 'Even

Lúthien! And of her I was thinking that morning, and of Beren the Man.'

To that Thingol said nothing, and he smiled no longer, but waited until Nellas should speak again.

'For Túrin reminded me of Beren,' she said at last. 'They are akin, I am told, and their kinship can be seen by some: by some that look close.'

Then Thingol grew impatient. 'That may be,' he said. 'But Túrin son of Húrin is gone in scorn of me, and you will see him no more to read his kindred. For now I will speak my judgement.'

'Lord King!' she cried then. 'Bear with me, and let me speak first. I sat in a tree to look on Túrin as he went away; and I saw Saeros come out from the wood with sword and shield, and spring on Túrin at unawares.'

At that there was a murmur in the hall; and the King lifted his hand, saying: 'You bring graver news to my ear than seemed likely. Take heed now to all that you say; for this is a court of doom.'

'So Beleg has told me,' she answered, 'and only for that have I dared to come here, so that Túrin shall not be ill judged. He is valiant, but he is merciful. They fought, lord, these two, until Túrin had bereft Saeros of both shield and sword; but he did not slay him. Therefore I do not believe that he willed his death in the end. If Saeros were put to shame, it was shame that he had earned.'

'Judgement is mine,' said Thingol. 'But what you have told shall govern it.' Then he questioned Nellas closely; and at last he turned to Mablung, saying: 'It is strange to me that Túrin said nothing of this to you.'

'Yet he did not,' said Mablung. 'And had he spoken of it, otherwise would my words have been to him at parting.'

'And otherwise shall my doom now be,' said Thingol. 'Hear me! Such fault as can be found in Túrin I now pardon, holding him wronged and provoked. And since it was indeed, as he said, one of my council who so misused him, he shall not seek for this pardon, but I will send it to him, wherever he may be found; and I will recall him in honour to my halls.'

But when the doom was pronounced, suddenly Nellas wept. 'Where can he be found?' she said. 'He has left our land, and the world is wide.'

'He shall be sought,' said Thingol. Then he rose, and Beleg led Nellas forth from Menegroth; and he said to her: 'Do not weep; for if Túrin lives or walks still abroad, I shall find him, though all others fail.'

On the next day Beleg came before Thingol and Melian, and the King said to him: 'Counsel me, Beleg; for I am grieved. I took Húrin's son as my son, and so he shall remain, unless Húrin himself should return out of the shadows to claim his own. I would not have any say that Túrin was driven forth unjustly into the wild, and gladly would I welcome him back; for I loved him well.'

And Beleg answered: 'I will seek Túrin until I find him, and I will bring him back to Menegroth, if I can; for I love him also.' Then he departed; and far across Beleriand he sought in vain for tidings of Túrin, through many perils; and that winter passed away, and the spring after.

### Túrin among the Outlaws

Now the tale turns again to Túrin. He, believing himself an outlaw whom the king would pursue, did not return to Beleg on the north-marches of Doriath, but went away westward, and passing secretly out of the Guarded Realm came into the woodlands south of Teiglin. There before the Nirnaeth many Men had dwelt in scattered home-steads; they were of Haleth's folk for the most part, but owned no lord, and they lived both by hunting and by husbandry, keeping swine in the mast-lands, and tilling clearings in the forest which were fenced from the wild. But most were now destroyed, or had fled into Brethil, and all that region lay under the fear of Orcs, and of outlaws. For in that time of ruin houseless and desperate Men went astray: remnants of battle and defeat, and lands laid waste; and some were Men driven into the wild for evil deeds. They hunted and gathered such food as they could; but in winter when hunger drove them they were to be feared as wolves, and Gaurwaith, the Wolf-men, they were called by those who still defended their homes. Some fifty of these Men had joined in one band, wandering in the woods beyond the western marches of Doriath; and they were hated scarcely less than Orcs, for there were among them outcasts hard of heart, bearing a grudge against their own kind. The grimmest among them was one named Andróg, hunted from Dor-lómin for the slaying of a woman; and others also came from that land: old Algund, the oldest of the fellowship, who had fled from the Nirnaeth, and Forweg, as he named himself, the captain of the band, a man with fair hair and unsteady glittering eyes, big and bold, but far fallen from the ways of the Edain of the people of Hador. They were become very wary, and they set scouts or a watch about them, whether moving or at rest; and thus they were quickly aware of Túrin when he strayed into their haunts. They trailed him, and they drew a ring about him; and suddenly, as he came out into a glade beside a stream, he found himself within a circle of men with bent bows and drawn swords.

Then Túrin halted, but he showed no fear. 'Who are you?' he said. 'I thought that only Orcs waylaid Men; but I see that I am mistaken.'

'You may rue the mistake,' said Forweg, 'for these are our haunts, and we do not allow other Men to walk in them. We take their lives as forfeit, unless they can ransom them.'

Then Túrin laughed. 'You will get no ransom from me,' he said, 'an outcast and an outlaw. You may search me when I am dead, but it will cost you dearly to prove my words true.'

Nonetheless his death seemed near, for many arrows were notched to the string, waiting for the word of the captain; and none of his enemies stood within reach of a leap with drawn sword. But Túrin, seeing some stones at the stream's edge before his feet, stooped suddenly; and in that instant one of the men, angered by his words, let fly a shaft. But it passed over Túrin, and he springing up cast a stone at the bowman with great force and true aim; and he fell to the ground with broken skull.

'I might be of more service to you alive, in the place of that luckless man,' said Túrin; and turning to Forweg he said: 'If you are the captain here, you should not allow your men to shoot without command.'

'I do not,' said Forweg; 'but he has been rebuked swiftly enough. I will take you in his stead, if you will heed my words better.'

Then two of the outlaws cried out against him; and one was a friend of the fallen man. Ulrad was his name. 'A strange way to gain entry to a fellowship,' he said: 'the slaying of one of the best men.'

'Not unchallenged,' said Túrin. 'But come then! I will endure you both together, with weapons or with strength alone; and then you shall see if I am fit to replace one of your best men.' Then he strode towards them; but Ulrad gave back and would not fight. The other threw down his bow, and looked Túrin up and down; and this man was Andróg of Dor-lómin.

'I am not your match,' he said at length, shaking his head. 'There is none here, I think. You may join us, for my part. But there is a strange look about you; you are a dangerous man. What is your name?'

'Neithan, the Wronged, I call myself,' said Túrin, and Neithan he was afterwards called by the outlaws; but though he told them that he had suffered injustice (and to any who claimed the like he ever lent too ready an ear), no more would he reveal concerning his life or his home. Yet they saw that he had fallen from some high state, and that though he had nothing but his arms, those were made by elvensmiths. He soon won their praise, for he was strong and valiant, and had more skill in the woods than they, and they trusted him, for he was not greedy, and took little thought for himself; but they feared him, because of his sudden angers, which they seldom understood. To Doriath Túrin could not, or in pride would not, return; to Nargothrond since the fall of Felagund none were admitted. To the lesser folk of Haleth in Brethil he did not deign to go; and to Dor-lómin he did not dare, for it was closely beset, and one man alone could not hope at that time, as he thought, to come through the passes of the Mountains of Shadow. Therefore Túrin abode with the outlaws, since the company of any men made the hardship of the wild more easy to endure; and because he wished to live and could not be ever at strife with them, he did little to restrain their evil deeds. Yet at times pity and shame would wake in him, and then he was perilous in his anger. In this way he lived to that year's end, and through the need and hunger of winter, until Stirring came and then a fair spring.

Now in the woods south of Teiglin, as has been told, there were still some homesteads of Men, hardy and wary, though now few in number. Though they loved them not at all and pitied them little, they would in bitter winter put out such food as they could well spare where the Gaurwaith might find it; and so they hoped to avoid the banded attack of the famished. But they earned less gratitude so from the outlaws than from beasts and birds, and they were saved rather by their dogs and their fences. For each homestead had great hedges about its cleared land, and about the houses was a ditch and a stockade; and there were paths from stead to stead, and men could summon help and need by horn-calls.

But when spring was come it was perilous for the Gaurwaith to linger so near to the houses of the Woodmen, who might gather and hunt them down; and Túrin wondered therefore that Forweg did not lead them away. There was more food and game, and less peril, away South where no Men remained. Then one day Túrin missed Forweg, and also Andróg his friend; and he asked where they were, but his companions laughed.

'Away on business of their own, I guess,' said Ulrad. 'They will be back before long, and then we shall move. In haste, maybe; for we shall be lucky if they do not bring the hive-bees after them.'

The sun shone and the young leaves were green; and Túrin was irked by the squalid camp of the outlaws, and he wandered away alone far into the forest. Against his will be remembered the Hidden Kingdom, and he seemed to hear the names of the flowers of Doriath as echoes of an old tongue almost forgotten. But on a sudden he heard cries, and from a hazel-thicket a young women ran out; her clothes were rent by thorns, and she was in great fear, and stumbling she fell gasping to the ground. Then Túrin springing towards the thicket with drawn sword hewed down a man that burst from the hazels in pursuit; and he saw only in the very stroke that it was Forweg.

But as he stood looking down in amaze at the blood upon the grass, Andróg came out, and halted also astounded. 'Evil work, Neithan!' he cried, and drew his sword; but Túrin's mood ran cold, and he said to Andróg: 'Where are the Orcs, then? Have you outrun them to help her?'

'Orcs?' said Andróg. 'Fool! You call yourself an outlaw. Outlaws know no law but their needs. Look to your own, Neithan, and leave us to mind ours.'

'I will do so,' said Túrin. 'But today our paths have crossed. You will leave the woman to me, or you will join Forweg.'

Andróg laughed. 'If that is the way of it, have your will,' he said. 'I make no claim to match you, alone; but our fellows may take this slaying ill.'

Then the woman rose to her feet and laid her hand on Túrin's arm. She looked at the blood and she looked at Túrin, and there was delight in her eyes. 'Kill him, lord!' she said. 'Kill him too! And then come with me. If you bring their heads, Larnach my father will not be displeased. For two "wolf-heads" he has rewarded men well.'

But Túrin said to Andróg: 'Is it far to her home?'

'A mile or so,' he answered, 'in a fenced homestead yonder. She was straying outside.'

'Go then quickly,' said Túrin, turning back to the woman. 'Tell your father to keep you better. But I will not cut off the heads of my fellows to buy his favour, or aught else.'

Then he put up his sword. 'Come!' he said to Andróg. 'We will return. But if you wish to bury your captain, you must do so yourself. Make haste, for a hue and cry may be raised. Bring his weapons!'

Then Túrin went on his way without more words, and Andróg watched him go, and he frowned as one pondering a riddle.

When Túrin came back to the camp of the outlaws he found

them restless and ill at ease; for they had stayed too long already
in one place, near to homesteads well-guarded, and they murmured
against Forweg. 'He runs hazards to our cost,' they said; 'and others
may have to pay for his pleasures.'

'Then choose a new captain!' said Túrin, standing before them.
'Forweg can lead you no longer; for he is dead.'

'How do you know that?' said Ulrad. 'Did you seek honey from
the same hive? Did the bees sting him?'

'No,' said Túrin. 'One sting was enough. I slew him. But I
spared Andróg, and he will soon return.' Then he told all that was
done, rebuking those that did such deeds; and while he yet spoke
Andróg returned bearing Forweg's weapons. 'See, Neithan!' he
cried. 'No alarm has been raised. Maybe she hopes to meet you
again.'

'If you jest with me,' said Túrin, 'I shall regret that I grudged
her your head. Now tell your tale, and be brief.'

Then Andróg told truly enough all that had befallen. 'What
business Neithan had there I now wonder,' he said. 'Not ours, it
seems: For when I came up, he had already slain Forweg. The
woman liked that well, and offered to go with him, begging our heads
as a bride-price. But he did not want her, and sped her off; so what
grudge he had against the captain I cannot guess. He left my head
on my shoulders, for which I am grateful, though much puzzled.'

'Then I deny your claim to come of the People of Hador,' said
Túrin. 'To Uldor the Accursed you belong rather, and should seek
service with Angband. But hear me now!' he cried to them all.
'These choices I give you. You must take me as your captain in
Forweg's place, or else let me go. I will govern this fellowship now,
or leave it. But if you wish to kill me, set to! I will fight you all
until I am dead – or you.'

Then many men seized their weapons, but Andróg cried out:
'Nay! The head that he spared is not witless. If we fight, more than
one will die needlessly, before we kill the best man among us.'
Then he laughed. 'As it was when he joined us, so it is again. He
kills to make room. If it proved well before, so may it again; and he
may lead us to better fortune than prowling about other men's
middens.'

And old Algund said: 'The best man among us. Time was when
we would have done the same, if we dared; but we have forgotten
much. He may bring us home in the end.'

At that the thought came to Túrin that from this small band he
might rise to build himself a free lordship of his own. But he looked

at Algund and Andróg, and he said: 'Home, do you say? Tall and cold stand the Mountains of Shadow between. Behind them are the people of Uldor, and about them the legions of Angband. If such things do not daunt you, seven times seven men, then I may lead you homewards. But how far, before we die?'

All were silent. Then Túrin spoke again. 'Do you take me to be your captain? Then I will lead you first away into the wild, far from the homes of Men. There we may find better fortune, or not; but at the least we shall earn less hatred of our own kind.'

Then all those that were of the People of Hador gathered to him, and took him as their captain; and the others with less good will agreed. And at once he led them away out of that country.[10]

Many messengers had been sent out by Thingol to seek Túrin within Doriath and in the lands near its borders; but in the year of his flight they searched for him in vain, for none knew or could guess that he was with the outlaws and enemies of Men. When winter came on they returned to the king, save Beleg only. After all others had departed still he went on alone.

But in Dimbar and along the north-marches of Doriath things had gone ill. The Dragon-helm was seen there in battle no longer, and the Strongbow also was missed; and the servants of Morgoth were heartened and increased ever in numbers and in daring. Winter came and passed, and with Spring their assault was renewed: Dimbar was overrun, and the Men of Brethil were afraid, for evil roamed now upon all their borders, save in the south.

It was now almost a year since Túrin had fled, and still Beleg sought for him, with ever lessening hope. He passed northwards in his wanderings to the Crossings of Teiglin, and there, hearing ill news of a new inroad of Orcs out of Taur-nu-Fuin, he turned back, and came as it chanced to the homes of the Woodmen soon after Túrin had left that region. There he heard a strange tale that went among them. A tall and lordly Man, or an Elf-warrior, some said, had appeared in the woods, and had slain one of the Gaurwaith, and rescued the daughter of Larnach whom they were pursuing. 'Very proud he was,' said Larnach's daughter to Beleg, 'with bright eyes that scarcely deigned to look at me. Yet he called the Wolf-men his fellows, and would not slay another that stood by, and knew his name. Neithan, he called him.'

'Can you read this riddle?' asked Larnach of the Elf.

'I can, alas,' said Beleg. 'The Man that you tell of is one whom I seek.' No more of Túrin did he tell the Woodmen; but he warned them of evil gathering northwards. 'Soon the Orcs will come ravening in this country in strength too great for you to withstand,' he said. 'This year at last you must give up your freedom or your lives. Go to Brethil while there is time!'

Then Beleg went on his way in haste, and sought for the lairs of the outlaws, and such signs as might show him whither they had gone. These he soon found; but Túrin was now several days ahead, and moved swiftly, fearing the pursuit of the Woodmen, and he used all the arts that he knew to defeat or mislead any that tried to follow them. Seldom did they remain two nights in one camp, and they left little trace of their going or staying. So it was that even Beleg hunted them in vain. Led by signs that he could read, or by the rumour of the passing of Men among the wild things with whom he could speak, he came often near, but always their lair was deserted when he came to it; for they kept a watch about them by day and night, and at any rumour of approach they were swiftly up and away. 'Alas!' he cried. 'Too well did I teach this child of Men craft in wood and field! An Elvish band almost one might think this to be.' But they for their part became aware that they were trailed by some tireless pursuer, whom they could not see, and yet could not shake off; and they grew uneasy.[11]

Not long afterwards, as Beleg had feared, the Orcs came across the Brithiach, and being resisted with all the force that he could muster by Handir of Brethil they passed south over the Crossings of Teiglin in search of plunder. Many of the Woodmen had taken Beleg's counsel and sent their women and children to ask for refuge in Brethil. These and their escort escaped, passing over the Crossings in time; but the armed men that came behind were met by the Orcs, and the men were worsted. A few fought their way through and came to Brethil, but many were slain or captured; and the Orcs passed on to the homesteads, and sacked them and burned them. Then at once they turned back westwards, seeking the Road, for they wished now to return North as swiftly as they could with their booty and their captives.

But the scouts of the outlaws were soon aware of them; and though they cared little enough for the captives, the plunder of the Woodmen aroused their greed. To Túrin it seemed perilous to reveal themselves to the Orcs, until their numbers were known; but the outlaws would not heed him, for they had need of many things in the wild, and already some began to regret his leading. Therefore taking one Orleg as his only companion Túrin went forth to spy upon the Orcs; and giving command of the band to Andróg he charged him to lie close and well hid while they were gone.

Now the Orc-host was far greater than the band of the outlaws, but they were in lands to which Orcs had seldom dared to come, and they knew also that beyond the Road lay the Talath Dirnen, the Guarded Plain, upon which the scouts and spies of Nargothrond kept watch; and fearing danger they were wary, and their scouts went creeping through the trees on either side of the marching lines. Thus it was that Túrin and Orleg were discovered, for three scouts stumbled upon them as they lay hid; and though they slew two the third escaped, crying as he ran *Golug! Golug!* Now that was a name which they had for the Noldor. At once the forest was filled with Orcs, scattering silently and hunting far and wide. Then Túrin, seeing that there was small hope of escape, thought at least to deceive them and to lead them away from the hiding-place of his men; and perceiving from the cry of *Golug!* that they feared the spies of Nargothrond, he fled with Orleg westward. The pursuit came swiftly after them, until turn and dodge as they would they were driven at last out of the forest; and then they were espied, and as they sought to cross the Road Orleg was shot down by many arrows. But Túrin was saved by his elven-mail, and escaped alone into the wilds beyond; and by speed and craft he eluded his enemies, fleeing far into lands that were strange to him. Then the Orcs, fearing that the Elves of Nargothrond might be aroused, slew their captives and made haste away into the North.

Now when three days had passed, and yet Túrin and Orleg did not return, some of the outlaws wished to depart from the cave where they lay hid; but Andróg spoke against it. And while they were in the midst of this debate, suddenly a grey figure stood before them. Beleg had found them at last. He came forward with no weapon in his hands, and held the palms turned towards them; but they leapt up in fear, and Andróg coming behind cast a noose over him, and drew it so that it pinioned his arms.

'If you do not wish for guests, you should keep better watch,' said Beleg. 'Why do you welcome me thus? I come as a friend, and seek only a friend. Neithan I hear that you call him.'

'He is not here,' said Ulrad. 'But unless you have long spied on us, how know you that name?'

'He has long spied on us,' said Andróg. 'This is the shadow that has dogged us. Now perhaps we shall learn his true purpose.' Then he bade them tie Beleg to a tree beside the cave; and when he was hard bound hand and foot they questioned him. But to all their questions Beleg would give one answer only: 'A friend I have been to this Neithan since I first met him in the woods, and he was then but a child. I seek him only in love, and to bring him good tidings.'

'Let us slay him, and be rid of his spying,' said Andróg in wrath; and he looked on the great bow of Beleg and coveted it, for he was an archer. But some of better heart spoke against him, and Algund said to him: 'The captain may return yet; and then you will rue it, if he learns that he has been robbed at once of a friend and of good tidings.'

'I do not believe the tale of this Elf,' said Andróg. 'He is a spy of the King of Doriath. But if he has indeed any tidings, he shall tell them to us; and we shall judge if they give us reason to let him live.'

'I shall wait for your captain,' said Beleg.

'You shall stand there until you speak,' said Andróg.

Then at the egging of Andróg they left Beleg tied to the tree without food or water, and they sat near eating and drinking; but he said no more to them. When two days and nights had passed in this way they became angry and fearful, and were eager to be gone; and most were now ready to slay the Elf. As night drew down they were all gathered about him, and Ulrad brought a brand from the little fire that was lit in the cave-mouth. But at that moment Túrin returned. Coming silently, as was his custom, he stood in the shadows beyond the ring of men, and he saw the haggard face of Beleg in the light of the brand.

Then he was stricken as with a shaft, and as if at the sudden melting of a frost tears long unshed filled his eyes. He sprang out and ran to the tree. 'Beleg! Beleg!' he cried. 'How have you come hither? And why do you stand so?' At once he cut the bonds from his friend, and Beleg fell forward into his arms.

When Túrin heard all that the men would tell, he was angry and grieved; but at first he gave heed only to Beleg. While he tended him with what skill he had, he thought of his life in the woods, and his anger turned upon himself. For often strangers had been slain, when caught near the lairs of the outlaws, or waylaid by them, and he had not hindered it; and often he himself had spoken ill of King Thingol and of the Grey-elves, so that he must share the blame, if they were treated as foes. Then with bitterness he turned to the men. 'You were cruel,' he said, 'and cruel without need. Never until now have we tormented a prisoner; but to such Orc-work such a life as we lead has brought us. Lawless and fruitless all our deeds have been, serving only ourselves, and feeding hate in our hearts.'

But Andróg said: 'Whom shall we serve, if not ourselves? Whom shall we love, when all hate us?'

'At least my hands shall not again be raised against Elves or Men,' said Túrin. 'Angband has servants enough. If others will not take this vow with me, I will walk alone.'

Then Beleg opened his eyes and raised his head. 'Not alone!' he said. 'Now at last I can tell my tidings. You are no outlaw, and Neithan is a name unfit. Such fault as was found in you is pardoned. For a year you have been sought, to recall you to honour and to the service of the king. The Dragon-helm has been missed too long.'

But Túrin showed no joy in this news, and sat long in silence; for at Beleg's words a shadow fell upon him again. 'Let this night pass,' he said at length. 'Then I will choose. However it goes, we must leave this lair tomorrow; for not all who seek us wish us well.'

'Nay, none,' said Andróg, and he cast an evil look at Beleg.

In the morning Beleg, being swiftly healed of his pains, after the manner of the Elven-folk of old, spoke to Túrin apart.

'I looked for more joy at my tidings,' he said. 'Surely you will return now to Doriath?' And he begged Túrin to do this in all ways that he could; but the more he urged it, the more Túrin hung back. Nonetheless he questioned Beleg closely concerning the judgement of Thingol. Then Beleg told him all that he knew, and at the last Túrin said: 'Then Mablung proved my friend, as he once seemed?'

'The friend of truth, rather,' said Beleg, 'and that was best, in the end. But why, Túrin, did you not speak to him of Saeros' assault upon you? All otherwise might things have gone. And,' he said, looking at the men sprawled near the mouth of the cave, 'you might have held your helm still high, and not fallen to this.'

'That may be, if fall you call it,' said Túrin. 'That may be. But so it went; and words stuck in my throat. There was reproof in his eyes, without question asked of me, for a deed I had not done. My Man's heart was proud, as the Elf-king said. And so it still is, Beleg Cúthalion. Not yet will it suffer me to go back to Menegroth and bear looks of pity and pardon, as for a wayward boy amended. I should give pardon, not receive it. And I am a boy no longer, but a man, according to my kind; and a hard man by my fate.'

Then Beleg was troubled. 'What will you do, then?' he asked.

'Fare free,' said Túrin. 'That wish Mablung gave me at our parting. The grace of Thingol will not stretch to receive these companions of my fall, I think; but I will not part with them now, if they do not wish to part with me. I love them in my way, even the worst a little. They are of my own kind, and there is some good in each that might grow. I think that they will stand by me.'

'You see with other eyes than mine,' said Beleg. 'If you try to wean them from evil, they will fail you. I doubt them, and one most of all.'

'How shall an Elf judge of Men?' said Túrin.

'As he judges all deeds, by whomsoever done,' answered Beleg, but he said no more, and did not speak of Andróg's malice, to which his evil handling had been chiefly due; for perceiving Túrin's mood he feared to be disbelieved and to hurt their old friendship, driving Túrin back to his evil ways.

'Fare free, you say, Túrin, my friend,' he said. 'What is your meaning?'

'I would lead my own men, and make war in my own way,' Túrin answered. 'But in this at least my heart is changed: I repent every stroke save those dealt against the Enemy of Men and Elves. And above all else I would have you beside me. Stay with me!'

'If I stayed beside you, love would lead me, not wisdom,' said Beleg. 'My heart warns me that we should return to Doriath.'

'Nonetheless, I will not go there,' said Túrin.

Then Beleg strove once more to persuade him to return to the service of King Thingol, saying that there was great need of his strength and valour on the north-marches of Doriath, and he spoke to him of the new inroads of the Orcs, coming down into Dimbar out of Taur-nu-Fuin by the Pass of Anach. But all his words were of no avail, and at last he said: 'A hard man you have called yourself, Túrin. Hard you are, and stubborn. Now the turn is mine. If you wish indeed to have the Strongbow beside you, look for me in Dimbar; for thither I shall return.'

Then Túrin sat in silence, and strove with his pride, which would not let him turn back; and he brooded on the years that lay behind him. But coming suddenly out of his thought he said to Beleg: 'The elf-maiden whom you named: I owe her well for her timely witness; yet I cannot recall her. Why did she watch my ways?'

Then Beleg looked strangely at him. 'Why indeed?' he said. 'Túrin, have you lived always with your heart and half your mind far away? You walked with Nellas in the woods of Doriath, when you were a boy.'

'That was long ago,' said Túrin. 'Or so my childhood now seems, and a mist is over it – save only the memory of my father's house in Dor-lómin. But why should I have walked with an elf-maiden?'

'To learn what she could teach, maybe,' said Beleg. 'Alas, child

of Men! There are other griefs in Middle-earth than yours, and
wounds made by no weapon. Indeed, I begin to think that Elves
and Men should not meet or meddle.'

Túrin said nothing, but looked long in Beleg's face, as if he would
read in it the riddle of his words. But Nellas of Doriath never saw
him again, and his shadow passed from her.[12]

### Of Mîm the Dwarf

After the departure of Beleg (and that was in the second summer
after the flight of Túrin from Doriath)[13] things went ill for the outlaws. There were rains out of season, and Orcs in greater numbers
than before came down from the North and along the old South
Road over Teiglin, troubling all the woods on the west borders of
Doriath. There was little safety or rest, and the company were more
often hunted than hunters.

One night as they lay lurking in the fireless dark, Túrin looked
on his life, and it seemed to him that it might well be bettered. 'I
must find some secure refuge,' he thought, 'and make provision
against winter and hunger'; and the next day he led his men away,
further than they had yet come from the Teiglin and the marches
of Doriath. After three days' journeying they halted at the western
edge of the woods of Sirion's Vale. There the land was drier and
more bare, as it began to climb up into the moorlands.

Soon after, it chanced that as the grey light of a day of rain was
failing Túrin and his men were sheltering in a holly-thicket; and
beyond it was a treeless space, in which there were many great
stones, leaning or tumbled together. All was still, save for the drip
of rain from the leaves. Suddenly a watchman gave a call, and
leaping up they saw three hooded shapes, grey-clad, going stealthily
among the stones. They were burdened each with a great sack, but
they went swiftly for all that.

Túrin cried out to them to halt, and the men ran out on them
like hounds; but they held on their way, and though Andróg shot
arrows after them two vanished in the dusk. One lagged behind,
being slower or more heavily burdened; and he was soon seized and
thrown down, and held by many hard hands, though he struggled and
bit like a beast. But Túrin came up, and rebuked his men. 'What
have you there?' he said. 'What need to be so fierce? It is old and
small. What harm is in it?'

'It bites,' said Andróg, showing his hand that bled. 'It is an Orc,
or of Orc-kin. Kill it!'

'It deserved no less, for cheating our hope,' said another, who had taken the sack. 'There is nothing here but roots and small stones.'

'Nay,' said Túrin, 'it is bearded. It is only a dwarf, I guess. Let him up, and speak.'

So it was that Mîm came in to the Tale of the Children of Húrin. For he stumbled up on his knees before Túrin's feet and begged for his life. 'I am old,' he said, 'and poor. Only a dwarf, as you say, and not an Orc. Mîm is my name. Do not let them slay me, lord, for no cause, as would the Orcs.'

Then Túrin pitied him in his heart, but he said: 'Poor you seem, Mîm, though that is strange in a dwarf; but we are poorer, I think: houseless and friendless Men. If I said that we do not spare for pity's sake only, being in great need, what would you offer for ransom?'

'I do not know what you desire, lord,' said Mîm warily.

'At this time, little enough!' said Túrin, looking about him bitterly with rain in his eyes. 'A safe place to sleep in out of the damp woods. Doubtless you have such for yourself.'

'I have,' said Mîm; 'but I cannot give it in ransom. I am too old to live under the sky.'

'You need grow no older,' said Andróg, stepping up with a knife in his unharmed hand. 'I can spare you that.'

'Lord!' cried Mîm then in great fear. 'If I lose my life, you will lose the dwelling; for you will not find it without Mîm. I cannot give it, but I will share it. There is more room in it than once there was: so many have gone for ever,' and he began to weep.

'Your life is spared, Mîm,' said Túrin.

'Till we come to his lair, at least,' said Andróg.

But Túrin turned upon him, and said: 'If Mîm brings us to his home without trickery, and it is good, then his life is ransomed; and he shall not be slain by any man who follows me. So I swear.'

Then Mîm clasped Túrin about his knees, saying: 'Mîm will be your friend, lord. At first I thought you were an Elf, by your speech and your voice; but if you are a Man, that is better. Mîm does not love Elves.'

'Where is this house of yours?' said Andróg. 'It must be good indeed if Andróg is to share it with a Dwarf. For Andróg does not like Dwarves. His people brought few good tales of that race out of the East.'

'Judge my home when you see it,' said Mîm. 'But you will need light on the way, you stumbling Men. I will return in good time and lead you.'

'No, no!' said Andróg. 'You will not allow this, surely, captain?
You would never see the old rascal again.'

'It is growing dark,' said Túrin. 'Let him leave us some pledge.
Shall we keep your sack and its load, Mîm?'

But at this the Dwarf fell on his knees again in great trouble. 'If
Mîm did not mean to return, he would not return for an old sack of
roots,' he said. 'I will come back. Let me go!'

'I will not,' said Túrin. 'If you will not part with your sack, you
must stay with it. A night under the leaves will make you pity us in
your turn, maybe.' But he marked, and others also, that Mîm set
more value on his load than it seemed worth to the eye.

They led the old Dwarf away to their dismal camp, and as he went
he muttered in a strange tongue that seemed harsh with ancient
hatred; but when they put bonds on his legs he went suddenly quiet.
And those who were on the watch saw him sitting on through the
night silent and still as stone, save for his sleepless eyes that glinted
as they roved in the dark.

Before morning the rain ceased, and a wind stirred in the trees.
Dawn came more brightly than for many days, and light airs from the
South opened the sky, pale and clear about the rising of the sun.
Mîm sat on without moving, and he seemed as if dead; for now the
heavy lids of his eyes were closed, and the morning-light showed him
withered and shrunken with age. Túrin stood and looked down on
him. 'There is light enough now,' he said.

Then Mîm opened his eyes and pointed to his bonds; and when
he was released he spoke fiercely. 'Learn this, fools!' he said. 'Do
not put bonds on a Dwarf! He will not forgive it. I do not wish to
die, but for what you have done my heart is hot. I repent my promise.'

'But I do not,' said Túrin. 'You will lead me to your home. Till
then we will not speak of death. That is *my* will.' He looked stead-
fastly in the eyes of the Dwarf, and Mîm could not endure it; few
indeed could challenge the eyes of Túrin in set will or in wrath. Soon
he turned away his head, and rose. 'Follow me, lord!' he said.

'Good!' said Túrin. 'But now I will add this: I understand your
pride. You may die, but you shall not be set in bonds again.'

Then Mîm led them back to the place where he had been captured,
and he pointed westward. 'There is my home!' he said. 'You have
often seen it, I guess, for it is tall. Sharbhund we called it, before
the Elves changed all the names.' Then they saw that he was pointing
to Amon Rûdh, the Bald Hill, whose bare head watched over many
leagues of the wild.

'We have seen it, but never nearer,' said Andróg. 'For what safe lair can be there, or water, or any other thing that we need? I guessed that there was some trick. Do men hide on a hill-top?'

'Long sight may be safer than lurking,' said Túrin. 'Amon Rûdh gazes far and wide. Well, Mîm, I will come and see what you have to show. How long will it take us, stumbling Men, to come thither?'

'All this day until dusk,' Mîm answered.

The company set out westward, and Túrin went at the head with Mîm at his side. They walked warily when they left the woods, but all the land was empty and quiet. They passed over the tumbled stones, and began to climb; for Amon Rûdh stood upon the eastern edge of the high moorlands that rose between the vales of Sirion and Narog, and even above the stony heath at its base its crown was reared up a thousand feet and more. Upon the eastern side a broken land climbed slowly up to the high ridges among knots of birch and rowan, and ancient thorn-trees rooted in rock. About the lower slopes of Amon Rûdh there grew thickets of *aeglos*; but its steep grey head was bare, save for the red *seregon* that mantled the stone.[14]

As the afternoon was waning the outlaws drew near to the roots of the hill. They came now from the north, for so Mîm had led them, and the light of the westering sun fell upon the crown of Amon Rûdh, and the *seregon* was all in flower.

'See! There is blood on the hill-top,' said Andróg.

'Not yet,' said Túrin.

The sun was sinking and light was failing in the hollows. The hill now loomed up before them and above them, and they wondered what need there could be of a guide to so plain a mark. But as Mîm led them on, and they began to climb the last steep slopes, they perceived that he was following some path by secret signs or old custom. Now his course wound to and fro, and if they looked aside they saw that at either hand dark dells and chines opened, or the land ran down into wastes of great stones, with falls and holes masked by bramble and thorn. There without a guide they might have laboured and clambered for days to find a way.

At length they came to steeper but smoother ground. They passed under the shadows of ancient rowan-trees into aisles of long-legged *aeglos*: a gloom filled with a sweet scent.[15] Then suddenly there was a rock-wall before them, flat-faced and sheer, towering high above them in the dusk.

'Is this the door of your house?' said Túrin. 'Dwarves love stone, it is said.' He drew close to Mîm, lest he should play them some trick at the last.

'Not the door of the house, but the gate of the garth,' said Mîm. Then he turned to the right along the cliff-foot, and after twenty paces halted suddenly; and Túrin saw that by the work of hands or of weather there was a cleft so shaped that two faces of the wall overlapped, and an opening ran back to the left between them. Its entrance was shrouded by long-trailing plants rooted in crevices above, but within there was a steep stony path going upwards in the dark. Water trickled down it, and it was dank. One by one they filed up. At the top the path turned right and south again, and brought them through a thicket of thorns out upon a green flat, through which it ran on into the shadows. They had come to Mîm's house, Bar-en-Nibin-noeg,[16] which only ancient tales in Doriath and Nargothrond remembered, and no Men had seen. But night was falling, and the east was starlit, and they could not yet see how this strange place was shaped.

Amon Rûdh had a crown: a great mass like a steep cap of stone with a bare flattened top. Upon its north side there stood out from it a shelf, level and almost square, which could not be seen from below; for behind it stood the hill-crown like a wall, and west and east from its brink sheer cliffs fell. Only from the north, as they had come, could it be reached with ease by those who knew the way.[17] From the cleft a path led, and passed soon into a little grove of dwarfed birches growing about a clear pool in a rock-hewn basin. This pool was fed by a spring at the foot of the wall behind, and through a runnel it spilled like a white thread over the western brink of the shelf. Behind the screen of the trees near the spring, between two tall buttresses of rock, there was a cave. No more than a shallow grot it looked, with a low broken arch; but further in it had been deepened and bored far under the hill by the slow hands of the Petty-dwarves, in the long years that they had dwelt there, untroubled by the Grey-elves of the woods.

Through the deep dusk Mîm led them past the pool, where now the faint stars were mirrored among the shadows of the birch-boughs. At the mouth of the cave he turned and bowed to Túrin. 'Enter,' he said, 'Bar-en-Danwedh, the House of Ransom; for so it shall be called.'

'That may be,' said Túrin. 'I will look first.' Then he went in with Mîm, and the others, seeing him unafraid, followed behind, even Andróg, who most misdoubted the Dwarf. They were soon in a black dark; but Mîm clapped his hands, and a little light appeared, coming round a corner: from a passage at the back of the outer grot there stepped another Dwarf bearing a small torch.

'Ha! I missed him, as I feared!' said Andróg. But Mîm spoke quickly with the other in their own harsh tongue, and seeming troubled or angered by what he heard, he darted into the passage and disappeared. Then Andróg was all for going forward. 'Attack first!' he said. 'There may be a hive of them; but they are small.'

'Three only, I guess,' said Túrin; and he led the way, while behind him the outlaws groped along the passage by the feel of the rough walls. Many times it bent this way and that at sharp angles; but at last a faint light gleamed ahead, and they came into a small but lofty hall, dim-lit by lamps hanging down out of the roof-shadow upon fine chains. Mîm was not there, but his voice could be heard, and led by it Túrin came to the door of a chamber opening at the back of the hall. Looking in, he saw Mîm kneeling on the floor. Beside him stood silent the Dwarf with the torch; but on a stone couch by the further wall there lay another. 'Khîm, Khîm, Khîm!' the old Dwarf wailed, tearing at his beard.

'Not all your shafts went wild,' said Túrin to Andróg. 'But this may prove an ill hit. You loose shaft too lightly; but you may not live long enough to learn wisdom.' Then entering softly Túrin stood behind Mîm, and spoke to him. 'What is the trouble, Mîm?' he said. 'I have some healing arts. Can I give you aid?'

Mîm turned his head, and there was a red light in his eyes. 'Not unless you can turn back time, and then cut off the cruel hands of your men,' he answered. 'This is my son, pierced by an arrow. Now he is beyond speech. He died at sunset. Your bonds held me from healing him.'

Again pity long hardened welled in Túrin's heart as water from rock. 'Alas!' he said. 'I would recall that shaft, if I could. Now Bar-en-Danwedh, House of Ransom, shall this be called in truth. For whether we dwell here or no, I will hold myself in your debt; and if ever I come to any wealth, I will pay you a ransom of heavy gold for your son, in token of sorrow, though it gladden your heart no more.'

Then Mîm rose, and looked long at Túrin. 'I hear you,' he said. 'You speak like a dwarf-lord of old; and at that I marvel. Now my heart is cooled, though it is not glad. My own ransom I will pay, therefore: you may dwell here, if you will. But this I will add: he that loosed the shaft shall break his bow and his arrows and lay them at my son's feet; and he shall never take arrow nor bear bow again. If he does, he shall die by it. That curse I lay on him.'

Andróg was afraid when he heard of this curse; and though he did so with great grudge, he broke his bow and his arrows and laid them at the dead Dwarf's feet. But as he came out from the chamber, he glanced evilly at Mîm, and muttered: 'The curse of a Dwarf never dies, they say; but a Man's too may come home. May he die with a dart in his throat!'[18]

That night they lay in the hall and slept uneasily for the wailing of Mîm and of Ibun, his other son. When that ceased they could not tell; but when they woke at last the Dwarves were gone, and the chamber was closed by a stone. The day was fair again, and in the morning sun the outlaws washed in the pool and prepared such food as they had; and as they ate Mîm stood before them.

He bowed to Túrin. 'He is gone, and all is done,' he said. 'He lies with his fathers. Now we turn to such life as is left, though the days before us may be short. Does Mîm's home please you? Is the ransom paid and accepted?'

'It is,' said Túrin.

'Then all is yours, to order your dwelling here as you will, save this: the chamber that is closed, none shall open it but me.'

'We hear you,' said Túrin. 'But as for our life here, we are secure, or so it seems; but still we must have food, and other things. How shall we go out; or still more, how shall we return?'

To their disquiet Mîm laughed in his throat. 'Do you fear that you have followed a spider to the heart of his web?' he said. 'Mîm does not eat Men! And a spider could ill deal with thirty wasps at a time. See, you are armed, and I stand here bare. No, we must share, you and I: house, food, and fire, and maybe other winnings. The house, I think, you will guard and keep secret for your own good, even when you know the ways in and out. You will learn them in time. But in the meanwhile Mîm must guide you, or Ibun his son.'

To this Túrin agreed, and he thanked Mîm, and most of his men were glad; for under the sun of morning, while summer was yet high, it seemed a fair place to dwell in. Andróg alone was ill-content. 'The sooner we are masters of our goings and comings the better,' he said. 'Never before have we taken a prisoner with a grievance to and fro on our ventures.'

That day they rested, and cleaned their arms and mended their gear; for they had food to last for a day or two yet, and Mîm added to what they had. Three great cooking-pots he lent to them, and firing also; and he brought out a sack. 'Rubbish,' he said. 'Not worth the stealing. Only wild roots.'

But when they were cooked these roots proved good to eat, somewhat like bread; and the outlaws were glad of them, for they had long lacked bread save when they could steal it. 'Wild Elves know them not; Grey-elves have not found them; the proud ones from over the Sea are too proud to delve,' said Mîm.

'What is their name?' said Túrin.

Mîm looked at him sidelong. 'They have no name, save in the dwarf-tongue, which we do not teach,' he said. 'And we do not teach Men to find them, for Men are greedy and thriftless, and would not spare till all the plants had perished; whereas now they pass them by as they go blundering in the wild. No more will you learn of me; but you may have enough of my bounty, as long as you speak fair and do not spy or steal.' Then again he laughed in his throat. 'They are of great worth,' he said. 'More than gold in the hungry winter, for they may be hoarded like the nuts of a squirrel, and already we were building our store from the first that are ripe. But you are fools, if you think that I would not be parted from one small load even for the saving of my life.'

'I hear you,' said Ulrad, who had looked in the sack when Mîm was taken. 'Yet you would not be parted, and your words only make me wonder the more.'

Mîm turned and looked at him darkly. 'You are one of the fools that spring would not mourn if you perished in winter,' he said. 'I had spoken my word, and so must have returned, willing or not, with sack or without, let a lawless and faithless man think what he will! But I like not to be parted from my own by force of the wicked, be it no more than a shoe-thong. Do I not remember that your hands were among those that put bonds on me, and so held me that I did not speak again with my son? Ever when I deal out the earth-bread from my store you shall be counted out, and if you eat it, you shall eat by the bounty of your fellows, not of me.'

Then Mîm went away; but Ulrad, who had quailed under his anger, spoke to his back: 'High words! Nonetheless the old rogue had other things in his sack, of like shape but harder and heavier. Maybe there are other things beside earth-bread in the wild which Elves have not found and Men must not know!'[19]

'That may be,' said Túrin. 'Nonetheless the Dwarf spoke the truth in one point at least, calling you a fool. Why must you speak your thoughts? Silence, if fair words stick in your throat, would serve all our ends better.'

The day passed in peace, and none of the outlaws desired to go abroad. Túrin paced much upon the green sward of the shelf, from brink to brink; and he looked out east, and west, and north, and wondered to find how far were the views in the clear air. Northward he looked, and descried the Forest of Brethil climbing green about Amon Obel in its midst, and thither his eyes were drawn ever and again, he knew not why; for his heart was set rather to the north-west, where league upon league away on the skirts of the sky it seemed to him that he could glimpse the Mountains of Shadow, the walls of his home. But at evening Túrin looked west into the sunset, as the sun rode down red into the hazes above the distant coasts, and the Vale of Narog lay deep in the shadows between.

So began the abiding of Túrin son of Húrin in the halls of Mîm, in Bar-en-Danwedh, the House of Ransom.

---

*For the story of Túrin from his coming to Bar-en-Danwedh to the fall of Nargothrond see The Silmarillion, pp. 204–15, and the Appendix to the Narn i Hîn Húrin, p. 150 below.*

---

### The Return of Túrin to Dor-lómin

At last worn by haste and the long road (for forty leagues and more had he journeyed without rest) Túrin came with the first ice of winter to the pools of Ivrin, where before he had been healed. But they were now only a frozen mire, and he could drink there no more.

Thence he came to the passes into Dor-lómin;[20] and snow came bitterly from the North, and the ways were perilous and cold. Though three and twenty years were gone since he had trodden that path it was graven in his heart, so great was the sorrow of each step at the parting from Morwen. Thus at last he came back to the land of his childhood. It was bleak and bare; and the people there were few and churlish, and they spoke the harsh tongue of the Easterlings, and the old tongue was become the language of serfs, or of foes.

Therefore Túrin walked warily, hooded and silent, and he came at last to the house that he sought. It stood empty and dark, and no living thing dwelt near it; for Morwen was gone, and Brodda the Incomer (he that took by force Aerin, Húrin's kinswoman, to wife) had plundered her house, and taken all that was left to her of goods or of servants. Brodda's house stood nearest to the old house of Húrin, and thither Túrin came, spent with wandering and grief, begging for shelter; and it was granted to him, for some of the kindlier manners of old were still kept there by Aerin. He was given a seat by a fire among the servants, and a few vagabonds well-nigh as grim and wayworn as he; and he asked news of the land.

At that the company fell silent, and some drew away, looking askance at the stranger. But one old vagabond man, with a crutch, said: 'If you must speak the old tongue, master, speak it softer, and ask for no tidings. Would you be beaten for a rogue, or hung for a spy? For both you may well be by the looks of you. Which is but to say,' he said, coming near and speaking low in Túrin's ear, 'one of the kindly folk of old that came with Hador in the days of gold, before heads wore wolf-hair. Some here are of that sort, though now made beggars and slaves, and but for the Lady Aerin would get neither this fire nor this broth. Whence are you, and what news would you have?'

'There was a lady called Morwen,' answered Túrin, 'and long ago I lived in her house. Thither after far wandering I came to seek welcome, but neither fire nor folk are there now.'

'Nor have been this long year and more,' answered the old man. 'But scant were both fire and folk in that house since the deadly war; for she was of the old people – as doubtless you know, the widow of our lord, Húrin Galdor's son. They dared not touch her, though, for they feared her; proud and fair as a queen, before sorrow marred her. Witchwife they called her, and shunned her. Witchwife: it is but "elf-friend" in the new language. Yet they robbed her. Often would she and her daughter have gone hungry, but for the Lady Aerin. She aided them in secret, it is said, and was often beaten for it by the churl Brodda, her husband by need.'

'And this long year and more?' said Túrin. 'Are they dead or made thralls? Or have the Orcs assailed her?'

'It is not known for sure,' said the old man. 'But she is gone with her daughter; and this Brodda has plundered her and stripped what remained. Not a dog is left, and her few folk made his slaves; save some that have gone begging, as have I. I served her many a year, and the great Master before, Sador Onefoot: a cursed axe in the woods long ago, or I would be lying in the Great Mound now. Well I remember the day Húrin's boy was sent away, and how he wept; and she, when he was gone. To the Hidden Kingdom he went, it was said.'

With that the old man stayed his tongue, and eyed Túrin doubt-
fully. 'I am old and I babble,' he said. 'Mind me not! But though it
is pleasant to speak the old tongue with one that speaks it fair as in
time past, the days are ill, and one must be wary. Not all that speak
the fair tongue are fair at heart.'

'Truly,' said Túrin. 'My heart is grim. But if you fear that I am
a spy of the North or the East, then you have little more wisdom
than you had long ago, Sador Labadal.'

The old man eyed him agape; then trembling he spoke. 'Come
outside! It is colder, but safer. You speak too loud, and I too much,
for an Easterling's hall.'

When they were come into the court he clutched at Túrin's cloak.
'Long ago you dwelt in that house, you say. Lord Túrin, son of
Húrin, why have you come back? My eyes are opened, and my ears
at last; you have the voice of your father. But young Túrin alone ever
gave me that name, Labadal. He meant no ill: we were merry friends
in those days. What does he seek here now? Few are we left; and we
are old and weaponless. Happier are those in the Great Mound.'

'I did not come with thought of battle,' said Túrin, 'though your
words have waked the thought in me now, Labadal. But it must
wait. I came seeking the Lady Morwen and Nienor. What can you
tell me, and swiftly?'

'Little, lord,' said Sador. 'They went away secretly. It was
whispered among us that they were summoned by the Lord Túrin;
for we did not doubt that he had grown great in the years, a king or
a lord in some south country. But it seems that is not so.'

'It is not,' answered Túrin. 'A lord I was in a south country,
though now I am a vagabond. But I did not summon them.'

'Then I know not what to tell you,' said Sador. 'But the Lady
Aerin will know, I doubt not. She knew all the counsel of your mother.'

'How can I come to her?'

'That I know not. It would cost her much pain were she caught
whispering at a door with a wandering wretch of the downtrod
people, even could any message call her forth. And such a beggar
as you are will not walk far up the hall towards the high board, before
the Easterlings seize him and beat him, or worse.'

Then in anger Túrin cried: 'May I not walk up Brodda's hall,
and will they beat me? Come, and see!'

Thereupon he went into the hall, and cast back his hood, and
thrusting aside all in his path he strode towards the board where sat
the master of the house and his wife, and other Easterling lords.
Then some ran to seize him, but he flung them to the ground, and

cried: 'Does no one rule this house, or is it an Orc-hold? Where is the master?'

Then Brodda rose in wrath. 'I rule this house,' said he.

But before he could say more, Túrin said: 'Then you have not learned the courtesy that was in this land before you. Is it now the manner of men to let lackeys mishandle the kinsmen of their wives? Such am I, and I have an errand to the Lady Aerin. Shall I come freely, or shall I come as I will?'

'Come!' said Brodda, and he scowled; but Aerin turned pale.

Then Túrin strode to the high board, and stood before it, and bowed. 'Your pardon, Lady Aerin,' he said, 'that I break in upon you thus; but my errand is urgent and has brought me far. I seek Morwen, Lady of Dor-lómin, and Nienor her daughter. But her house is empty and plundered. What can you tell me?'

'Nothing,' said Aerin in great fear, for Brodda watched her narrowly. 'Nothing, save that she is gone.'

'That I do not believe,' said Túrin.

Then Brodda sprang forth, and he was red with drunken rage. 'No more!' he cried. 'Shall my wife be gainsaid before me, by a beggar that speaks the serf-tongue? There is no Lady of Dor-lómin. But as for Morwen, she was of the thrall-folk, and has fled as thralls will. Do you likewise, and swiftly, or I will have you hung on a tree!'

Then Túrin leapt at him, and drew his black sword, and seized Brodda by the hair and laid back his head. 'Let no one stir,' said he, 'or this head will leave its shoulders! Lady Aerin, I would beg your pardon once more, if I thought that this churl had ever done you anything but wrong. But speak now, and do not deny me! Am I not Túrin, Lord of Dor-lómin? Shall I command you?'

'Command me,' she answered.

'Who plundered the house of Morwen?'

'Brodda,' she answered.

'When did she flee, and whither?'

'A year and three months gone,' said Aerin. 'Master Brodda and others of the Incomers of the East hereabout oppressed her sorely. Long ago she was bidden to the Hidden Kingdom; and she went forth at last. For the lands between were then free of evil for a while, because of the prowess of the Blacksword of the south country, it is said; but that now is ended. She looked to find her son there awaiting her. But if you are he, then I fear that all has gone awry.'

Then Túrin laughed bitterly. 'Awry, awry?' he cried. 'Yes, ever awry: as crooked as Morgoth!' And suddenly a black wrath shook him; for his eyes were opened, and the spell of Glaurung loosed its last threads, and he knew the lies with which he had been cheated. 'Have I been cozened, that I might come and die here dishonoured, who might at least have ended valiantly before the Doors of Nargothrond?' And out of the night about the hall it seemed to him that he heard the cries of Finduilas.

'Not first will I die here!' he cried. And he seized Brodda, and with the strength of his great anguish and wrath he lifted him on high and shook him, as if he were a dog. 'Morwen of the thrall-folk, did you say? You son of dastards, thief, slave of slaves!' Thereupon he flung Brodda head foremost across his own table, full in the face of an Easterling that rose to assail Túrin.

In that fall Brodda's neck was broken; and Túrin leapt after his cast and slew three more that cowered there, for they were caught weaponless. There was tumult in the hall. The Easterlings that sat there would have come against Túrin, but many others were gathered there of the elder people of Dor-lómin: long had they been tame servants, but now they rose with shouts in rebellion. Soon there was great fighting in the hall, and though the thralls had but meat-knives and such things as they could snatch up against daggers and swords, many were quickly slain on either hand, before Túrin leapt down among them and slew the last of the Easterlings that remained in the hall.

Then he rested, leaning against a pillar, and the fire of his rage was as ashes. But old Sador crept up to him and clutched him about the knees, for he was wounded to the death. 'Thrice seven years and more, it was long to wait for this hour,' he said. 'But now go, go, lord! Go, and do not come back, unless with greater strength. They will raise the land against you. Many have run from the hall. Go, or you will end here. Farewell!' Then he slipped down and died.

'He speaks with the truth of death,' said Aerin. 'You have learned what you would. Now go swiftly! But go first to Morwen and comfort her, or I will hold all the wrack you have wrought here hard to forgive. For ill though my life was, you have brought death to me with your violence. The Incomers will avenge this night on all that were here. Rash are your deeds, son of Húrin, as if you were still but the child that I knew.'

'And faint heart is yours, Aerin Indor's daughter, as it was when I called you aunt, and a rough dog frightened you,' said Túrin. 'You were made for a kinder world. But come away! I will bring you to Morwen.'

'The snow lies on the land, but deeper upon my head,' she answered. 'I should die as soon in the wild with you, as with the brute

Easterlings. You cannot mend what you have done. Go! To stay will make all the worse, and rob Morwen to no purpose. Go, I beg you!'

Then Túrin bowed low to her, and turned, and left the hall of Brodda; but all the rebels that had the strength followed him. They fled towards the mountains, for some among them knew well the ways of the wild, and they blessed the snow that fell behind them and covered their trail. Thus though soon the hunt was up, with many men and dogs and braying of horses, they escaped south into the hills. Then looking back they saw a red light far off in the land they had left.

'They have fired the hall,' said Túrin. 'To what purpose is that?'

'They? No, lord: she, I guess,' said one, Asgon by name. 'Many a man of arms misreads patience and quiet. She did much good among us at much cost. Her heart was not faint, and patience will break at the last.'

Now some of the hardiest that could endure the winter stayed with Túrin and led him by strange paths to a refuge in the mountains, a cave known to outlaws and runagates; and some store of food was hidden there. There they waited until the snow ceased, and then they gave him food and took him to a pass little used that led south to Sirion's Vale, where the snow had not come. On the downward path they parted.

'Farewell now, Lord of Dor-lómin,' said Asgon. 'But do not forget us. We shall be hunted men now; and the Wolf-folk will be crueller because of your coming. Therefore go, and do not return, unless you come with strength to deliver us. Farewell!'

### The Coming of Túrin into Brethil

Now Túrin went down towards Sirion, and he was torn in mind. For it seemed to him that whereas before he had two bitter choices, now there were three, and his oppressed people called him, upon whom he had brought only increase of woe. This comfort only he had: that beyond doubt Morwen and Nienor had come long since to Doriath, and only by the prowess of the Blacksword of Nargothrond had their road been made safe. And he said in his thought: 'Where else better might I have bestowed them, had I come indeed sooner? If the Girdle of Melian be broken, then is all ended. Nay, it is better as things be; for by my wrath and rash deeds I cast a shadow wherever I dwell. Let Melian keep them! And I will leave them in peace unshadowed for a while.'

But too late Túrin now sought for Finduilas, roaming the woods under the eaves of Ered Wethrin, wild and wary as a beast; and he waylaid all the roads that went north to the Pass of Sirion. Too late. For all trails had been washed away by the rains and the snows. But thus it was that Túrin passing down Teiglin came upon some of the People of Haleth from the Forest of Brethil. They were dwindled now by war to a small people, and dwelt for the most part secretly within a stockade upon Amon Obel deep in the forest. Ephel Brandir that place was named; for Brandir son of Handir was now their lord, since his father was slain. And Brandir was no man of war, being lamed by a leg broken in a misadventure in childhood; and he was moreover gentle in mood, loving wood rather than metal, and the knowledge of things that grow in the earth rather than other lore.

But some of the woodmen still hunted the Orcs on their borders; and thus it was that as Túrin came thither he heard the sound of an affray. He hastened towards it, and coming warily through the trees he saw a small band of men surrounded by Orcs. They defended themselves desperately, with their backs to a knot of trees that grew apart in a glade; but the Orcs were in great number, and they had little hope of escape, unless help came. Therefore, out of sight in the underwood, Túrin made a great noise of stamping and crashing, and then he cried in a loud voice, as if leading many men: 'Ha! Here we find them! Follow me all! Out now, and slay!'

At that many of the Orcs looked back in dismay, and then out came Túrin leaping, waving as if to men behind, and the edges of Gurthang flickered like flame in his hand. Too well was that blade known to the Orcs, and even before he sprang among them many scattered and fled. Then the woodmen ran to join him, and together they hunted their foes into the river: few came across.

At last they halted on the bank, and Dorlas, leader of the woodmen, said: 'You are swift in the hunt, lord; but your men are slow to follow.'

'Nay,' said Túrin, 'we all run together as one man, and will not be parted.'

Then the Men of Brethil laughed, and said: 'Well, one such is worth many. And we owe you great thanks. But who are you, and what do you here?'

'I do but follow my trade, which is Orc-slaying,' said Túrin. 'And I dwell where my trade is. I am Wildman of the Woods.'

'Then come and dwell with us,' said they. 'For we dwell in the woods, and we have need of such craftsmen. You would be welcome!'

Then Túrin looked at them strangely, and said: 'Are there then any left who will suffer me to darken their doors? But, friends, I have still a grievous errand: to find Finduilas, daughter of Orodreth of Nargothrond, or at least to learn news of her. Alas! Many weeks is it since she was taken from Nargothrond, but still I must go seeking.'

Then they looked on him with pity, and Dorlas said: 'Seek no more. For an Orc-host came up from Nargothrond towards the Crossings of Teiglin, and we had long warning of it: it marched very slow, because of the number of captives that were led. Then we thought to deal our small stroke in the war, and we ambushed the Orcs with all the bowmen we could muster, and hoped to save some of the prisoners. But alas! as soon as they were assailed the foul Orcs slew first the women among their captives; and the daughter of Orodreth they fastened to a tree with a spear.'

Túrin stood as one mortally stricken. 'How do you know this?' he said.

'Because she spoke to me, before she died,' said Dorlas. 'She looked upon us as though seeking one whom she had expected, and she said: "Mormegil. Tell the Mormegil that Finduilas is here." She said no more. But because of her latest words we laid her where she died. She lies in a mound beside Teiglin. It is a month now ago.'

'Bring me there,' said Túrin; and they led him to a hillock by the Crossings of Teiglin. There he laid himself down, and a darkness fell on him, so that they thought he was dead. But Dorlas looked down at him as he lay, and then he turned to his men and said: 'Too late! This is a piteous chance. But see: here lies the Mormegil himself, the great captain of Nargothrond. By his sword we should have known him, as did the Orcs.' For the fame of the Blacksword of the South had gone far and wide, even into the deeps of the wood.

Now therefore they lifted him with reverence and bore him to Ephel Brandir; and Brandir coming out to meet them wondered at the bier that they bore. Then drawing back the coverlet he looked on the face of Túrin son of Húrin; and a dark shadow fell on his heart.

'O cruel Men of Haleth!' he cried. 'Why did you hold back death from this man? With great labour you have brought hither the last bane of our people.'

But the woodmen said: 'Nay, it is the Mormegil of Nargothrond,[21] a mighty Orc-slayer, and he shall be a great help to us, if he lives. And were it not so, should we leave a man woe-stricken to lie as carrion by the way?'

'You should not indeed,' said Brandir. 'Doom willed it not so.' And he took Túrin into his house and tended him with care.

But when at last Túrin shook off the darkness, spring was returning;

and he awoke and saw sun on the green buds. Then the courage of
the House of Hador awoke in him also, and he arose, and said in his
heart: 'All my deeds and past days were dark and full of evil. But a
new day is come. Here I will stay at peace, and renounce name and
kin; and so I will put my shadow behind me, or at the least not lay
it upon those that I love.'

Therefore he took a new name, calling himself Turambar, which
in the High-elven speech signified Master of Doom; and he dwelt
among the woodmen, and was loved by them, and he charged them
to forget his name of old, and to count him as born in Brethil. Yet
with the change of a name he could not change wholly his temper,
nor wholly forget his old griefs against the servants of Morgoth; and
he would go hunting the Orcs with a few of the same mind, though
this was displeasing to Brandir. For he hoped rather to preserve his
people by silence and secrecy.

'The Mormegil is no more,' said he, 'yet have a care lest the valour
of Turambar bring a like vengeance on Brethil!'

Therefore Turambar laid his black sword by, and took it no more
to battle, and wielded rather the bow and the spear. But he would
not suffer the Orcs to use the Crossings of Teiglin or draw near the
mound where Finduilas was laid. Haudh-en-Elleth it was named, the
Mound of the Elfmaid, and soon the Orcs learned to dread that place,
and shunned it. And Dorlas said to Turambar: 'You have renounced
the name, but the Blacksword you are still; and does not rumour
say truly that he was the son of Húrin of Dor-lómin, lord of the
House of Hador?'

And Turambar answered: 'So I have heard. But publish it not, I
beg you, as you are my friend.'

### The Journey of Morwen and Nienor to Nargothrond

When the Fell Winter withdrew new tidings of Nargothrond came to
Doriath. For some that escaped from the sack, and had survived the
winter in the wild, came at last seeking refuge with Thingol, and the
march-wards brought them to the King. And some said that all the
enemy had withdrawn northwards, and others that Glaurung abode
still in the halls of Felagund; and some said that the Mormegil was
slain, and others that he was cast under a spell by the Dragon and
dwelt there yet, as one changed to stone. But all declared that it was
known in Nargothrond ere the end that the Blacksword was none
other than Túrin son of Húrin of Dor-lómin.

Then great was the fear and sorrow of Morwen and of Nienor;

and Morwen said: 'Such doubt is the very work of Morgoth! May
we not learn the truth, and know surely the worst that we must
endure?'

Now Thingol himself desired greatly to know more of the fate of
Nargothrond, and had in mind already the sending out of some that
might go warily thither, but he believed that Túrin was indeed slain
or beyond rescue, and he was loath to see the hour when Morwen
should know this clearly. Therefore he said to her: 'This is a perilous
matter, Lady of Dor-lómin, and must be pondered. Such doubt may
in truth be the work of Morgoth, to draw us on to some rashness.'

But Morwen being distraught cried: 'Rashness, lord! If my son
lurks in the woods hungry, if he lingers in bonds, if his body lies un-
buried, then I would be rash. I would lose no hour to go to seek him.'

'Lady of Dor-lómin,' said Thingol, 'that surely the son of Húrin
would not desire. Here would he think you better bestowed than in
any other land that remains: in the keeping of Melian. For Húrin's
sake and Túrin's I will not have you wander abroad in the black
peril of these days.'

'You did not hold Túrin from peril, but me you will hold from
him,'.cried Morwen. 'In the keeping of Melian! Yes, a prisoner of the
Girdle. Long did I hold back before I entered it, and now I rue it.'

'Nay, if you speak so, Lady of Dor-lómin,' said Thingol, 'know
this: the Girdle is open. Free you came hither; free you shall stay
– or go.'

Then Melian, who had remained silent, spoke: 'Go not hence,
Morwen. A true word you said: this doubt is of Morgoth. If you go,
you go at his will.'

'Fear of Morgoth will not withhold me from the call of my kin,'
Morwen answered. 'But if you fear for me, lord, then lend me some
of your people.'

'I command you not,' said Thingol. 'But my people are my own
to command. I will send them at my own advice.'

Then Morwen said no more, but wept; and she left the presence
of the King. Thingol was heavy-hearted, for it seemed to him that
the mood of Morwen was fey; and he asked Melian whether she
would not restrain her by her power.

'Against the coming in of evil I may do much,' she answered. 'But
against the going out of those who will go, nothing. That is your part.
If she is to be held here, you must hold her with strength. Yet
maybe thus you will overthrow her mind.'

Now Morwen went to Nienor, and said: 'Farewell, daughter of

Húrin. I go to seek my son, or true tidings of him, since none here will do aught, but will tarry until too late. Await me here until haply I return.'

Then Nienor in dread and distress would restrain her, but Morwen answered nothing, and went to her chamber; and when morning came she had taken horse and gone.

Now Thingol had commanded that none should stay her, or seem to waylay her. But as soon as she went forth, he gathered a company of the hardiest and most skilled of his march-wards, and he set Mablung in charge.

'Follow now speedily,' he said, 'yet let her not be aware of you. But when she is come into the wild, if danger threatens, then show yourselves; and if she will not return, then guard her as you may. But some of you I would have go forward as far as you can, and learn all that you may.'

Thus it was that Thingol sent out a larger company than he had at first intended, and there were ten riders among them with spare horses. They followed after Morwen, and she went south through Region, and so came to the shores of Sirion above the Twilit Meres; there she halted, for Sirion was wide and swift, and she did not know the way. Therefore now the guards must needs reveal themselves; and Morwen said: 'Will Thingol stay me? Or late does he send me the help that he denied?'

'Both,' answered Mablung. 'Will you not return?'

'No!' she said.

'Then I must help you,' said Mablung, 'though it is against my own will. Wide and deep here is Sirion, and perilous to swim for beast or man.'

'Then bring me over by whatever way the Elven-folk are used to cross,' said Morwen; 'or else I will try the swimming.'

Therefore Mablung led her to the Twilit Meres. There amid the creeks and reeds ferries were kept hidden and guarded on the east shore; for by that way messengers would pass to and fro between Thingol and his kin in Nargothrond.[22] Now they waited until the starlit night was late, and they passed over in the white mists before the dawn. And even as the sun rose red beyond the Blue Mountains, and a strong morning-wind blew and scattered the mists, the guards went up on to the west shore, and left the Girdle of Melian. Tall Elves of Doriath they were, grey-clad, and cloaked over their mail. Morwen from the ferry watched them as they passed silently, and then suddenly she gave a cry, and pointed to the last of the company that went by.

'Whence came he?' she said. 'Thrice ten you came to me. Thrice ten and one you go ashore!'

Then the others turned, and saw that the sun shone upon a head of gold: for it was Nienor, and her hood was blown back by the wind. Thus it was revealed that she had followed the company, and joined them in the dark before they crossed the river. They were dismayed, and none more than Morwen. 'Go back, go back! I command you!' she cried.

'If the wife of Húrin can go forth against all counsel at the call of kindred,' said Nienor, 'then so also can Húrin's daughter. Mourning you named me, but I will not mourn alone, for father, brother, and mother. But of these you only have I known, and above all do I love. And nothing that you fear not do I fear.'

In truth little fear was seen in her face or her bearing. Tall and strong she seemed; for of great stature were those of Hador's House, and thus clad in Elvish raiment she matched well with the guards, being smaller only than the greatest among them.

'What would you do?' said Morwen.

'Go where you go,' said Nienor. 'This choice indeed I bring. To lead me back and bestow me safely in the keeping of Melian; for it is not wise to refuse her counsel. Or to know that I shall go into peril, if you go.' For in truth Nienor had come most in the hope that for fear and love of her her mother would turn back; and Morwen was indeed torn in mind.

'It is one thing to refuse counsel,' said she. 'It is another to refuse the command of your mother. Go now back!'

'No,' said Nienor. 'It is long since I was a child. I have a will and wisdom of my own, though until now it has not crossed yours. I go with you. Rather to Doriath, for reverence of those that rule it; but if not, then westward. Indeed, if either of us should go on, it is I rather, in the fullness of strength.'

Then Morwen saw in the grey eyes of Nienor the steadfastness of Húrin; and she wavered, but she could not overcome her pride, and would not seem thus (save the fair words) to be led back by her daughter, as one old and doting.

'I go on, as I have purposed,' she said. 'Come you also, but against my will.'

'Let it be so,' said Nienor.

Then Mablung said to his company: 'Truly, it is by lack of counsel not of courage that Húrin's folk bring woe to others! Even so with Túrin; yet not so with his fathers. But now they are all fey, and I like it not. More do I dread this errand of the King than the hunting of the Wolf. What is to be done?'

But Morwen, who had come ashore and now drew near, heard the last of his words. 'Do as you are bidden by the King,' said she. 'Seek for tidings of Nargothrond, and of Túrin. For this end are we all come together.'

'It is yet a long way and dangerous,' said Mablung. 'If you go further, you shall both be horsed and go among the riders, and stray no foot from them.'

Thus it was that with the full day they set forth, and passed slowly and warily out of the country of reeds and low willows, and came to the grey woods that covered much of the southern plain before Nargothrond. All day they went due west, and saw nothing but desolation, and heard nothing; for the lands were silent, and it seemed to Mablung that a present fear lay upon them. That same way had Beren trodden years before, and then the woods were filled with the hidden eyes of the hunters; but now all the people of Narog were gone, and the Orcs, as it seemed, were not yet roaming so far south-ward. That night they encamped in the grey wood without fire or light.

The next two days they went on, and by evening of the third day from Sirion they were come across the plain and were drawing near to the east shores of Narog. Then so great an unease came upon Mablung that he begged Morwen to go no further. But she laughed, and said: 'You will be glad soon to be rid of us, as is likely enough. But you must endure us a little longer. We are come too near now to turn back in fear.'

Then Mablung cried: 'Fey are you both, and foolhardy. You help not but hinder any gathering of news. Now hear me! I was bidden not to stay you with strength; but I was bidden also to guard you, as I might. In this pass, one only can I do. And I will guard you. Tomorrow I will lead you to Amon Ethir, the Spyhill, which is near; and there you shall sit under guard, and go no further while I command here.'

Now Amon Ethir was a mound as great as a hill that long ago Felagund had caused to be raised with great labour in the plain before his Doors, a league east of Narog. It was tree-grown, save on the summit, where a wide view might be had all ways, of the roads that led to the great bridge of Nargothrond, and of the lands round about. To this hill they came late in the morning and climbed up from the east. Then looking out towards the High Faroth, brown and bare beyond the river,[23] Mablung saw with elven-sight the terraces of Nargothrond on the steep west bank, and as a small black hole in the hill-wall the gaping Doors of Felagund. But he could hear no sound, and he could see no sign of any foe, nor any token of the Dragon, save the burning about the Doors that he had wrought in the day of the sack. All lay quiet under a pale sun.

Now therefore Mablung, as he had said, commanded his ten riders to keep Morwen and Nienor on the hill-top, and not to stir thence until he returned, unless some great peril arose: and if that befell, the riders should set Morwen and Nienor in their midst and flee as swiftly as they might, east-away towards Doriath, sending one ahead to bring news and seek aid.

Then Mablung took the other score of his company, and they crept down from the hill; and then passing into the fields westward, where trees were few, they scattered and made each his way, daring but stealthy, to the banks of Narog. Mablung himself took the middle way, going towards the bridge, and so came to its hither end and found it all broken down; and the deep-cloven river, running wild after rains far away northward, was foaming and roaring among the fallen stones.

But Glaurung lay there, just within the shadow of the great passage that led inward from the ruined Doors, and he had long been aware of the spies, though few other eyes in Middle-earth would have discerned them. But the glance of his fell eyes was keener than that of eagles, and outreached the far sight of the Elves; and indeed he knew also that some remained behind and sat upon the bare top of Amon Ethir.

Thus, even as Mablung crept among the rocks seeking whether he could ford the wild river upon the fallen stones of the bridge, suddenly Glaurung came forth with a great blast of fire, and crawled down into the stream. Then straightway there was a vast hissing and huge vapours arose, and Mablung and his followers that lurked near were engulfed in a blinding steam and foul stench; and the most fled as best they could guess towards the Spyhill. But as Glaurung was passing over Narog, Mablung drew aside and lay under a rock, and remained; for it seemed to him that he had an errand yet to do. He knew now indeed that Glaurung abode in Nargothrond, but he was bidden also to learn the truth concerning Húrin's son, if he might; and in the stoutness of his heart, therefore, he purposed to cross the river, as soon as Glaurung was gone, and search the halls of Felagund. For he thought that all had been done that could be for the keeping of Morwen and Nienor: the coming of Glaurung would be marked, and even now the riders should be speeding towards Doriath.

Glaurung therefore passed Mablung by, a vast shape in the mist; and he went swiftly, for he was a mighty Worm, and yet lithe. Then

Mablung behind him forded Narog in great peril; but the watchers
upon Amon Ethir beheld the issuing of the Dragon, and were dismayed. At once they bade Morwen and Nienor mount, without
debate, and prepared to flee eastward as they were bidden. But even
as they came down from the hill into the plain, an ill wind blew the
great vapours upon them, bringing a stench that no horses would
endure. Then, blinded by the fog and in mad terror of the dragon-
reek, the horses soon became ungovernable, and went wildly this
way and that; and the guards were dispersed, and were dashed
against trees to great hurt, or sought vainly one for another. The
neighing of the horses and the cries of the riders came to the ears of
Glaurung; and he was well pleased.

One of the Elf-riders, striving with his horse in the fog, saw the
Lady Morwen passing near, a grey wraith upon a mad steed; but she
vanished into the mist, crying *Nienor*, and they saw her no more.

But when the blind terror came upon the riders, Nienor's horse,
running wild, stumbled, and she was thrown. Falling softly into grass
she was unhurt; but when she got to her feet she was alone: lost in
the mist without horse or companion. Her heart did not fail her, and
she took thought; and it seemed to her vain to go towards this cry or
that, for cries were all about her, but growing ever fainter. Better it
seemed to her in such case to seek again for the hill: thither doubtless
Mablung would come before he went away, if only to be sure that
none of his company had remained there.

Therefore walking at guess she found the hill, which was indeed
close at hand, by the rising of the ground before her feet; and slowly
she climbed the path that led up from the east. And as she climbed
so the fog grew thinner, until she came at last out into the sunlight
on the bare summit. Then she stepped forward and looked westward.
And there right before her was the great head of Glaurung, who had
even then crept up from the other side; and before she was aware
her eyes looked in his eyes, and they were terrible, being filled with
the fell spirit of Morgoth, his master.

Then Nienor strove against Glaurung, for she was strong in will;
but he put forth his power against her. 'What seek you here?' he said.

And constrained to answer she said: 'I do but seek one Túrin that
dwelt here a while. But he is dead, maybe.'

'I know not,' said Glaurung. 'He was left here to defend the women
and weaklings; but when I came he deserted them, and fled. A boaster
but a craven, it seems. Why seek you such a one?'

'You lie,' said Nienor. 'The children of Húrin at least are not
craven. We fear you not.'

Then Glaurung laughed, for so was Húrin's daughter revealed to his malice. 'Then you are fools, both you and your brother,' said he. 'And your boast shall be made vain. For I am Glaurung!'

Then he drew her eyes unto his, and her will swooned. And it seemed to her that the sun sickened and all became dim about her; and slowly a great darkness drew down on her and in that darkness there was emptiness; she knew nothing, and heard nothing, and remembered nothing.

Long Mablung explored the halls of Nargothrond, as well he might for the darkness and the stench; but he found no living thing there: nothing stirred amid the bones, and none answered his cries. At last, being oppressed by the horror of the place, and fearing the return of Glaurung, he came back to the Doors. The sun was sinking west, and the shadows of the Faroth behind lay dark on the terraces and the wild river below; but away beneath Amon Ethir he descried, as it seemed, the evil shape of the Dragon. Harder and more perilous was the return over Narog in such haste and fear; and scarcely had he reached the east shore and crept aside under the bank when Glaurung drew nigh. But he was slow now and stealthy; for all the fires in him were burned low: great power had gone out of him, and he would rest and sleep in the dark. Thus he writhed through the water and slunk up to the Doors like a huge snake, ashen-grey, sliming the ground with his belly.

But he turned before he went in and looked back eastward, and there came from him the laughter of Morgoth, dim but horrible, as an echo of malice out of the black depths far away. And this voice, cold and low, came after: 'There you lie like a vole under the bank, Mablung the mighty! Ill do you run the errands of Thingol. Haste you now to the hill and see what is become of your charge!'

Then Glaurung passed into his lair, and the sun went down and grey evening came chill over the land. But Mablung hastened back to Amon Ethir; and as he climbed to the top the stars came out in the East. Against them he saw there standing, dark and still, a figure as it were an image of stone. Thus Nienor stood, and heard nothing that he said, and made him no answer. But when at last he took her hand, she stirred, and suffered him to lead her away; and while he held her she followed, but if he loosed her, she stood still.

Then great was Mablung's grief and bewilderment; but no other choice had he but to lead Nienor so upon the long eastward way, without help or company. Thus they passed away, walking like dreamers, out into the night-shadowed plain. And when morning returned Nienor stumbled and fell, and lay still; and Mablung sat beside her in despair.

'Not for nothing did I dread this errand,' he said. 'For it will be my last, it seems. With this unlucky child of Men I shall perish in the wilderness, and my name shall be held in scorn in Doriath: if any tidings indeed are ever heard of our fate. All else doubtless are slain, and she alone spared, but not in mercy.'

Thus they were found by three of the company that had fled from Narog at the coming of Glaurung, and after much wandering when the mist had passed went back to the hill; and finding it empty they had begun to seek their way home. Hope then returned to Mablung; and they went on now together steering northward and eastward, for there was no road back into Doriath in the south, and since the fall of Nargothrond the ferry-wards were forbidden to set any across save those that came from within.

Slow was their journey, as for those that lead a weary child. But ever as they passed further from Nargothrond and drew nearer to Doriath, so little by little strength returned to Nienor, and she would walk hour by hour obediently, led by the hand. Yet her wide eyes saw nothing, and her ears heard no words, and her lips spoke no words.

And now at length after many days they came nigh to the west border of Doriath, somewhat south of Teiglin; for they intended to pass the fences of the little land of Thingol beyond Sirion and so come to the guarded bridge near the inflowing of Esgalduin. There a while they halted; and they laid Nienor on a couch of grass, and she closed her eyes as she had not yet done, and it seemed that she slept. Then the Elves rested also, and for very weariness were unheedful. Thus they were assailed at unawares by a band of Orc-hunters, such as now roamed much in that region, as nigh to the fences of Doriath as they dared to go. In the midst of the affray suddenly Nienor leapt up from her couch, as one waking out of sleep to an alarm by night, and with a cry she sped away into the forest. Then the Orcs turned and gave chase, and the Elves after them. But a strange change came upon Nienor and now she outran them all, flying like a deer among the trees with her hair streaming in the wind of her speed. The Orcs indeed Mablung and his companions swiftly overtook and they slew them one and all, and hastened on. But by then Nienor had passed away like a wraith; and neither sight nor slot of her could they find, though they hunted for many days.

Then at last Mablung returned to Doriath bowed with grief and with shame. Choose you a new master of your hunters, lord,' he said to the King. 'For I am dishonoured.'

But Melian said: 'It is not so, Mablung. You did all that you could, and none other among the King's servants would have done so much. But by ill chance you were matched against a power too great for you: too great indeed for all that now dwell in Middle-earth.'

'I sent you to win tidings, and that you have done,' said Thingol. 'It is no fault of yours that those whom the tidings touch nearest are now beyond hearing. Grievous indeed is this end of all Húrin's kin, but it lies not at your door.'

For not only was Nienor now run witless into the wild, but Morwen also was lost. Neither then nor after did any certain news of her fate come to Doriath or to Dor-lómin. Nonetheless Mablung would not rest, and with a small company he went out into the wild and for three years wandered far, from Ered Wethrin even to the Mouths of Sirion, seeking for sign or tidings of the lost.

*Nienor in Brethil*

But as for Nienor, she ran on into the wood, hearing the shouts of pursuit come behind; and her clothing she tore off, casting away her garments as she fled, until she went naked; and all that day still she ran, as a beast that is hunted to heart-bursting, and dare not stay or draw breath. But at evening suddenly her madness passed. She stood still a moment as in wonder, and then, in a swoon of utter weariness, she fell as one stricken down into a deep brake of fern. And there amid the old bracken and the swift fronds of spring she lay and slept, heedless of all.

In the morning she woke, and rejoiced in the light as one first called to life; and all things that she saw seemed to her new and strange, and she had no names for them. For behind her lay only an empty darkness, through which came no memory of anything she had ever known, nor any echo of any word. A shadow of fear only she remembered, and so she was wary, and sought ever for hidings: she would climb into trees or slip into thickets, swift as squirrel or fox, if any sound or shadow frightened her; and thence she would peer long through the leaves before she went on again.

Thus going forward in the way she first ran, she came to the river Teiglin, and stayed her thirst; but no food she found, nor knew how to seek it, and she was famished and cold. And since the trees across the water seemed closer and darker (as indeed they were, being the

eaves of Brethil forest) she crossed over at last, and came to a green
mound and there cast herself down: for she was spent, and it seemed
to her that the darkness that lay behind her was overtaking her again,
and the sun going dark.

But indeed it was a black storm that came up out of the South,
laden with lightning and great rain; and she lay there cowering in
terror of the thunder, and the dark rain smote her nakedness.

Now it chanced that some of the woodmen of Brethil came by in
that hour from a foray against Orcs, hastening over the Crossings of
Teiglin to a shelter that was near; and there came a great flash of
lightning, so that the Haudh-en-Elleth was lit as with a white flame.
Then Turambar who led the men started back and covered his eyes,
and trembled; for it seemed that he saw the wraith of a slain maiden
that lay upon the grave of Finduilas.

But one of the men ran to the mound, and called to him: 'Hither,
lord! Here is a young woman lying, and she lives!' and Turambar
coming lifted her, and the water dripped from her drenched hair,
but she closed her eyes and quivered and strove no more. Then
marvelling that she lay thus naked Turambar cast his cloak about
her and bore her away to the hunters' lodge in the woods. There
they lit a fire and wrapped coverlets about her, and she opened her
eyes and looked upon them; and when her glance fell on Turambar
a light came in her face and she put out a hand towards him, for it
seemed to her that she had found at last something that she had
sought in the darkness, and she was comforted. But Turambar took
her hand, and smiled, and said: 'Now, lady, will you not tell us your
name and your kin, and what evil has befallen you?'

Then she shook her head, and said nothing, but began to weep;
and they troubled her no more, until she had eaten hungrily of what
food they could give her. And when she had eaten she sighed, and
laid her hand again in Turambar's; and he said: 'With us you are
safe. Here you may rest this night, and in the morning we will lead
you to our homes up in the high forest. But we would know your
name and your kin, so that we may find them, maybe, and bring
them news of you. Will you not tell us?'

But again she made no answer, and wept.

'Do not be troubled!' said Turambar. 'Maybe the tale is too sad
yet to tell. But I will give you a name, and call you Níniel, Maid of
Tears.' And at that name she looked up, and she shook her head, but
said: Níniel. And that was the first word that she spoke after her
darkness, and it was her name among the woodmen ever after.

In the morning they bore Níniel towards Ephel Brandir, and the

road went steeply upward towards Amon Obel until it came to a
place where it must cross the tumbling stream of Celebros. There
a bridge of wood had been built, and below it the stream went over a
lip of worn stone, and fell down by many foaming steps into a rocky
bowl far below; and all the air was filled with spray like rain. There
was a wide greensward at the head of the falls, and birches grew
about it, but over the bridge there was a wide view towards the
ravines of Teiglin some two miles to the west. There the air was cool
and there wayfarers in summer would rest and drink of the cold
water. Dimrost, the Rainy Stair, those falls were called, but after
that day Nen Girith, the Shuddering Water; for Turambar and his
men halted there, but as soon as Níniel came to that place she grew
cold and shivered, and they could not warm her or comfort her.[24]
Therefore they hastened on their way; but before they came to
Ephel Brandir Níniel was already wandering in a fever.

Long she lay in her sickness, and Brandir used all his skill in her
healing, and the wives of the woodmen watched over her by night
and by day. But only when Turambar stayed near her would she lie
at peace, or sleep without moaning; and this thing all marked that
watched her: throughout all her fever, though often she was much
troubled, she murmured never a word in any tongue of Elves or of
Men. And when health slowly returned to her, and she walked and
began to eat again, then as with a child the women of Brethil must
teach her to speak, word by word. But in this learning she was quick
and took great delight, as one that finds again treasures great and
small that were mislaid; and when at length she had learned enough
to speak with her friends she would say: 'What is the name of this
thing? For in my darkness I lost it.' And when she was able to go
about again, she would seek the house of Brandir; for she was most
eager to learn the names of all living things, and he knew much of such
matters; and they would walk together in the gardens and the glades.

Then Brandir grew to love her; and when she grew strong she
would lend him an arm for his lameness, and she called him her
brother. But to Turambar her heart was given, and only at his coming
would she smile, and only when he spoke gaily would she laugh.

One evening of the golden autumn they sat together, and the sun
set the hillside and the houses of Ephel Brandir aglow, and there was
a deep quiet. Then Níniel said to him: 'Of all things I have now
asked the name, save you. What are you called?'

'Turambar,' he answered.

Then she paused as if listening for some echo; but she said: 'And
what does that say, or is it just the name for you alone?'

'It means,' said he, 'Master of the Dark Shadow. For I also, Níniel, had my darkness, in which dear things were lost; but now I have overcome it, I deem.'

'And did you also flee from it, running, until you came to these fair woods?' she said. 'And when did you escape, Turambar?'

'Yes,' he answered, 'I fled for many years. And I escaped when you did so. For it was dark when you came, Níniel, but ever since it has been light. And it seems to me that what I long sought in vain has come to me.' And as he went back to his house in the twilight, he said to himself: 'Haudh-en-Elleth! From the green mound she came. Is that a sign, and how shall I read it?'

Now that golden year waned and passed to a gentle winter, and there came another bright year. There was peace in Brethil, and the woodmen held themselves quiet and went not abroad, and they heard no tidings of the lands that lay about them. For the Orcs that at that time came southward to the dark reign of Glaurung, or were sent to spy on the borders of Doriath, shunned the Crossings of Teiglin, and passed westward far beyond the river.

And now Níniel was fully healed, and was grown fair and strong; and Turambar restrained himself no longer, but asked her in marriage. Then Níniel was glad; but when Brandir learned of it his heart was sick within him, and he said to her: 'Be not in haste! Think me not unkindly, if I counsel you to wait.'

'Nothing that you do is done unkindly,' she said. 'But why then do you give me such counsel, wise brother?'

'Wise brother?' he answered. 'Lame brother, rather, unloved and unlovely. And I scarce know why. Yet there lies a shadow on this man, and I am afraid.'

'There was a shadow,' said Níniel, 'for so he told me. But he has escaped from it, even as I. And is he not worthy of love? Though he now holds himself at peace, was he not once the greatest captain, from whom all our enemies would flee, if they saw him?'

'Who told you this?' said Brandir.

'It was Dorlas,' she said. 'Does he not speak truth?'

'Truth indeed,' said Brandir, but he was ill pleased, for Dorlas was chief of that party that wished for war on the Orcs. And yet he sought still for reasons to delay Níniel; and he said therefore: 'The truth, but not the whole truth; for he was the Captain of Nargothrond, and came before out of the North, and was (it is said) son of Húrin of Dor-lómin of the warlike House of Hador.' And Brandir, seeing the shadow that passed over her face at that name, misread her, and said more: 'Indeed, Níniel, well may you think that such a one is likely ere long to go back to war, far from this land, maybe. And if so, how will you endure it? Have a care, for I forebode that if Turambar goes again to battle, then not he but the Shadow shall have the mastery.'

'Ill would I endure it,' she answered; 'but unwedded no better than wedded. And a wife, maybe, would better restrain him, and hold off the shadow.' Nonetheless she was troubled by the words of Brandir, and she bade Turambar wait yet a while. And he wondered and was downcast; but when he learned from Níniel that Brandir had counselled her to wait, he was ill pleased.

But when the next spring came he said to Níniel: 'Time passes. We have waited, and now I will wait no longer. Do as your heart bids you, Níniel most dear, but see: this is the choice before me. I will go back now to war in the wild; or I will wed you, and go never to war again – save only to defend you, if some evil assails our home.'

Then she was glad indeed, and she plighted her troth, and at the mid-summer they were wedded; and the woodmen made a great feast, and they gave them a fair house which they had built for them upon Amon Obel. There they dwelt in happiness, but Brandir was troubled, and the shadow on his heart grew deeper.

## The Coming of Glaurung

Now the power and malice of Glaurung grew apace, and he waxed fat, and he gathered Orcs to him, and ruled as a dragon-King, and all the realm of Nargothrond that had been was laid under him. And before this year ended, the third of Turambar's dwelling among the woodmen, he began to assail their land, which for a while had had peace; for indeed it was well known to Glaurung and to his Master that in Brethil there abode still a remnant of free men, the last of the Three Houses to defy the power of the North. And this they would not brook; for it was the purpose of Morgoth to subdue all Beleriand and to search out its every corner, so that none in any hole or hiding might live that were not thrall to him. Thus, whether Glaurung guessed where Túrin was hidden, or whether (as some hold) he had indeed for that time escaped from the eye of Evil that pursued him, is of little matter. For in the end the counsels of Brandir must prove vain, and at the last two choices only could there be for Turambar: to sit deedless until he was found, driven forth like a rat; or to go forth soon to battle, and be revealed.

But when tidings of the coming of the Orcs were first brought to Ephel Brandir, he did not go forth and yielded to the prayers of Níniel. For she said: 'Our homes are not yet assailed, as your word was. It is said that the Orcs are not many. And Dorlas has told me that before you came such affrays were not seldom, and the woodmen held them off.'

But the woodmen were worsted, for these Orcs were of a fell breed, fierce and cunning; and they came indeed with a purpose to invade the Forest of Brethil, not as before passing through its eaves on other errands, or hunting in small bands. Therefore Dorlas and his men were driven back with loss, and the Orcs came over Teiglin and roamed far into the woods. And Dorlas came to Turambar and showed his wounds, and he said: 'See, lord, now is the time of our need come upon us, after a false peace, even as I foreboded. Did you not ask to be counted one of our people, and no stranger? Is this peril not yours also? For our homes will not remain hidden, if the Orcs come further into our land.'

Therefore Turambar arose, and took up again his sword Gurthang, and he went to battle; and when the woodmen learned this they were greatly heartened, and they gathered to him, till he had a force of many hundreds. Then they hunted through the forest and slew all the Orcs that crept there, and hung them on the trees near the Crossings of Teiglin. And when a new host came against them, they trapped it, and being surprised both by the numbers of the woodmen and by the terror of the Black Sword that had returned, the Orcs were routed and slain in great number. Then the woodmen made great pyres and burned the bodies of the soldiers of Morgoth in heaps, and the smoke of their vengeance rose black into heaven, and the wind bore it away westward. But few living went back to Nargothrond with these tidings.

Then Glaurung was wrathful indeed; but for a while he lay still and pondered what he had heard. Thus the winter passed in peace, and men said: 'Great is the Black Sword of Brethil, for all our enemies are overcome.' And Níniel was comforted, and she rejoiced in the renown of Turambar; but he sat in thought, and he said in his heart: 'The die is cast. Now comes the test, in which my boast shall be made good, or fail utterly. I will flee no more. Turambar indeed I will be, and by my own will and prowess I will surmount my doom – or fall. But falling or riding, Glaurung at least I will slay.'

Nonetheless he was unquiet, and he sent out men of daring as scouts far afield. For indeed though no word was said he now ordered things as he would, as if he were lord of Brethil, and no man heeded Brandir.

Spring came hopefully, and men sang at their work. But in that spring Níniel conceived, and she became pale and wan, and all her happiness was dimmed. And soon there came strange tidings, from the men that had gone abroad beyond Teiglin, that there was a great burning far out in the woods of the plain towards Nargothrond, and men wondered what it might be.

Before long there came more reports: that the fires drew ever northward, and that indeed Glaurung himself made them. For he had left Nargothrond, and was abroad again on some errand. Then the more foolish or more hopeful said: 'His army is destroyed, and now at last he sees wisdom and is going back whence he came.' And others said: 'Let us hope that he will pass us by.' But Turambar had no such hope, and knew that Glaurung was coming to seek him. Therefore though he masked his mind because of Níniel, he pondered ever by day and by night what counsel he should take; and spring turned towards summer.

A day came when two men returned to Ephel Brandir in terror, for they had seen the Great Worm himself. 'In truth, lord,' they said to Turambar, 'he draws now near to Teiglin, and turns not aside. He lay in the midst of a great burning, and the trees smoked about him. The stench of him is scarce to be endured. And all the long leagues back to Nargothrond his foul swath lies, we deem, in a line that swerves not, but points straight to us. What is to be done?'

'Little,' said Turambar, 'but to that little I have already given thought. The tidings you bring give me hope rather than dread; for if indeed he goes straight, as you say, and will not swerve, then I have some counsel for hardy hearts.' The men wondered, for he said no more at that time; but they took heart from his steadfast bearing.[25]

Now the river Teiglin ran in this manner. It flowed down from Ered Wethrin swift as Narog, but at first between low shores, until after the Crossings, gathering power from other streams, it clove a way through the feet of the highlands upon which stood the Forest of Brethil. Thereafter it ran in deep ravines, whose great sides were like walls of rock, but pent at the bottom the waters flowed with great force and noise. And right in the path of Glaurung there lay now one of these gorges, by no means the deepest, but the narrowest, just north of the inflow of Celebros. Therefore Turambar sent out three hardy men to keep watch from the brink on the movements of the Dragon; but he himself would ride to the high fall of Nen Girith, where news could find him swiftly, and whence he himself could look far across the lands.

But first he gathered the woodmen together in Ephel Brandir and spoke to them, saying:

'Men of Brethil, a deadly peril has come upon us which only great hardihood shall turn aside. But in this matter numbers will avail little; we must use cunning, and hope for good fortune. If we went up against the Dragon with all our strength, as against an army of Orcs, we should but offer ourselves all to death, and so leave our wives and kin defenceless. Therefore I say that you should stay here, and prepare for flight. For if Glaurung comes, then you must abandon this place, and scatter far and wide; and so may some escape and live. For certainly, if he can, he will come to our stronghold and dwelling, and he will destroy it, and all that he espies; but afterwards he will not abide here. In Nargothrond lies all his treasure, and there are the deep halls in which he can lie safe, and grow.'

Then the men were dismayed, and were utterly downcast, for they trusted in Turambar, and had looked for more hopeful words. But he said: 'Nay, that is the worst. And it shall not come to pass, if my counsel and fortune is good. For I do not believe that this Dragon is unconquerable, though he grows greater in strength and malice with the years. I know somewhat of him. His power is rather in the evil spirit that dwells within him than in the might of his body, great though that be. For hear now this tale that I was told by some that fought in the year of the Nirnaeth, when I and most that hear me were children. In that field the Dwarves withstood him and Azaghâl of Belegost pricked him so deep that he fled back to Angband. But here is a thorn sharper and longer than the knife of Azaghâl.'

And Turambar swept Gurthang from its sheath and stabbed with it up above his head, and it seemed to those that looked on that a flame leapt from Turambar's hand many feet into the air. Then they gave a great cry: 'The Black Thorn of Brethil!'

'The Black Thorn of Brethil,' said Turambar: 'well may he fear it. For know this: it is the doom of this Dragon (and all his brood, it is said) that how great so ever be his armour of horn, harder than iron, below he must go with the belly of a snake. Therefore, Men of Brethil, I go now to seek the belly of Glaurung, by what means I may. Who will come with me? I need but a few with strong arms and stronger hearts.'

Then Dorlas stood forth and said: 'I will go with you, lord; for I would ever go forward rather than wait for a foe.'

But no others were so swift to the call, for the dread of Glaurung lay on them, and the tale of the scouts that had seen him had gone about and grown in the telling. Then Dorlas cried out: 'Hearken, Men of Brethil, it is now well seen that for the evil of our times the counsels of Brandir were vain. There is no escape by hiding. Will none of you take the place of the son of Handir, that the House of Haleth be not put to shame?' Thus Brandir, who sat indeed in the high-seat of the lord of the assembly, but unheeded, was scorned, and he was bitter in his heart; for Turambar did not rebuke Dorlas. But one Hunthor, Brandir's kinsman, arose and said: 'You do evilly, Dorlas, to speak thus to the shame of your lord, whose limbs by ill hazard cannot do as his heart would. Beware lest the contrary be seen in you at some turn! And how can it be said that his counsels were vain, when they were never taken? You, his liege, have ever set them at naught. I say to you that Glaurung comes now to us, as to Nargothrond before, because our deeds have betrayed us, as he feared. But since this woe is now come, with your leave, son of Handir, I will go on behalf of Haleth's house.'

Then Turambar said: 'Three is enough! You twain will I take. But, lord, I do not scorn you. See! We must go in great haste, and our task will need strong limbs. I deem that your place is with your people. For you are wise, and are a healer; and it may be that there will be great need of wisdom and healing ere long.' But these words, though fair spoken, did but embitter Brandir the more, and he said to Hunthor: 'Go then, but not with my leave. For a shadow lies on this man, and it will lead you to evil.'

Now Turambar was in haste to go; but when he came to Níniel, to bid her farewell, she clung to him, weeping grievously. 'Go not forth, Turambar, I beg!' she said. 'Challenge not the shadow that you have fled from! Nay, nay, flee still, and take me with you, far away!'

'Níniel most dear,' he answered, 'we cannot flee further, you and I. We are hemmed in this land. And even should I go, deserting the people that befriended us, I could but take you forth into the houseless wild, to your death and the death of our child. A hundred leagues lie between us and any land that is yet beyond the reach of the Shadow. But take heart, Níniel. For I say to you: neither you nor I shall be slain by this Dragon, nor by any foe of the North.' Then Níniel ceased to weep and fell silent, but her kiss was cold as they parted.

Then Turambar with Dorlas and Hunthor went away hotfoot to Nen Girith, and when they came there the sun was westering and shadows were long; and the last two of the scouts were there awaiting them.

'You come not too soon, lord,' said they. 'For the Dragon has come on, and already when we left he had reached the brink of Teiglin, and glared across the water. He moves ever by night, and we may look then for some stroke before tomorrow's dawn.'

Turambar looked out over the falls of Celebros and saw the sun going down to its setting, and black spires of smoke rising by the borders of the river. 'There is no time to lose,' he said; 'yet these tidings are good. For my fear was that he would seek about; and if he passed northward and came to the Crossings and so to the old road in the lowland, then hope would be dead. But now some fury of pride and malice drives him headlong.' But even as he spoke, he wondered, and mused in his mind: 'Or can it be that one so evil and fell shuns the Crossings, even as the Orcs? Haudh-en-Elleth! Does Finduilas lie still between me and my doom?'

Then he turned to his companions and said: 'This task now lies before us. We must wait yet a little; for too soon in this case were as ill as too late. When dusk falls, we must creep down, with all stealth, to Teiglin. But beware! For the ears of Glaurung are as keen as his eyes – and they are deadly. If we reach the river unmarked, we must climb then down into the ravine, and cross the water, and so come in the path that he will take when he stirs.'

'But how can he come forward so?' said Dorlas. 'Lithe he may be, but he is a great Dragon, and how shall he climb down the one cliff and up the other, when part must again be climbing before the hinder is yet descended? And if he can so, what will it avail us to be in the wild water below?'

'Maybe he can so,' answered Turambar, 'and indeed if he does, it will go ill with us. But it is my hope from what we learn of him, and from the place where he now lies, that his purpose is otherwise. He is come to the brink of Cabed-en-Aras, over which, as you tell, a deer once leaped from the huntsmen of Haleth. So great is he now that I think he will seek to cast himself across there. That is all our hope, and we must trust to it.'

Dorlas' heart sank at these words; for he knew better than any all the land of Brethil, and Cabed-en-Aras was a grim place indeed. On the east side was a sheer cliff of some forty feet, bare but tree-grown at the crown; on the other side was a bank somewhat less sheer and less high, shrouded with hanging trees and bushes, but between them the water ran fiercely among rocks, and though a man bold and sure-footed might ford it by day, it was perilous to dare it at night. But this was the counsel of Turambar, and it was useless to gainsay him.

They set out therefore at dusk, and they did not go straight towards the Dragon, but took first the path to the Crossings; then, before they came so far, they turned southward by a narrow track and passed into the twilight of the woods above Teiglin.[26] And as they drew near to Cabed-en-Aras, step by step, halting often to listen, the reek of burning came to them, and a stench that sickened them. But all was deadly still, and there was no stir of air. The first stars glimmered in the East behind them, and faint spires of smoke rose straight and unwavering against the last light in the West.

Now when Turambar was gone Níniel stood silent as stone; but Brandir came to her and said: 'Níniel, fear not the worst until you must. But did I not counsel you to wait?'

'You did so,' she answered. 'Yet how would that profit me now? For love may abide and suffer unwedded.'

'That I know,' said Brandir. 'Yet wedding is not for nothing.'

'I am two months gone with his child,' said Níniel. 'But it does not seem to me that my fear of loss is the more heavy to bear. I understand you not.'

'Nor I myself,' said he. 'And yet I am afraid.'

'What a comforter are you!' she cried. 'But Brandir, friend: wedded or unwedded, mother or maid, my dread is beyond enduring. The Master of Doom is gone to challenge his doom far hence, and how shall I stay here and wait for the slow coming of tidings, good or ill? This night, it may be, he will meet with the Dragon, and how shall I stand, or sit, or pass the dreadful hours?'

'I know not,' said he, 'but somehow the hours must pass, for you and for the wives of those that went with him.'

'Let them do as their hearts bid!' she cried. 'But for me, I shall go. The miles shall not lie between me and my lord's peril. I will go to meet the tidings!'

Then Brandir's dread grew black at her words, and he cried: 'That you shall not do, if I may hinder it. For thus will you endanger all counsel. The miles that lie between may give time for escape, if ill befall.'

'If ill befall, I shall not wish to escape,' she said. 'And now your wisdom is vain, and you shall not hinder me.' And she stood forth before the people that were still gathered in the open place of the Ephel, and she cried: 'Men of Brethil! I will not wait here. If my lord fails, then all hope is false. Your land and woods shall be burned utterly, and all your houses laid in ashes, and none, none, shall escape. Therefore why tarry here? Now I go to meet the tidings and whatever doom may send. Let all those of like mind come with me!'

Then many were willing to go with her: the wives of Dorlas and Hunthor because those whom they loved were gone with Turambar; others for pity of Níniel and desire to befriend her; and many more that were lured by the very rumour of the Dragon, in their hardihood or their folly (knowing little of evil) thinking to see strange and glorious deeds. For indeed so great in their minds had the Black Sword become that few could believe that even Glaurung could conquer him. Therefore they set forth soon in haste, a great company, towards a peril that they did not understand; and going with little rest they came wearily at last, just at nightfall, to Nen Girith but a little while after Turambar had departed. But night is a cold counsellor, and many were now amazed at their own rashness; and when they heard from the scouts that remained there how near Glaurung was come, and the desperate purpose of Turambar, their hearts were chilled, and they dared go no further. Some looked out towards Cabed-en-Aras with anxious eyes, but nothing could they see, and nothing hear save the cold voice of the falls. And Níniel sat apart, and a great shuddering seized her.

When Níniel and her company had gone, Brandir said to those that remained: 'Behold how I am scorned, and all my counsel disdained! Let Turambar be your lord in name, since already he has taken all my authority. For here I renounce both lordship and people. Let none seek of me ever again either counsel or healing!' And he broke his staff. To himself he thought: 'Now nothing is left to me, save only my love of Níniel: therefore where she goes, in wisdom or folly, I must go. In this dark hour nothing can be foreseen; but it may well chance that even I could ward off some evil from her, if I were near.'

He girt himself therefore with a short sword, as seldom before, and took his crutch, and went with what speed he might out of the gate of the Ephel, limping after the others down the long path to the west march of Brethil.

### The Death of Glaurung

At last, even as full night closed over the land, Turambar and his companions came to Cabed-en-Aras, and they were glad of the great noise of the water; for though it promised peril below, it covered all other sounds. Then Dorlas led them a little aside, southwards, and they climbed down by a cleft to the cliff-foot; but there his heart quailed, for many rocks and great stones lay in the river, and the water ran wild about them, grinding its teeth. 'This is a sure way to death,' said Dorlas.

'It is the only way, to death or to life,' said Turambar, 'and delay will not make it seem more hopeful. Therefore follow me!' And he went on before them, and by skill and hardihood, or by fate, he came across, and in the deep dark he turned to see who came after. A dark form stood beside him. 'Dorlas?' he said.

'No, it is I,' said Hunthor. 'Dorlas failed at the crossing. For a man may love war, and yet dread many things. He sits shivering on the shore, I guess; and may shame take him for his words to my kinsman.'

Now Turambar and Hunthor rested a little, but soon the night chilled them, for they were both drenched with water, and they began to seek a way along the stream northwards towards the lodgement of Glaurung. There the chasm grew darker and narrower, and as they felt their way forward they could see a flicker above them as of smouldering fire, and they heard the snarling of the Great Worm in his watchful sleep. Then they groped for a way up, to come nigh under the brink; for in that lay all their hope to come at their enemy beneath his guard. But so foul now was the reek that their heads were dizzy, and they slipped as they clambered, and clung to the tree-stems, and retched, forgetting in their misery all fear save the dread of falling into the teeth of Teiglin.

Then Turambar said to Hunthor: 'We spend our waning strength to no avail. For till we be sure where the Dragon will pass, it is vain to climb.'

'But when we know,' said Hunthor, 'then there will be no time to seek a way up out of the chasm.'

'Truly,' said Turambar. 'But where all lies on chance, to chance we must trust.' They halted therefore and waited, and out of the dark ravine they watched a white star far above creep across the faint strip of sky; and then slowly Turambar sank into a dream, in which all his will was given to clinging, though a black tide sucked and gnawed at his limbs.

Suddenly there was a great noise and the walls of the chasm quivered and echoed. Turambar roused himself, and said to Hunthor: 'He stirs. The hour is upon us. Strike deep, for two must strike now for three!'

And with that Glaurung began his assault upon Brethil; and all passed much as Turambar had hoped. For now the Dragon crawled with slow weight to the edge of the cliff, and he did not turn aside, but made ready to spring over the chasm with his great forelegs and then draw his bulk after. Terror came with him; for he did not begin his passage right above, but a little to the northward, and the watchers from beneath could see the huge shadow of his head against the stars; and his jaws gaped, and he had seven tongues of fire. Then he sent forth a blast, so that all the ravine was filled with a red light, and black shadows flying among the rocks; but the trees before him withered and went up in smoke, and stones crashed down into the river. And thereupon he hurled himself forward, and grappled the further cliff with his mighty claws, and began to heave himself across.

Now there was need to be bold and swift, for though Turambar and Hunthor had escaped the blast, since they were not standing right in Glaurung's path, they yet had to come at him, before he passed over, or all their hope failed. Heedless of peril Turambar clambered along the water-edge to come beneath him; but there so deadly was the heat and the stench that he tottered and would have fallen if Hunthor, following stoutly behind, had not seized his arm and steadied him.

'Great heart!' said Turambar. 'Happy was the choice that took you for a helper!' But even as he spoke, a great stone hurtled from above and smote Hunthor on the head, and he fell into the water, and so ended: not the least valiant of the House of Haleth. Then Turambar cried: 'Alas! It is ill to walk in my shadow! Why did I seek aid? For now you are alone, O Master of Doom, as you should have known it must be. Now conquer alone!'

Then he summoned to him all his will, and all his hatred of the Dragon and his Master, and it seemed that suddenly he found a strength of heart and of body that he had not known before; and he climbed the cliff, from stone to stone, and root to root, until he seized at last a slender tree that grew a little beneath the lip of the chasm, and though its top was blasted, it held still fast by its roots. And even as he steadied himself in a fork of its boughs, the midmost parts of the Dragon came above him, and swayed down with their weight almost upon his head, ere Glaurung could heave them up. Pale and wrinkled was their underside, and all dank with a grey slime, to which clung all manner of dropping filth; and it stank of death. Then Turambar drew the Black Sword of Beleg and stabbed upwards with all the might of his arm, and of his hate, and the deadly blade, long and greedy, went into the belly even to its hilts.

Then Glaurung, feeling his death-pang, gave forth a scream,

whereat all the woods were shaken, and the watchers at Nen Girith were aghast. Turambar reeled as from a blow, and slipped down, and his sword was torn from his grasp, and clave to the belly of the Dragon. For Glaurung in a great spasm bent up all his shuddering bulk and hurled it over the ravine, and there upon the further shore he writhed, screaming, lashing and coiling himself in his agony, until he had broken a great space all about him, and lay there at last in a smoke and a ruin, and was still.

Now Turambar clung to the roots of the tree, stunned and well-nigh overcome. But he strove against himself and drove himself on, and half sliding and half climbing he came down to the river, and dared again the perilous crossing, crawling now on hands and feet, clinging, blinded with spray, until he came over at last, and climbed wearily up by the cleft by which they had descended. Thus he came at length to the place of the dying Dragon, and he looked on his stricken enemy without pity, and was glad.

There now Glaurung lay, with jaws agape; but all his fires were burned out, and his evil eyes were closed. He was stretched out in his length, and had rolled upon one side, and the hilts of Gurthang stood in his belly. Then the heart of Turambar rose high within him, and though the Dragon still breathed he would recover his sword, which if he prized it before was now worth to him all the treasure of Nargothrond. True proved the words spoken at its forging that nothing, great or small, should live that once it had bitten.

Therefore going up to his foe he set foot upon his belly, and seizing the hilts of Gurthang he put forth his strength to withdraw it. And he cried in mockery of Glaurung's words at Nargothrond: 'Hail, Worm of Morgoth! Well met again! Die now and the darkness have thee! Thus is Túrin son of Húrin avenged.' Then he wrenched out the sword, and even as he did so a spout of black blood followed it, and fell upon his hand, and his flesh was burned by the venom, so that he cried aloud at the pain. Thereat Glaurung stirred and opened his baleful eyes and looked upon Turambar with such malice that it seemed to him that he was smitten by an arrow; and for that and for the anguish of his hand he fell in a swoon, and lay as one dead beside the Dragon, and his sword was beneath him.

Now the screams of Glaurung came to the people at Nen Girith, and they were filled with terror; and when the watchers beheld from afar the great breaking and burning that the Dragon made in his throes, they believed that he was trampling and destroying those that had assailed him. Then indeed they wished the miles longer that lay between them; but they dared not leave the high place where they were gathered, for they remembered the words of Turambar that, if Glaurung conquered, he would go first to Ephel Brandir. Therefore they watched in fear for any sign of his movement, but none were so hardy as to go down and seek for tidings in the place of the battle. And Níniel sat, and did not move, save that she shuddered and could not still her limbs; for when she heard the voice of Glaurung her heart died within her, and she felt her darkness creeping upon her again.

Thus Brandir found her. For he came at last to the bridge over Celebros, slow and weary; all the long way alone he had limped on his crutch, and it was five leagues at the least from his home. Fear for Níniel had driven him on, and now the tidings that he learned were no worse than he had dreaded. 'The Dragon has crossed the river,' men told him, 'and the Black Sword is surely dead, and those that went with him.' Then Brandir stood by Níniel, and guessed her misery, and he yearned to her; but he thought nonetheless: 'The Black Sword is dead, and Níniel lives.' And he shuddered, for suddenly it seemed cold by the waters of Nen Girith; and he cast his cloak about Níniel. But he found no words to say; and she did not speak.

Time passed, and still Brandir stood silent beside her, peering into the night and listening; but he could see nothing, and could hear no sound but the falling of the waters of Nen Girith, and he thought: 'Now surely Glaurung is gone and has passed into Brethil.' But he pitied his people no more, fools that had flouted his counsel, and had scorned him. 'Let the Dragon go to Amon Obel, and there will be time then to escape, to lead Níniel away.' Whither, he scarce knew, for he had never journeyed beyond Brethil.

At last he bent down and touched Níniel on the arm, and said to her: 'Time passes, Níniel! Come! It is time to go. If you will let me, I will lead you.'

Then silently she arose, and took his hand, and they passed over the bridge and went down the path that led to the Crossings of Teiglin. But those that saw them moving as shadows in the dark knew not who they were, and cared not. And when they had gone some little way through the silent trees, the moon rose beyond Amon Obel, and the glades of the forest were filled with a grey light. Then Níniel halted and said to Brandir: 'Is this the way?'

And he answered: 'What is the way? For all our hope in Brethil is ended. We have no way, save to escape the Dragon, and flee far from him while there is yet time.'

Níniel looked at him in wonder and said: 'Did you not offer to lead me to him? Or would you deceive me? The Black Sword was my beloved and my husband, and only to find him do I go. What else could you think? Now do as you will, but I must hasten.'

And even as Brandir stood a moment amazed, she sped from him; and he called after her, crying: 'Wait, Níniel! Go not alone! You know not what you will find. I will come with you!' But she paid no heed to him, and went now as though her blood burned her, which before had been cold; and though he followed as he could she passed soon out of his sight. Then he cursed his fate and his weakness; but he would not turn back.

Now the moon rose white in the sky, and was near the full, and as Níniel came down from the upland towards the land near the river, it seemed to her that she remembered it, and feared it. For she was come to the Crossings of Teiglin, and Haudh-en-Elleth stood there before her, pale in the moonlight, with a black shadow cast athwart it; and out of the mound came a great dread.

Then she turned with a cry and fled south along the river, and cast her cloak as she ran, as though casting off a darkness that clung to her; and beneath she was all clad in white, and she shone in the moon as she flitted among the trees. Thus Brandir above on the hill-side saw her, and turned to cross her course, if he could; and finding by fortune the narrow path that Turambar had used, for it left the more beaten road and went steeply down southward to the river, he came at last close behind her again. But though he called, she did not heed, or did not hear, and soon once more she passed on ahead; and so they drew near to the woods beside Cabed-en-Aras and the place of the agony of Glaurung.

The moon then was riding in the South unclouded, and the light was cold and clear. Coming to the edge of the ruin that Glaurung had wrought, Níniel saw his body lying there, and his belly grey in the moon-sheen; but beside him lay a man. Then forgetting her fear she ran on amid the smouldering wrack and so came to Turambar. He was fallen on his side, and his sword lay beneath him, but his face was wan as death in the white light. Then she threw herself down by him weeping, and kissed him; and it seemed to her that he breathed faintly, but she thought it but a trickery of false hope, for he was cold, and did not move, nor did he answer her. And as she caressed him she found that his hand was blackened as if it had been scorched, and she washed it with her tears, and tearing a strip from her raiment she bound it about. But still he did not move at her touch, and she kissed him again, and cried aloud: 'Turambar,

Turambar, come back! Hear me! Awake! For it is Níniel. The Dragon is dead, dead, and I alone am here by you.' But he answered nothing.

Her cry Brandir heard, for he had come to the edge of the ruin; but even as he stepped forward towards Níniel, he was halted, and stood still. For at the cry of Níniel Glaurung stirred for the last time, and a quiver ran through all his body; and he opened his baleful eyes a slit, and the moon gleamed in them, as gasping he spoke:

'Hail, Nienor, daughter of Húrin. We meet again ere the end. I give thee joy that thou hast found thy brother at last. And now thou shalt know him: a stabber in the dark, treacherous to foes, faithless to friends, and a curse unto his kin, Túrin son of Húrin! But the worst of all his deeds thou shalt feel in thyself.'

Then Nienor sat as one stunned, but Glaurung died; and with his death the veil of his malice fell from her, and all her memory grew clear before her, from day unto day, neither did she forget any of those things that had befallen her since she lay on Haudh-en-Elleth. And her whole body shook with horror and anguish. But Brandir, who had heard all, was stricken, and leaned against a tree.

Then suddenly Nienor started to her feet, and stood pale as a wraith in the moon, and looked down on Túrin, and cried: 'Farewell, O twice beloved! *A Túrin Turambar turún' ambartanen*: master of doom by doom mastered! O happy to be dead!' Then distraught with woe and the horror that had overtaken her she fled wildly from that place; and Brandir stumbled after her, crying: 'Wait! Wait, Níniel!'

One moment she paused, looking back with staring eyes. 'Wait?' she cried. 'Wait? That was ever your counsel. Would that I had heeded! But now it is too late. And now I will wait no more upon Middle-earth.' And she sped on before him.[27]

Swiftly she came to the brink of Cabed-en-Aras, and there stood and looked on the loud water crying: 'Water, water! Take now Níniel Nienor daughter of Húrin; Mourning, Mourning daughter of Morwen! Take me and bear me down to the Sea!' With that she cast herself over the brink: a flash of white swallowed in the dark chasm, a cry lost in the roaring of the river.

The waters of Teiglin flowed on, but Cabed-en-Aras was no more: Cabed Naeramarth thereafter it was named by men; for no deer would ever leap there again, and all living things shunned it, and no man would walk upon its shore. Last of men to look down into its darkness was Brandir son of Handir; and he turned away in horror, for his heart quailed, and though he hated now his life, he could not there take the death that he desired.[28] Then his thought turned to

Túrin Turambar, and he cried: 'Do I hate you, or do I pity you? But you are dead. I owe you no thanks, taker of all that I had or would have. But my people owe you a debt. It is fitting that from me they should learn it.'

And so he began to limp back to Nen Girith, avoiding the place of the Dragon with a shudder; and as he climbed the steep path again he came on a man that peered through the trees, and seeing him drew back. But he had marked his face in a gleam of the sinking moon.

'Ha, Dorlas!' he cried. 'What news can you tell? How came you off alive? And what of my kinsman?'

'I know not,' answered Dorlas sullenly.

'Then that is strange,' said Brandir.

'If you will know,' said Dorlas, 'the Black Sword would have us ford the races of Teiglin in the dark. Is it strange that I could not? I am a better man with an axe than some, but I am not goat-footed.'

'So they went on without you to come at the Dragon?' said Brandir. 'But how when he passed over? At the least you would stay near, and would see what befell.'

Bur Dorlas made no answer, and stared only at Brandir with hatred in his eyes. Then Brandir understood, perceiving suddenly that this man had deserted his companions, and unmanned by shame had then hidden in the woods. 'Shame on you, Dorlas!' he said. 'You are the begetter of our woes: egging on the Black Sword, bringing the Dragon upon us, putting me to scorn, drawing Hunthor to his death, and then you flee to skulk in the woods!' And as he spoke another thought entered his mind, and he said in great anger: 'Why did you not bring tidings? It was the least penance that you could do. Had you done so, the Lady Níniel would have had no need to seek them herself. She need never have seen the Dragon. She might have lived. Dorlas, I hate you!'

'Keep your hate!' said Dorlas. 'It is as feeble as all your counsels. But for me the Orcs would have come and hung you as a scarecrow in your own garden. Take the name skulker to yourself!' And with that, being for his shame the readier to wrath, he aimed a blow at Brandir with his great fist, and so ended his life, before the look of amazement left his eyes: for Brandir drew his sword and hewed him his death-blow. Then for a moment he stood trembling, sickened by the blood; and casting down his sword he turned, and went on his way, bowed upon his crutch.

As Brandir came to Nen Girith the pallid moon was gone down, and the night was fading; morning was opening in the East. The

people that cowered there still by the bridge saw him come like a
grey shadow in the dawn, and some called to him in wonder: 'Where
have you been? Have you seen her? For the Lady Níniel is gone.'

'Yes, she is gone,' he said. 'Gone, gone, never to return! But I
am come to bring you tidings. Hear now, people of Brethil, and say
if there was ever such a tale as the tale that I bear! The Dragon is
dead, but dead also is Turambar at his side. And those are good
tidings: yes, both are good indeed.'

Then the people murmured, wondering at his speech, and some
said that he was mad; but Brandir cried: 'Hear me to the end!
Níniel too is dead, Níniel the fair whom you loved, whom I loved
dearest of all. She leaped from the brink of the Deer's Leap,[29] and
the teeth of Teiglin have taken her. She is gone, hating the light of
day. For this she learned before she fled: Húrin's children were they
both, sister and brother. The Morgemil he was called, Turambar he
named himself, hiding his past: Túrin son of Húrin. Níniel we named
her, not knowing her past: Nienor she was, daughter of Húrin. To
Brethil they brought their dark doom's shadow. Here their doom has
fallen, and of grief this land shall never again be free. Call it not
Brethil, not the land of the Halethrim, but *Sarch nia Hîn Húrin*,
Grave of the Children of Húrin!'

Then though they did not understand yet how this evil had come
to pass, the people wept as they stood, and some said: 'A grave there
is in Teiglin for Níniel the beloved, a grave there shall be for Turambar,
most valiant of men. Our deliverer shall not be left to lie under the
sky. Let us go to him.'

### The Death of Túrin

Now even as Níniel fled away, Túrin stirred, and it seemed to him
that out of his deep darkness he heard her call to him far away; but
as Glaurung died, the black swoon left him, and he breathed deep
again, and sighed, and passed into a slumber of great weariness. But
ere dawn it grew bitter cold, and he turned in his sleep, and the
hilts of Gurthang drove into his side, and suddenly he awoke. Night
was going, and there was a breath of morning in the air; and he
sprang to his feet, remembering his victory, and the burning venom
on his hand. He raised it up, and looked at it, and marvelled. For it
was bound about with a strip of white cloth, yet moist, and it was
at ease; and he said to himself: 'Why should one tend me so, and
yet leave me here to lie cold amid the wrack and the dragon-stench?
What strange things have chanced?'

Then he called aloud, but there was no answer. All was black and drear about him, and there was a reek of death. He stooped and lifted his sword, and it was whole, and the light of its edges was undimmed. 'Foul was the venom of Glaurung,' he said, 'but you are stronger than I, Gurthang! All blood will you drink. Yours is the victory. But come! I must go seek for aid. My body is weary, and there is a chill in my bones.'

Then he turned his back upon Glaurung and left him to rot; but as he passed from that place each step seemed more heavy, and he thought: 'At Nen Girith, maybe, I will find one of the scouts awaiting me. But would I were soon in my own house, and might feel the gentle hands of Níniel, and the good skill of Brandir!' And so at last, walking wearily, leaning on Gurthang, through the grey light of early day he came to Nen Girith, and even as men were setting forth to seek his dead body, he stood before the people.

Then they gave back in terror, believing that it was his unquiet spirit, and the women wailed and covered their eyes. But he said: 'Nay, do not weep, but be glad! See! Do I not live? And have I not slain the Dragon that you feared?'

Then they turned upon Brandir, and cried: 'Fool, with your false tales, saying that he lay dead. Did we not say that you were mad?' But Brandir was aghast, and stared at Túrin with fear in his eyes, and he could say nothing.

But Túrin said to him: 'It was you then that were there, and tended my hand? I thank you. But your skill is failing, if you cannot tell swoon from death.' Then he turned to the people: 'Speak not so to him, fools all of you. Which of you would have done better? At least he had the heart to come down to the place of battle, while you sit wailing!

'But now, son of Handir, come! There is more that I would learn. Why are you here, and all this people, whom I left at the Ephel? If I may go into the peril of death for your sakes, may I not be obeyed when I am gone? And where is Níniel? At the least I may hope that you did not bring her hither, but left her where I bestowed her, in my house, with true men to guard it?'

And when no one answered him, 'Come, say where is Níniel?' he cried. 'For her first I would see; and to her first will I tell the tale of the deeds in the night.'

But they turned their faces from him, and Brandir said at last: 'Níniel is not here.'

'That is well then,' he said. 'Then I will go to my home. Is there a horse to bear me? Or a bier would be better. I faint with my labours.'

'Nay, nay!' said Brandir in anguish. 'Your house is empty. Níniel is not there. She is dead.'

But one of the women – the wife of Dorlas, who loved Brandir little – cried shrilly: 'Pay no heed to him, lord! For he is crazed. He came crying that you were dead, and called it good tidings. But you live. Why then should his tale of Níniel be true: that she is dead, and yet worse?'

Then Túrin strode towards Brandir: 'So my death was good tidings?' he cried. 'Yes, ever you did begrudge her to me, that I knew. Now she is dead, you say. And yet worse? What lie have you begotten in your malice, Club-foot? Would you slay us then with foul words, since you can wield no other weapon?'

Then anger drove pity from Brandir's heart, and he cried: 'Crazed? Nay, crazed are you, Black Sword of black doom! And all this dotard people. I do not lie! Níniel is dead, dead, dead! Seek her in Teiglin!'

Then Túrin stood still and cold. 'How do you know?' he said softly. 'How did you contrive it?'

'I know because I saw her leap,' answered Brandir. 'But the contriving was yours. She fled from you, Túrin son of Húrin, and in Cabed-en-Aras she cast herself, that she might never see you again. Níniel! Níniel? Nay, Nienor daughter of Húrin.'

Then Túrin seized him and shook him; for in those words he heard the feet of his doom overtaking him, but in horror and fury his heart would not receive them, as a beast hurt to death that will wound ere it dies all that are near it.

'Yes, I am Túrin son of Húrin,' he cried. 'So long ago you guessed. But nothing do you know of Nienor my sister. Nothing! She dwells in the Hidden Kingdom, and is safe. It is a lie of your own vile mind, to drive my wife witless, and now me. You limping evil – would you dog us both to death?'

But Brandir shook him off. 'Touch me not!' he said. 'Stay your raving. She that you name wife came to you and tended you, and you did not answer her call. But one answered for you. Glaurung the Dragon, who I deem bewitched you both to your doom. So he spoke, before he ended: "Nienor daughter of Húrin, here is thy brother: treacherous to foes, faithless to friends, a curse unto his kin, Túrin son of Húrin".' Then suddenly a fey laughter seized on Brandir. 'On their deathbed men will speak true, they say,' he cackled. 'And even a Dragon too, it seems! Túrin son of Húrin, a curse unto thy kin and unto all that harbour thee!'

Then Túrin grasped Gurthang and a fell light was in his eyes. 'And what shall be said of you, Club-foot?' he said slowly. 'Who told

her secretly behind my back my right name? Who brought her to the
malice of the Dragon? Who stood by and let her die? Who came
hither to publish this horror at the swiftest? Who would now gloat
upon me? Do men speak true before death? Then speak it now
quickly.'

Then Brandir, seeing his death in Túrin's face, stood still and did
not quail, though he had no weapon but his crutch; and he said:
'All that has chanced is a long tale to tell, and I am weary of you.
But you slander me, son of Húrin. Did Glaurung slander you? If
you slay me, then all shall see that he did not. Yet I do not fear to
die, for then I will go to seek Níniel whom I loved, and perhaps I
may find her again beyond the Sea.'

'Seek Níniel!' cried Túrin. 'Nay, Glaurung you shall find, and
breed lies together. You shall sleep with the Worm, your soul's mate,
and rot in one darkness!' Then he lifted up Gurthang and hewed
Brandir, and smote him to death. But the people hid their eyes from
that deed, and as he turned and went from Nen Girith they fled
from him in terror.

Then Túrin went as one witless through the wild woods, now
cursing Middle-earth and all the life of Men, now calling upon
Níniel. But when at last the madness of his grief left him he sat
awhile and pondered all his deeds, and he heard himself crying: 'She
dwells in the Hidden Kingdom, and is safe!' And he thought that
now, though all his life was in ruin, he must go thither; for all the
lies of Glaurung had ever led him astray. Therefore he arose and
went to the Crossings of Teiglin, and as he passed by Haudh-en-
Elleth he cried: 'Bitterly have I paid, O Finduilas! that ever I gave
heed to the Dragon. Send me now counsel!'

But even as he cried out he saw twelve huntsmen well-armed that
came over the Crossings, and they were Elves; and as they drew near
he knew one, for it was Mablung, chief huntsman of Thingol. And
Mablung hailed him, crying: 'Túrin! Well met at last. I seek you,
and glad I am to see you living, though the years have been heavy
on you.'

'Heavy!' said Túrin. 'Yes, as the feet of Morgoth. But if you are
glad to see me living, you are the last in Middle-earth. Why so?'

'Because you were held in honour among us,' answered Mablung;
'and though you have escaped many perils, I feared for you at the
last. I watched the coming forth of Glaurung, and I thought that he
had fulfilled his wicked purpose and was returning to his Master.
But he turned towards Brethil, and at the same time I learned from
wanderers in the land that the Black Sword of Nargothrond had

appeared there again, and the Orcs shunned its borders as death. Then I was filled with dread, and I said: "Alas! Glaurung goes where his Orcs dare not, to seek out Túrin. Therefore I came hither as swift as might be, to warn you and aid you." '

'Swift, but not swift enough,' said Túrin. 'Glaurung is dead.'

Then the Elves looked at him in wonder, and said: 'You have slain the Great Worm! Praised for ever shall your name be among Elves and Men!'

'I care not,' said Túrin. 'For my heart also is slain. But since you come from Doriath, give me news of my kin. For I was told in Dor-lómin that they had fled to the Hidden Kingdom.'

The Elves made no answer, but at length Mablung spoke: 'They did so indeed, in the year before the coming of the Dragon. But they are not there now, alas!' Then Túrin's heart stood still, hearing the feet of doom that would pursue him to the end. 'Say on!' he cried. 'And be swift!'

'They went out into the wild seeking you,' said Mablung. 'It was against all counsel; but they would go to Nargothrond, when it was known that you were the Black Sword; and Glaurung came forth, and all their guard were scattered. Morwen none have seen since that day; but Nienor had a spell of dumbness upon her, and fled north into the woods like a wild deer, and was lost.' Then to the wonder of the Elves Túrin laughed loud and shrill. 'Is not that a jest?' he cried. 'O the fair Nienor! So she ran from Doriath to the Dragon, and from the Dragon unto me. What a sweet grace of fortune! Brown as a berry she was, dark was her hair; small and slim as an Elf-child, none could mistake her!'

Then Mablung was amazed, and he said: 'But some mistake is here. Not such was your sister. She was tall, and her eyes were blue, her hair fine gold, the very likeness in woman's form of Húrin her father. You cannot have seen her!'

'Can I not, can I not, Mablung?' cried Túrin. 'But why no! For see, I am blind! Did you not know? Blind, blind, groping since childhood in a dark mist of Morgoth! Therefore leave me! Go, go! Go back to Doriath, and may winter shrivel it! A curse upon Menegroth! And a curse on your errand! This only was wanting. Now comes the night!'

Then he fled from them, like the wind, and they were filled with wonder and fear. But Mablung said: 'Some strange and dreadful thing has chanced that we know not. Let us follow him and aid him if we may: for now he is fey and witless.'

But Túrin sped far before them, and came to Cabed-en-Aras, and stood still; and he heard the roaring of the water, and saw that all the trees near and far were withered, and their sere leaves fell mournfully, as though winter had come in the first days of summer.

'Cabed-en-Aras, Cabed Naeramarth!' he cried. 'I will not defile your waters where Níniel was washed. For all my deeds have been ill, and the latest the worst.'

Then he drew forth his sword, and said: 'Hail Gurthang, iron of death, thou alone now remainest! But what lord or loyalty dost thou know, save the hand that wieldeth thee? From no blood wilt thou shrink! Wilt thou take Túrin Turambar? Wilt thou slay me swiftly?'

And from the blade rang a cold voice in answer: 'Yea, I will drink thy blood, that I may forget the blood of Beleg my master, and the blood of Brandir slain unjustly. I will slay thee swiftly.'

Then Túrin set the hilts upon the ground, and cast himself upon the point of Gurthang, and the black blade took his life.

But Mablung came and looked on the hideous shape of Glaurung lying dead, and he looked upon Túrin and was grieved, thinking of Húrin as he had seen him in the Nirnaeth Arnoediad, and the dreadful doom of his kin. As the Elves stood there, men came down from Nen Girith to look upon the Dragon, and when they saw to what end the life of Túrin Turambar had come they wept; and the Elves learning at last the reason of Túrin's words to them were aghast. Then Mablung said bitterly: 'I also have been meshed in the doom of the Children of Húrin, and thus with words have slain one that I loved.'

Then they lifted up Túrin, and saw that his sword was broken asunder. So passed all that he possessed.

With toil of many hands they gathered wood and piled it high and made a great burning, and destroyed the body of the Dragon, until he was but black ash and his bones beaten to dust, and the place of that burning was ever bare and barren thereafter. But Túrin they laid in a high mound where he had fallen, and the shards of Gurthang were set beside him. And when all was done, and the minstrels of Elves and Men had made lament, telling of the valour of Turambar and the beauty of Níniel, a great grey stone was brought and set upon the mound; and thereon the Elves carved in the Runes of Doriath:

TÚRIN TURAMBAR DAGNIR GLAURUNGA

and beneath they wrote also:

NIENOR NÍNIEL

But she was not there, nor was it ever known whither the cold waters of Teiglin had taken her.

Thus ends the Tale of the Children of Húrin, longest of all the lays of Beleriand.

## NOTES

In an introductory note, existing in different forms, it is said that though made in Elvish speech and using much Elvish lore, especially of Doriath, the *Narn i Hîn Húrin* was the work of a Mannish poet, Dírhavel, who lived at the Havens of Sirion in the days of Eärendil, and there gathered all the tidings that he could of the House of Hador, whether among Men or Elves, remnants and fugitives of Dor-lómin, of Nargothrond, of Gondolin, or of Doriath. In one version of this note Dírhavel is said to have come himself of the House of Hador. This lay, longest of all the lays of Beleriand, was all that he ever made, but it was prized by the Eldar, for Dírhavel used the Grey-elven tongue, in which he had great skill. He used that mode of Elvish verse which was called *Minlamed thent / estent*, and was of old proper to the *narn* (a tale that is told in verse, but to be spoken and not sung). Dírhavel perished in the raid of the Sons of Fëanor upon the Havens of Sirion.

1   At this point in the text of the *Narn* there is a passage describing the sojourn of Húrin and Huor in Gondolin. This is very closely based on the story told in one of the 'constituent texts' of *The Silmarillion* – so closely as to be no more than a variant, and I have not given it again here. The story can be read in *The Silmarillion* pp. 158–9.

2   Here in the text of the *Narn* there is a passage, giving an account of the Nirnaeth Arnoediad, that I have excluded for the same reason as that given in Note 1; see *The Silmarillion* pp. 190–5.

3   In another version of the text it is made explicit that Morwen did indeed have dealings with the Eldar who had secret dwellings in the mountains not far from her house. 'But they could tell her no news. None had seen Húrin's fall. "He was not with Fingon," they said; "he was driven south with Turgon, but if any of his folk escaped it was in the wake of the host of Gondolin. But who knows? For the Orcs have piled all the slain together, and search is vain, even if any dared to go to the Haudh-en-Nirnaeth." '

4   With this description of the Helm of Hador compare the 'great masks hideous to look upon' worn by the Dwarves of Belegost in the Nirnaeth Arnoediad, which 'stood them in good stead against the dragons' (*The Silmarillion* p. 193). Túrin afterwards wore a dwarf-mask when he went into battle out of Nargothrond, 'and his enemies fled before his face' (*ibid.* p. 210). See further the Appendix to the *Narn*, pp. 154–5 below.

5  The Orc-raid into East Beleriand in which Maedhros saved Azaghâl is nowhere else referred to.

6  Elsewhere my father remarked that the speech of Doriath, whether of the King or others, was even in the days of Túrin more antique than that used elsewhere; and also that Mîm observed (though the extant writings concerning Mîm do not mention this) that one thing of which Túrin never rid himself, despite his grievance against Doriath, was the speech he had acquired during his fostering.

7  A marginal note in one text says here: 'Always he sought in all faces of women the face of Lalaith.'

8  In one variant text of this section of the narrative Saeros is said to have been the kinsman of Daeron, and in another Daeron's brother; the text printed is probably the latest.

9  *Woodwose*: 'wild man of the woods'; see note 14 to *The Drúedain*, p. 387 below.

10 In a variant text of this part of the story Túrin at this time declared to the outlaws his true name; and he claimed that, being by right the lord and judge of the People of Hador, he had slain Forweg justly, since he was a man of Dor-lómin. Then Algund, the old outlaw who had fled down Sirion from the Nirnaeth Arnoediad, said that Túrin's eyes had long reminded him of another whom he could not recall, and that now he knew him for the son of Húrin. ' "But he was a smaller man, small for his kin, though filled with fire; and his hair gold-red. You are dark, and tall. I see your mother in you, now that I look closer; she was of Bëor's people. What fate was hers, I wonder." "I do not know," said Túrin. "No word comes out of the North." ' In this version it was the knowledge that Neithan was Túrin son of Húrin that led those outlaws who came originally from Dor-lómin to accept him as the leader of the band.

11 The last-written versions of this part of the story agree that when Túrin became captain of the outlaw band he led them away from the homes of the Woodmen in the forest south of Teiglin, and that Beleg came there soon after they had gone; but the geography is unclear and the accounts of the outlaws' movements conflicting. It seems necessary to suppose, in view of the subsequent course of the narrative, that they remained in the Vale of Sirion, and indeed that they were not far from their previous haunts at the time of the Orc-raid on the homes of the Woodmen. In one tentative version they went away southwards and came to the country 'above the Aelin-uial and the Fens of Sirion'; but the men becoming discontented in that 'harbourless land', Túrin was persuaded to lead them back to the woodlands south of Teiglin where he first encountered them. This would fit the requirements of the narrative.

12 In *The Silmarillion* the narrative continues (pp. 201–2) with Beleg's farewell to Túrin, Túrin's strange foreknowledge that his fate would

lead him to Amon Rûdh, Beleg's coming to Menegroth (where he received the sword Anglachel from Thingol and *lembas* from Melian), and his return to warfare against the Orcs in Dimbar. There is no other text to supplement this, and the passage is omitted here.

13  Túrin fled from Doriath in the summer; he passed the autumn and winter among the outlaws, and he slew Forweg and became their captain in the spring of the next year. The events described here took place in the summer following.

14  *Aeglos*, 'snowthorn', is said to have been like furze (gorse), but larger, and with white flowers. *Aeglos* was also the name of the spear of Gil-galad. *Seregon*, 'blood of stone', was a plant of the kind called in English 'stonecrop'; it had flowers of a deep red.

15  So also the yellow-flowered gorse bushes encountered by Frodo, Sam and Gollum in Ithilien were 'gaunt and leggy below but thick above', so that they could walk upright under them, 'passing through long dry aisles', and they bore flowers that 'glimmered in the gloom and gave a faint sweet scent' (*The Two Towers* IV 7).

16  Elsewhere the Sindarin name of the Petty-Dwarves is given as *Noegyth Nibin* (so in *The Silmarillion* p. 204) and *Nibin-Nogrim*. The 'high moorlands that rose between the Vales of Sirion and Narog', north-east of Nargothrond (p. 99 above) are more than once referred to as the Moors of the Nibin-noeg (or variants of this name).

17  The tall cliff through which Mîm led them by the cleft that he called 'the gate of the garth' was (it appears) the north edge of the shelf; the cliffs on the eastern and western sides were much more precipitous.

18  Andróg's curse is also recorded in the form: 'May he lack a bow at need ere his end.' In the event Mîm met his death from Húrin's sword before the Doors of Nargothrond (*The Silmarillion* p. 230).

19  The mystery of the other things in Mîm's sack is not explained. The only other statement on the subject is in a hastily scribbled note, which suggests that there were ingots of gold disguised as roots, and refers to Mîm seeking 'for old treasures of a dwarf-house near the "flat stones"'. These were no doubt those referred to in the text (p. 96) as 'great stones, leaning or tumbled together', at the place where Mîm was captured. But there is nowhere any indication of what part this treasure was to play in the story of Bar-en-Danwedh.

20  It is said on p. 69 that the pass over the shoulder of Amon Darthir was the only pass 'between Serech and far westward where Dor-lómin marched with Nevrast'.

21  In the story as told in *The Silmarillion* (p. 216) Brandir's foreboding of evil came upon him after he had heard 'the tidings that Dorlas brought', and therefore (as it appears) after he knew that the man

on the bier was the Black Sword of Nargothrond, rumoured to be the son of Húrin of Dor-lómin.

22 See p. 153, where there is a reference to Orodreth's exchanging messages with Thingol 'by secret ways'.

23 In *The Silmarillion* (p. 122) the High Faroth, or Taur-en-Faroth, are 'great wooded highlands'. The description of them here as 'brown and bare' perhaps refers to the leaflessness of the trees in the beginning of spring.

24 One might suppose that it was only when all was over, and Túrin and Nienor dead, that her shuddering fit was recalled and its meaning seen, and Dimrost renamed Nen Girith; but in the legend Nen Girith is used as the name throughout.

25 If Glaurung's intention had indeed been to return to Angband it might be thought that he would have taken the old road to the Crossings of Teiglin, a course not greatly different from that which brought him to Cabed-en-Aras. Perhaps the assumption was that he would return to Angband by the way that he came south to Nargothrond, going up Narog to Ivrin. Cf. also Mablung's words (p. 143): 'I watched the coming forth of Glaurung, and I thought that he . . . was returning to his Master. But he turned towards Brethil . . .'

When Turambar spoke of his hope that Glaurung would go straight and not swerve, he meant that if the Dragon went up along Teiglin to the Crossings he would be able to enter Brethil without having to pass over the gorge, where he would be vulnerable: see his words to the men at Nen Girith, p. 130.

26 I have found no map to illustrate my father's conception of the lie of the land in detail, but this sketch seems at least to fit the references in the narrative:

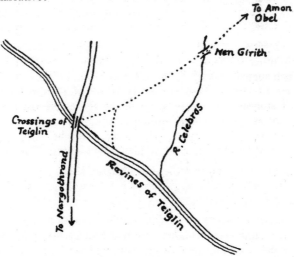

27  The phrases 'fled wildly from that place' and 'sped on before him'
    suggest that there was some distance between the place where Túrin
    lay beside Glaurung's corpse and the edge of the ravine. It may be
    that the Dragon's death-leap carried him some way beyond the further
    brink.

28  Later in the narrative (p. 145) Túrin himself, before his death,
    called the place Cabed Naeramarth, and it may be supposed that it
    was from the tradition of his last words that the later name was
    derived.

    The apparent discrepancy that, although Brandir is said (both
    here and in *The Silmarillion*) to have been the last man to look on
    Cabed-en-Aras, Túrin came there soon afterwards, and indeed the
    Elves also and all those who raised the mound over him, may perhaps
    be explained by taking the words of the *Narn* concerning Brandir in
    a narrow sense: he was the last man actually to 'look down into its
    darkness'. It was indeed my father's intention to alter the narrative
    so that Túrin slew himself not at Cabed-en-Aras but on the mound
    of Finduilas by the Crossings of Teiglin; but this never received
    written form.

29  It seems from this that 'The Deer's Leap' was the original name of
    the place, and indeed the meaning of Cabed-en-Aras.


# APPENDIX

From the point in the story where Túrin and his men established themselves in the ancient dwelling of the Petty-dwarves on Amon Rûdh there
is no completed narrative on the same detailed plan, until the *Narn* takes
up again with Túrin's journey northwards after the fall of Nargothrond.
From many tentative or exploratory outlines and notes, however, some
further glimpses can be gained beyond the more summary account in
*The Silmarillion*, and even some short stretches of connected narrative on
the scale of the *Narn*.

An isolated fragment describes the life of the outlaws on Amon Rûdh
in the time that followed their settlement there, and gives some further
description of Bar-en-Danwedh.

For a long while the life of the outlaws went well to their liking.
Food was not scarce, and they had good shelter, warm and dry, with
room enough and to spare; for they found that the caves could have
housed a hundred or more at need. There was another smaller hall
further in. It had a hearth at one side, above which a smoke-shaft ran
up through the rock to a vent cunningly hidden in a crevice on the
hillside. There were also many other chambers, opening out of the halls
or the passage between them, some for dwelling, some for works or for

stores. In storage Mîm had more arts than they, and he had many vessels and chests of stone and wood that looked to be of great age. But most of the chambers were now empty: in the armouries hung axes and other gear rusted and dusty, shelves and aumbries were bare; and the smithies were idle. Save one: a small room that led out of the inner hall and had a hearth which shared the smoke-vent of the hearth in the hall. There Mîm would work at times, but would not allow others to be with him.

During the rest of that year they went on no more raids, and if they stirred abroad for hunting or gathering of food they went for the most part in small parties. But for a long while they found it hard to retrace their road, and beside Túrin not more than six of his men became ever sure of the way. Nonetheless, seeing that those skilled in such things could come to their lair without Mîm's help, they set a watch by day and night near to the cleft in the north-wall. From the south they expected no enemies, nor was there fear of any climbing Amon Rûdh from that quarter; but by day there was at most times a watchman set on the top of the crown, who could look far all about. Steep as were the sides of the crown, the summit could be reached, for to the east of the cave-mouth rough steps had been hewn leading up to slopes where men could clamber unaided.

So the year wore on without hurt or alarm. But as the days drew in, and the pool became grey and cold and the birches bare, and great rains returned, they had to pass more time in shelter. Then they soon grew weary of the dark under hill, or the dim halflight of the halls; and to most it seemed that life would be better if it were not shared with Mîm. Too often he would appear out of some shadowy corner or doorway when they thought him elsewhere; and when Mîm was near unease fell on their talk. They took to speaking one to another ever in whispers.

Yet, and strange it seemed to them, with Túrin it went otherwise; and he became ever more friendly with the old Dwarf, and listened more and more to his counsels. In the winter that followed he would sit for long hours with Mîm, listening to his lore and the tales of his life; nor did Túrin rebuke him if he spoke ill of the Eldar. Mîm seemed well pleased, and showed much favour to Túrin in return; him only would he admit to his smithy at times, and there they would talk softly together. Less pleased were the Men; and Andróg looked on with a jealous eye.

The text followed in *The Silmarillion* gives no indication of how Beleg found his way into Bar-en-Danwedh: he 'appeared suddenly among them' 'in the dim dusk of a winter's day'. In other brief outlines the story is that through the improvidence of the outlaws food became short in Bar-en-Danwedh during the winter, and Mîm begrudged them the edible roots from his store; therefore in the beginning of the year they went out on a hunting foray from the stronghold. Beleg, approaching Amon Rûdh, came upon their tracks, and either trailed them to a camp which they were forced to make in a sudden snowstorm, or followed them back to Bar-en-Danwedh and slipped in after them.

At this time Andróg, seeking for Mîm's secret store of food, became lost in the caves, and found a hidden stair that led out on to the flat summit of Amon Rûdh (it was by this stair that some of the outlaws fled from Bar-en-Danwedh when it was attacked by the Orcs: *The Silmarillion* p. 206). And either during the foray just mentioned, or on a later occasion, Andróg, having taken up again bow and arrows in defiance of Mîm's curse, was wounded by a poisoned shaft – in one only of several references to the event said to have been an Orc-arrow.

Andróg was cured of this wound by Beleg, but it seems that his dislike and distrust of the Elf was not thereby mitigated; and Mîm's hatred of Beleg became all the fiercer, for he had thus 'undone' his curse upon Andróg. 'It will bite again,' he said. It came into Mîm's mind that if he also ate the *lembas* of Melian he would renew his youth and grow strong again; and since he could not come at it by stealth he feigned sickness and begged it of his enemy. When Beleg refused it to him the seal was set upon Mîm's hatred, and all the more because of Túrin's love for the Elf.

It may be mentioned here that when Beleg brought out the *lembas* from his pack (see *The Silmarillion* pp. 202, 204) Túrin refused it:

The silver leaves were red in the firelight; and when Túrin saw the seal his eyes darkened. 'What have you there?' he said.

'The greatest gift that one who loves you still has to give,' answered Beleg. 'Here is *lembas*, the waybread of the Eldar, that no Man yet has tasted.'

'The Helm of my fathers I take,' said Túrin, 'with good will for your keeping; but I will not receive gifts out of Doriath.'

'Then send back your sword and your arms,' said Beleg. 'Send back also the teaching and fostering of your youth. And let your men die in the desert to please your mood. Nonetheless, this waybread was a gift not to you but to me, and I may do with it as I will. Eat it not, if it sticks in your throat; but others here may be more hungry and less proud.'

Then Túrin was abashed, and in that matter overcame his pride.

Some slight further indications are found concerning Dor-Cúarthol, the Land of Bow and Helm, where Beleg and Túrin for a time became from their stronghold on Amon Rûdh the leaders of a strong force in the lands south of Teiglin (*The Silmarillion* p. 205).

Túrin received gladly all who came to him, but by the counsel of

Beleg he admitted no newcomer to his refuge upon Amon Rûdh (and that was now named Echad i Sedryn, Camp of the Faithful); the way thither only those of the Old Company knew and no others were admitted. But other guarded camps and forts were established round about: in the forest eastward, or in the highlands, or in the southward fens, from Methed-en-glad ('the End of the Wood') to Bar-erib some leagues south of Amon Rûdh; and from all these places men could see the summit of Amon Rûdh, and by signals receive tidings and commands.

In this way, before the summer had passed, the following of Túrin was swelled to a great force; and the power of Angband was thrown back. Word of this came even to Nargothrond, and many there grew restless, saying that if an Outlaw could do such hurt to the Enemy, what might not the Lord of Narog do. But Orodreth would not change his counsels. In all things he followed Thingol, with whom he exchanged messengers by secret ways; and he was a wise lord, according to the wisdom of those who considered first their own people, and how long they might preserve their life and wealth against the lust of the North. Therefore he allowed none of his people to go to Túrin, and he sent messengers to say to him that in all that he might do or devise in his war he should not set foot in the land of Nargothrond, nor drive Orcs thither. But help other than in arms he offered to the Two Captains, should they have need (and in this, it is thought, he was moved by Thingol and Melian).

It is several times emphasized that Beleg remained throughout opposed to Túrin's grand design, although he supported him; that it seemed to him that the Dragon-helm had worked otherwise with Túrin than he had hoped; and that he foresaw with a troubled mind what the days to come would bring. Scraps of his words with Túrin on these matters are preserved. In one of these, they sat in the stronghold of Echad i Sedryn together, and Túrin said to Beleg:

'Why are you sad, and thoughtful? Does not all go well, since you returned to me? Has not my purpose proved good?'

'All is well now,' said Beleg. 'Our enemies are still surprised, and afraid. And still good days lie before us; for a while.'

'And what then?'

'Winter. And after that another year, for those who live to see it.'

'And what then?'

'The wrath of Angband. We have burned the finger tips of the Black Hand – no more. It will not withdraw.'

'But is not the wrath of Angband our purpose and delight?' said Túrin. 'What else would you have me do?'

'You know full well,' said Beleg. 'But of that road you have forbidden me to speak. But hear me now. The lord of a great host has many needs. He must have a secure refuge; and he must have wealth, and many whose work is not in war. With numbers comes the need of food, more than the wild will furnish; and there comes the passing of secrecy. Amon Rûdh is a good place for a few – it has eyes and ears. But it stands alone, and is seen far off; and no great force is needed to surround it.'

'Nonetheless, I will be the captain of my own host,' said Túrin; 'and if I fall, then I fall. Here I stand in the path of Morgoth, and while I so stand he cannot use the southward road. For that in Nargothrond there should be some thanks; and even help with needful things.'

In another brief passage of speech between them Túrin replied to Beleg's warnings of the frailty of his power in these words:

'I wish to rule a land; but not this land. Here I desire only to gather strength. To my father's land in Dor-lómin my heart turns, and thither I shall go when I may.'

It is also asserted that Morgoth for a time withheld his hand and made mere feints of attack, 'so that by easy victory the confidence of these rebels might become overweening; as it proved indeed'.

Andróg appears again in an outline of the course of the assault on Amon Rûdh. It was only then that he revealed to Túrin the existence of the inner stair; and he was one of those who came by that way to the summit. There he is said to have fought more valiantly than any, but he fell at last mortally wounded by an arrow; and thus the curse of Mîm was fulfilled.

To the tale in *The Silmarillion* of Beleg's journey in pursuit of Túrin, his meeting with Gwindor in Taur-nu-Fuin, the rescue of Túrin, and Beleg's death at Túrin's hands, there is nothing of any moment to add. For Gwindor's possession of one of the blue-shining 'Fëanorian lamps' and the part that this lamp played in a version of the story see p. 51 above, Note 2.

It may be noted here that it was my father's intention to extend the history of the Dragon-helm of Dor-lómin into the period of Túrin's sojourn in Nargothrond and even beyond; but this was never incorporated into the narratives. In the existing versions the Helm disappears with the end of Dor-Cúarthol, in the destruction of the outlaws' stronghold on Amon Rûdh; but in some way it was to reappear in Túrin's possession at Nargothrond. It could only have come there if it had been taken by the Orcs that carried Túrin off to Angband; but its recovery from them at the time of Túrin's rescue by Beleg and Gwindor would have required some development of the narrative at that point.

An isolated scrap of writing tells that in Nargothrond Túrin would not wear the Helm again 'lest it reveal him', but that he wore it when he went

to the Battle of Tumhalad (*The Silmarillion* p. 212, where he is said to
have worn the dwarf-mask that he found in the armouries of Nargothrond).
This note continues:

 For fear of that helm all foes avoided him, and thus it was that he
came off unhurt from that deadly field. It was thus that he came back
to Nargothrond wearing the Dragon-helm, and Glaurung, desiring to
rid Túrin of its aid and protection (since he himself feared it), taunted
him, saying that surely Túrin claimed to be his vassal and retainer,
since he bore his master's likeness on the crest of his helm.
 But Túrin answered: 'Thou liest, and knowest it. For this image
was made in scorn of thee; and while there is one to bear it doubt shall
ever assail thee, lest the bearer deal thee thy doom.'
 'Then it must await a master of another name,' said Glaurung; 'for
Túrin son of Húrin I do not fear. Otherwise is it. For he has not the
hardihood to look me in the face, openly.'
 And indeed so great was the terror of the Dragon that Túrin dared
not look straight upon his eye, but had kept the visor of his helmet
down, shielding his face, and in his parley had looked no higher than
Glaurung's feet. But being thus taunted, in pride and rashness he
thrust up the visor and looked Glaurung in the eye.

In another place there is a note that it was when Morwen heard in
Doriath of the appearance of the Dragon-helm at the Battle of Tumhalad
that she knew that the tale was true that the Mormegil was indeed Túrin
her son.
 Finally, there is a suggestion that Túrin was to wear the Helm when
he slew Glaurung, and would taunt the Dragon at his death with his words
at Nargothrond about 'a master of another name'; but there is no indication
of how the narrative was to be managed to bring this about.

There is an account of the nature and substance of Gwindor's opposition
to Túrin's policies in Nargothrond, which in *The Silmarillion* is only very
briefly referred to (p. 211). This account is not fully formed into narrative,
but may be represented thus:

 Gwindor spoke ever against Túrin in the council of the King, saying
that he had been in Angband, and knew somewhat of the might of
Morgoth, and of his designs. 'Petty victories will prove profitless at
the last,' he said; 'for thus Morgoth learns where the boldest of his
enemies are to be found, and gathers strength great enough to destroy
them. All the might of the Elves and the Edain united sufficed only to
contain him, and to gain the peace of a siege; long indeed, but only so
long as Morgoth bided his time before he broke the leaguer; and never
again can such a union be made. In secrecy only lies now any hope;
until the Valar come.'

'The Valar!' said Túrin. 'They have forsaken you, and they hold Men in scorn. What use to look westward across the endless Sea? There is but one Vala with whom we have to do, and that is Morgoth; and if in the end we cannot overcome him, at the least we can hurt him and hinder him. For victory is victory, however small, nor is its worth only in what follows from it. But it is expedient also; for if you do nothing to halt him, all Beleriand will fall beneath his shadow before many years are passed, and then one by one he will smoke you out of your earths. And what then? A pitiable remnant will fly south and west, to cower on the shores of the Sea, caught between Morgoth and Ossë. Better then to win a time of glory, though it be shortlived; for the end will be no worse. You speak of secrecy, and say that therein lies the only hope; but could you ambush and waylay every scout and spy of Morgoth to the last and least, so that none came ever back with tidings to Angband, yet from that he would learn that you lived and guess where. And this also I say: though mortal Men have little life beside the span of the Elves, they would rather spend it in battle than fly or submit. The defiance of Húrin Thalion is a great deed; and though Morgoth slay the doer he cannot make the deed not to have been. Even the Lords of the West will honour it; and is it not written into the history of Arda, which neither Morgoth nor Manwë can unwrite?'

'You speak of high things,' Gwindor answered, 'and plain it is that you have lived among the Eldar. But a darkness is on you if you set Morgoth and Manwë together, or speak of the Valar as the foes of Elves or Men; for the Valar scorn nothing, and least of all the Children of Ilúvatar. Nor do you know all the hopes of the Eldar. It is a prophecy among us that one day a messenger from Middle-earth will come through the shadows to Valinor, and Manwë will hear, and Mandos relent. For that time shall we not attempt to preserve the seed of the Noldor, and of the Edain also? And Círdan dwells now in the South, and there is building of ships; but what know you of ships, or of the Sea? You think of yourself and of your own glory, and bid us each do likewise; but we must think of others beside ourselves, for not all can fight and fall, and those we must keep from war and ruin, while we can.'

'Then send them to your ships, while there is yet time,' said Túrin.

'They will not be parted from us,' said Gwindor, 'even could Círdan sustain them. We must abide together as long as we may, and not court death.'

'All this I have answered,' said Túrin. 'Valiant defence of the borders and hard blows ere the enemy gathers: in that course lies the best hope of your long abiding together. And do those that you speak of love such skulkers in the woods, hunting always like a wolf, better than one who puts on his helm and figured shield, and drives away the foe, be they far greater than all his host? At least the women of the Edain do not. They did not hold back the men from the Nirnaeth Arnoediad.'

'But they suffered greater woe than if that field had not been fought,' said Gwindor.

The love of Finduilas for Túrin was also to be more fully treated:

Finduilas the daughter of Orodreth was golden-haired after the manner of the house of Finarfin, and Túrin began to take pleasure in the sight of her and in her company; for she reminded him of his kindred and the women of Dor-lómin in his father's house. At first he met her only when Gwindor was by; but after a while she sought him out, and they met at times alone, though it seemed to be chance. Then she would question him about the Edain, of whom she had seen few and seldom, and about his country and his kin.

Then Túrin spoke freely to her concerning these things, though he did not name the land of his birth nor any of his kindred; and on a time he said to her: 'I had a sister, Lalaith, or so I named her; and of her you put me in mind. But Lalaith was a child, a yellow flower in the green grass of spring; and had she lived she would now, maybe, have become dimmed with grief. But you are queenly, and as a golden tree; I would I had a sister so fair.'

'But you are kingly,' said she, 'even as the lords of the people of Fingolfin; I would I had a brother so valiant. And I do not think that Agarwaen is your true name, nor is it fit for you, Adanedhel. I call you Thurin, the Secret.'

At this Túrin started, but he said: 'That is not my name; and I am not a king, for our kings are of the Eldar, as I am not.'

Now Túrin marked that Gwindor's friendship grew cooler towards him; and he wondered also that whereas at first the woe and horror of Angband had begun to be lifted from him, now he seemed to slip back into care and sorrow. And he thought, it may be that he is grieved that I oppose his counsels, and have overcome him; I would it were not so. For he loved Gwindor as his guide and healer, and was filled with pity for him. But in those days the radiance of Finduilas also became dimmed, her footsteps slow and her face grave; and Túrin perceiving this surmised that the words of Gwindor had set fear in her heart of what might come to pass.

In truth Finduilas was torn in mind. For she honoured Gwindor and pitied him, and wished not to add one tear to his suffering; but against her will her love for Túrin grew day by day, and she thought of Beren and Lúthien. But Túrin was not like Beren! He did not scorn her, and was glad in her company; yet she knew that he had no love of the kind she wished. His mind and heart were elsewhere, by rivers in springs long past.

Then Túrin spoke to Finduilas, and said: 'Do not let the words of Gwindor affright you. He has suffered in the darkness of Angband;

and it is hard for one so valiant to be thus crippled and backward perforce. He needs all solace, and a longer time for healing.'

'I know it well,' she said.

'But we will win that time for him!' said Túrin. 'Nargothrond shall stand! Never again will Morgoth the Craven come forth from Angband, and all his reliance must be on his servants; thus says Melian of Doriath. They are the fingers of his hands; and we will smite them, and cut them off, till he draws back his claws. Nargothrond shall stand!'

'Perhaps,' said Finduilas. 'It shall stand, if you can achieve it. But have a care, Adenedhel; my heart is heavy when you go out to battle, lest Nargothrond be bereaved.'

And afterwards Túrin sought out Gwindor, and said to him: 'Gwindor, dear friend, you are falling back into sadness; do not so! For your healing will come in the houses of your kin, and in the light of Finduilas.'

Then Gwindor stared at Túrin, but he said nothing, and his face was clouded.

'Why do you look upon me so?' said Túrin. 'Often your eyes have gazed strangely at me of late. How have I grieved you? I have opposed your counsels; but a man must speak as he sees, nor hide the truth that he believes, for any private cause. I would that we were one in mind; for to you I owe a great debt, and I shall not forget it.'

'Will you not?' said Gwindor. 'Nonetheless your deeds and your counsels have changed my home and my kin. Your shadow lies upon them. Why should I be glad, who have lost all to you?'

But Túrin did not understand these words, and did but guess that Gwindor begrudged him his place in the heart and counsels of the King.

A passage follows in which Gwindor warned Finduilas against her love for Túrin, telling her who Túrin was, and this is closely based on the text given in *The Silmarillion* (pp. 210–11). But at the end of Gwindor's speech Finduilas answers him at greater length than in the other version:

'Your eyes are dimmed, Gwindor,' she said. 'You do not see or understand what is here come to pass. Must I now be put to double shame to reveal the truth to you? For I love you, Gwindor, and I am ashamed that I love you not more, but have taken a love even greater, from which I cannot escape. I did not seek it, and long I put it aside. But if I have pity for your hurts, have pity on mine. Túrin loves me not; nor will.'

'You say this,' said Gwindor, 'to take the blame from him whom you love. Why does he seek you out, and sit long with you, and come ever more glad away?'

'Because he also needs solace,' said Finduilas, 'and is bereaved of his kin. You both have your needs. But what of Finduilas? Now is it not enough that I must confess myself to you unloved, but that you should say that I speak so to deceive?'

'Nay, a woman is not easily deceived in such a case,' said Gwindor. 'Nor will you find many who will deny that they are loved, if that is true.'

'If any of us three be faithless, it is I: but not in will. But what of your doom and rumours of Angband? What of death and destruction? The Adanedhel is mighty in the tale of the World, and his stature shall reach yet to Morgoth in some far day to come.'

'He is proud,' said Gwindor.

'But also he is merciful,' said Finduilas. 'He is not yet awake, but still pity can ever pierce his heart, and he will never deny it. Pity maybe shall be ever the only entry. But he does not pity me. He holds me in awe, as were I both his mother and a queen!'

Maybe Finduilas spoke truly, seeing with the keen eyes of the Eldar. And now Túrin, not knowing what had passed between Gwindor and Finduilas, was ever gentler towards her as she seemed more sad. But on a time Finduilas said to him: 'Thurin Adanedhel, why did you hide your name from me? Had I known who you were I should not have honoured you less, but I should better have understood your grief.'

'What do you mean?' he said. 'Whom do you make me?'

'Túrin son of Húrin Thalion, captain of the North.'

Then Túrin rebuked Gwindor for revealing his true name, as is told in *The Silmarillion* (p. 211).

One other passage in this part of the narrative exists in a fuller form than in *The Silmarillion* (of the battle of Tumhalad and the sack of Nargothrond there is no other account; while the speeches of Túrin and the Dragon are so fully recorded in *The Silmarillion* that it seems unlikely that they would have been further expanded). This passage is a much fuller account of the coming of the Elves Gelmir and Arminas to Nargothrond in the year of its fall (*The Silmarillion* pp. 211–12); for their earlier encounter with Tuor in Dor-lómin, which is referred to here, see pp. 21–2 above.

In the spring there came two Elves, and they named themselves Gelmir and Arminas of the people of Finarfin, and said that they had an errand to the Lord of Nargothrond. They were brought before Túrin; but Gelmir said: 'It is to Orodreth, Finarfin's son, that we would speak.'

And when Orodreth came, Gelmir said to him: 'Lord, we were of Angrod's people, and we have wandered far since the Dagor Bragollach; but of late we have dwelt among Círdan's following by the Mouths of

Sirion. And on a day he called us, and bade us go to you; for Ulmo himself, the Lord of Waters, had appeared to him and warned him of great peril that draws near to Nargothrond.'

But Orodreth was wary, and he answered: 'Why then do you come hither out of the North? Or perhaps you had other errands also?'

Then Arminas said: 'Lord, ever since the Nirnaeth I have sought for the hidden kingdom of Turgon, and I have found it not; and in this search I fear now that I have delayed our errand hither over long. For Círdan sent us along the coast by ship, for secrecy and speed, and we were put ashore in Drengist. But among the sea-folk were some that came south in past years as messengers from Turgon, and it seemed to me from their guarded speech that maybe Turgon dwells still in the North, and not in the South, as most believe. But we have found neither sign nor rumour of what we sought.'

'Why do you seek Turgon?' said Orodreth.

'Because it is said that his kingdom shall stand longest against Morgoth,' answered Arminas. And those words seemed to Orodreth ill-omened, and he was displeased.

'Then tarry not in Nargothrond,' he said; 'for here you will hear no news of Turgon. And I need none to teach me that Nargothrond stands in peril.'

'Be not angered, lord,' said Gelmir, 'if we answer your questions with truth. And our wandering from the straight path hither has not been fruitless, for we have passed beyond the reach of your furthest scouts; we have traversed Dor-lómin and all the lands under the eaves of Ered Wethrin, and we have explored the Pass of Sirion, spying out the ways of the Enemy. There is a great gathering of Orcs and evil creatures in those regions, and a host is mustering about Sauron's Isle.'

'I know it,' said Túrin. 'Your news is stale. If the message of Círdan was to any purpose, it should have come sooner.'

'At least, lord, you shall hear the message now,' said Gelmir to Orodreth. 'Hear then the words of the Lord of Waters! Thus he spoke to Círdan the Shipwright: "The Evil of the North has defiled the springs of Sirion, and my power withdraws from the fingers of the flowing waters. But a worse thing is yet to come forth. Say therefore to the Lord of Nargothrond: Shut the doors of the fortress and go not abroad. Cast the stones of your pride into the loud river, that the creeping evil may not find the gate."'

These words seemed dark to Orodreth, and he turned as he ever did to Túrin for counsel. But Túrin mistrusted the messengers, and he said in scorn: 'What does Círdan know of our wars, who dwell nigh to the Enemy? Let the mariner look to his ships! But if in truth the Lord of Waters would send us counsel, let him speak more plainly. For otherwise it will seem better in our case to muster our strength, and go boldly to meet our foes, ere they come too nigh.'

Then Gelmir bowed before Orodreth, and said: 'I have spoken as I was bidden, lord'; and he turned away. But Arminas said to Túrin: 'Are you indeed of the House of Hador, as I have heard said?'

'Here I am named Agarwaen, the Black Sword of Nargothrond,' said Túrin. 'You deal much, it seems, in guarded speech, friend Arminas; and it is well that Turgon's secret is hid from you, or soon it would be heard in Angband. A man's name is his own, and should the son of Húrin learn that you have betrayed him when he would be hid, then may Morgoth take you and burn out your tongue!'

Then Arminas was dismayed by the black wrath of Túrin; but Gelmir said: 'He shall not be betrayed by us, Agarwaen. Are we not in council behind closed doors, where speech may be plainer? And Arminas asked this thing, I deem, because it is known to all that dwell by the Sea that Ulmo has great love for the House of Hador, and some say that Húrin and Huor his brother came once into the Hidden Realm.'

'If that were so, then he would speak of it to none, neither the great nor the less, and least of all to his son in childhood,' answered Túrin. 'Therefore I do not believe that Arminas asked this of me in hope to learn aught of Turgon. I mistrust such messengers of mischief.'

'Save your mistrust!' said Arminas in anger. 'Gelmir mistakes me. I asked because I doubted what here seems believed; for little indeed do you resemble the kin of Hador, whatever your name.'

'And what do you know of them?' said Túrin.

'Húrin I have seen,' answered Arminas, 'and his fathers before him. And in the wastes of Dor-lómin I met with Tuor, son of Huor, Húrin's brother; and he is like his fathers, as you are not.'

'That may be,' said Túrin, 'though of Tuor I have heard no word ere now. But if my head be dark and not golden, of that I am not ashamed. For I am not the first of sons in the likeness of his mother; and I come through Morwen Eledhwen of the House of Bëor and the kindred of Beren Camlost.'

'I spoke not of the difference between the black and the gold,' said Arminas. 'But others of the House of Hador bear themselves otherwise, and Tuor among them. For they use courtesy, and they listen to good counsel, holding the Lords of the West in awe. But you, it seems, will take counsel with your own wisdom, or with your sword only; and you speak haughtily. And I say to you, Agarwaen Mormegil, that if you do so, other shall be your doom than one of the Houses of Hador and Bëor might look for.'

'Other it has ever been,' answered Túrin. 'And if, as it seems, I must bear the hate of Morgoth because of the valour of my father, shall I also endure the taunts and ill-boding of a runagate, though he claim the kinship of kings? I counsel you: get you back to the safe shores of the Sea.'

Then Gelmir and Arminas departed, and went back to the South:

but despite Túrin's taunts they would gladly have awaited battle beside
their kin, and they went only because Círdan had bidden them under
the command of Ulmo to bring back word to him of Nargothrond and
of the speeding of their errand there. And Orodreth was much troubled
by the words of the messengers; but all the more fell became the mood
of Túrin, and he would by no means listen to their counsels, and least
of all would he suffer the great bridge to be cast down. For so much
at least of the words of Ulmo were read aright.

It is nowhere explained why Gelmir and Arminas on an urgent errand to
Nargothrond were sent by Círdan all the length of the coast to the Firth
of Drengist. Arminas said that it was done for speed and secrecy; but
greater secrecy could surely have been achieved by journeying up Narog
from the South. It might be supposed that Círdan did this in obedience
to Ulmo's command (so that they should meet Tuor in Dor-lómin and
guide him through the Gate of the Noldor), but this is nowhere suggested.

# PART TWO

---

# THE SECOND AGE

# I

## A DESCRIPTION OF
## THE ISLAND OF NÚMENOR

The account of the Island of Númenor that here follows is derived from descriptions and simple maps that were long preserved in the archives of the Kings of Gondor. These represent indeed but a small part of all that was once written, for many natural histories and geographies were composed by learned men in Númenor; but these, like nearly all else of the arts and sciences of Númenor at its high tide, disappeared in the Downfall.

Even such documents as were preserved in Gondor, or in Imladris (where in the care of Elrond were deposited the surviving treasures of the Northern Númenórean kings) suffered from loss and destruction by neglect. For though the survivors in Middle-earth 'yearned', as they said, for Akallabêth, the Downfallen, and never even after long ages ceased to regard themselves as in a measure exiles, when it became clear that the Land of Gift was taken away and that Númenor had disappeared for ever, all but a few regarded study of what was left of its history as vain, breeding only useless regret. The story of Ar-Pharazôn and his impious armada was all that remained generally known in later ages.

★

The land of Númenor resembled in outline a five-pointed star, or pentangle, with a central portion some two hundred and fifty miles across, north and south, and east and west, from which extended five large peninsular promontories. These promontories were regarded as separate regions, and they were named Forostar (Northlands), Andustar (Westlands), Hyarnustar (Southwestlands), Hyarrostar (Southeastlands), and Orrostar (Eastlands). The central portion was called Mittalmar (Inlands), and it had no coast, except the land about Rómenna and the head of its firth. A small part of the Mittalmar was, however, separated from the rest, and called Arandor, the Kingsland. In Arandor were the haven of Rómenna, the Meneltarma, and Armenelos, the City of the Kings; and it was at all times the most populous region of Númenor.

The Mittalmar was raised above the promontories (not reckoning the height of their mountains and hills); it was a region of grasslands and low downs, and few trees grew there. Near to the centre of the Mittalmar stood the tall mountain called Meneltarma, Pillar of the Heavens, sacred to the worship of Eru Ilúvatar. Though the lower slopes of the mountain were gentle and grass-covered, it grew ever steeper, and towards the summit it could not be scaled; but a winding spiral road was made upon it, beginning at its foot upon the south, and ending below the lip of the summit upon the north. For the summit was somewhat flattened and depressed, and could contain a great multitude; but it remained untouched by hands throughout the history of Númenor. No building, no raised altar, not even a pile of undressed stones, ever stood there; and no other likeness of a temple did the Númenóreans possess in all the days of their grace, until the coming of Sauron. There no tool or weapon had ever been borne; and there none might speak any word, save the King only. Thrice only in each year the King spoke, offering prayer for the coming year at the *Erukyermë* in the first days of spring, praise of Eru Ilúvatar at the *Erulaitalë* in midsummer, and thanksgiving to him at the *Eruhantalë* at the end of autumn. At these times the King ascended the mountain on foot followed by a great concourse of the people, clad in white and garlanded, but silent. At other times the people were free to climb to the summit alone or in company; but it is said that the silence was so great that even a stranger ignorant of Númenor and all its history, if he were transported thither, would not have dared to speak aloud. No bird ever came there, save only eagles. If anyone approached the summit, at once three eagles would appear and alight upon three rocks near to the western edge; but at the times of the Three Prayers they did not descend, remaining in the sky and hovering above the people. They were called the Witnesses of Manwë, and they were believed to be sent by him from Aman to keep watch upon the Holy Mountain and upon all the land.

The base of the Meneltarma sloped gently into the surrounding plain, but it extended, after the fashion of roots, five long low ridges outwards in the direction of the five promontories of the land; and these were called Tarmasundar, the Roots of the Pillar. Along the crest of the south-western ridge the climbing road approached the mountain; and between this ridge and that on the south-east the land went down into a shallow valley. That was named Noirinan, the Valley of the Tombs; for at its head chambers were cut in the rock at the base of the mountain, in which were the tombs of the Kings and Queens of Númenor.

But for the most part the Mittalmar was a region of pastures. In the south-west there were rolling downs of grass; and there, in the Emerië, was the chief region of the Shepherds.

The Forostar was the least fertile part; stony, with few trees, save that on the westward slopes of the high heather-covered moors there were woods of fir and larch. Towards the North Cape the land rose to rocky heights, and there great Sorontil rose sheer from the sea in tremendous cliffs. Here was the abode of many eagles; and in this region Tar-Meneldur Elentirmo built a tall tower, from which he could observe the motions of the stars.

The Andustar was also rocky in its northern parts, with high fir-woods looking out upon the sea. Three small bays it had, facing west, cut back into the highlands; but here the cliffs were in many places not at the sea's edge, and there was a shelving land at their feet. The northmost of these was called the Bay of Andúnië, for there was the great haven of Andúnië (Sunset), with its town beside the shore and many other dwellings climbing up the steep slopes behind. But much of the southerly part of the Andustar was fertile, and there also were great woods, of birch and beech upon the upper ground, and in the lower vales of oaks and elms. Between the promontories of the Andustar and the Hyarnustar was the great Bay that was called Eldanna, because it faced towards Eressëa; and the lands about it, being sheltered from the north and open to the western seas, were warm, and the most rain fell there. At the centre of the Bay of Eldanna was the most beautiful of all the havens of Númenor, Eldalondë the Green; and hither in the earlier days the swift white ships of the Eldar of Eressëa came most often.

All about that place, up the seaward slopes and far into the land, grew the evergreen and fragrant trees that they brought out of the West, and so throve there that the Eldar said that almost it was fair as a haven in Eressëa. They were the greatest delight of Númenor, and they were remembered in many songs long after they had perished for ever, for few ever flowered east of the Land of Gift: *oiolairë* and *lairelossë*, *nessamelda*, *vardarianna*, *taniquelassë*, and *yavannamirë* with its globed and scarlet fruits. Flower, leaf, and rind of those trees exuded sweet scents, and all that country was full of blended fragrance; therefore it was called Nísimaldar, the Fragrant Trees. Many of them were planted and grew, though far less abundantly, in other regions of Númenor; but only here grew the mighty golden tree *malinornë*, reaching after five centuries a height scarce less than it achieved in Eressëa itself. Its bark was silver and smooth, and its boughs somewhat upswept after the manner of the beech; but it never grew save with a single trunk. Its leaves, like those of the beech but greater, were pale green above and beneath were silver, glistering in the sun; in the autumn they did not fall, but turned to pale gold. In the spring it bore golden blossom in clusters like a cherry, which bloomed on during the summer; and as soon as the flowers opened the leaves fell, so that through spring and summer a grove of *malinorni* was carpeted and roofed with gold, but its pillars were of grey silver.[1] Its fruit was a nut with a silver shale; and some were given as a gift by Tar-Aldarion, the sixth King of Númenor, to King Gil-galad of Lindon. They did not take root in that land; but Gil-galad gave some to his kinswoman Galadriel, and under her power they grew and flourished in the guarded land of Lothlórien beside the River Anduin, until the High Elves at last left Middle-earth; but they did not reach the height or girth of the great groves of Númenor.

The river Nunduinë flowed into the sea at Eldalondë, and on its way made the little lake of Nísinen, that was so named from the abundance of sweet-smelling shrubs and flowers that grew upon its banks.

The Hyarnustar was in its western part a mountainous region, with great cliffs on the western and southern coasts; but eastwards were great vineyards in a warm and fertile land. The promontories of the Hyarnustar and the Hyarrostar were splayed wide apart, and on those long shores sea and land came gently together, as nowhere else in Númenor. Here flowed down Siril, the chief river of the land (for all others, save for the Nunduinë in the west, were short and swift torrents hurrying to the sea), that rose in springs under the Meneltarma in the valley of Noirinan, and running through the Mittalmar southwards became in its lower course a slow and winding stream. It issued at last into the sea amid wide marshes and reedy flats, and its many small mouths found their changing paths through great sands; for many miles on either side were wide white beaches and grey shingles, and here the fisherfolk mostly dwelt, in villages upon the hards among the marshes and meres, of which the chief was Nindamos.

In the Hyarrostar grew an abundance of trees of many kinds, and among them the *laurinquë* in which the people delighted for its flowers, for it had no other use. This name they gave it because of its long-hanging clusters of yellow flowers; and some who had heard from the Eldar of Laurelin, the Golden Tree of Valinor, believed that it came from that great Tree, being brought in seed thither by the Eldar; but it was not so. From the days of Tar-Aldarion there were great plantations in the Hyarrostar to furnish timber for shipbuilding.

The Orrostar was a cooler land, but it was protected from the cold north-east winds by highlands that rose towards the end of the promontory; and in the inner regions of the Orrostar much grain was grown, especially in those parts near to the borders of Arandor.

The whole land of Númenor was so posed as if it had been thrust upward out of the sea, but tilted southward and a little eastward; and save upon the south the land in nearly all places fell towards the sea in steep cliffs. In Númenor birds that dwell near the sea, and swim or dive in it, abode in multitudes beyond reckoning. The mariners said that were they blind they still would know that their ship was drawing near to Númenor because of the great clamour of the birds of the shore; and when any ship approached the land seabirds in great flocks would arise and fly above it in welcome and gladness, for they were never killed or molested by intent. Some would accompany ships on their voyages, even those that went to Middle-earth. Likewise within the lands the birds of Númenor were beyond count, from the *kirinki* that were no bigger than wrens, but all scarlet, with piping voices on the edge of human hearing, to the great eagles that were held sacred to Manwë, and never afflicted, until the days of evil and the hatred of the Valar began. For two thousand years, from the days of Elros Tar-Minyatur until the time of Tar-Ancalimon son of Tar-Atanamir, there was an eyrie in the summit of the tower of the King's palace in Armenelos; and there one pair ever dwelt and lived on the bounty of the King.

In Númenor all journeyed from place to place on horseback; for in riding the Númenóreans, both men and women, took delight, and all the people of the land loved horses, treating them honourably and housing them nobly. They were trained to hear and answer calls from a great distance, and it is said in old tales that where there was great love between men and women and their favourite steeds they could be summoned at need by thought alone. Therefore the roads of Númenor were for the most part unpaved, made and tended for riding, since coaches and carriages were little used in the earlier centuries, and heavy cargoes were borne by sea. The chief and most ancient road, suitable for wheels, ran from the greatest port, Rómenna in the east, to the royal city of Armenelos, and thence on to the Valley of the Tombs and the Meneltarma; and this road was early extended to Ondosto within the borders of the Forostar, and thence to Andúnië in the west. Along it passed wains bearing stone from the Northlands that was most esteemed for building, and timber in which the Westlands were rich.

The Edain brought with them to Númenor the knowledge of many crafts, and many craftsmen who had learned from the Eldar, besides preserving lore and traditions of their own. But they could bring with them few materials, save for the tools of their crafts; and for long all metals in Númenor were precious metals. They brought with them many treasures of gold and silver, and gems also; but they did not find these things in Númenor. They loved them for their beauty, and it was this love that first aroused in them cupidity, in later days when they fell under the Shadow and became proud and unjust in their dealings with lesser folk of Middle-earth. Of the Elves of Eressëa in the days of their friendship they had at times gifts of gold and silver and jewels; but such things were rare and prized in all the earlier centuries, until the power of the Kings was spread to the coasts of the East.

Some metals they found in Númenor, and as their cunning in mining and in smelting and smithying swiftly grew things of iron and copper became common. Among the wrights of the Edain were weaponsmiths, and they had with the teaching of the Noldor acquired great skill in the forging of swords, of axe-blades, and of spearheads and knives. Swords the Guild of Weaponsmiths still made, for the preservation of the craft, though most of their labour was spent on the fashioning of tools for the uses of peace. The King and most of the great chieftains possessed swords as heirlooms of their fathers;[2] and at times they would still give a sword as a gift to their heirs. A new sword was made for the King's Heir to be given to him on the day on which this title was conferred. But no man wore a sword in Númenor, and for long years few indeed were the weapons of warlike intent that were made in the land. Axes and spears and bows they had, and shooting with bows on foot and on horseback was a chief sport and pastime of the Númenóreans. In later days, in the wars upon Middle-earth, it was the bows of the Númenóreans that were most greatly feared. 'The Men of the Sea', it was said, 'send before them a great cloud, as a rain turned to serpents, or a black hail tipped with steel'; and in those days the great cohorts of the King's Archers used bows made of hollow steel, with black-feathered arrows a full ell long from point to notch.

But for long the crews of the great Númenórean ships came unarmed among the men of Middle-earth; and though they had axes and bows aboard for the felling of timber and the hunting for food upon wild shores owned by no man, they did not bear these when they sought out the men of the lands. It was indeed their grievance, when the Shadow crept along the coasts and men whom they had befriended became afraid or hostile, that iron was used against them by those to whom they had revealed it.

Beyond all other pursuits the strong men of Númenor took delight in the Sea, in swimming, in diving, or in small craft for contests of speed in rowing or sailing. The hardiest of the people were the fisherfolk; fish were abundant all about the coasts, and were at all times a chief source of food in Númenor; and all the towns where many people congregated were set by the shores. From the fisherfolk were mostly drawn the Mariners, who as the years passed grew greatly in importance and esteem. It is said that when the Edain first set sail upon the Great Sea, following the Star to Númenor, the Elvish ships that bore them were each steered and captained by one of the Eldar deputed by Círdan; and after the Elvish steersmen departed and took with them the most part of their ships it was long before the Númenóreans themselves ventured far to sea. But there were shipwrights among them who had been instructed by the Eldar; and by their own study and devices they improved their art until they dared to sail ever further into the deep waters. When six hundred years had passed from the beginning of the Second Age Vëantur, Captain of the King's Ships under Tar-Elendil, first achieved the voyage to Middle-earth. He brought his ship *Entulessë* (which signifies 'Return') into Mithlond on the spring winds blowing from the west; and he returned in the autumn of the following year. Thereafter seafaring became the chief enterprise for daring and hardihood among the men of Númenor; and Aldarion son of Meneldur, whose wife was Vëantur's daughter, formed the Guild of Venturers, in which were joined all the tried mariners of Númenor; as is told in the tale that follows here.

## NOTES

1 This description of the mallorn is much like that given by Legolas to his companions as they approached Lothlórien (*The Fellowship of the Ring* II 6).

2 The King's sword was indeed Aranrúth, the sword of Elu Thingol of Doriath in Beleriand, that had descended to Elros from Elwing his mother. Other heirlooms there were beside: the Ring of Barahir; the great Axe of Tuor, father of Eärendil; and the Bow of Bregor of the House of Bëor. Only the Ring of Barahir father of Beren One-hand survived the Downfall; for it was given by Tar-Elendil to his daughter Silmarien and was preserved in the House of the Lords of Andúnië, of whom the last was Elendil the Faithful who fled from the wrack of

Númenor to Middle-earth. [Author's note.] – The story of the Ring of Barahir is told in *The Silmarillion*, Chapter 19, and its later history in *The Lord of the Rings* Appendix A (I, iii and v). Of 'the great Axe of Tuor' there is no mention in *The Silmarillion*, but it is named and described in the original 'Fall of Gondolin' (1916–17, see p. 4), where it is said that in Gondolin Tuor carried an axe rather than a sword, and that he named it in the speech of the people of Gondolin *Dramborleg*. In a list of names accompanying the tale *Dramborleg* is translated 'Thudder-Sharp': 'the axe of Tuor that smote both a heavy dint as of a club and cleft as a sword'.

# II

# ALDARION AND ERENDIS

## *The Mariner's Wife*

Meneldur was the son of Tar-Elendil, the fourth King of Númenor. He was the King's third child, for he had two sisters, named Silmarien and Isilmë. The elder of these was wedded to Elatan of Andúnië, and their son was Valandil, Lord of Andúnië, from whom came long after the lines of the Kings of Gondor and Arnor in Middle-earth.

Meneldur was a man of gentle mood, without pride, whose exercise was rather in thought than in deeds of the body. He loved dearly the land of Númenor and all things in it, but he gave no heed to the Sea that lay all about it; for his mind looked further than Middle-earth: he was enamoured of the stars and the heavens. All that he could gather of the lore of the Eldar and Edain concerning Eä and the deeps that lay about the Kingdom of Arda he studied, and his chief delight was in the watching of the stars. He built a tower in the Forostar (the northernmost region of the island) where the airs were clearest, from which by night he would survey the heavens and observe all the movements of the lights of the firmament.[1]

When Meneldur received the Sceptre he removed, as he must, from the Forostar, and dwelt in the great house of the Kings in Armenelos. He proved a good and wise king, though he never ceased to yearn for days in which he might enrich his knowledge of the heavens. His wife was a woman of great beauty, named Almarian. She was the daughter of Vëantur, Captain of the King's Ships under Tar-Elendil; and though she herself loved ships and the sea no more than most women of the land her son followed after Vëantur her father, rather than after Meneldur.

The son of Meneldur and Almarian was Anardil, afterwards renowned among the Kings of Númenor as Tar-Aldarion. He had two sisters, younger than he: Ailinel and Almiel, of whom the elder married Orchaldor, a descendant of the House of Hador, son of Hatholdir, who was close in friendship with Meneldur; and the son of Orchaldor and Ailinel was Soronto, who comes later into the tale.[2]

Aldarion, for so he is called in all tales, grew swiftly to a man of great stature, strong and vigorous in mind and body, golden-haired as his mother, ready to mirth and generous, but prouder than his father and ever more bent on his own will. From the first he loved the Sea, and his mind was turned to the craft of ship-building. He had little liking for the north country, and spent all the time that his father would grant by the shores of the sea, especially near Rómenna, where was the chief haven of Númenor, the greatest shipyards, and the most skilled shipwrights. His father did little to hinder him for many years, being well-pleased that Aldarion should have exercise for his hardihood and work for thought and hand.

Aldarion was much loved by Vëantur his mother's father, and he dwelt often in Vëantur's house on the southern side of the firth of Rómenna. That house had its own quay, to which many small boats were always moored, for Vëantur would never journey by land if he could by water; and there as a child Aldarion learned to row, and later to manage sail. Before he was full grown he could captain a ship of many men, sailing from haven to haven.

It happened on a time that Vëantur said to his grandson: 'Anardilya, the spring is drawing nigh, and also the day of your full age' (for in that April Aldarion would be twenty-five years old). 'I have in mind a way to mark it fittingly. My own years are far greater, and I do not think that I shall often again have the heart to leave my fair house and the blest shores of Númenor; but once more at least I would ride the Great Sea and face the North wind and the East. This year you shall come with me, and we will go to Mithlond and see the tall blue mountains of Middle-earth and the green land of the Eldar at their feet. Good welcome you will find from Círdan the Shipwright and from King Gil-galad. Speak of this to your father.'[3]

When Aldarion spoke of this venture, and asked leave to go as soon as the spring winds should be favourable, Meneldur was loath to grant it. A chill came upon him, as though his heart guessed that more hung upon this than his mind could foresee. But when he looked upon the eager face of his son he let no sign of this be seen. 'Do as your heart calls, *onya*,' he said. 'I shall miss you sorely; but with Vëantur as captain, under the grace of the Valar, I shall live in good hope of your return. But do not become enamoured of the Great Lands, you who one day must be King and Father of this Isle!'

Thus it came to pass that on a morning of fair sun and white wind, in the bright spring of the seven hundred and twenty-fifth year of the Second Age, the son of the King's Heir of Númenor[4] sailed from the land; and ere day was over he saw it sink shimmering into the sea, and last of all the peak of the Meneltarma as a dark finger against the sunset.

It is said that Aldarion himself wrote records of all his journeys to Middle-earth, and they were long preserved in Rómenna, though all were afterwards lost. Of his first journey little is known, save that he made the friendship of Círdan and Gil-galad, and journeyed far in Lindon and the west of Eriador, and marvelled at all that he saw. He did not return for more than two years, and Meneldur was in great disquiet. It is said that his delay was due to the eagerness he had to learn all that he could of Círdan, both in the making and management of ships, and in the building of walls to withstand the hunger of the sea.

There was joy in Rómenna and Armenelos when men saw the great ship *Númerrámar* (which signifies 'West-wings') coming up from the sea, her golden sails reddened in the sunset. The summer was nearly over and the *Eruhantalë* was nigh.[5] It seemed to Meneldur when he welcomed his son in the house of Vëantur that he had grown in stature, and his eyes were brighter; but they looked far away.

'What did you see, *onya*, in your far journeys that now lives most in memory?'

But Aldarion, looking east towards the night, was silent. At last he answered, but softly, as one that speaks to himself: 'The fair people of the Elves? The green shores? The mountains wreathed in cloud? The regions of mist and shadow beyond guess? I do not know.' He ceased, and Meneldur knew that he had not spoken his full mind. For Aldarion had become enamoured of the Great Sea, and of a ship riding there alone without sight of land, borne by the winds with foam at its throat to coasts and havens unguessed; and that love and desire never left him until his life's end.

Vëantur did not again voyage from Númenor; but the *Númerrámar* he gave in gift to Aldarion. Within three years Aldarion begged leave to go again, and he set sail for Lindon. He was three years abroad; and not long after another voyage he made, that lasted for four years, for it is said that he was no longer content to sail to Mithlond, but began to explore the coasts southwards, past the mouths of Baranduin and Gwathló and Angren, and he rounded the dark cape of Ras Morthil and beheld the great Bay of Belfalas, and the mountains of the country of Amroth where the Nandor Elves still dwell.[6]

In the thirty-ninth year of his age Aldarion returned to Númenor, bringing gifts from Gil-galad to his father; for in the following year, as he had long proclaimed, Tar-Elendil relinquished the Sceptre to his son, and Tar-Meneldur became the King. Then Aldarion restrained his desire, and remained at home for a while for the comfort of his father; and in those days he put to use the knowledge he had gained of Círdan concerning the making of ships, devising much anew of his own thought, and he began also to set men to the improvement of the havens and the quays, for he was ever eager to build greater vessels. But the sea-longing came upon him anew, and he departed again and yet again from Númenor; and his mind turned now to ventures that might not be compassed with one vessel's company. Therefore he formed the Guild of Venturers, that afterwards was renowned; to that brotherhood were joined all the hardiest and most eager mariners, and young men sought admission to it even from the inland regions of Númenor, and Aldarion they called the Great Captain. At that time he, having no mind to live upon land in Armenelos, had a ship built that should serve as his dwelling-place; he named it therefore *Eämbar*, and at times he would sail in it from haven to haven of Númenor, but for the most part it lay at anchor off Tol Uinen: and that was a little isle in the bay of Rómenna that was set there by Uinen the Lady of the Seas.[7] Upon Eämbar was the guildhouse of the Venturers, and there were kept the records of their great voyages;[8] for Tar-Meneldur looked coldly on the enterprises of his son, and cared not to hear the tale of his journeys, believing that he sowed the seeds of restlessness and the desire of other lands to hold.

In that time Aldarion became estranged from his father, and ceased to speak openly of his designs and his desires; but Almarian the Queen supported her son in all that he did, and Meneldur perforce let matters go as they must. For the Venturers grew in numbers and in the esteem of men, and they called them *Uinendili*, the lovers of Uinen; and their Captain became the less easy to rebuke or restrain. The ships of the Númenóreans became ever larger and of greater draught in those days, until they could make far voyages, carrying many men and great cargoes; and Aldarion was often long gone from Númenor. Tar-Meneldur ever opposed his son, and he set a curb on the felling of trees in Númenor for the building of vessels; and it came therefore into Aldarion's mind that he would find timber in Middle-earth, and seek there for a haven for the repair of his ships. In his voyages down the coasts he looked with wonder on the great forests; and at the mouth of the river that the Númenóreans called Gwathir, River of Shadow, he established Vinyalondë, the New Haven.[9]

But when nigh on eight hundred years had passed since the

beginning of the Second Age, Tar-Meneldur commanded his son to
remain now in Númenor and to cease for a time his eastward voyaging;
for he desired to proclaim Aldarion the King's Heir, as had been
done at that age of the Heir by the Kings before him. Then Meneldur
and his son were reconciled, for that time, and there was peace
between them; and amid joy and feasting Aldarion was proclaimed
Heir in the hundredth year of his age, and received from his father
the title and power of Lord of the Ships and Havens of Númenor.
To the feasting in Armenelos came one Beregar from his dwelling
in the west of the Isle, and with him came Erendis his daughter.
There Almarian the Queen observed her beauty, of a kind seldom
seen in Númenor; for Beregar came of the House of Bëor by ancient
descent, though not of the royal line of Elros, and Erendis was dark-
haired and of slender grace, with the clear grey eyes of her kin.[10] But
Erendis looked upon Aldarion as he rode by, and for his beauty and
splendour of bearing she had eyes for little else. Thereafter Erendis
entered the household of the Queen, and found favour also with the
King; but little did she see of Aldarion, who busied himself in the
tending of the forests, being concerned that in days to come timber
should not lack in Númenor. Ere long the mariners of the Guild of
Venturers became restless, for they were ill content to voyage more
briefly and more rarely under lesser commanders; and when six
years had passed since the proclamation of the King's Heir Aldarion
determined to sail again to Middle-earth. Of the King he got but
grudging leave, for he refused his father's urging that he abide in
Númenor and seek a wife; and he set sail in the spring of the year.
But coming to bid farewell to his mother he saw Erendis amid the
Queen's company; and looking on her beauty he divined the strength
that lay concealed in her.

Then Almarian said to him: 'Must you depart again, Aldarion, my
son? Is there nothing that will hold you in the fairest of all mortal lands?'

'Not yet,' he answered; 'but there are fairer things in Armenelos
than a man could find elsewhere, even in the lands of the Eldar.
But mariners are men of two minds, at war with themselves; and the
desire of the Sea still holds me.'

Erendis believed that these words were spoken also for her ears;
and from that time forth her heart was turned wholly to Aldarion,
though not in hope. In those days there was no need, by law or custom,
that those of the royal house, not even the King's Heir, should wed
only with descendants of Elros Tar-Minyatur; but Erendis deemed
that Aldarion was too high. Yet she looked on no man with favour
thereafter, and every suitor she dismissed.

Seven years passed before Aldarion came back, bringing with him ore of silver and gold; and he spoke with his father of his voyage and his deeds. But Meneldur said: 'Rather would I have had you beside me, than any news or gifts from the Dark Lands. This is the part of merchants and explorers, not of the King's Heir. What need have we of more silver and gold, unless to use in pride where other things would serve as well? The need of the King's house is for a man who knows and loves this land and people, which he will rule.'

'Do I not study men all my days?' said Aldarion. 'I can lead and govern them as I will.'

'Say rather, some men, of like mind with yourself,' answered the King. 'There are also women in Númenor, scarce fewer than men; and save your mother, whom indeed you can lead as you will, what do you know of them? Yet one day you must take a wife.'

'One day!' said Aldarion. 'But not before I must; and later, if any try to thrust me towards marriage. Other things I have to do more urgent to me, for my mind is bent on them. "Cold is the life of a mariner's wife"; and the mariner who is single of purpose and not tied to the shore goes further, and learns better how to deal with the sea.'

'Further, but not with more profit,' said Meneldur. 'And you do not "deal with the sea", Aldarion, my son. Do you forget that the Edain dwell here under the grace of the Lords of the West, that Uinen is kind to us, and Ossë is restrained? Our ships are guarded, and other hands guide them than ours. So be not overproud, or the grace may wane; and do not presume that it will extend to those who risk themselves without need upon the rocks of strange shores or in the lands of men of darkness.'

'To what purpose then is the gracing of our ships,' said Aldarion, 'if they are to sail to no shores, and may seek nothing not seen before?'

He spoke no more to his father of such matters, but passed his days upon the ship Eämbar in the company of the Venturers, and in the building of a vessel greater than any made before: that ship he named *Palarran*, the Far-Wanderer. Yet now he met Erendis often (and that was by contrivance of the Queen); and the King learning of their meetings felt disquiet, yet he was not displeased. 'It would be more kind to cure Aldarion of his restlessness,' said he, 'before he win the heart of any woman.' 'How else will you cure him, if not by love?' said the Queen. 'Erendis is yet young,' said Meneldur. But Almarian answered: 'The kin of Erendis have not the length of life that is granted to the descendants of Elros; and her heart is already won.'[11]

Now when the great ship Palarran was built Aldarion would depart once more. At this Meneldur became wrathful, though by the persuasions of the Queen he would not use the King's power to stay him. Here must be told of the custom that when a ship departed from Númenor over the Great Sea to Middle-earth a woman, most often of the captain's kin, should set upon the vessel's prow the Green Bough of Return; and that was cut from the tree *oiolairë*, that signifies 'Ever-summer', which the Eldar gave to the Númenóreans,[12] saying that they set it upon their own ships in token of friendship with Ossë and Uinen. The leaves of that tree were evergreen, glossy and fragrant; and it throve upon sea-air. But Meneldur forbade the Queen and the sisters of Aldarion to bear the bough of *oiolairë* to Rómenna where lay the Palarran, saying that he refused his blessing to his son, who was venturing forth against his will; and Aldarion hearing this said: 'If I must go without blessing or bough, then so I will go.'

Then the Queen was grieved; but Erendis said to her: '*Tarinya*, if you will cut the bough from the Elven-tree, I will bear it to the haven, by your leave; for the King has not forbidden it to me.'

The mariners thought it an ill thing that the Captain should depart thus; but when all was made ready and men prepared to weigh anchor Erendis came there, little though she loved the noise and bustle of the great harbour and the crying of the gulls. Aldarion greeted her with amazement and joy; and she said: 'I have brought you the Bough of Return, lord: from the Queen.' 'From the Queen?' said Aldarion, in a changed manner. 'Yes, lord,' said she; 'but I asked for her leave to do so. Others beside your own kin will rejoice at your return, as soon as may be.'

At that time Aldarion first looked on Erendis with love; and he stood long in the stern looking back as the Palarran passed out to sea. It is said that he hastened his return, and was gone less time than he had designed; and coming back he brought gifts for the Queen and the ladies of her house, but the richest gift he brought for Erendis, and that was a diamond. Cold now were the greetings between the King and his son; and Meneldur rebuked him, saying that such a gift was unbecoming in the King's Heir unless it were a betrothal gift, and he demanded that Aldarion declare his mind.

'In gratitude I brought it,' said he, 'for a warm heart amid the coldness of others.'

'Cold hearts may not kindle others to give them warmth at their goings and comings,' said Meneldur; and again he urged Aldarion to take thought of marriage, though he did not speak of Erendis. But Aldarion would have none of it, for he was ever and in every course the more opposed as those about him urged it; and treating Erendis now with greater coolness he determined to leave Númenor and further his designs in Vinyalondë. Life on land was irksome to him, for aboard his ship he was subject to no other will, and the Venturers who accompanied him knew only love and admiration for the Great Captain. But now Meneldur forbade his going; and Aldarion, before the winter was fully gone, set sail with a fleet of seven ships and the greater part of the Venturers in defiance of the King. The Queen did not dare incur Meneldur's wrath; but at night a cloaked woman came to the haven bearing a bough, and she gave it into the hands of Aldarion, saying: 'This comes from the Lady of the Westlands' (for so they called Erendis), and went away in the dark.

At the open rebellion of Aldarion the King rescinded his authority as Lord of the Ships and Havens of Númenor; and he caused the Guildhouse of the Venturers on Eämbar to be shut, and the shipyards of Rómenna to be closed, and forbade the felling of all trees for shipbuilding. Five years passed; and Aldarion returned with nine ships, for two had been built in Vinyalondë, and they were laden with fine timber from the forests of the coasts of Middle-earth. The anger of Aldarion was great when he found what had been done; and to his father he said: 'If I am to have no welcome in Númenor, and no work for my hands to do, and if my ships may not be repaired in its havens, then I will go again and soon; for the winds have been rough,[13] and I need refitment. Has not a King's son aught to do but study women's faces to find a wife? The work of forestry I took up, and I have been prudent in it; there will be more timber in Númenor ere my day ends than there is under your sceptre.' And true to his word Aldarion left again in the same year with three ships and the hardiest of the Venturers, going without blessing or bough; for Meneldur set a ban on all the women of his house and of the Venturers, and put a guard about Rómenna.

On that voyage Aldarion was away so long that the people feared for him; and Meneldur himself was disquieted, despite the grace of the Valar that had ever protected the ships of Númenor.[14] When ten years were gone since his sailing Erendis at last despaired, and believing that Aldarion had met with disaster, or else that he had determined to dwell in Middle-earth, and also in order to escape the importuning of suitors, she asked the Queen's leave, and departing from Armenelos she returned to her own kindred in the Westlands. But after four years more Aldarion at last returned, and his ships were battered and broken by the seas. He had sailed first to the haven of Vinyalondë, and thence he had made a great coastwise journey southwards, far beyond any place yet reached by the ships of the Númenóreans; but returning northwards he had met contrary winds and great storms, and scarce escaping shipwreck in the Harad found Vinyalondë overthrown by great seas and plundered by hostile men. Three times he was driven back from the crossing of the Great Sea by high winds out of the West, and his own ship was struck by lightning and dismasted; and only with labour and hardship in the deep waters did he come at last to haven in Númenor. Greatly was Meneldur comforted at Aldarion's return; but he rebuked him for his rebellion against king and father, thus forsaking the guardianship of the Valar, and risking the wrath of Ossë not only for himself but for men whom he had bound to himself in devotion. Then Aldarion was chastened in mood, and he received the pardon of Meneldur, who restored to him the Lordship of the Ships and Havens, and added thereto the title of Master of the Forests.

Aldarion was grieved to find Erendis gone from Armenelos, but he was too proud to seek her; and indeed he could not well do so save to ask for her in marriage, and he was still unwilling to be bound. He set himself to the repairing of the neglects of his long absence, for he had been nigh on twenty years away; and at that time great harbour works were put in hand, especially at Rómenna. He found that there had been much felling of trees for building and the making of many things, but all was done without foresight, and little had been planted to replace what was taken; and he journeyed far and wide in Númenor to view the standing woods.

Riding one day in the forests of the Westlands he saw a woman, whose dark hair flowed in the wind, and about her was a green cloak clasped at the throat with a bright jewel; and he took her for one of the Eldar, who came at times to those parts of the Island. But she approached, and he knew her for Erendis, and saw that the jewel was the one that he had given her; then suddenly he knew in himself the love that he bore her, and he felt the emptiness of his days. Erendis seeing him turned pale and would ride off, but he was too quick, and he said: 'Too well have I deserved that you should flee from me, who have fled so often and so far! But forgive me, and stay now.' They rode then together to the house of Beregar her father, and there Aldarion made plain his desire for betrothal to Erendis; but now Erendis was reluctant, though according to custom and the life of her people it was now full time for her marriage. Her love for him was not lessened, nor did she retreat out of guile; but she feared now in her heart that in the war between herself and the Sea for the keeping of Aldarion she would not conquer. Never would Erendis take less, that she might not lose all; and fearing the Sea, and begrudging to all ships the felling of trees which she loved, she determined that she must utterly defeat the Sea and the ships, or else be herself defeated utterly.

But Aldarion wooed Erendis in earnest, and wherever she went he would go; he neglected the havens and the shipyards and all the concerns of the Guild of Venturers, felling no trees but setting himself to their planting only, and he found more contentment in those days than in any others of his life, though he did not know it until he looked back long after when old age was upon him. At length he sought to persuade Erendis to sail with him on a voyage about the Island in the ship Eämbar; for one hundred years had now passed since Aldarion founded the Guild of Venturers, and feasts were to be held in all the havens of Númenor. To this Erendis consented, concealing her distaste and fear; and they departed from Rómenna and came to Andúnië in the west of the Isle. There Valandil, Lord of Andúnië and close kin of Aldarion,[15] held a great feast; and at that feast he drank to Erendis, naming her *Uinéniel*, Daughter of Uinen, the new Lady of the Sea. But Erendis, who sat beside the wife of Valandil, said aloud: 'Call me by no such name! I am no daughter of Uinen: rather is she my foe.'

Thereafter for a while doubt again assailed Erendis, for Aldarion turned his thoughts again to the works at Rómenna, and busied himself with the building of great sea-walls, and the raising of a tall tower upon Tol Uinen: *Calmindon*, the Light-tower, was its name. But when these things were done Aldarion returned to Erendis and besought her to be betrothed; yet still she delayed, saying: 'I have journeyed with you by ship, lord. Before I give you my answer, will you not journey with me ashore, to the places that I love? You know too little of this land, for one who shall be its King.' Therefore they departed together, and came to Emerië, where were rolling downs of grass, and it was the chief place of sheep pasturage in Númenor; and they saw the white houses of the farmers and shepherds, and heard the bleating of the flocks.

There Erendis spoke to Aldarion and said: 'Here could I be at ease!'

'You shall dwell where you will, as wife of the King's Heir,' said Aldarion. 'And as Queen in many fair houses, such as you desire.'

'When you are King, I shall be old,' said Erendis. 'Where will the King's Heir dwell meanwhile?'

'With his wife,' said Aldarion, 'when his labours allow, if she cannot share in them.'

'I will not share my husband with the Lady Uinen,' said Erendis.

'That is a twisted saying,' said Aldarion. 'As well might I say that I would not share my wife with the Lord Oromë of Forests, because she loves trees that grow wild.'

'Indeed you would not,' said Erendis; 'for you would fell any wood as a gift to Uinen, if you had a mind.'

'Name any tree that you love and it shall stand till it dies,' said Aldarion.

'I love all that grow in this Isle,' said Erendis.

Then they rode a great while in silence; and after that day they parted, and Erendis returned to her father's house. To him she said nothing, but to her mother Núneth she told the words that had passed between herself and Aldarion.

'All or nothing, Erendis,' said Núneth. 'So you were as a child. But you love this man, and he is a great man, not to speak of his rank; and you will not cast out your love from your heart so easily, nor without great hurt to yourself. A woman must share her husband's love with his work and the fire of his spirit, or make him a thing not loveable. But I doubt that you will ever understand such counsel. Yet I am grieved, for it is full time that you were wed; and having borne a fair child I had hoped to see fair grandchildren; nor if they were cradled in the King's house would that displease me.'

This counsel did not indeed move the mind of Erendis; nevertheless she found that her heart was not under her will, and her days were empty: more empty than in the years when Aldarion had been gone. For he still abode in Númenor, and yet the days passed, and he did not come again into the west.

Now Almarian the Queen, being acquainted by Núneth with what had passed, and fearing lest Aldarion should seek solace in voyaging again (for he had been long ashore), sent word to Erendis asking that she return to Armenelos; and Erendis being urged by Núneth and by her own heart did as she was bid. There she was reconciled to Aldarion; and in the spring of the year, when the time of the *Erukyermë* was come, they ascended in the retinue of the King to the summit of the Meneltarma, which was the Hallowed Mountain of the Númenóreans.[16] When all had gone down again Aldarion and Erendis remained behind; and they looked out, seeing all the Isle of Westernesse laid green beneath them in the spring, and they saw

the glimmer of light in the West where far away was Avallónë,[17] and
the shadows in the East upon the Great Sea; and the Menel was blue
above them. They did not speak, for no one, save only the King,
spoke upon the height of Meneltarma; but as they came down
Erendis stood a moment, looking towards Emerië, and beyond,
towards the woods of her home.

'Do you not love the Yôzâyan?' she said.

'I love it indeed,' he answered, 'though I think that you doubt it.
For I think also of what it may be in time to come, and the hope
and splendour of its people; and I believe that a gift should not lie
idle in hoard.'

But Erendis denied his words, saying: 'Such gifts as come from
the Valar, and through them from the One, are to be loved for
themselves now, and in all nows. They are not given for barter, for
more or for better. The Edain remain mortal Men, Aldarion, great
though they be: and we cannot dwell in the time that is to come, lest
we lose our now for a phantom of our own design.' Then taking
suddenly the jewel from her throat she asked him: 'Would you have
me trade this to buy me other goods that I desire?'

'No!' said he. 'But you do not lock it in hoard. Yet I think you
set it too high; for it is dimmed by the light of your eyes.' Then he
kissed her on the eyes, and in that moment she put aside fear, and
accepted him; and their troth was plighted upon the steep path of
the Meneltarma.

They went back then to Armenelos, and Aldarion presented
Erendis to Tar-Meneldur as the betrothed of the King's Heir; and
the King was rejoiced, and there was merrymaking in the city and
in all the Isle. As betrothal gift Meneldur gave to Erendis a fair
portion of land in Emerië, and there he had built for her a white
house. But Aldarion said to her: 'Other jewels I have in hoard, gifts
of kings in far lands to whom the ships of Númenor have brought aid.
I have gems as green as the light of the sun in the leaves of trees
which you love.'

'No!' said Erendis. 'I have had my betrothal gift, though it came
beforehand. It is the only jewel that I have or would have; and I will
set it yet higher.' Then he saw that she had caused the white gem to
be set as a star in a silver fillet; and at her asking he bound it on
her forehead. She wore it so for many years, until sorrow befell;
and thus she was known far and wide as Tar-Elestirnë, the Lady of
the Star-brow.[18] Thus there was for a time peace and joy in Armenelos
in the house of the King, and in all the Isle, and it is recorded in
ancient books that there was great fruitfulness in the golden summer

of that year, which was the eight hundred and fifty-eighth of the Second Age.

But alone among the people the mariners of the Guild of Venturers were not well content. For fifteen years Aldarion had remained in Númenor, and led no expedition abroad; and though there were gallant captains who had been trained by him, without the wealth and authority of the King's son their voyages were fewer and more brief, and went but seldom further than the land of Gil-galad. Moreover timber was become scarce in the shipyards, for Aldarion neglected the forests; and the Venturers besought him to turn again to this work. At their prayer Aldarion did so, and at first Erendis would go about with him in the woods; but she was saddened by the sight of trees felled in their prime, and afterwards hewn and sawn. Soon therefore Aldarion went alone, and they were less in company.

Now the year came in, in which all looked for the marriage of the King's Heir; for it was not the custom that betrothal should last much longer than three years. One morning in that spring Aldarion rode up from the haven of Andúnië, to take the road to the house of Beregar; for there he was to be guest, and thither Erendis had preceded him, going from Armenelos by the roads of the land. As he came to the top of the great bluff that stood out from the land and sheltered the haven from the north, he turned and looked back over the sea. A west wind was blowing, as often at that season, beloved by those who had a mind to sail to Middle-earth, and white-crested waves marched towards the shore. Then suddenly the sea-longing took him as though a great hand had been laid on his throat, and his heart hammered, and his breath was stopped. He strove for the mastery, and at length turned his back and continued on his journey; and by design he took his way through the wood where he had seen Erendis riding as one of the Eldar, now fifteen years gone. Almost he looked to see her so once more; but she was not there, and desire to see her face again hastened him, so that he came to Beregar's house before evening.

There she welcomed him gladly, and he was merry; but he said nothing touching their wedding, though all had thought that this was a part of his errand to the Westlands. As the days passed Erendis marked that he now often fell silent in company when others were gay; and if she looked towards him suddenly she saw his eyes upon her. Then her heart was shaken; for the blue eyes of Aldarion seemed to her now grey and cold, yet she perceived as it were a hunger in his gaze. That look she had seen too often before, and feared what it boded; but she said nothing. At that Núneth, who marked all that passed, was glad; for 'words may open wounds', as she said. Ere long Aldarion and Erendis rode away, returning to Armenelos, and as they drew further from the sea he grew merrier again. Still he said nothing to her of his trouble: for indeed he was at war within himself, and irresolute.

So the year drew on, and Aldarion spoke neither of the sea nor of wedding; but he was often in Rómenna, and in the company of the Venturers. At length, when the next year came in, the King called him to his chamber; and they were at ease together, and the love they bore one another was no longer clouded.

'My son,' said Tar-Meneldur, 'when will you give me the daughter that I have so long desired? More than three years have now passed, and that is long enough. I marvel that you could endure so long a delay.'

Then Aldarion was silent, but at length he said: 'It has come upon me again, Atarinya. Eighteen years is a long fast. I can scarce lie still in a bed, or hold myself upon a horse, and the hard ground of stone wounds my feet.'

Then Meneldur was grieved, and pitied his son; but he did not understand his trouble, for he himself had never loved ships, and he said: 'Alas! But you are betrothed. And by the laws of Númenor and the right ways of the Eldar and Edain a man shall not have two wives. You cannot wed the Sea, for you are affianced to Erendis.'

Then Aldarion's heart was hardened, for these words recalled his speech with Erendis as they passed through Emerië; and he thought (but untruly) that she had consulted with his father. It was ever his mood, if he thought that others combined to urge him on some path of their choosing, to turn away from it. 'Smiths may smithy, and horsemen ride, and miners delve, when they are betrothed,' said he. 'Therefore why may not mariners sail?'

'If smiths remained five years at the anvil few would be smiths' wives,' said the King. 'And mariners' wives are few, and they endure what they must, for such is their livelihood and their necessity. The King's Heir is not a mariner by trade, nor is he under necessity.'

'There are other needs than livelihood that drive a man,' said Aldarion. 'And there are yet many years to spare.'

'Nay, nay,' said Meneldur, 'you take your grace for granted: Erendis has shorter hope than you, and her years wane swifter. She is not of the line of Elros; and she has loved you now many years.'

'She held back well nigh twelve years, when I was eager,' said Aldarion. 'I do not ask for a third of such a time.'

'She was not then betrothed,' said Meneldur. 'But neither of you are now free. And if she held back, I doubt not that it was in fear of what now seems likely to befall, if you cannot master yourself. In some way you must have stilled that fear; and though you may have spoken no plain word, yet you are beholden, as I judge.'

Then Aldarion said in anger: 'It were better to speak with my betrothed myself, and not hold parley by proxy.' And he left his father. Not long after he spoke to Erendis of his desire to voyage again upon the great waters, saying that he was robbed of all sleep and rest. But she sat pale and silent. At length she said: 'I thought that you were come to speak of our wedding.'

'I will,' said Aldarion. 'It shall be as soon as I return, if you will wait.' But seeing the grief in her face he was moved, and a thought came to him. 'It shall be now,' he said. 'It shall be before this year is done. And then I will fit out such a ship as the Venturers made never yet, a Queen's house on the water. And you shall sail with me, Erendis, under the grace of the Valar, of Yavanna and of Oromë whom you love; you shall sail to lands where I shall show you such woods as you have never seen, where even now the Eldar sing; or forests wider than Númenor, free and wild since the beginning of days, where still you may hear the great horn of Oromë the Lord.'

But Erendis wept. 'Nay, Aldarion,' she said. 'I rejoice that the world yet holds such things as you tell of; but I shall never see them. For I do not desire it: to the woods of Númenor my heart is given. And, alas! if for love of you I took ship, I should not return. It is beyond my strength to endure; and out of sight of land I should die. The Sea hates me; and now it is revenged that I kept you from it and yet fled from you. Go, my lord! But have pity, and take not so many years as I lost before.'

Then Aldarion was abashed; for as he had spoken in heedless anger to his father, so now she spoke with love. He did not sail that year; but he had little peace or joy. 'Out of sight of land she will die!' he said. 'Soon I shall die, if I see it longer. Then if we are to spend any years together I must go alone, and go soon.' He made ready therefore at last for sailing in the spring; and the Venturers were glad, if none else in the Isle who knew of what was done. Three ships were manned, and in the month of Víressë they departed. Erendis herself set the green bough of *oiolairë* on the prow of the Palarran, and hid her tears, until it passed out beyond the great new harbour-walls.

Six years and more passed away before Aldarion returned to Númenor. He found even Almarian the Queen colder in welcome, and the Venturers were fallen out of esteem; for men thought that he had treated Erendis ill. But indeed he was longer gone than he had purposed; for he had found the haven of Vinyalondë now wholly ruined, and great seas had brought to nothing all his labours to restore it. Men near the coasts were growing afraid of the Númenóreans, or were become openly hostile; and Aldarion heard rumours of some lord in Middle-earth who hated the men of the ships. Then when he would turn for home a great wind came out of the south, and he was borne far to the northward. He tarried a while at Mithlond, but when his ships stood out to sea once more they were again swept away north, and driven into wastes perilous with ice, and they suffered cold. At last the sea and wind relented, but even as Aldarion looked out in longing from the prow of the Palarran and saw far off the Meneltarma, his glance fell upon the green bough, and he saw that it was withered. Then Aldarion was dismayed, for such a thing had never befallen the bough of *oiolairë*, so long as it was washed with the spray. 'It is frosted, Captain,' said a mariner who stood beside him. 'It has been too cold. Glad am I to see the Pillar.'

When Aldarion sought out Erendis she looked at him keenly but did not come forward to meet him; and he stood for a while at a loss for words, as was not his wont. 'Sit, my lord,' said Erendis, 'and first tell me of all your deeds. Much must you have seen and done in these long years!'

Then Aldarion began haltingly, and she sat silent, listening, while he told all the tale of his trials and delays; and when he ended she said: 'I thank the Valar by whose grace you have returned at last. But I thank them also that I did not come with you; for I should have withered sooner than any green bough.'

'Your green bough did not go into the bitter cold by will,' he answered. 'But dismiss me now, if you will, and I think that men will not blame you. Yet dare I not to hope that your love will prove stronger to endure even than fair *oiolairë*?'

'So it does prove indeed,' said Erendis. 'It is not yet chilled to the death, Aldarion. Alas! How can I dismiss you, when I look on you again, returning as fair as the sun after winter!'

'Then let spring and summer now begin!' he said.

'And let not winter return,' said Erendis.

Then to the joy of Meneldur and Almarian the wedding of the King's Heir was proclaimed for the next spring; and so it came to pass. In the eight hundred and seventieth year of the Second Age

Aldarion and Erendis were wedded in Armenelos, and in every house there was music, and in all the streets men and women sang. And afterwards the King's Heir and his bride rode at their leisure through all the Isle, until at midsummer they came to Andúnië, where the last feast was prepared by Valandil its lord; and all the people of the Westlands were gathered there, for love of Erendis and pride that a Queen of Númenor should come from among them.

In the morning before the feast Aldarion gazed out from the window of the bedchamber, which looked west-over-sea. 'See, Erendis!' he cried. 'There is a ship speeding to haven; and it is no ship of Númenor, but one such as neither you nor I shall ever set foot upon, even if we would.' Then Erendis looked forth, and she saw a tall white ship, with white birds turning in the sunlight all about it; and its sails glimmered with silver as with foam at the stem it rode towards the harbour. Thus the Eldar graced the wedding of Erendis, for love of the people of the Westlands, who were closest in their friendship.[19] Their ship was laden with flowers for the adornment of the feast, so that all that sat there, when evening was come, were crowned with *elanor*[20] and sweet *lissuin* whose fragrance brings heart's ease. Minstrels they brought also, singers who re-membered songs of Elves and Men in the days of Nargothrond and Gondolin long ago; and many of the Eldar high and fair were seated among Men at the tables. But the people of Andúnië, looking upon the blissful company, said that none were more fair than Erendis; and they said that her eyes were as bright as were the eyes of Morwen Eledhwen of old,[21] or even as those of Avallónë.

Many gifts the Eldar brought also. To Aldarion they gave a sapling tree, whose bark was snow-white, and its stem straight, strong and pliant as it were of steel; but it was not yet in leaf. 'I thank you,' said Aldarion to the Elves. 'The wood of such a tree must be precious indeed.'

'Maybe; we know not,' said they. 'None has ever been hewn. It bears cool leaves in summer, and flowers in winter. It is for this that we prize it.'

To Erendis they gave a pair of birds, grey, with golden beaks and feet. They sang sweetly one to another with many cadences never repeated through a long thrill of song; but if one were separated from the other, at once they flew together, and they would not sing apart.

'How shall I keep them?' said Erendis.

'Let them fly and be free,' answered the Eldar. 'For we have spoken to them and named you; and they will stay wherever you dwell. They mate for their life, and that is long. Maybe there will be many such birds to sing in the gardens of your children.'

That night Erendis awoke, and a sweet fragrance came through the lattice; but the night was light, for the full moon was westering. Then leaving their bed Erendis looked out and saw all the land sleeping in silver; but the two birds sat side by side upon her sill.

When the feasting was ended Aldarion and Erendis went for a while to her home; and the birds again perched upon the sill of her window. At length they bade Beregar and Núneth farewell, and they rode back at last to Armenelos; for there by the King's wish his Heir would dwell, and a house was prepared for them amidst a garden of trees. There the Elven-tree was planted, and the Elven-birds sang in its boughs.

Two years later Erendis conceived, and in the spring of the year after she bore to Aldarion a daughter. Even from birth the child was fair, and grew ever in beauty: the woman most beautiful, as old tales tell, that ever was born in the line of Elros, save Ar-Zimraphel, the last. When her first naming was due they called her Ancalimë. In heart Erendis was glad, for she thought: 'Surely now Aldarion will desire a son, to be his heir; and he will abide with me long yet.' For in secret she still feared the Sea and its power upon his heart; and though she strove to hide it, and would talk with him of his old ventures and of his hopes and designs, she watched jealously if he went to his house-ship or was much with the Venturers. To Eämbar Aldarion once asked her to come, but seeing swiftly in her eyes that she was not full-willing he never pressed her again. Not without cause was Erendis' fear. When Aldarion had been five years ashore he began to be busy again with his Mastership of Forests, and was often many days away from his house. There was now indeed sufficient timber in Númenor (and that was chiefly owing to his prudence); yet since the people were now more numerous there was ever need of wood for building and for the making of many things beside. For in those ancient days, though many had great skill with stone and with metals (since the Edain of old had learned much of the Noldor), the Númenóreans loved things fashioned of wood, whether for daily use, or for beauty of carving. At that time Aldarion again gave most heed to the future, planting always where there was felling, and he had new woods set to grow where there was room, a free land that was suited to trees of different kinds. It was then that he became most widely known as Aldarion, by which name he is remembered among those who held the sceptre in Númenor. Yet to many beside Erendis it seemed that he had little love for trees in themselves, caring for them rather as timber that would serve his designs.

Not far otherwise was it with the Sea. For as Núneth had said to Erendis long before: 'Ships he may love, my daughter, for those are made by men's minds and hands; but I think that it is not the winds or the great waters that so burn his heart, nor yet the sight of strange lands, but some heat in his mind, or some dream that pursues him.' And it may be that she struck near the truth; for Aldarion was a man long-sighted, and he looked forward to days when the people would need more room and greater wealth; and whether he himself knew this clearly or no, he dreamed of the glory of Númenor and the power of its kings, and he sought for footholds whence they could step to wider dominion. So it was that ere long he turned again from forestry to the building of ships, and a vision came to him of a mighty vessel like a castle with tall masts and great sails like clouds, bearing men and stores enough for a town. Then in the yards of Rómenna the saws and hammers were busy, while among many lesser craft a great ribbed hull took shape; at which men wondere l. *Turuphanto*, the Wooden Whale, they called it, but that was not its name.

Erendis learned of these things, though Aldarion had not spoken to her of them, and she was unquiet. Therefore one day she said to him: 'What is all this busyness with ships, Lord of the Havens? Have we not enough? How many fair trees have been cut short of their lives in this year?' She spoke lightly, and smiled as she spoke.

'A man must have work to do upon land,' he answered, 'even though he have a fair wife. Trees spring and trees fall. I plant more than are felled.' He spoke also in a light tone, but he did not look her in the face; and they did not speak again of these matters.

But when Ancalimë was close on four years old Aldarion at last declared openly to Erendis his desire to sail again from Númenor. She sat silent, for he said nothing that she did not already know; and words were in vain. He tarried until the birthday of Ancalimë, and made much of her that day. She laughed and was merry, though others in that house were not so; and as she went to her bed she said to her father: 'Where will you take me this summer, *tatanya*? I should like to see the white house in the sheep-land that *mamil* tells of.' Aldarion did not answer; and the next day he left the house, and was gone for some days. When all was ready he returned, and bade Erendis farewell. Then against her will tears were in her eyes. They grieved him, and yet irked him, for his mind was resolved, and he hardened his heart. 'Come, Erendis!' he said. 'Eight years I have stayed. You cannot bind for ever in soft bonds the son of the King, of the blood of Tuor and Eärendil! And I am not going to my death. I shall soon return.'

'Soon?' she said. 'But the years are unrelenting, and you will not bring them back with you. And mine are briefer than yours. My youth runs away; and where are my children, and where is your heir? Too long and often of late is my bed cold.'[22]

'Often of late I have thought that you preferred it so,' said Aldarion. 'But let us not be wroth, even if we are not of like mind. Look in your mirror, Erendis. You are beautiful, and no shadow of age is there yet. You have time to spare to my deep need. Two years! Two years is all that I ask!'

But Erendis answered: 'Say rather: "Two years I will take, whether you will or no." Take two years, then! But no more. A King's son of the blood of Eärendil should also be a man of his word.'

Next morning Aldarion hastened away. He lifted up Ancalimë and kissed her; but though she clung to him he set her down quickly and rode off. Soon after the great ship set sail from Rómenna. *Hirilondë* he named it, Haven-finder; but it went from Númenor without the blessing of Tar-Meneldur; and Erendis was not at the harbour to set the green Bough of Return, nor did she send. Aldarion's face was dark and troubled as he stood at the prow of Hirilondë, where the wife of his captain had set a great branch of *oiolairë*; but he did not look back until the Meneltarma was far off in the twilight.

All that day Erendis sat in her chamber alone, grieving; but deeper in her heart she felt a new pain of cold anger, and her love of Aldarion was wounded to the quick. She hated the Sea; and now even trees, that once she had loved, she desired to look upon no more, for they recalled to her the masts of great ships. Therefore ere long she left Armenelos, and went to Emerië in the midst of the Isle, where ever, far and near, the bleating of sheep was borne upon the wind. 'Sweeter it is to my ears than the mewing of gulls,' she said, as she stood at the doors of her white house, the gift of the King; and that was upon a downside, facing west, with great lawns all about that merged without wall or hedge into the pastures. Thither she took Ancalimë, and they were all the company that either had. For Erendis would have only servants in her household, and they were all women; and she sought ever to mould her daughter to her own mind, and to feed her upon her own bitterness against men. Ancalimë seldom indeed saw any man, for Erendis kept no state, and her few farm-servants and shepherds had a homestead at a distance. Other men did not come there, save rarely some messenger from the King; and he would ride away soon, for to men there seemed a chill in the house that put them to flight, and while there they felt constrained to speak half in whisper.

One morning soon after Erendis came to Emerië she awoke to the song of birds, and there on the sill of her window were the Elven-birds that long had dwelt in her garden in Armenelos, but which she had left behind forgotten. 'Sweet fools, fly away!' she said. 'This is no place for such joy as yours.'

Then their song ceased, and they flew up over the trees; thrice they wheeled above the roofs, and then they went away westwards. That evening they settled upon the sill of the chamber in the house of her father, where she had lain with Aldarion on their way from the feast in Andúnië; and there Núneth and Beregar found them on the morning of the next day. But when Núneth held out her hands to them they flew steeply up and fled away, and she watched them until they were specks in the sunlight, speeding to the sea, back to the land whence they came.

'He has gone again, then, and left her,' said Núneth.

'Then why has she not sent news?' said Beregar. 'Or why has she not come home?'

'She has sent news enough,' said Núneth. 'For she has dismissed the Elven-birds, and that was ill done. It bodes no good. Why, why, my daughter? Surely you knew what you must face? But let her alone, Beregar, wherever she may be. This is her home no longer, and she will not be healed here. He will come back. And then may the Valar send her wisdom – or guile, at the least!'

When the second year after Aldarion's sailing came in, by the King's wish Erendis ordered the house in Armenelos to be arrayed and made ready; but she herself made no preparation for return. To the King she sent answer saying: 'I will come if you command me, *atar aranya*. But have I a duty now to hasten? Will it not be time enough when his sail is seen in the East?' And to herself she said: 'Will the King have me wait upon the quays like a sailor's lass? Would that I were, but I am so no longer. I have played that part to the full.'

But that year passed, and no sail was seen; and the next year came, and waned to autumn. Then Erendis grew hard and silent. She ordered that the house in Armenelos be shut, and she went never more than a few hours' journey from her house in Emerië. Such love as she had was all given to her daughter, and she clung to her, and would not have Ancalimë leave her side, not even to visit Núneth

and her kin in the Westlands. All Ancalimë's teaching was from her
mother; and she learned well to write and to read, and to speak the
Elven-tongue with Erendis, after the manner in which high men of
Númenor used it. For in the Westlands it was a daily speech in such
houses as Beregar's, and Erendis seldom used the Númenórean
tongue, which Aldarion loved the better. Much Ancalimë also learned
of Númenor and the ancient days in such books and scrolls as were
in the house which she could understand; and lore of other kinds,
of the people and the land, she heard at times from the women of
the household, though of this Erendis knew nothing. But the women
were chary of their speech to the child, fearing their mistress; and
there was little enough of laughter for Ancalimë in the white house
in Emerië. It was hushed and without music, as if one had died
there not long since; for in Númenor in those days it was the part
of men to play upon instruments, and the music that Ancalimë
heard in childhood was the singing of women at work, out of doors,
and away from the hearing of the White Lady of Emerië. But now
Ancalimë was seven years old, and as often as she could get leave she
would go out of the house and on to the wide downs where she could
run free; and at times she would go with a shepherdess, tending the
sheep, and eating under the sky.

One day in the summer of that year a young boy, but older than
herself, came to the house on an errand from one of the distant
farms; and Ancalimë came upon him munching bread and drinking
milk in the farm-courtyard at the rear of the house. He looked at her
without deference, and went on drinking. Then he set down his mug.
'Stare, if you must, great eyes!' he said. 'You're a pretty girl, but
too thin. Will you eat?' He took a loaf out of his bag.
'Be off, Îbal!' cried an old woman, coming from the dairy-door.
'And use your long legs, or you'll forget the message I gave you for
your mother before you get home!'
'No need for a watch-dog where you are, mother Zamîn!' cried
the boy, and with a bark and a shout he leapt over the gate and went
off at a run down the hill. Zamîn was an old country-woman, free-
tongued, and not easily daunted, even by the White Lady.
'What noisy thing was that?' said Ancalimë.
'A boy,' said Zamîn, 'if you know what that is. But how should
you? They're breakers and eaters, mostly. That one is ever eating –
but not to no purpose. A fine lad his father will find when he comes
back; but if that is not soon, he'll scarce know him. I might say
that of others.'

'Has the boy then a father too?' asked Ancalimë.

'To be sure,' said Zamîn. 'Ulbar, one of the shepherds of the great lord away south: the Sheep-lord we call him, a kinsman of the King.'

'Then why is the boy's father not at home?'

'Why, *hérinkë*,' said Zamîn, 'because he heard of those Venturers, and took up with them, and went away with your father, the Lord Aldarion: but the Valar know whither, or why.'

That evening Ancalimë said suddenly to her mother: 'Is my father also called the Lord Aldarion?'

'He was,' said Erendis. 'But why do you ask?' Her voice was quiet and cool, but she wondered and was troubled; for no word concerning Aldarion had passed between them before.

Ancalimë did not answer the question. 'When will he come back?' she said.

'Do not ask me!' said Erendis. 'I do not know. Never, perhaps. But do not trouble yourself; for you have a mother, and she will not run away, while you love her.'

Ancalimë did not speak of her father again.

The days passed bringing in another year, and then another; in that spring Ancalimë was nine years old. Lambs were born and grew; shearing came and passed; a hot summer burned the grass. Autumn turned to rain. Then out of the East upon a cloudy wind Hirilondë came back over the grey seas, bearing Aldarion to Rómenna; and word was sent to Emerië, but Erendis did not speak of it. There were none to greet Aldarion upon the quays. He rode through the rain to Armenelos; and he found his house shut. He was dismayed, but he would ask news of no man; first he would seek the King, for he thought he had much to say to him.

He found his welcome no warmer than he looked for; and Meneldur spoke to him as King to a captain whose conduct is in question. 'You have been long away,' he said coldly. 'It is more than three years now since the date that you set for your return.'

'Alas!' said Aldarion. 'Even I have become weary of the sea, and for long my heart has yearned westward. But I have been detained against my heart: there is much to do. And all things go backward in my absence.'

'I do not doubt it,' said Meneldur. 'You will find it true here also in your right land, I fear.'

'That I hope to redress,' said Aldarion. 'But the world is changing again. Outside nigh on a thousand years have passed since the Lords of the West sent their power against Angband; and those days are forgotten, or wrapped in dim legend among Men of Middle-earth. They are troubled again, and fear haunts them. I desire greatly to consult with you, to give account of my deeds, and my thought concerning what should be done.'

'You shall do so,' said Meneldur. 'Indeed I expect no less. But there are other matters which I judge more urgent. "Let a King first rule well his own house ere he correct others", it is said. It is true of all men. I will now give you counsel, son of Meneldur. You have also a life of your own. Half of yourself you have ever neglected. To you I say now: Go home!'

Aldarion stood suddenly still, and his face was stern. 'If you know, tell me,' he said. 'Where is my home?'

'Where your wife is,' said Meneldur. 'You have broken your word to her, whether by necessity or no. She dwells now in Emerië, in her own house, far from the sea. Thither you must go at once.'

'Had any word been left for me, whither to go, I would have gone directly from the haven,' said Aldarion. 'But at least I need not now ask tidings of strangers.' He turned then to go, but paused, saying: 'Captain Aldarion has forgotten somewhat that belongs to his other half, which in his waywardness he also thinks urgent. He has a letter that he was charged to deliver to the King in Armenelos.' Presenting it to Meneldur he bowed and left the chamber; and within an hour he took horse and rode away, though night was falling. With him he had but two companions, men from his ship: Henderch of the Westlands, and Ulbar who came from Emerië.

Riding hard they came to Emerië at nightfall of the next day, and men and horses were weary. Cold and white looked the house on the hill in a last gleam of sunset under cloud. He blew a horn-call as soon as he saw it from afar.

As he leapt from his horse in the forecourt he saw Erendis: clad in white she stood upon the steps that went up to the pillars before the door. She held herself high, but as he drew near he saw that she was pale and her eyes over-bright.

'You come late, my lord,' she said. 'I had long ceased to expect you. I fear that there is no such welcome prepared for you as I had made when you were due.'

'Mariners are not hard to please,' he said.

'That is well,' she said; and she turned back into the house and left him. Then two women came forward, and an old crone who went down the steps. As Aldarion went in she said to the men in a loud voice so that he could hear her: 'There is no lodging for you here. Go down to the homestead at the hill's foot!'

'No, Zamîn,' said Ulbar. 'I'll not stay. I am for home, by the Lord Aldarion's leave. Is all well there?'

'Well enough,' said she. 'Your son has eaten himself out of your memory. But go, and find your own answers! You'll be warmer there than your Captain.'

Erendis did not come to the table at his late evening-meal, and Aldarion was served by women in a room apart. But before he was done she entered, and said before the women: 'You will be weary, my lord, after such haste. A guest-room is made ready for you, when you will. My women will wait on you. If you are cold, call for fire.'

Aldarion made no answer. He went early to the bedchamber, and being now weary indeed he cast himself on the bed and forgot soon the shadows of Middle-earth and of Númenor in a heavy sleep. But at cockcrow he awoke to a great disquiet and anger. He rose at once, and thought to go without noise from the house: he would find his man Henderch and the horses, and ride to his kinsman Hallatan, the sheep-lord of Hyarastorni. Later he would summon Erendis to bring his daughter to Armenelos, and not have dealings with her upon her own ground. But as he went out towards the doors Erendis came forward. She had not lain in bed that night, and she stood before him on the threshold.

'You leave more promptly than you came, my lord,' she said. 'I hope that (being a mariner) you have not found this house of women irksome already, to go thus before your business is done. Indeed, what business brought you hither? May I learn it before you leave?'

'I was told in Armenelos that my wife was here, and had removed my daughter hither,' he answered. 'As to the wife I am mistaken, it seems, but have I not a daughter?'

'You had one some years ago,' she said. 'But my daughter has not yet risen.'

'Then let her rise, while I go for my horse,' said Aldarion.

Erendis would have withheld Ancalimë from meeting him at that time; but she feared to go so far as to lose the King's favour, and the Council[23] had long shown their displeasure at the upbringing of the child in the country. Therefore when Aldarion rode back, with Henderch beside him, Ancalimë stood beside her mother on the threshold. She stood erect and stiff as her mother, and made him no courtesy as he dismounted and came up the steps towards her. 'Who are you?' she said. 'And why do you bid me to rise so early, before the house is stirring?'

Aldarion looked at her keenly, and though his face was stern he smiled within: for he saw there a child of his own, rather than of Erendis, for all her schooling.

'You knew me once, Lady Ancalimë,' he said, 'but no matter. Today I am but a messenger from Armenelos, to remind you that you are the daughter of the King's Heir; and (so far as I can now see) you shall be his Heir in your turn. You will not always dwell here. But go back to your bed now, my lady, until your maidservant wakes, if you will. I am in haste to see the King. Farewell!' He kissed the hand of Ancalimë and went down the steps; then he mounted and rode away with a wave of his hand.

Erendis alone at a window watched him riding down the hill, and she marked that he rode towards Hyarastorni and not towards Armenelos. Then she wept, from grief, but still more from anger. She had looked for some penitence, that she might extend after rebuke pardon if prayed for; but he had dealt with her as if she were the offender, and ignored her before her daughter. Too late she remembered the words of Núneth long before, and she saw Aldarion now as something large and not to be tamed, driven by a fierce will, more perilous when chill. She rose, and turned from the window, thinking of her wrongs. 'Perilous!' she said. 'I am steel hard to break. So he would find even were he the King of Númenor.'

Aldarion rode on to Hyarastorni, the house of Hallatan his cousin; for he had a mind to rest there a while and take thought. When he came near, he heard the sound of music, and he found the shepherds making merry for the homecoming of Ulbar, with many marvellous tales and many gifts; and the wife of Ulbar garlanded was dancing with him to the playing of pipes. At first none observed him, and he sat on his horse watching with a smile; but then suddenly Ulbar cried out 'The Great Captain!' and Îbal his son ran forward to Aldarion's stirrup. 'Lord Captain!' he said eagerly.

'What is it? I am in haste,' said Aldarion; for now his mood was changed, and he felt wrathful and bitter.

'I would but ask,' said the boy, 'how old must a man be, before he may go over sea in a ship, like my father?'

'As old as the hills, and with no other hope in life,' said Aldarion. 'Or whenever he has a mind! But your mother, Ulbar's son: will she not greet me?'

When Ulbar's wife came forward Aldarion took her hand. 'Will you receive this of me?' he said. 'It is but little return for six years of a good man's aid that you gave me.' Then from a wallet under his tunic he took a jewel red like fire, upon a band of gold, and he pressed it into her hand. 'From the King of the Elves it came,' he said. 'But he will think it well-bestowed, when I tell him.' Then Aldarion bade farewell to the people there, and rode away, having no mind now to stay in that house. When Hallatan heard of his strange coming and going he marvelled, until more news ran through the countryside.

Aldarion rode only a short way from Hyarastorni and then he stayed his horse, and spoke to Henderch his companion. 'Whatever welcome awaits you, friend, out West, I will not keep you from it. Ride now home with my thanks. I have a mind to go alone.'

'It is not fitting, Lord Captain,' said Henderch.

'It is not,' said Aldarion. 'But that is the way of it. Farewell!'

Then he rode on alone to Armenelos, and never again set foot in Emerië.

When Aldarion left the chamber, Meneldur looked at the letter that his son had given him, wondering; for he saw that it came from King Gil-galad in Lindon. It was sealed and bore his device of white stars upon a blue rondure.[24] Upon the outer fold was written:

Given at Mithlond to the hand of the Lord Aldarion King's Heir of Númenórë, to be delivered to the High King at Armenelos in person.

Then Meneldur broke the seal and read:

Ereinion Gil-galad son of Fingon to Tar-Meneldur of the line of Eärendil, greeting: the Valar keep you and may no shadow fall upon the Isle of Kings.

Long I have owed you thanks, for you have so many times sent to me your son Anardil Aldarion: the greatest Elf-friend that now is among Men, as I deem. At this time I ask your pardon, if I have detained him overlong in my service; for I had great need of the knowledge of Men and their tongues which he alone possesses. He has dared many perils to bring me counsel. Of my need he will speak to you; yet he does not guess how great it is, being young and full of hope. Therefore I write this for the eyes of the King of Númenórë only.

A new shadow arises in the East. It is no tyranny of evil Men, as your son believes; but a servant of Morgoth is stirring, and evil things wake again. Each year it gains in strength, for most Men are ripe to its purpose. Not far off is the day, I judge, when it will become too great for the Eldar unaided to withstand. Therefore, whenever I behold a tall ship of the Kings of Men, my heart is eased. And now I make bold to seek your help. If you have any strength of Men to spare, lend it to me, I beg.

Your son will report to you, if you will, all our reasons. But in fine it is his counsel (and that is ever wise) that when assault comes, as it surely will, we should seek to hold the Westlands, where still the Eldar dwell, and Men of your race, whose hearts are not yet darkened. At the least we must defend Eriador about the long rivers west of the mountains that we name Hithaeglir: our chief defence. But in that mountain-wall there is a great gap southward in the land of Calenardhon; and by that way inroad from the East must come. Already enmity creeps along the coast towards it. It could be defended and assault hindered, did we hold some seat of power upon the nearer shore.

So the Lord Aldarion long has seen. At Vinyalondë by the mouth of Gwathló he has long laboured to establish such a haven, secure against sea and land; but his mighty works have been in vain. He has great knowledge in such matters, for he has learned much of Círdan, and he understands better than any the needs of your great ships. But he has never had men enough; whereas Círdan has no wrights or masons to spare.

The King will know his own needs; but if he will listen with favour to the Lord Aldarion, and support him as he may, then hope will be greater in the world. The memories of the First Age are dim, and all things in Middle-earth grow colder. Let not the ancient friendship of Eldar and Dúnedain wane also.

Behold! The darkness that is to come is filled with hatred for us, but it hates you no less. The Great Sea will not be too wide for its wings, if it is suffered to come to full growth.

Manwë keep you under the One, and send fair wind to your sails.

Meneldur let the parchment fall into his lap. Great clouds borne upon a wind out of the East brought darkness early, and the tall candles at his side seemed to dwindle in the gloom that filled his chamber.

'May Eru call me before such a time comes!' he cried aloud. Then to himself he said: 'Alas! that his pride and my coolness have kept our minds apart so long. But sooner now than I had resolved it will be the course of wisdom to resign the Sceptre to him. For these things are beyond my reach.

'When the Valar gave to us the Land of Gift they did not make us their vice-gerents: we were given the Kingdom of Númenor, not of the world. They are the Lords. Here we were to put away hatred and war; for war was ended, and Morgoth thrust forth from Arda. So I deemed, and so was taught.

'Yet if the world grows again dark, the Lords must know; and they have sent me no sign. Unless this be the sign. What then? Our fathers were rewarded for the aid they gave in the defeat of the Great Shadow. Shall their sons stand aloof, if evil finds a new head?

'I am in too great doubt to rule. To prepare or to let be? To prepare for war, which is yet only guessed: train craftsmen and tillers in the midst of peace for bloodspilling and battle: put iron in the hands of greedy captains who will love only conquest, and count the slain as their glory? Will they say to Eru: *At least your enemies were amongst them?* Or to fold hands, while friends die unjustly: let men live in blind peace, until the ravisher is at the gate? What then will they do: match naked hands against iron and die in vain, or flee leaving the cries of women behind them? Will they say to Eru: *At least I spilled no blood?*

'When either way may lead to evil, of what worth is choice? Let the Valar rule under Eru! I will resign the Sceptre to Aldarion. Yet that also is a choice, for I know well which road he will take. Unless Erendis . . .'

Then Meneldur's thought turned in disquiet to Erendis in Emerië. 'But there is little hope there (if it should be called hope). He will not bend in such grave matters. I know her choice – even were she to listen long enough to understand. For her heart has no wings beyond Númenor, and she has no guess of the cost. If her choice should lead to death in her own time, she would die bravely. But what will she do with life, and other wills? The Valar themselves, even as I, must wait to discover.'

Aldarion came back to Rómenna on the fourth day after Hirilondë had returned to haven. He was way-stained and weary, and he went at once to Eämbar, upon which he now intended to dwell. By that time, as he found to his embitterment, many tongues were already wagging in the City. On the next day he gathered men in Rómenna and brought them to Armenelos. There he bade some fell all the trees, save one, in his garden, and take them to the shipyards; others he commanded to raze his house to the ground. The white Elven-tree alone he spared; and when the woodcutters were gone he looked at it, standing amid the desolation, and he saw for the first time that it was in itself beautiful. In its slow Elven growth it was yet but twelve feet high, straight, slender, youthful, now budded with its winter flowers upon upheld branches pointing to the sky. It recalled to him his daughter, and he said: 'I will call you also Ancalimë. May you and she stand so in long life, unbent by wind or will, and unclipped!'

On the third day after his return from Emerië Aldarion sought the King. Tar-Meneldur sat still in his chair and waited. Looking at his son he was afraid; for Aldarion was changed: his face was become grey, cold, and hostile, as the sea when the sun is suddenly veiled in dull cloud. Standing before his father he spoke slowly with tone of contempt rather than of wrath.

'What part you have played in this you yourself know best,' he said. 'But a King should consider how much a man will endure, though he be a subject, even his son. If you would shackle me to this Island, then you choose your chain ill. I have now neither wife, nor love of this land, left. I will go from this misenchanted isle of daydreams where women in their insolence would have men cringe. I will use my days to some purpose, elsewhere, where I am not scorned, more welcome in honour. Another Heir you may find more fit for a house-servant. Of my inheritance I demand only this: the ship Hirilondë and as many men as it will hold. My daughter I would take also, were she older; but I will commend her to my mother. Unless you dote upon sheep, you will not hinder this, and will not suffer the child to be stunted, reared among mute women in cold insolence and contempt of her kin. She is of the Line of Elros, and no other descendant will you have through your son. I have done. I will go now about business more profitable.'

Thus far Meneldur had sat in patience with downcast eyes and made no sign. But now he sighed, and looked up. 'Aldarion, my son,' he said sadly, 'the King would say that you also show cold insolence and contempt of your kin, and yourself condemn others unheard; but your father who loves you and grieves for you will remit that. The fault is not mine only that I have not ere now understood your purposes. But as for what you have suffered (of which, alas! too many now speak): I am guiltless. Erendis I have loved, and since our hearts lean the same way I have thought that she had much to endure that was hard. Your purposes are now become clear to me, though if you are in mood to hear aught but praise I would say that at first your own pleasure also led you. And it may be that things would have been otherwise if you had spoken more openly long ago.'

'The King may have some grievance in this,' cried Aldarion, now more hotly, 'but not the one you speak of! To her at least I spoke long and often: to cold ears uncomprehending. As well might a truant boy talk of tree-climbing to a nurse anxious only about the tearing of clothes and the due time of meals! I love her, or I should care less. The past I will keep in my heart; the future is dead. She does not love me, or aught else. She loves herself with Númenor as a setting, and myself as a tame hound, to drowse by the hearth until she has a mind to walk in her own fields. But since hounds now seem too gross, she will have Ancalimë to pipe in a cage. But enough of this. Have I the King's leave to depart? Or has he some command?'

'The King,' answered Tar-Meneldur, 'has thought much about these matters, in what seem the long days since last you were in Armenelos. He has read the letter of Gil-galad, which is earnest and grave in tone. Alas! To his prayer and your wishes the King of Númenor must say *nay*. He cannot do otherwise, according to his understanding of the perils of either course: to prepare for war, or not to prepare.'

Aldarion shrugged his shoulders, and took a step as if to go. But Meneldur held up his hand commanding attention, and continued: 'Nevertheless, the King, though he has now ruled the land of Númenor for one hundred and forty-two years, has no certainty that his understanding of the matter is sufficient for a just decision in matters of such high import and peril.' He paused, and taking up a parchment written in his own hand he read from it in a clear voice:

Therefore: first for the honour of his well-beloved son; and second for the better direction of the realm in courses which his son more clearly understands, the King has resolved: that he will forthwith resign the Sceptre to his son, who shall now become Tar-Aldarion, the King.

'This,' said Meneldur, 'when it is proclaimed, will make known to all my thought concerning this present pass. It will raise you above scorn; and it will set free your powers so that other losses may seem more easy to endure. The letter of Gil-galad, when you are King, you shall answer as seems fit to the holder of the Sceptre.'

Aldarion stood still for a moment in amaze. He had braced himself to face the King's anger, which wilfully he had endeavoured to kindle. Now he stood confounded. Then, as one swept from his feet by a sudden wind from a quarter unexpected, he fell to his knees before his father; but after a moment he raised his bowed head and laughed – so he always did, when he heard of any deed of great generosity, for it gladdened his heart.

'Father,' he said, 'ask the King to forget my insolence to him. For he is a great King, and his humility sets him far above my pride. I am conquered: I submit myself wholly. That such a King should resign the Sceptre while in vigour and wisdom is not to be thought.'

'Yet so it is resolved,' said Meneldur. 'The Council shall be summoned forthwith.'

When the Council came together, after seven days had passed, Tar-Meneldur acquainted them with his resolve, and laid the scroll before them. Then all were amazed, not yet knowing what were the courses of which the King spoke; and all demurred, begging him to delay his decision, save only Hallatan of Hyarastorni. For he had long held his kinsman Aldarion in esteem, though his own life and likings were far otherwise; and he judged the King's deed to be noble, and timed with shrewdness, if it must be.

But to those others who urged this or that against his resolve Meneldur answered: 'Not without thought did I come to this resolution, and in my thought I have considered all the reasons that you wisely argue. Now and not later is the time most fit for my will to be published, for reasons which though none here has uttered all must guess. Forthwith then let this decree be proclaimed. But if you will, it shall not take effect until the time of the *Erukyermë* in the Spring. Till then, I will hold the Sceptre.'

When news came to Emerië of the proclamation of the decree Erendis was dismayed; for she read therein a rebuke by the King in whose favour she had trusted. In this she saw truly, but that anything else of greater import lay behind she did not conceive. Soon afterwards there came a message from Tar-Meneldur, a command indeed, though graciously worded. She was bidden to come to Armenelos and to bring with her the lady Ancalimë, there to abide at least until the *Erukyermë* and the proclamation of the new King.

'He is swift to strike,' she thought. 'So I should have foreseen. He will strip me of all. But myself he shall not command, though it be by the mouth of his father.'

Therefore she returned answer to Tar-Meneldur: 'King and father, my daughter Ancalimë must come indeed, if you command it. I beg that you will consider her years, and see to it that she is lodged in quiet. For myself, I pray you to excuse me. I learn that my house in Armenelos has been destroyed; and I would not at this time willingly be a guest, least of all upon a house-ship among mariners. Here then permit me to remain in my solitude, unless it be the King's will also to take back this house.'

This letter Tar-Meneldur read with concern, but it missed its mark in his heart. He showed it to Aldarion, to whom it seemed chiefly aimed. Then Aldarion read the letter; and the King, regarding the face of his son, said: 'Doubtless you are grieved. But for what else did you hope?'

'Not for this, at least,' said Aldarion. 'It is far below my hope of her. She has dwindled; and if I have wrought this, then black is my blame. But do the large shrink in adversity? This was not the way, not even in hate or revenge! She should have demanded that a great house be prepared for her, called for a Queen's escort, and come back to Armenelos with her beauty adorned, royally, with the star on her brow; then well nigh all the Isle of Númenor she might have bewitched to her part, and made me seem madman and churl. The Valar be my witness, I would rather have had it so: rather a beautiful Queen to thwart me and flout me, than freedom to rule while the Lady Elestirnë falls down dim into her own twilight.'

Then with a bitter laugh he gave back the letter to the King. 'Well: so it is,' he said. 'But if one has a distaste to dwell on a ship among mariners, another may be excused dislike of a sheep-farm among serving-women. But I will not have my daughter so schooled. At least she shall choose by knowledge.' He rose, and begged leave to go.


### The Further Course of the Narrative

From the point where Aldarion read the letter from Erendis, refusing to return to Armenelos, the story can only be traced in glimpses and snatches, from notes and jottings: and even those do not constitute the fragments of a wholly consistent story, being composed at different times and often at odds with themselves.

It seems that when Aldarion became King of Númenor in the year 883 he determined to revisit Middle-earth at once, and departed for Mithlond either in the same year or the next. It is recorded that on the prow of Hirilondë he set no bough of *orolairë*, but the image of an eagle with golden beak and jewelled eyes, which was the gift of Círdan.

It perched there, by the craft of its maker, as if poised for flight unerring to some far mark that it espied. 'This sign shall lead us to our aim,' he said. 'For our return let the Valar care – if our deeds do not displease them.'

It is also stated that 'no records are now left of the later voyages that Aldarion made', but that 'it is known that he went much on land as well as sea, and went up the River Gwathló as far as Tharbad, and there met Galadriel'. There is no mention elsewhere of this meeting; but at that time Galadriel and Celeborn were dwelling in Eregion, at no great distance from Tharbad (see p. 235).

But all Aldarion's labours were swept away. The works that he began again at Vinyalondë were never completed, and the sea gnawed them.[25] Nevertheless he laid the foundation for the achievement of Tar-Minastir long years after, in the first war with Sauron, and but for his works the fleets of Númenor could not have brought their power in time to the right place – as he foresaw. Already the hostility was growing and dark men out of the mountains were thrusting into Enedwaith. But in Aldarion's day the Númenóreans did not yet desire more room, and his Venturers remained a small people, admired but little emulated.

There is no mention of any further development of the alliance with Gil-galad, or of the sending of the aid that he requested in his letter to Tar-Meneldur; it is said indeed that

Aldarion was too late, or too early. Too late: for the power that hated Númenor had already waked. Too early: for the time was not yet ripe for Númenor to show its power or to come back into the battle for the world.

There was a stir in Númenor when Tar-Aldarion determined to return to Middle-earth in 883 or 884, for no King had ever before left the Isle, and the Council had no precedent. It seems that Meneldur was offered but refused the regency, and that Hallatan of Hyarastorni became regent, either appointed by the Council or by Tar-Aldarion himself.

Of the history of Ancalimë during those years when she was growing up there is no certain form. There is less doubt concerning her somewhat ambiguous character, and the influence that her mother exerted on her. She was less prim than Erendis, and natively liked display, jewels, music, admiration, and deference; but she liked them at will and not unceasingly, and she made her mother and the white house in Emerië an excuse for escape. She approved, as it were, both Erendis' treatment of Aldarion on his late return, but also Aldarion's anger, impenitence, and subsequent relentless dismissal of Erendis from his heart and concern. She had a profound dislike of obligatory marriage, and in marriage of any constraint on her will. Her mother had spoken unceasingly against men, and indeed a remarkable example of Erendis' teaching in this respect is preserved:

Men in Númenor are half-Elves (said Erendis), especially the high men; they are neither the one nor the other. The long life that they were granted deceives them, and they dally in the world, children in mind, until age finds them – and then many only forsake play out of doors for play in their houses. They turn their play into great matters and great matters into play. They would be craftsmen and loremasters and heroes all at once; and women to them are but fires on the hearth – for others to tend, until they are tired of play in the evening. All things were made for their service: hills are for quarries, rivers to furnish water or to turn wheels, trees for boards, women for their body's need, or if fair to adorn their table and hearth; and children to be teased when nothing else is to do – but they would as soon play with their hounds' whelps. To all they are gracious and kind, merry as larks in the morning (if the sun shines); for they are never wrathful if they can avoid it. Men should be gay, they hold, generous as the rich, giving away what they do not need. Anger they show only when they become aware, suddenly, that there are other wills in the world beside their own. Then they will be as ruthless as the seawind if anything dare to withstand them.

Thus it is, Ancalimë, and we cannot alter it. For men fashioned Númenor: men, those heroes of old that they sing of – of their women we hear less, save that they wept when their men were slain. Númenor was to be a rest after war. But if they weary of rest and the plays of peace, soon they will go back to their great play, manslaying and war. Thus it is; and we are set here among them. But we need not assent. If we love Númenor also, let us enjoy it before they ruin it. We also are daughters of the great, and we have wills and courage of our own. Therefore do not bend, Ancalimë. Once bend a little, and they will bend you further until you are bowed down. Sink your roots into the rock, and face the wind, though it blow away all your leaves.

Moreover, and more potently, Erendis had made Ancalimë accustomed to the society of women: the cool, quiet, gentle life of Emerië without interruptions or alarms. Boys, like Îbal, shouted. Men rode up blowing horns at strange hours, and were fed with great noise. They begot children and left them in the care of women when they were troublesome. And though childbirth had less of ills and peril, Númenor was not an 'earthly paradise', and the weariness of labour or of all making was not taken away.

Ancalimë, like her father, was resolute in pursuing her policies; and like him she was obstinate, taking the opposite course to any that was counselled. She had something of her mother's coldness and sense of personal injury; and deep in her heart, almost but not quite forgotten, was the firmness with which Aldarion had unclasped her hand and set her down when he was in haste to be gone. She loved dearly the downlands of her home, and never (as she said) in her life could she sleep at peace far from the sound of sheep. But she did not refuse the Heirship, and determined that when her day came she would be a powerful Ruling Queen; and when so, to live where and how she pleased.

It seems that for some eighteen years after Aldarion became King he was often gone from Númenor; and during that time Ancalimë passed her days both in Emerië and in Armenelos, for Queen Almarian took a great liking to her, and indulged her as she had indulged Aldarion in his youth. In Armenelos she was treated with deference by all, and not least by Aldarion; and though at first she was ill at ease, missing the wide airs of her home, in time she ceased to be abashed, and became aware that men looked with wonder upon her beauty, now come to its full. As she grew older she became ever more wilful, and she found irksome the company of Erendis, who behaved like a widow and would not be Queen; but she continued to return to Emerië, both as a retreat from Armenelos and because she desired thus to vex Aldarion. She was clever, and malicious, and saw promise of sport as the prize for which her mother and her father did battle.

Now in the year 892, when Ancalimë was nineteen years old, she was proclaimed the King's Heir (at a far earlier age than had previously been the case, see p. 177); and at that time Tar-Aldarion caused the law of succession in Númenor to be changed. It is said specifically that Tar-Aldarion did this 'for reasons of private concern, rather than policy', and out of 'his long resolve to defeat Erendis'. The change of the law is referred to in *The Lord of the Rings*, Appendix A (I i):

The sixth King [Tar-Aldarion] left only one child, a daughter. She became the first Queen [i.e. Ruling Queen]; for it was then made a law of the royal house that the eldest child of the King, whether man or woman, should receive the sceptre.

But elsewhere the new law is formulated differently from this. The fullest and clearest account states in the first place that the 'old law', as it was afterwards called, was not in fact a Númenórean 'law', but an inherited custom which circumstances had not yet called in question; and according to that custom the Ruler's eldest son inherited the Sceptre. It was understood that if there were no son the nearest male kinsman *of male descent* from Elros Tar-Minyatur would be the Heir. Thus if Tar-Meneldur had had no son the Heir would not have been Valandil his nephew (son of his sister Silmarien), but Malantur his cousin (grandson of Tar-Elendil's younger brother Eärendur). But by the 'new law' the (eldest) daughter of the Ruler inherited the Sceptre, if he had no son (this being, of course, in contradiction to what is said in *The Lord of the Rings*). By the advice of the Council it was added that she was free to refuse.[26] In such a case, according to the 'new law', the heir of the Ruler was the nearest male kinsman whether by male or female descent. Thus if Ancalimë had refused the Sceptre Tar-Aldarion's heir would have been Soronto, the son of his sister Ailinel; and if Ancalimë had resigned the Sceptre or died childless Soronto would likewise have been her heir.

It was also ordained at the instance of the Council that a female heir must resign, if she remained unwed beyond a certain time; and to these provisions Tar-Aldarion added that the King's Heir should not wed save in the Line of Elros, and that any who did so should cease to be eligible for the Heirship. It is said that this ordinance arose directly from Aldarion's disastrous marriage to Erendis and his reflections upon it; for she was not of the Line of Elros, and had a lesser life-span, and he believed that therein lay the root of all their troubles.

Beyond question these provisions of the 'new law' were recorded in such detail because they were to bear closely on the later history of these reigns; but unhappily very little can now be said of it.

At some later date Tar-Aldarion rescinded the law that a Ruling Queen must marry, or resign (and this was certainly due to Ancalimë's reluctance to countenance either alternative); but the marriage of the Heir to another member of the Line of Elros remained the custom ever after.[27]

At all events, suitors for Ancalimë's hand soon began to appear in Emerië, and not only because of the change in her position, for the fame of her beauty, of her aloofness and disdain, and of the strangeness of her upbringing had run through the land. In that time the people began to speak of her as Emerwen Aranel, the Princess Shepherdess. To escape from importunity Ancalimë, aided by the old woman Zamîn, went into hiding at a farm on the borders of the lands of Hallatan of Hyarastorni, where she lived for a time the life of a shepherdess. The accounts (which are indeed no more than hasty jottings) vary as to how her parents responded to this state of affairs. According to one, Erendis herself knew where Ancalimë was, and approved the reason for her flight, while Aldarion prevented the Council from searching for her, since it was to his mind that his daughter should act thus independently. According to another, however, Erendis was disturbed at Ancalimë's flight and the King was wrathful; and at this time Erendis attempted some reconciliation with him, at least in respect of Ancalimë. But Aldarion was unmoved, declaring that the King had no wife, but that he had a daughter and an heir; and that he did not believe that Erendis was ignorant of her hiding-place.

What is certain is that Ancalimë fell in with a shepherd who was minding flocks in the same region; and to her this man named himself Mámandil. Ancalimë was all unused to such company as his, and she took delight in his singing, in which he was skilled; and he sang to her songs that came out of far-off days, when the Edain pastured their flocks in Eriador long ago, before ever they met the Eldar. They met thus in the pastures often and often, and he altered the songs of the lovers of old and brought into them the names of Emerwen and Mámandil; and Ancalimë feigned not to understand the drift of the words. But at length he declared his love for her openly, and she drew back, and refused him, saying that her fate lay between them, for she was the Heir of the King. But Mámandil was

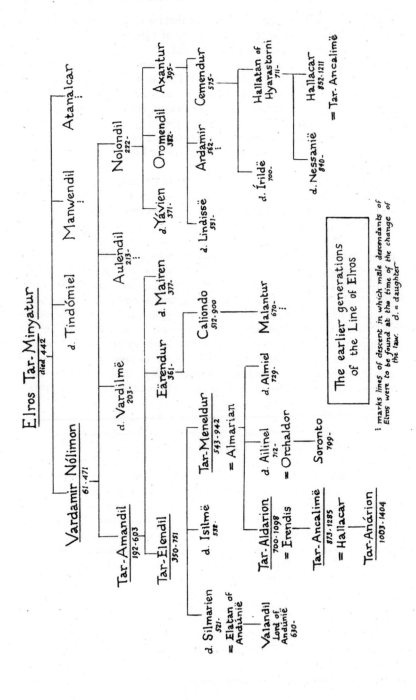

Elros Tar-Minyatur
*died 442*

The earlier generations
of the Line of Elros

: marks lines of descent in which male descendants of
Elros were to be found at the time of the change of
the law.   d. = daughter

not abashed, and he laughed, and told her that his right name was Hallacar, son of Hallatan of Hyarastorni, of the line of Elros Tar-Minyatur. 'And how else could any wooer find you?' he said.

Then Ancalimë was angry, because he had deceived her, knowing from the first who she was; but he answered: 'That is true in part. I contrived indeed to meet the Lady whose ways were so strange that I was curious to see more of her. But then I loved Emerwen, and I care not now who she may be. Do not think that I pursue your high place; for far rather would I have it that you were Emerwen only. I rejoice but in this, that I also am of the Line of Elros, because otherwise I deem that we could not wed.'

'We could,' said Ancalimë, 'if I had any mind to such a state. I could lay down my royalty, and be free. But if I were to do so, I should be free to wed whom I will; and that would be Úner (which is "Noman"), whom I prefer above all others.'

It was however to Hallacar that Ancalimë was wedded in the end. From one version it appears that the persistence of Hallacar in his suit despite her rejection of him, and the urging of the Council that she choose a husband for the quiet of the realm, led to their marriage not many years after their first meeting among the flocks in Emerië. But elsewhere it is said that she remained unmarried so long that her cousin Soronto, relying on the provision of the new law, called upon her to surrender the Heirship, and that she then married Hallacar in order to spite Soronto. In yet another brief notice it is implied that she wedded Hallacar after Aldarion had rescinded the provision, in order to put an end to Soronto's hopes of becoming King if Ancalimë died childless.

However this may be, the story is clear that Ancalimë did not desire love, nor did she wish for a son; and she said: 'Must I become like Queen Almarian, and dote upon him?' Her life with Hallacar was unhappy, and she begrudged him her son Anárion, and there was strife between them thereafter. She sought to subject him, claiming to be the owner of his land, and forbidding him to dwell upon it, for she would not, as she said, have her husband a farm-steward. From this time comes the last tale that is recorded of those unhappy things. For Ancalimë would let none of her women wed, and although for fear of her most were restrained, they came from the country about and had lovers whom they wished to marry. But Hallacar in secret arranged for them to be wedded; and he declared that he would give a last feast at his own house, before he left it. To this feast he invited Ancalimë, saying that it was the house of his kindred, and should be given a farewell of courtesy.

Ancalimë came, attended by all her women, for she did not care to be waited on by men. She found the house all lit and arrayed as for a great feast, and men of the household attired in garlands as for their weddings, and each with another garland in his hands for a bride. 'Come!' said Hallacar. 'The weddings are prepared, and the bride-chambers ready.

But since it cannot be thought that we should ask the Lady Ancalimë, King's Heir, to lie with a farm-steward, then, alas! she must sleep alone tonight.' And Ancalimë perforce remained there, for it was too far to ride back, nor would she go unattended. Neither men nor women hid their smiles; and Ancalimë would not come to the feast, but lay abed listening to the laughter far off and thinking it aimed at herself. Next day she rode off in a cold rage, and Hallacar sent three men to escort her. Thus he was revenged, for she came never back to Emerië, where the very sheep seemed to make scorn of her. But she pursued Hallacar with hatred afterwards.

Of the later years of Tar-Aldarion nothing can now be said, save that he seems to have continued his voyages to Middle-earth, and more than once left Ancalimë as his regent. His last voyage took place about the end of the first millennium of the Second Age; and in the year 1075 Ancalimë became the first Ruling Queen of Númenor. It is told that after the death of Tar-Aldarion in 1098 Tar-Ancalimë neglected all her father's policies and gave no further aid to Gil-galad in Lindon. Her son Anárion, who was afterwards the eighth Ruler of Númenor, first had two daughters. They disliked and feared the Queen, and refused the Heirship, remaining unwed, since the Queen would not in revenge allow them to marry.[28] Anárion's son Súrion was born the last, and was the ninth Ruler of Númenor.

Of Erendis it is said that when old age came upon her, neglected by Ancalimë and in bitter loneliness, she longed once more for Aldarion; and learning that he was gone from Númenor on what proved to be his last voyage but that he was soon expected to return, she left Emerië at last and journeyed unrecognised and unknown to the haven of Rómenna. There, it seems, she met her fate; but only the words 'Erendis perished in water in the year 985' remain to suggest how it came to pass.

# NOTES

## Chronology

Anardil (Aldarion) was born in the year 700 of the Second Age, and his first voyage to Middle-earth took place in 725–7. Meneldur his father became King of Númenor in 740. The Guild of Venturers was founded in 750, and Aldarion was proclaimed King's Heir in 800. Erendis was born in 771. Aldarion's seven year voyage (p. 178) covered the years 806–13, the first voyage of the Palarran (p. 179) 816–20, the voyage of seven ships in defiance of Tar-Meneldur (p. 180) 824–9, and the voyage of fourteen years that followed immediately on the last (pp. 180–1) 829–43.

Aldarion and Erendis were betrothed in 858; the years of the voyage undertaken by Aldarion after his betrothal (p. 187) were 863–9, and the wedding was in 870. Ancalimë was born in the Spring of 873. The Hirilondë sailed in the Spring of 877 and Aldarion's return, followed by the breach with Erendis, took place in 882; he received the Sceptre of Númenor in 883.

---

1  In the 'Description of Númenor' (p. 167) he is called Tar-Meneldur Elentirmo (Star-watcher). See also his entry in 'The Line of Elros' (p. 219).

2  Soronto's part in the story can now only be glimpsed; see p. 211.

3  As is told in the 'Description of Númenor' (p. 171) it was Vëantur who first achieved the voyage to Middle-earth in the year 600 of the Second Age (he was born in 451). In the Tale of Years in Appendix B to *The Lord of the Rings* the annal entry for the year 600 states: 'The first ships of the Númenóreans appear off the coasts.'

There is a description in a late philological essay of the first meeting of the Númenóreans with Men of Eriador at that time: 'It was six hundred years after the departure of the survivors of the Atani [Edain] over the sea to Númenor that a ship first came again out of the West to Middle-earth and passed up the Gulf of Lhûn. Its captain and mariners were welcomed by Gil-galad; and thus was begun the friendship and alliance of Númenor with the Eldar of Lindon. The news spread swiftly and Men in Eriador were filled with wonder. Although in the First Age they had dwelt in the East, rumours of the terrible war "beyond the Western Mountains" [i.e. Ered Luin] had reached them; but their traditions preserved no clear account of it, and they believed that all the Men who dwelt in the lands beyond had been destroyed or drowned in great tumults of fire and inrushing seas. But since it was still said among them that those Men had in years beyond memory been kinsmen of their own, they sent messages to Gil-galad asking leave to meet the shipmen "who had returned from death in the deeps of the Sea". Thus it came about that there was a meeting between them on the Tower Hills; and to that meeting with the Númenóreans came twelve Men only out of Eriador, Men of high heart and courage, for most of their people feared that the newcomers were perilous spirits of the Dead. But when they looked on the shipmen fear left them, though for a while they stood silent in awe; for mighty as they were themselves accounted among their kin, the shipmen resembled rather Elvish lords than mortal Men in bearing and apparel. Nonetheless they felt no doubt of their ancient kinship; and likewise the shipmen looked with glad surprise upon the Men of Middle-earth, for it had been believed in Númenor that the

Men left behind were descended from the evil Men who in the last days of the war against Morgoth had been summoned by him out of the East. But now they looked upon faces free from the Shadow and Men who could have walked in Númenor and not been thought aliens save in their clothes and their arms. Then suddenly, after the silence, both the Númenóreans and the Men of Eriador spoke words of welcome and greeting in their own tongues, as if addressing friends and kinsmen after a long parting. At first they were disappointed, for neither side could understand the other; but when they mingled in friendship they found that they shared very many words still clearly recognisable, and others that could be understood with attention, and they were able to converse haltingly about simple matters.' Elsewhere in this essay it is explained that these Men dwelt about Lake Evendim, in the North Downs and the Weather Hills, and in the lands between as far as the Brandywine, west of which they often wandered though they did not dwell there. They were friendly with the Elves, though they held them in awe; and they feared the Sea and would not look upon it. It appears that they were in origin Men of the same stock as the Peoples of Bëor and Hador who had not crossed the Blue Mountains into Beleriand during the First Age.

4  The son of the King's Heir: Aldarion son of Meneldur. Tar-Elendil did not resign the sceptre to Meneldur until a further fifteen years had passed.

5  *Eruhantalë*: 'Thanksgiving to Eru', the autumn feast in Númenor; see the 'Description of Númenor' p. 166.

6  (Sîr) Angren was the Elvish name of the river Isen. Ras Morthil, a name not otherwise found, must be the great headland at the end of the northern arm of the Bay of Belfalas, which was also called Andrast (Long Cape).

   The reference to 'the country of Amroth where the Nandor Elves still dwell' can be taken to imply that the tale of Aldarion and Erendis was written down in Gondor before the departure of the last ship from the haven of the Silvan Elves near Dol Amroth in the year 1981 of the Third Age; see pp. 240 ff.

7  For Uinen the spouse of Ossë (Maiar of the Sea) see *The Silmarillion* p. 30. There it is said that 'the Númenóreans lived long in her protection, and held her in reverence equal to the Valar'.

8  It is stated that the Guildhouse of the Venturers 'was confiscated by the Kings, and removed to the western haven of Andúnië; all its records perished' (i.e. in the Downfall), including all the accurate charts of Númenor. But it is not said when this confiscation of Eämbar took place.

9  The river was afterwards called Gwathló or Greyflood, and the haven Lond Daer; see pp. 261 ff.

10 Cf. *The Silmarillion* p. 148: 'The Men of that House [i.e. of Bëor]

were dark or brown of hair, with grey eyes.' According to a genealogical table of the House of Bëor Erendis was descended from Bereth,
who was the sister of Baragund and Belegund, and thus the aunt of
Morwen mother of Túrin Turambar and of Rían the mother of Tuor.

11 On different life-spans among the Númenóreans see Note 1 to 'The
Line of Elros', p. 224.

12 On the tree *oiolairë* see the 'Description of Númenor', p. 167.

13 This is to be understood as a portent.

14 Cf. the *Akallabêth* (*The Silmarillion* p. 277), where it is told that in
the days of Ar-Pharazôn 'ever and anon a great ship of the Númenóreans
would founder and not return to haven, though such a grief had
not till then befallen them since the rising of the Star'.

15 Valandil was Aldarion's cousin, for he was the son of Silmarien,
daughter of Tar-Elendil and sister of Tar-Meneldur. Valandil, first
of the Lords of Andúnië, was the ancestor of Elendil the Tall, father
of Isildur and Anárion.

16 *Erukyermë*: 'Prayer to Eru', the feast of the Spring in Númenor;
see the 'Description of Númenor' p. 166.

17 It is said in the *Akallabêth* (*The Silmarillion* pp. 262-3) that 'at times,
when all the air was clear and the sun was in the east, they would
look out and descry far off in the west a city white-shining on a
distant shore, and a great harbour and a tower. For in those days
the Númenóreans were far-sighted; yet even so it was only the keenest
eyes among them that could see this vision, from the Meneltarma
maybe, or from some tall ship that lay off their western coast. . . .
But the wise among them knew that this distant land was not indeed
the Blessed Realm of Valinor, but was Avallónë, the haven of the
Eldar upon Eressëa, easternmost of the Undying Lands.'

18 Thus came, it is said, the manner of the Kings and Queens afterward
to wear as a star a white jewel upon the brow, and they had no
crown. [Author's note.]

19 In the Westlands and in Andúnië the Elven-tongue [Sindarin] was
spoken by high and low. In that tongue Erendis was nurtured; but
Aldarion spoke the Númenórean speech, although as all high men
of Númenor he knew also the tongue of Beleriand. [Author's note.] –
Elsewhere, in a note on the languages of Númenor, it is said that
the general use of Sindarin in the north-west of the Isle was due to
the fact that those parts were largely settled by people of 'Bëorian'
descent; and the People of Bëor had in Beleriand early abandoned
their own speech and adopted Sindarin. (Of this there is no mention
in *The Silmarillion*, though it is said there (p. 148) that in Dor-lómin
in the days of Fingolfin the people of Hador did not forget their own
speech, 'and from it came the common tongue of Númenor'.) In
other regions of Númenor Adûnaic was the native language of the

people, though Sindarin was known in some degree to nearly all; and in the royal house, and in most of the houses of the noble or learned, Sindarin was usually the native tongue, until after the days of Tar-Atanamir. (It is said later in the present narrative (p. 194) that Aldarion actually preferred the Númenórean speech; it may be that in this he was exceptional.) This note further states that although Sindarin as used for a long period by mortal Men tended to become divergent and dialectal, this process was largely checked in Númenor, at least among the nobles and the learned, by their contact with the Eldar of Eressëa and Lindon. Quenya was not a spoken tongue in Númenor. It was known only to the learned and to the families of high descent, to whom it was taught in their early youth. It was used in official documents intended for preservation, such as the Laws, and the Scroll and Annals of the Kings (cf. the *Akallabêth* p. 267: 'in the Scroll of Kings the name Herunúmen was inscribed in the High-elven speech'), and often in more recondite works of lore. It was also largely used in nomenclature: the official names of all places, regions, and geographical features in the land were of Quenya form (though they usually had also local names, generally of the same meaning, in either Sindarin or Adúnaic). The personal names, and especially the official and public names, of all members of the royal house, and of the Line of Elros in general, were given in Quenya form.

In a reference to these matters in *The Lord of the Rings*, Appendix F, I (section *Of Men*), a somewhat different impression is given of the place of Sindarin among the languages of Númenor: 'The *Dúnedain* alone of all races of Men knew and spoke an Elvish tongue; for their forefathers had learned the Sindarin tongue, and this they handed on to their children as a matter of lore, changing little with the passing of the years.'

20  *Elanor* was a small golden star-shaped flower; it grew also upon the mound of Cerin Amroth in Lothlórien (*The Fellowship of the Ring* II 6). Sam Gamgee gave its name to his daughter, on Frodo's suggestion (*The Return of the King* VI 9).

21  See note 10 above for Erendis' descent from Bereth, the sister of Morwen's father Baragund.

22  It is stated that the Númenóreans, like the Eldar, avoided the begetting of children if they foresaw any separation likely between husband and wife between the conception of the child and at least its very early years. Aldarion stayed in his house for a very brief time after the birth of his daughter, according to the Númenóreans' idea of the fitness of things.

23  In a note on the 'Council of the Sceptre' at this time in the history of Númenor it is said that this Council had no powers to govern the King save by advice; and no such powers had yet been desired or dreamed of as needful. The Council was composed of members from

each of the divisions of Númenor; but the King's Heir when proclaimed was also a member, so that he might learn of the government of the land, and others also the King might summon, or ask to be chosen, if they had special knowledge of matters at any time in debate. At this time there were only two members of the Council (other than Aldarion) who were of the Line of Elros: Valandil of Andúnië for the Andustar, and Hallatan of Hyarastorni for the Mittalmar; but they owed their place not to their descent or their wealth, but to the esteem and love in which they were held in their countries. (In the *Akallabêth* (p. 268) it is said that 'the Lord of Andúnië was ever among the chief councillors of the Sceptre'.)

24 It is recorded that Ereinion was given the name Gil-galad 'Star of Radiance' 'because his helm and mail, and his shield overlaid with silver and set with a device of white stars, shone from afar like a star in sunlight or moonlight, and could be seen by Elvish eyes at a great distance if he stood upon a height'.

25 See p. 265.

26 A legitimate male heir, on the other hand, could not refuse; but since a King could always resign the Sceptre, a male heir could in fact immediately resign to *his* natural heir. He was then himself deemed also to have reigned for at least one year; and this was the case (the only case) with Vardamir, the son of Elros, who did not ascend the throne but gave the Sceptre to his son Amandil.

27 It is said elsewhere that this rule of 'royal marriage' was never a matter of law, but it became a custom of pride: 'a symptom of the growth of the Shadow, since it only became rigid when the distinction between the Line of Elros and other families, in life-span, vigour, or ability, had diminished or altogether disappeared.'

28 This is strange, because Anárion was the Heir in Ancalimë's lifetime. In 'The Line of Elros' (p. 220) it is said only that Anárion's daughters 'refused the sceptre'.

# III

# THE LINE OF ELROS:
# KINGS OF NÚMENOR

## *from the Founding of the City of Armenelos to the Downfall*

The Realm of Númenor is held to have begun in the thirty-second year of the Second Age, when Elros son of Eärendil ascended the throne in the City of Armenelos, being then ninety years of age. Thereafter he was known in the Scroll of the Kings by the name of Tar-Minyatur; for it was the custom of the Kings to take their titles in the forms of the Quenya or High-elven tongue, that being the noblest tongue of the world, and this custom endured until the days of Ar-Adûnakhôr (Tar-Herunúmen). Elros Tar-Minyatur ruled the Númenóreans for four hundred years and ten. For to the Númenóreans long life had been granted, and they remained unwearied for thrice the span of mortal Men in Middle-earth; but to Eärendil's son the longest life of any Man was given, and to his descendants a lesser span, and yet one greater than to others even of the Númenóreans; and so it was until the coming of the Shadow, when the years of the Númenóreans began to wane.[1]

I  *Elros Tar-Minyatur*
He was born fifty-eight years before the Second Age began: he remained unwearied until he was five hundred years old and then laid down his life, in the year 442, having ruled for 410 years.

II  *Vardamir Nólimon*
He was born in the year 61 of the Second Age and died in 471. He was called Nólimon for his chief love was for ancient lore, which he gathered from Elves and Men. Upon the departure of Elros, being then 381 years of age, he did not ascend the throne, but gave the sceptre to his son. He is nonetheless accounted the second of the Kings, and is deemed to have reigned one year.[2] It remained the custom thereafter until the days of Tar-Atanamir that the King should yield the sceptre to his successor before he died; and the Kings died of free will while yet in vigour of mind.

### III  Tar-Amandil

He was the son of Vardamir Nólimon, and he was born in the year 192. He ruled for 148 years,[3] and surrendered the sceptre in 590; he died in 603.

### IV  Tar-Elendil

He was the son of Tar-Amandil, and he was born in the year 350. He ruled for 150 years, and surrendered the sceptre in 740; he died in 751. He was also called Parmaitë, for with his own hand he made many books and legends of the lore gathered by his grandfather. He married late in his life, and his eldest child was a daughter, Silmarien, born in the year 521,[4] whose son was Valandil. Of Valandil came the Lords of Andúnië, of whom the last was Amandil father of Elendil the Tall, who came to Middle-earth after the Downfall. In Tar-Elendil's reign the ships of the Númenóreans first came back to Middle-earth.

### V  Tar-Meneldur

He was the only son and third child of Tar-Elendil, and he was born in the year 543. He ruled for 143 years, and surrendered the sceptre in 883; he died in 942. His 'right name' was Írimon; he took his title Meneldur from his love of star-lore. He married Almarian daughter of Vëantur, Captain of Ships under Tar-Elendil. He was wise, but gentle and patient. He resigned to his son, suddenly and long before due time, as a stroke of policy, in troubles that arose, owing to the disquiet of Gil-galad in Lindon, when he first became aware that an evil spirit, hostile to Eldar and Dúnedain, was stirring in Middle-earth.

### VI  Tar-Aldarion

He was the eldest child and only son of Tar-Meneldur, and he was born in the year 700. He ruled for 192 years, and surrendered the sceptre to his daughter in 1075; he died in 1098. His 'right name' was Anardil; but he was early known by the name of Aldarion, because he was much concerned with trees, and planted great woods to furnish timber for the ship-yards. He was a great mariner and ship-builder; and himself sailed often to Middle-earth, where he became the friend and counsellor of Gil-galad. Owing to his long absences abroad his wife Erendis became angered, and they separated in the year 882. His only child was a daughter, very beautiful, Ancalimë. In her favour Aldarion altered the law of succession, so that the (eldest) daughter of a King should succeed, if he had no sons. This change displeased the descendants of Elros, and especially the heir under the old law, Soronto, Aldarion's nephew, son of his elder sister Ailinel.[5]

## VII   *Tar-Ancalimë*
She was the only child of Tar-Aldarion, and the first Ruling Queen of Númenor. She was born in the year 873, and she reigned for 205 years, longer than any ruler after Elros; she surrendered the sceptre in 1280, and died in 1285. She long remained unwed; but when pressed by Soronto to resign, in his despite she married in the year 1000 Hallacar son of Hallatan, a descendant of Vardamir.[6] After the birth of her son Anárion there was strife between Ancalimë and Hallacar. She was proud and wilful. After Aldarion's death she neglected all his policies, and gave no further aid to Gil-galad.

## VIII   *Tar-Anárion*
He was the son of Tar-Ancalimë, and he was born in the year 1003. He ruled for 114 years, and surrendered the sceptre in 1394; he died in 1404.

## IX   *Tar-Súrion*
He was the third child of Tar-Anárion; his sisters refused the sceptre.[7] He was born in the year 1174, and ruled for 162 years; he surrendered the sceptre in 1556, and died in 1574.

## X   *Tar-Telperien*
She was the second Ruling Queen of Númenor. She was long-lived (for the women of the Númenóreans had the longer life, or laid down their lives less easily), and she would wed with no man. Therefore after her day the sceptre passed to Minastir; he was the son of Isilmo, the second child of Tar-Súrion.[8] Tar-Telperien was born in the year 1320; she ruled for 175 years, until 1731, and died in that same year.[9]

## XI   *Tar-Minastir*
This name he had because he built a high tower upon the hill of Oromet, nigh to Andúnië and the west shores, and thence would spend great part of his days gazing westward. For the yearning was grown strong in the hearts of the Númenóreans. He loved the Eldar but envied them. He it was who sent a great fleet to the aid of Gil-galad in the first war against Sauron. He was born in the year 1474, and ruled for 138 years; he surrendered the sceptre in 1869, and died in 1873.

## XII   Tar-Ciryatan

He was born in the year 1634, and ruled for 160 years; he surrendered
the sceptre in 2029, and died in 2035. He was a mighty King, but
greedy of wealth; he built a great fleet of royal ships, and his servants
brought back great store of metals and gems, and oppressed the men
of Middle-earth. He scorned the yearnings of his father, and eased
the restlessness of his heart by voyaging, east, and north, and south,
until he took the sceptre. It is said that he constrained his father to
yield to him ere of his free will he would. In this way (it is held)
might the first coming of the Shadow upon the bliss of Númenor be
seen.

## XIII   Tar-Atanamir the Great

He was born in the year 1800, and ruled for 192 years, until 2221,
which was the year of his death. Much is said of this King in the
Annals, such as now survive the Downfall. For he was like his father
proud and greedy of wealth, and the Númenóreans in his service
exacted heavy tribute from the men of the coasts of Middle-earth.
In his time the Shadow fell upon Númenor; and the King, and those
that followed his lore, spoke openly against the ban of the Valar,
and their hearts were turned against the Valar and the Eldar; but
wisdom they still kept, and they feared the Lords of the West, and
did not defy them. Atanamir is called also the Unwilling, for he was
the first of the Kings to refuse to lay down his life, or to renounce
the sceptre; and he lived until death took him perforce in dotage.[10]

## XIV   Tar-Ancalimon

He was born in the year 1986, and ruled for 165 years, until his
death in 2386. In his time the rift became wider between the King's
Men (the larger part) and those who maintained their ancient
friendship with the Eldar. Many of the King's Men began to forsake
the use of the Elven-tongues, and to teach them no longer to their
children. But the royal titles were still given in Quenya, out of ancient
custom rather than love, for fear lest the breaking of the old usage
should bring ill-fortune.

## XV   Tar-Telemmaitë

He was born in the year 2136, and ruled for 140 years, until his
death in 2526. Hereafter the Kings ruled in name from the death of
their father to their own death, though the actual power passed often
to their sons or counsellors; and the days of the descendants of
Elros waned under the Shadow. This King was so called because
of his love of silver, and he bade his servants to seek ever for *mithril*.

XVI   *Tar-Vanimeldë*
She was the third Ruling Queen; she was born in the year 2277, and
ruled for 111 years until her death in 2637. She gave little heed to
ruling, loving rather music and dance; and the power was wielded
by her husband Herucalmo, younger than she, but a descendant of
the same degree from Tar-Atanamir. Herucalmo took the sceptre
upon his wife's death, calling himself Tar-Anducal, and withholding
the rule from his son Alcarin; yet some do not reckon him in the
Line of Kings as seventeenth, and pass to Alcarin. Tar-Anducal was
born in the year 2286, and he died in 2657.

XVII   *Tar-Alcarin*
He was born in the year 2406, and he ruled for 80 years until his
death in 2737, being rightful King for one hundred years.

XVIII   *Tar-Calmacil*
He was born in the year 2516, and he ruled for 88 years until his
death in 2825. This name he took, for in his youth he was a great
captain, and won wide lands along the coasts of Middle-earth. Thus
he kindled the hate of Sauron, who nonetheless withdrew, and built
his power in the East, far from the shores, biding his time. In the
days of Tar-Calmacil the name of the King was first spoken in
Adûnaic; and by the King's Men he was called Ar-Belzagar.

XIX   *Tar-Ardamin*
He was born in the year 2618, and he ruled for 74 years until his
death in 2899. His name in Adûnaic was Ar-Abattârik.[11]

XX   *Ar-Adûnakhôr (Tar-Herunúmen)*
He was born in the year 2709, and he ruled for 63 years until his
death in 2962. He was the first King to take the sceptre with a title
in the Adûnaic tongue; though out of fear (as aforesaid) a name in
Quenya was inscribed in the Scrolls. But these titles were held by the
Faithful to be blasphemous, for they signified 'Lord of the West',
by which title they had been wont to name one of the great Valar
only, Manwë in especial. In this reign the Elven-tongues were no
longer used, nor permitted to be taught, but were maintained in
secret by the Faithful; and the ships from Eressëa came seldom and
secretly to the west shores of Númenor thereafter.

XXI   *Ar-Zimrathôn (Tar-Hostamir)*
He was born in the year 2798, and he ruled for 71 years until his
death in 3033.

XXII   *Ar-Sakalthôr (Tar-Falassion)*
He was born in the year 2876, and he ruled for 69 years until his death in 3102.

XXIII   *Ar-Gimilzôr (Tar-Telemnar)*
He was born in the year 2960, and he ruled for 75 years until his death in 3177. He was the greatest enemy of the Faithful that had yet arisen; and he forbade utterly the use of the Eldarin tongues, and would not permit any of the Eldar to come to the land, and punished those that welcomed them. He revered nothing, and went never to the Hallow of Eru. He was wedded to Inzilbêth, a lady descended from Tar-Calmacil;[12] but she was secretly of the Faithful, for her mother was Lindórië of the House of the Lords of Andúnië, and there was small love between them, and strife between their sons. For Inziladûn[13] the elder was beloved of his mother and of like mind with her; but Gimilkhâd the younger was his father's son, and him Ar-Gimilzôr would fain have appointed his Heir, had the laws allowed. Gimilkhâd was born in the year 3044, and he died in 3243.[14]

XXIV   *Tar-Palantir (Ar-Inziladûn)*
He was born in the year 3035, and he ruled for 78 years until his death in 3255. Tar-Palantir repented of the ways of the Kings before him, and would fain have returned to the friendship of the Eldar and the Lords of the West. This name Inziladûn took, because he was far-sighted both in eye and in mind, and even those who hated him feared his words as those of a true-seer. He also would spend much of his days in Andúnië, since Lindórië his mother's mother was of the kin of the Lords, being sister indeed of Eärendur, the fifteenth Lord and grandfather of Númendil, who was Lord of Andúnië in the days of Tar-Palantir his cousin; and Tar-Palantir would ascend often to the ancient tower of King Minastir, and gaze westward in yearning, hoping to see, maybe, some sail coming from Eressëa. But no ship came ever again out of the West, because of the insolence of the Kings, and because the hearts of the most part of the Númenóreans were still hardened. For Gimilkhâd followed the ways of Ar-Gimilzôr, and became leader of the King's Party, and resisted the will of Tar-Palantir as openly as he dared, and yet more in secret. But for a while the Faithful had peace; and the King went ever at due times to the Hallow upon the Meneltarma, and the White Tree was again given tendance and honour. For Tar-Palantir prophesied, saying that when the Tree died then the line of the Kings also would perish.

Tar-Palantir married late and had no son, and his daughter he named Míriel in the Elven-tongue. But when the King died, she was taken to wife by Pharazôn son of Gimilkhâd (who also was dead) against her will, and against the law of Númenor, since she was the child of his father's brother. And he then seized the sceptre into his own hand, taking the title of Ar-Pharazôn (Tar-Calion); and Míriel was named Ar-Zimraphel.[15]

## XXV  Ar-Pharazôn (Tar-Calion)

The mightiest and last King of Númenor. He was born in the year 3118, and ruled for 64 years, and died in the Downfall in the year 3319, usurping the sceptre of

## Tar-Míriel (Ar-Zimraphel)

She was born in the year 3117, and died in the Downfall.

Of the deeds of Ar-Pharazôn, of his glory and his folly, more is told in the tale of the Downfall of Númenor, which Elendil wrote, and which was preserved in Gondor.[16]

# NOTES

1   There are several references to the greater life-span of the descendants of Elros than that of any others among the Númenóreans, in addition to those in the tale of Aldarion and Erendis. Thus in the *Akallabêth* (*The Silmarillion* p. 261) it is said that all the line of Elros 'had long life even according to the measure of the Númenóreans'; and in an isolated note the difference in longevity is given a precise range: the 'end of vigour' for the descendants of Elros came (before the waning of their life-span set in) about the four hundredth year, or somewhat earlier, whereas for those not of that line it came towards the two hundredth year, or somewhat later. It may be noted that almost all the Kings from Vardamir to Tar-Ancalimon lived to or a little beyond their four hundredth year, and the three who did not died within one or two years of it.

But in the latest writing on this subject (which derives, however, from about the same time as the latest work on the tale of Aldarion and Erendis) the distinction in longevity is greatly diminished. To the Númenórean people as a whole is ascribed a life-span some five times the length of that of other Men (although this is in contradiction to the statement in *The Lord of the Rings* Appendix A (I, i) that the Númenóreans were granted a span 'in the beginning thrice that of lesser Men', a statement made again in the preface to the present text); and the difference of the Line of Elros from others in this respect is less a distinct mark and attribute than a mere tendency to live to a greater age. Though the case of Erendis, and the somewhat shorter lives of the 'Bëorians' of the West, are mentioned, there is no suggestion here, as there is in the tale of Aldarion and Erendis, that the difference in their expectation of life was both very great and also something inherent in their destinies, and recognised to be so.

In this account, only Elros was granted a peculiar longevity, and it is said here that he and his brother Elrond were not differently endowed in the physical potential of life, but that since Elros elected to remain among the kindred of Men he retained the chief characteristic of Men as opposed to the Quendi: the 'seeking elsewhither', as the Eldar called it, the 'weariness' or desire to depart from the world. It is further expounded that the increase in the Númenórean span was brought about by assimilation of their mode of life to that of the Eldar: though they were expressly warned that they had not become Eldar, but remained mortal Men, and had been granted only an extension of the period of their vigour of mind and body. Thus (as the Eldar) they grew at much the same rate as other Men, but when they had achieved 'full-growth' they then aged, or 'wore out', very much more slowly. The first approach of 'world-weariness' was indeed for them a sign that their period of vigour was nearing its end. When it came to an end, if they persisted in living, then decay would proceed, as growth had done, no more slowly than among other Men. Thus a Númenórean would pass quickly, in ten years maybe, from health and vigour of mind to decrepitude and senility. In the earlier generations they did not 'cling to life', but resigned it voluntarily. 'Clinging to life', and so in the end dying perforce and involuntarily, was one of the changes brought about by the Shadow and the rebellion of the Númenóreans; it was also accompanied by a shrinking of their natural life-span.

2   See p. 217, note 26.

3   The figure of 148 (rather than 147) must represent the years of Tar-Amandil's actual rule, and not take the notional year of Vardamir's reign into account.

4   There is no question but that Silmarien was the eldest child of Tar-Elendil; and her birth-date is several times given as Second Age 521, while that of her brother Tar-Meneldur is fixed at 543. In the Tale of Years (Appendix B to *The Lord of the Rings*), however, Silmarien's birth is given in the annal entry 548; a date that goes back to the first drafts of that text. I think it very likely that this should have been revised but escaped notice.

5   This is not in agreement with the account of the earlier and later laws of succession given on pp. 208–9, according to which Soronto only became Ancalimë's heir (if she died childless) by virtue of the new

law, for he was a descendant in the female line. – 'His elder sister' undoubtedly means 'the elder of his two sisters'.

6  See p. 211.

7  See p. 212 and note 28 on p. 217.

8  It is curious that the sceptre passed to Tar-Telperien when Tar-Súrion had a son, Isilmo. It may well be that the succession here depends on the formulation of the new law given in *The Lord of the Rings*, i.e. simple primogeniture irrespective of sex (see p. 208), rather than inheritance by a daughter only if the Ruler had no son.

9  The date 1731 here given for the end of the rule of Tar-Telperien and the accession of Tar-Minastir is strangely at variance with the dating, fixed by many references, of the first war against Sauron; for the great Númenórean fleet sent by Tar-Minastir reached Middle-earth in the year 1700. I cannot in any way account for the discrepancy.

10  In the Tale of Years (Appendix B to *The Lord of the Rings*) occurs the entry: '2251 Tar-Atanamir takes the sceptre. Rebellion and division of the Númenóreans begins.' This is altogether discrepant with the present text, according to which Tar-Atanamir died in 2221. This date 2221 is, however, itself an emendation from 2251; and his death is given elsewhere as 2251. Thus the same year appears in different texts as both the date of his accession and the date of his death; and the whole structure of the chronology shows clearly that the former must be wrong. Moreover, in the *Akallabêth* (*The Silmarillion* p. 266) it is said that it was in the time of Atanamir's son Ancalimon that the people of Númenor became divided. I have little doubt therefore that the entry in the Tale of Years is in error for a correct reading: '2251 Death of Tar-Atanamir. Tar-Ancalimon takes the sceptre. Rebellion and division of the Númenóreans begins.' But if so, it remains strange that the date of Atanamir's death should have been altered in 'The Line of Elros' if it were fixed by an entry in the Tale of Years.

11  In the list of the Kings and Queens of Númenor in Appendix A (I, i) to *The Lord of the Rings* the ruler following Tar-Calmacil (the eighteenth) was Ar-Adûnakhôr (the nineteenth). In the Tale of Years in Appendix B Ar-Adûnakhôr is said to have taken the sceptre in the year 2899; and on this basis Mr Robert Foster in *The Complete Guide to Middle-earth* gives the death-date of Tar-Calmacil as 2899. On the other hand, at a later point in the account of the rulers of Númenor in Appendix A, Ar-Adûnakhôr is called the twentieth king; and in 1964 my father replied to a correspondent who had enquired about this: 'As the genealogy stands he should be called the sixteenth king and nineteenth ruler. Nineteen should possibly be read for twenty; but it is also possible that a name has been left out.' He explained that he could not be certain because at the time of writing this letter his papers on the subject were not available to him.

When editing the *Akallabêth* I changed the actual reading 'And the twentieth king took the sceptre of his fathers, and he ascended the throne in the name of Adûnakhôr' to 'And the nineteenth king ...' (*The Silmarillion* p. 267), and similarly 'four and twenty' to 'three and twenty' (*ibid.* p. 270). At that time I had not observed that in 'The Line of Elros' the ruler following Tar-Calmacil was not Ar-Adûnakhôr but Tar-Ardamin; but it now seems perfectly clear, from the fact alone that Tar-Ardamin's death-date is here given as 2899, that he was omitted in error from the list in *The Lord of the Rings*.

On the other hand, it is a certainty of the tradition (stated in Appendix A, in the *Akallabêth*, and in 'The Line of Elros') that Ar-Adûnakhôr was the first King to take the sceptre in a name of the Adûnaic tongue. On the assumption that Tar-Ardamin dropped out of the list in Appendix A by a mere oversight, it is surprising that the change in the style of the royal names should there be attributed to the first ruler after Tar-Calmacil. It may be that a more complex textual situation underlies the passage than a mere error of omission.

12 In two genealogical tables her father is shown as Gimilzagar, the second son (born in 2630) of Tar-Calmacil, but this is clearly impossible: Inzilbêth must have been descended from Tar-Calmacil at more removes.

13 There is a highly formalised floral design of my father's, similar in style to that shown in *Pictures by J. R. R. Tolkien* (1979) no. 45, bottom right, which bears the title *Inziladûn*, and beneath it is written both in Fëanorian script and transliterated *Númellótë* ['Flower of the West'].

14 According to the *Akallabêth* (*The Silmarillion* p. 269) Gimilkhâd 'died two years before his two hundredth year, which was accounted an early death for one of Elros' line even in its waning'.

15 As noted in Appendix A to *The Lord of the Rings* Míriel should have been the fourth Ruling Queen.

A final discrepancy between 'The Line of Elros' and the Tale of Years arises in the dates of Tar-Palantir. It is said in the *Akallabêth* (p. 269) that 'when Inziladûn acceded to the sceptre, he took again a title in the Elven-tongue as of old, calling himself Tar-Palantir'; and in the Tale of Years occurs the entry: '3175 Repentance of Tar-Palantir. Civil war in Númenor.' It would seem almost certain from these statements that 3175 was the year of his accession; and this is borne out by the fact that in 'The Line of Elros' the death-date of his father Ar-Gimilzôr was originally given as 3175, and only later emended to 3177. As with the death-date of Tar-Atanamir (note 10 above) it is hard to understand why this small change was made, in contradiction to the Tale of Years.

16 The statement that Elendil was the author of the *Akallabêth* is made only here. It is also said, elsewhere, that the story of Aldarion and Erendis, 'one of the few detailed histories preserved from Númenor', owed its preservation to its being of interest to Elendil.

# IV

# THE HISTORY OF
# GALADRIEL AND CELEBORN

## *and of Amroth King of Lórien*

There is no part of the history of Middle-earth more full of problems than the story of Galadriel and Celeborn, and it must be admitted that there are severe inconsistencies 'embedded in the traditions'; or, to look at the matter from another point of view, that the role and importance of Galadriel only emerged slowly, and that her story underwent continual refashionings.

Thus, at the outset, it is certain that the earlier conception was that Galadriel went east over the mountains from Beleriand alone, before the end of the First Age, and met Celeborn in his own land of Lórien; this is explicitly stated in unpublished writing, and the same idea underlies Galadriel's words to Frodo in *The Fellowship of the Ring* II 7, where she says of Celeborn that 'He has dwelt in the West since the days of dawn, and I have dwelt with him years uncounted; for ere the fall of Nargothrond or Gondolin I passed over the mountains, and together through ages of the world we have fought the long defeat.' In all probability Celeborn was in this conception a Nandorin Elf (that is, one of the Teleri who refused to cross the Misty Mountains on the Great Journey from Cuiviénen).

On the other hand, in Appendix B to *The Lord of the Rings* appears a later version of the story; for it is stated there that at the beginning of the Second Age 'In Lindon south of the Lune dwelt for a time Celeborn, kinsman of Thingol; his wife was Galadriel, greatest of Elven women.' And in the notes to *The Road Goes Ever On* (1968, p. 60) it is said that Galadriel 'passed over the Mountains of Eredluin with her husband Celeborn (one of the Sindar) and went to Eregion'.

In *The Silmarillion* there is mention of the meeting of Galadriel and Celeborn in Doriath, and of his kinship with Thingol (p. 115); and of their being among the Eldar who remained in Middle-earth after the end of the First Age (p. 254).

The reasons and motives given for Galadriel's remaining in Middle-earth are various. The passage just cited from *The Road Goes Ever On* says explicitly: 'After the overthrow of Morgoth at the end of the First Age a ban was set upon her return, and she had replied proudly that she had no wish to do so.' There is no such explicit statement in *The Lord of the Rings*; but in a letter written in 1967 my father declared:

The Exiles were allowed to return – save for a few chief actors in the rebellion, of whom at the time of *The Lord of the Rings* only Galadriel remained. At the time of her Lament in Lórien she believed this to be perennial, as long as the Earth endured. Hence she concludes her lament with a wish or prayer that Frodo may as a special grace be granted a purgatorial (but not penal) sojourn in Eressëa, the solitary isle in sight of Aman, though for her the way is closed. Her prayer was granted – but also her personal ban was lifted, in reward for her services against Sauron, and above all for her rejection of the temptation to take the Ring when offered to her. So at the end we see her taking ship.

This statement, very positive in itself, does not however demonstrate that the conception of a ban on Galadriel's return into the West was present when the chapter 'Farewell to Lórien' was composed, many years before; and I am inclined to think that it was not (see p. 234).

In a very late and primarily philological essay, certainly written after the publication of *The Road Goes Ever On*, the story is distinctively different:

Galadriel and her brother Finrod were the children of Finarfin, the second son of Indis. Finarfin was of his mother's kind in mind and body, having the golden hair of the Vanyar, their noble and gentle temper, and their love of the Valar. As well as he could he kept aloof from the strife of his brothers and their estrangement from the Valar, and he often sought peace among the Teleri, whose language he learned. He wedded Eärwen, the daughter of King Olwë of Alqualondë, and his children were thus the kin of King Elu Thingol of Doriath in Beleriand, for he was the brother of Olwë; and this kinship influenced their decision to join in the Exile, and proved of great importance later in Beleriand. Finrod was like his father in his fair face and golden hair, and also in noble and generous heart, though he had the high courage of the Noldor and in his youth their eagerness and unrest; and he had also from his Telerin mother a love of the sea and dreams of far lands that he had never seen. Galadriel was the greatest of the Noldor, except Fëanor maybe, though she was wiser than he, and her wisdom increased with the long years.

Her mother-name was Nerwen ('man-maiden'),[1] and she grew to be tall beyond the measure even of the women of the Noldor; she was strong of body, mind, and will, a match for both the loremasters and the athletes of the Eldar in the days of their youth. Even among the Eldar she was accounted beautiful, and her hair was held a marvel unmatched. It was golden like the hair of her father and of her foremother Indis, but richer and more radiant, for its gold was touched by some memory of the starlike silver of her mother; and the Eldar said that the light of the Two Trees, Laurelin and Telperion, had been snared in her tresses. Many thought that this saying first gave to Fëanor the thought of imprisoning and blending the light of the Trees that later took shape in his hands as the Silmarils. For Fëanor beheld the hair of Galadriel with wonder and delight. He begged three times for a tress, but Galadriel would not give him even one hair. These two kinsfolk, the greatest of the Eldar of Valinor, were unfriends for ever.

Galadriel was born in the bliss of Valinor, but it was not long, in the reckoning of the Blessed Realm, before that was dimmed; and thereafter she had no peace within. For in that testing time amid the strife of the Noldor she was drawn this way and that. She was proud, strong, and selfwilled, as were all the descendants of Finwë save Finarfin; and like her brother Finrod, of all her kin the nearest to her heart, she had dreams of far lands and dominions that might be her own to order as she would without tutelage. Yet deeper still there dwelt in her the noble and generous spirit of the Vanyar, and a reverence for the Valar that she could not forget. From her earliest years she had a marvellous gift of insight into the minds of others, but judged them with mercy and understanding, and she withheld her goodwill from none save only Fëanor. In him she perceived a darkness that she hated and feared, though she did not perceive that the shadow of the same evil had fallen upon the minds of all the Noldor, and upon her own.

So it came to pass that when the light of Valinor failed, for ever as the Noldor thought, she joined the rebellion against the Valar who commanded them to stay; and once she had set foot upon that road of exile she would not relent, but rejected the last message of the Valar, and came under the Doom of Mandos. Even after the merciless assault upon the Teleri and the rape of their ships, though she fought fiercely against Fëanor in defence of her mother's kin, she did not turn back. Her pride was unwilling to return, a defeated suppliant for pardon; but now she burned with desire to follow Fëanor with her anger to whatever lands he might come, and to thwart him in all ways that she could. Pride still moved her when, at the end of the Elder Days after the final overthrow of Morgoth, she refused the pardon of the Valar for all who had fought against him, and remained in Middle-earth. It was not until two long ages more had passed, when at last all that she had desired in her youth came to her hand, the Ring of Power and the dominion of Middle-earth of which she had dreamed, that her wisdom was full grown and she rejected it, and passing the last test departed from Middle-earth for ever.

This last sentence relates closely to the scene in Lothlórien when Frodo offered the One Ring to Galadriel (*The Fellowship of the Ring* II 7): 'And now at last it comes. You will give me the Ring freely! In place of the Dark Lord you will set up a Queen.'
    In *The Silmarillion* it is told (p. 84) that at the time of the rebellion of the Noldor in Valinor Galadriel

was eager to be gone. No oaths she swore, but the words of Fëanor concerning Middle-earth had kindled in her heart, for she longed to see the wide unguarded lands and to rule there a realm at her own will.

There are however in the present account several features of which there is no trace in *The Silmarillion*: the kinship of Finarfin's children with Thingol as a factor influencing their decision to join in Fëanor's rebellion; Galadriel's peculiar dislike and distrust of Fëanor from the beginning, and the effect she had on him; and the fighting at Alqualondë among the Noldor themselves – Angrod asserted to Thingol in Menegroth no more than that the kin of Finarfin were guiltless of the slaying of the Teleri (*The Silmarillion* p. 129). Most notable however in the passage just cited is the explicit statement that Galadriel *refused the pardon of the Valar* at the end of the First Age.
    Later in this essay it is said that though called Nerwen by her mother and Artanis ('noble woman') by her father, the name she chose to be her Sindarin name was Galadriel, 'for it was the most beautiful of her names, and had been given to her by her lover, Teleporno of the Teleri, whom she wedded later in Beleriand'. Teleporno is Celeborn, here given a different history, as discussed further below (p. 233); on the name itself see Appendix E, p. 266.

A wholly different story, adumbrated but never told, of Galadriel's conduct at the time of the rebellion of the Noldor appears in a very late and partly illegible note: the last writing of my father's on the subject of Galadriel and Celeborn, and probably the last on Middle-earth and Valinor, set down in the last month of his life. In this he emphasized the commanding stature of Galadriel already in Valinor, the equal if unlike in endowments of Fëanor; and it is said here that so far from joining in

Fëanor's revolt she was in every way opposed to him. She did indeed wish to depart from Valinor and to go into the wide world of Middle-earth for the exercise of her talents; for 'being brilliant in mind and swift in action she had early absorbed all of what she was capable of the teaching which the Valar thought fit to give the Eldar', and she felt confined in the tutelage of Aman. This desire of Galadriel's was, it seems, known to Manwë, and he had not forbidden her; but nor had she been given formal leave to depart. Pondering what she might do Galadriel's thoughts turned to the ships of the Teleri, and she went for a while to dwell with her mother's kindred in Alqualondë. There she met Celeborn, who is here again a Telerin prince, the grandson of Olwë of Alqualondë and thus her close kinsman. Together they planned to build a ship and sail in it to Middle-earth; and they were about to seek leave from the Valar for their venture when Melkor fled from Valmar and returning with Ungoliant destroyed the light of the Trees. In Fëanor's revolt that followed the Darkening of Valinor Galadriel had no part: indeed she with Celeborn fought heroically in defence of Alqualondë against the assault of the Noldor, and Celeborn's ship was saved from them. Galadriel, despairing now of Valinor and horrified by the violence and cruelty of Fëanor, set sail into the darkness without waiting for Manwë's leave, which would undoubtedly have been withheld in that hour, however legitimate her desire in itself. It was thus that she came under the ban set upon all departure, and Valinor was shut against her return. But together with Celeborn she reached Middle-earth somewhat sooner than Fëanor, and sailed into the haven where Círdan was lord. There they were welcomed with joy, as being of the kin of Elwë (Thingol). In the years after they did not join in the war against Angband, which they judged to be hopeless under the ban of the Valar and without their aid; and their counsel was to withdraw from Beleriand and to build up a power to the eastward (whence they feared that Morgoth would draw reinforcement), befriending and teaching the Dark Elves and Men of those regions. But such a policy having no hope of acceptance among the Elves of Beleriand, Galadriel and Celeborn departed over Ered Lindon before the end of the First Age; and when they received the permission of the Valar to return into the West they rejected it.

This story, withdrawing Galadriel from all association with the rebellion of Fëanor, even to the extent of giving her a separate departure (with Celeborn) from Aman, is profoundly at variance with all that is said elsewhere. It arose from 'philosophical' (rather than 'historical') considerations, concerning the precise nature of Galadriel's disobedience in Valinor on the one hand, and her status and power in Middle-earth on the other. That it would have entailed a good deal of alteration in the narrative of *The Silmarillion* is evident; but that my father doubtless intended to do. It may be noted here that Galadriel did not appear in the original story of the rebellion and flight of the Noldor, which existed long before she did; and also, of course, that after her entry into the stories of the First Age her actions could still be transformed radically, since *The Silmarillion* had not been published. The book as published was however formed from completed narratives, and I could not take into account merely projected revisions.

On the other hand, the making of Celeborn into a Telerin Elf of Aman contradicts not only statements in *The Silmarillion*, but also those cited already (p. 228) from *The Road Goes Ever On* and Appendix B to *The Lord of the Rings*, where Celeborn is a Sindarin Elf of Beleriand. As to why this fundamental alteration in his history was to be made, it might be answered that it arose from the new narrative element of Galadriel's departure from Aman *separately* from the hosts of the rebel Noldor; but Celeborn is already transformed into a Telerin Elf in the text cited on p. 231, where Galadriel did take part in Fëanor's revolt and march from Valinor, and where there is no indication of how Celeborn came to Middle-earth.

The earlier story (apart from the question of the ban and the pardon), to which the statements in *The Silmarillion*, *The Road Goes Ever On*, and Appendix B to *The Lord of the Rings* refer, is fairly clear: Galadriel, coming to Middle-earth as one of the leaders of the second host of the Noldor, met Celeborn in Doriath, and was later wedded to him; he was the grandson of Thingol's brother Elmo – a shadowy figure about whom nothing is told save that he was the younger brother of Elwë (Thingol) and Olwë, and was 'beloved of Elwë with whom he remained'. (Elmo's son was named Galadhon, and his sons were Celeborn and Galathil; Galathil was the father of Nimloth, who wedded Dior Thingol's Heir and was the mother of Elwing. By this genealogy Celeborn was a kinsman of Galadriel, the grand-daughter of Olwë of Alqualondë, but not so close as by that in which he became Olwë's grandson.) It is a natural assumption that Celeborn and Galadriel were present at the ruin of Doriath (it is said in one place that Celeborn 'escaped the sack of Doriath'), and perhaps aided the escape of Elwing to the Havens of Sirion with the Silmaril – but this is nowhere stated. Celeborn is mentioned in Appendix B to *The Lord of the Rings* as dwelling for a time in Lindon south of the Lune;[2] but early in the Second Age they passed over the Mountains into Eriador. Their subsequent history, in the same phase (so to call it) of my father's writing, is told in the short narrative that follows here.

## Concerning Galadriel and Celeborn

The text bearing this title is a short and hasty outline, very roughly composed, which is nonetheless almost the sole narrative source for the events in the West of Middle-earth up to the defeat and expulsion of Sauron from Eriador in the year 1701 of the Second Age. Other than this there is little beyond the brief and infrequent entries in the Tale of Years, and the much more generalised and selective account in *Of the Rings of Power*

*and the Third Age* (published in *The Silmarillion*). It is certain that this
present text was composed after the publication of *The Lord of the Rings*,
both from there being a reference to the book and from the fact that
Galadriel is called the daughter of Finarfin and the sister of Finrod
Felagund (for these are the later names of those princes, introduced in
the revised edition: see p. 255, note 20). The text is much emended,
and it is not always possible to see what belongs to the time of composition
of the manuscript and what is indefinitely later. This is the case with
those references to Amroth that make him the son of Galadriel and Celeborn; but whenever these references were inserted, I think it is virtually
certain that this was a new construction, later than the writing of *The Lord
of the Rings*. Had he been supposed to be their son when it was written,
the fact would surely have been mentioned.

It is very notable that not only is there no mention in this text of a ban
on Galadriel's return into the West, but it even seems from a passage at
the beginning of the account that no such idea was present; while later in
the narrative Galadriel's remaining in Middle-earth after the defeat of
Sauron in Eriador is ascribed to her sense that it was her duty not to
depart while he was still finally unconquered. This is a chief support of
the (hesitant) view expressed above (p. 229) that the story of the ban was
later than the writing of *The Lord of the Rings*; cf. also a passage in the
story of the Elessar, given on p. 249.

What follows here is retold from this text, with some interspersed
comments, indicated by square brackets.

Galadriel was the daughter of Finarfin, and sister of Finrod Felagund.
She was welcome in Doriath, because her mother Eärwen, daughter of
Olwë, was Telerin and the niece of Thingol, and because the people of
Finarfin had had no part in the Kinslaying of Alqualondë; and she became
a friend of Melian. In Doriath she met Celeborn, grandson of Elmo the
brother of Thingol. For love of Celeborn, who would not leave Middle-
earth (and probably with some pride of her own, for she had been one of
those eager to adventure there), she did not go West at the Downfall of
Melkor, but crossed Ered Lindon with Celeborn and came into Eriador.
When they entered that region there were many Noldor in their following,
together with Grey-elves and Green-elves; and for a while they dwelt in
the country about Lake Nenuial (Evendim, north of the Shire). Celeborn
and Galadriel came to be regarded as Lord and Lady of the Eldar in
Eriador, including the wandering companies of Nandorin origin who had
never passed west over Ered Lindon and come down into Ossiriand [see
*The Silmarillion* p. 94]. During their sojourn near Nenuial was born, at
some time between the years 350 and 400, their son Amroth. [The time
and place of Celebrían's birth, whether here or later in Eregion, or even
later in Lórien, is not made definite.]

But eventually Galadriel became aware that Sauron again, as in the
ancient days of the captivity of Melkor [see *The Silmarillion* p. 51], had

been left behind. Or rather, since Sauron had as yet no single name, and his operations had not been perceived to proceed from a single evil spirit, prime servant of Melkor, she perceived that there was an evil controlling purpose abroad in the world, and that it seemed to proceed from a source further to the East, beyond Eriador and the Misty Mountains.

Celeborn and Galadriel therefore went eastwards, about the year 700 of the Second Age, and established the (primarily but by no means solely) Noldorin realm of Eregion. It may be that Galadriel chose it because she knew of the Dwarves of Khazad-dûm (Moria). There were and always remained some Dwarves on the eastern side of Ered Lindon,[3] where the very ancient mansions of Nogrod and Belegost had been – not far from Nenuial; but they had transferred most of their strength to Khazad-dûm. Celeborn had no liking for Dwarves of any race (as he showed to Gimli in Lothlórien), and never forgave them for their part in the destruction of Doriath; but it was only the host of Nogrod that took part in that assault, and it was destroyed in the battle of Sarn Athrad [*The Silmarillion* pp. 233–5]. The Dwarves of Belegost were filled with dismay at the calamity and fear for its outcome, and this hastened their departure eastwards to Khazad-dûm.[4] Thus the Dwarves of Moria may be presumed to have been innocent of the ruin of Doriath and not hostile to the Elves. In any case, Galadriel was more far-sighted in this than Celeborn; and she perceived from the beginning that Middle-earth could not be saved from 'the residue of evil' that Morgoth had left behind him save by a union of all the peoples who were in their way and in their measure opposed to him. She looked upon the Dwarves also with the eye of a commander, seeing in them the finest warriors to pit against the Orcs. Moreover Galadriel was a Noldo, and she had a natural sympathy with their minds and their passionate love of crafts of hand, a sympathy much greater than that found among many of the Eldar: the Dwarves were 'the Children of Aulë', and Galadriel, like others of the Noldor, had been a pupil of Aulë and Yavanna in Valinor.

Galadriel and Celeborn had in their company a Noldorin craftsman named Celebrimbor. [He is here said to have been one of the survivors of Gondolin, who had been among Turgon's greatest artificers; but the text is emended to the later story that made him a descendant of Fëanor, as is mentioned in Appendix B to *The Lord of the Rings* (in the revised edition only), and more fully detailed in *The Silmarillion* (pp. 176, 276), where he is said to have been the son of Curufin, the fifth son of Fëanor, who was estranged from his father and remained in Nargothrond when Celegorm and Curufin were driven forth.] Celebrimbor had 'an almost "dwarvish" obsession with crafts'; and he soon became the chief artificer of Eregion, entering into a close relationship with the Dwarves of Khazad-dûm, among whom his greatest friend was Narvi. [In the inscription on the West-gate of Moria Gandalf read the words: *Im Narvi hain echant: Celebrimbor o Eregion teithant i thiw hin:* 'I, Narvi, made them. Celebrimbor of Hollin drew these signs.' *The Fellowship of the Ring* II 4.] Both Elves

and Dwarves had great profit from this association: so that Eregion became
far stronger, and Khazad-dûm far more beautiful, than either would have
done alone.

[This account of the origin of Eregion agrees with what is told in *Of
the Rings of Power* (*The Silmarillion* p. 286), but neither there nor in the
brief references in Appendix B to *The Lord of the Rings* is there any
mention of the presence of Galadriel and Celeborn; indeed in the latter
(again, in the revised edition only) Celebrimbor is called the Lord of
Eregion.]

The building of the chief city of Eregion, Ost-in-Edhil, was begun in
about the year 750 of the Second Age [the date that is given in the Tale
of Years for the founding of Eregion by the Noldor]. News of these things
came to the ears of Sauron, and increased the fears that he felt concerning
the coming of the Númenóreans to Lindon and the coasts further south,
and their friendship with Gil-galad; and he heard tell also of Aldarion,
son of Tar-Meneldur the King of Númenor, now become a great ship-
builder who brought his vessels to haven far down into the Harad. Sauron
therefore left Eriador alone for a while, and he chose the land of Mordor,
as it was afterwards called, for a stronghold as a counter to the threat of
the Númenórean landings [this is dated c. 1000 in the Tale of Years].
When he felt himself to be secure he sent emissaries to Eriador, and finally,
in about the year 1200 of the Second Age, came himself, wearing the
fairest form that he could contrive.

But in the meantime the power of Galadriel and Celeborn had grown,
and Galadriel, assisted in this by her friendship with the Dwarves of
Moria, had come into contact with the Nandorin realm of Lórinand on
the other side of the Misty Mountains.[5] This was peopled by those Elves
who forsook the Great Journey of the Eldar from Cuiviénen and settled
in the woods of the Vale of Anduin [*The Silmarillion* p. 94]; and it extended into the forests on both sides of the Great River, including the
region where afterwards was Dol Guldur. These Elves had no princes or
rulers, and led their lives free of care while all Morgoth's power was
concentrated in the North-west of Middle-earth;[6] 'but many Sindar and
Noldor came to dwell among them, and their "Sindarizing" under the
impact of Beleriandic culture began'. [It is not made clear when this
movement into Lórinand took place; it may be that they came from
Eregion by way of Khazad-dûm and under the auspices of Galadriel.]
Galadriel, striving to counteract the machinations of Sauron, was successful
in Lórinand; while in Lindon Gil-galad shut out Sauron's emissaries and
even Sauron himself [as is more fully reported in *Of the Rings of Power*
(*The Silmarillion* p. 287)]. But Sauron had better fortune with the Noldor
of Eregion and especially with Celebrimbor, who desired in his heart to
rival the skill and fame of Fëanor. [The cozening of the smiths of Eregion
by Sauron, and his giving himself the name Annatar, Lord of Gifts, is
told in *Of the Rings of Power*; but there is there no mention of Galadriel.]

In Eregion Sauron posed as an emissary of the Valar, sent by them to

Middle-earth ('thus anticipating the Istari') or ordered by them to remain there to give aid to the Elves. He perceived at once that Galadriel would be his chief adversary and obstacle, and he endeavoured therefore to placate her, bearing her scorn with outward patience and courtesy. [No explanation is offered in this rapid outline of why Galadriel scorned Sauron, unless she saw through his disguise, or of why, if she did perceive his true nature, she permitted him to remain in Eregion.][7] Sauron used all his arts upon Celebrimbor and his fellow-smiths, who had formed a society or brotherhood, very powerful in Eregion, the Gwaith-i-Mírdain; but he worked in secret, unknown to Galadriel and Celeborn. Before long Sauron had the Gwaith-i-Mírdain under his influence, for at first they had great profit from his instruction in secret matters of their craft.[8] So great became his hold on the Mírdain that at length he persuaded them to revolt against Galadriel and Celeborn and to seize power in Eregion; and that was at some time between 1350 and 1400 of the Second Age. Galadriel thereupon left Eregion and passed through Khazad-dûm to Lórinand, taking with her Amroth and Celebrían; but Celeborn would not enter the mansions of the Dwarves, and he remained behind in Eregion, disregarded by Celebrimbor. In Lórinand Galadriel took up rule, and defence against Sauron.

Sauron himself departed from Eregion about the year 1500, after the Mírdain had begun the making of the Rings of Power. Now Celebrimbor was not corrupted in heart or faith, but had accepted Sauron as what he posed to be; and when at length he discovered the existence of the One Ring he revolted against Sauron, and went to Lórinand to take counsel once more with Galadriel. They should have destroyed all the Rings of Power at this time, 'but they failed to find the strength'. Galadriel counselled him that the Three Rings of the Elves should be hidden, never used, and dispersed, far from Eregion where Sauron believed them to be. It was at that time that she received Nenya, the White Ring, from Celebrimbor, and by its power the realm of Lórinand was strengthened and made beautiful; but its power upon her was great also and unforeseen, for it increased her latent desire for the Sea and for return into the West, so that her joy in Middle-earth was diminished.[9] Celebrimbor followed her counsel that the Ring of Air and the Ring of Fire should be sent out of Eregion; and he entrusted them to Gil-galad in Lindon. (It is said here that at this time Gil-galad gave Narya, the Red Ring, to Círdan Lord of the Havens, but later in the narrative there is a marginal note that he kept it himself until he set out for the War of the Last Alliance.)

When Sauron learned of the repentance and revolt of Celebrimbor his disguise fell and his wrath was revealed; and gathering a great force he moved over Calenardhon (Rohan) to the invasion of Eriador in the year 1695. When news of this reached Gil-galad he sent out a force under Elrond Half-elven; but Elrond had far to go, and Sauron turned north and made at once for Eregion. The scouts and vanguard of Sauron's host were already approaching when Celeborn made a sortie and drove them

back; but though he was able to join his force to that of Elrond they could
not return to Eregion, for Sauron's host was far greater than theirs, great
enough both to hold them off and closely to invest Eregion. At last the
attackers broke into Eregion with ruin and devastation, and captured the
chief object of Sauron's assault, the House of the Mírdain, where were
their smithies and their treasures. Celebrimbor, desperate, himself withstood Sauron on the steps of the great door of the Mírdain; but he was
grappled and taken captive, and the House was ransacked. There Sauron
took the Nine Rings and other lesser works of the Mírdain; but the Seven
and the Three he could not find. Then Celebrimbor was put to torment,
and Sauron learned from him where the Seven were bestowed. This
Celebrimbor revealed, because neither the Seven nor the Nine did he
value as he valued the Three; the Seven and the Nine were made with
Sauron's aid, whereas the Three were made by Celebrimbor alone, with
a different power and purpose. [It is not actually said here that Sauron at
this time took possession of the Seven Rings, though the implication
seems clear that he did so. In Appendix A (III) to *The Lord of the Rings*
it is said that there was a belief among the Dwarves of Durin's Folk that
the Ring of Durin III, King of Khazad-dûm, was given to him by the
Elven-smiths themselves, and not by Sauron; but nothing is said in the
present text about the way in which the Seven Rings came into the possession of the Dwarves.] Concerning the Three Rings Sauron could learn
nothing from Celebrimbor; and he had him put to death. But he guessed
the truth, that the Three had been committed to Elvish guardians: and
that must mean to Galadriel and Gil-galad.

In black anger he turned back to battle; and bearing as a banner
Celebrimbor's body hung upon a pole, shot through with Orc-arrows, he
turned upon the forces of Elrond. Elrond had gathered such few of the
Elves of Eregion as had escaped, but he had no force to withstand the
onset. He would indeed have been overwhelmed had not Sauron's host
been attacked in the rear; for Durin sent out a force of Dwarves from
Khazad-dûm, and with them came Elves of Lórinand led by Amroth.
Elrond was able to extricate himself, but he was forced away northwards,
and it was at that time [in the year 1697, according to the Tale of Years]
that he established a refuge and stronghold at Imladris (Rivendell).
Sauron withdrew the pursuit of Elrond and turned upon the Dwarves and
the Elves of Lórinand, whom he drove back; but the Gates of Moria
were shut, and he could not enter. Ever afterwards Moria had Sauron's
hate, and all Orcs were commanded to harry Dwarves whenever they
might.

But now Sauron attempted to gain the mastery of Eriador: Lórinand
could wait. But as he ravaged the lands, slaying or drawing off all the
small groups of Men and hunting the remaining Elves, many fled to
swell Elrond's host to the northward. Now Sauron's immediate purpose
was to take Lindon, where he believed that he had most chance of seizing
one, or more, of the Three Rings; and he called in therefore his scattered

forces and marched west towards the land of Gil-galad, ravaging as he went. But his force was weakened by the necessity of leaving a strong detachment to contain Elrond and prevent him coming down upon his rear.

Now for long years the Númenóreans had brought in their ships to the Grey Havens, and there they were welcome. As soon as Gil-galad began to fear that Sauron would come with open war into Eriador he sent messages to Númenor; and on the shores of Lindon the Númenóreans began to build up a force and supplies for war. In 1695, when Sauron invaded Eriador, Gil-galad called on Númenor for aid. Then Tar-Minastir the King sent out a great navy; but it was delayed, and did not reach the coasts of Middle-earth until the year 1700. By that time Sauron had mastered all Eriador, save only besieged Imladris, and had reached the line of the River Lhûn. He had summoned more forces, which were approaching from the south-east, and were indeed in Enedwaith at the Crossing of Tharbad, which was only lightly held. Gil-galad and the Númenóreans were holding the Lhûn in desperate defence of the Grey Havens, when in the very nick of time the great armament of Tar-Minastir came in; and Sauron's host was heavily defeated and driven back. The Númenórean admiral Ciryatur sent part of his ships to make a landing further to the south.

Sauron was driven away south-east after great slaughter at Sarn Ford (the crossing of the Baranduin); and though strengthened by his force at Tharbad he suddenly found a host of the Númenóreans again in his rear, for Ciryatur had put a strong force ashore at the mouth of the Gwathló (Greyflood), 'where there was a small Númenórean harbour'. [This was Vinyalondë of Tar-Aldarion, afterwards called Lond Daer; see Appendix D, p. 261.] In the Battle of the Gwathló Sauron was routed utterly and he himself only narrowly escaped. His small remaining force was assailed in the east of Calenardhon, and he with no more than a bodyguard fled to the region afterwards called Dagorlad (Battle Plain), whence broken and humiliated he returned to Mordor, and vowed vengeance upon Númenor. The army that was besieging Imladris was caught between Elrond and Gil-galad, and utterly destroyed. Eriador was cleared of the enemy, but lay largely in ruins.

At this time the first Council was held,[10] and it was there determined that an Elvish stronghold in the east of Eriador should be maintained at Imladris rather than in Eregion. At that time also Gil-galad gave Vilya, the Blue Ring, to Elrond, and appointed him to be his vice-regent in Eriador; but the Red Ring he kept, until he gave it to Círdan when he set out from Lindon in the days of the Last Alliance.[11] For many years the Westlands had peace, and time in which to heal their wounds; but the Númenóreans had tasted power in Middle-earth, and from that time forward they began to make permanent settlements on the western coasts [dated 'c. 1800' in the Tale of Years], becoming too powerful for Sauron to attempt to move west out of Mordor for a long time.

In its concluding passage the narrative returns to Galadriel, telling that the sea-longing grew so strong in her that (though she deemed it her duty to remain in Middle-earth while Sauron was still unconquered) she determined to leave Lórinand and to dwell near the sea. She committed Lórinand to Amroth, and passing again through Moria with Celebrían she came to Imladris, seeking Celeborn. There (it seems) she found him, and there they dwelt together for a long time; and it was then that Elrond first saw Celebrían, and loved her, though he said nothing of it. It was while Galadriel was in Imladris that the Council referred to above was held. But at some later time [there is no indication of the date] Galadriel and Celeborn together with Celebrían departed from Imladris and went to the little-inhabited lands between the mouth of the Gwathló and Ethir Anduin. There they dwelt in Belfalas, at the place that was afterwards called Dol Amroth; there Amroth their son at times visited them, and their company was swelled by Nandorin Elves from Lórinand. It was not until far on in the Third Age, when Amroth was lost and Lórinand was in peril, that Galadriel returned there, in the year 1981. Here the text 'Concerning Galadriel and Celeborn' comes to an end.

---

It may be noted here that the absence of any indication to the contrary in *The Lord of the Rings* had led commentators to the natural assumption that Galadriel and Celeborn passed the latter half of the Second Age and all the Third in Lothlórien; but this was not so, though their story as outlined in 'Concerning Galadriel and Celeborn' was greatly modified afterwards, as will be shown below.

### Amroth and Nimrodel

I have said earlier (p. 234) that if Amroth were indeed thought of as the son of Galadriel and Celeborn when *The Lord of the Rings* was written, so important a connection could hardly have escaped mention. But whether he was or not, this view of his parentage was later rejected. I give next a short tale (dating from 1969 or later) entitled 'Part of the Legend of Amroth and Nimrodel recounted in brief'.

Amroth was King of Lórien, after his father Amdír was slain in the Battle of Dagorlad [in the year 3434 of the Second Age]. His land had peace for many years after the defeat of Sauron. Though Sindarin in descent he lived after the manner of the Silvan Elves and housed in the tall trees of a great green mound, ever after called Cerin Amroth. This he did because of his love for Nimrodel. For long years he had loved her, and taken no wife, since she would not wed with him. She loved him indeed, for he was beautiful even for one of the Eldar, and valiant and wise; but she was of the Silvan Elves, and regretted the incoming of the Elves from the West, who (as she said) brought wars and destroyed the peace of old. She would speak only the Silvan tongue, even after it had fallen into disuse among the folk of Lórien;[12] and she dwelt alone beside the falls of the river Nimrodel to which she gave her name. But when the terror came out of Moria and the Dwarves were driven out, and in their stead Orcs crept in, she fled distraught alone south into empty lands [in the year 1981 of the Third Age]. Amroth followed her, and at last he found her under the eaves of Fangorn, which in those days drew much nearer to Lórien.[13] She dared not enter the wood, for the trees, she said, menaced her, and some moved to bar her way.

There Amroth and Nimrodel held a long debate; and at the last they plighted their troth. 'To this I will be true,' she said, 'and we shall be wedded when you bring me to a land of peace.' Amroth vowed that for her sake he would leave his people, even in their time of need, and with her seek for such a land. 'But there is none now in Middle-earth,' he said, 'and will not be for the Elven-folk ever again. We must seek for a passage over the Great Sea to the ancient West.' Then he told her of the haven in the south, where many of his own people had come long ago. 'They are now diminished, for most have set sail into the West; but the remnant of them still build ships and offer passage to any of their kin that come to them, weary of Middle-earth. It is said that the grace that the Valar gave to us to pass over the Sea is granted also now to any of those who made the Great Journey, even if they did not come in ages past to the shores and have not yet beheld the Blessed Land.'

There is not here the place to tell of their journey into the land of Gondor. It was in the days of King Eärnil the Second, the last but one of the Kings of the Southern Realm, and his lands were troubled. [Eärnil II reigned in Gondor from 1945 to 2043.] Elsewhere it is told [but not in any extant writing] how they became separated, and how Amroth after seeking her in vain went to the Elf-haven and found that only a few still lingered there. Less than a ship-load; and they had only one seaworthy ship. In this they were now preparing to depart, and to leave Middle-earth. They welcomed Amroth, being glad to strengthen their small company; but they were unwilling to await Nimrodel, whose coming seemed to them now beyond hope. 'If she came through the settled lands of Gondor,' they said, 'she would not be molested,

and might receive help; for the Men of Gondor are good, and
they are ruled by descendants of the Elf-friends of old who can
still speak our tongue, after a fashion; but in the mountains are
many unfriendly Men and evil things.'

The year was waning to autumn, and before long great winds
were to be expected, hostile and dangerous, even to Elven-ships
while they were still near to Middle-earth. But so great was the
grief of Amroth that nonetheless they stayed their going for many
weeks; and they lived on the ship, for their houses on the shore
were stripped and empty. Then in the autumn there came a great
night of storm, one of the fiercest in the annals of Gondor. It
came from the cold Northern Waste, and roared down through
Eriador into the lands of Gondor, doing great havoc; the White
Mountains were no shield against it, and many of the ships of Men
were swept out into the Bay of Belfalas and lost. The light Elven-
ship was torn from its moorings and driven into the wild waters
towards the coasts of Umbar. No tidings of it were ever heard in
Middle-earth; but the Elven-ships made for this journey did not
founder, and doubtless it left the Circles of the World and came
at last to Eressëa. But it did not bring Amroth thither. The storm
fell upon the coasts of Gondor just as dawn was peering through
the flying clouds; but when Amroth woke the ship was already far
from land. Crying aloud in despair *Nimrodel!* he leapt into the sea
and swam towards the fading shore. The mariners with their
Elvish sight for a long time could see him battling with the waves,
until the rising sun gleamed through the clouds and far off lit his
bright hair like a spark of gold. No eyes of Elves or Men ever saw
him again in Middle-earth. Of what befell Nimrodel nothing is
said here, though there were many legends concerning her fate.

The foregoing narrative was actually composed as an offshoot from an
etymological discussion of the names of certain rivers in Middle-earth,
in this case the Gilrain, a river of Lebennin in Gondor that flowed into
the Bay of Belfalas west of Ethir Anduin, and another facet of the legend
of Nimrodel emerges from the discussion of the element *rain*. This was
probably derived from the stem *ran-* 'wander, stray, go on uncertain
course' (as in *Mithrandir*, and in the name *Rána* of the Moon).

This would not seem suitable to any of the rivers of Gondor;
but the names of rivers may often apply only to part of their
course, to their source, or to their lower reaches, or to other
features that struck explorers who named them. In this case,
however, the fragments of the legend of Amroth and Nimrodel

offer an explanation. The Gilrain came swiftly down from the
mountains as did the other rivers of that region; but as it reached
the end of the outlier of Ered Nimrais that separated it from the
Celos [see the map accompanying Volume III of *The Lord of the
Rings*] it ran into a wide shallow depression. In this it wandered
for a while, and formed a small mere at the southern end before
it cut through a ridge and went on swiftly again to join the Serni.
When Nimrodel fled from Lórien it is said that seeking for the
sea she became lost in the White Mountains, until at last (by
what road or pass is not told) she came to a river that reminded
her of her own stream in Lórien. Her heart was lightened, and
she sat by a mere, seeing the stars reflected in its dim waters, and
listening to the waterfalls by which the river went again on its
journey down to the sea. There she fell into a deep sleep of weariness, and so long she slept that she did not come down into
Belfalas until Amroth's ship had been blown out to sea, and he
was lost trying to swim back to Belfalas. This legend was well
known in the Dor-en-Ernil (the Land of the Prince),[14] and no
doubt the name was given in memory of it.

The essay continues with a brief explanation of how Amroth as King of
Lórien related to the rule there of Celeborn and Galadriel:

The people of Lórien were even then [i.e. at the time of the loss
of Amroth] much as they were at the end of the Third Age:
Silvan Elves in origin, but ruled by princes of Sindarin descent
(as was the realm of Thranduil in the northern parts of Mirkwood;
though whether Thranduil and Amroth were akin is not now
known.)[15] They had however been much mingled with Noldor
(of Sindarin speech), who passed through Moria after the destruction of Eregion by Sauron in the year 1697 of the Second Age.
At that time Elrond went westward [*sic*; probably meaning simply
that he did not cross the Misty Mountains] and established the
refuge of Imladris; but Celeborn went at first to Lórien and
fortified it against any further attempts of Sauron to cross the
Anduin. When however Sauron withdrew to Mordor, and was
(as reported) wholly concerned with conquests in the East,
Celeborn rejoined Galadriel in Lindon.

Lórien had then long years of peace and obscurity under the
rule of its own king Amdír, until the Downfall of Númenor and
the sudden return of Sauron to Middle-earth. Amdír obeyed the
summons of Gil-galad and brought as large a force as he could
muster to the Last Alliance, but he was slain in the Battle of

Dagorlad and most of his company with him. Amroth, his son, became king.

This account is of course greatly at variance with that contained in 'Concerning Galadriel and Celeborn'. Amroth is no longer the son of Galadriel and Celeborn, but of Amdír, a prince of Sindarin origin. The older story of the relations of Galadriel and Celeborn with Eregion and Lórien seems to have been modified in many important respects, but how much of it would have been retained in any fully written narrative cannot be said. Celeborn's association with Lórien is now placed much further back (for in 'Concerning Galadriel and Celeborn' he never went to Lórien at all during the Second Age); and we learn here that many Noldorin Elves passed through Moria to Lórien *after* the destruction of Eregion. In the earlier account there is no suggestion of this, and the movement of 'Beleriandic' Elves into Lórien took place under peaceful conditions many years before (p. 236). The implication of the extract just given is that after Eregion's fall Celeborn led this migration to Lórien, while Galadriel joined Gil-galad in Lindon; but elsewhere, in a writing contemporary with this, it is said explicitly that they both at that time 'passed through Moria with a considerable following of Noldorin exiles and dwelt for many years in Lórien'. It is neither asserted nor denied in these late writings that Galadriel (or Celeborn) had relations with Lórien before 1697, and there are no other references outside 'Concerning Galadriel and Celeborn' to Celebrimbor's revolt (at some time between 1350 and 1400) against their rule in Eregion, nor to Galadriel's departure at that time to Lórien and her taking up rule there, while Celeborn remained behind in Eregion. It is not made clear in the late accounts where Galadriel and Celeborn passed the long years of the Second Age after the defeat of Sauron in Eriador; there are at any rate no further mentions of their agelong sojourn in Belfalas (p. 240).

The discussion of Amroth continues:

But during the Third Age Galadriel became filled with foreboding, and with Celeborn she journeyed to Lórien and stayed there long with Amroth, being especially concerned to learn all news and rumours of the growing shadow in Mirkwood and the dark stronghold in Dol Guldur. But his people were content with Amroth; he was valiant and wise, and his little kingdom was yet prosperous and beautiful. Therefore after long journeys of enquiry in Rhovanion, from Gondor and the borders of Mordor to Thranduil in the north, Celeborn and Galadriel passed over the mountains to Imladris, and there dwelt for many years; for Elrond was their kinsman, since he had early in the Third Age [in the year 109, according to the Tale of Years] wedded their daughter Celebrían.

After the disaster in Moria [in the year 1980] and the sorrows of Lórien, which was now left without a ruler (for Amroth was drowned in the sea in the Bay of Belfalas and left no heir), Celeborn and Galadriel returned to Lórien, and were welcomed by the people. There they dwelt while the Third Age lasted, but they took no title of King or Queen; for they said that they were only guardians of this small but fair realm, the last eastward outpost of the Elves.

Elsewhere there is one other reference to their movements during those years:

To Lórien Celeborn and Galadriel returned twice before the Last Alliance and the end of the Second Age; and in the Third Age, when the shadow of Sauron's recovery arose, they dwelt there again for a long time. In her wisdom Galadriel saw that Lórien would be a stronghold and point of power to prevent the Shadow from crossing the Anduin in the war that must inevitably come before it was again defeated (if that were possible); but that it needed a rule of greater strength and wisdom than the Silvan folk possessed. Nevertheless, it was not until the disaster in Moria, when by means beyond the foresight of Galadriel Sauron's power actually crossed the Anduin and Lórien was in great peril, its king lost, its people fleeing and likely to leave it deserted to be occupied by Orcs, that Galadriel and Celeborn took up their permanent abode in Lórien, and its government. But they took no title of King or Queen, and were the guardians that in the event brought it unviolated through the War of the Ring.

In another etymological discussion of the same period the name Amroth is explained as being a nickname derived from his living in a high *talan* or *flet*, the wooden platforms built high up in the trees of Lothlórien in which the Galadhrim dwelt (see *The Fellowship of the Ring* II 6): it meant 'upclimber, high climber'.[16] It is said here that the custom of dwelling in trees was not a habit of the Silvan Elves in general, but was developed in Lórien by the nature and situation of the land: a flat land with no good stone, except what might be quarried in the mountains westward and brought with difficulty down the Silverlode. Its chief wealth was in its trees, a remnant of the great forests of the Elder Days. But the dwelling in trees was not universal even in Lórien, and the *telain* or *flets* were in origin either refuges to be used in the event of attack, or most often (especially those high up in great trees) outlook posts from which the land and its borders could be surveyed by Elvish eyes: for Lórien after the end of the first millennium of the Third Age became a land of uneasy vigilance, and Amroth must have dwelt in growing disquiet ever since Dol Guldur was established in Mirkwood.

Such an outlook post, used by the wardens of the north marches, was the *flet* in which Frodo spent the night. The abode of Celeborn in Caras Galadhon was also of the same origin: its highest *flet*, which the Fellowship of the Ring did not see, was the highest point in the land. Earlier the *flet* of Amroth at the top of the great mound or hill of Cerin Amroth, piled by the labour of many hands, had been the highest, and was principally designed to watch Dol Guldur across the Anduin. The conversion of these *telain* into permanent dwellings was a later development, and only in Caras Galadhon were such dwellings numerous. But Caras Galadhon was itself a fortress, and only a small part of the Galadhrim dwelt within its walls. Living in such lofty houses was no doubt at first thought remarkable, and Amroth was probably the first to do so. It was thus from his living in a high *talan* that his name – the only one that was later remembered in legend – was most probably derived.

A note to the words 'Amroth was probably the first to do so' states:

Unless it was Nimrodel. Her motives were different. She loved the waters and the falls of Nimrodel from which she would not long be parted; but as times darkened the stream was too near the north borders, and in a part where few of the Galadhrim now dwelt. Maybe it was from her that Amroth took the idea of living in a high *flet*.[17]

Returning to the legend of Amroth and Nimrodel given above, what was the 'haven in the south' where Amroth awaited for Nimrodel, and where (as he told her) 'many of his own people had come long ago' (p. 241)? Two passages in *The Lord of the Rings* bear on this question. One is in *The Fellowship of the Ring* II 6, where Legolas, after singing the song of Amroth and Nimrodel, speaks of 'the Bay of Belfalas, whence the Elves of Lórien set sail'. The other is in *The Return of the King* V 9, where Legolas, looking on Prince Imrahil of Dol Amroth, saw that he was 'one who had elven-blood in his veins', and said to him: 'It is long since the people of Nimrodel left the woodlands of Lórien, and yet still one may see that not all sailed from Amroth's haven west over water.' To which Prince Imrahil replied: 'So it is said in the lore of my land.'

Late and fragmentary notes go some way to explaining these references. Thus in a discussion of linguistic and political interrelations in Middle-earth (dating from 1969 or later) there is a passing reference to the fact

that in the days of the earlier settlements of Númenor the shores of the
Bay of Belfalas were still mainly desolate 'except for a haven and small
settlement of Elves at the south of the confluence of Morthond and
Ringló' (i.e. just north of Dol Amroth).

This, according to the traditions of Dol Amroth, had been
established by seafaring Sindar from the west havens of Beleriand
who fled in three small ships when the power of Morgoth overwhelmed the Eldar and the Atani; but it was later increased by
adventurers of the Silvan Elves seeking for the sea who came down
Anduin.

The Silvan Elves (it is remarked here) 'were never wholly free of an
unquiet and a yearning for the Sea which at times drove some of them to
wander from their homes'. To relate this story of the 'three small ships'
to the traditions recorded in *The Silmarillion* we would probably have to
assume that they escaped from Brithombar or Eglarest (the Havens of
the Falas on the west coast of Beleriand) when they were destroyed in the
year after the Nirnaeth Arnoediad (*The Silmarillion* p. 196), but that
whereas Círdan and Gil-galad made a refuge on the Isle of Balar these
three ships' companies sailed far further south down the coasts, to
Belfalas.

But a quite different account, making the establishment of the Elvish
haven later, is given in an unfinished scrap on the origin of the name
*Belfalas*. It is said here that while the element *Bel-* is certainly derived
from a pre-Númenórean name, its source was in fact Sindarin. The note
peters out before any further information is given about *Bel-*, but the
reason given for its Sindarin origin is that 'there was one small but important element in Gondor of quite exceptional kind: an Eldarin settlement'. After the breaking of Thangorodrim the Elves of Beleriand, if
they did not take ship over the Great Sea or remain in Lindon, wandered
east over the Blue Mountains into Eriador; but there appears nonetheless
to have been a group of Sindar who in the beginning of the Second Age
went south. They were a remnant of the people of Doriath who harboured
still their grudge against the Noldor; and having remained a while at the
Grey Havens, where they learned the craft of shipbuilding, 'they went in
the course of years seeking a place for lives of their own, and at last they
settled at the mouth of the Morthond. There was already a primitive
harbour there of fisherfolk, but these in fear of the Eldar fled into the
mountains.'[18]

In a note written in December 1972 or later, and among the last writings
of my father's on the subject of Middle-earth, there is a discussion of the
Elvish strain in Men, as to its being observable in the beardlessness of
those who were so descended (it was a characteristic of all Elves to be
beardless); and it is here noted in connection with the princely house of

Dol Amroth that 'this line had a special Elvish strain, according to its own legends' (with a reference to the speeches between Legolas and Imrahil in *The Return of the King* V 9, cited above).

As Legolas' mention of Nimrodel shows, there was an ancient Elvish port near Dol Amroth, and a small settlement of Silvan Elves there from Lórien. The legend of the prince's line was that one of their earliest fathers had wedded an Elf-maiden: in some versions it was indeed (evidently improbably) said to have been Nimrodel herself. In other tales, and more probably, it was one of Nimrodel's companions who was lost in the upper mountain glens.

This latter version of the legend appears in more detailed form in a note appended to an unpublished genealogy of the line of Dol Amroth from Angelimar, the twentieth prince, father of Adrahil, father of Imrahil, prince of Dol Amroth at the time of the War of the Ring:

In the tradition of his house Angelimar was the twentieth in unbroken descent from Galador, first Lord of Dol Amroth (c. Third Age 2004–2129). According to the same traditions Galador was the son of Imrazôr the Númenórean, who dwelt in Belfalas, and the Elven-lady Mithrellas. She was one of the companions of Nimrodel, among many of the Elves that fled to the coast about the year 1980 of the Third Age, when evil arose in Moria; and Nimrodel and her maidens strayed in the wooded hills, and were lost. But in this tale it is said that Imrazôr harboured Mithrellas, and took her to wife. But when she had borne him a son, Galador, and a daughter, Gilmith, she slipped away by night and he saw her no more. But though Mithrellas was of the lesser Silvan race (and not of the High Elves or the Grey) it was ever held that the house and kin of the Lords of Dol Amroth was noble by blood as they were fair in face and mind.

## The Elessar

In unpublished writing there is little else to be found concerning the history of Celeborn and Galadriel, save for a very rough manuscript of four pages titled 'The Elessar'. It is in the first stage of composition, but bears a few pencilled emendations; there are no other versions. It reads, with some very slight editorial emendation, as follows:

There was in Gondolin a jewel-smith named Enerdhil, the greatest of that craft among the Noldor after the death of Fëanor.

Enerdhil loved all green things that grew, and his greatest joy was to see the sunlight through the leaves of trees. And it came into his heart to make a jewel within which the clear light of the sun should be imprisoned, but the jewel should be green as leaves. And he made this thing, and even the Noldor marvelled at it. For it is said that those who looked through this stone saw things that were withered or burned healed again or as they were in the grace of their youth, and that the hands of one who held it brought to all that they touched healing from hurt. This gem Enerdhil gave to Idril the King's daughter, and she wore it upon her breast; and so it was saved from the burning of Gondolin. And before Idril set sail she said to Eärendil her son: 'The Elessar I leave with thee, for there are grievous hurts to Middle-earth which thou maybe shalt heal. But to none other shalt thou deliver it.' And indeed at Sirion's Haven there were many hurts to heal both of Men and Elves, and of beasts that fled thither from the horror of the North; and while Eärendil dwelt there they were healed and prospered, and all things were for a while green and fair. But when Eärendil began his great voyages upon the Sea he wore the Elessar upon his breast, for amongst all his searchings the thought was always before him: that he might perhaps find Idril again; and his first memory of Middle-earth was the green stone above her breast, as she sang above his cradle while Gondolin was still in flower. So it was that the Elessar passed away, when Eärendil returned no more to Middle-earth.

In ages after there was again an Elessar, and of this two things are said, though which is true only those Wise could say who now are gone. For some say that the second was indeed only the first returned, by the grace of the Valar; and that Olórin (who was known in Middle-earth as Mithrandir) brought it with him out of the West. And on a time Olórin came to Galadriel, who dwelt now under the trees of Greenwood the Great; and they had long speech together. For the years of her exile began to lie heavy on the Lady of the Noldor, and she longed for news of her kin and for the blessed land of her birth, and yet was unwilling to forsake Middle-earth [this sentence was changed to read: but was not permitted yet to forsake Middle-earth]. And when Olórin had told her many tidings she sighed, and said: 'I grieve in Middle-earth, for leaves fall and flowers fade; and my heart yearns, remembering trees and grass that do not die. I would have these in my home.' Then Olórin said: 'Would you then have the Elessar?'

And Galadriel said: 'Where now is the Stone of Eärendil?

And Enerdhil is gone who made it.' 'Who knows?' said Olórin.
'Surely,' said Galadriel, 'they have passed over Sea, as almost all
fair things beside. And must Middle-earth then fade and perish
for ever?' 'That is its fate,' said Olórin. 'Yet for a little while
that might be amended, if the Elessar should return. For a little,
until the Days of Men are come.' 'If – and yet how could that be,'
said Galadriel. 'For surely the Valar are now removed and Middle-
earth is far from their thought, and all who cling to it are under a
shadow.'

'It is not so,' said Olórin. 'Their eyes are not dimmed nor
their hearts hardened. In token of which look upon this!' And he
held before her the Elessar, and she looked on it and wondered.
And Olórin said: 'This I bring to you from Yavanna. Use it as
you may, and for a while you shall make the land of your dwelling
the fairest place in Middle-earth. But it is not for you to possess.
You shall hand it on when the time comes. For before you grow
weary, and at last forsake Middle-earth one shall come who is to
receive it, and his name shall be that of the stone: Elessar he shall
be called.'[19]

*The other tale runs so:* that long ago, ere Sauron deluded the
smiths of Eregion, Galadriel came there, and she said to Celebrimbor, the chief of the Elven-smiths: 'I am grieved in Middle-earth,
for leaves fall and flowers fade that I have loved, so that the land
of my dwelling is filled with regret that no Spring can redress.'

'How otherwise can it be for the Eldar, if they cling to Middle-
earth?' said Celebrimbor. 'Will you then pass over Sea?'

'Nay,' she said. 'Angrod is gone, and Aegnor is gone, and
Felagund is no more. Of Finarfin's children I am the last.[20] But
my heart is still proud. What wrong did the golden house of
Finarfin do that I should ask the pardon of the Valar, or be
content with an isle in the sea whose native land was Aman the
Blessed? Here I am mightier.'

'What would you then?' said Celebrimbor.

'I would have trees and grass about me that do not die – here
in the land that is mine,' she answered. 'What has become of the
skill of the Eldar?' And Celebrimbor said: 'Where now is the
Stone of Eärendil? And Enerdhil who made it is gone.' 'They
have passed over Sea,' said Galadriel, 'with almost all fair things
else. But must then Middle-earth fade and perish for ever?'

'That is its fate, I deem,' said Celebrimbor. 'But you know
that I love you (though you turned to Celeborn of the Trees),
and for that love I will do what I can, if haply by my art your

grief can be lessened.' But he did not say to Galadriel that he himself was of Gondolin long ago, and a friend of Enerdhil, though his friend in most things outrivalled him. Yet if Enerdhil had not been then Celebrimbor would have been more renowned. Therefore he took thought, and began a long and delicate labour, and so for Galadriel he made the greatest of his works (save the Three Rings only). And it is said that more subtle and clear was the green gem that he made than that of Enerdhil, but yet its light had less power. For whereas that of Enerdhil was lit by the Sun in its youth, already many years had passed ere Celebrimbor began his work, and nowhere in Middle-earth was the light as clear as it had been, for though Morgoth had been thrust out into the Void and could not enter again, his far shadow lay upon it. Radiant nonetheless was the Elessar of Celebrimbor; and he set it within a great brooch of silver in the likeness of an eagle rising upon outspread wings.[21] Wielding the Elessar all things grew fair about Galadriel, until the coming of the Shadow to the Forest. But afterwards when Nenya, chief of the Three,[22] was sent to her by Celebrimbor, she needed it (as she thought) no more, and she gave it to Celebrían her daughter, and so it came to Arwen and to Aragorn who was called Elessar.

At the end is written:

The Elessar was made in Gondolin by Celebrimbor, and so came to Idril and so to Eärendil. But that passed away. But the second Elessar was made also by Celebrimbor in Eregion at the request of the Lady Galadriel (whom he loved), and it was not under the One, being made before Sauron rose again.

This narrative goes with 'Concerning Galadriel and Celeborn' in certain features, and was probably written at about the same time, or a little earlier. Celebrimbor is here again a jewel-smith of Gondolin, rather than one of the Fëanorians (cf. p. 235); and Galadriel is spoken of as being *unwilling* to forsake Middle-earth (cf. p. 234) – though the text was later emended and the conception of the ban introduced, and at a later point in the narrative she speaks of the pardon of the Valar.

Enerdhil appears in no other writing; and the concluding words of the text show that Celebrimbor was to displace him as the maker of the Elessar in Gondolin. Of Celebrimbor's love for Galadriel there is no trace else-where. In 'Concerning Galadriel and Celeborn' the suggestion is that he came to Eregion with them (p. 235); but in that text, as in *The Silmarillion*, Galadriel met Celeborn in Doriath, and it is difficult to understand

Celebrimbor's words 'though you turned to Celeborn of the Trees'. Obscure
also is the reference to Galadriel's dwelling 'under the trees of Greenwood
the Great'. This might be taken as a loose use (nowhere else evidenced)
of the expression to include the woods of Lórien, on the other side of
Anduin; but 'the coming of the Shadow to the Forest' undoubtedly refers
to the arising of Sauron in Dol Guldur, which in Appendix A (III) to
*The Lord of the Rings* is called 'the Shadow in the Forest'. This may
imply that Galadriel's power at one time extended into the southern parts
of Greenwood the Great; and support for this may be found in 'Concerning
Galadriel and Celeborn', p. 236, where the realm of Lórinand (Lórien)
is said to have 'extended into the forests on both sides of the Great River,
including the region where afterwards was Dol Guldur'. It is possible,
also, that the same conception underlay the statement in Appendix B to
*The Lord of the Rings*, in the headnote to the Tale of Years of the Second
Age, as it appeared in the first edition: 'many of the Sindar passed eastward and established realms in the forests far away. The chief of these
were Thranduil in the north of Greenwood the Great, and Celeborn in
the south of the forest.' In the revised edition this remark about Celeborn
was omitted, and instead there appears a reference to his dwelling in
Lindon (cited above, p. 228).

Lastly, it may be remarked that the healing power here ascribed to
the Elessar at the Havens of Sirion is in *The Silmarillion* (p. 247) attributed
to the Silmaril.


# NOTES

1   See Appendix E, p. 266.

2   In a note in unpublished material the Elves of Harlindon, or Lindon
    south of the Lune, are said to have been largely of Sindarin origin,
    and the region to have been a fief under the rule of Celeborn. It is
    natural to associate this with the statement in Appendix B; but the
    reference may possibly be to a later period, for the movements and
    dwelling-places of Celeborn and Galadriel after the fall of Eregion in
    1697 are extremely obscure.

3   Cf. *The Fellowship of the Ring* I 2: 'The ancient East–West Road ran
    through the Shire to its end at the Grey Havens, and dwarves had
    always used it on their way to their mines in the Blue Mountains.'

4   It is said in Appendix A (III) to *The Lord of the Rings* that the
    ancient cities of Nogrod and Belegost were ruined in the breaking of
    Thangorodrim; but in the Tale of Years in Appendix B: 'c. 40 Many
    Dwarves leaving their old cities in Ered Luin go to Moria and swell
    its numbers.'

5   In a note to the text it is explained that *Lórinand* was the Nandorin
    name of this region (afterwards called *Lórien* and *Lothlórien*), and

contained the Elvish word meaning 'golden light': 'valley of gold'. The Quenya form would be *Laurenandë*, the Sindarin *Glornan* or *Nan Laur*. Both here and elsewhere the meaning of the name is explained by reference to the golden mallorn-trees of Lothlórien; but they were brought there by Galadriel (for the story of their origin see pp. 167–8), and in another, later, discussion the name *Lórinand* is said to have been itself a transformation, after the introduction of the mallorns, of a yet older name *Lindórinand*, 'Vale of the Land of the Singers'. Since the Elves of this land were in origin Teleri, there is here no doubt present the name by which the Teleri called themselves, *Lindar*, 'the Singers'. From many other discussions of the names of Lothlórien, to some extent at variance among themselves, it emerges that all the later names were probably due to Galadriel herself, combining different elements: *laurë* 'gold', *nan(d)* 'valley', *ndor* 'land', *lin-* 'sing'; and in *Laurelindórinan* 'Valley of Singing Gold' (which Treebeard told the Hobbits was the earlier name) deliberately echoing the name of the Golden Tree that grew in Valinor, 'for which, as is plain, Galadriel's longing increased year by year to, at last, an overwhelming regret'.

*Lórien* itself was originally the Quenya name of a region in Valinor, often used as the name of the Vala (Irmo) to whom it belonged: 'a place of rest and shadowy trees and fountains, a retreat from cares and griefs'. The further change from *Lórinand* 'Valley of Gold' to *Lórien* 'may well be due to Galadriel herself', for 'the resemblance cannot be accidental. She had endeavoured to make Lórien a refuge and an island of peace and beauty, a memorial of ancient days, but was now filled with regret and misgiving, knowing that the golden dream was hastening to a grey awakening. It may be noted that Treebeard interpreted *Lothlórien* as "Dreamflower".'

In 'Concerning Galadriel and Celeborn' I have retained the name *Lórinand* throughout, although when it was written Lórinand was intended as the original and ancient Nandorin name of the region, and the story of the introduction of the mallorns by Galadriel had not yet been devised.

6  This is a later emendation; the text as originally written stated that Lórinand was ruled by native princes.

7  In an isolated and undateable note it is said that although the name *Sauron* is used earlier than this in the Tale of Years, his name, implying identity with the great lieutenant of Morgoth in *The Silmaril-lion*, was not actually known until about the year 1600 of the Second Age, the time of the forging of the One Ring. The mysterious power of hostility, to Elves and Edain, was perceived soon after the year 500, and among the Númenóreans first by Aldarion towards the end of the eighth century (about the time when he established the haven of Vinyalondë, p. 176). But it had no known centre. Sauron

endeavoured to keep distinct his two sides: *enemy* and *tempter*. When he came among the Noldor he adopted a specious fair form (a kind of simulated anticipation of the later Istari), and a fair name: *Artano* 'high-smith', or *Aulendil*, meaning one who is devoted to the service of the Vala Aulë. (In *Of the Rings of Power*, p. 287, the name that Sauron gave to himself at this time was *Annatar*, the Lord of Gifts; but that name is not mentioned here.) The note goes on to say that Galadriel was not deceived, saying that this *Aulendil* was not in the train of Aulë in Valinor; 'but this is not decisive, since Aulë existed before the "Building of Arda", and the probability is that Sauron was in fact one of the Aulëan Maiar, corrupted "before Arda began" by Melkor'. With this compare the opening sentences in *Of the Rings of Power:* 'Of old there was Sauron the Maia. . . . In the beginning of Arda Melkor seduced him to his allegiance.'

8   In a letter written in September 1954 my father said: 'At the beginning of the Second Age he [Sauron] was still beautiful to look at, or could still assume a beautiful visible shape – and was not indeed wholly evil, not unless all "reformers" who want to hurry up with "reconstruction" and "reorganization" are wholly evil, even before pride and the lust to exert their will eat them up. The particular branch of the High Elves concerned, the Noldor or Loremasters, were always vulnerable on the side of "science and technology", as we should call it: they wanted to have the knowledge that Sauron genuinely had, and those of Eregion refused the warnings of Gil-galad and Elrond. The particular "desire" of the Eregion Elves – an "allegory" if you like of a love of machinery, and technical devices – is also symbolized by their special friendship with the Dwarves of Moria.'

9   Galadriel cannot have made use of the powers of Nenya until a much later time, after the loss of the Ruling Ring; but it must be admitted that the text does not at all suggest this (although she is said just above to have advised Celebrimbor that the Elven Rings should never be used).

10  The text was emended to read 'the first White Council'. In the Tale of Years the formation of the White Council is given under the year 2463 of the Third Age; but it may be that the name of the Council of the Third Age deliberately echoed that of this Council held long before, the more especially as several of the chief members of the one had been members of the other.

11  Earlier in this narrative (p. 237) it is said that Gil-galad gave Narya, the Red Ring, to Círdan as soon as he himself received it from Celebrimbor, and this agrees with the statements in Appendix B to *The Lord of the Rings* and in *Of the Rings of Power*, that Círdan held it from the beginning. The statement here, at variance with the others, was added in the margin of the text.

12  On the Silvan Elves and their speech see Appendix A, p. 256.

13  See Appendix C, p. 260, on the boundaries of Lórien.

14  The origin of the name *Dor-en-Ernil* is nowhere given; its only other occurrence is on the large map of Rohan, Gondor, and Mordor in *The Lord of the Rings*. On that map it is placed on the other side of the mountains from Dol Amroth, but its occurrence in the present context suggests that *Ernil* was the Prince of Dol Amroth (which might be supposed in any case).

15  See Appendix B, p. 257, on the Sindarin princes of the Silvan Elves.

16  The explanation supposes that the first element in the name *Amroth* is the same Elvish word as Quenya *amba* 'up', found also in Sindarin *amon*, a hill or mountain with steep sides; while the second element is a derivative from a stem *rath-* meaning 'climb' (whence also the noun *rath*, which in the Númenórean Sindarin used in Gondor in the naming of places and persons was applied to all the longer roadways and streets of Minas Tirith, nearly all of which were on an incline: so *Rath Dínen*, the Silent Street, leading down from the Citadel to the Tombs of the Kings).

17  In the 'Brief Recounting' of the legend of Amroth and Nimrodel it is said that Amroth dwelt in the trees of Cerin Amroth 'because of his love for Nimrodel' (p. 240).

18  The place of the Elvish haven in Belfalas is marked with the name *Edhellond* ('Elf-haven', see the Appendix to *The Silmarillion* under *edhel* and *lond*) on the decorated map of Middle-earth by Pauline Baynes; but I have found no other occurrence of this name. See Appendix D, p. 261. Cf. *The Adventures of Tom Bombadil* (1962), p. 8: 'In the Langstrand and Dol Amroth there were many traditions of the ancient Elvish dwellings, and of the haven at the mouth of the Morthond from which "westward ships" had sailed as far back as the fall of Eregion in the Second Age.'

19  This chimes with the passage in *The Fellowship of the Ring* II 8, where Galadriel, giving the green stone to Aragorn, said: 'In this hour take the name that was foretold for you, Elessar, the Elfstone of the house of Elendil!'

20  The text here and again immediately below has *Finrod*, which I have changed to *Finarfin* to avoid confusion. Before the revised edition of *The Lord of the Rings* was published in 1966 my father changed Finrod to Finarfin, while his son Felagund, previously called Inglor Felagund, became Finrod Felagund. Two passages in the Appendices B and F were accordingly emended for the revised edition. – It is noteworthy that Orodreth, King of Nargothrond after Finrod Felagund, is not here named by Galadriel among her brothers. For a reason unknown to me, my father displaced the second King of Nargothrond and made him a member of the same family in the next generation; but this and associated genealogical changes were never incorporated in the narratives of *The Silmarillion*.

21   Compare the description of the Elfstone in *The Fellowship of the Ring*
      II 8: 'Then [Galadriel] lifted from her lap a great stone of a clear green,
      set in a silver brooch that was wrought in the likeness of an eagle
      with outspread wings; and as she held it up the gem flashed like the
      sun through the leaves of spring.'

22   But in *The Return of the King* VI 9, where the Blue Ring is seen on
      Elrond's finger, it is called 'Vilya, the mightiest of the Three'.


# APPENDICES


## APPENDIX A

## THE SILVAN ELVES AND THEIR SPEECH

According to *The Silmarillion* (p. 94) some of the Nandor, the Telerin
Elves who abandoned the march of the Eldar on the eastern side of the
Misty Mountains, 'dwelt age-long in the woods of the Vale of the Great
River' (while others, it is said, went down Anduin to its mouths, and yet
others entered Eriador: from these last came the Green-elves of Ossiriand).

In a late etymological discussion of the names Galadriel, Celeborn, and
Lórien the Silvan Elves of Mirkwood and Lórien are specifically declared
to be descended from the Telerin Elves who remained in the Vale of
Anduin:

> The Silvan Elves (*Tawarwaith*) were in origin Teleri, and so remoter
> kin of the Sindar, though even longer separated from them than the
> Teleri of Valinor. They were descended from those of the Teleri who,
> on the Great Journey, were daunted by the Misty Mountains and
> lingered in the Vale of Anduin, and so never reached Beleriand or the
> Sea. They were thus closer akin to the Nandor (otherwise called the
> Green-elves) of Ossiriand, who eventually crossed the mountains and
> came at last into Beleriand.

The Silvan Elves hid themselves in woodland fastnesses beyond the Misty
Mountains, and became small and scattered peoples, hardly to be distinguished from Avari;

> but they still remembered that they were in origin Eldar, members
> of the Third Clan, and they welcomed those of the Noldor and especially
> the Sindar who did not pass over the Sea but migrated eastward [i.e.
> at the beginning of the Second Age]. Under the leadership of these
> they became again ordered folk and increased in wisdom. Thranduil
> father of Legolas of the Nine Walkers was Sindarin, and that tongue
> was used in his house, though not by all his folk.

In Lórien, where many of the people were Sindar in origin, or Noldor, survivors from Eregion [see p. 243], Sindarin had become the language of all the people. In what way their Sindarin differed from the forms of Beleriand – see *The Fellowship of the Ring* II 6, where Frodo reports that the speech of the Silvan folk that they used among themselves was unlike that of the West – is not of course now known. It probably differed in little more than what would now be popularly called 'accent': mainly differences of vowel-sounds and intonation sufficient to mislead one who, as Frodo, was not well acquainted with purer Sindarin. There may of course also have been some local words and other features ultimately due to the influence of the former Silvan tongue. Lórien had long been much isolated from the outside world. Certainly some names preserved from its past, such as *Amroth* and *Nimrodel*, cannot be fully explained from Sindarin, though fitting it in form. *Caras* seems to be an old word for a moated fortress, not found in Sindarin. *Lórien* is probably an alteration of an older name now lost [though earlier the original Silvan or Nandorin name was stated to be *Lórinand*; see p. 252, note 5].

With these remarks on Silvan names compare Appendix F (I) to *The Lord of the Rings*, section 'Of the Elves', footnote (appearing only in the revised edition).

Another general statement concerning Silvan Elvish is found in a linguistic-historical discussion dating from the same late period as that just cited:

Although the dialects of the Silvan Elves, when they again met their long separated kindred, had so far diverged from Sindarin as to be hardly intelligible, little study was needed to reveal their kinship as Eldarin tongues. Though the comparison of the Silvan dialects with their own speech greatly interested the loremasters, especially those of Noldorin origin, little is now known of the Silvan Elvish. The Silvan Elves had invented no forms of writing, and those who learned this art from the Sindar wrote in Sindarin as well as they could. By the end of the Third Age the Silvan tongues had probably ceased to be spoken in the two regions that had importance at the time of the War of the Ring: Lórien and the realm of Thranduil in northern Mirkwood. All that survived of them in the records was a few words and several names of persons and places.

## APPENDIX B

## THE SINDARIN PRINCES OF THE SILVAN ELVES

In Appendix B to *The Lord of the Rings*, in the headnote to the Tale of Years of the Second Age, it is said that 'before the building of the Barad-

dûr many of the Sindar passed eastward, and some established realms in
the forests far away, where their people were mostly Silvan Elves.
Thranduil, king in the north of Greenwood the Great, was one of these.'

Something more of the history of these Sindarin princes of the Silvan
Elves is found in my father's late philological writings. Thus in one essay
Thranduil's realm is said to have

> extended into the woods surrounding the Lonely Mountain and growing
> along the west shores of the Long Lake, before the coming of the
> Dwarves exiled from Moria and the invasion of the Dragon. The
> Elvish folk of this realm had migrated from the south, being the kin
> and neighbours of the Elves of Lórien; but they had dwelt in Greenwood
> the Great east of Anduin. In the Second Age their king, Oropher [the
> father of Thranduil, father of Legolas], had withdrawn northward beyond
> the Gladden Fields. This he did to be free from the power and en-
> croachments of the Dwarves of Moria, which had grown to be the
> greatest of the mansions of the Dwarves recorded in history; and also
> he resented the intrusions of Celeborn and Galadriel into Lórien.
> But as yet there was little to fear between the Greenwood and the
> Mountains and there was constant intercourse between his people and
> their kin across the River, until the War of the Last Alliance.
>
> Despite the desire of the Silvan Elves to meddle as little as might
> be in the affairs of the Noldor and Sindar, or of any other peoples,
> Dwarves, Men, or Orcs, Oropher had the wisdom to foresee that
> peace would not return unless Sauron was overcome. He therefore
> assembled a great army of his now numerous people, and joining with
> the lesser army of Malgalad of Lórien he led the host of the Silvan
> Elves to battle. The Silvan Elves were hardy and valiant, but ill-
> equipped with armour or weapons in comparison with the Eldar of the
> West; also they were independent, and not disposed to place themselves
> under the supreme command of Gil-galad. Their losses were thus more
> grievous than they need have been, even in that terrible war. Malgalad
> and more than half his following perished in the great battle of the
> Dagorlad, being cut off from the main host and driven into the Dead
> Marshes. Oropher was slain in the first assault upon Mordor, rushing
> forward at the head of his most doughty warriors before Gil-galad had
> given the signal for the advance. Thranduil his son survived, but when
> the war ended and Sauron was slain (as it seemed) he led back home
> barely a third of the army that had marched to war.

Malgalad of Lórien occurs nowhere else, and is not said here to be the
father of Amroth. On the other hand, Amdír father of Amroth is twice
(pp. 240 and 243 above) said to have been slain in the Battle of Dagorlad,
and it seems therefore that Malgalad can be simply equated with Amdír.
But which name replaced the other I cannot say. This essay continues:

> A long peace followed in which the numbers of the Silvan Elves grew

again; but they were unquiet and anxious, feeling the change of the world that the Third Age would bring. Men also were increasing in numbers and in power. The dominion of the Númenórean kings of Gondor was reaching out northwards towards the borders of Lórien and the Greenwood. The Free Men of the North (so called by the Elves because they were not under the rule of the Dúnedain, and had not for the most part been subjected by Sauron or his servants) were spreading southwards: mostly east of the Greenwood, though some were establishing themselves in the eaves of the forest and the grasslands of the Vales of Anduin. More ominous were rumours from the further East: the Wild Men were restless. Former servants and worshippers of Sauron, they were released now from his tyranny, but not from the evil and darkness that he had set in their hearts. Cruel wars raged among them, from which some were withdrawing westward, with minds filled with hatred, regarding all that dwelt in the West as enemies to be slain and plundered. But there was in Thranduil's heart a still deeper shadow. He had seen the horror of Mordor and could not forget it. If ever he looked south its memory dimmed the light of the Sun, and though he knew that it was now broken and deserted and under the vigilance of the Kings of Men, fear spoke in his heart that it was not conquered for ever: it would arise again.

In another passage written at the same time as the foregoing it is said that when a thousand years of the Third Age had passed and the Shadow fell upon Greenwood the Great, the Silvan Elves ruled by Thranduil

retreated before it as it spread ever northward, until at last Thranduil established his realm in the north-east of the forest and delved there a fortress and great halls underground. Oropher was of Sindarin origin, and no doubt Thranduil his son was following the example of King Thingol long before, in Doriath; though his halls were not to be compared with Menegroth. He had not the arts nor the wealth nor the aid of the Dwarves; and compared with the Elves of Doriath his Silvan folk were rude and rustic. Oropher had come among them with only a handful of Sindar, and they were soon merged with the Silvan Elves, adopting their language and taking names of Silvan form and style. This they did deliberately; for they (and other similar adventurers forgotten in the legends or only briefly named) came from Doriath after its ruin, and had no desire to leave Middle-earth, nor to be merged with the other Sindar of Beleriand, dominated by the Noldorin Exiles for whom the folk of Doriath had no great love. They wished indeed to become Silvan folk and to return, as they said, to the simple life natural to the Elves before the invitation of the Valar had disturbed it.

Nowhere (I believe) is it made clear how the adoption of the Silvan speech by the Sindarin rulers of the Silvan Elves of Mirkwood, as described here, is to be related to the statement cited on p. 257 that by the end of the Third Age Silvan Elvish had ceased to be spoken in Thranduil's realm. See further note 14 to 'The Disaster of the Gladden Fields', p. 280.

## APPENDIX C

## THE BOUNDARIES OF LÓRIEN

In Appendix A (I, iv) to *The Lord of the Rings* the kingdom of Gondor at the summit of its power in the days of King Hyarmendacil I (Third Age 1015–1149) is said to have extended northwards 'to Celebrant and the southern eaves of Mirkwood'. This my father stated several times to be in error: the correct reading should be 'to the Field of Celebrant'. According to his late writing on the interrelations of the languages of Middle-earth,

> The river Celebrant (Silverlode) was within the borders of the realm of Lórien, and the effective bounds of the kingdom of Gondor in the north (west of Anduin) was the river Limlight. The whole of the grass-lands between Silverlode and Limlight, into which the woods of Lórien formerly extended further south, were known in Lórien as Parth Celebrant (i.e. the field, or enclosed grassland, of Silverlode) and regarded as part of its realm, though not inhabited by its Elvish folk beyond the eaves of the woods. In later days Gondor built a bridge over the upper Limlight, and often occupied the narrow land between the lower Limlight and Anduin as part of its eastern defences, since the great loops of the Anduin (where it came down swiftly past Lórien and entered low flat lands before its descent again into the chasm of the Emyn Muil) had many shallows and wide shoals over which a determined and well-equipped enemy could force a crossing by rafts or pontoons, especially in the two westward bends, known as the North and South Undeeps. It was to this land that the name Parth Celebrant was applied in Gondor; hence its use in defining the ancient northern boundary. In the time of the War of the Ring, when all the land north of the White Mountains (save Anórien) as far as the Limlight had become part of the Kingdom of Rohan, the name Parth (Field of) Celebrant was only used of the great battle in which Eorl the Young destroyed the invaders of Gondor [see p. 299].

In another essay my father noted that whereas east and west the land of Lórien was bounded by Anduin and by the mountains (and he says nothing about any extension of the realm of Lórien across the Anduin, see p. 252), it had no clearly defined borders northward and southward.

Of old the Galadhrim had claimed to govern the woods as far as the falls in the Silverlode where Frodo was bathed; southward it had extended far beyond the Silverlode into more open woodland of smaller trees that merged into Fangorn Forest, though the heart of the realm had always been in the angle between Silverlode and Anduin where Caras Galadhon stood. There were no visible borders between Lórien and Fangorn, but neither the Ents nor the Galadhrim ever passed them. For legend reported that Fangorn himself had met the King of the Galadhrim in ancient days, and Fangorn had said: 'I know mine, and you know yours; let neither side molest what is the other's. But if an Elf should wish to walk in my land for his pleasure he will be welcome; and if an Ent should be seen in your land fear no evil.' Long years had passed, however, since Ent or Elf had set foot in the other land.

## APPENDIX D

## THE PORT OF LOND DAER

It was told in 'Concerning Galadriel and Celeborn' that in the war against Sauron in Eriador at the end of the seventeenth century of the Second Age the Númenórean admiral Ciryatur put a strong force ashore at the mouth of the Gwathló (Greyflood), where there was 'a small Númenórean harbour' (p. 239). This seems to be the first reference to that port, of which a good deal is told in later writings.

The fullest account is in the philological essay concerning the names of rivers which has already been cited in connection with the legend of Amroth and Nimrodel (pp. 242 ff.). In this essay the name Gwathló is discussed as follows:

The river Gwathló is translated 'Greyflood'. But *gwath* is a Sindarin word for 'shadow', in the sense of dim light, owing to cloud or mist, or in deep valleys. This does not seem to fit the geography. The wide lands divided by the Gwathló into the regions called by the Númenóreans Minhiriath ('Between the Rivers', Baranduin and Gwathló) and Enedwaith ('Middle-folk') were mainly plains, open and mountainless. At the point of the confluence of Glanduin and Mitheithel [Hoarwell] the land was almost flat, and the waters became sluggish and tended to spread into fenland.* But some hundred miles below Tharbad the slope

---

* The Glanduin ('border-river') flowed down from the Misty Mountains south of Moria to join the Mitheithel above Tharbad. On the original map to *The Lord of the Rings* the name was not marked (it only occurs once in the book, in Appendix A (I, iii)). It seems that in 1969 my father communicated to Miss Pauline Baynes certain additional names for inclusion in her decorated map of Middle-earth: 'Edhellond' (referred to above, p. 255, note 18), 'Andrast', 'Drúwaith Iaur (Old Púkel-land)', 'Lond Daer (ruins)',

increased. The Gwathló, however, never became swift, and ships of smaller draught could without difficulty sail or be rowed as far as Tharbad.

The origin of the name Gwathló must be sought in history. In the time of the War of the Ring the lands were still in places well-wooded, especially in Minhiriath and in the south-east of Enedwaith; but most of the plains were grasslands. Since the Great Plague of the year 1636 of the Third Age Minhiriath had been almost entirely deserted, though a few secretive hunter-folk lived in the woods. In Enedwaith the remnants of the Dunlendings lived in the east, in the foothills of the Misty Mountains; and a fairly numerous but barbarous fisher-folk dwelt between the mouths of the Gwathló and the Angren (Isen).

But in the earlier days, at the time of the first explorations of the Númenóreans, the situation was quite different. Minhiriath and Enedwaith were occupied by vast and almost continuous forests, except in the central region of the Great Fens. The changes that followed were largely due to the operations of Tar-Aldarion, the Mariner-king, who formed a friendship and alliance with Gil-galad. Aldarion had a great hunger for timber, desiring to make Númenor into a great naval power; his felling of trees in Númenor had caused great dissensions. In voyages down the coasts he saw with wonder the great forests, and he chose the estuary of the Gwathló for the site of a new haven entirely under Númenórean control (Gondor of course did not yet exist). There he began great works, that continued to be extended after his days. This entry into Eriador later proved of great importance in the war against Sauron (Second Age 1693–1701); but it was in origin a timber-port and ship-building harbour. The native people were fairly numerous and warlike, but they were forest-dwellers, scattered communities without central leadership. They were in awe of the Númenóreans, but they did not become hostile until the tree-felling became devastating. Then they attacked and ambushed the Númenóreans when they could, and the Númenóreans treated them as enemies, and became ruthless in their fellings, giving no thought to husbandry or replanting. The fellings had at first been along both banks of the Gwathló, and timber had been floated down to the haven (Lond Daer); but now the Númenóreans drove great tracks and roads into the forests northwards and southwards from the Gwathló, and the native folk that survived fled from Minhiriath into the dark woods of the great Cape of Eryn Vorn, south of the mouth of the Baranduin, which they dared not

---

'Eryn Vorn', 'R.Adorn', 'Swanfleet', and 'R.Glanduin'. The last three of these names were then written into the original map that accompanies the book, but why this was done I have been unable to discover; and while 'R.Adorn' is correctly placed, 'Swanfleet' and 'River Glandin' [sic] are blunderingly placed against the upper course of the Isen. For the correct interpretation of the relation between the names Glanduin and Swanfleet see pp. 264-5.

cross, even if they could, for fear of the Elvenfolk. From Enedwaith they took refuge in the eastern mountains where afterwards was Dunland; they did not cross the Isen nor take refuge in the great promontory between Isen and Lefnui that formed the north arm of the Bay of Belfalas [Ras Morthil or Andrast: see p. 214, note 6], because of the 'Púkel-men'. . . . [For the continuation of this passage see p. 383.]

The devastation wrought by the Númenóreans was incalculable. For long years these lands were their chief source of timber, not only for their ship-yards at Lond Daer and elsewhere, but also for Númenor itself. Shiploads innumerable passed west over the sea. The denuding of the lands was increased during the war in Eriador; for the exiled natives welcomed Sauron and hoped for his victory over the Men of the Sea. Sauron knew of the importance to his enemies of the Great Haven and its ship-yards, and he used these haters of Númenor as spies and guides for his raiders. He had not enough force to spare for any assault upon the forts at the Haven or along the banks of the Gwathló, but his raiders made much havoc on the fringe of the forests, setting fire in the woods and burning many of the great wood-stores of the Númenóreans.

When Sauron was at last defeated and driven east out of Eriador most of the old forests had been destroyed. The Gwathló flowed through a land that was far and wide on either bank a desert, treeless but un-tilled. That was not so when it first received its name from the hardy explorers of Tar-Aldarion's ship who ventured to pass up the river in small boats. As soon as the seaward region of salt airs and great winds was passed the forest drew down to the river-banks, and wide though the waters were the huge trees cast great shadows on the river, under which the boats of the adventurers crept silently up into the unknown land. So the first name they gave to it was 'River of Shadow', *Gwath-hír*, *Gwathir*. But later they penetrated northward as far as the beginning of the great fenlands; though it was still long before they had the need or sufficient men to undertake the great works of drainage and dyke-building that made a great port on the site where Tharbad stood in the days of the Two Kingdoms. The Sindarin word that they used for the fenland was *ló*, earlier *loga* [from a stem *log-* meaning 'wet, soaked, swampy']; and they thought at first that it was the source of the forest-river, not yet knowing the Mitheithel that came down out of the mountains in the north, and gathering the waters of the Bruinen [Loudwater] and Glanduin poured flood-waters into the plain. The name *Gwathir* was thus changed to *Gwathló*, the shadowy river from the fens.

The Gwathló was one of the few geographical names that became generally known to others than mariners in Númenor, and received an Adûnaic translation. This was *Agathurush*.

The history of Lond Daer and Tharbad is also mentioned in this same essay in a discussion of the name *Glanduin*:

*Glanduin* means 'border-river'. It was the name first given (in the
Second Age), since the river was the southern boundary of Eregion,
beyond which pre-Númenórean and generally unfriendly peoples lived,
such as the ancestors of the Dunlendings. Later it, with the Gwathló
formed by its confluence with the Mitheithel, formed the southern
boundary of the North Kingdom. The land beyond, between the
Gwathló and the Isen (Sîr Angren) was called Enedwaith ('Middle-
folk'); it belonged to neither kingdom and received no permanent
settlements of men of Númenórean origin. But the great North–South
Road, which was the chief route of communication between the Two
Kingdoms except by sea, ran through it from Tharbad to the Fords of
Isen (Ethraid Engrin). Before the decay of the North Kingdom and
the disasters that befell Gondor, indeed until the coming of the Great
Plague in Third Age 1636, both kingdoms shared an interest in this
region, and together built and maintained the Bridge of Tharbad and
the long causeways that carried the road to it on either side of the
Gwathló and Mitheithel across the fens in the plains of Minhiriath and
Enedwaith.* A considerable garrison of soldiers, mariners and engineers
had been kept there until the seventeenth century of the Third Age.
But from then onwards the region fell quickly into decay; and long
before the time of *The Lord of the Rings* had gone back into wild fenlands. When Boromir made his great journey from Gondor to Rivendell
– the courage and hardihood required is not fully recognized in the
narrative – the North–South Road no longer existed except for the
crumbling remains of the causeways, by which a hazardous approach
to Tharbad might be achieved, only to find ruins on dwindling mounds,
and a dangerous ford formed by the ruins of the bridge, impassable if
the river had not been there slow and shallow – but wide.

If the name Glanduin was remembered at all it would only be in
Rivendell; and it would apply only to the upper course of the river
where it still ran swiftly, soon to be lost in the plains and disappear in
the fens: a network of swamps, pools, and eyots, where the only inhabitants were hosts of swans, and many other water-birds. If the
river had any name it was in the language of the Dunlendings. In

---

* In the early days of the kingdoms the most expeditious route from one
to the other (except for great armaments) was found to be by sea to the
ancient port at the head of the estuary of the Gwathló and so to the river-
port of Tharbad, and thence by the Road. The ancient sea-port and its
great quays were ruinous, but with long labour a port capable of receiving
seagoing vessels had been made at Tharbad, and a fort raised there on great
earthworks on both sides of the river, to guard the once famed Bridge of
Tharbad. The ancient port was one of the earliest ports of the Númenóreans,
begun by the renowned mariner-king Tar-Aldarion, and later enlarged and
fortified. It was called Lond Daer Enedh, the Great Middle Haven (as
being between Lindon in the North and Pelargir on the Anduin). [Author's
note.]

*The Return of the King* VI 6 it is called the Swanfleet river (not River), simply as being the river that went down into Nîn-in-Eilph, 'the Waterlands of the Swans'.*

It was my father's intention to enter, in a revised map of *The Lord of the Rings*, *Glanduin* as the name of the upper course of the river, and to mark the fens as such, with the name *Nîn-in-Eilph* (or *Swanfleet*). In the event his intention came to be misunderstood, for on Pauline Baynes' map the lower course is marked as 'R.Swanfleet', while on the map in the book, as noted above (p. 262), the names are placed against the wrong river.

It may be noted that Tharbad is referred to as 'a ruined town' in *The Fellowship of the Ring* II 3, and that Boromir in Lothlórien told that he lost his horse at Tharbad, at the fording of the Greyflood (*ibid.* II 8). In the Tale of Years the ruining and desertion of Tharbad is dated to the year 2912 of the Third Age, when great floods devastated Enedwaith and Minhiriath.

From these discussions it can be seen that the conception of the Númenórean harbour at the mouth of the Gwathló had been expanded since the time when 'Concerning Galadriel and Celeborn' was written, from 'a small Númenórean harbour' to Lond Daer, the Great Haven. It is of course the Vinyalondë or New Haven of 'Aldarion and Erendis' (p. 176), though that name does not appear in the discussions just cited. It is said in 'Aldarion and Erendis' (p. 206) that the works that Aldarion began again at Vinyalondë after he became King 'were never completed'. This probably means no more than that they were never completed by him; for the later history of Lond Daer presupposes that the haven was at length restored, and made secure from the assaults of the sea, and indeed the same passage in 'Aldarion and Erendis' goes on to say that Aldarion 'laid the foundation for the achievement of Tar-Minastir long years after, in the first war with Sauron, and but for his works the fleets of Númenor could not have brought their power in time to the right place – as he foresaw'.

The statement in the discussion of *Glanduin* above that the port was called Lond Daer Enedh 'the Great Middle Haven', as being between the havens of Lindon in the North and Pelargir on the Anduin, must refer to a time long after the Númenórean intervention in the war against Sauron in Eriador; for according to the Tale of Years Pelargir was not built until the year 2350 of the Second Age, and became the chief haven of the Faithful Númenóreans.

* Sindarin *alph*, a swan, plural *eilph*; Quenya *alqua*, as in *Alqualondë*. The Telerin branch of Eldarin shifted original *kw* to *p* (but original *p* remained unshifted). The much-changed Sindarin of Middle-earth turned the stops to spirants after *l* and *r*. Thus original *alkwa* became *alpa* in Telerin, and *alf* (transcribed *alph*) in Sindarin.

## APPENDIX E

## THE NAMES OF CELEBORN AND GALADRIEL

It is said in an essay concerning the customs of name-giving among the Eldar in Valinor that they had two 'given names' (*essi*), of which the first was given at birth by the father; and this one usually recalled the father's own name, resembling it in sense or form, or might even be actually the same as the father's, to which some distinguishing prefix might be added later, when the child was full-grown. The second name was given later, sometimes much later but sometimes soon after the birth, by the mother; and these mother-names had great significance, for the mothers of the Eldar had insight into the characters and abilities of their children, and many also had the gift of prophetic foresight. In addition, any of the Eldar might acquire an *epessë* ('after-name'), not necessarily given by their own kin, a nickname – mostly given as a title of admiration or honour; and an *epessë* might become the name generally used and recognised in later song and history (as was the case, for instance, with Ereinion, always known by his *epessë* Gil-galad).

Thus the name *Alatáriel*, which, according to the late version of the story of their relationship (p. 231), was given to Galadriel by Celeborn in Aman, was an *epessë* (for its etymology see the Appendix to *The Silmarillion*, entry *kal-*), which she chose to use in Middle-earth, rendered into Sindarin as *Galadriel*, rather than her 'father-name' *Artanis*, or her 'mother-name' *Nerwen*.

It is only of course in the late version that Celeborn appears with a High-elven, rather than Sindarin, name: *Teleporno*. This is stated to be actually Telerin in form; the ancient stem of the Elvish word for 'silver' was *kyelep-*, becoming *celeb* in Sindarin, *telep-*, *telpe* in Telerin, and *tyelep-*, *tyelpe* in Quenya. But in Quenya the form *telpe* became usual, through the influence of Telerin; for the Teleri prized silver above gold, and their skill as silversmiths was esteemed even by the Noldor. Thus *Telperion* was more commonly used than *Tyelperion* as the name of the White Tree of Valinor. (*Alatáriel* was also Telerin; its Quenya form was *Altáriel*.)

The name Celeborn when first devised was intended to mean 'Silver Tree'; it was also the name of the Tree of Tol Eressëa (*The Silmarillion* p. 59). Celeborn's close kin had 'tree-names' (p. 233): Galadhon his father, Galathil his brother, and Nimloth his niece, who bore the same name as the White Tree of Númenor. In my father's latest philological writings, however, the meaning 'Silver Tree' was abandoned: the second element of *Celeborn* (as the name of a person) was derived from the ancient adjectival form *ornā* 'uprising, tall', rather than from the related noun *ornë* 'tree'. (*Ornë* was originally applied to straighter and more slender trees such as birches, whereas stouter, more spreading trees such as oaks and beeches were called in the ancient language *galadā* 'great growth';

but this distinction was not always observed in Quenya and disappeared in Sindarin, where all trees came to be called *galadh*, and *orn* fell out of common use, surviving only in verse and songs and in many names both of persons and of trees.) That Celeborn was tall is mentioned in a note to the discussion of Númenórean Linear Measures, p. 286.

On occasional confusion of Galadriel's name with the word *galadh* my father wrote:

> When Celeborn and Galadriel became the rulers of the Elves of Lórien (who were mainly in origin Silvan Elves and called themselves the Galadhrim) the name of Galadriel became associated with trees, an association that was aided by the name of her husband, which also appeared to contain a tree-word; so that outside Lórien among those whose memories of the ancient days and Galadriel's history had grown dim her name was often altered to Galadhriel. Not in Lórien itself.

It may be mentioned here that *Galadhrim* is the correct spelling of the name of the Elves of Lórien, and similarly *Caras Galadhon*. My father originally altered the voiced form of *th* (as in Modern English *then*) in Elvish names to *d*, since (as he wrote) *dh* is not used in English and looks uncouth. Afterwards he changed his mind on the point, but *Galadrim* and *Caras Galadon* remained uncorrected until after the appearance of the revised edition of *The Lord of the Rings* (in recent reprints the change has been made). These names are wrongly spelt in the entry *alda* in the Appendix to *The Silmarillion*.

# PART THREE

---

# THE THIRD AGE

# I

# THE DISASTER OF
# THE GLADDEN FIELDS

After the fall of Sauron, Isildur, the son and heir of Elendil, returned to Gondor. There he assumed the Elendilmir[1] as King of Arnor, and proclaimed his sovereign lordship over all the Dúnedain in the North and in the South; for he was a man of great pride and vigour. He remained for a year in Gondor, restoring its order and defining its bounds;[2] but the greater part of the army of Arnor returned to Eriador by the Númenórean road from the Fords of Isen to Fornost.

When he at last felt free to return to his own realm he was in haste, and he wished to go first to Imladris; for he had left his wife and youngest son there,[3] and he had moreover an urgent need for the counsel of Elrond. He therefore determined to make his way north from Osgiliath up the Vales of Anduin to Cirith Forn en Andrath, the high-climbing pass of the North, that led down to Imladris.[4] He knew the land well, for he had journeyed there often before the War of the Alliance, and had marched that way to the war with men of eastern Arnor in the company of Elrond.[5]

It was a long journey, but the only other way, west and then north to the road-meeting in Arnor, and then east to Imladris, was far longer.[6] As swift, maybe, for mounted men, but he had no horses fit for riding;[7] safer, maybe, in former days, but Sauron was vanquished, and the people of the Vales had been his allies in victory. He had no fear, save for weather and weariness, but these men must endure whom need sends far abroad in Middle-earth.[8]

So it was, as is told in the legends of later days, that the second year of the Third Age was waning when Isildur set forth from Osgiliath early in Ivanneth,[9] expecting to reach Imladris in forty days, by mid-Narbeleth, ere winter drew nigh in the North. At the Eastgate of the Bridge on a bright morning Meneldil[10] bade him farewell. 'Go now with good speed, and may the Sun of your setting out not cease to shine on your road!'

With Isildur went his three sons, Elendur, Aratan, and Ciryon,[11] and his Guard of two hundred knights and soldiers, stern men of Arnor and war-hardened. Of their journey nothing is told until they had passed over the Dagorlad, and on northward into the wide and empty lands south of Greenwood the Great. On the twentieth day, as they came within far sight of the forest crowning the highlands before them with a distant gleam of the red and gold of Ivanneth, the sky became overcast and a dark wind came up from the Sea of Rhûn laden with rain. The rain lasted for four days; so when they came to the entrance to the Vales, between Lórien and Amon Lanc,[12] Isildur turned away from the Anduin, swollen with swift water, and went up the steep slopes on its eastern side to gain the ancient paths of the Silvan Elves that ran near the eaves of the Forest.

So it came to pass that late in the afternoon of the thirtieth day of their journey they were passing the north borders of the Gladden Fields,[13] marching along a path that led to Thranduil's realm,[14] as it then was. The fair day was waning; above the distant mountains clouds were gathering, reddened by the misty sun as it drew down towards them; the deeps of the valley were already in grey shadow. The Dúnedain were singing, for their day's march was near its end, and three parts of the long road to Imladris were behind them. To their right the Forest loomed above them at the top of steep slopes running down to their path, below which the descent into the valley-bottom was gentler.

Suddenly as the sun plunged into cloud they heard the hideous cries of Orcs, and saw them issuing from the Forest and moving down the slopes, yelling their war-cries.[15] In the dimmed light their number could only be guessed, but the Dúnedain were plainly many times, even to ten times, outnumbered. Isildur commanded a *thangail*[16] to be drawn up, a shield-wall of two serried ranks that could be bent back at either end if outflanked, until at need it became a closed ring. If the land had been flat or the slope in his favour he would have formed his company into a *dírnaith*[16] and charged the Orcs, hoping by the great strength of the Dúnedain and their weapons to cleave a way through them and scatter them in dismay; but that could not now be done. A shadow of foreboding fell upon his heart.

'The vengeance of Sauron lives on, though he may be dead,' he said to Elendur, who stood beside him. 'There is cunning and design here! We have no hope of help: Moria and Lórien are now far behind, and Thranduil four days' march ahead.' 'And we bear burdens of worth beyond all reckoning,' said Elendur; for he was in his father's confidence.

The Orcs were now drawing near. Isildur turned to his esquire: 'Ohtar,'[17] he said, 'I give this now into your keeping'; and he delivered to him the great sheath and the shards of Narsil, Elendil's sword. 'Save it from capture by all means that you can find, and at

all costs; even at the cost of being held a coward who deserted me.
Take your companion with you and flee! Go! I command you!'
Then Ohtar knelt and kissed his hand, and the two young men fled
down into the dark valley.[18]

If the keen-eyed Orcs marked their flight they took no heed. They
halted briefly, preparing their assault. First they let fly a hail of
arrows, and then suddenly with a great shout they did as Isildur
would have done, and hurled a great mass of their chief warriors
down the last slope against the Dúnedain, expecting to break up
their shield-wall. But it stood firm. The arrows had been unavailing
against the Númenórean armour. The great Men towered above the
tallest Orcs, and their swords and spears far outreached the weapons
of their enemies. The onslaught faltered, broke, and retreated, leaving
the defenders little harmed, unshaken, behind piles of fallen Orcs.

It seemed to Isildur that the enemy was withdrawing towards the
Forest. He looked back. The red rim of the sun gleamed out from the
clouds as it went down behind the mountains; night would soon be
falling. He gave orders to resume the march at once, but to bend
their course down towards the lower and flatter ground where the
Orcs would have less advantage.[19] Maybe he believed that after their
costly repulse they would give way, though their scouts might follow
him during the night and watch his camp. That was the manner of Orcs,
who were most often dismayed when their prey could turn and bite.

But he was mistaken. There was not only cunning in the attack,
but fierce and relentless hatred. The Orcs of the Mountains were
stiffened and commanded by grim servants of Barad-dûr, sent out
long before to watch the passes,[20] and though it was unknown to
them the Ring, cut from his black hand two years before, was still
laden with Sauron's evil will and called to all his servants for their
aid. The Dúnedain had gone scarcely a mile when the Orcs moved
again. This time they did not charge, but used all their forces. They
came down on a wide front, which bent into a crescent and soon
closed into an unbroken ring about the Dúnedain. They were silent
now, and kept at a distance out of the range of the dreaded steel-
bows of Númenor,[21] though the light was fast failing, and Isildur
had all too few archers for his need.[22] He halted.

There was a pause, though the most keen-eyed among the Dúnedain
said that the Orcs were moving inwards, stealthily, step by step.
Elendur went to his father, who was standing dark and alone, as if
lost in thought. '*Atarinya*,' he said, 'what of the power that would
cow these foul creatures and command them to obey you? Is it then
of no avail?'

'Alas, it is not, *senya*. I cannot use it. I dread the pain of touching it.[23] And I have not yet found the strength to bend it to my will. It needs one greater than I now know myself to be. My pride has fallen. It should go to the Keepers of the Three.'

At that moment there came a sudden blast of horns, and the Orcs closed in on all sides, flinging themselves against the Dúnedain with reckless ferocity. Night had come, and hope faded. Men were falling; for some of the greater Orcs leaped up, two at a time, and dead or alive with their weight bore down a Dúnedan, so that other strong claws could drag him out and slay him. The Orcs might pay five to one in this exchange, but it was too cheap. Ciryon was slain in this way and Aratan mortally wounded in an attempt to rescue him.

Elendur, not yet harmed, sought Isildur. He was rallying the men on the east side where the assault was heaviest, for the Orcs still feared the Elendilmir that he bore on his brow and avoided him. Elendur touched him on the shoulder and he turned fiercely, thinking an Orc had crept behind.

'My King,' said Elendur, 'Ciryon is dead and Aratan is dying. Your last counsellor must advise, nay command you, as you commanded Ohtar. Go! Take your burden, and at all costs bring it to the Keepers: even at the cost of abandoning your men and me!'

'King's son,' said Isildur, 'I knew that I must do so; but I feared the pain. Nor could I go without your leave. Forgive me, and my pride that has brought you to this doom.'[24] Elendur kissed him. 'Go! Go now!' he said.

Isildur turned west, and drawing up the Ring that hung in a wallet from a fine chain about his neck, he set it upon his finger with a cry of pain, and was never seen again by any eye upon Middle-earth. But the Elendilmir of the West could not be quenched, and suddenly it blazed forth red and wrathful as a burning star. Men and Orcs gave way in fear; and Isildur, drawing a hood over his head, vanished into the night.[25]

Of what befell the Dúnedain only this was later known: ere long they all lay dead, save one, a young esquire stunned and buried under fallen men. So perished Elendur, who should afterwards have been King, and as all foretold who knew him, in his strength and wisdom, and his majesty without pride, one of the greatest, the fairest of the seed of Elendil, most like to his grandsire.[26]

Now of Isildur it is told that he was in great pain and anguish of heart, but at first he ran like a stag from the hounds, until he came to the bottom of the valley. There he halted, to make sure that he was not pursued; for Orcs could track a fugitive in the dark by scent, and needed no eyes. Then he went on more warily, for wide flats stretched on into the gloom before him, rough and pathless, with many traps for wandering feet.

So it was that he came at last to the banks of Anduin at the dead of night, and he was weary; for he had made a journey that the Dúnedain on such ground could have made no quicker, marching without halt and by day.[27] The river was swirling dark and swift before him. He stood for a while, alone and in despair. Then in haste he cast off all his armour and weapons, save a short sword at his belt,[28] and plunged into the water. He was a man of strength and endurance that few even of the Dúnedain of that age could equal, but he had little hope to gain the other shore. Before he had gone far he was forced to turn almost north against the current; and strive as he might he was ever swept down towards the tangles of the Gladden Fields. They were nearer than he had thought,[29] and even as he felt the stream slacken and had almost won across he found himself struggling among great rushes and clinging weeds. There suddenly he knew that the Ring had gone. By chance, or chance well used, it had left his hand and gone where he could never hope to find it again. At first so overwhelming was his sense of loss that he struggled no more, and would have sunk and drowned. But swift as it had come the mood passed. The pain had left him. A great burden had been taken away. His feet found the river bed, and heaving himself up out of the mud he floundered through the reeds to a marshy islet close to the western shore. There he rose up out of the water: only a mortal man, a small creature lost and abandoned in the wilds of Middle-earth. But to the night-eyed Orcs that lurked there on the watch he loomed up, a monstrous shadow of fear, with a piercing eye like a star. They loosed their poisoned arrows at it, and fled. Needlessly, for Isildur unarmed was pierced through heart and throat, and without a cry he fell back into the water. No trace of his body was ever found by Elves or Men. So passed the first victim of the malice of the masterless Ring: Isildur, second King of all the Dúnedain, lord of Arnor and Gondor, and in that age of the World the last.

## The sources of the legend of Isildur's death

There were eye-witnesses of the event. Ohtar and his companion escaped, bearing with them the shards of Narsil. The tale mentions a young man who survived the slaughter: he was Elendur's esquire, named Estelmo, and was one of the last to fall, but was stunned by a club, and not slain, and was found alive under Elendur's body. He heard the words of Isildur and Elendur at their parting. There were rescuers who came on the scene too late, but in time to disturb the Orcs and prevent their mutilation of the bodies: for there were certain Woodmen who got news to Thranduil by runners, and also themselves gathered a force to ambush the Orcs – of which they got wind, and scattered, for though victorious their losses had been great, and almost all of the great Orcs had fallen: they attempted no such attack again for long years after.

The story of the last hours of Isildur and his death was due to surmise: but well-founded. The legend in its full form was not composed until the reign of Elessar in the Fourth Age, when other evidence was discovered. Up to then it had been known, firstly, that Isildur had the Ring, and had fled towards the River; secondly, that his mail, helm, shield and great sword (but nothing else) had been found on the bank not far above the Gladden Fields; thirdly, that the Orcs had left watchers on the west bank armed with bows to intercept any who might escape the battle and flee to the River (for traces of their camps were found, one close to the borders of the Gladden Fields); and fourthly, that Isildur and the Ring, separately or together, must have been lost in the River, for if Isildur had reached the west shore wearing the Ring he should have eluded the watch, and so hardy a man of great endurance could not have failed to come then to Lórien or Moria before he foundered. Though it was a long journey, each of the Dúnedain carried in a sealed wallet on his belt a small phial of cordial and wafers of a waybread that would sustain life in him for many days – not indeed the *miruvor*[30] or the *lembas* of the Eldar, but like them, for the medicine and other arts of Númenor were potent and not yet forgotten. No belt or wallet was among the gear discarded by Isildur.

Long afterwards, as the Third Age of the Elvish World waned and the War of the Ring approached, it was revealed to the Council of Elrond that the Ring had been found, sunk near the edge of the Gladden Fields and close to the western bank; though no trace of Isildur's body was ever discovered. They were also then aware that Saruman had been secretly searching in the same region; but though he had not found the Ring (which had long before been carried off), they did not yet know what else he might have discovered.

But King Elessar, when he was crowned in Gondor, began the re-ordering of his realm, and one of his first tasks was the restoration of Orthanc, where he proposed to set up again the *palantír* recovered from Saruman. Then all the secrets of the tower were searched. Many things of worth were found, jewels and heirlooms of Eorl, filched from Edoras by the agency of Wormtongue during King Théoden's decline, and other such things, more ancient and beautiful, from mounds and tombs far and wide. Saruman in his degradation had become not a dragon but a jackdaw. At last behind a hidden door that they could not have found or opened had not Elessar had the aid of Gimli the Dwarf a steel closet was revealed. Maybe it had been intended to receive the Ring; but it was almost bare. In a casket on a high shelf two things were laid. One was a small case of gold, attached to a fine chain; it was empty, and bore no letter or token, but beyond all doubt it had once borne the Ring about Isildur's neck. Next to it lay a treasure without price, long mourned as lost for ever: the Elendilmir itself, the white star of Elvish crystal upon a fillet of *mithril*[31] that had descended from Silmarien to Elendil, and had been taken by him as the token of royalty in the North Kingdom.[32] Every king and the chieftains that followed them in Arnor had borne the Elendilmir down even to Elessar himself; but though it was a jewel of great beauty, made by Elven-smiths in Imladris for Valandil Isildur's son, it had not the ancientry nor potency of the one that had been lost when Isildur fled into the dark and came back no more.

Elessar took it up with reverence, and when he returned to the North and took up again the full kingship of Arnor Arwen bound it upon his brow, and men were silent in amaze to see its splendour. But Elessar did not again imperil it, and wore it only on high days in the North Kingdom. Otherwise, when in kingly raiment he bore the Elendilmir which had descended to him. 'And this also is a thing of reverence,' he said, 'and above my worth; forty heads have worn it before.'[33]

When men considered this secret hoard more closely, they were dismayed. For it seemed to them that these things, and certainly the Elendilmir, could not have been found, unless they had been upon Isildur's body when he sank; but if that had been in deep water of strong flow they would in time have been swept far away. Therefore Isildur must have fallen not into the deep stream but into shallow water, no more than shoulder-high. Why then, though an Age had passed, were there no traces of his bones? Had Saruman found them, and scorned them – burned them with dishonour in one of his furnaces? If that were so, it was a shameful deed; but not his worst.

## NOTES

1  The Elendilmir is named in a footnote to Appendix A (I, iii) to *The Lord of the Rings*: the Kings of Arnor wore no crown, 'but bore a single white gem, the Elendilmir, Star of Elendil, bound on their brows with a silver fillet'. This note gives references to other mentions of the Star of Elendil in the course of the narrative. There were in fact not one but two gems of this name; see p. 277.

2  As is related in the Tale of Cirion and Eorl, drawing on older histories, now mostly lost, for its account of the events that led to the Oath of Eorl and the alliance of Gondor with the Rohirrim. [Author's note.] – See p. 308.

3  Isildur's youngest son was Valandil, third King of Arnor: see *Of the Rings of Power* in *The Silmarillion*, pp. 295–6. In Appendix A (I, ii) to *The Lord of the Rings* it is stated that he was born in Imladris.

4  This pass is named only here by an Elvish name. At Rivendell long after Gimli the Dwarf referred to it as the High Pass: 'If it were not for the Beornings, the passage from Dale to Rivendell would long ago have become impossible. They are valiant men and keep open the High Pass and the Ford of Carrock.' (*The Fellowship of the Ring* II 1.) It was in this pass that Thorin Oakenshield and his company were captured by Orcs (*The Hobbit* Chapter 4). *Andrath* no doubt means 'long climb': see p. 255, note 16.

5  Cf. *Of the Rings of Power* in *The Silmarillion*, p. 295: '[Isildur] marched north from Gondor by the way that Elendil had come.'

6  Three hundred leagues and more [i.e., by the route which Isildur intended to take], and for the most part without made roads; in those days the only Númenórean roads were the great road linking Gondor and Arnor, through Calenardhon, then north over the Gwathló at Tharbad, and so at last to Fornost; and the East–West Road from the Grey Havens to Imladris. These roads crossed at a point [Bree] west of Amon Sûl (Weathertop), by Númenórean road-measurements three hundred and ninety-two leagues from Osgiliath, and then east to Imladris one hundred and sixteen: five hundred and eight leagues in all. [Author's note.] – See the Appendix on Númenórean Linear Measures, p. 285.

7  The Númenóreans in their own land possessed horses, which they esteemed [see the 'Description of Númenor', p. 169]. But they did not use them in war; for all their wars were overseas. Also they were of great stature and strength, and their fully-equipped soldiers were accustomed to bear heavy armour and weapons. In their settlements on the shores of Middle-earth they acquired and bred horses, but used them little for riding, except in sport and pleasure. In war they were used only by couriers, and by bodies of light-armed archers (often not of Númenórean race). In the War of the Alliance such

horses as they used had suffered great losses, and few were available in Osgiliath. [Author's note.]

8  They needed some baggage and provisions in houseless country; for they did not expect to find any dwellings of Elves or Men, until they reached Thranduil's realm, almost at their journey's end. On the march each man carried with him two days' provisions (other than the 'need-wallet' mentioned in the text [p. 276]); the rest, and other baggage, was carried by small sturdy horses, of a kind, it was said, that had first been found, wild and free, in the wide plains south and east of the Greenwood. They had been tamed; but though they would carry heavy burdens (at walking pace), they would not allow any man to ride them. Of these they had only ten. [Author's note.]

9  *Yavannië* 5, according to the Númenórean 'King's Reckoning', still kept with little change in the Shire Calendar. *Yavannië* (*Ivanneth*) thus corresponded to *Halimath*, our September; and *Narbeleth* to our October. Forty days (till *Narbeleth* 15) was sufficient, if all went well. The journey was probably at least three hundred and eight leagues as marched; but the soldiers of the Dúnedain, tall men of great strength and endurance, were accustomed to move fully-armed at eight leagues a day 'with ease': when they went in eight spells of a league, with short breaks at the end of each league (*lár*, Sindarin *daur*, originally meaning a stop or pause), and one hour near midday. This made a 'march' of about ten and a half hours, in which they were walking eight hours. This pace they could maintain for long periods with adequate provision. In haste they could move much faster, at twelve leagues a day (or in great need more), but for shorter periods. At the date of the disaster, in the latitude of Imladris (which they were approaching), there were at least eleven hours of daylight in open country; but at midwinter less than eight. Long journeys were not, however, undertaken in the North between the beginning of *Hithui* (*Hísimë*, November) and the end of *Nínui* (*Nénimë*, February) in time of peace. [Author's note.] – A detailed account of the Calendars in use in Middle-earth is given in Appendix D to *The Lord of the Rings*.

10 Meneldil was the nephew of Isildur, son of Isildur's younger brother Anárion, slain in the siege of Barad-dûr. Isildur had established Meneldil as King of Gondor. He was a man of courtesy, but far-seeing, and he did not reveal his thoughts. He was in fact well-pleased by the departure of Isildur and his sons, and hoped that affairs in the North would keep them long occupied. [Author's note.] – It is stated in unpublished annals concerning the Heirs of Elendil that Meneldil was the fourth child of Anárion, that he was born in the year 3318 of the Second Age, and that he was the last man to be born in Númenor. The note just cited is the only reference to his character.

11 All three had fought in the War of the Alliance, but Aratan and

Ciryon had not been in the invasion of Mordor and the siege of Barad-dûr, for Isildur had sent them to man his fortress of Minas Ithil, lest Sauron should escape Gil-galad and Elendil and seek to force a way through Cirith Dúath (later called Cirith Ungol) and take vengeance on the Dúnedain before he was overcome. Elendur, Isildur's heir and dear to him, had accompanied his father throughout the war (save the last challenge upon Orodruin) and he was in Isildur's full confidence. [Author's note.] – It is stated in the annals mentioned in the last note that Isildur's eldest son was born in Númenor in the year 3299 of the Second Age (Isildur himself was born in 3209).

12  *Amon Lanc*, 'Naked Hill,' was the highest point in the highland at the south-west corner of the Greenwood, and was so called because no trees grew on its summit. In later days it was Dol Guldur, the first stronghold of Sauron after his awakening. [Author's note.]

13  The Gladden Fields (*Loeg Ningloron*). In the Elder Days, when the Silvan Elves first settled there, they were a lake formed in a deep depression into which the Anduin poured from the North down the swiftest part of its course, a long descent of some seventy miles, and there mingled with the torrent of the Gladden River (Sîr Ninglor) hastening from the Mountains. The lake had been wider west of Anduin, for the eastern side of the valley was steeper; but on the east it probably reached as far as the feet of the long slopes down from the Forest (then still wooded), its reedy borders being marked by the gentler slope, just below the path that Isildur was following. The lake had become a great marsh, through which the river wandered in a wilderness of islets, and wide beds of reed and rush, and armies of yellow iris that grew taller than a man and gave their name to all the region and to the river from the Mountains about whose lower course they grew most thickly. But the marsh had receded to the east, and from the foot of the lower slopes there were now wide flats, grown with grass and small rushes, on which men could walk. [Author's note.]

14  Long before the War of the Alliance, Oropher, King of the Silvan Elves east of Anduin, being disturbed by rumours of the rising power of Sauron, had left their ancient dwellings about Amon Lanc, across the river from their kin in Lórien. Three times he had moved northwards, and at the end of the Second Age he dwelt in the western glens of the Emyn Duir, and his numerous people lived and roamed in the woods and vales westward as far as Anduin, north of the ancient Dwarf-Road (*Men-i-Naugrim*). He had joined the Alliance, but was slain in the assault upon the Gates of Mordor. Thranduil his son had returned with the remnant of the army of the Silvan Elves in the year before Isildur's march.

The Emyn Duir (Dark Mountains) were a group of high hills in the north-east of the Forest, so called because dense fir-woods grew upon their slopes; but they were not yet of evil name. In later days when the shadow of Sauron spread through Greenwood the Great, and changed its name from Eryn Galen to Taur-nu-Fuin (translated Mirkwood), the Emyn Duir became a haunt of many of his most evil creatures, and were called Emyn-nu-Fuin, the Mountains of Mirkwood. [Author's note.] – On Oropher see Appendix B to 'The History of Galadriel and Celeborn'; in one of the passages there cited Oropher's retreat northwards within the Greenwood is ascribed to his desire to move out of range of the Dwarves of Khazad-dûm and of Celeborn and Galadriel in Lórien.

The Elvish names of the Mountains of Mirkwood are not found elsewhere. In Appendix F (II) to *The Lord of the Rings* the Elvish name of Mirkwood is Taur-e-Ndaedelos 'forest of the great fear'; the name given here, Taur-nu-Fuin 'forest under night', was the later name of Dorthonion, the forested highland on the northern borders of Beleriand in the Elder Days. The application of the same name, Taur-nu-Fuin, to both Mirkwood and Dorthonion is notable, in the light of the close relation of my father's pictures of them: see *Pictures by J. R. R. Tolkien*, 1979, note to no. 37. – After the end of the War of the Ring Thranduil and Celeborn renamed Mirkwood once more, calling it Eryn Lasgalen, the Wood of Greenleaves (Appendix B to *The Lord of the Rings*).

*Men-i-Naugrim*, the Dwarf Road, is the Old Forest Road described in *The Hobbit*, Chapter 7. In the earlier draft of this section of the present narrative there is a note referring to 'the ancient Forest Road that led down from the Pass of Imladris and crossed Anduin by a bridge (that had been enlarged and strengthened for the passage of the armies of the Alliance), and so over the eastern valley into the Greenwood. The Anduin could not be bridged at any lower point; for a few miles below the Forest Road the land fell steeply and the river became very swift, until it reached the great basin of the Gladden Fields. Beyond the Fields it quickened again, and was then a great flood fed by many streams, of which the names are forgotten save those of the larger: the Gladden (Sîr Ninglor), Silverlode (Celebrant), and Limlight (Limlaith).' In *The Hobbit* the Forest Road traversed the great river by the Old Ford, and there is no mention of there having once been a bridge at the crossing.

15   A different tradition of the event is represented in the brief account given in *Of the Rings of Power* (*The Silmarillion* p. 295): 'Isildur was overwhelmed by a host of Orcs that lay in wait in the Misty Mountains; and they descended upon him at unawares in his camp between the Greenwood and the Great River, nigh to Loeg Ningloron, the Gladden Fields, for he was heedless and set no guard, deeming that all his foes were overthrown.'

16   *Thangail* 'shield-fence' was the name of this formation in Sindarin,

the normal spoken language of Elendil's people; its 'official' name in Quenya was *sandastan* 'shield-barrier', derived from primitive *thandā* 'shield' and *stama-* 'bar, exclude'. The Sindarin word used a different second element: *cail*, a fence or palisade of spikes and sharp stakes. This, in primitive form *keglē*, was derived from a stem *keg-* 'snag, barb', seen also in the primitive word *kegyā* 'hedge', whence Sindarin *cai* (cf. the *Morgai* in Mordor).

The *dírnaith*, Quenya *nernehta* 'man-spearhead', was a wedge-formation, launched over a short distance against an enemy massing but not yet arrayed, or against a defensive formation on open ground. Quenya *nehte*, Sindarin *naith* was applied to any formation or projection tapering to a point: a spearhead, gore, wedge, narrow promontory (root *nek* 'narrow'); cf. the Naith of Lórien, the land at the angle of the Celebrant and Anduin, which at the actual junction of the rivers was narrower and more pointed than can be shown on a small-scale map. [Author's note.]

17  *Ohtar* is the only name used in the legends; but it is probably only the title of address that Isildur used at this tragic moment, hiding his feelings under formality. *Ohtar* 'warrior, soldier' was the title of all who, though fully trained and experienced, had not yet been admitted to the rank of *roquen*, 'knight'. But Ohtar was dear to Isildur and of his own kin. [Author's note.]

18  In the earlier draft Isildur directed Ohtar to take two companions with him. In *Of the Rings of Power* (*The Silmarillion* p. 295) and in *The Fellowship of the Ring* II 2 it is told that 'three men only came ever back over the mountains'. In the text given here the implication is that the third was Estelmo, Elendur's esquire, who survived the battle (see pp. 275–6).

19  They had passed the deep depression of the Gladden Fields, beyond which the ground on the east side of Anduin (which flowed in a deep channel) was firmer and drier, for the lie of the land changed. It began to climb northwards until as it neared the Forest Road and Thranduil's country it was almost level with the eaves of the Greenwood. This Isildur knew well. [Author's note.]

20  There can be no doubt that Sauron, well-informed of the Alliance, had sent out such Orc-troops of the Red Eye as he could spare, to do what they could to harry any forces that attempted to shorten their road by crossing the Mountains. In the event the main might of Gil-galad, together with Isildur and part of the Men of Arnor, had come over the Passes of Imladris and Caradhras, and the Orcs were dismayed and hid themselves. But they remained alert and watchful, determined to attack any companies of Elves or Men that they outnumbered. Thranduil they had let pass, for even his diminished army was far too strong for them; but they bided their time, for the most part hidden in the Forest, while others lurked along the river-

banks. It is unlikely that any news of Sauron's fall had reached them, for he had been straitly besieged in Mordor and all his forces had been destroyed. If any few had escaped, they had fled far to the East with the Ringwraiths. This small detachment in the North, of no account, was forgotten. Probably they thought that Sauron had been victorious, and the war-scarred army of Thranduil was retreating to hide in fastnesses of the Forest. Thus they would be emboldened and eager to win their master's praise, though they had not been in the main battles. But it was not his praise they would have won, if any had lived long enough to see his revival. No tortures would have satisfied his anger with the bungling fools who had let slip the greatest prize in Middle-earth; even though they could know nothing of the One Ring, which save to Sauron himself was known only to the Nine Ringwraiths, its slaves. Yet many have thought that the ferocity and determination of their assault on Isildur was in part due to the Ring. It was little more than two years since it had left his hand, and though it was swiftly cooling it was still heavy with his evil will, and seeking all means to return to its lord (as it did again when he recovered and was re-housed). So, it is thought, although they did not understand it the Orc-chiefs were filled with a fierce desire to destroy the Dúnedain and capture their leader. Nonetheless it proved in the event that the War of the Ring was lost at the Disaster of the Gladden Fields. [Author's note.]

21 On the bows of the Númenóreans see the 'Description of Númenor', p. 170.

22 No more than twenty, it is said; for no such need had been expected. [Author's note.]

23 Compare the words of the scroll which Isildur wrote concerning the Ring before he departed from Gondor on his last journey, and which Gandalf reported to the Council of Elrond in Rivendell: 'It was hot when I first took it, hot as a glede, and my hand was scorched, so that I doubt if ever again I shall be free of the pain of it. Yet even as I write it is cooled and seemeth to shrink . . .' (*The Fellowship of the Ring* II 2).

24 The pride that led him to keep the Ring against the counsel of Elrond and Círdan that it should be destroyed in the fires of Orodruin (*The Fellowship of the Ring* II 2, and *Of the Rings of Power*, in *The Silmarillion*, p. 295).

25 The meaning, sufficiently remarkable, of this passage appears to be that the light of the Elendilmir was proof against the invisibility conferred by the One Ring when worn, if its light would be visible were the Ring not worn; but when Isildur covered his head with a hood its light was extinguished.

26 It is said that in later days those (such as Elrond) whose memories recalled him were struck by the great likeness to him, in body and

mind, of King Elessar, the victor in the War of the Ring, in which both the Ring and Sauron were ended for ever. Elessar was according to the records of the Dúnedain the descendant in the thirty-eighth degree of Elendur's brother Valandil. So long was it before he was avenged. [Author's note.]

27 Seven leagues or more from the place of battle. Night had fallen when he fled; he reached Anduin at midnight or near it. [Author's note.]

28 This was of a kind called *eket*: a short stabbing sword with a broad blade, pointed and two-edged, from a foot to one and a half feet long. [Author's note.]

29 The place of the last stand had been a mile or more beyond their northern border, but maybe in the dark the fall of the land had bent his course somewhat to the south. [Author's note.]

30 A flask of *miruvor*, 'the cordial of Imladris', was given to Gandalf by Elrond when the company set out from Rivendell (*The Fellowship of the Ring* II 3); see also *The Road Goes Ever On*, p. 61.

31 For that metal was found in Númenor. [Author's note.] – In 'The Line of Elros' (p. 221) Tar-Telemmaitë, the fifteenth Ruler of Númenor, is said to have been called so (i.e. 'silver-handed') because of his love of silver, 'and he bade his servants to seek ever for *mithril*'. But Gandalf said that *mithril* was found in Moria 'alone in the world' (*The Fellowship of the Ring* II 4).

32 It is told in 'Aldarion and Erendis' (p. 184) that Erendis caused the diamond which Aldarion brought to her from Middle-earth 'to be set as a star in a silver fillet; and at her asking he bound it on her forehead'. For this reason she was known as Tar-Elestirnë, the Lady of the Star-brow; 'and thus came, it is said, the manner of the Kings and Queens afterward to wear as a star a white jewel upon the brow, and they had no crown' (p. 215, note 18). This tradition cannot be unconnected with that of the Elendilmir, a star-like gem borne on the brow as a token of royalty in Arnor; but the original Elendilmir itself, since it belonged to Silmarien, was in existence in Númenor (whatever its origin may have been) before Aldarion brought Erendis' jewel from Middle-earth, and they cannot be the same.

33 The actual number was thirty-eight, since the second Elendilmir was made for Valandil (cf. note 26 above). – In the Tale of Years in Appendix B to *The Lord of the Rings* the entry for the year 16 of the Fourth Age (given under Shire Reckoning 1436) states that when King Elessar came to the Brandywine Bridge to greet his friends he gave the Star of the Dúnedain to Master Samwise, while his daughter Elanor was made a maid of honour to Queen Arwen. On the basis of this record Mr Robert Foster says in *The Complete Guide to Middle-earth* that 'the Star [of Elendil] was worn on the brow of the Kings of the North-kingdom until Elessar gave it to Sam Gamgee in

Fourth Age 16'. The clear implication of the present passage is that King Elessar retained indefinitely the Elendilmir that was made for Valandil; and it seems to me in any case out of the question that he would have made a gift of it to the Mayor of the Shire, however greatly he esteemed him. The Elendilmir is called by several names: the Star of Elendil, the Star of the North, the Star of the North-kingdom; and the Star of the Dúnedain (occurring only in this entry in the Tale of Years) is assumed to be yet another both in Robert Foster's *Guide* and in J. E. A. Tyler's *Tolkien Companion.* I have found no other reference to it; but it seems to me to be almost certain that it was not, and that Master Samwise received some different (and more suitable) distinction.


# APPENDIX

## NÚMENÓREAN LINEAR MEASURES

A note associated with the passage in 'The Disaster of the Gladden Fields' concerning the different routes from Osgiliath to Imladris (pp. 271 and 278, note 6) runs as follows:

Measures of distance are converted as nearly as possible into modern terms. 'League' is used because it was the longest measurement of distance: in Númenórean reckoning (which was decimal) five thousand *rangar* (full paces) made a *lár*, which was very nearly three of our miles. *Lár* meant 'pause', because except in forced marches a brief halt was usually made after this distance had been covered [see note 9 above]. The Númenórean *ranga* was slightly longer than our yard, approximately thirty-eight inches, owing to their greater stature. Therefore five thousand *rangar* would be almost exactly the equivalent of 5280 yards, our 'league': 5277 yards, two feet and four inches, supposing the equivalence to be exact. This cannot be determined, being based on the lengths given in histories of various things and distances that can be compared with those of our time. Account has to be taken both of the great stature of the Númenóreans (since hands, feet, fingers and paces are likely to be the origin of names of units of length), and also of the variations from these averages or norms in the process of fixing and organising a measurement system both for daily use and for exact calculations. Thus two *rangar* was often called 'man-high', which at thirty-eight inches gives an average height of six feet four inches; but this was at a later date, when the stature of the Dúnedain appears to have decreased, and also was not intended to be an accurate statement of the observed average of male stature among them, but was an approximate length expressed in the well-known unit *ranga.* (The *ranga* is often said to have been the length of the stride, from rear heel to front toe, of a full-grown man marching swiftly but at ease; a full stride 'might be well nigh a *ranga* and a half'.) It is however said of the great people of the past that they were more than man-high. Elendil was said to be 'more than man-high by nearly half a *ranga*'; but he was accounted the tallest of all the Númenóreans who escaped the Downfall [and was indeed generally known as Elendil the Tall]. The Eldar of the Elder Days were also very tall. Galadriel, 'the tallest of all the women of the Eldar of whom tales tell', was said to be man-high, but it is noted 'according to the measure of the Dúnedain and the men of old', indicating a height of about six feet four inches.

The Rohirrim were generally shorter, for in their far-off ancestry they had been mingled with men of broader and heavier build. Éomer was said to have been tall, of like height with Aragorn; but he with other descendants of King Thengel were taller than the norm of Rohan, deriving this characteristic (together in some cases with darker hair) from Morwen, Thengel's wife, a lady of Gondor of high Númenórean descent.

A note to the foregoing text adds some information concerning Morwen to what is given in *The Lord of the Rings* (Appendix A (II), 'The Kings of the Mark'):

She was known as Morwen of Lossarnach, for she dwelt there; but she did not belong to the people of that land. Her father had removed thither, for love of its flowering vales, from Belfalas; he was a descendant of a former Prince of that fief, and thus a kinsman of Prince Imrahil. His kinship with Éomer of Rohan, though distant, was recognised by Imrahil, and great friendship grew between them. Éomer wedded Imrahil's daughter [Lothíriel], and their son, Elfwine the Fair, had a striking likeness to his mother's father.

Another note remarks of Celeborn that he was 'a Linda of Valinor' (that is, one of the Teleri, whose own name for themselves was Lindar, the Singers), and that

he was held by them to be tall, as his name indicated ('silver-tall'); but the Teleri were in general somewhat less in build and stature than the Noldor.

This is the late version of the story of Celeborn's origin, and of the meaning of his name; see pp. 233, 266.

In another place my father wrote of Hobbit stature in relation to that of the Númenóreans, and of the origin of the name Halflings:

The remarks [on the stature of Hobbits] in the Prologue to *The Lord of the Rings* are unnecessarily vague and complicated, owing to the inclusion of references to survivals of the race in later times; but as far as *The Lord of the Rings* is concerned they boil down to this: the Hobbits of the Shire were in height between three and four feet, never less and seldom more. They did not of course call themselves Halflings; this was the Númenórean name for them. It evidently referred to their height in comparison with Númenórean men, and was approximately accurate when given. It was applied first to the Harfoots, who became known to the rulers of Arnor in the eleventh century [cf. the entry for 1050 in the Tale of Years], and then later also to Fallohides and Stoors. The Kingdoms of the North and the South remained in close communication at that time, and indeed until much later, and each was well informed of all events in the other region, especially of the migration of peoples of all kinds. Thus though no 'halfling', so far as is known, had ever actually appeared in Gondor before Peregrin Took, the existence of this people within the kingdom of Arthedain was known in Gondor, and they were given the name Halfling, or in Sindarin *perian*. As soon as Frodo was brought to Boromir's notice [at the Council of Elrond] he recognised him as a member of this race. He had probably until then regarded them as creatures of what we should call fairy-tales or folklore. It seems plain from Pippin's reception in Gondor that in fact 'halflings' were remembered there.

In another version of this note more is said of the diminishing stature of both Halflings and Númenóreans:

The dwindling of the Dúnedain was not a normal tendency, shared by peoples whose proper home was Middle-earth; but due to the loss of their ancient land far in the West, nearest of all mortal lands to the Undying Realm. The much later dwindling of hobbits must be due to a change in their state and way of life; they became a fugitive and secret people, driven (as Men, the Big Folk, became more and more numerous, usurping the more fertile and habitable lands) to refuge in forest or wilderness: a wandering and poor folk, forgetful of their arts, living a precarious life absorbed in the search for food, and fearful of being seen.

# II

# CIRION AND EORL
# AND THE FRIENDSHIP OF
# GONDOR AND ROHAN

## (i)

### *The Northmen and the Wainriders*

The Chronicle of Cirion and Eorl[1] begins only with the first meeting of Cirion, Steward of Gondor, and Eorl, Lord of the Éothéod, after the Battle of the Field of Celebrant was over and the invaders of Gondor destroyed. But there were lays and legends of the great ride of the Rohirrim from the North both in Rohan and in Gondor, from which accounts that appear in later Chronicles,[2] together with much other matter concerning the Éothéod, were taken. These are here drawn together briefly in chronicle form.

The Éothéod were first known by that name in the days of King Calimehtar of Gondor (who died in the year 1936 of the Third Age), at which time they were a small people living in the Vales of Anduin between the Carrock and the Gladden Fields, for the most part on the west side of the river. They were a remnant of the Northmen, who had formerly been a numerous and powerful confederation of peoples living in the wide plains between Mirkwood and the River Running, great breeders of horses and riders renowned for their skill and endurance, though their settled homes were in the eaves of the Forest, and especially in the East Bight, which had largely been made by their felling of trees.[3]

These Northmen were descendants of the same race of Men as those who in the First Age passed into the West of Middle-earth and became the allies of the Eldar in their wars with Morgoth.[4] They were therefore from afar off kinsmen of the Dúnedain or Númenóreans, and there was great friendship between them and the people of Gondor. They were in fact a bulwark of Gondor, keeping its northern and eastern frontiers from invasion; though that was not fully realised by the Kings until the bulwark was weakened and at last destroyed. The waning of the Northmen of Rhovanion began with the Great Plague, which appeared there in the winter of the year 1635 and soon spread to Gondor. In Gondor the mortality was great, especially among those who dwelt in cities. It was greater

in Rhovanion, for though its people lived mostly in the open and had
no great cities, the Plague came with a cold winter when horses and
men were driven into shelter and their low wooden houses and stables
were thronged; moreover they were little skilled in the arts of healing
and medicine, of which much was still known in Gondor, preserved
from the wisdom of Númenor. When the Plague passed it is said
that more than half of the folk of Rhovanion had perished, and of
their horses also.

They were slow to recover; but their weakness was not tested for
a long time. No doubt the peoples further east had been equally
afflicted, so that the enemies of Gondor came chiefly from the south
or over sea. But when the invasions of the Wainriders began and
involved Gondor in wars that lasted for almost a hundred years, the
Northmen bore the brunt of the first assaults. King Narmacil II
took a great army north into the plains south of Mirkwood, and
gathered all that he could of the scattered remnants of the Northmen;
but he was defeated, and himself fell in battle. The remnant of his
army retreated over the Dagorlad into Ithilien, and Gondor abandoned all lands east of the Anduin save Ithilien.[5]

As for the Northmen, a few, it is said, fled over the Celduin
(River Running) and were merged with the folk of Dale under
Erebor (with whom they were akin), some took refuge in Gondor,
and others were gathered by Marhwini son of Marhari (who fell
in the rearguard action after the Battle of the Plains).[6] Passing north
between Mirkwood and Anduin they settled in the Vales of Anduin,
where they were joined by many fugitives who came through the
Forest. This was the beginning of the Éothéod,[7] though nothing
was known of it in Gondor for many years. Most of the Northmen
were reduced to servitude, and all their former lands were occupied
by the Wainriders.[8]

But at length King Calimehtar, son of Narmacil II, being free from
other dangers,[9] determined to avenge the defeat of the Battle of the
Plains. Messengers came to him from Marhwini warning him that
the Wainriders were plotting to raid Calenardhon over the Undeeps;[10]
but they said also that a revolt of the Northmen who had been enslaved was being prepared and would burst into flame if the Wainriders
became involved in war. Calimehtar therefore, as soon as he could,
led an army out of Ithilien, taking care that its approach should be
well known to the enemy. The Wainriders came down with all the
strength that they could spare, and Calimehtar gave way before them,
drawing them away from their homes. At length battle was joined

upon the Dagorlad, and the result was long in doubt. But at its height horsemen that Calimehtar had sent over the Undeeps (left unguarded by the enemy) joined with a great *éored*[11] led by Marhwini assailed the Wainriders in flank and rear. The victory of Gondor was overwhelming – though not in the event decisive. When the enemy broke and were soon in disordered flight north towards their homes Calimehtar, wisely for his part, did not pursue them. They had left well nigh a third of their host dead to rot upon the Dagorlad among the bones of other and nobler battles of the past. But the horsemen of Marhwini harried the fugitives and inflicted great loss upon them in their long rout over the plains, until they were within far sight of Mirkwood. There they left them, taunting them: 'Fly east not north, folk of Sauron! See, the homes you stole are in flames!' For there was a great smoke going up.

The revolt planned and assisted by Marhwini had indeed broken out; desperate outlaws coming out of the Forest had roused the slaves, and together had succeeded in burning many of the dwellings of the Wainriders, and their storehouses, and their fortified camps of wagons. But most of them had perished in the attempt; for they were ill-armed, and the enemy had not left their homes undefended: their youths and old men were aided by the younger women, who in that people were also trained in arms and fought fiercely in defence of their homes and their children. Thus in the end Marhwini was obliged to retire again to his land beside the Anduin, and the Northmen of his race never again returned to their former homes. Calimehtar withdrew to Gondor, which enjoyed for a time (from 1899 to 1944) a respite from war before the great assault in which the line of its kings came near to its end.

Nonetheless the alliance of Calimehtar and Marhwini had not been in vain. If the strength of the Wainriders of Rhovanion had not been broken, that assault would have come sooner and in greater force, and the realm of Gondor might have been destroyed. But the greatest effect of the alliance lay far in the future which none could then foresee: the two great rides of the Rohirrim to the salvation of Gondor, the coming of Eorl to the Field of Celebrant, and the horns of King Théoden upon the Pelennor but for which the return of the King would have been in vain.[12]

In the meanwhile the Wainriders licked their wounds, and plotted their revenge. Beyond the reach of the arms of Gondor, in lands east of the Sea of Rhûn from which no tidings came to its Kings, their kinsfolk spread and multiplied, and they were eager for conquests and booty and filled with hatred of Gondor which stood in their way. It was long, however, before they moved. On the one hand they feared the might of Gondor, and knowing nothing of what passed west of Anduin they believed that its realm was larger and more populous than it was in truth at that time. On the other hand the eastern Wainriders had been spreading southward, beyond Mordor, and were in conflict with the peoples of Khand and their neighbours further south. Eventually a peace and alliance was agreed between these enemies of Gondor, and an attack was prepared that should be made at the same time from north and south.

Little or nothing, of course, was known of these designs and movements in Gondor. What is here said was deduced from the events long afterwards by historians, to whom it was also clear that the hatred of Gondor, and the alliance of its enemies in concerted action (for which they themselves had neither the will nor the wisdom) was due to the machinations of Sauron. Forthwini, son of Marhwini, indeed warned King Ondoher (who succeeded his father Calimehtar in the year 1936) that the Wainriders of Rhovanion were recovering from their weakness and fear, and that he suspected that they were receiving new strength from the East, for he was much troubled by raids into the south of his land that came both up the river and through the Narrows of the Forest.[13] But Gondor could do no more at that time than gather and train as great an army as it could find or afford. Thus when the assault came at last it did not find Gondor unprepared, though its strength was less than it needed.

Ondoher was aware that his southern enemies were preparing for war, and he had the wisdom to divide his forces into a northern army and a southern. The latter was the smaller, for the danger from that quarter was held to be less.[14] It was under the command of Eärnil, a member of the Royal House, being a descendant of King Telumehtar, father of Narmacil II. His base was at Pelargir. The northern army was commanded by King Ondoher himself. This had always been the custom of Gondor, that the King, if he willed, should command his army in a major battle, provided that an heir with undisputed claim to the throne was left behind. Ondoher came of a warlike line, and was loved and esteemed by his army, and he had two sons, both of age to bear arms: Artamir the elder, and Faramir some three years younger.

News of the oncoming of the enemy reached Pelargir on the ninth day of Cermië in the year 1944. Eärnil had already made his dispositions: he had crossed the Anduin with half his force, and leaving by design the Fords of the Poros undefended had encamped some forty miles north in South Ithilien. King Ondoher had purposed to lead his host north through Ithilien and deploy it on the Dagorlad, a field of ill omen for the enemies of Gondor. (At that time the forts upon the line of the Anduin north of Sarn Gebir that had been built by Narmacil I were still in repair and manned by sufficient soldiers from Calenardhon to prevent any attempt of an enemy to cross the river at the Undeeps.) But the news of the northern assault did not reach Ondoher until the morning of the twelfth day of Cermië, by which time the enemy was already drawing near, whereas the army of Gondor had been moving more slowly than it would if Ondoher had received earlier warning, and its vanguard had not yet reached the Gates of Mordor. The main force was leading with the King and his Guards, followed by the soldiers of the Right Wing and the Left Wing which would take up their places when they passed out of Ithilien and approached the Dagorlad. There they expected the assault to come from the North or North-east, as it had before in the Battle of the Plains and in the victory of Calimehtar on the Dagorlad.

But it was not so. The Wainriders had mustered a great host by the southern shores of the inland Sea of Rhûn, strengthened by men of their kinsfolk in Rhovanion and from their new allies in Khand. When all was ready they set out for Gondor from the East, moving with all the speed they could along the line of the Ered Lithui, where their approach was not observed until too late. So it came to pass that the head of the army of Gondor had only drawn level with the Gates of Mordor (the Morannon) when a great dust borne on a wind from the East announced the oncoming of the enemy vanguard.[15] This was composed not only of the war-chariots of the Wainriders but also of a force of cavalry far greater than any that had been expected. Ondoher had only time to turn and face the assault with his right flank close to the Morannon, and to send word to Minohtar, Captain of the Right Wing behind, to cover his left flank as swiftly as he could, when the chariots and horsemen crashed into his disordered line. Of the confusion of the disaster that followed few clear reports were ever brought to Gondor.

Ondoher was utterly unprepared to meet a charge of horsemen and chariots in great weight. With his Guard and his banner he had hastily taken up a position on a low knoll, but this was of no avail.[16] The main charge was hurled against his banner, and it was captured, his Guard was almost annihilated, and he himself was slain and his son Artamir at his side. Their bodies were never recovered. The assault of the enemy passed over them and about both sides of the knoll, driving deep into the disordered ranks of Gondor, hurling them back in confusion upon those behind, and scattering and pursuing many others westward into the Dead Marshes.

Minohtar took command. He was a man both valiant and war-wise. The first fury of the onslaught was spent, with far less loss and greater success than the enemy had looked for. The cavalry and chariots now withdrew, for the main host of the Wainriders was approaching. In such time as he had Minohtar, raising his own banner, rallied the remaining men of the Centre and those of his own command that were at hand. He at once sent messengers to Adrahil of Dol Amroth,[17] the Captain of the Left Wing, commanding him to withdraw with all the speed he could both his own command and those at the rear of the Right Wing who had not yet been engaged. With these forces he was to take up a defensive position between Cair Andros (which was manned) and the mountains of Ephel Dúath, where owing to the great eastward loop of the Anduin the land was at its narrowest, to cover as long as he could the approaches to Minas Tirith. Minohtar himself, to allow time for this retreat, would form a rearguard and attempt to stem the advance of the main host of the Wainriders. Adrahil should at once send messengers to find Eärnil, if they could, and inform him of the disaster of the Morannon and of the position of the retreating northern army.

When the main host of the Wainriders advanced to the attack it was then two hours after noon, and Minohtar had withdrawn his line to the head of the great North Road of Ithilien, half a mile beyond the point where it turned east to the Watch-towers of the Morannon. The first triumph of the Wainriders was now the begin-ning of their undoing. Ignorant of the numbers and ordering of the defending army they had launched their first onslaught too soon, before the greater part of that army had come out of the narrow land of Ithilien, and the charge of their chariots and cavalry had met with a success far swifter and more overwhelming than they had expected. Their main onslaught was then too long delayed, and they could no longer use their greater numbers with full effect according to the tactics they had intended, being accustomed to warfare in open lands. It may well be supposed that elated by the fall of the King and the rout of a large part of the opposing Centre, they believed that they had already overthrown the defending army, and that their own main army had little more to do than advance to the invasion and occupation of Gondor. If that were so, they were deceived.

The Wainriders came on in little order, still exultant and singing songs of victory, seeing as yet no signs of any defenders to oppose them, until they found that the road into Gondor turned south into a narrow land of trees under the shadow of the dark Ephel Dúath, where an army could march, or ride, in good order only down a great highway. Before them it ran on through a deep cutting . . .

Here the text abruptly breaks off, and the notes and jottings for its continuation are for the most part illegible. It is possible to make out, however, that men of the Éothéod fought with Ondoher; and also that Ondoher's second son Faramir was ordered to remain in Minas Tirith as regent, for it was not permitted by the law that both his sons should go into battle at the same time (a similar observation is made earlier in the narrative, p. 291). But Faramir did not do so; he went to the war in disguise, and was slain. The writing is here almost impossible to decipher, but it seems that Faramir joined the Éothéod and was caught with a party of them as they retreated towards the Dead Marshes. The leader of the Éothéod (whose name is indecipherable after the first element Marh-) came to their rescue, but Faramir died in his arms, and it was only when he searched his body that he found tokens that showed that he was the Prince. The leader of the Éothéod then went to join Minohtar at the head of the North Road in Ithilien, who at that very moment was giving an order for a message to be taken to the Prince in Minas Tirith, who was now the King. It was then that the leader of the Éothéod gave him the news that the Prince had gone disguised to the battle, and had been slain.

The presence of the Éothéod and the part played by their leader may explain the inclusion in this narrative, ostensibly to be an account of the beginnings of the friendship of Gondor and the Rohirrim, of this elaborate story of the battle between the army of Gondor and the Wainriders.

The concluding passage of the fully-written text gives the impression that the host of the Wainriders were about to receive a check to their exaltation and elation as they came down the highway into the deep cutting; but the notes at the end show that they were not long held up by the rearguard defence of Minohtar. 'The Wainriders poured relentlessly into Ithilien', and 'late on the thirteenth day of Cermië they overwhelmed Minohtar', who was slain by an arrow. He is here said to have been King Ondoher's sister-son. 'His men carried him out of the fray, and all that remained of the rearguard fled southwards to find Adrahil.' The chief commander of the Wainriders then called a halt to the advance, and held a feast. Nothing more can be made out; but the brief account in Appendix A to *The Lord of the Rings* tells how Eärnil came up from the south and routed them:

In 1944 King Ondoher and both his sons, Artamir and Faramir, fell in battle north of the Morannon, and the enemy poured into Ithilien.

But Eärnil, Captain of the Southern Army, won a great victory in South Ithilien and destroyed the army of Harad that had crossed the River Poros. Hastening north, he gathered to him all that he could of the retreating Northern Army and came up against the main camp of the Wainriders, while they were feasting and revelling, believing that Gondor was overthrown and that nothing remained but to take the spoil. Eärnil stormed the camp and set fire to the wains, and drove the enemy in a great rout out of Ithilien. A great part of those who fled before him perished in the Dead Marshes.

In the Tale of Years the victory of Eärnil is called the Battle of the Camp. After the deaths of Ondoher and both his sons at the Morannon Arvedui, last king of the northern realm, laid claim to the crown of Gondor; but his claim was rejected, and in the year following the Battle of the Camp Eärnil became King. His son was Eärnur, who died in Minas Morgul after accepting the challenge of the Lord of the Nazgûl, and was the last of the Kings of the southern realm.

(ii)

*The Ride of Eorl*

While the Éothéod still dwelt in their former home[18] they were well-known to Gondor as a people of good trust, from whom they received news of all that passed in that region. They were a remnant of the Northmen, who were held to be akin in ages past to the Dúnedain, and in the days of the great Kings had been their allies and contributed much of their blood to the people of Gondor. It was thus of great concern to Gondor when the Éothéod removed into the far North, in the days of Eärnil II, last but one of the Kings of the southern realm.[19]

The new land of the Éothéod lay north of Mirkwood, between the Misty Mountains westward and the Forest River eastward. Southward it extended to the confluence of the two short rivers that they named Greylin and Langwell. Greylin flowed down from Ered Mithrin, the Grey Mountains, but Langwell came from the Misty Mountains, and this name it bore because it was the source of Anduin, which from its junction with Greylin they called Langflood.[20]

Messengers still passed between Gondor and the Éothéod after their departure; but it was some four hundred and fifty of our miles between the confluence of Greylin and Langwell (where was their only fortified *burg*) and the inflow of Limlight into Anduin, in a direct line as a bird might fly, and much more for those who journeyed on earth; and in like manner some eight hundred miles to Minas Tirith.

The Chronicle of Cirion and Eorl reports no events before the Battle of the Field of Celebrant; but from other sources they may be made out to have been of this sort.

The wide lands south of Mirkwood, from the Brown Lands to the Sea of Rhûn, which offered no obstacle to invaders from the East until they came to Anduin, were a chief source of concern and unease to the rulers of Gondor. But during the Watchful Peace[21] the forts along the Anduin, especially on the west shore of the Undeeps, had been unmanned and neglected.[22] After that time Gondor was assailed both by Orcs out of Mordor (which had long been unguarded) and by the Corsairs of Umbar, and had neither men nor opportunity for manning the line of Anduin north of the Emyn Muil.

Cirion became Steward of Gondor in the year 2489. The menace from the North was ever in his mind, and he gave much thought to ways that might be devised against the threat of invasion from that quarter, as the strength of Gondor diminished. He put a few men into the old forts to keep watch on the Undeeps, and sent scouts and spies into the lands between Mirkwood and Dagorlad. He was thus soon aware that new and dangerous enemies coming out of the East were steadily drifting in from beyond the Sea of Rhûn. They were slaying or driving north up the River Running and into the Forest the remnant of the Northmen, friends of Gondor that still dwelt east of Mirkwood.[23] But he could do nothing to aid them, and it became more and more dangerous to gather news; too many of his scouts never returned.

It was thus not until the winter of the year 2509 was past that Cirion became aware that a great movement against Gondor was being prepared: hosts of men were mustering all along the southern eaves of Mirkwood. They were only rudely armed, and had no great number of horses for riding, using horses mainly for draught, since they had many large wains, as had the Wainriders (to whom they were no doubt akin) that assailed Gondor in the last days of the Kings. But what they lacked in gear of war they made up in numbers, so far as could be guessed.

In this peril Cirion's thought turned at last in desperation to the Éothéod, and he determined to send messengers to them. But they would have to go through Calenardhon and over the Undeeps, and then through lands already watched and patrolled by the Balchoth[24] before they could reach the Vales of Anduin. This would mean a ride of some four hundred and fifty miles to the Undeeps, and more

than five hundred thence to the Éothéod, and from the Undeeps
they would be forced to go warily and mostly by night until they had
passed the shadow of Dol Guldur. Cirion had little hope that any
of them would get through. He called for volunteers, and choosing
six riders of great courage and endurance he sent them out in pairs
with a day's interval between them. Each bore a message learned by
heart, and also a small stone incised with the seal of the Stewards,[25]
that he should deliver to the Lord of the Éothéod in person, if he
succeeded in reaching that land. The message was addressed to Eorl
son of Léod, for Cirion knew that he had succeeded his father some
years before, when he was but a youth of sixteen, and though now
no more than five and twenty was praised in all such tidings as
reached Gondor as a man of great courage and wise beyond his years.
Yet Cirion had but faint hope that even if the message were received
it would be answered. He had no claim on the Éothéod beyond their
ancient friendship with Gondor to bring them from so far away with
any strength that would avail. The tidings that the Balchoth were
destroying the last of their kin in the South, if they did not know
it already, might give weight to his appeal, if the Éothéod themselves
were not threatened by any attack. Cirion said no more,[26] and ordered
what strength he had to meet the storm. He gathered as great a force
as he could, and taking command of it himself made ready as swiftly
as might be to lead it north to Calenardhon. Hallas his son he left
in command at Minas Tirith.

The first pair of messengers left on the tenth day of Súlimë; and
in the event it was one of these, alone of all the six, who got through
to the Éothéod. He was Borondir, a great rider of a family that
claimed descent from a captain of the Northmen in the service of
the Kings of old.[27] Of the others no tidings were ever heard, save
of Borondir's companion. He was slain by arrows in ambush as they
passed near Dol Guldur, from which Borondir escaped by fortune
and the speed of his horse. He was pursued as far north as the Gladden
Fields, and often waylaid by men that came out of the Forest and
forced him to ride far out of the direct way. He came at last to the
Éothéod after fifteen days, for the last two without food; and he was
so spent that he could scarce speak his message to Eorl.

It was then the twenty-fifth day of Súlimë. Eorl took counsel
with himself in silence; but not for long. Soon he rose, and he
said: 'I will come. If the Mundburg falls, whither shall we flee
from the Darkness?' Then he took Borondir's hand in token of his
promise.

Eorl at once summoned his council of Elders, and began to prepare for the great riding. But this took many days, for the host had to be gathered and mustered, and thought taken for the ordering of the people and the defence of the land. At that time the Éothéod were at peace and had no fear of war: though it might prove otherwise when it became known that their lord had ridden away to battle far off in the South. Nonetheless Eorl saw well that nothing less than his full strength would serve, and he must risk all or draw back and break his promise.

At last the whole host was assembled; and only a few hundreds were left behind to support the men unfitted for such a desperate venture by youth or age. It was then the sixth day of the month of Víressë. On that day in silence the great *éohere* set out, leaving fear behind, and taking with them small hope; for they knew not what lay before them, either on the road or at its end. It is said that Eorl led forth some seven thousand fully-armed riders and some hundreds of horsed archers. At his right hand rode Borondir, to serve as guide so far as he might, since he had lately passed through the lands. But this great host was not threatened or assailed during its long journey down the Vales of Anduin. Such folk of good or evil kind as saw it approach fled out of its path for fear of its might and splendour. As it drew southward and passed by southern Mirkwood (below the great East Bight), which was now infested by the Balchoth, still there was no sign of men, in force or in scouting parties, to bar their road or to spy upon their coming. In part this was due to events unknown to them, which had come to pass since Borondir set out; but other powers also were at work. For when at last the host drew near to Dol Guldur, Eorl turned away westward for fear of the dark shadow and cloud that flowed out from it, and then he rode on within sight of Anduin. Many of the riders turned their eyes thither, half in fear and half in hope to glimpse from afar the shimmer of the Dwimordene, the perilous land that in legends of their people was said to shine like gold in the springtime. But now it seemed shrouded in a gleaming mist; and to their dismay the mist passed over the river and flowed over the land before them.

Eorl did not halt. 'Ride on!' he commanded. 'There is no other way to take. After so long a road shall we be held back from battle by a river-mist?'

As they drew nearer they saw that the white mist was driving back the glooms of Dol Guldur, and soon they passed into it, riding slowly at first and warily; but under its canopy all things were lit with a clear and shadowless light, while to left and right they were guarded as it were by white walls of secrecy.

'The Lady of the Golden Wood is on our side, it seems,' said Borondir.

'Maybe,' said Eorl. 'But at least I will trust the wisdom of Felaróf.[28] He scents no evil. His heart is high, and his weariness is healed: he strains to be given his head. So be it! For never have I had more need of secrecy and speed.'

Then Felaróf sprang forward, and all the host behind followed like a great wind, but in a strange silence, as if their hooves did not beat upon the ground. So they rode on, as fresh and eager as on the morning of their setting-out, during that day and the next; but at dawn of the third day they rose from their rest, and suddenly the mist was gone, and they saw that they were far out in the open lands. On their right the Anduin lay near, but they had almost passed its great eastward loop,[29] and the Undeeps were in sight. It was the morning of the fifteenth day of Víressë, and they had come there at a speed beyond hope.[30]

Here the text ends, with a note that a description of the Battle of the Field of Celebrant was to follow. In Appendix A (II) to *The Lord of the Rings* there is a summary account of the war:

A great host of wild men from the North-east swept over Rhovanion and coming down out of the Brown-lands crossed the Anduin on rafts. At the same time by chance or design the Orcs (who at that time before their war with the Dwarves were in great strength) made a descent from the Mountains. The invaders overran Calenardhon, and Cirion, Steward of Gondor, sent north for help . . .

When Eorl and his Riders came to the Field of Celebrant

the northern army of Gondor was in peril. Defeated in the Wold and cut off from the south, it had been driven across the Limlight, and was then suddenly assailed by the Orc-host that pressed it towards the Anduin. All hope was lost when, unlooked for, the Riders came out of the North and broke upon the rear of the enemy. Then the fortunes of battle were reversed, and the enemy was driven with slaughter over Limlight. Eorl led his men in pursuit, and so great was the fear that went before the horsemen of the North that the invaders of the Wold were also thrown into panic, and the Riders hunted them over the plains of Calenardhon.

A similar, briefer, account is given elsewhere in Appendix A (I, iv). From neither is the course of the battle perhaps perfectly clear, but it seems certain that the Riders, having passed over the Undeeps, then crossed the Limlight (see note 27, p. 313) and fell upon the rear of the enemy at the Field of Celebrant; and that 'the enemy was driven with slaughter over Limlight' means that the Balchoth were driven back southwards into the Wold.

### (iii)

### *Cirion and Eorl*

The story is preceded by a note on the Halifirien, westernmost of the beacons of Gondor along the line of Ered Nimrais.

The Halifirien[31] was the highest of the beacons, and like Eilenach, the next in height, appeared to stand up alone out of a great wood; for behind it there was a deep cleft, the dark Firien-dale, in the long northward spur of Ered Nimrais, of which it was the highest point. Out of the cleft it rose like a sheer wall, but its outer slopes, especially northwards, were long and nowhere steep, and trees grew upon them almost to its summit. As they descended the trees became ever more dense, especially along the Mering Stream (which rose in the cleft) and northwards out into the plain through which the Stream flowed into the Entwash. The great West Road passed through a long cutting in the wood, to avoid the wet land beyond its northern eaves; but this road had been made in ancient days,[32] and after the departure of Isildur no tree was ever felled in the Firien Wood, except only by the Beacon-wardens whose task it was to keep open the great road and the path towards the summit of the hill. This path turned from the Road near to its entrance into the Wood, and wound its way up to the end of the trees, beyond which there was an ancient stairway of stone leading to the beacon-site, a wide circle levelled by those who had made the stair. The Beacon-wardens were the only inhabitants of the Wood, save wild beasts; they housed in lodges in the trees near the summit, but they did not stay long, unless held there by foul weather, and they came and went in turns of duty. For the most part they were glad to return home. Not because of the peril of the wild beasts, nor did any evil shadow out of dark days lie upon the Wood; but beneath the sounds of the winds, the cries of birds and beasts, or at times the noise of horsemen riding in haste upon the Road, there lay a silence, and a man would find himself speaking to his comrades in a whisper, as if he expected to hear the echo of a great voice that called from far away and long ago.

The name Halifirien meant in the language of the Rohirrim 'holy mountain'.[33] Before their coming it was known in Sindarin as Amon Anwar, 'Hill of Awe'; for what reason was not known in Gondor, except only (as later appeared) to the ruling King or Steward. For the few men who ever ventured to leave the Road and wander under the trees the Wood itself seemed reason enough: in the Common Speech it was called 'the Whispering Wood'. In the great days of Gondor no beacon was built on the Hill while the *palantíri* still maintained communication between Osgiliath and the three towers of the realm[34] without need of messages or signals. In later days little aid could be expected from the North as the people of Calenardhon declined, nor was armed force sent thither as Minas Tirith became more and more hard put to it to hold the line of the Anduin and guard its southern coast. In Anórien many people still dwelt and had the task of guarding the northern approaches, either out of Calenardhon or across the Anduin at Cair Andros. For communication with them the three oldest beacons (Amon Dîn, Eilenach, and Min-Rimmon) were built and maintained,[35] but though the line of the Mering Stream was fortified (between the impassable marshes of its confluence with the Entwash and the bridge where the Road passed westward out of the Firien Wood) it was not permitted that any fort or beacon should be set upon Amon Anwar.


In the days of Cirion the Steward there came a great assault by the Balchoth, who allied with Orcs crossed the Anduin into the Wold and began the conquest of Calenardhon. From this deadly peril, which would have brought ruin upon Gondor, the coming of Eorl the Young and the Rohirrim rescued the realm.

When the war was over men wondered in what way the Steward would honour Eorl and reward him, and expected that a great feast would be held in Minas Tirith at which this would be revealed. But Cirion was a man who kept his own counsel. As the diminished army of Gondor made its way south he was accompanied by Eorl and an *éored*[36] of the Riders of the North. When they came to the Mering Stream Cirion turned to Eorl and said, to men's wonder:

'Farewell now, Eorl, son of Léod. I will return to my home, where much needs to be set in order. Calenardhon I commit to your care for this time, if you are not in haste to return to your own realm. In three months' time I will meet you here again, and then we will take counsel together.'

'I will come,' Eorl answered; and so they parted.

As soon as Cirion came to Minas Tirith he summoned some of his most trusted servants. 'Go now to the Whispering Wood,' he said. 'There you must re-open the ancient path to Amon Anwar. It is long overgrown; but the entrance is still marked by a standing stone beside the Road, at that point where the northern region of the Wood closes in upon it. The path turns this way and that, but at each turn there is a standing stone. Following these you will come at length to the end of the trees and find a stone stair that leads on upwards. I charge you to go no further. Do this work as swiftly as you may and then return to me. Fell no trees; only clear a way by which a few men on foot can easily pass upwards. Leave the entrance by the Road still shrouded, so that none that use the Road may be tempted to use the path before I come there myself. Tell no one whither you go or what you have done. If any ask, say only that the Lord Steward wishes for a place to be made ready for his meeting with the Lord of the Riders.'

In due time Cirion set out with Hallas his son and the Lord of Dol Amroth, and two others of his Council; and he met Eorl at the crossing of the Mering Stream. With Eorl were three of his chief captains. 'Let us go now to the place that I have prepared,' said Cirion. Then they left a guard of Riders at the bridge and turned back into the tree-shadowed Road, and came to the standing stone. There they left their horses and another strong guard of soldiers of Gondor; and Cirion standing by the stone turned to his companions and said: 'I go now to the Hill of Awe. Follow me, if you will. With me shall come an esquire, and another with Eorl, to bear our arms; all others shall go unarmed as witnesses of our words and deeds in the high place. The path has been made ready, though none have used it since I came here with my father.'

Then Cirion led Eorl into the trees and the others followed in order; and after they had passed the first of the inner stones their voices were stilled and they walked warily as if unwilling to make any sound. So they came at last to the upper slopes of the Hill and passed through a belt of white birches and saw the stone stair going up to the summit. After the shadow of the Wood the sun seemed hot and bright, for it was the month of Úrimë; yet the crown of the Hill was green, as if the year were still in Lótessë.

At the foot of the stair there was a small shelf or cove made in the hillside with low turf-banks. There the company sat for a while, until Cirion rose and from his esquire took the white wand of office and the white mantle of the Stewards of Gondor. Then standing on the first step of the stair he broke the silence, saying in a low but clear voice:

'I will now declare what I have resolved, with the authority of the Stewards of the Kings, to offer to Eorl son of Léod, Lord of the Éothéod, in recognition of the valour of his people and of the help beyond hope that he brought to Gondor in time of dire need. To Eorl I will give in free gift all the great land of Calenardhon from Anduin to Isen. There, if he will, he shall be king, and his heirs after him, and his people shall dwell in freedom while the authority of the Stewards endures, until the Great King returns.[37] No bond shall be laid upon them other than their own laws and will, save in this only: they shall live in perpetual friendship with Gondor and its enemies shall be their enemies while both realms endure. But the same bond shall be laid also on the people of Gondor.'

Then Eorl stood up, but remained for some time silent. For he was amazed by the great generosity of the gift and the noble terms in which it had been offered; and he saw the wisdom of Cirion both on his own behalf as ruler of Gondor, seeking to protect what remained of his realm, and as a friend of the Éothéod of whose needs he was aware. For they were now grown to a people too numerous for their land in the North and longed to return south to their former home, but they were restrained by the fear of Dol Guldur. But in Calenardhon they would have room beyond hope, and yet be far from the shadows of Mirkwood.

Yet beyond wisdom and policy both Cirion and Eorl were moved at that time by the great friendship that bound their peoples together, and by the love that was between them as true men. On the part of Cirion the love was that of a wise father, old in the cares of the world, for a son in the strength and hope of his youth; while in Cirion Eorl saw the highest and noblest man of the world that he knew, and the wisest, on whom sat the majesty of the Kings of Men of long ago.

At last, when Eorl had swiftly passed all these things through his thought, he spoke, saying: 'Lord Steward of the Great King, the gift that you offer I accept for myself and for my people. It far exceeds any reward that our deeds could have earned, if they had not themselves been a free gift of friendship. But now I will seal that friendship with an oath that shall not be forgotten.'

'Then let us go now to the high place,' said Cirion, 'and before these witnesses take such oaths as seem fitting.'

Then Cirion went up the stair with Eorl and the others followed; and when they came to the summit they saw there a wide oval place of level turf, unfenced, but at its eastern end there stood a low mound on which grew the white flowers of *alfirin*,[38] and the westering sun touched them with gold. Then the Lord of Dol Amroth, chief of those in the company of Cirion, went towards the mound and saw, lying on the grass before it and yet unmarred by weed or weather, a black stone; and on the stone three letters were engraved. Then he said to Cirion:

'Is this then a tomb? But what great man of old lies here?'

'Have you not read the letters?' said Cirion.

'I have,' said the Prince,[39] 'and therefore I wonder; for the letters are *lambe, ando, lambe*, but there is no tomb for Elendil, nor has any man since his day dared to use that name.'[40]

'Nonetheless this is his tomb,' said Cirion; 'and from it comes the awe that dwells on this hill and in the woods below. From Isildur who raised it to Meneldil who succeeded him, and so down all the line of the Kings, and down the line of the Stewards even to myself, this tomb has been kept a secret by Isildur's command. For he said: "Here is the mid-point of the Kingdom of the South,[41] and here shall the memorial of Elendil the Faithful abide in the keeping of the Valar, while the Kingdom endures. This hill shall be a hallow, and let no man disturb its peace and silence, unless he be an heir of Elendil." I have brought you here, so that the oaths here taken may seem of deepest solemnity to ourselves and to our heirs upon either side.'

Then all those present stood a while in silence with bowed heads, until Cirion said to Eorl: 'If you are ready, take now your oath in such manner as seems to you fitting according to the customs of your people.'

Eorl then stood forth, and taking his spear from his esquire he set it upright in the ground. Then he drew his sword and cast it up shining in the sun, and catching it again he stepped forward and laid the blade upon the mound, but with his hand still about the hilts. He spoke then in a great voice the Oath of Eorl. This he said in the tongue of the Éothéod, which in the Common Speech is interpreted:[42]

Hear now all peoples who bow not to the Shadow in the East, by the gift of the Lord of the Mundburg we will come to dwell in the land that he names Calenardhon, and therefore I vow in my own name and on behalf of the Éothéod of the North that between us and the Great People of the West there shall be friendship for ever: their enemies shall be our enemies, their need shall be our need, and whatsoever evil, or threat, or assault may come upon them we will aid them to the utmost end of our strength. This vow shall descend to my heirs, all such as may come after me in our new land, and let them keep it in faith unbroken, lest the Shadow fall upon them and they become accursed.

Then Eorl sheathed his sword and bowed and went back to his captains.

Cirion then made answer. Standing to his full height he laid his hand upon the tomb and in his right hand held up the white wand of the Stewards, and spoke words that filled those who heard them with awe. For as he stood up the sun went down in flame in the West and his white robe seemed to be on fire; and after he had vowed that Gondor should be bound by a like bond of friendship and aid in all need, he lifted up his voice and said in Quenya:

*Vanda sina termaruva Elenna·nóreo alcar enyalien ar Elendil Vorondo voronwë. Nai tiruvantes i hárar mahalmassen mi Númen ar i Eru i or ilyë mahalmar eä tennoio.*[43]

And again he said the Common Speech:

This oath shall stand in memory of the glory of the Land of the Star, and of the faith of Elendil the Faithful, in the keeping of those who sit upon the thrones of the West and of the One who is above all thrones for ever.

Such an oath had not been heard in Middle-earth since Elendil himself had sworn alliance with Gil-galad King of the Eldar.[44]

When all was done and the shadows of evening were falling Cirion and Eorl with their company went down again in silence through the darkling Wood, and came back to the camp by the Mering Stream where tents had been prepared for them. After they had eaten Cirion and Eorl, with the Prince of Dol Amroth and Éomund the chief captain of the host of the Éothéod, sat together and defined the boundaries of the authority of the King of the Éothéod and the Steward of Gondor.

The bounds of the realm of Eorl were to be: in the West the river Angren from its junction with the Adorn and thence northwards to the outer fences of Agrenost, and thence westwards and northwards along the eaves of Fangorn Forest to the river Limlight; and that river was its northern boundary, for the land beyond had never been claimed by Gondor.[45] In the east its bounds were the Anduin and the west-cliff of the Emyn Muil down to the marshes of the Mouths of Onodló, and beyond that river the stream of the Glanhír that flowed through the Wood of Anwar to join the Onodló; and in the south its bounds were the Ered Nimrais as far as the end of their northward arm, but all those vales and inlets that opened northwards were to belong to the Éothéod, as well as the land south of the Hithaeglir that lay between the rivers Angren and Adorn.[46]

In all these regions Gondor still retained under its own command only the fortress of Angrenost, within which was the third Tower of Gondor, the impregnable Orthanc where was held the fourth of the *palantíri* of the southern realm. In the days of Cirion Angrenost was still manned by a guard of Gondorians, but these had become a small settled people, ruled by an hereditary Captain, and the keys of Orthanc were in the keeping of the Steward of Gondor. The 'outer fences' named in the description of the bounds of the realm of Eorl were a wall and dyke running some two miles south of the gates of Angrenost, between the hills in which the Misty Mountains ended; beyond them were the tilled lands of the people of the fortress.

It was agreed also that the Great Road which had formerly run through Anórien and Calenardhon to Athrad Angren (the Fords of Isen),[47] and thence northwards on its way to Arnor, should be open to all travellers of either people without hindrance in time of peace, and its maintenance should from the Mering Stream to the Fords of Isen be in the care of the Éothéod.

By this pact only a small part of the Wood of Anwar, west of the Mering Stream, was included in the realm of Eorl; but Cirion declared that the Hill of Anwar was now a hallowed place of both peoples, and the Eorlings and the Stewards should henceforward share its guard and maintenance. In later days, however, as the Rohirrim grew in power and numbers, while Gondor declined and was ever threatened from the East and by sea, the wardens of Anwar were provided entirely by the people of Eastfold, and the Wood became by custom part of the royal domain of the Kings of the Mark. The Hill they named the Halifirien, and the Wood the Firienholt.[48]

In later times the day of the Oath-taking was reckoned as the first day of the new kingdom, when Eorl took the title of King of the Mark of the Riders. But in the event it was some while before the Rohirrim took possession of the land, and during his life Eorl was known as Lord of the Éothéod and King of Calenardhon. The term Mark signified a borderland, especially one serving as a defence of the inner lands of a realm. The Sindarin names Rohan for the Mark and Rohirrim for the people were devised first by Hallas, son and successor of Cirion, but were often used not only in Gondor but by the Éothéod themselves.[49]

The day after the Oath-taking Cirion and Eorl embraced and took their leave unwillingly. For Eorl said: 'Lord Steward, I have much to do in haste. This land is now rid of enemies; but they are not destroyed at the root, and beyond Anduin and under the eaves of Mirkwood we know not yet what peril lurks. I sent yestereve three messengers north, riders brave and skilled, in the hope that one at least will reach my home before me. For I must now return myself, and with some strength; my land was left with few men, those too young and those too old; and if they are to make so great a journey our women and children, with such goods as we cannot spare, must be guarded, and only the Lord of the Éothéod himself will they follow. I will leave behind me all the strength that I can spare, well nigh half of the host that is now in Calenardhon. Some companies of horsed archers there shall be, to go where need calls, if any bands of the enemy still lurk in the land; but the main force shall remain in the North-east to guard above all the place where the Balchoth made a crossing of the Anduin out of the Brown Lands; for there is still the greatest danger, and there also is my chief hope, if I return, of leading my people into their new land with as little grief and loss as may be. If I return, I say: but be assured that I shall return, for the keeping of my oath, unless disaster befall us and I perish with my people on the long road. For that must be on the east side of Anduin ever under the threat of Mirkwood, and at last must pass through the vale that is haunted by the shadow of the hill that you name Dol Guldur. On the west side there is no road for horsemen, nor for a great host of people and wains, even were not the Mountains infested by Orcs; and none can pass, few or many, through the Dwimordene where dwells the White Lady and weaves nets that no mortal can pass.[50] By the east road will I come, as I came to Celebrant; and may those whom we called in witness of our oaths have us in their keeping. Let us part now in hope! Have I your leave?'

'Indeed you have my leave,' said Cirion, 'since I see now that it cannot be otherwise. I perceive that in our peril I have given too little thought to the dangers that you have faced and the wonder of your coming beyond hope over the long leagues from the North. The reward that I offered in joy and fullness of heart at our deliverance now seems little. But I believe that the words of my oath, which I had not forethought ere I spoke them, were not put into my mouth in vain. We will part then in hope.'

After the manner of the Chronicles no doubt much of what is here put into the mouths of Eorl and Cirion at their parting was said and considered in the debate of the night before; but it is certain that Cirion said at parting his words concerning the inspiration of his oath, for he was a man of little pride and of great courage and generosity of heart, the noblest of the Stewards of Gondor.

(iv)

## The Tradition of Isildur

It is said that when Isildur returned from the War of the Last Alliance he remained for a time in Gondor, ordering the realm and instructing Meneldil his nephew, before he himself departed to take up the kingship of Arnor. With Meneldil and a company of trusted friends he made a journey about the borders of all the lands to which Gondor laid claim; and as they were returning from the northern bound to Anórien they came to the high hill that was then called Eilenaer but was afterwards called Amon Anwar, 'Hill of Awe'.[51] That was near to the centre of the lands of Gondor. They made a path through the dense woods of its northward slopes, and so came to its summit, which was green and treeless. There they made a level space, and at its eastward end they raised a mound; within the mound Isildur laid a casket that he bore with him. Then he said: 'This is a tomb and memorial of Elendil the Faithful. Here it shall stand at the mid-point of the Kingdom of the South in the keeping of the Valar, while the Kingdom endures; and this place shall be a hallow that none shall profane. Let no man disturb its silence and peace, unless he be an heir of Elendil.'

They made a stone stair from the fringe of the woods up to the crown of the hill; and Isildur said: 'Up this stair let no man climb, save the King, and those that he brings with him, if he bids them follow him.' Then all those present were sworn to secrecy; but Isildur gave this counsel to Meneldil, that the King should visit the hallow from time to time, and especially when he felt the need of wisdom in days of danger or distress; and thither also he should bring his heir, when he was full-grown to manhood, and tell him of the making of the hallow, and reveal to him the secrets of the realm and other matters that he should know.

Meneldil followed Isildur's counsel, and all the Kings that came after him, until Rómendacil I (the fifth after Meneldil). In his time Gondor was first assailed by Easterlings;[52] and lest the tradition should be broken because of war or sudden death or other misfortune, he caused the 'Tradition of Isildur' to be set down in a sealed scroll, together with other things that a new King should know; and this scroll was delivered by the Steward to the King before his crowning.[53] This delivery was from then onwards always performed, though the custom of visiting the hallow of Amon Anwar with his heir was maintained by nearly all the Kings of Gondor.

When the days of the Kings came to an end and Gondor was ruled by the Stewards descended from Húrin, the steward of King Minardil, it was held that all the rights and duties of the Kings were theirs 'until the Great King returns'. But in the matter of the 'Tradition of Isildur' they alone were the judges, since it was known only to them. They judged that by the words 'an heir of Elendil' Isildur had meant one of the royal line descended from Elendil who had inherited the throne: but that he did not foresee the rule of the Stewards. If then Mardil had exercised the authority of the King in his absence,[54] the heirs of Mardil who had inherited the Stewardship had the same right and duty until a King returned; each Steward therefore had the right to visit the hallow when he would and to admit to it those who came with him, as he thought fit. As for the words 'while the Kingdom endures', they said that Gondor remained a 'kingdom', ruled by a vice-regent, and that the words must therefore be held to mean 'as long as the state of Gondor endures'.

Nonetheless, the Stewards, partly from awe, and partly from the cares of the kingdom, went very seldom to the hallow on the Hill of Anwar, except when they took their heir to the hill-top, according to the custom of the Kings. Sometimes it remained for several years unvisited, and as Isildur had prayed it was in the keeping of the Valar; for though the woods might grow tangled and be avoided by men because of the silence, so that the upward path was lost, still when the way was re-opened the hallow was found unweathered and unprofaned, ever-green and at peace under the sky, until the Kingdom of Gondor was changed.

For it came to pass that Cirion, the twelfth of the Ruling Stewards, was faced by a new and great danger: invaders threatened the conquest of all the lands of Gondor north of the White Mountains, and if that were to happen the downfall and destruction of the whole kingdom must soon follow. As is known in the histories, this peril was averted only by the aid of the Rohirrim; and to them Cirion with great wisdom granted all the northern lands, save Anórien, to be under their own rule and king, though in perpetual alliance with Gondor. There were no longer sufficient men in the realm to people the northward region, nor even to maintain in force the line of forts along the Anduin that had guarded its eastward boundary. Cirion gave long thought to this matter before he granted Calenardhon to the Horsemen of the North; and he judged that its cession must change wholly the 'Tradition of Isildur' with regard to the hallow of Amon Anwar. To that place he brought the Lord of the Rohirrim, and there by the mound of Elendil he with the greatest solemnity took the Oath of Eorl, and was answered by the Oath of Cirion, confirming for ever the alliance of the Kingdoms of the Rohirrim and of Gondor. But when this was done, and Eorl had returned to the North to bring back all his people to their new dwelling, Cirion removed the tomb of Elendil. For he judged that the 'Tradition of Isildur' was now made void. The hallow was no longer 'at the mid-point of the Kingdom of the South', but on the borders of another realm; and moreover the words 'while the Kingdom endures' referred to the Kingdom as it was when Isildur spoke, after surveying its bounds and defining them. It was true that other parts of the Kingdom had been lost since that day: Minas Ithil was in the hands of the Nazgûl, and Ithilien was desolate; but Gondor had not relinquished its claim to them. Calenardhon it had resigned for ever under oath. The casket therefore that Isildur had set within the mound Cirion removed to the Hallows of Minas Tirith; but the green mound remained as the memorial of a memorial. Nonetheless, even when it had become the site of a great beacon, the Hill of Anwar was still a place of reverence to Gondor and to the Rohirrim, who named it in their own tongue Halifirien, the Holy Mount.

# NOTES

1   No writing is extant with this title, but no doubt the narrative given in the third section ('Cirion and Eorl', p. 300) represents a part of it.

2   Such as the Book of the Kings. [Author's note.] – This work was referred to in the opening passage of Appendix A to *The Lord of the Rings*, as being (with *The Book of the Stewards* and the *Akallabêth*) among the records of Gondor that were opened to Frodo and Peregrin by King Elessar; but in the revised edition the reference was removed.

3   The East Bight, not named elsewhere, was the great indentation in the eastern border of Mirkwood seen in the map to *The Lord of the Rings*.

4   The Northmen appear to have been most nearly akin to the third and greatest of the peoples of the Elf-friends, ruled by the House of Hador. [Author's note.]

5   The escape of the army of Gondor from total destruction was in part
    due to the courage and loyalty of the horsemen of the Northmen under
    Marhari (a descendant of Vidugavia 'King of Rhovanion') who acted
    as rearguard. But the forces of Gondor had inflicted such losses on
    the Wainriders that they had not strength enough to press their
    invasion, until reinforced from the East, and were content for the
    time to complete their conquest of Rhovanion. [Author's note.] – It
    is told in Appendix A (I, iv) to *The Lord of the Rings* that Vidugavia,
    who called himself King of Rhovanion, was the most powerful of
    the princes of the Northmen; he was shown favour by Rómendacil II
    King of Gondor (died 1366), whom he had aided in war against the
    Easterlings, and the marriage of Rómendacil's son Valacar to Vidu-
    gavia's daughter Vidumavi led to the destructive Kin-strife in Gondor
    in the fifteenth century.

6   It is an interesting fact, not referred to I believe in any of my father's
    writings, that the names of the early kings and princes of the Northmen
    and the Éothéod are Gothic in form, not Old English (Anglo-Saxon)
    as in the case of Léod, Eorl, and the later Rohirrim. *Vidugavia* is
    Latinized in spelling, representing Gothic *Widugauja* ('wood-dweller'),
    a recorded Gothic name, and similarly *Vidumavi* Gothic *Widumawi*
    ('wood-maiden'). *Marhwini* and *Marhari* contain the Gothic word
    *marh* 'horse', corresponding to Old English *mearh*, plural *mearas*,
    the word used in *The Lord of the Rings* for the horses of Rohan;
    *wini* 'friend' corresponds to Old English *winë*, seen in the names of
    several of the Kings of the Mark. Since, as is explained in Appendix
    F (II), the language of Rohan was 'made to resemble ancient English',
    the names of the ancestors of the Rohirrim are cast into the forms of
    the earliest recorded Germanic language.

7   As was the form of the name in later days. [Author's note.] – This is
    Old English, 'horse-people'; see note 36.

8   The foregoing narrative does not contradict the accounts in Appendix
    A (I, iv and II) to *The Lord of the Rings*, though it is much briefer.
    Nothing is said here of the war fought against the Easterlings in
    the thirteenth century by Minalcar (who took the name of Rómendacil
    II), the absorption of many Northmen into the armies of Gondor by
    that king, or of the marriage of his son Valacar to a princess of the
    Northmen and the Kin-strife of Gondor that resulted from it; but
    it adds certain features which are not mentioned in *The Lord of the
    Rings*: that the waning of the Northmen of Rhovanion was due to the
    Great Plague; that the battle in which King Narmacil II was slain
    in the year 1856, said in Appendix A to have been 'beyond Anduin',
    was in the wide lands south of Mirkwood, and was known as the
    Battle of the Plains; and that his great army was saved from annihilation
    by the Wainriders through the rearguard defence of Marhari, descen-
    dant of Vidugavia. It is also made clearer here that it was after the

Battle of the Plains that the Éothéod, a remnant of the Northmen, became a distinct people, dwelling in the Vales of Anduin between the Carrock and the Gladden Fields.

9   His grandfather Telumehtar had captured Umbar and broken the power of the Corsairs, and the peoples of Harad were at this period engaged in wars and feuds of their own. [Author's note.] – The taking of Umbar by Telumehtar Umbardacil was in the year 1810.

10   The great westward bends of the Anduin east of Fangorn Forest; see the first citation given in Appendix C to 'The History of Galadriel and Celeborn', p. 260.

11   On the word éored see note 36.

12   This story is very much fuller than the summary account in Appendix A (I, iv) to The Lord of the Rings: 'Calimehtar, son of Narmacil II, helped by a revolt in Rhovanion, avenged his father with a great victory over the Easterlings upon Dagorlad in 1899, and for a while the peril was averted.'

13   The Narrows of the Forest must refer to the narrow 'waist' of Mirkwood in the south, caused by the indentation of the East Bight (see note 3).

14   Justly. For an attack proceeding from Near Harad – unless it had assistance from Umbar, which was not at that time available – could more easily be resisted and contained. It could not cross the Anduin, and as it went north passed into a narrowing land between the river and the mountains. [Author's note.]

15   An isolated note associated with the text remarks that at this period the Morannon was still in the control of Gondor, and the two Watch-towers east and west of it (the Towers of the Teeth) were still manned. The road through Ithilien was still in full repair as far as the Morannon; and there it met a road going north towards the Dagorlad, and another going east along the line of Ered Lithui. [Neither of these roads is marked on the maps to The Lord of the Rings.] The eastward road extended to a point north of the site of Barad-dûr; it had never been completed further, and what had been made was now long neglected. Nonetheless its first fifty miles, which had once been fully constructed, greatly speeded the Wainriders' approach.

16   Historians surmised that it was the same hill as that upon which King Elessar made his stand in the last battle against Sauron with which the Third Age ended. But if so it was still only a natural upswelling that offered little obstacle to horsemen and had not yet been piled up by the labour of Orcs. [Author's note.] – The passages in The Return of the King (V 10) here referred to tell that 'Aragorn now set the host in such array as could best be contrived, and they were drawn up on two great hills of blasted stone and earth that orcs had piled in years of labour,' and that Aragorn with Gandalf stood

on the one while the banners of Rohan and Dol Amroth were raised on the other.

17   On the presence of Adrahil of Dol Amroth see note 39.

18   Their former home: in the Vales of Anduin between the Carrock and the Gladden Fields, see p. 289.

19   The cause of the northward migration of the Éothéod is given in Appendix A (II) to *The Lord of the Rings*: '[The forefathers of Eorl] loved best the plains, and delighted in horses and all feats of horseman-ship, but there were many men in the middle vales of Anduin in those days, and moreover the shadow of Dol Guldur was lengthening; when therefore they heard of the overthrow of the Witch-king [in the year 1975], they sought more room in the North, and drove away the remnants of the people of Angmar on the east side of the Mountains. But in the days of Léod, father of Eorl, they had grown to be a numerous people and were again somewhat straitened in the land of their home.' The leader of the migration of the Éothéod was named Frumgar; and in the Tale of Years its date is given as 1977.

20   These rivers, unnamed, are marked on the map to *The Lord of the Rings*. The Greylin is there shown as having two tributary branches.

21   The Watchful Peace lasted from the years 2063 to 2460, when Sauron was absent from Dol Guldur.

22   For the forts along the Anduin see p. 292, and for the Undeeps p. 260.

23   From an earlier passage in this text (p. 290) one gains the impression that there were no Northmen left in the lands east of Mirkwood after the victory of Calimehtar over the Wainriders on the Dagorlad in the year 1899.

24   So these people were then called in Gondor: a mixed word of popular speech, from Westron *balc* 'horrible' and Sindarin *hoth* 'horde', applied to such peoples as the Orcs. [Author's note.] – See the entry *hoth* in the Appendix to *The Silmarillion*.

25   The letters R · ND · R surmounted by three stars, signifying *arandur* (king's servant), steward. [Author's note.]

26   He did not speak of the thought that he had also in mind: that the Éothéod were, as he had learned, restless, finding their northern lands too narrow and infertile to support their numbers, which had much increased. [Author's note.]

27   His name was long remembered in the song of *Rochon Methestel* (Rider of the Last Hope) as Borondir Udalraph (Borondir the Stirrup-less), for he rode back with the *éoherë* at the right hand of Eorl, and was the first to cross the Limlight and cleave a path to the aid of Cirion. He fell at last on the Field of Celebrant defending his lord, to the great grief of Gondor and the Éothéod, and was afterwards laid in tomb in the Hallows of Minas Tirith. [Author's note.]

28  Eorl's horse. In Appendix A (II) to *The Lord of the Rings* it is told
that Eorl's father Léod, who was a tamer of wild horses, was thrown
by Felaróf when he dared to mount him, and so he met his death.
Afterwards Eorl demanded of the horse that he surrender his freedom
till his life's end in wergild for his father; and Felaróf submitted,
though he would allow no man but Eorl to mount him. He understood
all that men said, and was as long-lived as they, as were his descendants, the *mearas*, 'who would bear no one but the King of the Mark
or his sons, until the time of Shadowfax'. *Felaróf* is a word of the
Anglo-Saxon poetic vocabulary, though not in fact recorded in the
extant poetry: 'very valiant, very strong'.

29  Between the inflow of the Limlight and the Undeeps. [Author's note.]
– This seems certainly in contradiction to the first citation given in
Appendix C to 'The History of Galadriel and Celeborn', p. 260,
where 'the North and South Undeeps' are 'the two westward bends'
of the Anduin, into the northmost of which the Limlight flowed in.

30  In nine days they had covered more than five hundred miles in a
direct line, probably more than six hundred as they rode. Though
there were no great natural obstacles on the east side of Anduin,
much of the land was now desolate, and roads or horse-paths running
southward were lost or little used; only for short periods were they
able to ride at speed, and they needed also to husband their own
strength and their horses', since they expected battle as soon as they
reached the Undeeps. [Author's note.]

31  The Halifirien is twice mentioned in *The Lord of the Rings*. In *The
Return of the King* I 1, when Pippin, riding with Gandalf on Shadowfax to Minas Tirith, cried out that he saw fires, Gandalf replied: 'The
beacons of Gondor are alight, calling for aid. War is kindled. See,
there is fire on Amon Dîn, and flame on Eilenach; and there they go
speeding west: Nardol, Erelas, Min-Rimmon, Calenhad, and the
Halifirien on the borders of Rohan.' In I 3 the Riders of Rohan on
their way to Minas Tirith passed through the Fenmarch 'where to
their right great oakwoods climbed on the skirts of the hills under the
shades of dark Halifirien by the borders of Gondor'. See the large-
scale map of Gondor and Rohan in *The Lord of the Rings*.

32  It was the great Númenórean road linking the Two Kingdoms,
crossing the Isen at the Fords of Isen and the Greyflood at Tharbad
and then on northwards to Fornost; elsewhere called the North–
South Road. See p. 264.

33  This is a modernized spelling for Anglo-Saxon *hálig-firgen*; similarly
Firien-dale for *firgen-dæl*, Firien Wood for *firgen-wudu*. [Author's
note.] – The *g* in the Anglo-Saxon word *firgen* 'mountain' came to be
pronounced as a modern *y*.

34  Minas Ithil, Minas Anor, and Orthanc.

35  It is said elsewhere, in a note on the names of the beacons, that 'the full beacon system, that was still operating in the War of the Ring, can have been no older than the settlement of the Rohirrim in Calenardhon some five hundred years before; for its principal function was to warn the Rohirrim that Gondor was in danger, or (more rarely) the reverse'.

36  According to a note on the ordering of the Rohirrim, the *éored* 'had no precisely fixed number, but in Rohan it was only applied to Riders, fully trained for war: men serving for a term, or in some cases permanently, in the King's Host. Any considerable body of such men, riding as a unit in exercise or on service, was called an *éored*. But after the recovery of the Rohirrim and the reorganization of their forces in the days of King Folcwine, a hundred years before the War of the Ring, a "full *éored*" in battle order was reckoned to contain not less than 120 men (including the Captain), and to be one hundredth part of the Full Muster of the Riders of the Mark, not including those of the King's Household. [The *éored* with which Éomer pursued the Orcs, *The Two Towers* III 2, had 120 Riders: Legolas counted 105 when they were far away, and Éomer said that fifteen men had been lost in battle with the Orcs.] No such host, of course, had ever ridden all together to war beyond the Mark; but Théoden's claim that he might, in this great peril, have led out an expedition of ten thousand Riders (*The Return of the King* V 3) was no doubt justified. The Rohirrim had increased since the days of Folcwine, and before the attacks of Saruman a Full Muster would probably have produced many more than twelve thousand Riders, so that Rohan would not have been denuded entirely of trained defenders. In the event, owing to losses in the western war, the hastiness of the Muster, and the threat from North and East, Théoden only led out a host of some six thousand spears, though this was still the greatest riding of the Rohirrim that was recorded since the coming of Eorl.'

The full muster of the cavalry was called *éoherë* (see note 49). These words, and also *Éothéod*, are of course Anglo-Saxon in form, since the true language of Rohan is everywhere thus translated (see note 6 above): they contain as their first element *eoh* 'horse'. *Éored*, *éorod* is a recorded Anglo-Saxon word, its second element derived from *rád* 'riding'; in *éoherë* the second element is *herë* 'host, army'. *Éothéod* has *théod* 'people' or 'land', and is used both of the Riders themselves and of their country. (Anglo-Saxon *eorl* in the name Eorl the Young is a wholly unrelated word.)

37  This was always said in the days of the Stewards, in any solemn pronouncement, though by the time of Cirion (the twelfth Ruling Steward) it had become a formula that few believed would ever come to pass. [Author's note.]

38  *alfirin*: the *simbelmynë* of the Kings' mounds below Edoras, and the *uilos* that Tuor saw in the great ravine of Gondolin in the Elder Days; see p. 55, note 27. *Alfirin* is named, but apparently of a different flower, in a verse that Legolas sang in Minas Tirith (*The Return of the King* V 9): 'The golden bells are shaken of mallos and alfirin / In the green fields of Lebennin.'

39  The Lord of Dol Amroth had this title. It was given to his ancestors by Elendil, with whom they had kinship. They were a family of the Faithful who had sailed from Númenor before the Downfall and had settled in the land of Belfalas, between the mouths of Ringló and Gilrain, with a stronghold upon the high promontory of Dol Amroth (named after the last King of Lórien). [Author's note.] – Elsewhere it is said (p. 248) that according to the tradition of their house the first Lord of Dol Amroth was Galador (c. Third Age 2004–2129), the son of Imrazôr the Númenórean, who dwelt in Belfalas, and the Elven-lady Mithrellas, one of the companions of Nimrodel. The note just cited seems to suggest that this family of the Faithful settled in Belfalas with a stronghold on Dol Amroth before the Downfall of Númenor; and if that is so, the two statements can only be reconciled on the supposition that the line of the Princes, and indeed the place of their dwelling, went back more than two thousand years before Galador's day, and that Galador was called the first Lord of Dol Amroth because it was not until his time (after the drowning of Amroth in the year 1981) that Dol Amroth was so named. A further difficulty is the presence of an Adrahil of Dol Amroth (clearly an ancestor of Adrahil the father of Imrahil, Lord of Dol Amroth at the time of the War of the Ring) as a commander of the forces of Gondor in the battle against the Wainriders in the year 1944 (pp. 293–4); but it may be supposed that this earlier Adrahil was not called 'of Dol Amroth' at that time.

    While not impossible, these explanations to save consistency seem to me to be less likely that than of two distinct and independent 'traditions' of the origins of the Lords of Dol Amroth.

40  The letters were ᴄᴘᴄ (L · ND · L): Elendil's name without vowel-marks, which he used as a badge, and a device upon his seals. [Author's note.]

41  Amon Anwar was in fact the high place nearest to the centre of a line from the inflow of the Limlight down to the southern cape of Tol Falas; and the distance from it to the Fords of Isen was equal to its distance from Minas Tirith. [Author's note.]

42  Though imperfectly; for it was in ancient terms and made in the forms of verse and high speech that were used by the Rohirrim, in which Eorl had great skill. [Author's note.] – There seems not to be any other version of the Oath of Eorl extant apart from that in the Common Speech given in the text.

43 *Vanda*: an oath, pledge, solemn promise. *ter-maruva*: *ter* 'through', *mar-* 'abide, be settled or fixed'; future tense. *Elenna·nóreo*: genitive case, dependent on *alcar*, of *Elenna·nórë* 'the land named Starwards'. *alcar*: 'glory'. *enyalien*: *en-* 'again', *yal-* 'summon', in infinitive (or gerundial) form *en-yalië*, here in dative 'for the re-calling', but governing a direct object, *alcar*: thus 'to recall or "commemorate" the glory'. *Vorondo*: genitive of *voronda* 'steadfast in allegiance, in keeping oath or promise, faithful'; adjectives used as a 'title' or frequently used attribute of a name are placed after the name, and as is usual in Quenya in the case of two declinable names in apposition only the last is declined. [Another reading gives the adjective as *vórimo* genitive of *vórima*, with the same meaning as *voronda*.] *voronwë*: 'steadfastness, loyalty, faithfulness', the object of *enyalien*.

    *Nai*: 'be it that, may it be that'; *Nai tiruvantes*: 'be it that they will guard it', i.e. 'may they guard it' (*-nte*, inflexion of 3 plural where no subject is previously mentioned). *i hárar*: 'they who are sitting upon'. *mahalmassen*: locative plural of *mahalma* 'throne'. *mi*: 'in the'. *Númen*: 'West'. *i Eru i*: 'the One who'. *eä*: 'is'. *tennoio*: *tenna* 'up to, as far as', *oio* 'an endless period'; *tennoio* 'for ever'. [Author's notes.]

44 And was not used again until King Elessar returned and renewed the bond in that same place with the King of the Rohirrim, Éomer the eighteenth descended from Eorl. It had been held lawful only for the King of Númenor to call Eru to witness, and then only on the most grave and solemn occasions. The line of the Kings had come to an end in Ar-Pharazôn who perished in the Downfall; but Elendil Voronda was descended from Tar-Elendil the fourth King, and was held to be the rightful lord of the Faithful, who had taken no part in the rebellion of the Kings and had been preserved from destruction. Cirion was the Steward of the Kings descended from Elendil, and so far as Gondor was concerned had as regent all their powers – until the King should come again. Nonetheless his oath astounded those who heard it, and filled them with awe, and was alone (over and above the venerable tomb) sufficient to hallow the place where it was spoken. [Author's note.] – Elendil's name Voronda, 'the Faithful', which appears also in Cirion's Oath, was in this note first written Voronwë, which in the Oath is a noun, meaning 'faithfulness, steadfastness'. But in Appendix A (I, ii) to *The Lord of the Rings* Mardil, the first Ruling Steward of Gondor, is called 'Mardil Voronwë "the Steadfast" '; and in the First Age the Elf of Gondolin who guided Tuor from Vinyamar was named Voronwë, which in the Index to *The Silmarillion* I likewise translated 'the Steadfast'.

45 See the first citation in Appendix C to 'The History of Galadriel and Celeborn', p. 260.

46 These names are given in Sindarin according to the usage of Gondor;

but many of them were named anew by the Éothéod, being alterations
of the older names to fit their own tongue, or translations of them,
or names of their own making. In the narrative of *The Lord of the
Rings* the names in the language of the Rohirrim are mostly used.
Thus Angren=Isen; Angrenost=Isengard; Fangorn (which is also
used)=Entwood; Onodló=Entwash; Glanhír=Mering Stream (both
mean 'boundary stream'). [Author's note.] – The name of the river
Limlight is perplexed. There are two versions of the text and note
at this point, from one of which it seems that the Sindarin name was
*Limlich*, adapted in the language of Rohan as *Limliht* ('modernized'
as *Limlight*). In the other (later) version, *Limlich* is emended, puzzlingly,
to *Limliht* in the text, so that this becomes the Sindarin form. Elsewhere (p. 281) the Sindarin name of this river is given as *Limlaith*.
In view of this uncertainty I have given *Limlight* in the text. Whatever
the original Sindarin name may have been, it is at least clear that the
Rohan form was an alteration of it and not a translation, and that
its meaning was not known (although in a note written much earlier
than any of the foregoing the name *Limlight* is said to be a partial
translation of Elvish *Limlint* 'swift-light'). The Sindarin names of
the Entwash and the Mering Stream are only found here; with
Onodló compare *Onodrim*, *Enyd*, the Ents (*The Lord of the Rings*,
Appendix F, 'Of Other Races').

47  *Athrad Angren*: see p. 264, where the Sindarin name for the Fords
of Isen is given as Ethraid Engrin. It seems then that both singular
and plural forms of the name of the Ford(s) existed.

48  Elsewhere the wood is always called the Firien Wood (a shortening
from Halifirien Wood). Firienholt – a word recorded in Anglo-Saxon
poetry (*firgenholt*) – means the same: 'mountain wood'. See note 33.

49  Their proper form was *Rochand* and *Rochir-rim*, and they were spelt
as *Rochand*, or *Rochan*, and *Rochirrim* in the records of Gondor. They
contain Sindarin *roch* 'horse', translating the *éo-* in *Éothéod* and in
many personal names of the Rohirrim [see note 36]. In *Rochand* the
Sindarin ending *-nd* (*-and, -end, -ond*) was added; it was commonly
used in the names of regions or countries, but the *-d* was usually
dropped in speech, especially in long names, such as *Calenardhon*,
*Ithilien*, *Lamedon*, etc. *Rochirrim* was modelled on *éo-herë*, the term
used by the Éothéod for the full muster of their cavalry in time of
war; it was made from *roch*+Sindarin *hír* 'lord, master' (entirely
unconnected with [the Anglo-Saxon word] *herë*). In the names of
peoples Sindarin *rim* 'great number, host' (Quenya *rimbë*) was
commonly used to form collective plurals, as in *Eledhrim* (*Edhelrim*)
'all Elves', *Onodrim* 'the Ent-folk', *Nogothrim* 'all Dwarves, the
Dwarf-people'. The language of the Rohirrim contained the sound
here represented by *ch* (a back spirant as *ch* in Welsh), and, though
it was infrequent in the middle of words between vowels, it presented

them with no difficulty. But the Common Speech did not possess it, and in pronouncing Sindarin (in which it was very frequent) the people of Gondor, unless learned, represented it by *h* in the middle of words and by *k* at the end of them (where it was most forcibly pronounced in correct Sindarin). Thus arose the names *Rohan* and *Rohirrim* as used in *The Lord of the Rings*. [Author's note.]

50  Eorl appears to have been unconvinced by the token of the White Lady's goodwill; see p. 299.

51  *Eilenaer* was a name of pre-Númenórean origin, evidently related to *Eilenach*. [Author's note.] – According to a note on the beacons, Eilenach was 'probably an alien name: not Sindarin, Númenórean, or Common Speech. . . . Both Eilenach and Eilenaer were notable features. Eilenach was the highest point of the Drúadan Forest. It could be seen far to the West, and its function in the days of the beacons was to transmit the warning of Amon Dîn; but it was not suitable for a large beacon-fire, there being little space on its sharp summit. Hence the name Nardol "Fire-hilltop" of the next beacon westward; it was on the end of a high ridge, originally part of the Drúadan Forest, but long deprived of trees by masons and quarriers who came up the Stonewain Valley. Nardol was manned by a guard, who also protected the quarries; it was well-stored with fuel and at need a great blaze could be lit, visible on a clear night even as far as the last beacon (Halifirien) some hundred and twenty miles to the westward.'

In the same note it is stated that 'Amon Dîn "the silent hill" was perhaps the oldest, with the original function of a fortified outpost of Minas Tirith, from which its beacon could be seen, to keep watch over the passage into North Ithilien from Dagorlad and any attempt by enemies to cross the Anduin at or near Cair Andros. Why it was given this name is not recorded. Probably because it was distinctive, a rocky and barren hill standing out and isolated from the heavily wooded hills of the Drúadan Forest (Tawar-in-Drúedain), little visited by men, beasts or birds.'

52  According to Appendix A (I, iv) to *The Lord of the Rings* it was in the days of Ostoher, the fourth king after Meneldil, that Gondor was first attacked by wild men out of the East; 'but Tarostar, his son, defeated them and drove them out, and took the name Rómendacil "East-victor" '.

53  It was also Rómendacil I who established the office of Steward (*Arandur* 'king's servant'), but he was chosen by the King as a man of high trust and wisdom, usually advanced in years since he was not permitted to go to war or to leave the realm. He was never a member of the Royal House. [Author's note.]

54  Mardil was the first of the Ruling Stewards of Gondor. He was the Steward to Eärnur the last King, who disappeared in Minas Morgul

in the year 2050. 'It was believed in Gondor that the faithless enemy had trapped the King, and that he had died in torment in Minas Morgul; but since there were no witnesses of his death, Mardil the Good Steward ruled Gondor in his name for many years' (*The Lord of the Rings*, Appendix A (I, iv)).

# III

# THE QUEST OF EREBOR

This story depends for its full understanding on the narrative given in Appendix A (III, *Durin's Folk*) to *The Lord of the Rings*, of which this is an outline:

The Dwarves Thrór and his son Thráin (together with Thráin's son Thorin, afterwards called Oakenshield) escaped from the Lonely Mountain (Erebor) by a secret door when the dragon Smaug descended upon it. Thrór returned to Moria, after giving to Thráin the last of the Seven Rings of the Dwarves, and was killed there by the Orc Azog, who branded his name on Thrór's brow. It was this that led to the War of the Dwarves and the Orcs, which ended in the great Battle of Azanulbizar (Nanduhirion) before the East-gate of Moria in the year 2799. Afterwards Thráin and Thorin Oakenshield dwelt in the Ered Luin, but in the year 2841 Thráin set out from there to return to the Lonely Mountain. While wandering in the lands east of Anduin he was captured and imprisoned in Dol Guldur, where the ring was taken from him. In 2850 Gandalf entered Dol Guldur and discovered that its master was indeed Sauron; and there he came upon Thráin before he died.

There is more than one version of 'The Quest of Erebor', as is explained in an Appendix following the text, where also substantial extracts from an earlier version are given.

I have not found any writing preceding the opening words of the present text ('He would say no more that day'). The 'He' of the opening sentence is Gandalf, 'we' are Frodo, Peregrin, Meriadoc, and Gimli, and 'I' is Frodo, the recorder of the conversation; the scene is a house in Minas Tirith, after the coronation of King Elessar (see p. 329).

He would say no more that day. But later we brought the matter up again, and he told us the whole strange story; how he came to arrange the journey to Erebor, why he thought of Bilbo, and how he persuaded the proud Thorin Oakenshield to take him into his company. I cannot remember all the tale now, but we gathered that to begin with Gandalf was thinking only of the defence of the West against the Shadow.

'I was very troubled at that time,' he said, 'for Saruman was hindering all my plans. I knew that Sauron had arisen again and would soon declare himself, and I knew that he was preparing for a great war. How would he begin? Would he try first to re-occupy Mordor, or would he first attack the chief strongholds of his enemies? I thought then, and I am sure now, that to attack Lórien and Rivendell, as soon as he was strong enough, was his original plan. It would have been a much better plan for him, and much worse for us.

'You may think that Rivendell was out of his reach, but I did not think so. The state of things in the North was very bad. The Kingdom under the Mountain and the strong Men of Dale were no more. To resist any force that Sauron might send to regain the northern passes in the mountains and the old lands of Angmar there were only the Dwarves of the Iron Hills, and behind them lay a desolation and a Dragon. The Dragon Sauron might use with terrible effect. Often I said to myself: "I must find some means of dealing with Smaug. But a direct stroke against Dol Guldur is needed still more. We must disturb Sauron's plans. I must make the Council see that."

'Those were my dark thoughts as I jogged along the road. I was tired, and I was going to the Shire for a short rest, after being away from it for more than twenty years. I thought that if I put them out of my mind for a while I might perhaps find some way of dealing with these troubles. And so I did indeed, though I was not allowed to put them out of my mind.

'For just as I was nearing Bree I was overtaken by Thorin Oakenshield,[1] who lived then in exile beyond the north-western borders of the Shire. To my surprise he spoke to me; and it was at that moment that the tide began to turn.

'He was troubled too, so troubled that he actually asked for my advice. So I went with him to his halls in the Blue Mountains, and I listened to his long tale. I soon understood that his heart was hot with brooding on his wrongs, and the loss of the treasure of his fore-fathers, and burdened too with the duty of revenge upon Smaug that he had inherited. Dwarves take such duties very seriously.

'I promised to help him if I could. I was as eager as he was to see the end of Smaug, but Thorin was all for plans of battle and war, as if he were really King Thorin the Second, and I could see no hope in that. So I left him and went off to the Shire, and picked up the threads of news. It was a strange business. I did no more than follow the lead of "chance", and made many mistakes on the way.

'Somehow I had been attracted by Bilbo long before, as a child, and a young hobbit: he had not quite come of age when I had last seen him. He had stayed in my mind ever since, with his eagerness and his bright eyes, and his love of tales, and his questions about the wide world outside the Shire. As soon as I entered the Shire I heard news of him. He was getting talked about, it seemed. Both his parents had died early for Shire-folk, at about eighty; and he had never married. He was already growing a bit queer, they said, and went off for days by himself. He could be seen talking to strangers, even Dwarves.

'"Even Dwarves!" Suddenly in my mind these three things came together: the great Dragon with his lust, and his keen hearing and scent; the sturdy heavy-booted Dwarves with their old burning grudge; and the quick, soft-footed Hobbit, sick at heart (I guessed) for a sight of the wide world. I laughed at myself; but I went off at once to have a look at Bilbo, to see what twenty years had done to him, and whether he was as promising as gossip seemed to make out. But he was not at home. They shook their heads in Hobbiton when I asked after him. "Off again," said one hobbit. It was Holman, the gardener, I believe.[2] "Off again. He'll go right off one of these days, if he isn't careful. Why, I asked him where he was going, and when he would be back, and *I don't know* he says; and then he looks at me queerly. *It depends if I meet any, Holman*, he says. *It's the Elves' New Year tomorrow!*[3] A pity, and him so kind a body. You wouldn't find a better from the Downs to the River."

'"Better and better!" I thought. "I think I shall risk it." Time was getting short. I had to be with the White Council in August at the latest, or Saruman would have his way and nothing would be done. And quite apart from greater matters, that might prove fatal to the quest: the power in Dol Guldur would not leave any attempt on Erebor unhindered, unless he had something else to deal with.

'So I rode off back to Thorin in haste, to tackle the difficult task of persuading him to put aside his lofty designs and go secretly – and take Bilbo with him. Without seeing Bilbo first. It was a mistake, and nearly proved disastrous. For Bilbo had changed, of course. At least, he was getting rather greedy and fat, and his old desires had dwindled down to a sort of private dream. Nothing could have been more dismaying than to find it actually in danger of coming true! He was altogether bewildered, and made a complete fool of himself. Thorin would have left in a rage, but for another strange chance, which I will mention in a moment.

'But you know how things went, at any rate as Bilbo saw them. The story would sound rather different, if I had written it. For one thing he did not realize at all how fatuous the Dwarves thought him, nor how angry they were with me. Thorin was much more indignant and contemptuous than he perceived. He was indeed contemptuous from the beginning, and thought then that I had planned the whole affair simply so as to make a mock of him. It was only the map and the key that saved the situation.

'But I had not thought of them for years. It was not until I got to the Shire and had time to reflect on Thorin's tale that I suddenly remembered the strange chance that had put them in my hands; and it began now to look less like chance. I remembered a dangerous journey of mine, ninety-one years before, when I had entered Dol Guldur in disguise, and had found there an unhappy Dwarf dying in the pits. I had no idea who he was. He had a map that had belonged to Durin's folk in Moria, and a key that seemed to go with it, though he was too far gone to explain it. And he said that he had possessed a great Ring.

'Nearly all his ravings were of that. *The last of the Seven* he said over and over again. But all these things he might have come by in many ways. He might have been a messenger caught as he fled, or even a thief trapped by a greater thief. But he gave the map and the key to me. "For my son," he said; and then he died, and soon after I escaped myself. I stowed the things away, and by some warning of my heart I kept them always with me, safe, but soon almost forgotten. I had other business in Dol Guldur more important and perilous than all the treasure of Erebor.

'Now I remembered it all again, and it seemed clear that I had heard the last words of Thráin the Second,[4] though he did not name himself or his son; and Thorin, of course, did not know what had become of his father, nor did he ever mention "the last of the Seven Rings". I had the plan and the key of the secret entrance to Erebor, by which Thrór and Thráin had escaped, according to Thorin's tale. And I had kept them, though without any design of my own, until the moment when they would prove most useful.

'Fortunately, I did not make any mistake in my use of them. I kept them up my sleeve, as you say in the Shire, until things looked quite hopeless. As soon as Thorin saw them he really made up his mind to follow my plan, as far as a secret expedition went at any rate. Whatever he thought of Bilbo he would have set out himself. The existence of a secret door, only discoverable by Dwarves, made it seem at least possible to find out something of the Dragon's doings, perhaps even to recover some gold, or some heirloom to ease his heart's longings.

'But that was not enough for me. I knew in my heart that Bilbo must go with him, or the whole quest would be a failure – or, as I should say now, the far more important events by the way would not come to pass. So I had still to persuade Thorin to take him. There were many difficulties on the road afterwards, but for me this was the most difficult part of the whole affair. Though I argued with him far into the night after Bilbo had retired, it was not finally settled until early the next morning.

'Thorin was contemptuous and suspicious. "He is soft," he snorted. "Soft as the mud of his Shire, and silly. His mother died too soon. You are playing some crooked game of your own, Master Gandalf. I am sure that you have other purposes than helping me."

'"You are quite right," I said. "If I had no other purposes, I should not be helping you at all. Great as your affairs may seem to you, they are only a small strand in the great web. I am concerned with many strands. But that should make my advice more weighty, not less." I spoke at last with great heat. "Listen to me, Thorin Oakenshield!" I said. "If this hobbit goes with you, you will succeed. If not, you will fail. A foresight is on me, and I am warning you."

'"I know your fame," Thorin answered. "I hope it is merited. But this foolish business of your hobbit makes me wonder whether it is foresight that is on you, and you are not crazed rather than foreseeing. So many cares may have disordered your wits."

'"They have certainly been enough to do so," I said. "And among them I find most exasperating a proud Dwarf who seeks advice from me (without claim on me that I know of), and then rewards me with insolence. Go your own ways, Thorin Oakenshield, if you will. But if you flout my advice, you will walk to disaster. And you will get neither counsel nor aid from me again until the Shadow falls on you. And curb your pride and your greed, or you will fall at the end of whatever path you take, though your hands be full of gold."

'He blenched a little at that; but his eyes smouldered. "Do not threaten me!" he said. "I will use my own judgement in this matter, as in all that concerns me."

'"Do so then!" I said. "I can say no more – unless it is this: I do not give my love or trust lightly, Thorin; but I am fond of this hobbit, and wish him well. Treat him well, and you shall have my friendship to the end of your days."

'I said that without hope of persuading him; but I could have said nothing better. Dwarves understand devotion to friends and gratitude to those who help them. "Very well," Thorin said at last after a silence. "He shall set out with my company, if he dares (which I doubt). But if you insist on burdening me with him, you must come too and look after your darling.''

' "Good!" I answered. "I will come, and stay with you as long as I can: at least until you have discovered his worth." It proved well in the end, but at the time I was troubled, for I had the urgent matter of the White Council on my hands.

'So it was that the Quest of Erebor set out. I do not suppose that when it started Thorin had any real hope of destroying Smaug. There was no hope. Yet it happened. But alas! Thorin did not live to enjoy his triumph or his treasure. Pride and greed overcame him in spite of my warning." '

'But surely,' I said, 'he might have fallen in battle anyway? There would have been an attack of Orcs, however generous Thorin had been with his treasure.'

'That is true,' said Gandalf. 'Poor Thorin! He was a great Dwarf of a great House, whatever his faults; and though he fell at the end of the journey, it was largely due to him that the Kingdom under the Mountain was restored, as I desired. But Dáin Ironfoot was a worthy successor. And now we hear that he fell fighting before Erebor again, even while we fought here. I should call it a heavy loss, if it was not a wonder rather that in his great age[5] he could still wield his axe as mightily as they say he did, standing over the body of King Brand before the Gate of Erebor until the darkness fell.

'It might all have gone very differently indeed. The main attack was diverted southwards, it is true; and yet even so with his far-stretched right hand Sauron could have done terrible harm in the North, while we defended Gondor, if King Brand and King Dáin had not stood in his path. When you think of the great Battle of Pelennor, do not forget the Battle of Dale. Think of what might have been. Dragon-fire and savage swords in Eriador! There might be no Queen in Gondor. We might now only hope to return from the victory here to ruin and ash. But that has been averted – because I met Thorin Oakenshield one evening on the edge of spring not far from Bree. A chance-meeting, as we say in Middle-earth.'

## NOTES

1   The meeting of Gandalf with Thorin is related also in Appendix A
    (III) to *The Lord of the Rings*, and there the date is given: 15 March,
    2941. There is the slight difference between the two accounts that
    in Appendix A the meeting took place in the inn at Bree and not on

the road. Gandalf had last visited the Shire twenty years before, thus in 2921, when Bilbo was thirty-one: Gandalf says later that he had not quite come of age [at thirty-three] when he last saw him.

2 Holman the gardener: Holman Greenhand, to whom Hamfast Gamgee (Sam's father, the Gaffer) was apprenticed: *The Fellowship of the Ring* I 1, and Appendix C.

3 The Elvish solar year (*loa*) began with the day called *yestarë*, which was the day before the first day of *tuilë* (Spring); and in the Calendar of Imladris *yestarë* 'corresponded more or less with Shire April 6'. (*The Lord of the Rings*, Appendix D.)

4 Thráin the Second: Thráin the First, Thorin's distant ancestor, escaped from Moria in the year 1981 and became the first King under the Mountain. (*The Lord of the Rings*, Appendix A (III).)

5 Dáin II Ironfoot was born in the year 2767; at the Battle of Azanulbizar (Nanduhirion) in 2799 he slew before the East-gate of Moria the great Orc Azog, and so avenged Thrór, Thorin's grandfather. He died in the Battle of Dale in 3019. (*The Lord of the Rings*, Appendices A (III) and B.) Frodo learnt from Glóin at Rivendell that 'Dáin was still King under the Mountain, and was now old (having passed his two hundred and fiftieth year), venerable, and fabulously rich'. (*The Fellowship of the Ring* II 1.)


# APPENDIX

## *Note on the texts of 'The Quest of Erebor'*

The textual situation in this piece is complex and hard to unravel. The earliest version is a complete but rough and much-emended manuscript, which I will here call A; it bears the title 'The History of Gandalf's Dealings with Thráin and Thorin Oakenshield'. From this a typescript, B, was made, with a great deal of further alteration, though mostly of a very minor kind. This is entitled 'The Quest of Erebor', and also 'Gandalf's Account of how he came to arrange the Expedition to Erebor and send Bilbo with the Dwarves'. Some extensive extracts from the typescript text are given below.

In addition to A and B ('the earlier version'), there is another manuscript, C, untitled, which tells the story in a more economical and tightly-constructed form, omitting a good deal from the first version and introducing some new elements, but also (particularly in the latter part) largely retaining the original writing. It seems to me to be quite certain that C is later than B, and C is the version that has been given above, although some writing has apparently been lost from the beginning, setting the scene in Minas Tirith for Gandalf's recollections.

The opening paragraphs of B (given below) are almost identical with a passage in Appendix A (III, *Durin's Folk*) to *The Lord of the Rings*, and obviously depend on the narrative concerning Thrór and Thráin that precedes them in Appendix A; while the ending of 'The Quest of Erebor' is also found in almost exactly the same words in Appendix A (III), here again in the mouth of Gandalf, speaking to Frodo and Gimli in Minas Tirith. In view of the letter cited in the Introduction (p. 11) it is clear that my father wrote 'The Quest of Erebor' to stand as part of the narrative of *Durin's Folk* in Appendix A.

## *Extracts from the earlier version*

The typescript B of the earlier version begins thus:

So Thorin Oakenshield became the Heir of Durin, but an heir without hope. At the sack of Erebor he had been too young to bear arms, but at Azanulbizar he had fought in the van of the assault; and when Thráin was lost he was ninety-five, a great Dwarf of proud bearing. He had no Ring, and (for that reason maybe) he seemed content to remain in Eriador. There he laboured long, and gained such wealth as he could; and his people were increased by many of the wandering Folk of Durin that heard of his dwelling and came to him. Now they had fair halls in the mountains, and store of goods, and their days did not seem so hard, though in their songs they spoke ever of the Lonely Mountain far away, and the treasure and the bliss of the Great Hall in the light of the Arkenstone.

The years lengthened. The embers in the heart of Thorin grew hot again, as he brooded on the wrongs of his House and of the vengeance upon the Dragon that was bequeathed to him. He thought of weapons and armies and alliances, as his great hammer rang in the forge; but the armies were dispersed and the alliances broken and the axes of his people were few; and a great anger without hope burned him, as he smote the red iron on the anvil.

Gandalf had not yet played any part in the fortunes of Durin's House. He had not had many dealings with the Dwarves; though he was a friend to those of good will, and liked well the exiles of Durin's Folk who lived in the West. But on a time it chanced that he was passing through Eriador (going to the Shire, which he had not seen for some years) when he fell in with Thorin Oakenshield, and they talked together on the road, and rested for the night at Bree.

In the morning Thorin said to Gandalf: 'I have much on my mind, and they say you are wise and know more than most of what goes on in the world. Will you come home with me and hear me, and give me your counsel?'

To this Gandalf agreed, and when they came to Thorin's hall he sat long with him and heard all the tale of his wrongs.

From this meeting there followed many deeds and events of great moment: indeed the finding of the One Ring, and its coming to the Shire, and the choosing of the Ringbearer. Many therefore have supposed that Gandalf foresaw all these things, and chose his time for the meeting with Thorin. Yet we believe that it was not so. For in his tale of the War of the Ring Frodo the Ringbearer left a record of Gandalf's words on this very point. This is what he wrote:

In place of the words 'This is what he wrote' A, the earliest manuscript, has: 'That passage was omitted from the tale, since it seemed long; but most of it we now set out here.'

After the crowning we stayed in a fair house in Minas Tirith with Gandalf, and he was very merry, and though we asked him questions about all that came into our minds his patience seemed as endless as his knowledge. I cannot now recall most of the things that he told us; often we did not understand them. But I remember this conversation very clearly. Gimli was there with us, and he said to Peregrin:

'There is a thing I must do one of these days: I must visit that Shire of yours.* Not to see more Hobbits! I doubt if I could learn anything about them that I do not know already. But no Dwarf of the House of Durin could fail to look with wonder on that land. Did not the recovery of the Kingship under the Mountain, and the fall of Smaug, begin there? Not to mention the end of Barad-dûr, though both were strangely woven together. Strangely, very strangely,' he said, and paused.

Then looking hard at Gandalf he went on: 'But who wove the web? I do not think I have ever considered that before. Did you plan all this then, Gandalf? If not, why did you lead Thorin Oakenshield to such an unlikely door? To find the Ring and bring it far away into the West for hiding, and then to choose the Ringbearer – and to restore the Mountain Kingdom as a mere deed by the way: was not that your design?'

Gandalf did not answer at once. He stood up, and looked out of the window, west, seawards; and the sun was then setting, and a glow was in his face. He stood so a long while silent. But at last he turned to Gimli and said: 'I do not know the answer. For I have changed since those days, and I am no longer trammelled by the burden of Middle-earth as I was then. In those days I should have answered you with words like those I used to Frodo, only last year in the spring. Only last year! But such measures are meaningless. In that far distant time I said to a small and frightened hobbit: Bilbo was *meant* to find the

* Gimli must at least have passed through the Shire on journeys from his original home in the Blue Mountains (see p. 336).

Ring, and *not* by its maker, and you therefore were *meant* to bear it. And I might have added: and I was *meant* to guide you both to those points.

'To do that I used in my waking mind only such means as were allowed to me, doing what lay to my hand according to such reasons as I had. But what I knew in my heart, or knew before I stepped on these grey shores: that is another matter. Olórin I was in the West that is forgotten, and only to those who are there shall I speak more openly.'

A has here: 'and only to those who are there (or who may, perhaps, return thither with me) shall I speak more openly.'

Then I said: 'I understand you a little better now, Gandalf, than I did before. Though I suppose that, whether *meant* or not, Bilbo might have refused to leave home, and so might I. You could not compel us. You were not even allowed to try. But I am still curious to know why you did what you did, as you were then, an old grey man as you seemed.'

Gandalf then explained to them his doubts at that time concerning Sauron's first move, and his fears for Lórien and Rivendell (cf. p. 322). In this version, after saying that a direct stroke against Sauron was even more urgent than the question of Smaug, he went on:

'That is why, to jump forward, I went off as soon as the expedition against Smaug was well started, and persuaded the Council to attack Dol Guldur first, before he attacked Lórien. We did, and Sauron fled. But he was always ahead of us in his plans. I must confess that I thought he really had retreated again, and that we might have another spell of watchful peace. But it did not last long. Sauron decided to take the next step. He returned at once to Mordor, and in ten years he declared himself.

'Then everything grew dark. And yet that was not his original plan; and it was in the end a mistake. Resistance still had somewhere where it could take counsel free from the Shadow. How could the Ringbearer have escaped, if there had been no Lórien or Rivendell? And those places might have fallen, I think, if Sauron had thrown all his power against them first, and not spent more than half of it in the assault on Gondor.

'Well, there you have it. That was my chief reason. But it is one thing to see what needs doing, and quite another to find the means. I was beginning to be seriously troubled about the situation in the North when I met Thorin Oakenshield one day: in the middle of March 2941, I think. I heard all his tale, and I thought: "Well, here is an enemy of Smaug at any rate! And one worthy of help. I must do what I can. I should have thought of Dwarves before."

'And then there was the Shire-folk. I began to have a warm place in my heart for them in the Long Winter, which none of you can remember.* They were very hard put to it then: one of the worst pinches they have been in, dying of cold, and starving in the dreadful dearth that followed. But that was the time to see their courage, and their pity one for another. It was by their pity as much as by their tough uncomplaining courage that they survived. I wanted them still to survive. But I saw that the Westlands were in for another very bad time again, sooner or later, though of quite a different sort: pitiless war. To come through that I thought they would need something more than they now had. It is not easy to say what. Well, they would want to know a bit more, understand a bit clearer what it was all about, and where they stood.

'They had begun to forget: forget their own beginnings and legends, forget what little they had known about the greatness of the world. It was not yet gone, but it was getting buried: the memory of the high and the perilous. But you cannot teach that sort of thing to a whole people quickly. There was not time. And anyway you must begin at some point, with some one person. I dare say he was "chosen" and I was only chosen to choose him; but I picked out Bilbo.'

'Now that is just what I want to know,' said Peregrin. 'Why did you do that?'

'How would you select any one Hobbit for such a purpose?' said Gandalf. 'I had not time to sort them all out; but I knew the Shire very well by that time, although when I met Thorin I had been away for more than twenty years on less pleasant business. So naturally thinking over the Hobbits that I knew, I said to myself: "I want a dash of the Took" (but not too much, Master Peregrin) "and I want a good foundation of the stolider sort, a Baggins perhaps." That pointed at once to Bilbo. And I had known him once very well, almost up to his coming of age, better than he knew me. I liked him then. And now I found that he was "unattached" – to jump on again, for of course I did not know all this until I went back to the Shire. I learned that he had never married. I thought that odd, though I guessed why it was; and the reason that I guessed was *not* the one that most of the Hobbits gave me: that he had early been left very well off and his own master. No, I guessed that he wanted to remain "unattached" for some reason deep down which he did not understand himself – or would not acknowledge, for it alarmed him. He wanted, all the same, to be free to go when the chance came, or he had made up his courage. I remembered how he used to pester me with questions when he was a youngster about the Hobbits that had occasionally "gone off", as they said in the Shire. There were at least two of his uncles on the Took side that had done so.'

* There is an account of the Long Winter of 2758-9 as it affected Rohan in Appendix A (II) to *The Lord of the Rings*; and the entry in the Tale of Years mentions that 'Gandalf came to the aid of the Shirefolk'.

These uncles were Hildifons Took, who 'went off on a journey and never returned', and Isengar Took (the youngest of the Old Took's twelve children), who was 'said to have "gone to sea" in his youth' (*The Lord of the Rings* Appendix C, Family Tree of Took of Great Smials).

When Gandalf accepted Thorin's invitation to go with him to his home in the Blue Mountains

'we actually passed through the Shire, though Thorin would not stop long enough for that to be useful. Indeed I think it was annoyance with his haughty disregard of the Hobbits that first put into my head the idea of entangling him with them. As far as he was concerned they were just food-growers who happened to work the fields on either side of the Dwarves' ancestral road to the Mountains.'

In this earlier version Gandalf gave a long account of how, after his visit to the Shire, he returned to Thorin and persuaded him 'to put aside his lofty designs and go secretly – and take Bilbo with him' – which sentence is all that is said of it in the later version (p. 323).

'At last I made up my mind, and I went back to Thorin. I found him in conclave with some of his kinsfolk. Balin and Glóin were there, and several others.

' "Well, what have you got to say?" Thorin asked me as soon as I came in.

' "This first," I answered. "Your own ideas are those of a king, Thorin Oakenshield; but your kingdom is gone. If it is to be restored, which I doubt, it must be from small beginnings. Far away here, I wonder if you fully realize the strength of a great Dragon. But that is not all: there is a Shadow growing fast in the world far more terrible. They will help one another." And they certainly would have done so, if I had not attacked Dol Guldur at the same time. "Open war would be quite useless; and anyway it is impossible for you to arrange it. You will have to try something simpler and yet bolder, indeed something desperate."

' "You are both vague and disquieting," said Thorin. "Speak more plainly!"

' "Well, for one thing," I said, "you will have to go on this quest yourself, and you will have to go *secretly*. No messengers, heralds, or challenges for you, Thorin Oakenshield. At most you can take with you a few kinsmen or faithful followers. But you will need something more, something unexpected."

' "Name it!" said Thorin.

' "One moment!" I said. "You hope to deal with a Dragon; and he is not only very great, but he is now also old and very cunning. From the beginning of your adventure you must allow for this: his memory, and his sense of smell."

' "Naturally," said Thorin. "Dwarves have had more dealings with

Dragons than most, and you are not instructing the ignorant."

'"Very good," I answered; "but your own plans did not seem to me to consider this point. My plan is one of stealth. *Stealth.* * Smaug does not lie on his costly bed without dreams, Thorin Oakenshield. He dreams of Dwarves! You may be sure that he explores his hall day by day, night by night, until he is sure that no faintest air of a Dwarf is near, before he goes to his sleep: his half-sleep, prick-eared for the sound of – Dwarf-feet."

'"You make your *stealth* sound as difficult and hopeless as any open attack," said Balin. "Impossibly difficult!"

'"Yes, it is difficult," I answered. "But not *impossibly* difficult, or I would not waste my time here. I would say *absurdly* difficult. So I am going to suggest an absurd solution to the problem. Take a Hobbit with you! Smaug has probably never heard of Hobbits, and he has certainly never smelt them."

'"What!" cried Glóin. "One of those simpletons down in the Shire? What use on earth, or under it, could he possibly be? Let him smell as he may, he would never dare to come within smelling distance of the nakedest dragonet new from the shell!"

'"Now, now!" I said, "that is quite unfair. You do not know much about the Shire-folk, Glóin. I suppose you think them simple, because they are generous and do not haggle; and think them timid because you never sell them any weapons. You are mistaken. Anyway, there is one that I have my eye on as a companion for you, Thorin. He is neat-handed and clever, though shrewd, and far from rash. And I think he has courage. Great courage, I guess, according to the way of his people. They are, you might say, 'brave at a pinch'. You have to put these Hobbits in a tight place before you find out what is in them."

'"The test cannot be made," Thorin answered. "As far as I have observed, they do all that they can to avoid tight places."

'"Quite true," I said. "They are a very sensible people. But this Hobbit is rather unusual. I think he could be persuaded to go into a tight place. I believe that in his heart he really desires to – to have, as he would put it, an adventure."

'"Not at my expense!" said Thorin, rising and striding about angrily. "This is not advice, it is foolery! I fail to see what any Hobbit, good or bad, could do that would repay me for a day's keep, even if he could be persuaded to start."

'"Fail to see! You would fail to hear it, more likely," I answered. "Hobbits move without effort more quietly than any Dwarf in the world could manage, though his life depended on it. They are, I suppose, the

---

* At this point a sentence in the manuscript, A, was perhaps unintentionally omitted in the typescript, in view of Gandalf's subsequent remark about Smaug's never having smelt a Hobbit: 'Also a scent that cannot be placed, at least not by Smaug, the enemy of Dwarves.'

most soft-footed of all mortal kinds. You do not seem to have observed that, at any rate, Thorin Oakenshield, as you tramped through the Shire, making a noise (I may say) that the inhabitants could hear a mile away. When I said that you would need stealth, I meant it: professional stealth."

'"Professional stealth?" cried Balin, taking up my words rather differently than I had meant them. "Do you mean a trained treasure-seeker? Can they still be found?"

'I hesitated. This was a new turn, and I was not sure how to take it. "I think so," I said at last. "For a reward they will go in where you dare not, or at any rate cannot, and get what you desire."

'Thorin's eyes glistened as the memories of lost treasures moved in his mind; but "A paid thief, you mean," he said scornfully. "That might be considered, if the reward was not too high. But what has all this to do with one of those villagers? They drink out of clay, and they cannot tell a gem from a bead of glass."

'"I wish you would not always speak so confidently without knowledge," I said sharply. "These villagers have lived in the Shire some fourteen hundred years, and they have learned many things in the time. They had dealings with the Elves, and with the Dwarves, a thousand years before Smaug came to Erebor. None of them are wealthy as your forefathers reckoned it, but you will find some of their dwellings have fairer things in them than you can boast here, Thorin. The Hobbit that I have in mind has ornaments of gold, and eats with silver tools, and drinks wine out of shapely crystal."

'"Ah! I see your drift at last," said Balin. "He is a thief, then? That is why you recommend him?"

'At that I fear I lost my temper and my caution. This Dwarvish conceit that no one can have or make anything "of value" save themselves, and that all fine things in other hands must have been got, if not stolen, from the Dwarves at some time, was more than I could stand at that moment. "A thief?" I said, laughing. "Why yes, a professional thief, of course! How else would a Hobbit come by a silver spoon? I will put the thief's mark on his door, and then you will find it." Then being angry I got up, and I said with a warmth that surprised myself: "You must look for that door, Thorin Oakenshield! I am *serious*." And suddenly I felt that I was indeed in hot earnest. This queer notion of mine was not a joke, it was *right*. It was desperately important that it should be carried out. The Dwarves must bend their stiff necks.

'"Listen to me, Durin's Folk!" I cried. "If you persuade this Hobbit to join you, you will succeed. If you do not, you will fail. If you refuse even to try, then I have finished with you. You will get no more advice or help from me until the Shadow falls on you!"

'Thorin turned and looked at me in astonishment, as well he might. "Strong words!" he said. "Very well, I will come. Some foresight is on you, if you are not merely crazed."

' "Good!" I said. "But you must come with good will, not merely in
the hope of proving me a fool. You must be patient and not easily put
off, if neither the courage nor the desire for adventure that I speak of
are plain to see at first sight. He will deny them. He will try to back
out; but *you must not* let him." '

' "Haggling will not help him, if that is what you mean," said Thorin.
"I will offer him a fair reward for anything that he recovers, and no
more." '

'It was not what I meant, but it seemed useless to say so. "There
is one other thing," I went on; "you must make all your plans and
preparations beforehand. Get everything ready! Once persuaded he
must have no time for second thoughts. You must go straight from the
Shire, east on your quest." '

' "He sounds a very strange creature, this thief of yours," said a
young Dwarf called Fíli (Thorin's nephew, as I afterwards learned).
"What is his name, or the one that he uses?" '

' "Hobbits use their real names," I said. "The only one that he has
is Bilbo Baggins." '

' "What a name!" said Fíli, and laughed. '

' "He thinks it very respectable," I said. "And it fits well enough; for
he is a middle-aged bachelor, and getting a bit flabby and fat. Food is
perhaps at present his main interest. He keeps a very good larder, I
am told, and maybe more than one. At least you will be well entertained." '

' "That is enough," said Thorin. "If I had not given my word, I
would not come now. I am in no mood to be made a fool of. For I am
serious also. Deadly serious, and my heart is hot within me." '

'I took no notice of this. "Look now, Thorin," I said, "April is
passing and Spring is here. Make everything ready as soon as you can.
I have some business to do, but I shall be back in a week. When I
return, if all is in order, I will ride on ahead to prepare the ground.
Then we will all visit him together on the following day." '

'And with that I took my leave, not wishing to give Thorin more
chance of second thoughts than Bilbo was to have. The rest of the story
is well known to you – from Bilbo's point of view. If I had written the
account, it would have sounded rather different. He did not know all
that went on: the care, for instance, that I took so that the coming of a
large party of Dwarves to Bywater, off the main road and their usual
beat, should not come to his ears too soon.

'It was on the morning of Tuesday, April the 25th, 2941, that I
called to see Bilbo; and though I knew more or less what to expect, I
must say that my confidence was shaken. I saw that things would be
far more difficult than I had thought. But I persevered. Next day,
Wednesday, April the 26th, I brought Thorin and his companions to
Bag End; with great difficulty so far as Thorin was concerned – he hung
back at the last. And of course Bilbo was completely bewildered and
behaved ridiculously. Everything in fact went extremely badly for me

from the beginning; and that unfortunate business about the "professional thief", which the Dwarves had got firmly into their heads, only made matters worse. I was thankful that I had told Thorin we should all stay the night at Bag End, since we should need time to discuss ways and means. It gave me a last chance. If Thorin had left Bag End before I could see him alone, my plan would have been ruined.'

It will be seen that some elements of this conversation were in the later version taken up into the argument between Gandalf and Thorin at Bag End.

From this point the narrative in the later version follows the earlier very closely, which is not therefore further cited here, except for a passage at the end. In the earlier, when Gandalf ceased speaking, Frodo records that Gimli laughed.

'It still sounds absurd,' he said, 'even now that all has turned out more than well. I knew Thorin, of course; and I wish I had been there, but I was away at the time of your first visit to us. And I was not allowed to go on the quest: too young, they said, though at sixty-two I thought myself fit for anything. Well, I am glad to have heard the full tale. If it is full. I do not really suppose that even now you are telling us all you know.'

'Of course not,' said Gandalf.

And after this Meriadoc questioned Gandalf further about Thráin's map and key; and in the course of his reply (most of which is retained in the later version, at a different point in the narrative) Gandalf said:

'It was nine years after Thráin had left his people that I found him, and he had then been in the pits of Dol Guldur for five years at least. I do not know how he endured so long, nor how he had kept these things hidden through all his torments. I think that the Dark Power had desired nothing from him except the Ring only, and when he had taken that he troubled no further, but just flung the broken prisoner into the pits to rave until he died. A small oversight; but it proved fatal. Small oversights often do.'

# IV

# THE HUNT FOR THE RING

## (i)

### *Of the Journey of the Black Riders according to the account that Gandalf gave to Frodo*

Gollum was captured in Mordor in the year 3017 and taken to Barad-dûr, and there questioned and tormented. When he had learned what he could from him, Sauron released him and sent him forth again. He did not trust Gollum, for he divined something indomitable in him, which could not be overcome, even by the Shadow of Fear, except by destroying him. But Sauron perceived the depth of Gollum's malice towards those that had 'robbed' him, and guessing that he would go in search of them to avenge himself, Sauron hoped that his spies would thus be led to the Ring.

Gollum, however, was before long captured by Aragorn, and taken to Northern Mirkwood; and though he was followed, he could not be rescued before he was in safe keeping. Now Sauron had never paid heed to the 'halflings', even if he had heard of them, and he did not yet know where their land lay. From Gollum, even under pain, he could not get any clear account, both because Gollum indeed had no certain knowledge himself, and because what he knew he falsified. Ultimately indomitable he was, except by death, as Sauron guessed, both from his halfling nature, and from a cause which Sauron did not fully comprehend, being himself consumed by lust for the Ring. Then he became filled with a hatred of Sauron even greater than his terror, seeing in him truly his greatest enemy and rival. Thus it was that he dared to pretend that he believed that the land of the Halflings was near to the places where he had once dwelt beside the banks of the Gladden.

Now Sauron learning of the capture of Gollum by the chiefs of his enemies was in great haste and fear. Yet all his ordinary spies and emissaries could bring him no tidings. And this was due largely both to the vigilance of the Dúnedain and to the treachery of Saruman, whose own servants either waylaid or misled the servants of Sauron.

Of this Sauron became aware, but his arm was not yet long enough to reach Saruman in Isengard. Therefore he hid his knowledge of Saruman's double-dealing and concealed his wrath, biding his time, and preparing for the great war in which he planned to sweep all his enemies into the western sea. At length he resolved that no others would serve him in this case but his mightiest servants, the Ringwraiths, who had no will but his own, being each utterly subservient to the ring that had enslaved him, which Sauron held.

Now few could withstand even one of these fell creatures, and (as Sauron deemed) none could withstand them when gathered together under their terrible captain, the Lord of Morgul. Yet this weakness they had for Sauron's present purpose: so great was the terror that went with them (even invisible and unclad) that their coming forth might soon be perceived and their mission be guessed by the Wise.

So it was that Sauron prepared two strokes – in which many after saw the beginnings of the War of the Ring. They were made together. The Orcs assailed the realm of Thranduil, with orders to recapture Gollum; and the Lord of Morgul was sent forth openly to battle against Gondor. These things were done towards the end of June 3018. Thus Sauron tested the strength and preparedness of Denethor, and found them more than he had hoped. But that troubled him little, since he had used little force in the assault, and his chief purpose was that the coming forth of the Nazgûl should appear only as part of his policy of war against Gondor.

Therefore when Osgiliath was taken and the bridge broken Sauron stayed the assault, and the Nazgûl were ordered to begin the search for the Ring. But Sauron did not underesteem the powers and vigilance of the Wise, and the Nazgûl were commanded to act as secretly as they could. Now at that time the Chieftain of the Ringwraiths dwelt in Minas Morgul with six companions, while the second to the Chief, Khamûl the Shadow of the East, abode in Dol Guldur as Sauron's lieutenant, with one other as his messenger.[1]

The Lord of Morgul therefore led his companions over Anduin, unclad and unmounted, and invisible to eyes, and yet a terror to all living things that they passed near. It was, maybe, on the first day of July that they went forth. They passed slowly and in stealth, through Anórien, and over the Entwade, and so into the Wold, and rumour of darkness and a dread of men knew not what went before them. They reached the west-shores of Anduin a little north of Sarn Gebir, as they had trysted; and there received horses and raiment that were secretly ferried over the River. This was (it is thought) about the seventeenth of July. Then they passed northward seeking for the Shire, the land of the Halflings.

About the twenty-second of July they met their companions, the Nazgûl of Dol Guldur, in the Field of Celebrant. There they learned that Gollum had eluded both the Orcs that recaptured him, and the Elves that pursued them, and had vanished.[2] They were told also by Khamûl that no dwelling of Halflings could be discovered in the Vales of Anduin, and that the villages of the Stoors by the Gladden had long been deserted. But the Lord of Morgul, seeing no better counsel, determined still to seek northward, hoping maybe to come upon Gollum as well as to discover the Shire. That this would prove to be not far from the hated land of Lórien seemed to him not unlikely, if it was not indeed within the fences of Galadriel. But the power of the White Ring he would not defy, nor enter yet into Lórien. Passing therefore between Lórien and the Mountains the Nine rode ever on into the North; and terror went before them and lingered behind them; but they did not find what they sought nor learn any news that availed them.

At length they returned; but the summer was now far waned, and the wrath and fear of Sauron was mounting. When they came back to the Wold September had come; and there they met messengers from Barad-dûr conveying threats from their Master that filled even the Morgul-lord with dismay. For Sauron had now learned of the words of prophecy heard in Gondor, and the going forth of Boromir, of Saruman's deeds, and the capture of Gandalf. From these things he concluded indeed that neither Saruman nor any other of the Wise had possession yet of the Ring, but that Saruman at least knew where it might be hidden. Speed alone would now serve, and secrecy must be abandoned.

The Ringwraiths therefore were ordered to go straight to Isengard. They rode then through Rohan in haste, and the terror of their passing was so great that many folk fled from the land, and went wildly away north and west, believing that war out of the East was coming on the heels of the black horses.

Two days after Gandalf had departed from Orthanc, the Lord of Morgul halted before the Gate of Isengard. Then Saruman, already filled with wrath and fear by the escape of Gandalf, perceived the peril of standing between enemies, a known traitor to both. His dread was great, for his hope of deceiving Sauron, or at the least of receiving his favour in victory, was utterly lost. Now either he himself must gain the Ring or come to ruin and torment. But he was wary and cunning still, and he had ordered Isengard against just such an evil chance. The Circle of Isengard was too strong for even the Lord of Morgul and his company to assail without great force of war. Therefore to his challenge and demands he received only the answer of the voice of Saruman, that spoke by some art as though it came from the Gate itself.

'It is not a land that you look for,' it said. 'I know what you seek, though you do not name it. I have it not, as surely its servants perceive without telling; for if I had it, then you would bow before me and call me Lord. And if I knew where this thing was hid, I should not be here, but long gone before you to take it. There is one only whom I guess to have this knowledge: Mithrandir, enemy of Sauron. And since it is but two days since he departed from Isengard, seek him nearby.'

Such was still the power of the voice of Saruman that even the Lord of the Nazgûl did not question what it said, whether it was false or short of the full truth; but straightway he rode from the Gate and began to hunt for Gandalf in Rohan. Thus it was that on the evening of the next day the Black Riders came upon Gríma Wormtongue as he hastened to bring word to Saruman that Gandalf was come to Edoras, and had warned King Théoden of the treacherous designs of Isengard. In that hour the Wormtongue came near to death by terror; but being inured to treachery he would have told all that he knew under less threat.

'Yea, yea, verily I can tell you, Lord,' he said. 'I have overheard their speech together in Isengard. The land of the Halflings: it was thence that Gandalf came, and desires to return. He seeks now only a horse.

'Spare me! I speak as swiftly as I may. West through the Gap of Rohan yonder, and then north and a little west, until the next great river bars the way; the Greyflood it is called. Thence from the crossing at Tharbad the old road will lead you to the borders. "The Shire", they call it.

'Yea, verily, Saruman knows of it. Goods came to him from that land down the road. Spare me, Lord! Indeed I will say naught of our meeting to any that live.'

The Lord of the Nazgûl spared the life of the Wormtongue, not out of pity, but because he deemed that so great a terror was upon him that he would never dare to speak of their encounter (as proved true), and he saw that the creature was evil and was likely to do great harm yet to Saruman, if he lived. So he left him lying on the ground, and rode away, and did not trouble to go back to Isengard. Sauron's vengeance could wait.

Now he divided his company into four pairs, and they rode separately, but he himself went ahead with the swiftest pair. Thus they passed west out of Rohan, and explored the desolation of Enedwaith, and came at last to Tharbad. Thence they rode through Minhiriath, and even though they were not yet assembled a rumour of dread spread about them, and the creatures of the wild hid themselves, and lonely men fled away. But some fugitives on the road they captured; and to the delight of the Captain two proved to be spies and servants of Saruman. One of them had been used much in the traffic between Isengard and the Shire, and though he had not himself been beyond the Southfarthing he had charts prepared by Saruman which clearly depicted and described the Shire. These the Nazgûl took, and then sent him on to Bree to continue spying; but warned him that he was now in the service of Mordor, and that if ever he tried to return to Isengard they would slay him with torture.

Night was waning on the twenty-second day of September when drawing together again they came to Sarn Ford and the southernmost borders of the Shire. They found them guarded, for the Rangers barred their way. But this was a task beyond the power of the Dúnedain; and maybe it would still have proved so even if their captain, Aragorn, had been with them. But he was away to the north, upon the East Road near Bree; and the hearts even of the Dúnedain misgave them. Some fled northward, hoping to bear news to Aragorn, but they were pursued and slain or driven away into the wild. Some still dared to bar the ford, and held it while day lasted, but at night the Lord of Morgul swept them away, and the Black Riders passed into the Shire; and ere the cocks crowed in the small hours of the twenty-third day of September some were riding north through the land, even as Gandalf upon Shadowfax was riding over Rohan far behind.

(ii)

*Other Versions of the Story*

I have chosen to give the version printed above as being the most finished as a narrative; but there is much other writing that bears on these events, adding to or modifying the story in important particulars. These manuscripts are confusing and their relations obscure, though they all doubtless derive from the same period, and it is sufficient to note the existence of two other primary accounts beside the one printed (here called for convenience 'A'). A second version ('B') agrees very largely with A in its narrative structure, but a third ('C'), in the form of a plot-outline beginning at a later point in the story, introduces some substantial differences, and this I am inclined to think is the latest in order of composition. In addition there is some material ('D') more particularly concerned with Gollum's part in the events, and various other notes bearing on this part of the history.

In D it is said that what Gollum revealed to Sauron of the Ring and the place of its finding was sufficient to warn Sauron that this was indeed the One, but that of its present whereabouts he could only discover that it was stolen by a creature named *Baggins* in the Misty Mountains, and that *Baggins* came from a land called *Shire*. Sauron's fears were much allayed when he perceived from Gollum's account that *Baggins* must have been a creature of the same sort.

Gollum would not know the term 'Hobbit', which was local and not a universal Westron word. He would probably not use 'Halfling' since he was one himself, and Hobbits disliked the name. That is why the Black Riders seem to have had two main pieces of information only to go on: *Shire* and *Baggins*.

From all the accounts it is clear that Gollum did at least know in which direction the Shire lay; but though no doubt more could have been wrung from him by torture, Sauron plainly had no inkling that *Baggins* came from a region far removed from the Misty Mountains or that Gollum knew where it was, and assumed that he would be found in the Vales of Anduin, in the same region as Gollum himself had once lived.

This was a very small and natural error – but possibly the most important mistake that Sauron made in the whole affair. But for it, the Black Riders would have reached the Shire weeks sooner.

In the text B more is told of the journey of Aragorn with the captive Gollum northwards to the realm of Thranduil, and more consideration is given to Sauron's doubts about the use of the Ringwraiths in the search for the Ring.

[After his release from Mordor] Gollum soon disappeared into the Dead Marshes, where Sauron's emissaries could not or would not follow him. No other spies of Sauron could bring him any news. (Sauron probably had very little power yet in Eriador, and few agents there; and such as he sent were often hindered or misled by the servants of Saruman). At length therefore he resolved to use the Ringwraiths. He had been reluctant to do so, until he knew precisely where the Ring was, for several reasons. They were by far the most powerful of his servants, and the most suitable for such a mission, since they were entirely enslaved to their Nine Rings, which he now himself held; they were quite incapable of acting against his will, and if one of them, even the Witch-king their captain, had seized the One Ring, he would have brought it back to his Master. But they had disadvantages, until open war began (for which Sauron was not yet ready). All except the Witch-king were apt to stray when alone by daylight; and all, again save the Witch-king, feared water, and were unwilling, except in dire need, to enter it or to cross streams unless dryshod by a bridge.[3] Moreover, their chief weapon was terror. This was actually greater when they were unclad and invisible; and it was greater also when they were gathered together. So any mission on which they were sent could hardly be conducted with secrecy; while the passage of Anduin and other rivers presented an obstacle. For such reasons Sauron long hesitated, since he did not desire that his chief enemies should become aware of his servants' errand. It must be supposed that Sauron did not know at first that anyone save Gollum and 'the thief Baggins' had any knowledge of the Ring. Until Gandalf came and questioned him[4] Gollum did not know that Gandalf had any connexion with Bilbo, he had not even known of Gandalf's existence.

But when Sauron learned of Gollum's capture by his enemies the situation was drastically changed. When and how this happened cannot of course be known for certain. Probably long after the event. According to Aragorn Gollum was taken at nightfall on February 1st. Hoping to escape detection by any of Sauron's spies he drove Gollum through the north end of the Emyn Muil, and crossed Anduin just above Sarn Gebir. Driftwood was often cast up there on the shoals by the east shore, and binding Gollum to a log he swam across with him, and continued his journey north by tracks as westerly as he could find, through the skirts of Fangorn, and so over Limlight, then over Nimrodel and Silverlode through the eaves of Lórien,[5] and then on, avoiding Moria and Dimrill Dale, over Gladden until he came near the Carrock. There he crossed Anduin again, with the help of the Beornings, and passed into the Forest. The whole journey, on foot, was not much short of nine hundred miles, and this Aragorn accomplished with weariness in fifty days, reaching Thranduil on the twenty-first of March.[6]

It is thus most likely that the first news of Gollum would be learned by the servants of Dol Guldur after Aragorn entered the Forest; for though the power of Dol Guldur was supposed to come to an end at the Old Forest Road, its spies were many in the wood. The news evidently did not reach the Nazgûl commander of Dol Guldur for some time, and he probably did not inform Barad-dûr until he had tried to learn more of Gollum's whereabouts. It would then no doubt be late in April before Sauron heard that Gollum had been seen again, apparently captive in the hands of a Man. This might mean little. Neither Sauron nor any of his servants yet knew of Aragorn or who he was. But evidently later (since the lands of Thranduil would now be closely watched), possibly a month later, Sauron heard the disquieting news that the Wise were aware of Gollum, and that Gandalf had passed into Thranduil's realm.

Sauron must then have been filled with anger and alarm. He resolved to use the Ringwraiths as soon as he could, for speed rather than secrecy was now important. Hoping to alarm his enemies and disturb their counsels with the fear of war (which he did not intend to make for some time), he attacked Thranduil and Gondor at about the same time.[7] He had these two additional objects: to capture or kill Gollum, or at least to deprive his enemies of him; and to force the passage of the bridge of Osgiliath, so that the Nazgûl could cross, while testing the strength of Gondor.

In the event Gollum escaped. But the passage of the bridge was effected. The forces there used were probably much less than men in Gondor thought. In the panic of the first assault, when the Witch-king was allowed to reveal himself briefly in his full terror,[8] the Nazgûl crossed the bridge at night and dispersed northwards. Without belittling the valour of Gondor, which indeed Sauron found greater far than he had hoped, it is clear that Boromir and Faramir were able to drive back the enemy and destroy the bridge, only because the attack had now served its main purpose.

My father nowhere explained the Ringwraiths' fear of water. In the account just cited it is made a chief motive in Sauron's assault on Osgiliath, and it reappears in detailed notes on the movements of the Black Riders in the Shire: thus of the Rider (who was in fact Khamûl of Dol Guldur, see note 1) seen on the far side of Bucklebury Ferry just after the Hobbits had crossed (*The Fellowship of the Ring* I 5) it is said that 'he was well aware that the Ring had crossed the river; but the river was a barrier to his sense of its movement', and that the Nazgûl would not touch the 'Elvish' waters of Baranduin. But it is not made clear how they crossed other rivers that lay in their path, such as the Greyflood, where there was only 'a dangerous ford formed by the ruins of the bridge' (p. 264). My father did indeed note that the idea was difficult to sustain.

The account of the vain journey of the Nazgûl up the Vales of
Anduin is much the same in version B as in that printed in full above
(A), but with the difference that in B the Stoor settlements were not
entirely deserted at that time; and such of the Stoors as dwelt there
were slain or driven away by the Nazgûl.[9] In all the texts the precise
dates are slightly at variance both with each other and with those given
in the Tale of Years; these differences are here neglected.

In D is found an account of how Gollum fared after his escape from
the Orcs of Dol Guldur and before the Fellowship entered the West-gate
of Moria. This is in a rough state and has required some slight editorial
revision.

It seems clear that pursued both by Elves and Orcs Gollum crossed
the Anduin, probably by swimming, and so eluded the hunt of
Sauron; but being still hunted by Elves, and not yet daring to pass
near Lórien (only the lure of the Ring itself made him dare to do this
afterwards), he hid himself in Moria.[10] That was probably in the
autumn of the year; after which all trace of him was lost.

What then happened to Gollum cannot of course be known for
certain. He was peculiarly fitted to survive in such straits, though at
cost of great misery; but he was in great peril of discovery by the
servants of Sauron that lurked in Moria,[11] especially since such bare
necessity of food as he must have he could only get by thieving
dangerously. No doubt he had intended to use Moria simply as a
secret passage westward, his purpose being to find 'Shire' himself as
quickly as he could; but he became lost, and it was a very long time
before he found his way about. It thus seems probable that he had
not long made his way towards the West-gate when the Nine Walkers
arrived. He knew nothing, of course, about the action of the doors.
To him they would seem huge and immovable; and though they
had no lock or bar and opened outwards to a thrust, he did not
discover that. In any case he was now far away from any source of
food, for the Orcs were mostly in the East-end of Moria, and was
become weak and desperate, so that even if he had known all about
the doors he still could not have thrust them open.[12] It was thus a
piece of singular good fortune for Gollum that the Nine Walkers
arrived when they did.

The story of the coming of the Black Riders to Isengard in September
3018, and their subsequent capture of Gríma Wormtongue, as told in
A and B, is much altered in version C, which takes up the narrative
only at their return southward over the Limlight. In A and B it was

two days after Gandalf's escape from Orthanc that the Nazgûl came to Isengard; Saruman told them that Gandalf was gone, and denied all knowledge of the Shire,[13] but was betrayed by Gríma whom they captured on the following day as he hastened to Isengard with news of Gandalf's coming to Edoras. In C, on the other hand, the Black Riders arrived at the Gate of Isengard while Gandalf was still a prisoner in the tower. In this account, Saruman, in fear and despair, and perceiving the full horror of service to Mordor, resolved suddenly to yield to Gandalf, and to beg for his pardon and help. Temporizing at the Gate, he admitted that he had Gandalf within, and said that he would go and try to discover what he knew; if that were unavailing, he would deliver Gandalf up to them. Then Saruman hastened to the summit of Orthanc – and found Gandalf gone. Away south against the setting moon he saw a great Eagle flying towards Edoras.

Now Saruman's case was worse. If Gandalf had escaped there was still a real chance that Sauron would not get the Ring, and would be defeated. In his heart Saruman recognized the great power and the strange 'good fortune' that went with Gandalf. But now he was left alone to deal with the Nine. His mood changed, and his pride reasserted itself in anger at Gandalf's escape from impenetrable Isengard, and in a fury of jealousy. He went back to the Gate, and he lied, saying that he had made Gandalf confess. He did not admit that this was his own knowledge, not being aware of how much Sauron knew of his mind and heart.[14] 'I will report this myself to the Lord of Barad-dûr,' he said loftily, 'to whom I speak from afar on great matters that concern us. But all that you need to know on the mission that he has given you is where "the Shire" lies. That, says Mithrandir, is northwest from here some six hundred miles, on the borders of the seaward Elvish country.' To his pleasure Saruman saw that even the Witch-king did not relish that. 'You must cross Isen by the Fords, and then rounding the Mountains' end make for Tharbad upon Greyflood. Go with speed, and I will report to your Master that you have done so.'

This skilful speech convinced even the Witch-king for the moment that Saruman was a faithful ally, high in Sauron's confidence. At once the Riders left the Gate and rode in haste to the Fords of Isen. Behind them Saruman sent out wolves and Orcs in vain pursuit of Gandalf; but in this he had other purposes also, to impress his power upon the Nazgûl, perhaps also to prevent them from lingering near, and in his anger he wished to do some injury to Rohan, and to increase the fear of him which his agent Wormtongue was building up in Théoden's heart. Wormtongue had been in Isengard not long since, and was then on his way back to Edoras; among the pursuers were some bearing messages to him.

When he was rid of the Riders Saruman retired to Orthanc, and sat in earnest and dreadful thought. It seems that he resolved still to temporize, and still to hope to get the Ring for himself. He thought that the direction of the Riders to the Shire might hinder them rather than help them, for he knew of the guard of the Rangers, and he believed also (knowing of the oracular dream-words and of Boromir's mission) that the Ring had gone and was already on the way to Rivendell. At once he marshalled and sent out into Eriador all the spies, spy-birds, and agents that he could muster.

In this version the element of Gríma's capture by the Ringwraiths and his betrayal of Saruman is thus absent; for of course there is insufficient time by this account for Gandalf to reach Edoras and attempt to warn King Théoden, and for Gríma in his turn to set out for Isengard to warn Saruman, before the Black Riders were already gone from Rohan.[15] The revelation of Saruman's lying to them here comes about through the man whom they captured and found to be bearing maps of the Shire (p. 341); and more is told of this man and of Saruman's dealings with the Shire.

When the Black Riders were far across Enedwaith and drawing near at last to Tharbad, they had what was for them a great stroke of good fortune, but disastrous for Saruman,[16] and deadly perilous for Frodo.

Saruman had long taken an interest in the Shire – because Gandalf did, and he was suspicious of him; and because (again in secret imitation of Gandalf) he had taken to the 'Halflings' leaf', and needed supplies, but in pride (having once scoffed at Gandalf's use of the weed) kept this as secret as he could. Latterly other motives were added. He liked to extend his power, especially into Gandalf's province, and he found that the money he could provide for the purchase of 'leaf' was giving him power, and was corrupting some of the Hobbits, especially the Bracegirdles, who owned many plantations, and so also the Sackville-Bagginses.[17] But also he had begun to feel certain that in some way the Shire was connected with the Ring in Gandalf's mind. Why this strong guard upon it? He therefore began to collect detailed information about the Shire, its chief persons and families, its roads, and other matters. For this he used Hobbits within the Shire, in the pay of the Bracegirdles and the Sackville-Bagginses, but his agents were Men, of Dunlendish origin. When Gandalf had refused to treat with him Saruman had redoubled his efforts. The Rangers were suspicious, but did not actually refuse entry to the servants of Saruman – for Gandalf was not at liberty to warn them, and when he had gone off to Isengard Saruman was still recognised as an ally.

Some while ago one of Saruman's most trusted servants (yet a ruffianly fellow, an outlaw driven from Dunland, where many said that he had Orc-blood) had returned from the borders of the Shire, where he had been negotiating for the purchase of 'leaf' and other supplies. Saruman was beginning to store Isengard against war. This man was now on his way back to continue the business, and to arrange for the transport of many goods before autumn failed.[18] He had orders also to get into the Shire if possible and learn if there had been any departures of persons well-known recently. He was well supplied with maps, lists of names, and notes concerning the Shire.

This Dunlending was overtaken by several of the Black Riders as they approached the Tharbad crossing. In an extremity of terror he was haled to the Witch-king and questioned. He saved his life by betraying Saruman. The Witch-king thus learned that Saruman knew well all along where the Shire was, and knew much about it, which he could and should have told to Sauron's servants if he had been a true ally. The Witch-king also obtained much information, including some about the only name that interested him: *Baggins*. It was for this reason that Hobbiton was singled out as one of the points for immediate visit and enquiry.

The Witch-king had now a clearer understanding of the matter. He had known something of the country long ago, in his wars with the Dúnedain, and especially of the Tyrn Gorthad of Cardolan, now the Barrow-downs, whose evil wights had been sent there by himself.[19] Seeing that his Master suspected some move between the Shire and Rivendell, he saw also that Bree (the position of which he knew) would be an important point, at least for information.[20] He put therefore the Shadow of Fear on the Dunlending, and sent him on to Bree as an agent. He was the squint-eyed southerner at the Inn.[21]

In version B it is noted that the Black Captain did not know whether the Ring was still in the Shire; that he had to find out. The Shire was too large for a violent onslaught such as he had made on the Stoors; he must use as much stealth and as little terror as he could, and yet also guard the eastern borders. Therefore he sent some of the Riders into the Shire, with orders to disperse while traversing it; and of these Khamûl was to find Hobbiton (see note 1), where 'Baggins' lived, according to Saruman's papers. But the Black Captain established a camp at Andrath, where the Greenway passed in a defile between the Barrow-downs and the South Downs;[22] and from there some others were sent to watch and patrol the eastern borders, while he himself visited the Barrow-downs. In notes on the movements of the Black Riders at that time it is said that the Black Captain stayed there for some days, and the Barrow-wights were roused, and all things of evil spirit, hostile to Elves and Men, were on the watch with malice in the Old Forest and on the Barrow-downs.

(iii)

*Concerning Gandalf, Saruman and the Shire*

Another set of papers from the same period consists of a large number of unfinished accounts of Saruman's earlier dealings with the Shire, especially as they concerned the 'Halflings' leaf', a matter that is touched on in connection with the 'squint-eyed southerner' (see pp. 347–8). The following text is one version among many, but though briefer than some is the most finished.

Saruman soon became jealous of Gandalf, and this rivalry turned at last to a hatred, the deeper for being concealed, and the more bitter in that Saruman knew in his heart that the Grey Wanderer had the greater strength, and the greater influence upon the dwellers in Middle-earth, even though he hid his power and desired neither fear nor reverence. Saruman did not revere him, but he grew to fear him, being ever uncertain how much Gandalf perceived of his inner mind, troubled more by his silences than by his words. So it was that openly he treated Gandalf with less respect than did others of the Wise, and was ever ready to gainsay him or to make little of his counsels; while secretly he noted and pondered all that he said, setting a watch, so far as he was able, upon all his movements.

It was in this way that Saruman came to give thought to the Halflings and the Shire, which otherwise he would have deemed beneath his notice. He had at first no thought that the interest of his rival in this people had any connexion with the great concerns of the Council, least of all with the Rings of Power. For indeed in the beginning it had no such connexion, and was due only to Gandalf's love for the Little People, unless his heart had some deep premonition beyond his waking thought. For many years he visited the Shire openly, and would speak of its people to any who would listen; and Saruman would smile, as at the idle tales of an old land-rover, but he took heed nonetheless.

Seeing then that Gandalf thought the Shire worth visiting, Saruman himself visited it, but disguised and in the utmost secrecy, until he had explored and noted all its ways and lands, and thought then he had learned all that there was to know of it. And even when it seemed to him no longer wise nor profitable to go thither, he still had spies and servants that went in or kept an eye upon its borders. For he was still suspicious. He was himself so far fallen that he believed all others of the Council had each their deep and far-reaching policies for their own enhancement, to which all that they did must in some way refer. So when long after he learned something of the finding of Gollum's Ring by the Halfling, he could believe only that Gandalf had known of this all the time; and this was his greatest grievance, since all that concerned the Rings he deemed his especial province. That Gandalf's mistrust of him was merited and just in no way lessened his anger.

Yet in truth Saruman's spying and great secrecy had not in the beginning any evil purpose, but was no more than a folly born of pride. Small matters, unworthy it would seem to be reported, may yet prove of great moment ere the end. Now truth to tell, observing Gandalf's love of the herb that he called 'pipe-weed' (for which, he said, if for nothing else, the Little People should be honoured), Saruman had affected to scoff at it, but in private he made trial of it, and soon began to use it; and for this reason the Shire remained important to him. Yet he dreaded lest this should be discovered, and his own mockery turned against him, so that he would be laughed at for imitating Gandalf, and scorned for doing so by stealth. This then was the reason for his great secrecy in all his dealings with the Shire, even from the first before any shadow of doubt had fallen upon it, and it was little guarded, free for those who wished to enter. For this reason also Saruman ceased to go thither in person; for it came to his knowledge that he had not been all unobserved by the keen-eyed Halflings, and some, seeing the figure as it were of an old man clad in grey or russet stealing through the woods or passing through the dusk, had mistaken him for Gandalf.

After that Saruman went no more to the Shire, fearing that such tales might spread and come maybe to the ears of Gandalf. But Gandalf knew of these vists, and guessed their object, and he laughed, thinking this the most harmless of Saruman's secrets; but he said nothing to others, for it was never his wish that any one should be put to shame. Nonetheless he was not ill-pleased when the visits of Saruman ceased, doubting him already, though he could not himself yet foresee that a time would come when Saruman's knowledge of the Shire would prove perilous and of the greatest service to the Enemy, bringing victory to within a nail's breadth of his grasp.

In another version there is a description of the occasion when Saruman openly scoffed at Gandalf's use of the 'pipe-weed':

Now because of his dislike and fear, in the later days Saruman avoided Gandalf, and they seldom met, except at the assemblies of the White Council. It was at the great Council held in 2851 that the 'Halflings' leaf' was first spoken of, and the matter was noted with amusement at the time, though it was afterwards remembered in a different light. The Council met in Rivendell, and Gandalf sat apart, silent, but smoking prodigiously (a thing he had never done before on such an occasion), while Saruman spoke against him, and urged that contrary to Gandalf's advice Dol Guldur should not yet be molested. Both the silence and the smoke seemed greatly to annoy Saruman, and before the Council dispersed he said to Gandalf: 'When weighty matters are in debate, Mithrandir, I wonder a little that you should play with your toys of fire and smoke, while others are in earnest speech.'

But Gandalf laughed, and replied: 'You would not wonder, if you used this herb yourself. You might find that smoke blown out cleared your mind of shadows within. Anyway, it gives patience, to listen to error without anger. But it is not one of my toys. It is an art of the Little People away in the West: merry and worthy folk, though not of much account, perhaps, in your high policies.'

Saruman was little appeased by this answer (for he hated mockery, however gentle), and he said then coldly: 'You jest, Lord Mithrandir, as is your way. I know well enough that you have become a curious explorer of the small: weeds, wild things, and childish folk. Your time is your own to spend, if you have nothing worthier to do; and your friends you may make as you please. But to me the days are too dark for wanderers' tales, and I have no time for the simples of peasants.'

Gandalf did not laugh again; and he did not answer, but looking keenly at Saruman he drew on his pipe and sent out a great ring of smoke with many smaller rings that followed it. Then he put up his hand, as if to grasp·them, and they vanished. With that he got up and left Saruman without another word; but Saruman stood for some time silent, and his face was dark with doubt and displeasure.

This story appears in half a dozen different manuscripts, and in one of them it is said that Saruman was suspicious,

doubting whether he read rightly the purport of Gandalf's gesture with the rings of smoke (above all whether it showed any connexion between the Halflings and the great matter of the Rings of Power, unlikely though that might seem); and doubting that one so great could concern himself with such a people as the Halflngs for their own sake merely.

In another (struck through) Gandalf's purpose is made explicit:

It was a strange chance, that being angered by his insolence Gandalf chose this way of showing to Saruman his suspicion that desire to possess them had begun to enter into his policies and his study of the lore of the Rings; and of warning him that they would elude him.

For it cannot be doubted that Gandalf had as yet no thought that the Halflings (and still less their smoking) had any connection with the Rings.[23] If he had had any such thought, then certainly he would not have done then what he did. Yet later when the Halflings did indeed become involved in this greatest matter, Saruman could believe only that Gandalf had known or foreknown this, and had concealed the knowledge from him and from the Council – for just such a purpose as Saruman would conceive: to gain possession and to forestall him.

In the Tale of Years the entry for 2851 refers to the meeting of the White Council in that year, when Gandalf urged an attack on Dol Guldur but was overruled by Saruman; and a footnote to the entry reads: 'It afterwards became clear that Saruman had then begun to desire to possess the One Ring himself, and hoped that it might reveal itself, seeking its master, if Sauron were let be for a time.' The foregoing story shows that Gandalf himself suspected Saruman of this at the time of the Council of 2851; though my father afterwards commented that it appears from Gandalf's story to the Council of Elrond of his meeting with Radagast that he did not seriously suspect Saruman of treachery (or of desiring the Ring for himself) until he was imprisoned in Orthanc.

## NOTES

1  According to the entry in the Tale of Years for 2951 Sauron sent three, not two, of the Nazgûl to reoccupy Dol Guldur. The two statements can be reconciled on the assumption that one of the Ringwraiths of Dol Guldur returned afterwards to Minas Morgul, but I think it more likely that the formulation of the present text was superseded when the Tale of Years was compiled; and it may be noted that in a rejected version of the present passage there was only one Nazgûl in Dol Guldur (not named as Khamûl, but referred to as 'the Second Chief (the Black Easterling)'), while one remained with Sauron as his chief messenger. – From notes recounting in detail the movements of the Black Riders in the Shire it emerges that it was Khamûl who came to Hobbiton and spoke to Gaffer Gamgee, who followed the Hobbits along the road to Stock, and who narrowly missed them at the Bucklebury Ferry (see p. 344). The Rider who accompanied him, whom he summoned by cries on the ridge above Woodhall, and with whom he visited Farmer Maggot, was 'his companion from Dol Guldur'. Of Khamûl it is said here that he was the most ready of all the Nazgûl, after the Black Captain himself,

to perceive the presence of the Ring, but also the one whose power was most confused and diminished by daylight.

2  He had indeed in his terror of the Nazgûl dared to hide in Moria. [Author's note.]

3  At the Ford of Bruinen only the Witch-king and two others, with the lure of the Ring straight before them, had dared to enter the river; the others were driven into it by Glorfindel and Aragorn. [Author's note.]

4  Gandalf, as he recounted to the Council of Elrond, questioned Gollum while he was imprisoned by the Elves of Thranduil.

5  Gandalf told the Council of Elrond that after he left Minas Tirith 'messages came to me out of Lórien that Aragorn had passed that way, and that he had found the creature called Gollum'.

6  Gandalf arrived two days later, and left on the 29th of March early in the morning. After the Carrock he had a horse, but he had the High Pass over the Mountains to cross. He got a fresh horse at Rivendell, and making the greatest speed he could he reached Hobbiton late on the 12th of April, after a journey of nearly eight hundred miles. [Author's note.]

7  Both here and in the Tale of Years the assault on Osgiliath is dated the 20th of June.

8  This statement no doubt relates to Boromir's account of the battle at Osgiliath which he gave to the Council of Elrond: 'A power was there that we have not felt before. Some said that it could be seen, like a great black horseman, a dark shadow under the moon.'

9  In a letter written in 1959 my father said: 'Between 2463 [when Déagol the Stoor found the One Ring, according to the Tale of Years] and the beginning of Gandalf's special enquiries concerning the Ring (nearly 500 years later) they [the Stoors] appear indeed to have died out altogether (except of course for Sméagol); or to have fled from the shadow of Dol Guldur.'

10  According to the author's note given in Note 2 above, Gollum fled into Moria from terror of the Nazgûl; cf. also the suggestion on p. 339 that one of the purposes of the Lord of Morgul in riding on northward beyond the Gladden was the hope of finding Gollum.

11  These were in fact not very numerous, it would seem; but sufficient to keep any intruders out, if no better armed or prepared than Balin's company, and not in great numbers. [Author's note.]

12  According to the Dwarves this needed usually the thrust of two; only a very strong Dwarf could open them single-handed. Before the desertion of Moria doorwards were kept inside the West-gate, and one at least was always there. In this way a single person (and so any intruder or person trying to escape) could not get out without permission. [Author's note.]

13   In A Saruman denied knowledge of where the Ring was hid; in B he 'denied all knowledge of the land that they sought'. But this is probably no more than a difference of wording.

14   Earlier in this version it is said that Sauron had at this time, by means of the *palantíri*, at last begun to daunt Saruman, and could in any case often read his thought even when he withheld information. Thus Sauron was aware that Saruman had some guess at the place where the Ring was; and Saruman actually revealed that he had got as his prisoner Gandalf, who knew the most.

15   The entry for the 18th of September 3018 in the Tale of Years reads: 'Gandalf escapes from Orthanc in the early hours. The Black Riders cross the Fords of Isen.' Laconic as this entry is, giving no hint that the Riders visited Isengard, it seems to be based on the story told in version C.

16   No indication is given in any of these texts of what passed between Sauron and Saruman as a result of the latter's unmasking.

17   Lobelia Bracegirdle married Otho Sackville-Baggins; their son was Lotho, who seized control of the Shire at the time of the War of the Ring, and was then known as 'the Chief'. Farmer Cotton referred in conversation with Frodo to Lotho's property in leaf-plantations in the Southfarthing (*The Return of the King* VI 8).

18   The usual way was by the crossing of Tharbad to Dunland (rather than direct to Isengard), whence goods were sent more secretly on to Saruman. [Author's note.]

19   Cf. *The Lord of the Rings*, Appendix A (I, iii, *The North-kingdom and the Dúnedain*): 'It was at this time [during the Great Plague that reached Gondor in 1636] that an end came of the Dúnedain of Cardolan, and evil spirits out of Angmar and Rhudaur entered into the deserted mounds and dwelt there.'

20   Since the Black Captain knew so much, it is perhaps strange that he had had so little idea of where the Shire, the land of the Halflings, lay; according to the Tale of Years there were already Hobbits settled in Bree at the beginning of the fourteenth century of the Third Age, when the Witch-king came north to Angmar.

21   See *The Fellowship of the Ring* I, 9. When Strider and the Hobbits left Bree (*ibid.* I, 11) Frodo caught a glimpse of the Dunlending ('a sallow face with sly, slanting eyes') in Bill Ferny's house on the outskirts of Bree, and thought: 'He looks more than half like a goblin.'

22   Cf. Gandalf's words at the Council of Elrond: 'Their Captain remained in secret away south of Bree.'

23   As the concluding sentence of this quotation shows, the meaning is: 'Gandalf had as yet no thought that the Halflings would have in the future any connexion with the Rings.' The meeting of the White Council in 2851 took place ninety years before Bilbo found the Ring.

# V

# THE BATTLES OF
# THE FORDS OF ISEN

The chief obstacles to an easy conquest of Rohan by Saruman were
Théodred and Éomer: they were vigorous men, devoted to the King,
and high in his affections, as his only son and his sister-son; and
they did all that they could to thwart the influence over him that
Gríma gained when the King's health began to fail. This occurred
early in the year 3014, when Théoden was sixty-six; his malady may
thus have been due to natural causes, though the Rohirrim commonly
lived till near or beyond their eightieth year. But it may well have
been induced or increased by subtle poisons, administered by Gríma.
In any case Théoden's sense of weakness and dependence on Gríma
was largely due to the cunning and skill of this evil counsellor's
suggestions. It was his policy to bring his chief opponents into dis-
credit with Théoden, and if possible to get rid of them. It proved
impossible to set them at odds with one another: Théoden before
his 'sickness' had been much loved by all his kin and people, and the
loyalty of Théodred and Éomer remained steadfast, even in his
apparent dotage. Éomer also was not an ambitious man, and his love
and respect for Théodred (thirteen years older than he) was only
second to his love of his foster-father.[1] Gríma therefore tried to play
them one against the other in the mind of Théoden, representing
Éomer as ever eager to increase his own authority and to act without
consulting the King or his Heir. In this he had some success, which
bore fruit when Saruman at last succeeded in achieving the death of
Théodred.

   It was clearly seen in Rohan, when the true accounts of the battles
at the Fords were known, that Saruman had given special orders that
Théodred should at all costs be slain. At the first battle all his
fiercest warriors were engaged in reckless assaults upon Théodred
and his guard, disregarding other events of the battle, which might
otherwise have resulted in a much more damaging defeat for the
Rohirrim. When Théodred was at last slain Saruman's commander
(no doubt under orders) seemed satisfied for the time being, and
Saruman made the mistake, fatal as it proved, of not immediately

throwing in more forces and proceeding at once to a massive invasion of Westfold;[2] though the valour of Grimbold and Elfhelm contributed to his delay. If the invasion of Westfold had begun five days earlier, there can be little doubt that the reinforcements from Edoras would never have come near Helm's Deep, but would have been surrounded and overwhelmed in the open plain; if indeed Edoras had not itself been attacked and captured before the arrival of Gandalf.[3]

It has been said that the valour of Grimbold and Elfhelm contributed to Saruman's delay, which proved disastrous for him. The above account perhaps underestimates its importance.

The Isen came down swiftly from its sources above Isengard, but in the flat land of the Gap it became slow until it turned west; then it flowed on through country falling by long slopes down into the low-lying coast-lands of furthest Gondor and the Enedwaith, and it became deep and rapid. Just above this westward bend were the Fords of Isen. There the river was broad and shallow, passing in two arms about a large eyot, over a stony shelf covered with stones and pebbles brought down from the north. Only here, south of Isengard, was it possible for large forces, especially those heavily armed or mounted, to cross the river. Saruman thus had this advantage: he could send his troops down either side of the Isen and attack the Fords, if they were held against him, from both sides. Any force of his west of Isen could if necessary retreat upon Isengard. On the other hand, Théodred might send men across the Fords, either in sufficient strength to engage Saruman's troops or to defend the western bridgehead; but if they were worsted, they would have no retreat except back over the Fords with the enemy at their heels, and possibly also awaiting them on the eastern bank. South and west along the Isen they had no way home,[4] unless they were provisioned for a long journey into Western Gondor.

Saruman's attack was not unforeseen, but it came sooner than was expected. Théodred's scouts had warned him of a mustering of troops before the Gates of Isengard, mainly (as it seemed) on the west side of Isen. He therefore manned the approaches, east and west, to the Fords with sturdy men on foot from the levies of Westfold. Leaving three companies of Riders, together with horse-herds and spare mounts, on the east bank, he himself passed over with the main strength of his cavalry: eight companies and a company of archers, intending to overthrow Saruman's army before it was fully prepared.

But Saruman had not revealed his intentions nor the full strength of his forces. They were already on the march when Théodred set out. Some twenty miles north of the Fords he encountered their

vanguard and scattered it with loss. But when he rode on to attack
the main host the resistance stiffened. The enemy was in fact in
positions prepared for the event, behind trenches manned by pike-
men, and Théodred in the leading *éored* was brought to a stand and
almost surrounded, for new forces hastening from Isengard were
now outflanking him upon the west.

He was extricated by the onset of the companies coming up behind
him; but as he looked eastward he was dismayed. It had been a dim
and misty morning, but the mists were now rolling back through the
Gap on a breeze from the west, and away east of the river he descried
other forces now hasting towards the Fords, though their strength
could not be guessed. He at once ordered a retreat. This the Riders,
well trained in the manoeuvre, managed in good order and with little
further loss; but the enemy was not shaken off or long outdistanced,
for the retreat was often delayed, when the rearguard under Grimbold
was obliged to turn at bay and drive back the most eager of their
pursuers.

When Théodred gained the Fords the day was waning. He set
Grimbold in command of the garrison of the west bank, stiffened
with fifty dismounted Riders. The rest of his Riders and all the
horses he at once sent across the river, save his own company: with
these on foot he manned the eyot, to cover the retreat of Grimbold
if he was driven back. This was barely done when disaster came.
Saruman's eastern force came down with unexpected speed; it was
much smaller than the western force, but more dangerous. In its
van were some Dunlending horsemen and a great pack of the dreadful
Orcish wolfriders, feared by horses.[5] Behind them came two battalions
of the fierce Uruks, heavily armed but trained to move at great speed
for many miles. The horsemen and wolfriders fell on the horse-herds
and picketed horses and slew or dispersed them. The garrison of
the east bank, surprised by the sudden assault of the massed Uruks,
was swept away, and the Riders that had just crossed from the west
were caught still in disarray, and though they fought desperately
they were driven from the Fords along the line of the Isen with the
Uruks in pursuit.

As soon as the enemy had gained possession of the eastern end of
the Fords there appeared a company of men or orc-men (evidently
dispatched for the purpose), ferocious, mail-clad, and armed with
axes. They hastened to the eyot and assailed it from both sides. At
the same time Grimbold on the west bank was attacked by Saruman's
forces on that side of the Isen. As he looked eastward, dismayed by
the sounds of battle and the hideous orc-cries of victory, he saw the

axe-men driving Théodred's men from the shores of the eyot towards
the low knoll in its centre, and he heard Théodred's great voice
crying *To me, Eorlingas!* At once Grimbold, taking a few men that
stood near him, ran back to the eyot. So fierce was his onset from
the rear of the attackers that Grimbold, a man of great strength and
stature, clove his way through, till with two others he reached
Théodred standing at bay on the knoll. Too late. As he came to his
side Théodred fell, hewn down by a great orc-man. Grimbold slew
him and stood over the body of Théodred, thinking him dead; and
there he would himself soon have died, but for the coming of Elfhelm.

Elfhelm had been riding in haste along the horse-road from Edoras,
leading four companies in answer to Théodred's summons; he was
expecting battle, but not yet for some days. But near the junction of
the horse-road with the road down from the Deeping[6] his outriders
on the right flank reported that two wolfriders had been seen abroad
on the fields. Sensing that things were amiss, he did not turn aside
to Helm's Deep for the night as he had intended but rode with all
speed towards the Fords. The horse-road turned north-west after
its meeting with the Deeping-road, but again bent sharply west when
level with the Fords, which it approached by a straight path of some
two miles long. Elfhelm thus heard and saw nothing of the fighting
between the retreating garrison and the Uruks south of the Fords.
The sun had sunk and light was failing when he drew near the last
bend in the road, and there encountered some horses running wild
and a few fugitives who told him of the disaster. Though his men
and horses were now weary he rode as fast as he could along the
straight, and as he came in sight of the east bank he ordered his
companies to charge.

It was the turn of the Isengarders to be surprised. They heard the
thunder of hooves, and saw coming like black shadows against the
darkening East a great host (as it seemed) with Elfhelm at its head,
and beside him a white standard borne as a guide to those that
followed. Few stood their ground. Most fled northwards, pursued
by two of Elfhelm's companies. The others he dismounted to guard
the east bank, but at once with the men of his own company rushed
to the eyot. The axemen were now caught between the surviving
defenders and the onslaught of Elfhelm, with both banks still held
by the Rohirrim. They fought on, but before the end were slain to
a man. Elfhelm himself, however, sprang up towards the knoll;
and there he found Grimbold fighting two great axemen for possession
of Théodred's body. One Elfhelm at once slew, and the other fell
before Grimbold.

They stooped then to lift the body, and found that Théodred still breathed; but he lived only long enough to speak his last words: *Let me lie here – to keep the Fords till Éomer comes!* Night fell. A harsh horn sounded, and then all was silent. The attack on the west bank ceased, and the enemy there faded away into the dark. The Rohirrim held the Fords of Isen; but their losses were heavy, not least in horses; the King's son was dead, and they were leaderless, and did not know what might yet befall.

When after a cold and sleepless night the grey light returned there was no sign of the Isengarders, save those many that they left dead upon the field. Wolves were howling far off, waiting for the living men to depart. Many men scattered by the sudden assault of the Isengarders began to return, some still mounted, some leading horses recaptured. Later in the morning most of Théodred's Riders that had been driven south down the river by a battalion of black Uruks came back battle-worn but in good order. They had a like tale to tell. They came to a stand on a low hill and prepared to defend it. Though they had drawn off part of the attacking force of Isengard, retreat south unprovisioned was in the end hopeless. The Uruks had resisted any attempt to burst eastwards, and were driving them towards the now hostile country of the Dunlendish 'west-march'. But as the Riders prepared to resist their assault, though it was now full night, a horn was sounded; and soon they discovered that the enemy had gone. They had too few horses to attempt any pursuit, or even to act as scouts, so far as that would have availed by night. After some time they began cautiously to advance north again, but met no opposition. They thought that the Uruks had gone back to reinforce their hold on the Fords, and expected there to meet in battle again, and they wondered much to find the Rohirrim in command. It was not till later that they discovered whither the Uruks had gone.

So ended the First Battle of the Fords of Isen. Of the Second Battle no such clear accounts were ever made, owing to the much greater events that immediately followed. Erkenbrand of Westfold assumed command of the West-mark when news of the fall of Théodred reached him in the Hornburg on the next day. He sent errand-riders to Edoras to announce this and to bear to Théoden his son's last words, adding his own prayer that Éomer should be sent at once with all help that could be spared.[7] 'Let the defence of Edoras be made here in the West,' he said, 'and not wait till it is itself besieged.' But Gríma used the curtness of this advice to further his policy of delay. It was not until his defeat by Gandalf that any action was taken. The reinforcements with Éomer and the King himself set out in the afternoon of March the 2nd, but that night the Second Battle of the Fords was fought and lost, and the invasion of Rohan began.

Erkenbrand did not at once himself proceed to the battle-field. All was in confusion. He did not know what forces he could muster in haste; nor could he yet estimate the losses that Théodred's troops had actually suffered. He judged rightly that invasion was imminent, but that Saruman would not dare to pass on eastward to attack Edoras while the fortress of the Hornburg was unreduced, if it was manned and well stored. With this business and the gathering of such men of Westfold as he could, he was occupied for three days. The command in the field he gave to Grimbold, until he could come himself; but he assumed no command over Elfhelm and his Riders, who belonged to the Muster of Edoras. The two commanders were, however, friends and both loyal and wise men, and there was no dissension between them; the ordering of their forces was a compromise between their differing opinions. Elfhelm held that the Fords were no longer important, but rather a snare to entrap men better placed elsewhere, since Saruman could clearly send forces down either side of the Isen as suited his purpose; and his immediate purpose would undoubtedly be to overrun Westfold and invest the Hornburg, before any effective help could come from Edoras. His army, or most of it, would therefore come down the east side of the Isen; for though by that way, over rougher ground without roads, their approach would be slower, they would not have to force the passage of the Fords. Elfhelm therefore advised that the Fords should be abandoned; all the available men on foot should be assembled on the east side, and placed in a position to hold up the advance of the enemy: a long line of rising ground running from west to east some few miles north of the Fords; but the cavalry should be withdrawn eastward to a point from which, when the advancing enemy was engaged with the defence, a charge with the greatest impact could be delivered on their flank and drive them into the river. 'Let Isen be their snare and not ours!'

Grimbold on the other hand was not willing to abandon the Fords. This was in part due to the tradition of Westfold in which he and Erkenbrand had been bred; but was not without some reason. 'We do not know,' he said, 'what force Saruman has still at his command. But if it is indeed his purpose to ravage Westfold and drive its defenders into Helm's Deep and there contain them, then it must be very great. He is unlikely to display it all at once. As soon as he guesses or discovers how we have disposed our defence, he will certainly send great strength at all speed down the road from Isengard, and crossing the undefended Fords come in our rear, if we are all gathered northwards.'

In the end Grimbold manned the western end of the Fords with the greater part of his foot-soldiers; there they were in a strong position in the earth-forts that guarded the approaches. He remained with the rest of his men, including what remained to him of Théodred's cavalry, on the east bank. The eyot he left bare.[8] Elfhelm however withdrew his Riders and took up his position on the line where he had wished the main defence to stand; his purpose was to descry as soon as could be any attack coming down on the east of the river and to disperse it before it could reach the Fords.

All went ill, as most likely it would have done in any case: Saruman's strength was too great. He began his attack by day, and before noon of March the 2nd a strong force of his best fighters, coming down by the Road from Isengard, attacked the forts on the west of the Fords. This force was in fact only a small part of those that he had in hand, no more than he deemed sufficient to dispose of the weakened defence. But the garrison of the Fords, though greatly outnumbered, resisted stubbornly. At length, however, when both the forts were heavily engaged, a troop of Uruks forced the passage between them and began to cross the Fords. Grimbold, trusting in Elfhelm to hold off attack on the east side, came across with all the men he had left and flung them back – for a while. But the enemy commander then threw in a battalion that had not been committed, and broke the defences. Grimbold was obliged to withdraw across the Isen. It was then near sunset. He had suffered much loss, but had inflicted far heavier losses on the enemy (mostly Orcs), and he still held the east bank strongly. The enemy did not attempt to cross the Fords and fight their way up the steep slopes to dislodge him; not yet.

Elfhelm had been unable to take part in this action. In the dusk he withdrew his companies and retired towards Grimbold's camp, setting his men in groups at some distance from it to act as a screen against attack from north and east. From southwards they expected no evil, and hoped for succour. After the retreat across the Fords errand-riders had been dispatched at once to Erkenbrand and to Edoras telling of their plight. Fearing, indeed knowing, that greater evil would befall them ere long, unless help beyond hope reached them swiftly, the defenders prepared to do what they could to hold up Saruman's advance before they were overwhelmed.[9] The greater part stood to arms, only a few at a time attempting to snatch such brief rest and sleep as they could. Grimbold and Elfhelm were sleepless, awaiting the dawn and dreading what it might bring.

They did not have to wait so long. It was not yet midnight when points of red light were seen coming from the north and already drawing near on the west of the river. It was the vanguard of the whole remaining forces of Saruman that he was now committing to battle for the conquest of Westfold.[10] They came on at great speed, and suddenly all the host burst into flame, as it seemed. Hundreds of torches were kindled from those borne by the leaders of troops, and gathering into their stream the forces already manning the west bank they swept over the Fords like a river of fire with a great clamour of hate. A great company of bowmen might have made them rue the light of their torches, but Grimbold had only a handful of archers. He could not hold the east bank, and withdrew from it, forming a great shieldwall about his camp. Soon it was surrounded, and the attackers cast torches among them, and some they sent high over the heads of the shieldwall, hoping to kindle fires among the stores and terrify such horses as Grimbold still had. But the shieldwall held. Then, since the Orcs were of less avail in such fighting because of their stature, fierce companies of the Dunlendish hillmen were thrown against it. But for all their hatred the Dunlendings were still afraid of the Rohirrim if they met face to face, and they were also less skilled in warfare and less well armed.[11] The shieldwall still held.

In vain Grimbold looked for help to come from Elfhelm. None came. At last then he determined to carry out if he could the plan that he had already made, if he should find himself in just such a desperate position. He had at length recognised the wisdom of Elfhelm, and understood that though his men might fight on till all were slain, and would if he ordered it, such valour would not help Erkenbrand: any man that could break out and escape southwards would be more useful, though he might seem inglorious.

The night had been overcast and dark, but now the waxing moon began to glimmer through drifting cloud. A wind was moving from the East: the forerunner of the great storm that when day came would pass over Rohan and burst over Helm's Deep the next night. Grimbold was aware suddenly that most of the torches had been extinguished and the fury of the assault had abated.[12] He therefore at once mounted those riders for whom horses were available, not many more than half an *éored*, and placed them under the command of Dúnhere.[13] The shieldwall was opened on the east side and the Riders passed through, driving back their assailants on that side;

then dividing and wheeling round they charged the enemy to the north and south of the camp. The sudden manoeuvre was for a space successful. The enemy was confused and dismayed; many thought at first that a large force of Riders had come from the east. Grimbold himself remained on foot with a rearguard of picked men, already chosen, and covered for the moment by these and the Riders under Dúnhere the remainder retreated with what speed they could. But Saruman's commander soon perceived that the shieldwall was broken and the defenders in flight. Fortunately the moon was overtaken by cloud and all was dark again, and he was in haste. He did not allow his troops to press the pursuit of the fugitives far into the darkness, now that the Fords were captured. He gathered his force as best he could and made for the road southward. So it was that the greater part of Grimbold's men survived. They were scattered in the night, but, as he had ordered, they made their ways away from the Road, east of the great turn where it bent west towards the Isen. They were relieved but amazed to encounter no enemies, not knowing that a large army had already some hours before passed southward and that Isengard was now guarded by little but its own strength of wall and gate.[14]

It was for this reason that no help had come from Elfhelm. More than half of Saruman's force had actually been sent down east of Isen. They came on more slowly than the western division, for the land was rougher and without roads; and they bore no lights. But before them, swift and silent, went several troops of the dreaded wolfriders. Before Elfhelm had any warning of the approach of enemies on his side of the river the wolfriders were between him and Grimbold's camp; and they were also attempting to surround each of his small groups of Riders. It was dark and all his force was in disarray. He gathered all that he could into a close body of horsemen, but he was obliged to retreat eastward. He could not reach Grimbold, though he knew that he was in straits and had been about to come to his aid when attacked by the wolfriders. But he also guessed rightly that the wolfriders were only the forerunners of a force far too great for him to oppose that would make for the southward road. The night was wearing away; he could only await the dawn.

What followed is less clear, since only Gandalf had full knowledge of it. He received news of the disaster only in the late afternoon of March the 3rd.[15] The King was then at a point not far east of the junction of the Road with the branch going to the Hornburg. From there it was about ninety miles in a direct line to Isengard; and

Gandalf must have ridden there with the greatest speed that Shadowfax could command. He reached Isengard in the early darkness,[16]
and left again in no more than twenty minutes. Both on the outward
journey, when his direct route would take him close to the Fords,
and on his return south to find Erkenbrand, he must have met
Grimbold and Elfhelm. They were convinced that he was acting for
the King, not only by his appearance on Shadowfax, but also by his
knowledge of the name of the errand-rider, Ceorl, and the message
that he brought; and they took as orders the advice that he gave.[17]
Grimbold's men he sent southward to join Erkenbrand . . .

# NOTES

1   Éomer was the son of Théoden's sister Théodwyn, and of Éomund of
Eastfold, chief Marshal of the Mark. Éomund was slain by Orcs in
3002, and Théodwyn died soon after; their children Éomer and
Éowyn were then taken to live in King Théoden's house, together
with Théodred, the King's only child. (*The Lord of the Rings*,
Appendix A (II).)

2   The Ents are here left out of account, as they were by all save
Gandalf. But unless Gandalf could have brought about the rising
of the Ents several days earlier (as from the narrative was plainly
not possible), it would not have saved Rohan. The Ents might have
destroyed Isengard, and even captured Saruman (if after victory he
had not himself followed his army). The Ents and Huorns, with
the aid of such Riders of the East-mark as had not yet been engaged,
might have destroyed the forces of Saruman in Rohan, but the Mark
would have been in ruins, and leaderless. Even if the Red Arrow
had found any one with authority to receive it, the call from Gondor
would not have been heeded – or at most a few companies of weary
men would have reached Minas Tirith, too late except to perish
with it. [Author's note.] – For the Red Arrow see *The Return of the
King* I 3, where it was brought to Théoden by an errand-rider from
Gondor as a token of the need of Minas Tirith.

3   The first battle of the Fords of Isen, in which Théodred was slain,
was fought on the 25th of February; Gandalf reached Edoras seven
days later, on the 2nd of March. (*The Lord of the Rings*, Appendix B,
year 3019.) See note 7.

4   Beyond the Gap the land between Isen and Adorn was nominally
part of the realm of Rohan; but though Folcwine had reclaimed it,
driving out the Dunlendings that had occupied it, the people that
remained were largely of mixed blood, and their loyalty to Edoras
was weak: the slaying of their lord, Freca, by King Helm was still

remembered. Indeed at this time they were more disposed to side with Saruman, and many of their warriors had joined Saruman's forces. In any case there was no way into their land from the west except for bold swimmers. [Author's note.] – The region between Isen and Adorn was declared to be a part of the realm of Eorl at the time of the Oath of Cirion and Eorl: see p. 305.

In the year 2754 Helm Hammerhand, King of the Mark, slew with his fist his arrogant vassal Freca, lord of lands on either side of the Adorn; see *The Lord of the Rings*, Appendix A (II).

5  They were very swift and skilled in avoiding ordered men in close array, being used mostly to destroy isolated groups or to hunt down fugitives; but at need they would pass with reckless ferocity through any gaps in companies of horsemen, slashing at the bellies of the horses. [Author's note.]

6  The Deeping: this is so written and is clearly correct, since it occurs again later. My father noted elsewhere that the Deeping-coomb (and Deeping-stream) should be so spelt, rather than Deeping Coomb, 'since *Deeping* is not a verbal ending but one indicating relationship: the coomb or deep valley belonging to the *Deep* (*Helm's Deep*) to which it led up'. (Notes on Nomenclature to assist translators, published in *A Tolkien Compass*, edited by Jared Lobdell, 1975, page 181.)

7  The messages did not reach Edoras until about noon on February the 27th. Gandalf came there early in the morning of March the 2nd (February had thirty days!): it was thus, as Gríma said, not then fully five days since news of Théodred's death had reached the King. [Author's note.] – The reference is to *The Two Towers*, III 6.

8  It is told that he set up on stakes all about the eyot the heads of the axemen that had been slain there, but above the hasty mound of Théodred in the middle was set his banner. 'That will be defence enough,' he said. [Author's note.]

9  This, it is said, was Grimbold's resolve. Elfhelm would not desert him, but had he himself been in command, he would have abandoned the Fords under cover of night and withdrawn southwards to meet Erkenbrand and swell the forces still available for the defence of the Deeping-coomb and the Hornburg. [Author's note.]

10 This was the great host that Meriadoc saw leaving Isengard, as he related afterwards to Aragorn, Legolas and Gimli (*The Two Towers* III 9): 'I saw the enemy go: endless lines of marching Orcs; and troops of them mounted on great wolves. And there were battalions of Men, too. Many of them carried torches, and in the flare I could see their faces. . . . They took an hour to pass out of the gates. Some went off down the highway to the Fords, and some turned away and went eastward. A bridge has been built down there, about a mile away, where the river runs in a very deep channel.'

11   They were without body-armour, having only among them a few
     hauberks gained by theft or in loot. The Rohirrim had the advantage
     in being supplied by the metal-workers of Gondor. In Isengard as
     yet only the heavy and clumsy mail of the Orcs was made, by them
     for their own uses. [Author's note.]

12   It seems that Grimbold's valiant defence had not been altogether
     unavailing. It had been unexpected, and Saruman's commander was
     late: he had been delayed for some hours, whereas it was intended
     that he should sweep over the Fords, scatter the weak defences, and
     without waiting to pursue them hasten to the road and proceed then
     south to join in the assault on the Deeping. He was now in doubt.
     He awaited, maybe, some signal from the other army that had been
     sent down the east side of the Isen. [Author's note.]

13   A valiant captain, nephew of Erkenbrand. By courage and skill in
     arms he survived the disaster of the Fords, but fell in the Battle of
     the Pelennor, to the great grief of Westfold. [Author's note.] –
     Dúnhere was Lord of Harrowdale (*The Return of the King* V 3).

14   This sentence is not very clear, but in view of what follows it seems
     to refer to that part of the great army out of Isengard that came down
     the east side of the Isen.

15   The news was brought by the Rider named Ceorl, who returning
     from the Fords fell in with Gandalf, Théoden and Éomer as they
     rode west with reinforcements from Edoras: *The Two Towers* III 7.

16   As the narrative suggests, Gandalf must already have made contact
     with Treebeard, and knew that the patience of the Ents was at an
     end; and he had also read the meaning of Legolas' words (*The Two
     Towers* III 7, at the beginning of the chapter): Isengard was veiled
     in an impenetrable shadow, the Ents had already surrounded it.
     [Author's note.]

17   When Gandalf came with Théoden and Éomer to the Fords of Isen
     after the Battle of the Hornburg he explained to them: 'Some men
     I sent with Grimbold of Westfold to join Erkenbrand. Some I set
     to make this burial. They have now followed your marshal, Elfhelm.
     I sent him with many Riders to Edoras.' (*The Two Towers* III 8.)
     The present text ends in the middle of the next sentence.


# APPENDIX

## (i)

In writing associated with the present text some further particulars are
given concerning the Marshals of the Mark in the year 3019 and after
the end of the War of the Ring:

Marshal of the Mark (or Riddermark) was the highest military rank and the title of the King's lieutenants (originally three), commanders of the royal forces of fully equipped and trained Riders. The First Marshal's ward was the capital, Edoras, and the adjacent King's Lands (including Harrowdale). He commanded the Riders of the Muster of Edoras, drawn from this ward, and from some parts of the West-mark and East-mark* for which Edoras was the most convenient place of assembly. The Second and Third Marshals were assigned commands according to the needs of the time. In the beginning of the year 3019 the threat from Saruman was the most urgent, and the Second Marshal, the King's son Théodred, had command over the West-mark with his base at Helm's Deep; the Third Marshal, the King's nephew Éomer, had as his ward the East-mark with his base at his home, Aldburg in the Folde.†

In the days of Théoden there was no man appointed to the office of First Marshal. He came to the throne as a young man (at the age of thirty-two), vigorous and of martial spirit, and a great horseman. If war came, he would himself command the Muster of Edoras; but his kingdom was at peace for many years, and he rode with his knights and his Muster only on exercises and in displays; though the shadow of Mordor reawakened grew ever greater from his childhood to his old age. In this peace the Riders and other armed men of the garrison of Edoras were governed by an officer of the rank of marshal (in the years 3012–19 this was Elfhelm). When Théoden became, as it seemed, prematurely old, this situation continued, and there was no effective central command: a state of affairs encouraged by his counsellor Gríma. The King, becoming decrepit and seldom leaving his house, fell into the habit of issuing orders to Háma, Captain of his Household, to Elfhelm, and even to the Marshals of the Mark, by the mouth of Gríma Wormtongue. This was resented, but the orders were obeyed, within Edoras. As far as fighting was concerned, when the war with Saruman began Théodred without orders assumed general command. He summoned a muster of Edoras, and drew away a large part of its Riders, under Elfhelm, to strengthen the Muster of Westfold and help it to resist the invasion.

In times of war or unquiet each Marshal of the Mark had under his immediate orders, as part of his 'household' (that is, quartered under arms at his residence) an *éored* ready for battle which he could use in

---

* These were terms only used with reference to military organisation. Their boundary was the Snowbourn River to its junction with the Entwash, and thence north along the Entwash. [Author's note.]

† Here Eorl had his house; it passed after Brego son of Eorl removed to Edoras into the hands of Eofor, third son of Brego, from whom Éomund, father of Éomer, claimed descent. The Folde was part of the King's Lands, but Aldburg remained the most convenient base for the Muster of the East-mark. [Author's note.]

an emergency at his own discretion. This was what Éomer had in fact done;* but the charge against him, urged by Gríma, was that the King had in this case forbidden him to take any of the still uncommitted forces of the East-mark from Edoras, which was insufficiently defended; that he knew of the disaster at the Fords of Isen and the death of Théodred before he pursued the Orcs into the remote Wold; and that he had also against general orders allowed strangers to go free, and had even lent them horses.

After the fall of Théodred command in the West-mark (again without orders from Edoras) was assumed by Erkenbrand, Lord of Deeping-coomb and of much other land in Westfold. He had in youth been, as most lords, an officer in the King's Riders, but he was so no longer. He was, however, the chief lord in the West-mark, and since its people were in peril it was his right and duty to gather all those among them able to bear arms to resist invasion. He thus took command also of the Riders of the Western Muster; but Elfhelm remained in independent command of the Riders of the Muster of Edoras that Théodred had summoned to his assistance.

After the healing of Théoden by Gandalf, the situation changed. The King again took command in person. Éomer was reinstated, and became virtually First Marshal, ready to take command if the King fell or his strength failed; but the title was not used, and in the presence of the King in arms he could only advise and not issue orders. The part he actually played was thus much the same as that of Aragorn: a redoubtable champion among the companions of the King.†

When the Full Muster was made in Harrowdale, and the 'line of journey' and order of battle considered and as far as possible determined,‡ Éomer remained in this position, riding with the King (as commander of the leading *éored*, the King's Company) and acting as his chief counsellor. Elfhelm became a Marshal of the Mark, leading the first *éored* of the Muster of the East-mark. Grimbold (not previously mentioned in the narrative) had the function, but not the title, of the

---

* I.e., when Éomer pursued the Orcs, captors of Meriadoc and Peregrin, who had come down into Rohan from the Emyn Muil. The words that Éomer used to Aragorn were: 'I led forth my *éored*, men of my own household' (*The Two Towers* III 2).

† Those who did not know of the events at court naturally assumed that the reinforcements sent west were under Éomer's command as the only remaining Marshal of the Mark. [Author's note.] – The reference here is to the words of Ceorl, the Rider who met the reinforcements coming from Edoras and told them what had happened in the Second Battle of the Fords of Isen (*The Two Towers* III 7).

‡ Théoden called a council of 'the marshals and captains' at once, and before he took a meal; but it is not described, since Meriadoc was not present ('I wonder what they are all talking about.'). [Author's note.] – The reference is to *The Return of the King* V 3.

Third Marshal, and commanded the Muster of the Westmark.* Grimbold fell in the Battle of the Pelennor Fields, and Elfhelm became the lieutenant of Éomer as King; he was left in command of all the Rohirrim in Gondor when Éomer went to the Black Gate, and he routed the hostile army that had invaded Anórien (*The Return of the King* V, end of chapter 9 and beginning of 10). He is named as one of the chief witnesses of Aragorn's coronation (*ibid.* VI 5).

It is recorded that after Théoden's funeral, when Éomer reordered his realm, Erkenbrand was made Marshal of the West-mark, and Elfhelm Marshal of the East-mark, and these titles were maintained, instead of Second and Third Marshal, neither having precedence over the other. In time of war a special appointment was made to the office of Underking: its holder either ruled the realm in the King's absence with the army, or took command in the field if for any reason the King remained at home. In peace the office was only filled when the King because of sickness or old age deputed his authority; the holder was then naturally the Heir to the throne, if he was a man of sufficient age. But in war the Council was unwilling that an old King should send his Heir to battle beyond the realm, unless he had at least one other son.

### (ii)

A long note to the text (at the place where the differing views of the commanders on the importance of the Fords of Isen is discussed, pages 360-1) is given here. The first part of it largely repeats history that is given elsewhere in this book, but I have thought it best to give it in full.

In ancient days the southern and eastern bounds of the North Kingdom had been the Greyflood; the western bounds of the South Kingdom was the Isen. To the land between (the Enedwaith or 'middle region') few Númenóreans had ever come, and none had settled there. In the days of the Kings it was part of the realm of Gondor,† but it was of little concern to them, except for the patrolling and upkeep of the great Royal Road. This went all the way from Osgiliath and Minas Tirith to Fornost in the far North, crossed the Fords of Isen and

---

* Grimbold was a lesser marshal of the Riders of West-mark in Théodred's command, and was given this position, as a man of valour in both the battles at the Fords, because Erkenbrand was an older man, and the King felt the need of one of dignity and authority to leave behind in command of such forces as could be spared for the defence of Rohan. [Author's note.]–Grimbold is not mentioned in the narrative of *The Lord of the Rings* until the final ordering of the Rohirrim before Minas Tirith (*The Return of the King*, V 5).

† The statement that Enedwaith was in the days of the Kings part of the realm of Gondor seems to conflict with that immediately preceding, that 'the western bounds of the South Kingdom was the Isen'. Elsewhere (see p. 264) it is said that Enedwaith 'belonged to neither kingdom'.

passed through Enedwaith, keeping to the higher land in the centre
and north-east until it had to descend to the west lands about the lower
Greyflood, which it crossed on a raised causeway leading to a great
bridge at Tharbad. In those days the region was little peopled. In the
marshlands of the mouths of Greyflood and Isen lived a few tribes of
'Wild Men', fishers and fowlers, but akin in race and speech to the
Drúedain of the woods of Anórien.* In the foothills of the western side
of the Misty Mountains lived the remnants of the people that the
Rohirrim later called the Dunlendings: a sullen folk, akin to the ancient
inhabitants of the White Mountain valleys whom Isildur cursed.†
They had little love of Gondor, but though hardy and bold enough
were too few and too much in awe of the might of the Kings to trouble
them, or to turn their eyes away from the East, whence all their chief
perils came. The Dunlendings suffered, like all the peoples of Arnor
and Gondor, in the Great Plague of the years 1636-7 of the Third
Age, but less than most, since they dwelt apart and had few dealings
with other men. When the days of the Kings ended (1975-2050) and
the waning of Gondor began, they ceased in fact to be subjects of
Gondor; the Royal Road was unkept in Enedwaith, and the Bridge of
Tharbad becoming ruinous was replaced only by a dangerous ford.
The bounds of Gondor were the Isen, and the Gap of Calenardhon
(as it was then called). The Gap was watched by the fortresses of
Aglarond (the Hornburg) and Angrenost (Isengard), and the Fords of
Isen, the only easy entrance to Gondor, were ever guarded against any
incursion from the 'Wild Lands'.

But during the Watchful Peace (from 2063 to 2460) the people of
Calenardhon dwindled: the more vigorous, year by year, went eastward
to hold the line of the Anduin; those that remained became rustic and
far removed from the concerns of Minas Tirith. The garrisons of the
forts were not renewed, and were left to the care of local hereditary

---

* Cf. p. 262, where it is said that 'a fairly numerous but barbarous fisher-
folk dwelt between the mouths of the Gwathló and the Angren (Isen)'. No
mention is made there of any connection between these people and the
Drúedain, though the latter are said to have dwelt (and to have survived
there into the Third Age) in the promontory of Andrast, south of the mouths
of Isen (p. 384 and note 13).

† Cf. *The Lord of the Rings* Appendix F (Of Men): 'The Dunlendings
were a remnant of the peoples that had dwelt in the vales of the White
Mountains in ages past. The Dead Men of Dunharrow were of their kin.
But in the Dark Years others'had removed to the southern dales of the Misty
Mountains, and thence some had passed into the empty lands as far north
as the Barrow-downs. From them came the Men of Bree; but long before
these had become subjects of the North Kingdom of Arnor and had taken
up the Westron tongue. Only in Dunland did Men of this race hold to their
old speech and manners: a secret folk, unfriendly to the Dúnedain, hating
the Rohirrim.'

chieftains whose subjects were of more and more mixed blood. For the Dunlendings drifted steadily and unchecked over the Isen. Thus it was, when the attacks on Gondor from the East were renewed, and Orcs and Easterlings overran Calenardhon and besieged the forts, which would not have long held out. Then the Rohirrim came, and after the victory of Eorl on the Field of Celebrant in the year 2510 his numerous and warlike people with great wealth of horses swept into Calenardhon, driving out or destroying the eastern invaders. Cirion the Steward gave them possession of Calenardhon, which was thenceforth called the Riddermark, or in Gondor Rochand (later Rohan). The Rohirrim at once began the settlement of this region, though during the reign of Eorl their eastern bounds along the Emyn Muil and Anduin were still under attack. But under Brego and Aldor the Dunlendings were rooted out again and driven away beyond the Isen, and the Fords of Isen were guarded. Thus the Rohirrim earned the hatred of the Dunlendings, which was not appeased until the return of the King, then far off in the future. Whenever the Rohirrim were weak or in trouble the Dunlendings renewed their attacks.

No alliance of peoples was ever more faithfully kept on both sides than the alliance of Gondor and Rohan under the Oath of Cirion and Eorl; nor were any guardians of the wide grassy plains of Rohan more suited to their land than the Riders of the Mark. Nonetheless there was a grave weakness in their situation, as was most clearly shown in the days of the War of the Ring when it came near to causing the ruin of Rohan and of Gondor. This was due to many things. Above all, the eyes of Gondor had ever been eastward, whence all their perils came; the enmity of the 'wild' Dunlendings seemed of small account to the Stewards. Another point was that the Stewards retained under their own rule the Tower of Orthanc and the Ring of Isengard (Angrenost); the keys of Orthanc were taken to Minas Tirith, the Tower was shut, and the Ring of Isengard remained manned only by an hereditary Gondorian chieftain and his small people, to whom were joined the old hereditary guards of Aglarond. The fortress there was repaired with the aid of masons of Gondor and then committed to the Rohirrim.* From it the guards of the Fords were supplied. For the most part their settled dwellings were about the feet of the White Mountains and in the glens and valleys of the south. To the northern bounds of the Westfold they went seldom and only at need, regarding the eaves of Fangorn (the Entwood) and the frowning walls of Isengard with dread. They meddled little with the 'Lord of Isengard' and his secret folk, whom they believed to be dealers in dark magic. And to

* By whom it was called *Glǽmscrafu*, but the fortress Súthburg, and after King Helm's day the Hornburg. [Author's note.] – *Glǽmscrafu* (in which the *sc* is pronounced as *sh*) is Anglo-Saxon, 'caves of radiance', with the same meaning as *Aglarond*.

Isengard the emissaries from Minas Tirith came ever more seldom, until they ceased; it seemed that amidst their cares the Stewards had forgotten the Tower, though they held the keys.

Yet the western frontier and the line of the Isen was naturally commanded by Isengard, and this had evidently been well understood by the Kings of Gondor. The Isen flowed down from its sources along the eastern wall of the Ring, and as it went on southwards it was still a young river that offered no great obstacle to invaders, though its waters were still very swift and strangely cold. But the Great Gate of Angrenost opened west of Isen, and if the fortress were well manned enemies from the westlands must be in great strength if they thought to pass on into Westfold. Moreover Angrenost was less than half the distance of Aglarond from the Fords, to which a wide horseroad ran from the Gates, for most of the way over level ground. The dread that haunted the great Tower, and fear of the glooms of Fangorn that lay behind, might protect it for a while, but if it were unmanned and neglected, as it was in the latter days of the Stewards, that protection would not long avail.

So it proved. In the reign of King Déor (2699 to 2718) the Rohirrim found that to keep a watch on the Fords was not enough. Since neither Rohan nor Gondor gave heed to this far corner of the realm, it was not known until later what had happened there. The line of the Gondorian chieftains of Angrenost had failed, and the command of the fortress passed into the hands of a family of the people. These, as has been said, were already long before of mixed blood, and they were now more friendly disposed to the Dunlendings than to the 'wild Northmen' who had usurped the land; with Minas Tirith far away they no longer had any concern. After the death of King Aldor, who had driven out the last of the Dunlendings and even raided their lands in Enedwaith by way of reprisal, the Dunlendings unmarked by Rohan but with the connivance of Isengard began to filter into northern Westfold again, making settlements in the mountain glens west and east of Isengard and even in the southern eaves of Fangorn. In the reign of Déor they became openly hostile, raiding the herds and studs of the Rohirrim in Westfold. It was soon clear to the Rohirrim that these raiders had not crossed the Isen either by the Fords or at any point far south of Isengard, for the Fords were guarded.* Déor therefore led an expedition north- wards, and was met by a host of Dunlendings. These he overcame; but he was dismayed to find that Isengard was also hostile. Thinking that he had relieved Isengard of a Dunlendish siege, he sent messengers to its Gates with words of good will, but the Gates were shut upon them and the only answer they got was by bowshot. As was later known,

* Attacks were often made on the garrison of the west bank, but these were not pressed: they were in fact only made to distract the attention of the Rohirrim from the north. [Author's note.]

the Dunlendings, having been admitted as friends, had seized the Ring of Isengard, slaying the few survivors of its ancient guards who were not (as were most) willing to merge with the Dunlendish folk. Déor sent word at once to the Steward in Minas Tirith (at that time, in the year 2710, Egalmoth), but he was unable to send help, and the Dunlendings remained in occupation of Isengard until, reduced by the great famine after the Long Winter (2758–9) they were starved out and capitulated to Fréaláf (afterwards first King of the Second Line). But Déor had no power to storm or besiege Isengard, and for many years the Rohirrim had to keep a strong force of Riders in the north of Westfold; this was maintained until the great invasions of 2758.*

It can thus be readily understood that when Saruman offered to take command of Isengard and repair it and reorder it as part of the defences of the West he was welcomed both by King Fréaláf and by Beren the Steward. So when Saruman took up his abode in Isengard, and Beren gave to him the keys of Orthanc, the Rohirrim returned to their policy of guarding the Fords of Isen, as the most vulnerable point in their western frontier.

There can be little doubt that Saruman made his offer in good faith, or at least with good will towards the defence of the West, so long as he himself remained the chief person in that defence, and the head of its council. He was wise, and perceived clearly that Isengard with its position and its great strength, natural and by craft, was of utmost importance. The line of the Isen, between the pincers of Isengard and the Hornburg, was a bulwark against invasion from the East (whether incited and guided by Sauron, or otherwise), either aiming at encircling Gondor or at invading Eriador. But in the end he turned to evil and became an enemy; and yet the Rohirrim, though they had warnings of his growing malice towards them, continued to put their main strength in the west at the Fords, until Saruman in open war showed them that the Fords were small protection without Isengard and still less against it.

* An account of these invasions of Gondor and Rohan is given in *The Lord of the Rings* Appendix A (I, iv and II).

# PART FOUR

# I

# THE DRÚEDAIN

The Folk of Haleth were strangers to the other Atani, speaking an
alien language; and though united with them in alliance with the
Eldar, they remained a people apart. Among themselves they adhered
to their own language, and though of necessity they learned Sindarin
for communication with the Eldar and the other Atani, many spoke
it haltingly, and some of those who seldom went beyond the borders
of their own woods did not use it at all. They did not willingly adopt
new things or customs, and retained many practices that seemed
strange to the Eldar and the other Atani, with whom they had few
dealings except in war. Nonetheless they were esteemed as loyal
allies and redoubtable warriors, though the companies that they sent
to battle beyond their borders were small. For they were and remained
to their end a small people, chiefly concerned to protect their own
woodlands, and they excelled in forest warfare. Indeed for long even
those Orcs specially trained for this dared not set foot near their
borders. One of the strange practices spoken of was that many of
their warriors were women, though few of these went abroad to fight
in the great battles. This custom was evidently ancient;[1] for their
chieftainess Haleth was a renowned Amazon with a picked bodyguard
of women.[2]

The strangest of all the customs of the Folk of Haleth was the
presence among them of people of a wholly different kind,[3] the like
of which neither the Eldar in Beleriand nor the other Atani had ever
seen before. They were not many, a few hundreds maybe, living
apart in families or small tribes, but in friendship, as members of
the same community.[4] The Folk of Haleth called them by the name
*drûg*, that being a word of their own language. To the eyes of Elves
and other Men they were unlovely in looks: they were stumpy (some
four foot high) but very broad, with heavy buttocks and short thick
legs; their wide faces had deep-set eyes with heavy brows, and flat
noses, and grew no hair below their eyebrows, except in a few men
(who were proud of the distinction) a small tail of black hair in the
midst of the chin. Their features were usually impassive, the most
mobile being their wide mouths; and the movement of their wary

eyes could not be observed save from close at hand, for they were
so black that the pupils could not be distinguished, but in anger they
glowed red. Their voices were deep and guttural, but their laughter
was a surprise: it was rich and rolling, and set all who heard it,
Elves or Men, laughing too for its pure merriment untainted by scorn
or malice.[5] In peace they often laughed at work or play when other
Men might sing. But they could be relentless enemies, and when
once aroused their red wrath was slow to cool, though it showed no
sign save the light in their eyes; for they fought in silence and did
not exult in victory, not even over Orcs, the only creatures for whom
their hatred was implacable.

The Eldar called them Drúedain, admitting them to the rank of
Atani,[6] for they were much loved while they lasted. Alas! they were
not long-lived, and were ever few in number, and their losses were
heavy in their feud with the Orcs, who returned their hatred and
delighted to capture them and torture them. When the victories of
Morgoth destroyed all the realms and strongholds of Elves and Men
in Beleriand, it is said that they had dwindled to a few families,
mostly of women and children, some of whom came to the last
refuges at the Mouths of Sirion.[7]

In their earlier days they had been of great service to those among
whom they dwelt, and they were much sought after; though few
would ever leave the land of the Folk of Haleth.[8] They had a marvellous skill as trackers of all living creatures, and they taught to
their friends what they could of their craft; but their pupils did not
equal them, for the Drúedain used their scent, like hounds save that
they were also keen-eyed. They boasted that they could smell an
Orc to windward further away than other Men could see them, and
could follow its scent for weeks except through running water.
Their knowledge of all growing things was almost equal to that of
the Elves (though untaught by them); and it is said that if they
removed to a new country they knew within a short time all things
that grew there, great or minute, and gave names to those that were
new to them, discerning those that were poisonous, or useful as
food.[9]

The Drúedain, as also the other Atani, had no form of writing
until they met the Eldar; but the runes and scripts of the Eldar were
never learned by them. They came no nearer to writing by their own
invention than the use of a number of signs, for the most part
simple, for the marking of trails or the giving of information and
warning. In the far distant past they appear already to have had small
tools of flint for scraping and cutting, and these they still used,

although the Atani had a knowledge of metals and some smith-craft before they came to Beleriand,[10] for metals were hard to come by and forged weapons and tools very costly. But when in Beleriand by association with the Eldar and in traffic with the Dwarves of Ered Lindon these things became more common, the Drúedain showed great talent for carving in wood or stone. They already had a know-ledge of pigments, derived chiefly from plants, and they drew pictures and patterns on wood or flat surfaces of stone; and sometimes they would scrape knobs of wood into faces that could be painted. But with sharper and stronger tools they delighted in carving figures of men and beasts, whether toys and ornaments or large images, to which the most skilled among them could give vivid semblance of life. Sometimes these images were strange and fantastic, or even fearful: among the grim jests to which they put their skill was the making of Orc-figures which they set at the borders of the land, shaped as if fleeing from it, shrieking in terror. They made also images of themselves and placed them at the entrances to tracks or at turnings of woodland paths. These they called 'watch-stones'; of which the most notable were set near the Crossings of Teiglin, each representing a Drúadan, larger than the life, squatting heavily upon a dead Orc. These figures served not merely as insults to their enemies; for the Orcs feared them and believed them to be filled with the malice of the *Oghor-hai* (for so they named the Drúedain), and able to hold communication with them. Therefore they seldom dared to touch them, or to try to destroy them, and unless in great numbers would turn back at a 'watch-stone' and go no further.

But among the powers of this strange people perhaps most to be remarked was their capacity of utter silence and stillness, which they could at times endure for many days on end, sitting with their legs crossed, their hands upon their knees or in their laps, and their eyes closed or looking at the ground. Concerning this a tale was related among the Folk of Haleth:

On a time, one of the most skilled in stone-carving among the Drûgs made an image of his father, who had died; and he set it up by a pathway near to their dwelling. Then he sat down beside it and passed into a deep silence of recollection. It chanced that not long after a forester came by on a journey to a distant village, and seeing two Drûgs he bowed and wished them good day. But he received no answer, and he stood for some time in surprise, looking closely at them. Then he went on his way, saying to himself: 'Great skill have they in stone-work, but I have never

seen any more lifelike.' Three days later he returned, and being
very weary he sat down and propped his back against one of the
figures. His cloak he cast about its shoulders to dry, for it had been
raining, but the sun was now shining hot. There he fell asleep; but
after a while he was wakened by a voice from the figure behind him.
'I hope you are rested,' it said, 'but if you wish for more sleep, I
beg you to move to the other one. He will never need to stretch
his legs again; and I find your cloak too hot in the sun.'

It is said that the Drúedain would often sit thus in times of grief
or loss, but sometimes for pleasure in thought, or in the making of
plans. But they could also use this stillness when on guard; and then
they would sit or stand, hidden in shadow, and though their eyes
might seem closed or staring with a blank gaze nothing passed or
came near that was not marked and remembered. So intense was
their unseen vigilance that it could be felt as a hostile menace by
intruders, who retreated in fear before any warning was given; but
if any evil thing passed on, then they would utter as a signal a shrill
whistle, painful to endure close at hand and heard far off. The
service of the Drúedain as guards was much esteemed by the Folk
of Haleth in times of peril; and if such guards were not to be had
they would have figures carved in their likeness to set near their
houses, believing that (being made by the Drúedain themselves for
the purpose) they would hold some of the menace of the living men.
Indeed, though they held the Drúedain in love and trust, many
of the Folk of Haleth believed that they possessed uncanny and
magical powers; and among their tales of marvels there were several
that told of such things. One of these is recorded here.

### The Faithful Stone

On a time there was a Drûg named Aghan, well-known as a leech.
He had a great friendship with Barach, a forester of the Folk, who
lived in a house in the woods two miles or more from the nearest
village. The dwellings of Aghan's family were nearer, and he spent
most of his time with Barach and his wife, and was much loved by
their children. There came a time of trouble, for a number of
daring Orcs had secretly entered the woods nearby, and were
scattered in twos and threes, waylaying any that went abroad alone,
and at night attacking houses far from neighbours. The household
of Barach were not much afraid, for Aghan stayed with them at
night and kept watch outside. But one morning he came to Barach

and said: 'Friend, I have ill news from my kin, and I fear I must leave you a while. My brother has been wounded, and he lies now in pain and calls for me, since I have skill in treating Orc-wounds. I will return as soon as I may.' Barach was greatly troubled, and his wife and children wept, but Aghan said: 'I will do what I can. I have had a watch-stone brought here and set near your house.' Barach went out with Aghan and looked at the watch-stone. It was large and heavy and sat under some bushes not far from his doors. Aghan laid his hand upon it, and after a silence said: 'See, I have left with it some of my powers. May it keep you from harm!'

Nothing untoward happened for two nights, but on the third night Barach heard the shrill warning call of the Drûgs – or dreamed that he heard it, for it roused no one else. Leaving his bed he took his bow from the wall and went to a narrow window; and he saw two Orcs setting fuel against his house and preparing to kindle it. Then Barach was shaken with fear, for marauding Orcs carried with them brimstone or some other devilish stuff that was quickly inflamed and not quenched with water. Recovering himself he bent his bow, but at that moment, just as the flames leapt up, he saw a Drûg come running up behind the Orcs. One he felled with a blow of his fist, and the other fled; then he plunged barefoot into the fire, scattering the burning fuel and stamping on the Orc-flames that ran along the ground. Barach made for the doors, but when he had unbarred them and sprang out the Drûg had disappeared. There was no sign of the smitten Orc. The fire was dead, and there remained only a smoke and a stench.

Barach went back indoors to comfort his family, who had been roused by the noises and the burning reek; but when it was daylight he went out again and looked about. He found that the watch-stone had gone, but he kept that to himself. 'Tonight I must be the watchman,' he thought; but later in the day Aghan came back, and was welcomed with joy. He was wearing high buskins such as the Drûgs sometimes wore in hard country, among thorns or rocks, and he was weary. But he was smiling, and seemed pleased; and he said: 'I bring good news. My brother is no longer in pain and will not die, for I came in time to withstand the venom. And now I learn that the marauders have been slain, or else fled. How have you fared?'

'We are still alive,' said Barach. 'But come with me, and I will show you and tell you more.' Then he led Aghan to the place of the fire and told him of the attack in the night. 'The watch-stone has gone – Orc-work, I guess. What have you to say to that?'

'I will speak, when I have looked and thought longer,' said Aghan; and then he went hither and thither scanning the ground, and Barach followed him. At length Aghan led him to a thicket at the edge of the clearing in which the house stood. There the watch-stone was, sitting on a dead Orc; but its legs were all blackened and cracked, and one of its feet had split off and lay loose at its side. Aghan looked grieved; but he said: 'Ah well! He did what he could. And better that his legs should trample Orc-fire than mine.'

Then he sat down and unlaced his buskins, and Barach saw that under them there were bandages on his legs. Aghan undid them. 'They are healing already,' he said. 'I had kept vigil by my brother for two nights, and last night I slept. I woke before morning came, and I was in pain, and found my legs blistered. Then I guessed what had happened. Alas! If some power passes from you to a thing that you have made, then you must take a share in its hurts.'[11]

### Further notes on the Drúedain

My father was at pains to emphasize the radical difference between the Drúedain and the Hobbits. They were of quite different physical shape and appearance. The Drúedain were taller, and of heavier and stronger build. Their facial features were unlovely (judged by general human standards); and while the head-hair of the Hobbits was abundant (but close and curly) the Drúedain had only sparse and lank hair on their heads and none at all on their legs and feet. They were at times merry and gay, like Hobbits, but they had a grimmer side to their nature and could be sardonic and ruthless; and they had, or were credited with, strange or magical powers. They were moreover a frugal people, eating sparingly even in times of plenty and drinking nothing but water. In some ways they resembled rather the Dwarves: in build and stature and endurance; in their skill in carving stone; in the grim side of their character; and in their strange powers. But the 'magic' skills with which the Dwarves were credited were quite different; and the Dwarves were far grimmer, and also long-lived, whereas the Drúedain were short-lived compared with other kinds of Men.

Only once, in an isolated note, is anything said explicitly concerning the relationship between the Drúedain of Beleriand in the First Age, who guarded the houses of the Folk of Haleth in the Forest of Brethil, and the remote ancestors of Ghân-buri-Ghân, who guided the Rohirrim down the Stonewain Valley on their way to Minas Tirith (*The Return of the King* V 5), or the makers of the images on the road to Dunharrow (*ibid.* V 3).[12] This note states:

An emigrant branch of the Drúedain accompanied the Folk of Haleth at the end of the First Age, and dwelt in the Forest [of Brethil] with them. But most of them had remained in the White Mountains, in spite of their persecution by later-arrived Men, who had relapsed into the service of the Dark.

It is also said here that the identity of the statues of Dunharrow with the remnants of the Drúath (perceived by Meriadoc Brandybuck when he first set eyes on Ghân-buri-Ghân) was originally recognized in Gondor, though at the time of the establishment of the Númenórean kingdom by Isildur they survived only in the Drúadan Forest and in the Drúwaith Iaur (see below).

We can thus if we wish elaborate the ancient legend of the coming of the Edain in *The Silmarillion* (pp. 140–3) by the addition of the Drúedain, descending out of Ered Lindon into Ossiriand with the Haladin (the Folk of Haleth). Another note says that historians in Gondor believed that the first Men to cross the Anduin were indeed the Drúedain. They came (it was believed) from lands south of Mordor, but before they reached the coasts of Haradwaith they turned north into Ithilien, and eventually finding a way across the Anduin (probably near Cair Andros) settled in the vales of the White Mountains and the wooded lands at their northern feet. 'They were a secretive people, suspicious of other kinds of Men by whom they had been harried and persecuted as long as they could remember, and they had wandered west seeking a land where they could be hidden and have peace.' But nothing more is said, here or elsewhere, concerning the history of their association with the Folk of Haleth.

In an essay, cited previously, on the names of rivers in Middle-earth there is a glimpse of the Drúedain in the Second Age. It is said here (see p. 263) that the native people of Enedwaith, fleeing from the devastations of the Númenóreans along the course of the Gwathló,

did not cross the Isen nor take refuge in the great promontory between Isen and Lefnui that formed the north arm of the Bay of Belfalas, because of the 'Púkel-men', who were a secret and fell people, tireless and silent hunters, using poisoned darts. They said that they had always been there, and had formerly lived also in the White Mountains. In ages past they had paid no heed to the Great Dark One (Morgoth), nor did they later ally themselves with Sauron; for they hated all invaders from the East. From the East, they said, had come the tall Men who drove them from the White Mountains, and they were wicked at heart. Maybe even in the days of the War of the Ring some of the Drû-folk lingered in the mountains of Andrast, the western outlier of the White Mountains, but only the remnant in the woods of Anórien were known to the people of Gondor.

This region between Isen and Lefnui was the Drúwaith Iaur, and in yet another scrap of writing on this subject it is stated that the word *Iaur* 'old' in this name does not mean 'original' but 'former':

The 'Púkel-men' occupied the White Mountains (on both sides) in the First Age. When the occupation of the coastlands by the Númenóreans began in the Second Age they survived in the mountains of the promontory [of Andrast], which was never occupied by the Númenóreans. Another remnant survived at the eastern end of the range [in Anórien]. At the end of the Third Age the latter, much reduced in numbers, were believed to be the only survivors; hence the other region was called 'the Old Púkel-wilderness' (Drúwaith Iaur). It remained a 'wilderness' and was not inhabited by Men of Gondor or of Rohan, and was seldom entered by any of them; but Men of the Anfalas believed that some of the old 'Wild Men' still lived there secretly.[13]

But in Rohan the identity of the statues of Dunharrow called 'Púkel-men' with the 'Wild Men' of the Drúadan Forest was not recognized, neither was their 'humanity': hence the reference by Ghân-buri-Ghân to persecution of the 'Wild Men' by the Rohirrim in the past ['leave Wild Men alone in the woods and do not hunt them like beasts any more']. Since Ghân-buri-Ghân was attempting to use the Common Speech he called his people 'Wild Men' (not without irony); but this was not of course their own name for themselves.[14]

## NOTES

1  Not due to their special situation in Beleriand, and maybe rather a cause of their small numbers than its result. They increased in numbers far more slowly than the other Atani, hardly more than was sufficient to replace the wastage of war; yet many of their women (who were fewer than the men) remained unwed. [Author's note.]

2  In *The Silmarillion* Bëor described the Haladin (afterwards called the People or Folk of Haleth) to Felagund as 'a people from whom we are sundered in speech' (p. 142). It is said also that 'they remained a people apart' (p. 146), and that they were of smaller stature than the men of the House of Bëor; 'they used few words, and did not love great concourse of men; and many among them delighted in solitude,

wandering free in the greenwoods while the wonder of the lands of the Eldar was new upon them' (p. 148). Nothing is said in *The Silmarillion* about the Amazonian element in their society, other than that the Lady Haleth was a warrior and the leader of the people, nor of their adherence to their own language in Beleriand.

3  Though they spoke the same language (after their fashion). They retained however a number of words of their own. [Author's note.]

4  After the fashion in which in the Third Age the Men and Hobbits of Bree lived together; though there was no kinship between the Drûg-folk and the Hobbits. [Author's note.]

5  To the unfriendly who, not knowing them well, declared that Morgoth must have bred the Orcs from such a stock the Eldar answered: 'Doubtless Morgoth, since he can make no living thing, bred Orcs from various kinds of Men, but the Drúedain must have escaped his Shadow; for their laughter and the laughter of Orcs are as different as is the light of Aman from the darkness of Angband.' But some thought, nonetheless, that there had been a remote kinship, which accounted for their special enmity. Orcs and Drûgs each regarded the other as renegades. [Author's note.] – In *The Silmarillion* the Orcs are said to have been bred by Melkor from captured Elves in the beginning of their days (p. 50; cf. pp. 93–4); but this was only one of several diverse speculations on the origin of the Orcs. It may be noted that in *The Return of the King* V 5 the laughter of Ghân-buri-Ghân is described: 'At that old Ghân made a curious gurgling noise, and it seemed that he was laughing.' He is described as having a scanty beard that 'straggled on his lumpy chin like dry moss', and dark eyes that showed nothing.

6  It is stated in isolated notes that their own name for themselves was *Drughu* (in which the *gh* represents a spirantal sound). This name adopted into Sindarin in Beleriand became *Drû* (plurals *Drúin* and *Drúath*); but when the Eldar discovered that the Drû-folk were steadfast enemies of Morgoth, and especially of the Orcs, the 'title' *adan* was added, and they were called *Drúedain* (singular *Drúadan*), to mark both their humanity and friendship with the Eldar, and their racial difference from the people of the Three Houses of the Edain. *Drû* was then only used in compounds such as *Drúnos* 'a family of the Drû-folk', *Drúwaith* 'the wilderness of the Drû-folk'. In Quenya *Drughu* became *Rú*, and *Rúatan*, plural *Rúatani*. For their other names in later times (Wild Men, Woses, Púkel-men) see p. 384 and note 14.

7  In the annals of Númenor it is said that this remnant was permitted to sail over sea with the Atani, and in the peace of the new land throve and increased again, but took no more part in war, for they dreaded the sea. What happened to them later is only recorded in one of the few legends that survived the Downfall, the story of the

first sailings of the Númenóreans back to Middle-earth, known as
*The Mariner's Wife*. In a copy of this written and preserved in
Gondor there is a note by the scribe on a passage in which the
Drúedain in the household of King Aldarion the Mariner are mentioned: it relates that the Drúedain, who were ever noted for their
strange foresight, were disturbed to hear of his voyages, foreboding
that evil would come of them, and begged him to go no more. But
they did not succeed, since neither his father nor his wife could
prevail on him to change his courses, and the Drúedain departed
in distress. From that time onward the Drúedain of Númenor became
restless, and despite their fear of the sea one by one, or in twos and
threes, they would beg for passages in the great ships that sailed to
the North-western shores of Middle-earth. If any asked 'Why would
you go, and whither?' they answered: 'The Great Isle no longer
feels sure under our feet, and we wish to return to the lands whence
we came.' Thus their numbers dwindled again slowly through the
long years, and none were left when Elendil escaped from the Downfall: the last had fled the land when Sauron was brought to it.
[Author's note.] – There is no trace, either in the materials relating to
the story of Aldarion and Erendis or elsewhere, of the presence of
Drúedain in Númenor apart from the foregoing, save for a detached
note which says that 'the Edain who at the end of the War of the
Jewels sailed over sea to Númenor contained few remnants of the
Folk of Haleth, and the very few Drúedain that accompanied them
died out long before the Downfall'.

8   A few lived in the household of Húrin of the House of Hador, for
he had dwelt among the Folk of Haleth in his youth and had kinship
with their lord. [Author's note.] – On the relationship of Húrin to the
Folk of Haleth see *The Silmarillion* p. 158. – It was my father's
intention ultimately to transform Sador, the old serving-man in
Húrin's house in Dor-lómin, into a Drûg.

9   They had a law against the use of all poisons for the hurt of any
living creatures, even those who had done them injury – save only
Orcs, whose poisoned darts they countered with others more deadly.
[Author's note.] – Elfhelm told Meriadoc Brandybuck that the Wild
Men used poisoned arrows (*The Return of the King* V 5), and the
same was believed of them by the inhabitants of Enedwaith in the
Second Age (p. 383). At a later point in this essay something is told
of the dwellings of the Drúedain, which it is convenient to cite here.
Living among the Folk of Haleth, who were a woodland people,
'they were content to live in tents or shelters, lightly built round the
trunks of large trees, for they were a hardy race. In their former
homes, according to their own tales, they had used caves in the
mountains, but mainly as store-houses, only occupied as dwellings
and sleeping-places in severe weather. They had similar refuges in

Beleriand to which all but the most hardy retreated in times of storm or bitter winter; but these places were guarded and not even their closest friends among the Folk of Haleth were welcomed there.'

10 Acquired according to their legends from the Dwarves. [Author's note.]

11 Of this story my father remarked: 'The tales, such as *The Faithful Stone*, that speak of their transferring part of their "powers" to their artefacts, remind one in miniature of Sauron's transference of power to the foundations of the Barad-dûr and to the Ruling Ring.'

12 'At each turn of the road there were great standing stones that had been carved in the likeness of men, huge and clumsy-limbed, squatting cross-legged with their stumpy arms folded on fat bellies. Some in the wearing of the years had lòst all features save the dark holes of their eyes that still stared sadly at the passers-by.'

13 The name *Drúwaith Iaur* (*Old Púkel-land*) appears on Miss Pauline Baynes' decorated map of Middle-earth (see p. 261), placed well to the north of the mountains of the promontory of Andrast. My father stated however that the name was inserted by him and was correctly placed. – A marginal jotting states that after the Battles of the Fords of Isen it was found that many Drúedain did indeed survive in the Drúwaith Iaur, for they came forth from the caves where they dwelt to attack remnants of Saruman's forces that had been driven away southwards. – In a passage cited on p. 370 there is a reference to tribes of 'Wild Men', fishers and fowlers, on the coasts of Enedwaith, who were akin in race and speech to the Drúedain of Anórien.

14 Once in *The Lord of the Rings* the term 'Woses' is used, when Elfhelm said to Meriadoc Brandybuck: 'You hear the Woses, the Wild Men of the Woods.' *Wose* is a modernization (in this case, the form that the word would have had now if it still existed in the language) of an Anglo-Saxon word *wása*, which is actually found only in the compound *wudu-wása* 'wild man of the woods'. (Saeros the Elf of Doriath called Túrin a 'woodwose', pp. 80–1 above. The word survived long in English and was eventually corrupted into 'wood-house'.) The actual word employed by the Rohirrim (of which 'wose' is a translation, according to the method employed throughout) is once mentioned: *róg*, plural *rógin*.

It seems that the term 'Púkel-men' (again a translation: it represents Anglo-Saxon *púcel* 'goblin, demon', a relative of the word *púca* from which *Puck* is derived) was only used in Rohan of the images of Dunharrow.

# II

# THE ISTARI

The fullest account of the Istari was written, as it appears, in 1954 (see the Introduction, p. 12, for an account of its origin). I give it here in full, and will refer to it subsequently as 'the essay on the Istari'.

*Wizard* is a translation of Quenya istar (Sindarin *ithron*): one of the members of an 'order' (as they called it), claiming to possess, and exhibiting, eminent knowledge of the history and nature of the World. The translation (though suitable in its relation to 'wise' and other ancient words of knowing, similar to that of *istar* in Quenya) is not perhaps happy, since the *Heren Istarion* or 'Order of Wizards' was quite distinct from the 'wizards' and 'magicians' of later legend; they belonged solely to the Third Age and then departed, and none save maybe Elrond, Círdan, and Galadriel discovered of what kind they were or whence they came.

Among Men they were supposed (at first) by those that had dealings with them to be Men who had acquired lore and arts by long and secret study. They first appeared in Middle-earth about the year 1000 of the Third Age, but for long they went about in simple guise, as it were of Men already old in years but hale in body, travellers and wanderers, gaining knowledge of Middle-earth and all that dwelt therein, but revealing to none their powers and purposes. In that time Men saw them seldom and heeded them little. But as the shadow of Sauron began to grow and take shape again, they became more active, and sought ever to contest the growth of the Shadow, and to move Elves and Men to beware of their peril. Then far and wide rumour of their comings and goings, and their meddling in many matters, was noised among Men; and Men perceived that they did not die, but remained the same (unless it were that they aged somewhat in looks), while the fathers and sons of Men passed away. Men, therefore, grew to fear them, even when they loved them, and they were held to be of the Elven-race (with whom, indeed, they often consorted).

Yet they were not so. For they came from over the Sea out of the Uttermost West; though this was for long known only to Círdan,

Guardian of the Third Ring, master of the Grey Havens, who saw their landings upon the western shores. Emissaries they were from the Lords of the West, the Valar, who still took counsel for the governance of Middle-earth, and when the shadow of Sauron began first to stir again took this means of resisting him. For with the consent of Eru they sent members of their own high order, but clad in bodies as of Men, real and not feigned, but subject to the fears and pains and weariness of earth, able to hunger and thirst and be slain; though because of their noble spirits they did not die, and aged only by the cares and labours of many long years. And this the Valar did, desiring to amend the errors of old, especially that they had attempted to guard and seclude the Eldar by their own might and glory fully revealed; whereas now their emissaries were forbidden to reveal themselves in forms of majesty, or to seek to rule the wills of Men or Elves by open display of power, but coming in shapes weak and humble were bidden to advise and persuade Men and Elves to good, and to seek to unite in love and understanding all those whom Sauron, should he come again, would endeavour to dominate and corrupt.

Of this Order the number is unknown; but of those that came to the North of Middle-earth, where there was most hope (because of the remnant of the Dúnedain and of the Eldar that abode there), the chiefs were five. The first to come was one of noble mien and bearing, with raven hair, and a fair voice, and he was clad in white; great skill he had in works of hand, and he was regarded by well-nigh all, even by the Eldar, as the head of the Order.[1] Others there were also: two clad in sea-blue, and one in earthen brown; and last came one who seemed the least, less tall than the others, and in looks more aged, grey-haired and grey-clad, and leaning on a staff. But Círdan from their first meeting at the Grey Havens divined in him the greatest spirit and the wisest; and he welcomed him with reverence, and he gave to his keeping the Third Ring, Narya the Red.

'For,' said he, 'great labours and perils lie before you, and lest your task prove too great and wearisome, take this Ring for your aid and comfort. It was entrusted to me only to keep secret, and here upon the West-shores it is idle; but I deem that in days ere long to come it should be in nobler hands than mine, that may wield it for the kindling of all hearts to courage.'[2] And the Grey Messenger took the Ring, and kept it ever secret; yet the White Messenger (who was skilled to uncover all secrets) after a time became aware of this gift, and begrudged it, and it was the beginning of the hidden ill-will that he bore to the Grey, which afterwards became manifest.

Now the White Messenger in later days became known among Elves as Curunír, the Man of Craft, in the tongues of Northern Men Saruman; but that was after he returned from his many journeys and came into the realm of Gondor and there abode. Of the Blue little was known in the West, and they had no names save *Ithryn Luin* 'the Blue Wizards'; for they passed into the East with Curunír, but they never returned, and whether they remained in the East, pursuing there the purposes for which they were sent; or perished; or as some hold were ensnared by Sauron and became his servants, is not now known.[3] But none of these chances were impossible to be; for, strange indeed though this may seem, the Istari, being clad in bodies of Middle-earth, might even as Men and Elves fall away from their purposes, and do evil, forgetting the good in the search for power to effect it.

A separate passage written in the margin no doubt belongs here:

For it is said indeed that being embodied the Istari had need to learn much anew by slow experience, and though they knew whence they came the memory of the Blessed Realm was to them a vision from afar off, for which (so long as they remained true to their mission) they yearned exceedingly. Thus by enduring of free will the pangs of exile and the deceits of Sauron they might redress the evils of that time.

Indeed, of all the Istari, one only remained faithful, and he was the last-comer. For Radagast, the fourth, became enamoured of the many beasts and birds that dwelt in Middle-earth, and forsook Elves and Men, and spent his days among the wild creatures. Thus he got his name (which is in the tongue of Númenor of old, and signifies, it is said, 'tender of beasts').[4] And Curunír 'Lân, Saruman the White, fell from his high errand, and becoming proud and impatient and enamoured of power sought to have his own will by force, and to oust Sauron; but he was ensnared by that dark spirit, mightier than he.

But the last-comer was named among the Elves Mithrandir, the Grey Pilgrim, for he dwelt in no place, and gathered to himself neither wealth nor followers, but ever went to and fro in the Westlands from Gondor to Angmar, and from Lindon to Lórien, befriending all folk in times of need. Warm and eager was his spirit (and it was enhanced by the ring Narya), for he was the Enemy of Sauron, opposing the fire that devours and wastes with the fire that kindles, and succours in wanhope and distress; but his joy, and his swift wrath, were veiled in garments grey as ash, so that only those that knew him well glimpsed the flame that was within. Merry he could be, and kindly to the young and simple, and yet quick at times to sharp speech and the rebuking of folly; but he was not proud, and sought neither power nor praise, and thus far and wide he was beloved among all those that were not themselves proud. Mostly he journeyed unwearyingly on foot, leaning on a staff; and so he was called among Men of the North Gandalf, 'the Elf of the Wand'. For they deemed him (though in error, as has been said) to be of Elven-kind, since he would at times work wonders among them, loving especially the beauty of fire; and yet such marvels he wrought mostly for mirth and delight, and desired not that any should hold him in awe or take his counsels out of fear.

Elsewhere it is told how it was that when Sauron rose again, he also arose and partly revealed his power, and becoming the chief mover of the resistance to Sauron was at last victorious, and brought all by vigilance and labour to that end which the Valar under the One that is above them had designed. Yet it is said that in the ending of the task for which he came he suffered greatly, and was slain, and being sent back from death for a brief while was clothed then in white, and became a radiant flame (yet veiled still save in great need). And when all was over and the Shadow of Sauron was removed, he departed for ever over the Sea. Whereas Curunír was cast down, and utterly humbled, and perished at last by the hand of an oppressed slave; and his spirit went whithersoever it was doomed to go, and to Middle-earth, whether naked or embodied, came never back.

In *The Lord of the Rings* the only general statement about the Istari is found in the headnote to the Tale of Years of the Third Age in Appendix B:

When maybe a thousand years had passed, and the first shadow had fallen on Greenwood the Great, the *Istari* or Wizards appeared in Middle-earth. It was afterwards said that they came out of the Far West and were messengers sent to contest the power of Sauron, and to unite all those who had the will to resist him; but they were forbidden to match his power with power, or to seek to dominate Elves or Men by force or fear.

They came therefore in the shape of Men, though they were

never young and aged only slowly, and they had many powers of mind and hand. They revealed their true names to few, but used such names as were given to them. The two highest of this order (of whom it is said there were five) were called by the Eldar Curunír, 'the Man of Skill', and Mithrandir, 'the Grey Pilgrim', but by Men in the North Saruman and Gandalf. Curunír journeyed often into the East, but dwelt at last in Isengard. Mithrandir was closest in friendship with the Eldar, and wandered mostly in the West, and never made for himself any lasting abode.

There follows an account of the guardianship of the Three Rings of the Elves, in which it is said that Círdan gave the Red Ring to Gandalf when he first came to the Grey Havens from over the Sea ('for Círdan saw further and deeper than any other in Middle-earth').

The essay on the Istari just cited thus tells much about them and their origin that does not appear in *The Lord of the Rings* (and also contains some incidental remarks of great interest about the Valar, their continuing concern for Middle-earth, and their recognition of ancient error, which cannot be discussed here). Most notable are the description of the Istari as 'members of their own high order' (the order of the Valar), and the statements about their physical embodiment.[5] But also to be remarked are the coming of the Istari to Middle-earth at different times; Círdan's perception that Gandalf was the greatest of them; Saruman's knowledge that Gandalf possessed the Red Ring, and his jealousy; the view taken of Radagast, that he did not remain faithful to his mission; the two other 'Blue Wizards', unnamed, who passed with Saruman into the East, but unlike him never returned into the Westlands; the number of the order of the Istari (said here to be unknown, though 'the chiefs' of those that came to the North of Middle-earth were five); the explanation of the names Gandalf and Radagast; and the Sindarin word *ithron*, plural *ithryn*.

The passage concerning the Istari in *Of the Rings of Power* (in *The Silmarillion*, p. 300) is very close indeed to the statement in Appendix B to *The Lord of the Rings* cited above, even in wording; but it does include this sentence, agreeing with the essay on the Istari:

Curunír was the eldest and came first, and after him came Mithrandir and Radagast, and others of the Istari who went into the East of Middle-earth, and do not come into these tales.

Most of the remaining writings about the Istari (as a group) are unhappily no more than very rapid jottings, often illegible. Of major

interest, however, is a brief and very hasty sketch of a narrative, telling
of a council of the Valar, summoned it seems by Manwë ('and maybe
he called upon Eru for counsel?'), at which it was resolved to send out
three emissaries to Middle-earth. 'Who would go? For they must be
mighty, peers of Sauron, but must forgo might, and clothe themselves
in flesh so as to treat on equality and win the trust of Elves and Men.
But this would imperil them, dimming their wisdom and knowledge,
and confusing them with fears, cares, and wearinesses coming from the
flesh.' But two only came forward: Curumo, who was chosen by Aulë,
and Alatar, who was sent by Oromë. Then Manwë asked, where was
Olórin? And Olórin, who was clad in grey, and having just entered
from a journey had seated himself at the edge of the council, asked
what Manwë would have of him. Manwë replied that he wished Olórin
to go as the third messenger to Middle-earth (and it is remarked in
parentheses that 'Olórin was a lover of the Eldar that remained',
apparently to explain Manwë's choice). But Olórin declared that he
was too weak for such a task, and that he feared Sauron. Then Manwë
said that that was all the more reason why he should go, and that he
commanded Olórin (illegible words follow that seem to contain the
word 'third'). But at that Varda looked up and said: 'Not as the third';
and Curumo remembered it.

The note ends with the statement that Curumo [Saruman] took
Aiwendil [Radagast] because Yavanna begged him, and that Alatar
took Pallando as a friend.[6]

On another page of jottings clearly belonging to the same period it
is said that 'Curumo was obliged to take Aiwendil to please Yavanna
wife of Aulë'. There are here also some rough tables relating the names
of the Istari to the names of the Valar: Olórin to Manwë and Varda,
Curumo to Aulë, Aiwendil to Yavanna, Alatar to Oromë, and Pallando
also to Oromë (but this replaces Pallando to Mandos and Nienna).

The meaning of these relations between Istari and Valar is clearly,
in the light of the brief narrative just cited, that each Istar was chosen
by each Vala for his innate characteristics – perhaps even that they were
members of the 'people' of that Vala, in the same sense as is said of
Sauron in the *Valaquenta* (*The Silmarillion* p. 32) that 'in his beginning
he was of the Maiar of Aulë, and he remained mighty in the lore of
that people'. It is thus very notable that Curumo (Saruman) was chosen
by Aulë. There is no hint of an explanation of why Yavanna's evident
desire that the Istari should include in their number one with a particular love of the things of her making could only be achieved by imposing
Radagast's company on Saruman; while the suggestion in the essay on
the Istari (p. 390) that in becoming enamoured of the wild creatures of
Middle-earth Radagast neglected the purpose for which he was sent is
perhaps not perfectly in accord with the idea of his being specially
chosen by Yavanna. Moreover both in the essay on the Istari and in
*Of the Rings of Power* Saruman came first and he came alone. On the

other hand it is possible to see a hint of the story of Radagast's unwelcome
company in Saruman's extreme scorn for him, as related by Gandalf to
the Council of Elrond:

' "Radagast the Brown!" laughed Saruman, and he no longer concealed his scorn. "Radagast the Bird-tamer! Radagast the Simple!
Radagast the Fool! Yet he had just the wit to play the part that I
set him." '

Whereas in the essay on the Istari it is said that the two who passed
into the East had no names save *Ithryn Luin* 'the Blue Wizards' (meaning
of course that they had no names in the West of Middle-earth), here
they are named, as Alatar and Pallando, and are associated with Oromë,
though no hint is given of the reason for this relationship. It might be
(though this is the merest guess) that Oromë of all the Valar had the
greatest knowledge of the further parts of Middle-earth, and that the Blue
Wizards were destined to journey in those regions and to remain there.

Beyond the fact that these notes on the choosing of the Istari certainly
date from after the completion of *The Lord of the Rings* I can find no
evidence of their relation, in time of composition, to the essay on the
Istari.[7]

I know of no other writings about the Istari save some very rough
and in part uninterpretable notes that are certainly much later than any
of the foregoing, and probably date from 1972:

We must assume that they [the Istari] were all Maiar, that is persons
of the 'angelic' order, though not necessarily of the same rank. The
Maiar were 'spirits', but capable of self-incarnation, and could take
'humane' (especially Elvish) forms. Saruman is said (e.g. by Gandalf
himself) to have been the chief of the Istari – that is, higher in
Valinórean stature than the others. Gandalf was evidently the next
in order. Radagast is presented as a person of much less power and
wisdom. Of the other two nothing is said in published work save the
reference to the Five Wizards in the altercation between Gandalf
and Saruman [*The Two Towers* III 10]. Now these Maiar were
sent by the Valar at a crucial moment in the history of Middle-earth
to enhance the resistance of the Elves of the West, waning in power,
and of the uncorrupted Men of the West, greatly outnumbered by
those of the East and South. It may be seen that they were free each
to do what they could in this mission; that they were not commanded
or supposed to act *together* as a small central body of power and
wisdom; and that each had different powers and inclinations and
were chosen by the Valar with this in mind.

Other writings are concerned exclusively with Gandalf (Olórin, Mithrandir). On the reverse of the isolated page containing the narrative of the choice of the Istari by the Valar appears the following very remarkable note:

Elendil and Gil-galad were partners; but this was 'the Last Alliance' of Elves and Men. In Sauron's final overthrow, Elves were not effectively concerned at the point of action. Legolas probably achieved least of the Nine Walkers. Galadriel, the greatest of the Eldar surviving in Middle-earth, was potent mainly in wisdom and goodness, as a director or counsellor in the struggle, unconquerable in *resistance* (especially in mind and spirit) but incapable of punitive *action*. In her scale she had become like Manwë with regard to the greater total action. Manwë, however, even after the Downfall of Númenor and the breaking of the old world, even in the Third Age when the Blessed Realm had been removed from the 'Circles of the World', was still not a mere observer. It is clearly from Valinor that the emissaries came who were called the Istari (or Wizards), and among them Gandalf, who proved to be the director and coordinator both of attack and defence.

Who was 'Gandalf'? It is said that in later days (when again a shadow of evil arose in the Kingdom) it was believed by many of the 'Faithful' of that time that 'Gandalf' was the last appearance of Manwë himself, before his final withdrawal to the watchtower of Taniquetil. (That Gandalf said that his name 'in the West' had been Olórin was, according to this belief, the adoption of an incognito, a mere by-name.) I do not (of course) know the truth of the matter, and if I did it would be a mistake to be more explicit than Gandalf was. But I think it was not so. Manwë will not descend from the Mountain until the Dagor Dagorath, and the coming of the End, when Melkor returns.[8] To the overthrow of Morgoth he sent his herald Eönwë. To the defeat of Sauron would he not then send some lesser (but mighty) spirit of the angelic people, one coëval and equal, doubtless, with Sauron in their beginnings, but not more? Olórin was his name. But of Olórin we shall never know more than he revealed in Gandalf.

This is followed by sixteen lines of a poem in alliterative verse:

Wilt thou learn the lore.    that was long secret
of the Five that came    from a far country?
One only returned.    Others never again

under Men's dominion     Middle-earth shall seek
until Dagor Dagorath      and the Doom cometh.
How hast thou heard it:    the hidden counsel
of the Lords of the West    in the land of Aman?
The long roads are lost      that led thither,
and to mortal Men      Manwë speaks not.
From the West-that-was     a wind bore it
to the sleeper's ear,     in the silences
under night-shadow,       when news is brought
from lands forgotten     and lost ages
over seas of years      to the searching thought.
Not all are forgotten      by the Elder King.
Sauron he saw      as a slow menace. . . .

There is much here that bears on the larger question of the concern
of Manwë and the Valar with the fate of Middle-earth after the Downfall
of Númenor, which must fall quite outside the scope of this book.

After the words 'But of Olórin we shall never know more than he
revealed in Gandalf' my father added later:

save that Olórin is a High-elven name, and must therefore have been
given to him in Valinor by the Eldar, or be a 'translation' meant to
be significant to them. In either case, what was the significance of
the name, given or assumed? *Olor* is a word often translated 'dream',
but that does not refer to (most) human 'dreams', certainly not the
dreams of sleep. To the Eldar it included the vivid contents of their
*memory*, as of their *imagination*: it referred in fact to *clear vision*, in
the mind, of things not physically present at the body's situation.
But not only to an idea, but to a full clothing of this in particular
form and detail.

An isolated etymological note explains the meaning similarly:

*olo-s*: vision, 'phantasy': Common Elvish name for 'construction of
the mind' not actually (pre)existing in Eä apart from the construction,
but by the Eldar capable of being by Art (*Karmë*) made visible and
sensible. *Olos* is usually applied to *fair* constructions having solely
an artistic object (i.e. not having the object of deception, or of
acquiring power).

Words deriving from this root are cited: Quenya *olos* 'dream, vision',
plural *olozi/olori*; *ōla-* (impersonal) 'to dream'; *olosta* 'dreamy'. A
reference is then made to *Olofantur*, which was the earlier 'true' name

of Lórien, the Vala who was 'master of visions and dreams', before it was changed to *Irmo* in *The Silmarillion* (as *Nurufantur* was changed to *Námo* (Mandos): though the plural *Fëanturi* for these two 'brethren' survived in the *Valaquenta*).

These discussions of *olos*, *olor* are clearly to be connected with the passage in the *Valaquenta* (*The Silmarillion* pp. 30–1) where it is said that Olórin dwelt in Lórien in Valinor, and that

though he loved the Elves, he walked among them unseen, or in form as one of them, and they did not know whence came the fair visions or the promptings of wisdom that he put into their hearts.

In an earlier version of this passage it is said that Olórin was 'counsellor of Irmo', and that in the hearts of those who hearkened to him awoke thoughts 'of fair things that had not yet been but might yet be made for the enrichment of Arda'.

There is a long note to elucidate the passage in *The Two Towers* IV 5 where Faramir at Henneth Annûn told that Gandalf had said:

Many are my names in many countries. Mithrandir among the Elves, Tharkûn to the Dwarves; Olórin I was in my youth in the West that is forgotten,[9] in the South Incánus, in the North Gandalf; to the East I go not.

This note dates from before the publication of the second edition of *The Lord of the Rings* in 1966, and reads as follows:

The date of Gandalf's arrival is uncertain. He came from beyond the Sea, apparently at about the same time as the first signs were noted of the re-arising of 'the Shadow': the reappearance and spread of evil things. But he is seldom mentioned in any annals or records during the second millennium of the Third Age. Probably he wandered long (in various guises), engaged not in deeds and events but in exploring the hearts of Elves and Men who had been and might still be expected to be opposed to Sauron. His own statement (or a version of it, and in any case not fully understood) is preserved that his name in youth was Olórin in the West, but he was called Mithrandir by the Elves (Grey Wanderer), Tharkûn by the Dwarves (said to mean 'Staff-man'), Incánus in the South, and Gandalf in the North, but 'to the East I go not'.

'The West' here plainly means the Far West beyond the Sea, not part of Middle-earth; the name Olórin is of High-Elven form. 'The

North' must refer to the North-western regions of Middle-earth, in which most of the inhabitants or speaking-peoples were and remained uncorrupted by Morgoth or Sauron. In those regions resistance would be strongest to the evils left behind by the Enemy, or to Sauron his servant, if he should reappear. The bounds of this region were naturally vague; its eastern frontier was roughly the River Carnen to its junction with Celduin (the River Running), and so to Núrnen, and thence south to the ancient confines of South Gondor. (It did not originally exclude Mordor, which was occupied by Sauron, although outside his original realms 'in the East', as a deliberate threat to the West and the Númenóreans.) 'The North' thus includes all this great area: roughly West to East from the Gulf of Lune to Núrnen, and North and South from Carn Dûm to the southern bounds of ancient Gondor between it and Near Harad. Beyond Núrnen Gandalf had never gone.

This passage is the only evidence that survives for his having extended his travels further South. Aragorn claims to have penetrated 'the far countries of Rhûn and Harad where the stars are strange' (*The Fellowship of the Ring* II 2).[10] It need not be supposed that Gandalf did so. These legends are North-centred – because it is represented as an historical fact that the struggle against Morgoth and his servants occurred mainly in the North, and especially the North-west, of Middle-earth, and that was so because the movement of Elves, and of Men afterwards escaping from Morgoth, had been inevitably *westward*, towards the Blessed Realm, and *north-westward* because at that point the shores of Middle-earth were nearest to Aman. *Harad* 'South' is thus a vague term, and although before its downfall Men of Númenor had explored the coasts of Middle-earth far southward, their settlements beyond Umbar had been absorbed, or being made by men already in Númenor corrupted by Sauron had become hostile and parts of Sauron's dominions. But the southern regions in touch with Gondor (and called by men of Gondor simply Harad 'South', Near or Far) were probably both more convertible to the 'Resistance', and also places where Sauron was most busy in the Third Age, since it was a source to him of man-power most readily used against Gondor. Into these regions Gandalf may well have journeyed in the earlier days of his labours.

But his main province was 'the North', and within it above all the North-west, Lindon, Eriador, and the Vales of Anduin. His alliance was primarily with Elrond and the northern Dúnedain (Rangers). Peculiar to him was his love and knowledge of the 'Halflings', because his wisdom had presage of their ultimate importance, and at the same time he perceived their inherent worth. Gondor attracted his attention less, for the same reason that made it more interesting to Saruman: it was a centre of knowledge and power. Its rulers by ancestry and all their traditions were irrevocably opposed to Sauron, certainly politically: their realm arose as a threat to him, and continued to exist only in so far and so long as his threat to them could be resisted by armed force. Gandalf could do little to guide their proud rulers or to instruct them, and it was only in the decay of their power, when they were ennobled by courage and steadfastness in what seemed a losing cause, that he began to be deeply concerned with them.

The name *Incánus* is apparently 'alien', that is neither Westron, nor Elvish (Sindarin or Quenya), nor explicable by the surviving tongues of Northern Men. A note in the Thain's Book says that it is a form adapted to Quenya of a word in the tongue of the Haradrim meaning simply 'North-spy' (*Inkā + nūs*).[11]

*Gandalf* is a substitution in the English narrative on the same lines as the treatment of Hobbit and Dwarf names. It is an actual Norse name (found applied to a Dwarf in *Völuspá*)[12] used by me since it appears to contain *gandr*, a staff, especially one used in 'magic', and might be supposed to mean 'Elvish wight with a (magic) staff'. Gandalf was not an Elf, but would be by Men associated with them, since his alliance and friendship with Elves was well-known. Since the name is attributed to 'the North' in general, *Gandalf* must be supposed to represent a Westron name, but one made up of elements not derived from Elvish tongues.

A wholly different view of the meaning of Gandalf's words 'in the South Incánus', and of the etymology of the name, is taken in a note written in 1967:

It is very unclear what was meant by 'in the South'. Gandalf disclaimed ever visiting 'the East', but actually he appears to have confined his journeys and guardianship to the western lands, inhabited by Elves and peoples in general hostile to Sauron. At any rate it seems unlikely that he ever journeyed or stayed long enough in the Harad (or Far Harad!) to have there acquired a special name in any of the alien languages of those little known regions. The South should thus mean Gondor (at its widest those lands under the suzerainty of Gondor at the height of its power). At the time of this Tale, however, we find Gandalf always called Mithrandir in Gondor (by men of rank or Númenórean origin, as Denethor, Faramir, etc.).

This is Sindarin, and given as the name used by the Elves; but men
of rank in Gondor knew and used this language. The 'popular' name
in the Westron or Common Speech was evidently one meaning
'Greymantle', but having been devised long before was now in an
archaic form. This is maybe represented by the *Greyhame* used by
Éomer in Rohan.

> My father concluded here that 'in the South' did refer to Gondor, and
> that Incánus was (like Olórin) a Quenya name, but one devised in
> Gondor in earlier times while Quenya was still much used by the
> learned, and was the language of many historical records, as it had been
> in Númenor.

Gandalf, it is said in the Tale of Years, appeared in the West early
in the eleventh century of the Third Age. If we assume that he first
visited Gondor, sufficiently often and for long enough to acquire a
name or names there – say in the reign of Atanatar Alcarin, about
1800 years before the War of the Ring – it would be possible to take
Incánus as a Quenya name devised for him which later became
obsolete, and was remembered only by the learned.

> On this assumption an etymology is proposed from the Quenya elements
> *in(id)*- 'mind' and *kan-* 'ruler', especially in *cáno, cánu* 'ruler, governor,
> chieftain' (which latter constitutes the second element in the names
> *Turgon* and *Fingon*). In this note my father referred to the Latin word
> *incánus* 'grey-haired' in such a way as to suggest that this was the
> actual origin of this name of Gandalf's when *The Lord of the Rings* was
> written, which if true would be very surprising; and at the end of the
> discussion he remarked that the coincidence in form of the Quenya
> name and the Latin word must be regarded as an 'accident', in the same
> way that Sindarin *Orthanc* 'forked height' happens to coincide with the
> Anglo-Saxon word *orþanc* 'cunning device', which is the translation of
> the actual name in the language of the Rohirrim.

## NOTES

1   In *The Two Towers* III 8 it is said that Saruman was 'accounted by
    many the chief of Wizards', and at the Council of Elrond (*The
    Fellowship of the Ring* II 2) Gandalf explicitly stated this: 'Saruman
    the White is the greatest of my order.'

2   Another version of Círdan's words to Gandalf on giving him the
    Ring of Fire at the Grey Havens is found in *Of the Rings of Power*
    (*The Silmarillion* p. 304), and in closely similar words in Appendix B

to *The Lord of the Rings* (headnote to the Tale of Years of the Third Age).

3   In a letter written in 1958 my father said that he knew nothing clearly about 'the other two', since they were not concerned in the history of the North-west of Middle-earth. 'I think,' he wrote, 'they went as emissaries to distant regions, East and South, far out of Númenórean range: missionaries to enemy-occupied lands, as it were. What success they had I do not know; but I fear that they failed, as Saruman did, though doubtless in different ways; and I suspect they were founders or beginners of secret cults and "magic" traditions that outlasted the fall of Sauron.'

4   In a very late note on the names of the Istari Radagast is said to be a name deriving from the Men of the Vales of Anduin, 'not now clearly interpretable'. Rhosgobel, called 'the old home of Radagast' in *The Fellowship of the Ring* II 3, is said to have been 'in the forest borders between the Carrock and the Old Forest Road'.

5   It appears indeed from the mention of Olórin in the *Valaquenta* (*The Silmarillion* pp 30–1) that the Istari were Maiar; for Olórin was Gandalf.

6   *Curumo* would seem to be Saruman's name in Quenya, recorded nowhere else; *Curunír* was the Sindarin form. *Saruman,* his name among Northern men, contains the Anglo-Saxon word *searu, saru* 'skill, cunning, cunning device'. *Aiwendil* must mean 'lover of birds'; cf. *Linaewen* 'lake of birds' in Nevrast (see the Appendix to *The Silmarillion,* entry *lin (I)*.) For the meaning of *Radagast* see p. 390· and note 4. *Pallando,* despite the spelling, perhaps contains *palan* 'afar', as in *palantír* and in *Palarran* 'Far Wanderer', the name of Aldarion's ship.

7   In a letter written in 1956 my father said that 'There is hardly any reference in *The Lord of the Rings* to things that do not actually *exist*, on its own plane (of secondary or sub-creational reality)', and added in a footnote to this: 'The cats of Queen Berúthiel and the names of the other two wizards (five minus Saruman, Gandalf, Radagast) are all that I recollect.' (In Moria Aragorn said of Gandalf that 'He is surer of finding the way home in a blind night than the cats of Queen Berúthiel' (*The Fellowship of the Ring* II 4).)
    Even the story of Queen Berúthiel does exist, however, if only in a very 'primitive' outline, in one part illegible. She was the nefarious, solitary, and loveless wife of Tarannon, twelfth King of Gondor (Third Age 830–913) and first of the 'Ship-kings', who took the crown in the name of Falastur 'Lord of the Coasts', and was the first childless king (*The Lord of the Rings,* Appendix A, I, ii and iv). Berúthiel lived in the King's House in Osgiliath, hating the sounds and smells of the sea and the house that Tarannon built below

Pelargir 'upon arches whose feet stood deep in the wide waters of Ethir Anduin'; she hated all making, all colours and elaborate adornment, wearing only black and silver and living in bare chambers, and the gardens of the house in Osgiliath were filled with tormented sculptures beneath cypresses and yews. She had nine black cats and one white, her slaves, with whom she conversed, or read their memories, setting them to discover all the dark secrets of Gondor, so that she knew those things 'that men wish most to keep hidden', setting the white cat to spy upon the black, and tormenting them. No man in Gondor dared touch them; all were afraid of them, and cursed when they saw them pass. What follows is almost wholly illegible in the unique manuscript, except for the ending, which states that her name was erased from the Book of the Kings ('but the memory of men is not wholly shut in books, and the cats of Queen Berúthiel never passed wholly out of men's speech'), and that King Tarannon had her set on a ship alone with her cats and set adrift on the sea before a north wind. The ship was last seen flying past Umbar under a sickle moon, with a cat at the masthead and another as a figure-head on the prow.

8    This is a reference to 'the Second Prophecy of Mandos', which does not appear in *The Silmarillion*; its elucidation cannot be attempted here, since it would require some account of the history of the mythology in relation to the published version.

9    Gandalf said again 'Olórin I was in the West that is forgotten' when he spoke to the Hobbits and Gimli in Minas Tirith after the coronation of King Elessar: see 'The Quest of Erebor', p. 330.

10   The 'strange stars' apply strictly only to the Harad, and must mean that Aragorn travelled or voyaged some distance into the southern hemisphere. [Author's note.]

11   A mark over the last letter of *Inkā-nūs* suggests that the final consonant was *sh*.

12   One of the poems of the collection of very ancient Norse poetry known as the 'Poetic Edda' or the 'Elder Edda'.

# III

# THE PALANTÍRI

The *palantíri* were no doubt never matters of common use or common knowledge, even in Númenor. In Middle-earth they were kept in guarded rooms, high in strong towers, only kings and rulers, and their appointed wardens, had access to them, and they were never consulted, nor exhibited, publicly. But until the passing of the Kings they were not sinister secrets. Their use involved no peril, and no king or other person authorized to survey them would have hesitated to reveal the source of his knowledge of the deeds or opinions of distant rulers, if obtained through the Stones.[1]

After the days of the Kings, and the loss of Minas Ithil, there is no further mention of their open and official use. There was no answering Stone left in the North after the shipwreck of Arvedui Last-king in the year 1975.[2] In 2002 the Ithil-stone was lost. There then remained only the Anor-stone in Minas Tirith and the Orthanc-stone.[3]

Two things contributed then to the neglect of the Stones, and their passing out of the general memory of the people. The first was ignorance of what had happened to the Ithil-stone: it was reasonably assumed that it was destroyed by the defenders before Minas Ithil was captured and sacked;[4] but it was clearly possible that it had been seized and had come into the possession of Sauron, and some of the wiser and more farseeing may have considered this. It would appear that they did so, and realized that the Stone would be of little use to him for the damage of Gondor, unless it made contact with another Stone that was in accord with it.[5] It was for this reason, it may be supposed, that the Anor-stone, about which all the records of the Stewards are silent until the War of the Ring, was kept as a closely-guarded secret, accessible only to the Ruling Stewards and never by them used (it seems) until Denethor II.

The second reason was the decay of Gondor, and the waning of interest in or knowledge of ancient history among all but a few even of the high men of the realm, except in so far as it concerned their genealogies: their descent and kinship. Gondor after the Kings declined into a 'Middle Age' of fading knowledge, and simpler skills.

Communications depended on messengers and errand-riders, or in times of urgency upon beacons, and if the Stones of Anor and Orthanc were still guarded as treasures out of the past, known to exist only by a few, the Seven Stones of old were by the people generally forgotten, and the rhymes of lore that spoke of them were if remembered no longer understood; their operations were transformed in legend into the Elvish powers of the ancient kings with their piercing eyes, and the swift birdlike spirits that attended on them, bringing them news or bearing their messages.

The Orthanc-stone appears to have been at this time long disregarded by the Stewards: it was no longer of any use to them, and was secure in its impregnable tower. Even if it too had not been overshadowed by the doubt concerning the Ithil-stone, it stood in a region with which Gondor became less and less directly concerned. Calenardhon, never densely populated, had been devastated by the Dark Plague of 1636, and thereafter steadily denuded of inhabitants of Númenórean descent by migration to Ithilien and lands nearer Anduin. Isengard remained a personal possession of the Stewards, but Orthanc itself became deserted, and eventually it was closed and its keys removed to Minas Tirith. If Beren the Steward considered the Stone at all when he gave these to Saruman, he probably thought that it could be in no safer hands than those of the head of the Council opposed to Sauron.

Saruman had no doubt from his investigations[6] gained a special knowledge of the Stones, things that would attract his attention, and had become convinced that the Orthanc-stone was still intact in its tower. He acquired the keys of Orthanc in 2759, nominally as warden of the tower and lieutenant of the Steward of Gondor. At that time the matter of the Orthanc-stone would hardly concern the White Council. Only Saruman, having gained the favour of the Stewards, had yet made sufficient study of the records of Gondor to perceive the interest of the *palantíri* and the possible uses of those that survived; but of this he said nothing to his colleagues. Owing to Saruman's jealousy and hatred of Gandalf he ceased to cooperate with the Council, which last met in 2953. Without any formal declaration Saruman then seized Isengard as his own domain and paid no further attention to Gondor. The Council no doubt disapproved of this; but Saruman was a free agent, and had the right, if he wished, to act independently according to his own policy in the resistance to Sauron.[7]

The Council in general must independently have known of the

Stones and their ancient dispositions, but they did not regard them as of much present importance: they were things that belonged to the history of the Kingdoms of the Dúnedain, marvellous and admirable, but mostly now lost or rendered of little use. It must be remembered that the Stones were originally 'innocent', serving no evil purpose. It was Sauron who made them sinister, and instruments of domination and deceit.

Though (warned by Gandalf) the Council may have begun to doubt Saruman's designs as regarded the Rings, not even Gandalf knew that he had become an ally, or servant, of Sauron. This Gandalf only discovered in July 3018. But, although Gandalf had in latter years enlarged his own and the Council's knowledge of Gondor's history by study of its documents, his and their chief concern was still with the Ring: the possibilities latent in the Stones were not realized. It is evident that at the time of the War of the Ring the Council had not long become aware of the doubt concerning the fate of the Ithil-stone, and failed (understandably even in such persons as Elrond, Galadriel, and Gandalf, under the weight of their cares) to appreciate its significance, to consider what might be the result if Sauron became possessed of one of the Stones, and anyone else should then make use of another. It needed the demonstration on Dol Baran of the effects of the Orthanc-stone on Peregrin to reveal suddenly that the 'link' between Isengard and Barad-dûr (seen to exist after it was discovered that forces of Isengard had been joined with others directed by Sauron in the attack on the Fellowship at Parth Galen) was in fact the Orthanc-stone – and one other *palantír*.

In his talk to Peregrin as they rode on Shadowfax from Dol Baran (*The Two Towers* III 11) Gandalf's immediate object was to give the Hobbit some idea of the history of the *palantíri*, so that he might begin to realize the ancientry, dignity, and power of things that he had presumed to meddle with. He was not concerned to exhibit his own processes of discovery and deduction, except in its last point: to explain how Sauron came to have control of them, so that they were perilous for *anyone*, however exalted, to use. But Gandalf's mind was at the same time earnestly busy with the Stones, considering the bearings of the revelation at Dol Baran upon many things that he had observed and pondered: such as the wide knowledge of events far away possessed by Denethor, and his appearance of premature old age, first observable when he was not much above sixty years old, although he belonged to a race and family that still normally had longer lives than other men. Undoubtedly Gandalf's haste to reach

Minas Tirith, in addition to the urgency of the time and the imminence of war, was quickened by his sudden fear that Denethor also had made use of a *palantír*, the Anor-stone, and his desire to judge what effect this had had on him: whether in the crucial test of desperate war it would not prove that he (like Saruman) was no longer to be trusted and might surrender to Mordor. Gandalf's dealings with Denethor on arrival in Minas Tirith, and in the following days, and all things that they are reported to have said to one another, must be viewed in the light of this doubt in Gandalf's mind.[8]

The importance of the *palantír* of Minas Tirith in his thoughts thus dated only from Peregrin's experience on Dol Baran. But his knowledge or guesses concerning its existence were, of course, much earlier. Little is known of Gandalf's history until the end of the Watchful Peace (2460) and the formation of the White Council (2463), and his special interest in Gondor seems only to have been shown after Bilbo's finding of the Ring (2941) and Sauron's open return to Mordor (2951).[9] His attention was then (as was Saruman's) concentrated on the Ring of Isildur; but in his reading in the archives of Minas Tirith he may be assumed to have learned much about the *palantíri* of Gondor, though with less immediate appreciation of their possible significance than that shown by Saruman, whose mind was in contrast to Gandalf's always more attracted by artefacts and instruments of power than by persons. Gandalf all the same probably at that time already knew more than did Saruman about the nature and ultimate origin of the *palantíri*, since all that concerned the ancient realm of Arnor and the later history of those regions was his special province, and he was in close alliance with Elrond.

But the Anor-stone had become a secret: no mention of its fate after the fall of Minas Ithil appeared in any of the annals or records of the Stewards. History would indeed make it clear that neither Orthanc nor the White Tower in Minas Tirith had ever been captured or sacked by enemies, and it might therefore be supposed that the Stones were most probably intact and remained in their ancient sites; but it could not be certain that they had not been removed by the Stewards, and perhaps 'buried deep'[10] in some secret treasure-chamber, even one in some last hidden refuge in the mountains, comparable to Dunharrow.

Gandalf should have been reported as saying that he did not *think* that Denethor had presumed to use it, until his wisdom failed.[11] He could not state it as a known fact, for when and why Denethor had dared to use the Stone was and remains a matter of conjecture.

Gandalf might well think as he did on the matter, but it is probable, considering Denethor and what is said about him, that he began to use the Anor-stone many years before 3019, and earlier than Saruman ventured or thought it useful to use the Stone of Orthanc. Denethor succeeded to the Stewardship in 2984, being then fifty-four years old: a masterful man, both wise and learned beyond the measure of those days, and strong-willed, confident in his own powers, and dauntless. His 'grimness' was first observable to others after his wife Finduilas died in 2988, but it seems fairly plain that he had *at once* turned to the Stone as soon as he came to power, having long studied the matter of the *palantíri* and the traditions regarding them and their use preserved in the special archives of the Stewards, available beside the Ruling Steward only to his heir. During the end of the rule of his father, Ecthelion II, he must have greatly desired to consult the Stone, as anxiety in Gondor increased, while his own position was weakened by the fame of 'Thorongil'[12] and the favour shown to him by his father. At least one of his motives must have been jealousy of Thorongil, and hostility to Gandalf, to whom, during the ascendancy of Thorongil, his father paid much attention; Denethor desired to surpass these 'usurpers' in knowledge and information, and also if possible to keep an eye on them when they were elsewhere.

The breaking strain of Denethor's confrontation of Sauron must be distinguished from the general strain of using the Stone.[13] The latter Denethor thought that he could endure (and not without reason); confrontation with Sauron almost certainly did not occur for many years, and was probably never originally contemplated by Denethor. For the uses of the *palantíri*, and the distinction between their solitary use for 'seeing' and their use for communication with another respondent Stone and its 'surveyor', see pp. 410–11. Denethor could, after he had acquired the skill, learn much of distant events by the use of the Anor-stone alone, and even after Sauron became aware of his operations he could still do so, as long as he retained the strength to control his Stone to his own purposes, in spite of Sauron's attempt to 'wrench' the Anor-stone always towards himself. It must also be considered that the Stones were only a small item in Sauron's vast designs and operations: a means of dominating and deluding two of his opponents, but he would not (and could not) have the Ithil-stone under perpetual observation. It was not his way to commit such instruments to the use of subordinates; nor had he any servant whose mental powers were superior to Saruman's or even Denethor's.

In the case of Denethor, the Steward was strengthened, even against Sauron himself, by the fact that the Stones were far more amenable to legitimate users: most of all to true 'Heirs of Elendil' (as Aragorn), but also to one with inherited authority (as Denethor), as compared to Saruman, or Sauron. It may be noted that the effects were different. Saruman fell under the domination of Sauron and desired his victory, or no longer opposed it. Denethor remained steadfast in his rejection of Sauron, but was made to believe that his victory was inevitable, and so fell into despair. The reasons for this difference were no doubt that in the first place Denethor was a man of great strength of will, and maintained the integrity of his personality until the final blow of the (apparently) mortal wound of his only surviving son. He was proud, but this was by no means merely personal: he loved Gondor and its people, and deemed himself appointed by destiny to lead them in this desperate time. And in the second place the Anor-stone was his *by right*, and nothing but expediency was against his use of it in his grave anxieties. He must have guessed that the Ithil-stone was in evil hands, and risked contact with it, trusting his strength. His trust was not entirely unjustified. Sauron failed to dominate him and could only influence him by deceits. Probably he did not at first look towards Mordor, but was content with such 'far views' as the Stone would afford; hence his surprising knowledge of events far off. Whether he ever thus made contact with the Orthanc-stone and Saruman is not told; probably he did, and did so with profit to himself. Sauron could not break in on these conferences: only the surveyor using the Master Stone of Osgiliath could 'eavesdrop'. While two of the other Stones were in response, the third would find them both blank.[14]

There must have been a considerable lore concerning the *palantíri* preserved in Gondor by the Kings and Stewards, and handed down even after use was no longer made of them. These Stones were an inalienable gift to Elendil and his heirs, to whom alone they belonged by right; but this does not mean that they could only be used rightfully by one of these 'heirs'. They could be used lawfully by anyone authorized by either the 'heir of Anárion' or the 'heir of Isildur', that is, a lawful King of Gondor or Arnor. Actually they must normally have been used by such deputies. Each Stone had its own warden, one of whose duties was to 'survey the Stone' at regular intervals, or when commanded, or in times of need. Other persons also were appointed to visit the Stones, and ministers of the Crown concerned with 'intelligence' made regular and special inspections of them, reporting the information so gained to the King and Council, or to the King privately, as the matter demanded. In Gondor latterly, as the office of Steward rose in importance and became hereditary, providing as it were a permanent 'understudy' to the King, and an immediate viceroy at need, the command and use of the Stones seems mainly to have been in the hands of the Stewards, and the traditions concerning their nature and use to have been guarded and transmitted in their House. Since the Stewardship had become hereditary from 1998 onwards,[15] so the authority to use, or again to depute the use, of the Stones, was lawfully transmitted in their line, and belonged therefore fully to Denethor.[16]

It must however be noted with regard to the narrative of *The Lord of the Rings* that over and above such deputed authority, even hereditary, any 'heir of Elendil' (that is, a recognized descendant occupying a throne or lordship in the Númenórean realms by virtue of this descent) had the *right* to use any of the *palantíri*. Aragorn thus claimed the right to take the Orthanc-stone into his possession, since it was now, for the time being, without owner or warden; and also because he was *de jure* the rightful King of both Gondor and Arnor, and could, if he willed, for just cause withdraw all previous grants to himself.

The 'lore of the Stones' is now forgotten, and can only be partly recovered by conjecture and from things recorded about them. They were perfect spheres, appearing when at rest to be made of solid glass or crystal deep black in hue. At smallest they were about a foot in diameter, but some, certainly the Stones of Osgiliath and Amon Sûl, were much larger and could not be lifted by one man. Originally they were placed in sites suitable to their sizes and intended uses, standing on low round tables of black marble in a central cup or depression, in which they could at need be revolved by hand. They were very heavy but perfectly smooth, and would suffer no damage if by accident or malice they were unseated and rolled off their tables. They were indeed unbreakable by any violence then controlled by men, though some believed that great heat, such as that of Orodruin, might shatter them, and surmised that this had been the fate of the Ithil-stone in the fall of Barad-dûr.

Though without any external markings of any kind they had permanent *poles*, and were originally so placed in their sites that they stood 'upright': their diameters from pole to pole pointed to the earth's centre, but the permanent nether pole must then be at the bottom. The faces along the circumference in this position were the viewing faces, receiving the visions from the outside, but transmitting them to the eye of a 'surveyor' upon the far side. A surveyor, therefore,

who wished to look west would place himself on the east side of the
Stone, and if he wished to shift his vision northward must move to
his left, southward. But the minor Stones, those of Orthanc, Ithil,
and Anor, and probably Annúminas, had also fixed orientation in
their original situation, so that (for example) their west face would
only look west and turned in other directions was blank. If a Stone
became unseated or disturbed it could be re-set by observation, and
it was then useful to revolve it. But when removed and cast down,
as was the Orthanc-stone, it was not so easy to set right. So it was
'by chance' as Men call it (as Gandalf would have said) that Peregrin,
fumbling with the Stone, must have set it on the ground more or less
'upright', and sitting westward of it have had the fixed east-looking
face in the proper position. The major Stones were not so fixed:
their circumference could be revolved and they could still 'see' in
any direction.[17]

Alone the *palantíri* could only 'see': they did not transmit sound.
Ungoverned by a directing mind they were wayward, and their
'visions' were (apparently at least) haphazard. From a high place
their westward face, for instance, would look to vast distance, its
vision blurred and distorted to either side and above and below, and
its foreground obscured by things behind receding in ever-diminishing
clarity. Also, what they 'saw' was directed or hindered by chance,
by darkness, or by 'shrouding' (see below). The vision of the
*palantíri* was not 'blinded' or 'occluded' by physical obstacles, but
only by darkness; so they could look *through* a mountain as they
could look *through* a patch of dark or shadow, but see nothing within
that did not receive some light. They could see through walls but
see nothing within rooms, caves, or vaults unless some light fell on
it; and they could not themselves provide or project light. It was
possible to guard against their sight by the process called 'shrouding',
by which certain things or areas would be seen in a Stone only as
a shadow or a deep mist. How this was done (by those aware of the
Stones and the possibility of being watched by them) is one of the
lost mysteries of the *palantíri*.[18]

A viewer could by his will cause the vision of the Stone to *concentrate* on some point, on or near its direct line.[19] The uncontrolled
'visions' were small, especially in the minor Stones, though they were
much larger to the eye of a beholder who placed himself at some
distance from the surface of the *palantír* (about three feet at best).
But controlled by the will of a skilled and strong surveyor, remoter
things could be enlarged, brought as it were nearer and clearer,
while their background was almost suppressed. Thus a man at a

considerable distance might be seen as a tiny figure, half an inch high, difficult to pick out against a landscape or a concourse of other men; but concentration could enlarge and clarify the vision till he was seen in clear if reduced detail like a picture apparently a foot or more in height, and recognized if he was known to the surveyor. Great concentration might even enlarge some detail that interested the surveyor, so that it could be seen (for instance) if he had a ring on his hand.

But this 'concentration' was very tiring and might become exhausting. Consequently it was only undertaken when information was urgently desired, and chance (aided by other information maybe) enabled the surveyor to pick out items (significant for him and his immediate concern) from the welter of the Stone's visions. For example, Denethor sitting before the Anor-stone anxious about Rohan, and deciding whether or not at once to order the kindling of the beacons and the sending out of the 'arrow', might place himself in a direct line looking north-west by west through Rohan, passing close to Edoras and on towards the Fords of Isen. At that time there might be visible movements of men in that line. If so, he could concentrate on (say) a group, see them as Riders, and finally discover some figure known to him: Gandalf, for instance, riding with the reinforcements to Helm's Deep, and suddenly breaking away and racing northwards.[20]

The *palantíri* could not themselves survey men's minds, at unawares or unwilling; for the transference of thought depended on the *wills* of the user on either side, and thought (received as speech)[21] was only transmittable by one Stone to another in accord.

## NOTES

1  Doubtless they were used in the consultations between Arnor and Gondor in the year 1944 concerning the succession to the Crown. The 'messages' received in Gondor in 1973, telling of the dire straits of the Northern Kingdom, was possibly their last use until the approach of the War of the Ring. [Author's note.]

2  With Arvedui were lost the Stones of Annúminas and Amon Sûl (Weathertop). The third *palantír* of the North was that in the tower Elostirion on Emyn Beraid, which had special properties (see note 16).

3  The Stone of Osgiliath had been lost in the waters of Anduin in 1437, during the civil war of the Kin-strife.

4  On the destructibility of the *palantíri* see p. 409. In the entry in the Tale of Years for 2002, and also in Appendix A (I, iv), it is stated as

a fact that the *palantír* was captured in the fall of Minas Ithil; but my father noted that these annals were made after the War of the Ring, and that the statement, however certain, was a deduction. The Ithil-stone was never found again, and probably perished in the ruin of Barad-dûr; see p. 409.

5  By themselves the Stones could only *see*: scenes or figures in distant places, or in the past. These were without explanation; and at any rate for men of later days it was difficult to direct what visions should be revealed by the will or desire of a surveyor. But when another mind occupied a Stone in accord, thought could be 'transferred' (received as 'speech'), and visions of the things in the mind of the surveyor of one Stone could be seen by the other surveyor. [See further pp. 410–11 and note 21.] These powers were originally used mainly in consultation, for the purpose of exchanging news necessary to government, or advice and opinions; less often in simple friendship and pleasure or in greetings and condolence. It was only Sauron who used a Stone for the transference of his superior will, dominating the weaker surveyor and forcing him to reveal hidden thought and to submit to commands. [Author's note.]

6  Cf. Gandalf's remarks to the Council of Elrond concerning Saruman's long study of the scrolls and books of Minas Tirith.

7  For any more 'worldly' policy of power and warlike strength Isengard was well placed, being the key to the Gap of Rohan. This was a weak point in the defences of the West, especially since the decay of Gondor. Through it hostile spies and emissaries could pass in secret, or eventually, as in the former Age, forces of war. The Council seems to have been unaware, since for many years Isengard had been closely guarded, of what went on within its Ring. The use, and possibly special breeding, of Orcs was kept secret, and cannot have begun much before 2990 at earliest. The orc-troops seem never to have been used beyond the territory of Isengard before the attack on Rohan. Had the Council known of this they would, of course, at once have realized that Saruman had become evil. [Author's note.]

8  Denethor was evidently aware of Gandalf's guesses and suspicions, and at once both angered and sardonically amused by them. Note his words to Gandalf at their meeting in Minas Tirith (*The Return of the King* V i): 'I know already sufficient of these deeds for my own counsel against the menace of the East', and especially his mocking words that followed: 'Yea; for though the Stones be lost, they say, still the lords of Gondor have keener sight than lesser men, and many messages come to them.' Quite apart from the *palantíri*, Denethor was a man of great mental powers, and a quick reader of thoughts behind faces and words, but he may well also have actually seen in the Anor-stone visions of events in Rohan and Isengard. [Author's note.] – See further p. 411.

9   Note the passage in *The Two Towers* IV 5 where Faramir (who was
    born in 2983) recollected seeing Gandalf in Minas Tirith when he
    was a child, and again two or three times later; and said that it was
    interest in records that brought him. The last time would have been
    in 3017, when Gandalf found the scroll of Isildur. [Author's note.]

10  This is a reference to Gandalf's words to Peregrin (*The Two Towers*
    III 11): 'Who knows where the lost Stones of Arnor and Gondor now
    lie, buried, or drowned deep?'

11  This is a reference to Gandalf's words after the death of Denethor
    in *The Return of the King* V 7, at the end of the chapter. My father's
    emendation (arising from the present discussion) of 'Denethor did
    not presume to use it' to 'Denethor would not presume to use it'
    was (apparently by mere oversight) not incorporated in the revised
    edition. See the Introduction, p. 13.

12  Thorongil ('Eagle of the Star') was the name given to Aragorn when
    he served in disguise Ecthelion II of Gondor; see *The Lord of the
    Rings*, Appendix A (I, iv, *The Stewards*).

13  The use of the *palantíri* was a mental strain, especially on men of
    later days not trained to the task, and no doubt in addition to his
    anxieties this strain contributed to Denethor's 'grimness'. It was
    probably felt earlier by his wife than by others and increased her
    unhappiness, to the hastening of her death. [Author's note.]

14  An unplaced marginal note observes that Saruman's integrity 'had
    been undermined by purely personal pride and lust for the domination
    of his own will. His study of the Rings had caused this, for his pride
    believed that he could use them, or It, in defiance of any other will.
    He, having lost any devotion to other persons or causes, was open to
    the domination of a superior will, to its threats, and to its display of
    power.' And moreover he had himself no *right* to the Orthanc-stone.

15  1998 was the year of the death of Pelendur, Steward of Gondor. 'After
    the days of Pelendur the Stewardship became hereditary as a kingship,
    from father to son or nearest kin,' *The Lord of the Rings*, Appendix
    A, I, iv, *The Stewards*.

16  The case was different in Arnor. Lawful possession of the Stones
    belonged to the King (who normally used the Stone of Annúminas);
    but the Kingdom became divided and the high-kingship was in
    dispute. The Kings of Arthedain, who were plainly those with the
    just claim, maintained a special warden at Amon Sûl, whose Stone
    was held to be the chief of the Northern *palantíri*, being the largest
    and most powerful and the one through which communication with
    Gondor was mainly conducted. After the destruction of Amon Sûl
    by Angmar in 1409 both Stones were placed at Fornost, where the
    King of Arthedain dwelt. These were lost in the shipwreck of
    Arvedui, and no deputy was left with any authority direct or inherited

to use the Stones. One only remained in the North, the Elendil Stone on Emyn Beraid, but this was one of special properties, and not employable in communications. Hereditary right to use it would no doubt still reside in the 'heir of Isildur', the recognized chieftain of the Dúnedain, and descendant of Arvedui. But it is not known whether any of them, including Aragorn, ever looked into it, desiring to gaze into the lost West. This Stone and its tower were maintained and guarded by Círdan and the Elves of Lindon. [Author's note.] – It is told in Appendix A (I, iii) to *The Lord of the Rings* that the *palantír* of Emyn Beraid 'was unlike the others and not in accord with them; it looked only to the Sea. Elendil set it there so that he could look back with "straight sight" and see Eressëa in the vanished West; but the bent seas below covered Númenor for ever.' Elendil's vision of Eressëa in the *palantír* of Emyn Beraid is told of also in *Of the Rings of Power* (*The Silmarillion* p. 292); 'it is believed that thus he would at whiles see far away even the Tower of Avallónë upon Eressëa, where the Master-stone abode, and yet abides'. It is notable that in the present account there is no reference to this Master-stone.

17  A later, detached note denies that the *palantíri* were polarized or oriented, but gives no further detail.

18  The later note referred to in note 17 treats some of these aspects of the *palantíri* slightly differently; in particular the concept of 'shrouding' seems differently employed. This note, very hasty and somewhat obscure, reads in part: 'They retained the images received, so that each contained within itself a multiplicity of images and scenes, some from a remote past. They could not "see" in the dark; that is, things that were in the dark were not recorded by them. They themselves could be and usually were kept in the dark, because it was much easier then to see the scenes that they presented, and as the centuries passed to limit their "overcrowding". How they were thus "shrouded" was kept secret and so is now unknown. They were not "blinded" by physical obstacles, as a wall, a hill, or a wood, so long as the distant objects were themselves in light. It was said, or guessed, by later commentators that the Stones were placed in their original sites in spherical cases that were locked to prevent their misuse by the unauthorized; but that this casing also performed the office of shrouding them and making them quiescent. The cases must therefore have been made of some metal or other substance not now known.' Marginal jottings associated with this note are partly illegible, but so much can be made out, that the remoter the past the clearer the view, while for distant viewing there was a 'proper distance', varying with the Stones, at which distant objects were clearer. The greater *palantíri* could look much further than the lesser; for the lesser the 'proper distance' was of the order of five hundred miles, as between the Orthanc-stone and that of Anor. 'Ithil was too near, but was

largely used for [illegible words], not for personal contacts with
Minas Anor.'

19  The orientation was not, of course, divided into separate 'quarters'
    but continuous; so that its *direct* line of vision to a surveyor sitting
    south-east would be to the north-west, and so on. [Author's note.]

20  See *The Two Towers* III 7.

21  In a detached note this aspect is more explicitly described: 'Two
    persons, each using a Stone "in accord" with the other, could
    converse, but not by sound, which the Stones did not transmit.
    Looking one at the other they would exchange "thought" – not their
    full or true thought, or their intentions, but "silent speech", the
    thoughts they wished to transmit (already formalized in linguistic
    form in their minds or actually spoken aloud), which would be
    received by their respondents and of course immediately transformed
    into "speech", and only reportable as such.'

# INDEX

This Index, as noted in the Introduction, covers not only the main texts but also the Notes and Appendices, since much original material appears in these latter. As a result a good many references are trivial, but I have thought it more useful, as it is certainly easier, to aim at completeness. The only intentional exceptions are a very few cases (as *Morgoth, Númenor*) where I have used the word *passim* to cover certain sections of the book, and the absence of references for *Elves, Men, Orcs,* and *Middle-earth.* In many cases the references include pages where a person or place is mentioned but not by name (thus the mention on p. 232 of 'the haven where Círdan was lord' is given under *Mithlond*). Asterisks are used to indicate names, nearly a quarter of the total, that have not been published in my father's works (they are thus also set against the names, listed in the footnote on pp. 261–2, that appeared on Miss Pauline Baynes' map of Middle-earth). The brief defining statements are not restricted to matters actually mentioned in the book; and occasionally I have added notes on the meaning of hitherto untranslated names.

This Index is not a model of consistency in presentation, but its deficiency in this respect may be partly excused in view of the interlacing ramification of names (including variant translations, partial translations, names that are equivalent in reference but not in meaning), which makes such consistency extremely difficult or impossible to achieve: as may be seen from such a series as *Eilenaer, Halifirien, Amon Anwar, Anwar, Hill of Anwar, Hill of Awe, Wood of Anwar, Firienholt, Firien Wood, Whispering Wood.* As a general rule I have included references for translations of Elvish names under the Elvish entry (as *Langstrand* under *Anfalas*), with a cross-reference, but I have departed from this in particular cases, where the 'translated' names (as *Mirkwood, Isengard*) are generally used and familiar.

*Amdír*   King of Lórien, slain in the Battle of Dagorlad; father of Amroth.
240, 243–4, 258. See *Malgalad.*

*Amon Anwar*   Sindarin name of Halifirien, seventh of the beacons of
Gondor in Ered Nimrais. 301–2, 308–10, 316. Translated *Hill of Awe*
301–2, 308, and partially as *Hill of Anwar* 306, 309–10; also simply
*Anwar* 306. See *Eilenaer, Halifirien, Wood of Anwar.*

*Amon Darthir*   A peak in the range of Ered Wethrin south of Dor-lómin.
68, 148.

*Amon Dîn*   'The Silent Hill', first of the beacons of Gondor in Ered
Nimrais. 301, 314, 319

*Amon Ereb*   'The Lonely Hill' in East Beleriand. 77

*Amon Ethir*   The great earthwork raised by Finrod Felagund to the east
of the Doors of Nargothrond. 116–19. Translated *the Spyhill* 116–17.

*Amon Lanc*   'The Naked Hill' in the south of Greenwood the Great,
afterwards called *Dol Guldur*, q.v. 272, 280

*Amon Obel*   A hill in the Forest of Brethil, on which was built Ephel
Brandir. 104, 110, 123, 125, 136

*Amon Rûdh*   'The Bald Hill', a lonely height in the lands south of Brethil;
abode of Mîm, and lair of Túrin's outlaw band. 98–100, 148, 150–4.
See *Sharbhund.*

*Amon Sûl*   'Hill of the Wind', a round bare hill at the southern end of
the Weather Hills in Eriador. 278, 409, 411, 413. Called in Bree
*Weathertop* 278, 411

*Amon Uilos*   Sindarin name of *Oiolossë*, q.v. 55

*Amroth*   Sindarin Elf, King of Lórien, lover of Nimrodel; drowned in the
Bay of Belfalas. 234, 237–8, 240–6, 255, 257–8, 261, 316. *The country
of Amroth* (coast of Belfalas near Dol Amroth) 175, 214. *Amroth's
Haven*, see *Edhellond.*

*Anach*   Pass leading down from Taur-nu-Fuin (Dorthonion) at the
western end of Ered Gorgoroth. 54, 95

*Anar*   Quenya name of the Sun. 22, 29–30

*Anárion* (*1*)   See *Tar-Anárion.*

*Anárion* (*2*)   Younger son of Elendil, who with his father and his brother
Isildur escaped from the Drowning of Númenor and founded in
Middle-earth the Númenórean realms in exile; lord of Minas Anor;
slain in the siege of Barad-dûr. 215, 279. *Heir of Anárion* 408

*Anardil*   The given name of Tar-Aldarion. 173, 199, 212, 219; with
suffix of endearment, *Anardilya* 174. [The sixth King of Gondor was
also named *Anardil.*]

*Ancalimë*   See *Tar-Ancalimë*. The name was also given by Aldarion to the
tree from Eressëa that he planted in Armenelos 202

*Andrast*   'Long Cape', the mountainous promontory between the rivers
Isen and Lefnui. 214, 261, 263, 370, 383–4, 387. See *Ras Morthil,
Drúwaith Iaur.*

*Andrath*   'Long Climb', defile between the Barrow-downs and the South
Downs through which the North–South Road (Greenway) passed. 348

*Andróg  Man of Dor-lómin, a leader of the outlaw-band (*Gaurwaith*) that Túrin joined. 85–90, 92–102, 148, 151–2, 154

Androth  Caves in the hills of Mithrim where Tuor dwelt with the Grey-elves and afterwards as a solitary outlaw. 18–19

Anduin  'The Long River' east of the Misty Mountains; also *the River*, *the Great River*. Frequently in *the Vale(s) of Anduin*. 168, 236, 243, 245–7, 252, 256, 258–61, 264–5, Part 3 §§ I and II *passim*, 321, 338–9, 342–3, 345–6, 370–1, 383, 398, 401, 404, 411. See *Ethir Anduin, Langflood*.

Andúnië  'Sunset', city and haven on the west coast of Númenor. 167, 169, 173, 182, 185, 189, 193, 214–15, 217, 220, 223. *Bay of Andúnië* 167. *Lord(s) of Andúnië* 171, 173, 182, 215, 217, 219, 223

*Andustar  The western promontory of Númenor. 165, 167, 217. Translated *the Westlands* 165, 169, 181, 185, 189, 194, 196, 215. *Lady of the Westlands*, Erendis, 180

Anfalas  Fief of Gondor; coastal region between the mouths of the rivers Lefnui and Morthond. 384. In Westron translated *Langstrand* 255

Anfauglith  Name of the plain of Ard-galen after its desolation by Morgoth in the Dagor Bragollach. 17, 58

Angband  The great fortress of Morgoth in the North-west of Middle-earth. 18, 37, 51, 55, 58, 66–7, 75, 78–9, 81, 89–90, 94, 128, 149, 153–9, 161, 195, 232, 385. *The Siege of Angband* 34, 53, 155

*Angelimar  Twentieth Prince of Dol Amroth, grandfather of Imrahil. 248

Anglachel  Beleg's sword. 148. See *Gurthang*.

Angmar  The Witch-realm ruled by the Lord of the Nazgûl at the northern end of the Misty Mountains. 313, 322, 354, 390, 413

*Angren  Sindarin name of the Isen, q.v. (also *Sîr Angren*, River Isen). 175, 214, 262, 264, 305–6, 318, 370. See *Athrad Angren*.

Angrenost  Sindarin name of Isengard, q.v. 305–6, 318, 370–2

Angrod  Noldorin prince, the third son of Finarfin; slain in the Dagor Bragollach. 52, 159, 231, 250

Annael  Grey-elf of Mithrim, fosterfather of Tuor. 17–21, 25, 56

Annatar  'Lord of Gifts', name given to himself by Sauron in the Second Age. 236, 254. See *Artano, Aulendil*.

Annon-in-Gelydh  Entrance to a subterranean watercourse in the western hills of Dor-lómin, leading to Cirith Ninniach. 18. Translated *Gate of the Noldor* 18–21, 51, 162

Annúminas  'Tower of the West', ancient seat of the Kings of Arnor beside Lake Nenuial; afterwards restored by King Elessar. 410–11, 413

Anórien  Region of Gondor north of Ered Nimrais. 260, 301, 306, 308–9, 338, 369–70, 384, 387

Anor-stone, Stone of Anor  The *palantír* of Minas Anor. 403–4, 406–8, 410–12, 414

*Anwar  See *Amon Anwar*.

*Ar-Abattârik  Adûnaic name of Tar-Ardamin. 222

*Ar-Adûnakhôr*   Twentieth Ruler of Númenor; named in Quenya *Tar-Herunúmen*. 218, 222, 226–7

*Aragorn*   Thirty-ninth Heir of Isildur in the direct line; King of the reunited realms of Arnor and Gondor after the War of the Ring; wedded Arwen, daughter of Elrond. 251, 255, 286, 312, 337, 341–4, 353, 365, 368–9, 398, 401–2, 408–9, 413–14. See *Elessar, Elfstone, Strider, Thorongil.*

\*Arandor*   The 'Kingsland' of Númenor. 165, 169

\*Arandur*   'King's servant, minister', Quenya term for the Stewards of Gondor. 313, 319

*Aranrúth*   'King's Ire', Thingol's sword. 171

*Aranwë*   Elf of Gondolin, father of Voronwë. 32, 45. *Aranwion*, son of Aranwë. 50

*Aratan*   Second son of Isildur, slain at the Gladden Fields. 271, 274, 279

\*Ar-Belzagar*   Adûnaic name of Tar-Calmacil. 222

*Arda*   'The Realm', name of the Earth as the Kingdom of Manwë. 67–8, 156, 173, 201, 254, 397

*Aredhel*   Sister of Turgon and mother of Maeglin. 54

*Ar-Gimilzôr*   Twenty-third Ruler of Númenor; named in Quenya *Tar-Telemnar*. 223, 227

*Ar-Inziladûn*   Adûnaic name of Tar-Palantir. 223, 227

*Arkenstone*   The great jewel of the Lonely Mountain. 328

*Armenelos*   City of the Kings in Númenor. 165, 169, 173, 175–7, 181, 183–6, 189–90, 192–3, 195–9, 201, 203–5, 208, 218

*Arminas*   Noldorin Elf, who with Gelmir came upon Tuor at Annon-in-Gelydh, and afterwards went to Nargothrond to warn Orodreth of its peril. 21–2, 51–2, 159–62

*Arnor*   The northern realm of the Númenóreans in Middle-earth. 173, 271, 275, 277–8, 282, 284, 287, 306, 308, 370, 406, 408–9, 411, 413. *The North(ern) Kingdom, Northern Realm* 264, 277, 284–5, 287, 295, 369–70, 411

*Aros*   The southern river of Doriath. 77

*Ar-Pharazôn*   Twenty-fifth and last Ruler of Númenor, who perished in the Downfall; named in Quenya *Tar-Calion*. 165, 215, 224, 317

\*Arroch*   The horse of Húrin of Dor-lómin. 70

*Ar-Sakalthôr*   Twenty-second Ruler of Númenor; named in Quenya *Tar-Falassion*. 223

*Artamir*   Elder son of Ondoher King of Gondor; slain in battle with the Wainriders. 291–2, 294–5

\*Artanis*   Name given to Galadriel by her father. 231, 266

\*Artano*   'High-smith', name given to himself by Sauron in the Second Age. 254. See *Annatar, Aulendil.*

*Arthedain*   One of the three kingdoms into which Arnor was divided in the ninth century of the Third Age; bounded by the rivers Baranduin and Lhûn, extending eastwards to the Weather Hills, and with its chief place at Fornost. 287, 413

Ring between Riders of Rohan and Saruman's forces out of Isengard. *The First Battle* described 355–9, referred to 364; *the Second Battle* described 359–63, referred to 368; other references 355, 366, 368–9, 387

*Bauglir* 'The Constrainer', a name of Morgoth. 66

*Bay of Balar* See *Balar.*

*Bay of Belfalas* See *Belfalas.*

*Beacons of Gondor* 300–1, 314–15, 319

*Beleg* Elf of Doriath; a great archer, and chief of Thingol's march-wardens; friend and companion of Túrin, by whom he was slain. 37, 51, 54, 73–4, 77, 79–80, 82–5, 90–6, 134, 145, 147–8, 151–4. Called *Cúthalion* 79, 94, translated (*the*) *Strongbow* 73, 77, 82, 90, 95

*Belegaer* 'The Great Sea' of the West, between Middle-earth and Aman. 24, 34. *The Great Sea* 20, 24–5, 30, 35, 171, 174–5, 179, 181, 184, 200, 241, 247; in many other passages called simply *the Sea.*

*Belegost* One of the two cities of the Dwarves in the Blue Mountains. 55, 75, 128, 146, 235, 252

*Belegund* Father of Rían wife of Huor; nephew of Barahir and one of his twelve companions on Dorthonion. 58, 215

*Beleriand* Lands west of the Blue Mountains in the Elder Days. 17, 20, 22, 25–6, 33, 44, 58, 63, 67–8, 73, 85, 125, 146, 156, 171, 214–15, 228–9, 231–3, 247, 256–7, 259, 281, 377–9, 382, 384–5, 387. *East Beleriand* (divided from West Beleriand by the river Sirion) 75, 147. *Tongue of Beleriand,* see *Sindarin. First Battle of Beleriand* 77. Adjective *Beleriandic* 236, 244

*Belfalas* Fief of Gondor; coastal region looking on to the great bay of the same name. 240, 243, 247–8, 255, 286, 316. *Bay of Belfalas* 175, 214, 242, 245–7, 263, 383

*Bëor* Leader of the first Men to enter Beleriand, progenitor of the First House of the Edain. 384. *House of, People of, Bëor* 57, 63–4, 147, 161, 171, 177, 214–15, 384; *Bëorian(s)* 215, 225

*Beornings* Men of the upper Vales of Anduin. 278, 343

\*Beregar* Man from the Westlands of Númenor, descended from the House of Bëor; father of Erendis. 177, 181, 183, 185, 190, 193–4

*Beren* (*1*) Man of the House of Bëor, who cut the Silmaril from Morgoth's crown, and alone of mortal Men returned from the dead. 57–8, 63, 74, 77, 79, 84, 116, 157, 161, 171. Called after his return from Angband *Erchamion* 77, translated *One-hand* 57, 171; and *Camlost* 'Empty-handed' 161

*Beren* (*2*) Nineteenth Ruling Steward of Gondor, who gave the keys of Orthanc to Saruman. 373, 404

\*Bereth* Sister of Baragund and Belegund and ancestress of Erendis. 215–16

*Berúthiel* Queen of Tarannon Falastur, twelfth King of Gondor. 401–2

*Bilbo Baggins* Hobbit of the Shire, finder of the One Ring. 321–7, 329–35, 343, 354, 406. See *Baggins.*

*Black Captain*   See *Lord of the Nazgûl*.
\**Black Easterling*   See *Khamûl*.
*Black Gate*   See *Morannon*.
\**Black King*   See *Morgoth*.
*Black Riders*   See *Nazgûl*.
*Blacksword, Black Sword*   See *Gurthang, Mormegil*.
*Blessed Realm*   See *Aman*.
*Blue Mountains*   See *Ered Lindon* and *Ered Luin*.
*Blue Ring*   See *Vilya*.
*Blue Wizards*   See *Ithryn Luin*.
*Book of the Kings*   One of the chronicles of Gondor. 310, 402
*Book of the Stewards*   See *Stewards of Gondor*.
*Boromir*   Elder son of Denethor II, Steward of Gondor; one of the
    Fellowship of the Ring. 264-5, 287, 339, 344, 347, 353
\**Borondir*   Called *Udalraph* 'the Stirrupless'; rider of Minas Tirith who
    brought the message of Cirion to Eorl asking for his aid. 297-9, 313
\**Bough of Return*   See *Oiolairë*.
*Bracegirdles*   A family of Hobbits of the Shire. 347. *Lobelia Bracegirdle* 354
*Bragollach*   See *Dagor Bragollach*.
*Brand*   Third King of Dale, grandson of Bard the Bowman; slain in the
    Battle of Dale. 326
*Brandir*   Ruler of the People of Haleth in Brethil at the time of the
    coming of Túrin Turambar, by whom he was slain. 110-12, 123-5,
    127, 129, 131-2, 136-43, 145, 148, 150. Called by Túrin *Club-foot* 142
*Brandywine*   See *Baranduin*.
*Bree*   The principal village of the Bree-land at the crossing of the
    Númenórean roads in Eriador. 278, 322, 326, 328, 341, 348, 354.
    *Men of Bree* 370, 385; *Hobbits of Bree* 385
*Brego*   Second King of Rohan, son of Eorl the Young. 367, 371
*Bregolas*   Brother of Barahir and father of Baragund and Belegund. 57-8
*Bregor*   Father of Barahir and Bregolas. 63. *The Bow of Bregor*, preserved
    in Númenor, 171
*Brethil*   Forest between the rivers Teiglin and Sirion in Beleriand,
    dwelling-place of the People of Haleth. 41, 54, 63, 68, 73, 85, 87, 91,
    104, 110, 112, 122-7, 130, 132-3, 136, 140, 143, 149, 382-3. *Men of*,
    *People of, Brethil* 57, 90, 110, 128-9, 131, 140; and see *Woodmen*.
    *Black Thorn of Brethil*, see *Gurthang*.
*Brithiach*   Ford over Sirion north of the Forest of Brethil. 41-2, 54, 91
*Brithombar*   The northernmost of the Havens of the Falas on the coast of
    Beleriand. 33, 51, 53-4, 247
*Brithon*   River flowing into the Great Sea at Brithombar. 54
*Brodda*   Easterling in Hithlum after the Nirnaeth Arnoediad who took as
    wife Aerin, kinswoman of Húrin; slain by Túrin. 69, 104-9. Called
    *the Incomer* 104
*Brown Lands*   The desolate region between Mirkwood and the Emyn Muil.
    296, 299, 307

*Ciryatur* Númenórean admiral commanding the fleet sent by Tar-Minastir to the aid of Gil-galad against Sauron. 239, 261

*Ciryon* Third son of Isildur, slain at the Gladden Fields. 271, 274, 280

*Common Speech* See *Westron.*

*Corsairs of Umbar* 296, 312. See *Umbar.*

*Cotton, Farmer* Tolman Cotton, Hobbit of Bywater. 354

*Council of Elrond* Council held at Rivendell before the departure of the Fellowship of the Ring. 276, 283, 287, 352–4, 394, 400, 412

*Council, The* In various references: the Council of the Sceptre (the King's Council of Númenor, see especially 216–17) 197, 204, 208–9, 211, 216–17; the Council of Gondor 408; the White Council, q.v.

*Crissaegrim* The mountain-peaks south of Gondolin, where were the eyries of Thorondor. 42, 55

*Crossings, The* See *Teiglin.*

*Cuiviénen* 'Water of Awakening', the lake in Middle-earth where the first Elves awoke. 228, 236

*Curufin* The fifth son of Fëanor, father of Celebrimbor. 54, 235

*Curumo* The name of Curunír (Saruman) in Quenya. 393, 401

*Curunír* 'The one of cunning devices', Sindarin name of Saruman, q.v.; also *Curunir 'Lân*, Saruman the White. 390–2, 401. See *Curumo.*

*Cúthalion* 'Strongbow', see *Beleg.*


*Daeron* Minstrel of Doriath; enamoured of Lúthien and twice betrayed her; friend (or kinsman) of Saeros. 77, 147

*Dagor Bragollach* 'The Battle of Sudden Flame' (also simply *the Bragollach*), fourth of the great battles in the Wars of Beleriand, in which the Siege of Angband was ended. 34, 52–3, 57–8, 60, 159

*Dagor Dagorath* 395–6; see 402, note 8.

*Dagorlad* 'Battle Plain', east of Emyn Muil and near the Dead Marshes, site of the great battle between Sauron and the Last Alliance of Elves and Men at the end of the Second Age. 235, 271, 289–90, 292, 296, 312–13, 319. *Battle of Dagorlad* 240, 243–4, 258. Later battles on the Dagorlad: the victory in Third Age 1899 of King Calimehtar over the Wainriders, 289–90; the defeat and death of King Ondoher in Third Age 1944, 292

*Dáin Ironfoot* Lord of the Dwarves of the Iron Hills, afterwards King under the Mountain; slain in the Battle of Dale. 326–7

*Dale* Country of the Bardings about the feet of Mount Erebor, allied with the Kingdom of the Dwarves under the Mountain. 278, 289, 322. See *Battle of Dale.*

*Dark Elves* See *Avari.*

*Dark Lands* Term for Middle-earth in Númenor. 178

*Dark Lord* Morgoth, 79; Sauron, 231

*Dark Plague* See *Great Plague.*

*Dark Power* See *Sauron.*

*Dark Years* The years of the dominion of Sauron in the Second Age. 370

*Dead Marshes*  Wide stagnant marshes south-east of Emyn Muil, in which the slain of the Battle of Dagorlad were seen. 258, 293–5, 342

*Dead Men of Dunharrow*  See *Dunharrow*.

*Déagol*  A Stoor of the Vales of Anduin, finder of the One Ring. 353

\*Deeping, The  Apparently synonymous with *Deeping-coomb*. 358, 365–6

*Deeping-coomb*  The valley leading up to Helm's Deep. 365, 368

\*Deeping-road  Road running northwards from the Deeping-coomb to join the Great Road east of the Fords of Isen. 358 (cf. 'the branch going to the Hornburg', 363)

*Deeping-stream*  Stream flowing out of Helm's Deep down into Westfold. 365

\*Deer's Leap  See *Cabed-en-Aras*.

*Denethor* (1)  Leader of the Nandorin Elves that came over the Blue Mountains and dwelt in Ossiriand; slain on Amon Ereb in the First Battle of Beleriand. 77

*Denethor* (2)  Twenty-sixth and last Ruling Steward of Gondor, the second of the name; Lord of Minas Tirith at the time of the War of the Ring; father of Boromir and Faramir. 338, 399, 403, 405–9, 411–13

*Déor*  Seventh King of Rohan. 372–3

*Dimbar*  The land between the rivers Sirion and Mindeb. 41, 43–4, 54, 90, 95, 148

*Dimrill Dale*  See *Nanduhirion*.

*Dimrost*  The falls of Celebros in the Forest of Brethil, afterwards called *Nen Girith*, q.v.; translated *the Rainy Stair*. 123, 149

*Dior Thingol's Heir*  Son of Beren and Lúthien; King of Doriath after Thingol; possessor of the Silmaril; slain by the Sons of Fëanor. 233

*Dírhavel*  Man of Dor-lómin, author of the *Narn i Hîn Húrin*. 146

\*dirnaith  Wedge-shaped battle-formation used by the Dúnedain. 272, 282

*Dol Amroth*  Stronghold on a promontory of Belfalas, named after Amroth King of Lórien. 214, 240, 247–8, 255, 313, 316. With reference to the Lords or Princes of Dol Amroth, 246–8, 255, 302, 304–5, 313, 316. See *Angelimar, Adrahil, Imrahil*.

*Dol Baran*  'Gold-brown Hill', a hill at the southern end of the Misty Mountains, where Peregrin Took looked into the *palantír* of Orthanc. 405–6

*Dol Guldur*  'Hill of Sorcery', a treeless height in the south-west of Mirkwood, fastness of the Necromancer before he was revealed as Sauron returned. 236, 244, 246, 252, 280, 297–8, 303, 307, 313, 321–4, 330, 332, 336, 338–9, 343–5, 350, 352–3. See *Amon Lanc*.

*Dor-Cúarthol*  'Land of Bow and Helm', name of the country defended by Beleg and Túrin from their lair on Amon Rûdh. 152, 154

*Dor-en-Ernil*  'Land of the Prince', in Gondor west of the river Gilrain. 243, 255

*Doriath*  'Land of the Fence' (*Dor Iâth*), referring to the Girdle of Melian; the kingdom of Thingol and Melian in the forests of Neldoreth and Region, ruled from Menegroth on the river Esgalduin.

Morthond and Ringló, north of Dol Amroth. 255, 261. Called *Amroth's Haven* 246; other references 241, 246-8

\*Edhelrim, Eledhrim*  'The Elves'; Sindarin *edhel, eledh* and collective plural ending *rim* (see Appendix to *The Simarillion*, entry *êl, elen*). 318

*Edoras*  'The Courts', name in the Mark-speech of the royal town of Rohan on the northern edge of Ered Nimrais. 55, 277, 316, 340, 346–7, 356, 358–61, 364–8, 411. *Muster of Edoras* 360, 367–8

*Egalmoth*  Eighteenth Ruling Steward of Gondor. 373

*Eglarest*  The southernmost of the Havens of the Falas on the coast of Beleriand. 34, 51, 53, 247

*Eilenach*  Second of the beacons of Gondor in Ered Nimrais, the highest point of the Drúadan Forest. 300–1, 314, 319

\*Eilenaer*  Pre-Númenórean name (related to *Eilenach*) of *Amon Anwar* (*Halifirien*), q.v. 308, 319

*Eithel Sirion*  'Sirion's Well', in the eastern face of Ered Wethrin; used with reference to the Noldorin fortress (*Barad Eithel*) at that place. 60, 75

\*eket*  Short broad-bladed sword. 284

*elanor* (*1*)  A small golden star-shaped flower that grew both in Tol Eressëa and in Lothlórien. 189, 216

*Elanor* (*2*)  Daughter of Samwise Gamgee, named after the flower. 216, 284

\*Elatan of Andúnië*  Númenórean, husband of Silmarien, father of Valandil first Lord of Andúnië. 173

\*Eldalondë*  'Haven of the Eldar' in the Bay of Eldanna at the mouth of the river Nunduinë in Númenor; called 'the Green'. 167–8

\*Eldanna*  Great bay in the west of Númenor, so called 'because it faced towards Eressëa' (i.e. *Elda(r)*+suffix *-(n)na* of movement towards, cf. *Elenna, Rómenna*). 167

*Eldar*  The Elves of the Three Kindreds (Vanyar, Noldor, and Teleri). 25, 29, 34, 38, 41, 54, 57–9, 61–2, 66–8, 81, 146, 151–2, 156–7, 159, 167–8, 170–1, 173–4, 177, 179, 181, 185–7, 189, 200, 209, 213, 215–16, 219–21, 223, 225, 228–30, 232, 234–6, 241, 247, 250, 256, 258, 266, 276, 286, 288, 305, 377–9, 385, 389, 392–3, 395–6. *Eldarin* (*tongues*) 223, 257, 265. *Elves of Beleriand* 232, 247, *Elves of Eressëa* 170; in many other passages *Elves* used alone implies *Eldar*.

*Elder Children*  See *Children of Ilúvatar*.

*Elder King*  See *Manwë*. (Title claimed by Morgoth, 67.)

\*Eledhrim*  See *Edhelrim*.

*Eledhwen*  Name of Morwen. 57, 62, 68, 161, 189

\*Elemmakil*  Elf of Gondolin, captain of the guard of the outer gate. 45–50

*Elendil*  Son of Amandil, last Lord of Andúnië, descended from Eärendil and Elwing but not of the direct line of the Kings of Númenor; escaped with his sons Isildur and Anárion from the Drowning of Númenor and founded the Númenórean realms in Middle-earth; slain with Gil-galad in the otherthrow of Sauron at the end of the

*Elu Thingol*   Sindarin form of *Elwë Singollo*. 171, 229. See *Thingol*.

*Elves' New Year*   323, 327

*Elwë*   232–3; see *Thingol*.

*Elwing*   Daughter of Dior Thingol's Heir, who escaping from Doriath with the Silmaril wedded Eärendil at the Mouths of Sirion and went with him to Aman; mother of Elrond and Elros. 171, 233

\*Emerië   Region of sheep pasturage in the Mittalmar (Inlands) of Númenor. 166, 182, 184, 186, 192–6, 199, 201–2, 204, 206–9, 211–12. *The White Lady of Emerië*, Erendis, 194

\*Emerwen   (*Aranel*)   '(Princess) Shepherdess', name given to Tar-Ancalimë in her youth. 209, 211

*Emyn Beraid*   Hills in the west of Eriador on which were built the White Towers. 411, 414. Translated *Tower Hills* 213. See *Elostirion*.

\*Emyn Duir   'Dark Mountains', the Mountains of Mirkwood. 280. See *Emyn-nu-Fuin*.

*Emyn Muil*   'Drear Hills', folded, rocky, and (especially on the east side) barren hill-country about Nen Hithoel ('Mist-cool Water') above Rauros falls. 260, 296, 306, 343, 368, 371

\*Emyn-nu-Fuin   'Mountains under Night', later name of the Mountains of Mirkwood. 281. See *Emyn Duir*.

*Enchanted Isles*   The islands set by the Valar in the Great Sea eastwards of Tol Eressëa, at the time of the Hiding of Valinor. 52. See *Shadowy Isles*.

*Encircling Mountains*   See *Echoriath*.

*Enedwaith*   'Middle-folk', between the rivers Greyflood (Gwathló) and Isen (see especially 262–4). 206, 239, 261–5, 341, 347, 356, 369–70, 372, 383, 386–7

*Enemy, The*   Name given to Morgoth, q.v.; and to Sauron, 350

\*Enerdhil   Jewel-smith of Gondolin. 248–51

*Ents*   261, 318, 364, 366. See *Enyd, Onodrim*.

*Entulessë*   'Return', the ship in which Vëantur the Númenórean achieved the first voyage to Middle-earth. 171

*Entwade*   Ford over the Entwash. 338

*Entwash*   River flowing through Rohan from Fangorn Forest to the Nindalf. 300–1, 318, 367. See *Onodló*.

*Entwood*   Name in Rohan of Fangorn Forest. 318, 371

*Enyd*   Sindarin name for Ents (plural of *Onod*, see *Onodló, Onodrim*). 318

\*Eofor   Third son of Brego the second king of Rohan; ancestor of Éomer. 367

\*éoherë   Term used by the Rohirrim for the full muster of their cavalry (for the meaning see 315). 298, 313, 315, 318

*Eöl*   The 'Dark Elf' of Nan Elmoth, father of Maeglin. 54

*Éomer*   Nephew and fosterson of King Théoden; at the time of the War of the Ring Third Marshal of the Mark; after Théoden's death eighteenth King of Rohan; friend of King Elessar. 286, 315, 317, 355, 359–60, 364, 366–9, 400

*Éomund (1)   Chief captain of the host of the Éothéod at the time of the Ride of Eorl. 305

Éomund (2)   Chief Marshal of the Mark of Rohan; wedded Théodwyn sister of Théoden; father of Éomer and Éowyn. 364, 367

Eönwë   One of the mightiest of the Maiar, called the Herald of Manwë; leader of the host of the Valar in the attack on Morgoth at the end of the First Age. 395

éored   A body of the Riders of the Éothéod (for a detailed account of the word's meaning in Rohan see 315). 290, 301, 315, 357, 362, 367–8

Eorl the Young   Lord of the Éothéod; rode from his land in the far North to the aid of Gondor against the invasion of the Balchoth; received Calenardhon in gift from Cirion Steward of Gondor; first King of Rohan. 260, 277–8, 288, 290, 297–9, 301–8, 310–11, 313–16, 319, 365, 367, 371. Called *Lord of the Éothéod, Lord of the Riders, Lord of the Rohirrim, King of Calenardhon, King of the Mark of the Riders*, 297, 302–3, 305–7, 310. *Chronicle of, Tale of, Cirion and Eorl* 278, 288, 296; *Oath of Eorl* 278, 304, 310, 316, 365, 371; words of the oath 304–5

Eorlings   The people of Eorl, the Rohirrim. 306; with Anglo-Saxon plural ending, *Eorlingas* 358

Éothéod   Name of the people afterwards called the Rohirrim, and also of their land (see 315). 288–9, 294–8, 303–7, 311–13, 315, 318. *Riders, Horsemen, of the North* 299–302, 310

Éowyn   Sister of Éomer, wife of Faramir; slayer of the Lord of the Nazgûl in the Battle of the Pelennor Fields. 364

*epessë   An 'after-name' received by one of the Eldar in addition to the given names (*essi*). 266

Ephel Brandir   'The encircling fence of Brandir', dwellings of the Men of Brethil upon Amon Obel. 110–11, 122–3, 126–8, 136. *The Ephel* 131–2, 141

Ephel Dúath   'Fence of Shadow', the mountain-range between Gondor and Mordor. 293–4, 312

Erchamion   See *Beren (1)*.

Erebor   An isolated mountain to the east of the northernmost parts of Mirkwood, where was the Kingdom of the Dwarves under the Mountain and the lair of Smaug. 289, 321, 323–4, 326–8, 334. *The Lonely Mountain* 258, 321, 328

Ered Lindon   'Mountains of Lindon', another name for *Ered Luin*, q.v. 232, 234–5, 379, 383

Ered Lithui   'Ash Mountains', forming the northern border of Mordor. 292, 312

Ered Lómin   'Echoing Mountains', forming the west-fence of Hithlum. 20, 52. *The Echoing Mountains of Lammoth* 23

Ered Luin   The great mountain-chain (also called *Ered Lindon*, q.v.) separating Beleriand from Eriador in the Elder Days, and after the destruction at the end of the First Age forming the north-western coastal range of Middle-earth. 213, 228, 252, 321. Translated *the*

*Esgalduin* The river of Doriath, dividing the forests of Neldoreth and Region and flowing into Sirion. 74, 82, 120

*\*Estelmo* Elendur's esquire, who survived the disaster of the Gladden Fields. 276, 282

*Estolad* The land south of Nan Elmoth in East Beleriand where the Men of the followings of Bëor and Marach dwelt after they had crossed the Blue Mountains. 77

*Ethir Anduin* 'Outflow of Anduin', the delta of the Great River in the Bay of Belfalas. 240, 242, 402

*\*Ethraid Engrin* Sindarin name (also in singular form *Athrad Angren*) of the Fords of Isen, q.v. 264, 318

*Evendim* See *Nenuial.*

*Evermind* See *simbelmynë.*

*\*Evil Breath* A wind out of Angband that brought sickness to Dor-lómin, from which Túrin's sister Urwen (Lalaith) died. 58–9, 61

*Exiles, The* The rebellious Noldor who returned to Middle-earth from Aman. 20, 55, 229, 259

*Faelivrin* Name given to Finduilas by Gwindor. 37, 54

*Fair Folk* The Eldar. 72

*Faithful, The* (i) Those Númenóreans who were not estranged from the Eldar and continued to reverence the Valar in the days of Tar-Ancalimon and later kings. 222–3, 265, 316–17. (ii) 'The Faithful' of the Fourth Age. 395

*Falas* The western coasts of Beleriand, south of Nevrast. 33–4, 51. *Havens of the Falas* 247

*Falastur* 'Lord of the Coasts', name of Tarannon, twelfth King of Gondor. 401

*Falathrim* Telerin Elves of the Falas, whose lord was Círdan. 33

*Fallohides* One of the three peoples into which the Hobbits were divided, described in the Prologue (i) to *The Lord of the Rings.* 287

*Fangorn* (i) The oldest of the Ents and the guardian of Fangorn Forest. 261. Translated *Treebeard* 253, 366. (ii) The Forest of Fangorn, at the south-eastern end of the Misty Mountains, about the upper waters of the rivers Entwash and Limlight. 241, 261, 305, 312, 318, 343, 371–2. See *Entwood.*

*Faramir (1)* Younger son of Ondoher King of Gondor; slain in battle with the Wainriders. 291, 294–5

*Faramir (2)* Younger son of Denethor II, Steward of Gondor; Captain of the Rangers of Ithilien; after the War of the Ring Prince of Ithilien and Steward of Gondor. 344, 397, 399, 408, 413

*Far Harad* See *Harad.*

*Faroth* See *Taur-en-Faroth.*

*Fëanor* Eldest son of Finwë, half-brother of Fingolfin and Finarfin; leader of the Noldor in their rebellion against the Valar; maker of the

266, 280, 282, 305, 395. Called *King of the Elves* 199. *Land of Gil-galad*, Lindon, 185. See *Ereinion.*

*\*Gilmith*  Sister of Galador, first Lord of Dol Amroth. 248

*Gilrain*  River of Lebennin in Gondor flowing into the Bay of Belfalas west of Ethir Anduin. 242-3, 316

*Gimilkhâd*  Younger son of Ar-Gimilzôr and Inzilbêth; father of Ar-Pharazôn, last King of Númenor. 223-4, 227

*\*Gimilzagar*  Second son of Tar-Calmacil. 227

*Gimli*  Dwarf of the House of Durin, son of Glóin; one of the Fellowship of the Ring. 235, 277-8, 321, 328-9, 336, 365, 402

*Gladden*  River flowing down from the Misty Mountains and joining Anduin at the Gladden Fields; translation of Sindarin *Sîr Ninglor*, q.v. 280-1, 337, 339, 343, 353

*Gladden Fields*  Partial translation of Sindarin *Loeg Ningloron*, q.v.; the great stretches of reed and iris (gladden) where the Gladden River joined Anduin; see especially 280. 258, 272, 275-6, 280-3, 288, 297, 312-13

*\*Glǽmscrafu*  'Caves of Radiance', name in Rohan of *Aglarond*, q.v. 371

*Glamdring*  Gandalf's sword. 54

*Glamhoth*  Sindarin word for Orcs. 39, 54

*Glanduin*  'Border-river', flowing westwards from the Misty Mountains; forming in the Second Age the southern boundary of Eregion and in the Third a part of the southern boundary of Arnor. 261-5. See *Nîn-in-Eilph.*

*\*Glanhír*  'Boundary-stream', Sindarin name of the *Mering Stream*, q.v. 306, 318

*Glaurung*  The first of the Dragons of Morgoth; in the Dagor Bragollach, the Nirnaeth Arnoediad, and the sack of Nargothrond; cast his spell upon Túrin and Nienor; slain by Túrin at Cabed-en-Aras. In many references called *the Dragon.* 75, 107, 112, 117-20, 124-45, 149-50, 155, 159. *The (Great) Worm* 127, 133, 143-4; *Worm of Morgoth* 135; *Great Worm of Angband* 37; *Gold-worm of Angband* 75

*\*Glithui*  River flowing down from Ered Wethrin, a tributary of Teiglin. 38, 54, 68

*Glóin*  Dwarf of the House of Durin, companion of Thorin Oakenshield; father of Gimli. 327, 332-3

*Glóredhel*  Daughter of Hador Goldenhead of Dor-lómin and sister of Galdor. 57, 68

*Glorfindel*  Elf of Rivendell. 353

*\*Glornan*  See *Lórien* (2)

*Golden Tree (of Valinor)*  See *Laurelin.*

*Golden Wood*  See *Lórien* (2)

*Gollum*  148, 337-9, 342-5, 349, 353. See *Sméagol.*

*\*Golug*  Orc name for the Noldor. 92

*Gondolin*  The hidden city of King Turgon, destroyed by Morgoth. 51-6, 63, 66, 146, 172, 189, 228, 235, 248-9, 251, 316-17. Called *the Hidden*

to the lands west of Sirion. 130, 377, 385. *House of, People of, Folk of, Men of, Haleth* 63, 85, 87, 110–11, 129, 134, 377–80, 382–4, 386–7. See *Brethil, Halethrim.*

*\*Halethrim*   The People of Haleth. 140

*Halflings*   Hobbits; translation of Sindarin *periannath.* 286–7, 337, 339, 342, 349–52, 354, 398. *Land of the Halflings* 339–40, 354; *Halflings' Leaf* 347–8, 350. See *Perian.*

*Halifirien*   'Holy Mount', name in Rohan of *Amon Anwar,* q.v. 300–1, 306, 310, 314, 319. *Halifirien Wood* 318. See *Eilenaer.*

*Halimath*   The ninth month in the Shire Calendar. 279. See *Yavannië, Ivanneth.*

*\*Hallacar*   Son of Hallatan of Hyarastorni; wedded Tar-Ancalimë, first Ruling Queen of Númenor, with whom he was at strife. 211–12, 220. See *Mámandil.*

*Hallas*   Son of Cirion; thirteenth Ruling Steward of Gondor; deviser of the names *Rohan* and *Rohirrim.* 297, 302, 307

*\*Hallatan*   Lord of Hyarastorni in the Mittalmar (Inlands) of Númenor; cousin of Tar-Aldarion. 197–9, 204, 206, 209, 211, 217, 220. Called *the Sheep-lord* 195

*Halmir*   Lord of the Haladin, father of Haldir. 57

*Háma*   Captain of the household of King Théoden. 367

*Hamfast Gamgee*   Sam Gamgee's father. (The name *Hamfast* is Anglo-Saxon *hām-fæst,* literally 'home-fixed', 'home-firm'.) 327. Called *Gaffer Gamgee* and *the Gaffer,* 327, 352

*Handir*   Lord of the Haladin, son of Haldir and Glóredhel. 91. *Son of Handir,* Brandir the Lame, 110, 129, 138, 141

*Harad*   'The South', used vaguely of countries far south of Gondor and Mordor. 181, 236, 295, 312, 398–9, 402. *Near Harad* 312, 398; *Far Harad* 398–9

*Haradrim*   Men of the Harad. 399

*Haradwaith*   'South-folk', the Harad. 383

*Hareth*   Daughter of Halmir of Brethil, wedded Galdor of Dor-lómin; mother of Húrin and Huor. 57, 63

*Harfoots*   One of the three peoples into which the Hobbits were divided (see *Fallohides*). 287

*Harlindon*   Lindon south of the Gulf of Lhûn. 252

*Harrowdale*   Valley at the head of the Snowbourn, under the walls of Dunharrow. 366–8

*\*Hatholdir*   Man of Númenor, friend of Tar-Meneldur; father of Orchaldor. 173

*Haudh-en-Elleth*   The mound in which Finduilas of Nargothrond was buried near the Crossings of Teiglin. (It is not clear what relation *Elleth,* rendered 'Elf-maid' and always so spelt, bears to *Eledh* 'Elda' seen in Morwen's name *Eledhwen.*) 112, 122, 124, 130, 137–8, 143. Translated *Mound of the Elf-maid* 112

*Haudh-en-Ndengin*   'Mound of the Slain' in the desert of Anfauglith,

*Îbal  A boy of Emerië in Númenor, son of Ulbar, a mariner of Tar-Aldarion. 194, 198, 207

Ibun  One of the sons of Mîm the Petty-dwarf. 101–2

Idril  (Celebrindal), daughter of Turgon of Gondolin, wife of Tuor, mother of Eärendil. 56, 249, 251

Ilúvatar  'Father of All', Eru. 166 (Eru Ilúvatar). See Children of Ilúvatar.

Imladris  Sindarin name of Rivendell, q.v. 165, 238–40, 243–4, 271–2, 277–9, 284–5, 327. Pass of Imladris, see Cirith Forn en Andrath.

Imrahil  Lord of Dol Amroth at the time of the War of the Ring. 246, 248, 286, 316

*Imrazôr  Called 'the Númenórean'; took to wife the Elf Mithrellas; father of Galador first Lord of Dol Amroth. 248, 316

Incánus  Name given to Gandalf 'in the South'. 397, 399–400, 402

*Incomers  See Easterlings, Brodda.

Indis  Vanyarin Elf; second wife of Finwë, mother of Fingolfin and Finarfin. 229–30

*Indor  Man of Dor-lómin, father of Aerin. 108

*Inglor  Rejected name of Finrod. 255

Inziladûn  See Ar-Inziladûn. As name of a formal design, 227; see Númellótë.

Inzilbêth  Queen of Ar-Gimilzôr; of the house of the Lords of Andúnië; mother of Inziladûn (Tar-Palantir). 223, 227

*Írimon  The given name of Tar-Meneldur. 219

Irmo  Vala, 'master of visions and dreams', commonly called Lórien from the name of his dwelling in Valinor. 253, 397. See Fëanturi, Olofantur.

Iron Hills  Range east of the Lonely Mountain and north of the Sea of Rhûn. 322

Isen  River flowing from the Misty Mountains through Nan Curunír (the Wizard's Vale) and across the Gap of Rohan; translation (to represent the language of Rohan) of Sindarin Angren, q.v. 214, 262–4, 303, 314, 318, 346, 356–7, 360–1, 363–6, 369–73, 383–4. See Fords of Isen.

Isengard  Númenórean stronghold in the valley called, after its occupation by the wizard Curunír (Saruman), Nan Curunír, at the southern end of the Misty Mountains; translation (to represent the language of Rohan) of Sindarin Angrenost, q.v. 318, 338–41, 345–7, 354, 356–7, 359–61, 363–6, 370–3, 392, 404–5, 412. Ring of Isengard 371–3, 412, Circle of Isengard 340, referring to the great circular wall surrounding the inner plain, in the centre of which was Orthanc. Isengarders 358–9

Isengar Took  One of Bilbo Baggins' uncles. 332

Isildur  Elder son of Elendil, who with his father and his brother Anárion escaped from the Drowning of Númenor and founded in Middle-earth the Númenórean realms in exile; lord of Minas Ithil; cut the Ruling Ring from Sauron's hand; slain by Orcs in the Anduin when the Ring slipped from his finger. 215, 271–83, 300, 304, 308–10, 370, 383. Heir of Isildur 280, 408, 414; Ring of Isildur 406; Scroll of Isildur 283, 413; 'Tradition of Isildur' 309–10; Isildur's wife 271

*Lindórinand* 'Vale of the Land of Singers' 253; *Laurelindórinan* 'Valley of Singing Gold' 253. Called *the Golden Wood* 299; and see. *Dwimordene, Lothlórien.*

\*Lórinand See *Lórien* (2).

*Lossarnach* Region in the north-east of Lebennin about the sources of the river Erui. (The name is stated to mean 'Flowery Arnach', Arnach being a pre-Númenórean name.) 286

*Lótessë* Quenya name of the fifth month according to the Númenórean calendar, corresponding to May. 302. See *Lothron.*

*Lothíriel* Daughter of Imrahil of Dol Amroth; wife of King Éomer of Rohan and mother of Elfwine the Fair. 286

*Lothlórien* The name *Lórien* with the Sindarin word *loth* 'flower' prefixed. 56, 168, 171, 216, 231, 235, 240, 245, 252-3, 265

*Lothron* Sindarin name of the fifth month. 65. See *Lótessë.*

*Loudwater* See *Bruinen.*

*Lune* Spelling of *Lhûn,* q.v. 228, 233, 252, 398

*Lúthien* Daughter of Thingol and Melian, who after the fulfilment of the Quest for the Silmaril and the death of Beren chose to become mortal and to share his fate. 57-8, 79, 84, 157. Called *Tinúviel* 'Nightingale' 57

*Mablung* Called *the Hunter* 80; Elf of Doriath, chief captain of Thingol, friend of Túrin. 80-2, 84, 94, 114-21, 143-5, 149

*Maedhros* Eldest son of Fëanor. 58, 75, 147

*Maeglin* Son of Eöl and Aredhel Turgon's sister; became mighty in Gondolin, and betrayed it to Morgoth; slain in the sack of the city by Tuor. 49, 54, 56

*Maggot, Farmer* Hobbit of the Shire, farming in the Marish near the Bucklebury Ferry. 352

*Maiar* (Singular *Maia*). Ainur of lesser degree than the Valar. 214, 254, 393-4, 401

\*Malantur Númenórean, descendant of Tar-Elendil. 208

*Malduin* A tributary of the Teiglin. 38, 54

\*Malgalad King of Lórien, slain in the Battle of Dagorlad; apparently identical with *Amdír,* q.v. 258

\*malinornë Quenya form of Sindarin *mallorn,* q.v.

*mallorn* Name of the great trees with golden flowers brought from Tol Eressëa to Eldalondë in Númenor, and afterwards grown in Lothlórien. 56, 171, 253. Quenya *malinornë,* plural *malinorni,* 167-8

*mallos* A golden flower of Lebennin. 316

\*Mámandil Name given to himself by Hallacar in his first encounters with Ancalimë. 209

*Mandos* The name of the dwelling in Aman of the Vala properly called Námo, but who was usually himself called Mandos. 30, 82, 156, 393, 397. *Curse of Mandos* 29; *Doom of Mandos* 29-30, 230; *Second Prophecy of Mandos* 402

*Manwë*  The chief of the Valar. 55, 67, 156, 169, 200, 222, 232, 393, 395-6. Called *the Elder King* 67, 396. See *Witnesses of Manwë*.

*Mardil*  First Ruling Steward of Gondor. 309, 317, 319-20. Called *Voronwë* 'the Steadfast' 317, and *the Good Steward* 320

\*Marhari  Leader of the Northmen in the Battle of the Plains, where he was slain; father of Marhwini. 289, 311

\*Marhwini  'Horse-friend', leader of the Northmen (Éothéod) who settled in the Vales of Anduin after the Battle of the Plains, and ally of Gondor against the Wainriders. 289-91, 311

*Mark, The*  Name among the Rohirrim for their own country. 306, 311, 314-15, 364-5, 371. *Riddermark* 367, 371; *Mark of the Riders* 306; *Marshals of the Mark* 364, 366-9. See *East-mark, West-mark*.

*Master of Doom*  See *Turambar*.

mearas  The horses of Rohan. 311, 314

*Melian*  Maia, Queen of King Thingol of Doriath, about which she set a girdle of enchantment; mother of Lúthien and foremother of Elrond and Elros. 73-6, 78-9, 83, 85, 109, 113, 115, 121, 148, 152-3, 158, 234. *Girdle of Melian* 41, 63, 78, 109, 113-14

*Melkor*  The great rebellious Vala, the beginning of evil, in his origin the mightiest of the Ainur; afterwards named *Morgoth*, q.v. 29, 67-8, 232, 234-5, 254, 385, 395

*Menegroth*  'The Thousand Caves', the hidden halls of Thingol and Melian on the river Esgalduin in Doriath. 74, 76-9, 81-5, 94, 144, 148, 231, 259

*Menel*  High heaven, the region of the stars. 67, 184

*Meneldil*  Son of Anárion and third King of Gondor. 271, 279, 304, 308, 319

*Meneldur*  See *Tar-Meneldur*.

*Meneltarma*  Mountain in the midst of Númenor, on whose summit was the Hallow of Eru Ilúvatar (see *Eru*). 31 (unnamed, in Tuor's dream), 165-6, 168-9, 175, 183-4, 188, 192, 215, 223. Translated *Pillar of the Heavens* 166 (*the Pillar* 188). Called also *the Holy Mountain* 166, *the Hallowed Mountain of the Númenóreans* 183

\*Men-i-Naugrim  'Way of the Dwarves', a name of the Old Forest Road. 280-1. Translated *Dwarf Road* 280-1

*Men of the Sea*  See *Númenóreans*.

*Meriadoc Brandybuck*  Hobbit of the Shire, one of the Fellowship of the Ring. 321, 336, 365, 368, 383, 386-7

*Mering Stream*  'Boundary Stream', flowing down from Ered Nimrais to join the Entwash, and forming the boundary between Rohan and Gondor; in Sindarin called *Glanhír*, q.v. 300-2, 305-6, 318

\*Methed-en-Glad  'End of the Wood', a stronghold in Dor-Cúarthol at the edge of the forest south of Teiglin. 153

*Middle-earth*  Passim. Called *the Dark Lands* 178, *the Great Lands* 174

*Mîm*  The Petty-dwarf, in whose house (*Bar-en-Danwedh*) on Amon Rûdh Túrin dwelt with the outlaw-band, and by whom their lair was

*Northern Waste*   Region of cold in the far North of Middle-earth (also called *Forodwaith*, see Introduction p. 14). 242

*\*Northlands (of Númenor)*   See *Forostar*.

Northmen   The horsemen of Rhovanion, allies of Gondor, ancestrally related to the Edain; from them derived the *Éothéod*, q.v. 288–90, 295–7, 310–13; with reference to the Rohirrim 372. *Free Men of the North* 258

*North–South Road*   See *Roads*.

*\*Núath, Woods of*   Woods extending westward from the upper waters of the river Narog. 36, 53

*\*Númellótë*   'Flower of the West' = *Inziladûn*. 227

*\*Númendil*   Seventeenth Lord of Andúnië. 223

Númenor   (In full Quenya form *Númenórë*, 199.) 'Westernesse', 'Westland', the great island prepared by the Valar as a dwelling-place for the Edain after the ending of the First Age. 52, 56, Part 2 §§ I-III *passim*, 236, 239, 247, 262–3, 265, 272, 276, 279–80, 284, 287–8, 316–17, 385–6, 398, 400, 403, 414. Called *the Great Isle* 386, *Isle of Kings* 199, *Isle of Westernesse* 183, *Land of Gift* 165, 167, 201, *Land of the Star* 305; and see *Akallabêth, Elenna·nórë, Yôzâyan*. References to the *Downfall of Númenor* are given in a separate entry.

Númenóreans   The Men of Númenor. (The following references include *Númenórean* used as an adjective.) Part 2 §§ I-III *passim* (see especially 206–7, 224–5), 236, 239, 247–8, 253, 255, 258, 261–5, 273, 278–9, 283, 285–8, 314, 369, 383–4, 386, 398–9, 401, 404, 409. *Kings of Men* 27, 200, 259, 303; *Men of the Sea* 170, 263; and see *Dúnedain*. *Númenórean tongue, speech*, see *Adûnaic*.

*\*Númerrámar*   'West-wings', the ship of Vëantur in which Aldarion made his first voyage to Middle-earth. 175

*\*Nunduinë*   River in the west of Númenor, flowing into the sea at Eldalondë. 168

*\*Núneth*   Mother of Erendis. 183, 186, 190–1, 193, 198

Núrnen   'Sad Water', inland sea in the south of Mordor. 398

*\*Nurufantur*   One of the *Fëanturi*, q.v.; the earlier 'true' name of Mandos, before it was replaced by Námo. 397. See *Olofantur*.

Ohtar   Esquire of Isildur, who brought the shards of Narsil to Imladris. (On the name *Ohtar* 'warrior' see 282). 272–5, 282

*\*Oghor-hai*   Name given to the Drúedain by Orcs. 379

*\*oiolairë*   'Ever-summer', an evergreen tree brought to Númenor by the Eldar of Eressëa, from which was cut the Bough of Return set upon the Númenórean ships. (*Corollairë*, the Green Mound of the Trees in Valinor, was also called *Coron Oiolairë*: Appendix to *The Silmarillion*, entry *coron*). 167, 179, 187–8, 192, 205, 215. *Bough of Return* 179–80, 192

Oiolossë   'Ever-snow-white', the Mountain of Manwë in Aman. 55. See *Amon Uilos, Taniquetil*.

*\*Old Company*   Name given to the original members of Túrin's band in Dor-Cúarthol. 153

was continued to the sea after its confluence with Gilrain. Its mouth
was blocked with shingles, and at any rate in later times ships approaching Anduin and making for Pelargir went by the eastern side of Tol
Falas and took the sea-way passage made by the Númenóreans in the
midst of the Delta of Anduin.') 243

*Shadowfax*   The great horse of Rohan ridden by Gandalf in the War of
the Ring. 314, 341, 364, 405

*Shadowy Isles*   Probably a name for the *Enchanted Isles*, q.v. 30, 52

*Shadowy Mountains*   See *Ered Wethrin*.

*\*Sharbhund*   Name among the Petty-dwarves for *Amon Rûdh*, q.v. 98

*Shire, The*   The chief dwelling-place of Hobbits in the west of Eriador.
234, 252, 287, 322–5, 327–9, 331–5, 339–42, 344–50, 352, 354. *Shire
Calendar, Reckoning*, 279, 284. *Shire-folk* 323, 331, 333

*Silmarien*   Daughter of Tar-Elendil; mother of Valandil first Lord of
Andúnië and ancestress of Elendil the Tall. 171, 173, 208, 215, 219,
225, 277, 284

*Silmarils*   The three jewels made by Fëanor before the destruction of the
Two Trees of Valinor, and filled with their light. 52, 230, 233, 252.
See *War of the Jewels*.

*Silvan Elves*   Nandorin Elves who never passed west of the Misty
Mountains but remained in the Vale of Anduin and in Greenwood the
Great. 214, 240–1, 243, 245, 247–8, 256–60, 267, 272, 280. *Silvan
Elvish, Silvan tongue* 241, 257, 259–60. See *Tawarwaith*.

*Silverlode*   See *Celebrant*.

*simbelmynë*   A small white flower, also called *alfirin* and *uilos*, q.v. 55, 316.
Translated *Evermind* 48, 55

*Sindar*   The Grey-elves; name applied to all the Elves of Telerin origin
whom the returning Noldor found in Beleriand, save for the Green-
elves of Ossiriand. 48, 228, 236, 247, 252, 256–9. *Grey-elves* 17–19, 21,
34, 68, 93, 100, 103, 234, 248

*Sindarin*   Of the Sindar: 233, 240, 243–4, 252, 256, 258–60. Of the tongue
of the Sindar: 54–5, 76, 148, 215–16, 231, 243, 247, 253, 255, 257, 261,
263, 265–7, 279, 281–2, 287, 301, 306, 313, 317–19, 377, 385, 388,
392, 399–400. *Tongue of Beleriand* 44, 215, *Grey-elven tongue* 146

*\*Sîr Angren*   See *Angren*.

*\*Siril*   The chief river of Númenor, flowing southwards from the
Meneltarma. 168

*Sirion*   The great river of Beleriand. 34–5, 38, 40–2, 54, 56, 78, 109, 114,
116, 120, 147. *Fens of Sirion* 147; *Havens of Sirion, Sirion's Haven*,
see *Havens*; *Mouths of Sirion* 20, 34, 51, 53, 121, 159–60, 378;
*Pass(es) of Sirion* 18, 110, 160; *Springs of Sirion* 160; *Vale (Valley)
of Sirion* 28, 39, 43, 73, 96, 99, 109, 147–8

*\*Sîr Ninglor*   Sindarin name of the *Gladden River*, q.v. 280–1

*Smaug*   The great Dragon of Erebor. In many references called *the
Dragon*. 258, 321–4, 326, 328–30, 332–4

*Sméagol*   Gollum. 353

*Vilya* One of the Three Rings of the Elves, borne by Gil-galad and after-wards by Elrond. 239, 256. Called *the Ring of Air* 237, *the Blue Ring* 239, 256

\*Vinyalondë 'New Haven', Númenórean harbour established by Tar-Aldarion at the mouth of the river Gwathló; afterwards called *Lond Daer*, q.v. 176, 180–1, 188, 200, 206, 239, 253, 265

*Vinyamar* 'New Dwelling', the house of Turgon in Nevrast. 26–8, 31, 46, 51–2, 54, 317

*Víressë* Quenya name of the fourth month according to the Númenórean calendar, corresponding to April. 187, 298–9

*Voronwë (1)* Elf of Gondolin, the only mariner to survive from the seven ships sent into the West after the Nirnaeth Arnoediad; met with Tuor at Vinyamar and guided him to Gondolin. 30–50, 53–5, 317

*Voronwë (2)* Name of Mardil Steward of Gondor. 317

*Wainriders* An Easterling people who invaded Gondor in the nineteenth and twentieth centuries of the Third Age. 289–96, 311–13, 316

*War of the Dwarves and the Orcs* 299, 321

*War of the Jewels* The wars of Beleriand fought by the Noldor for the recovery of the Silmarils. 386

*War of the (Last) Alliance* See *Last Alliance*.

*War of the Ring* See *Rings of Power*.

*Watchful Peace* The period lasting from Third Age 2063, when Sauron left Dol Guldur, until 2460, when he returned. 296, 313, 370, 406

*Weather Hills* Hills in Eriador, of which Amon Sûl (Weathertop) was the southernmost. 214

*Weathertop* See *Amon Sûl*.

*Westernesse* Translation of *Númenor*; *Isle of Westernesse* 183

*Westfold* Region of Rohan, the slopes and fields between Thrihyrne (the peaks above the Hornburg) and Edoras. 356, 359–60, 362, 366, 368, 371–3. *Muster of Westfold* 367

*Westlands* (i) Of Númenor, see *Andustar*. (ii) Of Middle-earth, a very general expression, referring broadly to the lands west of Anduin. 200, 239, 331, 390, 392

\*West-mark The western half of Rohan in the military organisation of the Rohirrim (see *East-mark*). 359, 367–9. *Muster of the West-mark* 369; *Marshal of the West-mark* 369

*West Road* See *Roads*.

*Westron* The common tongue of the North-west of Middle-earth, described in Appendix F to *The Lord of the Rings*, and represented by modern English. 313, 342, 370, 399–400. *Common Speech* 301, 304–5, 316, 319, 384, 400

\*Whispering Wood See *Firien Wood*.

*White Council* The deliberations of *the Wise* (q.v.), meeting at intervals from Third Age 2463 to 2953; usually referred to as *the Council*. 254, 322–3, 326, 330, 349–52, 354, 373, 404–6, 412. For a much earlier Council of the Wise also called *the White Council* see 239–40, 254

THE WEST OF
**MIDDLE-EARTH**
AT THE END OF
**THE THIRD AGE**

Miles

50    100    150    200